JOSEPH CONRAD

JOSEPH CONRAD

Lord Jim
The Nigger of the 'Narcissus'
Typhoon
Nostromo
The Secret Agent

Octopus/Heinemann

Lord Jim was first published in Great Britain in 1900; in the United States in 1899.
Nostromo was first published in Great Britain and in the United States in 1904.
The Secret Agent was first published in Great Britain in 1907; in the United States in 1906.
The Nigger of the Narcissus was first published in Great Britain in 1897; in the
United States (as *Children of the Sea*) in 1897.
Typhoon was first published in Great Britain and in the United States in 1902.

This edition first published in the United States of America
in 1979 jointly by

William Heinemann Inc
450 Park Avenue,
New York, NY 10022

and

Octopus Books Inc
The Olympic Towers,
645 Fifth Avenue,
New York, NY 10022

This edition first published in Great Britain
jointly by

William Heinemann Ltd
10 Upper Grosvenor Street,
London W1X 9PA

Martin Secker & Warburg Ltd
54 Poland Street,
London W1V 3DF

and

Octopus Books Ltd
59 Grosvenor Street,
London W1X 9DA

ISBN 0 905712 40 4

The Secret Agent Copyright 1906 by Ridgway & Co,
Copyright 1907 by Doubleday & Co Inc

Printed in the United States of America
by R. R. Donnelley and Sons Company

CONTENTS

LORD JIM

A Tale

AUTHOR'S NOTE

When this novel first appeared in book form a notion got about that I had been bolted away with. Some reviewers maintained that the work starting as a short story had got beyond the writer's control. One or two discovered internal evidence of the fact, which seemed to amuse them. They pointed out the limitations of the narrative form. They argued that no man could have been expected to talk all that time, and other men to listen so long. It was not, they said, very credible.

After thinking it over for something like sixteen years I am not so sure about that. Men have been known, both in the tropics and in the temperate zone, to sit up half the night 'swapping yarns'. This, however, is but one yarn, yet with interruptions affording some measure of relief; and in regard to the listeners' endurance, the postulate must be accepted that the story *was* interesting. It is the necessary preliminary assumption. If I hadn't believed that it *was* interesting I could never have begun to write it. As to the mere physical possibility we all know that some speeches in Parliament have taken nearer six than three hours in delivery; whereas all that part of the book which is Marlow's narrative can be read through aloud, I should say, in less than three hours. Besides – though I have kept strictly all such insignificant details out of the tale – we may presume that there must have been refreshments on that night, a glass of mineral water of some sort to help the narrator on.

But, seriously, the truth of the matter is, that my first thought was of a short story, concerned only with the pilgrim ship episode; nothing more. And that was a legitimate conception. After writing a few pages, however, I became for some reason discontented and I laid them aside for a time. I didn't take them out of the drawer till the late Mr William Blackwood suggested I should give something again to his magazine.

It was only then that I perceived that the pilgrim ship episode was a good starting-point for a free and wandering tale; that it was an event, too, which could conceivably colour the whole 'sentiment of existence' in a simple and sensitive character. But all these preliminary moods and stirrings of spirit were rather obscure at the time, and they do not appear clearer to me now after the lapse of so many years.

The few pages I had laid aside were not without their weight in the choice of subject. But the whole was re-written deliberately. When I sat down to it I knew it would be a long book, though I didn't foresee that it would spread itself over thirteen numbers of *Maga*.

I have been asked at times whether this was not the book of mine I liked best. I am a great foe to favouritism in public life, in private life, and even in the delicate relationship of an author to his works. As a matter of principle

Author's Note

I will have no favourites; but I don't go so far as to feel grieved and annoyed by the preference some people give to my Lord Jim. I won't even say that I 'fail to understand . . .' No! But once I had occasion to be puzzled and surprised.

A friend of mine returning from Italy had talked with a lady there who did not like the book. I regretted that, of course, but what surprised me was the ground of her dislike. 'You know,' she said, 'it is all so morbid.'

The pronouncement gave me food for an hour's anxious thought. Finally I arrived at the conclusion that, making due allowances for the subject itself being rather foreign to women's normal sensibilities, the lady could not have been an Italian. I wonder whether she was European at all? In any case, no Latin temperament would have perceived anything morbid in the acute consciousness of lost honour. Such a consciousness may be wrong, or it may be right, or it may be condemned as artificial; and, perhaps, my Jim is not a type of wide commonness. But I can safely assure my readers that he is not the product of coldly perverted thinking. He's not a figure of Northern Mists either. One sunny morning in the commonplace surroundings of an Eastern roadstead, I saw his form pass by – appealing – significant – under a cloud – perfectly silent. Which is as it should be. It was for me, with all the sympathy of which I was capable, to seek fit words for his meaning. He was 'one of us'.

J.C.

June, 1917

CHAPTER 1

He was an inch, perhaps two, under six feet, powerfully built, and he advanced straight at you with a slight stoop of the shoulders, head forward, and a fixed from-under stare which made you think of a charging bull. His voice was deep, loud, and his manner displayed a kind of dogged self-assertion which had nothing aggressive in it. It seemed a necessity, and it was directed apparently as much at himself as at anybody else. He was spotlessly neat, apparelled in immaculate white from shoes to hat, and in the various Eastern ports where he got his living as ship-chandler's water-clerk he was very popular.

A water-clerk need not pass an examination in anything under the sun, but he must have Ability in the abstract and demonstrate it practically. His work consisted in racing under sail, steam, or oars against other water-clerks for any ship about to anchor, greeting her captain cheerily, forcing upon him a card – the business card of the ship-chandler – and on his first visit on shore piloting him firmly but without ostentation to a vast, cavern-like shop which is full of things that are eaten and drunk on board ship; where you can get everything to make her sea-worthy and beautiful, from a set of chain-hooks for her cable to a book of gold-leaf for the carvings of her stern; and where her commander is received like a brother by a ship-chandler he has never seen before. There is a cool parlour, easy-chairs, bottles, cigars, writing implements, a copy of harbour regulations, and a warmth of welcome that melts the salt of a three months' passage out of a seaman's heart. The connexion thus begun is kept up, as long as the ship remains in harbour, by the daily visits of the water-clerk. To the captain he is faithful like a friend and attentive like a son, with the patience of Job, the unselfish devotion of a woman, and the jollity of a boon companion. Later on the bill is sent in. It is a beautiful and humane occupation. Therefore good water-clerks are scarce. When a water-clerk who possesses Ability in the abstract has also the advantage of having been brought up to the sea, he is worth to his employer a lot of money and some humouring. Jim had always good wages and as much humouring as would have bought the fidelity of a fiend. Nevertheless, with black ingratitude he would throw up the job suddenly and depart. To his employers the reasons he gave were obviously inadequate. They said 'Confounded fool!' as soon as his back was turned. This was their criticism of his exquisite sensibility.

To the white men in the waterside business and to the captains of ships he was just Jim – nothing more. He had, of course, another name, but he was anxious that it should not be pronounced. His incognito, which had as many holes as a sieve, was not meant to hide a personality but a fact. When the fact broke through the incognito he would leave suddenly the seaport where he happened to be at the time and go to another – generally farther east. He kept to seaports because he was a seaman in exile from the sea, and had Ability in the abstract, which is good for no other work but that of a water-clerk. He retreated in good order towards the rising sun, and the fact followed him casually but inevitably. Thus in the course of years he was known successively in Bombay, in Calcutta, in Rangoon, in Penang, in Batavia – and in each of these halting-places was just Jim the water-clerk. Afterwards, when his keen perception of the Intolerable drove him away for good from seaports and white men, even into the virgin forest, the Malays of the jungle village, where he had elected to conceal his deplorable faculty, added a word to the monosyllable of his incognito. They called him Tuan Jim: as one might say – Lord Jim.

Originally he came from a parsonage. Many commanders of fine merchant-ships come from these abodes of piety and peace. Jim's father possessed such certain knowledge of the Unknowable as made for the righteousness of people in cottages without disturbing the ease of mind of those whom an unerring Providence enables to live in mansions. The little church on a hill had the mossy greyness of a rock seen through a ragged screen of leaves. It had stood there for centuries, but the trees around probably remembered the laying of the first stone. Below, the red front of the rectory gleamed with a warm tint in the midst of grass-plots, flower-beds, and fir-trees, with an orchard at the back, a paved stable-yard to the left, and the sloping glass of green-houses tacked along a wall of bricks. The living had belonged to the family for generations; but Jim was one of five sons, and when after a course of light holiday literature his vocation for the sea had declared itself, he was sent at once to a 'training-ship for officers of the mercantile marine'.

He learned there a little trigonometry and how to cross top-gallant yards. He was generally liked. He had the third place in navigation and pulled stroke in the first cutter. Having a steady head with an excellent physique, he was very smart aloft. His station was in the fore-top, and often from there he looked down, with the contempt of a man destined to shine in the midst of dangers, at the peaceful multitude of roofs cut in two by the brown tide of the stream, while scattered on the outskirts of the surrounding plain the factory chimneys rose perpendicular against a grimy sky, each slender like a pencil, and belching out smoke like a volcano. He could see the big ships departing, the broad-beamed ferries constantly on the move, the little boats floating far below his feet, with the hazy splendour of the sea in the distance, and the hope of a stirring life in the world of adventure.

On the lower deck in the babel of two hundred voices he would forget himself, and beforehand live in his mind the sea-life of light literature. He saw himself saving people from sinking ships, cutting away masts in a hurricane, swimming through a surf with a line; or as a lonely castaway, barefooted and half-naked, walking on uncovered reefs in search of shellfish to stave off starvation. He confronted savages on tropical shores, quelled mutinies on the high seas, and in a small boat upon the ocean kept up the hearts of despairing men – always an example of devotion to duty, and as unflinching as a hero in a book.

'Something's up. Come along.'

He leapt to his feet. The boys were streaming up the ladders. Above could be heard a great scurrying about and shouting, and when he got through the hatchway he stood still – as if confounded.

It was the dusk of a winter's day. The gale had freshened since noon, stopping the traffic on the river and now blew with the strength of a hurricane in fitful bursts that boomed like salvoes of great guns firing over the ocean. The rain slanted in sheets that flicked and subsided, and between whiles Jim had threatening glimpses of the tumbling tide, the small craft jumbled and tossing along the shore, the motionless buildings in the driving mist, the broad ferry-boats pitching ponderously at anchor, the vast landing-stages heaving up and down and smothered in sprays. The next gust seemed to blow all this away. The air was full of flying water. There was a fierce purpose in the gale, a furious earnestness in the screech of the wind, in the brutal tumult of earth and sky, that seemed directed at him, and made him hold his breath in awe. He stood still. It seemed to him he was whirled around.

He was jostled. 'Man the cutter!' Boys rushed past him. A coaster running in for shelter had crashed through a schooner at anchor, and one of the ship's instructors had seen the accident. A mob of boys clambered on the rails, clustered round the davits. 'Collision. Just ahead of us. Mr Symons saw it.' A push made him stagger against the mizzen-mast, and he caught hold of a rope. The old training-ship chained to her moorings quivered all over, bowing gently head to wind, and with her scanty rigging humming in a deep bass the breathless song of her youth at sea. 'Lower away!' He saw the boat, manned, drop swiftly below the rail, and rushed after her. He heard a splash. 'Let go; clear the falls!' He learned over. The river alongside seethed in frothy streaks. The cutter could be seen in the falling darkness under the spell of tide and wind, that for a moment held her bound, and tossing abreast of the ship. A yelling voice in her reached him faintly: 'Keep stroke, you young whelps, if you want to save anybody! Keep stroke!' And suddenly she lifted high her bow, and, leaping with raised oars over a wave, broke the spell cast upon her by the wind and tide.

Jim felt his shoulder gripped firmly. 'Too late, youngster.' The captain of the ship laid a restraining hand on that boy, who seemed on the point of leaping overboard, and Jim looked up with the pain of conscious defeat in his eyes. The captain smiled sympathetically. 'Better luck next time. This will teach you to be smart.'

A shrill cheer greeted the cutter. She came dancing back half full of water, and with two exhausted men washing about on her bottom boards. The tumult and the menace of wind and sea now appeared very contemptible to Jim, increasing the regret of his awe at their inefficient menace. Now he knew what to think of it. It seemed to him he cared nothing for the gale. He could affront greater perils. He would do so – better than anybody. Not a particle of fear was left. Nevertheless he brooded that evening while the bowman of the cutter – a boy with a face like a girl's and big grey eyes – was the hero of the lower deck. Eager questioners crowded round him. He narrated: 'I just saw his head bobbing, and I dashed my boat-hook in the water. It caught in his breeches and I nearly went overboard, as I thought

I would, only old Symons let go the tiller and grabbed my legs – the boat nearly swamped. Old Symons is a fine old chap. I don't mind a bit him being grumpy with us. He swore at me all the time he held my leg, but that was only his way of telling me to stick to the boat-hook. Old Symons is awfully excitable – isn't he? No – not the little fair chap – the other, the big one with a beard. When we pulled him in he groaned, "Oh, my leg! oh, my leg!" and turned up his eyes. Fancy such a big chap fainting like a girl. Would any of you fellows faint for a jab with a boat-hook? – I wouldn't. It went into his leg so far.' He showed the boat-hook, which he had carried below for the purpose, and produced a sensation. 'No, silly! It was not his flesh that held him – his breeches did. Lots of blood, of course.'

Jim thought it a pitiful display of vanity. The gale had ministered to a heroism as spurious as its own pretence of terror. He felt angry with the brutal tumult of earth and sky for taking him unawares and checking unfairly a generous readiness for narrow escapes. Otherwise he was rather glad he had not gone into the cutter, since a lower achievement had served the turn. He had enlarged his knowledge more than those who had done the work. When all men flinched, then – he felt sure – he alone would know how to deal with the spurious menace of wind and seas. He knew what to think of it. Seen dispassionately, it seemed contemptible. He could detect no trace of emotion in himself, and the final effect of a staggering event was that, unnoticed and apart from the noisy crowd of boys, he exulted with fresh certitude in his avidity for adventure, and in a sense of many-sided courage.

CHAPTER 2

After two years of training he went to sea, and entering the regions so well known to his imagination, found them strangely barren of adventure. He made many voyages. He knew the magic monotony of existence between sky and water: he had to bear the criticism of men, the exactions of the sea, and the prosaic severity of the daily task that gives bread – but whose only reward is in the perfect love of the work. This reward eluded him. Yet he could not go back, because there is nothing more enticing, disenchanting, and enslaving than the life at sea. Besides, his prospects were good. He was gentlemanly, steady, tractable, with a thorough knowledge of his duties; and in time, when yet very young, he became chief mate of a fine ship, without ever having been tested by those events of the sea that show in the light of day the inner worth of a man, the edge of his temper, and the fibre of his stuff; that reveal the quality of his resistance and the secret truth of his pretences, not only to others but also to himself.

Only once in all that time he had again the glimpse of the earnestness in the anger of the sea. That truth is not so often made apparent as people might think. There are many shades in the danger of adventures and gales, and it is only now and then that there appears on the face of facts a sinister violence of intention – that indefinable something which forces it upon the mind and the heart of a man, that this complication of accidents or these elemental furies are coming at him with a purpose of malice, with a strength beyond control, with an unbridled cruelty that means to tear out of him his hope and his fear, the pain of his fatigue and his longing for rest: which means to smash, to destroy, to annihilate all he has seen, known, loved, enjoyed, or hated; all that is priceless and necessary – the sunshine, the memories, the future, – which means to sweep the whole precious world utterly away from his sight by the simple and appalling act of taking his life.

Jim, disabled by a falling spar at the beginning of a week of which his Scottish captain used to say afterwards, 'Man! it's a pairfect meeracle to me how she lived through it!', spent many days stretched on his back, dazed, battered, hopeless, and tormented as if at the bottom of an abyss of unrest. He did not care what the end would be, and in his lucid moments over-valued his indifference. The danger, when not seen, has the imperfect vagueness of human thought. The fear grows shadowy; and Imagination, the enemy of men, the father of all terrors, unstimulated, sinks to rest in the dullness of exhausted emotion. Jim saw nothing but the disorder of his tossed cabin. He lay there battered down in the midst of a small devastation, and felt secretly glad he had not to go on deck. But now and again an uncon-trollable rush of anguish would grip him bodily, make him gasp and writhe under the blankets, and then the unintelligent brutality of an existence liable to the agony of such sensations filled him with a despairing desire to escape at any cost. Then fine weather returned, and he thought no more about it.

His lameness, however, persisted, and when the ship arrived at an Eastern port he had to go to the hospital. His recovery was slow, and he was left behind.

There were only two other patients in the white men's ward: the purser of a gunboat, who had broken his leg falling down a hatchway; and a kind of railway contractor from a neighbouring province, afflicted by some mysterious tropical disease, who held the doctor for an ass, and indulged in secret debaucheries of patent medicine which his Tamil servant used to smuggle in with unwearied devotion. They told each other the story of their lives, played cards a little, or, yawning and in pyjamas, lounged through the day in easy-chairs without saying a word. The hospital stood on a hill, and a gentle breeze entering through the windows, always flung wide open, brought into the bare room the softness of the sky, the langour of the earth, the bewitching breath of the Eastern waters. There were perfumes in it, suggestions of infinite repose, the gift of endless dreams. Jim looked every day over the thickets of gardens, beyond the roofs of the town, over the fronds of palms growing on the shore, at that roadstead which is a thoroughfare to the East, – at the roadstead, dotted by garlanded islets, lighted by festal sunshine, its ships like toys, its brilliant activity resembling a holiday pageant, with the eternal serenity of the Eastern sky overhead and the smiling peace of the Eastern seas possessing the space as far as the horizon.

Directly he could walk without a stick, he descended into the town to look for some opportunity to get home. Nothing offered just then, and, while waiting, he associated naturally with the men of his calling in the port. These were of two kinds. Some, very few and seen there but seldom, led mysterious lives, had preserved an undefaced energy with the temper of buccaneers and the eyes of dreamers. They appeared to live in a crazy maze of plans, hopes, dangers, enterprises, ahead of civilization, in the dark places of the sea; and their death was the only event of their fantastic existence that seemed to have a reasonable certitude of achievement. The majority were men who, like himself, thrown there by some accident, had remained as officers of country ships. They had now a horror of the home service, with its harder conditions, severer view of duty, and the hazard of stormy oceans. They were attuned to the eternal peace of Eastern sky and sea. They loved short passages, good deck-chairs, large native crews, and the distinction of being white. They shuddered at the thought of hard work, and led precariously easy lives, always on the verge of dismissal, always on the verge of engagement, serving Chinamen, Arabs, half-castes – would have served the devil himself had he made it easy enough. They talked everlastingly of turns of luck; how So-and-so got charge of a boat on the coast of China – a soft thing; how this one had an easy billet in Japan somewhere, and that one was doing well in the Siamese navy; and in all they said – in their actions, in their looks, in their persons – could be detected the soft spot, the place of decay, the determination to lounge safely through existence.

To Jim that gossiping crowd, viewed as seamen, seemed at first more unsubstantial than so many shadows. But at length he found a fascination in the sight of those men, in their appearance of doing so well on such a small allowance of danger and toil. In time, beside the original disdain there grew up slowly another sentiment; and suddenly, giving up the idea of going home, he took a berth as chief mate of the *Patna*.

The *Patna* was a local steamer as old as the hills, lean like a greyhound, and eaten up with rust worse than a condemned water-tank. She was owned by a Chinaman, chartered by an Arab, and commanded by a sort of renegade New South Wales German, very anxious to curse publicly his native country, but who, apparently on the strength of Bismark's victorious policy, brutalized all those he was not afraid of, and wore a 'blood-and-iron' air, combined with a purple nose and a red moustache. After she had been painted outside and whitewashed inside, eight hundred pilgrims (more or less) were driven on board of her as she lay with steam up alongside a wooden jetty.

They streamed abroad over three gangways, they streamed in urged by faith and the hope of paradise, they streamed in with a continuous tramp and shuffle of bare feet, without a word, a murmur, or a look back; and when clear of confining rails spread on all sides over the deck, flowed forward and aft, overflowed down the yawning hatchways, filled the inner recesses of the ship – like water filling a cistern, like water flowing into crevices and crannies, like water rising silently even with the rim. Eight hundred men and women with faith and hopes, with affections and memories, they had collected there, coming from north and south and from the outskirts of the East, after treading the jungle paths, descending the rivers, coasting in praus along the shallows, crossing in small canoes from island to island, passing through suffering, meeting strange sights, beset by strange fears, upheld by one desire. They came from solitary huts in the wilderness, from populous campongs, from villages by the sea. At the call of an idea they had left their forests, their clearings, the protection of their rulers, their prosperity, their poverty, the surroundings of their youth, and the graves of their fathers. They came covered with dust, with sweat, with grime, with rags – the strong men at the head of family parties, the lean old men pressing forward without hope of return; young boys with fearless eyes glancing curiously, shy little girls with tumbled long hair; the timid women muffled up and clasping to their breasts, wrapped in loose ends of soiled head-cloths, their sleeping babies, the unconscious pilgrims of an exacting belief.

'Look at dese cattle,' said the German skipper to his new chief mate.

An Arab, the leader of that pious voyage, came last. He walked slowly aboard, handsome and grave in his white gown and large turban. A string of servants followed, loaded with his luggage; the *Patna* cast off and backed away from the wharf.

She was headed between two small islets, crossed obliquely the anchoring-ground of sailing-ships, swung through half a circle in the shadow of a hill, then ranged close to a ledge of foaming reefs. The Arab, standing up aft, recited aloud the prayer of travellers by sea. He invoked the favour of the Most High upon that journey, implored His blessing on men's toil and on the secret purposes of their hearts; the steamer pounded in the dusk the calm water of the Strait; and far astern of the pilgrim ship a screw-pile lighthouse, planted by unbelievers on a treacherous shoal, seemed to wink at her its eye of flame, as if in derision of her errand of faith.

She cleared the Strait, crossed the bay, continued on her way through the 'One-degree' passage. She held on straight for the Red Sea under a serene sky, under a sky scorching and unclouded, enveloped in a fulgor of sunshine that killed all thought, oppressed the heart, withered all impulses of strength and energy. And under the sinister splendour of that sky the sea, blue and profound, remained still, without a stir, without a ripple, without a wrinkle – viscous, stagnant, dead. The *Patna*, with a slight hiss, passed over that plain luminous and smooth, unrolled a black ribbon of smoke across the sky, left behind her on the water a white ribbon of foam that vanished at once, like the phantom of a track drawn upon a lifeless sea by the phantom of a steamer.

Every morning the sun, as if keeping pace in his revolutions with the progress of the pilgrimage, emerged with a silent burst of light at exactly the same distance astern of the ship, caught up with her at noon, pouring the concentrated fire of his rays on the pious purposes of the men, glided past on his descent, and sank mysteriously into the sea evening after evening, preserving the same distance ahead of her advancing bows. The five whites on board lived amidships, isolated from the human cargo. The awnings covered the deck with a white roof from stem to stern, and a faint hum, a low murmur of sad voices, alone revealed the presence of a crowd of people upon the great blaze of the ocean. Such were the days, still, hot, heavy, disappearing one by one into the past, as if falling into an abyss for ever open in the wake of the ship; and the ship, lonely under a wisp of smoke, held on her steadfast way black and smouldering in a luminous immensity, as if scorched by a flame flicked at her from a heaven without pity.

The nights descended on her like a benediction.

CHAPTER 3

A marvellous stillness pervaded the world, and the stars, together with the serenity of their rays, seemed to shed upon the earth the assurance of everlasting security. The young moon recurved, and shining low in the west, was like a slender shaving thrown up from a bar of gold, and the Arabian Sea, smooth and cool to the eye like a sheet of ice, extended its perfect level to the perfect circle of a dark horizon. The propeller turned without a check, as though its beat had been part of the scheme of a safe universe; and on each side of the *Patna* two deep folds of water, permanent and sombre on the unwrinkled shimmer, enclosed within their straight and diverging ridges a few white swirls of foam bursting in a low hiss, a few wavelets, a few ripples, a few undulations that, left behind, agitated the surface of the sea for an instant after the passage of the ship, subsided splashing gently, calmed down at last into the circular stillness of water and sky with the black speck of the moving hull remaining everlastingly in its centre.

Jim on the bridge was penetrated by the great certitude of unbounded safety and peace that could be read on the silent aspect of nature like the certitude of fostering love upon the placid tenderness of a mother's face. Below the roof awnings, surrendered to the wisdom of white men and to their courage, trusting the power of their unbelief and the iron shell of their fire-ship, the pilgrims of an exacting faith slept on mats, on blankets, on bare planks, on every deck, in all the dark corners, wrapped in dyed cloths, muffled in soiled rags, with their heads resting on small bundles, with their faces pressed to bent forearms: the men, the women, the children; the old with the young, the decrepit with the lusty – all equal before sleep, death's brother.

A draught of air, fanned from forward by the speed of the ship, passed steadily through the long gloom between the high bulwarks, swept over the rows of prone bodies; a few dim flames in globe-lamps were hung short here and there under the ridge-poles, and in the blurred circles of light thrown down and trembling slightly to the unceasing vibration of the ship appeared a chin upturned, two closed eyelids, a dark hand with silver rings, a meagre limb draped in a torn covering, a head bent back, a naked foot, a throat bared and stretched as if offering itself to the knife. The well-to-do had made for their families shelters with heavy boxes and dusty mats; the poor reposed side by side with all they had on earth tied up in a rag under their heads; the lone old men slept, with drawn-up legs, upon their prayer-carpets, with their hands over their ears and one elbow on each side of the face; a father, his shoulders up and his knees under his forehead, dozed dejectedly by a boy who slept on his back with tousled hair and one arm commandingly extended; a woman covered from head to foot, like a corpse, with a piece of white sheeting, had a naked child in the hollow of each arm; the Arab's belongings, piled right aft, made a heavy mound of broken outlines, with a cargo-lamp swung above and a great confusion of vague forms behind: gleams of paunchy brass pots, the foot-rest of a deck-chair, blades of spears, the straight scabbard of an old sword leaning against a heap of pillows, the spout of a tin coffee-pot. The patent log on the taffrail periodically rang a single tinkling stroke for every mile traversed on an errand of faith. Above the mass of sleepers a faint and patient sigh at times floated, the exhalation of a troubled dream; and short metallic clangs bursting out suddenly in the depths of the ship, the harsh scrape of a shovel, the violent slam of a furnace-door, exploded brutally, as if the man handling the mysterious things below had their breasts full of fierce anger: while the slim high hull of the steamer went on evenly ahead, without a sway of her bare masts, cleaving continuously the great calm of the waters under the inaccessible serenity of the sky.

Jim paced athwart, and his footsteps in the vast silence were loud to his own ears, as if echoed by the watchful stars: his eyes roaming about the line of the horizon, seemed to gaze hungrily into the unattainable, and did not see the shadow of the coming event. The only shadow on the sea was the shadow of the black smoke pouring heavily from the funnel its immense streamer, whose end was constantly dissolving in the air. Two Malays, silent and almost motionless, steered, one on each side of the wheel, whose brass rim shone fragmentarily in the oval of light thrown out by the binnacle. Now and then a hand, with black fingers alternately letting go and catching hold of revolving spokes, appeared in the illumined part; the links of wheel-chains ground heavily in the grooves of the barrel. Jim would glance at the compass, would glance around the unattainable horizon, would stretch himself till his joints cracked with a leisurely twist of the body, in the very excess of well-being; and, as if made audacious by the invincible aspect of the peace, he felt he cared for nothing that could happen to him to the end of his days. From time to time he glanced idly at a chart pegged out with four drawing-pins on a low three-legged table abaft the steering-gear case. The sheet of paper portraying the depths of the sea presented a shiny surface under the light of a bull's eye lamp lashed to a stanchion, a surface as level and smooth as the glimmering surface of the waters. Parallel rulers with a pair of dividers reposed on it; the ship's position at last noon was marked with a small black cross, and the straight pencil-line drawn firmly as far as Perim figured the course of the ship – the path of souls towards the holy place, the promise of salvation, the reward of eternal life – while the pencil with its sharp end touching the Somali coast lay round and still like a naked ship's spar floating in the pool of a sheltered dock. 'How steady she goes,' thought Jim with wonder, with something like gratitude for this high peace of ease and sky. At such times his thoughts would be full of valorous deeds: he loved these dreams and the success of his imaginary achievements. They were the best parts of life, its secret truth, its hidden reality. They had a gorgeous virility, the charm of vagueness, they passed before him with a heroic tread; they carried his soul away with them and made it drunk with the divine philtre of an unbounded confidence in itself. There was nothing he could not face. He was so pleased with the idea that he smiled, keeping perfunctorily his eyes ahead; and when he happened to glance back he saw the white streak of the wake drawn as straight by the ship's keel upon the sea as the black line drawn by the pencil upon the chart.

The ash-buckets racketed, clanking up and down the stokehold ventilators, and this tin-pot clatter warned him the end of his watch was near. He sighed with content, with regret as well at having to part from that serenity which fostered the adventurous freedom of his thoughts. He was a little sleepy, too, and felt a pleasurable languor running through every limb as though all the blood in his body had turned to warm milk. His skipper had come up noiselessly, in pyjamas and with his sleeping-jacket flung wide open. Red of face, only half awake, the left eye partly closed, the right staring stupid and glassy, he hung his big head over the chart and scratched his ribs sleepily. There was something obscene in the sight of his naked flesh. His bared breast glistened soft and greasy as though he had sweated out his fat in his sleep. He pronounced a professional remark in a voice harsh and dead, resembling the rasping sound of a wood-file on the edge of a plank; the fold of his double chin hung like a bag triced up close under the hinge of his jaw. Jim started, and his answer was full of deference; but the odious and fleshy figure, as though seen for the first time in a revealing moment, fixed itself in his memory for ever as the incarnation of everything vile and base that lurks in the world we love: in our own hearts we trust for our salvation in the men that surround us, in the sights that fill our eyes, in the sounds that fill our ears, and in the air that fills our lungs.

The thin gold shaving of the moon floating slowly downwards had lost itself on the darkened surface of the waters, and the eternity beyond the sky seemed to come down nearer to the earth, with the augmented glitter of the stars, with the more profound sombreness in the lustre of the half-transparent dome covering the flat disc of an opaque sea. The ship moved so smoothly that her onward motion was imperceptible to the senses of men, as though she had been a crowded planet speeding through the dark spaces of ether behind the swarm of suns, in the apalling and calm solitudes awaiting the breath of future creations. 'Hot is no name for it down below,' said a voice.

Jim smiled without looking round. The skipper presented an unmoved breadth of back: it was the renegade's trick to appear pointedly unaware of your existence unless it suited his purpose to turn at you with a devouring glare before he let loose a torrent of foamy, abusive jargon that came like a gush from a sewer. Now he emitted only a sulky grunt; the second engineer at the head of the bridge-ladder, kneading with damp palms a dirty sweat-rag, unabashed, continued the tale of his complaints. The sailors had a good time of it up here, and what was the use of them in the world he would be blowed if he could see. The poor devils of engineers had to get the ship along anyhow, and they could very well do the rest too; by gosh they – 'Shut up,' growled the German stolidly. 'Oh yes! Shut up – and when anything goes wrong you fly to us, don't you?' went on the other. He was more than half cooked, he expected; but anyway, now, he did not mind how much he sinned, because these last three days he had passed through a fine course of training for the place where the bad boys go when they die – b'gosh, he had – besides being made jolly well deaf by the blasted racket below. The durned, compound, surface-condensing, rotten scrapheap rattled and banged down there like an old deck-winch, only more so; and what made him risk his life every night and day that God made amongst the refuse of a breaking-up yard flying round at fifty-seven revolutions, was more than *he* could tell. He must have been born reckless, b'gosh. He . . . 'Where did you get drink?' inquired the German, very savage, but motionless in the light of the binnacle, like a clumsy effigy of a man cut out of a block of fat. Jim went on smiling at the retreating horizon; his heart was full of generous impulses, and his thought was contemplating his own superiority. 'Drink!' repeated the engineer with amiable scorn: he was hanging on with both hands to the rail, a shadowy figure with flexible legs. 'Not from you, captain. You're far too mean, b'gosh. You would let a good man die sooner than give him a drop of schnapps. That's what you Germans call economy. Penny wise, pound foolish.' He became sentimental. The chief had given him a four-finger nip about ten o'clock – 'only one, s'elp me!' – good old chief; but as to getting the old fraud out of this bunk – a five-ton crane couldn't do it. Not it. Not to-night anyhow. He was sleeping sweetly like a little child, with a bottle of prime brandy under his pillow. From the thick throat of the commander of the *Patna* came a low rumble, on which the sound of the word *schwein* fluttered high and low like a capricious feather in a faint stir of air. He and the chief engineer had been cronies for a good few years – serving the same jovial, crafty, old Chinaman, with horn-rimmed goggles and strings of red silk plaited into the venerable grey hairs of his pigtail. The quay-side opinion in the *Patna*'s home-port was that these two in the way of brazen peculation 'had done together pretty well everything you can think of'. Outwardly they were badly matched: one dull-eyed, malevolent, and of soft fleshy curves; the other lean, all hollows, with a head long and bony like the head of an old horse, with sunken cheeks, with sunken temples, with an indifferent glazed glance of sunken eyes. He had been stranded out East somewhere – in Canton, in Shanghai, or perhaps in Yokohama; he probably did not care to remember himself the exact locality, nor yet the cause of his shipwreck. He had been, in mercy to his youth, kicked quietly out of his ship twenty years ago or more, and it might have been so much worse for him that the memory of the episode had in it hardly a trace of misfortune. Then, steam navigation expanding in these seas and men of his craft being scarce at first, he had 'got on' after a sort. He was eager to let strangers know in a dismal mumble that he was 'an old stager out here'. When he moved, a skeleton seemed to sway loose in his clothes; his walk was mere wandering, and he was given to wander thus around the engine-room skylight, smoking, without relish, doctored tobacco in a brass bowl at the end of a cherrywood stem four feet long, with the imbecile gravity of a thinker evolving a system of philosophy from the hazy glimpse of a truth. He was usually anything but free with his private store of liquor; but on that night he had departed from his principles, so that his second, a weak-headed child of Wapping, what with the unexpectedness of the treat and the strength of the stuff, had become very happy, cheeky, and talkative. The fury of the New South Wales German was extreme; he puffed like an exhaust-pipe, and Jim, faintly amused by the scene, was impatient for the time when he could get below: the last ten minutes of the watch were irritating like a gun that hangs fire; those men did not belong to the world of heroic adventure; they weren't bad chaps though. Even the skipper himself ... His gorge rose at the mass of panting flesh from which issued gurgling mutters, a cloudy trickle of filthy expressions; but he was too pleasurably languid to dislike actively this or any other thing. The quality of these men did not matter; he rubbed shoulders with them, but they could not touch him; he shared the air they breathed, but he was different ... Would the skipper go for the engineer? ... The life was easy and he was too sure of himself – too sure of himself to ... The line dividing his meditation from a surreptitious doze on his feet was thinner than a thread in a spider's web.

The second engineer was coming by easy transitions to the consideration of his finances and of his courage.

'Who's drunk? I? No, no, captain! That won't do. You ought to know by this time the chief ain't free-hearted enough to make a sparrow drunk, b'gosh. I've never been the worse for liquor in my life; the stuff ain't made yet that would make *me* drunk. I could drink liquid fire against your whisky peg for peg, b'gosh, and keep as cool as a cucumber. If I thought I was drunk I would jump overboard – do away with myself, b'gosh. I would! Straight! And I won't go off the bridge. Where do you expect me to take the air on a night like this, eh? On deck amongst that vermin down there? Likely – ain't it! And I am not afraid of anything you can do.'

The German lifted two heavy fists to heaven and shook them a little without a word.

'I don't know what fear is,' pursued the engineer, with the enthusiasm of sincere conviction. 'I am not afraid of doing all the bloomin' work in this rotten hooker, b'gosh! And a jolly good thing for you that there are some of us about the world that aren't afraid of their lives, or where would you be – you and this old thing here with her plates like brown paper – brown paper, s'elp me? It's all very fine for you – you get a power of pieces out of her one way and another; but what about me – what do I get? A measly hundred and fifty dollars a month and find yourself. I wish to ask you respectfully – respectfully, mind – who wouldn't chuck a dratted job like this? 'Tain't safe, s'elp me, it ain't! Only I am one of them fearless fellows. ...'

He let go the rail and made ample gestures as if demonstrating in the air the shape and extent of his valour; his thin voice darted in prolonged squeaks upon the sea, he tiptoed back and forth for the better emphasis of utterance, and suddenly pitched down head-first as though he had been clubbed from behind. He said 'Damn!' as he tumbled; an instant of silence followed upon his screeching: Jim and the skipper staggered forward by common accord, and catching themselves up, stood very stiff and still gazing, amazed, at the undisturbed level of the sea. Then they looked upwards at the stars.

What had happened? The wheezy thump of the engines went on. Had the earth been checked in her course? They could not understand; and suddenly the calm sea, the sky without a cloud, appeared formidably insecure in their immobility, as it poised on the brow of yawning destruction. The engineer rebounded vertically full length and collapsed again into a vague heap. This heap said 'What's that?' in the muffled accents of profound grief. A faint noise as of thunder, of thunder infinitely remote, less than a sound, hardly more than a vibration, passed slowly, and the ship quivered in response, as if the thunder had growled deep down in the water. The eyes of the two Malays at the wheel glittered towards the white men, but their dark hands remained closed on the spokes. The sharp hull driving on its way seemed to rise a few inches in succession through its whole length, as though it had become pliable, and settled down again rigidly to its work of cleaving the smooth surface of the sea. Its quivering stopped, and the faint noise of thunder ceased all at once, as though the ship had steamed across a narrow belt of vibrating water and of humming air.

CHAPTER 4

A month or so afterwards, when Jim, in answer to pointed questions, tried to tell honestly the truth of this experience, he said, speaking of the ship: 'She went over whatever it was as easy as a snake crawling over a stick.' The illustration was good: the questions were aiming at facts, and the official Inquiry was being held in the police court of an Eastern port. He stood elevated in the witness-box, with burning cheeks in a cool, lofty room: the big framework of punkahs moved gently to and fro high above his head, and from below many eyes were looking at him out of dark faces, out of white faces, out of red faces, out of faces attentive, spellbound, as if all these people sitting in orderly rows upon narrow benches had been enslaved by the fascination of his voice. It was very loud, it rang startling in his own ears, it was the only sound audible in the world, for the terribly distinct questions that extorted his answers seemed to shape themselves in anguish and pain within his breast – came to him poignant and silent like the terrible questioning of one's conscience. Outside the court the sun blazed – within was the wind of great punkahs that made you shiver, the shame that made you burn, the attentive eyes whose glance stabbed. The face of the presiding magistrate, clean shaved and impassable, looked at him deadly pale between the red faces of the two nautical assessors. The light of a broad window under the ceiling fell from above on the heads and shoulders of the three men, and they were fiercely distinct in the half-light of the big court-room where the audience seemed composed of staring shadows. They wanted facts. Facts! They demanded facts from him, as if facts could explain anything!

'After you had concluded you had collided with something floating awash, say a water-logged wreck, you were ordered by your captain to go forward

and ascertain if there was any damage done. Did you think it likely from
the force of the blow?' asked the assessor sitting to the left. He had a thin
horseshoe beard, salient cheek-bones and with both elbows on the desk
clasped his rugged hands before his face, looking at Jim with thoughtful
blue eyes; the other, a heavy, scornful man, thrown back in his seat, his left
arm extended full length, drummed delicately with his finger-tips on a
blotting-pad: in the middle the magistrate upright in the roomy arm-chair,
his head inclined slightly on the shoulder, had his arms crossed on his breast
and a few flowers in a glass vase by the side of his inkstand.

'I did not,' said Jim. 'I was told to call no one and to make no noise for
fear of creating a panic. I thought the precaution reasonable. I took one of
the lamps that were hung under the awnings and went forward. After
opening the forepeak hatch I heard splashing in there. I lowered then the
lamp the whole drift of its lanyard, and saw that the forepeak was more
than half full of water already. I knew then there must be a big hole below
the waterline.' He paused.

'Yes,' said the big assessor, with a dreamy smile at the blotting-pad; his
fingers played incessantly, touching the paper without noise.

'I did not think of danger just then. I might have been a little startled: all
this happened in such a quiet way and so very suddenly. I knew there was
no other bulkhead in the ship but the collision bulkhead separating the
forepeak from the forehold. I went back to tell the captain. I came upon the
second engineer getting up at the foot of the bridge-ladder: he seemed dazed,
and told me he thought his left arm was broken; he had slipped on the top
step when getting down while I was forward. He exclaimed, "My God!
That rotten bulkhead 'll give way in a minute, and the damned thing will
go down under us like a lump of lead." He pushed me away with his right
arm and ran before me up the ladder, shouting as he climbed. His left arm
hung by his side. I followed up in time to see the captain rush at him and
knock him down flat on his back. He did not strike him again: he stood
bending over him and speaking angrily but quite low. I fancy he was asking
him why the devil he didn't go and stop the engines, instead of making a
row about it on deck. I heard him say, "Get up! Run! Fly!" He swore also.
The engineer slid down the starboard ladder and bolted round the skylight
to the engine-room companion which was on the port-side. He moaned as
he ran.T...'

He spoke slowly; he remembered swiftly and with extreme vividness; he
could have reproduced like an echo the moaning of the engineer for the better
information of these men who wanted facts. After his first feeling of revolt
he had come round to the view that only a meticulous precision of statement
would bring out the true horror behind the appalling face of things. The
facts those men were so eager to know had been visible, tangible, open to the
senses, occupying their place in space and time, requiring for their existence
a fourteen-hundred-ton steamer and twenty-seven minutes by the watch;
they made a whole that had features, shades of expression, a complicated
aspect that could be remembered by the eye, and something else besides,
something invisible, a directing spirit of perdition that dwelt within, like a
malevolent soul in a detestable body. He was anxious to make this clear.

This had not been a common affair, everything in it had been of the utmost importance, and fortunately he remembered everything. He wanted to go on talking for truth's sake, perhaps for his own sake also; and while his utterance was deliberate, his mind positively flew round and round the serried circle of facts that had surged up all about him to cut him off from the rest of his kind: it was like a creature that, finding itself imprisoned within an enclosure of high stakes, dashes round and round, distracted in the night, trying to find a weak spot, a crevice, a place to scale, some opening through which it may squeeze itself and escape. This awful activity of mind made him hesitate at times in his speech. T . . .

'The captain kept on moving here and there on the bridge; he seemed calm enough, only he stumbled several times; and once as I stood speaking to him he walked right into me as though he had been stone-blind. He made no definite answer to what I had to tell. He mumbled to himself; all I heard of it were a few words that sounded like "confounded steam!" and "infernal steam" – something about steam. I thought. . . .'

He was becoming irrelevant; a question to the point cut short his speech, like a pang of pain, and he felt extremely discouraged and weary. He was coming to that, he was coming to that – and now, checked brutally, he had to answer by yes or no. He answered truthfully by a curt 'Yes, I did'; and fair of face, big of frame, with young, gloomy eyes, he held his shoulders upright above the box while his soul writhed within him. He was made to answer another question so much to the point and so useless, then waited again. His mouth was tastelessly dry as though he had been eating dust, then salt and bitter as after a drink of sea-water. He wiped his damp forehead, passed his tongue over parched lips, felt a shiver run down his back. The big assessor had dropped his eyelids, and drummed on without a sound, careless and mournful; the eyes of the other above the sunburnt, clasped fingers seemed to glow with kindliness; the magistrate had swayed forwards; his pale face hovered near the flowers, and then dropping sideways over the arm of his chair, he rested his temple in the palm of his hand. The wind of the punkahs eddied down on the heads, on the dark-faced natives wound about in voluminous draperies, on the Europeans sitting together very hot and in drill suits that seemed to fit them as close as their skins, and holding their round pith hats on their knees; while gliding along the walls the court peons, buttoned tight in long white coats, flitted rapidly to and fro, running on bare toes, red-sashed, red turban on head, as noiseless as ghosts, and on the alert like so many retrievers.

Jim's eyes, wandering in the intervals of his answers, rested upon a white man who sat apart from the others, with his face worn and clouded, but with quiet eyes that glanced straight, interested and clear. Jim answered another question and was tempted to cry out, 'What's the good of this! what's the good!' He tapped with his foot slightly, bit his lip, and looked away over the heads. He met the eyes of the white man. The glance directed at him was not the fascinated stare of the others. It was an act of intelligent volition. Jim between two questions forgot himself so far as to find leisure for a thought. This fellow – ran the thought – looks at me as though he could see somebody or something past my shoulder. He had come across that man before – in the street perhaps. He was positive he had never spoken to him. For days, for many days, he had spoken to no one, but had held silent, incoherent, and endless converse with himself, like a prisoner alone in his cell or like a wayfarer lost in a wilderness. At present he was answering questions that did not matter though they had a purpose, but he doubted whether he would ever again speak out as long as he lived. The sound of his own truthful statements confirmed his deliberate opinion that speech was of no use to him any longer. That man there seemed to be aware of his hopeless difficulty. Jim looked at him, then turned away resolutely, as after a final parting.

And later on, many times, in distant parts of the world, Marlow showed himself willing to remember Jim, to remember him at length, in detail and audibly.

Perhaps it would be after dinner, on a veranda draped in motionless foliage and crowned with flowers, in the deep dusk speckled by fiery cigar-ends. The elongated bulk of each cane-chair harboured a silent listener. Now and then a small red glow would move abruptly, and expanding light up the fingers of a languid hand, part of a face in profound repose, or flash a crimson gleam into a pair of pensive eyes overshadowed by a fragment of an unruffled forehead; and with the very first word uttered Marlow's body, extended at rest in the seat, would become very still, as though his spirit had winged its way back into the lapse of time and were speaking through his lips from the past.

CHAPTER 5

'Oh yes. I attended the inquiry,' he would say, 'and to this day I haven't left off wondering why I went. I am willing to believe each of us has a guardian angel, if you fellows will concede to me that each of us has a familiar devil as well. I want you to own up, because I don't like to feel exceptional in any way, and I know I have him – the devil, I mean. I haven't seen him, of course, but I go upon circumstantial evidence. He is there right enough, and, being malicious, he lets me in for that kind of thing. What kind of thing, you ask? Why, the inquiry thing, the yellow-dog thing – you wouldn't think a mangy, native tyke would be allowed to trip up people in the veranda of a magistrate's court, would you? – the kind of thing that by devious, unexpected, truly diabolical ways causes me to run up against men with soft spots, with hard spots, with hidden plague spots, by Jove! and loosens their tongues at the sight of me for their infernal confidences; as though, forsooth, I had no confidences to make to myself, as though – God help me! – I didn't have enough confidential information about myself to harrow my own soul till the end of my appointed time. And what I have done to be thus favoured I want to know. I declare I am as full of my own concerns as the next man, and I have as much memory as the average pilgrim in this valley, so you see I am not particularly fit to be a receptacle of confessions. Then why? Can't tell – unless it be to make time pass away after dinner. Charley, my dear chap, your dinner was extremely good, and in consequence these men here look upon a quiet rubber as a tumultuous occupation. They wallow in your good chairs and think to themselves, "Hang exertion. Let that Marlow talk."

'Talk! So be it. And it's easy enough to talk of Master Jim, after a good spread, two hundred feet above the sea-level, with a box of decent cigars handy, on a blessed evening of freshness and starlight that would make the best of us forget we are only on sufferance here and got to pick our way in cross lights, watching every precious minute and every irremediable step, trusting we shall manage yet to go out decently in the end – but not so sure of it after all – and with dashed little help to expect from those we touch elbows with right and left. Of course there are men here and there to whom the whole of life is like an after-dinner hour with a cigar; easy, pleasant, empty, perhaps enlivened by some fable of strife to be forgotten before the end is told – before the end is told – even if there happens to be any end to it.

'My eyes met his for the first time at that inquiry. You must know that everybody connected in any way with the sea was there, because the affair had been notorious for days, ever since that mysterious cable message came from Aden to start us all cackling. I say mysterious, because it was so in a sense though it contained a naked fact, about as naked and ugly as a fact can well be. The whole waterside talked of nothing else. First thing in the morning as I was dressing in my state-room, I would hear through the bulkhead my Parsee Dubash jabbering about the *Patna* with the steward, while he drank a cup of tea, by favour, in the pantry. No sooner on shore I would meet some acquaintance, and the first remark would be, "Did you ever hear of anything to beat this?" and according to his kind the man would smile cynically, or look sad, or let out a swear or two. Complete strangers would accost each other familiarly, just for the sake of easing their minds on the subject: every confounded loafer in the town came in for a harvest of drinks over this affair: you heard of it in the harbour office, at every ship-broker's, at your agent's, from whites, from natives, from half-castes, from the very boatman squatting half-naked on the stone steps as you went up – by Jove! There was some indignation, not a few jokes, and no end of discussions as to what had become of them, you know. This went on for a couple of weeks or more, and the opinion that whatever was mysterious in this affair would turn out to be tragic as well, began to prevail, when one fine morning, as I was standing in the shade by the steps of the harbour office, I perceived four men walking towards me along the quay. I wondered for a while where that queer lot had sprung from, and suddenly, I may say, I shouted to myself, "Here they are!"

'There they were, sure enough, three of them as large as life, and one much larger of girth than any living man has a right to be, just landed with a good breakfast inside of them from an outward-bound Dale Line steamer that had come in about an hour after sunrise. There could be no mistake; I spotted the jolly skipper of the *Patna* at the first glance: the fattest man in the whole blessed tropical belt clear round that good old earth of ours. Moreover, nine months or so before, I had come across him in Samarang. His steamer was loading in the Roads, and he was abusing the tyrannical institutions of the German empire, and soaking himself in beer all day long and day after day in De Jongh's back-shop, till De Jongh, who charged a guilder for every bottle without as much as the quiver of an eyelid, would beckon me aside, and, with his little leathery face all puckered up, declare confidentially, "Business is business, but this man, captain, he make me very sick. Tfui!"

'I was looking at him from the shade. He was hurrying on a little in advance, and the sunlight beating on him brought out his bulk in a startling way. He made me think of a trained baby elephant walking on hind-legs. He was extravagantly gorgeous too – got up in a soiled sleeping-suit, bright green and deep orange vertical stripes, with a pair of ragged straw slippers on his bare feet, and somebody's cast-off pith hat, very dirty and two sizes too small for him, tied up with a manilla rope-yarn on the top of his big head. You understand a man like that hasn't the ghost of a chance when it comes to borrowing clothes. Very well. On he came in hot haste, without a look right or left, passed within three feet of me, and in the innocence of his heart went on pelting upstairs in the harbour office to make his deposition, or report, or whatever you like to call it.

'It appears he addressed himself in the first instance to the principal shipping-master. Archie Ruthvel had just come in, and, as his story goes, was about to begin his arduous day by giving a dressing-down to his chief clerk. Some of you might have known him – an obliging little Portuguese half-caste with a miserably skinny neck, and always on the hop to get something from the shipmasters in the way of eatables – a piece of salt pork, a bag of biscuits, a few potatoes, or what not. One voyage, I recollect, I tipped him a live sheep out of the remnant of my sea-stock: not that I wanted him to do anything for me – he couldn't, you know – but because his childlike belief in the sacred right to perquisites quite touched my heart. It was so strong as to be almost beautiful. The race – the two races rather – and the climate . . . However, never mind. I know where I have a friend for life.

'Well, Ruthvel says he was giving him a severe lecture – on official morality, I suppose – when he heard a kind of subdued commotion at his back, and turning his head he saw, in his own words, something round and enormous, resembling a sixteen-hundred-weight sugar-hogshead wrapped in striped flannelette, up-ended in the middle of the large floor space in the office. He declares he was so taken aback that for quite an appreciable time he did not realize the thing was alive, and sat still wondering for what purpose and by what means that object had been transported in front of his desk. The archway from the anteroom was crowded with punkah-pullers, sweepers, police peons, the coxswain and crew of the harbour steam-launch, all craning their necks and almost climbing on each other's backs. Quite a riot. By that time the fellow had managed to tug and jerk his hat clear off his head, and advanced in slight bows at Ruthvel, who told me the sight was so discomposing that for some time he listened quite unable to make out what that apparition wanted. It spoke in a voice harsh and lugubrious but intrepid, and little by little it dawned upon Archie that this was a development of the *Patna* case. He says that as soon as he understood who it was before him he felt quite unwell – Archie is so sympathetic and easily upset – but pulled himself together and shouted "Stop! I can't listen to you. You must go to the Master Attendant. I can't possibly listen to you. Captain Elliot is the man you want to see. This way, this way." He jumped up, ran round that long counter, pulled, shoved: the other let him, surprised but obedient at first, and only at the door of the private office some sort of animal instinct made him hang back and snort like a frightened bullock. "Look here! what's up? Let go! Look here!" Archie flung open the door without knocking. "The master of the *Patna*, sir," he shouts. "Go in, captain." He saw the old man lift his head from some writing so sharp that his nose-nippers fell off, banged the door to, and fled to his desk, where he had some papers waiting for his signature: but he says the row that burst out in there was so awful that he couldn't collect his senses sufficiently to remember the spelling of his own name. Archie's the most sensitive shipping-master in the two hemispheres. He declares he felt as though he had thrown a man to a hungry lion. No doubt the noise was great. I heard it down below, and I have every reason to believe it was heard clear across the Esplanade as far as the band-stand. Old father Elliot had a great stock of words and could shout – and didn't mind who he shouted at either. He would have shouted at the Viceroy himself. As he used to tell me: "I am as high as I can get; my pension is safe. I've a few pounds laid by, and if they don't like my notions of duty I would just as soon go home as not. I am an old man, and I have always spoken my mind. All I care for now is to see my girls married before I die." He was a little crazy on that point. His three daughters were awfully nice, though they resembled him amazingly, and on the mornings he woke up with a gloomy view of their matrimonial prospects the office would read it in his eye and tremble, because, they said, he was sure to have somebody for breakfast. However, that morning he did not eat the renegade, but, if I may be allowed to carry on the metaphor, chewed him up very small, so to speak, and – ah! ejected him again.

'Thus in a very few moments I saw his monstrous bulk descend in haste and stand still on the outer steps. He had stopped close to me for the purpose of profound meditation: his large purple cheeks quivered. He was biting his thumb, and after a while noticed me with a sidelong vexed look. The other three chaps that had landed with him made a little group waiting at some distance. There was a sallow-faced, mean little chap with his arm in a sling, and a long individual in a blue flannel coat, as dry as a chip and no stouter than a broomstick, with drooping grey moustaches, who looked about him with an air of jaunty imbecility. The third was an upstanding, broad-shouldered youth, with his hands in his pockets, turning his back on the other two who appeared to be talking together earnestly. He stared across the empty Esplanade. A ramshackle gharry, all dust and venetian blinds, pulled up short opposite the group, and the driver, throwing up his right foot over his knee, gave himself up to the critical examination of his toes. The young chap, making no movement, not even stirring his head, just stared into the sunshine. This was my first view of Jim. He looked as unconcerned and unapproachable as only the young can look. There he stood, clean-limbed, clean-faced, firm on his feet, as promising a boy as the sun ever shone on; and, looking at him, knowing all he knew and a little more too, I was as angry as though I had detected him trying to get something out of me by false pretences. He had no business to look so sound. I thought to myself – well, if this sort can go wrong like that ... and I felt as though I could fling down my hat and dance on it from sheer mortification, as I once saw the skipper of an Italian barque do because his duffer of a mate got into a mess with his anchors when making a flying moor in a roadstead full of ships. I asked myself, seeing him there apparently so much at ease – is he silly? is he callous? He seemed ready to start whistling a tune. And note, I did not care a rap about the behaviour of the other two. Their persons somehow fitted the tale that was public property, and was going to be the subject of an official inquiry. "That old mad rogue upstairs called me a hound," said the captain of the *Patna*. I can't tell whether he recognized me – I rather think he did; but at any rate our glances met. He glared – I smiled; hound was the very mildest epithet that had reached me through the open window. "Did he?" I said from some strange inability to hold my tongue. He nodded, bit his thumb again, swore under his breath: then lifting his head and looking at me with sullen and passionate impudence – "Bah! the Pacific is big, my friendt. You damned Englishmen can do your worst: I know where there's plenty room for a man like me: I am well aguaindt in Apia, in Honolulu, in ..." He paused reflectively, while without effort I could depict to myself the sort of people he was "aguaindt" with in those places. I won't make a secret of it that I had been "aguaindt" with not a few of that sort myself. There are times when a man must act as though life were equally sweet in any company. I've known such a time, and, what's more, I shan't now pretend to pull a long face over my necessity, because a good many of that bad company from want of moral – moral – what shall I say? – posture, or from some other equally profound cause, were twice as instructive and twenty times more amusing than the usual respectable thief of commerce you fellows ask to sit at your table without any real necessity – from habit, from cowardice, from good-nature, from a hundred sneaking and inadequate reasons.

' "You Englishmen are all rogues," went on my patriotic Flensborg or Stettin Australian, I really don't recollect now what decent little port on the shores of the Baltic was defiled by being the nest of that precious bird. "What are you to shout? Eh? You tell me? You no better than other people, and that old rogue he make Gottam fuss with me." His thick carcass trembled on its legs that were like a pair of pillars; it trembled from head to foot. "That's what you English always make – make a tam' fuss – for any little thing, because I was not born in your tam' country. Take away my certificate. Take it. I don't want the certificate. A man like me don't want your verfluchte certificate. I shpit on it." He spat. "I vill an Amerigan citizen begome," he cried, fretting and fuming and shuffling his feet as if to free his ankles from some invisible and mysterious grasp that would not let him get away from that spot. He made himself so warm that the top of his bullet head positively smoked. Nothing mysterious prevented me from going away: curiosity is the most obvious of sentiments, and it held me there to see the effect of a full information upon the young fellow who, hands in pockets, and turning his back upon the sidewalk, gazed across the grass-plots of the Esplanade at the yellow portico of the Malabar Hotel with the air of a man about to go for a walk as soon as his friend is ready. That's how he looked, and it was odious. I waited to see him overwhelmed, confounded, pierced through and through, squirming like an impaled beetle – and I was half afraid to see it too – if you understand what I mean. Nothing more awful than to watch a man who has been found out, not in a crime but in a more than criminal weakness. The commonest sort of fortitude prevents us from becoming criminals in a legal sense; it is from weakness, unknown, but perhaps suspected, as in some parts of the world you suspect a deadly snake in every bush – from weakness that may lie hidden, watched or unwatched, prayed against or manfully scorned, repressed or maybe ignored more than half a lifetime, not one of us is safe. We are snared into doing things for which we get called names, and things for which we get hanged, and yet the spirit may well survive – survive the condemnations, survive the halter, by Jove! And there are things – they look small enough sometimes too – by which some of us are totally and completely undone. I watched the youngster there. I liked his appearance; I knew his appearance; he came from the right place; he was one of us. He stood there for all the parentage of his kind, for men and women by no means clever or amusing, but whose very existence is based upon honest faith, and upon the instinct of courage. I don't mean military courage, or civil courage or any special kind of courage. I mean just that inborn ability to look temptations straight in the face – a readiness unintellectual enough, goodness knows, but without pose – a power of resistance, don't you see, ungracious if you like, but priceless – an unthinking and blessed stiffness before the outward and inward terrors, before the might of nature, and the seductive corruption of men – backed by a faith invulnerable to the strength of facts to the contagion of example, to the solicitation of ideas. Hang ideas! They are tramps, vagabonds, knocking at the backdoor of your mind, each taking a little of your substance, each carrying away some crumb of that belief in a few simple notions you must cling to if you want to live decently and would like to die easy!

'This has nothing to do with Jim, directly; only he was outwardly so typical of that good, stupid kind we like to feel marching right and left of us in life, of the kind that is not disturbed by the vagaries of intelligence and the perversions of – of nerves, let us say. He was the kind of fellow you would, on the strength of his looks, leave in charge of the deck – figuratively and professionally speaking. I say I would, and I ought to know. Haven't I turned out youngsters enough in my time, for the service of the Red Rag, to the craft of the sea, to the craft whose whole secret could be expressed in one short sentence, and yet must be driven afresh every day into young heads till it becomes the component part of every working thought – till it is present in every dream of their young sleep! The sea has been good to me, but when I remember all these boys that passed through my hands, some grown up now and some drowned by this time, but all good stuff for the sea, I don't think I have done badly by it either. Were I to go home tomorrow, I bet that before two days passed over my head some sunburnt young chief mate would overtake me at some dock gateway or other, and a fresh deep voice speaking above my hat would ask: "Don't you remember me, sir? Why! little So-and-so. Such and such a ship. It was my first voyage." And I would remember a bewildered little shaver, no higher than the back of this chair, with a mother and perhaps a big sister on the quay, very quiet but too upset to wave their handkerchiefs at the ship that glides out gently between the pier-heads: or perhaps some decent middle-aged father who had come early with his boy to see him off, and stays all the morning because he is interested in the windlass apparently, and stays too long, and has got to scramble ashore at last with no time at all to say good-bye. The mud pilot on the poop sings out to me in a drawl, "Hold her with the check line for a moment, Mister Mate. There's a gentleman wants to get shore . . . Up with you, sir. Nearly got carried off to Talcahuano, didn't you? Now's your time; easy does it . . . All right. Slack away again forward there." The tugs, smoking like the pit of perdition, get hold and churn the old river into fury; the gentleman ashore is dusting his knees – the benevolent steward has shied his umbrella after him. All very proper. He has offered his bit of sacrifice to the sea, and now he may go home pretending he thinks nothing of it; and the little willing victim shall be very sea-sick before the next morning. By-and-by, when he has learned all the little mysteries and the one great secret of the craft, he shall be fit to live or die as the sea may decree; and the man who had taken a hand in this fool game, in which the sea wins every toss, will be pleased to have his back slapped by a heavy young hand, and to hear a cheery sea-puppy voice: "Do you remember me, sir? The little So-and-so."

'I tell you this is good; it tells you that once in your life at least you have gone the right way to work. I have been thus slapped, and I have winced, for the slap was heavy, and I have glowed all day long and gone to bed feeling less lonely in the world by virtue of that hearty thump. Don't I remember the little So-and-so's! I tell you I ought to know the right kind of looks. I would have trusted the deck to that youngster on the strength of a single glance, and gone to sleep with both eyes – and, by Jove! it wouldn't have been safe. There are depths of horror in that thought. He looked as genuine as a new sovereign, but there was some infernal alloy in his metal. How much? The least thing – the least drop of something rare and accursed; the least drop! – but he made you – standing there with his don't-care-hang air – he made you wonder whether perchance he were nothing more rare than brass.

'I couldn't believe it. I tell you I wanted to see him squirm for the honour of the craft. The other two no-account chaps spotted their captain, and began to move slowly towards us. They chatted together as they strolled, and I did not care any more than if they had not been visible to the naked eye. They grinned at each other – might have been exchanging jokes, for all I know. I saw that with one of them it was the case of a broken arm; and as to the long individual with grey moustaches he was the chief engineer, and in various ways a pretty notorious personality. They were nobodies. They approached. The skipper gazed in an inanimate way between his feet: he seemed to be swollen to an unnatural size by some awful disease, by the mysterious action of an unknown poison. He lifted his head, saw the two before him waiting, opened his mouth with an extraordinary, sneering contortion of his puffed face – to speak to them, I suppose – and then a thought seemed to strike him. His thick, purplish lips came together without a sound, he went off in a resolute waddle to the gharry and began to jerk at the door-handle with such a blind brutality of impatience that I expected to see the whole concern overturned on its side, pony and all. The driver, shaken out of his meditation over the sole of his foot, displayed at once all the signs of intense terror, and held with both hands, looking round from his box at this vast carcass forcing its way into his conveyance. The little machine shook and rocked tumultuously, and the crimson nape of that lowered neck, the size of those straining thighs, the immense heaving of that dingy, striped green-and-orange back, the whole burrowing effort of that gaudy and sordid mass troubled one's sense of probability with a droll and fearsome effect, like one of those grotesque and distinct visions that scare and fascinate one in a fever. He disappeared. I half expected the roof to split in two, the little box on wheels to burst open in the manner of a ripe cotton-pod – but it only sank with a click of flattened springs, and suddenly one venetian blind rattled down. His shoulders reappeared, jammed in the small opening; his head hung out, distended and tossing like a captive balloon, perspiring, furious, spluttering. He reached for the gharry-wallah with vicious flourishes of a fist as dumpy and red as a lump of raw meat. He roared at him to be off, to go on. Where? Into the Pacific, perhaps. The driver lashed; the pony snorted, reared once, and darted off at a gallop. Where? To Apia? to Honolulu? He had 6,000 miles of tropical belt to disport himself in, and I did not hear the precise address. A snorting pony snatched him into "ewigkeit" in the twinkling of an eye, and I never saw him again; and, what's more, I don't know of anybody that ever had a glimpse of him after he departed from my knowledge sitting inside a ramshackle little gharry that fled round the corner in a white smother of dust. He departed, disappeared, vanished, absconded; and absurdly enough it looked as though he had taken that gharry with him, for never again did I come across a sorrel pony with a slit ear and a lackadaisical Tamil driver afflicted by a sore foot. The Pacific is indeed big; but whether he found a place for a display of his talents in it or not, the fact remains he had flown into space like a witch on a broomstick. The little chap with his arm in a sling started to run after the carriage, bleating, "Captain! I say, Captain! I sa-a-ay!" – but after a few steps stopped short, hung his head, and walked back slowly. At the sharp rattle of the wheels the young fellow spun round where he stood. He made no other movement, no gesture, no sign, and remained facing in the new direction after the gharry had swung out of sight.

'All this happened in much less time than it takes to tell, since I am trying to interpret for you into slow speech the instantaneous effect of visual impressions. Next moment the half-caste clerk, sent by Archie to look a little after the poor castaways of the *Patna*, came upon the scene. He ran out eager and bareheaded, looking right and left, and very full of his mission.

It was doomed to be a failure as far as the principal person was concerned, but he approached the others with fussy importance, and, almost immediately, found himself involved in a violent altercation with the chap that carried his arm in a sling and who turned out to be extremely anxious for a row. He wasn't going to be ordered about – "not he, b'gosh". He wouldn't be terrified with a pack of lies by a cocky half-bred little quill-driver. He was not going to be bullied by "no object of that sort", if the story were true "ever so!" He bawled his wish, his desire, his determination to go to bed. "If you weren't a God-forsaken Portuguee," I heard him yell, "you would know that the hospital is the right place for me." He pushed the fist of his sound arm under the other's nose; a crowd began to collect; the half-caste, flustered, but doing his best to appear dignified, tried to explain his intentions. I went away without waiting to see the end.

'But it so happened that I had a man in the hospital at the time, and going there to see about him the day before the opening of the Inquiry, I saw in the white men's ward that little chap tossing on his back, with his arm in splints, and quite light-headed. To my great surprise the other one, the long individual with drooping white moustaches, had also found his way there. I remembered I had seen him slinking away during the quarrel, in a half prance, half shuffle, and trying very hard not to look scared. He was no stranger to the port, it seems, and in his distress was able to make tracks straight for Mariani's billiard-room and grog-shop near the bazaar. That unspeakable vagabond, Mariani, who had known the man and had minis-tered to his vices in one or two other places, kissed the ground, in a manner of speaking, before him, and shut him up with a supply of bottles in an upstairs room of his infamous hovel. It appears he was under some hazy apprehension as to his personal safety, and wished to be concealed. However, Mariani told me a long time after (when he came on board one day to dun my steward for the price of some cigars) that he would have done more for him without asking any questions, from gratitude for some unholy favour received very many years ago – as far as I could make out. He thumped twice his brawny chest, rolled enormous black and white eyes glistening with tears: "Antonio never forget – Antonio never forget!" What was the precise nature of the immoral obligation I never learned, but be it what it may, he had every facility given him to remain under lock and key, with a chair, a table, a mattress in a corner, and a litter of fallen plaster on the floor, in an irrational state of funk, and keeping up his pecker with such tonics as Mariani dispensed. This lasted till the evening of the third day, when, after letting out a few horrible screams, he found himself compelled to seek safety in flight from a legion of centipedes. He burst the door open, made one leap for dear life down the crazy little stairway, landed bodily on Mariani's stomach, picked himself up, and bolted like a rabbit into the streets. The police plucked him off a garbage-heap in the early morning. At first he had a notion they were carrying him off to be hanged, and fought for liberty like a hero, but when I sat down by his bed he had been very quiet for two days. His lean bronzed head, with white moustaches, looked fine and calm on the pillow, like the head of a war-worn soldier with a child-like soul, had it not been for a hint of spectral alarm that lurked in the blank glitter of his glance, resembling a nondescript form of a terror crouching silently behind a pane of glass. He was so extremely calm, that I began to indulge in the eccentric hope of hearing something explanatory of the famous affair from his point of view. Why I longed to go grubbing into the deplorable details of an occurrence which, after all, concerned me no more than as a member of an obscure body of men held together by a community of inglorious toil and by fidelity to a certain standard of conduct, I can't explain. You may call it an unhealthy curiosity if you like; but I have a distinct notion I wished to find something. Perhaps, unconsciously, I hoped I would find that something, some profound and redeeming cause, some merciful explanation, some convincing shadow of an excuse. I see well enough now that I hoped for the impossible – for the laying of what is the most obstinate ghost of man's creation, of the uneasy doubt uprising like a mist, secret and gnawing like a worm, and more chilling than the certitude of death – the doubt of the sovereign power enthroned in a fixed standard of conduct. It is the hardest thing to stumble against; it is the thing that breeds yelling panics and good little quiet villainies; it's the true shadow of calamity. Did I believe in a miracle? and why did I desire it so ardently? Was it for my own sake that I wished to find some shadow of an excuse for that young fellow whom I had never seen before, but whose appearance alone added a touch of personal concern to the thoughts suggested by the knowledge of his weakness – made it a thing of mystery and terror – like a hint of a destructive fate ready for us all whose youth – in its day – had resembled his youth? I fear that such was the secret motive of my prying. I was, and no mistake, looking for a miracle. The only thing that at this distance of time strikes me as miraculous is the extent of my imbecility. I positively hoped to obtain from that battered and shady invalid some exorcism against the ghost of doubt. I must have been pretty desperate too, for, without a loss of time, after a few indifferent and friendly sentences which he answered with languid readiness, just as any decent sick man would do, I produced the word *Patna* wrapped up in delicate question as in a wisp of floss silk. I was delicate selfishly; I did not want to startle him; I had no solicitude for him; I was not furious with him and sorry for him: his experience was of no importance, his redemption would have had no point for me. He had grown old in minor iniquities, and could no longer inspire aversion or pity. He repeated *Patna?* interrogatively, seemed to make a short effort of memory and said: "Quite right. I am an old stager out here. I saw her go down." I made ready to vent my indignation at such a stupid lie, when he added smoothly, "She was full of reptiles."

'This made me pause. What did he mean? The uneasy phantom of terror behind his glassy eyes seemed to stand still and look into mine wistfully. "They turned me out of my bunk in the middle watch to look at her sinking," he pursued in a reflective tone. His voice sounded alarmingly strong all at once. I was sorry for my folly. There was no snowy-winged coif of a nursing sister to be seen flitting in the perspective of the ward; but away in the middle of a long row of empty iron bedsteads an accident case from some ship in the Roads sat up brown and gaunt with a white bandage set rakishly on the forehead. Suddenly my interesting invalid shot out an arm thin like a tentacle and clawed my shoulder. "Only my eyes were good enough to see.

I am famous for my eyesight. That's why they called me, I expect. None of them was quick enough to see her go, but they saw that she was gone right enough, and sang out together – like this." . . . A wolfish howl searched the very recesses of my soul. "Oh, make 'im dry up," whined the accident case irritably. "You don't believe me, I suppose," went on the other, with an air of ineffable conceit. "I tell you there are no such eyes as mine this side of the Persian Gulf. Look under the bed."

'Of course I stooped instantly. I defy anybody not to have done so. "What can you see?" he asked. "Nothing," I said, feeling awfully ashamed of myself. He scrutinized my face with wild and withering contempt. "Just so," he said, "but if I were to look I could see – there's no eyes like mine, I tell you." Again he clawed, pulling me downwards in his eagerness to relieve himself by confidential communication. "Millions of pink toads. There's no eyes like mine. Millions of pink toads. It's worse than seeing a ship sink. I could look at sinking ships and smoke my pipe all day long. Why don't they give me back my pipe? I would get a smoke while I watched these toads. The ship was full of them. They've got to be watched, you know." He winked facetiously. The perspiration dripped on him off my head, my drill coat clung to my wet back: the afternoon breeze swept impetuously over the row of bedsteads, the stiff folds of curtains stirred perpendicularly, rattling on brass rods, the covers of empty beds blew about noiselessly near the bare floor all along the line, and I shivered to the very marrow. The soft wind of the tropics played in that naked ward as bleak as a winter's gale in an old barn at home. "Don't you let him start his hollering, mister," hailed from afar the accident case in a distressed angry shout that came ringing between the walls like a quavering call down a tunnel. The clawing hand hauled at my shoulder; he leered at me knowingly. "The ship was full of them, you know, and we had to clear out on the strict Q.T.," he whispered with extreme rapidity. "All pink. All pink – as big as mastiffs, with an eye on the top of the head and claws all round their ugly mouths. Ough! Ough!" Quick jerks as of galvanic shocks disclosed under the flat coverlet the outlines of meagre and agitated legs; he let go my shoulder and reached after something in the air; his body trembled tensely like a released harp-spring; and while I looked down, the spectral horror in him broke through his glassy gaze. Instantly his face of an old soldier, with its noble and calm outlines, became decomposed before my eyes by the corruption of stealthy cunning, of an abominable caution, and of desperate fear. He restrained a cry – "Ssh! what are they doing now down there?" he asked, pointing to the floor with fantastic precautions of voice and gesture, whose meaning, borne upon my mind in a lurid flash, made me very sick of my cleverness. "They are all asleep," I answered, watching him narrowly. That was it. That's what he wanted to hear; these were the exact words that could calm him. He drew a long breath. "Ssh! Quiet, steady. I am an old stager out here. I know them brutes. Bash in the head of the first that stirs. There's too many of them, and she won't swim more than ten minutes." He panted again. "Hurry up," he yelled suddenly and went on in a steady scream: "They are all awake – millions of them. They are trampling on me! Wait! Oh, wait! I'll smash them in heaps like flies. Wait for me! Help!

H-e-l-p!" An interminable and sustained howl completed my discomfiture. I saw in the distance the accident case raise deplorably both his hands to his bandaged head; a dresser, aproned to the chin, showed himself in the vista of the ward, as if seen in the small end of a telescope. I confessed myself fairly routed, and without more ado, stepping out through one of the long windows, escaped into the outside gallery. The howl pursued me like a vengeance. I turned into a deserted landing, and suddenly all became very still and quiet round me, and I descended the bare and shiny staircase in a silence that enabled me to compose my distracted thoughts. Down below I met one of the resident surgeons who was crossing the courtyard and stopped me. "Been to see your man, Captain? I think we may let him go tomorrow. These fools have no notion of taking care of themselves, though. I say, we've got the chief engineer of that pilgrim ship here. A curious case. D.T.'s of the worst kind. He has been drinking hard in that Greek's or Italian's grog-shop for three days. What can you expect. Four bottles of that kind of brandy a day, I am told. Wonderful, if true. Sheeted with boiler-iron inside, I should think. The head, ah! the head, of course, gone, but the curious part is there's some sort of method in his raving. I am trying to find out. Most unusual – that thread of logic in such a delirium. Traditionally he ought to see snakes, but he doesn't. Good old tradition's at a discount nowadays. Eh! His – er – visions are batrachian. Ha! ha! No, seriously, I never remember being so interested in a case of jim-jams before. He ought to be dead, don't you know, after such a festive experiment. Oh! he is a tough object. Four-and-twenty years of the tropics too. You ought really to take a peep at him. Noble-looking old boozer. Most extraordinary man I ever met – medically, of course. Won't you?"

'I had been all along exhibiting the usual polite signs of interest, but now assuming an air of regret I murmured of want of time, and shook hands in a hurry. "I say," he cried after me, "he can't attend that inquiry. Is his evidence material, you think?"

' "Not in the least," I called back from the gateway.'

CHAPTER 6

'The authorities were evidently of the same opinion. The inquiry was not adjourned. It was held on the appointed day to satisfy the law, and it was well attended because of its human interest, no doubt. There was no incertitude as to facts – as to the one material fact, I mean. How the *Patna* came by her hurt it was impossible to find out; the court did not expect to find out; and in the whole audience there was not a man who cared. Yet, as I've told you, all the sailors in the port attended, and the waterside business was fully represented. Whether they knew it or not, the interest that drew them there was purely psychological – the expectation of some essential disclosure as to the strength, the power, the horror, of human emotions. Naturally nothing of the kind could be disclosed. The examination of the only man able and willing to face it was beating futilely round the well-known fact, and the play of questions upon it was as instructive as the tapping with a hammer on an iron box, were the object to find out what's inside. However, an official inquiry could not be any other thing. Its object was not the fundamental why, but the superficial how, of this affair.

'The young chap could have told them, and, though that very thing was the thing that interested the audience, the questions put to him necessarily led him away from what to me, for instance, would have been the only truth worth knowing. You can't expect the constituted authorities to inquire into the state of a man's soul – or is it only of his liver? Their business was to come down upon the consequences and, frankly, a casual police magistrate and two nautical assessors are not much good for anything else. I don't mean to imply these fellows were stupid. The magistrate was very patient. One of the assessors was a sailing-ship skipper with a reddish beard, and of a pious disposition. Brierly was the other. Big Brierly. Some of you must have heard of Big Brierly – the captain of the crack ship of the Blue Star line. That's the man.

'He seemed consumedly bored by the honour thrust upon him. He had never in his life made a mistake, never had an accident, never a mishap, never a check in his steady rise, and he seemed to be one of those lucky fellows who know nothing of indecision, much less of self-mistrust. At thirty-two he had one of the best commands going in the Eastern trade – and, what's more, he thought a lot of what he had. There was nothing like it in the world, and I suppose if you had asked him point-blank he would have confessed that in his opinion there was not such another commander. The choice had fallen upon the right man. The rest of mankind that did not command the sixteen-knot steel steamer *Ossa* were rather poor creatures. He had saved lives at sea, had rescued ships in distress, had a gold chronometer presented to him by the underwriters, and a pair of binoculars with a suitable inscription from some foreign Government, in commemoration of these services. He was acutely aware of his merits and of his rewards. I liked him well enough, though some I know – meek, friendly men at that – couldn't stand him at any price. I haven't the slightest doubt he considered himself vastly my superior – indeed, had you been Emperor of East and West, you could not have ignored your inferiority in his presence – but I couldn't get up any real sentiment of offence. He did not despise me for anything I could help, for anything I was – don't you know? I was a negligible quantity simply because I was not *the* fortunate man of the earth, not Montague Brierly in command of the *Ossa*, not the owner of an inscribed gold chronometer and of silver-mounted binoculars testifying to the excellence of my seamanship and to my indomitable pluck; not possessed of an acute sense of my merits and of my rewards, besides the love of worship of a black retriever, the most wonderful of its kind – for never was such a man loved thus by such a dog. No doubt, to have all this forced upon you was exasperating enough; but when I reflected that I was associated in these fatal disadvantages with twelve hundred millions of other more or less human beings, I found I could bear my share of his good-natured and contemptuous pity for the sake of something indefinite and attractive in the man. I have never defined to myself this attraction, but there were moments when I envied him. The sting of life could do no more to his complacent soul than the scratch of a pin to the smooth face of a rock. This was enviable. As I looked at him flanking on one side of the unassuming pale-faced magistrate who presided at the inquiry, his self-satisfaction presented to me and to the world a surface as hard as granite. He committed suicide very soon after.

'No wonder Jim's case bored him, and while I thought with something akin to fear of the immensity of his contempt for the young man under examination, he was probably holding silent inquiry into his own case. The verdict must have been of unmitigated guilt, and he took the secret of the evidence with him in that leap into the sea. If I understand anything of men, the matter was no doubt of the gravest import, one of those trifles that awaken ideas – start into life some thought with which a man unused to such a companionship finds it impossible to live. I am in a position to know that it wasn't money, and it wasn't drink, and it wasn't woman. He jumped overboard at sea barely a week after the end of the inquiry, and less than three days after leaving port on his outward passage; as though on that exact spot in the midst of waters he had suddenly perceived the gates of the other world flung open wide for his reception.

'Yet it was not a sudden impulse. His grey-headed mate, a first-rate sailor and a nice old chap with strangers, but in his relations with his commander the surliest chief-officer I've ever seen, would tell the story with tears in his eyes. It appears that when he came on deck in the morning Brierly had been writing in the chart-room. "It was ten minutes to four," he said, "and the middle watch was not relieved yet of course. He heard my voice on the bridge speaking to the second mate, and called me in. I was loth to go, and that's the truth, Captain Marlow – I couldn't stand poor Captain Brierly, I tell you with shame; we never know what a man is made of. He had been promoted over too many heads, not counting my own, and he had a damnable trick of making you feel small, nothing but by the way he said 'Good morning'. I never addressed him, sir, but on matters of duty, and then it was as much as I could do to keep a civil tongue in my head." (He flattered himself there. I often wondered how Brierly could put up with his manners for more than half a voyage.) "I've a wife and children," he went on, "and I had been ten years in the Company, always expecting the next command – more fool I. Says he, just like this: 'Come in here, Mr Jones,' in that swagger voice of his – 'Come in here, Mr Jones.' In I went. 'We'll lay down her position,' says he, stooping over the chart, a pair of dividers in hand. By the standing orders, the officer going off duty would have done that at the end of his watch. However, I said nothing, and looked on while he marked off the ship's position with a tiny cross and wrote the date and the time. I can see him this moment writing his neat figures: seventeen, eight, four a.m. The year would be written in red ink at the top of the chart. He never used his charts more than a year, Captain Brierly didn't. I've the chart now. When he had done he stands looking down at the mark he had made and smiling to himself, then looks up at me. 'Thirty-two miles more as she goes,' says he, 'and then we shall be clear, and you may alter the course twenty degrees to the southward.'

' "We were passing to the north of the Hector Bank that voyage. I said, 'All right, sir,' wondering what he was fussing about, since I had to call him before altering the course anyhow. Just then eight bells were struck: we came out on the bridge, and the second mate before going off mentions in his usual way – 'Seventy-one on the log.' Captain Brierly looks at the compass and then all round. It was dark and clear, and all the stars were out as plain as on a frosty night in high latitudes. Suddenly he says with a sort of little sigh: 'I am going aft, and shall set the log at zero for you myself, so that there can be no mistake. Thirty-two miles more on this course and then you are safe. Let's see – the correction on the log is six per cent additive; say, then, thirty by the dial to run, and you may come twenty degrees to starboard at once. No use losing any distance – is there?' I had never heard him talk so much at a stretch, and to no purpose as it seemed to me. I said nothing. He went down the ladder, and the dog, that was always at his heels whenever he moved, night or day, followed, sliding nose first, after him. I heard his boot-heels tap, tap on the after-deck, then he stopped and spoke to the dog – 'Go back, Rover. On the bridge, boy! Go on – get.' Then he calls out to me from the dark, 'Shut that dog up in the chart-room, Mr Jones – will you?'

' "This was the last time I heard his voice, Captain Marlow. These are the last words he spoke in the hearing of any living human being, sir." At this point the old chap's voice got quite unsteady. "He was afraid the poor brute would jump after him, don't you see?" he pursued with a quaver. "Yes, Captain Marlow. He set the log for me; he – would you believe it? – he put a drop of oil in it too. There was the oil-feeder where he left it near by. The boatswain's mate got the hose along aft to wash down at half past five; by-and-by he knocks off and runs up on the bridge – 'Will you please come aft, Mr Jones,' he says. 'There's a funny thing. I don't like to touch it.' It was Captain Brierly's gold chronometer watch carefully hung under the rail by its chain.

' "As soon as my eyes fell on it something struck me, and I knew, sir. My legs got soft under me. It was as if I had seen him go over; and I could tell how far behind he was left too. The taffrail-log marked eighteen miles and three-quarters, and four iron belaying-pins were missing round the main-mast. Put them in his pockets to help him down, I suppose; but, Lord! what's four pins to a powerful man like Captain Brierly. Maybe his confidence in himself was just shook a bit at the last. That's the only sign of fluster he gave in his whole life, I should think; but I am ready to answer for him, that once over he did not try to swim a stroke, the same as he would have had pluck enough to keep up all day long on the bare chance had he fallen over-board accidentally. Yes, sir. He was second to none – if he said so himself, as I heard him once. He had written two letters in the middle watch, one to the Company and the other to me. He gave me a lot of instructions as to the passage – I had been in the trade before he was out of his time – and no end of hints as to my conduct with our people in Shanghai, so that I should keep the command of the *Ossa*. He wrote like a father would to a favourite son, Captain Marlow, and I was five-and-twenty years his senior and had tasted salt water before he was fairly breeched. In his letter to the owners – it was left open for me to see – he said that he had always done his duty by them – up to that moment – and even now he was not betraying their confidence, since he was leaving the ship to as competent a seaman as could be found – meaning me, sir, meaning me! He told them that if the last act of his life didn't take away all his credit with them, they would give weight to my faithful service and to his warm recommendation, when about to fill the vacancy made by his death. And much more like this, sir. I couldn't believe my eyes. It made me feel queer all over," went on the old chap in great perturbation, and squashing something in the corner of his right eye with the end of a thumb as broad as a spatula. "You would think, sir, he had jumped overboard only to give an unlucky man a last show to get on. What with the shock of him going in this awful rash way, and thinking myself a made man by that chance, I was nearly off my chump for a week. But no fear. The captain of the *Pelion* was shifted into the *Ossa* – came aboard in Shanghai – a little popinjay, sir, in a grey check suit, with his hair parted in the middle. 'Aw – I am – aw – your new captain, Mister – mister – aw – Jones.' He was drowned in scent – fairly stunk with it, Captain Marlow. I daresay it was the look I gave him that made him stammer. He mumbled something about my natural disappointment – I had better know at once that his chief officer got the promotion to the *Pelion* – he had nothing to do with it, of course – supposed the office knew best – sorry. . . . Says I, 'Don't you mind old Jones, sir; damn his soul, he's used to it.' I could see directly I had shocked his delicate ear, and while we sat at our first tiffin together he began to find fault in a nasty manner with this and that in the ship. I never heard such a voice out of a Punch and Judy show. I set my teeth hard, and glued my eyes to my plate, and held my peace as long as I could; but at last I had to say something: up he jumps tiptoeing, ruffling all his pretty plumes, like a little fighting cock. 'You'll find you have a different person to deal with than the late Captain Brierly.' 'I've found it,' says I, very glum, but pretending to be mighty busy with my steak. 'You are an old ruffian, Mr – aw – Jones; and what's more, you are known for an old ruffian in the employ,' he squeaks at me. The damned bottle-washers stood about listening with their mouths stretched from ear to ear. 'I may be a hard case,' answers I, 'but I ain't so far gone as to put up with the sight of you sitting in Captain Brierly's chair.' With that I lay down my knife and fork. 'You would like to sit in it yourself – that's where the shoe pinches,' he sneers. I left the saloon, got my rags together, and was on the quay with all my dunnage about my feet before the stevedores had turned to again. Yes. Adrift – on shore – after ten years' service – and with a poor woman and four children six thousand miles off depending on my half-pay for every mouthful they ate. Yes, sir! I chucked it rather than hear Captain Brierly abused. He left me his night-glasses – here they are; and he wished me to take care of the dog – here he is. Hallo, Rover, poor boy. Where's the captain, Rover?" The dog looked up at us with mournful yellow eyes, gave one desolate bark, and crept under the table.

'All this was taking place, more than two years afterwards, on board that nautical ruin the *Fire-Queen* this Jones had got charge of – quite by a funny accident, too – from Matherson – mad Matherson they generally called him – the same who used to hang out in Haï-phong, you know, before the occupation days. The old chap snuffled on —

' "Ay, sir, Captain Brierly will be remembered here, if there's no other place on earth. I wrote fully to his father and did not get a word in reply – neither Thank you, nor Go to the devil! – nothing! Perhaps they did not want to know."

'The sight of that watery-eyed old Jones mopping his bald head with a red cotton handkerchief, the sorrowing yelp of the dog, the squallor of that fly-blown cuddy which was the only shrine of his memory, threw a veil of inexpressibly mean pathos over Brierly's remembered figure, the posthumous revenge of fate for that belief in his own splendour which had almost cheated his life of its legitimate terrors. Almost! Perhaps wholly. Who can tell what flattering view he had induced himself to take of his own suicide?

' "Why did he commit the rash act, Captain Marlow – can you think?" asked Jones, pressing his palms together. "Why? It beats me! Why?" He slapped his low and wrinkled forehead. "If he had been poor and old and in debt – and never a show – or else mad. But he wasn't of the kind that goes mad, not he. You trust me. What a mate don't know about his skipper isn't worth knowing. Young, healthy, well off, no cares ... I sit here sometimes thinking, thinking, till my head fairly begins to buzz. There was some reason."

' "You may depend on it, Captain Jones," said I, "it wasn't anything that would have disturbed much either of us two," I said; and then, as if a light had been flashed into the muddle of his brain, poor old Jones found a last word of amazing profundity. He blew his nose, nodding at me dolefully: "Ay, ay! neither you nor I, sir, had ever thought so much of ourselves."

'Of course the recollection of my last conversation with Brierly is tinged with the knowledge of his end that followed so close upon it. I spoke with him for the last time during the progress of the inquiry. It was after the first adjournment, and he came up with me in the street. He was in a state of irritation, which I noticed with surprise, his usual behaviour when he condescended to converse being perfectly cool, with a trace of amused tolerance, as if the existence of his interlocutor had been a rather good joke. "They caught me for that inquiry, you see," he began, and for a while enlarged complainingly upon the inconveniences of daily attendance in court. "And goodness knows how long it will last. Three days, I suppose." I heard him out in silence; in my then opinion it was a way as good as another of putting on side. "What's the use of it? It is the stupidest set out you can imagine," he pursued, hotly. I remarked that there was no option. He interrupted me with a sort of pent-up violence. "I feel like a fool all the time." I looked up at him. This was going very far – for Brierly – when talking of Brierly. He stopped short, and seizing the lapel of my coat, gave it a slight tug. "Why are we tormenting that young chap?" he asked. This question chimed in so well to the tolling of a certain thought of mine that, with the image of the absconding renegade in my eye, I answered at once, "Hanged if I know, unless it be that he lets you." I was astonished to see him fall into line, so to speak, with that utterance, which ought to have been tolerably cryptic. He said angrily, "Why, yes. Can't he see that wretched skipper of his has cleared out? What does he expect to happen? Nothing can save him. He's done for." We walked on in silence a few steps. "Why eat all that dirt?" he exclaimed, with an oriental energy of expression – about the only sort of energy you can find a trace of east of the fiftieth meridian. I wondered greatly at the direction of his thoughts, but now I strongly suspect it was strictly in character: at bottom poor Brierly must have been thinking of himself. I pointed out to him that the skipper of the *Patna* was known to have feathered his nest pretty well, and could procure almost anywhere the means of getting away. With Jim it was otherwise: the Government was keeping him in the Sailors' Home for the time being, and probably he hadn't a penny in his pocket to bless himself with. It costs some money to run away. "Does it? Not always," he said, with a bitter laugh, and to some further remark of mine – "Well, then, let him creep twenty feet underground and stay there! By heavens! *I* would." I don't know why his tone provoked me, and I said, "There is a kind of courage in facing it out as he does, knowing very well that if he went away nobody would trouble to run after him." "Courage be hanged!" growled Brierly. "That sort of courage is of no use to keep a man straight, and I don't care a snap for such courage. If you were to say it was a kind of cowardice now – of softness. I tell you what, I will put up two hundred rupees if you put up another hundred and undertake to make the beggar clear out early tomorrow morning. The fellow's a gentleman if he ain't fit to be touched – he will understand. He must! This infernal publicity is too shocking: there he sits while all these confounded natives, serangs, lascars, quartermasters, are giving evidence that's enought to burn a man to ashes with shame. This is abominable. Why, Marlow, don't you think, don't you feel, that this is abominable; don't you now – come – as a seaman? If he went away, all this would stop at once." Brierly said these words with a most unusual animation, and made as if to reach after his pocket-book. I restrained him, and declared coldly that the cowardice of these four men did not seem to me a matter of such great importance. "And you call yourself a seaman, I suppose," he pronounced angrily. I said that's what I called myself, and I hoped I was too. He heard me out, and made a gesture with his big arm that seemed to deprive me of my individuality, to push me away into the crowd. "The worst of it," he said, "is that all you fellows have no sense of dignity; you don't think enough of what you are supposed to be."

'We had been walking slowly meantime, and now stopped opposite the harbour office, in sight of the very spot from which the immense captain of the *Patna* had vanished as utterly as a tiny feather blown away in a hurricane. I smiled. Brierly went on: "This is a disgrace. We've got all kinds amongst us – some anointed scoundrels in the lot: but, hang it, we must preserve professional decency or we become no better than so many tinkers going about loose. We are trusted. Do you understand? – trusted! Frankly, I don't care a snap for all the pilgrims that ever came out of Asia, but a decent man would not have behaved like this to a full cargo of old rags in bales. We aren't an organized body of men, and the only thing that holds us together is just the name for that kind of decency. Such an affair destroys one's confidence. A man may go pretty near through his whole sea-life without any call to show a stiff upper lip. But when the call comes . . . Aha! . . . If I . . ."

'He broke off, and in a changed tone, "I'll give you two hundred rupees now, Marlow, and you just talk to that chap. Confound him! I wish he had never come out here. Fact is, I rather think some of my people know this. The old man's a parson, and I remember now I met him once when staying with my cousin in Essex last year. If I am not mistaken, the old chap seemed rather to fancy his sailor son. Horrible. I can't do it myself – but you . . ."

'Thus, apropos of Jim, I had a glimpse of the real Brierly a few days before he committed his reality and his sham together to the keeping of the sea. Of course I declined to meddle. The tone of this last "but you" (poor Brierly couldn't help it), that seemed to imply I was no more noticeable than an insect, caused me to look at the proposal with indignation, and on account of that provocation, or for some other reason, I became positive in my mind that the inquiry was a severe punishment to that Jim, and that his facing it – practically of his own free will – was a redeeming feature in his abominable case. I hadn't been so sure of it before. Brierly went off in a huff. At the time his state of mind was more of a mystery to me than it is now.

'Next day, coming into court late, I sat by myself. Of course I could not forget the conversation I had with Brierly, and now I had them both under my eyes. The demeanour of one suggested gloomy impudence and of the other a contemptuous boredom; yet one attitude might not have been truer than the other, and I was aware that one was not true. Brierly was not bored – he was exasperated; and if so, then Jim might not have been impudent. According to my theory he was not. I imagined he was hopeless. Then it was that our glances met. They met, and the look he gave me was discouraging of any intention I might have had to speak to him. Upon either hypothesis – insolence or despair – I felt I could be of no use to him. This was the second day of the proceedings. Very soon after that exchange of glances the inquiry was adjourned again to the next day. The white men began to troop out at once. Jim had been told to stand down some time before, and was able to leave amongst the first. I saw his broad shoulders and his head outlined in the light of the door, and while I made my way slowly out talking with someone – some stranger who had addressed me casually – I could see him from within the court-room resting both elbows on the balustrade of the veranda and turning his back on the small stream of people trickling down the few steps. There was a murmur of voices and a shuffle of boots.

'The next case was that of assault and battery committed upon a money-lender, I believe; and the defendant – a venerable villager with a straight white beard – sat on a mat just outside the door with his sons, daughters, sons-in-law, their wives, and, I should think, half the population of his village besides, squatting or standing around him. A slim dark woman, with part of her back and one black shoulder bared, and with a thin gold ring in her nose, suddenly began to talk in a high-pitched, shrewish tone. The man with me instinctively looked up at her. We were then just through the door, passing behind Jim's burly back.

'Whether those villagers had brought the yellow dog with them, I don't know. Anyhow, a dog was there, weaving himself in and out amongst people's legs in that mute stealthy way native dogs have, and my companion stumbled over him. The dog leaped away without a sound; the man, raising his voice a little, said with a slow laugh, "Look at that wretched cur," and directly afterwards we became separated by a lot of people pushing in. I stood back for a moment against the wall while the stranger managed to get down the steps and disappeared. I saw Jim spin round. He made a step forward and barred my way. We were alone; he glared at me with an air of stubborn resolution. I became aware I was being held up, so to speak, as if in a wood. The veranda was empty by then, and the noise and movement in court had ceased: a great silence fell upon the building, in which, somewhere far within, an Oriental voice began to whine abjectly. The dog in the very act of trying to sneak in at the door, sat down hurriedly to hunt for fleas.

' "Did you speak to me?" asked Jim very low, and bending forward, not so much towards me but at me, if you know what I mean. I said "No" at once. Something in the sound of that quiet tone of his warned me to be on my defence. I watched him. It was very much like a meeting in a wood, only more uncertain in its issue, since he could possibly want neither my money nor my life – nothing that I could simply give up or defend with a clear conscience. "You say you didn't," he said, very sombre. "But I heard." "Some mistake," I protested, utterly at a loss, and never taking my eyes off him. To watch his face was like watching a darkening sky before a clap of thunder, shade upon shade imperceptibly coming on, the gloom growing mysteriously intense in the calm of maturing violence.

' "As far as I know, I haven't opened my lips in your hearing," I affirmed with perfect truth. I was getting a little angry, too, at the absurdity of this encounter. It strikes me now I have never in my life been so near a beating – I mean it literally; a beating with fists. I suppose I had some hazy prescience of that eventuality being in the air. Not that he was actively threatening me. On the contrary, he was strangely passive – don't you know? but he was lowering, and, though not exceptionally big, he looked generally fit to demolish a wall. The most reassuring symptom I noticed was a kind of slow and ponderous hesitation, which I took as a tribute to the evident sincerity of my manner and of my tone. We faced each other. In the court the assault case was proceeding. I caught the words: "Well – buffalo – stick – in the greatness of my fear. . . ."

' "What did you mean by staring at me all the morning?" said Jim at last. He looked up and looked down again. "Did you expect us all to sit with downcast eyes out of regard for your susceptibilities?" I retorted sharply. I was not going to submit meekly to any of his nonsense. He raised his eyes again, and this time continued to look me straight in the face. "No. That's all right," he pronounced with an air of deliberating with himself upon the truth of this statement – "that's all right. I am going through with that. Only" – and there he spoke a little faster – "I won't let any man call me

names outside this court. There was a fellow with you. You spoke to him
– oh, yes – I know; 'tis all very fine. You spoke to him, but you meant me
to hear. ...."

'I assured him he was under some extraordinary delusion. I had no
conception how it came about. "You thought I would be afraid to resent
this," he said, with a faint tinge of bitterness. I was interested enough to
discern the slightest shades of expression, but I was not in the least enlightened; yet I don't know what in these words, or perhaps just the intonation
of that phrase, induced me suddenly to make all possible allowances for
him. I ceased to be annoyed at any unexpected predicament. It was some
mistake on his part; he was blundering and I had an intuition that the
blunder was of an odious, of an unfortunate nature. I was anxious to end
this scene on grounds of decency, just as one is anxious to cut short some
unprovoked and abominable confidence. The funniest part was, that in the
midst of all these considerations of the higher order I was conscious of a
certain trepidation as to the possibility – nay, likelihood – of this encounter
ending in some disreputable brawl which could not possibly be explained,
and would make me ridiculous. I did not hanker after a three days' celebrity
as the man who got a black eye or something of the sort from the mate of
the *Patna*. He, in all probability, did not care what he did, or at any rate
would be fully justified in his own eyes. It took no magician to see he was
amazingly angry about something, for all his quiet and even torpid demeanour. I don't deny I was extremely desirous to pacify him at all costs, had I
only known what to do. But I didn't know, as you may well imagine. It was
blackness without a single gleam. We confronted each other in silence. He
hung fire for about fifteen seconds, then made a step nearer, and I made
ready to ward off a blow, though I don't think I moved a muscle. "If you
were as big as two men and as strong as six," he said very softly, "I would
tell you what I think of you. You ...." "Stop!" I exclaimed. This checked
him for a second. "Before you tell me what you think of me," I went on,
quickly, "will you kindly tell me what it is I've said or done?" During the
pause that ensued he surveyed me with indignation, while I made supernatural efforts of memory, in which I was hindered by the Oriental voice
within the court-room expostulating with impassioned volubility against a
charge of falsehood. Then we spoke almost together. "I will soon show you
I am not," he said, in a tone suggestive of a crisis. "I declare I don't know,"
I protested earnestly at the same time. He tried to crush me by the scorn of
his glance. "Now that you see I am not afraid you try to crawl out of it,"
he said. "Who's a cur now – hey?" Then, at last, I understood.

'He had been scanning my features as though looking for a place, where
he would plant his fist. "I will allow no man," ... he mumbled, threaten-
ingly. It was, indeed, a hideous mistake; he had given himself away utterly.
I can't give you an idea how shocked I was. I suppose he saw some reflection
of my feelings in my face, because his expression changed just a little. "Good
God!" I stammered, "you don't think I ...." "But I am sure I've heard," he
persisted, raising his voice for the first time since the beginning of this
deplorable scene. Then with a shade of disdain he added, "It wasn't you,
then? Very well; I'll find the other." "Don't be a fool," I cried in exasperation;

"it wasn't that at all." "I've heard," he said again with an unshaken and sombre perseverance.

'There may be those who could have laughed at his pertinacity. I didn't. Oh, I didn't! There had never been a man so mercilessly shown up by his own natural impulse. A single word had stripped him of his discretion – of that discretion which is more necessary to the decencies of our inner being than clothing is to the decorum of our body. "Don't be a fool," I repeated. "But the other man said it, you don't deny that?" he pronounced, distinctly, and looking in my face without flinching. "No, I don't deny," said I, returning his gaze. At last his eyes followed downwards the direction of my pointing finger. He appeared at first uncomprehending, then confounded, and at last amazed and scared as though a dog had been a monster and he had never seen a dog before. "Nobody dreamt of insulting you," I said.

'He contemplated the wretched animal, that moved no more than an effigy: it sat with ears pricked and its sharp muzzle pointed into the doorway, and suddenly snapped at a fly like a piece of mechanism.

'I looked at him. The red of his fair sunburnt complexion deepened suddenly under the down of his cheeks, invaded his forehead, spread to the roots of his curly hair. His ears became intensely crimson, and even the clear blue of his eyes was darkened many shades by the rush of blood to his head. His lips pouted a little, trembling as though he had been on the point of bursting into tears. I perceived he was incapable of pronouncing a word from the excess of his humiliation. From disappointment too – who knows? Perhaps he looked forward to that hammering he was going to give me for rehabilitation, for appeasement? Who can tell what relief he expected from this chance of a row? He was naïve enough to expect anything; but he had given himself away for nothing in this case. He had been frank with himself – let alone with me – in the wild hope of arriving in that way at some effective refutation, and the stars had been ironically unpropitious. He made an inarticulate noise in his throat like a man imperfectly stunned by a blow on the head. It was pitiful.

'I didn't catch up again with him till well outside the gate. I had even to trot a bit at the last, but when, out of breath at elbow, I taxed him with running away, he said, "Never!" and at once turned at bay. I explained I never meant to say he was running away from *me*. "From no man – from not a single man on earth," he affirmed with a stubborn mien. I forebore to point out the one obvious exception which would hold good for the bravest of us; I thought he would find out by himself very soon. He looked at me patiently while I was thinking of something to say, but I could find nothing on the spur of the moment, and he began to walk on. I kept up, and anxious not to lose him, I said hurriedly that I couldn't think of leaving him under a false impression of my – of my – I stammered. The stupidity of the phrase appalled me while I was trying to finish it, but the power of sentences has nothing to do with their sense or the logic of their construction. My idiotic mumble seemed to please him. He cut it short by saying, with courteous placidity that argued an immense power of self-control or else a wonderful elasticity of spirits – "Altogether my mistake." I marvelled greatly at this expression: he might have been alluding to some trifling occurrence. Hadn't he understood its deplorable meaning? "You may well forgive me," he continued, and went on a little moodily. "All these staring people in court seemed such fools that – that it might have been as I supposed."

'This opened suddenly a new view of him to my wonder. I looked at him curiously and met his unabashed and impenetrable eyes. "I can't put up with this kind of thing," he said, very simply, "and I don't mean to. In court it's different; I've got to stand that – and I can do it too."

'I don't pretend I understood him. The views he let me have of himself were like those glimpses through the shifting rents in a thick fog – bits of vivid and vanishing detail, giving no connected idea of the general aspect of a country. They fed one's curiosity without satisfying it; they were no good for purposes of orientation. Upon the whole he was misleading. That's how I summed him up to myself after he left me late in the evening. I had been staying at the Malabar House for a few days, and on my pressing invitation he dined with me there.'

CHAPTER 7

'An outward-bound mail-boat had come in that afternoon, and the big dining-room of the hotel was more than half full of people with a hundred pounds round-the-world tickets in their pockets. There were married couples looking domesticated and bored with each other in the midst of their travels; there were small parties and large parties, and lone individuals dining solemnly or feasting boisterously, but all thinking, conversing, joking, or scowling as was their wont at home; and just as intelligently receptive of new impressions as their trunks upstairs. Henceforth they would be labelled as having passed through this and that place, and so would be their luggage. They would cherish this distinction of their persons, and preserve the gummed tickets on their portmanteaux as documentary evidence, as the only permanent trace of their improving enterprise. The dark-faced servants tripped without noise over the vast and polished floor; now and then a girl's laugh would be heard, as innocent and empty as her mind, or, in a sudden hush of crockery, a few words in an affected drawl from some wit embroidering for the benefit of a grinning tableful the last funny story of shipboard scandal. Two nomadic old maids, dressed up to kill, worked acrimoniously through the bill of fare, whispering to each other with faded lips, wooden-faced and bizarre, like two sumptuous scarecrows. A little wine opened Jim's heart and loosened his tongue. His appetite was good, too, I noticed. He seemed to have buried somewhere the opening episode of our acquaintance. It was like a thing of which there would be no more question in this world. And all the time I had before me these blue, boyish eyes looking straight into mine, this young face, these capable shoulders, the open bronzed forehead with a white line under the roots of clustering fair hair, this appearance appealing at sight to all my sympathies; this frank aspect, the artless smile, the youthful seriousness. He was of the right sort; he was one of us. He talked soberly, with a sort of composed unreserve, and with a quiet bearing that might have been the outcome of manly self-control, of impudence, of callousness, of a colossal unconsciousness, of a gigantic deception. Who can tell! From our tone we might have been discussing a third person, a football match, last year's weather. My mind floated in a sea of conjectures till the turn of the conversation enabled me, without being offensive, to remark that, upon the whole, this inquiry must have been pretty trying to him. He darted his arm across the tablecloth, and clutching my hand by the side of my plate, glared fixedly. I *was* startled. "It must be awfully hard," I stammered, confused by this display of speechless feeling. "It is – hell," he burst out in a muffled voice.

'This movement and these words caused two well-groomed male globe-trotters at a neighbouring table to look up in alarm from their iced pudding. I rose, and we passed into the front gallery for coffee and cigars.

'On little octagon tables candles burned in glass globes; clumps of stiff-leaved plants separated sets of cosy wicker chairs; and between the pairs of columns, whose reddish shafts caught in a long row the sheen from the tall windows, the night, glittering and sombre, seemed to hang like a splendid drapery. The riding lights of ships winked afar like setting stars, and the hills across the roadstead resembled rounded black masses of arrested thunder-clouds.

' "I couldn't clear out," Jim began. "The skipper did – that's all very well for him. I couldn't, and I wouldn't. They all got out of it in one way or another, but it wouldn't do for me."

'I listened with concentrated attention, not daring to stir in my chair; I wanted to know – and to this day I don't know, I can only guess. He would be confident and depressed all in the same breath, as if some conviction of innate blamelessness had checked the truth writhing within him at every turn. He began by saying, in the tone in which a man would admit his inability to jump a twenty-foot wall, that he could never go home now; and this declaration recalled to my mind what Brierly had said, "that the old parson in Essex seemed to fancy his sailor son not a little".

'I can't tell you whether Jim knew he was especially "fancied", but the tone of his references to "my Dad" was calculated to give me a notion that the good old rural dean was about the finest man that ever had been worried by the cares of a large family since the beginning of the world. This, though never stated, was implied with an anxiety that there should be no mistake about it, which was really very true and charming, but added a poignant sense of lives far off to the other elements of the story. "He has seen it all in the home papers by this time," said Jim. "I can never face the poor old chap." I did not dare to lift my eyes at this till I heard him add, "I could never explain. He wouldn't understand." Then I looked up. He was smoking reflectively, and after a moment, rousing himself, began to talk again. He discovered at once a desire that I should not confound him with his partners in – crime, let us call it. He was not one of them; he was altogether of another sort. I gave no sign of dissent. I had no intention, for the sake of barren truth, to rob him of the smallest particle of any saving grace that would come in his way. I didn't know how much of it he believed himself. I didn't know what he was playing up to – if he was playing up to anything at all – and I suspect he did not know either; for it is my belief no man ever understands quite his own artful dodges to escape from the grim shadow of self-knowledge. I made no sound all the time he was wondering what he had better do after "that stupid inquiry was over".

'Apparently he shared Brierly's contemptuous opinion of these proceedings ordained by law. He would not know where to turn, he confessed, clearly thinking aloud rather than talking to me. Certificate gone, career broken, no money to get away, no work that he could obtain as far as he could see. At home he could perhaps get something; but it meant going to his people for help, and that he would not do. He saw nothing for it but ship before the mast – could get perhaps a quartermaster's billet in some steamer. Would do for a quartermaster.... "Do you think you would?" I asked, pitilessly. He jumped up, and going to the stone balustrade looked out into the night. In a moment he was back, towering above my chair with his youthful face clouded yet by the pain of a conquered emotion. He had understood very well I did not doubt his ability to steer a ship. In a voice that quavered a bit he asked me, "Why did I say that? I had been 'no end kind' to him. I had not even laughed at him when" – here he began to mumble – "that mistake, you know – made a confounded ass of myself." I broke in by saying rather warmly that for me such a mistake was not a matter to laugh at. He sat down and drank deliberately some coffee, emptying the small cup to the last drop. "That does not mean I admit for a moment the cap fitted," he declared, distinctly. "No?" I said. "No," he affirmed with quiet decision. "Do you know what *you* would have done? Do you? And you don't think yourself" ... he gulped something ... "you don't think yourself a – a – cur?"

'And with this – upon my honour! – he looked up at me inquisitively. It was a question it appears – a *bona-fide* question! However, he didn't wait for an answer. Before I could recover he went on, with his eyes straight before him, as if reading off something written on the body of the night. "It is all in being ready. I wasn't; not – not then. I don't want to excuse myself; but I would like to explain – I would like somebody to understand – somebody – one person at least! You! Why not you?"

'It was solemn, and a little ridiculous, too, as they always are, those struggles of an individual trying to save from the fire his idea of what his moral identity should be, this precious notion of a convention, only one of the rules of the game, nothing more, but all the same so terribly effective by its assumption of unlimited power over natural instincts, by the awful penalties of its failure. He began his story quiety enough. On board that Dale Line steamer that had picked up these four floating in a boat upon the discreet sunset glow of the sea, they had been after the first day looked askance upon. The fat skipper told some story, the others had been silent, and at first it had been accepted. You don't cross-examine poor castaways you had the good luck to save, if not from cruel death, then at least from cruel suffering. Afterwards, with time to think it over, it might have struck the officers of the *Avondale* that there was "something fishy" in the affair;

but of course they would keep their doubts to themselves. They had picked up the captain, the mate, and two engineers of the steamer *Patna* sunk at sea, and that, very properly, was enough for them. I did not ask Jim about the nature of his feelings during the ten days he spent on board. From the way he narrated that part I was at liberty to infer he was partly stunned by the discovery he had made – the discovery about himself – and no doubt was at work trying to explain it away to the only man who was capable of appreciating all its tremendous magnitude. You must understand he did not try to minimize its importance. Of that I am sure; and therein lies his distinction. As to what sensations he experienced when he got ashore and heard the unforeseen conclusion of the tale in which he had taken such a pitiful part, he told me nothing of them, and it is difficult to imagine. I wonder whether he felt the ground cut from under his feet? I wonder? But no doubt he managed to get a fresh foothold very soon. He was ashore a whole fortnight waiting in the Sailors' Home, and as there were six or seven men staying there at the time, I had heard of him a little. Their languid opinion seemed to be that in addition to his other shortcomings, he was a sulky brute. He had passed these days on the veranda, buried in a long chair, and coming out of his place of sepulture only at meal-times or late at night, when he wandered on the quays all by himself, detached from his surroundings, irresolute and silent, like a ghost without a home to haunt. "I don't think I've spoken three words to a living soul in all that time," he said, making me very sorry for him; and directly he added, "One of these fellows would have been sure to blurt out something I had made up my mind not to put up with, and I didn't want a row. No! Not then. I was too – too ... I had no heart for it." "So that bulkhead held out after all," I remarked, cheerfully. "Yes," he murmured, "it held. And yet I swear to you I felt it bulge under my hand." "It's extraordinary what strains old iron will stand sometimes," I said. Thrown back in his seat, his legs stiffly out and arms hanging down, he nodded slightly several times. You could not conceive a sadder spectacle. Suddenly he lifted his head; he sat up; he slapped his thigh. "Ah! what a chance missed! My God! what a chance missed!" he blazed out, but the ring of the last "missed" resembled a cry wrung out by pain.

'He was silent again with a still, far-away look of fierce yearning after that missed distinction, with his nostrils for an instant dilated, sniffing the intoxicating breath of that wasted opportunity. If you think I was either surprised or shocked you do me an injustice in more ways than one! Ah, he was an imaginative beggar! He would give himself away; he would give himself up. I could see in his glance darted into the night all his inner being carried on, projected headlong into the fanciful realm of recklessly heroic aspirations. He had no leisure to regret what he had lost, he was so wholly and naturally concerned for what he had failed to obtain. He was very far away from me who watched him across three feet of space. With every instant he was penetrating deeper into the impossible world of romantic achievements. He got to the heart of it at last! A strange look of beatitude overspread his features, his eyes sparkled in the light of the candle burning between us; he positively smiled! He had penetrated to the very heart – to the very heart. It was an ecstatic smile that your faces – or mine either – will never wear, my dear boys. I whisked him back by saying, "If you had stuck to the ship, you mean!"

'He turned upon me, his eyes suddenly amazed and full of pain, with a bewildered, startled, suffering face, as though he had stumbled down from a star. Neither you nor I will ever look like this on any man. He shuddered profoundly, as if a cold finger-tip had touched his heart. Last of all he sighed.

'I was not in a merciful mood. He provoked one by his contradictory indiscretions. "It is unfortunate you didn't know beforehand!" I said with every unkind intention; but the perfidious shaft fell harmless – dropped at his feet like a spent arrow, as it were, and he did not think of picking it up. Perhaps he had not even seen it. Presently, lolling at ease, he said, "Dash it all! I tell you it bulged. I was holding up my lamp along the angle-iron in the lower deck when a flake of rust as big as the palm of my hand fell off the plate, all of itself." He passed his hand over his forehead. "The thing stirred and jumped off like something alive while I was looking at it." "That made you feel pretty bad," I observed, casually. "Do you suppose," he said, "that I was thinking of myself, with a hundred and sixty people at my back, all fast asleep in that fore-'tween-deck alone – and more of them aft; more on the deck – sleeping – knowing nothing about it – three times as many as there were boats for, even if there had been time? I expected to see the iron open out as I stood there and the rush of water going over them as they lay.... What could I do – what?"

'I can easily picture him to myself in the peopled gloom of the cavernous place, with the light of the bulk-lamp falling on a small portion of the bulkhead that had the weight of the ocean on the other side, and the breathing of unconscious sleepers in his ears. I can see him glaring at the iron, startled by the falling rust, overburdened by the knowledge of an imminent death. This, I gathered, was the second time he had been sent forward by that skipper of his, who, I rather think, wanted to keep him away from the bridge. He told me that his first impulse was to shout and straight away make all those people leap out of sleep in terror; but such an overwhelming sense of his helplessness came over him that he was not able to produce a sound. This is, I suppose, what people mean by the tongue cleaving to the roof of the mouth. "Too dry," was the concise expression he used in reference to this state. Without a sound, then, he scrambled out on deck through the number one hatch. A wind-sail rigged down there swung against him accidentally, and he remembered that the light touch of the canvas on his face nearly knocked him off the hatchway ladder.

'He confessed that his knees wobbled a good deal as he stood on the foredeck looking at another sleeping crowd. The engines having been stopped by that time, the steam was blowing off. Its deep rumble made the whole night vibrate like a bass string. The ship trembled to it.

'He saw here and there a head lifted off a mat, a vague form uprise in sitting posture, listen sleepily for a moment, sink down again into the billowy confusion of boxes, steam-winches, ventilators. He was aware all these people did not know enough to take intelligent notice of that strange noise. The ship of iron, the men with white faces, all the sights, all the sounds, everything on board to that ignorant and pious multitude was strange alike, and as trustworthy as it would for ever remain incomprehensible. It occurred to him that the fact was fortunate. The idea of it was simply terrible.

'You must remember he believed, as any other man would have done in his place, that the ship would go down at any moment; the bulging, rust-eaten plates that kept back the ocean, fatally must give way, all at once like an undermined dam, and let in a sudden and overwhelming flood. He stood still looking at these recumbent bodies, a doomed man aware of his fate, surveying the silent company of the dead. They *were* dead! Nothing could save them! There were boats enough for half of them perhaps, but there was no time. No time! No time! It did not seem worth while to open his lips, to stir hand or foot. Before he could shout three words, or make three steps, he would be floundering in a sea whitened awfully by the desperate struggles of human beings, clamorous with the distress of cries for help. There was no help. He imagined what would happen perfectly; he went through it all motionless by the hatchway with the lamp in his hand – he went through it to the very last harrowing detail. I think he went through it again while he was telling me these things he could not tell the court.

' "I saw as clearly as I see you now that there was nothing I could do. It seemed to take all life out of my limbs. I thought I might just as well stand where I was and wait. I did not think I had many seconds . . ." Suddenly the steam ceased blowing off. The noise, he remarked, had been distracting, but the silence at once became intolerably oppressive.

' "I thought I would choke before I got drowned," he said.

'He protested he did not think of saving himself. The only distinct thought formed, vanishing, and reforming in his brain, was: eight hundred people and seven boats; eight hundred people and seven boats.

' "Somebody was speaking aloud inside my head," he said a little wildly. "Eight hundred people and seven boats – and no time! Just think of it." He leaned towards me across the little table, and I tried to avoid his stare. "Do you think I was afraid of death?" he asked in a voice very fierce and low. He brought down his open hand with a bang that made the coffee-cups dance. "I am ready to swear I was not – I was not. . . . By God – no!" He hitched himself upright and crossed his arms; his chin fell on his breast.

'The soft clashes of crockery reached us faintly through the high windows. There was a burst of voices, and several men came out in high good-humour into the gallery.They were exchanging jocular reminiscences of the donkeys in Cairo. A pale anxious youth stepping softly on long legs was being chaffed by a strutting and rubicund globe-trotter about his purchases in the bazaar. "No, really – do you think I've been done to that extent?" he inquired very earnest and deliberate. The band moved away, dropping into chairs as they went; matches flared, illuminating for a second faces without the ghost of an expression and the flat gaze of white shirt-fronts; the hum of many conversations animated with the ardour of feasting sounded to me absurd and infinitely remote.

' "Some of the crew were sleeping on the number one hatch within reach of my arm," began Jim again.

'You must know they kept Kalashee watch in that ship, all hands sleeping through the night, and only the reliefs of quartermasters and look-out men being called. He was tempted to grip and shake the shoulder of the nearest lascar, but he didn't. Something held his arms down along his sides. He was not afraid – oh no! he just couldn't – that's all. He was not afraid of death perhaps, but I'll tell you what, he was afraid of the emergency. His confounded imagination had evoked for him all the horrors of panic, the trampling rush, the pitiful screams, boats swamped – all the appalling incidents of a disaster at sea he had ever heard of. He might have been resigned to die but I suspect he wanted to die without added terrors, quietly, in a sort of peaceful trance. A certain readiness to perish is not so very rare, but it is seldom that you meet men whose souls, steeled in the impenetrable armour of resolution, are ready to fight a losing battle to the last, the desire of peace waxes stronger as hope declines, till at last it conquers the very desire of life. Which of us here has not observed this, or maybe experienced something of that feeling in his own person – this extreme weariness of emotions, the vanity of effort, the yearning for rest? Those striving with unreasonable forces know it well, – the shipwrecked castaways in boats, wanderers lost in a desert, men battling against the unthinking might of nature, or the stupid brutality of crowds.'

CHAPTER 8

'How long he stood stock-still by the hatch expecting every moment to feel the ship dip under his feet and the rush of water to take him at the back and toss him like a chip, I cannot say. Not very long – two minutes perhaps. A couple of men he could not make out began to converse drowsily, and also, he could not tell where, he detected a curious noise of shuffling feet. Above these faint sounds there was that awful stillness preceding a catastrophe, that trying silence of the moment before the crash; then it came into his head that perhaps he would have time to rush along and cut all the lanyards of the gripes, so that the boats would float off as the ship went down.

'The *Patna* had a long bridge, and all the boats were up there, four on one side and three on the other – the smallest of them on the port-side and nearly abreast of the steering gear. He assured me, with evident anxiety to be believed, that he had been most careful to keep them ready for instant service. He knew his duty. I dare say he was a good enough mate as far as that went. "I always believed in being prepared for the worst," he commented, staring anxiously in my face. I nodded my approval of the sound principle, averting my eyes before the subtle unsoundness of the man.

'He started unsteadily to run. He had to step over legs, avoid stumbling against the heads. Suddenly someone caught hold of his coat from below, and a distressed voice spoke under his elbow. The light of the lamp he carried in his right hand fell upon an upturned dark face whose eyes entreated him together with the voice. He had picked up enough of the language to understand the word water, repeated several times in a tone of insistence, of prayer, almost of despair. He gave a jerk to get away, and felt an arm embrace his leg.

' "The beggar clung to me like a drowning man," he said, impressively. "Water, water! What water did he mean? What did he know? As calmly as I could I ordered him to let go. He was stopping me, time was pressing, other men began to stir; I wanted time – time to cut the boats adrift. He got hold of my hand now, and I felt that he would begin to shout. It flashed upon me it was enough to start a panic, and I hauled off with my free arm and slung the lamp in his face. The glass jingled, the light went out, but the blow made him let go, and I ran off – I wanted to get at the boats; I wanted to get at the boats. He leaped after me from behind. I turned on him. He would not keep quiet; he tried to shout; I had half throttled him before I made out what he wanted. He wanted some water – water to drink; they were on strict allowance, you know, and he had with him a young boy I had noticed several times. His child was sick – and thirsty. He had caught sight of me as I passed by, and was begging for a little water. That's all. We were under the bridge in the dark. He kept on snatching at my wrists; there was no getting rid of him. I dashed into my berth, grabbed my water-bottle, and thrust it into his hands. He vanished. I didn't find out till then how much I was in want of a drink myself." He leaned on one elbow with a hand over his eyes.

'I felt a creepy sensation all down my backbone; there was something peculiar in all this. The fingers of the hand that shaded his brow trembled slightly. He broke the short silence.

' "These things happen only once to a man and . . . Ah! well! When I got on the bridge at last the beggars were getting one of the boats off the chocks. A boat! I was running up the ladder when a heavy blow fell on my shoulder, just missing my head. It didn't stop me, and the chief engineer – they had got him out of his bunk by then – raised the boat-stretcher again. Somehow I had no mind to be surprised at anything. All this seemed natural – and awful – and awful. I dodged that miserable maniac, lifted him off the deck as though he had been a little child, and he started whispering in my arms: 'Don't! Don't! I thought you were one of them niggers.' I flung him away, he skidded along the bridge and knocked the legs from under the little chap – the second. The skipper, busy about the boat, looked round and came at me head down, growling like a wild beast. I flinched no more than a stone. I was as solid standing there as this," he tapped lightly with his knuckles the wall beside his chair. "It was as though I had heard it all, seen it all, gone through it all twenty times already. I wasn't afraid of them. I drew back my fist and he stopped short, muttering –

' " 'Ah! it's you. Lend me a hand quick.'

' "That's what he said. Quick! As if anybody could be quick enough. 'Aren't you going to do something?' I asked. 'Yes. Clear out,' he snarled over his shoulder.

' "I don't think I understood then what he meant. The other two had picked themselves up by that time, and they rushed together to the boat.

They tramped, they wheezed, they shoved, they cursed the boat, the ship, each other – cursed me. All in mutters. I didn't move, I didn't speak. I watched the slant of the ship. She was as still as if landed on the blocks in a dry dock – only she was like this." He held up his hand, palm under, the tips of the fingers inclined downwards. "Like this," he repeated. "I could see the line of the horizon before me, as clear as a bell, above her stem-head; I could see the water far off there black and sparkling, and still – still as a pond, deadly still, more still than ever sea was before – more still than I could bear to look at. Have you watched a ship floating head down, checked in sinking by a sheet of old iron too rotten to stand being shored up. Have you? Oh yes, shored up? I thought of that – I thought of every mortal thing; but can you shore up a bulkhead in five minutes – or in fifty for that matter? Where was I going to get men that would go down below? And the timber – the timber! Would you have had the courage to swing the maul for the first blow if you had seen that bulkhead? Don't say you would: you had not seen it; nobody would. Hang it – to do a thing like that you must believe there is a chance, one in a thousand, at least, some ghost of a chance; and you would not have believed. Nobody would have believed. You think me a cur for standing there, but what would you have done? What! You can't tell – nobody can tell. One must have time to turn round. What would you have me do? Where was the kindness in making crazy with fright all those people I could not save single-handed – that nothing could save? Look here! As true as I sit on this chair before you . . . ."

'He drew quick breaths at every few words and shot quick glances at my face, as though in his anguish he was watchful of the effect. He was not speaking to me, he was only speaking before me, in a dispute with an invisible personality, an antagonistic and inseparable partner of his existence – another possessor of his soul. These were issues beyond the competency of a court of inquiry: it was a subtle and momentous quarrel as to the true essence of life, and did not want a judge. He wanted an ally, a helper, an accomplice. I felt the risk I ran of being circumvented, blinded, decoyed, bullied, perhaps, into taking a definite part in a dispute impossible of decision if one had to be fair to all the phantoms in possession – to the reputable that had its claims and to the disreputable that had its exigencies. I can't explain to you who haven't seen him and who hear his words only at second hand the mixed nature of my feelings. It seemed to me I was being made to comprehend the Inconceivable – and I know of nothing to compare with the discomfort of such a sensation. I was made to look at the convention that lurks in all truth and on the essential sincerity of falsehood. He appealed to all sides at once – to the side turned perpetually to the light of day, and to that side of us which, like the other hemisphere of the moon, exists stealthily in perpetual darkness, with only a fearful ashy light falling at times on the edge. He swayed me. I own to it, I own up. The occasion was obscure, insignificant – what you will: a lost youngster, one in a million – but then he was one of us; an incident as completely devoid of importance as the flooding of an ant-heap, and yet the mystery of his attitude got hold of me as though he had been an individual in the forefront of his kind, as if the obscure truth involved were momentous enough to affect mankind's conception of itself. . . .'

Marlow paused to put new life into his expiring cheroot, seemed to forget all about the story, and abruptly began again.

'My fault of course. One has no business really to get interested. It's a weakness of mine. His was of another kind. My weakness consists in not having a discriminating eye for the incidental – for the externals – no eye for the hod of the rag-picker or the fine linen of the next man. Next man – that's it. I have met so many men," he pursued, with momentary sadness – 'met them, too, with a certain – certain – impact, let us say; like this fellow, for instance – and in each case all I could see was merely the human being. A confounded democratic quality of vision which may be better than total blindness, but has been of no advantage to me, I can assure you. Men expect one to take into account their fine linen. But I never could get up any enthusiasm about these things. Oh! it's a failing; it's a failing; and then comes a soft evening; a lot of men too indolent for whist – and a story . . .'

He paused again to wait for an encouraging remark perhaps, but nobody spoke; only by the host, as if reluctantly performing a duty, murmured –

'You are so subtle, Marlow.'

'Who? I?' said Marlow in a low voice. 'Oh, no! But *he* was; and try as I may for the success of this yarn, I am missing innumerable shades – they were so fine, so difficult to render in colourless words. Because he complicated matters by being so simple, too – the simplest poor devil! . . . By Jove! he was amazing. There he sat telling me that just as I saw him before my eyes he wouldn't be afraid to face anything – and believing in it, too. I tell you it was fabulously innocent and it was enormous, enormous! I watched him covertly, just as though I had suspected him of an intention to take a jolly good rise out of me. He was confident that, on the square, "on the square, mind!" there was nothing he couldn't meet. Ever since he had been "so high" – "quite a little chap", he had been preparing himself for all the difficulties that can beset one on land and water. He confessed proudly to this kind of foresight. He had been elaborating dangers and defences, expecting the worst, rehearsing his best. He must have led a most exalted existence. Can you fancy it? A succession of adventures, so much glory, such a victorious progress! and the deep sense of his sagacity crowning every day of his inner life. He forgot himself; his eyes shone; and with every word my heart, searched by the light of his absurdity, was growing heavier in my breast. I had no mind to laugh, and lest I should smile I made for myself a stolid face. He gave signs of irritation.

' "It is always the unexpected that happens," I said in a propitiatory tone. My obtuseness provoked him into a contemptuous "Pshaw!" I suppose he meant that the unexpected couldn't touch him; nothing less than the unconceivable itself could get over his perfect state of preparation. He had been taken unawares – and he whispered to himself a malediction upon the waters and the firmament, upon the ship, upon the men. Everything had betrayed him! He had been tricked into that sort of high-minded resignation which prevented him lifting as much as his little finger, while these others who had a very clear perception of the actual necessity were tumbling against each other and sweating desperately over that boat business. Something had gone wrong there at the last moment. It appears that in their flurry they had contrived in some mysterious way to get the sliding bolt of the foremost boat-chock jammed tight, and forthwith had gone out of the remnants of their minds over the deadly nature of that accident. It must have been a pretty sight, the fierce industry of these beggars toiling on a motionless ship that floated quietly in the silence of a world asleep, fighting against time for the freedom of that boat, grovelling on all-fours, standing up in despair, tugging, pushing, snarling at each other venomously, ready to kill, ready to weep, and only kept from flying at each other's throats by the fear of death that stood silent behind them like an inflexible and cold-eyed taskmaster. Oh, yes! It must have been a pretty sight. He saw it all, he could talk about it with scorn and bitterness; he had a minute knowledge of it by means of some sixth sense, I conclude, because he swore to me he had remained apart without a glance at them and at the boat – without one single glance. And I believe him. I should think he was too busy watching the threatening slant of the ship, the suspended menace discovered in the midst of the most perfect security – fascinated by the sword hanging by a hair over his imaginative head.

'Nothing in the world moved before his eyes, and he could depict to himself without hindrance the sudden swing upwards of the dark sky-line, the sudden tilt up of the vast plain of the sea, the swift still rise, the brutal fling, the grasp of the abyss, the struggle without hope, the starlight closing over his head for ever like the vault of a tomb – the revolt of his young life – the black end. He could! By Jove! who couldn't? And you must remember he was a finished artist in that peculiar way, he was a gifted poor devil with the faculty of swift and forestalling vision. The sights it showed him had turned him into cold stone from the soles of his feet to the nape of his neck; but there was a hot dance of thoughts in his head, a dance of lame, blind, mute thoughts – a whirl of awful cripples. Didn't I tell you he confessed himself before me as though I had the power to bind and to loose? He burrowed deep, deep, in the hope of my absolution, which would have been of no good to him. This was one of those cases which no solemn deception can palliate, which no man can help; where his very Maker seems to abandon a sinner to his own devices.

'He stood on the starboard side of the bridge, as far as he could get from the struggle for the boat, which went on with the agitation of madness and the stealthiness of a conspiracy. The two Malays had meantime remained holding to the wheel. Just picture to yourselves the actors in that, thank God! unique, episode of the sea, four beside themselves with fierce and secret exertions, and three looking on in complete immobility, above the awnings covering the profound ignorance of hundreds of human beings, with their weariness, with their dreams, with their hopes, arrested, held by an invisible hand on the brink of annihilation. For that they were so, makes no doubt to me: given the state of the ship, this was the deadliest possible description of accident that could happen. These beggars by the boat had every reason to go distracted with funk. Frankly, had I been there I would not have given as much as a counterfeit farthing for the ship's chance to keep above water to the end of each successive second. And still she floated! These sleeping pilgrims were destined to accomplish their whole pilgrimage to the bitterness of some other end. It was as if the Omnipotence whose mercy they confessed had needed their humble testimony on earth for a while longer, and had looked down to make a sign, "Thou shalt not!" to the ocean. Their escape would trouble me as a prodigiously inexplicable event, did I not know how tough old iron can be – as tough sometimes as the spirit of some men we meet now and then, worn to a shadow and breasting the weight of life. Not in the least wonder of these twenty minutes, to my mind, is the behaviour of the two helmsmen. They were amongst the native batch of all sorts brought over from Aden to give evidence at the inquiry. One of them, labouring under intense bashfulness, was very young, and with his smooth, yellow, cheery countenance looked even younger than he was. I remember perfectly Brierly asking him, through the interpreter, what he thought of it at the time, and the interpreter, after a short colloquy, turning to the court with an important air –

' "He says he thought nothing."

'The other with patient blinking eyes, a blue cotton handkerchief, faded with much washing, bound with a smart twist over a lot of grey wisps, his face shrunk into grim hollows, his brown skin made darker by a mesh of wrinkles, explained that he had a knowledge of some evil thing befalling the ship, but there had been no order; he could not remember an order; why should he leave the helm? To some further questions he jerked back his spare shoulders, and declared it never came into his mind then that the white men were about to leave the ship through fear of death. He did not believe it now. There might have been secret reasons. He wagged his old chin knowingly. Aha! secret reasons. He was a man of great experience, and he wanted *that* white Tuan to know – he turned towards Brierly, who didn't raise his head – that he had acquired a knowledge of many things by serving white men on the sea for a great number of years – and, suddenly, with shaky excitement he poured upon our spellbound attention a lot of queer-sounding names, names of dead-and-gone skippers, names of forgotten country ships, names of familiar and distorted sound, as if the hand of dumb time had been at work on them for ages. They stopped him at last. A silence fell upon the court, – a silence that remained unbroken for at least a minute, and passed gently into a deep murmur. This episode was *the* sensation of the second day's proceedings – affecting all the audience, affecting everybody except Jim, who was sitting moodily at the end of the first bench, and never looked up at this extraordinary and damning witness that seemed possessed of some mysterious theory of defence.

'So these two lascars stuck to the helm of that ship without steerage-way, where death would have found them if such had been their destiny. The whites did not give them half a glance, had probably forgotten their existence. Assuredly Jim did not remember it. He remembered he could do nothing; he could do nothing, now he was alone. There was nothing to do but to sink with the ship. No use making a disturbance about it. Was there? He waited upstanding, without a sound, stiffened in the idea of some sort of heroic discretion. The first engineer ran cautiously across the bridge to tug at his sleeve.

' "Come and help! For God's sake, come and help!"

'He ran back to the boat on the points of his toes, and returned directly to worry at his sleeve, begging and cursing at the same time.

' "I believe he would have kissed my hands," said Jim, savagely, "and, next moment, he starts foaming and whispering in my face, 'If I had the time I would like to crack your skull for you.' I pushed him away. Suddenly he caught hold of me round the neck. Damn him! I hit him. I hit out without looking. 'Won't you save your own life – you infernal coward?' he sobs. Coward! He called me an infernal coward! Ha! ha! ha! ha! He called me – ha! ha! ha . . ."

'He had thrown himself back and was shaking with laughter. I had never in my life heard anything so bitter as that noise. It fell like a blight on all the merriment about donkeys, pyramids, bazaars, or what not. Along the whole dim length of the gallery the voices dropped, the pale blotches of faces turned our way with one accord, and the silence became so profound that the clear tinkle of a teaspoon falling on the tessellated floor of the veranda rang out like a tiny and silvery scream.

' "You mustn't laugh like this, with all these people about," I remonstrated. "It isn't nice for them, you know."

'He gave no sign of having heard at first, but after a while, with a stare that, missing me altogether, seemed to probe the heart of some awful vision, he muttered carelessly – "Oh, they'll think I am drunk."

'And after that you would have thought from his appearance he would never make a sound again. But – no fear! He could no more stop telling now than he could have stopped living by the mere exertion of his will.'

CHAPTER 9

' "I was saying to myself, 'Sink – curse you! Sink!" ' These were the words with which he began again. He wanted it over. He was severely left alone, and he formulated in his head this address to the ship in a tone of imprecation, while at the same time he enjoyed the privilege of witnessing scenes – as far as I can judge – of low comedy. They were still at that bolt. The skipper was ordering. "Get under and try to lift"; and the others naturally shirked. You understand that to be squeezed flat under the keel of a boat wasn't a desirable position to be caught in if the ship went down suddenly. "Why don't you – you the strongest?" whined the little engineer. "Gott-for-dam! I am too thick," spluttered the skipper in despair. It was funny enough to make angels weep. They stood idle for a moment, and suddenly the chief engineer rushed again at Jim.

' "Come and help, man! Are you mad to throw your only chance away? Come and help, man! Man! Look there – look!"

'And at last Jim looked astern where the other pointed with maniacal insistence. He saw a silent black squall which had eaten up already one-third of the sky. You know how these squalls come up there about that time of the year. First you see a darkening of the horizon – no more; then a cloud rises opaque like a wall. A straight edge of vapour lined with sickly whitish gleams flies up from the southwest, swallowing the stars in whole constellations; its shadow flies over the waters, and confounds sea and sky into one abyss of obscurity. And all is still. No thunder, no wind, no sound; not a flicker of lightning. Then in the tenebrous immensity a livid arch appears; a swell or two like undulations of the very darkness run past, and suddenly, wind and rain strike together with a peculiar impetuosity as if they had burst through something solid. Such a cloud had come up while they weren't looking. They had just noticed it, and were perfectly justified in surmising that if in absolute stillness there was some chance for the ship to keep afloat a few minutes longer, the least disturbance of the sea would make an end of her instantly. Her first nod to the swell that precedes the burst of such a squall would be also her last, would become a plunge, would, so to speak, be prolonged into a long dive, down, down to the bottom. Hence these new capers of their fright, these new antics in which they displayed their extreme aversion to die.

' "It was black, black," pursued Jim with moody steadiness. "It had sneaked upon us from behind. The infernal thing! I suppose there had been at the back of my head some hope yet. I don't know. But that was all over anyhow. It maddened me to see myself caught like this. I was angry, as though I had been trapped. I *was* trapped! The night was hot, too, I remember. Not a breath of air."

'He remembered so well that, gasping in the chair, he seemed to sweat and choke before my eyes. No doubt it maddened him; it knocked him over afresh – in a manner of speaking – but it made him also remember that important purpose which had sent him rushing on that bridge only to slip clean out of his mind. He had intended to cut the life-boats clear of the ship. He whipped out his knife and went to work slashing as though he had seen nothing, had heard nothing, had known of no one on board. They thought him hopelessly wrong-headed and crazy, but dared not protest noisily against this useless loss of time. When he had done he returned to the very same spot from which he had started. The chief was there, ready with a clutch at him to whisper close to his head, scathingly, as though he wanted to bite his ear —

' "You silly fool! do you think you'll get the ghost of a show when all that lot of brutes is in the water? Why, they will batter your head for you from these boats."

'He wrung his hands, ignored, at Jim's elbow. The skipper kept up a nervous shuffle in one place and mumbled, "Hammer! hammer! Mein Gott! Get a hammer."

'The little engineer whimpered like a child, but broken arm and all, he turned out the least craven of the lot as it seems, and, actually, mustered enough pluck to run an errand to the engine-room. No trifle it must be owned in fairness to him. Jim told me he darted desperate looks like a cornered man, gave one low wail, and dashed off. He was back instantly clambering, hammer in hand, and without a pause flung himself at the bolt. The others gave up Jim at once and ran off to assist. He heard the tap, tap of the hammer, the sound of the released chock falling over. The boat was clear. Only then he turned to look – only then. But he kept his distance – he kept his distance. He wanted me to know he had kept his distance; that there was nothing in common between him and these men – who had the hammer. Nothing whatever. It is more than probable he thought himself cut off from them by a space that could not be traversed, by an obstacle that could not be overcome, by a chasm without bottom. He was as far as he could get from them – the whole breadth of the ship.

'His feet were glued to that remote spot and his eyes to their indistinct group bowed together and swaying strangely in the common torment of fear. A hand-lamp lashed to a stanchion above a little table rigged up on the bridge – the *Patna* had no chart-room amidships – threw a light on their labouring shoulders, on their arched and bobbing backs. They pushed at the bow of the boat; they pushed out into the night; they pushed, and would no more look back at him. They had given him up as if indeed he had been too far, too hopelessly separated from themselves, to be worth an appealing word, a glance, or a sign. They had no leisure to look back upon his passive heroism, to feel the sting of his abstention. The boat was heavy; they pushed at the bow with no breath to spare for an encouraging word: but the turmoil of terror that had scattered their self-control like chaff before the wind, converted their desperate exertions into a bit of fooling, upon my word fit for knockabout clowns in a farce. They pushed with their hands, with their heads, they pushed for dear life with all the weight of their bodies, they pushed with all the might of their souls – only no sooner had they succeeded in canting the stem clear of the davit than they would leave off like one man and start a wild scramble into her. As a natural consequence the boat would swing in abruptly, driving them back, helpless and jostling against each other. They would stand nonplussed for a while, exchanging in fierce whispers all the infamous names they could call to mind, and go at it again. Three times this occurred. He described it to me with morose thoughtfulness. He hadn't lost a single movement of that comic business. "I loathed them. I hated them. I had to look at all that," he said without emphasis, turning upon me a sombrely watchful glance. "Was ever there any one so shamefully tried!"

'He took his head in his hands for a moment, like a man driven to distraction by some unspeakable outrage. These were things he could not explain to the court – and not even to me; but I would have been little fitted for the reception of his confidences had I not been able at times to understand the pauses between the words. In this assault upon his fortitude there was the jeering intention of a spiteful and vile vengeance; there was an element of burlesque in his ordeal – a degradation of funny grimaces in the approach of death or dishonour.

'He related facts which I have not forgotten, but at this distance of time

I couldn't recall his very words: I only remember that he managed wonderfully to convey the brooding rancour of his mind into the bare recital of events. Twice, he told me, he shut his eyes in the certitude that the end was upon him already, and twice he had to open them again. Each time he noted the darkening of the great stillness. The shadow of the silent cloud had fallen upon the ship from the zenith, and seemed to have extinguished every sound of her teeming life. He could no longer hear the voices under the awnings. He told me that each time he closed his eyes a flash of thought showed him that crowd of bodies, laid out for death, as plain as daylight. When he opened them, it was to see the dim struggle of four men fighting like mad with a stubborn boat. "They would fall back before it time after time, stand swearing at each other, and suddenly make another rush in a bunch.... Enough to make you die laughing," he commented with downcast eyes; then raising them for a moment to my face with a dismal smile, "I ought to have a merry life of it, by God! for I shall see that funny sight a good many times yet before I die." His eyes fell again. "See and hear ... See and hear," he repeated twice, at long intervals, filled by vacant staring.

'He roused himself.

' "I made up my mind to keep my eyes shut," he said, "and I couldn't. I couldn't, and I don't care who knows it. Let them go through that kind of thing before they talk. Just let them – and do better – that's all. The second time my eyelids flew open and my mouth too. I had felt the ship move. She just dipped her bows – and lifted them gently – and slow! everlastingly slow; and ever so little. She hadn't done that much for days. The cloud had raced ahead, and this first swell seemed to travel upon a sea of lead. There was no life in that stir. It managed, though, to knock over something in my head. What would you have done? You are sure of yourself – aren't you? What would you do if you felt now – this minute – the house here move, just move a little under your chair. Leap! By heavens! you would take one spring from where you sit and land in the clump of bushes yonder."

'He flung his arm out at the night beyond the stone balustrade. I held my peace. He looked at me very steadily, very severe. There could be no mistake: I was being bullied now, and it behoved me to make no sign lest by gesture or a word I should be drawn into a fatal admission about myself which would have had some bearing on the case. I was not disposed to take any risk of that sort. Don't forget I had him before me, and really he was too much like one of us not to be dangerous. But if you want to know I don't mind telling you that I did, with a rapid glance, estimate the distance to the mass of denser blackness in the middle of the grass-plot before the veranda. He exaggerated. I would have landed short by several feet – and that's the only thing of which I am fairly certain.

'The last moment had come, as he thought, and he did not move. His feet remained glued to the planks if his thoughts were knocking about loose in his head. It was at this moment, too, that he saw one of the men around the boat step backwards suddenly, clutch at the air with raised arms, totter and collapse. He didn't exactly fall, he only slid gently into a sitting posture, all hunched up and with his shoulders propped against the side of the engine-room skylight. "That was the donkey-man. A haggard, white-faced chap with a ragged moustache. Acted third engineer," he explained.

' "Dead," I said. We had heard something of that in court.

' "So they say," he pronounced with sombre indifference. "Of course I never knew. Weak heart. The man had been complaining of being out of sorts for some time before. Excitement. Over-exertion. Devil only knows. Ha! ha! ha! It was easy to see he did not want to die either. Droll, isn't it? May I be shot if he hadn't been fooled into killing himself! Fooled – neither more nor less. Fooled into it, by heavens! just as I . . . Ah! If he had only kept still; if he had only told them to go to the devil when they came to rush him out of his bunk because the ship was sinking! If he had only stood by with his hands in his pockets and called them names!"

'He got up, shook his fist, glared at me, and sat down.

' "A chance missed, eh?" I murmured.

' "Why don't you laugh?" he said. "A joke hatched in hell. Weak heart! . . . I wish sometimes mine had been."

'This irritated me. "Do you?" I exclaimed with deep-rooted irony. "Yes! Can't *you* understand?" he cried. "I don't know what more you could wish for," I said, angrily. He gave me an utterly uncomprehending glance. This shaft had also gone wide of the mark, and he was not the man to bother about stray arrows. Upon my word, he was too unsuspecting; he was not fair game. I was glad that my missile had been thrown away, that he had not even heard the twang of the bow.

'Of course he could not know at the time the man was dead. The next minute – his last on board – was crowded with a tumult of events and sensations which beat about him like the sea upon a rock. I used the simile advisedly, because from his relation I am forced to believe he had preserved through it all a strange illusion of passiveness, as though he had not acted but had suffered himself to be handled by the infernal powers who had selected him for the victim of their practical joke. The first thing that came to him was the grinding surge of the heavy davits swinging out at last – a jar which seemed to enter his body from the deck through the soles of his feet, and travel up his spine to the crown of his head. Then, the squall being very near now, another and a heavier swell lifted the passive hull in a threatening heave that checked his breath, while his brain and his heart together were pierced as with daggers by panic-stricken screams. "Let go! For God's sake, let go! Let go! She's going." Following upon that the boat-falls ripped through the blocks, and a lot of men began to talk in startled tones under the awnings. "When these beggars did break out, their yelps were enough to wake the dead," he said. Next after the splashing shock of the boat literally dropped in the water, came the hollow noises of stamping and tumbling in her, mingled with confused shouts: "Unhook! Unhook! Shove! Unhook! Shove for your life! Here's a squall coming down on us. . . ." He heard, high above his head, the faint muttering of the wind; he heard below his feet a cry of pain. A lost voice alongside started cursing a swivel hook. The ship began to buzz fore and aft like a disturbed hive, and, as quietly as he was telling me all of this – because just then he was very quiet in attitude, in face, in voice – he went on to say without the slightest warning as it were, "I stumbled over his legs."

'This was the first I heard of his having moved at all. I could not restrain a grunt of surprise. Something had started him off at last, but of the exact moment, of the cause that tore him out of his immobility, he knew no more than the uprooted tree knows of the wind that laid it low. All this had come to him: the sounds, the sights, the legs of the dead man – by Jove! The infernal joke was being crammed devilishly down his throat, but – look you – he was not going to admit of any sort of swallowing motion in his gullet. It's extraordinary how he could cast upon you the spirit of his illusion. I listened as if to a tale of black magic at work upon a corpse.

' "He went over sideways, very gently, and this is the last thing I remember seeing on board," he continued. "I did not care what he did. It looked as though he were picking himself up: I thought he was picking himself up, of course: I expected him to bolt past me over the rail and drop into the boat after the others. I could hear them knocking about, down there, and a voice as if crying up a shaft called out 'George'. Then three voices together raised a yell. They came to me separately: one bleated, another screamed, one howled. Ough!"

'He shivered a little, and I beheld him rise slowly as if a steady hand from above had been pulling him out of the chair by his hair. Up, slowly – to his full height, and when his knees had locked stiff the hand let him go, and he swayed on his feet. There was a suggestion of awful stillness in his face, in his movements, in his very voice when he said "They shouted" – and involuntarily I pricked up my ears for the ghost of that shout that would be heard directly through the false effect of silence. "There were eight hundred people in that ship," he said, impaling me to the back of my seat with that awful blank stare. "Eight hundred living people, and they were yelling after the one dead man to come down and be saved. 'Jump, George! Jump! Oh, jump!' I stood by with my hand on the davit. I was very quiet. It had come over pitch dark. You could see neither sky nor sea. I heard the boat alongside go bump, bump, and not another sound down there for a while, but the ship under me was full of talking noises. Suddenly the skipper howled, 'Mein Gott! The squall! The squall! Shove off!' With the first hiss of rain, and the first gust of wind, they screamed, 'Jump, George! We'll catch you! Jump!' The ship began a slow plunge; the rain swept over her like a broken sea; my cap flew off my head; my breath was driven back into my throat. I heard as if I had been on the top of a tower another wild screech, 'Geo-o-o-orge! Oh, jump!' She was going down, down, head first under me...."

'He raised his hand deliberately to his face, and made picking motions with his fingers as though he had been bothered with cobwebs, and afterwards he looked into the open palm for quite half a second before he blurted out—

' "I had jumped ..." He checked himself, averted his gaze. ... "It seems," he added.

'His clear blue eyes turned to me with a piteous stare, and looking at him standing before me, dumbfounded and hurt, I was oppressed by a sad sense of resigned wisdom, mingled with the amused and profound pity of an old man helpless before a childish disaster.

' "Looks like it," I muttered.

' "I knew nothing about it till I looked up," he explained, hastily. And that's possible, too. You had to listen to him as you would to a small boy in trouble. He didn't know. It had happened somehow. It would never happen again. He had landed partly on somebody and fallen across a thwart. He felt as though all his ribs on his left side must be broken; then he rolled over, and saw vaguely the ship he had deserted uprising above him, with the red side-light glowing large in the rain like a fire on the brow of a hill seen through a mist. "She seemed higher than a wall; she loomed like a cliff over the boat. . . . I wished I could die," he cried. "There was no going back. It was as if I had jumped into a well – into an everlasting deep hole. . . ." '

CHAPTER 10

'He locked his fingers together and tore them apart. Nothing could be more true: he had indeed jumped into an everlasting deep hole. He had tumbled from a height he could never scale again. By that time the boat had gone driving forward past the bows. It was too dark just then for them to see each other, and, moreover, they were blinded and half drowned with rain. He told me it was like being swept by a flood through a cavern. They turned their backs to the squall; the skipper, it seems, got an oar over the stern to keep the boat before it, and for two or three minutes the end of the world had come through a deluge in a pitchy blackness. The sea hissed "like twenty thousand kettles". That's his simile, not mine. I fancy there was not much wind after the first gust; and he himself had admitted at the inquiry that the sea never got up that night to any extent. He crouched down in the bows and stole a furtive glance back. He saw just one yellow gleam of the masthead light high up and blurred like a last star ready to dissolve. "It terrified me to see it, still there," he said. That's what he said. What terrified him was the thought that the drowning was not yet over. No doubt he wanted to be done with that abomination as quickly as possible. Nobody in the boat made a sound. In the dark she seemed to fly, but of course she could not have had much way. Then the shower swept ahead, and the great, distracting, hissing noise followed the rain into the distance and died out. There was nothing to be heard then but the slight wash about the boat's sides. Somebody's teeth were chattering violently. A hand touched his back. A faint voice said, "You there?" Another cried out, shakily, "She's gone!" and they all stood up together to look astern. They saw no lights. All was black. A thin cold drizzle was driving into their faces. The boat lurched slightly. The teeth chattered faster, stopped, and began again twice before the man could master his shiver sufficiently to say, "Ju-ju-st in ti-ti-me. . . . Brrrr." He recognized the voice of the chief engineer saying surlily, "I saw her go down. I happened to turn my head." The wind had dropped almost completely.

'They watched in the dark with their heads half turned to windward as if expecting to hear cries. At first he was thankful the night had covered up the scene before his eyes, and then to know of it and yet to have seen and heard nothing appeared somehow the culminating-point of an awful misfortune. "Strange, isn't it?" he murmured, interrupting himself in his disjointed narrative.

'It did not seem so strange to me. He must have had an unconscious conviction that the reality could not be half as bad, not half as anguishing, appalling, and vengeful as the created terror of his imagination. I believe that, in this first moment, his heart was wrung with all the suffering, that his soul knew the accumulated savour of all the fear, all the horror, all the despair of eight hundred human beings pounced upon in the night by a sudden and violent death, else why should he have said, "It seemed to me that I must jump out of that accursed boat and swim back to see – half a mile – more – any distance – to the very spot . . ."? Why this impulse? Do you see the significance? Why back to the very spot? Why not drown alongside – if he meant drowning? why back to the very spot, to see – as if his imagination had to be soothed by the assurance that all was over before death could bring relief? I defy any one of you to offer another explanation. It was one of those bizarre and exciting glimpses through the fog. It was an extraordinary disclosure. He let it out as the most natural thing one could say. He fought down that impulse and then he became conscious of the silence. He mentioned this to me. A silence of the sea, of the sky, merged into one indefinite immensity still as death around these saved, palpitating lives. "You might have heard a pin drop in the boat," he said with a queer contraction of his lips, like a man trying to master his sensibilities while relating some extremely moving fact. A silence! God alone, who had willed him as he was, knows what he made of it in his heart. "I didn't think any spot on earth could be so still," he said. "You couldn't distinguish the sea from the sky; there was nothing to see and nothing to hear. Not a glimmer, not a shape, not a sound. You could have believed that every bit of dry land had gone to the bottom; that every man on earth but I and these beggars in the boat had got drowned." He leaned over the table with his knuckles propped amongst coffee-cups, liqueur-glasses, cigar-ends. "I seemed to believe it. Everything was gone and – all was over . . ." he fetched a deep sigh . . . "with me." '

Marlow sat up abruptly and flung away his cheroot with force. It made a darting red trail like a toy rocket fired through the drapery of creepers. Nobody stirred.

'Hey, what do you think of it?' he cried with sudden animation. 'Wasn't he true to himself, wasn't he? His saved life was over for want of ground under his feet, for want of sights for his eyes, for want of voices in his ears. Annihilation – hey! And all the time it was only a clouded sky, a sea that did not break, the air that did not stir. Only a night; only a silence.

'It lasted for a while, and then they were suddenly and unanimously moved to make a noise over their escape. "I knew from the first she would go." "Not a minute too soon." "A narrow squeak, b'gosh!" He said nothing, but the breeze that had dropped came back, a gentle draught freshened steadily, and the sea joined its murmuring voice to this talkative reaction succeeding the dumb moments of awe. She was gone! She was gone! Not a doubt of it. Nobody could have helped. They repeated the same words over and over again as though they couldn't stop themselves. Never doubted she would go. The lights were gone. No mistake. The lights were gone. Couldn't expect anything else. She had to go.... He noticed that they talked as though they had left behind them nothing but an empty ship. They concluded she would not have been long when she once started. It seemed to cause them some sort of satisfaction. They assured each other that she couldn't have been long about it – "Just shot down like a flat-iron". The chief engineer declared that the masthead light at the moment of sinking seemed to drop "like a lighted match you throw down". At this the second laughed hysterically. "I am g-g-glad, I am gla-a-a-d." His teeth went on "like an electric rattle," said Jim, "and all at once he began to cry. He wept and blubbered like a child, catching his breath and sobbing 'Oh, dear! oh, dear! oh, dear!' He would be quiet for a while and start suddenly, 'Oh, my poor arm! oh, my poor a-a-a-arm!' I felt I could knock him down. Some of them sat in the stern sheets. I could just make out their shapes. Voices came to me, mumble, mumble, grunt, grunt. All this seemed very hard to bear. I was cold, too. And I could do nothing. I thought that if I moved I would have to go over the side and ..."

'His hand groped stealthily, came in contact with a liqueur-glass and was withdrawn suddenly as if it had touched a red-hot coal. I pushed the bottle slightly. "Won't you have some more?" I asked. He looked at me angrily. "Don't you think I can tell you what there is to tell without screwing myself up?" he asked. The squad of globe-trotters had gone to bed. We were alone but for a vague white form erect in the shadow, that, being looked at, cringed forward, hesitated, backed away silently. It was getting late, but I did not hurry my guest.

'In the midst of his forlorn state he heard his companions begin to abuse someone. "What kept you from jumping, you lunatic?" said a scolding voice. The chief engineer left the sternsheets, and could be heard clambering forward as if with hostile intentions against "the greatest idiot that ever was". The skipper shouted with rasping effort offensive epithets from where he sat at the oars. He lifted his head at that uproar, and heard the name "George", while a hand in the dark struck him on the breast. "What have you got to say for yourself, you fool?" queried somebody, with a sort of virtuous fury. "They were after me," he said. "They were abusing me – abusing me ... by the name of George."

'He paused to stare, tried to smile, turned his eyes away and went on. "That little second puts his head right under my nose, 'Why, it's that blasted mate!' 'What!' howls the skipper from the other end of the boat. 'No!' shrieks the chief. And he, too, stopped to look at my face."

'The wind had left the boat suddenly. The rain began to fall again, and the soft, uninterrupted, a little mysterious sound with which the sea receives a shower arose on all sides in the night. "They were too taken aback to say anything more at first," he narrated steadily, "and what could I have to say to them?" He faltered for a moment, and made an effort to go on. "They called me horrible names." His voice sinking to a whisper, now and then would leap up suddenly, hardened by the passion of scorn, as though he had been talking of secret abominations, "Never mind what they called me," he said, grimly. "I could hear hate in their voices. A good thing, too. They could not forgive me for being in that boat. They hated it. It made them mad.... " He laughed short.... "But it kept me from – Look! I was sitting with my arms crossed, on the gunwale! ... " He perched himself smartly on the edge of the table and crossed his arms.... "Like this – see? One little tilt backwards and I would have been gone – after the others. One little tilt – the least bit – the least bit." He frowned, and tapping his forehead with the tip of his middle finger, "It was there all the time," he said, impressively. "All the time – that notion. And the rain – cold, thick, cold as melted snow – colder – on my thin cotton clothes – I'll never be so cold again in my life, I know. And the sky was black, too – all black. Not a star, not a light anywhere. Nothing outside that confounded boat and those two yapping before me like a couple of mean mongrels at a tree'd thief. Yap! yap! What you doing here? You're a fine sort! Too much of a bloomin' gentleman to put his hand to it. Come out of your trance, did you? To sneak in? Did you? Yap! yap! You ain't fit to live! Yap! yap! Two of them together trying to out-bark each other. The other would bay from the stern through the rain – couldn't see him – couldn't make out – some of his filthy jargon. Yap! yap! Bow-ow-ow-ow-ow! Yap! yap! It was sweet to hear them; it kept me alive, I tell you. It saved my life. At it they went, as if trying to drive me overboard with the noise! ... I wonder you had pluck enough to jump. You ain't wanted here. If I had known who it was, I would have tipped you over – you skunk. What have you done with the other? Where did you get the pluck to jump – you coward? What's to prevent us three from firing you overboard? ... They were out of breath; the shower passed away upon the sea. Then nothing. There was nothing round the boat, not even a sound. Wanted to see me overboard, did they? Upon my soul! I think they would have had their wish if they had only kept quiet. Fire me overboard! Would they? 'Try,' I said. 'I would for twopence.' 'Too good for you,' they screeched together. It was so dark that it was only when one or the other of them moved that I was quite sure of seeing him. By heavens! I only wish they had tried."

'I couldn't help exclaiming, "What an extraordinary affair!"

' "Not bad – eh?" he said, as if in some sort astounded. "They pretended to think I had done away with that donkey-man for some reason or other. Why should I? And how the devil was I to know? Didn't I get, somehow into that boat? into that boat – I ... " The muscles round his lips contracted into an unconscious grimace that tore through the mask of his usual expression – something violent, short-lived, and illuminating like a twist of lightning that admits the eye for an instant into the secret convolutions of a cloud. "I did. I was plainly there with them – wasn't I? Isn't it awful a man should be driven to do a thing like that – and be responsible? What did I know about their George they were howling after? I remembered I had seen him curled up on the deck. 'Murdering coward!' the chief kept on calling me. He didn't seem able to remember any other two words. I didn't care, only his noise began to worry me. 'Shut up,' I said. At that he collected himself for a confounded screech. 'You killed him. You killed him.' 'No,' I shouted, 'but I will kill you directly.' I jumped up, and he fell backwards over a thwart with an awful loud thump. I don't know why. Too dark. Tried to step back, I suppose. I stood still facing aft, and the wretched little second began to whine, 'You ain't going to hit a chap with a broken arm – and you call yourself a gentleman, too.' I heard a heavy tramp – one – two – and wheezy grunting. The other beast was coming at me, clattering his oar over the stern. I saw him moving, big, big – as you see a man in a mist, in a dream. 'Come on,' I cried. I would have tumbled him over like a bale of shakings. He stopped, muttered to himself, and went back. Perhaps he had heard the wind. I didn't. It was the last heavy gust we had. He went back to his oar. I was sorry. I would have tried to – to ..."

'He opened and closed his curved fingers, and his hands had an eager and cruel flutter. "Steady, steady," I murmured.

' "Eh? What? I am not excited," he remonstrated, awfully hurt, and with a convulsive jerk of his elbow knocked over the cognac-bottle. I started forward, scraping my chair. He bounced off the table as if a mine had been exploded behind his back, and half turned before he alighted, crouching on his feet to show me a startled pair of eyes and a face white about the nostrils. A look of intense annoyance succeeded. "Awfully sorry. How clumsy of me!" he mumbled very vexed, while the pungent odour of spilt alcohol enveloped us suddenly with an atmosphere of a low drinking-bout in the cool, pure darkness of the night. The lights had been put out in the dining-hall; our candle glimmered solitary in the long gallery, and the columns had turned black from pediment to capital. On the vivid stars the high corner of the Harbour Office stood out distinct across the Esplanade, as though the sombre pile had glided nearer to see and hear.

'He assumed an air of indifference.

' "I dare say I am less calm now than I was then. I was ready for anything. These were trifles...."

' "You had a lively time of it in that boat," I remarked.

' "I was ready," he repeated. "After the ship's lights had gone, anything might have happened in that boat – anything in the world – and the world no wiser. I felt this, and I was pleased. It was just dark enough, too. We were like men walled up quick in a roomy grave. No concern with anything on earth. Nobody to pass an opinion. Nothing mattered." For the third time during this conversation he laughed harshly, but there was no one about to suspect him of being only drunk. "No fear, no law, no sounds, no eyes – not even our own, till – till sunrise at least."

'I was struck by the suggestive truth of his words. There is something peculiar in a small boat upon the wide sea. Over the lives borne from under the shadow of death there seems to fall the shadow of madness. When your ship fails you, your whole world seems to fail you; the world that made you, restrained you, taken care of you. It is as if the souls of men floating on an abyss and in touch with immensity had been set free for any excess of heroism, absurdity, or abomination. Of course, as with belief, thought, love, hate, conviction, or even the visual aspect of material things, there are as many shipwrecks as there are men, and in this one there was something abject which made the isolation more complete – there was a villainy of circumstances that cut these men off more completely from the rest of mankind, whose ideal of conduct had never undergone the trial of a fiendish and appalling joke. They were exasperated with him for being a half-hearted shirker: he focussed on them his hatred of the whole thing; he would have liked to take a signal revenge for the abhorrent opportunity they had put in his way. Trust a boat on the high seas to bring out the Irrational that lurks at the bottom of every thought, sentiment, sensation, emotion. It was part of the burlesque meanness pervading that particular disaster at sea that they did not come to blows. It was all threats, all a terribly effective feint, a sham from beginning to end, planned by the tremendous disdain of the Dark Powers whose real terrors, always on the verge of triumph, are perpetually foiled by the steadfastness of men. I asked, after waiting for a while, "Well, what happened?" A futile question. I knew too much already to hope for the grace of a single uplifting touch, for the favour of hinted madness, of shadowed horror. "Nothing," he said. "I meant business, but they meant noise only. Nothing happened."

'And the rising sun found him just as he had jumped up first in the bows of the boat. What a persistence of readiness! He had been holding the tiller in his hand, too, all the night. They had dropped the rudder overboard while attempting to ship it, and I suppose the tiller got kicked forward somehow while they were rushing up and down that boat trying to do all sorts of things at once so as to get clear of the side. It was a long heavy piece of hard wood, and apparently he had been clutching it for six hours or so. If you don't call that being ready! Can you imagine him, silent and on his feet half the night, his face to the gusts of rain, staring at sombre forms, watchful of vague movements, straining his ears to catch rare low murmurs in the sternsheets! Firmness of courage or effort of fear? What do you think? And the endurance is undeniable, too. Six hours more or less on the defensive; six hours of alert immobility while the boat drove slowly or floated arrested according to the caprice of the wind; while the sea, calmed, slept at last; while the clouds passed above his head; while the sky from an immensity lustreless and black, diminished to a sombre and lustrous vault, scintillated with a greater brilliance, faded to the east, paled at the zenith; while the dark shapes blotting the low stars astern got outlines, relief; became shoulders, heads, faces, features – confronted him with dreary stares, had dishevelled hair, torn clothes, blinked red eyelids at the white dawn. "They looked as though they had been knocking about drunk in gutters for a week," he described graphically; and then he muttered something about the sunrise being of a kind that foretells a calm day. You know that sailor habit of referring to the weather in every connexion. And on my side his few mumbled words were enough to make me see the lower limb of the sun clearing the line of the horizon, the tremble of a vast ripple running over all the visible expanse of the sea, as if the waters had shuddered, giving birth to the globe of light, while the last puff of the breeze would stir the air in a sigh of relief.

' "They sat in the stern shoulder to shoulder, with the skipper in the middle, like three dirty owls, and stared at me," I heard him say with an intention of hate that distilled a corrosive virtue into the common-place words like a drop of powerful poison falling into a glass of water; but my thoughts dwelt upon that sunrise. I could imagine under the pellucid emptiness of the sky these four men imprisoned in the solitude of the sea, the lonely sun, regardless of the speck of life, ascending the clear curve of the heaven as if to gaze ardently from a great height at his own splendour reflected in the still ocean. "They called out to me from aft," said Jim, "as though we had been chums together. I heard them. They were begging me to be sensible and drop that 'blooming piece of wood'. Why *would* I carry on so? They hadn't done me any harm – had they? There had been no harm.... No harm!"

'His face crimsoned as though he could not get rid of the air in his lungs.

' "No harm!" he burst out. "I leave it to you. You can understand. Can't you? You see it – don't you? No harm! Good God! What more could they have done? Oh, yes, I know very well – I jumped. Certainly. I jumped! I told you I jumped; but I tell you they were too much for any man. It was their doing as plainly as if they had reached up with a boat-hook and pulled me over. Can't you see it? You must see it? Come. Speak – straight out."

' "His uneasy eyes fastened upon mine, questioned, begged, challenged, entreated. For the life of me I couldn't help murmuring, "You've been tried." "More than is fair," he caught up, swiftly. "I wasn't given half a chance – with a gang like that. And now they were friendly – oh, so damnably friendly! Chums, shipmates. All in the same boat. Make the best of it. They hadn't meant anything. They didn't care a hang for George. George had gone back to his berth for something at the last moment and got caught. The man was a manifest fool. Very sad, of course.... Their eyes looked at me; their lips moved; they wagged their heads at the other end of the boat – three of them; they beckoned – to me. Why not? Hadn't I jumped? I said nothing. There are no words for the sort of things I wanted to say. If I had opened my lips just then I would have simply howled like an animal. I was asking myself when I would wake up. They urged me aloud to come aft and hear quietly what the skipper had to say. We were sure to be picked up before the evening – right in the track of all the Canal traffic; there was smoke to the north-west now.

' "It gave me an awful shock to see this faint, faint blur, this low trail of brown mist through which you could see the boundary of sea and sky. I called out to them that I could hear very well where I was. The skipper started swearing, as hoarse as a crow. He wasn't going to talk at the top of his voice for *my* accommodation. 'Are you afraid they will hear you on shore?' I asked. He glared as if he would have liked to claw me to pieces. The chief engineer advised him to humour me. He said I wasn't right in my head yet. The other rose astern, like a thick pillar of flesh – and talked – talked...."

'Jim remained thoughtful. "Well? I said. "What did I care what story they agreed to make up?" he cried, recklessly. "They could tell what they jolly well liked. It was their business. I knew the story. Nothing they could make people believe could alter it for me. I let him talk, argue – talk, argue. He went on and on and on. Suddenly I felt my legs give way under me. I was sick, tired – tired to death. I let fall the tiller, turned my back on them, and sat down on the foremost thwart. I had enough. They called to me to know if I understood – wasn't it true, every word of it? It was true, by God! after their fashion. I did not turn my head. I heard them palavering together. 'The silly ass won't say anything.' 'Oh, he understands well enough.' 'Let him be; he will be all right.' 'What can he do?' What could I do? Weren't we all in the same boat? I tried to be deaf. The smoke had disappeared to the northward. It was a dead calm. They had a drink from the water-breaker, and I drank, too. Afterwards they made a great business of spreading the boat-sail over the gunwales. Would I keep a look-out? They crept under, out of my sight, thank God! I felt weary, weary, done up, as if I hadn't had one hour's sleep since the day I was born. I couldn't see the water for the glitter of the sunshine. From time to time one of them would creep out, stand up to take a look all round, and get under again. I could hear spells of snoring below the sail. Some of them could sleep. One of them at least. I couldn't! All was light, light, and the boat seemed to be falling through it. Now and then I would feel quite surprised to find myself sitting on a thwart. . . ."

'He began to walk with measured steps to and fro before my chair, one hand in his trousers-pocket, his head bent thoughtfully, and his right arm at long intervals raised for a gesture that seemed to put out of his way an invisible intruder.

' "I suppose you think I was going mad," he began in a changed tone. "And well you may, if you remember I had lost my cap. The sun crept all the way from east to west over my bare head, but that day I could not come to any harm, I suppose. The sun could not make me mad. . . ." His right arm put aside the idea of madness. . . . "Neither could it kill me. . . ." Again his arm repulsed a shadow. . . . "*That* rested with me."

' "Did it?" I said, inexpressibly amazed at this new turn, and I looked at him with the same sort of feeling I might be fairly conceived to experience had he, after spinning round on his heel, presented an altogether new face.

' "I didn't get brain fever, I did not drop dead either," he went on. "I didn't bother myself at all about the sun over my head. I was thinking as coolly as any man that ever sat thinking in the shade. That greasy beast of a skipper poked his big cropped head from under the canvas and screwed his fishy eyes up at me. 'Donnerwetter! you will die,' he growled, and drew in like a turtle. I had seen him. I had heard him. He didn't interrupt me. I was thinking just then that I wouldn't."

'He tried to sound my thought with an attentive glance dropped on me in passing. "Do you mean to say you had been deliberating with yourself whether you would die?" I asked in as impenetrable a tone as I could command. He nodded without stopping. "Yes, it had come to that as I sat there alone," he said. He passed on a few steps to the imaginary end of his beat, and when he flung round to come back both his hands were thrust deep into his pockets. He stopped short in front of my chair and looked down. "Don't you believe it?" he inquired with tense curiosity. I was moved to make a solemn declaration of my readiness to believe implicitly anything he thought fit to tell me.'

CHAPTER 11

'He heard me out with his head on one side, and I had another glimpse through a rent in the mist in which he moved and had his being. The dim candle spluttered within the ball of glass, and that was all I had to see him by; at his back was the dark night with the clear stars, whose distant glitter disposed in retreating planes lured the eye into the depths of a greater darkness; and yet a mysterious light seemed to show me his boyish head, as if in that moment the youth within him had, for a moment, gleamed and expired. "You are an awful good sort to listen like this," he said. "It does me good. You don't know what it is to me. You don't . . ." words seemed to fail him. It was a distinct glimpse. He was a youngster of the sort you like to see about you; of the sort you like to imagine yourself to have been; of the sort whose appearance claims the fellowship of these illusions you had thought gone out, extinct, cold, and which, as if rekindled at the approach of another flame, give a flutter deep, deep down somewhere, give a flutter of light . . . of heat! . . . Yes; I had a glimpse of him then . . . and it was not the last of that kind . . . "You don't know what it is for a fellow in my position to be believed – make a clean breast of it to an elder man. It is so difficult – so awfully unfair – so hard to understand."

'The mists were closing again. I don't know how old I appeared to him – and how much wise. Not half as old as I felt just then; not half as uselessly wise as I knew myself to be. Surely in no other craft as in that of the sea do the hearts of those already launched to sink or swim go out so much to the youth on the brink, looking with shining eyes upon that glitter of the vast surface which is only a reflection of his own glances full of fire. There is such magnificent vagueness in the expectations that had driven each of us to sea, such a glorious indefiniteness, such a beautiful greed of adventures that are their own and only reward! What we get – well, we won't talk of that; but can one of us restrain a smile? In no other kind of life is the illusion more wide of reality – in no other is the beginning *all* illusion – the disenchantment more swift – the subjugation more complete. Hadn't we all commenced with the same desire, ended with the same knowledge, carried the memory of the same cherished glamour through the sordid days of imprecation? What wonder that when some heavy prod gets home the bond is found to be close; that besides the fellowship of the craft there is felt the strength of a wider feeling – the feeling that binds a man to a child. He was there before me, believing that age and wisdom can find a remedy against the pain of truth, giving me a glimpse of himself as a young fellow in a scrape that is the very devil of a scrape, the sort of scrape greybeards wag at solemnly while they hide a smile. And he had been deliberating upon death – confound him! He had found *that* to meditate about because he thought he had saved his life, while all its glamour had gone with the ship in the night. What more natural! It was tragic enough and funny enough in all conscience to call aloud for compassion, and in what was I better than the rest of us to refuse him my pity? And even as I looked at him the mists rolled into the tent, and his voice spoke –

' "I was so lost, you know. It was the sort of thing one does not expect to happen to one. It was not like a fight, for instance."

' "It was not," I admitted. He appeared changed as if he had suddenly matured.

' "One couldn't be sure," he muttered.

' "Ah! You were not sure," I said, and was placated by the sound of a faint sigh that passed between us like the flight of a bird in the night.

' "Well, I wasn't," he said, courageously. "It was something like that wretched story they made up. It was not a lie – but it wasn't truth all the same. It was something.... One knows a downright lie. There was not the thickness of a sheet of paper between the right and wrong of this affair."

' "How much more did you want?" I asked; but I think I spoke so low that he did not catch what I said. He had advanced his argument as though life had been a network of paths separated by chasms. His voice sounded reasonable.

' "Suppose I had not – I mean to say, suppose I had stuck to the ship? Well. How much longer? Say a minute – half a minute. Come. In thirty seconds, as it seemed certain then, I would have been overboard; and do you think I would not have laid hold of the first thing that came in my way – oar, life-buoy, grating – anything? Wouldn't you?"

' "And be saved," I interjected.

' "I would have meant to be," he retorted. "And that's more than I meant when I" ... he shivered as if about to swallow some nauseous drug ... "jumped," he pronounced with a convulsive effort, whose stress, as if propagated by the waves of the air, made my body stir a little in the chair. He fixed me with lowering eyes. "Don't you believe me?" he cried. "I swear! ... Confound it! You got me here to talk, and ... You must! ... You said you would believe." "Of course I do," I protested in a matter-of-fact tone which produced a calming effect. "Forgive me," he said. "Of course I wouldn't have talked to you about all this if you had not been a gentleman. I ought to have known ... I am – I am – a gentleman, too ..." "Yes, yes," I said, hastily. He was looking me squarely in the face and withdrew his gaze slowly. "Now you understand why I didn't after all ... didn't go out in that way. I wasn't going to be frightened at what I had done. And, anyhow, if I had stuck to the ship I would have done my best to be saved. Men have been known to float for hours – in the open sea – and be picked up not much the worse for it. I might have lasted it out better than many others. There's nothing the matter with *my* heart." He withdrew his right fist from his pocket, and the blow he struck on his chest resounded like a muffled detonation in the night.

' "No," I said. He meditated, with his legs slightly apart and his chin sunk. "A hair's-breadth," he muttered. "Not the breadth of a hair between this and that. And at the time ..."

' "It is difficult to see a hair at midnight," I put in, a little viciously I fear. Don't you see what I mean by the solidarity of the craft? I was aggrieved against him, as though he had cheated me – me! – of a splendid opportunity to keep up the illusion of my beginnings, as though he had robbed our common life of the last spark of its glamour. "And so you cleared out – at once."

' "Jumped," he corrected me incisively. "Jumped – mind!" he repeated, and I wondered at the evident but obscure intention. "Well, yes! Perhaps I could not see then. But I had plenty of time and any amount of light in that boat. And I could think, too. Nobody would know, of course, but this did not make it any easier for me. You've got to believe that, too. I did not want all this talk.... No ... Yes ... I won't lie ... I wanted it: it is the very thing I wanted – there. Do you think you or anybody could have made me if I ... I am – I am not afraid to tell. And I wasn't afraid to think either. I looked it in the face. I wasn't going to run away. At first – at night, if it hadn't been for these fellows I might have ... No! by heavens! I was not going to give them that satisfaction. They had done enough. They made up a story, and believed it for all I know. But I knew the truth, and I would live it down – alone, with myself. I wasn't going to give in to such a beastly unfair thing. What did it prove after all? I was confoundedly cut up. Sick of life – to tell you the truth; but what would have been the good to shirk it – in – in – that way? That was not the way. I believe – I believe it would have – it would have ended – nothing." '

'He had been walking up and down, but with the last word he turned short at me.

"What do *you* believe?" he asked with violence. A pause ensued, and suddenly I felt myself overcome by a profound and hopeless fatigue, as though his voice had startled me out of a dream of wandering through empty spaces whose immensity had harassed my soul and exhausted my body.

' "... Would have ended nothing," he muttered over me obstinately, after a little while. "No! the proper thing was to face it out – alone for myself – wait for another chance – find out ..." '

CHAPTER 12

'All around everything was still as far as the ear could reach. The mist of his feelings shifted between us, as if disturbed by his struggles, and in the rifts of the immaterial veil he would appear to my staring eyes distinct of form and pregnant with vague appeal like a symbolic figure in a picture. The chill air of the night seemed to lie on my limbs as heavy as a slab of marble.

' "I see," I murmured, more to prove to myself that I could break my state of numbness than for any other reason.

' "The *Avondale* picked us up just before sunset," he remarked, moodily. "Steamed right straight for us. We had only to sit and wait."

'After a long interval, he said, "They told their story." And again there was that oppressive silence. "Then only I knew what it was I had made up my mind to," he added.

' "You said nothing," I whispered.

' "What could I say?" he asked, in the same low tone. . . "Shock slight. Stopped the ship. Ascertained the damage. Took measures to get the boats out without creating a panic. As the first boat was lowered ship went down in a squall. Sank like lead. . . . What could be more clear" . . . he hung his head . . . "and more awful?" His lips quivered while he looked straight into my eyes. "I had jumped – hadn't I?" he asked, dismayed. "That's what I had to live down. The story didn't matter." . . . He clasped his hands for an instant, glanced right and left into the gloom: "It was like cheating the dead," he stammered.

' "And there were no dead," I said.

'He went away from me at this. That is the only way I can describe it. In a moment I saw his back close to the balustrade. He stood there for some time, as if admiring the purity and the peace of the night. Some flowering-shrub in the garden below spread its powerful scent through the damp air. He returned to me with hasty steps.

' "And that did not matter," he said, as stubbornly as you please.

' "Perhaps not," I admitted. I began to have a notion he was too much for me. After all, what did I know?

' "Dead or not dead, I could not get clear," he said. "I had to live; hadn't I?"

' "Well, yes – if you take it in that way," I mumbled.

' "I was glad, of course," he threw out carelessly with his mind fixed on something else. "The exposure," he pronounced, slowly, and lifted his head. "Do you know what was my first thought when I heard? I was relieved. I was relieved to learn that those shouts – did I tell you I had heard shouts? No? Well, I did. Shouts for help . . . blown along with the drizzle. Imagination I suppose. And yet I can hardly . . . How stupid . . . The others did not. I asked them afterwards. They all said No. No? And I was hearing them even then! I might have known – but I didn't think – I only listened. Very faint screams – day after day. Then that little half-caste chap here came up and spoke to me. 'The *Patna* . . . French gunboat . . . towed successfully to Aden . . . Investigation . . . Marine Office . . . Sailors' Home. . . arrangements made for your board and lodging!' I walked along with him, and I enjoyed the silence. So there had been no shouting. Imagination. I had to believe him. I could hear nothing any more. I wonder how long I could have stood it. It was getting worse, too . . . I mean – louder."

'He fell into thought.

' "And I heard nothing! Well – so be it. But the lights. The lights did go! We did not see them. They were not there. If they had been, I would have swum back – I would have gone back and shouted alongside – I would have begged them to take me on board. . . . I would have had my chance. . . . You doubt me? ... How do you know how I felt? ... What right have you to doubt? ... I very nearly did it as it was – do you understand?" His voice fell. "There was not a glimmer – not a glimmer," he protested, mournfully. "Don't you understand that if there had been, you would not have seen me here? You see me – and you doubt."

'I shook my head negatively. This question of the lights being lost sight of when the boat could not have been more than a quarter of a mile from the ship was a matter for much discussion. Jim stuck to it that there was nothing to be seen after the first shower had cleared away; and the others had affirmed the same thing to the officers of the *Avondale*. Of course people shook their heads and smiled. One old skipper who sat near me in court tickled my ear with his white beard to murmur, "Of course they would lie." As a matter of fact nobody lied; not even the chief engineer with his story of the masthead light dropping like a match you throw down. Not consciously, at least. A man with his liver in such a state might very well have seen a floating spark in the corner of his eye when stealing a hurried glance over his shoulder. They had seen no light of any sort though they were well within range, and they could only explain this one way: the ship had gone down. It was obvious and comforting. The foreseen fact coming so swiftly had justified their haste. No wonder they did not cast about for any other explanation. Yet the true one was very simple, and as soon as Brierly suggested it the court ceased to bother about the question. If you remember, the ship had been stopped and was lying with her head on the course steered through the night, with her stern canted high and her bows brought low down in the water through the filling of the fore-compartment. Being thus out of trim, when the squall struck her a little on the quarter, she swung head to wind as sharply as though she had been at anchor. By this change in her position all her lights were in a very few moments shut off from the boat to leeward. It may very well be that, had they been seen, they would have had the effect of a mute appeal – that their glimmer lost in the darkness of the cloud would have had the mysterious power of the human glance that can awaken the feelings of remorse and pity. It would have said, "I am here – still here" ... and what more can the eye of the most forsaken of human beings say? But she turned her back on them as if in disdain of their fate: she had swung round, burdened, to glare stubbornly at the new danger of the open sea which she so strangely survived to end her days in a breaking-up yard, as if it had been her recorded fate to die obscurely under the blows of many hammers. What were the various ends their destiny provided for the pilgrims I am unable to say; but the immediate future brought, at about nine o'clock next morning, a French gunboat homeward bound from Réunion. The report of her commander was public property. He had swept a little out of his course to ascertain what was the matter with that steamer floating dangerously by the head upon a still and hazy sea. There was an ensign, union down, flying at her main gaff (the serang had the sense to make a signal of distress at daylight); but the cooks were preparing the food in the cooking-boxes forward as usual. The decks were packed as close as a sheep-pen: there were people perched all along the rails, jammed on the bridge in a solid mass; hundreds of eyes stared, and not a sound was heard when the gunboat ranged abreast, as if all that multitude of lips had been sealed by a spell.

'The Frenchman hailed, could get no intelligible reply, and after ascertaining through his binoculars that the crowd on deck did not look plague-stricken, decided to send a boat. Two officers came on board, listened to the serang, tried to talk with the Arab, couldn't make head or tail of it: but of course the nature of the emergency was obvious enough. They were also very much struck by discovering a white man dead and curled up peacefully on the bridge. "*Fort intrigués par ce cadavre,*" as I was informed a long time after by an elderly French lieutenant whom I came across one afternoon in Sydney, by the merest chance, in a sort of café, and who remembered the affair perfectly. Indeed this affair, I may notice in passing, had an extraordinary power of defying the shortness of memories and the length of time: it seemed to live, with a sort of uncanny vitality, in the minds of men, on the tips of their tongues. I've had the questionable pleasure of meeting it often, years afterwards, thousands of miles away, emerging from the remotest possible talk, coming to the surface of the most distant allusions. Has it not turned up tonight between us? And I am the only seaman here. I am the only one to whom it is a memory. And yet it has made its way out! But if two men who, unknown to each other, knew of this affair met accidentally on any spot of this earth, the thing would pop up between them as sure as fate, before they parted. I had never seen that Frenchman before, and at the end of an hour we had done with each other for life: he did not seem particularly talkative either; he was a quiet, massive chap in a creased uniform sitting drowsily over a tumbler half full of some dark liquid. His shoulder-straps were a bit tarnished, his clean-shaved cheeks were large and sallow; he looked like a man who would be given to taking snuff – don't you know? I won't say he did; but the habit would have fitted that kind of man. It all began by his handing me a number of *Home News*, which I didn't want, across the marble table. I said, "*Merci.*" We exchanged a few apparently innocent remarks, and suddenly, before I knew how it had come about, we were in the midst of it, and he was telling me how much they had been "intrigued by that corpse". It turned out he had been one of the boarding officers.

'In the establishment where we sat one could get a variety of foreign drinks which were kept for the visiting naval officers, and he took a sip of the dark medical-looking stuff, which probably was nothing more nasty than *cassis à l'eau*, and glancing with one eye into the tumbler, shook his head slightly. "*Impossible de comprendre – vous concevez,*" he said, with a curious mixture of unconcern and thoughtfulness. I could very easily conceive how impossible it had been for them to understand. Nobody in the gunboat knew enough English to get hold of the story as told by the serang. There was a good deal of noise, too, round the two officers. "They crowded upon us. There was a circle round that dead man (*autour de ce mort*)," he described. "One had to attend to the most pressing. These people were beginning to agitate themselves – *Parbleu!* A mob like that – don't you see?" he interjected with philosophic indulgence. As to the bulkhead, he had advised his commander that the safest thing was to leave it alone, it was so villainous to look at. They got two hawsers on board promptly (*en toute hâte*) and took the *Patna* in tow – stern foremost at that – which, under the circumstances, was not so foolish, since the rudder was too much out of the water to be of any great use for steering, and this manoeuvre eased the strain on the bulkhead, whose state, he expounded with stolid glibness, demanded the greatest care (*éxigeait les plus grands ménagements*). I could not help thinking that my new acquaintance must have had a voice in most of these arrangements: he looked a reliable officer, no longer very active, and he was seamanlike, too, in a way, though as he sat there, with his thick fingers clasped lightly on his stomach, he reminded you of one of those snuffy, quiet village priests, into whose ears are poured the sins, the sufferings, the remorse of peasant generations, on whose faces the placid and simple expression is like a veil thrown over the mystery of pain and distress. He ought to have had a threadbare black *soutane* buttoned smoothly up to his ample chin, instead of a frockcoat with shoulder-straps and brass buttons. His broad bosom heaved regularly while he went on telling me that it had been the very devil of a job, as doubtless (*sans doute*) I could figure to myself in my quality of a seaman (*en votre qualité de marin*). At the end of the period he inclined his body slightly towards me, and, pursing his shaved lips, allowed the air to escape with a gentle hiss. "Luckily," he continued, "the sea was level like this table, and there was no more wind than there is here." . . . The place struck me as indeed intolerably stuffy, and very hot; my face burned as though I had been young enough to be embarrassed and blushing. They had directed their course, he pursued, to the nearest English port "*naturellement*", where their responsibility ceased "*Dieu merci*". . . . He blew out his flat cheeks a little. . . . 'Because, mind you (*notez bien*), all the time of towing we had two quartermasters stationed with axes by the hawsers, to cut us clear of our tow in case she . . ." He fluttered downwards his heavy eyelids, making his meaning as plain as possible. . . . "What would you! One does what one can (*on fait ce qu'on peut*)," and for a moment he managed to invest his ponderous immobility with an air of resignation. "Two quartermasters – thirty hours – always there. Two!" he repeated, lifting up his right hand a little, and exhibiting two fingers. This was absolutely the first gesture I saw him make. It gave me the opportunity to "note" a starred scar on the back of his hand – effect of a gunshot clearly; and, as if my sight had been made more acute by this discovery, I perceived also the seam of an old wound, beginning a little below the temple and going out of sight under the short grey hair at the side of his head – the graze of a spear or the cut of a sabre. He clasped his hands on his stomach again. "I remained on board that – that – my memory is going (*s'en va*). Ah! *Patt-nà*. C'est bien ça. Patt-nà. Merci. It is droll how one forgets. I stayed on that ship thirty hours. . . ."

' "You did!" I exclaimed. Still gazing at his hands, he pursed his lips a little, but this time made no hissing sound. "It was judged proper," he said, lifting his eyebrows dispassionately, "that one of the officers should remain to keep an eye open (*pour ouvrir l'oeil*)" . . . he sighed idly . . . "and for communicating by signals with the towing ship – do you see? – and so on. For the rest, it was my opinion, too. We made our boats ready to drop over – and I also on that ship took measures. . . . *Enfin!* One has done one's possible. It was a delicate position. Thirty hours. They prepared me some food. As for the wine – go and whistle for it – not a drop." In some extraordinary way, without any marked change in his inert attitude and in the placid expression of his face, he managed to convey the idea of profound disgust. "I – you know – when it comes to eating without my glass of wine – I am nowhere."

'I was afraid he would enlarge upon the grievance, for though he didn't stir a limb or twitch a feature, he made one aware how much he was irritated by the recollection. But he seemed to forget all about it. They delivered their charge to the "port authorities", as he expressed it. He was struck by the calmness with which it had been received. "One might have thought they had such a droll find (*drôle de trouvaille*) brought them every day. You are extraordinary – you others," he commented, with his back propped against the wall, and looking himself as incapable of an emotional display as a sack of meal. There happened to be a man-of-war and an Indian Marine steamer in the harbour at the time, and he did not conceal his admiration of the efficient manner in which the boats of these two ships cleared the *Patna* of her passengers. Indeed his torpid demeanour concealed nothing: it had that mysterious, almost miraculous, power of producing striking effects by means impossible of detection which is the last word of the highest art. "Twenty-five minutes – watch in hand – twenty-five, no more." . . . He unclasped and clasped again his fingers without removing his hands from his stomach, and made it infinitely more effective than if he had thrown up his arms to heaven in amazement. . . . "All that lot (*tout ce monde*) on shore – with their little affairs – nobody left but a guard of seamen (*marins de l'État*) and that interesting corpse (*cet intéressant cadavre*). Twenty-five minutes." . . . With downcast eyes and his head tilted slightly on one side he seemed to roll knowingly on his tongue the savour of a smart bit of work. He persuaded one without any further demonstration that his approval was eminently worth having, and resuming his hardly interrupted immobility, he went on to inform me that, being under orders to make the best of their way to Toulon, they left in two hours' time, "so that (*de sorte que*) there are many things in this incident of my life (*dans cet épisode de ma vie*) which have remained obscure." '

CHAPTER 13

'After these words, and without a change of attitude, he, so to speak, submitted himself passively to a state of silence. I kept him company; and suddenly, but not abruptly, as if the appointed time had arrived for his moderate and husky voice to come out of his immobility, he pronounced, "*Mon Dieu!* how the time passes!" Nothing could have been more common-place than this remark; but its utterance coincided for me with a moment of vision. It's extraordinary how we go through life with eyes half shut, with dull ears, with dormant thoughts. Perhaps it's just as well; and it may be that it is this very dullness that makes life to the incalculable majority so supportable and so welcome. Nevertheless, there can be but few of us who had never known one of these rare moments of awakening when we see, hear, understand ever so much – everything – in a flash – before we fall back again into our agreeable somnolence. I raised my eyes when he spoke, and I saw him as though I had never seen him before. I saw his chin sunk on his breast, the clumsy folds of his coat, his clasped hands, his motionless pose, so curiously suggestive of his having been simply left there. Time had passed indeed: it had overtaken him and gone ahead. It had left him hopelessly behind with a few poor gifts: the iron-grey hair, the heavy fatigue of the tanned face, two scars, a pair of tarnished shoulder-straps; one of those steady, reliable men who are the raw material of great reputations, one of those uncounted lives that are buried without drums and trumpets under the foundations of monumental successes. "I am now third lieutenant of the *Victorieuse*" (she was the flagship of the French Pacific squadron at the time), he said, detaching his shoulders from the wall a couple of inches to introduce himself. I bowed slightly on my side of the table, and told him I commanded a merchant vessel at present anchored in Rushcutters' Bay. He had "remarked" her, – a pretty little craft. He was very civil about it in his impassive way. I even fancy he went the length of tilting his head in compliment as he repeated, breathing visibly the while, "Ah, yes. A little craft painted black – very pretty – very pretty (*très coquet*)" After a time he twisted his body slowly to face the glass door on our right. "A dull town (*triste ville*)," he observed, staring into the street. It was a brilliant day; a southerly buster was raging, and we could see the passers-by, men and women, buffeted by the wind on the side-walks, the sunlit fronts of the houses across the road blurred by the tall whirls of dust. "I descended on shore," he said, "to stretch my legs a little, but . . ." He didn't finish, and sank into the depths of his repose. "Pray – tell me," he began, coming up ponderously, "what was there at the bottom of this affair – precisely (*au juste*)? It is curious. That dead man, for instance – and so on."

' "There were living men, too," I said; "much more curious."

' "No doubt, no doubt," he agreed half audibly, then, as if after mature consideration, murmured, "Evidently." I made no difficulty in communicating to him what had interested me most in this affair. It seemed as though he had a right to know: hadn't he spent thirty hours on board the *Patna* – had he not taken the succession, so to speak, had he not done "his possible"? He listened to me, looking more priest-like than ever, and with what – probably on account of his downcast eyes – had the appearance of devout concentration. Once or twice he elevated his eyebrows (but without raising his eyelids), as one would say "The devil!" Once he calmly exclaimed, "Ah, bah!" under his breath, and when I had finished he pursed his lips in a deliberate way and emitted a sort of sorrowful whistle.

'In any one else it might have been an evidence of boredom, a sign of indifference; but he, in his occult way, managed to make his immobility appear profoundly responsive, and as full of valuable thoughts as an egg is of meat. What he said at last was nothing more than a "very interesting", pronounced politely, and not much above a whisper. Before I got over my disappointment he added, but as if speaking to himself, "That's it. That *is* it." His chin seemed to sink lower on his breast, his body to weigh heavier on his seat. I was about to ask him what he meant when a sort of preparatory tremor passed over his whole person, as a faint ripple may be seen upon stagnant water even before the wind is felt. "And so that poor young man ran away along with the others," he said, with grave tranquillity.

'I don't know what made me smile: it is the only genuine smile of mine I can remember in connexion with Jim's affair. But somehow this simple statement of the matter sounded funny in French. . . . "*S'est enfui avec les autres*," had said the lieutenant. And suddenly I began to admire the discrimination of the man. He had made out the point at once: he did get hold of the only thing I cared about. I felt as though I were taking professional opinion on the case. His imperturbable and mature calmness was that of an expert in possession of the facts, and to whom one's perplexities are mere child's-play. "Ah! The young, the young," he said, indulgently. "And after all, one does not die of it." "Die of what?" I asked, swiftly. "Of being afraid." He elucidated his meaning and sipped his drink.

'I perceived that the last three fingers of his wounded hand were stiff and could not move independently of each other, so that he took up his tumbler with an ungainly clutch. "One is always afraid. One may talk, but . . ." He put down the glass awkwardly. . . . "The fear, the fear – look you – it is always there." . . . He touched his breast near a brass button on the very spot where Jim had given a thump to his own when protesting that there was nothing the matter with his heart. I suppose I made some sign of dissent, because he insisted, "Yes! yes! One talks, one talks; this is all very fine; but at the end of the reckoning one is no cleverer than the next man – and no more brave. Brave! This is always to be seen. I have rolled my hump (*roulé ma bosse*)," he said, using the slang expression with imperturbable serious-ness, "in all parts of the world; I have known brave men – famous ones! *Allez!*" . . . He drank carelessly. . . . "Brave – you conceive – in the Service – one has got to be – the trade demands it (*le métier veut ça*). Is it not so?" he appealed to me reasonably. "*Eh bien!* Each of them – I say each of them, if he were an honest man – *bien entendu* – would confess that there is a point – there is a point – for the best of us – there is somewhere a point when you let go everything (*vous lachez tout*). And you have got to live with that truth – do you see? Given a certain combination of circumstances, fear is sure to come. Abominable funk (*un trac épouvantable*). And even for those who do not believe this truth there is fear all the same – the fear of themselves. Absolutely so. Trust me. Yes. Yes. . . . At my age one knows what one is talking about – *que diable!*" . . . He had delivered himself of all this as immovably as though he had been the mouthpiece of abstract wisdom, but at this point he heightened the effect of detachment by beginning to twirl his thumbs slowly. "It's evident – *parbleu!*" he continued; "for, make up your mind as much as you like, even a simple headache or a fit of indigestion (*un dérangement d'estomac*) is enough to . . . Take me, for instance – I have made my proofs. *Eh bien!* I, who am speaking to you, once . . ."

'He drained his glass and returned to his twirling. "No, no; one does not die of it," he pronounced, finally, and when I found he did not mean to proceed with the personal anecdote, I was extremely disappointed; the more so as it was not the sort of story, you know, one could very well press him for. I sat silent, and he too, as if nothing could please him better. Even his thumbs were still now. Suddenly his lips began to move. "That is so," he resumed, placidly. "Man is born a coward (*L'homme est né poltron*). It is a difficulty – *parbleu!* It would be too easy otherwise. But habit – habit – necessity – do you see? – the eye of others – *voilà*. One puts up with it. And then the example of others who are no better than yourself, and yet make good countenance. . . ."

'His voice ceased.

' "That young man – you will observe – had none of these inducements – at least at the moment," I remarked.

'He raised his eyebrows forgivingly: "I don't say: I don't say. The young man in question might have had the best dispositions – the best dispositions," he repeated, wheezing a little.

' "I am glad to see you taking a lenient view," I said. 'His own feeling in the matter was – ah! – hopeful, and . . ."

'The shuffle of his feet under the table interrupted me. He drew up his heavy eyelids. Drew up, I say – no other expression can describe the steady deliberation of the act – and at last was disclosed completely to me. I was confronted by two narrow grey circlets, like two tiny steel rings around the profound blackness of the pupils. The sharp glance, coming from that massive body, gave a notion of extreme efficiency, like a razor-edge on a battle-axe. "Pardon," he said, punctiliously. His right hand went up, and he swayed forward. "Allow me . . . I contended that one may get on knowing very well that one's courage does not come of itself (*ne vient pas tout seul*). There's nothing much in that to get upset about. One truth the more ought not to make life impossible. . . . But the honour – the honour, monsieur! . . . The honour . . . that is real – that is! And what life may be worth when" . . . he got on his feet with a ponderous impetuosity, as a startled ox might scramble up from the grass . . . "when the honour is gone – *ah çal par exemple* – I can offer no opinion I can offer no opinion – because – monsieur – I know nothing of it."

'I had risen, too, and, trying to throw infinite politeness into our attitudes, we faced each other mutely, like two china dogs on a mantelpiece. Hang the fellow! he had pricked the bubble. The blight of futility that lies in wait for men's speeches had fallen upon our conversation, and made it a thing of empty sounds. "Very well," I said, with a disconcerted smile, "but couldn't it reduce itself to not being found out?" He made as if to retort readily, but when he spoke he had changed his mind. "This, monsieur, is too fine for me – much above me – I don't think about it." He bowed heavily over his cap, which he held before him by the peak, between the thumb and the forefinger of his wounded hand. I bowed too. We bowed together: we scraped our feet at each other with much ceremony, while a dirty specimen of a waiter looked on critically, as though he had paid for the performance. "Serviteur," said the Frenchman. Another scrape. "Monsieur" . . . "Monsieur." . . . The glass door swung behind his burly back. I saw the southerly buster get hold of him and drive him down wind with his hand to his head, his shoulders braced, and the tails of his coat blown hard against his legs.

'I sat down again alone and discouraged – discouraged about Jim's case. If you wonder that after more than three years it had preserved its actuality, you must know that I had seen him only very lately. I had come straight from Samarang, where I had loaded a cargo for Sydney: an utterly uninteresting bit of business, – what Charley here would call one of my rational transactions – and in Samarang I had seen something of Jim. He was then working for De Jongh, on my recommendation. Water-clerk. "My representative afloat", as De Jongh called him. You can't imagine a mode of life more barren of consolation, less capable of being invested with a spark of glamour – unless it be the business of an insurance canvasser. Little Bob Stanton – Charley here knew him well – had gone through that experience. The same who got drowned afterwards trying to save a lady's-maid in the *Sephora* disaster. A case of collision on a hazy morning off the Spanish coast you may remember. All the passengers had been packed tidily into the boats and shoved clear of the ship when Bob sheered alongside again and scrambled back on deck to fetch that girl. How she had been left behind I can't make out; anyhow, she had gone completely crazy – wouldn't leave the ship – held to the rail like grim death. The wrestling-match could be seen plainly from the boats; but poor Bob was the shortest chief mate in the merchant service, and the woman stood five feet ten in her shoes and was as strong as a horse, I've been told. So it went on, pull devil, pull baker, the wretched girl screaming all the time and Bob letting out a yell now and then to warn his boat to keep well clear of the ship. One of the hands told me, hiding a smile at the recollection, "It was for all the world, sir, like a naughty youngster fighting with his mother." The same old chap said that "At the last we could see that Mr Stanton had given up hauling at the gal, and just stood by looking at her, watchful like. We thought afterwards he must' ve been reckoning that, maybe, the rush of water would tear her away from the rail by and by and give him a show to save her. We daren't come alongside for our life; and after a bit the old ship went down all on a sudden with a lurch to starboard – plop. The suck in was something awful. We never saw anything alive or dead come up." Poor Bob's spell of shore life had been one of the complications of a love affair, I believe. He fondly hoped he had done with the sea for ever, and made sure he had got hold of all the bliss on earth, but it came to canvassing in the end. Some cousin of his in Liverpool put him up to it. He used to tell us his experiences in that line. He made us laugh till we cried, and, not altogether displeased at the effect, undersized and bearded to the waist like a gnome, he would tiptoe amongst us and say, "It's all very well for you beggars to laugh, but my immortal soul was shrivelled down to the size of a parched pea after a week of that work." I don't know how Jim's soul accommodated itself to the new conditions of his life – I was kept too busy in getting him something to do that would keep body and soul together – but I am pretty certain his adventurous fancy was

suffering all the pangs of starvation. It had certainly nothing to feed upon
in this new calling. It was distressing to see him at it, though he tackled it
with a stubborn serenity for which I must give him full credit. I kept my eye
on his shabby plodding with a sort of notion that it was a punishment for
the heroics of his fancy – an expiation for his craving after more glamour
than he could carry. He had loved too well to image himself a glorious
racehorse, and now he was condemned to toil without honour like a
costermonger's donkey. He did it very well. He shut himself in, put his head
down, said never a word. Very well; very well indeed – except for certain
fantastic and violent outbreaks, on the deplorable occasions when the irrepressible *Patna* case cropped up. Unfortunately that scandal of the Eastern
seas would not die out. And this is the reason why I could never feel I had
done with Jim for good.

'I sat thinking of him after the French lieutenant had left, not, however,
in connexion with De Jongh's cool and gloomy backshop, where we had
hurriedly shaken hands not very long ago, but as I had seen him years before
in the last flickers of the candle, alone with me in the long gallery of the
Malabar House, with the chill and the darkness of the night at his back.
The respectable sword of his country's law was suspended over his head.
Tomorrow – or was it today? (midnight had slipped by long before we
parted) – the marble-faced police magistrate, after distributing fines and
terms of imprisonment in the assault-and-battery case, would take up the
awful weapon and smite his bowed neck. Our communion in the night was
uncommonly like a last vigil with a condemned man. He was guilty, too. He
was guilty – as I had told myself repeatedly, guilty and done for; nevertheless,
I wished to spare him the mere detail of a formal execution. I don't pretend
to explain the reasons of my desire – I don't think I could; but if you haven't
got a sort of notion by this time, then I must have been very obscure in my
narrative, or you too sleepy to seize upon the sense of my words. I don't
defend my morality. There was no morality in the impulse which induced
me to lay before him Brierly's plan of evasion – I may call it – in all its
primitive simplicity. There were the rupees – absolutely ready in my pocket
and very much at his service. Oh! a loan; a loan of course – and if an
introduction to a man (in Rangoon) who could put some work in his way . . .
Why! with the greatest pleasure. I had pen, ink, and paper in my room on
the first floor. And even while I was speaking I was impatient to begin the
letter: day, month, year, 2.30 a.m. . . . for the sake of our old friendship I
ask you to put some work in the way of Mr James So-and-so, in whom,
&c., &c. . . . I was even ready to write in that strain about him. If he had not
enlisted my sympathies he had done better for himself – he had gone to the
very fount and origin of that sentiment, he had reached the secret sensibility
of my egoism. I am concealing nothing from you, because were I to do so
my action would appear more unintelligible than any man's action has the
right to be, and – in the second place – tomorrow you shall forget my
sincerity along with the other lessons of the past. In this transaction, to speak
grossly and precisely, I was the irreproachable man; but the subtle intentions
of my immorality were defeated by the moral simplicity of the criminal. No
doubt he was selfish, too, but his selfishness had a higher origin, a more

lofty aim. I discovered that, say what I would, he was eager to go through the ceremony of execution; and I didn't say much, for I felt that in argument his youth would tell against me heavily: he believed where I had already ceased to doubt. There was something fine in the wildness of his unexpressed, hardly formulated hope. "Clear out! Couldn't think of it," he said, with a shake of his head. "I make you an offer for which I neither demand nor expect any sort of gratitude," I said; "you shall repay the money when convenient, and . . ." "Awfully good of you," he muttered without looking up. I watched him narrowly: the future must have appeared horribly uncertain to him; but he did not falter, as though indeed there had been nothing wrong with his heart. I felt angry – not for the first time that night. "The whole wretched business," I said, "is bitter enough, I should think, for a man of your kind . . ." "It is, it is," he whispered twice, with his eyes fixed on the floor. It was heartrending. He towered above the light, and I could see the down on his cheek, the colour mantling warm under the smooth skin of his face. Believe me or not, I say it was outrageously heartrending. It provoked me to brutality. "Yes," I said; "and allow me to confess that I am totally unable to imagine what advantage you can expect from this licking of the dregs." "Advantage!" he murmured out of his stillness. "I am dashed if I do," I said enraged. "I've been trying to tell you all there is in it," he went on, slowly, as if meditating something unanswerable. "But after all, it is *my* trouble." I opened my mouth to retort, and discovered suddenly that I'd lost all confidence in myself; and it was as if he, too, had given me up, for he mumbled like a man thinking half aloud. "Went away . . . went into hospitals . . . Not one of them would face it. . . . They! . . ." He moved his hand slightly to imply disdain. "But I've got to get over this thing, and I mustn't shirk any of it or . . . I won't shirk any of it." He was silent. He gazed as though he had been haunted. His unconscious face reflected the passing expressions of scorn, of despair, of resolution, – reflected them in turn, as a magic mirror would reflect the gliding passage of unearthly shapes. He lived surrounded by deceitful ghosts, by austere shades. "Oh! nonsense, my dear fellow," I began. He had a movement of impatience. "You don't seem to understand," he said, incisively; then looking at me without a wink, "I may have jumped, but I don't run away." "I meant no offence," I said; and added stupidly, "Better men than you have found it expedient to run, at times." He coloured all over, while in my confusion I half-choked myself with my own tongue. "Perhaps so," he said at last, "I am not good enough; I can't afford it. I am bound to fight this thing down – I am fighting it *now*." I got out of my chair and felt stiff all over. The silence was embarrassing, and to put an end to it I imagined nothing better but to remark, "I had no idea it was so late," in an airy tone. . . . "I daresay you have had enough of this," he said, brusquely: "and to tell you the truth" – he began to look round for his hat – "so have I."

'Well! he had refused this unique offer. He had struck aside my helping hand; he was ready to go now, and beyond the balustrade the night seemed to wait for him very still, as though he had been marked down for its prey. I heard his voice. "Ah! here it is." He had found his hat. For a few seconds we hung in the wind. "What will you do after – after . . ." I asked very low.

"Go to the dogs as likely as not," he answered in a gruff mutter. I had recovered my wits in a measure, and judged best to take it lightly. "Pray remember," I said, "that I should like very much to see you again before you go." "I don't know what's to prevent you. The damned thing won't make me invisible," he said with intense bitterness, – "no such luck." And then at the moment of taking leave he treated me to a ghastly muddle of dubious stammers and movements, to an awful display of hesitations. God forgive him – me! He had taken it into his fanciful head that I was likely to make some difficulty as to shaking hands. It was too awful for words. I believe I shouted suddenly at him as you would bellow to a man you saw about to walk over a cliff; I remember our voices being raised, the appearance of a miserable grin on his face, a crushing clutch on my hand, a nervous laugh. The candle spluttered out, and the thing was over at last, with a groan that floated up to me in the dark. He got himself away somehow. The night swallowed his form. He was a horrible bungler. Horrible. I heard the quick crunch-crunch of the gravel under his boots. He was running. Absolutely running, with nowhere to go to. And he was not yet four-and-twenty'.

CHAPTER 14

'I slept little, hurried over my breakfast, and after a slight hesitation gave up my early morning visit to my ship. It was really very wrong of me, because, though my chief mate was an excellent man all round, he was the victim of such black imaginings that if he did not get a letter from his wife at the expected time he would go quite distracted with rage and jealousy, lose all grip on the work, quarrel with all hands, and either weep in his cabin or develop such a ferocity of temper as all but drove the crew to the verge of mutiny. The thing had always seemed inexplicable to me: they had been married thirteen years; I had a glimpse of her once, and, honestly, I couldn't conceive a man abandoned enough to plunge into sin for the sake of such an unattractive person. I don't know whether I have not done wrong by refraining from putting that view before poor Selvin: the man made a little hell on earth for himself, and I also suffered indirectly, but some sort of, no doubt, false delicacy prevented me. The marital relations of seamen would make an interesting subject, and I could tell you instances. . . . However, this is not the place, nor the time, and we are concerned with Jim – who was unmarried. If his imaginative conscience or his pride; if all the extravagant ghosts and austere shades that were the disastrous familiars of his youth would not let him run away from the block, I, who of course can't be suspected of such familiars, was irresistibly impelled to go and see his head roll off. I wended my way towards the court. I didn't hope to be very much impressed or edified, or interested or even frightened – though, as long as there is any life before one, a jolly good fright now and then is a salutary discipline. But neither did I expect to be so awfully depressed. The bitterness of his punishment was in its chill and mean atmosphere. The real significance of crime is in its being a breach of faith with the community of mankind, and from that point of view he was no mean traitor, but his execution was a hole-and-corner affair. There was no high scaffolding, no scarlet cloth (did they have scarlet cloth on Tower Hill? They should have had), no awe-stricken multitude to be horrified at his guilt and be moved to tears at his fate – no air of sombre retribution. There was, as I walked along, the clear sunshine, a brilliance too passionate to be consoling, the streets full of jumbled bits of colour like a damaged kaleidoscope: yellow, green, blue, dazzling white, the brown nudity of an undraped shoulder, a bullock-cart with a red canopy, a company of native infantry in a drab body with dark heads marching in dusty laced boots, a native policeman in a sombre uniform of scanty cut and belted in patent leather, who looked up at me with orientally pitiful eyes as though his migrating spirit were suffering exceed-ingly from that unforeseen – what d'ye call 'em? – avatar – incarnation. Under the shade of a lonely tree in the courtyard, the villagers connected with the assault case sat in a picturesque group, looking like a chromo-lithograph of a camp in a book of Eastern travel. One missed the obligatory thread of smoke in the foreground and the pack-animals grazing. A blank yellow wall rose behind overtopping the trees, reflecting the glare. The court-room was sombre, seemed more vast. High up in the dim space the punkahs were swaying short to and fro, to and fro. Here and there a draped figure, dwarfed by the bare walls, remained without stirring amongst the rows of empty benches, as if absorbed in pious meditation. The plaintiff, who had been beaten, an obese chocolate-coloured man with shaved head, one fat breast bare and a bright yellow caste-mark above the bridge of his nose, sat in pompous immobility: only his eyes glittered, rolling in the gloom, and the nostrils dilated and collapsed violently as he breathed. Brierly dropped into his seat looking done up, as though he had spent the night in sprinting on a cinder-track. The pious sailing-ship skipper appeared excited and made uneasy movements, as if restraining with difficulty an impulse to stand up and exhort us earnestly to prayer and repentance. The head of the magistrate, delicately pale under the neatly arranged hair, resembled the head of a hopeless invalid after he had been washed and brushed and propped up in bed. He moved aside the vase of flowers – a bunch of purple with a few pink blossoms on long stalks – and seizing in both hands a long sheet of bluish paper, ran his eye over it, propped his forearms on the edge of the desk, and began to read aloud in an even, distinct, and careless voice.

'By Jove! For all my foolishness about scaffolds and heads rolling off – I assure you it was infinitely worse than a beheading. A heavy sense of finality brooded over all this, unrelieved by the hope of rest and safety following the fall of the axe. These proceedings had all the cold vengefulness of a death-sentence, had all the cruelty of a sentence of exile. This is how I looked at it that morning – and even now I seem to see an undeniable vestige of truth in that exaggerated view of a common occurrence. You may imagine how strongly I felt this at the time. Perhaps it is for that reason that I could not bring myself to admit the finality. The thing was always with me, I was always eager to take opinion on it, as though it had not been practically settled: individual opinion – international opinion – by Jove! That Frenchman's, for instance. His own country's pronouncement was uttered in passionless and definite phraseology a machine would use, if machines could speak. The head of the magistrate was half hidden by the paper, his brow was like alabaster.

'There were several questions before the Court. The first as to whether the ship was in every respect fit and seaworthy for the voyage. The court found she was not. The next point, I remember, was, whether up to the time of the accident the ship hàd been navigated with proper and seamanlike care. They said Yes to that, goodness knows why, and then they declared that there was no evidence to show the exact cause of the accident. A floating derelict probably. I myself remember that a Norwegian barque bound out with a cargo of pitch-pine had been given up as missing about that time, and it was just the sort of craft that would capsize in a squall and float bottom up for months – a kind of maritime ghoul on the prowl to kill ships in the dark. Such wandering corpses are common enough in the North Atlantic, which is haunted by all the terrors of the sea, – fogs, icebergs, dead ships bent upon mischief, and long sinister gales that fasten upon one like a vampire till all the strength and the spirit and even hope are gone, and one feels like the empty shell of a man. But there – in those seas – the incident was rare enough to resemble a special arrangement of a malevolent providence, which, unless it had for its object the killing of a donkeyman and the bringing of worse than death upon Jim, appeared an utterly aimless piece of devilry. This view occurring to me took off my attention. For a time I was aware of the magistrate's voice as a sound merely; but in a moment it shaped itself into distinct words . . . "in utter disregard of their plain duty," it said. The next sentence escaped me somehow, and then . . . "abandoning in the moment of danger the lives and property confided to their charge" . . . went on the voice evenly, and stopped. A pair of eyes under the white forehead shot darkly a glance above the edge of the paper. I looked for Jim hurriedly, as though I had expected him to disappear. He was very still – but he was there. He sat pink and fair and extremely attentive. "Therefore . . ." began the voice emphatically. He stared with parted lips, hanging upon the words of the man behind the desk. These came out into the stillness wafted on the wind made by the punkahs, and I, watching for their effect upon him, caught only the fragments of official language . . . "The Court . . . Gustav So-and-so master . . . native of Germany . . . James So-and-so . . . mate . . . certificates cancelled." A silence fell. The magistrate had dropped the paper, and leaning sideways on the arm of his chair, began to talk with Brierly easily. People started to move out; others were pushing in, and I also made for the door. Outside I stood still, and when Jim passed me on his way to the gate, I caught at his arm and detained him. The look he gave discomposed me, as though I had been responsible for his state: he looked at me as if I had been the embodied evil of life. "It's all over," I stammered. "Yes," he said, thickly. "And now let no man . . ." He jerked his arm out of my grasp. I watched his back as he went away. It was a long street, and he remained in sight for some time. He walked rather slow, and straddling his legs a little, as if he had found it difficult to keep a straight line. Just before I lost him I fancied he staggered a bit.

' "Man overboard," said a deep voice behind me. Turning round, I saw a fellow I knew slightly, a West Australian; Chester was his name. He, too, had been looking after Jim. He was a man with an immense girth of chest, a rugged, clean-shaved face of mahogany colour, and two blunt tufts of iron-grey, thick wiry hairs on his upper lip. He had been pearler, wrecker, trader, whaler, too, I believe; in his own words – anything and everything a man may be at sea, but a pirate. The Pacific, north and south, was his proper hunting-ground; but he had wandered so far afield looking for a cheap steamer to buy. Lately he had discovered – so he said – a guano island somewhere, but its approaches were dangerous, and the anchorage, such as it was, could not be considered safe, to say the least of it. "As good as a gold-mine," he would exclaim. "Right bang in the middle of the Walpole Reefs, and if it's true enough that you can get no holding-ground anywhere in less than forty fathom, then what of that? There are the hurricanes, too. But it's a first-rate thing. As good as a gold-mine – better! Yet there's not a fool of them that will see it. I can't get a skipper or a shipowner to go near the place. So I made up my mind to cart the blessed stuff myself." ... This was what he required a steamer for, and I knew he was just then negotiating enthusiastically with a Parsee firm for an old, brig-rigged, sea-anachronism of ninety horse-power. We had met and spoken together several times. He looked knowingly after Jim. "Takes it to heart?" he asked scornfully. "Very much," I said. "Then he's no good," he opined. "What's all the to-do about? A bit of ass's skin. That never yet made a man. You must see things exactly as they are – if you don't, you may just as well give in at once. You will never do anything in this world. Look at me. I made it a practice never to take anything to heart." "Yes," I said, "you see things as they are." "I wish I could see my partner coming along, that's what I wish to see," he said. "Know my partner? Old Robinson. Yes; *the* Robinson. Don't *you* know? The notorious Robinson. The man who smuggled more opium and bagged more seals in his time than any loose Johnny now alive. They say he used to board the sailing-schooners up Alaska way when the fog was so thick that the Lord God, He alone, could tell one man from another. Holy-Terror Robinson. That's the man. He is with me in that guano thing. The best chance he ever came across in his life." He put his lips to my ear. "Cannibal? – well, they used to give him the name years and years ago. You remember the story? A shipwreck on the west side of Stewart Island; that's right; seven of them got ashore, and it seems they did not get on very well together. Some men are too cantankerous for anything – don't know how to make the best of a bad job – don't see things as they are – as they *are*, my boy! And then what's the consequence? Obvious! Trouble, trouble; as likely as not a knock on the head; and serve 'em right, too. That sort is the most useful when it's dead. The story goes that a boat of Her Majesty's ship *Wolverine* found him kneeling on the kelp, naked as the day he was born, and chanting some psalm-tune or other; light snow was falling at the time. He waited till the boat was an oar's length from the shore, and then up and away. They chased him for an hour up and down the boulders, till a marine flung a stone that took him behind the ear providentially and knocked him senseless. Alone? Of course. But that's like that tale of sealing-schooners; the Lord God knows the right and the wrong of that story. The cutter did not investigate much. They wrapped him in a boat-cloak and took him off as quick as they could, with a dark night coming on, the weather threatening, and the ship firing recall guns every fives minutes. Three weeks afterwards he was as well as ever. He didn't allow any fuss that was made on shore to upset him; he just shut his lips tight, and let people screech. It was bad enough to have lost his ship, and all he was worth besides, without paying attention to the hard names they called him. That's the man for me." He lifted his arm for a signal to someone down the street. "He's got a little money, so I have to let him into my thing. Had to! It would have been sinful to throw away such a find, and I was cleaned out myself. It cut me to the quick, but I could see the matter just as it was, and if I *must* share – thinks I – with any man, then give me Robinson. I left him at breakfast in the hotel to come to court, because I've an idea ... Ah! Good morning, Captain Robinson ... Friend of mine, Captain Robinson."

'An emaciated patriarch in a suit of white drill, a sola topee with a green-lined rim on a head trembling with age, joined us after crossing the street in a trotting shuffle, and stood propped with both hands on the handle of an umbrella. A white beard with amber streaks hung limply down to his waist. He blinked his creased eye-lids at me in a bewildered way. "How do you do? how do you do?" he piped, amiably, and tottered. "A little deaf," said Chester aside. "Did you drag him over six thousand miles to get a cheap steamer?" I asked. "I would have taken him twice round the world as soon as look at him," said Chester with immense energy. "The steamer will be the making of us, my lad. Is it my fault that every skipper and shipowner in the whole of blessed Australasia turns out a blamed fool? Once I talked for three hours to a man in Auckland. 'Send a ship,' I said, 'send a ship. I'll give you half of the first cargo for yourself, free gratis for nothing – just to make a good start.' Says he, 'I wouldn't do it if there was no other place on earth to send a ship to.' Perfect ass, of course. Rocks, currents, no anchorage, sheer cliff to lay to, no insurance company would take the risk, didn't see how he could get loaded under three years. Ass! I nearly went on my knees to him. 'But look at the thing as it is,' says I. 'Damn rocks and hurricanes. Look at it as it is. There's guano there, Queensland sugar-planters would fight for – fight for on the quay, I tell you.' ... What can you do with a fool? ... 'That's one of your little jokes, Chester,' he says ... Joke! I could have wept. Ask Captain Robinson here ... And there was another ship-owning fellow – a fat chap in a white waistcoat in Wellington, who seemed to think I was up to some swindle or other. 'I don't know what sort of fool you're looking for,' he says, 'but I am busy just now. Good morning.' I longed to take him in my two hands and smash him through the window of his own office. But I didn't. I was as mild as a curate. 'Think of it,' says I. '*Do* think it over. I'll call tomorrow.' He grunted something about being 'out all day'. On the stairs I felt ready to beat my head against the wall from vexation. Captain Robinson here can tell you. It was awful to think of all that lovely stuff lying waste under the sun – stuff that would send the sugar-cane shooting sky-high. The making of Queensland! The making of Queensland! And in Brisbane, where I went to have a last try, they gave me the name of a lunatic. Idiots! The only sensible man I came across was the cabman who drove me about. A broken-down swell he was, I fancy. Hey! Captain Robinson? You remember I told you about my cabby in Brisbane – don't you? The chap had a wonderful eye for things. He saw it in a jiffy. It was a real pleasure to talk with him. One evening after a devil of a day amongst shipowners I felt so bad that, says I, 'I must get drunk. Come along; I must get drunk, or I'll go mad.' 'I am your man,' he says; 'go ahead.' I don't know what I would have done without him. Hey! Captain Robinson."

'He poked the ribs of his partner. "He! he! he!" laughed the Ancient, looked aimlessly down the street, then peered at me doubtfully with sad, dim pupils ... "He! he! he!" ... He leaned heavier on the umbrella, and dropped his gaze on the ground. I needn't tell you I had tried to get away several times, but Chester had foiled every attempt by simply catching hold of my coat. "One minute, I've a notion." "What's your infernal notion?" I exploded at last. "If you think I am going in with you ..." "No, no, my boy. Too late, if you wanted ever so much. We've got a steamer." "You've got the ghost of a steamer," I said. "Good enough for a start – there's no superior nonsense about us. Is there, Captain Robinson?" "No! no! no!" croaked the old man without lifting his eyes, and the senile tremble of his head became almost fierce with determination. "I understand you know that young chap," said Chester, with a nod at the street from which Jim had disappeared long ago. "He's been having grub with you in the Malabar last night – so I was told."

'I said that was true, and after remarking that he, too, liked to live well and in style, only that, for the present, he had to be saving of every penny – "none too many for the business! Isn't that so, Captain Robinson?" – he squared his shoulders and stroked his dumpy moustache, while the notorious Robinson, coughing at his side, clung more than ever to the handle of the umbrella, and seemed ready to subside passively into a heap of old bones. "You, see, the old chap has all the money," whispered Chester, confidentially. "I've been cleaned out trying to engineer the dratted thing. But wait a bit, wait a bit. The good time is coming." ... He seemed suddenly astonished at the signs of impatience I gave. "Oh, crakee!" he cried; "I am telling you of the biggest thing that ever was, and you ..." "I have an appointment," I pleaded mildly. "What of that?" he asked with genuine surprise; "let it wait." "That's exactly what I am doing now," I remarked; "hadn't you better tell me what it is you want?" "Buy twenty hotels like that," he growled to himself; "and every joker boarding in them, too – twenty times over." He lifted his head smartly. "I want that young chap." "I don't understand," I said. "He's no good, is he?" said Chester, crisply. "I know nothing about it," I protested. "Why, you told me yourself he was taking it to heart," argued Chester. "Well, in my opinion a chap who ... Anyhow, he can't be much good; but then you see I am on the look-out for somebody, and I've just got a thing that will suit him. I'll give him a job on my island." He nodded significantly. "I'm going to dump forty coolies there – if I've got to steal 'em. Somebody must work the stuff. Oh! I mean to act square:

wooden shed, corrugated-iron roof – I know a man in Hobart who will take my bill at six months for the materials. I do. Honour bright. Then there's the water-supply. I'll have to fly round and get somebody to trust me for half-a-dozen second-hand iron tanks. Catch rain-water, hey? Let him take charge. Make him supreme boss over the coolies. Good idea, isn't it? What do you say?" "There are whole years when not a drop of rain falls on Walpole," I said, too amazed to laugh. He bit his lip and seemed bothered. "Oh, well, I will fix up something for them – or land a supply. Hang it all! That's not the question."

'I said nothing. I had a rapid vision of Jim perched on a shadowless rock, up to his knees in guano, with the screams of sea-birds in his ears, the incandescent ball of the sun above his head; the empty sky and the empty ocean all a-quiver, simmering together in the heat as far as the eye could reach. "I wouldn't advise my worst enemy . . ." I began. "What's the matter with you?" cried Chester; "I mean to give him a good screw – that is, as soon as the thing is set going, of course. It's as easy as falling off a log. Simply nothing to do; two six-shooters in his belt. . . . Surely he wouldn't be afraid of anything forty coolies could do – with two six-shooters and he the only armed man, too! It's much better than it looks. I want you to help me to talk him over." "No!" I shouted. Old Robinson lifted his bleared eyes dismally for a moment, Chester looked at me with infinite contempt. "So you wouldn't advise him?" he uttered, slowly. "Certainly not," I answered, as indignant as though he had requested me to help murder somebody; "moreover, I am sure he wouldn't. He is badly cut up, but he isn't mad as far as I know." "He is no earthly good for anything," Chester mused aloud. "He would just have done for me. If you only could see a thing as it is, you would see it's the very thing for him. And besides . . . Why! it's the most splendid, sure chance . . ." He got angry suddenly. "I must have a man. There! . . ." He stamped his foot and smiled unpleasantly. "Anyhow, I could guarantee the island wouldn't sink under him – and I believe he is a bit particular on that point." "Good morning," I said, curtly. He looked at me as though I had been an incomprehensible fool . . . "Must be moving, Captain Robinson," he yelled suddenly into the old man's ear. "These Parsee Johnnies are waiting for us to clinch the bargain." He took his partner under the arm with a firm grip, swung him round, and, unexpectedly, leered at me over his shoulder. "I was trying to do him a kindness," he asserted, with an air and tone that made my blood boil. "Thank you for nothing – in his name," I rejoined. "Oh! you are devilish smart," he sneered; "but you are like the rest of them. Too much in the clouds. See what *you* will do with him." "I don't know that I want to do anything with him." "Don't you?" he spluttered; his grey moustache bristled with anger, and by his side the notorious Robinson, propped on the umbrella, stood with his back to me, as patient and still as a worn-out cab-horse. "I haven't found a guano island," I said. "It's my belief you wouldn't know one if you were led right up to it by the hand," he riposted quickly; "and in this world you've got to see a thing first, before you can make use of it. Got to see it through and through at that, neither more nor less." "And get others to see it, too," I insinuated, with a glance at the bowed back by his side. Chester snorted at me. "His eyes are right enough – don't you worry. He ain't a puppy." "Oh, dear, no!" I said. "Come along, Captain Robinson," he shouted, with a sort of bullying deference under the rim of the old man's hat; the Holy Terror gave a submissive little jump. The ghost of a steamer was waiting for them. Fortune on that fair isle! They made a curious pair of Argonauts. Chester strode on leisurely, well set up, portly, and of conquering mien; the other, long, wasted, drooping, and hooked to his arm, shuffled his withered shanks with desperate haste.'

CHAPTER 15

'I did not start in search of Jim at once, only because I had really an appointment which I could not neglect. Then, as ill-luck would have it, in my agent's office I was fastened upon by a fellow fresh from Madagascar with a little scheme for a wonderful piece of business. It had something to do with cattle and cartridges and a Prince Ravonalo something; but the pivot of the whole affair was the stupidity of some admiral – Admiral Pierre, I think. Everything turned on that, and the chap couldn't find words strong enough to express his confidence. He had globular eyes starting out of his head with a fishy glitter, bumps on his forehead, and wore his long hair brushed back without a parting. He had a favourite phrase which he kept on repeating triumphantly, "The minimum of risk with the maximum of profit is my motto. What?" He made my head ache, spoiled my tiffin, but got his own out of me all right; and as soon as I had shaken him off I headed straight for the water-side. I caught sight of Jim leaning over the parapet of the quay. Three native boatmen quarrelling over five annas were making an awful row at his elbow. He didn't hear me come up, but spun round as if the slight contact of my finger had released a catch. "I was looking," he stammered. I don't remember what I said, not much anyhow, but he made no difficulty in following me to the hotel.

'He followed me as manageable as a little child, with an obedient air, with no sort of manifestation, rather as though he had been waiting for me there to come along and carry him off. I need not have been so surprised as I was at his tractability. On all the round earth, which to some seems so big and that others affect to consider as rather smaller than a mustard-seed, he had no place where he could – what shall I say? – where he could withdraw. That's it! Withdraw – be alone with his loneliness. He walked by my side very calm, glancing here and there, and once turned his head to look after a Sidiboy fireman in a cutaway coat and yellowish trousers, whose black face had silky gleams like a lump of anthracite coal. I doubt, however, whether he saw anything, or even remained all the time aware of my companionship, because if I had not edged him to the left here, or pulled him to the right there, I believe he would have gone straight before him in any direction till stopped by a wall or some other obstacle. I steered him into my bedroom, and sat down at once to write letters. This was the only place in the world (unless, perhaps, the Walpole Reef – but that was not so handy) where he could have it out with himself without being bothered by the rest of the universe. The damned thing – as he had expressed it – had not made him invisible, but I behaved exactly as though he were. No sooner in my chair I bent over my writing-desk like a medieval scribe, and, but for the movement of the hand holding the pen, remained anxiously quiet. I can't say I was frightened; but I certainly kept as still as if there had been something dangerous in the room, that at the first hint of a movement on my part would be provoked to pounce upon me. There was not much in the room – you know how these bedrooms are – a sort of four-poster bedstead under a mosquito-net, two or three chairs, the table I was writing at, a bare floor. A glass door opened on an upstairs veranda, and he stood with his face to it, having a hard time with all possible privacy. Dusk fell; I lit a candle with the greatest economy of movement and as much prudence as though it were an illegal proceeding. There is no doubt that he had a very hard time of it, and so had I, even to the point, I must own, of wishing him to the devil, or on Walpole Reef at least. It occurred to me once or twice that, after all, Chester was, perhaps, the man to deal effectively with such a disaster. That strange idealist had found a practical use for it at once – unerringly, as it were. It was enough to make one suspect that, maybe, he really could see the true aspect of things that appeared mysterious or utterly hopeless to less imaginative persons. I wrote and wrote; I liquidated all the arrears of my correspondence, and then went on writing to people who had no reason whatever to expect from me a gossipy letter about nothing at all. At times I stole a sidelong glance. He was rooted to the spot, but convulsive shudders ran down his back; his shoulders would heave suddenly. He was fighting, he was fighting – mostly for his breath, as it seemed. The massive shadows, cast all one way from the straight flame of the candle, seemed possessed of gloomy consciousness; the immobility of the furniture had to my furtive eye an air of attention. I was becoming fanciful in the midst of my industrious scribbling; and though, when the scratching of my pen stopped for a moment, there was complete silence and stillness in the room, I suffered from that profound disturbance and confusion of thought which is caused by a violent and menacing uproar – of a heavy gale at sea, for instance. Some of you may know what I mean, – that mingled anxiety, distress, and irritation with a sort of craven feeling creeping in – not pleasant to acknowledge, but which gives a quiet special merit to one's endurance. I don't claim any merit for standing the stress of Jim's emotions; I could take refuge in the letters; I could have written to strangers if necessary. Suddenly, as I was taking up a fresh sheet of notepaper, I heard a low sound, the first sound that, since we had been shut up together, had come to my ears in the dim stillness of the room. I remained with my head down, with my hand arrested. Those who have kept vigil by a sick-bed have heard such faint sounds in the stillness of the night watches, sounds wrung from a racked body, from a weary soul. He pushed the glass door with such force that all the panes rang: he stepped out, and I held my breath, straining my ears without knowing what else I expected to hear. He was really taking too much to heart an empty formality which to Chester's rigorous criticism seemed unworthy the notice of a man who could see things as they were. An empty formality; a piece of parchment. Well, well. As to the inaccessible guano deposit, that was another story altogether. One could intelligibly break one's heart over that. A feeble burst of many voices mingled with the tinkle of silver and glass floated up from the dining-room below; through the open door the outer edge of the light from my candle fell on his back faintly; beyond all was black; he stood on the brink of a vast obscurity, like a lonely figure by the shore of a sombre and hopeless ocean. There was the Walpole Reef in it – to be sure – a speck in the dark void, a straw for the drowning man. My compassion for him took the shape of the thought that I wouldn't have liked his people to see him at that moment. I found it trying myself. His back was no longer shaken by his gasps; he stood straight as an arrow, faintly visible and still; and the meaning of this stillness sank to the bottom of my soul like lead into the water, and made it so heavy that for a second I wished heartily that the only course left open for me were to pay for his funeral. Even the law had done with him. To bury him would have been such an easy kindness! It would have been so much in accordance with the wisdom of life, which consists in putting out of sight all the reminders of our folly, of our weakness, of our mortality; all that makes against our efficiency – the memory of our failures, the hints of our undying fears, the bodies of our dead friends. Perhaps he did take it too much to heart. And if so then – Chester's offer . . . At this point I took up a fresh sheet and began to write resolutely. There was nothing but myself between him and the dark ocean. I had a sense of responsibility. If I spoke, would that motionless and suffering youth leap into the obscurity – clutch at the straw? I found out how difficult it may be sometimes to make a sound. There is a weird power in a spoken word. And why the devil not? I was asking myself persistently while I drove on with my writing. All at once, on the blank page, under the very point of the pen, the two figures of Chester and his antique partner, very distinct and complete, would dodge into view with stride and gestures, as if reproduced in the field of some optical toy. I would watch them for a while. No! They were too phantasmal and extravagant to enter into anyone's fate. And a word carries far – very far – deals destruction through time as the bullets go flying through space. I said nothing; and he, out there with his back to the light, as if bound and gagged by all the invisible foes of man, made no stir and made no sound.'

CHAPTER 16

'The time was coming when I should see him loved, trusted, admired, with a legend of strength and prowess forming round his name as though he had been the stuff of a hero. It's true – I assure you; as true as I'm sitting here talking about him in vain. He, on his side, had that faculty of beholding at a hint the face of his desire and the shape of his dream, without which the earth would know no lover and no adventurer. He captured much honour and an Arcadian happiness (I won't say anything about innocence) in the bush, and it was as good to him as the honour and the Arcadian happiness of the streets to another man. Felicity, felicity – how shall I say it? – is quaffed out of a golden cup in every latitude: the flavour is with you – with you alone, and you can make it as intoxicating as you please. He was of the sort that would drink deep, as you may guess from what went before. I found him, if not exactly intoxicated, then at least flushed with the elixir at his lips. He had not obtained it at once. There had been, as you know, a period of probation amongst infernal ship-chandlers, during which he had suffered and I had worried about – about – my trust – you may call it. I don't know that I am completely reassured now, after beholding him in all his brilliance. That was my last view of him – in a strong light, dominating, and yet in complete accord with his surroundings – with the life of the forests and with the life of men. I own that I was impressed, but I must admit to myself that after all this is not the lasting impression. He was protected by his isolation, alone of his own superior kind, in close touch with Nature, that keeps faith on such easy terms with her lovers. But I cannot fix before my eye the image of his safety. I shall always remember him as seen through the open door of my room, taking, perhaps, too much to heart the mere consequences of his failure. I am pleased, of course, that some good – and even some splendour – came out of my endeavours; but at times it seems to me it would have been better for my peace of mind if I had not stood between him and Chester's confoundedly generous offer. I wonder what his exuberant imagination would have made of Walpole islet – that most hopelessly forsaken crumb of dry land on the face of the waters. It is not likely I would ever have heard, for I must tell you that Chester, after calling at some Australian port to patch up his brig-rigged sea-anachronism, steamed out into the Pacific with a crew of twenty-two hands all told, and the only news having a possible bearing upon the mystery of his fate was the news of a hurricane which is supposed to have swept in its course over the Walpole shoals, a month or so afterwards. Not a vestige of the Argonauts ever turned up; not a sound came out of the waste. Finis! The Pacific is the most discreet of live, hot-tempered oceans: the chilly Antarctic can keep a secret, too, but more in the manner of a grave.

'And there is a sense of blessed finality in such discretion, which is what we all more or less sincerely are ready to admit – for what else is it that makes the idea of death supportable? End! Finis! the potent word that exorcises from the house of life the haunting shadow of fate. This is what – notwithstanding the testimony of my eyes and his own earnest assurances – I miss when I look back upon Jim's success. While there's life there is hope, truly; but there is fear, too. I don't mean to say that I regret my action, nor will I pretend that I can't sleep o' nights in consequence; still the idea obtrudes itself that he made so much of his disgrace while it is the guilt alone that matters. He was not – if I may say so – clear to me. He was not clear. And there is a suspicion he was not clear to himself either. There were his fine sensibilities, his fine feelings, his fine longings – a sort of sublimated, idealized selfishness. He was – if you allow me to say so – very fine; very fine – and very unfortunate. A little coarser nature would not have borne the strain; it would have had to come to terms with itself – with a sigh, a grunt, or even with a guffaw; a still coarser one would have remained invulnerably ignorant and completely uninteresting.

'But he was too interesting or too unfortunate to be thrown to the dogs, or even to Chester. I felt this while I sat with my face over the paper and he fought and gasped, struggling for his breath in that terribly stealthy way, in my room; I felt it when he rushed out on the veranda as if to fling himself over – and didn't; I felt it more and more all the time he remained outside, faintly lighted on the background of night, as if standing on the shore of a sombre and hopeless sea.

'An abrupt heavy rumble made me lift my head. The noise seemed to roll away, and suddenly a searching and violent glare fell on the blind face of the night. The sustained and dazzling flickers seemed to last for an unconscionable time. The growl of the thunder increased steadily while I looked at him, distinct and black, planted solidly upon the shores of a sea of light. At the moment of greatest brilliance the darkness leaped back with a culminating crash, and he vanished before my dazzled eyes as utterly as though he had been blown to atoms. A blustering sigh passed; furious hands seemed to tear at the shrubs, shake the tops of the trees below, slam doors, break window-panes, all along the front of the building. He stepped in, closing the door behind him, and found me bending over the table: my sudden anxiety as to what he would say was very great, and akin to a fright. "May I have a cigarette?" he asked. I gave a push to the box without raising my head. "I want – want – tobacco," he muttered. I became extremely buoyant. "Just a moment," I grunted, pleasantly. He took a few steps here and there. "That's over," I heard him say. A single distant clap of thunder came from the sea like a gun of distress. "The monsoon breaks up early this year," he remarked, conversationally, somewhere behind me. This encouraged me to turn round, which I did as soon as I had finished addressing the last envelope. He was smoking greedily in the middle of the room, and though he heard the stir I made, he remained with his back to me for a time.

' "Come – I carried it off pretty well," he said, wheeling suddenly. "Something's paid off – not much. I wonder what's to come." His face did not show any emotion, only it appeared a little darkened and swollen, as though he had been holding his breath. He smiled reluctantly as it were, and went on while I gazed up at him mutely.... "Thank you, though – your room – jolly convenient – for a chap – badly hipped." ... The rain pattered and swished in the garden; a water-pipe (it must have had a hole in it) performed just outside the window a parody of blubbering woe with funny sobs and gurgling lamentations, interrupted by jerky spasms of silence.... "A bit of shelter," he mumbled and ceased.

'A flash of faded lightning darted in through the black framework of the windows and ebbed out without any noise. I was thinking how I had best approach him (I did not want to be flung off again) when he gave a little laugh. "No better than a vagabond now" ... the end of the cigarette smouldered between his fingers ... "without a single – single," he pronounced slowly; "and yet ..." He paused; the rain fell with redoubled violence. "Some day one's bound to come upon some sort of chance to get it all back again. Must!" he whispered, distinctly, glaring at my boots.

'I did not even know what it was he wished so much to regain, what it was he had so terribly missed. It might have been so much that it was impossible to say. A piece of ass's skin, according to Chester.... He looked up at me inquisitively. "Perhaps. If life's long enough," I muttered through my teeth with unreasonable animosity. "Don't reckon too much on it."

' "Jove! I feel as if nothing could ever touch me," he said in a tone of sombre conviction. "If this business couldn't knock me over, then there's no fear of there being not enough time to – climb out, and ..." He looked upwards.

'It struck me that it is from such as he that the great army of waifs and strays is recruited, the army that marches down, down into all the gutters of the earth. As soon as he left my room, that "bit of shelter", he would take his place in the ranks, and begin the journey towards the bottomless pit. I at least had no illusions; but it was I, too, who a moment ago had been so sure of the power of words, and now was afraid to speak, in the same way one dares not move for fear of losing a slippery hold. It is when we try to grapple with another man's intimate need that we perceive how incomprehensible, wavering, and misty are the beings that share with us the sight of the stars and the warmth of the sun. It is as if loneliness were a hard and absolute condition of existence; the envelope of flesh and blood on which our eyes are fixed melts before the outstretched hand, and there remains only the capricious, unconsolable, and elusive spirit that no eye can follow, no hand can grasp. It was the fear of losing him that kept me silent, for it was borne upon me suddenly and with unaccountable force that should I let him slip away into the darkness I would never forgive myself.

' "Well. Thanks – once more. You've been – er – uncommonly – really there's no word to ... Uncommonly! I don't know why, I am sure. I am afraid I don't feel as grateful as I would if the whole thing hadn't been so brutally sprung on me. Because at bottom ... you, yourself ..." He stuttered.

' "Possibly," I struck in. He frowned.

' "All the same, one is responsible." He watched me like a hawk.

' "And that's true, too," I said.

' "Well. I've gone with it to the end, and I don't intend to let any man cast it in my teeth without – without – resenting." He clenched his fist.

' "There's yourself," I said with a smile – mirthless enough, God knows – but he looked at me menacingly. "That's my business," he said. An air of indomitable resolution came and went upon his face like a vain and passing shadow. Next moment he looked a dear good boy in trouble, as before. He flung away the cigarette. "Good-bye," he said, with the sudden haste of a man who had lingered too long in view of a pressing bit of work waiting for him; and then for a second or so he made not the slightest movement. The downpour fell with the heavy uninterrupted rush of a sweeping flood, with a sound of unchecked overwhelming fury that called to one's mind the images of collapsing bridges, of uprooted trees, of undermined mountains. No man could breast the colossal and headlong stream that seemed to break and swirl against the dim stillness in which we were precariously sheltered as if on an island. The perforated pipe gurgled, choked, spat, and splashed in odious ridicule of a swimmer fighting for his life. "It is raining," I remonstrated, "and I ..." "Rain or shine," he began, brusquely, checked himself, and walked to the window. "Perfect deluge," he muttered after a while; he leaned his forehead on the glass. "It's dark, too."

' "Yes, it is very dark," I said.

'He pivoted on his heels, crossed the room, and had actually opened the door leading into the corridor before I leaped up from my chair. "Wait," I cried, "I want you to ..." "I can't dine with you again tonight," he flung at me, with one leg out of the room already. "I haven't the slightest intention to ask you," I shouted. At this he drew back his foot, but remained mistrustfully in the very doorway. I lost no time in entreating him earnestly not to be absurd; to come in and shut the door.'

CHAPTER 17

'He came in at last; but I believe it was mostly the rain that did it; it was falling just then with a devastating violence which quieted down gradually while we talked. His manner was very sober and set; his bearing was that of a naturally taciturn man possessed by an idea. My talk was of the material aspect of his position; it had the sole aim of saving him from the degradation, ruin, and despair that out there close so swiftly upon a friendly, homeless man; I pleaded with him to accept my help; I argued reasonably: and every time I looked up at that absorbed smooth face, so grave and youthful, I had a disturbing sense of being no help but rather an obstacle to some mysterious, inexplicable, impalpable striving of his wounded spirit.

' "I suppose you intend to eat and drink and to sleep under shelter in the usual way," I remember saying with irritation. "You say you won't touch the money that is due to you." ... He came as near as his sort can to making a gesture of horror. (There were three weeks and five days' pay owing to him as mate of the *Patna*.) "Well, that's too little to matter anyhow; but what will you do tomorrow? Where will you turn? You must live . . ." "That isn't the thing," was the comment that escaped him under his breath. I ignored it, and went on combating what I assumed to be the scruples of an exaggerated delicacy. "On every conceivable ground," I concluded, "you must let me help you." "You can't," he said very simply and gently, and holding fast to some deep idea which I could detect shimmering like a pool of water in the dark, but which I despaired of ever approaching near enough to fathom. I surveyed his well-proportioned bulk. "At any rate," I said, "I am able to help what I can see of you. I don't pretend to do more." He shook his head sceptically without looking at me. I got very warm. "But I can," I insisted. "I can do even more. I *am* doing more. I am trusting you . . ." "The money . . ." he began. "Upon my word you deserve being told to go to the devil," I cried, forcing the note of indignation. He was startled, smiled, and I pressed my attack home. "It isn't a question of money at all. You are too superficial," I said (and at the same time I was thinking to myself: Well, here goes! And perhaps he is after all). "Look at the letter I want you to take. I am writing to a man of whom I've never asked a favour, and I am writing about you in terms that one only ventures to use when speaking of an intimate friend. I make myself unreservedly responsible for you. That's what I am doing. And really if you will only reflect a little what that means. . . ."

'He lifted his head. The rain had passed away; only the waterpipe went on shedding tears with an absurd drip, drip outside the window. It was very quiet in the room, whose shadows huddled together in corners, away from the still flame of the candle flaring upright in the shape of a dagger; his face after a while seemed suffused by a reflection of a soft light as if the dawn had broken already.

' "Jove!" he gasped out. "It is noble of you!"

'Had he suddenly put out his tongue at me in derision, I could not have felt more humiliated. I thought to myself – Serve me right for a sneaking humbug. . . . His eyes shone straight into my face, but I perceived it was not a mocking brightness. All at once he sprang into jerky agitation, like one of those flat wooden figures that are worked by a string. His arms went up, then came down with a slap. He became another man altogether. "And I had never seen," he shouted; then suddenly bit his lip and frowned. "What a bally ass I've been," he said very slow in awed tone. . . . "You are a brick," he cried next in a muffled voice. He snatched my hand as though he had just then seen it for the first time, and dropped it at once. "Why! this is what I – you – I . . ." he stammered, and then with a return of his stolid, I may say mulish, manner he began heavily, "I would be a brute now if I . . ." and then his voice seemed to break. "That's all right," I said. I was almost alarmed by this display of feeling, through which pierced a strange elation. I had pulled the string accidentally, as it were; I did not fully understand the working of the toy. "I must go now," he said. "Jove! You *have* helped me. Can't sit still. The very thing . . ." He looked at me with puzzled admiration. "The very thing . . ."

'Of course it was the thing. It was ten to one that I had saved him from starvation – of that peculiar sort that is almost invariably associated with drink. This was all. I had not a single illusion on that score, but looking at him, I allowed myself to wonder at the nature of the one he had, within the last three minutes, so evidently taken into his bosom. I had forced into his hand the means to carry on decently the serious business of life, to get food, drink, and shelter of the customary kind while his wounded spirit, like a bird with a broken wing, might hop and flutter into some hole to die quietly of inanition there. This is what I had thrust upon him: a definitely small thing; and – behold! – by the manner of its reception it looked in the dim light of the candle like a big, indistinct, perhaps a dangerous shadow. "You don't mind me not saying anything appropriate," he burst out. "There isn't anything one could say. Last night already you had done me no end of good. Listening to me – you know. I give you my word I've thought more than once the top of my head would fly off...." He darted – positively darted – here and there, rammed his hands into his pockets, jerked them out again, flung his cap on his head. I had no idea it was in him to be so airily brisk. I thought of a dry leaf imprisoned in an eddy of wind, while a mysterious apprehension, a load of indefinite doubt, weighed me down in my chair. He stood stock-still, as if struck motionless by a discovery. "You have given me confidence," he declared, soberly. "Oh! for God's sake, my dear fellow – don't!" I entreated, as though he had hurt me. "All right. I'll shut up now and henceforth. Can't prevent me thinking though.... Never mind! ... I'll show yet ..." He went to the door in a hurry, paused with his head down, and came back, stepping deliberately. "I always thought that if a fellow could begin with a clean slate ... And now you ... in a measure ... yes ... clean slate." I waved my hand, and he marched out without looking back; the sound of his footfalls died out gradually behind the closed door – the unhesitating tread of a man walking in broad daylight.

'But as to me, left alone with the solitary candle, I remained strangely unenlightened. I was no longer young enough to behold at every turn the magnificence that besets our insignificant footsteps in good and in evil. I smiled to think that, after all, it was yet he, of us two, who had the light. And I felt sad. A clean slate, did he say? As if the initial word of each our destiny were not graven in imperishable characters upon the face of a rock.'

CHAPTER 18

'Six months afterwards my friend (he was a cynical, more than middle-aged bachelor, with a reputation for eccentricity, and owned a rice-mill) wrote to me, and judging, from the warmth of my recommendation, that I would like to hear, enlarged a little upon Jim's perfections. These were apparently of a quiet and effective sort. "Not having been able so far to find more in my heart than a resigned toleration for any individual of my kind, I have lived till now alone in a house that even in this steaming climate could be considered as too big for one man. I have had him to live with me for some time past. It seems I haven't made a mistake." It seemed to me on reading this letter that my friend had found in his heart more than tolerance for Jim – that there were the beginnings of active liking. Of course he stated his grounds in a characteristic way. For one thing, Jim kept his freshness in the climate. Had he been a girl – my friend wrote – one could have said he was blooming – blooming modestly – like a violet, not like some of these blatant tropical flowers. He had been in the house for six weeks, and had not as yet attempted to slap him on the back, or address him as "old boy", or try to make him feel a superannuated fossil. He had nothing of the exasperating young man's chatter. He was good-tempered, had not much to say for himself, was not clever by any means, thank goodness – wrote my friend. It appeared, however, that Jim was clever enough to be quietly appreciative of his wit, while, on the other hand, he amused him by his naïveness. "The dew is yet on him, and since I had the bright idea of giving him a room in the house and having him at meals I feel less withered myself. The other day he took it into his head to cross the room with no other purpose but to open a door for me; and I felt more in touch with mankind than I had been for years. Ridiculous, isn't it? Of course I guess there is something – some awful little scrape – which you know all about – but if I am sure that it is terribly heinous, I fancy one could manage to forgive it. For my part, I declare I am unable to imagine him guilty of anything much worse than robbing an orchard. Is *it* much worse? Perhaps you ought to have told me; but it is such a long time since we both turned saints that you may have forgotten we, too, had sinned in our time? It may be that some day I shall have to ask you, and then I shall expect to be told. I don't care to question him myself till I have some idea what it is. Moreover, it's too soon as yet. Let him open the door a few times more for me...." Thus my friend, I was trebly pleased – at Jim's shaping so well, at the tone of the letter, at my own cleverness. Evidently I had known what I was doing. I had read characters aright, and so on. And what if something unexpected and wonderful were to come of it? That evening, reposing in a deck-chair under the shade of my own poop awning (it was in Hong Kong harbour), I laid on Jim's behalf the first stone of a castle in Spain.

'I made a trip to the northward, and when I returned I found another letter from my friend waiting for me. It was the first envelope I tore open. "There are no spoons missing, as far as I know," ran the first line; "I haven't been interested enough to inquire. He is gone, leaving on the breakfast-table a formal little note of apology, which is either silly or heartless. Probably both – and it's all one to me. Allow me to say, lest you should have some more mysterious young men in reserve, that I have shut up shop, definitely and for ever. This is the last eccentricity I shall be guilty of. Do not imagine for a moment that I care a hang; but he is very much regretted at tennis-parties, and for my own sake I've told a plausible lie at the club...." I flung the letter aside and started looking through the batch on my table, till I came upon Jim's handwriting. Would you believe it? One chance in a hundred! But it is always that hundredth chance! That little second engineer of the *Patna* had turned up in a more or less destitute state, and got a temporary job of looking after the machinery of the mill. "I couldn't stand the familiarity of the little beast," Jim wrote from a seaport seven hundred miles south of the place where he should have been in clover. "I am now for the time with Egström & Blake, ship-chandlers, as their – well – runner, to call the thing by its right name. For reference I gave them your name, which they know of course, and if you could write a word in my favour it would be a permanent employment." I was utterly crushed under the ruins of my castle, but of course I wrote as desired. Before the end of the year my new charter took me that way, and I had an opportunity of seeing him.

'He was still with Egström & Blake, and we met in what they called "our parlour" opening out of the store. He had that moment come in from boarding a ship, and confronted me head down, ready for a tussle. "What have you got to say for yourself?" I began as soon as we had shaken hands. "What I wrote you – nothing more," he said stubbornly. "Did the fellow blab – or what?" I asked. He looked up at me with a troubled smile. "Oh, no! He didn't. He made it a kind of confidential business between us. He was most damnably mysterious whenever I came over to the mill; he would wink at me in a respectful manner – as much as to say, 'We know what we know.' Infernally fawning and familiar – and that sort of thing." He threw himself into a chair and stared down his legs. "One day we happened to be alone and the fellow had the cheek to say, 'Well, Mr James' – I was called Mr James there as if I had been the son – 'here we are together once more. This is better than the old ship – ain't it?' ... Wasn't it appalling, eh? I looked at him, and he put on a knowing air. 'Don't you be uneasy, sir,' he says. 'I know a gentleman when I sees one, and I know how a gentleman feels, I hope, though, you will be keeping me on this job. I had a hard time of it, too, along of that rotten old *Patna* racket.' Jove! It was awful. I don't know what I should have said or done if I had not just then heard Mr Denver calling me in the passage. It was tiffin-time, and we walked together across the yard and through the garden to the bungalow. He began to chaff me in his kindly way ... I believe he liked me...."

'Jim was silent for a while.

' "I know he liked me. That's what made it so hard. Such a splendid man! That morning he slipped his hand under my arm.... He, too, was familiar with me." He burst into a short laugh, and dropped his chin on his breast. "Pah! When I remembered how that mean little beast had been talking to me," he began suddenly in a vibrating voice, "I couldn't bear to think of myself ... I suppose you know ..." I nodded.... "More like a father," he cried; his voice sank. "I would have had to tell him. I couldn't let it go on – could I?" "Well?" I murmured, after waiting a while. "I preferred to go," he said, slowly; "this thing must be buried."

'We could hear in the shop Blake upbraiding Egström in an abusive, strained voice. They had been associated for many years, and every day from the moment the doors were opened to the last minute before closing, Blake, a little man with sleek, jetty hair and unhappy, beady eyes, could be heard rowing his partner incessantly with a sort of scathing and plaintive fury.

The sound of that everlasting scolding was part of the place like the other fixtures; even strangers would very soon come to disregard it completely unless it be perhaps to mutter "Nuisance", or to get up suddenly and shut the door of the "parlour". Egström himself, a raw-boned, heavy Scandinavian, with a busy manner and immense blonde whiskers, went on directing his people, checking parcels, making out bills or writing letters at a stand-up desk in the shop, and comported himself in that clatter exactly as though he had been stone-deaf. Now and again he would emit a bothered perfunctory "Sssh", which neither produced nor was expected to produce the slightest effect. "They are very decent to me here," said Jim. "Blake's a little cad, but Egström's all right." He stood up quickly, and walking with measured steps to a tripod telescope standing in the window and pointed at the roadstead, he applied his eye to it. "There's that ship which had been becalmed outside all the morning has got a breeze now and is coming in," he remarked, patiently; "I must go and board." We shook hands in silence, and he turned to go. "Jim!" I cried. He looked round with his hand on the lock. "You – you have thrown away something like a fortune." He came back to me all the way from the door. "Such a splendid old chap," he said. "How could I? How could I?" His lips twitched. "*Here* it does not matter." "Oh! you – you —" I began, and had to cast about for a suitable word, but before I became aware that there was no name that would just do, he was gone. I heard outside Egström's deep gentle voice saying cheerily, "That's the *Sarah W. Granger*, Jimmy. You must manage to be first aboard"; and directly Blake struck in, screaming after the manner of an outraged cockatoo, "Tell the captain we've got some of his mail here. That'll fetch him. D'ye hear, Mister What's-your-name?" And there was Jim answering Egström with something boyish in his tone. "All right. I'll make a race of it." He seemed to take refuge in the boat-sailing part of that sorry business.

'I did not see him again that trip, but on my next (I had a six months' charter) I went up to the store. Ten yards away from the door Blake's scolding met my ears, and when I came in he gave me a glance of utter wretchedness; Egström, all smiles, advanced, extending a large bony hand. "Glad to see you, captain.... Sssh.... Been thinking you were about due back here. What did you say, sir? ... Sssh.... Oh! him! He has left us. Come into the parlour." ... After the slam of the door Blake's strained voice became faint, as the voice of one scolding desperately in a wilderness.... "Put us to a great inconvenience, too. Used us badly – I must say...." "Where's he gone to? Do you know?" I asked. "No. It's no use asking either," said Egström, standing bewhiskered and obliging before me with his arms hanging down his sides clumsily and a thin silver watch-chain looped very low on a rucked-up blue serge waistcoat. "A man like that don't go anywhere in particular." I was too concerned at the news to ask for the explanation of that pronouncement, and he went on. "He left – let's see – the very day a steamer with returning pilgrims from the Red Sea put in here with two blades of her propeller gone. Three weeks ago now." "Wasn't there something said about the *Patna* case?" I asked, fearing the worst. He gave a start, and looked at me as if I had been a sorcerer. "Why, yes! How do you know? Some of them were talking about it here. There was a captain or two, the manager of Vanlo's engineering shop at the harbour, two or three others, and myself. Jim was in here, too, having a sandwich and a glass of beer; when we are busy – you see, captain – there's no time for a proper tiffin. He was standing by this table eating sandwiches, and the rest of us were round the telescope watching that steamer come in; and by and by Vanlo's manager began to talk about the chief of the *Patna*; he had done some repairs for him once, and from that he went on to tell us what an old ruin she was, and the money that had been made out of her. He came to mention her last voyage, and then we all struck in. Some said one thing and some another – not much – what you or any other man might say; and there was some laughing. Captain O'Brien of the *Sarah W. Granger*, a large, noisy old man with a stick – he was sitting listening to us in this arm-chair here – he let drive suddenly with his stick at the floor, and roars out, 'Skunks!' ... Made us all jump. Vanlo's manager winks at us and asks, 'What's the matter, Captain O'Brien?' 'Matter! matter!' the old man began to shout; 'what are you Injuns laughing at? It's no laughing matter. It's a disgrace to human natur' – that's what it is. I would despise being seen in the same room with one of those men. Yes, sir!' he seemed to catch my eye like, and I had to speak out of civility. 'Skunks!' says I, 'of course, Captain O'Brien, and I wouldn't care to have them here myself so you're quite safe in this room, Captain O'Brien. Have a little something cool to drink.' 'Dam' your drink, Egström,' says he, with a twinkle in his eye; 'when I want a drink I will shout for it. I am going to quit. It stinks here now.' At this all the others burst out laughing, and out they go after the old man. And then, sir, that blasted Jim he puts down the sandwich he had in his hand and walks round the table to me; there was his glass of beer poured out quite full. 'I am off,' he says – just like this. 'It isn't half past one yet,' says I; 'you might snatch a smoke first.' I thought he meant it was time for him to go down to his work. When I understood what he was up to, my arms fell – so! Can't get a man like that every day, you know, sir; a regular devil for sailing a boat; ready to go out miles to sea to meet ships in any sort of weather. More than once a captain would come in here full of it, and the first thing he would say would be, 'That's a reckless sort of lunatic you've got for water-clerk, Egström. I was feeling my way in at daylight under short canvas when there comes flying out of the mist right under my forefront a boat half under water, sprays going over the masthead, two frightened niggers on the bottom boards, a yelling fiend at the tiller. Hey! hey! Ship ahoy! ahoy! Captain! Hey! hey! Egström & Blake's man first to speak to you! Hey! hey! Egström & Blake! Hallo! hey! whoop! Kick the niggers – out reefs – a squall on at the time – shoots ahead whooping and yelling to me to make sail and he would give me a lead in – more like a demon than a man. Never saw a boat handled like that in all my life. Couldn't have been drunk – was he? Such a quiet, soft-spoken chap, too – blush like a girl when he came on board....' I tell you, Captain Marlow, nobody had a chance against us with a strange ship when Jim was out. The other ship-chandlers just keep their old customers, and ..."

'Egström appeared overcome with emotion.

' "Why, sir – it seems as though he wouldn't mind going a hundred miles out to sea in an old shoe to nab a ship for the firm. If the business had been his own and all to make yet, he couldn't have done more in that way. And now . . . all at once . . . like this! Thinks I to myself: 'Oho! a rise in the screw – that's the trouble – is it? All right,' says I, 'no need of all that fuss with me, Jimmy. Just mention your figure. Anything in reason.' He looks at me as if he wanted to swallow something that stuck in his throat. 'I can't stop with you.' 'What's that blooming joke?' I asks. He shakes his head, and I could see in his eye he was as good as gone already, sir. So I turned to him and slanged him till all was blue. 'What is it you're running away from?' I asks. 'Who has been getting at you? What scared you? You haven't as much sense as a rat; they don't clear out from a good ship. Where do you expect to get a better berth? – you this and you that.' I made him look sick, I can tell you. 'This business ain't going to sink,' says I. He gave a big jump. 'Good-bye,' he says, nodding at me like a lord; 'you ain't half a bad chap, Egström. I give you my word that if you knew my reasons you wouldn't care to keep me.' 'That's the biggest lie you ever told in your life,' says I; 'I know my own mind.' He made me so mad that I had to laugh. 'Can't you really stop long enough to drink this glass of beer here, you funny beggar, you?' I don't know what came over him; he didn't seem able to find the door; something comical, I can tell you, captain. I drank the beer myself. 'Well, if you're in such a hurry, here's luck to you in your own drink,' says I; 'only, you mark my words, if you keep up this game you'll very soon find that the earth ain't big enough to hold you – that's all.' He gave me one black look, and out he rushed with a face fit to scare little children."

'Egström snorted bitterly, and combed one auburn whisker with knotty fingers. "Haven't been able to get a man that was any good since. It's nothing but worry, worry, worry in business. And where might you have come across him, captain, if it's fair to ask?"

' "He was the mate of the *Patna* that voyage," I said, feeling that I owed some explanation. For a time Egström remained very still, with his fingers plunged in the hair at the side of his face, and then exploded. "And who the devil cares about that?" "I daresay no one," I began . . . "And what the devil is he – anyhow – for to go on like this?" He stuffed suddenly his left whisker into his mouth and stood amazed. "Jee!" he exclaimed, "I told him the earth wouldn't be big enough to hold his caper." '

CHAPTER 19

'I have told you these two episodes at length to show his manner of dealing with himself under the new conditions of his life. There were many others of the sort, more than I could count on the fingers of my two hands.

'They were all equally tinged by a high-minded absurdity of intention which made their futility profound and touching. To fling away your daily bread so as to get your hands free for a grapple with a ghost may be an act of prosaic heroism. Men had done it before (though we who have lived know full well that it is not the haunted soul but the hungry body that makes an outcast), and men who had eaten and meant to eat every day had applauded the creditable folly. He was indeed unfortunate, for all his recklessness could not carry him out from under the shadow. There was always a doubt of his courage. The truth seems to be that it is impossible to lay the ghost of a fact. You can face it or shirk it – and I have come across a man or two who could wink at their familiar shades. Obviously Jim was not of the winking sort; but what I could never make up my mind about was whether his line of conduct amounted to shirking his ghost or to facing him out.

'I strained my mental eyesight only to discover that, as with the complexion of all our actions, the shade of difference was so delicate that it was impossible to say. It might have been a fight and it might have been a mode of combat. To the common mind he became known as a rolling stone, because this was the funniest part; he did after a time become perfectly known, and even notorious, within the circle of his wanderings (which had a diameter of, say, three thousand miles), in the same way as an eccentric character is known to a whole countryside. For instance, in Bangkok, where he found employment with Yucker Brothers, charterers and teak merchants, it was almost pathetic to see him go about in sunshine hugging his secret, which was known to the very up-country logs on the river. Schomberg, the keeper of the hotel where he boarded, a hirsute Alsatian of manly bearing and an irrepressible retailer of all the scandalous gossip of the place, would, with both elbows on the table, impart an adorned version of the story to any guest who cared to imbibe knowledge along with the more costly liquors. "And, mind you, the nicest fellow you could meet," would be his generous conclusion; "quite superior." It says a lot for the casual crowd that frequented Schomberg's establishment that Jim managed to hang out in Bangkok for a whole six months. I remarked that people, perfect strangers, took to him as one takes to a nice child. His manner was reserved, but it was as though his personal appearance, his hair, his eyes, his smile, made friends for him wherever he went. And, of course, he was no fool. I heard Siegmund Yucker (native of Switzerland), a gentle creature ravaged by a cruel dyspepsia, and so frightfully lame that his head swung through a quarter of a circle at every step he took, declare appreciatively that for one so young he was "of great gabasidy", as though it had been a mere question of cubic contents. "Why not send him up country?" I suggested anxiously. (Yucker Brothers had concessions and teak forests in the interior.) "If he has capacity, as you say, he will soon get hold of the work. And physically he is very fit. His health is always excellent." "Ach! It's a great ting in dis goundry to be vree vrom tispep-shia," sighed poor Yucker enviously, casting a stealthy glance at the pit of his ruined stomach. I left him drumming pensively on his desk and muttering, "Es ist ein idee. Es ist ein idee." Unfortunately, that very evening an unpleasant affair took place in the hotel.

'I don't know that I blame Jim very much, but it was a truly regrettable incident. It belonged to the lamentable species of bar-room scuffles, and the other party to it was a cross-eyed Dane of sorts whose visiting card recited under his misbegotten name: first lieutenant in the Royal Siamese Navy. The fellow, of course, was utterly hopeless at billiards, but did not like to be beaten, I suppose. He had had enough to drink to turn nasty after the sixth game, and make some scornful remark at Jim's expense. Most of the people there didn't hear what was said, and those who had heard seemed to have had all precise recollection scared out of them by the appalling nature of the consequences that immediately ensued. It was very lucky for the Dane that he could swim, because the room opened on a veranda and the Menam flowerd below very wide and black. A boat-load of Chinamen, bound, as likely as not, on some thieving expedition, fished out the officer of the King of Siam, and Jim turned up at about midnight on board my ship without a hat. "Everybody in the room seemed to know," he said, gasping yet from the contest, as it were. He was rather sorry, on general principles, for what happened, though in this case there had been, he said, "no option". But what dismayed him was to find the nature of his burden as well known to everybody as though he had gone about all that time carrying it on his shoulders. Naturally after this he couldn't remain in the place. He was universally condemned for the brutal violence, so unbecoming a man in his delicate position; some maintained he had been disgracefully drunk at the time; others criticized his want of tact. Even Schomberg was very much annoyed. "He is a very nice young man," he said, argumentatively, to me, "but the lieutenant is a first-rate fellow, too. He dines every night at my *table d'hôte*, you know. And there's a billard-cue broken. I can't allow that. First thing this morning I went over with my apologies to the lieutenant, and I think I've made it all right for myself; but only think, captain, if everybody started such games! Why, the man might have been drowned! And here I can't run out into the next street and buy a new cue. I've got to write to Europe for them. No, no! A temper like that won't do!" . . . He was extremely sore on the subject.

'This was the worse incident of all in his – his retreat. Nobody could deplore it more than myself; for if, as somebody said hearing him mentioned, "Oh, yes! I know. He has knocked about a good deal out here," yet he had somehow avoided being battered and chipped in the process. This last affair, however, made me seriously uneasy, because if his exquisite sensibilities were to go the length of involving him in pot-house shindies, he would lose his name of an inoffensive, if aggravating, fool, and acquire that of a common loafer. For all my confidence in him I could not help reflecting that in such cases from the name to the thing itself is but a step. I suppose you will understand that by that time I could not think of washing my hands of him. I took him away from Bangkok in my ship, and we had a longish passage. It was pitiful to see how he shrank within himself. A seaman, even if a mere passenger, takes an interest in a ship, and looks at sea-life around him with the critical enjoyment of a painter, for instance, looking at another man's work. In every sense of the expression he is "on deck"; but my Jim, for the most part, skulked down below as though he had been a stowaway. He infected me so that I avoided speaking on professional matters, such as would suggest themselves naturally to two sailors during a passage. For whole days we did not exchange a word; I felt extremely unwilling to give orders to my officers in his presence. Often, when alone with him on deck or in the cabin, we didn't know what to do with our eyes.

'I placed him with De Jongh, as you know, glad enough to dispose of him in any way, yet persuaded that his position was now growing intolerable. He had lost some of that elasticity which had enabled him to rebound back into his uncompromising position after every overthrow. One day, coming ashore, I saw him standing on the quay; the water of the roadstead and the sea in the offing made one smooth ascending plane, and the outermost ships at anchor seemed to ride motionless in the sky. He was waiting for his boat, which was being loaded at our feet with packages of small stores for some vessel ready to leave. After exchanging greetings, we remained silent – side by side. "Jove!" he said, suddenly, "this is killing work."

'He smiled at me; I must say he generally could manage a smile. I made no reply. I knew very well he was not alluding to his duties; he had an easy time of it with De Jongh. Nevertheless, as soon as he had spoken I became completely convinced that the work was killing. I did not even look at him. "Would you like," said I, "to leave this part of the world altogether; try California or the West Coast? I'll see what I can do . . ." He interrupted me a little scornfully. "What difference would it make?" . . . I felt at once convinced that he was right. It would make no difference; it was not relief he wanted; I seemed to perceive dimly that what he wanted, what he was, as it were, waiting for, was something not easy to define – something in the nature of an opportunity. I had given him many opportunities, but they had been merely opportunities to earn his bread. Yet what more could any man do? The position struck me as hopeless, and poor Brierly's saying recurred to me, "Let him creep twenty feet underground and stay there." Better that, I thought, than this waiting above ground for the impossible. Yet one could not be sure even of that. There and then, before his boat was three oars' lengths away from the quay, I had made up my mind to go and consult Stein in the evening.

'This Stein was a wealthy and respected merchant. His "house" (because it was a house, Stein & Co., and there was some sort of partner who, as Stein said, "looked after the Moluccas") had a large inter-island business, with a lot of trading posts established in the most out-of-the-way places for collecting the produce. His wealth and his respectability were not exactly the reasons why I was anxious to seek his advice. I desired to confide my difficulty to him because he was one of the most trustworthy men I had ever known. The gentle light of a simple unwearied, as it were, and intelligent good-nature illuminated his long hairless face. It had deep downward folds, and was pale as of a man who had always led a sedentary life – which was indeed very far from being the case. His hair was thin, and brushed back from his massive and lofty forehead. One fancied that at twenty he must have looked very much like what he was now at threescore. It was a student's face; only the eyebrows nearly all white, thick and bushy, together with the resolute searching glance that came from under them, were not in accord with his, I may say, learned appearance. He was tall and loose-jointed; his slight stoop, together with an innocent smile, made him appear benevolently ready to lend you his ear; his long arms with pale big hands had rare deliberate gestures of a pointing out, demonstrating kind. I speak of him at length, because under this exterior, and in conjunction with an upright and indulgent nature, this man possessed an intrepidity of spirit and a physical courage that could have been called reckless had it not been like a natural function of the body – say good digestion, for instance – completely unconscious of itself. It is sometimes said of a man that he carries his life in his hand. Such a saying would have been inadequate if applied to him; during the early part of his existence in the East he had been playing ball with it. All this was in the past, but I knew the story of his life and the origin of his fortune. He was also a naturalist of some distinction, or perhaps I should say a learned collector. Entomology was his special study. His collection of *Buprestidae* and *Longicorns* – beetles all – horrible miniature monsters, looking malevolent in death and immobility, and his cabinet of butterflies, beautiful and hovering under the glass of cases of lifeless wings, had spread his fame far over the earth. The name of this merchant, adventurer, sometime adviser of a Malay sultan (to whom he never alluded otherwise than as "my poor Mohammed Bonso"), had, on account of a few bushels of dead insects, become known to learned persons in Europe, who could have no conception, and certainly would not have cared to know anything of his life or character. I, who knew, considered him an eminently suitable person to receive my confidences about Jim's difficulties as well as my own.'

CHAPTER 20

'Late in the evening I entered his study, after traversing an imposing but empty dining-room very dimly lit. The house was silent. I was preceded by an elderly grim Javanese servant in a sort of livery of white jacket and yellow sarong, who, after throwing the door open, exclaimed low, "O master!" and stepping aside, vanished in a mysterious way as though he had been a ghost only momentarily embodied for that particular service. Stein turned round with the chair, and in the same movement his spectacles seemed to get pushed up on his forehead. He welcomed me in his quiet and humorous voice. Only one corner of the vast room, the corner in which stood his writing-desk, was strongly lighted by a shaded reading-lamp, and the rest of the spacious apartment melted into shapeless gloom like a cavern. Narrow shelves filled with dark boxes of uniform shape and colour ran round the walls, not from floor to ceiling, but in a sombre belt about four feet broad. Catacombs of beetles. Wooden tablets were hung above at irregular intervals. The light reached one of them, and the word *Coleoptera* written in gold letters glittered mysteriously upon a vast dimness. The glass cases containing the collection of butterflies were ranged in three long rows upon slender-legged little tables. One of these cases had been removed from its place and stood on the desk, which was bestrewn with oblong slips of paper blackened with minute handwriting.

' "So you see me – so," he said. His hand hovered over the case where a butterfly in solitary grandeur spread out dark bronze wings, seven inches or more across, with exquisite white veinings and a gorgeous border of yellow spots. "Only one specimen like this they have in *your* London, and then – no more. To my small native town this my collection I shall bequeath. Something of me. The best."

'He bent forward in the chair and gazed intently, his chin over the front of the case. I stood at his back. "Marvellous," he whispered, and seemed to forget my presence. His history was curious. He had been born in Bavaria, and when a youth of twenty-two had taken an active part in the revolutionary movement of 1848. Heavily compromised, he managed to make his escape, and at first found refuge with a poor republican watchmaker in Trieste. From there he made his way to Tripoli with a stock of cheap watches to hawk about – not a very great opening truly, but it turned out lucky enough, because it was there he came upon a Dutch traveller – a rather famous man, I believe, but I don't remember his name. It was that naturalist who, engaging him as a sort of assistant, took him to the East. They travelled in the Archipelago together and separately, collecting insects and birds, for four years or more. Then the naturalist went home, and Stein, having no home to go to, remained with an old trader he had come across in his journeys in the interior of Celebes – if Celebes may be said to have an interior. This old Scotsman, the only white man allowed to reside in the country at the time, was a privileged friend of the chief ruler of Wajo States, who was a woman. I often heard Stein relate how that chap, who was slightly paralysed on one side, had introduced him to the native court a short time before another stroke carried him off. He was a heavy man with a patriarchal white beard, and of imposing stature. He came into the council-hall where all the rajahs, pangerans, and headmen were assembled, with the queen, a fat wrinkled woman (very free in her speech, Stein said), reclining on a high couch under a canopy. He dragged his leg, thumping with his stick, and grasped Stein's arm, leading him right up to the couch. "Look, queen, and you rajahs, this is my son," he proclaimed in a stentorian voice. "I have traded with your fathers, and when I die he shall trade with you and your sons."

'By means of this simple formality Stein inherited the Scotsman's privileged position and all his stock-in-trade, together with a fortified house on the banks of the only navigable river in the country. Shortly afterwards the old queen, who was so free in her speech, died, and the country became disturbed by various pretenders to the throne. Stein joined the party of the younger son, the one of whom thirty years later he never spoke otherwise but as "my poor Mohammed Bonso". They both became the heroes of innumerable exploits; they had wonderful adventures, and once stood a siege in the Scotsman's house for a month, with only a score of followers against a whole army. I believe the natives talk of that war to this day. Meantime, it seems, Stein never failed to annex on his own account every butterfly or beetle he could lay his hands on. After some eight years of war, negotiations, false truces, sudden outbreaks, reconciliation, treachery, and so on, and just as peace seemed at last permanently established, his "poor Mohammed Bonso" was assassinated at the gate of his own royal residence while dismounting in the highest spirits on his return from a successful deer-hunt. This event rendered Stein's position extremely insecure, but he would have stayed perhaps had it not been that a short time afterwards he lost Mohammed's sister ("my dear wife the princess," he used to say solemnly), by whom he had had a daughter – mother and child both dying within three days of each other from some infectious fever. He left the country, which this cruel loss had made unbearable to him. Thus ended the first and adventurous part of his existence. What followed was so different that, but for the reality of sorrow which remained with him, this strange part must have resembled a dream. He had a little money; he started life afresh, and in the course of years acquired a considerable fortune. At first he had travelled a good deal amongst the islands, but age had stolen upon him, and of late he seldom left his spacious house three miles out of town, with an extensive garden, and surrounded by stables, offices, and bamboo cottages for his servants and dependants, of whom he had many. He drove in his buggy every morning to town, where he had an office with white and Chinese clerks. He owned a small fleet of schooners and native craft, and dealt in island produce on a large scale. For the rest he lived solitary, but not misanthropic, with his books and his collection, classing and arranging specimens, corresponding with entomologists in Europe, writing up a descriptive catalogue of his treasures. Such was the history of the man whom I had come to consult upon Jim's case without any definite hope. Simply to hear what he would have to say would have been a relief. I was very anxious, but I respected the intense, almost passionate, absorption with which he looked at a butterfly, as though on the bronze sheen on these frail wings, in the white tracings, in the gorgeous markings, he could see other things, an image of something as perishable and defying destruction as these delicate and lifeless tissues displaying a splendour unmarred by death.

' "Marvellous!" he repeated, looking up at me. "Look! The beauty – but that is nothing – look at the accuracy, the harmony. And so fragile! And so strong! And so exact! This is Nature – the balance of colossal forces. Every star is so – and every blade of grass stands *so* – and the mighty Kosmos in perfect equilibrium produces – this. This wonder; this masterpiece of Nature – the great artist."

' "Never heard an entomologist go on like this," I observed, cheerfully. "Masterpiece! And what of man?"

' "Man is amazing, but he is not a masterpiece," he said, keeping his eyes fixed on the glass case. "Perhaps the artist was a little mad. Eh? What do you think? Sometimes it seems to me that man is come where he is not wanted, where there is no place for him; for if not, why should he want all the place? Why should he run about here and there making a great noise about himself, talking about the stars, disturbing the blades of grass? . . ."

' "Catching butterflies," I chimed in.

'He smiled, threw himself back in his chair, and stretched his legs. "Sit down," he said. "I captured this rare specimen myself one very fine morning.

And I had a very big emotion. You don't know what it is for a collector to capture such a rare specimen. You can't know."

'I smiled at my ease in a rocking-chair. His eyes seemed to look far beyond the wall at which they stared; and he narrated how, one night, a messenger arrived from his "poor Mohammed", requiring his presence at the "residenz" – as he called it – which was distant some nine or ten miles by a bridle-path over a cultivated plain, with patches of forest here and there. Early in the morning he started from his fortified house, after embracing his little Emma, and leaving the "princess", his wife, in command. He described how she came with him as far as the gate, walking with one hand on the neck of his horse; she had on a white jacket, gold pins in her hair, and a brown leather belt over her left shoulder with a revolver in it. "She talked as women will talk," he said, "telling me to be careful, and to try to get back before dark, and what a great wickedness it was for me to go alone. We were at war, and the country was not safe; my men were putting up bullet-proof shutters to the house and loading their rifles, and she begged me to have no fear for her. She could defend the house against anybody till I returned. And I laughed with pleasure a little. I liked to see her so brave and young and strong. I, too, was young then. At the gate she caught hold of my hand and gave it one squeeze and fell back. I made my horse stand still outside till I heard the bars of the gate put up behind me. There was a great enemy of mine, a great noble – and a great rascal, too – roaming with a band in the neighbourhood. I cantered for four or five miles; there had been rain in the night, but the mists had gone up, up – and the face of the earth was clean; it lay smiling to me, so fresh and innocent – like a little child. Suddenly somebody fires a volley – twenty shots at least it seemed to me. I hear bullets sing in my ear, and my hat jumps to the back of my head. It was a little intrigue, you understand. They got my poor Mohammed to send for me and then laid that ambush. I see it all in a minute, and I think – This wants a little management. My pony snort, jump, and stand, and I fall slowly forward with my head on his mane. He begins to walk, and with one eye I could see over his neck a faint cloud of smoke hanging in front of a clump of bamboos to my left. I think – Aha! my friends, why you not wait long enough before you shoot? This is not yet *gelungen*. Oh, no! I get hold of my revolver with my right hand – quiet – quiet. After all, there were only seven of these rascals. They get up from the grass and start running with their sarongs tucked up, waving spears above their heads, and yelling to each other to look out and catch the horse, because I was dead. I let them come as close as the door here, and then bang, bang, bang – take aim each time, too. One more shot I fire at a man's back, but I miss. Too far already. And then I sit alone on my horse with the clean earth smiling at me, and there are the bodies of three men lying on the ground. One was curled up like a dog, another on his back had an arm over his eyes as if to keep off the sun, and the third man he draws up his leg very slowly and makes it with one kick straight again. I watch him very carefully from my horse, but there is no more – *bleibt ganz ruhig* – keep still, so. And as I looked at his face for some sign of life I observed something like a faint shadow pass over his forehead. It was the shadow of this butterfly. Look at the form of the wing. This species fly high with a strong flight. I raised my eyes and I saw him fluttering away. I think – Can it be possible? And then I lost him. I dismounted and went on very slow, leading my horse and holding my revolver with one hand and my eyes darting up and down and right and left, everywhere! At last I saw him sitting on a small heap of dirt ten feet away. At once my heart began to beat quick. I let go my horse, keep my revolver in one hand, and with the other snatch my soft felt hat off my head. One step. Steady. Another step. Flop! I got him! When I got up I shook like a leaf with excitement, and when I opened these beautiful wings and made sure what a rare and so extraordinary perfect specimen I had, my head went round and my legs became so weak with emotion that I had to sit on the ground. I had greatly desired to possess myself of a specimen of that species when collecting for the professor. I took long journeys and underwent great privations; I had dreamed of him in my sleep, and here suddenly I had him in my fingers – for myself! In the words of the poet" (he pronounced it "boet") —

"So halt' ich's endlich denn in meinen Händen,
Und nenn' es in gewissem Sinne mein."

He gave to the last word the emphasis of a suddenly lowered voice, and withdrew his eyes slowly from my face. He began to charge a long-stemmed pipe busily and in silence, then, pausing with his thumb on the orifice of the bowl, looked again at me significantly.

' "Yes, my good friend. On that day I had nothing to desire; I had greatly annoyed my principal enemy; I was young, strong; I had friendship; I had the love" (he said "lof") "of woman, a child I had, to make my heart very full – and even what I had once dreamed in my sleep had come into my hand, too!"

'He struck a match, which flared violently. His thoughtful placid face twitched once.

' "Friend, wife, child," he said, slowly, gazing at the small flame – "phoo!" The match was blown out. He sighed and turned again to the glass case. The frail and beautiful wings quivered faintly, as if his breath had for an instant called back to life that gorgeous object of his dreams.

' "The work," he began, suddenly, pointing to the scattered slips, and in his usual gentle and cheery tone, "is making great progress. I have been this rare specimen describing . . . Na! And what is your good news?'

' "To tell you the truth, Stein," I said with an effort that surprised me, "I came here to describe a specimen. . . ."

' "Butterfly?" he asked, with an unbelieving and humorous eagerness.

' "Nothing so perfect," I answered, feeling suddenly dispirited with all sorts of doubts. "A man!"

' "Ach so?" he murmured, and his smiling countenance, turned to me, became grave. Then after looking at me for a while he said slowly. "Well – I am a man, too."

'Here you have him as he was; he knew how to be so generously encouraging as to make a scrupulous man hesitate on the brink of confidence; but if I did hesitate it was not for long.

'He heard me out, sitting with crossed legs. Sometimes his head would disappear completely in a great eruption of smoke, and a sympathetic growl would come out from the cloud. When I finished he uncrossed his legs, laid down his pipe, leaned forward towards me earnestly with his elbows on the arms of his chair, the tips of his fingers together.

' "I understand very well. He is romantic."

'He had diagnosed the case for me, and at first I was startled to find how simple it was; and indeed our conference resembled so much a medical consultation – Stein, of learned aspect, sitting in an arm-chair before his desk; I, anxious, in another, facing him, but a little to one side – that it seemed natural to ask —

' "What's good for it?"

'He lifted up a long forefinger.

' "There is only one remedy! One thing alone can us from being ourselves cure!" The finger came down on the desk with a smart rap. The case which he had made to look so simple before became if possible still simpler – and altogether hopeless. There was a pause. "Yes," said I, "strictly speaking, the question is not how to get cured, but how to live."

'He approved with his head, a little sadly as it seemed. *"Ja! Ja!* In general, adapting the words of your great poet: That is the question. . . ." He went on nodding sympathetically . . . "How to be! *Ach!* How to be."

'He stood up with the tips of his fingers resting on the desk.

' "We want in so many different ways to be," he began again. "This magnificent butterfly finds a little heap of dirt and sits still on it; but man will never on his heap of mud keep still. He want to be so, and again he want to be so. . . ." He moved his hand up, then down. . . . "He wants to be a saint, and he wants to be a devil – and every time he shuts his eyes he seems himself as a very fine fellow – so fine as he can never be. . . . In a dream. . . ."

'He lowered the glass lid, the automatic lock clicked sharply, and taking up the case in both hands he bore it religiously away to its place, passing out of the bright circle of the lamp into the ring of fainter light – into shapeless dusk at last. It had an odd effect – as if these few steps had carried him out of this concrete and perplexed world. His tall form, as though robbed of its substance, hovered noiselessly over invisible things with stooping and indefinite movements; his voice, heard in that remoteness where he could be glimpsed mysteriously busy with immaterial cares, was no longer incisive, seemed to roll voluminous and grave – mellowed by distance.

' "And because you not always can keep your eyes shut there comes the real trouble – the heart pain – the world pain. I tell you, my friend, it is not good for you to find you cannot make your dream come true, for the reason that you not strong enough are, or not clever enough. *Ja!* . . . And all the time you are such a fine fellow too! *Wie? Was! Gott in Himmel!* How can that be? Ha! ha! ha!"

'The shadow prowling amongst the graves of butterflies laughed boisterously.

' "Yes! Very funny this terrible thing is. A man that is born falls into a dream like a man who falls into the sea. If he tries to climb out into the air as inexperienced people endeavour to do, he drowns – *nicht wahr?* . . . No! I tell you! The way is to the destructive element submit yourself, and with the exertions of your hands and feet in the water make the deep, deep sea keep you up. So if you ask me – how to be?"

'His voice leaped up extraordinarily strong, as though away there in the dusk he had been inspired by some whisper of knowledge. "I will tell you! For that, too, there is only one way."

'With a hasty swish swish of his slippers he loomed up in the ring of faint light, and suddenly appeared in the bright circle of the lamp. His extended hand aimed at my breast like a pistol; his deep-set eyes seemed to pierce through me, but his twitching lips uttered no word, and the austere exaltation of a certitude seen in the dusk vanished from his face. The hand that had been pointing at my breast fell, and by-and-by, coming a step nearer, he laid it gently on my shoulder. There were things, he said mournfully, that perhaps could never be told, only he had lived so much alone that sometimes he forgot – he forgot. The light had destroyed the assurance which had inspired him in the distant shadows. He sat down and, with both elbows on the desk, rubbed his forehead. "And yet it is true – it is true. In the destructive element immerse." . . . He spoke in a subdued tone, without looking at me, one hand on each side of his face. "That was the way. To follow the dream, and again to follow the dream – and so – *ewig* – *usque ad finem*. . . ." The whisper of his conviction seemed to open before me a vast and uncertain expanse, as of a crepuscular horizon on a plain at dawn – or was it, perchance, at the coming of the night? One had not the courage to decide; but it was a charming and deceptive light, throwing the impalpable poesy of its dimness over pitfalls – over graves. His life had begun in sacrifice, in enthusiasm for generous ideas; he had travelled very far, on various ways, on strange paths, and whatever he followed it had been without faltering, and therefore without shame and without regret. In so far he was right. That was the way, no doubt. Yet for all that the great plain on which men wander amongst graves and pitfalls remained very desolate under the impalpable poesy of its crepuscular light, overshadowed in the centre, circled with a bright edge as if surrounded by an abyss full of flames. When at last I broke the silence it was to express the opinion that no one could be more romantic than himself.

'He shook his head slowly, and afterwards looked at me with a patient and inquiring glance. It was a shame, he said. There we were sitting and talking like two boys, instead of putting our heads together to find something practical – a practical remedy – for the evil – for the great evil – he repeated, with a humorous and indulgent smile. For all that, our talk did not grow more practical. We avoided pronouncing Jim's name as though we had tried to keep flesh and blood out of our discussion, or he were nothing but an erring spirit, a suffering and nameless shade. "Na!" said Stein, rising. "Tonight you sleep here, and in the morning we shall do something practical – practical. . . . He lit a two-branched candlestick and led the way. We passed through empty dark rooms, escorted by gleams from the lights Stein carried. They glided along the waxed floors, sweeping here and there over the polished surface of the table, leaped upon a fragmentary curve of a piece of furniture, or flashed perpendicularly in and out of distant mirrors, while the forms of two men and the flicker of two flames could be seen for a moment stealing silently across the depths of a crystalline void. He walked slowly a pace in advance with stooping courtesy, there was a profound, as it were a listening, quietude on his face, the long flaxen locks mixed with white threads were scattered thinly upon his slightly bowed neck.

' "He is romantic – romantic," he repeated. "And that is very bad – very bad. ... Very good, too," he added. "But *is he?*" I queried.

' "*Gewiss*," he said, and stood still holding up the candelabrum, but without looking at me. "Evident! What is it that by inward pain makes him know himself? What is it that for you and me makes him – exist?"

'At that moment it was difficult to believe in Jim's existence – starting from a country parsonage, blurred by crowds of men as by clouds of dust, silenced by the clashing claims of life and death in a material world – but his imperishable reality came to me with a convincing, with an irresistible force! I saw it vividly, as though in our progress through the lofty silent rooms amongst fleeting gleams of light and the sudden revelations of human figures stealing with flickering flames within unfathomable and pellucid depths, we had approached nearer to absolute Truth, which, like Beauty itself, floats elusive, obscure, half submerged, in the silent still waters of mystery. "Perhaps he is," I admitted with a slight laugh, whose unexpectedly loud reverberations made me lower my voice directly; "but I am sure you are." With his head dropping on his breast and the light held high he began to walk again. "Well – I exist, too," he said.

'He preceded me. My eyes followed his movements, but what I did see was not the head of the firm, the welcome guest at afternoon receptions, the correspondent of learned societies, the entertainer of stray naturalists; I saw only the reality of his destiny, which he had known how to follow with unfaltering footsteps, that life begun in humble surroundings, rich in generous enthusiasms, in friendship, love, war – in all the exalted elements of romance. At the door of my room he faced me. "Yes," I said, as though carrying on a discussion, "and amongst other things you dreamed foolishly of a certain butterfly; but when one fine morning your dream came in your way you did not let the splendid opportunity escape. Did you? Whereas he ..." Stein lifted his hand. "And do you know how many opportunities I let escape; how many dreams I had lost that had come in my way?" He shook his head regretfully. "It seems to me that some would have been very fine – if I had made them come true. Do you know how many? Perhaps I myself don't know." "Whether his were fine or not," I said, "he knows of one which he certainly did not catch." "Everybody knows of one or two like that," said Stein; "and that is the trouble – the great trouble. ..."

'He shook hands on the threshold, peered into my room under his raised arm. "Sleep well. And tomorrow we must do something practical – practical. ..."

'Though his own room was beyond mine I saw him return the way he came. He was going back to his butterflies.'

CHAPTER 21

'I don't suppose any of you had ever heard of Patusan?' Marlow resumed, after a silence occupied in the careful lighting of a cigar. 'It does not matter; there's many a heavenly body in the lot crowding upon us of a night that mankind had never heard of, it being outside the sphere of its activities and of no earthly importance to anybody but to the astronomers who are paid to talk learnedly about its composition, weight, path – the irregularities of its conduct, the aberrations of its light – a sort of scientific scandal-mongering. Thus with Patusan. It was referred to knowingly in the inner government circles in Batavia, especially as to its irregularities and aberrations, and it was known by name to some few, very few, in the mercantile world. Nobody, however, had been there, and I suspect no one desired to go there in person, just as an astronomer, I should fancy, would strongly object to being transported into a distant heavenly body, where, parted from his earthly emoluments, he would be bewildered by the view of an unfamiliar heaven. However, neither heavenly bodies nor astronomers have anything to do with Patusan. It was Jim who went there. I only meant you to understand that had Stein arranged to send him into a star of the fifth magnitude the change could not have been greater. He left his earthly failings behind him and that sort of reputation he had, and there was a totally new set of conditions for his imaginative faculty to work upon. Entirely new, entirely remarkable. And he got hold of them in a remarkable way.

'Stein was the man who knew more about Patusan than anybody else. More than was known in the government circles I suspect. I have no doubt he had been there, either in his butterfly-hunting days or later on, when he tried in his incorrigible way to season with a pinch of romance the fattening dishes of his commercial kitchen. There were very few places in the Archipelago he had not seen in the original dusk of their being, before light (and even electric light) had been carried into them for the sake of better morality and – and – well – the greater profit, too. It was at breakfast of the morning following our talk about Jim that he mentioned the place, after I had quoted poor Brierly's remark: "Let him creep twenty feet underground and stay there." He looked up at me with interested attention, as though I had been a rare insect. "This could be done, too," he remarked, sipping his coffee. "Bury him in some sort," I explained. "One doesn't like to do it of course, but it would be the best thing, seeing what he is." "Yes; he is young," Stein mused. "The youngest human being now in existence," I affirmed. "*Schön*. There's Patusan," he went on in the same tone. ... "And the woman is dead now," he added incomprehensibly.

'Of course I don't know that story; I can only guess that once before Patusan had been used as a grave for some sin, transgression, or misfortune.

It is impossible to suspect Stein. The only woman that had ever existed for him was the Malay girl he called "my wife the princess", or, more rarely in moments of expansion, "the mother of my Emma". Who was the woman he had mentioned in connexion with Patusan I can't say; but from his allusions I understood she had been an educated and very good-looking Dutch-Malay girl, with a tragic or perhaps only a pitiful history, whose most painful part no doubt was her marriage with a Malacca Portuguese who had been clerk in some commercial house in the Dutch colonies. I gathered from Stein that this man was an unsatisfactory person in more ways than one, all being more or less indefinite and offensive. It was solely for his wife's sake that Stein had appointed him manager of Stein & Co.'s trading post in Patusan; but commercially the arrangement was not a success, at any rate for the firm, and now the woman had died, Stein was disposed to try another agent there. The Portuguese, whose name was Cornelius, considered himself a very deserving but ill-used person, entitled by his abilities to a better position. This man Jim would have to relieve. "But I don't think he will go away from the place," remarked Stein. "That has nothing to do with me. It was only for the sake of the woman that I . . . But as I think there is a daughter left, I shall let him, if he likes to stay, keep the old house."

'Patusan is a remote district of a native-ruled State, and the chief settlement bears the same name. At a point on the river about forty miles from the sea, where the first houses come into view, there can be seen rising above the level of the forests the summits of two steep hills very close together, and separated by what looks like a deep fissure, the cleavage of some mighty stroke. As a matter of fact, the valley between is nothing but a narrow ravine; the appearance from the settlement is one of irregularly conical hill split in two, and with the two halves leaning slightly apart. On the third day after the full moon, as seen from the open space in front of Jim's house (he had a very fine house in the native style when I visited him), rose exactly behind these hills, its diffused light at first throwing the two masses into intensely black relief, and then the nearly perfect disc, glowing ruddily, appeared, gliding upwards between the sides of the chasm, till it floated away above the summits, as if escaping from a yawning grave in gentle triumph. "Wonderful effect," said Jim by my side. "Worth seeing. Is it not?"

'And this question was put with a note of personal pride that made me smile, as though he had had a hand in regulating that unique spectacle. He had regulated so many things in Patusan! Things that would have appeared as much beyond his control as the motions of the moon and the stars.

'It was inconceivable. That was the distinctive quality of the part into which Stein and I had tumbled him unwittingly, with no other notion than to get him out of the way; out of his own way, be it understood. That was our main purpose, though, I own, I might have had another motive which had influenced me a little. I was about to go home for a time; and it may be I desired, more than I was aware of myself, to dispose of him – to dispose of him, you understand – before I left. I was going home, and he had come to me from there, with his miserable trouble and his shadowy claim, like a man panting under a burden in a mist. I cannot say I had ever seen him distinctly – not even to this day, after I had my last view of him; but it seemed to me that the less I understood the more I was bound to him in the name of that doubt which is the inseparable part of our knowledge. I did not know so much more about myself. And then, I repeat, I was going home – to that home distant enough for all its hearthstones to be like one hearthstone, by which the humblest of us has the right to sit. We wander in our thousands over the face of the earth, the illustrious and the obscure, earning beyond the seas our fame, our money, or only a crust of bread; but it seems to me that for each of us going home must be like going to render an account. We return to face our superiors, our kindred, our friends – those whom we obey, and those whom we love; but even they who have neither, the most free, lonely, irresponsible and bereft of ties, – even those for whom home holds no dear face, no familiar voice, – even they have to meet the spirit that dwells within the land, under its sky, in its air, in its valleys, and on its rises, in its fields, in its waters and its trees – a mute friend, judge, and inspirer. Say what you like, to get its joy, to breath its peace, to face its truth, one must return with a clear consciousness. All this may seem to you sheer sentimentalism; and indeed very few of us have the will or the capacity to look consciously under the surface of familiar emotions. There are the girls we love, the men we look up to, the tenderness, the friendships, the opportunities, the pleasures! But the fact remains that you must touch your reward with clean hands, lest it turn to dead leaves, to thorns, in your grasp. I think it is the lonely, without a fireside or an affection they may call their own, those who return not to a dwelling but to the land itself, to meet its disembodied, eternal, and unchangeable spirit – it is those who understand best its severity, its saving power, the grace of its secular right to our fidelity, to our obedience. Yes! few of us understand, but we all feel it though, and I say *all* without exception, because those who do not feel do not count. Each blade of grass has its spot on earth whence it draws its life, its strength; and so is man rooted to the land from which he draws his faith together with his life. I don't know how much Jim understood; but I know he felt, he felt confusedly but powerfully, the demand of some such truth or some such illusion – I don't care how you call it, there is so little difference, and the difference means so little. The thing is that in virtue of his feelings he mattered. He would never go home now. Not he. Never. Had he been capable of picturesque manifestations he would have shuddered at the thought and made you shudder, too. But he was not of that sort, though he was expressive enough in his way. Before the idea of going home he would grow desperately stiff and immovable, with lowered chin and pouted lips, and with those candid blue eyes of his glowing darkly under a frown, as if before something unbearable, as if before something revolting. There was imagination in that hard skull of his, over which the thick clustering hair fitted like a cap. As to me, I have no imagination (I would be more certain about him today, if I had), and I do not mean to imply that I figured to myself the spirit of the land uprising above the white cliffs of Dover, to ask me what I – returning with no bones broken, so to speak – had done with my very young brother. I could not make such a mistake. I knew very well he was of those about whom there is no inquiry; I had seen better men go out, disappear, vanish utterly, without provoking a sound of curiosity or sorrow. The spirit of the land, as becomes the ruler of great enterprises, is careless of innumerable lives. Woe to the stragglers! We exist only in so far as we hang together. He had straggled in a way; he had not hung on; but he was aware of it with an intensity that made him touching, just as a man's more intense life makes his death more touching than the death of a tree. I happened to be handy, and I happened to be touched. That's all there is to it. I was concerned as to the way he would go out. It would have hurt me if, for instance, he had taken to drink. The earth is so small that I was afraid of, some day, being waylaid by a blear-eyed, swollen-faced, besmirched loafer, with no soles to his canvas shoes, and with a flutter of rags about the elbows, who, on the strength of old acquaintance, would ask for a loan of five dollars. You know the awful jaunty bearing of these scarecrows coming to you from a decent past, the rasping careless voice, the half-averted impudent glances – those meetings more trying to a man who believes in the solidarity of our lives than the sight of an impenitent deathbed to a priest. That, to tell you the truth, was the only danger I could see for him and for me; but I also mistrusted my want of imagination. It might even come to something worse, in some way it was beyond my powers of fancy to foresee. He wouldn't let me forget how imaginative he was, and your imaginative people swing farther in any direction, as if given a longer scope of cable in the uneasy anchorage of life. They do. They take to drink, too. It may be I was belittling him by such a fear. How could I tell? Even Stein could say no more than that he was romantic. I only knew he was one of us. And what business had he to be romantic? I am telling you so much about my own instinctive feelings and bemused reflections because there remains so little to be told of him. He existed for me, and after all it is only through me that he exists for you. I've led him out by the hand; I have paraded him before you. Were my commonplace fears unjust? I won't say – not even now. You may be able to tell better, since the proverb has it that the onlookers see most of the game. At any rate, they were superfluous. He did not go out, not at all; on the contrary, he came on wonderfully, came on straight as a die and in excellent form, which showed that he could stay as well as spurt. I ought to be delighted, for it is a victory in which I had taken my part; but I am not so pleased as I would have expected to be. I ask myself whether his rush had really carried him out of that mist in which he loomed interesting if not very big, with floating outlines – a straggler yearning inconsolably for his humble place in the ranks. And besides, the last word is not said – probably shall never be said. Are not our lives too short for that full utterance which through all our stammerings is of course our only and abiding intention? I have given up expecting those last words, whose ring, if they could only be pronounced, would shake both heaven and earth. There is never time to say our last word – the last word of our love, of our desire, faith, remorse, submission, revolt. The heaven and the earth must not be shaken. I suppose – at least, not by us who know so many truths about either. My last words about Jim shall be few. I affirm he had achieved greatness; but the thing would be dwarfed in the telling, or rather in the hearing. Frankly, it is not my words that I mistrust but your minds. I could be eloquent were I not afraid you fellows have starved your imaginations to feed your bodies. I do not mean to be offensive; it is respectable to have no illusions – and safe – and profitable – and dull. Yet you, too, in your time must have known the intensity of life, that light of glamour created in the shock of trifles, as amazing as the glow of sparks struck from a cold stone – and as short-lived, alas?'

CHAPTER 22

'The conquest of love, honour, men's confidence – the pride of it, the power of it, are fit materials for a heroic tale; only our minds are struck by the externals of such a success, and to Jim's successes, there were no externals. Thirty miles of forest shut it off from the sight of an indifferent world, and the noise of the white surf along the coast overpowered the voice of fame. The stream of civilization, as if divided on a headland a hundred miles north of Patusan, branches east and south-east, leaving its plains and valleys, its old trees and its old mankind, neglected and isolated, such as an insignificant and crumbling islet between the two branches of a mighty, devouring stream. You find the name of the country pretty often in collections of old voyages. The seventeenth-century traders went there for pepper, because the passion for pepper seemed to burn like a flame of love in the breast of Dutch and English adventurers about the time of James the First. Where wouldn't they go for pepper! For a bag of pepper they would cut each other's throats without hesitation, and would forswear their souls, of which they were so careful otherwise: the bizarre obstinacy of that desire made them defy death in a thousand shapes; the unknown seas, the loathsome and strange diseases; wounds, captivity, hunger, pestilence, and despair. It made them great! By heavens! it made them heroic; and it made them pathetic, too, in their craving for trade with the inflexible death levying its toll on young and old. It seems impossible to believe that mere greed could hold men to such a steadfastness of purpose, to such a blind persistence in endeavour and sacrifice. And indeed those who adventured their persons and lives risked all they had for a slender reward. They left their bones to lie bleaching on distant shores, so that wealth might flow to the living at home. To us, their less tried successors, they appear magnified, not as agents of trade but as instruments of a recorded destiny, pushing out into the unknown in obedience to an inward voice, to an impulse beating in the blood, to a dream of the future. They were wonderful; and it must be owned they were ready for the wonderful. They recorded it complacently in their sufferings, in the aspect of the seas, in the customs of strange nations, in the glory of splendid rulers.

'In Patusan they had found lots of pepper, and had been impressed by the magnificence and the wisdom of the Sultan; but somehow, after a century of checkered intercourse, the country seems to drop gradually out of the trade. Perhaps the pepper had given out. Be it as it may, nobody cares for it now; the glory has departed, the Sultan is an imbecile youth with two thumbs on his left hand and an uncertain and beggarly revenue extorted from a miserable population and stolen from him by his many uncles.

'This of course I have from Stein. He gave me their names and a short sketch of the life and character of each. He was as full of information about native States as an official report, but infinitely more amusing. He *had* to know. He traded in so many, and in some districts – as in Patusan, for instance – his firm was the only one to have an agency by special permit from the Dutch authorities. The Government trusted his discretion, and it was understood that he took all the risks. The men he employed understood that, too, but he made it worth their while apparently. He was perfectly frank with me over the breakfast-table in the morning. As far as he was aware (the last news was thirteen months old, he stated precisely), utter insecurity for life and property was the normal condition. There were in Patusan antagonistic forces, and one of them was Rajah Allang, the worst of the Sultan's uncles, the governor of the river, who did the extorting and the stealing, and ground down to the point of extinction the country-born Malays, who, utterly defenceless, had not even the resource of emigrating – "for indeed," as Stein remarked, "where could they go, and how could they get away?" No doubt they did not even desire to get away. The world (which is circumscribed by lofty impassable mountains) has been given into the hand of the high-born and *this* Rajah they knew: he was of their own royal house. I had the pleasure of meeting the gentleman later on. He was a dirty, little, used-up old man with evil eyes and a weak mouth, who swallowed an opium pill every two hours, and in defiance of common decency wore his hair uncovered and falling in wild stringy locks about his wizened grimy face. When giving audience he would clamber upon a sort of narrow stage erected in a hall like a ruinous barn with a rotten bamboo floor, through the cracks of which you could see twelve or fifteen feet below the heaps of refuse and garbage of all kinds lying under the house. That is where and how he received us when, accompanied by Jim, I paid him a visit of ceremony. There were about forty people in the room, and perhaps three times as many in the great courtyard below. There was constant movement, coming and going, pushing and murmuring, at our backs. A few youths in gay silks glared from the distance; the majority, slaves and humble dependants, were half naked, in ragged sarongs, dirty with ashes and mud-stains. I had never seen Jim look so grave, so self-possessed, in an impenetrable, impressive way. In the midst of these dark-faced men, his stalwart figure in white apparel, the gleaming clusters of his fair hair, seemed to catch all the sunshine that trickled through the cracks in the closed shutters of that dim hall, with its walls of mats and a roof of thatch. He appeared like a creature not only of another kind but of another essence. Had they not seen him come up in a canoe they might have thought he had descended upon them from the clouds. He did, however, come in a crazy dug-out, sitting (very still and with his knees together, for fear of overturning the thing) – sitting on a tin box – which I had lent him – nursing on his lap a revolver of the Navy pattern – presented by me on parting – which, through an interposition of

Providence, or through some wrong-headed notion, that was just like him, or else from sheer instinctive sagacity, he had decided to carry unloaded. That's how he ascended the Patusan river. Nothing could have been more prosaic and more unsafe, more extravagantly casual, more lonely. Strange, this fatality that would cast the complexion of a flight upon all his acts, of impulsive unreflecting desertion – of a jump into the unknown.

'It is precisely the casualness of it that strikes me most. Neither Stein nor I had a clear conception of what might be on the other side when we, metaphorically speaking, took him up and hove him over the wall with scant ceremony. At the moment I merely wished to achieve his disappearance. Stein characteristically enough had a sentimental motive. He had a notion of paying off (in kind, I suppose) the old debt he had never forgotten. Indeed he had been all his life especially friendly to anybody from the British Isles. His late benefactor, it is true, was a Scot – even to the length of being called Alexander M'Neil – and Jim came from a long way south of the Tweed; but at the distance of six or seven thousand miles Great Britain, though never diminished, looks foreshortened enough even to its own children to rob such details of their importance. Stein was excusable, and his hinted intentions were so generous that I begged him most earnestly to keep them secret for a time. I felt that no consideration of personal advantage should be allowed to influence Jim; that not even the risk of such influence should be run. We had to deal with another sort of reality. He wanted a refuge, and a refuge at the cost of danger should be offered him – nothing more.

'Upon every other point I was perfectly frank with him, and I even (as I believed at the time) exaggerated the danger of the undertaking. As a matter of fact I did not do it justice; his first day in Patusan was nearly his last – would have been his last if he had not been so reckless or so hard on himself and had condescended to load that revolver. I remember, as I unfolded our precious scheme for his retreat, how his stubborn but weary resignation was gradually replaced by surprise, interest, wonder, and by boyish eagerness. This was a chance he had been dreaming of. He couldn't think how he merited that I . . . He would be shot if he could see to what he owed. . . . And it was Stein, Stein the merchant, who . . . but of course it was me he had to . . . I cut him short. He was not articulate, and his gratitude caused me inexplicable pain. I told him that if he owed this chance to any one especially, it was to an old Scot of whom he had never heard, who had died many years ago, of whom little was remembered besides a roaring voice and a rough sort of honesty. There was really no one to receive his thanks. Stein was passing on to a young man the help he had received in his own young days, and I had done no more than to mention his name. Upon this he coloured, and, twisting a bit of paper in his fingers, he remarked bashfully that I had always trusted him.

'I admitted that such was the case, and added after a pause that I wished he had been able to follow my example. "You think I don't?" he asked uneasily, and remarked in a mutter that one had to get some sort of show first; then brightening up, and in a loud voice he protested he would give me no occasion to regret my confidence, which – which . . .

' "Do not misapprehend," I interrupted. "It is not in your power to make me regret anything." There would be no regrets; but if there were, it would be altogether my own affair; on the other hand, I wished him to understand clearly that this arrangement, this – this – experiment, was his own doing; he was responsible for it and no one else. "Why? Why?" he stammered, "this is the very thing that I ..." I begged him not to be dense, and he looked more puzzled than ever. He was in a fair way to make life intolerable to himself. ... "Do you think so?" he asked, disturbed; but in a moment added confidentially, "I was going on though. Was I not?" It was impossible to be angry with him: I could not help a smile, and told him that in the old days people who went on like this were on the way of becoming hermits in a wilderness. "Hermits be hanged!" he commented with engaging impulsiveness. Of course he didn't mind a wilderness. ... "I was glad of it," I said. That was where he would be going to. He would find it lively enough, I ventured to promise. "Yes, yes," he said, keenly. He had shown a desire, I continued inflexibly, to go out and shut the door after him. ... "Did I?" he interrupted in a strange access of gloom that seemed to envelop him from head to foot like the shadow of a passing cloud. He was wonderfully expressive after all. Wonderfully! "Did I?" he repeated, bitterly. "You can't say I made much noise about it. And I can keep it up, too – only, confound it! you show me a door." ... "Very well. Pass on," I struck in. I could make him a solemn promise that it would be shut behind him with a vengeance. His fate, whatever it was, would be ignored, because the country, for all its rotten state, was not judged ripe for interference. Once he got in, it would be for the outside world as though he had never existed. He would have nothing but the soles of his two feet to stand upon, and he would have first to find his ground at that. "Never existed – that's it, by Jove!" he murmured to himself. His eyes, fastened upon my lips, sparkled. If he had thoroughly understood the conditions, I concluded, he had better jump into the first gharry he could see and drive on to Stein's house for his final instructions. He flung out of the room before I had fairly finished speaking.'

CHAPTER 23

'He did not return till next morning. He had been kept to dinner and for the night. There never had been such a wonderful man as Mr Stein. He had in his pocket a letter for Cornelius ("the Johnnie who's going to get the sack," he explained with a momentary drop in his elation), and he exhibited with glee a silver ring, such as natives use, worn down very thin and showing faint traces of chasing.

'This was his introduction to an old chap called Doramin – one of the principal men out there – a big pot – who had been Mr Stein's friend in that country where he had all these adventures. Mr Stein called him "war-comrade". War-comrade was good. Wasn't it? And didn't Mr Stein speak

English wonderfully well? Said he had learned it in Celebes – of all places! That was awfully funny. Was it not? He did speak with an accent – a twang – did I notice? That chap Doramin had given him the ring. They had exchanged presents when they parted for the last time. Sort of promising eternal friendship. He called it fine – did I not? They had to make a dash for dear life out of the country when that Mohammed – Mohammed – What's-his-name had been killed. I knew the story, of course. Seemed a beastly shame, didn't it? . . .

'He ran on like this, forgetting his plate, with a knife and fork in hand (he had found me at tiffin), slightly flushed, and with his eyes darkened many shades, which was with him a sign of excitement. The ring was a sort of credential – ("It's like something you read of in books," he threw in appreciatively) and Doramin would do his best for him. Mr Stein had been the means of saving that chap's life on some occasion; purely by accident, Mr Stein had said, but he – Jim – had his own opinion about that. Mr Stein was just the man to look out for such accidents. No matter. Accident or purpose, this would serve his turn immensely. Hoped to goodness the jolly old beggar had not gone off the hooks meantime. Mr Stein could not tell. There had been no news for more than a year; they were kicking up no end of an all-fired row amongst themselves, and the river was closed. Jolly awkward, this; but, no fear; he would manage to find a crack to get in.

'He impressed, almost frightened, me with his elated rattle. He was voluble like a youngster on the eve of a long holiday with a prospect of delightful scrapes, and such an attitude of mind in a grown man and in this connexion had in it something phenomenal, a little mad, dangerous, unsafe. I was on the point of entreating him to take things seriously when he dropped his knife and fork (he had begun eating, or rather swallowing food, as it were, unconsciously), and began a search all round his plate. The ring! The ring! Where the devil . . . Ah! Here it was. . . . He closed his big hand on it, and tried all his pockets one after another. Jove! wouldn't do to lose the thing. He meditated gravely over his fist. Had it? Would hang the bally affair round his neck! And he proceeded to do this immediately, producing a string (which looked like a bit of cotton shoe-lace) for the purpose. There! That would do the trick! It would be the deuce if . . . He seemed to catch sight of my face for the first time, and it steadied him a little. I probably didn't realize, he said with a naïve gravity, how much importance he attached to that token. It meant a friend; and it is a good thing to have a friend. He knew something about that. He nodded at me expressively, but before my disclaiming gesture he leaned his head on his hand and for a while sat silent, playing thoughtfully with the bread-crumbs on the cloth. . . . "Slam the door – that was jolly well put," he cried, and jumping up, began to pace the room, reminding me by the set of the shoulders, the turn of his head, the head-long and uneven stride, of that night when he had paced thus, confessing, explaining – what you will – but, in the last instance, living – living before me, under his own little cloud, with all his unconscious subtlety which could draw consolation from the very source of sorrow. It was the same mood, the same and different, like a fickle companion that today guiding you on the true path, with the same eyes, the same step, the same impulse, tomorrow will lead you hopelessly astray. His tread was assured, his straying, darkened eyes seemed to search the room for something. One of his footfalls somehow sounded louder than the other – the fault of his boots probably – and gave a curious impression of an invisible halt in his gait. One of his hands was rammed deep into his trousers-pocket, the other waved suddenly above his head. "Slam the door!" he shouted. "I've been waiting for that. I'll show yet ... I'll ... I'm ready for any confounded thing. ... I've been dreaming of it ... Jove! Get out of this. Jove! This is luck at last. ... You wait. I'll ..."

'He tossed his head fearlessly, and I confess that for the first and last time in our acquaintance I perceived myself unexpectedly to be thoroughly sick of him. Why these vapourings? He was stumping about the room flourishing his arm absurdly, and now and then feeling on his breast for the ring under his clothes. Where was the sense of such exaltation in a man appointed to be a trading-clerk, and in a place where there was no trade – at that? Why hurl defiance at the universe? This was not a proper frame of mind to approach any undertaking; an improper frame of mind not only for him, I said, but for any man. He stood still over me. Did I think so? he asked, by no means subdued, and with a smile in which I seemed to detect suddenly something insolent. But then I am twenty years his senior. Youth *is* insolent; it is its right – its necessity; it has got to assert itself, and all assertion in this world of doubts is a defiance, is an insolence. He went off into a far corner, and coming back, he, figuratively speaking, turned to rend me. I spoke like that because I – even I, who had been no end kind to him – even I remembered – remembered – against him – what – what had happened. And what about others – the – the world? Where's the wonder he wanted to get out, meant to get out, meant to stay out – by heavens! And I talked about proper frames of mind!

' "It is not I or the world who remembers," I shouted. "It is you – you, who remember."

'He did not flinch, and went on with heat, "Forget everything, everybody, everybody." ... His voice fell. ... "But you," he added.

' "Yes – me, too – if it would help," I said, also in a low tone. After this we remained silent and languid for a time as if exhausted. Then he began again, composedly, and told me that Mr Stein had instructed him to wait for a month or so, to see whether it was possible for him to remain, before he began building a new house for himself, so as to avoid "vain expense". He did make use of funny expressions – Stein did. "Vain expense" was good. ... Remain? Why! of course. He would hang on. Let him only get in – that's all; he would answer for it he would remain. Never get out. It was easy enough to remain.

' "Don't be foolhardy," I said, rendered uneasy by his threatening tone. "If you only live long enough you will want to come back."

' "Come back to what?" he asked, absently, with his eyes fixed upon the face of a clock on the wall.

'I was silent for a while. "Is it to be never, then?" I said. "Never," he repeated, dreamily, without looking at me, and then flew into sudden activity. "Jove! Two o'clock, and I sail at four?"

'It was true. A brigantine of Stein's was leaving for the westward that afternoon, and he had been instructed to take his passage in her, only no orders to delay the sailing had been given. I suppose Stein forgot. He made a rush to get his things while I went aboard my ship, where he promised to call on his way to the outer roadster. He turned up accordingly in a great hurry and with a small leather valise in his hand. This wouldn't do, and I offered him an old tin trunk of mine supposed to be water-tight, or at least damp-tight. He effected the transfer by the simple process of shooting out the contents of his valise as you would empty a sack of wheat. I saw three books in the tumble; two small, in dark covers, and a thick green-and-gold volume – a half-crown complete Shakespeare. "You read this?" I asked. "Yes. Best thing to cheer up a fellow," he said hastily. I was struck by this appreciation, but there was no time for Shakespearian talk. A heavy revolver and two small boxes of cartridges were lying on the cuddy-table. "Pray take this," I said. "It may help you to remain." No sooner were these words out of my mouth than I perceived what grim meaning they could bear. "May help you to get in," I corrected myself, remorsefully. He, however, was not troubled by obscure meanings; he thanked me effusively and bolted out, calling Good-bye over his shoulder. I heard his voice through the ship's side urging his boatmen to give way, and looking out of the stern-port I saw the boat rounding under the counter. He sat in her leaning forward, exciting his men with voice and gestures; and as he had kept the revolver in his hand and seemed to be presenting it at their heads, I shall never forget the scared faces of the four Javanese, and the frantic swing of their stroke which snatched that vision from under my eyes. Then turning away, the first thing I saw were the two boxes of cartridges on the cuddy-table. He had forgotten to take them.

'I ordered my gig manned at once; but Jim's rowers, under the impression that their lives hung on a thread while they had that madman in the boat, made such excellent time that before I had traversed half the distance between the two vessels I caught sight of him clambering over the rail, and of his box being passed up. All the brigantine's canvas was loose, her mainsail was set, and the windlass was just beginning to clink as I stepped upon her deck: her master, a dapper little half-caste of forty or so, in a blue flannel suit, with lively eyes, his round face the colour of lemon-peel and with a thin little black moustache drooping on each side of his thick, dark lips, came forward smirking. He turned out, notwithstanding his self-satisfied and cheery exterior, to be of a careworn temperament. In answer to a remark of mine (while Jim had gone below for a moment) he said, "Oh, yes. Patusan." He was going to carry the gentleman to the mouth of the river, but would "never ascend." His flowing English seemed to be derived from a dictionary compiled by a lunatic. Had Mr Stein desired to "ascend", he would have "reverentially" – (I think he wanted to say respectfully – but devil only knows) – "reverentially made objects for the safety of properties." If disregarded, he would have presented "resignation to quit." Twelve months ago he had made his last voyage there, and though Mr Cornelius "propitiated many offertories" to Mr Rajah Allang and the "principal populations", on conditions which made the trade "a snare and ashes in the mouth", yet his ship had been fired upon from the woods by "irresponsive parties" all the way down the river; which causing his crew "from exposure to limb to remain silent in hidings," the brigantine was nearly stranded on a sandbank at the bar, where she "would have been perishable beyond the act of man". The angry disgust at the recollection, the pride of his fluency, to which he turned an attentive ear, struggled for the possession of his broad simple face. He scowled and beamed at me, and watched with satisfaction the undeniable effect of his phraseology. Dark frowns ran swiftly over the placid sea, and the brigantine, with her fore-topsail to the mast and her main-boom amidships, seemed bewildered amongst the cat's-paws. He told me further, gnashing his teeth, that the Rajah was a "laughable hyaena" (can't image how he got hold of hyaenas); while somebody else was many times falser than the "weapons of a crocodile." Keeping one eye on the movements of his crew forward, he let loose his volubility – comparing the place to a "cage of beasts made ravenous by long impenitence." I fancy he meant impunity. He had no intention, he cried, to "exhibit himself to be made attached purposefully to robbery." The long-drawn wails, giving the time for the pull of the men catting the anchor, came to an end, and he lowered his voice. "Plenty too much enough of Patusan," he concluded, with energy.

'I heard afterwards he had been so indiscreet as to get himself tied up by the neck with a rattan halter to a post planted in the middle of a mud-hole before the Rajah's house. He spent the best part of a day and a whole night in that unwholesome situation, but there is every reason to believe the thing had been meant as a sort of joke. He brooded for a while over that horrid memory, I suppose, and then addressed in a quarrelsome tone the man coming aft to the helm. When he turned to me again it was to speak judicially, without passion. He would take the gentleman to the mouth of the river at Batu Kring (Patusan town "being situated internally," he remarked, "thirty miles"). But in his eyes, he continued – a tone of bored, weary conviction replacing his previous voluble delivery – the gentleman was already "in the similitude of a corpse." "What? What did you say?" I asked. He assumed a startlingly ferocious demeanour, and imitated to perfection the act of stabbing from behind. "Already like the body of one deported," he explained, with the insufferably conceited air of his kind after what they imagine a display of cleverness. Behind him I perceived Jim smiling silently at me, and with a raised hand checking the exclamation on my lips.

'Then, while the half-caste, bursting with importance, shouted his orders, while the yards swung creaking and the heavy boom came surging over, Jim and I, alone as it were, to leeward of the mainsail, clasped each other's hands and exchanged the last hurried words. My heart was freed from that dull resentment which had existed side by side with interest in his fate. The absurd chatter of the half-caste had given more reality to the miserable dangers of his path than Stein's careful statements. On that occasion the sort of formality that had been always present in our intercourse vanished from our speech; I believe I called him "dear boy", and he tacked on the words "old man" to some half-uttered expression of gratitude, as though his risk set off against my years had made us more equal in age and in feeling. There was a moment of real and profound intimacy, unexpected and short-lived like a glimpse of some everlasting, of some saving truth. He exerted himself to soothe me as though he had been the more mature of the two. "All right, all right," he said, rapidly, and with feeling. "I promise to take care of myself. Yes; I won't take any risks. Not a single blessed risk. Of course not. I mean to hang out. Don't you worry. Jove! I feel as if nothing could touch me. Why! this is luck from the word Go. I wouldn't spoil such a magnificent chance!" . . . A magnificent chance! Well, it *was* magnificent, but chances are what men make them, and how was I to know? As he had said, even I – even I remembered – his – his misfortunes against him. It was true. And the best thing for him was to go.

'My gig had dropped in the wake of the brigantine, and I saw him aft detached upon the light of the westering sun, raising his cap high above his head. I heard an indistinct shout, "You – shall – hear – of – me." Of me, or from me, I don't know which. I think it must have been *of* me. My eyes were too dazzled by the glitter of the sea below his feet to see him clearly; I am fated never to see him clearly; but I can assure you no man could have appeared less "in the similitude of a corpse", as that half-caste croaker had put it. I could see the little wretch's face, the shape and colour of a ripe pumpkin, poked out somewhere under Jim's elbow. He, too, raised his arm as if for a downward thrust. *Absit omen!*'

CHAPTER 24

'The coast of Patusan (I saw it nearly two years afterwards) is straight and sombre, and faces a misty ocean. Red trails are seen like cataracts of rust streaming under the dark-green foliage of bushes and creepers clothing the low cliffs. Swampy plains open out at the mouth of rivers, with a view of jagged blue peaks beyond the vast forests. In the offing a chain of islands, dark, crumbling shapes, stand out in the everlasting sunlit haze like the remnants of a wall breached by the sea.

'There is a village of fisher-folk at the mouth of the Batu Kring branch of the estuary. The river, which had been closed so long, was open then, and Stein's little schooner, in which I had my passage, worked her way up in three tides without being exposed to a fusillade from "irresponsive parties". Such a state of affairs belonged already to ancient history, if I could believe the elderly headman of the fishing village, who came on board to act as a sort of pilot. He talked to me (the second white man he had ever seen) with confidence, and most of his talk was about the first white man he had ever seen. He called him Tuan Jim, and the tone of his references was made remarkable by a strange mixture of familiarity and awe. They, in the village, were under that lord's special protection, which showed that Jim bore no grudge. If he had warned me that I would hear of him it was perfectly true. I was hearing of him. There was already a story that the tide had turned two hours before its time to help him on his journey up the river. The talkative old man himself had steered the canoe and had marvelled at the phenomenon. Moreover, all the glory was in his family. His son and his son-in-law had paddled; but they were only youths without experience, who did not notice the speed of the canoe till he pointed out to them the amazing fact.

'Jim's coming to that fishing village was a blessing; but to them, as to many of us, the blessing came heralded by terrors. So many generations had been released since the last white man had visited the river that the very tradition had been lost. The appearance of the being that descended upon them and demanded inflexibly to be taken up to Patusan was discomposing; his insistence was alarming; his generosity more than suspicious. It was an unheard-of request. There was no precedent. What would the Rajah say to this? What would he do to them? The best part of the night was spent in consultation; but the immediate risk from the anger of that strange man seemed so great that at last a cranky dug-out was got ready. The women shrieked with grief as it put off. A fearless old hag cursed the stranger.

'He sat in it, as I've told you, on his tin box, nursing the unloaded revolver on his lap. He sat with precaution – than which there is nothing more fatiguing – and thus entered the land he was destined to fill with the fame of his virtues, from the blue peaks inland to the white ribbon of surf on the coast. At the first bend he lost sight of the sea with its labouring waves for ever rising, sinking, and vanishing to rise again – the very image of struggling mankind – and faced the immovable forests rooted deep in the soil, soaring towards the sunshine, everlasting in the shadowy might of their tradition, like life itself. And his opportunity sat veiled by his side like an Eastern bride waiting to be uncovered by the hand of the master. He, too, was the heir of a shadowy and mighty tradition! He told me, however, that he had never in his life felt so depressed and tired as in that canoe. All the movement he dared to allow himself was to reach, as it were by stealth, after the shell of half a coco-nut floating between his shoes, and bale some of the water out with a carefully restrained action. He discovered how hard the lid of a block-tin case was to sit upon. He had heroic health; but several times during that journey he experienced fits of giddiness, and between whiles he speculated hazily as to the size of the blister the sun was raising on his back. For amusement he tried by looking ahead to decide whether the muddy object he saw lying on the water's edge was a log of wood or an alligator. Only very soon he had to give that up. No fun in it. Always alligator. One of them flopped into the river and all but capsized the canoe. But this excitement was over directly. Then in a long empty reach he was very grateful to a troop of monkeys who came right down on the bank and made an insulting hullabaloo on his passage. Such was the way in which he was approaching greatness as genuine as any man ever achieved. Principally, he longed for sunset; and meantime his three paddlers were preparing to put into execution their plan of delivering him up to the Rajah.

' "I suppose I must have been stupid with fatigue, or perhaps I did doze off for a time," he said. The first thing he knew was his canoe coming to the bank. He became instantaneously aware of the forest having been left behind, of the first houses being visible higher up, of a stockade on his left, and of his boatmen leaping out together upon a low point of land and taking to their heels. Instinctively he leaped out after them. At first he thought himself deserted for some inconceivable reason, but he heard excited shouts, a gate swung open, and a lot of people poured out, making towards him. At the same time a boat full of armed men appeared on the river and came alongside his empty canoe, thus shutting off his retreat.

' "I was too startled to be quite cool – don't you know? and if that revolver had been loaded I would have shot somebody – perhaps two, three bodies, and that would have been the end of me. But it wasn't. ...." "Why not?" I asked. "Well, I couldn't fight the whole population, and I wasn't coming to them as if I were afraid of my life," he said, with just a faint hint of his stubborn sulkiness in the glance he gave me. I refrained from pointing out to him that they could not have known the chambers were actually empty. He had to satisfy himself in his own way. ... "Anyhow it wasn't," he repeated, good-humouredly, "and so I just stood still and asked them what was the matter. That seemed to strike them dumb. I saw some of these thieves going off with my box. That long-legged old scoundrel Kassim (I'll show him to you tomorrow) ran out fussing to me about the Rajah wanting to see me. I said, 'All right'; I, too, wanted to see the Rajah, and I simply walked in through the gate and – and – here I am." He laughed, and then with unexpected emphasis, "And do you know what's the best in it?" he asked. "I'll tell you. It's the knowledge that had I been wiped out it is this place that would have been the loser."

'He spoke thus to me before his house on that evening I've mentioned – after we had watched the moon float away above the chasm between the hills like an ascending spirit out of a grave; its sheen descended, cold and pale, like the ghost of dead sunlight. There is something haunting in the light of the moon; it has all the dispassionateness of a disembodied soul, and something of its inconceivable mystery. It is to our sunshine, which – say what you like – is all we have to live by, what the echo is to the sound: misleading and confusing whether the note be mocking or sad. It robs all forms of matter – which, after all, is our domain – of their substance, and gives a sinister reality to shadows alone. And the shadows were very real around us, but Jim by my side looked very stalwart, as though nothing – not even the occult power of moonlight – could rob him of his reality in my eyes. Perhaps, indeed, nothing could touch him since he had survived the assault of the dark powers. All was silent, all was still; even on the river the moonbeams slept as on a pool. It was the moment of high water, a moment of immobility that accentuated the utter isolation of this lost corner of the earth. The houses crowding along the wide shining sweep without ripple or glitter, stepping into the water in a line of jostling, vague, grey, silvery forms mingled with black masses of shadow, were like a spectral herd of shapeless creatures pressing forward to drink in a spectral and lifeless stream. Here and there a red gleam twinkled within the bamboo walls, warm, like a living spark, significant of human affections, of shelter, of repose.

'He confessed to me that he often watched these tiny warm gleams go out one by one, that he loved to see people go to sleep under his eyes, confident in the security of tomorrow. "Peaceful here, eh?" he asked. He was not eloquent, but there was a deep meaning in the words that followed. "Look at these houses; there's not one where I am not trusted. Jove! I told you I would hang on. Ask any man, woman, or child . . ." He paused. "Well, I am all right anyhow."

'I observed quickly that he had found that out in the end. I had been sure of it, I added. He shook his head. "Were you?" He pressed my arm lightly above the elbow. "Well, then – you were right."

'There was elation and pride, there was awe almost, in that low exclamation. "Jove!" he cried, "only think what it is to me." Again he pressed my arm. "And you asked me whether I thought of leaving. Good God! I! want to leave! Especially now after what you told me of Mr Stein's . . . Leave! Why! That's what I was afraid of. It would have been – it would have been harder than dying. No – on my word. Don't laugh. I must feel – every day, every time I open my eyes – that I am trusted – that nobody has a right – don't you know? Leave! For where? What for? To get what?"

'I had told him (indeed it was the main object of my visit) that it was Stein's intention to present him at once with the house and the stock of trading goods, on certain easy conditions which would make the transaction perfectly regular and valid. He began to snort and plunge at first. "Confound your delicacy!" I shouted. "It isn't Stein at all. It's giving you what you had made for yourself. And in any case keep your remarks for M'Neil – when you meet him in the other world. I hope it won't happen soon. . . ." He had to give in to my arguments, because all his conquests, the trust, the fame, the friendships, the love – all these things that made him master had made him a captive, too. He looked with an owner's eye at the peace of the evening, at the river, at the houses, at the everlasting life of the forests, at the life of the old mankind, at the secrets of the land, at the pride of his own heart: but it was they that possessed him and made him their own to the innermost thought, to the slightest stir of blood, to his last breath.

'It was something to be proud of. I, too, was proud – for him, if not so certain of the fabulous value of the bargain. It was wonderful. It was not so much of his fearlessness that I thought. It is strange how little account I took of it: as if it had been something too conventional to be at the root of the matter. No. I was more struck by the other gifts he had displayed. He had proved his grasp of the unfamiliar situation, his intellectual alertness in that field of thought. There was his readiness, too! Amazing. And all this had come to him in a manner like keen scent to a well-bred hound. He was not eloquent, but there was a dignity in this constitutional reticence, there was a high seriousness in his stammerings. He had still his old trick of stubborn blushing. Now and then, though, a word, a sentence, would escape him that showed how deeply, how solemnly, he felt about that work which had given him the certitude of rehabilitation. That is why he seemed to love the land and the people with a sort of fierce egoism, with a contemptuous tenderness.'

CHAPTER 25

' "This is where I was prisoner for three days," he murmured to me (it was on the occasion of our visit to the Rajah), while we were making our way slowly through a kind of awestruck riot of dependants across Tunku Allang's courtyard. "Filthy place, isn't it? And I couldn't get anything to eat either, unless I made a row about it, and then it was only a small plate of rice and a fried fish not much bigger than a stickleback – confound them! Jove! *I've* been hungry prowling inside this stinking enclosure with some of these vagabonds shoving their mugs right under my nose. I had given up that famous revolver of yours at the first demand. Glad to get rid of the bally thing. Look like a fool walking about with an empty shooting-iron in my hand." At that moment we came into the presence, and he became unflinchingly grave and complimentary with his late captor. Oh! magnificent! I want to laugh when I think of it. But I was impressed, too. The old disreputable Tunku Allang could not help showing his fear (he was no hero, for all the tales of his hot youth he was fond of telling); and at the same time there was a wistful confidence in his manner towards his late prisoner. Note! Even where he would be most hated he was still trusted. Jim – as far as I could follow the conversation – was improving the occasion by the delivery of a lecture. Some poor villagers had been waylaid and robbed while on their way to Doramin's house with a few pieces of gum or beeswax which they wished to exchange for rice. "It was Doramin who was a thief," burst out the Rajah. A shaking fury seemed to enter that old frail body. He writhed weirdly on his mat, gesticulating with his hands and feet, tossing the tangled strings of his mop – an important incarnation of rage. There were staring eyes and dropping jaws all around us. Jim began to speak. Resolutely, coolly, and for some time he enlarged upon the text that no man should be prevented from getting his food and his children's food honestly. The other sat like a tailor at his board, one palm on each knee, his head low, and fixing Jim through the grey hair that fell over his very eyes. When Jim had done there was a great stillness. Nobody seemed to breathe even; no one made a sound till the old Rajah sighed faintly, and looking up, with a toss of his head, said quickly, "You hear, my people! No more of these little games." This decree was received in profound silence. A rather heavy man, evidently in a position of confidence, with intelligent eyes, a bony, broad, very dark face, and a cheerily officious manner (I learned later on he was the executioner), presented to us two cups of coffee on a brass tray, which he took from the hands of an inferior attendant. "You needn't drink," muttered Jim very rapidly. I didn't perceive the meaning at first, and only looked at him. He took a good sip and sat composedly, holding the saucer in his left hand. In a moment I felt excessively annoyed. "Why the devil,"

I whispered, smiling at him amiably, "do you expose me to such a stupid risk?" I drank, of course, there was nothing for it, while he gave no sign, and almost immediately afterwards we took our leave. While we were going down the courtyard to our boat, escorted by the intelligent and cheery executioner, Jim said he was very sorry. It was the barest chance, of course. Personally he thought nothing of poison. The remotest chance. He was – he assured me – considered to be infinitely more useful than dangerous, and so ... "But the Rajah is afraid of you abominably. Anybody can see that," I argued, with, I own, a certain peevishness, and all the time watching anxiously for the first twist of some sort of ghastly colic. I was awfully disgusted. "If I am to do any good here and preserve my position," he said, taking his seat by my side in the boat, "I must stand the risk: I take it once every month, at least. Many people trust me to do that – for them. Afraid of me! That's just it. Most likely he is afraid of me because I am not afraid of his coffee." Then showing me a place on the north front of the stockade where the pointed tops of several stakes were broken, "This is where I leaped over on my third day in Patusan. They haven't put new stakes there yet. Good leap, eh?" A moment later we passed the mouth of a muddy creek. "This my second leap. I had a bit of a run and took this one flying, but fell short. Thought I would leave my skin there. Lost my shoes struggling. And all the time I was thinking to myself how beastly it would be to get a jab with a bally long spear while sticking in the mud like this. I remember how sick I felt wriggling in that slime. I mean really sick – as if I had bitten something rotten."

'That's how it was – and the opportunity ran by his side, leaped over the gap, floundered in the mud ... still veiled. The unexpectedness of his coming was the only thing, you understand, that saved him from being at once despatched with krises and flung into the river. They had him, but it was like getting hold of an apparition, a wraith, a portent. What did it mean? What to do with it? Was it too late to conciliate him? Hadn't he better be killed without delay? But what would happen then? Wretched old Allang went nearly mad with apprehension and through the difficulty of making up his mind. Several times the council was broken up, and the advisers made a break helter-skelter for the door and out on to the veranda. One – it is said – even jumped down to the ground – fifteen feet, I should judge – and broke his leg. The royal governor of Patusan had bizarre mannerisms, and one of them was to introduce boastful rhapsodies into every arduous discussion, when, getting gradually excited, he would end by flying off his perch with a kris in his hand. But, barring such interruptions, the deliberations upon Jim's fate went on night and day.

'Meanwhile he wandered about the courtyard, shunned by some, glared at by others, but watched by all, and practically at the mercy of the first casual ragamuffin with a chopper, in there. He took possession of a small tumble-down shed to sleep in; the effluvia of filth and rotten matter incommoded him greatly: it seems he had not lost his appetite though, because – he told me – he had been hungry all the blessed time. Now and again "some fussy ass" deputed from the council-room would come out running to him, and in honeyed tones would administer amazing interrogatories: "Were the

Dutch coming to take the country? Would the white man like to go back
down the river? What was the object of coming to such a miserable country?
The Rajah wanted to know whether the white man could repair a watch?"
They did actually bring out to him a nickel clock of New England make,
and out of sheer unbearable boredom he busied himself in trying to get the
alarum to work. It was apparently when thus occupied in his shed that the
true perception of his extreme peril dawned upon him. He dropped the thing
– he says – "like a hot potato", and walked out hastily, without the slightest
idea of what he would, or indeed could, do. He only knew that the position
was intolerable. He strolled aimlessly beyond a sort of ramshackle little
granary on posts, and his eyes fell on the broken stakes of the palisade; and
then – he says – at once, without any mental process as it were, without any
stir of emotion, he set about his escape as if executing a plan matured for
a month. He walked off carelessly to give himself a good run, and when he
faced about there was some dignitary, with two spearmen in attendance,
close at his elbow ready with a question. He started off "from under his very
nose", went over "like a bird", and landed on the other side with a fall that
jarred all his bones and seemed to split his head. He picked himself up
instantly. He never thought of anything at the time; all he could remember
– he said – was a great yell; the first houses of Patusan were before him four
hundred yards away; he saw the creek, and as it were mechanically put on
more pace. The earth seemed fairly to fly backwards under his feet. He took
off from the last dry spot, felt himself flying through the air, felt himself,
without any shock, planted upright in an extremely soft and sticky mudbank.
It was only when he tried to move his legs and found he couldn't that, in
his own words, "he came to himself". He began to think of the "bally long
spears". As a matter of fact, considering that the people inside the stockade
had to run to the gate, then get down to the landing-place, get into boats,
and pull round a point of land, he had more advance than he imagined.
Besides, it being low water, the creek was without water – you couldn't call
it dry – and practically he was safe for a time from everything but a very
long shot perhaps. The higher firm ground was about six feet in front of
him. "I thought I would have to die there all the same," he said. He reached
and grabbed desperately with his hands, and only succeeded in gathering a
horrible cold shiny heap of slime against his breast – up to his very chin. It
seemed to him he was burying himself alive, and then he struck out madly,
scattering the mud with his fists. It fell on his head, on his face, over his
eyes, into his mouth. He told me that he rememberd suddenly the courtyard,
as you remember a place where you had been very happy years ago. He
longed – so he said – to be back there again, mending the clock. Mending
the clock – that was the idea. He made efforts, tremendous sobbing, gasping
efforts, efforts that seemed to burst his eyeballs in their sockets and make
him blind, and culminating into one mighty supreme effort in the darkness
to crack the earth asunder, to throw it off his limbs – and he felt himself
creeping feebly up the bank. He lay full length on the firm ground and saw
the light, the sky. Then as a sort of happy thought the notion came to him
that he would go to sleep. He will have it that he *did* actually go to sleep;
that he slept – perhaps for a minute, perhaps for twenty seconds, or only for

one second, but he recollects distinctly the violent convulsive start of awakening. He remained lying still for a while, and then he arose muddy from head to foot and stood there, thinking he was alone of his kind for hundreds of miles, alone, with no help, no sympathy, no pity to expect from anyone, like a hunted animal. The first houses were not more than twenty yards away from him; and it was the desperate screaming of a frightened woman trying to carry off a child that started him again. He pelted straight on in his socks, beplastered with filth out of all semblance to a human being. He traversed more than half the length of the settlement. The nimbler women fled right and left, the slower men just dropped whatever they had in their hands, and remained petrified with dropping jaws. He was a flying terror. He says he noticed the little children trying to run for life, falling on their little stomachs and kicking. He swerved between two houses up a slope, clambered in desperation over a barricade of felled trees (there wasn't a week without some fight in Patusan at that time), burst through a fence into a maize-patch, where a scared boy flung a stick at him, blundered upon a path, and ran all at once into the arms of several startled men. He just had breath enough to gasp out, "Doramin! Doramin!" He remembers being half-carried, half-rushed to the top of the slope, and in a vast enclosure with palms and fruit-trees being run up to a large man sitting massively in a chair in the midst of the greatest possible commotion and excitement. He fumbled in mud and clothes to produce the ring, and, finding himself suddenly on his back, wondered who had knocked him down. They had simply let him go – don't you know? – but he couldn't stand. At the foot of the slope random shots were fired, and above the roofs of the settlement there rose a dull roar of amazement. But he was safe. Doramin's people were barricading the gate and pouring water down this throat; Doramin's old wife, full of business and commiseration, was issuing shrill orders to her girls. "The old woman," he said, softly, "made a to-do over me as if I had been her own son. They put me into an immense bed – her state bed – and she ran in and out wiping her eyes to give me pats on the back. I must have been a pitiful object. I just lay there like a log for I don't know how long."

'He seemed to have a great liking for Doramin's old wife. She on her side had taken a motherly fancy to him. She had a round, nut-brown, soft face, all fine wrinkles, large, bright red lips (she chewed betel assiduously), and screwed-up, winking, benevolent eyes. She was constantly in movement, scolding busily and ordering unceasingly a troop of young women with clear brown faces and big grave eyes, her daughters, her servants, her slave-girls. You know how it is in these households: it's generally impossible to tell the difference. She was very spare, and even her ample outer garment, fastened in front with jewelled clasps, had somehow a skimpy effect. Her dark bare feet were thrust into yellow straw slippers of Chinese make. I have seen her myself flitting about with her extremely thick, long, grey hair falling about her shoulders. She uttered homely shrewd sayings, was of noble birth, and was eccentric and arbitrary. In the afternoon she would sit in a very roomy arm-chair, opposite her husband, gazing steadily through a wide opening in the wall which gave an extensive view of the settlement and the river.

'She invariably tucked up her feet under her, but old Doramin sat squarely, sat imposingly as a mountain sits on a plain. He was only of the *nakhoda* or merchant class, but the respect shown to him and the dignity of his bearing were very striking. He was the chief of the second power in Patusan. The immigrants from Celebes (about sixty families that, with dependants and so on, could muster some two hundred men "wearing the kris") had elected him years ago for their head. The men of that race are intelligent, enterprising, revengeful, but with a more frank courage than the other Malays, and restless under oppression. They formed the party opposed to the Rajah. Of course the quarrels were for trade. This was the primary cause of faction fights, of the sudden outbreaks that would fill this or that part of the settlement with smoke, flame, the noise of shots and shrieks. Villages were burnt, men were dragged into the Rajah's stockade to be killed or tortured for the crime of trading with anybody else but himself. Only a day or two before Jim's arrival several heads of households in the very fishing village that was afterwards taken under his especial protection had been driven over the cliffs by a party of the Rajah's spearmen, on suspicion of having been collecting edible birds' nests for a Celebes trader. Rajah Allang pretended to be the only trader in his country, and the penalty for the breach of the monopoly was death; but his idea of trading was indistinguishable from the commonest forms of robbery. His cruelty and rapacity had no other bounds than his cowardice, and he was afraid of the organized power of the Celebes men, only – till Jim came – he was not afraid enough to keep quiet. He struck at them through his subjects, and thought himself pathetically in the right. The situation was complicated by a wandering stranger, an Arab half-breed, who, I believe, on purely religious grounds, had incited the tribes in the interior (the bush-folk, as Jim himself called them) to rise, and had established himself in a fortified camp on the summit of one of the twin hills. He hung over the town of Patusan like a hawk over a poultry-yard, but he devastated the open country. Whole villages, deserted, rotted on their blackened posts over the banks of clear streams, dropping piecemeal into the water the grass of their walls, the leaves of their roofs, with a curious effect of natural decay as if they had been a form of vegetation stricken by a blight at its very root. The two parties in Patusan were not sure which one this partisan most desired to plunder. The Rajah intrigued with him feebly. Some of the Bugis settlers, weary with endless insecurity, were half inclined to call him in. The younger spirits amongst them, chaffing, advised to "get Sherif Ali with his wild men and drive the Rajah Allang out of the country". Doramin restrained them with difficulty. He was growing old, and, though his influence had not diminished, the situation was getting beyond him. This was the state of affairs when Jim, bolting from the Rajah's stockade, appeared before the chief of the Bugis, produced the ring, and was received, in a manner of speaking, into the heart of the community.'

CHAPTER 26

'Doramin was one of the most remarkable men of his race I had ever seen. His bulk for a Malay was immense, but he did not look merely fat; he looked imposing, monumental. This motionless body, clad in rich stuffs, coloured silks, gold embroideries; this huge head, enfolded in a red-and-gold headkerchief; the flat, big, round face, wrinkled, furrowed, with two semi-circular heavy folds starting on each side of wide, fierce nostrils, and enclosing a thick-lipped mouth; the throat like a bull; the vast corrugated brow overhanging the staring proud eyes – made a whole that, once seen, can never be forgotten. His impassive repose (he seldom stirred a limb when once he sat down) was like a display of dignity. He was never known to raise his voice. It was a hoarse and powerful murmur, slightly veiled as if heard from a distance. When he walked, two short, sturdy young fellows, naked to the waist, in white sarongs and with black skull-caps on the backs of their heads, sustained his elbows; they would ease him down and stand behind his chair till he wanted to rise, when he would turn his head slowly, as if with difficulty, to the right and to the left, and then they would catch him under his armpits and help him up. For all that, there was nothing of a cripple about him; on the contrary, all his ponderous movements were like manifestations of a mighty deliberate force. It was generally believed he consulted his wife as to public affairs; but nobody, as far as I know, had ever heard them exchange a single word. When they sat in state by the wide opening it was in silence. They could see below them in the declining light the vast expanse of the forest country, a dark sleeping sea of sombre green undulating as far as the violet and purple range of mountains; the shining sinuosity of the river like an immense letter S of beaten silver; the brown ribbon of houses following the sweep of both banks, overtopped by the twin hills uprising above the nearer tree-tops. They were wonderfully contrasted: she, light, delicate, spare, quick, a little witch-like, with a touch of motherly fussiness in her repose; he, facing her, immense and heavy, like a figure of a man roughly fashioned of stone, with something magnanimous and ruthless in his immobility. The son of these old people was a most distinguished youth.

'They had him late in life. Perhaps he was not really so young as he looked. Four- or five-and-twenty is not so young when a man is already father of a family at eighteen. When he entered the large room, lined and carpeted with fine mats, and with a high ceiling of white sheeting, where the couple sat in state surrounded by a most deferential retinue, he would make his way straight to Doramin, to kiss his hand – which the other abandoned to him majestically – and then would step across to stand by his mother's chair. I suppose I may say they idolized him, but I never caught them giving him an overt glance. Those, it is true, were public functions. The room was generally thronged. The solemn formality of greetings and leave-takings, the profound respect expressed in gestures, on the faces, in the low whispers, is simply indescribable. "It's well worth seeing," Jim had assured me while we were crossing the river, on our way back. "They are like people in a book, aren't they?" he said triumphantly. "And Dain Waris – their son – is the best friend (barring you) I ever had. .What Mr Stein would call a good 'war-comrade'. I was in luck. Jove! I was in luck when I tumbled amongst them at my last gasp." He meditated with bowed head, then rousing himself he added:

' "Of course, I didn't go to sleep over it, but . . ." He paused again. "It seemed to come to me," he murmured. "All at once I saw what I had to do . . ."

'There was no doubt that it had come to him; and it had come through the war, too, as is natural, since this power that came to him was the power to make peace. It is in this sense alone that might so often *is* right. You must not think he had seen his way at once. When he arrived the Bugis community was in a most critical position. "They were all afraid," he said to me – "each man afraid for himself; while I could see as plain as possible that they must do something at once, if they did not want to go under one after another, what between the Rajah and that vagabond Sherif." But to see that was nothing. When he got his idea he had to drive it into reluctant minds, through the bulwarks of fear, of selfishness. He drove it in at last. And that was nothing. He had to devise the means. He devised them – an audacious plan; and his task was only half done. He had to inspire with his own confidence a lot of people who had hidden and absurd reasons to hang back; he had to conciliate imbecile jealousies, and argue away all sorts of senseless mistrusts. Without the weight of Doramin's authority, and his son's fiery enthusiasm, he would have failed. Dain Waris, the distinguished youth, was the first to believe in him; theirs was one of those strange, profound, rare friendships between brown and white, in which the very difference of race seems to draw two human beings closer by some mystic element of sympathy. Of Dain Waris, his own people said with pride that he knew how to fight like a white man. This was true; he had that sort of courage – the courage in the open, I may say – but he had also a European mind. You meet them sometimes like that, and are surprised to discover unexpectedly a familiar turn of thought, an unobscured vision, a tenacity of purpose, a touch of altruism. Of small stature, but admirably well proportioned, Dain Waris had a proud carriage, a polished, easy bearing, a temperament like a clear flame. His dusky face, with big black eyes, was in action expressive, and in repose thoughtful. He was of silent disposition; a firm glance, an ironic smile, a courteous deliberation of manner seemed to hint at great reserves of intelligence and power. Such beings open to the Western eye, so often concerned with mere surfaces, the hidden possibilities of races and lands over which hangs the mystery of unrecorded ages. He not only trusted Jim, he understood him, I firmly believe. I speak of him because he had captivated me. His – if I may say so – his caustic placidity, and, at the same time, his intelligent sympathy with Jim's aspirations, appealed to me. I seemed to behold the very origin of friendship. If Jim took the lead, the other had captivated his leader. In fact, Jim the leader was a captive in every sense. The land, the people, the friendship, the love, were like the jealous guardians of his body. Every day added a link to the fetters of that strange freedom. I felt convinced of it, as from day to day I learned more of the story.

'The story! Haven't I heard the story? I've heard it on the march, in camp (he made me scour the country after invisible game); I've listened to a good part of it on one of the twin summits, after climbing the last hundred feet or so on my hands and knees. Our escort (we had volunteer followers from village to village) had camped meantime on a bit of level ground half-way up the slope, and in the still breathless evening the smell of wood-smoke reached our nostrils from below with the penetrating delicacy of some choice scent. Voices also ascended, wonderful in their distinct and immaterial clearness. Jim sat on the trunk of a felled tree, and pulling out his pipe began to smoke. A new growth of grass and bushes was springing up; there were traces of an earthwork under a mass of thorny twigs. "It all started from here," he said, after a long and meditative silence. On the other hill, two hundred yards across a sombre precipice, I saw a line of high blackened stakes, showing here and there ruinously – the remnants of Sherif Ali's impregnable camp.

'But it had been taken though. That had been his idea. He had mounted Doramin's old ordnance on the top of that hill; two rusty iron 7-pounders, a lot of small brass cannon – currency cannon. But if the brass guns represent wealth, they can also, when crammed recklessly to the muzzle, send a solid shot to some little distance. The thing was to get them up there. He showed me where he had fastened the cables, explained how he had improvised a rude capstan out of a hollowed log turning upon a pointed stake, indicated with the bowl of his pipe the outline of the earthwork. The last hundred feet of the ascent had been the most difficult. He had made himself responsible for success on his own head. He had induced the war party to work hard all night. Big fires lighted at intervals blazed all down the slope, "but up here," he explained, "the hoisting gang had to fly around in the dark." From the top he saw men moving on the hillside like ants at work. He himself on that night had kept on rushing down and climbing up like a squirrel, directing, encouraging, watching all along the line. Old Doramin had himself carried up the hill in his arm-chair. They put him down on the level place upon the slope, and he sat there in the light of one of the big fires – "amazing old chap – real old chieftain," said Jim, "with his little fierce eyes – a pair of immense flintlock pistols on his knees. Magnificent things, ebony, silver-mounted, with beautiful locks and a calibre like an old blunderbuss. A present from Stein, it seems – in exchange for that ring, you know. Used to belong to good old M'Neil. God only knows how *he* came by them. There he sat, moving neither hand nor foot, a flame of dry brushwood behind him, and lots of people rushing about, shouting and pulling round him – the most solemn, imposing old chap you can imagine. *He* wouldn't have had much chance if Sherif Ali had let his infernal crew loose at us and stampeded my lot. Eh? Anyhow, he had come up there to die if anything went wrong. No mistake! Jove! It thrilled me to see him there – like a rock. But the Sherif must have thought us mad, and never troubled to come and see how we got on. Nobody believed it could be done. Why! I think the very chaps who pulled and shoved and sweated over it did not believe it could be done! Upon my word I don't think they did. . . ."

'He stood erect, the smouldering brier-wood in his clutch, with a smile on his lips and a sparkle in his boyish eyes. I sat on the stump of a tree at his feet, and below us stretched the land, the great expanse of the forests, sombre under the sunshine, rolling like a sea, with glints of winding rivers, the grey spots of villages, and here and there a clearing, like an islet of light amongst the dark waves of continuous tree-tops. A brooding gloom lay over this vast and monotonous landscape; the light fell on it as if into an abyss. The land devoured the sunshine; only far off, along the coast, the empty ocean, smooth and polished within the faint haze, seemed to rise up to the sky in a wall of steel.

'And there I was with him, high in the sunshine on the top of that historic hill of his. He dominated the forest, the secular gloom, the old mankind. He was like a figure set up on a pedestal, to represent in his persistent youth the power, and perhaps the virtues, of races that never grow old, that have emerged from the gloom. I don't know why he should always have appeared to me symbolic. Perhaps this is the real cause of my interest in his fate. I don't know whether it was exactly fair to him to remember the incident which had given a new direction to his life, but at that very moment I remembered very distinctly. It was like a shadow in the light.'

CHAPTER 27

'Already the legend had gifted him with supernatural powers. Yes, it was said, there had been many ropes cunningly disposed, and a strange contrivance that turned by the efforts of many men, and each gun went up tearing slowly through the bushes, like a wild pig rooting its way in the undergrowth, but . . . and the wisest shook their heads. There was something occult in all this, no doubt; for what is the strength of ropes and of men's arms? There is a rebellious soul in things which must be overcome by powerful charms and incantations. Thus old Sura – a very respectable householder of Patusan – with whom I had a quiet chat one evening. However, Sura was a professional sorcerer also, who attended all the rice sowings and reapings for miles around for the purpose of subduing the stubborn soul of things. This occupation he seemed to think a most arduous one, and perhaps the souls of things are more stubborn than the souls of men. As to the simple folk of outlying villages, they believed and said (as the most natural thing in the world) that Jim had carried the guns up the hill on his back – two at a time.

'This would make Jim stamp his foot in vexation and exclaim with an exasperated little laugh, "What can you do with such silly beggars? They will sit up half the night talking bally rot, and the greater the lie the more they seem to like it." You could trace the subtle influence of his surroundings in this irritation. It was part of his captivity. The earnestness of his denials was amusing, and at last I said, "My dear fellow, you don't suppose *I* believe this." He looked at me quite startled. "Well, no! I suppose not," he said, and burst into a Homeric peal of laughter. "Well, anyhow, the guns were there, and went off together at sunrise. Jove! You should have seen the splinters fly," he cried. By his side Dain Waris, listening with a quiet smile, dropped his eyelids and shuffled his feet a little. It appears that the success in mounting the guns had given Jim's people such a feeling of confidence that he ventured to leave the battery under charge of two elderly Bugis who had seen some fighting in their day, and went to join Dain Waris and the storming party who were concealed in the ravine. In the small hours they began creeping up, and when two-thirds of the way up, lay in the wet grass waiting for the appearance of the sun, which was the agreed signal. He told me with what impatient anguishing emotion he watched the swift coming of the dawn; how, heated with the work and the climbing, he felt the cold dew chilling his very bones; how afraid he was he would begin to shiver and shake like a leaf before the time came for the advance. "It was the slowest half-hour in my life," he declared. Gradually the silent stockade came out on the sky above him. Men scattered all down the slope were crouching amongst the dark stones and dripping bushes. Dain Waris was lying flattened by his side. "We looked at each other," Jim said, resting a gentle hand on his friend's shoulder. "He smiled at me as cheery as you please, and I dared not stir my lips for fear I would break out into a shivering fit. 'Pon my word, it's true! I had been streaming with perspiration when we took cover – so you may imagine . . ." He declared, and I believe him, that he had no fears as to the result. He was only anxious as to his ability to repress these shivers. He didn't bother about the result. He was bound to get to the top of that hill and stay there, whatever might happen. There could be no going back for him. Those people had trusted him implicitly. Him alone! His bare word. . . .

'I remember how, at this point, he paused with his eyes fixed upon me. "As far as he knew, they never had an occasion to regret it yet," he said. "Never. He hoped to God they never would. Meantime – worse luck! – they had got into the habit of taking his word for anything and everything. I could have no idea! Why? Only the other day an old fool he had never seen in his life came from some village miles away to find out if he should divorce his wife. Fact. Solemn word. That's the sort of thing. . . . He wouldn't have believed it. Would I? Squatted on the veranda chewing betel-nut, sighing and spitting all over the place for more than an hour, and as glum as an undertaker before he came out with that dashed conundrum. That's the kind of thing that isn't so funny as it looks. What was a fellow to say? – Good wife? – Yes. Good wife – old though; started a confounded long story about some brass pots. Been living together for fifteen years – twenty years – could not tell. A long, long time. Good wife. Beat her a little – not much – just a little, when she was young. Had to – for the sake of his honour. Suddenly in her old age she goes and lends three brass pots to her sister's son's wife, and begins to abuse him every day in a loud voice. His enemies jeered at him; his face was utterly blackened. Pots totally lost. Awfully cut up about it. Impossible to fathom a story like that; told him to go home, and promised to come along myself and settle it all. It's all very well to grin, but it was the dashedest nuisance! A day's journey through the forest, another day lost in coaxing a lot of silly villagers to get at the rights of the affair. There was the making of a sanguinary shindy in the thing. Every bally idiot took sides with one family or the other, and one half of the village was ready to go for the other half with anything that came handy. Honour bright! No joke! . . . Instead of attending to their bally crops. Got him the infernal pots back of course – and pacified all hands. No trouble to settle it. Of course not. Could settle the deadliest quarrel in the country by crooking his little finger. The trouble was to get at the truth of anything. Was not sure to this day whether he had been fair to all parties. It worried him. And the talk! Jove! There didn't seem to be any head or tail to it. Rather storm a twenty-foot-high old stockade any day. Much! Child's play to that other job. Wouldn't take so long either. Well, yes; a funny set out, upon the whole – the fool looked old enough to be his grandfather. But from another point of view it was no joke. His word decided everything – ever since the smashing of Sherif Ali. An awful responsibility," he repeated. "No, really – joking apart, had it been three lives instead of three rotten brass pots it would have been the same. . . ."

'Thus he illustrated the moral effect of his victory in war. It was in truth immense. It had led him from strife to peace, and through death into the innermost life of the people; but the gloom of the land spread out under the sunshine preserved its appearance of inscrutable, of secular repose. The sound of his fresh young voice – it's extraordinary how very few signs of wear he showed – floated lightly, and passed away over the unchanged face of the forests like the sound of the big guns on that cold dewy morning when he had no other concern on earth but the proper control of the chills in his body. With the first slant of sun-rays along these immovable tree-tops the summit of one hill wreathed itself, with heavy reports, in white clouds of smoke, and the other burst into an amazing noise of yells, war-cries, shouts of anger, of surprise, of dismay. Jim and Dain Waris were the first to lay their hands on the stakes. The popular story has it that Jim with a touch of one finger had thrown down the gate. He was, of course, anxious to disclaim this achievement. The whole stockade – he would insist on explaining to you – was a poor affair (Sherif Ali trusted mainly to the inaccessible position); and, anyway, the thing had been already knocked to pieces and only hung together by a miracle. He put his shoulder to it like a little fool and went in head over heels. Jove! If it hadn't been for Dain Waris, a pockmarked tattooed vagabond would have pinned him with his spear to a baulk of timber like one of Stein's beetles. The third man in, it seems, had been Tamb' Itam, Jim's own servant. This was a Malay from the north, a stranger who had wandered into Patusan, and had been forcibly detained by Rajah Allang as a paddler of one of the state boats. He had made a bolt of it at the first opportunity, and finding a precarious refuge (but very little to eat) amongst the Bugis settlers, had attached himself to Jim's person. His complexion was very dark, his face flat, his eyes prominent and injected with bile. There was something excessive, almost fanatical, in his devotion to his "white lord". He was inseparable from Jim like a morose shadow. On state occasions he would tread on his masters heels, one hand on the haft of his kris, keeping the common people at a distance by his truculent brooding glances. Jim had made him the headman of his establishment, and all Patusan respected and courted him as a person of much influence. At the taking of the stockade he had distinguished himself greatly by the methodical ferocity of his fighting. The storming-party had come on so quick – Jim said – that notwithstanding the panic of the garrison, there was a "hot five minutes hand-to-hand inside that stockade, till some bally ass set fire to the shelters of boughs and dry grass, and we all had to clear out for dear life."

'The rout, it seems, had been complete. Doramin waiting immovably in his chair on the hillside, with the smoke of the guns spreading slowly above his big head, received the news with a deep grunt. When informed that his son was safe and leading the pursuit, he, without another sound, made a mighty effort to rise; his attendants hurried to his help, and, held up reverently, he shuffled with great dignity into a bit of shade where he laid himself down to sleep covered entirely with a piece of white sheeting. In Patusan the excitement was intense. Jim told me that from the hill, turning his back on the stockade with its embers, black ashes, and half-consumed corpses, he could see time after time the open spaces between the houses on both sides of the stream fill suddenly with a seething rush of people and get empty in a moment. His ears caught feebly from below the tremendous din of gongs and drums; the wild shouts of the crowd reached him in bursts of faint roaring. A lot of streamers made a flutter as of little white, red, yellow birds amongst the brown ridges of roofs. "You must have enjoyed it," I murmured, feeling the stir of sympathetic emotion.

' "It was . . . it was immense! Immense!" he cried aloud, flinging his arms open. The sudden movement startled me as though I had seen him bare the secrets of his breast to the sunshine, to the brooding forests, to the steely sea. Below us the town reposed in easy curves upon the banks of a stream whose current seemed to sleep. "Immense!" he repeated for a third time, speaking in a whisper, for himself alone.

'Immense! No doubt it was immense; the seal of success upon his words, the conquered ground for the soles of his feet, the blind trust of men, the belief in himself snatched from the fire, the solitude of his achievement. All this, as I've warned you, gets dwarfed in the telling. I can't with mere words convey to you the impression of his total and utter isolation. I know, of course, he was in every sense alone of his kind there, but the unsuspected qualities of his nature had brought him in such close touch with his surroundings that this isolation seemed only the effect of his power. His loneliness added to his stature. There was nothing within sight to compare him with, as though he had been one of those exceptional men who can be only measured by the greatness of their fame; and his fame, remember, was the greatest thing around for many a day's journey. You would have to paddle, pole, or track a long weary way through the jungle before you pass beyond the reach of its voice. Its voice was not the trumpeting of the disreputable goddess we all know – not blatant – not brazen. It took its tone from the stillness and gloom of the land without a past, where his word was the one truth of every passing day. It shared something of the nature of that silence through which it accompanied you into unexplored depths, heard continuously by your side, penetrating, far-reaching – tinged with wonder and mystery on the lips of whispering men.'

CHAPTER 28

'The defeated Sherif Ali fled the country without making another stand, and when the miserable hunted villagers began to crawl out of the jungle back to their rotting houses, it was Jim who, in consultation with Dain Waris, appointed the headmen. Thus he became the virtual ruler of the land. As to old Tunku Allang, his fears at first had known no bounds. It is said that at the intelligence of the successful storming of the hill he flung himself, face down, on the bamboo floor of his audience-hall, and lay motionless for a whole night and a whole day, uttering stifled sounds of such an appalling nature that no man dared approach his prostrate form nearer than a spear's length. Already he could see himself driven ignominiously out of Patusan, wandering, abandoned, stripped, without opium, without his women, without followers, a fair game for the first comer to kill. After Sherif Ali his turn would come, and who could resist an attack led by such a devil? And indeed he owed his life and such authority as he still possessed at the time of my visit to Jim's idea of what was fair alone. The Bugis had been extremely anxious to pay off old scores, and the impassive old Doramin cherished the hope of yet seeing his son ruler of Patusan. During one of our interviews he deliberately allowed me to get a glimpse of this secret ambition. Nothing could be finer in its way than the dignified wariness of his approaches. He himself – he began by declaring – had used his strength in his young days, but now he had grown old and tired. ... With his imposing bulk and haughty little eyes darting sagacious, inquisitive glances, he reminded one irresistibly of a cunning old elephant; the slow rise and fall of his vast breast went on powerful and regular, like the heave of a calm sea. He, too, as he protested, had an unbounded confidence in Tuan Jim's wisdom. If he could only obtain a promise! One word would be enough! ... His breathing silences, the low rumblings of his voice, recalled the last efforts of a spent thunderstorm.

'I tried to put the subject aside. It was difficult, for there could be no question that Jim had the power; in his new sphere there did not seem to be anything that was not his to hold or to give. But that, I repeat, was nothing in comparison with the notion, which occurred to me, while I listened with a show of attention, that he seemed to have come very near at last to mastering his fate. Doramin was anxious about the future of the country, and I was struck by the turn he gave to the argument. The land remains where God had put it; but white men – he said – they come to us and in a little while they go. They go away. Those they leave behind do not know when to look for their return. They go to their own land, to their people, and so this white man, too, would. . . . I don't know what induced me to commit myself at this point by a vigorous "No, no." The whole extent of this indiscretion became apparent when Doramin, turning full upon me his face, whose expression, fixed in rugged deep folds, remained unalterable, like a huge brown mask, said that this was good news indeed, reflectively; and then wanted to know why.

'His little, motherly witch of a wife sat on my other hand, with her head covered and her feet tucked up, gazing through the great shutter-hole. I could only see a straying lock of grey hair, a high cheek-bone, the slight masticating motion of the sharp chin. Without removing her eyes from the vast prospect of forests stretching as far as the hills, she asked me in a pitying voice why was it that he so young had wandered from his home, coming so far, through so many dangers? Had he no household there, no kinsmen in his own country? Had he no old mother, who would always remember his face? . . .

'I was completely unprepared for this. I could only mutter and shake my head vaguely. Afterwards I am perfectly aware I cut a very poor figure trying to extricate myself out of this difficulty. From that moment, however, the old *nakhoda* became taciturn. He was not very pleased, I fear, and evidently I had given him food for thought. Strangely enough, on the evening of that very day (which was my last in Patusan) I was once more confronted with the same question, with the unanswerable why of Jim's fate. And this brings me to the story of his love.

'I suppose you think it is a story that you can imagine for yourselves. We have heard so many such stories, and the majority of us don't believe them to be stories of love at all. For the most part we look upon them as stories of opportunities: episodes of passion at best, or perhaps only of youth and temptation, doomed to forgetfulness in the end, even if they pass through the reality of tenderness and regret. This view mostly is right, and perhaps in this case, too. . . . Yet I don't know. To tell this story is by no means so easy as it should be – were the ordinary standpoint adequate. Apparently it is a story very much like the others: for me, however, there is visible in its background the melancholy figure of a woman, the shadow of a cruel wisdom buried in a lonely grave, looking on wistfully, helplessly, with sealed lips. The grave itself, as I came upon it during an early morning stroll, was a rather shapeless brown mound, with an inlaid neat border of white lumps of coral at the base, and enclosed within a circular fence made of split saplings, with the bark left on. A garland of leaves and flowers was woven about the heads of the slender posts – and the flowers were fresh.

'Thus, whether the shadow is of my imagination or not, I can at all events point out the significant fact of an unforgotten grave. When I tell you besides that Jim with his own hands had worked at the rustic fence, you will perceive directly the difference, the individual side of the story. There is in his espousal of memory and affection belonging to another human being something characteristic of his seriousness. He had a conscience, and it was a romantic conscience. Through her whole life the wife of the unspeakable Cornelius had no other companion, confidant, and friend but her daughter. How the poor woman had come to marry the awful Malacca Portuguese – after the separation from the father of her girl – and how that separation had been brought about, whether by death, which can be sometimes merciful, or by the merciless pressure of conventions, is a mystery to me. From the little which Stein (who knew so many stories) had let drop in my hearing, I am convinced that she was no ordinary woman. Her own father had been a white; a high official; one of the brilliantly endowed men who are not dull enough to nurse a success, and whose careers so often end under a cloud. I suppose she, too, must have lacked the saving dullness – and her career ended in Patusan. Our common fate ... for where is the man – I mean a real sentient man – who does not remember vaguely having been deserted in the fullness of possession by someone or something more precious than life? ... our common fate fastens upon the women with a peculiar cruelty. It does not punish like a master, but inflicts lingering torment, as if to gratify a secret, unappeasable spite. One would think that, appointed to rule on earth, it seeks to revenge itself upon the beings that come nearest to rising above the trammels of earthly caution; for it is only women who manage to put at times into their love an element just palpable enough to give one a fright – an extra-terrestrial touch. I ask myself with wonder – how the world can look to them – whether it has the shape and substance *we* know, the air *we* breathe! Sometimes I fancy it must be a region of unreasonable sublimities seething with the excitement of their adventurous souls, lighted by the glory of all possible risks and renunciations. However, I suspect there are very few women in the world, though of course I am aware of the multitudes of mankind and of the equality of sexes in point of numbers – that is. But I am sure that the mother was as much of a woman as the daughter seemed to be. I cannot help picturing to myself these two, at first the young woman and the child, then the old woman and the young girl, the awful sameness and the swift passage of time, the barrier of forest, the solitude and the turmoil round these two lonely lives, and every word spoken between them penetrated with sad meaning. There must have been confidences, not so much of fact, I suppose, as of innermost feelings – regrets – fears – warnings, no doubt: warnings that the younger did not fully understand till the elder was dead – and Jim came along. Then I am sure she understood much – not everything – the fear mostly it seems. Jim called her by a word that means precious, in the sense of a precious gem – jewel. Pretty, isn't it? But he was capable of anything. He was equal to his fortune, as he – after all – must have been equal to his misfortune. Jewel he called her; and he would say this as he might have said "Jane", don't you know – with a marital, homelike, peaceful effect. I heard the name for the first time ten minutes after I had landed in his courtyard, when, after nearly shaking my arm off, he darted up the steps and began to make a joyous, boyish disturbance at the door under the heavy eaves. "Jewel! O Jewel! Quick! Here's a friend come," ... and suddenly peering at me in the dim veranda, he mumbled earnestly, "You know – this – no confounded nonsense about it – can't tell you how much I owe to her – and so – you understand – I – exactly as if ..." His hurried, anxious whispers were cut short by the flitting of a white form within the house, a faint exclamation, and a childlike but energetic little face with delicate features and a profound, attentive glance peeped out of the inner gloom, like a bird out of the recess of a nest. I was struck by the name, of course; but it was not till later on that I connected it with an astonishing rumour that had met me on my journey, at a little place on the coast about 230 miles south of Patusan river. Stein's schooner, in which I had my passage, put in there, to collect some produce, and going ashore, I found to my great surprise that the wretched locality could boast of a third-class deputy-assistant resident, a big, fat, greasy, blinking fellow of mixed descent, with turned-out, shiny lips. I found him lying extended on his back in a cane chair, odiously unbuttoned, with a large green leaf of some sort on the top of his steaming head, and another in his hand which he used lazily as a fan. ... Going to Patusan? Oh, yes. Stein's Trading Company. He knew. Had a permission. No business of his. It was not so bad there now, he remarked negligently, and, he went on drawling, "There's some sort of white vagabond had got in there, I hear. ... Eh? What you say? Friends of yours? So! ... Then it was true there was one of these *verdammte* – What was he up to? Found his way in, the rascal. Eh? I had not been sure. Patusan – they cut throats there – no business of ours." He interrupted himself to groan. "Phoo! Almighty! The heat! The heat! Well, then, there might be something in the story, too, after all, and ..." He shut one of his beastly glassy eyes (the eyelid went on quivering), while he leered at me atrociously with the other. "Look here," says he, mysteriously, "if – do you understand? – if he has really got hold of something fairly good – none of your bits of green glass – understand? – I am a government official – you tell the rascal ... Eh? What? Friend of yours?" ... He continued wallowing calmly in the chair. ... "You said so; that's just it; and I am pleased to give you the hint. I suppose you, too, would like to get something out of it? Don't interrupt. You just tell him I've heard the tale, but to my government I have made no report. Not yet. See? Why make a report? Eh? Tell him to come to me if they let him get alive out of the country. He had better look out for himself. Eh? I promise to ask no questions. On the quiet – you understand? You, too – you shall get something from me. Small commission for the trouble. Don't interrupt. I am a government official, and make no report. That's business. Understand? I know some good people that will buy anything worth having, and can give him more money than the scoundrel ever saw in his life. I know his sort." He fixed me steadfastly with both his eyes open, while I stood over him utterly amazed, and asking myself whether he was mad or drunk. He perspired, puffed, moaning feebly, and scratching himself with such horrible composure that I could not bear the sight long enough to find out. Next day, talking casually with the people of the little native court of the place, I discovered that a story was travelling slowly down the coast about a mysterious white man in Patusan who had got hold of an extraordinary gem – namely, an emerald of an enormous size, and altogether priceless. The emerald seems to appeal more to the Eastern imagination than any other precious stone. The white man had obtained it,

I was told, partly by the exercise of his wonderful strength and partly by cunning, from the ruler of a distant country, whence he had fled instantly, arriving in Patusan in utmost distress, but frightening the people by his extreme ferocity, which nothing seemed able to subdue. Most of my inform-ants were of the opinion that the stone was probably unlucky – like the famous stone of the Sultan of Succadana, which in the old times had brought wars and untold calamities upon that country. Perhaps it was the same stone – one couldn't say. Indeed the story of a fabulously large emerald is as old as the arrival of the first white man in the Archipelago; and the belief in it is so persistent that less than forty years ago there had been an official Dutch inquiry into the truth of it. Such a jewel – it was explained to me by the old fellow from whom I heard most of this amazing Jim-myth – a sort of scribe to the wretched little Rajah of the place; such a jewel, he said, cocking his poor purblind eyes up at me (he was sitting on the cabin floor out of respect), is best preserved by being concealed about the person of a woman. Yet it is not every woman that would do. She must be young – he sighed deeply – and insensible to the seductions of love. He shook his head sceptically. But such a woman seemed to be actually in existence. He had been told of a tall girl, whom the white man treated with great respect and care, and who never went forth from the house unattended. People said the white man could be seen with her almost any day; they walked side by side, openly, he holding her arm under his – pressed to his side – thus – in a most extraordinary way. This might be a lie, he conceded, for it was indeed a strange thing for anyone to do: on the other hand, there could be no doubt she wore the white man's jewel concealed upon her bosom.'

CHAPTER 29

'This was the theory of Jim's marital evening walks. I made a third on more than one occasion, unpleasantly aware every time of Cornelius, who nursed the aggrieved sense of his legal paternity, slinking in the neighbourhood with that peculiar twist of his mouth as if he were perpetually on the point of gnashing his teeth. But do you notice how, three hundred miles beyond the end of telegraph cables and mail-boat lines, the haggard utilitarian lies of our civilization wither and die, to be replaced by pure exercises of imagi-nation, that have the futility, often the charm, and sometimes the deep hidden truthfulness, of works of art? Romance had singled Jim for its own – and that was the true part of the story, which otherwise was all wrong. He did not hide his jewel. In fact, he was extremely proud of it.

'It comes to me now that I had, on the whole, seen very little of her. What I remember best is the even, olive pallor of her complexion, and the intense blue-black gleams of her hair, flowing abundantly from under a small crimson cap she wore far back on her shapely head. Her movements were free, assured, and she blushed a dusky red. While Jim and I were talking, she would come and go with rapid glances at us, leaving on her passage an impression of grace and charm and a distinct suggestion of shyness and watchfulness. Her manner presented a curious combination of shyness and audacity. Every pretty smile was succeeded swiftly by a look of silent, repressed anxiety, as if put to flight by the recollection of some abiding danger. At times she would sit down with us and, with her soft cheek dimpled by the knuckles of her little hand, she would listen to our talk; her big clear eyes would remain fastened on our lips, as though each pronounced word had a visible shape. Her mother had taught her to read and write; she had learned a good bit of English from Jim, and she spoke it most amusingly, with his own clipping, boyish intonation. Her tenderness hovered over him like a flutter of wings. She lived so completely in his contemplation that she had acquired something of his outward aspect, something that recalled him in her movements, in the way she stretched her arm, turned her head, directed her glances. Her vigilant affection had an intensity that made it almost perceptible to the senses; it seemed actually to exist in the ambient matter of space, to envelop him like a peculiar fragrance, to dwell in the sunshine like a tremulous, subdued, and impassioned note. I suppose you think that I, too, am romantic, but it is a mistake. I am relating to you the sober impressions of a bit of youth, of a strange uneasy romance that had come in my way. I observed with interest the work of his – well – good fortune. He was jealously loved, but why she should be jealous, and of what, I could not tell. The land, the people, the forests were her accomplices, guarding him with vigilant accord, with an air of seclusion, of mystery, of invincible possession. There was no appeal, as it were; he was imprisoned within the very freedom of his power, and she, though ready to make a footstool of her head for his feet, guarded her conquest inflexibly – as though he were hard to keep. The very Tamb' Itam, marching on our journeys upon the heels of his white lord, with his head thrown back, truculent and be-weaponed like a janissary, with kris, chopper, and lance (besides carrying Jim's gun); even Tamb' Itam allowed himself to put on the airs of uncompromising guardianship, like a surly devoted jailer ready to lay down his life for his captive. On the evenings when we sat up late his silent, indistinct form would pass and repass under the veranda, with noiseless footsteps, or lifting my head I would unexpectedly make him out standing rigidly erect in the shadow. As a general rule he would vanish after a time, without a sound; but when we rose he would spring up close to us as if from the ground, ready for any orders Jim might wish to give. The girl, too, I believe, never went to sleep till we had separated for the night. More than once I saw her and Jim through the window of my room come out together quietly and lean on the rough balustrade – two white forms very close, his arm about her waist, her head on his shoulder. Their soft murmurs reached me, penetrating, tender, with a calm sad note in the stillness of the night, like a self-communication of one being carried on in two tones. Later on, tossing on my bed under the mosquito-net, I was sure to hear slight creakings, faint breathing, a throat cleared cautiously – and I would know that Tamb' Itam was still on the prowl. Though he had (by the favour of the white lord) a house in the compound, had "taken wife", and had lately been blessed with a child, I believe that, during my stay at all events, he slept on the veranda every night. It was very difficult to make this faithful and grim retainer talk. Even Jim himself was answered in jerky short sentences, under protest as it were. Talking, he seemed to imply, was no business of his. The longest speech I heard him volunteer was one morning when, suddenly extending his hand towards the courtyard, he pointed at Cornelius and said, "Here comes the Nazarene". I don't think he was addressing me, though I stood at his side, his object seemed rather to awaken the indignant attention of the universe. Some muttered allusions, which followed, to dogs and the smell of roast-meat, struck me as singularly felicitous. The courtyard, a large square space, was one torrid blaze of sunshine, and, bathed in intense light, Cornelius was creeping across in full view with an inexpressible effect of stealthiness, of dark and secret slinking. He reminded one of everything that is unsavoury. His slow laborious walk resembled the creeping of a repulsive beetle, the legs alone moving with horrid industry while the body glided evenly. I suppose he made straight enough for the place where he wanted to get to, but his progress with one shoulder carried forward seemed oblique. He was often seen circling slowly amongst the sheds, as if following a scent; passing before the veranda with upward stealthy glances; disappearing without haste round the corner of some hut. That he seemed free of the place demonstrated Jim's absurd carelessness or else his infinite disdain, for Cornelius had played a very dubious part (to say the least of it) in a certain episode which might have ended fatally for Jim. As a matter of fact, it had redounded to his glory. But everything redounded to his glory; and it was the irony of his good fortune that he, who had been too careful of it once, seemed to bear a charmed life.

'You must know he had left Doramin's place very soon after his arrival – much too soon, in fact, for his safety, and of course a long time before the war. In this he was actuated by a sense of duty; he had to look after Stein's business, he said. Hadn't he? To that end, with an utter disregard of his personal safety, he crossed the river and took up his quarters with Cornelius. How the latter had managed to exist through the troubled times I can't say. As Stein's agent, after all, he must have had Doramin's protection in a measure; and in one way or another he had managed to wriggle through all the 'deadly complications, while I have no doubt that his conduct, whatever line he was forced to take, was marked by that abjectness which was like the stamp of the man. That was his characteristic; he was fundamentally and outwardly abject, as other men are markedly of a generous, distinguished, or venerable appearance. It was the elements of his nature which permeated all his acts and passions and emotions; he raged abjectly, smiled abjectly, was abjectly sad; his civilities and his indignations were alike abject. I am sure his love would have been the most abject of sentiments – but can one imagine a loathsome insect in love? And his loathsomeness, too, was abject, so that a simply disgusting person would have appeared noble by his side. He has his place neither in the background nor in the foreground of the story; he is simply seen skulking on its outskirts, enigmatical and unclean, tainting the fragrance of its youth and of its naïveness.

'His position in any case could not have been other than extremely miserable, yet it may very well be that he found some advantages in it. Jim told me he had been received at first with an abject display of the most amicable sentiments. "The fellow apparently couldn't contain himself for joy," said Jim with disgust. "He flew at me every morning to shake both my hands – confound him! But I could never tell whether there would be any breakfast. If I got three meals in two days I considered myself jolly lucky, and he made me sign a chit for ten dollars every week. Said he was sure Mr Stein did not mean him to keep me for nothing. Well – he kept me on nothing as near as possible. Put it down to the unsettled state of the country, and made as if to tear his hair out, begging my pardon twenty times a day, so that I had at last to entreat him not to worry. It made me sick. Half the roof of his house had fallen in, and the whole place had a mangy look, with wisps of dry grass sticking out and the corners of broken mats flapping on every wall. He did his best to make out that Mr Stein owed him money on the last three years' trading, but his books were all torn, and some were missing. He tried to hint it was his late wife's fault. Disgusting scoundrel! At last I had to forbid him to mention his late wife at all. It made Jewel cry. I couldn't discover what became of all the trade-goods; there was nothing in the store but rats, having a high old time amongst a litter of brown paper and old sacking. I was assured on every hand that he had a lot of money buried somewhere, but of course could get nothing out of him. It was the most miserable existence I led there in that wretched house. I tried to do my duty by Stein, but I had also other matters to think of. When I escaped to Doramin old Tunku Allang got frightened and returned all my things. It was done in a roundabout way, and with no end of mystery, through a Chinaman who keeps a small shop here; but as soon as I left the Bugis quarter and went to live with Cornelius it began to be said openly that the Rajah had made up his mind to have me killed before long. Pleasant, wasn't it? And I couldn't see what there was to prevent him if he really *had* made up his mind. The worst of it was, I couldn't help feeling I wasn't doing any good either for Stein or for myself. Oh! it was beastly – the whole six weeks of it." '

CHAPTER 30

'He told me further that he did't know what made him hang on – but of course we may guess. He sympathized deeply with the defenceless girl, at the mercy of that "mean, cowardly scoundrel". It appears Cornelius led her an awful life, stopping only short of actual ill-usage, for which he had not the pluck, I suppose. He insisted upon her calling him father "and with respect, too – with respect", he would scream, shaking a little yellow fist in her face. "I am a respectable man, and what are you? Tell me – what are you? You think I am going to bring up somebody else's child and not to be treated with respect? You ought to be glad I let you. Come – say Yes, father. ... No? ... You wait a bit." Thereupon he would begin to abuse the dead woman, till the girl would run off with her hands to her head. He pursued her, dashing in and out and round the house and amongst the sheds, would drive her into some corner, where she would fall on her knees stopping her ears, and then he would stand at a distance and declaim filthy denunciations at her back for half an hour at a stretch. "Your mother was a devil, a deceitful devil – and you, too, are a devil," he would shriek in a final outburst, pick up a bit of dry earth or a handful of mud (there was plenty of mud around the house), and fling it into her hair. Sometimes, though, she would hold out full of scorn, confronting him in silence, her face sombre and contracted, and only now and then uttering a word or two that would make the other jump and writhe with the sting. Jim told me these scenes were terrible. It was indeed a strange thing to come upon in a wilderness. The endlessness of such a subtly cruel situation was appalling – if you think of it. The respectable Cornelius (Inchi 'Nelyus the Malays called him, with a grimace that meant many things) was a much-disappointed man. I don't know what he had expected would be done for him in consideration of his marriage; but evidently the liberty to steal, and embezzle, and appropriate to himself for many years and in any way that suited him best, the goods of Stein's Trading Company (Stein kept the supply up unfalteringly as long as he could get his skippers to take it there) did not seem to him a fair equivalent for the sacrifice of his honourable name. Jim would have enjoyed exceedingly thrashing Cornelius within an inch of his life; on the other hand, the scenes were of so painful a character, so abominable, that his impulse would be to get out of earshot, in order to spare the girl's feelings. They left her agitated, speechless, clutching her bosom now and then with a stony, desperate face, and then Jim would lounge up and say unhappily,"Now – come – really – what's the use – you must try to eat a bit," or give some such mark of sympathy. Cornelius would keep on slinking through the doorways, across the veranda and back again, as mute as a fish, and with malevolent, mistrustful, underhand glances. "I can stop his game," Jim said to her once. "Just say the word." And do you know what she answered? She said – Jim told me impressively – that if she had not been sure he was intensely wretched himself, she would have found the courage to kill him with her own hands. "Just fancy that! The poor devil of a girl, almost a child, being driven to talk like that," he exclaimed in horror. It seemed impossible to save her not only from that mean rascal but even from herself! It wasn't that he pitied her so much, he affirmed; it was more than pity; it was as if he had something on his conscience, while that life went on. To leave the house would have appeared a base desertion. He had understood at last that there was nothing to expect from a longer stay, neither accounts nor money, nor truth of any sort, but he stayed on, exasperating Cornelius to the verge, I won't say of insanity, but almost of courage. Meantime he felt all sorts of dangers gathering obscurely about him. Doramin had sent over twice a trusty servant to tell him seriously that he could do nothing for his safety unless he would recross the river again and live amongst the Bugis as at first. People of every condition used to call, often in the dead of night, in order to disclose to him plots for his assassination. He was to be poisoned. He was to be stabbed in the bath-house. Arrangements were being made to have him shot from a boat on the river. Each of these informants professed himself to be his very good friend. It was enough – he told me – to spoil a fellow's rest for ever. Something of the kind was extremely possible – nay, probable – but the lying warnings gave him only the sense of deadly scheming going on all around him, on all sides, in the dark. Nothing more calculated to shake the best of nerve. Finally, one night, Cornelius himself, with a great apparatus of alarm and secrecy, unfolded in solemn wheedling tones a little plan wherein for one hundred dollars – or even for eighty; let's say eighty – he, Cornelius, would procure a trustworthy man to smuggle Jim out of the river, all safe. There was nothing else for it now – if Jim cared a pin for his life. What's eighty dollars? A trifle. An insignificant sum. While he, Cornelius, who had to remain behind, was absolutely courting death by his proof of devotion to Mr Stein's young friend. The sight of his abject grimacing was – Jim told me – very hard to bear; he clutched at his hair, beat his breast, rocked himself to and fro with his hands pressed to his stomach, and actually pretended to shed tears. "Your blood be on your own head," he squeaked at last, and rushed out. It is a curious question how far Cornelius was sincere in that performance. Jim confessed to me that he did not sleep a wink after the fellow had gone. He lay on his back on a thin mat spread over the bamboo flooring, trying idly to make out the bare rafters, and listening to the rustlings in the torn thatch. A star suddenly twinkled through a hole in the roof. His brain was in a whirl; but, nevertheless, it was on that very night that he matured his plan for overcoming Sherif Ali. It had been the thought of all the moments he could spare from the hopeless investigation into Stein's affairs, but the notion – he says – came to him then all at once. He could see, as it were, the guns mounted on top of the hill. He got very hot and excited lying there; sleep was out of the question more than ever. He jumped up, and went out barefooted on the veranda. Walking silently, he came upon the girl, motionless against the wall, as if on the watch. In his then state of mind it did not surprise him to see her up, nor yet to hear her ask in an anxious whisper where Cornelius could be. He simply said he did not know. She moaned a little, and peered into the *campong*. Everything was very quiet. He was possessed by his new idea, and so full of it that he could not help telling the girl all about it at once. She listened, clapped her hands lightly, whispered softly her admiration, but was evidently on the alert all the time. It seems he had been used to make a confidant of her all along – and that she on her part could and did give him a lot of useful hints as to Patusan affairs there is no doubt. He assured me more than once that he had never found himself the worse for her advice. At any rate, he was proceeding to explain his plan fully to her there and then, when she pressed his arm once, and vanished from his side. Then Cornelius appeared from somewhere, and, perceiving Jim, ducked sideways, as though he had been shot at, and afterwards stood very still in the dusk. At last he came forward prudently, like a suspicious cat. "There were some fishermen there – with fish," he said in a shaky voice. "To sell fish – you understand." ... It must have been then two o'clock in the morning – a likely time for anybody to hawk fish about!

'Jim, however, let the statement pass, and did not give it a single thought. Other matters occupied his mind, and besides he had neither seen nor heard anything. He contented himself by saying, "Oh!" absently, got a drink of water out of a pitcher standing there, and leaving Cornelius a prey to some inexplicable emotion – that made him embrace with both arms the worm-eaten rail of the veranda as if his legs had failed – went in again and lay down on his mat to think. By-and-by he heard stealthy footsteps. They stopped. A voice whispered tremulously through the wall, "Are you asleep?" "No! What is it?" he answered, briskly, and there was an abrupt movement outside, and then all was still, as if the whisperer had been startled. Extremely annoyed at this, Jim came out impetuously, and Cornelius with a faint shriek fled along the veranda as far as the steps, where he hung on to the broken banister. Very puzzled, Jim called out to him from the distance to know what the devil he meant. "Have you given your consideration to what I spoke to you about?" asked Cornelius, pronouncing the words with difficulty, like a man in the cold fit of a fever. "No!" shouted Jim in a passion. "I did not, and I don't intend to. I am going to live here, in Patusan." "You shall d-d-die h-h-here," answered Cornelius, still shaking violently, and in a sort of expiring voice. The whole performance was so absurd and provoking that Jim didn't know whether he ought to be amused or angry. "Not till I have seen you tucked away, you bet," he called out, exasperated yet ready to laugh. Half seriously (being excited with his own thoughts, you know) he went on shouting, "Nothing can touch me! You can do your damnedest." Somehow the shadowy Cornelius far off there seemed to be the hateful embodiment of all the annoyances and difficulties he had found in his path. He let himself go – his nerves had been over-wrought for days – and called him many pretty names – swindler, liar, sorry rascal: in fact, carried on in an extraordinary way. He admits he passed all bounds, that he was quite beside himself – defied all Patusan to scare him away – declared he would make them all dance to his own tune yet, and so on, in a menacing, boasting strain. Perfectly bombastic and ridiculous, he said. His ears burned at the bare recollection. Must have been off his chump in some way. ...
The girl, who was sitting with us, nodded her little head at me quickly, frowning faintly, and said, "I heard him," with childlike solemnity. He laughed and blushed. What stopped him at last, he said, was the silence, the complete deathlike silence, of the indistinct figure far over there, that seemed to hang collapsed, doubled over the rail in a weird immobility. He came to his senses, and ceasing suddenly, wondered greatly at himself. He watched for a while. Not a stir, not a sound. "Exactly as if the chap had died while I had been making all that noise," he said. He was so ashamed of himself that he went indoors in a hurry without another word, and flung himself down again. The row seemed to have done him good though, because he went to sleep for the rest of the night like a baby. Hadn't slept like that for weeks. "But *I* didn't sleep," struck in the girl, one elbow on the table and nursing her cheek. "I watched." Her big eyes flashed, rolling a little, and then she fixed them on my face intently.'

CHAPTER 31

'You may imagine with what interest I listened. All these details were perceived to have some significance twenty-four hours later. In the morning Cornelius made no allusion to the events of the night. "I suppose you will come back to my poor house," he muttered, surlily, slinking up just as Jim was entering the canoe to go over to Doramin's *campong*. Jim only nodded, without looking at him. "You find it good fun, no doubt," muttered the other in a sour tone. Jim spent the day with the old *nakhoda*, preaching the necessity of vigorous action to the principal men of the Bugis community, who had been summoned for a big talk. He remembered with pleasure how very eloquent and persuasive he had been. "I managed to put some backbone into them that time, and no mistake," he said. Sherif Ali's last raid had swept the outskirts of the settlement, and some women belonging to the town had been carried off to the stockade. Sherif Ali's emissaries had been seen in the market-place the day before, strutting about haughtily in white cloaks, and boasting of the Rajah's friendship for their master. One of them stood forward in the shade of a tree, and, leaning on the long barrel of a rifle, exhorted the people to prayer and repentance, advising them to kill all the strangers in their midst, some of whom, he said, were infidels and others even worse – children of Satan in the guise of Moslems. It was reported that several of the Rajah's people amongst the listeners had loudly expressed their approbation. The terror amongst the common people was intense. Jim, immensely pleased with his day's work, crossed the river again before sunset.

'As he had got the Bugis irretrievably committed to action, and made himself responsible for success on his own head, he was so elated that in the lightness of his heart he absolutely tried to be civil with Cornelius. But Cornelius became wildly jovial in response, and it was almost more than he could stand, he says, to hear his little squeaks of false laughter, to see him wriggle and blink, and suddenly catch hold of his chin and crouch low over the table with a distracted stare. The girl did not show herself, and Jim retired early. When he rose to say good night, Cornelius jumped up, knocking his chair over, and ducked out of sight as if to pick up something he had dropped. His good night came huskily from under the table. Jim was amazed to see him emerge out with a dropping jaw, and staring, stupidly frightened eyes. He clutched the edge of the table. "What's the matter? Are you unwell?" asked Jim. "Yes, yes, yes, A great colic in my stomach," says the other; and it is Jim's opinion that it was perfectly true. If so, it was, in view of his contemplated action, an abject sign of a still imperfect callousness for which he must be given all due credit.

'Be it as it may, Jim's slumbers were disturbed by a dream of heavens like brass resounding with a great voice, which called upon him to Awake!

Awake! so loud that, notwithstanding his desperate determination to sleep on, he did wake up in reality. The glare of a red spluttering conflagration going on in mid-air fell on his eyes. Coils of black thick smoke curved round the head of some apparition, some unearthly being, all in white, with a severe, drawn, anxious face. After a second or so, he recognized the girl. She was holding a dammar torch at arm's-length aloft, and in a persistent, urgent monotone she was repeating, "Get up! Get up! Get up!"

'Suddenly he leapt to his feet; at once she put into his hand a revolver, his own revolver, which had been hanging on a nail, but loaded this time. He gripped it in silence, bewildered, blinking in the light. He wondered what he could do for her.

'She asked rapidly and very low,"Can you face four men with this?" He laughed while narrating this part at the recollection of his polite alacrity. It seems he made a great display of it. "Certainly – of course – certainly – command me." He was not properly awake, and had a notion of being very civil in these extraordinary circumstances, of showing his unquestioning, devoted readiness. She left the room, and he followed her; in the passage they disturbed an old hag who did the casual cooking of the household, though she was so decrepit as to be hardly able to understand human speech. She got up and hobbled behind them, mumbling toothlessly. On the veranda a hammock of sailcloth, belonging to Cornelius, swayed lightly to the touch of Jim's elbow. It was empty.

'The Patusan establishment, like all the posts of Stein's Trading Company, had originally consisted of four buildings. Two of them were represented by two heaps of sticks, broken bamboos, rotten thatch, over which the four corner-posts of hardwood leaned sadly at different angles: the principal storeroom, however, stood yet, facing the agent's house. It was an oblong hut, built of mud and clay; it had at one end a wide door of stout planking, which so far had not come off the hinges, and in one of the side walls there was a square aperture, a sort of window, with three wooden bars. Before descending the few steps the girl turned her face over her shoulder and said quickly, "You were to be set upon while you slept." Jim tells me he experienced a sense of deception. It was the old story. He was weary of these attempts upon his life. He had had his fill of these alarms. He was sick of them. He assured me he was angry with the girl for deceiving him. He had followed her under the impression that it was she who wanted his help, and now he had half a mind to turn on his heel and go back in disgust. "Do you know," he commented, profoundly, "I rather think I was not quite myself for whole weeks on end about that time." "Oh, yes. You were though," I couldn't help contradicting.

'But she moved on swiftly, and he followed her into the courtyard. All its fences had fallen in a long time ago; the neighbours' buffaloes would pace in the morning across the open space, snorting profoundly, without haste; the very jungle was invading it already. Jim and the girl stopped in the rank grass. The light in which they stood made a dense blackness all around, and only above their heads there was an opulent glitter of stars. He told me it was a beautiful night – quite cool, with a little stir of breeze from the river. It seems he noticed its friendly beauty. Remember this is a love-story I am telling you now. A lovely night that seemed to breathe on them a soft caress. The flame of the torch streamed now and then with a fluttering noise like a flag, and for a time this was the only sound. "They are in the storeroom waiting," whispered the girl; "they are waiting for the signal." "Who's to give it?" he asked. She shook the torch, which blazed up after a shower of sparks. "Only you have been sleeping so restlessly," she continued in a murmur. "I watched your sleep, too." "You!" he exclaimed, craning his neck to look about him. "You think I watched on this night only!" she said, with a sort of despairing indignation.

'He says it was as if he had received a blow on the chest. He gasped. He thought he had been an awful brute somehow, and he felt remorseful, touched, happy, elated. This, let me remind you again, is a love story; you can see it by the imbecility, not a repulsive imbecility, the exalted imbecility of these proceedings, this station in torchlight, as if they had come there on purpose to have it out for the edification of concealed murderers. If Sherif Ali's emissaries had been possessed – as Jim remarked – of a pennyworth of spunk, this was the time to make a rush. His heart was thumping – not with fear – but he seemed to hear the grass rustle, and he stepped smartly out of the light. Something dark, imperfectly seen, flitted rapidly out of sight. He called out in a strong voice, "Cornelius! O Cornelius!" A profound silence succeeded: his voice did not seem to have carried twenty feet. Again the girl was by his side. "Fly!" she said. The old woman was coming up; her broken figure hovered in crippled little jumps on the edge of the light; they heard her mumbling, and a light, moaning sigh. "Fly!" repeated the girl, excitedly. "They are frightened now – this light – the voices. They know you are awake now – they know you are big, strong, fearless ..." "If I am all that," he began, but she interrupted him. "Yes – tonight! But what of tomorrow night? Of the next night? Of the night after – of all the many, many nights? Can I always be watching?" A sobbing catch of her breath affected him beyond the power of words.

'He told me that he had never felt so small, so powerless – and as to courage, what was the good of it? he thought. He was so helpless that even flight seemed of no use: and though she kept on whispering, "Go to Doramin, go to Doramin," with feverish insistence, he realized that for him there was no refuge from that loneliness which centupled all his dangers except – in her. "I thought," he said to me, "that if I went away from her it would be the end of everything somehow." Only as they couldn't stop there for ever in the middle of that courtyard, he made up his mind to go and look into the storehouse. He let her follow him without thinking of any protest, as if they had been indissolubly united. "I am fearless – am I?" he muttered through his teeth. She restrained his arm. "Wait till you hear my voice," she said, and, torch in hand, ran lightly round the corner. He remained alone in the darkness, his face to the door: not a sound, not a breath came from the other side. The old hag let out a dreary groan somewhere behind his back. He heard a high-pitched almost screaming call from the girl. "Now! Push!" He pushed violently; the door swung with a creak and a clatter, disclosing to his intense astonishment the low dungeon-like interior illuminated by a lurid, wavering glare. A turmoil of smoke eddied down upon an empty wooden crate in the middle of the floor, a litter of rags and straw tried to soar, but only stirred feebly in the draught. She had thrust the light through the bars of the window. He saw her bare round arm extended and rigid, holding up the torch with the steadiness of an iron bracket. A conical ragged heap of old mats cumbered a distant corner almost to the ceiling, and that was all.

'He explained to me that he was bitterly disappointed at this. His fortitude had been tried by so many warnings, he had been for weeks surrounded by so many hints of danger, that he wanted the relief of some reality, of something tangible that he could meet. "It would have cleared the air for a couple of hours at least, if you know what I mean," he said to me. "Jove! I had been living for days with a stone on my chest." Now at last he had thought he would get hold of something, and – nothing! Not a trace, not a sign of anybody. He had raised his weapon as the door flew open, but now his arm fell. "Fire! Defend yourself," the girl outside cried in an agonizing voice. She, being in the dark and with her arm thrust in to the shoulder through the small hole, couldn't see what was going on, and she dared not withdraw the torch now to run round. "There's nobody here!" yelled Jim contemptuously, but his impulse to burst into a resentful exasperated laugh died without a sound: he had perceived in the very act of turning away that he was exchanging glances with a pair of eyes in the heap of mats. He saw a shifting gleam of whites. "Come out!" he cried in a fury, a little doubtful, and a dark-faced head, a head without a body, shaped itself in the rubbish, a strangely detached head, that looked at him with a steady scowl. Next moment the whole mound stirred, and with a low grunt a man emerged swiftly, and bounded towards Jim. Behind him the mats as it were jumped and flew, his right arm was raised with a crooked elbow, and the dull blade of a kris protruded from his fist held off, a little above his head. A cloth wound tight round his loins seemed dazzling white on his bronze skin; his naked body glistened as if wet.

'Jim noted all this. He told me he was experiencing a feeling of unutterable relief, of vengeful elation. He held his shot, he says, deliberately. He held it for the tenth part of a second, for three strides of the man – an unconscionable time. He held it for the pleasure of saying to himself, That's a dead man! He was absolutely positive and certain. He let him come on because it did not matter. A dead man, anyhow. He noticed the dilated nostrils, the wide eyes, the intent eager expression of the face, and then he fired.

'The explosion in that confined space was stunning. He stepped back a pace. He saw the man jerk his head up, fling his arms forward, and drop the kris. He ascertained afterwards that he had shot him through the mouth, a little upwards, the bullet coming out high at the back of the skull. With the impetus of his rush the man drove straight on, his face suddenly gaping disfigured, with his hands open before him gropingly, as though blinded, and landing with terrific violence on his forehead, just short of Jim's bare toes. Jim says he didn't lose the smallest detail of all this. He found himself calm, appeased, without rancour, without uneasiness, as if the death of that man had atoned for everything. The place was getting very full of sooty smoke from the torch, in which the unswaying flame burned blood-red without flickering. He walked in resolutely, striding over the dead body, and covered with his revolver another naked figure outlined vaguely at the other end. As he was about to pull the trigger, the man threw away with force a short heavy spear, and squatted submissively on his hams, his back to the wall and his clasped hands between his legs. "You want your life?" Jim said. The other made no sound. "How many of you?" asked Jim again. "Two more, Tuan," said the man very softly, looking with big fascinated eyes into the muzzle of the revolver. Accordingly two more crawled from under the mats, holding out ostentatiously their empty hands.'

CHAPTER 32

'Jim took up an advantageous position and shepherded them out in a bunch through the doorway: all that time the torch had remained vertical in the grip of a little hand, without so much as a tremble. The three men obeyed him, perfectly mute, moving automatically. He ranged them in a row. "Link arms!" he ordered. They did so. "The first who withdraws his arm or turns his head is a dead man," he said. "March!" They stepped out together, rigidly; he followed, and at the side the girl, in a trailing white gown, her black hair falling as low as her waist, bore the light. Erect and swaying, she seemed to glide without touching the earth; the only sound was the silky swish and rustle of the long grass. "Stop!" cried Jim.

'The river bank was steep; a great freshness ascended, the light fell on the edge of smooth dark water frothing without a ripple; right and left the shapes of the houses ran together below the sharp outlines of the roofs. "Take my greetings to Sherif Ali – till I come myself," said Jim. Not one head of the three budged. "Jump!" he thundered. The three splashes made one splash, a shower flew up, black heads bobbed convulsively, and disappeared; but a great blowing and spluttering went on, growing faint, for they were diving industriously, in great fear of a parting shot. Jim turned to the girl, who had been a silent and attentive observer. His heart seemed suddenly to grow too big for his breast and choke him in the hollow of his throat. This probably made him speechless for so long, and after returning his gaze she flung the burning torch with a wide sweep of the arm into the river. The ruddy fiery glare, taking a long flight through the night, sank with a vicious hiss, and the calm soft starlight descended upon them, unchecked.

'He did not tell me what it was he said when at last he recovered his voice. I don't suppose he could be very eloquent. The world was still, the night breathed on them, one of those nights that seem created for the sheltering of tenderness, and there are moments when our souls, as if freed from their dark envelope, glow with an exquisite sensibility that makes certain silences more lucid than speeches. As to the girl, he told me, "She broke down a bit. Excitement – don't you know. Reaction. Deucedly tired

she must have been – and all that kind of thing. And – and – hang it all –
she was fond of me, don't you see. . . . I, too . . . didn't know, of course . . .
never entered my head. . . ."

'There he got up and began to walk about in some agitation. "I – I love
her dearly. More than I could tell. Of course one cannot tell. You take a
different view of your actions when you come to understand, when you are
made to understand every day that your existence is necessary – you see,
absolutely necessary – to another person. I am made to feel that. Wonderful.
But only try to think what her life had been. It is too extravagantly awful!
Isn't it? And me finding her here like this – as you may go out for a stroll
and come suddenly upon somebody drowning in a lonely dark place. Jove!
No time to lose. Well, it is a trust, too . . . I believe I am equal to it. . . ."

'I must tell you the girl had left us to ourselves some time before. He
slapped his chest. "Yes! I feel that, but I believe I am equal to all my luck!"
He had the gift of finding a special meaning in everything that happened
to him. This was the view he took of his love-affair; it was idyllic, a little
solemn, and also true, since his belief had all the unshakable seriousness of
youth. Some time after, on another occasion, he said to me, "I've been only
two years here, and now, upon my word, I can't conceive being able to live
anywhere else. The very thought of the world outside is enough to give me
a fright; because, don't you see," he continued, with downcast eyes watching
the action of his boot busied in squashing thoroughly a tiny bit of dried mud
(we were strolling on the river-bank) – "because I have not forgotten why
I came here. Not yet!"

'I refrained from looking at him, but I think I heard a short sigh; we took
a turn or two in silence. "Upon my soul and conscience," he began again,
"if such a thing can be forgotten, then I think I have a right to dismiss it
from my mind. Ask any man here" . . . his voice changed. "Is it not strange,"
he went on in a gentle, almost yearning tone, "that all these people, all these
people who would do anything for me, can never be made to understand?
Never! If you disbelieve me I could not call them up. It seems hard, somehow.
I am stupid, am I not? What more can I want? If you ask them who is brave
– who is true – who is just – who is it they would trust with their lives? –
they would say, Tuan Jim. And yet they can never know the real, real
truth. . . ."

'That's what he said to me on my last day with him. I did not let a
murmur escape me: I felt he was going to say more, and come no nearer to
the root of the matter. The sun, whose concentrated glare dwarfs the earth
into a restless mote of dust, had sunk behind the forest, and the diffused
light from an opal sky seemed to cast upon a world without shadows and
without brilliance the illusion of a calm and pensive greatness. I don't know
why, listening to him, I should have noted so distinctly the gradual darkening
of the river, of the air; the irresistible slow work of the night settling silently
on all the visible forms, effacing the outlines, burying the shapes deeper and
deeper, like a steady fall of impalpable black dust.

' "Jove!" he began, abruptly, "there are days when a fellow is too absurd
for anything; only I know I can tell you what I like. I talk about being done
with it – with the bally thing at the back of my head. . . . Forgetting. . . .

Hang me if I know! I can think of it quietly. After all, what has it proved? Nothing. I suppose you don't think so. . . ."

'I made a protesting murmur.

' "No matter," he said. 'I am satisfied . . . nearly. I've got to look only at the face of the first man that comes along, to regain my confidence. They can't be made to understand what is going on in me. What of that? Come! I haven't done so badly."

' "Not so badly," I said.

' "But all the same, you wouldn't like to have me aboard your own ship – hey?"

' "Confound you!" I cried. "Stop this."

' "Aha! You see," he cried, crowing, as it were, over me placidly. "Only," he went on, "you just try to tell this to any of them here. They would think you a fool, a liar, or worse. And so I can stand it. I've done a thing or two for them, but this is what they have done for me."

' "My dear chap," I cried, "you shall always remain for them an insoluble mystery." Thereupon we were silent.

' "Mystery," he repeated, before looking up. "Well, then let me always remain here."

'After the sun had set, the darkness seemed to drive upon us, borne in every faint puff of the breeze. In the middle of a hedged path I saw the arrested, gaunt, watchful, and apparently one-legged silhouette of Tamb' Itam; and across the dusky space my eye detected something white moving to and fro behind the supports of the roof. As soon as Jim, with Tamb' Itam at his heels, had started upon his evening rounds, I went up to the house alone, and, unexpectedly, found myself waylaid by the girl, who had been clearly waiting for this opportunity.

'It is hard to tell you what it was precisely she wanted to wrest from me. Obviously it would be something very simple – the simplest impossibility in the world; as, for instance, the exact description of the form of a cloud. She wanted an assurance, a statement, a promise, an explanation – I don't know how to call it: the thing has no name. It was dark under the projecting roof, and all I could see were the flowing lines of her gown, the pale small oval of her face, with the white flash of her teeth, and, turned towards me, the big sombre orbits of her eyes, where there seemed to be a faint stir, such as you may fancy you can detect when you plunge your gaze to the bottom of an immensely deep well. What is it that moves there? you ask yourself. Is it a blind monster or only a lost gleam from the universe? It occurred to me – don't laugh – that all things being dissimilar, she was more inscrutable in her childish ignorance than the Sphinx propounding childish riddles to wayfarers. She had been carried off to Patusan before her eyes were open. She had grown up there; she had seen nothing, she had known nothing, she had no conception of anything. I ask myself whether she were sure that anything else existed. What notions she may have formed of the outside world is to me inconceivable: all that she knew of its inhabitants were a betrayed woman and a sinister pantaloon. Her lover also came to her from there, gifted with irresistible seductions; but what would become of her if he should return to these inconceivable regions that seemed always to claim back their own? Her mother had warned her of this with tears, before she died. . . .

'She had caught hold of my arm firmly, and as soon as I had stopped she had withdrawn her hand in haste. She was audacious and shrinking. She feared nothing, but she was checked by the profound incertitude and the extreme strangeness – a brave person groping in the dark. I belonged to this Unknown that might claim Jim for its own at any moment. I was, as it were, in the secret of its nature and of its intentions – the confidant of a threatening mystery – armed with its power perhaps! I believe she supposed I could with a word whisk Jim away out of her very arms; it is my sober conviction she went through agonies of apprehension during my long talks with Jim; through a real and intolerable anguish that might have conceivably driven her into plotting my murder, had the fierceness of her soul been equal to the tremendous situation it had created. This is my impression, and it is all I can give you: the whole thing dawned gradually upon me, and as it got clearer and clearer I was overwhelmed by a slow incredulous amazement. She made me believe her, but there is no word that on my lips could render the effect of the headlong and vehement whisper, of the soft, passionate tones, of the sudden breathless pause and the appealing movement of the white arms extended swiftly. They fell; the ghostly figure swayed like a slender tree in the wind, the pale oval of the face drooped; it was impossible to distinguish her features, the darkness of the eyes was unfathomable; two wide sleeves uprose in the dark like unfolding wings, and she stood silent, holding her head in her hands.'

CHAPTER 33

'I was immensely touched: her youth, her ignorance, her pretty beauty, which had the simple charm and the delicate vigour of a wild-flower, her pathetic pleading, her helplessness, appealed to me with almost the strength of her own unreasonable and natural fear. She feared the unknown as we all do, and her ignorance made the unknown infinitely vast. I stood for it, for myself, for you fellows, for all the world that neither cared for Jim nor needed him in the least. I would have been ready enough to answer for the indifference of the teeming earth but for the reflection that he, too, belonged to this mysterious unknown of her fears, and that, however much I stood for, I did not stand for him. This made me hesitate. A murmur of hopeless pain unsealed my lips. I began by protesting that I at least had come with no intention to take Jim away.

'Why did I come, then? After a slight movement she was as still as a marble statue in the night. I tried to explain briefly: friendship, business; if I had any wish in the matter it was rather to see him stay. . . . "They always leave us," she murmured. The breath of sad wisdom from the grave which her piety wreathed with flowers seemed to pass in a faint sigh. . . . Nothing, I said, could separate Jim from her.

'It is my firm conviction now; it was my conviction at the time; it was the only possible conclusion from the facts of the case. It was not made more certain by her whispering in a tone in which one speaks to oneself, "He swore this to me." "Did you ask him?" I said.

'She made a step nearer. "No. Never!" She had asked him only to go away. It was that night on the river-bank, after he had killed the man – after she had flung the torch in the water because he was looking at her so. There was too much light, and the danger was over then – for a little time – for a little time. He said then he would not abandon her to Cornelius. She had insisted. She wanted him to leave her. He said that he could not – that it was impossible. He trembled while he said this. She had felt him tremble. . . . One does not require much imagination to see the scene, almost to hear their whispers. She was afraid of him, too. I believe that then she saw in him only a predestined victim of dangers which she understood better than himself. Though by nothing but his mere presence he had mastered her heart, had filled all her thoughts, and had possessed himself of all her affections, she under-estimated his chances of success. It is obvious that at about that time everybody was inclined to under-estimate his chances. Strictly speaking, he didn't seem to have any. I know this was Cornelius's view. He confessed that much to me in extenuation of the shady part he had played in Sherif Ali's plot to do away with the infidel. Even Sherif Ali himself, as it seems certain now, had nothing but contempt for the white man. Jim was to be murdered mainly on religious grounds, I believe. A simple act of piety (and so far infinitely meritorious), but otherwise without much importance. In the last part of this opinion Cornelius concurred. "Honourable sir," he argued abjectly on the only occasion he managed to have me to himself – "Honourable sir, how was I to know? Who was he? What could he do to make people believe him? What did Mr Stein mean sending a boy like that to talk big to an old servant? I was ready to save him for eighty dollars. Only eighty dollars. Why didn't the fool go? Was I to get stabbed myself for the sake of a stranger?" He grovelled in spirit before me, with his body doubled up insinuatingly and his hands hovering about my knees, as though he were ready to embrace my legs. "What's eighty dollars? An insignificant sum to give a defenceless old man ruined for life by a deceased she-devil." Here he wept. But I anticipate. I didn't that night chance upon Cornelius till I had had it out with the girl.

'She was unselfish when she urged Jim to leave her, and even to leave the country. It was his danger that was foremost in her thoughts – even if she wanted to save herself, too – perhaps unconsciously; but then look at the warning she had, look at the lesson that could be drawn from every moment of the recently ended life in which all her memories were centred. She fell at his feet – she told me so – there by the river, in the discreet light of stars which showed nothing except great masses of silent shadows, indefinite open spaces, and trembling faintly upon the broad stream made it appear as wide as the sea. He had lifted her up. He lifted her up, and then she would struggle no more. Of course not. Strong arms, a tender voice, a stalwart shoulder to rest her poor lonely little head upon. The need – the infinite need – of all this for the aching heart, for the bewildered mind – the promptings of youth – the necessity of the moment. What would you have? One understands – unless one is incapable of understanding anything under the sun. And so she was content to be lifted up – and held. "You know – Jove! this is serious – no nonsense in it!" as Jim had whispered hurriedly with a troubled, concerned face on the threshold of his house. I don't know so much about nonsense, but there was nothing light-hearted in their romance: they came together under the shadow of a life's disaster, like knight and maiden meeting to exchange vows amongst haunted ruins. The starlight was good enough for that story, a light so faint and remote that it cannot resolve shadows into shapes, and show the other shore of a stream. I did look upon the stream that night and from the very place; it rolled silent and black as Styx: the next day I went away, but I am not likely to forget what it was she wanted to be saved from when she entreated him to leave her while there was time. She told me what it was, calmed – she was now too passionately interested for mere excitement – in a voice as quiet in the obscurity as her white half-lost figure. She told me, "I didn't want to die weeping." I thought I had not heard aright.

' "You did not want to die weeping?" I repeated after her. "Like my mother," she added readily. The outlines of her white shape did not stir in the least. "My mother had wept bitterly before she died," she explained. An inconceivable calmness seemed to have risen from the ground around us, imperceptibly, like the still rise of a flood in the night, obliterating the familiar landmarks of emotions. There came upon me, as though I had felt myself losing my footing in the midst of waters, a sudden dread, the dread of the unknown depths. She went on explaining that, during the last moments, being alone with her mother, she had to leave the side of the couch to go and set her back against the door, in order to keep Cornelius out. He desired to get in, and kept on drumming with both fists, only desisting now and again to shout huskily, "Let me in! Let me in! Let me in!" In a far corner upon a few mats the moribund woman, already speechless and unable to lift her arm, rolled her head over, and with a feeble movement of her hand seemed to command – "No! No!" and the obedient daughter, setting her shoulders with all her strength against the door, was looking on. "The tears fell from her eyes – and then she died," concluded the girl in an imperturbable monotone, which more than anything else, more than the white statuesque immobility of her person, more than mere words could do, troubled my mind profoundly with the passive, irremediable horror of the scene. It had the power to drive me out of my conception of existence, out of that shelter each of us makes for himself to creep under in moments of danger, as a tortoise withdraws within its shell. For a moment I had a view of a world that seemed to wear a vast and dismal aspect of disorder, while, in truth, thanks to our unwearied efforts, it is as sunny an arrangement of small conveniences as the mind of man can conceive. But still – it was only a moment: I went back into my shell directly. One *must* – don't you know? – though I seemed to have lost all my words in the chaos of dark thoughts I had contemplated for a second or two beyond the pale. These came back, too, very soon, for words also belong to the sheltering conception of light and order which is our refuge. I had them ready at my disposal before she whispered softly, "He swore he would never leave me, when we stood there alone! He swore to me!" ... "And it is possible that you – you! do not believe him?" I asked, sincerely reproachful, genuinely shocked. Why couldn't she believe? Wherefore this craving for incertitude, this clinging to fear, as if incertitude and fear had been the safeguards of her love. It was monstrous. She should have made for herself a shelter of inexpugnable peace out of that honest affection. She had not the knowledge – not the skill perhaps. The night had come on apace; it had grown pitch-dark where we were, so that without stirring she had faded like the intangible form of a wistful and perverse spirit. And suddenly I heard her quiet whisper again, "Other men have sworn the same thing." It was like a meditative comment on some thoughts full of sadness, of awe. And she added, still lower if possible, "My father did." She paused the time to draw an inaudible breath. "Her father, too." ... These were the things she knew! At once I said, "Ah! but he is not like that." This, it seemed, she did not intend to dispute; but after a time the strange still whisper wandering dreamily in the air stole into my ears. "Why is he different? Is he better? Is he ...?" "Upon my word of honour," I broke in, "I believe he is." We subdued our tones to a mysterious pitch. Amongst the huts of Jim's workmen (they were mostly liberated slaves from the Sherif's stockade) somebody started a shrill, drawling song. Across the river a big fire (at Doramin's, I think) made a glowing ball, completely isolated in the night. "Is he more true?" she murmured. "Yes," I said. "More true than any other man," she repeated in lingering accents. "Nobody here," I said, "would dream of doubting his word – nobody would dare – except you."

'I think she made a movement at this. "More brave," she went on in a changed tone. "Fear shall never drive him away from you," I said a little nervously. The song stopped short on a shrill note, and was succeeded by several voices talking in the distance. Jim's voice, too. I was struck by her silence. "What has he been telling you? He has been telling you something?" I asked. There was no answer. "What is it he told you?" I insisted.

' "Do you think I can tell you? How am I to know? How am I to understand?" she cried at last. There was a stir. I believe she was wringing her hands. "There is something he can never forget."

' "So much the better for you," I said, gloomily.

' "What is it? What is it?" She put an extraordinary force of appeal into her supplicating tone. "He says he had been afraid. How can I believe this? Am I a mad woman to believe this? You all remember something! You all go back to it. What is it! You tell me! What is this thing? Is it alive – is it dead? I hate it. It is cruel. Has it got a face and a voice – this calamity! Will he see it – will he hear it? In his sleep perhaps when he cannot see me – and then arise and go. Ah! I shall never forgive him. My mother had forgiven – but I, never! Will it be a sign – a call?"'

'It was a wonderful experience. She mistrusted his very slumbers – and she seemed to think I could tell her why! Thus a poor mortal seduced by the charm of an apparition might have tried to wring from another ghost the

tremendous secret of the claim the other world holds over a disembodied
soul astray amongst the passions of this earth. The very ground on which
I stood seemed to melt under my feet. And it was so simple, too; but if the
spirits evoked by our fears and our unrest have ever to vouch for each other's
constancy before the forlorn magicians that we are, then I – I alone of us
dwellers in the flesh – have shuddered in the hopeless chill of such a task.
A sign, a call! How telling in its expression was her ignorance. A few words!
How she came to know them, how she came to pronounce them, I can't
imagine. Women find their inspiration in the stress of moments that for us
are merely awful, absurd, or futile. To discover that she had a voice at all
was enough to strike awe into the heart. Had a spurned stone cried out in
pain it could not have appeared a greater and more pitiful miracle. These
few sounds wandering in the dark had made their two benighted lives tragic
to my mind. It was impossible to make her understand. I chafed silently at
my impotence. And Jim, too – poor devil! Who would need him? Who
would remember him? He had what he wanted. His very existence probably
had been forgotten by this time. They had mastered their fates. They were
tragic.

'Her immobility before me was clearly expectant, and my part was to
speak for my brother from the realm of forgetful shades. I was deeply moved
at my responsibility and at her distress. I would have given anything for the
power to soothe her frail soul, tormenting itself in its invincible ignorance
like a small bird beating about the cruel wires of a cage. Nothing easier than
to say, Have no fear! Nothing more difficult. How does one kill fear, I
wonder? How do you shoot a spectre through the heart, slash off its spectral
head, take it by its spectral throat? It is an enterprise you rush into while
you dream, and are glad to make your escape with wet hair and every limb
shaking. The bullet is not run, the blade not forged, the man not born; even
the winged words of truth drop at your feet like lumps of lead. You require
for such a desperate encounter an enchanted and poisoned shaft dipped in
a lie too subtle to be found on earth. An enterprise for a dream, my masters!

'I began my exorcism with a heavy heart, with a sort of sullen anger in
it, too. Jim's voice, suddenly raised with a stern intonation, carried across
the courtyard, reproving the carelessness of some dumb sinner by the riverside. Nothing – I said, speaking in a distinct murmur – there could be
nothing, in that unknown world she fancied so eager to rob her of her
happiness, there was nothing neither living nor dead, there was no face, no
voice, no power, that could tear Jim away from her side. I drew breath and
she whispered softly, "He told me so." "He told you the truth," I said.
"Nothing," she sighed out, and abruptly turned upon me with a barely
audible intensity of tone: "Why did you come to us from out there? He
speaks of you too often. You make me afraid. Do you – do you want him?"
A sort of stealthy fierceness had crept into our hurried mutters. "I shall
never come again," I said, bitterly. "And I don't want him. No one wants
him." "No one," she repeated in a tone of doubt. "No one," I affirmed,
feeling myself swayed by some strange excitement. "You think him strong,
wise, courageous, great – why not believe him to be true, too? I shall go
tomorrow – and that is the end. You shall never be troubled by a voice from

there again. This world you don't know is too big to miss him. You understand? Too big. You've got his heart in your hand. You must feel that. You must know that." "Yes, I know that," she breathed out, hard and still, as a statue might whisper.

'I felt I had done nothing. And what is it that I had wished to do? I am not sure now. At the time I was animated by an inexplicable ardour, as if before some great and necessary task – the influence of the moment upon my mental and emotional state. There are in all our lives such moments, such influences, coming from the outside, as it were, irresistible, incomprehensible – as if brought about by the mysterious conjunctions of the planets. She owned, as I had put it to her, his heart. She had that and everything else – if she could only believe it. What I had to tell her was that in the whole world there was no one who would need his heart, his mind, his hand. It was a common fate, and yet it seemed an awful thing to say of any man. She listened without a word, and her stillness now was like the protest of an invincible unbelief. What need she care for the world beyond the forests? I asked. From all the multitudes that peopled the vastness of that unknown there would come, I assured her, as long as he lived, neither a call nor a sign for him. Never. I was carried away. Never! Never! I remember with wonder the sort of dogged fierceness I displayed. I had the illusion of having got the spectre by the throat at last. Indeed the whole real thing has left behind the detailed and amazing impression of a dream. Why should she fear? She knew him to be strong, true, wise, brave. He was all that. Certainly. He was more. He was great – invincible – and the world did not want him, it had forgotten him, it would not even know him.

'I stopped; the silence over Patusan was profound, and the feeble dry sound of a paddle striking the side of a canoe somewhere in the middle of the river seemed to make it infinite. "Why?" she murmured. I felt that sort of rage one feels during a hard tussle. The spectre was trying to slip out of my grasp. "Why?" she repeated louder, "tell me!" And as I remained confounded, she stamped with her foot like a spoilt child. "Why? Speak." "You want to know?" I asked in a fury. "Yes!" she cried. "Because he is not good enough," I said, brutally. During the moment's pause I noticed the fire on the other shore blaze up, dilating the circle of its glow like an amazed stare, and contract suddenly to a red pin-point. I only knew how close to me she had been when I felt the clutch of her fingers on my forearm. Without raising her voice, she threw into it an infinity of scathing contempt, bitterness, and despair.

' "This is the very thing he said . . . You lie!"

'The last two words she cried at me in the native dialect. "Hear me out!" I entreated; she caught her breath tremulously, flung my arm away. "Nobody, nobody is good enough," I began with the greatest earnestness. I could hear the sobbing labour of her breath frightfully quickened. I hung my head. What was the use? Footsteps were approaching; I slipped away without another word. . . . '

CHAPTER 34

Marlow swung his legs out, got up quickly, and staggered a little, as though he had been set down after a rush through space. He leaned his back against the balustrade and faced a disordered array of long cane-chairs. The bodies prone in them seemed startled out of their torpor by his movement. One or two sat up as if alarmed; here and there a cigar glowed yet; Marlow looked at them all with the eyes of a man returning from the excessive remoteness of a dream. A throat was cleared; a calm voice encouraged negligently, 'Well.'

'Nothing,' said Marlow with a slight start. 'He had told her – that's all. She did not believe him – nothing more. As to myself, I do not know whether it be just, proper, decent for me to rejoice or to be sorry. For my part, I cannot say what I believed – indeed I don't know to this day, and never shall probably. But what did the poor devil believe himself? Truth shall prevail – don't you know *Magna est veritas et* . . . Yes, when it gets a chance. There is a law, no doubt – and likewise a law regulates your luck in the throwing of dice. It is not Justice the servant of men, but accident, hazard, Fortune – the ally of patient Time – that holds an even and scrupulous balance. Both of us had said the very same thing. Did we both speak the truth – or one of us did – or neither? . . .'

Marlow paused, crossed his arms on his breast, and in a changed tone —

'She said we lied. Poor soul. Well – let's leave it to chance, whose ally is Time, that cannot be hurried, and whose enemy is Death, that will not wait. I had retreated – a little cowed, I must own. I had tried a fall with fear itself and got thrown – of course. I had only succeeded in adding to her anguish the hint of some mysterious collusion, of an inexplicable and incomprehensible conspiracy to keep her for ever in the dark. And it had come easily, naturally, unavoidably, by his act, by her own act! It was as though I had been shown the working of the implacable destiny of which we are the victims – and the tools. It was appalling to think of the girl whom I had left standing there motionless; Jim's footsteps had a fateful sound as he tramped by, without seeing me, in his heavy laced boots. "What? No lights!" he said in a loud, surprised voice. "What are you doing in the dark – you two?" Next moment he caught sight of her, I suppose. "Hallo, girl!" he cried, cheerily. "Hallo, boy!" she answered at once, with amazing pluck.

'This was their usual greeting to each other, and the bit of swagger she would put into her rather high but sweet voice was very droll, pretty, and childlike. It delighted Jim greatly. This was the last occasion on which I heard them exchange this familiar hail, and it struck a chill into my heart. There was the high sweet voice, the pretty effort, the swagger; but it all seemed to die out prematurely, and the playful call sounded like a moan. It was too confoundedly awful. "What have you done with Marlow?" Jim was asking; and then, "Gone down – has he? Funny I didn't meet him. . . . You there, Marlow?"

'I didn't answer. I wasn't going in – not yet at any rate. I really couldn't. While he was calling me I was engaged in making my escape through a little gate leading out upon a stretch of newly cleared ground. No; I couldn't face them yet. I walked hastily with lowered head along a trodden path. The ground rose gently, the few big trees had been felled, the undergrowth had been cut down and the grass fired. He had a mind to try a coffee-plantation there. The big hill, rearing its double summit coal-black in the clear yellow glow of the rising moon, seemed to cast its shadow upon the ground prepared for that experiment. He was going to try ever so many experiments; I had admired his energy, his enterprise, and his shrewdness. Nothing on earth seemed less real now than his plans, his energy, and his enthusiasm; and raising my eyes, I saw part of the moon glittering through the bushes at the bottom of the chasm. For a moment it looked as though the smooth disc, falling from its place in the sky upon the earth, had rolled to the bottom of that precipice: its ascending movement was like a leisurely rebound; it disengaged itself from the tangle of twigs; the bare contorted limb of some tree, growing on the slope, made a black crack right across its face. It threw its level rays afar as if from a cavern, and in this mournful eclipse-like light the stumps of felled trees uprose very dark, the heavy shadows fell at my feet on all sides, my own moving shadow, and across my path the shadow of the solitary grave perpetually garlanded with flowers. In the darkened moonlight the interlaced blossoms took on shapes foreign to one's memory and colours indefinable to the eye, as though they had been special flowers gathered by no man, grown not in this world, and destined for the use of the dead alone. Their powerful scent hung in the warm air, making it thick and heavy like the fumes of incense. The lumps of white coral shone round the dark mound like a chaplet of bleached skulls, and everything around was so quiet that when I stood still all sound and all movements in the world seemed to come to an end.

'It was a great peace, as if the earth had been one grave, and for a time I stood there thinking mostly of the living who, buried in remote places out of the knowledge of mankind, still are fated to share in its tragic or grotesque miseries. In its noble struggles, too – who knows? The human heart is vast enough to contain all the world. It is valiant enough to bear the burden, but where is the courage that would cast it off?

'I suppose I must have fallen into a sentimental mood; I only know that I stood there long enough for the sense of utter solitude to get hold of me so completely that all I had lately seen, all I had heard, and the very human speech itself, seemed to have passed away out of existence, living only for a while longer in my memory, as though I had been the last of mankind. It was a strange and melancholy illusion, evolved half-consciously like all our illusions, which I suspect only to be visions of remote unattainable truth, seen dimly. This was, indeed, one of the lost, forgotten, unknown places of the earth; I had looked under its obscure surface; and I felt that when tomorrow I had left it for ever, it would slip out of existence, to live only in my memory till I myself passed into oblivion. I have that feeling about me now; perhaps it is that feeling which had incited me to tell you the story, to try to hand over to you, as it were, its very existence, its reality – the truth disclosed in a moment of illusion.

'Cornelius broke upon it. He bolted out, vermin-like, from the long grass growing in a depression of the ground. I believe his house was rotting somewhere near by, though I've never seen it, not having been far enough in that direction. He ran towards me upon the path; his feet, shod in dirty white shoes, twinkled on the dark earth; he pulled himself up, and began to whine and cringe under a tall stove-pipe hat. His dried-up little carcass was swallowed up, totally lost, in a suit of black broadcloth. That was his costume for holidays and ceremonies, and it reminded me that this was the fourth Sunday I had spent in Patusan. All the time of my stay I had been vaguely aware of his desire to confide in me, if he only could get me all to himself. He hung about with an eager craving look on his sour yellow little face; but his timidity had kept him back as much as my natural reluctance to have anything to do with such an unsavoury creature. He would have succeeded, nevertheless, had he not been so ready to slink off as soon as you looked at him. He would slink off before Jim's severe gaze, before my own, which I tried to make indifferent, even before Tamb' Itam's surly, superior glance. He was perpetually slinking away; whenever seen he was seen moving off deviously, his face over his shoulder, with either a mistrustful snarl or a woe-begone, piteous, mute aspect; but no assumed expression could conceal this innate irremediable abjectness of his nature, any more than an arrangement of clothing can conceal some monstrous deformity of the body.

'I don't know whether it was the demoralization of my utter defeat in my encounter with a spectre of fear less than an hour ago, but I let him capture me without even a show of resistance. I was doomed to be the recipient of confidences, and to be confronted with unanswerable questions. It was trying; but the contempt, the unreasoned contempt, the man's appearance provoked, made it easier to bear. He couldn't possibly matter. Nothing mattered, since I had made up my mind that Jim, for whom alone I cared, had at last mastered his fate. He had told me he was satisfied . . . nearly. This is going further than most of us dare. I – who have the right to think myself good enough – dare not. Neither does any of you here, I suppose? . . .'

Marlow paused, as if expecting an answer. Nobody spoke.

'Quite right,' he began again. 'Let no soul know, since the truth can be wrung out of us only by some cruel, little, awful catastrophe. But he is one of us, and he could say he was satisfied . . . nearly. Just fancy this! Nearly satisfied. One could almost envy him his catastrophe. Nearly satisfied. After this nothing could matter. It did not matter who suspected him, who trusted him, who loved him, who hated him – especially as it was Cornelius who hated him.

'Yet after all this was a kind of recognition. You shall judge of a man by his foes as well as by his friends, and this enemy of Jim was such as no decent man would be ashamed to own, without, however, making too much of him. This was the view Jim took, and in which I shared; but Jim disregarded him on general grounds. "My dear Marlow," he said, "I feel that if I go straight nothing can touch me. Indeed I do. Now you have been long enough here to have a good look round – and, frankly, don't you think I am pretty safe? It all depends upon me, and, by Jove! I have lots of confidence in myself. The worst thing he could do would be to kill me, I suppose. I don't think for a moment he would. He couldn't, you know – not if I were myself to hand him a loaded rifle for the purpose, and then turn my back on him. That's the sort of thing he is. And suppose he would – suppose he could? Well – what of that? I didn't come here flying for my life – did I? I came here to set my back against the wall, and I am going to stay here ..."

' "Till you are *quite* satisfied," I struck in.

'We were sitting at the time under the roof in the stern of his boat; twenty paddles flashed like one, ten on a side, striking the water with a single splash, while behind our backs Tamb' Itam dipped silently right and left, and stared right down the river, attentive to keep the long canoe in the greatest strength of the current. Jim bowed his head, and our last talk seemed to flicker out for good. He was seeing me off as far as the mouth of the river. The schooner had left the day before, working down and drifting on the ebb, while I had prolonged my stay overnight. And now he was seeing me off.

'Jim had been a little angry with me for mentioning Cornelius at all. I had not, in truth, said much. The man was too insignificant to be dangerous, though he was as full of hate as he could hold. He had called me "honourable sir" at every second sentence, and had whined at my elbow as he followed me from the grave of his "late wife" to the gate of Jim's compound. He declared himself the most unhappy of men, a victim, crushed like a worm; he entreated me to look at him. I wouldn't turn my head to do so; but I could see out of the corner of my eye his obsequious shadow gliding after mine, while the moon, suspended on our right hand, seemed to gloat serenely upon the spectacle. He tried to explain – as I've told you – his share in the events of the memorable night. It was a matter of expediency. How could he know who was going to get the upper hand? "I would have saved him, honourable sir! I would have saved him for eighty dollars," he protested in dulcet tones, keeping a pace behind me. "He has saved himself," I said, "and he has forgiven you." I heard a sort of tittering, and turned upon him; at once he appeared ready to take to his heels. "What are you laughing at?" I asked, standing still. "Don't be deceived, honourable sir!" he shrieked, seemingly losing all control over his feelings. "*He* save himself! He knows nothing, honourable sir – nothing whatever. Who is he? What does he want here – the big thief? What does he want here? He throws dust into everybody's eyes; he throws dust into your eyes, honourable sir; but he can't throw dust into my eyes. He is a big fool, honourable sir." I laughed contemptuously, and, turning on my heel, began to walk on again. He ran up to my elbow and whispered forcibly, "He's no more than a little child here – like a little child – a little child." Of course I didn't take the slightest notice, and seeing the time pressed, because we were approaching the bamboo fence that glittered over the blackened ground of the clearing, he came to the point. He commenced by being abjectly lachrymose. His great misfortunes had affected his head. He hoped I would kindly forget what nothing but his troubles made him say. He didn't mean anything by it; only the honourable sir did not know what it was to be ruined, broken down, trampled upon. After this introduction he approached the matter near his heart, but in such a rambling, ejaculatory, craven fashion, that for a long time I couldn't make out what he was driving at. He wanted me to intercede with Jim in his favour. It seemed, too, to be some sort of money affair. I heard time and again the words, "Moderate provision – suitable present". He seemed to be claiming value for something, and he even went the length of saying with some warmth that life was not worth having if a man were to be robbed of everything. I did not breathe a word, of course, but neither did I stop my ears. The gist of the affair, which became clear to me gradually, was in this, that he regarded himself as entitled to some money in exchange for the girl. He had brought her up. Somebody else's child. Great trouble and pains – old man now – suitable present. If the honourable sir would say a word. . . . I stood still to look at him with curiosity, and fearful lest I should think him extortionate, I suppose, he hastily brought himself to make a concession. In consideration of a "suitable present" given at once, he would, he declared, be willing to undertake the charge of the girl, "without any other provision – when the time came for the gentleman to go home". His yellow face, all crumpled as though it had been squeezed together, expressed the most anxious, eager avarice. His voice whined coaxingly, "No more trouble – natural guardian – a sum of money. . . ."

'I stood there and marvelled. That kind of thing, with him, was evidently a vocation. I discovered suddenly in his cringing attitude a sort of assurance, as though he had been all his life dealing in certitudes. He must have thought I was dispassionately considering his proposal, because he became as sweet as honey. "Every gentleman made a provision when the time came to go home," he began, insinuatingly. I slammed the little gate. "In this case, Mr Cornelius," I said, "the time shall never come." He took a few seconds to gather this in. "What!" he fairly squealed. "Why," I continued from my side of the gate, "haven't you heard him say so himself? He will never go home." "Oh! this is too much," he shouted. He would not address me as "honoured sir" any more. He was very still for a time, and then without a trace of humility began very low. "Never go – ah! He – he – he comes here devil knows from where – comes here – devil knows why – to trample on me till I die – ah – trample" (he stamped softly with both feet), "trample like this – nobody knows why – till I die. . . ." His voice became quite extinct; he was bothered by a little cough; he came up close to the fence and told me, dropping into a confidential and piteous tone, that he would *not* be trampled upon. "Patience – patience," he muttered, striking his breast. I had done laughing at him, but unexpectedly he treated me to a wild cracked burst of it. "Ha! ha! ha! We shall see! We shall see! What! Steal from me? Steal from me everything! Everything! Everything!" His head drooped on one shoulder, his hands were hanging before him lightly clasped. One would have thought he had cherished the girl with surpassing love, that his spirit had been crushed and his heart broken by the most cruel of spoliations.

Suddenly he lifted his head and shot out an infamous word. "Like her mother – she is like her deceitful mother. Exactly. In her face, too. In her face. The devil!" He leaned his forehead against the fence, and in that position uttered threats and horrible blasphemies in Portuguese in very weak ejaculations, mingled with miserable plaints and groans, coming out with a heave of the shoulders as though he had been overtaken by a deadly fit of sickness. It was an inexpressibly grotesque and vile performance, and I hastened away. He tried to shout something after me. Some disparagement of Jim, I believe – not too loud though, we were too near the house. All I heard distinctly was, "No more than a little child – a little child." '

CHAPTER 35

'But next morning, at the first bend of the river shutting off the houses of Patusan, all this dropped out of my sight bodily, with its colour, its design, and its meaning, like a picture created by fancy on a canvas, upon which, after long contemplation, you turn your back for the last time. It remains in the memory motionless, unfaded, with its life arrested, in an unchanging light. There are the ambitions, the fears, the hate, the hopes, and they remain in my mind just as I had seen them – intense and as if for ever suspended in their expression. I had turned away from the picture and was going back to the world where events move, men change, light flickers, life flows in a clear stream, no matter whether over mud or over stones. I wasn't going to dive into it; I would have enough to do to keep my head above the surface. But as to what I was leaving behind, I cannot imagine any alteration. The immense and magnanimous Doramin and his little motherly witch of a wife, gazing together upon the land and nursing secretly their dreams of parental ambition; Tunku Allang, wizened and greatly perplexed; Dain Waris, intelligent and brave, with his faith in Jim, with his firm glance and his ironic friendliness; the girl, absorbed in her frightened, suspicious adoration; Tamb' Itam, surly and faithful; Cornelius, leaning his forehead against the fence under the moonlight – I am certain of them. They exist as if under an enchanter's wand. But the figure round which all these are grouped – that one lives, and I am not certain of him. No magician's wand can immobilize him under my eyes. He is one of us.

'Jim, as I've told you, accompanied me on the first stage of my journey back to the world he had renounced, and the way at times seemed to lead through the very heart of untouched wilderness. The empty reaches sparkled under the high sun; between the high walls of vegetation the heat drowsed upon the water, and the boat, impelled vigorously, cut her way through the air that seemed to have settled dense and warm under the shelter of lofty trees.

'The shadow of the impending separation had already put an immense space between us, and when we spoke it was with an effort, as if to force our low voices across a vast and increasing distance. The boat fairly flew; we sweltered side by side in the stagnant superheated air; the smell of mud, of marsh, the primeval smell of fecund earth, seemed to sting our faces; till suddenly at a bend it was as if a great hand far away had lifted a heavy curtain, had flung open an immense portal. The light itself seemed to stir, the sky above our heads widened, a far-off murmur reached our ears, a freshness enveloped us, filled our lungs, quickened our thoughts, our blood, our regrets – and, straight ahead, the forests sank down against the dark-blue ridge of the sea.

'I breathed deeply, I revelled in the vastness of the opened horizon, in the different atmosphere that seemed to vibrate with a toil of life, with the energy of an impeccable world. This sky and this sea were open to me. The girl was right – there was a sign, a call in them – something to which I responded with every fibre of my being. I let my eyes roam through space, like a man released from bonds who stretches his cramped limbs, runs, leaps, responds to the inspiring elation of freedom. "This is glorious!" I cried, and then I looked at the sinner by my side. He sat with his head sunk on his breast and said, "Yes", without raising his eyes, as if afraid to see writ large on the clear sky of the offing the reproach of his romantic conscience.

'I remember the smallest details of that afternoon. We landed on a bit of white beach. It was backed by a low cliff wooded on the brow, draped in creepers to the very foot. Below us the plain of the sea, of a serene and intense blue, stretched with a slight upward tilt to the thread-like horizon drawn at the height of our eyes. Great waves of glitter blew lightly along the pitted dark surface, as swift as feathers chased by the breeze. A chain of islands sat broken and massive facing the wide estuary, displayed in a sheet of pale glassy water reflecting faithfully the contour of the shore. High in the colourless sunshine a solitary bird, all black, hovered, dropping and soaring above the same spot with a slight rocking motion of the wings. A ragged, sooty bunch of flimsy mat hovels was perched over its own inverted image upon a crooked multitude of high piles the colour of ebony. A tiny black canoe put off from amongst them with two tiny men, all black, who toiled exceedingly, striking down at the pale water: and the canoe seemed to slide painfully on a mirror. This bunch of miserable hovels was the fishing village that boasted of the white lord's especial protection, and the two men crossing over were the old headman and his son-in-law. They landed and walked up to us on the white sand, lean, dark-brown as if dried in smoke, with ashy patches on the skin of their naked shoulders and breasts. Their heads were bound in dirty but carefully folded handkerchiefs, and the old man began at once to state a complaint, voluble, stretching a lank arm, screwing up at Jim his old bleared eyes confidently. The Rajah's people would not leave them alone; there had been some trouble about a lot of turtles' eggs his people had collected on the islets there – and leaning at arm's-length upon his paddle, he pointed with a brown skinny hand over the sea. Jim listened for a time without looking up, and at last told him gently to wait. He would hear him by-and-by. They withdrew obediently to some little distance, and sat on their heels, with their paddles lying before them on the sand; the silvery gleams in their eyes followed our movements patiently; and the immensity of the outspread sea, the stillness of the coast, passing north and south beyond the limits of my vision, made up one colossal Presence watching us four dwarfs isolated on a strip of glistening sand.

' "The trouble is," remarked Jim, moodily, "that for generations these beggars of fishermen in that village there had been considered as the Rajah's personal slaves – and the old rip can't get it into his head that . . ."

'He paused. "That you have changed all that," I said.

' "Yes. I've changed all that," he muttered in a gloomy voice.

' "You have had your opportunity," I pursued.

' "Have I?" he said. "Well, yes, I suppose so. Yes. I have got back my confidence in myself – a good name – yet sometimes I wish . . . No! I shall hold what I've got. Can't expect anything more." He flung his arm out towards the sea. "Not out there anyhow." He stamped his foot upon the sand. "This is my limit, because nothing less will do."

'We continued pacing the beach. "Yes, I've changed all that," he went on, with a sidelong glance at the two patient squatting fishermen; "but only try to think what it would be if I went away. Jove! can't you see it? Hell loose. No! Tomorrow I shall go and take my chance of drinking that silly old Tunku Allang's coffee, and I shall make no end of fuss over these rotten turtles' eggs. No. I can't say – enough. Never. I must go on, go on for ever holding up my end, to feel sure that nothing can touch me. I must stick to their belief in me to feel safe and to – to" . . . He cast about for a word, seemed to look for it on the sea . . . "to keep in touch with" . . . His voice sank suddenly to a murmur . . . "with those whom, perhaps, I shall never see any more. With – with – you, for instance."

'I was profoundly humbled by his words. "For God's sake," I said, "don't set me up, my dear fellow; just look to yourself." I felt a gratitude, an affection, for that straggler whose eyes had singled me out, keeping my place in the ranks of an insignificant multitude. How little that was to boast of, after all! I turned my burning face away; under the low sun, glowing, darkened, and crimson, like an ember snatched from the fire, the sea lay outspread, offering all its immense stillness to the approach of the fiery orb. Twice he was going to speak, but checked himself: at last, as if he had found a formula —

' "I shall be faithful," he said, quietly. "I shall be faithful," he repeated, without looking at me, but for the first time letting his eyes wander upon the waters, whose blueness had changed to a gloomy purple under the fires of sunset. Ah! he was romantic, romantic. I recalled some words of Stein's. . . . "In the destructive element immerse! . . . To follow the dream, and again to follow the dream – and so – always – *usque ad finem* . . ." He was romantic, but none the less true. Who could tell what forms, what visions, what faces, what forgiveness he could see in the glow of the west! . . . A small boat, leaving the schooner, moved slowly, with a regular beat of two oars, towards the sandbank to take me off. "And then there's Jewel," he said, out of the great silence of earth, sky, and sea, which had mastered my very thoughts so that his voice made me start. "There's Jewel." "Yes," I murmured. "I need not tell you what she is to me," he pursued. "You've

seen. In time she will come to understand . . ." "I hope so," I interrupted.
"She trusts me, too," he mused, and then changed his tone. "When shall we
meet next, I wonder?" he said.

' "Never – unless you come out," I answered, avoiding his glance. He
didn't seem to be surprised; he kept very quiet for a while.

' "Good-bye, then," he said, after a pause. "Perhaps it's just as well."

'We shook hands, and I walked to the boat, which waited with her nose
on the beach. The schooner, her mainsail set and jib-sheet to windward,
curveted on the purple sea; there was a rosy tinge on her sails. "Will you
be going home again soon?" asked Jim, just as I swung my leg over the
gunwale. "In a year or so if I live," I said. The forefoot grated on the sand,
the boat floated, the wet oars flashed and dipped once, twice. Jim, at the
water's edge, raised his voice. "Tell them . . ." he began. I signed to the
men to cease rowing, and waited in wonder. Tell who? The half-submerged
sun faced him; I could see its red gleam in his eyes that looked dumbly at
me. . . . "No – nothing," he said, and with a slight wave of his hand
motioned the boat away. I did not look again at the shore till I had clambered
on board the schooner.

'By that time the sun had set. The twilight lay over the east, and the
coast, turned black, extended infinitely its sombre wall that seemed the very
stronghold of the night; the western horizon was one great blaze of gold and
crimson in which a big detached cloud floated dark and still, casting a slaty
shadow on the water beneath, and I saw Jim on the beach watching the
schooner fall off and gather headway.

'The two half-naked fishermen had arisen as soon as I had gone; they
were no doubt pouring the plaint of their trifling, miserable, oppressed lives
into the ears of the white lord, and no doubt he was listening to it, making
it his own, for was it not a part of his luck – the luck "from the word Go"
– the luck to which he had assured me he was so completely equal? They,
too, I should think, were in luck, and I was sure their pertinacity would be
equal to it. Their dark-skinned bodies vanished on the dark background
long before I had lost sight of their protector. He was white from head to
foot, and remained persistantly visible with the stronghold of the night at his
back, the sea at his feet, the opportunity by his side – still veiled. What do
you say? Was it still veiled? I don't know. For me that white figure in the
stillness of coast and sea seemed to stand at the heart of a vast enigma. The
twilight was ebbing fast from the sky above his head, the strip of sand had
sunk already under his feet, he himself appeared no bigger than a child –
then only a speck, a tiny white speck, that seemed to catch all the light left
in a darkened world. . . . And, suddenly, I lost him. . . .'

CHAPTER 36

With these words Marlow had ended his narrative, and his audience had broken up forthwith, under his abstract, pensive gaze. Men drifted off the veranda in pairs or alone without loss of time, without offering a remark, as if the last image of that incomplete story, its incompleteness itself, and the very tone of the speaker, had made discussion vain and comment impossible. Each of them seemed to carry away his own impression, to carry it away with him like a secret; but there was only one man of all these listeners who was ever to hear the last word of the story. It came to him at home, more than two years later, and it came contained in a thick packet addressed in Marlow's upright and angular handwriting.

The privileged man opened the packet, looked in, then, laying it down, went to the window. His rooms were in the highest flat of a lofty building, and his glance could travel afar beyond the clear panes of glass, as though he were looking out of the lantern of a lighthouse. The slopes of the roofs glistened, the dark broken ridges succeeded each other without end like sombre, uncrested waves, and from the depths of the town under his feet ascended a confused and unceasing mutter. The spires of churches, numerous, scattered haphazard, uprose like beacons on a maze of shoals without a channel; the driving rain mingled with the falling dusk of a winter's evening; and the booming of a big clock on a tower striking the hour, rolled past in voluminous, austere bursts of sound, with a shrill vibrating cry at the core. He drew the heavy curtains.

The light of his shaded reading-lamp slept like a sheltered pool, his footfalls made no sound on the carpet, his wandering days were over. No more horizons as boundless as hope, no more twilights within the forests as solemn as temples, in the hot quest of the Ever-undiscovered Country over the hill, across the stream, beyond the wave. The hour was striking! No more! No more! – but the opened packet under the lamp brought back the sounds, the visions, the very savour of the past – a multitude of fading faces, a tumult of low voices, dying away upon the shores of distant seas under a passionate and unconsoling sunshine. He sighed and sat down to read.

At first he saw three distinct enclosures. A good many pages closely blackened and pinned together; a loose square sheet of greyish paper with a few words traced in a handwriting he had never seen before, and an explanatory letter from Marlow. From this last fell another letter, yellowed by time and frayed on the folds. He picked it up and, laying it aside, turned to Marlow's message, ran swiftly over the opening lines, and, checking himself, thereafter read on deliberately, like one approaching with slow feet and alert eyes the glimpse of an undiscovered country.

'. . . I don't suppose you've forgotten,' went on the letter. 'You alone have

showed an interest in him that survived the telling of his story, though I
remember well you would not admit he had mastered his fate. You prophesied
for him the disaster of weariness and of disgust with acquired honour, with
the self-appointed task, with the love sprung from pity and youth. You had
said you knew so well "that kind of thing", its illusory satisfaction, its
unavoidable deception. You said also – I call to mind – that "giving your life
up to them" (*them* meaning all of mankind with skins brown, yellow, or
black in colour) "was like selling your soul to a brute." You contended that
"that kind of thing" was only endurable and enduring when based on a firm
conviction in the truth of ideas racially our own, in whose name are
established the order, the morality of an ethical progress. "We want its
strength at our backs," you had said. "We want a belief in its necessity and
its justice, to make a worthy and conscious sacrifice of our lives. Without it
the sacrifice is only forgetfulness, the way of offering is no better than the
way to perdition." In other words, you maintained that we must fight in the
ranks or our lives don't count. Possibly! You ought to know – be it said
without malice – you who have rushed into one or two places single-handed
and came out cleverly, without singeing your wings. The point, however, is
that of all mankind Jim had no dealings but with himself, and the question
is whether at the last he had not confessed to a faith mightier than the laws
of order and progress.

  'I affirm nothing. Perhaps you may pronounce – after you've read. There
is much truth – after all – in the common expression "under a cloud". It is
impossible to see him clearly – especially as it is through the eyes of others
that we take our last look at him. I have no hesitation in imparting to you
all I know of the last episode that, as he used to say, had "come to him".
One wonders whether this was perhaps that supreme opportunity, that last
and satisfying test for which I had always suspected him to be waiting,
before he could frame a message to the impeccable world. You remember
that when I was leaving him for the last time he had asked whether I would
be going home soon, and suddenly cried after me, "Tell them!" ... I had
waited – curious I'll own, and hopeful, too – only to hear him shout, "No.
Nothing." That was all then – and there shall be nothing more; there shall
be no message, unless such as each of us can interpret for himself from the
language of facts, that are so often more enigmatic than the craftiest
arrangement of words. He made, it is true, one more attempt to deliver
himself; but that, too, failed, as you may perceive if you look at the sheet of
greyish foolscap enclosed here. He had tried to write; do you notice the
commonplace hand? It is headed "The Fort, Patusan". I suppose he had
carried out his intention of making out of his house a place of defence. It
was an excellent plan: a deep ditch, and earth wall topped by a palisade,
and at the angles guns mounted on platforms to sweep each side of the
square. Doramin had agreed to furnish him the guns; and so each man of
his party would know there was a place of safety, upon which every faithful
partisan could rally in case of some sudden danger. All this showed his
judicious foresight, his faith in the future. What he called "my own people"
– the liberated captives of the Sherif – were to make a distinct quarter of
Patusan, with their huts and little plots of ground under the walls of the

stronghold. Within he would be an invincible host in himself. "The Fort, Patusan." No date, as you observe. What is a number and a name to a day of days? It is also impossible to say whom he had in his mind when he seized the pen: Stein – myself – the world at large – or was it only the aimless startled cry of a solitary man confronted by his fate? "An awful thing has happened," he wrote before he flung the pen down for the first time; look at the ink blot resembling the head of an arrow under these words. After a while he had tried again, scrawling heavily, as if with a hand of lead, another line. "I must now at once . . ." The pen had spluttered, and that time he gave it up. There's nothing more; he had seen a broad gulf that neither eye nor voice could span. I can understand this. He was overwhelmed by the inexplicable; he was overwhelmed by his own personality – the gift of that destiny which he had done his best to master.

'I send you also an old letter – a very old letter. It was found carefully preserved in his writing-case. It is from his father, and by the date you can see he must have received it a few days before he joined the *Patna*. Thus it must be the last letter he had ever had from home. He had treasured it all these years. The good old parson fancied his sailor-son. I've looked in at a sentence here and there. There is nothing in it except just affection. He tells his "dear James" that the last long letter from him was very "honest and entertaining". He would not have him "judge men harshly or hastily". There are four pages of it, easy morality and family news. Tom had "taken orders". Carrie's husband had "money losses". The old chap goes on equably trusting providence and the established order of the universe, but alive to its small dangers and its small mercies. One can almost see him, grey-haired and serene in the inviolable shelter of his book-lined, faded, and comfortable study, where for forty years he had conscientiously gone over and over again the round of his little thoughts about faith and virtue, about the conduct of life and the only proper manner of dying; where he had written so many sermons, where he sits talking to his boy, over there, on the other side of the earth. But what of the distance? Virtue is one all over the world, and there is only one faith, one conceivable conduct of life, one manner of dying. He hopes his "dear James" will never forget that "who once gives way to temptation, in the very instant hazards his total depravity and everlasting ruin. Therefore resolve fixedly never, through any possible motives, to do anything which you believe to be wrong." There is also some news of a favourite dog; and a pony, "which all you boys used to ride", had gone blind from old age and had to be shot. The old chap invokes Heaven's blessing; the mother and all the girls then at home send their love. . . . No, there is nothing much in that yellow frayed letter fluttering out of his cherishing grasp after so many years. It was never answered, but who can say what converse he may have held with all these placid, colourless forms of men and women peopling that quiet corner of the world as free of danger or strife as a tomb, and breathing equally the air of undisturbed rectitude. It seems amazing that he should belong to it, he to whom so many things "had come". Nothing ever came to them; they would never be taken unawares, and never be called upon to grapple with fate. Here they all are, evoked by the mild gossip of the father, all these brothers and sisters, bone of his bone and flesh of his flesh, gazing with clear unconscious eyes, while I seem to see him, returned at last, no longer a mere white speck at the heart of an immense mystery, but of full stature, standing disregarded amongst their untroubled shapes, with a stern and romantic aspect, but always mute, dark – under a cloud.

'The story of the last events you shall find in the few pages enclosed here. You must admit that it is romantic beyond the wildest dreams of his boyhood, and yet there is to my mind a sort of profound and terrifying logic in it, as if it were our imagination alone that could set loose upon us the might of an overwhelming destiny. The imprudence of our thoughts recoils upon our heads; who toys with the sword shall perish by the sword. This astounding adventure, of which the most astounding part is that it is true, comes on as an unavoidable consequence. Something of the sort had to happen. You repeat this to yourself while you marvel that such a thing could happen in the year of grace before last. But it has happened – and there is no disputing its logic.

'I put it down here for you as though I had been an eyewitness. My information was fragmentary, but I've fitted the pieces together, and there is enough of them to make an intelligible picture. I wonder how he would have related it himself. He has confided so much in me that at times it seems as though he must come in presently and tell the story in his own words, in his careless yet feeling voice, with his offhand manner, a little puzzled, a little bothered, a little hurt, but now and then by a word or a phrase giving one of these glimpses of his very own self that were never any good for purposes of orientation. It's difficult to believe he will never come. I shall never hear his voice again, nor shall I see his smooth tan-and-pink face with a white line on the forehead, and the youthful eyes darkened by excitement to a profound, unfathomable blue.'

CHAPTER 37

'It all begins with a remarkable exploit of a man called Brown, who stole with complete success a Spanish schooner out of a small bay near Zamboanga. Till I discovered the fellow my information was incomplete, but most unexpectedly I did come upon him a few hours before he gave up his arrogant ghost. Fortunately he was willing and able to talk between the choking fits of asthma, and his racked body writhed with malicious exultation at the bare thought of Jim. He exulted thus at the idea that he had "paid out the stuck-up beggar after all". He gloated over his action. I had to bear the sunken glare of his fierce crow-footed eyes if I wanted to know; and so I bore it, reflecting how much certain forms of evil are akin to madness, derived from intense egoism, inflamed by resistance, tearing the soul to pieces, and giving factitious vigour to the body. The story also reveals unsuspected depths of cunning in the wretched Cornelius, whose abject and intense hate acts like a subtle inspiration, pointing out an unerring way towards revenge.

' "I could see directly I set my eyes on him what sort of a fool he was," gasped the dying Brown. "He a man! Hell! He was a hollow sham. As if he couldn't have said straight out, 'Hands off my plunder!' blast him! That would have been like a man! Rot his superior soul! He had me there – but he hadn't devil enough in him to make an end of me. Not he! A thing like that letting me off as if I wasn't worth a kick! ..." Brown struggled desperately for breath. ... "Fraud. ... Letting me off. ... And so I did make an end of him after all. ..." He choked again. ... "I expect this thing'll kill me, but I shall die easy now. You ... you hear ... I don't know your name – I would give you a five-pound note if – if I had it – for the news – or my name's not Brown. ..." He grinned horribly. ... "Gentleman Brown."

'He said all these things in profound gasps, staring at me with his yellow eyes out of a long, ravaged brown face: he jerked his left arm; a pepper-and-salt matted beard hung almost into his lap; a dirty ragged blanket covered his legs. I had found him out in Bangkok through that busybody Schomberg, the hotel-keeper, who had, confidentially, directed me where to look. It appears that a sort of loafing, fuddled vagabond – a white man living among the natives with a Siamese woman – had considered it a great privilege to give a shelter to the last days of the famous Gentleman Brown. While he was talking to me in the wretched hovel, and, as it were, fighting for every minute of his life, the Siamese woman, with big bare legs and a stupid coarse face, sat in a dark corner chewing betel stolidly. Now and then she would get up for the purpose of shooing a chicken away from the door. The whole hut shook when she walked. An ugly yellow child, naked and pot-bellied, like a little heathen god, stood at the foot of the couch, finger in mouth, lost in a profound and calm contemplation of the dying man.

'He talked feverishly; but in the middle of a word, perhaps, an invisible hand would take him by the throat, and he would look at me dumbly with an expression of doubt and anguish. He seemed to fear that I would get tired of waiting and go away, leaving him with his tale untold, with his exultation unexpressed. He died during the night, I believe, but by that time I had nothing more to learn.

'So much as to Brown, for the present.

'Eight months before this, coming into Samarang, I went as usual to see Stein. On the garden side of the house a Malay on the veranda greeted me shyly, and I remembered that I had seen him in Patusan, in Jim's house, amongst other Bugis men who used to come in the evening to talk interminably over their war reminiscences and to discuss State affairs. Jim had pointed him out to me once as a respectable petty trader owning a small sea-going native craft, who had showed himself "one of the best at the taking of the stockade". I was not very surprised to see him, since any Patusan trader venturing as far as Samarang would naturally find his way to Stein's house. I returned his greeting and passed on. At the door of Stein's room I came upon another Malay in whom I recognized Tamb' Itam.

'I asked him at once what he was doing there; it occurred to me that Jim might have come on a visit. I own I was pleased and excited at the thought. Tamb' Itam looked as if he did not know what to say. "Is Tuan Jim inside?" I asked, impatiently. "No," he mumbled, hanging his head for a moment, and then with sudden earnestness, "He would not fight. He would not fight," he repeated twice. As he seemed unable to say anything else, I pushed him aside and went in.

'Stein, tall and stooping, stood alone in the middle of the room between the rows of butterfly cases. "Ach! is it you my friend?" he said, sadly peering through his glasses. A drab sack-coat of alpaca hung, unbuttoned down to his knees. He had a panama hat on his head, and there were deep furrows on his pale cheeks. "What's the matter now?" I asked, nervously. "There's Tamb' Itam there. . . ." "Come and see the girl. Come and see the girl. She is here," he said, with a half-hearted show of activity. I tried to detain him, but with gentle obstinacy he would take no notice of my eager questions. "She is here, she is here," he repeated, in great perturbation. "They came here two days ago. An old man like me, a stranger – *sehen sie* – cannot do much. . . . Come this way. . . . Young hearts are unforgiving. . . ." I could see he was in the utmost distress. . . . "The strength of life in them, the cruel strength of life. . . ." he mumbled, leading me round the house; I followed him, lost in dismal and angry conjectures. At the door of the drawing-room he barred my way. "He loved her very much," he said, interrogatively, and I only nodded, feeling so bitterly disappointed that I would not trust myself to speak. "Very frightful," he murmured. "She can't understand me. I am only a strange old man. Perhaps you . . . she knows you. Talk to her. We can't leave it like this. Tell her to forgive him. It was very frightful." "No doubt," I said, exasperated at being in the dark; "but have *you* forgiven him?" He looked at me queerly. "You shall hear," he said, and opening the door, absolutely pushed me in.

'You know Stein's big house and the two immense reception-rooms, uninhabited and uninhabitable, clean, full of solitude and of shining things that look as if never beheld by the eye of man? They are cool on the hottest days, and you enter them as you would a scrubbed cave underground. I passed through one, and in the other I saw the girl sitting at the end of a big mahogany table, on which she rested her head, the face hidden in her arms. The waxed floor reflected her dimly as though it had been a sheet of frozen water. The rattan screens were down, and through the strange greenish gloom made by the foliage of the trees outside, a strong wind blew in gusts, swaying the long draperies of windows and doorways. Her white figure seemed shaped in snow; the pendent crystals of a great chandelier clicked above her head like glittering icicles. She looked up and watched my approach. I was chilled as if these vast apartments had been the cold abode of despair.

'She recognized me at once, and as soon as I had stopped, looking down at her: "He has left me," she said, quietly; "you always leave us – for your own ends." Her face was set. All the heat of life seemed withdrawn within some inaccessible spot in her breast. "It would have been easy to die with him," she went on, and made a slight weary gesture as if giving up the incomprehensible. "He would not! It was like a blindness – and yet it was I who was speaking to him; it was I who stood before his eyes; it was at me that he looked all the time! Ah! you are hard, treacherous, without truth, without compassion. What makes you so wicked? Or is it that you are all mad?"

'I took her hand; it did not respond, and when I dropped it, it hung down to the floor. That indifference, more awful than tears, cries, and reproaches, seemed to defy time and consolation. You felt that nothing you could say would reach the seat of the still and benumbing pain.

'Stein had said, "You shall hear." I did hear. I heard it all, listening with amazement, with awe, to the tones of her inflexible weariness. She could not grasp the real sense of what she was telling me, and her resentment filled me with pity for her – for him, too. I stood rooted to the spot after she had finished. Leaning on her arm, she stared with hard eyes, and the wind passed in gusts, the crystals kept on clicking in the greenish gloom. She went on whispering to herself: "And yet he was looking at me! He could see my face, hear my voice, hear my grief! When I used to sit at his feet, with my cheek against his knees and his hand on my head, the curse of cruelty and madness was already within him, waiting for the day. The day came! ... and before the sun had set he could not see me any more – he was made blind and deaf and without pity, as you all are. He shall have no tears from me. Never, never. Not one tear. I will not! He went away from me as if I had been worse than death. He fled as if driven by some accursed thing he had heard or seen in his sleep. ..."

'Her steady eyes seemed to strain after the shape of a man torn out of her arms by the strength of a dream. She made no sign to my silent bow. I was glad to escape.

'I saw her once again, the same afternoon. On leaving her I had gone in search of Stein, whom I could not find indoors; and I wandered out, pursued by distressful thoughts into the gardens, those famous gardens of Stein, in which you can find every plant and tree of tropical lowlands. I followed the course of the canalized stream, and sat for a long time on a shaded bench near the ornamental pond, where some waterfowl with clipped wings were diving and splashing noisily. The branches of casuarina-trees behind me swayed lightly, incessantly, reminding me of the soughing of fir-trees at home.

'This mournful and restless sound was a fit accompaniment to my meditations. She had said he had been driven away from her by a dream – and there was no answer one could make her – there seemed to be no forgiveness for such a transgression. And yet is not mankind itself, pushing on its blind way, driven by a dream of its greatness and its power upon the dark paths of excessive cruelty and of excessive devotion? And what is the pursuit of truth, after all?

'When I rose to get back to the house I caught sight of Stein's drab coat through a gap in the foliage, and very soon at a turn of the path I came upon him walking with the girl. Her little hand rested on his forearm, and under the broad, flat rim of his panama hat he bent over her, greyhaired, paternal, with compassionate and chivalrous deference. I stood aside, but they stopped, facing me. His gaze was bent on the ground at his feet; the girl, erect and slight on his arm, stared sombrely beyond my shoulder with black, clear, motionless eyes. "*Schrecklich*", he murmured. "Terrible! Terrible! What can one do?" He seemed to be appealing to me, but her youth, the length of the days suspended over her head, appealed to me more; and suddenly, even as I realized that nothing could be said, I found myself pleading his cause for her sake. "You must forgive him," I concluded, and my own voice seemed to me muffled, lost in an irresponsive deaf immensity. "We all want to be forgiven," I added after a while.

‘ "What have I done?" she asked with her lips only.

‘ "You always mistrusted him," I said.

‘ "He was like the others," she pronounced slowly.

‘ "Not like the others," I protested, but she continued evenly, without any feeling —

‘ "He was false." And suddenly Stein broke in. "No! no! no! My poor child! . . ." He patted her hand lying passively on his sleeve. "No! no! Not false! True! true! true!" He tried to look into her stony face. "You don't understand. Ach! Why you do not understand? . . . Terrible," he said to me. "Some day she *shall* understand."

‘ "Will *you* explain?" I asked, looking hard at him. They moved on.

'I watched them. Her gown trailed on the path, her black hair fell loose. She walked upright and light by the side of the tall man, whose long shapeless coat hung in perpendicular folds from the stooping shoulders, whose feet moved slowly. They disappeared beyond that spinney (you may remember) where sixteen different kinds of bamboo grow together, all distinguishable to the learned eye. For my part I was fascinated by the exquisite grace and beauty of that fluted grove, crowned with pointed leaves and feathery heads, the lightness, the vigour, the charm as distinct as a voice of that unperplexed luxuriating life. I remember staying to look at it for a long time, as one would linger within reach of a consoling whisper. The sky was pearly grey. It was one of those overcast days so rare in the tropics, in which memories crowd upon one, memories of other shores, of other faces.

'I drove back to town the same afternoon, taking with me Tamb' Itam and the other Malay, in whose seagoing craft they had escaped in the bewilderment, fear, and gloom of the disaster. The shock of it seemed to have changed their natures. It had turned her passion into stone, and it made the surly taciturn Tamb' Itam almost loquacious. His surliness, too, was subdued into puzzled humility, as though he had seen the failure of a potent charm in a supreme moment. The Bugis trader, a shy hesitating man, was very clear in the little he had to say. Both were evidently overawed by a sense of deep inexpressible wonder, by the touch of an inscrutable mystery.'

There with Marlow's signature the letter proper ended. The privileged reader screwed up his lamp, and solitary above the billowy roofs of the town, like a lighthouse keeper above the sea, he turned to the pages of the story.

Chapter 38

'It all begins, as I've told you, with the man called Brown,' ran the opening sentence of Marlow's narrative. 'You who have knocked about in the Western Pacific must have heard of him. He was the show ruffian on the Australian coast – not that he was often to be seen there, but because he was always trotted out in the stories of lawless life a visitor from home is treated to; and the mildest of these stories which were told about him from Cape York to Eden Bay was more than enough to hang a man if told in the right place. They never failed to let you know, too, that he was supposed to be the son of a baronet. Be it as it may, it is certain he had deserted from a home ship in the early gold-digging days, and in a few years became talked about as the terror of this or that group of islands in Polynesia. He would kidnap natives, he would strip some lonely white trader to the very pyjamas he stood in, and after he had robbed the poor devil, he would as likely as not invite him to fight a duel with shot-guns on the beach – which would have been fair enough as these things go, if the other man hadn't been by that time already half-dead with fright. Brown was a latter-day buccaneer, sorry enough, like his more celebrated prototypes; but what distinguished him from his contemporary brother ruffians, like Bully Hayes or the mellifluous Pease, or that perfumed, Dundreary-whiskered, dandified scoundrel known as Dirty Dick, was the arrogant temper of his misdeeds and a vehement scorn for mankind at large and for his victims in particular. The others were merely vulgar and greedy brutes, but he seemed moved by some complex intention. He would rob a man as if only to demonstrate his poor opinion of the creature, and he would bring to the shooting or maiming of some quiet, unoffending stranger a savage and vengeful earnestness fit to terrify the most reckless of desperadoes. In the days of his greatest glory he owned an armed barque, manned by a mixed crew of Kanakas and runaway whalers, and boasted, I don't know with what truth, of being financed on the quiet by a most respectable firm of copra merchants. Later on he ran off – it was reported – with the wife of a missionary, a very young girl from Clapham way, who had married the mild, flat-footed fellow in a moment of enthusiasm, and suddenly transplanted to Melanesia, lost her bearings somehow. It was a dark story. She was ill at the time he carried her off, and died on board his ship. It is said – as the most wonderful part of the tale – that over her body he gave way to an outburst of sombre and violent grief. His luck left him, too, very soon after. He lost his ship on some rocks off Malaita, and disappeared for a time as though he had gone down with her. He is heard of next at Nuka-Hiva, where he bought an old French schooner out of Government service. What creditable enterprise he might have had in view when he made that purchase, I can't say, but it is evident that what with High Commissioners, consuls, men-of-war, and international control, the South Seas were getting too hot to hold gentlemen of his kidney. Clearly he must have shifted the scene of his operations farther west, because a year later he plays an incredibly audacious, but not a very profitable part, in a serio-comic business in Manila Bay, in which a peculating governor and an absconding treasurer are the principal figures; thereafter he seems to have hung around the Philippines in his rotten schooner, battling with an adverse fortune, till at last, running his appointed course, he sails into Jim's history, a blind accomplice of the Dark Powers.

'His tale goes that when a Spanish patrol cutter captured him he was simply trying to run a few guns for the insurgents. If so, then I can't understand what he was doing off the south coast of Mindanao. My belief, however, is that he was blackmailing the native villages along the coast. The principal thing is that the cutter, throwing a guard on board, made him sail in company towards Zamboanga. On the way, for some reason or other, both vessels had to call at one of these new Spanish settlements – which never came to anything in the end – where there was not only a civil official in charge on shore, but a good stout coasting schooner lying at anchor in the little bay; and this craft, in every way much better than his own, Brown made up his mind to steal.

'He was down on his luck – as he told me himself. The world he had bullied for twenty years with fierce, aggressive disdain, had yielded him nothing in the way of material advantage except a small bag of silver dollars, which was concealed in his cabin so that "the devil himself couldn't smell it out". And that was all – absolutely all. He was tired of his life, and not afraid of death. But this man, who would stake his existence on a whim with a bitter and jeering recklessness, stood in mortal fear of imprisonment. He had an unreasoning, cold-sweat, nerve-shaking, blood-to-water-turning sort of horror at the bare possibility of being locked up – the sort of terror a superstitious man would feel at the thought of being embraced by a spectre. Therefore the civil official who came on board to make a preliminary investigation into the capture, investigated arduously all day long, and only went ashore after dark, muffled up in a cloak, and taking great care not to let Brown's little all clink in its bag. Afterwards, being a man of his word, he contrived (the very next evening, I believe) to send off the Government cutter on some urgent bit of special service. As her commander could not spare a prize crew, he contented himself by taking away before he left all the sails of Brown's schooner to the very last rag, and took good care to tow his two boats on to the beach a couple of miles off.

'But in Brown's crew there was a Solomon Islander, kidnapped in his youth and devoted to Brown, who was the best man of the whole gang. That fellow swam off to the coaster – five hundred yards or so – with the end of a warp made up of all the running gear unrove for the purpose. The water was smooth, and the bay dark, "like the inside of a cow", as Brown described it. The Solomon Islander clambered over the bulwarks with the end of the rope in his teeth. The crew of the coaster – all Taglas – were ashore having a jollification in the native village. The two shipkeepers left on board woke up suddenly and saw the devil. It had glittering eyes and leaped quick as lightning about the deck. They fell on their knees, paralysed with fear, crossing themselves and mumbling prayers. With a long knife he found in the caboose the Solomon Islander, without interrupting their orisons, stabbed first one, then the other; with the same knife he set to sawing patiently at the coir cable till suddenly it parted under the blade with a splash. Then in the silence of the bay he let out a cautious shout, and Brown's gang, who meantime had been peering and straining their hopeful ears in the darkness, began to pull gently at their end of the warp. In less than five minutes the two schooners came together with a slight shock and a creak of spars.

'Brown's crowd transferred themselves without losing an instant, taking with them their firearms and a large supply of ammunition. They were sixteen in all: two runaway blue-jackets, a lanky deserter from a Yankee man-of-war, a couple of simple, blond Scandinavians, a mulatto of sorts, one bland Chinaman who cooked – and the rest of the nondescript spawn of the South Seas. None of them cared; Brown bent them to his will, and Brown, indifferent to gallows, was running away from the spectre of a Spanish prison. He didn't give them the time to trans-ship enough provisions; the weather was calm, the air was charged with dew, and when they cast off the ropes and set sail to a faint offshore draught there was no flutter in the damp canvas; their old schooner seemed to detach itself gently from the stolen craft and slip away silently, together with the black mass of the coast, into the night.

'They got clear away. Brown related to me in detail their passage down the Straits of Macassar. It is a harrowing and desperate story. They were short of food and water; they boarded several native craft and got a little from each. With a stolen ship Brown did not dare to put into any port, of course. He had no money to buy anything, no papers to show, and no lie plausible enough to get him out again. An Arab barque, under the Dutch flag, surprised one night at anchor off Poulo Laut, yielded a little dirty rice, a bunch of bananas, and a cask of water; three days of squally misty weather from the north-east shot the schooner across the Java Sea. The yellow muddy waves drenched that collection of hungry ruffians. They sighted mailboats moving on their appointed routes; passed well-founded home ships with rusty iron sides anchored in the shallow sea waiting for a change of weather or the turn of the tide; an English gunboat, white and trim, with two slim masts, crossed their bows one day in the distance; and on another occasion a Dutch corvette, black and heavily sparred, loomed upon their quarter, steaming dead slow in the mist. They slipped through unseen or disregarded, a wan, sallow-faced band of utter outcasts, enraged with hunger and hunted by fear. Brown's idea was to make for Madagascar, where he expected, on grounds not altogether illusory, to sell the schooner in Tamatave, and no questions asked, or perhaps obtain some more or less forged papers for her. Yet before he could face the long passage across the Indian Ocean food was wanted – water, too.

'Perhaps he had heard of Patusan – or perhaps he just only happened to see the name written in small letters on the chart – probably that of a largish village up a river in a native state, perfectly defenceless, far from the beaten tracks of the sea and from the ends of the submarine cables. He had done that kind of thing before – in the way of business; and this now was an absolute necessity, a question of life and death – rather of liberty. Of liberty! He was sure to get provisions – bullocks – rice – sweet-potatoes. The sorry gang licked their chops. A cargo of produce for the schooner perhaps could be extorted – and, who knows? – some real ringing coin money! Some of these chiefs and the village headmen can be made to part freely. He told me he would have roasted their toes rather than be baulked. I believe him. His men believed him too. They didn't cheer aloud, being a dumb pack, but made ready wolfishly.

'Luck served him as to weather. A few days of calm would have brought unmentionable horrors on board that schooner, but with the help of land and sea breezes, in less than a week after clearing the Sunda Straits, he anchored off the Batu Kring mouth within a pistol-shot of the fishing village.

'Fourteen of them packed into the schooner's long-boat (which was big, having been used for cargo-work) and started up the river, while two remained in charge of the schooner with food enough to keep starvation off for ten days. The tide and wind helped, and early one afternoon the big white boat under a ragged sail shouldered its way before the sea breeze into Patusan Reach, manned by fourteen assorted scarecrows glaring hungrily ahead, and fingering the breech-blocks of cheap rifles. Brown calculated upon the terrifying surprise of his appearance. They sailed in with the last of the flood; the Rajah's stockade gave no sign; the first houses on both sides of the stream seemed deserted. A few canoes were seen up the reach in full flight. Brown was astonished at the size of the place. A profound silence reigned. The wind dropped between the houses; two oars were got out and the boat held on upstream, the idea being to effect a lodgement in the centre of the town before the inhabitants could think of resistance.

'It seems, however, that the headman of the fishing village at Batu Kring had managed to send off a timely warning. When the long-boat came abreast of the mosque (which Doramin had built: a structure with gables and roof finials of carved coral) the open space before it was full of people A shout went up, and was followed by the clash of gongs all up the river. From a point above two little brass six-pounders were discharged, and the round-shot came skipping down the empty reach, spurting glittering jets of water in the sunshine. In front of the mosque a shouting lot of men began firing in volleys that whipped athwart the current of the river; an irregular, rolling fusillade was opened on the boat from both banks, and Brown's men replied with a wild, rapid fire. The oars had been got in.

'The turn of the tide at high water comes on very quick in that river, and the boat in midstream, nearly hidden in smoke, began to drift back stern foremost. Along both shores the smoke thickened also, lying below the roofs in a level streak as you may see a long cloud cutting the slope of a mountain. A tumult of war-cries, the vibrating clang of gongs, the deep snoring of drums, yells of rage, crashes of volley-firing, made an awful din, in which Brown sat confounded but steady at the tiller, working himself into a fury of hate and rage against those people who dared to defend themselves. Two of his men had been wounded, and he saw his retreat cut off below the town by some boats that had put off from Tunku Allang's stockade. There were six of them full of men. While he was thus beset he perceived the entrance of the narrow creek (the same which Jim had jumped at low water). It was then brim full. Steering the long-boat in, they landed, and, to make a long story short, they established themselves on a little knoll about 900 yards from the stockade, which, in fact, they commanded from that position. The slopes of the knoll were bare, but there were a few trees on the summit. They went to work cutting these down for a breastwork, and were fairly entrenched before dark; meantime the Rajah's boats remained in the river with curious neutrality. When the sun set the glare of many brushwood blazes lighted on the river-front, and between the double line of houses on the land side threw into black relief the roofs, the groups of slender palms, the heavy clumps of fruit-trees. Brown ordered the grass round his position to be fired; a low ring of thin flames under the slow, ascending smoke wriggled rapidly down the slopes of the knoll; here and there a dry bush caught with a tall, vicious roar. The conflagration made a clear zone of fire for the rifles of the small party, and expired smouldering on the edge of the forests and along the muddy bank of the creek. A strip of jungle luxuriating in a damp hollow between the knoll and the Rajah's stockade stopped it on that side with a great crackling and detonations of bursting bamboo stems. The sky was sombre, velvety, and swarming with stars. The blackened ground smoked quietly with low creeping wisps, till a little breeze came on and blew everything away. Brown expected an attack to be delivered as soon as the tide had flowed enough again to enable the war-boats which had cut off his retreat to enter the creek. At any rate he was sure there would be an attempt to carry off his long-boat, which lay below the hill, a dark high lump on the feeble sheen of a wet mud-flat. But no move of any sort was made by the boats in the river. Over the stockade and the Rajah's buildings Brown saw their lights on the water. They seemed to be anchored across the stream. Other lights afloat were moving in the reach, crossing and recrossing from side to side. There were also lights twinkling motionless upon the long walls of houses up the reach, as far as the bend, and more still beyond, others isolated inland. The loom of the big fires disclosed buildings, roofs, black piles as far as he could see. It was an immense place. The fourteen desperate invaders lying flat behind the felled trees raised their chins to look over at the stir of that town that seemed to extend up-river for miles and swarm with thousands of angry men. They did not speak to each other. Now and then they would hear a loud yell, or a single shot rang out, fired very far somewhere. But round their position everything was still, dark, silent. They seemed to be forgotten, as if the excitement keeping awake all the population had nothing to do with them, as if they had been dead already.'

Chapter 39

'All the events of that night have a great importance, since they brought about a situation which remained unchanged till Jim's return. Jim had been away in the interior for more than a week, and it was Dain Waris who had directed the first repulse. That brave and intelligent youth ("who knew how to fight after the manner of white men") wished to settle the business on hand, but his people were too much for him. He had not Jim's racial prestige and the reputation of invincible, supernatural power. He was not the visible, tangible incarnation of unfailing truth and of unfailing victory. Beloved, trusted, and admired as he was, he was still one of *them*, while Jim was one of *us*. Moreover, the white man, a tower of strength in himself, was invulnerable, while Dain Waris could be killed. Those unexpressed thoughts guided the opinions of the chief men of the town, who elected to assemble in Jim's fort for deliberation upon the emergency, as if expecting to find wisdom and courage in the dwelling of the absent white man. The shooting of Brown's ruffians was so far good, or lucky, that there had been half-a-dozen casualties amongst the defenders. The wounded were lying on the veranda tended by their women-folk. The women and children from the lower part of the town had been sent into the fort at the first alarm. There Jewel was in command, very efficient and high-spirited, obeyed by Jim's "own people", who, quitting in a body their little settlement under the stockade, had gone in to form the garrison. The refugees crowded round her; and through the whole affair, to the very disastrous last, she showed an extraordinary martial ardour. It was to her that Dain Waris had gone at once at the first intelligence of danger, for you must know that Jim was the only one in Patusan who possessed a store of gunpowder. Stein, with whom he had kept up intimate relations by letters, had obtained from the Dutch Government a special authorization to export five hundred kegs of it to Patusan. The powder-magazine was a small hut of rough logs covered entirely with earth, and in Jim's absence the girl had the key. In the council, held at eleven o'clock in the evening in Jim's dining-room, she backed up Waris's advice for immediate and vigorous action. I am told that she stood up by the side of Jim's empty chair at the head of the long table and made a warlike impassioned speech, which for the moment extorted murmurs of approbation from the assembled headmen. Old Doramin, who had not showed himself outside his own gate for more than a year, had been brought across with great difficulty. He was, of course, the chief man there. The temper of the council was very unforgiving, and the old man's word would have been decisive; but it is my opinion that, well aware of his son's fiery courage, he dared not pronounce the word. More dilatory counsels prevailed. A certain Haji Saman pointed out at great length that "these tyrannical and ferocious men had delivered themselves to a certain death in any case. They would stand fast on their hill and starve, or they would try to regain their boat and be shot from ambushes across the creek, or they would break and fly into the forest and perish singly there." He argued that by the use of proper stratagems these evil-minded strangers could be destroyed without the risk of a battle, and his words had a great weight, especially with the Patusan men proper. What unsettled the minds of the townsfolk was the failure of the Rajah's boats to act at the decisive moment. It was the diplomatic Kassim who represented the Rajah at the council. He spoke very little, listened smilingly, very friendly and impenetrable. During the sitting messengers kept arriving every few minutes almost, with reports of the invaders' proceedings. Wild and exaggerated rumours were flying: there was a large ship at the mouth of the river with big guns and many more men – some white, others with black skins and of bloodthirsty appearance. They were coming with many more boats to exterminate every living thing. A sense of near, incomprehensible danger affected the common people. At one moment there was a panic in the courtyard amongst the women; shrieking; a rush; children crying – Haji Saman went out to quiet them. Then a fort sentry fired at something moving on the river, and nearly killed a villager bringing in his women-folk in a canoe together with the best of his domestic utensils and a dozen fowls. This caused more confusion. Meantime the palaver inside Jim's house went on in the presence of the girl. Doramin sat fierce-faced, heavy, looking at the speakers in turn, and breathing slow like a bull. He didn't speak till the last, after Kassim had declared that the Rajah's boats would be called in because the men were required to defend his master's stockade. Dain Waris in his father's presence would offer no opinion, though the girl entreated him in Jim's name to speak out. She offered him Jim's own men in her anxiety to have these intruders driven out at once. He only shook his head, after a glance or two at Doramin. Finally, when the council broke up it had been decided that the houses nearest the creek should be strongly occupied to obtain the command of the enemy's boat. The boat itself was not to be interfered with openly, so that the robbers on the hill should be tempted to embark, when a well-directed fire would kill most of them, no doubt. To cut the escape of those who might survive, and to prevent more of them coming up, Dain Waris was ordered by Doramin to take an armed party of Bugis down the river to a certain spot ten miles below Patusan, and there form a camp on the shore and blockade the stream with the canoes. I don't believe for a moment that Doramin feared the arrival of fresh forces. My opinion is, that his conduct was guided solely by his wish to keep his son out of harm's way. To prevent a rush being made into the town the construction of a stockade was to be commenced at daylight at the end of the street on the left bank. The old *nakhoda* declared his intention to command there himself. A distribution of powder, bullets, and percussion caps was made immediately under the girl's supervision. Several messengers were to be despatched in different directions after Jim, whose exact whereabouts were unknown. These men started at dawn, but before that time Kassim had managed to open communications with the besieged Brown.

'That accomplished diplomatist and confidant of the Rajah, on leaving the fort to go back to his master, took into his boat Cornelius, whom he found slinking mutely amongst the people in the courtyard. Kassim had a little plan of his own and wanted him for an interpreter. Thus it came about that towards morning Brown, reflecting upon the desperate nature of his position, heard from the marshy overgrown hollow an amicable, quavering, strained voice crying – in English – for permission to come up, under a promise of personal safety and on a very important errand. He was overjoyed. If he was spoken to he was no longer a hunted wild beast. These friendly sounds took off at once the awful stress of vigilant watchfulness as of so many blind men not knowing whence the deathblow might come. He pretended a great reluctance. The voice declared itself "a white man. A poor, ruined, old man who had been living here for years." A mist, wet and chilly, lay on the slopes of the hill, and after some more shouting from one to the other, Brown called out, "Come on, then, but alone, mind!" As a matter of fact – he told me, writhing with rage at the recollection of his helplessness – it made no difference. They couldn't see more than a few yards before them, and no treachery could make their position worse. By-and-by Cornelius, in his week-day attire of a ragged dirty shirt and pants, barefooted, with a broken-rimmed pith hat on his head, was made out vaguely, sidling up to the defences, hesitating, stopping to listen in a peering posture. "Come along! You are safe," yelled Brown, while his men stared. All their hopes of life became suddenly centred in that dilapidated, mean new-comer, who in profound silence clambered clumsily over a felled tree-trunk, and shivering, with his sour mistrustful face, looked about at the knot of bearded, anxious, sleepless desperadoes.

'Half an hour's confidential talk with Cornelius opened Brown's eyes as to the home affairs of Patusan. He was on the alert at once. There were possibilities, immense possibilities; but before he would talk over Cornelius's proposals he demanded that some food should be sent up as a guarantee of good faith. Cornelius went off, creeping sluggishly down the hill on the side of the Rajah's palace, and after some delay a few of Tunku Allang's men came up, bringing a scanty supply of rice, chillies, and dried fish. This was immeasurably better than nothing. Later on Cornelius returned accompanying Kassim, who stepped out with an air of perfect good-humoured trustfulness, in sandals, and muffled up from neck to ankles in dark-blue sheeting. He shook hands with Brown discreetly, and the three drew aside for a conference. Brown's men, recovering their confidence, were slapping each other on the back, and cast knowing glances at their captain while they busied themselves with preparations for cooking.

'Kassim disliked Doramin and his Bugis very much, but he hated the new order of things still more. It had occurred to him that these whites, together with the Rajah's followers, could attack and defeat the Bugis before Jim's return. Then, he reasoned, general defection of the townsfolk was sure to follow, and the reign of the white man who protected poor people would be over. Afterwards the new allies could be dealt with. They would have no friends. The fellow was perfectly able to perceive the difference of character, and had seen enough of white men to know that these new-comers were outcasts, men without country. Brown preserved a stern and inscrutable demeanour. When he first heard Cornelius's voice demanding admittance, it brought merely the hope of a loophole for escape. In less than an hour other thoughts were seething in his head. Urged by an extreme necessity, he had come there to steal food, a few tons of rubber or gum maybe, perhaps a handful of dollars, and had found himself enmeshed by deadly dangers. Now in consequence of these overtures from Kassim he began to think of stealing the whole country. Some confounded fellow had apparently accomplished something of the kind – single-handed at that. Couldn't have done it very well though. Perhaps they could work together – squeeze everything dry and then go out quietly. In the course of his negotiations with Kassim he became aware that he was supposed to have a big ship with plenty of men outside. Kassim begged him earnestly to have this big ship with his many guns and men brought up the river without delay for the Rajah's service. Brown professed himself willing, and on this basis the negotiation was carried on with mutual distrust. Three times in the course of the morning the courteous and active Kassim went down to consult the Rajah and came up busily with his long stride. Brown, while bargaining, had a sort of grim enjoyment in thinking of his wretched schooner, with nothing but a heap of dirt in her hold, that stood for an armed ship, and a Chinaman and a lame ex-beachcomber of Levuka on board, who represented all his many men. In the afternoon he obtained further doles of food, a promise of some money, and a supply of mats for his men to make shelters for themselves. They lay down and snored, protected from the burning sunshine; but Brown, sitting fully exposed on one of the felled trees, feasted his eyes upon the view of the town and the river. There was much loot here. Cornelius, who had made himself at home in the camp, talked at his elbow, pointing out the localities, imparting advice, giving his own version of Jim's character, and commenting in his own fashion upon the events of the last three years. Brown, who, apparently indifferent and gazing away, listened with attention to every word, could not make out clearly what sort of man this Jim could be. "What's his name? Jim! Jim! That's not enough for a man's name." "They call him," said Cornelius, scornfully, "Tuan Jim here. As you may say Lord Jim." "What is he? Where does he come from?" inquired Brown. "What sort of man is he? Is he an Englishman?" "Yes, yes, he's an Englishman. I am an Englishman, too. From Malacca. He is a fool. All you have to do is to kill him and then you are king here. Everything belongs to him," explained Cornelius. "It strikes me he may be made to share with somebody before very long," commented Brown half aloud. "No, no. The proper way is to kill him the first chance you get, and then you can do what you like," Cornelius would insist earnestly. "I have lived for many years here, and I am giving you a friend's advice."

'In such converse and in gloating over the view of Patusan, which he had determined in his mind should become his prey, Brown whiled away most of the afternoon, his men, meantime, resting. On that day Dain Waris's fleet of canoes stole one by one under the shore farthest from the creek, and went down to close the river against his retreat. Of this Brown was not aware, and Kassim, who came up the knoll an hour before sunset, took good care not to enlighten him. He wanted the white man's ship to come up the river, and this news, he feared, would be discouraging. He was very pressing with Brown to send the "order", offering at the same time a trusty messenger, who for greater secrecy (as he explained) would make his way by land to the mouth of the river and deliver the "order" on board. After some reflection Brown judged it expedient to tear a page out of his pocket-book, on which he simply wrote, "We are getting on. Big job. Detain the man." The stolid youth selected by Kassim for that service performed it faithfully, and was rewarded by being suddenly tipped, head first, into the schooner's empty hold by the ex-beachcomber and the Chinaman, who thereupon hastened to put on the hatches. What become of him afterwards Brown did not say.'

Chapter 40

'Brown's object was to gain time by fooling with Kassim's diplomacy. For doing a real stroke of business he could not help thinking the white man was the person to work with. He could not imagine such a chap (who must be confoundedly clever after all to get hold of the natives like that) refusing a help that would do away with the necessity for slow, cautious, risky cheating, that imposed itself as the only possible line of conduct for a single-handed man. He, Brown, would offer him the power. No man could hesitate. Everything was coming to a clear understanding. Of course they would share. The idea of there being a fort – all ready to his hand – a real fort, with artillery (he knew this from Cornelius), excited him. Let him only once get in and ... He would impose modest conditions. Not too low, though. The man was no fool, it seemed. They would work like brothers till ... till the time came for a quarrel and a shot that would settle all accounts. With grim impatience of plunder he wished himself to be talking with the man now. The land already seemed to be his to tear to pieces, squeeze, and throw away. Meantime Kassim had to be fooled for the sake of food first – and for a second string. But the principal thing was to get something to eat from day to day. Besides, he was not averse to begin fighting on that Rajah's account, and teach a lesson to those people who had received him with shots. The lust of battle was upon him.

'I am sorry that I can't give you this part of the story, which of course I have mainly from Brown, in Brown's own words. There was in the broken, violent speech of that man, unveiling before me his thoughts with the very hand of Death upon his throat, an undisguised ruthlessness of purpose, a strange vengeful attitude towards his own past, and a blind belief in the righteousness of his will against all mankind, something of that feeling which could induce the leader of a horde of wandering cut-throats to call himself proudly the Scourge of God. No doubt the natural senseless ferocity which is the basis of such a character was exasperated by failure, ill-luck, and the recent privations, as well as by the desperate position in which he found himself; but what was most remarkable of all was this, that while he planned treacherous alliances, had already settled in his own mind the fate of the white man, and intrigued in an overbearing, offhand manner with Kassim, one could perceive that what he had really desired, almost in spite of himself, was to play havoc with that jungle town which had defied him, to see it strewn over with corpses and enveloped in flames. Listening to his pitiless, panting voice, I could imagine how he must have looked at it from the hillock, peopling it with images of murder and rapine. The part nearest to the creek wore an abandoned aspect, though as a matter of fact every house concealed a few armed men on the alert. Suddenly beyond the stretch of waste ground, interspersed with small patches of low dense bush, excavations, heaps of rubbish, with trodden paths between, a man, solitary and looking very small, strolled out into the deserted opening of the street between the shut-up, dark, lifeless buildings at the end. Perhaps one of the inhabitants, who had fled to the other bank of the river, coming back for some object of domestic use. Evidently he supposed himself quite safe at that distance from the hill on the other side of the creek. A light stockade, set up hastily, was just round the turn of the street, full of his friends. He moved leisurely. Brown saw him, and instantly called to his side the Yankee deserter, who acted as a sort of second in command. This lanky, loose-jointed fellow came forward, wooden-faced, trailing his rifle lazily. When he understood what was wanted from him a homicidal and conceited smile uncovered his teeth, making two deep folds down his sallow, leathery cheeks. He prided himself on being a dead shot. He dropped on one knee, and taking aim from a steady rest through the unlopped branches of a felled tree, fired, and at once stood up to look. The man, far away, turned his head to the report, made another step forward, seemed to hesitate, and abruptly got down on his hands and knees. In the silence that fell upon the sharp crack of the rifle, the dead shot, keeping his eyes fixed upon the quarry, guessed that "this there coon's health would never be a source of anxiety to his friends any more". The man's limbs were seen to move rapidly under his body in an endeavour to run on all-fours. In that empty space arose a multitudinous shout of dismay and surprise. The man sank flat, face down, and moved no more. "That showed them what we could do," said Brown to me. "Struck the fear of sudden death into them. That was what we wanted. They were two hundred to one, and this gave them something to think over for the night. Not one of them had an idea of such a long shot before. That beggar belonging to the Rajah scouted down-hill with his eyes hanging out of his head."

'As he was telling me this he tried with a shaking hand to wipe the thin foam on his blue lips. "Two hundred to one. Two hundred to one ... strike terror ... terror, terror, I tell you...." His own eyes were starting out of their sockets. He fell back, clawing the air with skinny fingers, sat up again, bowed and hairy, glared at me sideways like some man-beast of folklore, with open mouth in his miserable and awful agony before he got his speech back after that fit. There are sights one never forgets.

'Furthermore, to draw the enemy's fire and locate such parties as might have been hiding in the bushes along the creek, Brown ordered the Solomon

Islander to go down to the boat and bring an oar, as you send a spaniel after a stick into the water. This failed, and the fellow came back without a single shot having been fired at him from anywhere. "There's nobody," opined some of the men. It is "onnatural", remarked the Yankee. Kassim had gone, by that time, very much impressed, pleased, too, and also uneasy. Pursuing his tortuous policy, he had despatched a message to Dain Waris warning him to look out for the white men's ship, which, he had had information, was about to come up the river. He minimized its strength and exhorted him to oppose its passage. This double-dealing answered his purpose, which was to keep the Bugis forces divided and to weaken them by fighting. On the other hand, he had in the course of that day sent word to the assembled Bugis chiefs in town, assuring them that he was trying to induce the invaders to retire; his messages to the fort asked earnestly for powder for the Rajah's men. It was a long time since Tunku Allang had had ammunition for the score or so of old muskets rusting in their arm-racks in the audience-hall. The open intercourse between the hill and the palace unsettled all the minds. It was already time for men to take sides, it began to be said. There would soon be much bloodshed, and thereafter great trouble for many people. The social fabric of orderly, peaceful life, when every man was sure of tomorrow, the edifice raised by Jim's hands, seemed on that evening ready to collapse into a ruin reeking with blood. The poorer folk were already taking to the bush or flying up the river. A good many of the upper class judged it necessary to go and pay their court to the Rajah. The Rajah's youths jostled them rudely. Old Tunku Allang, almost out of his mind with fear and indecision, either kept a sullen silence or abused them violently for daring to come with empty hands: they departed very much frightened; only old Doramin kept his countrymen together and pursued his tactics inflexibly. Enthroned in a big chair behind the improvised stockade, he issued his orders in a deep veiled rumble, unmoved, like a deaf man, in the flying rumours.

'Dusk fell, hiding first the body of the dead man, which had been left lying with arms outstretched as if nailed to the ground, and then the revolving sphere of the night rolled smoothly over Patusan and came to a rest, showering the glitter of countless worlds upon the earth. Again, in the exposed part of the town big fires blazed along the only street, revealing from distance to distance upon their glares the falling straight lines of roofs, the fragments of wattled walls jumbled in confusion, here and there a whole hut elevated in the glow upon the vertical black stripes of a group of high piles; and all this line of dwellings, revealed in patches by the swaying flames, seemed to flicker tortuously away up-river into the gloom at the heart of the land. A great silence, in which the looms of successive fires played without noise, extended into the darkness at the foot of the hill; but the other bank of the river, all dark save for a solitary bonfire at the river-front before the fort, sent out into the air an increasing tremor that might have been the stamping of a multitude of feet, the hum of many voices, or the fall of an immensely distant waterfall. It was then, Brown confessed to me, while turning his back on his men, he sat looking at it all, that notwithstanding his disdain, his ruthless faith in himself, a feeling came over him that at last he had run his head against a stone wall. Had his boat been afloat at the time, he believed he would have tried to steal away, taking his chances of a long chase down the river and of starvation at sea. It was very doubtful whether he would have succeeded in getting away. However, he didn't try this. For another moment he had a passing thought of trying to rush the town, but he perceived very well that in the end he would find himself in the lighted street, where they would be shot down like dogs from the houses. They were two hundred to one – he thought, while his men, huddling round two heaps of smouldering embers, munched the last of the bananas and roasted the few yams they owed to Kassim's diplomacy. Cornelius sat amongst them dozing sulkily.

'Then one of the whites remembered that some tobacco had been left in the boat, and, encouraged by the impunity of the Solomon Islander, said he would go to fetch it. At this all the others shook off their despondency. Brown applied to, said, "Go, and be d—d to you," scornfully. He didn't think there was any danger in going to the creek in the dark. The man threw a leg over the tree-trunk and disappeared. A moment later he was heard clambering into the boat and then clambering out. "I've got it," he cried. A flash and a report at the very foot of the hill followed. "I am hit," yelled the man. "Look out, look out – I am hit," and instantly all the rifles went off. The hill squirted fire and noise into the night like a little volcano, and when Brown and the Yankee with curses and cuffs stopped the panic-stricken firing, a profound, weary groan floated up from the creek, succeeded by a plaint whose heart-rending sadness was like some poison turning the blood cold in the veins. Then a strong voice pronounced several distinct incomprehensible words somewhere beyond the creek. "Let no one fire," shouted Brown. "What does it mean?" ... "Do you hear on the hill? Do you hear? Do you hear?" repeated the voice three times. Cornelius translated, and then prompted the answer. "Speak," cried Brown, "we hear." Then the voice, declaiming in the sonorous inflated tone of a herald, and shifting continually on the edge of the vague waste-land, proclaimed that between the men of the Bugis nation living in Patusan and the white men on the hill and those with them, there would be no faith, no compassion, no speech, no peace. A bush rustled; a haphazard volley rang out. "Dam' foolishness," muttered the Yankee, vexedly grounding the butt. Cornelius translated. The wounded man below the hill, after crying out twice, "Take me up! take me up!" went on complaining in moans. While he had kept on the blackened earth of the slope and afterwards crouching in the boat, he had been safe enough. It seems that in his joy at finding tobacco he forgot himself and jumped out on her off-side, as it were. The white boat, lying high and dry, showed him up; the creek was no more than seven yards wide in that place, and there happened to be a man crouching in the bush on the other bank.

'He was a Bugis of Tondano only lately come to Patusan, and a relation of the man shot in the afternoon. That famous long shot had indeed appalled the beholders. The man in utter security had been struck down, in full view of his friends, dropping with a joke on his lips, and they seemed to see in the act an atrocity which had stirred a bitter rage. That relation of his, Si-Lapa by name, was then with Doramin in the stockade only a few feet away. You who know these chaps must admit that the fellow showed an unusual pluck by volunteering to carry the message, alone, in the dark. Creeping across the open ground, he had deviated to the left and found himself opposite the boat. He was startled when Brown's man shouted. He came to a sitting position with his gun to his shoulder, and when the other jumped out, exposing himself, he pulled the trigger and lodged three jagged slugs point-blank into the poor wretch's stomach. Then, lying flat on his face, he gave himself up for dead, while a thin hail of lead chopped and swished the bushes close on his right hand; afterwards he delivered his speech shouting, bent double, dodging all the time in cover. With the last word he leaped sideways, lay close for a while, and afterwards got back to the houses unharmed, having achieved on that night such a renown as his children will not willingly allow to die.

'And on the hill the forlorn band let the two little heaps of embers go out under their bowed heads. They sat dejected on the ground with compressed lips and downcast eyes, listening to their comrade below. He was a strong man and died hard, with moans now loud, now sinking to a strange confidential note of pain. Sometimes he shrieked, and again, after a period of silence, he could be heard muttering deliriously a long and unintelligible complaint. Never for a moment did he cease.

' "What's the good?" Brown had said unmoved once, seeing the Yankee, who had been swearing under his breath, prepare to go down. "That's so," assented the deserter, reluctantly desisting. "There's no encouragement for wounded men here. Only his noise is calculated to make all the others think too much of the hereafter, cap'n." "Water!" cried the wounded man in an extraordinarily clear vigorous voice, and then went off moaning feebly. "Ay, water. Water will do it," muttered the other to himself, resignedly. "Plenty by-and-by. The tide is flowing."

'At last the tide flowed, silencing the plaint and the cries of pain, and the dawn was near when Brown, sitting with his chin in the palm of his hand before Patusan, as one might stare at the unscaleable side of a mountain, heard the brief ringing bark of a brass six-pounder far away in town somewhere. "What's this?" he asked of Cornelius, who hung about him. Cornelius listened. A muffled roaring shout rolled down-river over the town; a big drum began to throb, and others responded, pulsating and droning. Tiny scattered lights began to twinkle in the dark half of the town, while the part lighted by the loom of fires hummed with a deep and prolonged murmur. "He has come," said Cornelius. "What? Already? Are you sure?" Brown asked. "Yes! yes! Sure. Listen to the noise." "What are they making that row about?" pursued Brown. "For joy," snorted Cornelius; "he is a very great man, but all the same, he knows no more than a child, and so they make a great noise to please him, because they know no better." "Look here," said Brown, "how is one to get at him?" "He shall come to talk to you," Cornelius declared. "What do you mean? Come down here strolling as it were?" Cornelius nodded vigorously in the dark. "Yes. He will come straight here and talk to you. He is just like a fool. You shall see what a fool he is." Brown was incredulous. "You shall see; you shall see," repeated Cornelius. "He is not afraid – not afraid of anything. He will come and order you to leave his people alone. Everybody must leave his people alone. He is like a little child. He will come to you straight." Alas! he knew Jim well – that "mean little skunk", as Brown called him to me. "Yes, certainly," he pursued with ardour, "and then, captain, you tell that tall man with a gun to shoot him. Just you kill him, and you shall frighten everybody so much that you can do anything you like with them afterwards – get what you like – go away when you like. Ha! ha! ha! Fine. . . ." He almost danced with impatience and eagerness; and Brown, looking over his shoulder at him, could see, shown up by the pitiless dawn, his men drenched with dew, sitting amongst the cold ashes and the litter of the camp, haggard, cowed, and in rags.'

CHAPTER 41

'To the very last moment, till the full day came upon them with a spring, the fires on the west bank blazed bright and clear; and then Brown saw in a knot of coloured figures motionless between the advanced houses a man in European clothes, in a helmet, all white. "That's him; look! look!" Cornelius said excitedly. All Brown's men had sprung up and crowded at his back with lustreless eyes. The group of vivid colours and dark faces with the white figure in the midst were observing the knoll. Brown could see naked arms being raised to shade the eyes and other brown arms pointing. What should he do? He looked around, and the forests that faced him on all sides walled the cock-pit of an unequal contest. He looked once more at his men. A contempt, a weariness, the desire of life, the wish to try for one more chance – for some other grave – struggled in his breast. From the outline the figure presented it seemed to him that the white man there, backed up by all the power of the land, was examining his position through binoculars. Brown jumped up on the log, throwing his arms up, the palms outwards. The coloured group closed round the white man, and fell back twice before he got clear of them, walking slowly alone. Brown remained standing on the log till Jim, appearing and disappearing between the patches of thorny scrub, had nearly reached the creek; then Brown jumped off and went down to meet him on his side.

'They met, I should think, not very far from the place, perhaps on the very spot, where Jim took the second desperate leap of his life – the leap that landed him into the life of Patusan, into the trust, the love, the confidence of the people. They faced each other across the creek, and with steady eyes tried to understand each other before they opened their lips. Their antagonism must have been expressed in their glances; I know that Brown hated Jim at first sight. Whatever hopes he might have had vanished at once. This was not the man he had expected to see. He hated him for this – and in a checked flannel shirt with sleeves cut off at the elbows, grey bearded, with a sunken, sun-blackened face – he cursed in his heart the other's youth and assurance, his clear eyes and his untroubled bearing. That fellow had got in a long way before him! He did not look like a man who would be willing to give anything for assistance. He had all the advantages on his side – possession, security, power; he was on the side of an overwhelming force! He was not hungry and desperate, and he did not seem in the least afraid. And there was something in the very neatness of Jim's clothes, from the white helmet to the canvas leggings and the pipe-clayed shoes, which in Brown's sombre, irritated eyes seemed to belong to things he had in the very shaping of his life condemned and flouted.

' "Who are you?" asked Jim at last, speaking in his usual voice. "My name's Brown," answered the other, loudly; "Captain Brown. What's yours?" and Jim after a little pause went on quietly, as if he had not heard: "What made you come here?" "You want to know," said Brown, bitterly. "It's easy to tell. Hunger. And what made you?"

' "The fellow started at this," said Brown, relating to me the opening of this strange conversation between those two men, separated only by the muddy bed of a creek, but standing on the opposite poles of that conception of life which includes all mankind – "The fellow started at this and got very red in the face. Too big to be questioned, I suppose. I told him that if he looked upon me as a dead man with whom you may take liberties, he himself was not a whit better off really. I had a fellow up there who had a bead drawn on him all the time, and only waited for a sign from me. There was nothing to be shocked at in this. He had come down of his own freewill. 'Let us agree,' said I, 'that we are both dead men, and let us talk on that basis, as equals. We are all equal before death,' I said. I admitted I was there like a rat in a trap, but we had been driven to it, and even a trapped rat can give a bite. He caught me up in a moment. 'Not if you don't go near the trap till the rat is dead.' I told him that sort of game was good enough for these native friends of his, but I would have thought him too white to serve even a rat so. Yes, I had wanted to talk with him. Not to beg for my life, though. My fellows were – well – what they were – men like himself, anyhow. All we wanted from him was to come on in the devil's name and have it out. 'God d—n it,' said I, while he stood there as still as a wooden post, 'you don't want to come out here every day with your glasses to count how many of us are left on our feet. Come. Either bring your infernal crowd along or let us go out and starve in the open sea, by God! You have been white once, for all your tall talk of this being your own people and you being one with them. Are you? And what the devil do you get for it; what is it you've found here that is so d—d precious? Hey? You don't want us to come down here perhaps – do you? You are two hundred to one. You don't want us to come down into the open. Ah! I promise you we shall give you some sport before you've done. You talk about me making a cowardly set upon unoffending people. What's that to me that they are unoffending when I am starving for next to no offence? But I am not a coward. Don't you be one. Bring them along or, by all the fiends, we shall yet manage to send half your unoffending town to heaven with us in smoke!' "

'He was terrible – relating this to me – this tortured skeleton of a man drawn up together with his face over his knees, upon a miserable bed in that wretched hovel, and lifting his head to look at me with malignant triumph.

' "That's what I told him – I knew what to say," he began again, feebly at first, but working himself up with incredible speed into a fiery utterance of his scorn. "We aren't going into the forest to wander like a string of living skeletons dropping one after another for ants to go to work upon us before we are fairly dead. Oh, no! . . . 'You don't deserve a better fate,' he said. 'And what do you deserve?' I shouted at him, 'you that I find skulking here with your mouth full of your responsibility, of innocent lives, of your infernal duty? What do you know more of me than I know of you? I came here for food. D'ye hear? – food to fill our bellies. And what did *you* come for? What did you ask for when you came here? We don't ask you for anything but to give us a fight or a clear road to go back whence we came. . . .' 'I would fight with you now,' says he, pulling at his little moustache. 'And I would let you shoot me, and welcome,' I said. 'This is as good a jumping-off place for me as another. I am sick of my infernal luck. But it would be too easy. There are my men in the same boat – and, by God, I am not the sort to jump out of trouble and leave them in a d—d lurch,' I said. He stood thinking for a while and then wanted to know what I had done ('out there', he says, tossing his head down-stream) to be hazed about so. 'Have we met to tell each other the story of our lives?' I asked him. 'Suppose you begin. No? Well, I am sure I don't want to hear. Keep it to yourself. I know it is no better than mine. I've lived – and so did you though you talk as if you were one of those people that should have wings so as to go about without touching the dirty earth. Well – it is dirty. I haven't got any wings. I am here because I was afraid once in my life. Want to know what of? Of a prison. That scares me, and you may know it – if it's any good to you. I won't ask you what scared you into this infernal hole, where you seem to have found pretty pickings. That's your luck and this is mine – the privilege to beg for the favour of being shot quickly, or else kicked out to go free and starve in my own way." ' . . .

'His debilitated body shook with an exultation so vehement, so assured, and so malicious that it seemed to have driven off the death waiting for him in that hut. The corpse of his mad self-love uprose from rags and destitution as from the dark horrors of a tomb. It is impossible to say how much he lied to Jim then, how much he lied to me now – and to himself always. Vanity plays lurid tricks with our memory, and the truth of every passion wants some pretence to make it live. Standing at the gate of the other world in the guise of a beggar, he had slapped this world's face, he had spat upon it, he had thrown upon it an immensity of scorn and revolt at the bottom of his misdeeds. He had overcome them all – men, women, savages, traders, ruffians, missionaries – and Jim – that beefy-faced beggar. I did not begrudge him this triumph *in articulo mortis*, this almost posthumous illusion of having trampled all the earth under his feet. While he was boasting to me, in his sordid and repulsive agony, I couldn't help thinking of the chuckling talk relating to the time of his greatest splendour when, during a year or more, Gentleman Brown's ship was to be seen, for many days on end, hovering off an islet befringed with green upon azure, with the dark dot of the mission-house on a white beach; while Gentleman Brown, ashore, was casting his spells over a romantic girl for whom Melanesia had been too much, and giving hopes of a remarkable conversion to her husband. The poor man, some time or other, had been heard to express the intention of winning "Captain Brown to a better way of life".... "Bag Gentleman Brown for Glory" – as a leery-eyed loafer expressed it once – "just to let them see up above what a Western Pacific trading skipper looks like." And this was the man, too, who had run off with a dying woman, and had shed tears over her body. "Carried on like a big baby," his then mate was never tired of telling, "and where the fun came in may I be kicked to death by diseased Kanakas if *I* know. Why, gents! she was too far gone when he brought her aboard to know him; she just lay there on her back in his bunk staring at the beam with awful shining eyes – and then she died. Dam' bad sort of fever, I guess...." I remembered all these stories while, wiping his matted lump of a beard with a livid hand, he was telling me from his noisome couch how he got round, got in, got home, on that confounded, immaculate, don't-you-touch-me sort of fellow. He admitted that he couldn't be scared, but there was a way, "as broad as a turnpike, to get in and shake his twopenny soul around and inside out and upside down – by God!" '

CHAPTER 42

'I don't think he could do more than perhaps look upon that straight path. He seemed to have been puzzled by what he saw, for he interrupted himself in his narrative more than once to exclaim, "He nearly slipped from me there. I could not make him out. Who was he?" And after glaring at me wildly he would go on, jubilating and sneering. To me the conversation of these two across the creek appears now as the deadliest kind of duel on which Fate looked on with her cold-eyed knowledge of the end. No, he didn't turn Jim's soul inside out, but I am much mistaken if the spirit so utterly out of his reach had not been made to taste to the full the bitterness of that contest. These were the emissaries with whom the world he had renounced was pursuing him in his retreat. White men from "out there" where he did not think himself good enough to live. This was all that came to him – a menace, a shock, a danger to his work. I suppose it is this sad, half-resentful, half-resigned feeling, piercing through the few words Jim said now and then, that puzzled Brown so much in the reading of his character. Some great men owe most of their greatness to the ability of detecting in those they desire for their tools the exact quality of strength that matters for their work, and Brown, as though he had been really great, had a satanic gift of finding out the best and the weakest spot in his victims. He admitted to me that Jim wasn't of the sort that can be got over by truckling, and accordingly he took care to show himself as a man confronting without dismay ill-luck, censure, and disaster. The smuggling of a few guns was no great crime, he pointed out. As to coming to Patusan, who had the right to say he hadn't come to beg? The infernal people here let loose at him from both banks without staying to ask questions. He made the point brazenly, for, in truth, Dain Waris's energetic action had prevented the greatest calamities; because Brown told me distinctly that, perceiving the size of the place, he had resolved instantly in his mind that as soon as he had gained a footing he would set fire right and left, and begin by shooting down everything living in sight, in order to cow and terrify the population. The disproportion of forces was so great that this was the only way giving him the slightest chance of attaining his ends – he argued in a fit of coughing. But he didn't tell Jim this. As to the hardships and starvation they had gone through, these had been very real; it was enough to look at his band. He made, at the sound of a shrill whistle, all his men appear standing in a row on the logs in full view, so that Jim could see them. For the killing of the man, it had been done – well, it had – but was not this war, bloody war – in a corner? and the fellow had been killed cleanly, shot through the chest, not like that poor devil of his lying now in the creek. They had to listen to him dying for six hours, with his entrails torn with slugs. At any rate this was a life for a life. . . . And all this was said with the weariness, with the recklessness of a man spurred on and on by ill-luck till he cares not where he runs. When he asked Jim, with a sort of brusque despairing frankness, whether he himself – straight now – didn't understand that when "it came to saving one's life in the dark, one didn't care who else went – three, thirty, three hundred people" – it was as if a demon had been whispering advice in his ear. "I made him wince," boasted Brown to me. "He very soon left off coming the righteous over me. He just stood there with nothing to say, and looking as black as thunder – not at me – on the ground." He asked Jim whether he had nothing fishy in his life to remember that he was so damnedly hard upon a man trying to get out of a deadly hole by the first means that came to hand – and so on, and so on. And there ran through the rough talk a vein of subtle reference to their common blood, an assumption of common experience; a sickening suggestion of common guilt, of secret knowledge that was like a bond of their minds and of their hearts.

'At last Brown threw himself down full length and watched Jim out of the corners of his eyes. Jim on his side of the creek stood thinking and switching his leg. The houses in view were silent, as if a pestilence had swept them clean of every breath of life; but many invisible eyes were turned, from within, upon the two men with the creek between them, a stranded white boat, and the body of the third man half sunk in the mud. On the river canoes were moving again, for Patusan was recovering its belief in the stability of earthly institutions since the return of the white lord. The right bank, the platforms of the houses, the rafts moored along the shores, even the roofs of bathing-huts, were covered with people that, far away out of earshot and almost out of sight, were straining their eyes towards the knoll beyond the Rajah's stockade. Within the wide irregular ring of forests broken in two places by the sheen of the river there was a silence. "Will you promise to leave the coast?" Jim asked. Brown lifted and let fall his hand, giving everything up as it were – accepting the inevitable. "And surrender your arms?" Jim went on. Brown sat up and glared across. "Surrender our arms! Not till you come to take them out of our stiff hands. You think I am gone crazy with funk? Oh, no! That and the rags I stand in is all I have got in the world, besides a few more breechloaders on board; and I expect to sell the lot in Madagascar, if I ever get so far – begging my way from ship to ship."

'Jim said nothing to this. At last, throwing away the switch he held in his hand, he said, as if speaking to himself. "I don't know whether I have the power." . . . "You don't know! And you wanted me just now to give up my arms! That's good, too," cried Brown. "Suppose they say one thing to you, and do the other thing to me." He calmed down markedly. "I daresay you have the power, or what's the meaning of all this talk?" he continued. "What did you come down here for? To pass the time of day?"

' "Very well," said Jim, lifting his head suddenly after a long silence. "You shall have a clear road or else a clear fight." He turned on his heel and walked away.

'Brown got up at once, but he did not go up the hill till he had seen Jim disappear between the first houses. He never set his eyes on him again. On his way back he met Cornelius slouching down with his head between his shoulders. He stopped before Brown. "Why didn't you kill him?" he demanded in a sour, discontented voice. "Because I could do better than that," Brown said with an amused smile. "Never! never!" protested Cornelius with energy. "Couldn't. I have lived here for many years." Brown looked up at him curiously. There were many sides to the life of that place in arms against him; things he would never find out. Cornelius slunk past dejectedly in the direction of the river. He was now leaving his new friends; he accepted the disappointing course of events with a sulky obstinacy which seemed to draw more together his little yellow old face; and as he went down he glanced askant here and there, never giving up his fixed idea.

'Henceforth events move fast without a check, flowing from the very hearts of men like a stream from a dark source, and we see Jim amongst them, mostly through Tamb' Itam's eyes. The girl's eyes had watched him, too, but her life is too much entwined with his: there is her passion, her wonder, her anger, and, above all, her fear and her unforgiving love. Of the faithful servant, uncomprehending as the rest of them, it is the fidelity alone that comes into play; a fidelity and a belief in his lord so strong that even amazement is subdued to a sort of saddened acceptance of a mysterious failure. He has eyes only for one figure, and through all the mazes of bewilderment he preserves his air of guardianship, of obedience, of care.

'His master came back from his talk with the white men, walking slowly towards the stockade in the street. Everybody was rejoiced to see him return, for while he was away every man had been afraid not only of him being killed, but also of what he would come after. Jim went into one of the houses, where old Doramin had retired, and remained alone for a long time with the head of the Bugis settlers. No doubt he discussed the course to follow with him then, but no man was present at the conversation. Only Tamb' Itam, keeping as close to the door as he could, heard his master say, "Yes.

I shall let all the people know that such is my wish; but I spoke to you, O Doramin, before all the others, and alone; for you know my heart as well as I know yours and its greatest desire. And you know well also that I have no thought but for the people's good." Then his master, lifting the sheeting in the doorway, went out, and he, Tamb' Itam, had a glimpse of old Doramin within, sitting in the chair with his hands on his knees, and looking between his feet. Afterwards he followed his master to the fort, where all the principal Bugis and Patusan inhabitants had been summoned for a talk. Tamb' Itam himself hoped there would be some fighting. "What was it but the taking of another hill?" he exclaimed regretfully. However, in the town many hoped that the rapacious strangers would be induced by the sight of so many brave men making ready to fight, to go away. It would be a good thing if they went away. Since Jim's arrival had been made known before daylight by the gun fired from the fort and the beating of the big drum there, the fear that had hung over Patusan had broken and subsided like a wave on a rock, leaving the seething foam of excitement, curiosity, and endless speculation. Half of the population had been ousted out of their homes for purposes of defence, and were living in the street on the left side of the river, crowding round the fort, and in momentary expectation of seeing their abandoned dwellings on the threatened bank burst into flames. The general anxiety was to see the matter settled quickly. Food, through Jewel's care, had been served out to the refugees. Nobody knew what their white man would do. Some remarked that it was worse than in Sherif Ali's war. Then many people did not care; now everybody had something to lose. The movements of canoes passing to and fro between the two parts of the town were watched with interest. A couple of Bugis war-boats lay anchored in the middle of the stream to protect the river, and a thread of smoke stood at the bow of each; the men in them were cooking their midday rice when Jim, after his interviews with Brown and Doramin, crossed the river and entered by the water-gate of his fort. The people inside crowded round him so that he could hardly make his way to the house. They had not seen him before, because on his arrival during the night he had only exchanged a few words with the girl, who had come down to the landing-stage for the purpose, and had then gone on at once to join the chiefs and the fighting men on the other bank. People shouted greetings after him. One old woman raised a laugh by pushing her way to the front madly and enjoining him in a scolding voice to see to it that her two sons, who were with Doramin, did not come to harm at the hands of the robbers. Several of the bystanders tried to pull her away, but she struggled and cried, "Let me go. What is this, O Muslims? This laughter is unseemly. Are they not cruel, bloodthirsty robbers bent on killing?" "Let her be," said Jim, and as a silence fell suddenly, he said slowly, "Everybody shall be safe." He entered the house before the great sigh, and the loud murmurs of satisfaction, had died out.

'There's no doubt his mind was made up that Brown should have his way clear back to the sea. His fate, revolted, was forcing his hand. He had for the first time to affirm his will in the face of out-spoken opposition. "There was much talk, and at first my master was silent," Tamb' Itam said.

"Darkness came, and then I lit the candles on the long tables. The chiefs sat on each side, and the lady remained by my master's right hand."

'When he began to speak the unaccustomed difficulty seemed only to fix his resolve more immovably. The white men were now waiting for his answer on the hill. Their chief had spoken to him in the language of his own people, making clear many things difficult to explain in any other speech. They were erring men whom suffering had made blind to right and wrong. It is true that lives had been lost already, but why lose more? He declared to his hearers, the assembled heads of the people, that their welfare was his welfare, their losses his losses, their mourning his mourning. He looked round the grave listening faces and told them to remember that they had fought and worked side by side. They knew his courage . . . Here a murmur interrupted him . . . And that he had never deceived them. For many years they had dwelt together. He loved the land and the people living in it with a very great love. He was ready to answer with his life for any harm that should come to them if the white men with beards were allowed to retire. They were evil-doers, but their destiny had been evil, too. Had he ever advised them ill? Had his words ever brought suffering to the people? he asked. He believed that it would be best to let these whites and their followers go with their lives. It would be a small gift. "I whom you have tried and found always true ask you to let them go." He turned to Doramin. The old *nakhoda* made no movement. "Then," said Jim, "call in Dain Waris, your son, my friend, for in this business I shall not lead." '

CHAPTER 43

'Tamb' Itam behind his chair was thunderstruck. The declaration produced an immense sensation. "Let them go because this is best in my knowledge which has never deceived you," Jim insisted. There was a silence. In the darkness of the courtyard could be heard the subdued whispering, shuffling noise of many people. Doramin raised his heavy head and said that there was no more reading of hearts than touching the sky with the hand, but – he consented. The others gave their opinion in turn. "It is best", "Let them go", and so on. But most of them simply said that they "believed Tuan Jim".

'In this simple form of assent to his will lies the whole gist of the situation; their creed, his truth; and the testimony to that faithfulness which made him in his own eyes the equal of the impeccable men who never fall out of the ranks. Stein's words, "Romantic! – Romantic!" seem to ring over those distances that will never give him up now to a world indifferent to his failing and his virtues, and to that ardent and clinging affection that refuses him the dole of tears in the bewilderment of a great grief and of eternal separation. From the moment the sheer truthfulness of his last three years of life carries the day against the ignorance, the fear, and the anger of men, he appears no longer to me as I saw him last – a white speck catching all the dim light left upon a sombre coast and the darkened sea – but greater and more pitiful in the loneliness of his soul, that remains even for her who loved him best a cruel and insoluble mystery.

'It is evident he did not mistrust Brown; there was no reason to doubt the story, whose truth seemed warranted by the rough frankness, by a sort of virile sincerity in accepting the morality and the consequences of his acts. But Jim did not know the almost inconceivable egotism of the man which made him, when resisted and foiled in his will, mad with the indignant and revengeful rage of a thwarted autocrat. But if Jim did not mistrust Brown, he was evidently anxious that some misunderstanding should not occur, ending perhaps in collision and bloodshed. It was for this reason that directly the Malay chiefs had gone he asked Jewel to get him something to eat, as he was going out of the fort to take command in the town. On her remonstrating against this on the score of his fatigue, he said that something might happen for which he would never forgive himself. "I am responsible for every life in the land," he said. He was moody at first; she served him with her own hands, taking the plates and dishes (of the dinner-service presented him by Stein) from Tamb' Itam. He brightened up after a while; told her she would again be in command of the fort for another night. "There is no sleep for us, old girl," he said, "while our people are in danger." Later on he said jokingly that she was the best man of them all. "If you and Dain Waris had done what you wanted, not one of those poor devils would be alive today." "Are they very bad?" she asked, leaning over his chair. "Men act badly sometimes without being much worse than others," he said after some hesitation.

'Tamb' Itam followed his master to the landing-stage outside the fort. The night was clear, but without a moon, and the middle of the river was dark, while the water under each bank reflected the light of many fires "as on the night of Ramadan," Tamb' Itam said. War-boats drifted silently in the dark lane or, anchored, floated motionless with a loud ripple. That night there was much paddling in a canoe and walking at his master's heels for Tamb' Itam: up and down the street they tramped, where the fires were burning, inland on the outskirts of the town where small parties of men kept guard in the fields. Tuan Jim gave his orders and was obeyed. Last of all they went to the Rajah's stockade, which a detachment of Jim's people manned on that night. The old Rajah had fled early in the morning with most of his women to a small house he had near a jungle village on a tributary stream. Kassim, left behind, had attended the council with his air of diligent activity to explain away the diplomacy of the day before. He was considerably cold-shouldered, but managed to preserve his smiling, quiet alertness, and professed himself highly delighted when Jim told him sternly that he proposed to occupy the stockade on that night with his own men. After the council broke up he was heard outside accosting this and that departing chief, and speaking in a loud, gratified tone of the Rajah's property being protected in the Rajah's absence.

'About ten or so Jim's men marched in. The stockade commanded the

mouth of the creek, and Jim meant to remain there till Brown had passed
below. A small fire was lit on the flat, grassy point outside the wall of stakes,
and Tabm' Itam placed a little folding stool for his master. Jim told him to
try and sleep. Tamb' Itam got a mat and lay down a little way off; but he
could not sleep, though he knew he had to go on an important journey before
the night was out. His master walked to and fro before the fire with bowed
head and with his hands behind his back. His face was sad. Whenever his
master approached him Tamb' Itam pretended to sleep, not wishing his
master to know he had been watched. At last his master stood still, looking
down on him as he lay, and said softly, "It is time."

'Tamb' Itam arose directly and made his preparations. His mission was
to go down the river, preceding Brown's boat by an hour or more, to tell
Dain Waris finally and formally that the whites were to be allowed to pass
out unmolested. Jim would not trust anybody else with that service. Before
starting Tamb' Itam, more as a matter of form (since his position about Jim
made him perfectly known), asked for a token. "Because Tuan," he said,
"the message is important, and these are thy very words I carry." His master
first put his hand into one pocket, then into another, and finally took off his
forefinger Stein's silver ring, which he habitually wore, and gave it to Tamb'
Itam. When Tamb' Itam left on his mission, Brown's camp on the knoll was
dark but for a single small glow shining through the branches of one of the
trees the white men had cut down.

'Early in the evening Brown had received from Jim a folded piece of paper
on which was written, "You get the clear road. Start as soon as your boat
floats on the morning tide. Let your men be careful. The bushes on both
sides of the creek and the stockade at the mouth are full of well-armed men.
You would have no chance, but I don't believe you want bloodshed." Brown
read it, tore the paper into small pieces, and, turning to Cornelius, who had
brought it, said jeeringly, "Good-bye, my excellent friend." Cornelius had
been in the fort, and had been sneaking around Jim's house during the
afternoon. Jim chose him to carry the note because he could speak English,
was known to Brown, and was not likely to be shot by some nervous mistake
of one of the men as a Malay, approaching in the dusk, perhaps might have
been.

'Cornelius didn't go away after delivering the paper. Brown was sitting
up over a tiny fire; all the others were lying down. "I could tell you something
you would like to know," Cornelius mumbled crossly. Brown paid no
attention. "You did not kill him," went on the other, "and what do you get
for it? You might have had money from the Rajah, besides the loot of all the
Bugis houses, and now you get nothing." "You had better clear out from
here," growled Brown, without even looking at him. But Cornelius let
himself drop by his side and began to whisper very fast, touching his elbow
from time to time. What he had to say made Brown sit up at first, with a
curse. He had simply informed him of Dain Waris's armed party down the
river. At first Brown saw himself completely sold and betrayed, but a
moment's reflection convinced him that there could be no treachery intended.
He said nothing, and after a while, Cornelius remarked, in a tone of complete
indifference, that there was another way out of the river which he knew

very well. "A good thing to know, too," said Brown, pricking up his ears; and Cornelius began to talk of what went on in town and repeated all that had been said in council, gossiping in an even undertone at Brown's ear as you talk amongst sleeping men you do not wish to wake. "He thinks he has made me harmless, does he?" mumbled Brown very low ... "Yes. He is a fool. A little child. He came here and robbed me," droned on Cornelius, "and he made all the people believe him. But if something happened that they did not believe him any more, where would he be? And the Bugis Dain who is waiting for you down the river there, captain, is the very man who chased you up here when you first came." Brown observed nonchalantly that it would be just as well to avoid him, and with the same detached, musing air, Cornelius declared himself acquainted with a backwater broad enough to take Brown's boat past Waris's camp. "You will have to be quiet," he said as an afterthought, "for in one place we pass close behind his camp. Very close. They are camped ashore with their boat hauled up." "Oh, we know how to be as quiet as mice; never fear," said Brown. Cornelius stipulated that in case he were to pilot Brown out, his canoe should be towed. "I'll have to get back quick," he explained.

'It was two hours before the dawn when word was passed to the stockade from outlying watchers that the white robbers were coming down to their boat. In a very short time every armed man from one end of Patusan to the other was on the alert, yet the banks of the river remained so silent that but for the fires burning with sudden blurred flares the town might have been asleep as if in peace-time. A heavy mist lay very low on the water, making a sort of illusive grey light that showed nothing. When Brown's long-boat glided out of the creek into the river, Jim was standing on the low point of land before the Rajah's stockade – on the very spot where for the first time he put his foot on Patusan shore. A shadow loomed up, moving in the greyness, solitary, very bulky, and yet constantly eluding the eye. A murmur of low talking came out of it. Brown at the tiller heard Jim speak calmly: "A clear road. You had better trust to the current while the fog lasts; but this will lift presently." "Yes, presently we shall see clear," replied Brown.

'The thirty or forty men standing with muskets at ready outside the stockade held their breath. The Bugis owner of the prau, whom I saw on Stein's veranda, and who was amongst them, told me that the boat, shaving the low point close, seemed for a moment to grow big and hang over it like a mountain. "If you think it worth your while to wait a day outside," called out Jim, "I'll try to send you down something – bullocks, some yams – what I can." The shadow went on moving. "Yes. Do," said a voice, blank and muffled out of the fog. Not one of the many attentive listeners understood what the words meant; and then Brown and his men in their boat floated away, fading spectrally without the slightest sound.

'Thus Brown, invisible in the mist, goes out of Patusan elbow to elbow with Cornelius in the sternsheets of the long-boat. "Perhaps you shall get a small bullock," said Cornelius. "Oh, yes. Bullock. Yam. You'll get it if *he* says so. He always speaks the truth. He stole everything I had. I suppose you like a small bullock better than the loot of many houses." "I would advise you to hold your tongue, or somebody here may fling you overboard into this damned fog," said Brown. The boat seemed to be standing still; nothing could be seen, not even the river alongside, only the water-dust flew and trickled, condensed, down their beards and faces. It was weird, Brown told me. Every individual man of them felt as though he were adrift alone in a boat, hunted by an almost imperceptible suspicion of sighing, muttering ghosts. "Throw me out, would you? But I would know where I was," mumbled Cornelius, surlily. "I've lived many years here." "Not long enough to see through a fog like this," Brown said, lolling back with his arm swinging to and fro on the useless tiller. "Yes. Long enough for that," snarled Cornelius. "That's very useful," commented Brown. "Am I to believe you could find that backway you spoke of blindfold, like this?" Cornelius grunted. "Are you too tired to row?" he asked after a silence. "No, by God!" shouted Brown suddenly. "Out with your oars there." There was a great knocking in the fog, which after a while settled into a regular grind of invisible sweeps against invisible thole-pins. Otherwise nothing was changed, and but for the slight splash of a dipped blade it was like rowing a balloon car in a cloud, said Brown. Thereafter Cornelius did not open his lips except to ask querulously for somebody to bale out his canoe, which was towing behind the long-boat. Gradually the fog whitened and became luminous ahead. To the left Brown saw a darkness as though he had been looking at the back of the departing night. All at once a big bough covered with leaves appeared above his head, and ends of twigs, dripping and still, curved slenderly close alongside. Cornelius, without a word, took the tiller from his hand.'

CHAPTER 44

'I don't think they spoke together again. The boat entered a narrow by-channel, where it was pushed by the oar-blades set into crumbling banks, and there was a gloom as if enormous black wings had been outspread above the mist that filled its depth to the summit of the trees. The branches overhead showered big drops through the gloomy fog. At a mutter from Cornelius, Brown ordered his men to load. "I'll give you a chance to get even with them before we're done, you dismal cripples you," he said to his gang. "Mind you don't throw it away – you hounds." Low growls answered that speech. Cornelius showed much fussy concern for the safety of his canoe.

'Meantime Tamb' Itam had reached the end of his journey. The fog delayed him a little, but he had paddled steadily, keeping in touch with the south bank. By-and-by daylight came like a glow in a ground glass globe. The shores made on each side of the river a dark smudge, in which one could detect hints of columnar forms and shadows of twisted branches high up. The mist was still thick on the water, but a good watch was being kept, for as Tamb' Itam approached the camp the figures of two men emerged out

of the white vapour, and voices spoke to him boisterously. He answered, and
presently a canoe lay alongside, and he exchanged news with the paddlers.
All was well. The trouble was over. Then the men in the canoe let go their
grip on the side of his dug-out and incontinently fell out of sight. He pursued
his way till he heard voices coming to him quietly over the water, and saw,
under the now lifting, swirling mist, the glow of many little fires burning
on a sandy stretch, backed by lofty thin timber and bushes. There again a
look-out was kept, for he was challenged. He shouted his name as the two
last sweeps of his paddle ran his canoe up on the strand. It was a big camp.
Men crouched in many knots under a subdued murmur of early morning
talk. Many thin threads of smoke curled slowly on the white mist. Little
shelters, elevated above the ground, had been built for the chiefs. Muskets
were stacked in small pyramids, and long spears were stuck singly into the
sand near the fires.

'Tamb' Itam, assuming an air of importance, demanded to be led to Dain
Waris. He found the friend of his white lord lying on a raised couch made
of bamboo, and sheltered by a sort of shed of sticks covered with mats. Dain
Waris was awake, and a bright fire was burning before his sleeping-place,
which resembled a rude shrine. The only son of Nakhoda Doramin answered
his greeting kindly. Tamb' Itam began by handing him the ring which
vouched for the truth of the messenger's words. Dain Waris, reclining on
his elbow, bade him speak and tell all the news. Beginning with the
consecrated formula, "The news is good," Tamb' Itam delivered Jim's own
words. The white men, departing with the consent of all the chiefs, were to
be allowed to pass down the river. In answer to a question or two Tamb'
Itam then reported the proceedings of the last council. Dain Waris listened
attentively to the end, toying with the ring which ultimately he slipped on
the forefinger of his right hand. After hearing all he had to say he dismissed
Tamb' Itam to have food and rest. Orders for the return in the afternoon
were given immediately. Afterwards Dain Waris lay down again, open-
eyed, while his personal attendants were preparing his food at the fire, by
which Tamb' Itam also sat talking to the men who lounged up to hear the
latest intelligence from the town. The sun was eating up the mist. A good
watch was kept upon the reach of the main stream where the boat of the
whites was expected to appear every moment.

'It was then that Brown took his revenge upon the world which, after
twenty years of contemptuous and reckless bullying refused him the tribute
of a common robber's success. It was an act of cold-blooded ferocity, and it
consoled him on his deathbed like a memory of an indomitable defiance.
Stealthily he landed his men on the other side of the island opposite to the
Bugis camp, and led them across. After a short but quite silent scuffle,
Cornelius who had tried to slink away at the moment of landing, resigned
himself to show the way where the undergrowth was most sparse. Brown
held both his skinny hands together behind his back in the grip of one vast
fist, and now and then impelled him forward with a fierce push. Cornelius
remained as mute as a fish, abject but faithful to his purpose, whose
accomplishment loomed before him dimly. At the edge of the patch of forest
Brown's men spread themselves out in cover and waited. The camp was

plain from end to end before their eyes, and no one looked their way. Nobody even dreamed that the white men could have any knowledge of the narrow channel at the back of the island. When he judged the moment come, Brown yelled, "Let them have it," and fourteen shots rang out like one.

'Tamb' Itam told me the surprise was so great that, except for those who fell dead or wounded, not a soul of them moved for quite an appreciable time after the first discharge. Then a man screamed, and after that scream a great yell of amazement and fear went up from all the throats. A blind panic drove these men in a surging swaying mob to and fro along the shore like a herd of cattle afraid of the water. Some few jumped into the river then, but most of them did so only after the last discharge. Three times Brown's men fired into the ruck, Brown, the only one in view, cursing and yelling, "Aim low! aim low!"

'Tamb' Itam says that, as for him, he understood at the first volley what had happened. Though untouched he fell down and lay as if dead, but with his eyes open. At the sound of the first shots Dain Waris, reclining on the couch, jumped up and ran out upon the open shore, just in time to receive a bullet in his forehead at the second discharge. Tamb' Itam saw him fling his arms wide open before he fell. Then, he says, a great fear came upon him – not before. The white men retired as they had come – unseen.

'Thus Brown balanced his account with the evil fortune. Notice that even in this awful outbreak there is a superiority as of a man who carries right – the abstract thing – within the envelope of his common desires. It was not a vulgar and treacherous massacre; it was a lesson, a retribution – a demonstration of some obscure and awful attribute of our nature which, I am afraid, is not so very far under the surface as we like to think.

'Afterwards the whites depart unseen by Tamb' Itam, and seem to vanish from before men's eyes altogether; and the schooner, too, vanishes after the manner of stolen goods. But a story is told of a white long-boat picked up a month later in the Indian Ocean by a cargo-steamer. Two parched, yellow, glassy-eyed whispering skeletons in her recognized the authority of a third, who declared that his name was Brown. His schooner, he reported, bound south with a cargo of Java sugar, had sprung a bad leak and sank under his feet. He and his companions were the survivors of a crew of six. The two died on board the steamer which rescued them. Brown lived to be seen by me, and I can testify that he had played his part to the last.

'It seems, however, that in going away they had neglected to cast off Cornelius's canoe, Cornelius himself Brown had let go at the beginning of the shooting, with a kick for a parting benediction. Tamb' Itam, after arising from amongst the dead, saw the Nazarene running up and down the shore amongst the corpses and the expiring fires. He uttered little cries. Suddenly he rushed to the water, and made frantic efforts to get one of the Bugis boats into the water. "Afterwards, till he had seen me," related Tamb' Itam, "he stood looking at the heavy canoe and scratching his head." "What became of him?" I asked. Tamb' Itam, staring at me, made an expressive gesture with his right arm. "Twice I struck, Tuan," he said. "When he beheld me approaching he cast himself violently on the ground and made a great outcry, kicking. He screeched like a frightened hen till he felt the point; then he was still, and lay staring at me while his life went out of his eyes."

'This done, Tamb' Itam did not tarry. He understood the importance of being the first with the awful news at the fort. There were, of course, many survivors of Dain Waris's party; but in the extremity of panic some had swum across the river, others had bolted into the bush. The fact is that they did not know really who struck that blow – whether more white robbers were not coming, whether they had not already got hold of the whole land. They imagined themselves to be the victims of a vast treachery, and utterly doomed to destruction. It is said that some small parties did not come in till three days afterwards. However, a few tried to make their way back to Patusan at once, and one of the canoes that were patrolling the river that morning was in sight of the camp at the very moment of the attack. It is true that at first the men in her leaped overboard and swam to the opposite bank, but afterwards they returned to their boat and started fearfully upstream. Of these Tamb' Itam had an hour's advance.'

CHAPTER 45

'When Tamb' Itam, paddling madly, came into the town-reach, the women, thronging the platforms before the houses, were looking out for the return of Dain Waris's little fleet of boats. The town had a festive air; here and there men, still with spears or guns in their hands, could be seen moving or standing on the shore in groups. Chinamen's shops had been opened early; but the market-place was empty, and a sentry, still posted at the corner of the fort, made out Tamb' Itam, and shouted to those within. The gate was wide open. Tamb' Itam jumped ashore and ran in headlong. The first person he met was the girl coming down from the house.

'Tamb' Itam, disordered, panting, with trembling lips and wild eyes, stood for a time before her as if a sudden spell had been laid on him. Then he broke out very quickly: "They have killed Dain Waris and many more." She clapped her hands, and her first words were, "Shut the gates." Most of the fort-men had gone back to their houses, but Tamb' Itam hurried on the few who remained for their turn of duty within. The girl stood in the middle of the courtyard while the others ran about. "Doramin," she cried despairingly, as Tamb' Itam passed her. Next time he went by he answered her thought rapidly, "Yes. But we have all the powder in Patusan." She caught him by the arm, and, pointing at the house, "Call him out," she whispered, trembling.

'Tamb' Itam ran up the steps. His master was sleeping. "It is I, Tamb' Itam,' he cried at the door, "with tidings that cannot wait." He saw Jim turn over on the pillow and open his eyes, and he burst out at once. "This, Tuan, is a day of evil, an accursed day." His master raised himself on his elbow to listen – just as Dain Waris had done. And then Tamb' Itam began his tale, trying to relate the story in order, calling Dain Waris Panglima, and saying: "The Panglima then called out to the chief of his own boatman, 'Give Tamb' Itam something to eat' " – when his master put his feet to the ground and looked at him with such a discomposed face that the words remained in his throat.

' "Speak out," said Jim. "Is he dead?" "May you live long," cried Tamb' Itam. "It was a most cruel treachery. He ran out at the first shots and fell" . . . His master walked to the window and with his fist struck at the shutter. The room was made light; and then in a steady voice, but speaking fast, he began to give him orders to assemble a fleet of boats for immediate pursuit, go to this man, to the other – send messengers; and as he talked he sat down on the bed, stopping to lace his boots hurriedly, and suddenly looked up. "Why do you stand here?" he asked, very red-faced. "Waste no time." Tamb' Itam did not move. "Forgive me, Tuan, but . . . but," he began to stammer. "What?" cried his master aloud, looking terrible, leaning forward with his hands gripping the edge of the bed. "It is not safe for thy servant to go out amongst the people," said Tamb' Itam, after hesitating a moment.

'Then Jim understood. He had retreated from one world, for a small matter of an impulsive jump, and now the other, the work of his own hands, had fallen in ruins upon his head. It was not safe for his servant to go out amongst his own people! I believe that in that very moment he had decided to defy the disaster in the only way it occurred to him such a disaster could be defied; but all I know is that, without a word, he came out of his room and sat before the long table, at the head of which he was accustomed to regulate the affairs of his world, proclaiming daily the truth that surely lived in his heart. The dark powers should not rob him twice of his peace. He sat like a stone figure. Tamb' Itam, deferential, hinted at preparations for defence. The girl he loved came in and spoke to him, but he made a sign with his hand, and she was awed by the dumb appeal for silence in it. She went out on the veranda and sat on the threshold, as if to guard him with her body from dangers outside.

'What thoughts passed through his head – what memories? Who can tell? Everything was gone, and he who had been once unfaithful to his trust had lost again all men's confidence. It was then, I believe, he tried to write – to somebody – and gave it up. Loneliness was closing on him. People had trusted him with their lives – only for that; and yet they could never, as he had said, never be made to understand him. Those without did not hear him make a sound. Later, towards the evening, he came to the door and called for Tamb' Itam. "Well?" he asked. "There is much weeping. Much anger, too," said Tamb' Itam. Jim looked up at him. "You know?" he murmured. "Yes, Tuan," said Tamb' Itam. "Thy servant does know, and the gates are closed. We shall have to fight." "Fight! What for?" he asked. "For our lives." "I have no life," he said. Tamb' Itam heard a cry from the girl at the door. "Who knows?" said Tamb' Itam. "By audacity and cunning we may even escape. There is much fear in men's hearts, too." He went out, thinking vaguely of boats and of open sea, leaving Jim and the girl together.

'I haven't the heart to set down here such glimpses as she had given me of the hour or more she had passed in there wrestling with him for the possession of her happiness. Whether he had any hope – what he expected, what he imagined – it is impossible to say. He was inflexible, and with the growing loneliness of his obstinacy his spirit seemed to rise above the ruins of his existence. She cried "Fight?" into his ear. She could not understand. There was nothing to fight for. He was going to prove his power in another way and conquer the fatal destiny itself. He came out into the courtyard, and behind him, with streaming hair, wild of face, breathless, she staggered out and leaned on the side of the doorway. "Open the gates," he ordered. Afterwards, turning to those of his men who were inside, he gave them leave to depart to their homes. "For how long, Tuan?" asked one of them timidly. "For all life," he said, in a sombre tone.

'A hush had fallen upon the town after the outburst of wailing and lamentation that had swept over the river, like a gust of wind from the opened abode of sorrow. But rumours flew in whispers, filling the hearts with consternation and horrible doubts. The robbers were coming back, bringing many others with them, in a great ship, and there would be no refuge in the land for anyone. A sense of utter insecurity as during an earthquake pervaded the minds of men, who whispered their suspicions, looking at each other as if in the presence of some awful portent.

'The sun was sinking towards the forests when Dain Waris's body was brought into Doramin's *campong*. Four men carried it in, covered decently with a white sheet which the old mother had sent out down to the gate to meet her son on his return. They laid him at Doramin's feet, and the old man sat still for a long time, one hand on each knee, looking down. The fronds of palms swayed gently, and the foliage of fruit-trees stirred above his head. Every single man of his people was there, fully armed, when the old *nakhoda* at last raised his eyes. He moved them slowly over the crowd, as if seeking for a missing face. Again his chin sank on his breast. The whispers of many men mingled with the slight rustling of the leaves.

'The Malay who had brought Tamb' Itam and the girl to Samarang was there, too. "Not so angry as many," he said to me, but struck with a great awe and wonder at the "suddenness of men's fate, which hangs over their heads like a cloud charged with thunder." He told me that when Dain Waris's body was uncovered at a sign of Doramin's, he whom they often called the white lord's friend was disclosed lying unchanged with his eyelids a little open as if about to wake. Doramin leaned forward a little more, like one looking for something fallen on the ground. His eyes searched the body from its feet to its head, for the wound maybe. It was in the forehead and small; and there was no word spoken while one of the bystanders, stooping, took off the silver ring from the cold stiff hand. In silence he held it up before Doramin. A murmur of dismay and horror ran through the crowd at the sight of that familiar token. The old *nakhoda* stared at it, and suddenly let out one great fierce cry, deep from the chest, a roar of pain and fury, as mighty as the bellow of a wounded bull, bringing great fear into men's hearts, by the magnitude of his anger and his sorrow that could be plainly discerned without words. There was a great stillness afterwards for a space, while the body was being borne aside by four men. They laid it down under a tree, and on the instant, with one long shriek, all the women of the household began to wail together; they mourned with shrill cries; the sun was setting, and in the intervals of screamed lamentations the high sing-song voices of two old men intoning the Koran chanted alone.

'About this time Jim, leaning on a gun-carriage, looked at the river, and turned his back on the house; and the girl, in the doorway, panting as if she had run herself to a standstill, was looking at him across the yard. Tamb' Itam stood not far from his master, waiting patiently for what might happen. All at once Jim, who seemed to be lost in quiet thought, turned to him and said, "Time to finish this."

' "Tuan?" said Tamb' Itam, advancing with alacrity. He did not know what his master meant, but as soon as Jim made a movement the girl started, too, and walked down into the open space. It seems that no one else of the people of the house was in sight. She tottered slightly, and about half-way down called out to Jim, who had apparently resumed his peaceful contemplation of the river. He turned round, setting his back against the gun. "Will you fight?" she cried. "There is nothing to fight for," he said; "nothing is lost." Saying this he made a step towards her. "Will you fly?" she cried again. "There is no escape," he said, stopping short, and she stood still also, silent, devouring him with her eyes. "And you shall go?" she said, slowly. He bent his head. "Ah!" she exclaimed, peering at him as it were, "you are mad or false. Do you remember the night I prayed you to leave me, and you said that you could not? That it was impossible! Impossible! Do you remember you said you would never leave me? Why? I asked you for no promise. You promised unasked – remember." "Enough, poor girl" he said. "I should not be worth having."

'Tamb' Itam said that while they were talking she would laugh loud and senselessly like one under the visitation of God. His master put his hands to his head. He was fully dressed as for every day, but without a hat. She stopped laughing suddenly. "For the last time," she cried, menacingly, "will you defend yourself?" "Nothing can touch me," he said in a last flicker of superb egoism. Tamb' Itam saw her lean forward where she stood, open her arms, and run at him swiftly. She flung herself upon his breast and clasped him round the neck.

' "Ah! but I shall hold thee thus," she cried. . . . "Thou art mine!"

'She sobbed on his shoulder. The sky over Patusan was blood-red, immense, streaming like an open vein. An enormous sun nestled crimson amongst the tree-tops, and the forest below had a black and forbidding face.

'Tamb' Itam tells me that on that evening the aspect of the heavens was angry and frightful. I may well believe it, for I know that on that very day a cyclone passed within sixty miles of the coast, though there was hardly more than a languid stir of air in the place.

'Suddenly Tamb' Itam saw Jim catch her arms, trying to unclasp her hands. She hung on them with her head fallen back; her hair touched the ground. "Come here!" his master called, and Tamb' Itam helped to ease her down. It was difficult to separate her fingers. Jim, bending over her, looked earnestly upon her face, and all at once ran to the landing-stage. Tamb'

Itam followed him, but turning his head, he saw that she had struggled up to her feet. She ran after them a few steps, then fell down heavily on her knees. "Tuan! Tuan!" called Tamb' Itam, "look back"; but Jim was already in a canoe, standing up paddle in hand. He did not look back. Tamb' Itam had just time to scramble in after him when the canoe floated clear. The girl was then on her knees, with clasped hands, at the watergate. She remained thus for a time in a supplicating attitude before she sprang up. "You are false!" she screamed out after Jim. "Forgive me," he cried. "Never! Never!" she called back.

'Tamb' Itam took the paddle from Jim's hands, it being unseemly that he should sit while his lord paddled. When they reached the other shore his master forbade him to come any farther; but Tamb' Itam did follow him at a distance, walking up the slope to Doramin's *campong.*

'It was beginning to grow dark. Torches twinkled here and there. Those they met seemed awestruck, and stood aside hastily to let Jim pass. The wailing of women came from above. The courtyard was full of armed Bugis with their followers, and of Patusan people.

'I do not know what this gathering really meant. Were these preparations for war, or for vengeance, or to repulse a threatened invasion? Many days elapsed before the people had ceased to look out, quaking, for the return of the white men with long beards and in rags, whose exact relation to their own white man they could never understand. Even for those simple minds poor Jim remains under a cloud.

'Doramin, alone, immense and desolate, sat in his arm-chair with the pair of flintlock pistols on his knees, faced by an armed throng. When Jim appeared, at somebody's exclamation, all the heads turned round together, and then the mass opened right and left, and he walked up a lane of averted glances. Whispers followed him; murmurs: "He has worked all the evil." "He hath a charm." . . . He heard them – perhaps!

'When he came up into the light of torches the wailing of the women ceased suddenly. Doramin did not lift his head, and Jim stood silent before him for a time. Then he looked to the left, and moved in that direction with measured steps. Dain Waris's mother crouched at the head of the body, and the grey dishevelled hair concealed her face. Jim came up slowly, looked at his dead friend, lifting the sheet, then dropped it without a word. Slowly he walked back.

' "He came! He came!" was running from lip to lip, making a murmur to which he moved. "He hath taken it upon his own head," a voice said aloud. He heard this and turned to the crowd. "Yes. Upon my head." A few people recoiled. Jim waited awhile before Doramin, and then said gently, "I am come in sorrow." He waited again. "I am come ready and unarmed," he repeated.

'The unwieldy old man, lowering his big forehead like an ox under a yoke, made an effort to rise, clutching at the flintlock pistols on his knees. From his throat came gurgling, choking, inhuman sounds, and his two attendants helped him from behind. People remarked that the ring which he had dropped on his lap fell and rolled against the foot of the white man, and that poor Jim glanced down at the talisman that had opened for him the door of fame, love, and success within the wall of forests fringed with white foam, within the coast that under the western sun looks like the very stronghold of the night. Doramin, struggling to keep his feet, made with his two supporters a swaying, tottering group; his little eyes stared with an expression of mad pain, of rage, with a ferocious glitter, which the bystanders noticed; and then, while Jim stood stiffened and with bared head in the light of torches, looking him straight in the face, he clung heavily with his left arm round the neck of a bowed youth, and lifting deliberately his right, shot his son's friend through the chest.

'The crowd, which had fallen apart behind Jim as soon as Doramin had raised his hand, rushed tumultuously forward after the shot. They say that the white man sent right and left at all those faces a proud and unflinching glance. Then with his hand over his lips he fell forward, dead.

'And that's the end. He passes away under a cloud, inscrutable at heart, forgotten, unforgiven, and excessively romantic. Not in the wildest days of his boyish visions could he have seen the alluring shape of such an extraordinary success! For it may very well be that in the short moment of his last proud and unflinching glance, he had beheld the face of that opportunity which, like an Eastern bride, had come veiled to his side.

'But we can see him, an obscure conqueror of fame, tearing himself out of the arms of a jealous love at the sign, at the call of his exalted egoism. He goes away from a living woman to celebrate his pitiless wedding with a shadowy ideal of conduct. Is he satisfied – quite, now, I wonder? We ought to know. He is one of us – and have I not stood up once, like an evoked ghost, to answer for his eternal constancy? Was I so very wrong after all? Now he is no more, there are days when the reality of his existence comes to me with an immense, with an overwhelming force; and yet upon my honour there are moments, too, when he passes from my eyes like a disembodied spirit astray amongst the passions of this earth, ready to surrender himself faithfully to the claim of his own world of shades.

'Who knows? He is gone, inscrutable at heart, and the poor girl is leading a sort of soundless, inert life in Stein's house. Stein has aged greatly of late. He feels it himself, and says often that he is "preparing to leave all this; preparing to leave ..." while he waves his hand sadly at his butterflies.'

September 1899–July 1900

THE NIGGER OF THE 'NARCISSUS'

A Tale of the Sea

PREFACE TO
THE NIGGER OF THE 'NARCISSUS'

A work that aspires, however humbly, to the condition of art should carry its justification in every line. And art itself may be defined as a single-minded attempt to render the highest kind of justice to the visible universe, by bringing to light the truth, manifold and one, underlying its every aspect. It is an attempt to find in its forms, in its colours, in its light, in its shadows, in the aspects of matter and in the facts of life what of each is fundamental, what is enduring and essential – their one illuminating and convincing quality – the very truth of their existence. The artist, then, like the thinker or the scientist, seeks the truth and makes his appeal. Impressed by the aspect of the world the thinker plunges into ideas, the scientists into facts – whence, presently, emerging they make their appeal to those qualities of our being that fit us best for the hazardous enterprise of living. They speak authoritatively to our common sense, to our intelligence, to our desire of peace, or to our desire of unrest; not seldom to our prejudices, sometimes to our fears, often to our egoism – but always to our credulity. And their words are heard with reverence, for their concern is with weighty matters: with the cultivation of our minds and the proper care of our bodies, with the attainment of our ambitions, with the perfection of the means and the glorification of our precious aims.

It is otherwise with the artist.

Confronted by the same enigmatical spectacle the artist descends within himself, and in that lonely region of stress and strife, if he be deserving and fortunate, he finds the terms of his appeal. His appeal is made to our less obvious capacities: to that part of our nature which, because of the warlike conditions of existence, is necessarily kept out of sight within the more resisting and hard qualities – like the vulnerable body within a steel armour. His appeal is less loud, more profound, less distinct, more stirring – and sooner forgotten. Yet its effect endures for ever. The changing wisdom of successive generations discards ideas, questions facts, demolishes theories. But the artist appeals to that part of our being which is not dependent on wisdom; to that in us which is a gift and not an acquisition – and, therefore, more permanently enduring. He speaks to our capacity for delight and wonder, to the sense of mystery surrounding our lives; to our sense of pity, and beauty, and pain; to the latent feeling of fellowship with all creation – and to the subtle but invincible conviction of solidarity that knits together the loneliness of innumerable hearts, to the solidarity in dreams, in joy, in sorrow, in aspirations, in illusions, in hope, in fear, which binds men to each other, which binds together all humanity – the dead to the living and the living to the unborn.

It is only some such train of thought or rather of feeling, that can in a measure explain the aim of the attempt, made in the tale which follows, to present an unrestful episode in the obscure lives of a few individuals out of all the disregarded multitude of the bewildered, the simple, and the voiceless. For, if any part of truth dwells in the belief confessed above, it becomes evident that there is not a place of splendour or a dark corner of the earth that does not deserve, if only a passing glance of wonder and pity. The motive then, may be held to justify the matter of the work; but this preface, which is simply an avowal of endeavour, cannot end here – for the avowal is not yet complete.

Fiction – if it at all aspires to be art – appeals to temperament. And in truth it must be, like painting, like music, like all art, the appeal of one temperament to all the other innumerable temperaments whose subtle and resistless power endows passing events with their true meaning, and creates the moral, the emotional atmosphere of the place and time. Such an appeal to be effective must be an impression conveyed through the senses; and, in fact, it cannot be made in any other way, because temperament, whether individual or collective, is not amenable to persuasion. All art, therefore, appeals primarily to the senses, and the artistic aim when expressing itself in written words must also make its appeal through the senses, if its high desire is to reach the secret spring of responsive emotions. It must strenuously aspire to the plasticity of sculpture, to the colour of painting, and to the magic suggestiveness of music – which is the art of arts. And it is only through complete, unswerving devotion to the perfect blending of form and substance; it is only through an unremitting never-discouraged care for the shape and ring of sentences that an approach can be made to plasticity, to colour, and that the light of magic suggestiveness may be brought to play for an evanescent instant over the commonplace surface of words: of the old, old words, worn thin, defaced by ages of careless usage.

The sincere endeavour to accomplish that creative task, to go as far on that road as his strength will carry him, to go undeterred by faltering, weariness, or reproach, is the only vaild justification for the worker in prose. And if his conscience is clear, his answer to those who in the fulness of a wisdom which looks for immediate profit, demand specifically to be edified, consoled, amused; who demand to be promptly improved, or encouraged, or frightened, or shocked, or charmed, must run thus: My task which I am trying to achieve is, by the power of the written word to make you hear, to make you feel – it is, before all, to make you *see*. That – and no more, and it is everything. If I succeed, you shall find there according to your deserts: encouragement, consolation, fear, charm – all you demand – and, perhaps, also that glimpse of truth for which you have forgotten to ask.

To snatch in a moment of courage, from the remorseless rush of time, a passing phase of life, is only the beginning of the task. The task approached in tenderness and faith is to hold up unquestioningly, without choice and without fear, the rescued fragment before all eyes in the light of a sincere mood. It is to show its vibration, its colour, its form; and through its movement, its form, and its colour, reveal the substance of its truth – disclose its inspiring secret: the stress and passion within the core of each convincing moment. In a single-minded attempt of that kind, if one be deserving and fortunate, one may perchance attain to such clearness of sincerity that at last the presented vision of regret or pity, of terror or mirth, shall awaken in the hearts of the beholders that feeling of unavoidable solidarity; of the solidarity in mysterious origin, in toil, in joy, in hope, in uncertain fate, which binds men to each other and all mankind to the visible world.

It is evident that he who, rightly or wrongly, holds by the convictions expressed above cannot be faithful to any one of the temporary formulas of his craft. The enduring part of them – the truth which each only imperfectly veils – should abide with him as the most precious of his possessions, but they all: Realism, Romanticism, Naturalism, even the unofficial sentimentalism (which like the poor, is exceedingly difficult to get rid of), all these gods must, after a short period of fellowship, abandon him – even on the very threshold of the temple – to the stammerings of his conscience and to the outspoken consciousness of the difficulties of his work. In that uneasy solitude the supreme cry of Art for Art itself loses the exciting ring of its apparent immorality. It sounds far off. It has ceased to be a cry, and is heard only as a whisper, often incomprehensible, but at times faintly encouraging.

Sometimes, stretched at ease in the shade of a roadside tree, we watch the motions of a labourer in a distant field, and after a time, begin to wonder languidly as to what the fellow may be at. We watch the movements of his body, the waving of his arms, we see him bend down, stand up, hesitate, begin again. It may add to the charm of an idle hour to be told the purpose of his exertions. If we know he is trying to lift a stone, to dig a ditch, to uproot a stump, we look with a more real interest at his efforts; we are disposed to condone the jar of his agitation upon the restfulness of the landscape; and even, if in a brotherly frame of mind, we may bring ourselves to forgive his failure. We understood his object, and, after all, the fellow has tried, and perhaps he had not the strength – and perhaps he had not the knowledge. We forgive, go on our way – and forget.

And so it is with the workman of art. Art is long and life is short, and success is very far off. And thus, doubtful of strength to travel so far, we talk a little about the aim – the aim of art, which, like life itself, is inspiring, difficult – obscured by mists. It is not in the clear logic of a triumphant conclusion; it is not in the unveiling of one of those heartless secrets which are called the Laws of Nature. It is not less great, but only more difficult.

To arrest, for the space of a breath, the hands busy about the work of the earth, and compel men entranced by the sight of distant goals to glance for a moment at the surrounding vision of form and colour, of sunshine and shadows; to make them pause for a look, for a sigh, for a smile – such is the aim, difficult and evanescent, and reserved only for a very few to achieve. But sometimes, by the deserving and the fortunate, even that task is accomplished. And when it is accomplished – behold! – all the truth of life is there: a moment of vision, a sigh, a smile – and the return to an eternal rest.

J.C.

1897

CHAPTER 1

Mr Baker, chief mate of the ship *Narcissus*, stepped in one stride out of his lighted cabin into the darkness of the quarter-deck. Above his head, on the break of the poop, the night-watchman rang a double stroke. It was nine o'clock. Mr Baker, speaking up to the man above him, asked: 'Are all the hands aboard, Knowles?'

The man limped down the ladder, then said reflectively:

'I think so, sir. All our old chaps are there, and a lot of new men has come . . . They must be all there.'

'Tell the boatswain to send all hands aft,' went on Mr Baker; 'and tell one of the youngsters to bring a good lamp here. I want to muster our crowd.'

The main deck was dark aft, but half-way from forward, through the open doors of the forecastle, two streaks of brilliant light cut the shadow of the quiet night that lay upon the ship. A hum of voices was heard there, while port and starboard, in the illuminated doorways, silhouettes of moving men appeared for a moment, very black, without relief, like figures cut out of sheet tin. The ship was ready for sea. The carpenter had driven in the last wedge of the main-hatch battens, and, throwing down his maul, had wiped his face with great deliberation, just on the stroke of five. The decks had been swept, the windlass oiled and made ready to heave up the anchor; the big tow-rope lay in long bights along one side of the main deck, with one end carried up and hung over the bows, in readiness for the tug that would come paddling and hissing noisily, hot and smoky, in the limpid, cool quietness of the early morning. The captain was ashore, where he had been engaging some new hands to make up his full crew; and, the work of the day over, the ship's officers had kept out of the way, glad of a little breathing-time. Soon after dark the few liberty-men and the new hands began to arrive in shore-boats rowed by white-clad Asiatics, who clamoured fiercely for payment before coming alongside the gangway-ladder. The feverish and shrill babble of Eastern language struggled against the masterful tones of tipsy seamen, who argued against brazen claims and dishonest hopes by profane shouts. The resplendent and bestarred peace of the East was torn into squalid tatters by howls of rage and shrieks of lament raised over sums ranging from five annas to half a rupee; and every soul afloat in Bombay Harbour became aware that the new hands were joining the *Narcissus*.

Gradually the distracting noise had subsided. The boats came no longer in splashing clusters of three or four together, but dropped alongside singly, in a subdued buzz of expostulation cut short by a 'Not a pice more! You go to the devil!' from some man staggering up the accommodation-ladder – a dark figure, with a long bag poised on the shoulder. In the forecastle the newcomers, upright and swaying amongst corded boxes and bundles of bedding, made friends with the old hands, who sat one above another in the two tiers of bunks, gazing at their future shipmates with glances critical but friendly. The two forecastle lamps were turned up high, and shed an intense hard glare; shore-going round hats were pushed far on the backs of heads, or rolled about on the deck amongst the chain-cables; white collars, undone, stuck out on each side of red faces; big arms in white sleeves gesticulated; the growling voices hummed steady amongst bursts of laughter and hoarse calls. 'Here, sonny take that bunk!' – 'Don't you do it!' – 'What's your last ship?' – 'I know her' – 'Three years ago, in Puget Sound' – 'This berth leaks, I tell you!' – 'Come on; give us a chance to swing that chest!' – 'Did you bring a bottle, any of you shore toffs?' – 'Give us a bit of baccy' – 'I know her; her skipper drank himself to death' – 'He was a dandy boy!' – 'Liked his lotion inside, he did!' – 'No!' – 'Hold your row, you chaps!' – 'I tell you, you came on board a hooker, where they get their money's worth out of poor Jack by—!'

A little fellow, called Craik and nicknamed Belfast, abused the ship violently, romancing on principle, just to give the new hands something to think over. Archie, sitting aslant on his sea-chest, kept his knees out of the way, and pushed the needle steadily through a white patch in a pair of blue trousers. Men in black jackets and stand-up collars, mixed with men bare-footed, bare-armed, with coloured shirts open on hairy chests, pushed against one another in the middle of the forecastle. The group swayed, reeled, turning upon itself with the motion of a scrimmage, in a haze of tobacco smoke. All were speaking together, swearing at every second word. A Russian Finn, wearing a yellow shirt with pink stripes, stared upwards, dreamy-eyed, from under a mop of tumbled hair. Two young giants with smooth, baby faces – two Scandinavians – helped each other to spread their bedding, silent, and smiling placidly at the tempest of good-humoured and meaningless curses. Old Singleton, the oldest able seaman in the ship, sat apart on the deck right under the lamps, stripped to the waist, tattooed like a cannibal chief all over his powerful chest and enormous biceps. Between the blue and red patterns his white skin gleamed like satin; his bare back was propped against the heel of the bowsprit, and he held a book at arm's length before his big, sunburnt face. With his spectacles and a venerable white beard, he resembled a learned and savage patriarch, the incarnation of barbarian wisdom serene in the blasphemous turmoil of the world. He was intensely absorbed, and as he turned the pages an expression of grave surprise would pass over his rugged features. He was reading *Pelham*. The popularity of Bulwer Lytton in the forecastles of southern-going ships is a wonderful and bizarre phenomenon. What ideas do his polished and so curiously insincere sentences awaken in the simple minds of the big children who people those dark and wandering places of the earth? What meaning their rough, inexperienced souls can find in the elegant verbiage of his pages? What excitement? – what forgetfulness? – what appeasement? Mystery! Is it the fascination of the incomprehensible? – is it the charm of the impossible? Or are those beings who exist beyond the pale of life stirred by his tales as by an enigmatical disclosure of a resplendent world that exists within the frontier of infamy and filth, within that border of dirt and hunger, of misery and dissipation, that comes down on all sides to the water's edge of the incorruptible ocean, and is the only thing they know of life, the only thing they see of surrounding land – those life-long prisoners of the sea? Mystery!

Singleton, who had sailed to the southward since the age of twelve, who in the last forty-five years had lived (as we had calculated from his papers) no more than forty months ashore – old Singleton, who boasted, with the mild composure of long years well spent, that generally from the day he was paid off from one ship till the day he shipped in another he seldom was in a condition to distinguish daylight – old Singleton sat unmoved in the clash of voices and cries, spelling through *Pelham* with slow labour, and lost in an absorption profound enough to resemble a trance. He breathed regularly. Every time he turned the book in his enormous blackened hands the muscles of his big white arms rolled slightly under the smooth skin. Hidden by the white moustache, his lips, stained with tobacco-juice that trickled down the long beard, moved in inward whisper. His bleared eyes gazed fixedly from behind the glitter of black-rimmed glasses. Opposite to him, and on a level with his face, the ship's cat sat on the barrel of the windlass in the pose of a crouching chimera, blinking its green eyes at its old friend. It seemed to meditate a leap on to the old man's lap over the bent back of the ordinary seaman who sat at Singleton's feet. Young Charley was lean and long-necked. The ridge of his backbone made a chain of small hills under the old shirt. His face of a street-boy – a face precocious, sagacious, and ironic, with deep downward folds on each side of the thin, wide mouth – hung low over his bony knees. He was learning to make a lanyard knot with a bit of an old rope. Small drops of perspiration stood out on his bulging forehead; he sniffed strongly from time to time, glancing out of the corners of his restless eyes at the old seaman, who took no notice of the puzzled youngster muttering at his work.

The noise increased. Little Belfast seemed, in the heavy heat of the forecastle, to boil with facetious fury. His eyes danced; in the crimson of his face, comical as a mask, the mouth yawned black, with strange grimaces. Facing him, a half-undressed man held his sides, and, throwing his head back, laughed with wet eyelashes. Others stared with amazed eyes. Men sitting doubled up in the upper bunks smoked short pipes, swinging bare brown feet above the heads of those who, sprawling below on sea-chests, listened, smiling stupidly or scornfully. Over the white rims of berths stuck out heads with blinking eyes; but the bodies were lost in the gloom of those places, that resembled narrow niches for coffins in a whitewashed and lighted mortuary. Voices buzzed louder. Archie, with compressed lips, drew himself in, seemed to shrink into a smaller space, and sewed steadily, industrious and dumb. Belfast shrieked like an inspired Dervish: '. . . So I seez to him, boys, seez I, "Beggin' yer pardon, sorr," seez I to that second mate of that steamer – "beggin' your-r-r pardon, sorr, the Board of Trade must 'ave been drunk when they granted you your certificate!" "What do you say, you—!" seez he, comin' at me like a mad bull . . . all in his white clothes; and I up with my tar-pot and capsizes it all over his blamed lovely face and his lovely jacket. . . . "Take that!" seez I. "I am a sailor, anyhow, you

nosing, skipper-licking, useless, sooperfloos bridge-stanchion you!" "That's
the kind of man I am!" shouts I. . . . You should have seed him skip, boys!
Drowned, blind with tar, he was! So . . .'

'Don't 'ee believe him! He never upset no tar; I was there!' shouted
somebody. The two Norwegians sat on a chest side by side, alike and placid,
resembling a pair of love-birds on a perch, and with round eyes stared
innocently; but the Russian Finn, in the racket of explosive shouts and
rolling laughter, remained motionless, limp, and dull, like a deaf man
without a backbone. Near him Archie smiled at his needle. A broad-chested,
slow-eyed newcomer spoke deliberately to Belfast during an exhausted lull
in the noise: 'I wonder any of the mates here are alive yet with such a chap
as you on board! I concloode they ain't that bad now, if you had the taming
of them, sonny.'

'Not bad! Not bad!' screamed Belfast. 'If it wasn't for us sticking
together. . . . Not bad! They ain't never bad when they ain't got a chawnce,
blast their black 'arts. . . .' He foamed, whirling his arms, then suddenly
grinned and, taking a tablet of black tobacco out of his pocket, bit a piece
off with a funny show of ferocity. Another new hand – a man with shifty
eyes and a yellow hatchet face, who had been listening open-mouthed in the
shadow of the midship locker – observed in a squeaky voice: 'Well, it's a
'omeward trip, anyhow. Bad or good, I can do it on my 'ed – s'long as I get
'ome. And I can look after my rights! I will show 'em!' All the heads turned
towards him. Only the ordinary seaman and the cat took no notice. He stood
with arms akimbo, a little fellow with white eyelashes. He looked as if he
had known all the degradations and all the furies. He looked as if he had
been cuffed, kicked, rolled in the mud; he looked as if he had been scratched,
spat upon, pelted with unmentionable filth . . . and he smiled with a sense
of security at the faces around. His ears were bending down under the
weight of his battered felt hat. The torn tails of his black coat flapped in
fringes about the calves of his legs. He unbuttoned the only two buttons that
remained and everyone saw that he had no shirt under it. It was his deserved
misfortune that those rags which nobody could possibly be supposed to own
looked on him as if they had been stolen. His neck was long and thin; his
eyelids were red; rare hairs hung about his jaws; his shoulders were peaked
and drooped like the broken wings of a bird; all his left side was caked with
mud which showed that he had lately slept in a wet ditch. He had saved his
inefficient carcass from violent destruction by running away from an American ship where, in a moment of forgetful folly, he had dared to engage
himself; and he had knocked about for a fortnight ashore in the native
quarter, cadging for drinks, starving, sleeping on rubbish-heaps, wandering
in sunshine: a startling visitor from a world of nightmares. He stood repulsive
and smiling in the sudden silence. This clean white forecastle was his refuge;
the place where he could be lazy; where he could wallow, and lie and eat
– and curse the food he ate; where he could display his talents for shirking
work, for cheating, for cadging; where he could find surely someone to
wheedle and someone to bully – and where he would be paid for doing all
this. They all knew him. Is there a spot on earth where such a man is
unknown, an ominous survival testifying to the eternal fitness of lies and

impudence? A taciturn long-armed shellback, with hooked fingers, who had been lying on his back smoking, turned in his bed to examine him dispassionately, then, over his head, sent a long jet of clear saliva towards the door. They all knew him! He was the man that cannot steer, that cannot splice, that dodges the work on dark nights; that, aloft, holds on frantically with both arms and legs, and swears at the wind, the sleet, the darkness; the man who curses the sea while others work. The man who is the last out and the first in when all hands are called. The man who can't do most things and won't do the rest. The pet of philanthropists and self-seeking landlubbers. The sympathetic and deserving creature that knows all about his rights, but knows nothing of courage, of endurance, and of the unexpressed faith, of the unspoken loyalty that knits together a ship's company. The independent offspring of the ignoble freedom of the slums full of disdain and hate for the austere servitude of the sea.

Someone cried at him: 'What's your name?' 'Donkin,' he said, looking round with cheerful effrontery. 'What are you?' asked another voice. 'Why, a sailor like you, old man,' he replied, in a tone that meant to be hearty but was impudent. 'Blamme if you don't look a blamed sight worse than a broken-down fireman,' was the comment in a convinced mutter. Charley lifted his head and piped in a cheeky voice: 'He is a man and a sailor' – then wiping his nose with the back of his hand, bent down industriously over his bit of rope. A few laughed. Others stared doubtfully. The ragged newcomer was indignant – 'That's a fine way to welcome a chap into a fo'c'sle,' he snarled. 'Are you men or a lot of 'artless cannybals?' 'Don't take your shirt off for a word, shipmate,' called out Belfast, jumping up in front, fiery, menacing, and friendly at the same time. 'Is that 'ere bloke blind?' asked the indomitable scarecrow, looking right and left with affected surprise. 'Can't 'ee see I 'aven't got no shirt?'

He held both his arms out crosswise and shook the rags that hung over his bones with dramatic effect.

"Cos why?' he continued very loud. 'The bloody Yankees been tryin' to jump my guts out 'cos I stood up for my rights like a good 'un. I am an Englishman, I am. They set upon me an' I 'ad to run. That's why. A'n't yer never seed a man 'ard up? Yah! What kind of blamed ship is this? I'm dead broke. I 'aven't got nothink. No bag, no bed, no blanket, no shirt – not a bloomin' rag but what I stand in. But I 'ad the 'art to stand up agin' them Yankees. 'As any of you 'art enough to spare a pair of old pants for a chum?'

He knew how to conquer the naïve instincts of that crowd. In a moment they gave him their compassion, jocularly, contemptuously, or surlily; and at first it took the shape of a blanket thrown at him as he stood there with the white skin of his limbs showing his human kinship through the black fantasy of his rags. Then a pair of old shoes fell at his muddy feet. With a cry: 'From under,' a rolled-up pair of canvas trousers, heavy with tar stains, struck him on the shoulder. The gust of their benevolence sent a wave of sentimental pity through their doubting hearts. They were touched by their own readiness to alleviate a shipmate's misery. Voices cried: 'We will fit you out, old man.' Murmurs: 'Never seed seech a hard case' – 'Poor beggar' – 'I've got an old singlet' – 'Will that be of any use to you?' – 'Take it, matey.'

Those friendly murmurs filled the forecastle. He pawed around with his naked foot, gathering the things in a heap, and looked about for more. Unemotional Archie perfunctorily contributed to the pile an old cloth cap with the peak torn off. Old Singleton, lost in the serene regions of fiction, read on unheeding. Charley, pitiless with the wisdom of youth, squeaked: 'If you want brass buttons for your new unyforms I've got two for you.' The filthy object of universal charity shook his fist at the youngster. 'I'll make you keep this 'ere fo'c'sle clean, young feller,' he snarled viciously. 'Never you fear. I will learn you to be civil to an able seaman, you ignerant ass.' He glared harmfully, but saw Singleton shut his book, and his little beady eyes began to roam from berth to berth. 'Take that bunk by the door there – it's pretty fair,' suggested Belfast. So advised, he gathered the gifts at his feet, pressed them in a bundle against his breast, then looked cautiously at the Russian Finn, who stood on one side with an unconscious gaze, contemplating, perhaps, one of those weird visions that haunt the men of his race. 'Get out of my road, Dutchy,' said the victim of Yankee brutality. The Finn did not move – did not hear. 'Get out, blast ye,' shouted the other, shoving him aside with his elbow. 'Get out, you blanked deaf and dumb fool. Get out.' The man staggered, recovered himself, and gazed at the speaker in silence. 'Those damned furriners should be kept under,' opined the amiable Donkin to the forecastle. 'If you don't teach 'em their place they put on you like anythink.' He flung all his worldly possessions into the empty bed-place, gauged with another shrewd look the risks of the proceeding, then leaped up to the Finn, who stood pensive and dull. 'I'll teach you to swell around,' he yelled. 'I'll plug your eyes for you, you blooming square-head.' Most of the men were now in their bunks and the two had the forecastle clear to themselves. The development of the destitute Donkin aroused interest. He danced all in tatters before the amazed Finn, squaring from a distance at the heavy, unmoved face. One or two men cried encouragingly: 'Go it, Whitechapel!' settling themselves luxuriously in their beds to survey the fight. Others shouted: 'Shut yer row! ... Go an' put yer 'ed in a bag! ...' The hubbub was recommencing. Suddenly many heavy blows struck with a handspike on the deck above boomed like discharges of small cannon through the forecastle. Then the boatswain's voice rose outside the door with an authoritative note in its drawl: 'D'ye hear, below there? Lay aft! Lay aft to muster all hands!'

There was a moment of surprised stillness. Then the forecastle floor disappeared under men whose bare feet flopped on the planks as they sprang clear out of their berths. Caps were rooted for amongst tumbled blankets. Some, yawning, buttoned waistbands. Half-smoked pipes were knocked hurriedly against woodwork and stuffed under pillows. Voices growled: 'What's up? ... Is there no rest for us?' Donkin yelped: 'If that's the way of this ship, we'll 'ave to change all that. ... You leave me alone. ... I will soon ...' None of the crowd noticed him. They were lurching in twos and threes through the doors, after the manner of merchant Jacks who cannot go out of a door fairly, like mere landsmen. The votary of change followed them. Singleton, struggling into his jacket, came last, tall and fatherly, bearing high his head of a weatherbeaten sage on the body of an old athlete.

Only Charley remained alone in the white glare of the empty place, sitting between the two rows of iron links that stretched into the narrow gloom forward. He pulled hard at the strands in a hurried endeavour to finish his knot. Suddenly he started up, flung the rope at the cat, and skipped after the black tom which went off leaping sedately over chain compressors, with its tail carried stiff and upright, like a small flagpole.

Outside the glare of the steaming forecastle the serene purity of the night enveloped the seamen with its soothing breath, with its tepid breath flowing under the stars that hung countless above the mastheads in a thin cloud of luminous dust. On the town side the blackness of the water was streaked with trails of light which undulated gently on slight ripples, similar to filaments that float rooted to the shore. Rows of other lights stood away in straight lines as if drawn up on parade between towering buildings; but on the other side of the harbour sombre hills arched high their black spines, on which, here and there, the point of a star resembled a spark fallen from the sky. Far off, Byculla way, the electric lamps at the dock gates shone on the end of lofty standards with a glow blinding and frigid like captive ghosts of some evil moons. Scattered all over the dark polish of the roadstead, the ships at anchor floated in perfect stillness under the feeble gleam of their riding-lights, looming up, opaque and bulky, like strange and monumental structures abandoned by men to an everlasting repose.

Before the cabin door Mr Baker was mustering the crew. As they stumbled and lurched along past the mainmast, they could see aft his round, broad face with a white paper before it, and beside his shoulder the sleepy head, with dropped eyelids, of the boy, who held, suspended at the end of his raised arm, the luminous globe of a lamp. Even before the shuffle of naked soles had ceased along the decks, the mate began to call over the names. He called distinctly in a serious tone befitting this roll-call to unquiet loneliness, to inglorious and obscure struggle, or to the more trying endurance of small privations and wearisome duties. As the chief mate read out a name, one of the men would answer: 'Yes, sir!' or 'Here!' and, detaching himself from the shadowy mob of heads visible above the blackness of starboard bulwarks, would step barefooted into the circle of light, and in two noiseless strides pass into the shadows on the port side of the quarter-deck. They answered in divers tones: in thick mutters, in clear, ringing voices; and some, as if the whole thing had been an outrage on their feelings, used an injured intonation: for discipline is not ceremonious in merchant ships, where the sense of hierarchy is weak, and where all feel themselves equal before the unconcerned immensity of the sea and the exacting appeal of the work.

Mr Baker read on steadily: 'Hansen – Campbell – Smith – Wamibo. Now, then, Wamibo. Why don't you answer? Always got to call your name twice.' The Finn emitted at last an uncouth grunt, and, stepping out, passed through the patch of light, weird and gaudy, with the face of a man marching through a dream. The mate went on faster: 'Craik – Singleton – Donkin. . . . O Lord!' he involuntarily ejaculated as the incredibly dilapidated figure appeared in the light. It stopped; it uncovered pale gums and long, upper teeth in a malevolent grin. 'Is there anything wrong with me, Mister Mate?' it asked, with a flavour of insolence in the forced simplicity of its tone. On both sides of the deck subdued titters were heard. 'That'll do. Go over,' growled Mr Baker, fixing the new hand with steady blue eyes. And Donkin vanished suddenly out of the light into the dark group of mustered men, to be slapped on the back and to hear flattering whispers: 'He ain't afeared, he'll give sport to 'em, see if he don't' – 'Reg'lar Punch and Judy show' – 'Did ye see the mate start at him?' – 'Well! Damme, if I ever!'

The last man had gone over, and there was a moment of silence while the mate peered at his list. 'Sixteen, seventeen,' he muttered. 'I am one hand short, bo'sen,' he said aloud. The big west-countryman at his elbow, swarthy and bearded like a gigantic Spaniard, said in a rumbling bass: 'There's no one left forward, sir. I had a look around. He ain't aboard, but he may turn up before daylight.' 'Ay. He may or he may not,' commented the mate, 'can't make out that last name. It's all a smudge. . . . That will do, men. Go below.'

The distinct and motionless group stirred, broke up, began to move forward.

'Wait!' cried a deep, ringing voice.

All stood still. Mr Baker, who had turned away yawning, spun round open-mouthed. At last, furious, he blurted out: 'What's this? Who said "Wait"? What . . .'

But he saw a tall figure standing on the rail. It came down and pushed through the crowd, marching with a heavy tread towards the light on the quarter-deck. Then again the sonorous voice said with insistence: 'Wait!' The lamplight lit up the man's body. He was tall. His head was away up in the shadows of lifeboats that stood on skids above the deck. The whites of his eyes and his teeth gleamed distinctly, but the face was indistinguishable. His hands were big and seemed gloved.

Mr Baker advanced intrepidly. 'Who are you? How dare you . . . ?' he began.

The boy, amazed like the rest, raised the light to the man's face. It was black. A surprised hum – a faint hum that sounded like the suppressed mutter of the word 'Nigger' – ran along the deck and escaped out into the night. The nigger seemed not to hear. He balanced himself where he stood in a swagger that marked time. After a moment he said calmly: 'My name is Wait – James Wait.'

'Oh!' said Mr Baker. Then, after a few seconds of smouldering silence, his temper blazed out. 'Ah! Your name is Wait. What of that? What do you want? What do you mean, coming shouting here?'

The nigger was calm, cool, towering superb. The men had approached and stood behind him in a body. He overtopped the tallest by half a head. He said: 'I belong to the ship.' He enunciated distinctly, with soft precision. The deep, rolling tones of his voice filled the deck without effort. He was naturally scornful, unaffectedly condescending, as if from his height of six foot three he had surveyed all the vastness of human folly and had made up his mind not to be too hard on it. He went on: 'The captain shipped me this morning. I couldn't get aboard sooner. I saw you all aft as I came up the ladder, and could see directly you were mustering the crew. Naturally I called out my name. I thought you had it on your list, and would understand.

You misapprehended.' He stopped short. The folly around him was confounded. He was right as ever, and as ever ready to forgive. The disdainful tones had ceased, and breathing heavily, he stood still, surrounded by all these white men. He held his head up in the glare of the lamp – a head vigorously modelled into deep shadows and shining lights – a head powerful and misshapen with a tormented and flattened face – a face pathetic and brutal: the tragic, the mysterious, the repulsive mask of a nigger's soul.

Mr Baker, recovering his composure, looked at the paper close. 'Oh, yes; that's so. All right. Wait. Take your gear forward,' he said.

Suddenly the nigger's eyes rolled wildly, became all whites. He put his hand to his side and coughed twice, a cough metallic, hollow, and tremendously loud; it resounded like two explosions in a vault; the dome of the sky rang to it, and the iron plates of the ship's bulwarks seemed to vibrate in unison, then he marched off forward with the others. The officers lingering by the cabin door could hear him say: 'Won't some of you chaps lend a hand with my dunnage? I've got a chest and a bag.' The words, spoken sonorously, with an even intonation, were heard all over the ship, and the question was put in a manner that made refusal impossible. The short, quick shuffle of men carrying something heavy went away forward, but the tall figure of the nigger lingered by the main hatch in a knot of smaller shapes. Again he was heard asking: 'Is your cook a coloured gentleman?' Then a disappointed and disapproving 'Ah! h'm?' was his comment upon the information that the cooked happened to be a mere white man. Yet, as they went all together towards the forecastle, he condescended to put his head through the galley door and boom out inside a magnificent 'Good evening, doctor!' that made all the saucepans ring. In the dim light the cook dozed on the coal locker in front of the captain's supper. He jumped up as if he had been cut with a whip, and dashed wildly on deck to see the backs of several men going away laughing. Afterwards, when talking about that voyage, he used to say: 'The poor fellow had scared me. I thought I had seen the devil.' The cook had been seven years in the ship with the same captain. He was a serious-minded man with a wife and three children, whose society he enjoyed on an average one month out of twelve. When on shore he took his family to church twice every Sunday. At sea he went to sleep every evening with his lamp turned up full, a pipe in his mouth, and an open Bible in his hand. Some one had always to go during the night to put out the light, take the book from his hand, and the pipe from between his teeth. 'For' – Belfast used to say, irritated and complaining – 'some night, you stupid cookie, you'll swallow your ould clay, and we will have no cook.' 'Ah! sonny, I am ready for my Maker's call ... wish you all were,' the other would answer with a benign serenity that was altogether imbecile and touching. Belfast outside the galley door danced with vexation. 'You holy fool! I don't want you to die,' he howled, looking up with furious, quivering face and tender eyes. 'What's the hurry? You blessed wooden-headed ould heretic, the divvle will have you soon enough. Think of Us ... of Us ... of Us!' And he would go away, stamping, spitting aside, disgusted, and worried; while the other, stepping out, saucepan in hand, hot, begrimed, and placid, watched with a superior, cock-sure smile the back of his 'queer little man' reeling in a rage. They were great friends.

Mr Baker, lounging over the after-hatch, sniffed the humid night in the company of the second mate. 'Those West India niggers run fine and large – some of them ... Ough! ... Don't they? A fine, big man that, Mr Creighton. Feel him on a rope. Hey? Ough! I will take him into my watch, I think.' The second mate, a fair, gentlemanly young fellow, with a resolute face and a splendid physique, observed quietly that it was just about what he expected. There could be felt in his tone some slight bitterness which Mr Baker very kindly set himself to argue away. 'Come, come, young man,' he said, grunting between the words. 'Come! Don't be too greedy. You had that big Finn in your watch all the voyage. I will do what's fair. You may have those two young Scandinavians and I ... Ough! ... I get the nigger, and will take that ... Ough! that cheeky costermonger chap in a black frock-coat. I'll make him ... Ough! ... make him toe the mark, or my ... Ough! ... name isn't Baker. Ough! Ough! Ough!'

He grunted thrice – furiously. He had that trick of grunting so between his words and at the end of sentences. It was a fine, effective grunt that went well with his menacing utterance, with his heavy, bullnecked frame, his jerky, rolling gait; with his big, seamed face, his steady eyes, and sardonic mouth. But its effect had been long ago discounted by the men. They liked him; Belfast – who was a favourite, and knew it – mimicked him, not quite behind his back. Charley – but with greater caution – imitated his rolling gait. Some of his sayings became established, daily quotations in the forecastle. Popularity can go no farther! Besides, all hands were ready to admit that on a fitting occasion the mate could 'jump down a fellow's throat in a reg'lar Western Ocean style'.

Now he was giving his last orders. 'Ough! ... You, Knowles! Call all hands at four. I want ... Ough! ... to heave short before the tug comes. Look out for the captain. I am going to lie down in my clothes ... Ough! ... Call me when you see the boat coming. Ough! Ough! ... The old man is sure to have something to say when he gets aboard,' he remarked to Creighton. 'Well, good night ... Ough! A long day before us tomorrow ... Ough! ... Better turn in now. Ough! Ough!'

Upon the dark deck a band of lights flashed, then a door slammed, and Mr Baker was gone into his neat cabin. Young Creighton stood leaning over the rail, and looked dreamily into the night of the East. And he saw in it a long country lane, a lane of waving leaves and dancing sunshine. He saw stirring boughs of old trees outspread, and framing in their arch the tender, the caressing blueness of an English sky. And through the arch a girl in a light dress, smiling under a sunshade, seemed to be stepping out of the tender sky.

At the other end of the ship the forecastle, with only one lamp burning now, was going to sleep in a dim emptiness traversed by loud breathings, by sudden short sighs. The double row of berths yawned black, like graves tenanted by uneasy corpses. Here and there a curtain of gaudy chintz, half drawn, marked the resting-place of a sybarite. A leg hung over the edge very white and lifeless. An arm stuck straight out with a dark palm turned up, and thick fingers half closed. Two light snores, that did not synchronize, quarrelled in funny dialogue. Singleton stripped again – the old man suffered much from prickly heat – stood cooling his back in the doorway, with his arms crossed on his bare and adorned chest. His head touched the beam of the deck above. The nigger, half undressed, was busy casting adrift the lashing of his box, and spreading his bedding in an upper berth. He moved about in his socks, tall and noiseless, with a pair of braces beating about his calves. Amongst the shadows of stanchions and bowsprit, Donkin munched a piece of hard ship's bread, sitting on the deck with upturned feet and restless eyes; he held the biscuit up before his mouth in the whole fist and snapped his jaws at it with a raging face. Crumbs fell between his outspread legs. Then he got up.

'Where's our water-cask?' he asked in a contained voice.

Singleton, without a word, pointed with a big hand that held a short smouldering pipe. Donkin bent over the cask, drank out of the tin, splashing the water, turned round, and noticed the nigger looking at him over the shoulder with calm loftiness. He moved up sideways.

'There's a blooming supper for a man,' he whispered bitterly. 'My dorg at 'ome wouldn't 'ave it. It's fit enouf for you an' me. 'Ere's a big ship's fo'c'sle! ... Not a blooming scrap of meat in the kids. I've looked in all the lockers. ...'

The nigger stared like a man addressed unexpectedly in a foreign language. Donkin changed his tone: 'Giv' us a bit of baccy, mate,' he breathed out confidentially, 'I 'aven't 'ad smoke or chew for the last month. I am rampin' mad for it. Come on, old man!'

'Don't be familiar,' said the nigger. Donkin started and sat down on a chest near by, out of sheer surprise. 'We haven't kept pigs together,' continued James Wait in a deep undertone. 'Here's your tobacco.' Then, after a pause, he inquired: 'What ship?' 'Golden State,' muttered Donkin indistinctly, biting the tobacco. The nigger whistled low. 'Ran?' he said curtly. Donkin nodded: one of his cheeks bulged out. 'In course I ran,' he mumbled. 'They booted the life hout of one Dago chap on the passage 'ere, then started oh me. I cleared hout 'ere.' 'Left your dunnage behind?' 'Yes, dunnage and money,' answered Donkin, raising his voice a little: 'I got nothink. No clothes, no bed. A bandy-legged little Hirish chap 'ere 'as give me a blanket ... Think I'll go an' sleep in the fore topmast staysail tonight.' ·

He went on deck trailing behind his back a corner of the blanket. Singleton, without a glance, moved slightly aside to let him pass. The nigger put away his short togs and sat in clean working clothes on his box, one arm stretched over his knees. After staring at Singleton for some time he asked without emphasis: 'What kind of ship is this? Pretty fair? Eh?'

Singleton didn't stir. A long while after he said, with unmoved face: 'Ship! ... Ships are all right. It is the men in them!'

He went on smoking in the profound silence. The wisdom of half a century spent in listening to the thunder of the waves had spoken unconsciously through his old lips. The cat purred on the windlass. Then James Wait had a fit of roaring, rattling cough, that shook him, tossed him like a hurricane, and flung him panting with staring eyes headlong on his sea-chest. Several men woke up. One said sleepily out of his bunk: "Struth! what a blamed row!' 'I have a cold on my chest,' gasped Wait. 'Cold! you call it,' grumbled the man; 'should think 'twas something more. . . . ' 'Oh! you think so,' said the nigger upright and loftily scornful again. He climbed into his berth and began coughing persistently while he put his head out to glare all round the forecastle.There was no further protest. He fell back on the pillow, and could be heard there wheezing regularly like a man oppressed in his sleep.

Singleton stood at the door with his face to the light and his back to the darkness. And alone in the dim emptiness of the sleeping forecastle he appeared bigger, colossal, very old; old as Father Time himself, who should have come there into this place as quiet as a sepulchre to contemplate with patient eyes the short victory of sleep, the consoler. Yet he was only a child of time, a lonely relic of a devoured and forgotten generation. He stood, still strong, as ever unthinking; a ready man with a vast empty past and with no future, with his childlike impulses and his man's passions already dead within his tattooed breast. The men who could understand his silence were gone – those men who knew how to exist beyond the pale of life and within sight of eternity. They had been strong, as those are strong who know neither doubts nor hopes. They had been impatient and enduring, turbulent and devoted, unruly and faithful. Well-meaning people had tried to represent those men as whining over every mouthful of their food; as going about their work in fear of their lives. But in truth they had been men who knew toil, privation, violence, debauchery – but knew not fear, and had no desire of spite in their hearts. Men hard to manage, but easy to inspire; voiceless men – but men enough to scorn in their hearts the sentimental voices that bewailed the hardness of their fate. It was a fate unique and their own; the capacity to bear it appeared to them the privilege of the chosen! Their generation lived inarticulate and indispensable, without knowing the sweetness of affections or the refuge of a home – and died free from the dark menace of a narrow grave. They were the everlasting children of the mysterious sea. Their successors are the grown-up children of a discontented earth. They are less naughty, but less innocent; less profane, but perhaps also less believing; and if they had learned how to speak they have also learned how to whine. But the others were strong and mute; they were effaced, bowed, and enduring, like stone caryatides that hold up in the night the lighted halls of a resplendent and glorious edifice. They are gone now – and it does not matter. The sea and the earth are unfaithful to their children: a truth, a faith, a generation of men goes – and is forgotten, and it does not matter! Except, perhaps, to the few of those who believed the truth, confessed the faith – or loved the men.

A breeze was coming. The ship that had been lying tide-rode swung to a heavier puff; and suddenly the slack of the chain cable between the windlass and the hawse-pipe clinked, slipped forward an inch, and rose gently off the deck with a startling suggestion as of unsuspected life that had been lurking stealthily in the iron. In the hawse-pipe the grinding links sent through the ship a sound like a low groan of a man sighing under a burden. The strain came on the windlass, the chain tautened like a string, vibrated – and the handle of the screwbrake moved in slight jerks. Singleton stepped forward.

Till then he had been standing meditative and unthinking, reposeful and hopeless, with a face grim and blank – a sixty-year-old child of the mysterious sea. The thoughts of all his lifetime could have been expressed in six words, but the stir of those things that were as much part of his existence as his beating heart called up a gleam of alert understanding upon the sterness of his aged face. The flame of the lamp swayed, and the old man, with knitted and bushy eyebrows, stood over the brake, watchful and motionless in the wild saraband of dancing shadows. Then the ship, obedient to the call of her anchor, forged ahead slightly and eased the strain. The cable relieved, hung down, and after swaying imperceptibly to and fro dropped with a loud tap on the hard wood planks. Singleton seized the high lever, and, by a violent throw forward of his body, wrung out another half-turn from the brake. He recovered himself, breathed largely, and remained for a while glaring down at the powerful and compact engine that squatted on the deck at his feet like some quiet monster – a creature amazing and tame.

'You . . . hold!' he growled at it masterfully, in the incult tangle of his white beard.

CHAPTER 2

Next morning, at daylight, the *Narcissus* went to sea.

A slight haze blurred the horizon. Outside the harbour the measureless expanse of smooth water lay sparkling like a floor of jewels, and as empty as the sky. The short black tug gave a pluck to windward, in the usual way, then let go the rope, and hovered for a moment on the quarter with her engines stopped; while the slim, long hull of the ship moved ahead slowly under lower topsails. The loose upper canvas blew out in the breeze with soft round contours, resembling small white clouds snared in the maze of ropes. Then the sheets were hauled home, the yards hoisted, and the ship became a high and lonely pyramid, gliding, all shining and white, through the sunlit mist. The tug turned short round and went away towards the land. Twenty-six pairs of eyes watched her low broad stern crawling languidly over the smooth swell between the two paddle-wheels that turned fast, beating the water with fierce hurry. She resembled an enormous and aquatic black beetle, surprised by the light, overwhelmed by the sunshine, trying to escape with ineffectual effort into the distant gloom of the land. She left a lingering smudge of smoke on the sky, and two vanishing trails of foam on the water. On the place where she had stopped a round black patch of soot remained, undulating on the swell – an unclean mark of the creature's rest.

The *Narcissus* left alone, heading south, seemed to stand resplendent and still upon the restless sea, under the moving sun. Flakes of foam swept past her sides; the water struck her with flashing blows; the land glided away slowly fading; a few birds screamed on motionless wings over the swaying mastheads. But soon the land disappeared, the birds went away; and to the west the pointed sail of an Arab dhow running for Bombay, rose triangular and upright above the sharp edge of the horizon, lingered and vanished like an illusion. Then the ship's wake, long and straight, stretched itself out through a day of immense solitude. The setting sun, burning on the level of the water, flamed crimson below the blackness of heavy rain clouds. The sunset squall, coming up from behind, dissolved itself into the short deluge of a hissing shower. It left the ship glistening from trucks to waterline, and with darkened sails. She ran easily before a fair monsoon, with her decks cleared for the night, and, moving along with her, was heard the sustained and monotonous swishing of the waves, mingled with the low whispers of men mustered aft for the setting of watches; the short plaint of some block aloft; or, now and then, a loud sigh of wind.

Mr Baker, coming out of his cabin, called out the first name sharply before closing the door behind him. He was going to take charge of the deck. On the homeward trip, according to an old custom of the sea, the chief officer takes the first night-watch – from eight till midnight. So Mr Baker after he had heard the last 'Yes, sir!' said moodily, 'Relieve the wheel and look-out'; and climbed with heavy feet the poop ladder to windward. Soon after Mr Creighton came down, whistling softly, and went into the cabin. On the doorstep the steward lounged, in slippers, meditative, and with his shirt-sleeves rolled up to the armpits. On the main deck the cook, locking up the galley doors, had an altercation with young Charley about a pair of socks. He could be heard saying impressively, in the darkness amidships: 'You don't deserve a kindness. I've been drying them for you, and now you complain about the holes – and you swear, too! Right in front of me! If I hadn't been a Christian – which you ain't, you young ruffian – I would give you a clout on the head. . . . Go away!' Men in couples or threes stood pensive or moved silently along the bulwarks in the waist. The first busy day of a homeward passage was sinking into the dull peace of resumed routine. Aft, on the high poop, Mr Baker walked shuffling and grunted to himself in the pauses of his thoughts. Forward, the look-out man, erect between the flukes of the two anchors, hummed an endless tune, keeping his eyes fixed dutifully ahead in a vacant stare. A multitude of stars coming out into the clear night peopled the emptiness of the sky. They glittered, as if alive above the sea; they surrounded the running ship on all sides; more intense than the eyes of a staring crowd, and as inscrutable as the souls of men.

The passage had begun, and the ship, a fragment detached from the earth, went on lonely and swift like a small planet. Round her the abysses of sky and sea met in an unattainable frontier. A great circular solitude moved with her, ever changing and ever the same, always monotonous and always imposing. Now and then another wandering white speck, burdened with life, appeared far off – disappeared; intent on its own destiny. The sun looked upon her all day, and every morning rose with a burning, round stare of undying curiosity. She had her own future; she was alive with the lives of those beings who trod her decks; like that earth which had given up to the sea, she had an intolerable load of regrets and hopes. On her lived timid truth and audacious lies; and, like the earth, she was unconscious, fair to see – and condemned by men to an ignoble fate. The august loneliness of her path lent dignity to the sordid inspiration of her pilgrimage. She drove foaming to the southward, as if guided by the courage of a high endeavour. The smiling greatness of the sea dwarfed the extent of time. The days raced after one another, brilliant and quick like the flashes of a lighthouse, and the nights, eventful and short, resembled fleeting dreams.

The men had shaken into their places, and the half-hourly voice of the bells ruled their life of unceasing care. Night and day the head and shoulders of a seaman could be seen aft by the wheel, outlined high against sunshine or starlight, very steady above the stir of revolving spokes. The faces changed, passing in rotation. Youthful faces, bearded faces, dark faces: faces serene, or faces moody, but all akin with the brotherhood of the sea; all with the same attentive expression of eyes, carefully watching the compass or the sails. Captain Allistoun, serious, and with an old red muffler round his throat, all day long pervaded the poop. At night, many times he rose out of the darkness of the companion, such as a phantom above a grave, and stood watchful and mute under the stars, his night-shirt fluttering like a flag – then, without a sound, sank down again. He was born on the shores of the Pentland Firth. In his youth he attained the rank of harpooner in Peterhead whalers. When he spoke of that time his restless grey eyes became still and cold, like the loom of ice. Afterwards he went into the East Indian trade for the sake of change. He had commanded the *Narcissus* since she was built. He loved his ship, and drove her unmercifully; for his secret ambition was to make her accomplish some day a brilliantly quick passage which would be mentioned in nautical papers. He pronounced his owner's name with a sardonic smile, spoke but seldom to his officers, and reproved errors in a gentle voice, with words that cut to the quick. His hair was iron-grey, his face hard and of the colour of pump-leather. He shaved every morning of his life – at six – but once (being caught in a fierce hurricane eighty miles south-west of Mauritius) he had missed three consecutive days. He feared naught but an unforgiving God, and wished to end his days in a little house, with a plot of ground attached – far in the country – out of sight of the sea.

He, the ruler of that minute world, seldom descended from the Olympian heights of his poop. Below him – at his feet, so to speak – common mortals led their busy and insignificant lives. Along the main deck, Mr Baker grunted in a manner bloodthirsty and innocuous; and kept all our noses to the grindstone, being – as he once remarked – paid for doing that very thing. The men working about the deck were healthy and contended – as most seamen are, when once well out to sea. The true peace of God begins at any spot a thousand miles from the nearest land; and when He sends there the messengers of His might it is not in terrible wrath against crime, presumption, and folly, but paternally, to chasten simple hearts – ignorant hearts that know nothing of life, and beat undisturbed by envy or greed.

In the evening the cleared decks had a reposeful aspect, resembling the autumn of the earth. The sun was sinking to rest, wrapped in a mantle of warm clouds. Forward, on the end of the spare spars, the boatswain and the carpenter sat together with crossed arms; two men friendly, powerful, and deep-chested. Beside them the short, dumpy, sailmaker – who had been in the Navy – related, between the whiffs of his pipe, impossible stories about Admirals. Couples tramped backwards and forwards, keeping step and balance without effort, in a confined space. Pigs grunted in the big pigsty. Belfast, leaning thoughtfully on his elbow, above the bars, communed with them through the silence of his meditation. Fellows with shirts open wide on sunburnt breasts sat upon the mooring bits, and all up the steps of the forecastle ladders. By the foremast a few discussed in a circle the characteristics of a gentleman. One said: 'It's money as does it.' Another maintained: 'No, it's the way they speak.' Lame Knowles stumped up with an unwashed face (he had the distinction of being the dirty man of the forecastle), and showing a few yellow fangs in a shrewd smile, explained craftily that he 'had seen some of their pants.' The backsides of them – he had observed – were thinner than paper from constant sitting down in offices, yet otherwise they looked first-rate and would last for years. It was all appearance. 'It was,' he said, 'bloomin' easy to be a gentleman when you had a clean job for life.' They disputed endlessly, obstinate and childish; they repeated in shouts and with inflamed faces their amazing arguments; while the soft breeze, eddying down the enormous cavity of the foresail, distended above their bare heads, stirred the tumbled hair with a touch passing and light like an indulgent caress.

They were forgetting their toil, they were forgetting themselves. The cook approached to hear, and stood by, beaming with the inward consciousness of his faith, like a conceited saint unable to forget his glorious reward; Donkin, solitary and brooding over his wrongs on the forecastle-head, moved closer to catch the drift of the discussion below him; he turned his sallow face to the sea, and his thin nostrils moved, sniffing the breeze, as he lounged negligently by the rail. In the glow of sunset faces shone with interest, teeth flashed, eyes sparkled. The walking couples stood still suddenly, with broad grins; a man, bending over a washtub, sat up, entranced, with the soapsuds flecking his wet arms. Even the three petty officers listened leaning back, comfortably propped, and with superior smiles. Belfast left off scratching the ear of his favourite pig, and, open mouthed, tried with eager eyes to have his say. He lifted his arms, grimacing and baffled. From a distance Charley screamed at the ring: 'I know about gentlemen morn'n any of you. I've been intermit with 'em. . . . I've blacked their boots.' The cook, craning his neck to hear better, was scandalized. 'Keep your mouth shut when your elders speak, you impudent young heathen – you.' 'All right, old Hallelujah, I'm done,' answered Charley, soothingly. At some opinion of dirty Knowles, delivered with an air of supernatural cunning, a ripple of laughter ran along, rose like a wave, burst with a startling roar. They stamped with both feet; they turned their shouting faces to the sky; many, spluttering, slapped their thighs; while one or two, bent double, gasped, hugging themselves with both arms like men in pain. The carpenter and the boatswain, without changing their attitude, shook with laughter where they sat; the sailmaker, charged with an anecdote about a Commodore, looked sulky; the cook was wiping his eyes with a greasy rag; and lame Knowles, astonished at his own success, stood in their midst showing a slow smile.

Suddenly the face of Donkin leaning high-shouldered over the after-rail became grave. Something like a weak rattle was heard through the forecastle door. It became a murmur; it ended in a sighing groan. The washerman plunged both his arms into the tub abruptly; the cook became more crestfallen than an exposed backslider; the boatswain moved his shoulders uneasily; the carpenter got up with a spring and walked away – while the sailmaker seemed mentally to give his story up, and began to puff at his pipe with sombre determination. In the blackness of the doorway a pair of eyes glimmered white, and big, and staring. Then James Wait's head protruding, became visible, as if suspended between the two hands that grasped a doorpost on each side of the face. The tassel of his blue woollen nightcap, cocked forward, danced gaily over his left eyelid. He stepped out in a tottering stride. He looked powerful as ever, but showed a strange and affected unsteadiness in his gait; his face was perhaps a trifle thinner, and his eyes appeared rather startlingly prominent. He seemed to hasten the retreat of departing light by his very presence; the setting sun dipped sharply, as though fleeing before our nigger; a black mist emanated from him; a subtle and dismal influence; a something cold and gloomy that floated out and settled on all the faces like a mourning veil. The circle broke up. The joy of laughter died on stiffened lips. There was not a smile left among all the ship's company. Not a word was spoken. Many turned their backs, trying to look unconcerned; others, with averted heads, sent half-reluctant glances out of the corners of their eyes. They resembled criminals conscious of misdeeds more than honest men distracted by doubt; only two or three stared frankly, but stupidly, with lips slightly open. All expected James Wait to say something, and, at the same time, had the air of knowing beforehand what he would say. He leaned his back against the doorpost, and with heavy eyes swept over them a glance domineering and pained, like a sick tyrant overawing a crowd of abject but untrustworthy slaves.

No one went away. They waited in fascinated dread. He said ironically, with gasps between the words:

'Thank you ... chaps. You ... are nice ... and ... quiet ... you are! Yelling so ... before ... the door. ....'

He made a longer pause, during which he worked his ribs in an exaggerated labour of breathing. It was intolerable. Feet were shuffled. Belfast let out a groan; but Donkin above blinked his red eyelids with invisible eyelashes, and smiled bitterly over the nigger's head.

The nigger went on again with surprising ease. He gasped no more, and his voice rang, hollow and loud, as though he had been talking in an empty cavern. He was contemptuously angry.

'I tried to get a wink of sleep. You know I can't sleep o' nights. And you come jabbering near the door here like a blooming lot of old women. ... You think yourselves good shipmates. Do you? ... Much you care for a dying man!'

Belfast spun away from the pigsty. 'Jimmy,' he cried tremulously, 'if you hadn't been sick I would—'

He stopped. The nigger waited awhile, then said, in a gloomy tone: 'You would . . . What? Go an' fight another such one as yourself. Leave me alone. It won't be for long. I'll soon die. . . . It's coming right enough!'

Men stood around very still and with exasperated eyes. It was just what they had expected, and hated to hear, that idea of a stalking death, thrust at them many times a day like a boast and like a menace by this obnoxious nigger. He seemed to take a pride in that death which, so far, had attended only upon the ease of his life; he was overbearing about it, as if no one else in the world had ever been intimate with such a companion; he paraded it unceasingly before us with an affectionate persistence that made its presence indubitable, and at the same time incredible. No man could be suspected of such monstrous friendship! Was he a reality – or was he a sham – this ever-expected visitor of Jimmy's? We hesitated between pity and mistrust, while, on the slightest provocation he shook before our eyes the bones of his bothersome and infamous skeleton. He was for ever trotting him out. He would talk of that coming death as though it had been already there, as if it had been walking the deck outside, as if it would presently come in to sleep in the only empty bunk; as if it had sat by his side at every meal. It interfered daily with our occupations, with our leisure, with our amusements. We had no songs and no music in the evening, because Jimmy (we all lovingly called him Jimmy, to conceal our hate of his accomplice) had managed, with that prospective decease of his, to disturb even Archie's mental balance. Archie was the owner of the concertina; but after a couple of stinging lecturers from Jimmy he refused to play any more. He said: 'Yon's an uncanny joker. I dinna ken what's wrang wi' him, but there's something verra wrang, verra wrang. It's nae manner of use asking me. I won't play.' Our singers became mute because Jimmy was a dying man. For the same reason no chap – as Knowles remarked – could 'drive in a nail to hang his few poor rags upon', without being made aware of the enormity he committed in disturbing Jimmy's interminable last moments. At night, instead of the cheerful yell, 'One bell! Turn out! Do you hear there? Hey! hey! hey! Show leg!' the watches were called man by man, in whispers, so as not to interfere with Jimmy's, possibly, last slumber on earth. True, he was always awake, and managed, as we sneaked out on deck, to plant in our backs some cutting remark that, for the moment, made us feel as if we had been brutes, and afterwards made us suspect ourselves of being fools. We spoke in low tones within that fo'c'sle as though it had been a church. We ate our meals in silence and dread, for Jimmy was capricious with his food, and railed bitterly at the salt meat, at the biscuits, at the tea, as at articles unfit for human consumption – 'let alone for a dying man!' He would say: 'Can't you find a better slice of meat for a sick man who's trying to get home to be cured – or buried? But there! If I had a chance, you fellows would do away with it. You would poison me. Look at what you have given me!' We served him in his bed with rage and humility, as though we had been the base courtiers of a hated prince; and he rewarded us by his unconciliating criticism. He had found the secret of keeping for ever on the run the fundamental imbecility of mankind; he had the secret of life, that confounded dying man, and he made himself master of every moment of our existence. We grew desperate, and remained submissive. Emotional little Belfast was for ever on the verge of assault or on the verge of tears. One evening he confided to Archie: 'For a ha'penny I would knock his ugly black head off – the skulking dodger!' And the straight-forward Archie pretended to be shocked! Such was the infernal spell which that casual St Kitt's nigger had cast upon our guileless manhood! But the same night Belfast stole from the galley the officers' Sunday fruit pie, to tempt the fastidious appetite of Jimmy. He endangered not only his long friendship with the cook but also – as it appeared – his eternal welfare. The cook was overwhelmed with grief; he did not know the culprit but he knew that wickedness flourished; he knew that Satan was abroad amongst those men, whom he looked upon as in some way under his spiritual care. Whenever he saw three or four of us standing together he would leave his stove, to run out and preach. We fled from him; and only Charley (who knew the thief) affronted the cook with a candid gaze which irritated the good man. 'It's you, I believe,' he groaned, sorrowful and with a patch of soot on his chin. 'It's you. You are a brand for the burning! No more of YOUR socks in my galley.' Soon, unofficially, the information was spread about that, should there be another case of stealing, our marmalade (an extra allowance: half a pound per man) would be stopped. Mr Baker ceased to heap jocular abuse upon his favourites, and grunted suspiciously at all. The captain's cold eyes, high up on the poop, glittered mistrustful, as he surveyed us trooping in a small mob from halyards to braces for the usual evening pull at all the ropes. Such stealing in a merchant ship is difficult to check, and may be taken as a declaration by men of their dislike for their officers. It is a bad symptom. It may end in God knows what trouble. The *Narcissus* was still a peaceful ship, but mutual confidence was shaken. Donkin did not conceal his delight. We were dismayed.

Then illogical Belfast reproached our nigger with great fury. James Wait, with his elbow on the pillow, choked, gasped out: 'Did I ask you to bone the dratted thing? Blow your blamed pie. It has made me worse – you little Irish lunatic, you!' Belfast, with scarlet face and trembling lips, made a dash at him. Every man in the forecastle rose with a shout. There was a moment of wild tumult. Someone shrieked piercingly: 'Easy, Belfast! Easy! . . .' We expected Belfast to strangle Wait without more ado. Dust flew. We heard through it the nigger's cough, metallic and explosive like a gong. Next moment we saw Belfast hanging over him. He was saying plaintively: 'Don't! Don't, Jimmy! Don't be like that. An angel couldn't put up with ye – sick as ye are.' He looked round at us from Jimmy's bedside, his comical mouth twitching, and through tearful eyes; then he tried to put straight the disarranged blankets. The unceasing whisper of the sea filled the forecastle. Was James Wait frightened, or touched, or repentant? He lay on his back with a hand to his side, and as motionless as if his expected visitor had come at last. Belfast fumbled about his feet, repeating with emotion: 'Yes. We know. Ye are bad, but . . . Just say what ye want done, and . . . We all know ye are bad – very bad. . . .' No! Decidedly James Wait was not touched or repentant. Truth to say, he seemed rather startled. He sat up with incredible suddenness and ease. 'Ah! You think I am bad do you?' he said gloomily, in his clearest baritone voice (to hear him speak sometimes you would never think there was anything wrong with that man). 'Do you? . . . Well, act according! Some of you haven't sense enough to put a blanket shipshape over a sick man. There! Leave it alone! I can die anyhow!' Belfast turned away limply with a gesture of discouragement. In the silence of the forecastle, full of interested men, Donkin pronounced distinctly: 'Well, I'm blowed!' and sniggered. Wait looked at him. He looked at him in a quite friendly manner. Nobody could tell what would please our incomprehensible invalid: but for us the scorn of that snigger was hard to bear.

Donkin's position in the forecastle was distinguished but unsafe. He stood on the bad eminence of a general dislike. He was left alone; and in his isolation he could do nothing but think of the gales of the Cape of Good Hope and envy us the possession of warm clothing and waterproofs. Our sea-boots, our oilskin coats, our well-filled sea-chests, were to him so many causes for bitter meditation: he had none of those things, and he felt instinctively that no man, when the need arose, would offer to share them with him. He was impudently cringing to us and systematically insolent to the officers. He anticipated the best results, for himself, from such a line of conduct – and was mistaken. Such natures forget that under extreme provocation men will be just – whether they want to be so or not. Donkin's insolence to long-suffering Mr Baker became at last intolerable to us, and we rejoiced when the mate, one dark night, tamed him for good. It was done neatly, with great decency and decorum, and with little noise. We had been called – just before midnight – to trim the yards, and Donkin – as usual – made insulting remarks. We stood sleepily in a row with the forebrace in our hands waiting for the next order, and heard in the darkness a scuffly trampling of feet, an exclamation of surprise, sounds of cuffs and slaps, suppressed, hissing whispers: 'Ah! Will you!' – 'Don't! . . . Don't!' – 'Then behave' – 'Oh! Oh! . . .' Afterwards there were soft thuds mixed with the rattle of iron things as if a man's body had been tumbling helplessly amongst the main-pump rods. Before we could realize the situation, Mr Baker's voice was heard very near and a little impatient: 'Haul away, men! Lay back on that rope!' And we did lay back on the rope with great alacrity. As if nothing had happened, the chief mate went on trimming the yards with his usual and exasperating fastidiousness. We didn't at the time see anything of Donkin, and did not care. Had the chief officer thrown him overboard, no man would have said as much as 'Hallo! he's gone!' But, in truth, no great harm was done – even if Donkin did lose one of his front teeth. We perceived this in the morning, and preserved a ceremonious silence: the etiquette of the forecastle commanded us to be blind and dumb in such a case, and we cherished the decencies of our life more than ordinary landsmen respect theirs. Charley, with unpardonable want of *savoir vivre*, yelled out: "'Ave you been to your dentyst? . . . Hurt ye, didn't it?' He got a box on the ear from one of his best friends. The boy was surprised and remained plunged in grief for at least three hours. We were sorry for him, but youth requires even more discipline than age. Donkin grinned venomously. From that day he became pitiless; told Jimmy that he was a 'black fraud'; hinted to us that we were an imbecile lot, daily taken in by a vulgar nigger. And Jimmy seemed to like the fellow!

Singleton lived untouched by human emotions. Taciturn and unsmiling, he breathed amongst us – in that alone resembling the rest of the crowd. We were trying to be decent chaps, and found it jolly difficult; we oscillated between the desire of virtue and the fear of ridicule; we wished to save ourselves from the pain of remorse, but did not want to be made the contemptible dupes of our sentiment. Jimmy's hateful accomplice seemed to have blown with his impure breath undreamt-of subtleties into our hearts. We were disturbed and cowardly. That we knew. Singleton seemed to know nothing, understand nothing. We had thought him till then as wise as he looked, but now we dared, at times, suspect him of being stupid – from old age. One day, however, at dinner, as we sat on our boxes round a tin dish that stood on the deck within the circle of our feet, Jimmy expressed his general disgust with men and things in words that were particularly disgusting. Singleton lifted his head. We became mute. The old man, addressing Jimmy, asked: 'Are you dying?' Thus interrogated, James Wait appeared horribly startled and confused. We all were startled. Mouths remained open; hearts thumped, eyes blinked; a dropped tin fork rattled in the dish; a man rose as if to go out, and stood still. In less than a minute Jimmy pulled himself together: 'Why? Can't you see I am?' he answered shakily. Singleton lifted a piece of soaked biscuit ('his teeth' – he declared – 'had no edge on them now') to his lips. 'Well, get on with your dying,' he said with venerable mildness; 'don't raise a blamed fuss with us over that job. We can't help you.' Jimmy fell back in his bunk, and for a long time lay very still wiping the perspiration off his chin. The dinner-tins were put away quickly. On deck we discussed the incident in whispers. Some showed a chuckling exultation. Many looked grave. Wamibo, after long periods of staring dreaminess, attempted abortive smiles; and one of the young Scandinavians, much tormented by doubt, ventured in the second dog-watch to approach Singleton (the old man did not encourage us much to speak to him) and ask sheepishly: 'You think he will die?' Singleton looked up. 'Why, of course he will die,' he said deliberately. This seemed decisive. It was promptly imparted to everyone by him who had consulted the oracle. Shy and eager, he would step up and with averted gaze recite his formula: 'Old Singleton says he will die.' It was a relief! At last we knew that our compassion would not be misplaced, and we could again smile without misgivings – but we reckoned without Donkin. Donkin 'didn't want to 'ave no truck with 'em dirty furriners'. When Nilsen came to him with the news: 'Singleton says he will die,' he answered him by a spiteful 'And so will you – you fat-headed Dutchman. Wish you Dutchmen were all dead – 'stead comin' takin' our money inter your starvin' country.' We were appalled. We perceived that after all Singleton's answer meant nothing. We began to hate him for making fun of us. All our certitudes were going; we were on doubtful terms with our officers; the cook had given us up for lost; we had overheard the boatswain's opinion that 'we were a crowd of softies'. We suspected Jimmy, one another, and even our very selves. We did not know what to do. At every insignificant turn of our humble life we met Jimmy overbearing and blocking the way, arm-in-arm with his awful and veiled familiar. It was a weird servitude.

It began a week after leaving Bombay and came on us stealthily like any other great misfortune. Everyone had remarked that Jimmy from the first was very slack at his work; but we thought it simply the outcome of his philosophy of life. Donkin said: 'You put no more weight on a rope than a bloody sparrer.' He disdained him. Belfast, ready for a fight, exclaimed provokingly: 'You don't kill yourself, old man!' 'Would YOU?' he retorted with extreme scorn – and Belfast retired. One morning, as we were washing decks, Mr Baker called to him: 'Bring your broom over here, Wait.' He strolled languidly. 'Move yourself! Ough!' grunted Mr Baker; 'what's the matter with your hind legs?' He stopped dead short. He gazed slowly with eyes that bulged out with an expression audacious and sad. 'It isn't my legs,' he said, 'it's my lungs.' Everybody listened. 'What's . . . Ough! . . . What's wrong with them?' inquired Mr Baker. All the watch stood around on the wet deck, grinning, and with brooms or buckets in their hands. He said mournfully: 'Going – or gone. Can't you see I'm a dying man? I know it!' Mr Baker was disgusted. 'Then why the devil did you ship aboard here?' 'I must live till I die – mustn't I?' he replied. The grins became audible. 'Go off the deck – get out of my sight,' said Mr Baker. He was nonplussed. It was an unique experience. James Wait, obedient, dropped his broom, and walked slowly forward. A burst of laughter followed him. It was too funny. All hands laughed. . . . They laughed! . . . Alas!

He became the tormentor of all our moments; he was worse than a nightmare. You couldn't see that there was anything wrong with him: a nigger does not show. He was not very fat – certainly – but then he was no leaner than other niggers we had known. He coughed often, but the most prejudiced person could perceive that, mostly, he coughed when it suited his purpose. He wouldn't, or couldn't, do his work – and he wouldn't lie-up. One day he would skip aloft with the best of them and next time we would be obliged to risk our lives to get his limp body down. He was reported, he was examined; he was remonstrated with, threatened, cajoled, lectured. He was called into the cabin to interview the captain. There were wild rumours. It was said he had cheeked the old man; it was said he had frightened him. Charley maintained that the 'skipper, weepin', 'as giv' 'im 'is blessin' an' a pot of jam'. Knowles had it from the steward that the unspeakable Jimmy had been reeling against the cabin furniture; that he had groaned; that he had complained of general brutality and disbelief; and had ended by coughing all over the old man's meteorological journals which were then spread on the table. At any rate, Wait returned forward supported by the steward, who, in a pained and shocked voice, entreated us: 'Here! Catch hold of him, one of you. He is to lie-up.' Jimmy drank a tin mugful of coffee, and, after bullying first one and then another, went to bed. He remained there most of the time, but when it suited him would come on deck and appear amongst us. He was scornful and brooding; he looked ahead upon the sea, and no one could tell what was the meaning of that black man sitting apart in meditative attitude and as motionless as a carving.

He refused steadily all medicine; he threw sago and cornflour overboard till the steward got tired of bringing it to him. He asked for paregoric. They sent him a big bottle; enough to poison a wilderness of babies. He kept it between his mattress and the deal lining of the ship's side; and nobody ever saw him take a dose. Donkin abused him to his face, jeered at him while he gasped; and the same day Wait would lend him a warm jersey. Once Donkin reviled him for half an hour; reproached him with the extra work his malingering gave to the watch; and ended by calling him 'a black-faced swine'. Under the spell of our accursed perversity we were horror-struck. But Jimmy positively seemed to revel in that abuse. It made him look cheerful – and Donkin had a pair of old sea boots thrown at him. 'Here, you East End trash,' boomed Wait, 'you may have that.'

At last Mr Baker had to tell the captain that James Wait was disturbing the peace of the ship. 'Knock discipline on the head – he will, Ough,' grunted Mr Baker. As a matter of fact, the starboard watch came as near as possible to refusing duty, when ordered one morning by the boatswain to wash out their forecastle. It appears Jimmy objected to a wet floor – and that morning we were in a compassionate mood. We thought the boatswain a brute, and, practically, told him so. Only Mr Baker's delicate tact prevented an all-fired row: he refused to take us seriously. He came bustling forward, and called us many unpolite names but in such a hearty and seamanlike manner that we began to feel ashamed of ourselves. In truth, we thought him much too good a sailor to annoy him willingly: and after all Jimmy might have been a fraud – probably was! The forecastle got a clean up that morning; but in the afternoon a sick-bay was fitted up in the deck-house. It was a nice little cabin opening on deck, and with two berths. Jimmy's belongings were transported there, and then – notwithstanding his protests – Jimmy himself. He said he couldn't walk. Four men carried him on a blanket. He complained that he would have to die there alone, like a dog. We grieved for him, and were delighted to have him removed from the forecastle. We attended him as before. The galley was next door, and the cook looked in many times a day. Wait became a little more cheerful. Knowles affirmed having heard him laugh to himself in peals one day. Others had seen him walking about on deck at night. His little place, with the door ajar on a long hook, was always full of tobacco smoke. We spoke through the crack cheerfully, sometimes abusively, as we passed by, intent on our work. He fascinated us. He would never let doubt die. He overshadowed the ship. Invulnerable in his promise of speedy corruption he trampled on our self-respect, he demonstrated to us daily our want of moral courage; he tainted our lives. Had we been a miserable gang of wretched immortals, unhallowed alike by hope and fear, he could not have lorded it over us with a more pitiless assertion of his sublime privilege.

CHAPTER 3

Meantime the *Narcissus*, with square yards, ran out of the fair monsoon. She drifted slowly, swinging round and round the compass, through a few days of baffling light airs. Under the patter of short warm showers, grumbling men whirled the heavy yards from side to side; they caught hold of the soaked ropes with groans and sighs, while their officers, sulky and dripping with rain water, unceasingly ordered them about in wearied voices. During the short respites they looked with disgust into the smarting palms of their stiff hands, and asked one another bitterly: 'Who would be a sailor if he could be a farmer?' All the tempers were spoilt, and no man cared what he said. One black night, when the watch, panting in the heat and half-drowned with the rain, had been through four mortal hours hunted from brace to brace, Belfast declared that he would 'chuck the sea for ever and go in a steamer'. This was excessive, no doubt. Captain Allistoun, with great self-control, would mutter sadly to Mr Baker: 'It is not so bad – not so bad,' when he had managed to shove, and dodge, and manoeuvre his smart ship through sixty miles in twenty-four hours. From the doorstep of the little cabin, Jimmy, chin in hand, watched our distasteful labours with insolent and melancholy eyes. We spoke to him gently – and out of his sight exchanged sour smiles.

Then, again, with a fair wind and under a clear sky, the ship went on piling up the South Latitude. She passed outside Madagascar and Mauritius without a glimpse of the land. Extra lashings were put on the spare spars. Hatches were looked to. The steward in his leisure moments and with a worried air tried to fit washboards to the cabin doors. Stout canvas was bent with care. Anxious eyes looked to the westward, towards the cape of storms. The ship began to dip into a south-west swell, and the softly luminous sky of low latitudes took on a harder sheen from day to day above our heads: it arched high above the ship, vibrating and pale, like an immense dome of steel, resonant with the deep voice of freshening gales. The sunshine gleamed cold on the white curls of black waves. Before the strong breath of westerly squalls the ship, with reduced sail, lay slowly over, obstinate and yielding. She drove to and fro in the unceasing endeavour to fight her way through the invisible violence of the winds: she pitched headlong into dark smooth hollows; she struggled upwards over the snowy ridges of great running seas; she rolled, restless, from side to side, like a thing in pain. Enduring and valiant, she answered to the call of men; and her slim spars waving for ever in abrupt semicircles, seemed to beckon in vain for help towards the stormy sky.

It was a bad winter off the Cape that year. The relieved helmsmen came off flapping their arms, or ran stamping hard and blowing into swollen, red fingers. The watch on deck dodged the sting of cold sprays, or, crouching in sheltered corners, watched dismally the high and merciless seas boarding the ship time after time in unappeasable fury. Water tumbled in cataracts over the forecastle doors. You had to dash through a waterfall to get into your damp bed. The men turned in wet and turned out stiff to face the redeeming and ruthless exactions of their glorious and obscure fate. Far aft, and peering watchfully to windward, the officers could be seen through the mist of squalls. They stood by the weather-rail, holding on grimly, straight and glistening in their long coats; and in the disordered plunges of the hard-driven ship, they appeared high up, attentive, tossing violently above the grey line of a clouded horizon in motionless attitudes.

They watched the weather and the ship as men on shore watch the momentous chances of fortune. Captain Allistoun never left the deck, as though he had been part of the ship's fittings. Now and then the steward, shivering, but always in shirt sleeves, would struggle towards him with some hot coffee, half of which the gale blew out of the cup before it reached the master's lips. He drank what was left gravely in one long gulp, while heavy sprays pattered loudly on his oilskin coat, the seas swishing broke about his high boots; and he never took his eyes off the ship. He kept his gaze riveted upon her as a loving man watches the unselfish toil of a delicate woman upon the slender thread of whose existence is hung the whole meaning and joy of the world. We all watched her. She was beautiful and had a weakness. We loved her no less for that. We admired her qualities aloud, we boasted of them to one another, as though they had been our own, and the consciousness of her only fault we kept buried in the silence of our profound affection. She was born in the thundering peal of hammers beating upon iron, in black eddies of smoke, under a grey sky, on the banks of the Clyde. The clamorous and sombre stream gives birth to things of beauty that float away into the sunshine of the world to be loved by men. The *Narcissus* was one of that perfect brood. Less perfect than many perhaps, but she was ours, and, consequently, incomparable. We were proud of her. In Bombay, ignorant landlubbers alluded to her as that 'pretty grey ship'. Pretty! A scurvy meed of commendation! We knew she was the most magnificent sea-boat ever launched. We tried to forget that, like many good sea-boats, she was at times rather crank. She was exacting. She wanted care in loading and handling, and no one knew exactly how much care would be enough. Such are the imperfections of mere men! The ship knew, and sometimes would correct the presumptuous human ignorance by the wholesome discipline of fear. We had heard ominous stories about past voyages. The cook (technically a seaman, but in reality no sailor) – the cook, when unstrung by some misfortune, such as the rolling over of a saucepan, would mutter gloomily while he wiped the floor: 'There! Look at what she has done! Some voy'ge she will drown all hands! You'll see if she won't.' To which the steward, snatching in the galley a moment to draw breath in the hurry of his worried life, would remark philosophically: 'Those that see won't tell, anyhow. I don't want to see it.' We derided those fears. Our hearts went out to the old man when he pressed her hard so as to make her hold her own, hold to every inch gained to windward; when he made her, under reefed sails, leap obliquely at enormous waves. The men, knitted together aft into a ready group by the first sharp order of an officer coming to take charge of the deck in bad weather: 'Keep handy the watch', stood admiring her valiance. Their eyes blinked in the wind; their dark faces were wet with drops of water more salt and bitter than human tears; beards and moustaches, soaked, hung straight and dripping like fine seaweed. They were fantastically misshapen; in high boots, in hats like helmets, and swaying clumsily, stiff and bulky in glistening oilskins, they resembled men strangely equipped for some fabulous adventure. Whenever she rose easily to a towering green sea, elbows dug ribs, faces brightened, lips murmured: 'Didn't she do it cleverly,' and all the heads turning like one watched with sardonic grins the foiled wave go roaring to leeward, white with the foam of a monstrous rage. But when she had not been quick enough and, struck heavily, lay over trembling under the blow, we clutched at ropes, and looking up at the narrow bands of drenched and strained sails waving desperately aloft, we thought in our hearts: 'No wonder. Poor thing!'

The thirty-second day out of Bombay began inauspiciously. In the morning a sea smashed one of the galley doors. We dashed in through lots of steam and found the cook very wet and indignant with the ship: 'She's getting worse every day. She's trying to drown me in front of my own stove!' He was very angry. We pacified him, and the carpenter, though washed away twice from there, managed to repair the door. Through that accident our dinner was not ready till late, but it didn't matter in the end because Knowles, who went to fetch it, got knocked down by a sea and the dinner went over the side. Captain Allistoun, looking more hard and thin-lipped than ever, hung on to full topsails and foresail, and would not notice that the ship, asked to do too much, appeared to lose heart altogether for the first time since we knew her. She refused to rise, and bored her way sullenly through the seas. Twice running, as though she had been blind or weary of life, she put her nose deliberately into a big wave and swept the decks from end to end. As the boatswain observed with marked annoyance, while we were splashing about in a body to try and save a worthless wash-tub: 'Every blooming thing in the ship is going overboard this afternoon.' Venerable Singleton broke his habitual silence and said with a glance aloft: 'The old man's in a temper with the weather, but it's no good bein' angry with the winds of heaven.' Jimmy had shut his door, of course. We knew he was dry and comfortable within his little cabin, and in our absurd way were pleased one moment, exasperated the next, by that certitude. Donkin skulked shamelessly, uneasy and miserable. He grumbled: 'I'm perishin' with cold outside in bloomin' wet rags, an' that 'ere black sojer sits dry on a blamed chest full of bloomin' clothes; blank his black soul!' We took no notice of him; we hardly gave a thought to Jimmy and his bosom friend. There was no leisure for idle probing of hearts. Sails blew adrift. Things broke loose. Cold and wet, we were washed about the deck while trying to repair damages. The ship tossed about, shaken furiously, like a toy in the hand of a lunatic. Just at sunset there was a rush to shorten sail before the menace of a sombre hail cloud. The hard gust of wind came brutal like the blow of a fist. The ship relieved of her canvas in time received it pluckily: she yielded reluctantly to the violent onset; then, coming up with a stately and irresistible motion, brought her spars to windward in the teeth of the screeching squall. Out of the abysmal darkness of the black cloud overhead white hail streamed on her, rattled on the rigging, leaped in handfuls off the yards, rebounded on the deck – round and gleaming in the murky turmoil like a shower of pearls. It passed away. For a moment a livid sun shot horizontally the last rays of sinister light between the hills of steep, rolling waves. Then a wild night rushed in – stamped out in a great howl that dismal remnant of a stormy day.

There was no sleep on board that night. Most seamen remember in their life one or two such nights of a culminating gale. Nothing seems left of the whole universe but darkness, clamour, fury – and the ship. And like the last vestige of a shattered creation she drifts, bearing an anguished remnant of sinful mankind, through the distress, tumult, and pain of an avenging terror. No one slept in the forecastle. The tin oil-lamp suspended on a long string, smoking, described wide circles; wet clothing made dark heaps on the glistening floor; a thin layer of water rushed to and fro. In the bed-places men lay booted, resting on elbows and with open eyes. Hung-up suits of oilskin swung out and in, lively and disquieting like reckless ghosts of decapitated seamen dancing in a tempest. No one spoke and all listened. Outside the night moaned and sobbed to the accompaniment of a continuous loud tremor as of innumerable drums beating far off. Shrieks passed through the air. Tremendous dull blows made the ship tremble while she rolled under the weight of the seas toppling on her deck. At times she soared up swiftly as if to leave this earth for ever, then during interminable moments fell through a void with all the hearts on board of her standing still, till a frightful shock, expected and sudden, started them off again with a big thump. After every dislocating jerk of the ship, Wamibo, stretched full length, his face on the pillow, groaned slightly with the pain of his tormented universe. Now and then, for the fraction of an intolerable second, the ship, in the fiercer burst of a terrible uproar, remained on her side, vibrating and still, with a stillness more appalling than the wildest motion. Then upon all those prone bodies a stir would pass, a shiver of suspense. A man would protrude his anxious head and a pair of eyes glistened in the sway of light glaring wildly. Some moved their legs a little as if making ready to jump out. But several, motionless on their backs and with one hand gripping hard the edge of the bunk, smoked nervously with quick puffs, staring upwards; immobilized in a great craving for peace.

At midnight, orders were given to furl the fore and mizen topsails. With immense efforts men crawled aloft through a merciless buffeting, saved the canvas and crawled down almost exhausted, to bear in panting silence the cruel battering of the seas. Perhaps for the first time in the history of the merchant service the watch, told to go below, did not leave the deck, as if compelled to remain there by the fascination of a venomous violence. At every heavy gust men, huddled together, whispered to one another: 'It can blow no harder' – and presently the gale would give them the lie with a piercing shriek, and drive their breath back into their throats. A fierce squall seemed to burst asunder the thick mass of sooty vapours; and above the wrack of torn clouds glimpses could be caught of the high moon rushing backwards with frightful speed over the sky, right into the wind's eye. Many hung their heads, muttering that it 'turned their inwards out' to look at it. Soon the clouds closed up and the world again became a raging, blind darkness that howled, flinging at the lonely ship salt sprays and sleet.

About half past seven the pitchy obscurity round us turned a ghastly grey, and we knew that the sun had risen. This unnatural and threatening daylight, in which we could see one another's wild eyes and drawn faces, was only an added tax on our endurance. The horizon seemed to have come on all sides within arm's length of the ship. Into that narrowed circle furious seas leaped in, struck, and leaped out. A rain of salt, heavy drops flew aslant like mist. The main-topsail had to be goose-winged, and with stolid resignation every one prepared to go aloft once more; but the officers yelled, pushed back, and at last we understood that no more men would be allowed to go on the yard than were absolutely necessary for the work. As at any moment the masts were likely to be jumped out or blown overboard, we concluded that the captain didn't want to see all his crowd go over the side at once. That was reasonable. The watch then on duty, led by Mr Creighton, began to struggle up the rigging. The wind flattened them against the ratlines; then, easing a little, would let them ascend a couple of steps; and again, with a sudden gust, pin all up the shrouds the whole crawling line in attitudes of crucifixion. The other watch plunged down on the main deck to haul up the sail. Men's heads bobbed up as the water flung them irresistibly from side to side. Mr Baker grunted encouragingly in our midst, spluttering and blowing amongst the tangled ropes like an energetic porpoise. Favoured by an ominous and untrustworthy lull, the work was done without anyone being lost either off the deck or from the yard. For the moment the gale seemed to take off, and the ship, as if grateful for our efforts, plucked up heart and made better weather of it.

At eight the men off duty, watching their chance, ran forward over the flooded deck to get some rest. The other half of the crew remained aft for their turn of 'seeing her through her trouble', as they expressed it. The two mates urged the master to go below. Mr Baker grunted in his ear: 'Ough! surely now ... Ough! ... confidence in us ... nothing more to do ... she must lay it out or go. Ough! Ough!' Tall young Mr Creighton smiled down at him cheerfully: '... She's as right as a trivet! Take a spell, sir.' He looked at them stonily with bloodshot, sleepless eyes. The rims of his eyelids were scarlet, and he moved his jaw unceasingly with a slow effort, as though he had been masticating a lump of india-rubber. He shook his head. He repeated: 'Never mind me. I must see it out – I must see it out,' but he consented to sit down for a moment on the skylight, with his hard face turned unflinchingly to windward. The sea spat at it – and stoical, it streamed with water as though he had been weeping. On the weather side of the poop the watch, hanging on to the mizen rigging and to one another, tried to exchange encouraging words. Singleton, at the wheel, yelled out: 'Look out for yourselves!' His voice reached them in a warning whisper. They were startled.

A big, foaming sea came out of the mist; it made for the ship, roaring wildly, and in its rush it looked as mischievous and discomposing as a madman with an axe. One or two, shouting, scrambled up the rigging; most, with a convulsive catch of the breath, held on where they stood. Singleton dug his knees under the wheel-box, and carefully eased the helm to the headlong pitch of the ship, but without taking his eyes off the coming wave. It towered close-to and high, like a wall of green glass topped with snow. The ship rose to it as though she had soared on wings, and for a moment rested poised upon the foaming crest as if she had been a great sea-bird. Before we could draw breath a heavy gust struck her, another roller took her unfairly under the weather bow, she gave a toppling lurch, and filled her decks. Captain Allistoun leaped up, and fell; Archie rolled over him, screaming: 'She will rise!' She gave another lurch to leeward; the lower deadeyes dipped heavily; the men's feet flew from under them, and they hung kicking above the slanting poop. They could see the ship putting her side in the water, and shouted all together: 'She's going!' Forward the forecastle doors flew open, and the watch below were seen leaping out one after another, throwing their arms up; and, falling on hands and knees, scrambled aft on all fours along the high side of the deck, sloping more than the roof of a house. From leeward the seas rose, pursuing them; they looked wretched in a hopeless struggle, like vermin fleeing before a flood; they fought up the weather ladder of the poop one after another, half naked and staring wildly; and as soon as they got up they shot to leeward in clusters, with closed eyes, till they brought up heavily with their ribs against the iron stanchions of the rail: then, groaning, they rolled in a confused mass. The immense volume of water thrown forward by the last scend of the ship had burst the lee door of the forecastle. They could see their chests, pillows, blankets, clothing, come out floating upon the sea. While they struggled back to windward they looked in dismay. The straw beds swam high, the blankets, spread out, undulated; while the chests, waterlogged and with a heavy list, pitched heavily like dismasted hulks, before they sank; Archie's big coat passed with outspread arms, resembling a drowned seaman floating with his head under water. Men were slipping down while trying to dig their fingers into the planks: others, jammed in corners, rolled enormous eyes. They all yelled unceasingly: 'The masts! Cut! Cut! . . .' A black squall howled low over the ship, that lay on her side with the weather yard-arms pointing to the clouds; while the tall masts, inclined nearly to the horizon, seemed to be of an immeasurable length. The carpenter let go his hold, rolled against the skylight, and began to crawl to the cabin entrance, where a big axe was kept ready for just such an emergency. At that moment the topsail sheet parted, the end of the heavy chain racketed aloft, and sparks of red fire streamed down through the flying sprays. The sail flapped once with a jerk that seemed to tear our hearts out through our teeth, and instantly changed into a bunch of fluttering narrow ribbons that tied themselves into knots and became quiet along the yard. Captain Allistoun struggled, managed to stand up with his face near the deck, upon which men swung on the ends of ropes, like nest robbers upon a cliff. One of his feet was on somebody's chest; his face was purple; his lips moved. He yelled also; he yelled, bending down: 'No! No!' Mr Baker, one leg over the binnacle-stand, roared out: 'Did you

say no? Not cut?' He shook his head madly. 'No! No!' Between his legs the
crawling carpenter heard, collapsed at once, and lay full length in the angle
of the skylight. Voices took up the shout – 'No! No!' Then all became still.
They waited for the ship to turn over altogether, and shake them out into
the sea; and upon the terrific noise of wind and sea not a murmur of
remonstrance came out from those men, who each would have given ever so
many years of life to see 'them damned sticks go overboard!' They all believed
it their only chance: but a little hard-faced man shook his grey head and
shouted 'No!' without giving them as much as a glance. They were silent,
and gasped. They gripped rails, they had wound ropes'-ends under their
arms; they clutched ringbolts, they crawled in heaps where there was
foothold; they held on with both arms, hooked themselves to anything to
windward with elbows, with chins, almost with their teeth: and some, unable
to crawl away from where they had been flung, felt the sea leap up, striking
against their backs as they struggled upwards. Singleton had stuck to the
wheel. His hair flew out in the wind; the gale seemed to take its life-long
adversary by the beard and shake his old head. He wouldn't let go, and,
with his knees forced between the spokes, flew up and down like a man on
a bough. As Death appeared unready, they began to look about. Donkin,
caught by one foot in a loop of some rope, hung, head down, below us, and
yelled, with his face to the deck: 'Cut! Cut!' Two men lowered themselves
cautiously to him; others hauled on the rope. They caught him up, shoved
him into a safer place, held him. He shouted curses at the master, shook his
fist at him with horrible blasphemies, called upon us in filthy words to 'Cut!
Don't mind that murdering fool! Cut, some of you!' One of his rescuers
struck him a back-handed blow over the mouth; his head banged on the
deck, and he became suddenly very quiet, with a white face, breathing hard,
and with a few drops of blood trickling from his cut lip. On the lee side
another man could be seen stretched out as if stunned; only the washboard
prevented him from going over the side. It was the steward. We had to sling
him up like a bale for he was paralysed with fright. He had rushed up out
of the pantry when he felt the ship go over, and had rolled down helplessly,
clutching a china mug. It was not broken. With difficulty we tore it away
from him, and when he saw it in our hands he was amazed. 'Where did you
get that thing?' he kept on asking us in a trembling voice. His shirt was
blown to shreds; the ripped sleeves flapped like wings. Two men made him
fast, and, doubled over the rope that held him, he resembled a bundle of wet
rags. Mr Baker crawled along the line of men, asking: 'Are you all there?'
and looking them over. Some blinked vacantly, others shook convulsively;
Wamibo's head hung over his breast; and in painful attitudes, cut by lashings,
exhausted with clutching, screwed up in corners, they breathed heavily.
Their lips twitched, and at every sickening heave of the overturned ship they
opened them wide as if to shout. The cook, embracing a wooden stanchion,
unconsciously repeated a prayer. In every short interval of the fiendish noises
around he could be heard there, without cap or slippers, imploring in that
storm the Master of our lives not to lead him into temptation. Soon he also
became silent. In all that crowd of cold and hungry men, waiting wearily

for a violent death, not a voice was heard; they were mute, and in sombre thoughtfulness listened to the horrible imprecations of the gale.

Hours passed. They were sheltered by the heavy inclination of the ship from the wind that rushed in one long unbroken moan above their heads, but cold rain showers fell at times into the uneasy calm of their refuge. Under the torment of that new infliction a pair of shoulders would writhe a little. Teeth chattered. The sky was clearing, and bright sunshine gleamed over the ship. After every burst of battering seas, vivid and fleeting rainbows arched over the drifting hull in the flick of sprays. The gale was ending in a clear blow, which gleamed and cut like a knife. Between two bearded shellbacks Charley, fastened with somebody's long muffler to a deck ringbolt, wept quietly, with rare tears wrung out by bewilderment, cold, hunger, and general misery. One of his neighbours punched him in the ribs asking roughly: 'What's the matter with your cheek? In fine weather there's no holding you, youngster.' Turning about with prudence he worked himself out of his coat and threw it over the boy. The other man closed up, muttering: "Twill make a bloomin' man of you, sonny.' They flung their arms over and pressed against him. Charley drew his feet up and his eyelids dropped. Sighs were heard, as men, perceiving that they were not to be 'drowned in a hurry', tried easier positions. Mr Creighton, who had hurt his leg, lay amongst us with compressed lips. Some fellows belonging to his watch set about securing him better. Without a word or a glance he lifted his arms one after another to facilitate the operation, and not a muscle moved in his stern, young face. They asked him with solicitude: 'Easier now, sir?' He answered with a curt: 'That'll do.' He was a hard young officer, but many of his watch used to say they liked him well enough because he had 'such a gentlemanly way of damning us up and down the deck'. Others unable to discern such fine shades of refinement, respected him for his smartness. For the first time since the ship had gone on her beam ends Captain Allistoun gave a short glance down at his men. He was almost upright – one foot against the side of the skylight, one knee on the deck; and with the end of the vang round his waist swung back and forth with his gaze fixed ahead, watchful, like a man looking out for a sign. Before his eyes the ship, with half her deck below water, rose and fell on heavy seas that rushed from under her flashing in the cold sunshine. We began to think she was wonderfully buoyant – considering. Confident voices were heard shouting: 'She'll do, boys!' Belfast exclaimed with fervour: 'I would giv' a month's pay for a draw at a pipe!' One or two, passing dry tongues on their salt lips, muttered something about a 'drink of water'. The cook, as if inspired, scrambled up with his breast against the poop water-cask and looked in. There was a little at the bottom. He yelled, waving his arms, and two men began to crawl backwards and forwards with the mug. We had a good mouthful all round. The master shook his head impatiently, refusing. When it came to Charley one of his neighbours shouted: 'That bloomin' boy's asleep.' He slept as though he had been dosed with narcotics. They let him be. Singleton held to the wheel with one hand while he drank, bending down to shelter his lips from the wind. Wamibo had to be poked and yelled at before he saw the mug held before his eyes. Knowles said sagaciously: 'It's better'n a tot o' rum.' Mr Baker grunted: 'Thank ye.' Mr Creighton drank and nodded. Donkin gulped greedily, glaring over the rim. Belfast made us laugh when with grimacing mouth he shouted: 'Pass it this way. We're all taytottlers here.' The master, presented with the mug again by a crouching man, who screamed up at him: 'We all had a drink, captain,' groped for it without ceasing to look ahead, and handed it back stiffly as though he could not spare half a glance away from the ship. Faces brightened. We shouted to the cook: 'Well done, doctor!' He sat to leeward, propped by the water-cask and yelled back abundantly, but the seas were breaking in thunder just then, and we only caught snatches that sounded like: 'Providence' and 'born again'. He was at his old game of preaching. We made friendly but derisive gestures at him, and from below he lifted one arm, holding on with the other, moved his lips; he beamed up to us, straining his voice – earnest, and ducking his head before the sprays.

Suddenly someone cried: 'Where's Jimmy?' and we were appalled once more. On the end of the row the boatswain shouted hoarsely: 'Has anyone seed him come out?' Voices exclaimed dismally: 'Drowned – is he? ... No! In his cabin! ... Good Lord! ... Caught like a bloomin' rat in a trap.... Couldn't open his door ... Aye! She went over too quick and the water jammed it ... Poor beggar! ... No help for 'im.... Let's go and see ...' 'Damn him, who could go?' screamed Donkin. 'Nobody expects you to,' growled the man next to him: 'you're only a thing.' 'Is there half a chance to get at 'im?' inquired two or three men together. Belfast untied himself with blind impetuosity, and all at once shot down to leeward quicker than a flash of lightning. We shouted all together with dismay; but with his legs overboard he held and yelled for a rope. In our extremity nothing could be terrible; so we judged him funny kicking there, and with his scared face. Someone began to laugh, and, as if hysterically infected with screaming merriment, all those haggard men went off laughing, wild-eyed, like a lot of maniacs tied up on a wall. Mr Baker swung off the binnacle-stand and tendered him one leg. He scrambled up rather scared, and consigning us with abominable words to the 'divvle'. 'You are.... Ough! You're a foul-mouthed beggar. Craik,' grunted Mr Baker. He answered, stuttering with indignation: 'Look at 'em, sorr. The bloomin' dirty images! laughing at a chum going overboard. Call themselves men, too.' But from the break of the poop the boatswain called out: 'Come along,' and Belfast crawled away in a hurry to join him. The five men, poised and gazing over the edge of the poop, looked for the best way to get forward. They seemed to hesitate. The others, twisting in their lashings, turning painfully, stared with open lips. Captain Allistoun saw nothing; he seemed with his eyes to hold the ship up in a superhuman concentration of effort. The wind screamed loud in sunshine; columns of spray rose straight up; and in the glitter of rainbows bursting over the trembling hull the men went over cautiously, disappearing from sight with deliberate movements.

They went swinging from belaying pin to cleat above the seas that beat the half-submerged deck. Their toes scraped the planks. Lumps of green cold water toppled over the bulwark and on their heads. They hung for a moment on strained arms, with the breath knocked out of them, and with closed eyes – then, letting go with one hand, balanced with lolling heads, trying to grab some rope or stanchion further forward. The long-armed and athletic boatswain swung quickly, gripping things with a fist hard as iron, and remembering suddenly snatches of the last letter from his 'old woman'. Little Belfast scrambled in a rage spluttering 'cursed nigger'. Wamibo's tongue hung out with excitement; and Archie, intrepid and calm, watched his chance to move with intelligent coolness.

When above the side of the house, they let go one after another, and falling heavily, sprawled, pressing their palms to the smooth teak wood. Round them the backwash of waves seethed white and hissing. All the doors had become trapdoors, of course. The first was the galley door. The galley extended from side to side, and they could hear the sea splashing with hollow noises in there. The next door was that of the carpenter's shop. They lifted it, and looked down. The room seemed to have been devastated by an earthquake. Everything in it had tumbled on the bulkhead facing the door, and on the other side of that bulkhead there was Jimmy, dead or alive. The bench, a half-finished meat-safe, saws, chisels, wire rods, axes, crowbars, lay in a heap besprinkled with loose nails. A sharp adze stuck up with a shining edge that gleamed dangerously down there like a wicked smile. The men clung to one another peering. A sickening, sly lurch of the ship nearly sent them overboard in a body. Belfast howled 'Here goes!' and leaped down. Archie followed cannily, catching at shelves that gave way with him, and eased himself in a great crash of ripped wood. There was hardly room for three men to move. And in the sunshiny blue square of the door, the boatswain's face, bearded and dark, Wamibo's face, wild and pale, hung over – watching.

Together they shouted: 'Jimmy! Jim!' From above the boatswain contributed a deep growl: 'You . . . Wait!' In a pause, Belfast entreated: 'Jimmy, darlin', are ye aloive?' The boatswain said: 'Again! All together, boys!' All yelled excitedly. Wamibo made noises resembling loud barks. Belfast drummed on the side of the bulkhead with a piece of iron. All ceased suddenly. The sound of screaming and hammering went on thin and distinct – like a solo after a chorus. He was alive. He was screaming and knocking below us with the hurry of a man prematurely shut up in a coffin. We went to work. We attacked with desperation the abominable heap of things heavy, of things sharp, of things clumsy to handle. The boatswain crawled away to find somewhere a flying end of a rope: and Wamibo, held back by shouts: 'Don't jump! . . . Don't come in here, muddle-head!' – remained glaring above us – all shining eyes, gleaming fangs, tumbled hair; resembling an amazed and half-witted fiend gloating over the extraordinary agitation of the damned. The boatswain adjured us to 'bear a hand', and a rope descended. We made things fast to it and they went up spinning, never to be seen by man again. A rage to fling things overboard possessed us. We worked fiercely, cutting our hands and speaking brutally to one another. Jimmy kept up a distracting row; he screamed piercingly, without drawing breath, like a tortured woman; he banged with hands and feet. The agony of his fear wrung our hearts so terribly that we longed to abandon him, to get out of that place deep as a well and swaying like a tree, to get out of his hearing, back on the poop where we could wait passively for death in incomparable repose. We shouted to him to 'shut up, for God's sake'. He redoubled his cries. He must have fancied we could not hear him. Probably he heard his own clamour but faintly. We could picture him crouching on the edge of the upper berth, letting out with both fists at the wood, in the dark, and with his mouth wide open for that unceasing cry. Those were loathsome moments. A cloud driving across the sun would darken the doorway menacingly. Every movement of the ship was pain. We scrambled about with no room to breathe, and felt frightfully sick. The boatswain yelled down at us: 'Bear a hand! Bear a hand! We two will be washed away from here directly if you ain't quick!' Three times a sea leaped over the high side and flung bucketfuls of water on our heads. Then Jimmy, startled by the shock, would stop his noise for a moment – waiting for the ship to sink, perhaps – and began again, distressingly loud, as if invigorated by the gust of fear. At the bottom the nails lay in a layer several inches thick. It was ghastly. Every nail in the world, not driven in firmly somewhere, seemed to have found its way into that carpenter's shop. There they were, of all kinds, the remnants of stores from seven voyages. Tin-tacks, copper tacks (sharp as needles), pump nails, with big heads, like tiny iron mushrooms; nails without any heads (horrible); French nails polished and slim. They lay in a solid mass more inabordable than a hedgehog. We hesitated, yearning for a shovel, while Jimmy below us yelled as though he had been flayed. Groaning, we dug our fingers in, and very much hurt, shook our hands, scattering nails and drops of blood.We passed up our hats full of assorted nails to the boatswain, who, as if performing a mysterious and appeasing rite, cast them wide upon a raging sea.

We got to the bulkhead at last. Those were stout planks. She was a ship, well finished in every detail – the *Narcissus* was. They were the stoutest planks ever put into a ship's bulkhead – we thought – and then we perceived that, in our hurry, we had sent all the tools overboard. Absurd little Belfast wanted to break it down with his own weight, and with both feet leaped straight up like a springbok, cursing the Clyde shipwrights for not scamping their work. Incidentally he reviled all North Britain, the rest of the earth, the sea – and all his companions. He swore, as he alighted heavily on his heels, that he would never, never any more associate with any fool that 'hadn't savee enough to know his knee from his elbow'. He managed by his thumping to scare the last remnant of wits out of Jimmy. We could hear the object of our exasperated solicitude darting to and fro under the planks. He had cracked his voice at last, and could only squeak miserably. His back or else his head rubbed the planks, now here, now there, in a puzzling manner. He squeaked as he dodged the invisible blows. It was more heartrending even than his yells. Suddenly Archie produced a crowbar. He had kept it back; also a small hatchet. We howled with satisfaction. He struck a mighty blow and small chips flew at our eyes. The boatswain above shouted: 'Look out! Look out there. Don't kill the man. Easy does it!' Wamibo, maddened with excitement, hung head down and insanely urged us: 'Hoo! Strook 'im! Hoo! Hoo!' We were afraid he would fall in and kill one of us and, hurriedly, we entreated the boatswain to 'shove the blamed Finn overboard'. Then, all together, we yelled down at the planks: 'Stand from under! Get forward,' and listened. We only heard the deep hum and moan of the wind above us, the mingled roar and hiss of the seas. The ship, as if overcome with despair, wallowed lifelessly, and our heads swam with that unnatural motion. Belfast clamoured: 'For the love of God, Jimmy, where are ye? . . . Knock! Jimmy darlint! . . . Knock! You bloody black beast! Knock!' He was as quiet as a dead man inside a grave; and, like men standing above a grave, we were on the verge of tears – but with vexation, the strain, the fatigue; with the great longing to be done with it, to get away, and lay down to rest somewhere where we could see our danger and breathe. Archie shouted: 'Gi'e me room!' We crouched behind him, guarding our heads, and he struck time after time in the joint of planks. They cracked. Suddenly the crowbar went half-way in through a splintered oblong hole. It must have missed Jimmy's head by less than an inch. Archie withdrew it quickly, and that infamous nigger rushed at the hole, put his lips to it, and whispered 'Help' in an almost extinct voice; he pressed his head to it, trying madly to get out through that opening one inch wide and three inches long. In our disturbed state we were absolutely paralysed by his incredible action. It seemed impossible to drive him away. Even Archie at last lost his composure. 'If ye don't clear oot I'll drive the crowbar thro' your head,' he shouted in a determined voice. He meant what he said, and his earnestness seemed to make an impression on Jimmy. He disappeared suddenly, and we set to prising and tearing at the planks with the eagerness of men trying to get at a mortal enemy, and spurred by the desire to tear him limb from limb. The wood split, cracked, gave way. Belfast plunged in head and shoulders and groped viciously. 'I've got 'im! Got 'im,' he shouted. 'Oh! There! . . . He's gone; I've got 'im! . . . Pull at my legs! . . . Pull!' Wamibo hooted unceasingly. The boatswain shouted directions: 'Catch hold of his hair, Belfast; pull straight up, you two! . . . Pull fair!' We pulled fair. We pulled Belfast out with a jerk, and dropped him with disgust. In a sitting posture, purple-faced, he sobbed despairingly: 'How can I hold on to 'is blooming short wool?' Suddenly Jimmy's head and shoulders appeared. He stuck half-way, and with rolling eyes foamed at our feet. We flew at him with brutal impatience, we tore the shirt of his back, we tugged at his ears, we panted over him; and all at once he came away in our hands as though somebody had let go his legs. With the same movement, without a pause, we swung him up. His breath whistled, he kicked our upturned faces, he grasped two pairs of arms above his head, and he squirmed up with such precipitation that he seemed positively to escape from our hands like a bladder full of gas. Streaming with perspiration, we swarmed up the rope, and, coming into the blast of cold wind, gasped like men plunged into icy water. With burning faces we shivered to the very marrow of our bones. Never before had the gale seemed to us more furious, the sea more mad, the sunshine more merciless and mocking, and the position of the ship more hopeless and appalling. Every movement of her was ominous of the end of her agony and of the beginning of ours. We staggered away from the door, and, alarmed by a sudden roll, fell down in a bunch. It appeared to us that the side of the house was more smooth than glass and more slippery than ice. There was nothing to hang on to but a long brass hook used sometimes to keep back an open door. Wamibo held on to it and we held on to Wamibo, clutching our Jimmy. He had completely collapsed now. He did not seem to have the strength to close his hand. We stuck to him blindly in our fear. We were not afraid of Wamibo letting go (we remembered that the brute was stronger than any three men in the ship), but we were afraid of the hook giving way, and we also believed that the ship had made up her mind to turn over at last. But she didn't. A sea swept over us. The boatswain spluttered: 'Up and away. There's a lull. Away aft with you, or we will all go to the devil here.' We stood up surrounding Jimmy. We begged him to hold up, to hold on, at least. He glared with his bulging eyes, mute as a fish, and with all the stiffening knocked out of him. He wouldn't stand; he wouldn't even as much as clutch at our necks; he was only a cold black skin loosely stuffed with soft cotton wool; his arms and legs swung jointless and pliable; his head rolled about; the lower lip hung down, enormous and heavy. We pressed round him, bothered and dismayed; sheltering him we swung here and there in a body; and on the very brink of eternity we tottered all together with concealing and absurd gestures, like a lot of drunken men embarrassed with a stolen corpse.

Something had to be done. We had to get him aft. A rope was tied slack under his armpits, and, reaching up at the risk of our lives, we hung him on the foresheet cleet. He emitted no sound; he looked as ridiculously lamentable as a doll that had lost half its sawdust, and we started on our perilous journey over the main deck, dragging along with care that pitiful, that limp, that hateful burden. He was not very heavy, but had he weighed a ton he could not have been more awkward to handle. We literally passed him from hand to hand. Now and then we had to hang him up on a handy belaying-pin, to draw a breath and re-form the line. Had the pin broken he would have irretrievably gone into the Southern Ocean, but he had to take his chance of that; and after a little while, becoming apparently aware of it, he groaned slightly, and with a great effort whispered a few words. We listened eagerly. He was reproaching us with our carelessness in letting him run such risks; 'Now, after I got myself out from there,' he breathed out weakly. 'There' was his cabin. And he got himself out. We had nothing to do with it apparently! . . . No matter. . . . We went on and let him take his chances, simply because we could not help it; for though at that time we hated him more than ever – more than anything under heaven – we did not want to lose him. We had so far saved him; and it had become a personal matter between us and the sea. We meant to stick to him. Had we (by an incredible hypothesis) undergone similar toil and trouble for an empty cask, that cask would have become as precious to us as Jimmy was. More precious, in fact, because we would have had no reason to hate the cask. And we hated James Wait. We could not get rid of the monstrous suspicion that this astounding black-man was shamming sick, had been malingering heartlessly in the face of our toil, of our scorn, of our patience – and now was malingering in the face of our devotion – in the face of death. Our vague and imperfect morality rose with disgust at his unmanly lie. But he stuck to it manfully – amazingly. No! It couldn't be. He was at all extremity. His cantankerous temper was only the result of the provoking invincibleness of that death he felt by his side. Any man may be angry with such a masterful chum. But, then, what kind of men were we – with our thoughts! Indignation and doubt grappled within us in a scuffle that trampled upon the finest of our feelings. And we hated him because of the suspicion; we detested him because of the doubt. We could not scorn him safely – neither could we pity him without risk to our dignity. So we hated him, and passed him carefully from hand to hand. We cried, 'Got him?' 'Yes. All right. Let go.' And he swung from one enemy to another, showing about as much of life as an old bolster would do. His eyes made two narrow white slits in the black face. The air escaped through his lips with a noise like the sound of bellows. We reached the poop ladder at last, and it being a comparatively safe place, we lay for a moment in an exhausted heap to rest a little. He began to mutter. We were always incurably anxious to hear what he had to say. This time he mumbled peevishly, 'It took you some time to come. I began to think the whole smart lot of you had been washed overboard. What kept you back? Hey? Funk?' We said nothing. With sighs we started again to drag him up. The secret and ardent desire of our hearts was the desire to beat him viciously with our fists about the head; and we handled him as tenderly as though he had been made of glass. . . .

The return on the poop was like the return of wanderers after many years amongst people marked by the desolation of time. Eyes were turned slowly in their sockets glancing at us. Faint murmurs were heard, 'Have you got 'im after all?' The well-known faces looked strange and familiar; they seemed faded and grimy; they had a mingled expression of fatigue and eagerness. They seemed to have become much thinner during our absence, as if all these men had been starving for a long time in their abandoned attitudes. The captain, with a round turn of a rope on his wrist, and kneeling on one knee, swung with a face cold and stiff; but with living eyes he was still holding the ship up, heeding no one, as if lost in the unearthly effort of that endeavour. We fastened up James Wait in a safe place. Mr Baker scrambled along to lend a hand. Mr Creighton, on his back, and very pale, muttered, 'Well done,' and gave us, Jimmy, and the sky, a scornful glance, then closed his eyes slowly. Here and there a man stirred a little, but most of them remained apathetic, in cramped positions, muttering between shivers. The sun was setting. A sun enormous, unclouded and red, declining low as if bending down to look into their faces. The wind whistled across long sunbeams that, resplendent and cold, struck full on the dilated pupils of staring eyes without making them wink. The wisps of hair and the tangled beards were grey with the salt of the sea. The faces were earthy, and the dark patches under the eyes extended to the ears, smudged into the hollows of sunken cheeks. The lips were livid and thin, and when they moved it was with difficulty, as though they had been glued to the teeth. Some grinned sadly in the sunlight, shaking with cold. Others were sad and still. Charley, subdued by the sudden disclosure of the insignificance of his youth, darted fearful glances. The two smooth-faced Norwegians resembled decrepit children, staring stupidly. To leeward, on the edge of the horizon, black seas leaped up towards the glowing sun. It sank slowly, round and blazing, and the crests of waves splashed on the edge of the luminous circle. One of the Norwegians appeared to catch sight of it, and, after giving a violent start, began to speak. His voice, startling the others, made them stir. They moved their heads stiffly, or turning with difficulty, looked at him with surprise, with fear, or in grave silence. He chattered at the setting sun, nodding his head, while the big seas began to roll across the crimson disc; and over miles of turbulent waters the shadows of high waves swept with a running darkness the faces of men. A crested roller broke with a loud hissing roar, and the sun, as if put out, disappeared. The chattering voice faltered, went out together with the light. There were sighs. In the sudden lull that follows the crash of a broken sea a man said wearily, 'Here's that blooming Dutchman gone off his chump.' A seaman, lashed by the middle, tapped the deck with his open hand with unceasing quick flaps. In the gathering greyness of twilight a bulky form was seen rising aft, and began marching on all fours with the movements of some big cautious beast. It was Mr Baker passing along the line of men. He grunted encouragingly over every one, felt their fastenings. Some, with half-open eyes, puffed like men oppressed by heat; others mechanically and in dreamy voices answered him, 'Aye! aye! sir!' He went from one to another grunting, 'Ough! . . . See her through it yet'; and unexpectedly, with loud angry outbursts, blew up Knowles for cutting off a long piece from the fall of the relieving tackle. 'Ough! . . . Ashamed of yourself . . . Relieving tackle . . . Don't you know better! . . . Ough! . . . Able seaman! Ough!' The lame man was crushed. He muttered, 'Get som'think for a lashing for myself, sir.' 'Ough! Lashing . . . yourself. Are you a tinker or a sailor . . . What? Ough! . . . May want that tackle directly. . . . Ough! . . . More use to the ship than your lame carcass. Ough! . . . Keep it! . . . Keep it, now you've done it.' He crawled away slowly, muttering to himself about some men being 'worse than children'. It had been a comforting row. Low exclamations were heard: 'Hallo . . . Hallo.' . . . Those who had been painfully dozing asked with convulsive starts, 'What's up? . . . What is it?' The answers came with unexpected cheerfulness: 'The mate is going bald-headed for lame Jack about something or other' – 'No!' – 'What 'as he done?' Someone even chuckled. It was like a whiff of hope, like a reminder of safe days. Donkin, who had been stupefied with fear, revived suddenly and began to shout: "Ear 'im; that's the way they tawlk to us. Vy donch 'ee 'it 'im – one ov yer? 'It 'im. 'It 'im! Comin' the mate over us. We are as good men as 'ee! We're all goin' to 'ell now. We 'ave been starved in this rotten ship, an' now we're goin' to be drowned for them black 'earted bullies! 'It 'im!' He shrieked in the deepening gloom, he blubbered and sobbed, screaming: "It im!' 'It 'im!' The rage and fear of his disregarded right to live tried the steadfastness of hearts more than the menacing shadows of the night that advanced through the unceasing clamour of the gale. From aft Mr Baker was heard: 'Is one of you men going to stop him – must I come along?' 'Shut up!' . . . 'Keep quiet!' cried various voices, exasperated, trembling with cold. 'You'll get one across the mug from me directly,' said an invisible seaman, in a weary tone. 'I won't let the mate have the trouble.' He ceased and lay still with the silence of despair. On the black sky the stars, coming out, gleamed over an inky sea that, speckled with foam, flashed back at them the evanescent and pale light of a dazzling whiteness born from the black turmoil of the waves. Remote in the eternal calm they glittered hard and cold above the uproar of the earth; they surrounded the vanquished and tormented ship on all sides; more pitiless than the eyes of a triumphant mob, and as unapproachable as the hearts of men.

The icy south wind howled exultingly under the sombre splendour of the sky. The cold shook the men with a resistless violence as though it had tried to shake them to pieces. Short moans were swept unheard off the stiff lips. Some complained in mutters of 'not feeling themselves below the waist'; while those who had closed their eyes, imagined they had a block of ice on their chests. Others, alarmed at not feeling any pain in their fingers, beat the deck feebly with their hands – obstinate and exhausted. Wamibo stared vacant and dreamy. The Scandinavians kept on a meaningless mutter through chattering teeth. The spare Scotchmen, with determined efforts, kept their lower jaws still. The West-country men lay big and stolid in an invulnerable surliness. A man yawned and swore in turns. Another breathed with a rattle in his throat. Two elderly hard-weather shellbacks, fast side by side, whispered dismally to one another about the landlady of a boarding-house in Sunderland, whom they both knew. They extolled her motherliness and her liberality; they tried to talk about the joint of beef and the big fire in the downstairs kitchen. The words dying faintly on their lips, ended in light sighs. A sudden voice cried into the cold night. 'Oh Lord!' No one changed his position or took any notice of the cry. One or two passed, with a repeated and vague gesture, their hand over their faces, but most of them kept very still. In the benumbed immobility of their bodies they were excessively wearied by their thoughts, which rushed with the rapidity and vividness of dreams. Now and then, by an abrupt and startling exclamation, they answered the weird hail of some illusion; then, again, in silence contemplated the vision of known faces and familiar things. They recalled the aspect of forgotten shipmates and heard the voice of dead and gone skippers. They remembered the noise of gaslit streets, the steamy heat of tap-rooms or the scorching sunshine of calm days at sea.

Mr Baker left his insecure place, and crawled, with stop-pages, along the poop. In the dark and on all fours he resembled some carnivorous animal prowling amongst corpses. At the break, propped to windward of a stanchion, he looked down on the main deck. It seemed to him that the ship had a tendency to stand up a little more. The wind had eased a little, he thought, but the sea ran as high as ever. The waves foamed viciously, and the lee side of the deck disappeared under a hissing whiteness as of boiling milk, while the rigging sang steadily with a deep vibrating note, and, at every upward swing of the ship, the wind rushed with a long-drawn clamour amongst the spars. Mr Baker watched very still. A man near him began to make a blabbing noise with his lips, all at once and very loud, as though the cold had broken brutally through him. He went on: 'Ba – ba – ba – brrr – brr – ba – ba.' 'Stop that!' cried Mr Baker, groping in the dark. 'Stop it!' He went on shaking the leg he found under his hand. 'What is it, sir?' called out Belfast, in the tone of a man awakened suddenly; 'we are looking after that 'ere Jimmy.' 'Are you? Ough! Don't make that row then. Who's that near you?' 'It's me – the boatswain, sir,' growled the West-country man;

'we are trying to keep life in that poor devil.' 'Aye, aye!' said Mr Baker. 'Do it quietly, can't you.' 'He wants us to hold him up above the rail,' went on the boatswain, with irritation, 'says he can't breathe here under our jackets.' 'If we lift 'im, we drop 'im overboard,' said another voice, 'we can't feel our hands with cold' 'I don't care. I am choking!' exclaimed James Wait in a clear tone. 'Oh, no, my son,' said the boatswain, desperately, 'you don't go till we all go on this fine night.' 'You will see yet many a worse,' said Mr Baker, cheerfully. 'It's no child's play, sir!' answered the boatswain. 'Some of us further aft, here, are in a pretty bad way.' 'If the blamed sticks had been cut out of her she would be running along on her bottom now like any decent ship, an' giv' us all a chance,' said someone, with a sigh. 'The old man wouldn't have it . . . much he cares for us,' whispered another. 'Care for you!' exclaimed Mr Baker, angrily. 'Why should he care for you? Are you a lot of women passengers to be taken care of? We are here to take care of the ship – and some of you ain't up to that. Ough! . . . What have you done so very smart to be taken care of? Ough! . . . Some of you can't stand a bit of a breeze without crying over it.' 'Come, sorr. We ain't so bad,' protested Belfast, in a voice shaken by shivers; 'we ain't . . . brrr . . .' 'Again,' shouted the mate, grabbing at the shadowy form; 'again! . . . Why, you're in your shirt! What have you done?' 'I've put my oilskin and jacket over that half-dead nayggur – and he says he chokes,' said Belfast, com-plainingly. 'You wouldn't call me nigger if I wasn't half dead, you Irish begger!' boomed James Wait, vigorously. 'You . . . brrr . . . You wouldn't be white if you were ever so well . . . I will fight you . . . brrrr . . . in fine weather . . . brrr . . . with one hand tied behind my back . . . brrrrrr . . .' 'I don't want your rags – I want air,' gasped out the other faintly, as if suddenly exhausted.

The sprays swept over whistling and pattering. Men disturbed in their peaceful torpor by the pain of quarrelsome shouts, moaned, muttering curses. Mr Baker crawled off a little way to leeward where a watercask loomed up big, with something white against it. 'Is it you, Podmore?' asked Mr Baker. He had to repeat the question twice before the cook turned, coughing feebly. 'Yes, sir. I've been praying in my mind for a quick deliverance; for I am prepared for any call. . . . I—' 'Look here, cook,' interrupted Mr Baker, 'the men are perishing with cold.' 'Cold!' said the cook, mournfully; 'they will be warm enough before long.' 'What?' asked Mr Baker, looking along the deck into the faint sheen of frothing water. 'They are a wicked lot,' continued the cook solemnly, but in an unsteady voice, 'about as wicked as any ship's company in this sinful world! Now, I' – he trembled so that he could hardly speak; his was an exposed place, and in a cotton shirt, a thin pair of trousers, and with his knees under his nose, he received, quaking, the flicks of stinging, salt drops; his voice sounded exhausted – 'now, I – any time . . . My eldest youngster, Mr Baker . . . a clever boy . . . last Sunday on shore before this voyage he wouldn't go to church, sir. Says I, "You go and clean yourself, or I'll know the reason why!" What does he do? . . . Pond Mr Baker – fell into the pond in his best rig, sir! . . . Accident? . . . "Nothing will save you, fine scholar though you are!" says I. . . . Acci-dent! . . . I whopped him, sir, till I couldn't lift my arm. . . .' His voice faltered. 'I whopped 'im!' he repeated, rattling his teeth; then, after a while, let out a mournful sound that was half a groan, half a snore. Mr Baker shook him by the shoulders. 'Hey! Cook! Hold up, Podmore! Tell me – is there any fresh water in the galley tank? The ship is lying along less, I think; I would try to get forward. A little water would do them good. Hallo! Look out! Look out!' The cook struggled. 'Not you, sir – not you!' He began to scramble to windward. 'Galley! . . . my business!' he shouted. 'Cook's going crazy now,' said several voices. He yelled: 'Crazy, am I? I am more ready to die than any of you, officers incloosive – there! As long as she swims I will cook! I will get you coffee.' 'Cook, ye are a gentleman!' cried Belfast. But the cook was already going over the weather-ladder. He stopped for a moment to shout back on the poop: 'As long as she swims I will cook!' and disappeared as though he had gone overboard. The men who had heard sent after him a cheer that sounded like a wail of sick children. An hour or more afterwards some one said distinctly: 'He's gone for good.' 'Very likely,' assented the boatswain; 'even in fine weather he was as smart about the deck as a milch-cow on her first voyage. We ought to go and see.' Nobody moved. As the hours dragged slowly through the darkness Mr Baker crawled back and forth along the poop several times. Some men fancied they had heard him exchange murmurs with the master, but at that time the memories were incomparably more vivid than anything actual, and they were not certain whether the murmurs were heard now or many years ago. They did not try to find out. A mutter more or less did not matter. It was too cold for curiosity, and almost for hope. They could not spare a moment or a thought from the great mental occupation of wishing to live. And the desire of life kept them alive, apathetic and enduring, under the cruel persistence of wind and cold; while the bestarred black dome of the sky revolved slowly above the ship, that drifted, bearing their patience and their suffering, through the stormy solitude of the sea.

Huddled close to one another, they fancied themselves utterly alone. They heard sustained loud noises, and again bore the pain of existence through long hours of profound silence. In the night they saw sunshine, felt warmth, and suddenly, with a start, thought that the sun would never rise upon a freezing world. Some heard laughter, listened to songs; others, near the end of the poop, could hear loud human shrieks, and opening their eyes, were surprised to hear them still, though very faint, and far away. The boatswain said: 'Why, it's the cook, hailing from forward, I think.' He hardly believed his own words or recognized his own voice. It was a long time before the man next to him gave a sign of life. He punched hard his other neighbour and said: 'The cook's shouting!' Many did not understand, others did not care; the majority further aft did not believe. But the boatswain and another man had the pluck to crawl away forward to see. They seemed to have been gone for hours, and were very soon forgotten. Then suddenly men who had been plunged in a hopeless resignation became as if possessed with a desire to hurt. They belaboured one another with fists. In the darkness they struck persistently anything soft they could feel near, and, with a greater effort than for a shout, whispered excitedly: 'They've got some hot coffee. . . . Bos'n got it. . . .' 'No! . . . Where?' – 'It's coming! Cook made it.' James

Wait moaned. Donkin scrambled viciously, caring not where he kicked, and anxious that the officers should have none of it. It came in a pot, and they drank in turns. It was hot, and while it blistered the greedy palates, it seemed incredible. The men sighed out parting with the mug: 'How 'as he done it?' Some cried weakly: 'Bully for you, doctor!'

He had done it somehow. Afterwards Archie declared that the thing was 'meeraculous'. For many days we wondered, and it was the one ever-interesting subject of conversation to the end of the voyage. We asked the cook, in fine weather, how he felt when he saw his stove 'reared up on end'. We inquired, in the north-east trade and on serene evenings, whether he had to stand on his head to put things right somewhat. We suggested he had used his bread-board for a raft, and from there comfortably had stoked his grate; and we did our best to conceal our admiration under the wit of fine irony. He affirmed not to know anything about it, rebuked our levity, declared himself, with solemn animation, to have been the object of a special mercy for the saving of our unholy lives. Fundamentally he was right, no doubt; but he need not have been so offensively positive about it – he need not have hinted so often that it would have gone hard with us had he not been there, meritorious and pure, to receive the inspiration and the strength for the work of grace. Had we been saved by his recklessness or his agility, we could have at length become reconciled to the fact; but to admit our obligation to anybody's virtue and holiness alone was as difficult for us as for any other handful of mankind. Like many benefactors of humanity, the cook took himself too seriously, and reaped the reward of irreverence. We were not ungrateful, however. He remained heroic. His saying – *the* saying of his life – became proverbial in the mouths of men as are the sayings of conquerors or sages. Later, whenever one of us was puzzled by a task and advised to relinquish it, he would express his determination to persevere and to succeed by the words: 'As long as she swims I will cook!'

The hot drink helped us through the bleak hours that precede the dawn. The sky low by the horizon took on the delicate tints of pink and yellow like the inside of a rare shell. And higher, where it glowed with a pearly sheen, a small black cloud appeared, like a forgotten fragment of the night set in a border of dazzling gold. The beams of light skipped on the crests of waves. The eyes of men turned to the eastward. The sunlight flooded their weary faces. They were giving themselves up to fatigue as though they had done for ever with their work. On Singleton's black oilskin coat the dried salt glistened like hoar frost. He hung on by the wheel, with open and lifeless eyes. Captain Allistoun, unblinking, faced the rising sun. His lips stirred, opened for the first time in twenty-four hours, and with a fresh firm voice he cried, 'Wear ship!'

The commanding sharp tones made all these torpid men start like a sudden flick of a whip. Then again, motionless where they lay, the force of habit made some of them repeat the order in hardly audible murmurs. Captain Allistoun glanced down at his crew, and several, with fumbling fingers and hopeless movements, tried to cast themselves adrift. He repeated impatiently, 'Wear ship. Now then, Mr Baker, get the men along. What's the matter with them?' 'Wear ship. Do you hear there? – Wear ship!'

thundered out the boatswain suddenly. His voice seemed to break through a deadly spell. Men began to stir and crawl. 'I want the fore-topmast stay-sail run up smartly,' said the master, very loudly; 'if you can't manage it standing up you must do it lying down – that's all. Bear a hand!' 'Come along! Let's give the old girl a chance,' urged the boatswain. 'Aye! aye! Wear ship!' exclaimed quavering voices. The forecastle men, with reluctant faces, prepared to go forward. Mr Baker pushed ahead grunting on all fours to show the way, and they followed him over the break. The others lay still with a vile hope in their hearts of not being required to move till they got saved or drowned in peace.

After some time they could be seen forward appearing on the forecastle head, one by one in unsafe attitudes; hanging on to the rails, clambering over the anchors; embracing the cross-head of the windlass or hugging the fore-capstan. They were restless with strange exertions, waved their arms, knelt, lay flat down, staggered up, seemed to strive their hardest to go overboard. Suddenly a small white piece of canvas fluttered amongst them, grew larger, beating. Its narrow head rose in jerks – and at last it stood distended and triangular in the sunshine. 'They have done it!' cried the voices aft. Captain Allistoun let go the rope he had round his wrist and rolled to leeward headlong. He could be seen casting the lee main braces off the pins while the backwash of waves splashed over him. 'Square the main yard!' he shouted up to us – who stared at him in wonder. We hesitated to stir. 'The main brace, men. Haul! haul anyhow! Lay on your backs and haul!' he screeched, half drowned down there. We did not believe we could move the main yard, but the strongest and the less discouraged tried to execute the order. Others assisted half-heartedly. Singleton's eyes blazed suddenly as he took a fresh grip of the spokes. Captain Allistoun fought his way up to windward. 'Haul men! Try to move it! Haul, and help the ship.' His hard face worked suffused and furious. 'Is she going off, Singleton?' he cried. 'Not a move yet, sir,' croaked the old seaman in a horribly hoarse voice. 'Watch the helm, Singleton,' spluttered the master. 'Haul men! Have you no more strength than rats? Haul, and earn your salt.' Mr Creighton, on his back, with a swollen leg and a face as white as a piece of paper, blinked his eyes; his bluish lips twitched. In the wild scramble men grabbed at him, crawled over his hurt leg, knelt on his chest. He kept perfectly still, setting his teeth without a moan, without a sigh. The master's ardour, the cries of that silent man inspired us. We hauled and hung in bunches on the rope. We heard him say with violence to Donkin, who sprawled abjectly on his stomach: 'I will brain you with this belaying pin if you don't catch hold of the brace,' and that victim of men's injustice, cowardly and cheeky, whimpered: 'Are you goin' to murder us now,' while with sudden desperation he gripped the rope. Men sighed, shouted, hissed meaningless words, groaned. The yards moved, came slowly square against the wind, that hummed loudly on the yard-arms. 'Going off, sir,' shouted Singleton, 'she's just started.' 'Catch a turn with that brace. Catch a turn!' clamoured the master. Mr Creighton, nearly suffocated and unable to move, made a mighty effort, and with his left hand managed to nip the rope. 'All fast!' cried someone. He closed his eyes as if going off into a swoon, while huddled together about the brace we watched with scared looks what the ship would do now.

She went off slowly as though she had been weary and disheartened like the men she carried. She paid off very gradually, making us hold our breath till we choked, and as soon as she had brought the wind abaft the beam she started to move, and fluttered our hearts. It was awful to see her, nearly overturned, begin to gather way and drag her submerged side through the water. The dead-eyes of the rigging churned the breaking seas. The lower half of the deck was full of mad whirlpools and eddies; and the long line of the lee rail could be seen showing black now and then in the swirls of a field of foam as dazzling and white as a field of snow. The wind sang shrilly amongst the spars; and at every slight lurch we expected her to slip to the bottom sideways from under our backs. When dead before it she made the first distinct attempt to stand up, and we encouraged her with a feeble and discordant howl. A great sea came running up aft and hung for a moment over us with a curling top; then crashed down under the counter and spread out on both sides into a great sheet of bursting froth. Above its fierce hiss we heard Singleton's croak: 'She is steering!' He had both his feet now planted firmly on the grating, and the wheel spun fast as he eased the helm. 'Bring the wind on the port quarter and steady her!' called out the master, staggering to his feet, the first man up from amongst our prostrate heap. One or two screamed with excitement: 'She rises!' Far away forward, Mr Baker and three others were seen erect and black on the clear sky, lifting their arms, and with open mouths as though they had been shouting all together. The ship trembled, trying to lift her side, lurched back, seemed to give up with a nerveless dip, and suddenly with an unexpected jerk swung violently to windward, as though she had torn herself out from a deadly grasp. The whole immense volume of water, lifted by her deck, was thrown bodily across to starboard. Loud cracks were heard. Iron ports breaking open thundered with ringing blows. The water topped over the starboard rail with the rush of a river falling over a dam. The sea on deck, and the seas on every side of her, mingled together in a deafening roar. She rolled violently. We got up and were helplessly run or flung about from side to side. Men, rolling over and over, yelled: 'The house will go!' – 'She clears herself!' Lifted by a towering sea she ran along with it for a moment, spouting thick streams of water through every opening of her wounded sides. The lee braces having been carried away or washed off the pins, all the ponderous yards on the fore swung from side to side and with appalling rapidity at every roll. The men forward were seen crouching here and there with fearful glances upwards at the enormous spars that whirled about over their heads. The torn canvas and the ends of broken gear streamed in the wind like wisps of hair. Through the clear sunshine, over the flashing turmoil and uproar of the seas, the ship ran blindly, dishevelled and headlong, as if fleeing for her life; and on the poop we spun, we tottered about, distracted and noisy. We all spoke at once in a thin babble; we had the aspect of invalids and the gestures of maniacs. Eyes shone, large and haggard, in smiling, meagre faces that seemed to have been dusted over with powdered chalk. We stamped, clapped our hands, feeling ready to jump and do anything; but in reality hardly able to keep on our feet. Captain Allistoun, hard and slim, gesticulated madly from the poop at Mr Baker: 'Steady these fore-yards! Steady them the best you can!' On the main deck, men excited by his cries, splashed, dashing aimlessly here and there with the foam swirling up to their waists. Apart, far aft, and alone by the helm, old Singleton had deliberately tucked his white beard under the top button of his glistening coat. Swaying upon the din and tumult of the seas, with the whole battered length of the ship launched forward in a rolling rush before his steady old eyes, he stood rigidly still, forgotten by all, and with an attentive face. In front of his erect figure only the two arms moved crosswise with a swift and sudden readiness, to check or urge again the rapid stir of circling spokes. He steered with care.

CHAPTER 4

On men reprieved by its disdainful mercy, the immortal sea confers in its justice the full privilege of desired unrest. Through the perfect wisdom of its grace they are not permitted to meditate at ease upon the complicated and acrid savour of existence. They must without pause justify their life to the eternal pity that commands toil to be hard and unceasing, from sunrise to sunset, from sunset to sunrise; till the weary succession of nights and days tainted by the obstinate clamour of sages, demanding bliss and an empty heaven, is redeemed at last by the vast silence of pain and labour, by the dumb fear and the dumb courage of men obscure, forgetful, and enduring.

The master and Mr Baker coming face to face stared for a moment, with the intense and amazed looks of men meeting unexpectedly after years of trouble. Their voices were gone, and they whispered desperately at one another. 'Anyone missing?' asked Captain Allistoun. 'No. All there.' 'Anybody hurt?' 'Only the second mate.' 'I will look after him directly. We're lucky.' 'Very,' articulated Mr Baker, faintly. He gripped the rail and rolled bloodshot eyes. The little grey man made an effort to raise his voice above a dull mutter, and fixed his chief mate with a cold gaze, piercing like a dart. 'Get sail on the ship,' he said, speaking authoritatively and with an inflexible snap of his thin lips. 'Get sail on her as soon as you can. This is a fair wind. At once, sir – Don't give the men time to feel themselves. They will get done up and stiff, and we will never ... We must get her along now ...' He reeled to a long heavy roll; the rail dipped into the glancing, hissing water. He caught a shroud, swung helplessly against the mate ... 'now we have a fair wind at last. ... Make ... sail.' His head rolled from shoulder to shoulder. His eyelids began to beat rapidly. 'And the pumps ... pumps, Mr Baker.' He peered as though the face within a foot of his eyes had been half a mile off. 'Keep the men on the move to ... to get her 'long,' he mumbled in a drowsy tone, like a man going off into a doze. He pulled himself together suddenly. 'Mustn't stand. Won't do,' he said with a painful attempt at a smile. He let go his hold, and, propelled by the dip of the ship, ran aft unwillingly, with small steps, till he brought up against the binnacle stand. Hanging on there he looked up in an objectless manner at Singleton, who, unheeding him, watched anxiously the end of the jib-boom. 'Steering gear works all right?' he asked. There was a noise in the old seaman's throat, as though the words had been rattling together before they could come out. 'Steers . . . like a little boat,' he said, at last, with hoarse tenderness, without giving the master as much as half a glance – then, watchfully, spun the wheel down, steadied, flung it back again. Captain Allistoun tore himself away from the delight of leaning against the binnacle, and began to walk the poop, swaying and reeling to preserve his balance. . . .

The pump-rods, clanking, stamped in short jumps while the fly-wheels turned smoothly, with great speed, at the foot of the mainmast, flinging back and forth with a regular impetuosity two limp clusters of men clinging to the handles. They abandoned themselves, swaying from the hip with twitching faces and stony eyes. The carpenter, sounding from time to time, exclaimed mechanically: 'Shake her up! Keep her going!' Mr Baker could not speak, but found his voice to shout; and under the goad of his objurgations, men looked to the lashings, dragged out new sails; and thinking themselves unable to move, carried heavy blocks aloft – overhauled the gear. They went up the rigging with faltering and desperate efforts. Their heads swam as they shifted their hold, stepped blindly on the yards like men in the dark; or trusted themselves to the first rope at hand with the negligence of exhausted strength. The narrow escapes from falls did not disturb the languid beat of their hearts; the roar of the seas seething far below them sounded continuous and faint like an indistinct noise from another world: the wind filled their eyes with tears, and with heavy gusts tried to push them off from where they swayed in insecure positions. With streaming faces and blowing hair they flew up and down between sky and water, bestriding the end of yard-arms, crouching on footropes, embracing lifts to have their hands free, or standing up against chain ties. Their thoughts floated vaguely between the desire of rest and the desire of life, while their stiffened fingers cast off head-earrings, fumbled for knives, or held with tenacious grip against the violent shocks of beating canvas. They glared savagely at one another, made frantic signs with one hand while they held their life in the other, looked down on the narrow strip of flooded deck, shouted along to leeward: 'Light-to!' . . . 'Haul out!' . . . 'Make fast!' Their lips moved, their eyes started, furious and eager with the desire to be understood, but the wind tossed their words unheard upon the disturbed sea. In an unendurable and unending strain they worked like men driven by a merciless dream to toil in an atmosphere of ice or flame. They burnt and shivered in turns. Their eyeballs smarted as if in the smoke of a conflagration; their heads were ready to burst with every shout. Hard fingers seemed to grip their throats. At every roll they thought: Now I must let go. It will shake us all off – and thrown about aloft they cried wildly: 'Look out there – catch the end.' . . . 'Reeve clear' . . . 'Turn this block. . . .' They nodded desperately; shook infuriated faces, 'No! No! From down up.' They seemed to hate one another with a deadly hate. The longing to be done with it all gnawed their breasts, and the wish to do things well was a burning pain. They cursed their fate, contemned their life, and wasted their breath in deadly imprecations upon one another. The sailmaker, with his bald head bared, worked feverishly, forgetting his intimacy with so many admirals. The boatswain, climbing up with marlinspikes and bunches of spunyarn rovings, or kneeling on the yard and ready to take a turn with the midship-stop, had acute and fleeting visions of his old woman and the youngsters in a moorland village. Mr Baker, feeling very weak, tottered here and there, grunting and inflexible, like a man of iron. He waylaid those who, coming from aloft, stood gasping for breath. He ordered, encouraged, scolded. 'Now then – to the main topsail now! Tally on to that gantline. Don't stand about there!' 'Is there no rest for us?' muttered voices. He spun round fiercely, with a sinking heart. 'No! No rest till the work is done. Work till you drop. That's what you're here for.' A bowed seaman at his elbow gave a short laugh. 'Do or die,' he croaked bitterly, then spat into his broad palms, swung up his long arms, and grasping the rope high above his head sent out a mournful, wailing cry for a pull all together. A sea boarded the quarter-deck and sent the whole lot sprawling to leeward. Caps, handspikes floated. Clenched hands, kicking legs, with here and there a spluttering face, stuck out of the white hiss of foaming water. Mr Baker, knocked down with the rest, screamed: 'Don't let go that rope! Hold on to it! Hold!' And sorely bruised by the brutal fling, they held on to it, as though it had been the fortune of their life. The ship ran, rolling heavily, and the topping crests glanced past port and starboard flashing their white heads. Pumps were freed. Braces were rove. The three topsails and foresail were set. She spurted faster over the water, outpacing the swift rush of waves. The menacing thunder of distanced seas rose behind her – filled the air with the tremendous vibrations of its voice. And devastated, battered, and wounded she drove foaming to the northward, as though inspired by the courage of a high endeavour. . . .

The forecastle was a place of damp desolation. They looked at their dwelling with dismay. It was slimy, dripping; it hummed hollow with the wind, and was strewn with shapeless wreckage like a half-tide cavern in a rocky and exposed coast. Many had lost all they had in the world, but most of the starboard watch had preserved their chests; thin streams of water trickled out of them, however. The beds were soaked; the blankets spread out and saved by some nail squashed under foot. They dragged wet rags from evil-smelling corners, and wringing the water out, recognized their property. Some smiled stiffly. Others looked round blank and mute. There were cries of joy over old waistcoats, and groans of sorrow over shapeless things found among the splinters of smashed bed boards. One lamp was discovered jammed under the bowsprit. Charley whimpered a little. Knowles stumped here and there, sniffing, examining dark places for salvage. He poured dirty water out of a boot, and was concerned to find the owner. Those who, overwhelmed by their losses, sat on the forepeak hatch, remained elbows on knees, and, with a fist against each cheek, disdained to look up. He pushed it under their noses. 'Here's a good boot. Yours?' They snarled, 'No – get out.' One snapped at him, 'Take it to hell out of this.' He seemed surprised. 'Why? It's a good boot,' but remembering suddenly that he had lost every stitch of his clothing, he dropped his find and began to swear. In the dim light cursing voices clashed. A man came in and, dropping his arms, stood still, repeating from the doorstep, 'Here's a bloomin' old go! Here's a bloomin' old go!' A few rooted anxiously in flooded chests for tobacco. They breathed hard, clamoured with heads down. 'Look at that Jack!' ... 'Here! Sam! Here's my shore-going rig spoilt for ever.' One blasphemed tearfully holding up a pair of dripping trousers. No one looked at him. The cat came out from somewhere. He had an ovation. They snatched him from hand to hand, caressed him in a murmur of pet names. They wondered where he had 'weathered it out'; disputed about it. A squabbling argument began. Two men brought in a bucket of fresh water, and all crowded round it; but Tom, lean and mewing, came up with every hair astir and had the first drink. A couple of hands went aft for oil and biscuits.

Then in the yellow light and in the intervals of mopping the deck they crunched hard bread, arranging to 'worry through somehow'. Men chummed as to beds. Turns were settled for wearing boots and having the use of oilskin coats. They called one another 'old man' and 'sonny' in cheery voices. Friendly slaps resounded. Jokes were shouted. One or two stretched on the wet deck, slept with heads pillowed on their bent arms, and several, sitting on the hatch, smoked. Their weary faces appeared through a thin blue haze, pacified and with sparkling eyes. The boatswain put his head through the door. 'Relieve the wheel, one of you' – he shouted inside – 'it's six. Blamme if that old Singleton hadn't been there more'n thirty hours. You are a fine lot.' He slammed the door again. 'Mate's watch on deck,' said someone. 'Hey, Donkin, it's your relief!' shouted three or four together. He had crawled into an empty bunk and on wet planks lay still. 'Donkin, your wheel.' He made no sound. 'Donkin's dead,' guffawed someone. 'Sell 'is bloomin' clothes,' shouted another. 'Donkin, if ye don't go to the bloomin' wheel they will sell your clothes – d'ye hear?' jeered a third. He groaned from his dark hole. He complained about pains in all his bones, he whimpered pitifully. 'He won't go,' exclaimed a contemptuous voice, 'your turn, Davis.' The young seaman rose painfully squaring his shoulders. Donkin stuck his head out, and it appeared in the yellow light, fragile and ghastly. 'I will giv' yer a pound of tobaccer,' he whined in a conciliating voice, 'so soon as I draw it from aft. I will – s'elp me. ...' Davis swung his arm backhanded and the head vanished. 'I'll go,' he said, 'but you will pay for it.' He walked unsteady but resolute to the door. 'So I will,' yelped Donkin, popping out behind him. 'So I will – s'elp me ... a pound ... three bob they chawrge.' Davis flung the door open. 'You will pay my price ... in fine weather,' he shouted over his shoulder. One of the men unbuttoned his wet coat rapidly, threw it at his head. 'Here, Taffy – take that, you thief!' 'Thank you!' he cried from the darkness above the swish of rolling water. He could be heard splashing; a sea came on board with a thump. 'He's got his bath already,' remarked a grim shellback. 'Aye, aye!' grunted others. Then, after a long silence, Wamibo made strange noises. 'Hallo, what's up with you?' said someone grumpily. 'He says he would have gone for Davy,' explained Archie, who was the Finn's interpreter generally. 'I believe him!' cried voices. . . . 'Never mind, Dutchy' . . . 'You'll do, muddle-head.' . . . 'Your turn will come soon enough.' . . . 'You don't know when ye're well off.' They ceased, and all together turned their faces to the door. Singleton stepped in, made two paces, and stood swaying slightly. The sea hissed, flowed roaring past the bows, and the forecastle trembled, full of deep murmurs; the lamp flared, swinging like a pendulum. He looked with a dreamy and puzzled stare, as though he could not distinguish the still men from their restless shadows. There were awestruck exclamations: 'Hallo, hallo' . . . 'How does it look outside now, Singleton?' Those who sat on the hatch lifted their eyes in silence, and the next oldest seaman in the ship (those two understood one another, though they hardly exchanged three words in a day) gazed up at his friend attentively for a moment, then taking a short clay pipe out of his mouth, offered it without a word. Singleton put out his arm towards it, missed, staggered, and suddenly fell forward, crashing down, stiff and headlong like an uprooted tree. There was a swift rush. Men pushed, crying: 'He's done!' . . . 'Turn him over!' . . . 'Stand clear there!' Under a crowd of startled faces bending over him he lay on his back, staring upwards in a continuous and intolerable manner. In the breathless silence of a general consternation, he said in a grating murmur: 'I am all right,' and clutched with his hands. They helped him up. He mumbled despondently: 'I am getting old . . . old.' 'Not you,' cried Belfast, with ready tact. Supported on all sides, he hung his head. 'Are you better?' they asked. He glared at them from under his eyebrows with large black eyes, spreading over his chest the bushy whiteness of a beard long and thick. 'Old! old!' he repeated sternly. Helped along, he reached his bunk. There was in it a slimy soft heap of something that smelt, as does at dead low water a muddy foreshore. It was his soaked straw bed. With a convulsive effort he pitched himself on it, and in the darkness of the narrow place could be heard growling angrily, like an irritated and savage animal uneasy in its den: 'Bit of breeze . . . small thing . . . can't stand up . . . old!' He slept at last, high-booted, sou'wester on head, and his oilskin clothes rustled, when with a deep sighing groan he turned over. Men conversed about him in quiet, concerned whispers. 'This will break 'im up' . . . 'Strong as a horse' . . . 'Aye. But he ain't what he used to be.' . . . In sad murmurs they gave him up. Yet at midnight he turned out to duty as if nothing had been the matter, and answered to his name with a mournful 'Here!' He brooded alone more than ever, in an impenetrable silence and with a saddened face. For many years he had heard himself called 'Old Singleton', and had serenely accepted the qualification, taking it as a tribute of respect due to a man who through half a century had measured his strength against the favours and the rages of the sea. He had never given a thought to his mortal self. He lived unscathed, as though he had been indestructible, surrendering to all the temptations, weathering many gales. He had panted in sunshine, shivered in the cold; suffered hunger, thirst, debauch; passed through many trials – known all the furies. Old! It seemed to him he was broken at last. And like a man bound treacherously while he sleeps, he woke up fettered by the long chain of disregarded years. He had to take up at once the burden of all his existence, and found it almost too heavy for his strength. Old! He moved his

arms, shook his head, felt his limbs. Getting old . . . and then? He looked
upon the immortal sea with the awakened and groping perception of its
heartless might; he saw it unchanged, black and foaming under the eternal
scrutiny of the stars; he heard its impatient voice calling for him out of a
pitless vastness full of unrest, of turmoil, and of terror. He looked afar upon
it, and he saw an immensity tormented and blind, moaning and furious, that
claimed all the days of his tenacious life, and, when life was over, would
claim the worn-out body of its slave. . . .

This was the last of the breeze. It veered quickly, changed to a black
south-easter, and blew itself out, giving the ship a famous shove to the
northward into the joyous sunshine of the trade. Rapid and white she ran
homewards in a straight path, under a blue sky and upon the plain of a blue
sea. She carried Singleton's completed wisdom, Donkin's delicate susceptibilities, and the conceited folly of us all. The hours of ineffective turmoil
were forgotten; the fear and anguish of these dark moments were never
mentioned in the glowing peace of fine days. Yet from that time our life
seemed to start afresh as though we had died and had been resuscitated. All
the first part of the voyage, the Indian Ocean on the other side of the Cape,
all that was lost in a haze, like an ineradicable suspicion of some previous
existence. It had ended – then there were blank hours: a livid blurr – and
again we lived! Singleton was possessed of sinister truth; Mr Creighton of
a damaged leg; the cook of fame – and shamefully abused the opportunities
of his distinction. Donkin had an added grievance. He went about repeating
with insistence: ''E said 'e would brain me – did yer 'ear? They are goin'
to murder us now for the least little thing.' We began at last to think it was
rather awful. And we were conceited! We boasted of our pluck, of our
capacity for work, of our energy. We remembered honourable episodes: our
devotion, our indomitable perseverance – and were proud of them as though
they had been the outcome of our unaided impulses. We remembered our
danger, our toil – and conveniently forgot our horrible scare. We decried
our officers – who had done nothing – and listened to the fascinating Donkin.
His care for our rights, his disinterested concern for our dignity, were not
discouraged by the invariable contumely of our words, by the disdain of our
looks. Our contempt for him was unbounded – and we could not but listen
with interest to that consummate artist. He told us we were good men – a
'bloomin' condemned lot of good men'. Who thanked us? Who took any
notice of our wrongs? Didn't we lead a 'dorg's loife for two poun' ten a
month?' Did we think that miserable pay enough to compensate us for the
risk to our lives and for the loss of our clothes? 'We've lost every rag!' he
cried. He made us forget that he, at any rate, had lost nothing of his own.
The younger men listened, thinking – this 'ere Donkin's a long-headed chap,
though no kind of man, anyhow. The Scandinavians were frightened at his
audacities; Wamibo did not understand; and the older seamen thoughtfully
nodded their heads making the thin gold earrings glitter in the fleshy lobes
of hairy ears. Severe, sunburnt faces were propped meditatively on tattooed
forearms. Veined, brown fists held in their knotted grip the dirty white clay
of smouldering pipes. They listened, impenetrable, broad-backed, with bent

shoulders, and in grim silence. He talked with ardour, despised and irre-
futable. His picturesque and filthy loquacity flowed like a troubled stream
from a poisoned source. His beady little eyes danced, glancing right and left,
ever on the watch for the approach of an officer. Sometimes Mr Baker going
forward to take a look at the head sheets would roll with his uncouth gait
through the sudden stillness of the men; or Mr Creighton limped along,
smooth-faced, youthful, and more stern than ever, piercing our short silence
with a keen glance of his clear eyes. Behind his back Donkin would begin
again darting stealthy, sidelong looks. "'Ere's one of 'em. Some of yer 'as
made 'im fast that day. Much thanks yer got for it. Ain't 'ee a-driven' yer
wusse'n ever? . . . Let 'im slip overboard. . . . Vy not? It would 'ave been
less trouble. Vy not?' He advanced confidentially, backed away with great
effect; he whispered, he screamed, waved his miserable arms no thicker than
pipe-stems – stretched his lean neck – spluttered – squinted. In the pauses
of his impassioned orations the wind sighed quietly aloft, the calm sea
unheeded murmured in a warning whisper along the ship's side. We
abominated the creature and could not deny the luminous truth of his
contentions. It was all so obvious. We were indubitably good men; our
deserts were great and our pay small. Through our exertions we had saved
the ship and the skipper would get the credit of it. What had he done? we
wanted to know. Donkin asked: 'What 'ee could do without hus?' and we
could not answer. We were oppressed by the injustice of the world, surprised
to perceive how long we had lived under its burden without realizing our
unfortunate state, annoyed by the uneasy suspicion of our undiscerning
stupidity. Donkin assured us it was all our 'good 'eartedness', but we would
not be consoled by such shallow sophistry. We were men enough to courageously admit to ourselves our intellectual shortcomings; though from that
time we refrained from kicking him, tweaking his nose, or from accidentally
knocking him about, which last, after we had weathered the Cape, had been
rather a popular amusement. Davis ceased to talk at him provokingly about
black eyes and flattened noses. Charley, much subdued since the gale, did
not jeer at him. Knowles deferentially and with a crafty air propounded
questions such as: 'Could we all have the same grub as the mates? Could
we all stop ashore till we got it? What would be the next thing to try for if
we got that?' He answered readily with contemptuous certitude; he strutted
with assurance in clothes that were much too big for him as though he had
tried to disguise himself. These were Jimmy's clothes mostly – though he
would accept anything from anybody; but nobody, except Jimmy, had
anything to spare. His devotion to Jimmy was unbounded. He was for ever
dodging in the little cabin, ministering to Jimmy's wants, humouring his
whims, submitting to his exacting peevishness, often laughing with him.
Nothing could keep him away from the pious work of visiting the sick,
especially when there was some heavy hauling to be done on deck. Mr Baker
had on two occasions jerked him out from there by the scruff of the neck to
our inexpressible scandal. Was a sick chap to be left without attendance?
Were we to be ill-used for attending a shipmate? 'What?' growled Mr
Baker, turning menacingly at the mutter, and the whole half-circle like one
man stepped back a pace. 'Set the topmast stunsail. Away aloft, Donkin,

overhaul the gear,' ordered the mate inflexibly. 'Fetch the sail along; bend the down-haul clear. Bear a hand.' Then, the sail set, he would go slowly aft and stand looking at the compass for a long time, careworn, pensive, and breathing hard as if stifled by the taint of unaccountable ill-will that pervaded the ship. 'What's up amongst them?' he thought. 'Can't make out this hanging back and growling. A good crowd, too, as they go nowadays.' On deck the men exchanged bitter words, suggested by a silly exasperation against something unjust and irremediable that would not be denied, and would whisper into their ears long after Donkin has ceased speaking. Our little world went on its curved and unswerving path carrying a discontented and aspiring population. They found comfort of a gloomy kind in an interminable and conscientious analysis of their unappreciated worth; and inspired by Donkin's hopeful doctrines they dreamed enthusiastically of the time when every lonely ship would travel over a serene sea, manned by a wealthy and well-fed crew of satisfied skippers.

It looked as if it would be a long passage. The south-east trades, light and unsteady, were left behind; and then, on the equator and under a low grey sky, the ship, in close heat, floated upon a smooth sea that resembled a sheet of ground glass. Thunder squalls hung on the horizon, circled round the ship, far off and growling angrily, like a troop of wild beasts afraid to charge home. The invisible sun, sweeping above the upright masts, made on the clouds a blurred stain of rayless light, and a similar patch of faded radiance kept pace with it from east to west over the unglittering level of the waters. At night, through the impenetrable darkness of earth and heaven, broad sheets of flame waved noiselessly; and for half a second the becalmed craft stood out with its masts and rigging, with every sail and every rope distinct and black in the centre of a fiery outburst, like a charred ship enclosed in a globe of fire. And, again, for long hours she remained lost in a vast universe of night and silence where gentle sighs wandering here and there like forlorn souls, made the still sails flutter as in sudden fear, and the ripple of a beshrouded ocean whisper its compassion afar – in a voice mournful, immense, and faint. . . .

When the lamp was put out, and through the door thrown wide open, Jimmy, turning on his pillow, could see vanishing beyond the straight line of top-gallant rail, the quick, repeated visions of a fabulous world made up of leaping fire and sleeping water. The lightning gleamed in his big sad eyes that seemed in a red flicker to burn themselves out in his black face, and then he would lie blinded and invisible in the midst of an intense darkness. He could hear on the quiet deck soft footfalls, the breathing of some man lounging on the doorstep; the low creak of swaying masts; or the calm voice of the watch-officer reverberating aloft, hard and loud, amongst the unstirring sails. He listened with avidity, taking a rest in the attentive perception of the slightest sound from the fatiguing wanderings of his sleeplessness. He was cheered by the rattling of blocks, reassured by the stir and murmur of the watch, soothed by the slow yawn of some sleepy and weary seaman settling himself deliberately for a snooze on the planks. Life seemed an indestructible thing. It went on in darkness, in sunshine, in sleep; tireless, it hovered affectionately round the imposture of his ready death. It was bright, like the twisted flare of lightning, and more full of surprises than the dark night. It made him safe, and the calm of its overpowering darkness was as precious as its restless and dangerous light.

But in the evening, in the dog-watches, and even far into the first night-watch, a knot of men could always be seen congregated before Jimmy's cabin. They leaned on each side of the door peacefully interested and with crossed legs; they stood astride the doorstep discoursing, or sat in silent couples on his sea-chest; while against the bulwark along the spare topmast, three or four in a row stared meditatively; with their simple faces lit up by the projected glare of Jimmy's lamp. The little place, repainted white, had, in the night, the brilliance of a silver shrine where a black idol, reclining stiffly under a blanket, blinked its weary eyes and received our homage. Donkin officiated. He had the air of a demonstrator showing a phenomenon, a manifestation bizarre, simple, and meritorious that, to the beholders, should be a profound and an everlasting lesson. 'Just look at 'im, 'ee knows what's what – never fear!' he exclaimed now and then, flourishing a hand hard and fleshless like the claw of a snipe. Jimmy, on his back, smiled with reserve and without moving a limb. He affected the languor of extreme weakness, so as to make it manifest to us that our delay in hauling him out from his horrible confinement, and then that night spent on the poop among our selfish neglect of his needs, had 'done for him'. He rather liked to talk about it, and of course we were always interested. He spoke spasmodically, in fast rushes with long pauses between, as a tipsy man walks. . . . 'Cook had just given me a pannikin of hot coffee. . . . Slapped it down there, on my chest – banged the door to. . . : I felt a heavy roll coming; tried to save my coffee, burnt my fingers . . . and fell out of my bunk. . . . She went over so quick. . . . Water came in through the ventilator. . . . I couldn't move the door . . . dark as a grave . . . tried to scramble up into the upper berth. . . . Rats . . . a rat bit my finger as I got up. . . . I could hear him swimming below me. . . . I thought you would never come. . . . I thought you were all gone overboard . . . of course . . . Could hear nothing but the wind. . . . Then you came . . . to look for the corpse, I suppose. A little more and . . .'

'Man! But ye made a rare lot of noise in here,' observed Archie, thoughtfully.

'You chaps kicked up such a confounded row above. . . . Enough to scare anyone. . . . I didn't know what you were up to. . . . Bash in the blamed planks . . . my head. . . . Just what a silly, scary gang of fools would do. . . . Not much good to me anyhow. . . . Just as well·. . . drown. . . . Pah.'

He groaned, snapped his big white teeth, and gazed with scorn. Belfast lifted a pair of dolorous eyes, with a broken-hearted smile, clenched his fists stealthily; blue-eyed Archie caressed his red whiskers with a hesitating hand; the boatswain at the door stared a moment, and brusquely went away with a loud guffaw. Wamibo dreamed. . . . Donkin felt all over his sterile chin for the few rare hairs, and said, triumphantly, with a sidelong glance at Jimmy: 'Look at 'im! Wish I was 'arf has 'ealthy as 'ee is – I do.' He jerked a short thumb over his shoulder towards the after end of the ship. 'That's the blooming way to do 'em!' he yelped, with forced heartiness. Jimmy said:

'Don't be a damn fool,' in a pleasant voice. Knowles, rubbing his shoulder against the doorpost, remarked shrewdly: 'We can't all go an' be took sick – it would be mutiny.' 'Mutiny – gawn!' jeered Donkin, 'there's no bloomin' law against bein' sick.' 'There's six weeks' hard for refoosing dooty,' argued Knowles. 'I mind I once seed in Cardiff the crew of an overloaded ship – leastways she weren't overloaded, only a fatherly old gentleman with a white beard and an umbreller came along the quay and talked to the hands. Said as how it was crool hard to be drownded in winter just for the sake of a few pounds more for the owner – he said. Nearly cried over them – he did; and he had a square mainsail coat, and a gaff-topsail hat too – all proper. So they chaps they said they wouldn't go to be drownded in winter – depending upon that 'ere Plimsoll man to see 'em through the court. They thought to have a bloomin' lark and two or three days' spree. And the beak giv' 'em six weeks – coss the ship warn't overloaded. Anyways they made it out in court that she wasn't. There wasn't one overloaded ship in Penarth Dock at all. 'Pears that old coon he was only on pay and allowance from some kind people, under orders to look for overloaded ships, and he couldn't see no further than the length of his umbreller. Some of us in the boarding-house, where I live when I'm looking for a ship in Cardiff, stood by to duck that old weeping spunger in the dock. We kept a good look-out, too – but he topped his boom directly he was outside the court. . . . Yes. They got six weeks' hard. . . .'

They listened, full of curiosity, nodding in the pauses their rough pensive faces. Donkin opened his mouth once or twice, but restrained himself. Jimmy lay still with open eyes and not at all interested. A seaman emitted the opinion that after a verdict of atrocious partiality 'the bloomin' beaks go an' drink at the skipper's expense'. Others assented. It was clear, of course. Donkin said: 'Well, six weeks ain't much trouble. You sleep all night in, reg'lar, in hokey. Do it on my 'ead.' 'You are used to it ainch'ee, Donkin?' asked somebody. Jimmy condescended to laugh. It cheered up everyone wonderfully. Knowles, with surprising mental agility, shifted his ground. 'If we all went sick what would become of the ship? eh?' He posed the problem and grinned all round. 'Let 'er go to 'ell,' sneered Donkin. 'Damn 'er. She ain't yourn.' 'What? Just let her drift?' insisted Knowles in a tone of unbelief. 'Aye! Drift, an' be blowed,' affirmed Donkin with fine reck-lessness. The other did not see it – meditated. 'The stores would run out,' he muttered, 'and . . . never get anywhere . . . and what about pay-day?' he added with greater assurance. 'Jack likes a good pay-day,' exclaimed a listener on the doorstep. 'Aye, because then the girls put one arm round his neck an' t'other in his pocket, and call him ducky. Don't they, Jack?' – 'Jack, you're a terror with the gals' – 'He takes three of 'em in tow to once, like one of 'em Watkinses two-funnel tugs waddling away with three schooners behind' – 'Jack, you're a lame scamp' – 'Jack, tell us about that one with a blue eye and a black eye. Do' – 'There's plenty of girls with one black eye along the Highway by . . .' – 'No, that's a speshul one – come Jack.' Donkin looked severe and disgusted; Jimmy very bored; a grey-haired sea-dog shook his head slightly, smiling at the bowl of his pipe, discreetly amused. Knowles turned about bewildered; stammered first at one, then at another. 'No! ... I never! ... can't talk sensible sense midst you.... Always on the kid.' He retired bashfully – muttering and pleased. They laughed hooting in the crude light, around Jimmy's bed, where on a white pillow his hollowed black face moved to and fro restlessly. A puff of wind came, made the flame of the lamp leap, and outside, high up, the sails fluttered, while near by the block of the foresheet struck a ringing blow on the iron bulwark. A voice far off cried, 'Helm up!' another, more faint, answered, 'Hard-up, sir!' They became silent – waited expectantly. The grey-haired seaman knocked his pipe on the doorstep and stood up. The ship leaned over gently and the sea seemed to wake up, murmuring drowsily. 'Here's a little wind comin',' said someone very low. Jimmy turned over slowly to face the breeze. The voice in the night cried loud and commanding: 'Haul the spanker out.' The group before the door vanished out of the light. They could be heard tramping aft while they repeated with varied intonations: 'Spanker out!' ... 'Out spanker, sir!' Donkin remained alone with Jimmy. There was a silence. Jimmy opened and shut his lips several times as if swallowing draughts of fresher air; Donkin moved the toes of his bare feet and looked at them thoughtfully.

'Ain't you going to give them a hand with the sail?' asked Jimmy.

'No. If six ov 'em ain't 'nough beef to set that blamed, rotten spanker, they ain't fit to live,' answered Donkin in a bored, far-away voice, as though he had been talking from the bottom of a hole. Jimmy considered the conical, fowl-like profile with a queer kind of interest; he was leaning out of his bunk with the calculating, uncertain expression of a man who reflects how best to lay hold of some strange creature that looks as though it could sting or bite. But he said only: 'The mate will miss you – and there will be ructions.'

Donkin got up to go. 'I will do for 'im some dark night; see if I don't,' he said over his shoulder.

Jimmy went on quickly: 'You're like a poll-parrot, like a screechin' poll-parrot.' Donkin stopped and cocked his head attentively on one side. His big ears stood out, transparent and veined, resembling the thin wings of a bat.

'Yuss?' he said, with his back towards Jimmy.

'Yes! Chatter out all you know – like ... like a dirty white cockatoo.'

Donkin waited. He could hear the other's breathing, long and slow; the breathing of a man with a hundredweight or so on the breastbone. Then he asked calmly: 'What do I know?'

'What? ... What I tell you ... not much. What do you want ... to talk about my health so....'

'It's a blooming imposyshun. A bloomin', stinkin', first-class imposyshun – but it don't tyke me in. Not it.'

Jimmy kept still. Donkin put his hands in his pockets, and in one slouching stride came up to the bunk.

'I talk – what's the odds. They ain't men 'ere – sheep they are. A driven lot of sheep. I 'old you up ... Vy not? You're well orf.'

'I am ... I don't say anything about that....'

'Well. Let 'em see it. Let 'em larn what a man can do. I am a man, I know all about yer....' Jimmy threw himself further away on the pillow;

the other stretched out his skinny neck, jerked his bird face down at him as though pecking at the eyes. 'I am a man. I've seen the inside of every chokey in the Colonies rather'n give up my rights....'

'You are a jail-prop,' said Jimmy, weakly.

'I am ... an' proud of it, too. You! You 'aven't the bloomin' nerve – so you inventyd this 'ere dodge....' He paused; then with marked afterthought accentuated slowly: 'Yer ain't sick – are yer?'

'No,' said Jimmy, firmly. 'Been out of sorts now and again this year,' he mumbled with a sudden drop in his voice.

Donkin closed one eye, amicable and confidential. He whispered: 'Ye 'ave done this afore 'aven'tchee?' Jimmy smiled – then as if unable to hold back he let himself go: 'Last ship – yes. I was out of sorts on the passage. See? It was easy. They paid me off in Calcutta, and the skipper made no bones about it either.... I got my money all right. Laid up fifty-eight days! The fools! O Lord! The fools! Paid right off.' He laughed spasmodically. Donkin chimed in giggling. Then Jimmy coughed violently. 'I am as well as ever,' he said, as soon as he could draw breath.

Donkin made a derisive gesture. 'In course,' he said, profoundly, 'anyone can see that.' 'They don't,' said Jimmy, gasping like a fish. 'They would swallow any yarn,' affirmed Donkin. 'Don't you let on too much,' admonished Jimmy in an exhausted voice. 'You're little gyme? Eh?' commented Donkin, jovially. Then with sudden disgust: 'Yer all for yerself, s'long as ye're right....'

So charged with egoism James Wait pulled the blanket up to his chin and lay still for awhile. His heavy lips protruded in an everlasting black pout. 'Why are you so hot on making trouble?' he asked without much interest.

''Cos it's a bloomin' shayme. We are put upon ... bad food, bad pay ... I want us to kick up a bloomin' row; a blamed 'owling row that would make 'em remember! Knocking people about ... brains us ... indeed! Ain't we men?' His altruistic indignation blazed. Then he said calmly: 'I've been airing yer clothes.' 'All right,' said Jimmy, languidly, 'bring them in.' 'Giv' us the key of your chest, I'll put 'em away for yer,' said Donkin with friendly eagerness. 'Bring 'em in, I will put them away myself,' answered James Wait with severity. Donkin looked down, muttering.... 'What d'you say? What d'you say?' inquired Wait anxiously. 'Nothing. The night's dry, let 'em 'ang out till the morning,' said Donkin, in a strangely trembling voice, as though restraining laughter or rage. Jimmy seemed satisfied. 'Give me a little water for the night in my mug – there,' he said. Donkin took a stride over the door-step. 'Git it yerself,' he replied in a surly tone. 'You can do it, unless you *are* sick.' 'Of course I can do it,' said Wait, 'only ...' 'Well, then, do it,' said Donkin, viciously, 'if yer can look after yer clothes, yer can look after yerself.' He went on deck without a look back.

Jimmy reached out for the mug. Not a drop. He put it back gently with a faint sigh – and closed his eyes. He thought: That lunatic Belfast will bring me some water if I ask. Fool. I am very thirsty.... It was very hot in the cabin, and it seemed to turn slowly round, detach itself from the ship, and swing out smoothly into a luminous, arid space where a black sun shone, spinning very fast. A place without any water! No water! A policeman with the face of Donkin drank a glass of beer by the side of an empty well, and flew away flapping vigorously. A ship whose mastheads protruded through the sky and could not be seen, was discharging grain, and the wind whirled the dry husks in spirals along the quay of a dock with no water in it. He whirled along with the husks – very tired and light. All his inside was gone. He felt lighter than the husks – and more dry. He expanded his hollow chest. The air streamed in carrying away in its rush a lot of strange things that resembled houses, trees, people, lamp-posts.... No more! There was no more air – and he had not finished drawing his long breath. But he was in jail! They were locking him up. A door slammed. They turned the key twice, flung a bucket of water over him – Phoo! What for?

He opened his eyes, thinking the fall had been very heavy for an empty man – empty – empty. He was in his cabin. Ah! All right! His face was streaming with perspiration, his arms heavier than lead. He saw the cook standing in the doorway, a brass key in one hand and a bright tin hook-pot in the other.

'I have locked up the galley for the night,' said the cook, beaming benevolently. 'Eight bells just gone. I brought you a pot of cold tea for your night's drinking, Jimmy. I sweetened it with some white cabin sugar, too. Well – it won't break the ship.'

He came in, hung the pot on the edge of the bunk, asked perfunctorily, 'How goes it?' and sat down on the box. 'H'm,' grunted Wait, inhospitably. The cook wiped his face with a dirty cotton rag, which, afterwards, he tied round his neck. 'That's how them firemen do in steamboats,' he said, serenely, and much pleased with himself. 'My work is as heavy as theirs – I'm thinking – and longer hours. Did you ever see them down the stokehold? Like fiends they look – firing – firing – firing – down there.'

He pointed his forefinger at the deck. Some gloomy thought darkened his shining face, fleeting, like the shadow of a travelling cloud over the light of a peaceful sea. The relieved watch tramped noisily forward, passing in a body across the sheen of the doorway. Someone cried, 'Good night!' Belfast stopped for a moment and looked at Jimmy, quivering and speechless with repressed emotion. He gave the cook a glance charged with dismal foreboding, and vanished. The cook cleared his throat. Jimmy stared upwards and kept as still as a man in hiding.

The night was clear, with a gentle breeze. Above the mastheads the resplendent curve of the Milky Way spanned the sky like a triumphal arch of eternal light, thrown over the dark pathway of the earth. On the forecastle head a man whistled with loud precision a lively jig, while another could be heard faintly, shuffling and stamping in time. There came from forward a confused murmur of voices, laughter – snatches of song. The cook shook his head, glanced obliquely at Jimmy, and began to mutter. 'Aye. Dance and sing. That's all they think of. I am surprised that Providence don't get tired.... They forget the day that's sure to come ... but you....'

Jimmy drank a gulp of tea, hurriedly, as though he had stolen it, and shrank under his blanket, edging away towards the bulkhead. The cook got up, closed the door, then sat down again and said distinctly:

'Whenever I poke my galley fire I think of you chaps – swearing, stealing, lying, and worse – as if there was no such thing as another world. . . . Not bad fellows, either, in a way,' he conceded, slowly; then, after a pause of regretful musing, he went on in a resigned tone: 'Well, well. They will have a hot time of it. Hot! Did I say? The furnaces of one of them White Star boats ain't nothing to it.'

He kept very quiet for a while. There was a great stir in his brain; an addled vision of bright outlines; an exciting row of rousing songs and groans of pain. He suffered, enjoyed, admired, approved. He was delighted, frightened, exalted – as on that evening (the only time in his life – twenty-seven years ago; he loved to recall the number of years) when as a young man he had – through keeping bad company – become intoxicated in an East End music-hall. A tide of sudden feeling swept him clean out of his body. He soared. He contemplated the secret of the hereafter. It commended itself to him. It was excellent; he loved it, himself, all hands, and Jimmy. His heart overflowed with tenderness, with comprehension, with the desire to meddle, with anxiety for the soul of that black man, with the pride of possessed eternity, with the feeling of might. Snatch him up in his arms and pitch him right into the middle of salvation. . . . The black soul – blacker – body – rot – Devil. No! Talk – strength – Samson. . . . There was a great din as of cymbals in his ears; he flashed through an ecstatic jumble of shining faces, lilies, prayer-books, unearthly joy, white shirts, gold harps, black coats, wings. He saw flowing garments, clean-shaved faces, a sea of light – a lake of pitch. There were sweet scents, a smell of sulphur – red tongues of flame licking a white mist. An awesome voice thundered! . . . It lasted three seconds.

'Jimmy!' he cried in an inspired tone. Then he hesitated. A spark of human pity glimmered yet through the infernal fog of his supreme conceit.

'What?' said James Wait, unwillingly. There was a silence. He turned his head just the least bit, and stole a cautious glance. The cook's lips moved without a sound; his face was rapt, his eyes turned up. He seemed to be mentally imploring deck beams, the brass hook of the lamp, two cockroaches.

'Look here,' said Wait, 'I want to go to sleep. I think I could.'

'This is no time for sleep!' exclaimed the cook, very loud. He had prayerfully divested himself of the last vestige of his humanity. He was a voice – a fleshless and sublime thing, as on that memorable night – the night when he went walking over the sea to make coffee for perishing sinners. 'This is no time for sleeping,' he repeated with exaltation. '*I* can't sleep.'

'Don't care damn,' said Wait, with factitious energy. 'I can. Go an' turn in.'

'Swear . . . in the very jaws! . . . In the very jaws! Don't you see the everlasting fire . . . don't you feel it? Blind, chock-full of sin! Repent, repent! I can't bear to think of you. I hear the call to save you. Night and day. Jimmy, let me save you!' The words of entreaty and menace broke out of him in a roaring torrent. The cockroaches ran away. Jimmy perspired, wriggling stealthily under his blanket. The cook yelled. . . . 'Your days are numbered! . . .' 'Get out of this,' boomed Wait, courageously. 'Pray with me! . . .' 'I won't! . . .' The little cabin was as hot as an oven. It contained an immensity of fear and pain; an atmosphere of shrieks and moans; prayers

vociferated like blasphemies and whispered curses. Outside, the men called
by Charley, who informed them in tones of delight that there was a holy
row going on in Jimmy's place, crowded before the closed door, too startled
to open it. All hands were there. The watch below had jumped out on deck
in their shirts, as after a collision. Men running up, asked: 'What is it?'
Others said: 'Listen!' The muffled screaming went on: 'On your knees! On
your knees!' – 'Shut up!' – 'Never! You are delivered into my hands....
Your life has been saved.... Purpose.... Mercy.... Repent.' 'You are a
crazy fool! ...' 'Account of you ... you ... Never sleep in this world, if
I ...' 'Leave off.' 'No! ... stokehold ... only think! ...' Then an impassioned screeching babble where words pattered like hail. 'No!' shouted Wait.
'Yes. You are! ... No help. ... Everybody says so.' 'You lie!' 'I see you
dying this minyt ... before my eyes ... as good as dead already.' 'Help!'
shouted Jimmy, piercingly. 'Not in this valley ... look upwards,' howled
the other. 'Go away! Murder! Help!' clamoured Jimmy. His voice broke.
There were moanings, low mutters, a few sobs.

'What's the matter now?' said a seldom-heard voice. 'Fall back, men! Fall
back, there!' repeated Mr Creighton, sternly, pushing through. 'Here's the
old man,' whispered some. 'The cook's in there, sir,' exclaimed several,
backing away. The door clattered open; a broad stream of light darted out
on wondering faces; a warm whiff of vitiated air passed. The two mates
towered head and shoulders above the spare, grey-haired man who stood
revealed between them, in shabby clothes, stiff and angular, like a small
carved agure, and with a thin, composed face. The cook got up from his
knees. Jimmy sat high in the bunk, clasping his drawn-up legs. The tassel
of the blue night-cap almost imperceptibly trembled over his knees. They
gazed astonished at his long, curved back, while the white corner of one eye
gleamed blindly at them. He was afraid to turn his head, he shrank within
himself; and there was an aspect astounding and animal-like in the perfection
of his expectant immobility. A thing of instinct – the unthinking stillness of
a scared brute.

'What are you doing here?' asked Mr Baker, sharply. 'My duty,' said the
cook, with ardour. 'Your ... what?' began the mate. Captain Allistoun
touched his arm lightly. 'I know his caper,' he said, in a low voice. 'Come
out of that, Podmore,' he ordered, aloud.

The cook wrung his hands, shook his fists above his head, and his arms
dropped as if too heavy. For a moment he stood distracted and speechless.
'Never,' he stammered, 'I ... he ... I.' 'What – do – you – say?' pronounced
Captain Allistoun. 'Come out at once – or ...' 'I am going,' said the cook,
with a hasty and sombre resignation. He strode over the doorstep firmly –
hesitated – made a few steps. They looked at him in silence. 'I make you
responsible!' he cried, desperately, turning half round. 'That man is dying.
I make you ...' 'You there yet?' called the master in a threatening tone.
'No, sir,' he exclaimed, hurriedly, in a startled voice. The boatswain led him
away by the arm; someone laughed; Jimmy lifted his head for a stealthy
glance, and in one unexpected leap sprang out of his bunk; Mr Baker made
a clever catch and felt him very limp in his arms; the group at the door
grunted with surprise. 'He lies,' gasped Wait, 'he talked about black devils

– he is a devil – a white devil – I am all right.' He stiffened himself, and Mr Baker, experimentally, let him go. He staggered a pace or two; Captain Allistoun watched him with a quiet and penetrating gaze; Belfast ran to his support. He did not appear to be aware of anyone near him; he stood silent for a moment, battling single-handed with a legion of nameless terrors, amidst the eager looks of excited men who watched him far off, utterly alone in the impenetrable solitude of his fear. The sea gurgled through the scuppers as the ship heeled over to a short puff of wind.

'Keep him away from me,' said James Wait at last in his fine baritone voice, and leaning with all his weight on Belfast's neck. 'I've been better this last week . . . I am well . . . I was going back to duty . . . tomorrow – now if you like – Captain.' Belfast hitched his shoulders to keep him upright.

'No,' said the master, looking at him, fixedly.

Under Jimmy's armpit Belfast's red face moved uneasily. A row of eyes gleaming stared on the edge of light. They pushed one another with elbows, turned their heads, whispered. Wait let his chin fall on his breast and, with lowered eyelids, looked round in a suspicious manner.

'Why not?' cried a voice from the shadows, 'the man's all right, sir.'

'I am all right,' said Wait, with eagerness. 'Been sick . . . better . . . turn-to now.' He sighed. 'Howly Mother!' exclaimed Belfast with a heave of the shoulders, 'stand up, Jimmy.' 'Keep away from me then,' said Wait, giving Belfast a petulant push, and reeling fetched against the doorpost. His cheekbones glistened as though they had been varnished. He snatched off his night-cap, wiped his perspiring face with it, flung it on the deck. 'I am coming out,' he declared without stirring.

'No. You don't,' said the master, curtly. Bare feet shuffled, disapproving voices murmured all round; he went on as if he had not heard: 'You have been skulking nearly all the passage and now you want to come out. You think you are near enough to the pay-table now. Smell the shore, hey?'

'I've been sick . . . now – better,' mumbled Wait, glaring in the light. 'You have been shamming sick,' retorted Captain Allistoun with severity; 'Why . . .' he hesitated for less than half a second. 'Why, anybody can see that. There's nothing the matter with you, but you choose to lie-up to please yourself – and now you shall lie-up to please me. Mr Baker, my orders are that this man is not to be allowed on deck to the end of the passage.'

There were exclamations of surprise, triumph, indignation. The dark group of men swung across the light. 'What for?' – 'Told you so . . .' – 'Bloomin' shame. . . .' 'We've got to say somethink about that,' screeched Donkin from the rear. 'Never mind, Jim – we will see you righted,' cried several together. An elderly seaman stepped to the front. 'D'ye mean to say, sir,' he asked, ominously, 'that a sick chap ain't allowed to get well in this 'ere hooker?' Behind him Donkin whispered excitedly amongst a staring crowd where no one spared him a glance, but Captain Allistoun shook a forefinger at the angry bronzed face of the speaker. 'You – you hold your tongue,' he said, warningly. 'This isn't the way,' clamoured two or three younger men. 'Are we bloomin' masheens?' inquired Donkin in a piercing tone, and dived under the elbows of the front rank. 'Soon show 'im we ain't boys . . .' – 'The man's a man if he is black' – 'We ain't goin' to work this bloomin' ship shorthanded if Snowball's all right . . .' – 'He says he is' – 'Well then, strike, boys, strike!' – 'That's the bloomin' ticket.' Captain Allistoun said sharply to the second mate: 'Keep quiet, Mr Creighton,' and stood composed in the tumult, listening with profound attention to mixed growls and screeches, to every exclamation and every curse of the sudden outbreak. Somebody slammed the cabin door to with a kick; the darkness full of menacing mutters leaped with a short clatter over the streak of light, and the men became gesticulating shadows that growled, hissed, laughed excitedly. Mr Baker whispered: 'Get away from them, sir.' The big shape of Mr Creighton hovered silently about the slight figure of the master. 'We have been hymposed upon all this voyage,' said a gruff voice, 'but this 'ere fancy takes the cake.' 'That man is a shipmate' – 'Are we bloomin' kids?' – 'The port watch will refuse duty.' Charley carried away by his feeling whistled shrilly, then yelped: 'Giv' us our Jimmy!' This seemed to cause a variation in the disturbance. There was a fresh burst of squabbling uproar. A lot of quarrels were set going at once. 'Yes' – 'No' – 'Never been sick' – 'Go for them to once' – 'Shut yer mouth, youngster – this is men's work.' 'Is it?' muttered Captain Allistoun, bitterly. Mr Baker grunted: 'Ough! They're gone silly. They've been simmering for the last month.' 'I did notice,' said the master. 'They have started a row amongst themselves now,' said Mr Creighton with disdain, 'better get aft, sir. We will soothe them.' 'Keep your temper, Creighton,' said the master. And the three men began to move slowly towards the cabin door.

In the shadows of the fore rigging a dark mass stamped, eddied, advanced, retreated. There were words of reproach, encouragement, unbelief, execration. The elder seamen, bewildered and angry, growled their determination to go through with something or other; but the younger school of advanced thought exposed their and Jimmy's wrongs with confused shouts, arguing amongst themselves. They clustered round that moribund carcass, the fit emblem of their aspirations, and encouraging one another they swayed, they tramped on one spot, shouting that they would not be 'put upon'. Inside the cabin, Belfast, helping Jimmy into his bunk, twitched all over in his desire not to miss all the row, and with difficulty restrained the tears of his facile emotion. James Wait, flat on his back under the blanket, gasped complaints. 'We will back you up, never fear,' assured Belfast, busy about his feet. 'I'll come out tomorrow morning . . . take my chance . . . you fellows must . . .' mumbled Wait, 'I come out tomorrow . . . skipper or no skipper.' He lifted one arm with great difficulty, passed the hand over his face; 'Don't you let that cook . . .' he breathed out. 'No, no,' said Belfast, turning his back on the bunk, 'I will put a head on him if he comes near you.' 'I will smash his mug!' exclaimed Wait faintly, enraged and weak; 'I don't want to kill a man, but . . .' He panted fast like a dog after a run in sunshine. Someone just outside the door shouted, 'He's as fit as any ov us!' Belfast put his hand on the door-handle. 'Here!' called James Wait, hurriedly, and in such a clear voice that the other spun round with a start. James Wait, stretched out black and deathlike in the dazzling light, turned his head on the pillow. His eyes stared at Belfast, appealing and impudent. 'I am rather weak from lying-up so long,' he said, distinctly. Belfast nodded. 'Getting quite well now,' insisted Wait. 'Yes. I noticed you getting better this . . . last month,' said Belfast, looking down. 'Hallo! What's this?' he shouted and ran out.

He was flattened directly against the side of the house by two men who lurched against him. A lot of disputes seemed to be going on all around. He got clear and saw three indistinct figures standing alone in the fainter darkness under the arched foot of the mainsail, that rose above their heads like a convex wall of a high edifice. Donkin hissed: 'Go for them . . . it's dark!' The crowd took a short run aft in a body – then there was a check. Donkin, agile and thin, flitted past with his right arm going like a windmill – and then stood still suddenly with his arm pointing rigidly above his head. The hurtling flight of some heavy object was heard; it passed between the heads of the two mates, bounded heavily along the deck, struck the after hatch with a ponderous and deadened blow. The bulky shape of Mr Baker grew distinct. 'Come to your senses, men!' he cried, advancing at the arrested crowd. 'Come back, Mr Baker!' called the master's quiet voice. He obeyed unwillingly. There was a minute of silence, then a deafening hubbub arose. Above it Archie was heard energetically: 'If ye do oot ageen I wull tell!' There were shouts. 'Don't!' – 'Drop it!' – 'We ain't that kind!' The black cluster of human forms reeled against the bulwark, back again towards the house. Ringbolts rang under stumbling feet. 'Drop it!' – 'Let me!' – 'No!' – 'Curse you . . . hah!' Then sounds as of someone's face being slapped; a piece of iron fell on the deck; a short scuffle, and someone's shadowy body scuttled rapidly across the main hatch before the shadow of a kick. A raging voice sobbed out a torrent of filthy language. . . . 'Throwing things – good God!' grunted Mr Baker in dismay. 'That was meant for me,' said the master, quietly; 'I felt the wind of that thing; what was it – an iron belaying-pin?' 'By Jove!' muttered Mr Creighton. The confused voices of men talking amidships mingled with the wash of the sea, ascended between the silent and distended sails – seemed to flow away into the night, further than the horizon, higher than the sky. The stars burned steadily over the inclined mastheads. Trails of light lay on the water, broke before the advancing hull, and, after she had passed, trembled for a long time as if in awe of the murmuring sea.

Meantime the helmsman, anxious to know what the row was about, had let go the wheel, and, bent double, ran with long, stealthy footsteps to the break of the poop. The *Narcissus*, left to herself, came up gently to the wind without anyone being aware of it. She gave a slight roll, and the sleeping sails woke suddenly, coming all together with a mighty flap against the masts, then filled again one after another in a quick succession of loud reports that ran down the lofty spars, till the collapsed mainsail flew out last with a violent jerk. The ship trembled from trucks to keel; the sails kept on rattling like a discharge of musketry; the chain sheets and loose shackles jingled aloft in a thin peal; the gin blocks groaned. It was as if an invisible hand had given the ship an angry shake to recall the men that peopled her decks to the sense of reality, vigilance, and duty. 'Helm up!' cried the master, sharply. 'Run aft, Mr Creighton, and see what that fool there is up to.' 'Flatten in the head sheets. Stand by the weather fore-braces,' growled Mr Baker. Startled men ran swiftly repeating the orders. The watch below, abandoned all at once by the watch on deck, drifted towards the forecastle in twos and threes, arguing noisily as they went: 'We shall see tomorrow!' cried a loud voice, as if to cover with a menacing hint an inglorious retreat. And then only orders were heard, the falling of heavy coils of rope, the rattling of blocks. Singleton's white head flitted here and there in the night, high above the deck, like the ghost of a bird. 'Going off, sir!' shouted Mr Creighton from aft. 'Full again' – 'All right....' 'Ease off the head sheets. That will do the braces. Coil the ropes up,' grunted Mr Baker, bustling about.

Gradually the tramping noises, the confused sound of voices, died out, and the officers, coming together on the poop, discussed the events. Mr Baker was bewildered and grunted; Mr Creighton was calmly furious; but Captain Allistoun was composed and thoughtful. He listened to Mr Baker's growling argumentation, to Creighton's interjected and severe remarks, while looking down on the deck he weighed in his hand the iron belaying-pin – that a moment ago had just missed his head – as if it had been the only tangible fact of the whole transaction. He was one of those commanders who speak little, seem to hear nothing, look at no one – and know everything, hear every whisper, see every fleeting shadow of their ship's life. His two big officers towered above his lean, short figure; they talked over his head; they were dismayed, surprised, and angry, while between them the little quiet man seemed to have found his taciturn serenity in the profound depths of a larger experience. Lights were burning in the forecastle; now and then a loud gust of babbling chatter came from forward, swept over the decks, and became faint, as if the unconscious ship, gliding gently through the great peace of the sea, had left behind and for ever the foolish noise of turbulent mankind. But it was renewed again and again. Gesticulating arms, profiles of heads with open mouths appeared for a moment in the illuminated squares of doorways; black fists darted – withdrew ... 'Yes. It was most damnable to have such an unprovoked row sprung on one,' assented the master.... A tumult of yells rose in the light, abruptly ceased.... He didn't think there would be any further trouble just then.... A bell was struck aft, another, forward, answered in a deeper tone, and the clamour of ringing metal spread round the ship in a circle of wide vibrations that ebbed away into the immeasurable night of an empty sea.... Didn't he know them! Didn't he! In past years. Better men, too. Real men to stand by one in a tight place. Worse than devils too sometimes – down-right, horned devils. Pah! This – nothing. A miss as good as a mile.... The wheel was being relieved in the usual way. 'Full and by,' said, very loud, the man going off. 'Full and by,' repeated the other, catching hold of the spokes. 'This head wind is my trouble,' exclaimed the master, stamping his foot in sudden anger; 'head wind! all the rest is nothing.' He was calm again in a moment. 'Keep them on the move tonight, gentlemen; just to let them feel we've got hold all the time – quietly, you know. Mind you keep your hands off them, Creighton. Tomorrow I will talk to them like a Dutch Uncle. A crazy crowd of tinkers! Yes, tinkers! I could count the real sailors amongst them on the fingers of one hand. Nothing will do but a row – if – you – please.' He paused. 'Did you think I had gone wrong there, Mr Baker?' He tapped his forehead, laughed short. 'When I saw him standing there, three parts dead and so scared – black amongst that gaping lot – no grit to face what's coming to us all – the notion came to me all at once, before I could think. Sorry for him – like you would be for a sick brute. If ever creature was in a mortal funk to die! . . . I thought I would let him go out in his own way. Kind of impulse. It never came into my head, those fools.... H'm! Stand to it now – of course.' He stuck the belaying-pin in his pocket, seemed ashamed of himself, then sharply: 'If you see Podmore at his tricks again tell him I will have him put under the pump. Had to do it once before. The fellow breaks out like that now and then. Good cook tho'.' He walked away quickly, came back to the companion. The two mates followed him through the starlight with amazed eyes. He went down three steps, and changing his tone, spoke with his head near the deck: 'I shan't turn in tonight, in case of anything; just call out if . . . Did you see the eyes of that sick nigger, Mr Baker? I fancied he begged me for something. What? Past all help. One lone black beggar amongst the lot of us, and he seemed to look through me into the very hell. Fancy, this wretched Podmore! Well, let him die in peace. I am master here after all. Let him be. He might have been half a man once.... Keep a good look-out.' He disappeared down below, leaving his mates facing one another, and more impressed than if they had seen a stone image shed a miraculous tear of compassion over the incertitudes of life and death....

In the blue mist spreading from twisted threads that stood upright in the bowls of pipes, the forecastle appeared as vast as a hall. Between the beams a heavy cloud stagnated; and the lamps surrounded by halos burned each at the core of a purple glow in two lifeless flames without rays. Wreaths drifted in denser wisps. Men sprawled about on the deck, sat in negligent poses, or, bending a knee, drooped with one shoulder against a bulkhead. Lips moved, eyes flashed, waving arms made sudden eddies in the smoke. The murmur of voices seemed to pile itself higher and higher as if unable to run out quick enough through the narrow doors. The watch below in their shirts, and striding on long white legs, resembled raving somnambulists; while now and then one of the watch on deck would rush in, looking strangely over-dressed, listen a moment, fling a rapid sentence into the noise, and run out again; but a few remained near the door, fascinated, and with one ear turned to the deck. 'Stick together, boys,' roared Davis. Belfast tried to make himself heard. Knowles grinned in a slow, dazed way. A short fellow with a thick clipped beard kept on yelling periodically: 'Who's afeard? Who's afeard?' Another one jumped up, excited, with glazing eyes, sent out a string of unattached curses and sat down quietly. Two men discussed familiarly, striking one another's breast in turn, to clinch arguments. Three others, with their heads in a bunch, spoke all together with a confidential air, and at the top of their voices. It was a stormy chaos of speech where intelligible fragments tossing, struck the ear. One could hear: 'In the last ship' – 'Who cares? Try it on any one of us if —' – 'Knock under' – 'Not a hand's turn' – 'He says he is all right' – 'I always thought' – 'Never mind....' Donkin, crouching all in a heap against the bowsprit, hunched his shoulderblades as high as his ears, and hanging a peaked nose, resembled a sick vulture with ruffled plumes. Belfast, straddling his legs, had a face red

with yelling, and with arms thrown up, figured a Maltese cross. The two
Scandinavians, in a corner, had the dumbfounded and distracted aspect of
men gazing at a cataclysm. And, beyond the light, Singleton stood in the
smoke, monumental, indistinct, with his head touching the beam; like a
statue of heroic size in the gloom of a crypt.

He stepped forward, impassive and big. The noise subsided like a broken
wave: but Belfast cried once more with uplifted arms: 'The man is dying I
tell ye?' then sat down suddenly on the hatch and took his head between his
hands. All looked at Singleton, gazing upwards from the deck, staring out
of dark corners, or turning their heads with curious glances. They were
expectant and appeased as if that old man, who looked at no one, had
possessed the secret of their uneasy indignations and desires, a sharper vision,
a clearer knowledge. And indeed standing there amongst them, he had the
uninterested appearance of one who had seen multitudes of ships, had
listened many times to voices such as theirs, had already seen all that could
happen on the wide seas. They heard his voice rumble in his broad chest as
though the words had been rolling towards them out of a rugged past. 'What
do you want to do?' he asked. No one answered. Only Knowles muttered
– 'Aye, aye,' and somebody said low: 'It's a bloomin' shame.' He waited,
made a contemptuous gesture. 'I have seen rows aboard ship before some of
you were born,' he said, slowly, 'for something or nothing; but never for
such a thing.' 'The man is dying, I tell ye,' repeated Belfast, woefully, sitting
at Singleton's feet. 'And a black fellow, too,' went on the old seaman, 'I have
seen them die like flies.' He stopped, thoughtful, as if trying to recollect
gruesome things, details, of horrors, hecatombs of niggers. They looked at
him fascinated. He was old enough to remember slavers, bloody mutinies,
pirates perhaps; who could tell through what violences and terrors he had
lived! What would he say? He said: 'You can't help him; die he must.' He
made another pause. His moustache and beard stirred. He chewed words,
mumbled behind tangled white hairs; incomprehensible and exciting, like
an oracle behind a veil.... 'Stop ashore ... sick.... Instead ... bringing
all this head wind. Afraid. The sea will have her own. ... Die in sight of
land. Always so. They know it ... long passage ... more days, more
dollars.... You keep quiet.... What do you want? Can't help him.' He
seemed to wake up from a dream. 'You can't help yourselves,' he said,
austerely. 'Skipper's no fool. He has something in his mind. Look out – I
say! I know 'em!' With eyes fixed in front he turned his head from right to
left, from left to right, as if inspecting a long row of astute skippers. ''Ee
said 'ee would brain me!' cried Donkin in a heartrending tone. Singleton
peered downwards with puzzled attention, as though he couldn't find him.
'Damn you!' he said, vaguely, giving it up. He radiated unspeakable wisdom,
hard unconcern, the chilling air of resignation. Round him all the listeners
felt themselves somehow completely enlightened by their disappointment,
and mute, they lolled about with the careless ease of men who can discern
perfectly the irremediable aspect of their existence. He, profound and
unconscious, waved his arm once, and strode out on deck without another
word.

Belfast was lost in a round-eyed meditation. One or two vaulted heavily into upper berths, and, once there, sighed; others dived head first inside lower bunks – swift, and turning round instantly upon themselves, like animals going into lairs. The grating of a knife scraping burnt clay was heard. Knowles grinned no more. Davis said, in a tone of ardent conviction: 'Then our skipper's looney.' Archie muttered: 'My faith! we haven't heard the last of it yet!' Four bells were struck. 'Half our watch below gone!' cried Knowles in alarm, then reflected. 'Well, two hours' sleep is something towards a rest,' he observed, consolingly. Some already pretended to slumber; and Charley, sound asleep, suddenly said a few slurred words in an arbitrary, blank voice. 'This blamed boy has worrums!' commented Knowles from under a blanket, in a learned manner. Belfast got up and approached Archie's berth. 'We pulled him out,' he whispered, sadly. 'What?' said the other, with sleepy discontent. 'And now we will have to chuck him overboard,' went on Belfast, whose lower lip trembled. 'Chuck what?' asked Archie. 'Poor Jimmy,' breathed out Belfast. 'He be blowed!' said Archie with untruthful brutality, and sat up in his bunk; 'It's all through him. If it hadn't been for me, there would have been murder on board this ship!' ''Tain't his fault, is it?' argued Belfast, in a murmur; 'I've put him to bed ... an' he ain't no heavier than an empty beef-cask,' he added, with tears in his eyes. Archie looked at him steadily, then turned his nose to the ship's side with determination. Belfast wandered about as though he had lost his way in the dim forecastle, and nearly fell over Donkin. He contemplated him from on high for a while. 'Ain't ye going to turn in?' he asked. Donkin looked up hopelessly. 'That black 'earted Scotch son of a thief kicked me!' he whispered from the floor, in a tone of utter desolation. 'And a good job, too!' said Belfast, still very depressed; 'You were as near hanging as damn-it tonight, sonny. Don't you play any of your murthering games around my Jimmy! You haven't pulled him out. You just mind! 'Cos if I start to kick you' – he brightened up a bit – 'if I start to kick you, it will be Yankee fashion – to break something!' He tapped lightly with his knuckles the top of the bowed head. 'You moind that, my bhoy!' he concluded, cheerily. Donkin let it pass. 'Will they split on me?' he asked, with pained anxiety. 'Who – split?' hissed Belfast, coming back a step. 'I would split your nose this minyt if I hadn't Jimmy to look after! Who d'ye think we are?' Donkin rose and watched Belfast's back lurch through the doorway. On all sides invisible men slept, breathing calmly. He seemed to draw courage and fury from the peace around him. Venomous and thin-faced, he glared from the ample misfit of borrowed clothes as if looking for something he could smash. His heart leaped wildly in his narrow chest. They slept! He wanted to wring necks, gouge eyes, spit on faces. He shook a dirty pair of meagre fists at the smoking lights. 'Ye're no men!' he cried, in a deadened tone. No one moved. 'Yer 'aven't the pluck of a mouse!' His voice rose to a husky screech. Wamibo darted out a dishevelled head, and looked at him wildly. 'Ye're sweepings ov ships! I 'ope you will all rot before you die!' Wamibo blinked, uncomprehending but interested. Donkin sat down heavily; he blew with force through quivering nostrils, he ground and snapped his teeth, and, with the chin pressed hard against the breast, he seemed busy gnawing his way through it, as if to get at the heart within....

In the morning the ship, beginning another day of her wandering life, had an aspect of sumptuous freshness, like the spring-time of the earth. The washed decks glistened in a long clear stretch; the oblique sunlight struck the yellow brasses in dazzling splashes, darted over the polished rods in lines of gold, and the single drops of salt water forgotten here and there along the rail were as limpid as drops of dew, and sparkled more than scattered diamonds. The sails slept, hushed by a gentle breeze. The sun, rising lonely and splendid in the blue sky, saw a solitary ship gliding close-hauled on the blue sea.

The men pressed three deep abreast of the mainmast and opposite the cabin-door. They shuffled, pushed, had an irresolute mien and stolid faces. At every slight movement Knowles lurched heavily on his short leg. Donkin glided behind backs, restless and anxious, like a man looking for an ambush. Captain Allistoun came out on the quarter-deck suddenly. He walked to and fro before the front. He was grey, slight, alert, shabby in the sunshine, and as hard as adamant. He had his right hand in the side-pocket of his jacket, and also something heavy in there that made folds all down that side. One of the seamen cleared his throat ominously. 'I haven't till now found fault with you men,' said the master, stopping short. He faced them with his worn, steely gaze, that by an universal illusion looked straight into every individual pair of the twenty pairs of eyes before his face. At his back Mr Baker, gloomy, and bull-necked, grunted low; Mr Creighton, fresh as paint, had rosy cheeks and a ready, resolute bearing. 'And I don't now,' continued the master; 'but I am here to drive this ship and keep every man-jack aboard of her up to the mark. If you knew your work as well as I do mine, there would be no trouble. You've been braying in the dark about "See tomorrow morning!" Well, you see me now. What do you want?' He waited, stepping quickly to and fro, giving them searching glances. What did they want? They shifted from foot to foot, they balanced their bodies; some, pushing back their caps, scratched their heads. What did they want? Jimmy was forgotten; no one thought of him, alone forward in his cabin, fighting great shadows, clinging to brazen lies, chuckling painfully over his transparent deceptions. No, not Jimmy; he was more forgotten than if he had been dead. They wanted great things. And suddenly all the simple words they knew seemed to be lost for ever in the immensity of their vague and burning desire. They knew what they wanted, but they could not find anything worth saying. They stirred on one spot, swinging, at the end of muscular arms, big tarry hands with crooked fingers. A murmur died out. 'What is it – food?' asked the master, 'you know the stores have been spoiled off the Cape.' 'We know that, sir,' said a bearded shell-back in the front rank. 'Work too hard – eh? Too much for your strength?' he asked again. There was an offended silence. 'We don't want to go shorthanded, sir,' began at last Davis in a wavering voice, 'and this 'ere black . . .' 'Enough!' cried the master. He stood scanning them for a moment, then walking a few steps this way and that began to storm at them coldly, in gusts violent and cutting like the gales of those icy seas that had known his youth. 'Tell you what's the matter? Too big for your boots. Think yourselves damn good men. Know half your work. Do half your duty. Think it too much. If you did ten times as much it wouldn't be enough.' 'We did our best by her, sir,' cried someone with shaky exasperation. 'Your best,' stormed on the master: 'You hear a lot on shore, don't you? They don't tell you there your best isn't much to boast of. I tell you – your best is no better than bad. You can do no more? No, I know, and say nothing. But you stop your caper or I will stop it for you. I am ready for you! Stop it!' He shook a finger at the crowd. 'As to that man,' he raised his voice very much; 'as to that man, if he puts his nose out on deck without my leave I will clap him in irons. There!' The cook heard him forward, ran out of the galley lifting his arms, horrified, unbelieving, amazed, and ran in again. There was a moment of profound silence during which a bow-legged seaman, stepping aside, expectorated decorously into the scupper. 'There is another thing,' said the master, calmly. He made a quick stride and with a swing took an iron belaying-pin out of his pocket. 'This!' His movement was so unexpected and sudden that the crowd stepped back. He gazed fixedly at their faces, and some at once put on a surprised air as though they had never seen a belaying-pin before. He held it up. 'This is my affair. I don't ask you any questions, but you all know it; it has got to go where it came from.' His eyes became angry. The crowd stirred uneasily. They looked away from the piece of iron, they appeared shy, they were embarrassed and shocked as though it had been something horrid, scandalous, or indelicate, that in common decency should not have been flourished like this in broad daylight. The master watched them attentively. 'Donkin,' he called out in a short, sharp tone.

Donkin dodged behind one, then behind another, but they looked over their shoulders and moved aside. The ranks kept on opening before him, closing behind, till at last he appeared alone before the master as though he had come up through the deck. Captain Allistoun moved close to him. They were much of a size, and at short range the master exchanged a deadly glance with the beady eyes. They wavered. 'You know this,' asked the master. 'No, I don't,' answered the other with cheeky trepidation. 'You are a cur. Take it,' ordered the master. Donkin's arms seemed glued to his thighs; he stood, eyes front, as if drawn on parade. 'Take it,' repeated the master, and stepped closer; they breathed on one another. 'Take it,' said Captain Allistoun again, making a menacing gesture. Donkin tore away one arm from his side. 'Vy are yer down on me?' he mumbled with effort and as if his mouth had been full of dough. 'If you don't . . .' began the master. Donkin snatched at the pin as though his intention had been to run away with it, and remained stock still holding it like a candle. 'Put it back where you took it from,' said Captain Allistoun, looking at him fiercely. Donkin stepped back opening wide eyes. 'Go, you blackguard, or I will make you,' cried the master, driving him slowly backwards by a menacing advance. He dodged, and with the dangerous iron tried to guard his head from a threatening fist. Mr Baker ceased grunting for a moment. 'Good! By Jove,' murmured appreciatively Mr Creighton in the tone of a connoisseur. 'Don't tech me,' snarled Donkin, backing away. 'Then go. Go faster.' 'Don't yer 'it me. . . . I will pull yer up afore the magistryt. . . . I'll show yer up.' Captain Allistoun made a long stride, and Donkin, turning his back fairly, ran off a little, then stopped and over his shoulder showed yellow teeth.

'Further on, fore-rigging,' urged the master, pointing with his arm. 'Are yer goin' to stand by and see me bullied,' screamed Donkin at the silent crowd that watched him. Captain Allistoun walked at him smartly. He started off again with a leap, dashed at the fore-rigging, rammed the pin into its hole violently. 'I'll be even with yer yet,' he screamed at the ship at large and vanished beyond the foremast. Captain Allistoun spun round and walked back aft with a composed face, as though he had already forgotten the scene. Men moved out of his way. He looked at no one. 'That will do, Mr Baker. Send the watch below,' he said, quietly. 'And you men try to walk straight for the future,' he added in a calm voice. He looked pensively for a while at the backs of the impressed and retreating crowd. 'Breakfast, steward,' he called in a tone of relief through the cabin door. 'I didn't like to see you – Ough! – give that pin to that chap, sir,' observed Mr Baker; 'he could have bust – Ough! – bust your head like an eggshell with it.' 'O! he!' muttered the master absently. 'Queer lot,' he went on in a low voice. 'I suppose it's all right now. Can never tell tho', nowadays, with such a . . . Years ago; I was a young master then – one China voyage I had a mutiny; real mutiny, Baker. Different men tho'. I knew what they wanted: they wanted to broach the cargo and get at the liquor. Very simple. . . . We knocked them about for two days, and when they had enough – gentle as lambs. Good crew. And a smart trip I made.' He glanced aloft at the yards braced sharp up. 'Head wind day after day,' he exclaimed, bitterly. 'Shall we never get a decent slant this passage?' 'Ready, sir,' said the steward, appearing before them as if by magic and with a stained napkin in his hand. 'Ah! All right. Come along, Mr Baker – it's late – with all this nonsense.'

CHAPTER 5

A heavy atmosphere of oppressive quietude pervaded the ship. In the afternoon men went about washing clothes and hanging them out to dry in the unprosperous breeze with the meditative languor of disenchanted philosophers. Very little was said. The problem of life seemed too voluminous for the narrow limits of human speech, and by common consent it was abandoned to the great sea that had from the beginning enfolded it in its immense grip; to the sea that knew all, and would in time infallibly unveil to each the wisdom hidden in all the errors, the certitude that lurks in doubts, the realm of safety and peace beyond the frontiers of sorrow and fear. And in the confused current of impotent thoughts that set unceasingly this way and that through bodies of men, Jimmy bobbed up upon the surface, compelling attention, like a black buoy chained to the bottom of a muddy stream. Falsehood triumphed. It triumphed through doubt, through stupidity, through pity, through sentimentalism. We set ourselves to bolster it up, from compassion, from recklessness, from a sense of fun. Jimmy's steadfastness to his untruthful attitude in the face of the inevitable truth had the proportions of a colossal enigma – of a manifestation grand and incomprehensible that at times inspired a wondering awe; and there was also, to many, something exquisitely droll in fooling him thus to the top of his bent. The latent egoism of tenderness to suffering appeared in the developing anxiety not to see him die. His obstinate non-recognition of the only certitude whose approach we could watch from day to day was as disquieting as the failure to some law of nature. He was so utterly wrong about himself that one could not but suspect him of having access to some source of supernatural knowledge. He was absurd to the point of inspiration. He was unique, and as fascinating as only something inhuman could be; he seemed to shout his denials already from beyond the awful border. He was becoming immaterial like an apparition; his cheekbones rose, the forehead slanted more; the face was all hollows, patches of shade; and the fleshless head resembled a disinterred black skull, fitted with two restless globes of silver in the sockets of eyes. He was demoralizing. Through him we were becoming highly humanized, tender, complex, excessively decadent: we understood the subtlety of his fear, sympathized with all his repulsions, shrinkings, evasions, delusions – as though we had been over-civilized, and rotten, and without any knowledge of the meaning of life. We had the air of being initiated in some infamous mysteries; we had the profound grimaces of conspirators, exchanged meaning glances, significant short words. We were inexpressibly vile and very much pleased with ourselves. We lied to him with gravity, with emotion, with unction, as if performing some moral trick with a view to an eternal reward. We made a chorus of affirmation to his wildest assertions, as though he had been a millionaire, a politician, or a reformer – and we a crowd of ambitious lubbers. When we ventured to question his statements we did it after the manner of obsequious sycophants, to the end that his glory should be augmented by the flattery of our dissent. He influenced the moral tone of our world as though he had it in his power to distribute honours, treasures, or pain; and he could give us nothing but his contempt. It was immense; it seemed to grow gradually larger, as his body day by day shrank a little more, while we looked. It was the only thing about him – of him – that gave the impression of durability and vigour. It lived within him with an unquenchable life. It spoke through the eternal pout of his black lips; it looked at us through the impertinent mournfulness of his languid and enormous stare. We watched him intently. He seemed unwilling to move, as if distrustful of his own solidity. The slightest gesture must have disclosed to him (it could not surely be otherwise) his bodily weakness, and caused a pang of mental suffering. He was chary of movements. He lay stretched out, chin on blanket, in a kind of sly, cautious immobility. Only his eyes roamed over faces: his eyes disdainful, penetrating, and sad.

It was at that time that Belfast's devotion – and also his pugnacity – secured universal respect. He spent every moment of his spare time in Jimmy's cabin. He tended him, talked to him; was as gentle as a woman, as tenderly gay as an old philanthropist, as sentimentally careful of his nigger as a model slaveowner. But outside he was irritable, explosive as gunpowder, sombre, suspicious, and never more brutal than when most sorrowful. With him it was a tear and a blow; a tear for Jimmy, a blow for anyone who did not seem to take a scrupulously orthodox view of Jimmy's case. We talked about nothing else. The two Scandinavians, even, discussed the situation – but it was impossible to know in what spirit, because they quarrelled in their own language. Belfast suspected one of them of irreverence, and in this incertitude thought that there was no option but to fight them both. They became very much terrified by his truculence, and henceforth lived amongst us, dejected, like a pair of mutes. Wamibo never spoke intelligibly, but he was as smileless as an animal – seemed to know much less about it all than the cat – and consequently was safe. Moreover, he had belonged to the chosen band of Jimmy's rescuers, and was above suspicion. Archie was silent generally, but often spent an hour or so talking to Jimmy quietly with an air of proprietorship. At any time of the day and often through the night some man could be seen sitting on Jimmy's box. In the evening, between six and eight, the cabin was crowded, and there was an interested group at the door. Everyone stared at the nigger.

He basked in the warmth of our interest. His eyes gleamed ironically, and in a weak voice he reproached us with our cowardice. He would say, 'If you fellows had stuck out for me I would be now on deck.' We hung our heads. 'Yes, but if you think I am going to let them put me in irons just to show you sport . . . Well, no . . . It ruins my health, this lying-up, it does. You don't care.' We were as abashed as if it had been true. His superb impudence carried all before it. We would not have dared to revolt. We didn't want to, really. We wanted to keep him alive till home – to the end of the voyage.

Singleton as usual held aloof, appearing to scorn the insignificant events of an ended life. Once only he came along, and unexpectedly stopped in the doorway. He peered at Jimmy in profound silence, as if desirous to add that black image to the crowd of Shades that peopled his old memory. We kept very quiet, and for a long time Singleton stood there as though he had come by appointment to call for someone, or to see some important event. James Wait lay perfectly still, and apparently not aware of the gaze scrutinizing him with a steadiness full of expectation. There was a sense of a contest in the air. We felt the inward strain of men watching a wrestling bout. At last Jimmy with perceptible apprehension turned his head on the pillow. 'Good evening,' he said in a conciliating tone. 'H'm,' answered the old seaman grumpily. For a moment longer he looked at Jimmy with severe fixity, then suddenly went away. It was a long time before anyone spoke in the little cabin, though we all breathed more freely as men do after an escape from some dangerous situation. We all knew the old man's ideas about Jimmy, and nobody dared to combat them. They were unsettling, they caused pain; and, what was worse, they might have been true for all we knew. Only once did he condescend to explain them fully, but the impression was lasting. He said that Jimmy was the cause of head winds. Mortally sick men – he maintained – linger till the first sight of land, and then die; and Jimmy knew that the very first land would draw his life from him. It is so in every ship. Didn't we know it? He asked us with austere contempt: what did we know? What would we doubt next? Jimmy's desire encouraged by us and aided by Wamibo's (he was a Finn – wasn't he? Very well!) by Wamibo's spells delayed the ship in the open sea. Only lubberly fools couldn't see it. Whoever heard of such a run of calms and head winds? It wasn't natural. . . . We could not deny that it was strange. We felt uneasy. The common saying, 'More days, more dollars', did not give the usual comfort because the stores were running short. Much had been spoiled off the Cape, and we were on half allowance of biscuit. Peas, sugar and tea had been finished long ago. Salt meat was giving out. We had plenty of coffee but very little water to make it with. We took up another hole in our belts and went on scraping, polishing, painting the ship from morning to night. And soon she looked as though she had come out of a band-box; but hunger lived on board of her. Not dead starvation, but steady, living hunger that stalked about the decks, slept in the forecastle; the tormentor of waking moments, the disturber of dreams. We looked to windward for signs of change. Every few hours of night and day we put her round with the hope that she would come up on that tack at last! She didn't. She seemed to have forgotten the way home; she rushed to and fro, heading north-west, heading east; she ran backwards and forwards, distracted like a timid creature at the foot of a wall. Sometimes, as if tired to death, she would wallow languidly for a day in the smooth swell of an unruffled sea. All up the swinging masts the sails trashed furiously through the hot stillness of the calm. We were weary, hungry, thirsty; we commenced to believe Singleton, but with unshaken fidelity dissembled to Jimmy. We spoke to him with jocose allusiveness, like cheerful accomplices in a clever plot; but we looked to the westward over the rail with longing eyes for a sign of hope, for a sign of fair wind; even if its first breath should bring death to our reluctant Jimmy. In vain! The universe conspired with James Wait. Light airs from the northward sprang up again; the sky remained clear; and round our weariness the glittering sea, touched by the breeze, basked voluptuously in the great sunshine, as though it had forgotten our life and trouble.

Donkin looked out for a fair wind along with the rest. No one knew the venom of his thoughts now. He was silent, and appeared thinner, as if consumed slowly by an inward rage at the injustice of men and of fate. He was ignored by all and spoke to no one, but his hate for every man dwelt in his furtive eyes. He talked with the cook only, having somehow persuaded the good man that he – Donkin – was a much calumniated and persecuted person. Together they bewailed the immorality of the ship's company. There could be no greater criminals than we, who by our lies conspired to send the unprepared soul of a poor ignorant black man to everlasting perdition. Podmore cooked what there was to cook, remorsefully, and felt all the time that by preparing the food of such sinners he imperilled his own salvation. As to the Captain – he had sailed with him for seven years, now, he said, and would not have believed it possible that such a man . . . 'Well. Well . . . There it was. . . . Can't get out of it. Judgement capsized all in a minute. . . . Struck in all his pride. . . . More like a sudden visitation than anything else.' Donkin, perched sullenly on the coal-locker, swung his legs and concurred. He paid in the coin of spurious assent for the privilege to sit in the galley; he was disheartened and scandalized; he agreed with the cook; could find no words severe enough to criticize our conduct; and when in the heat of reprobation he swore at us, Podmore, who would have liked to swear also if it hadn't been for his principles, pretended not to hear. So Donkin, unrebuked, cursed enough for two, cadged for matches, borrowed tobacco, loafed for hours and very much at home before the stove. From there he could hear us on the other side of the bulkhead, talking to Jimmy, The cook knocked the saucepans about, slammed the oven door, muttered prophesies of damnation for all the ship's company; and Donkin, who did not admit of any hereafter (except for purposes of blasphemy) listened, concentrated and angry, gloating fiercely over a called-up image of infinite torment – as men gloat over the accursed images of cruelty and revenge, of greed and of power. . . .

On clear evenings the silent ship, under the cold sheen of the dead moon, took on a false aspect of passionless repose resembling the winter of the earth. Under her a long band of gold barred the black disc of the sea. Footsteps echoed on her quiet decks. The moonlight clung to her like a frosted mist, and the white sails stood out in dazzling cones as of stainless snow. In the magnificence of the phantom rays the ship appeared pure like a vision of ideal beauty, illusive like a tender dream of serene peace. And nothing in her was real, nothing was distinct and solid but the heavy shadows that filled her decks with their unceasing and noiseless stir: the shadows darker than the night and more restless than the thoughts of men.

Donkin prowled spiteful and alone amongst the shadows, thinking that Jimmy too long delayed to die. That evening land had been reported from aloft, and the master, while adjusting the tubes of the long glass, had observed with quiet bitterness to Mr Baker that, after fighting our way inch by inch to the Western Islands, there was nothing to expect now but a spell of calm. The sky was clear and the barometer high. The light breeze dropped with the sun, and an enormous stillness, forerunner of a night without wind, descended upon the heated waters of the ocean. As long as daylight lasted, the hands collected on the forecastle-head watched on the eastern sky the island of Flores, that rose above the level expanse of the sea with irregular and broken outlines like a sombre ruin upon a vast and deserted plain. It was the first land seen for nearly four months. Charley was excited, and in the midst of general indulgence took liberties with his betters. Men strangely elated without knowing why, talked in groups, and pointed with bared arms. For the first time that voyage Jimmy's sham existence seemed for a moment forgotten in the face of a solid reality. We had got so far anyhow. Belfast discoursed, quoting imaginary examples of short homeward runs from the Islands. 'Them smart fruit schooners do it in five days,' he affirmed. 'What do you want? – only a good little breeze.' Archie maintained that seven days was the record passage, and they disputed amicably with insulting words. Knowles declared he could already smell home from there, and with a heavy list on his short leg laughed fit to split his sides. A group of grizzled sea-dogs looked out for a time in silence and with grim absorbed faces. One said suddenly: "Tain't far to London now.' 'My first night ashore, blamme if I haven't steak and onions for supper . . . and a pint of bitter,' said another. 'A barrel ye mean,' shouted someone. 'Ham an' eggs three times a day. That's the way I live!' cried an excited voice. There was a stir, appreciative murmurs; eyes began to shine; jaws champed; short, nervous laughs were heard. Archie smiled with reserve all to himself. Singleton came up, gave a careless glance, and went down again without saying a word, indifferent, like a man who had seen Flores an incalculable number of times. The night travelling from the East blotted out of the limpid sky the purple stain of the high land. 'Dead calm,' said somebody quietly. The murmur of lively talk suddenly wavered, died out; the clusters broke up; men began to drift away one by one, descending the ladders slowly and with serious faces as if sobered by that reminder of their dependence upon the invisible. And when the big yellow moon ascended gently above the sharp rim of the clear horizon it found the ship wrapped up in a breathless silence; a fearless ship that seemed to sleep profoundly, dreamlessly on the bosom of the sleeping and terrible sea.

Donkin chafed at the peace – at the ship – at the sea that stretching away on all sides merged into the illimitable silence of all creation. He felt himself pulled up sharp by unrecognized grievances. He had been physically cowed, but his injured dignity remained indomitable, and nothing could heal his lacerated feelings. Here was land already – home very soon – a bad pay-day – no clothes – more hard work. How offensive all this was. Land The land that draws away life from sick sailors. That nigger there had money – clothes – easy times; and would not die. Land draws life away. . . . He felt tempted to go and see whether it did. Perhaps already . . . It would be a bit of luck. There was money in the beggar's chest. He stepped briskly out of the shadows into the moonlight, and, instantly, his craving, hungry face from sallow became livid. He opened the door of the cabin and had a shock. Sure enough, Jimmy was dead! He moved no more than a recumbent figure with clasped hands, carved on the lid of a stone coffin. Donkin glared with avidity. Then Jimmy, without stirring, blinked his eyelids, and Donkin had another shock. Those eyes were rather startling. He shut the door behind his back with gentle care, looking intently the while at James Wait as though he had come in there at a great risk to tell some secret of startling importance. Jimmy did not move but glanced languidly out of the corners of his eyes. 'Calm?' he asked, 'Yuss,' said Donkin, very disappointed, and sat down on the box.

Jimmy was used to such visits at all times of night or day. Men succeeded one another. They spoke in clear voices, pronounced cheerful words, repeated old jokes, listened to him; and each, going out, seemed to leave behind a little of his own vitality, surrender some of his own strength, renew the assurance of life – the indestructible thing! He did not like to be alone in his cabin, because, when he was alone, it seemed to him as if he hadn't been there at all. There was nothing. No pain. Not now. Perfectly right – but he couldn't enjoy his healthful repose unless someone was by to see it. This man would do as well as anybody. Donkin watched him stealthily. 'Soon home now,' observed Wait. 'Vy d'yer whisper?' asked Donkin with interest, 'can't yer speak up?' Jimmy looked annoyed and said nothing for a while; then in a lifeless, unringing voice: 'Why should I shout? You ain't deaf that I know.' 'Oh! I can 'ear right enough,' answered Donkin in a low tone, and looked down. He was thinking sadly of going out when Jimmy spoke again. 'Time

we did get home . . . to get something decent to eat. . . . I am always hungry.'
Donkin felt angry all of a sudden. 'What about me,' he hissed, 'I am 'ungry
too an' got ter work. You, 'ungry!' 'Your work won't kill you,' commented
Wait, feebly; 'there's a couple of biscuits in the lower bunk there – you may
have one. I can't eat them.' Donkin dived in, groped in the corner and when
he came up again his mouth was full. He munched with ardour. Jimmy
seemed to doze with open eyes. Donkin finished his hard bread and got up.
'You're not going?' asked Jimmy, staring at the ceiling. 'No,' said Donkin,
impulsively, and instead of going out leaned his back against the closed door.
He looked at James Wait, and saw him long, lean, dried up, as though all
his flesh had shrivelled on his bones in the heat of a white furnace; the
meagre fingers of one hand moved lightly upon the edge of the bunk playing
an endless tune. To look at him was irritating and fatiguing; he could last
like this for days; he was outrageous – belonging wholly neither to death nor
life, and perfectly invulnerable in his apparent ignorance of both. Donkin
felt tempted to enlighten him. 'What are yer thinkin' of?' he asked, surlily.
James Wait had a grimacing smile that passed over the death-like impas-
siveness of his bony face, incredible and frightful as would, in a dream, have
been the sudden smile of a corpse.
  'There is a girl,' whispered Wait. . . . 'Canton Street girl. . . . She chucked
a third engineer of a Rennie boat . . . for me. Cooks oysters just as I like. . . .
She says . . . she would chuck . . . any toff . . . for a coloured gentleman. . . .
That's me. I am kind to wimmen,' he added, a shade louder.
  Donkin could hardly believe his ears. He was scandalized – 'Would she?
Yer wouldn't be any good to 'er,' he said with unrestrained disgust. Wait
was not there to hear him. He was swaggering up the East India Dock
Road; saying kindly, 'Come along for a treat,' pushing glass swing-doors,
posing with superb assurance in the gaslight above a mahogany counter.
'D'yer think yer will ever get ashore?' asked Donkin angrily. Wait came
back with a start. 'Ten days,' he said, promptly, and returned at once to the
regions of memory that know nothing of time. He felt untired, calm, and
safely withdrawn within himself beyond the reach of every grave incertitude.
There was something of the immutable quality of eternity in the slow
moments of his complete restfulness. He was very quiet and easy amongst
his vivid reminiscences which he mistook joyfully for images of an undoubted
future. He cared for no one. Donkin felt this vaguely like a blind man feeling
in his darkness the fatal antagonism of all the surrounding existences, that
to him shall for ever remain irrealizable, unseen and enviable. He had a
desire to assert his importance, to break, to crush; to be even with everybody
for everything; to tear the veil, unmask, expose, leave no refuge – a perfidious
desire of truthfulness! He laughed in a mocking splutter and said:
  'Ten days. Strike me blind if I ever! . . . You will be dead by this time
tomorrow p'r'aps. Ten days!' He waited for a while. 'D'ye 'ear me? Blamme
if yer don't look dead already.'
  Wait must have been collecting his strength for he said almost aloud:
'You're a stinking, cadging liar. Everyone knows you.' And sitting up,
against all probability, startled his visitor horribly. But very soon Donkin
recovered himself. He blustered:

'What? What? Who's a liar? You are – the crowd are – the skipper – everybody. I ain't! Putting on airs! Who's yer?' He nearly choked himself with indignation. 'Who's yer to put on airs,' he repeated, trembling. ''Ave one – 'ave one, says 'ee – an' cawn't eat 'em 'isself. Now I'll 'ave both. By Gawd – I will! Yer nobody!'

He plunged into the lower bunk, rooted in there, and brought to light another dusty biscuit. He held it up before Jimmy – then took a bite defiantly.

'What now?' he asked with feverish impudence. 'Yer may take one – says yer. Why not giv' me both? No. I'm a mangy dorg. One fur a mangy dorg. I'll tyke both. Can yer stop me? Try. Come on. Try.'

Jimmy was clasping his legs and hiding his face on the knees. His shirt clung to him. Every rib was visible. His emaciated back was shaken in repeated jerks by the panting catches of his breath.

'Yer won't? Yer can't! What did I say?' went on Donkin, fiercely. He swallowed another dry mouthful with a hasty effort. The other's silent helplessness, his weakness, his shrinking attitude exasperated him. 'Ye're done!' he cried. 'Who's yer to be lied to; to be waited on 'and an' foot like a bloomin' ymperor. Yer nobody. Yer no one at all!' he spluttered with such a strength of unerring conviction that it shook him from head to foot in coming out, and left him vibrating like a released string.

James Wait rallied again. He lifted his head and turned bravely at Donkin, who saw a strange face, an unknown face, a fantastic and grimacing mask of despair and fury. Its lips moved rapidly; and hollow, moaning, whistling sounds filled the cabin with a vague mutter full of menace, complaint, and desolation, like the far-off murmur of a rising wind. Wait shook his head; rolled his eyes; he denied, cursed, threatened – and not a word had the strength to pass beyond the sorrowful pout of those black lips. It was incomprehensible and disturbing; a gibberish of emotions, a frantic dumb show of speech pleading for impossible things, promising a shadowy vengeance. It sobered Donkin into a scrutinizing watchfulness.

'Yer can't oller. See? What did I tell yer?' he said, slowly, after a moment of attentive examination. The other kept on headlong and unheard, nodding passionately, grinning with grotesque and appalling flashes of big white teeth. Donkin, as if fascinated by the dumb eloquence and anger of that black phantom, approached, stretching his neck out with distrustful curiosity; and it seemed to him suddenly that he was looking only at the shadow of a man crouching high in the bunk on the level with his eyes. 'What? What?' he said. He seemed to catch the shape of some words in the continuous panting hiss. 'Yer will tell Belfast! Will yer? Are yer a bloomin' kid?' He trembled with alarm and rage, 'Tell yer gran'mother! Yer afeard! Who's yer ter be afeard more'n anyone?' His passionate sense of his own importance ran away with a last remnant of caution. 'Tell an' be damned! Tell, if yer can!' he cried. 'I've been treated worser'n a dorg by your blooming back-lickers. They 'as set me on, only to turn aginst me. I am the only man 'ere. They clouted me, kicked me – an' yer laffed – yer black, rotten incumbrance, you! You will pay fur it. They giv' yer their grub, their water – yer will pay fur it to me, by Gawd! Who axed me ter 'ave a drink of water? They put their bloomin' rags on yer that night, an' what did they giv' ter me – a clout on the bloomin' mouth – blast their ... S'elp me! ... Yer will pay fur it with yer money. I'm goin' ter 'ave it in a minyt; as soon has ye're dead, yer bloomin' useless fraud. That's the man I am. An' ye're a thing – a bloody thing. Yah – you corpse!'

He flung at Jimmy's head the biscuit he had been all the time clutching hard, but it only grazed, and striking with a loud crack the bulkhead beyond burst like a hand-grenade into flying pieces. James Wait, as if wounded mortally, fell back on the pillow. His lips ceased to move and the rolling eyes became quiet and stared upwards with an intense and steady persistence. Donkin was surprised; he sat suddenly on the chest, and looked down, exhausted and gloomy. After a moment, he began to mutter to himself, 'Die, you beggar – die. Somebody'll come in. ... I wish I was drunk. ... Ten days ... oysters ...' He looked up and spoke louder. 'No ... No more for yer ... no more bloomin' gals that cook oysters. ... Who's yer? It's my turn now. ... I wish I was drunk; I would soon giv' you a leg up. That's where yer bound to go. Feet fust, through a port. ... Splash! Never see yer any more. Overboard! Good 'nuff fur yer.'

Jimmy's head moved slightly and he turned his eyes to Donkin's face; a gaze unbelieving, desolated, and appealing, of a child frightened by the menace of being shut up alone in the dark. Donkin observed him from the chest with hopeful eyes; then, without rising, tried the lid. Locked. 'I wish I was drunk,' he muttered and getting up listened anxiously to the distant sound of footsteps on the deck. They approached – ceased. Someone yawned interminably just outside the door, and the footsteps went away shuffling lazily. Donkin's fluttering heart eased its pace, and when he looked towards the bunk again Jimmy was staring as before at the white beam. ''Ow d'yer feel now?' he asked. 'Bad,' breathed out Jimmy.

Donkin sat down patient and purposeful. Every half-hour the bells spoke to one another ringing along the whole length of the ship. Jimmy's respiration was so rapid that it couldn't be counted, so faint that it couldn't be heard. His eyes were terrified as though he had been looking at unspeakable horrors; and by his face one could see that he was thinking of abominable things. Suddenly with an incredibly strong and heart-breaking voice he sobbed out:

'Overboard! ... I! ... My God!'

Donkin writhed a little on the box. He looked unwillingly. James Wait was mute. His two long bony hands smoothed the blanket upwards, as though he had wished to gather it all up under his chin. A tear, a big solitary tear, escaped from the corner of his eye and, without touching the hollow cheek, fell on the pillow. His throat rattled faintly.

And Donkin, watching the end of that hateful nigger, felt the anguishing grasp of a great sorrow on his heart at the thought that he himself, some day, would have to go through it all – just like this – perhaps! His eyes became moist. 'Poor beggar,' he murmured. The night seemed to go by in a flash; it seemed to him he could hear the irremediable rush of precious minutes. How long would this blooming affair last? Too long surely. No luck. He could not restrain himself. He got up and approached the bunk.

Wait did not stir. Only his eyes appeared alive and his hands continued their smoothing movement with a horrible and tireless industry. Donkin bent over.

'Jimmy,' he called low. There was no answer, but the rattle stopped. 'D'yer see me?' he asked, trembling. Jimmy's chest heaved. Donkin, looking away, bent his ear to Jimmy's lips, and heard a sound like the rustle of a single dry leaf driven along the smooth sand of a beach. It shaped itself.

'Light ... the lamp ... and ... go,' breathed out Wait.

Donkin, instinctively, glanced over his shoulder at the brilliant flame; then, still looking away, felt under the pillow for a key. He got it at once and for the next few minutes remained on his knees shakily but swiftly busy inside the box. When he got up, his face – for the first time in his life – had a pink flush – perhaps of triumph.

He slipped the key under the pillow again, avoiding to glance at Jimmy, who had not moved. He turned his back squarely from the bunk, and started to the door as though he were going to walk a mile. At his second stride he had his nose against it. He clutched the handle cautiously, but at that moment he received the irresistible impression of something happening behind his back. He spun round as though he had been tapped on the shoulder. He was just in time to see Wait's eyes blaze up and go out at once, like two lamps overturned together by a sweeping blow. Something resembling a scarlet thread hung down his chin out of the corner of his lips – and he had ceased to breathe.

Donkin closed the door behind him gently but firmly. Sleeping men, huddled under jackets, made on the lighted deck shapeless dark mounds that had the appearance of neglected graves. Nothing had been done all through the night and he hadn't been missed. He stood motionless and perfectly astounded to find the world outside as he had left it; there was the sea, the ship – sleeping men; and he wondered absurdly at it, as though he had expected to find the men dead, familiar things gone for ever: as though, like a wanderer returning after many years, he had expected to see bewildering changes. He shuddered a little in the penetrating freshness of the air, and hugged himself forlornly. The declining moon drooped sadly in the western board as if withered by the cold touch of a pale dawn. The ship slept. And the immortal sea stretched away, immense and hazy, like the image of life, with a glittering surface and lightless depths. Donkin gave it a defiant glance and slunk off noiselessly as if judged and cast out by the august silence of its might.

Jimmy's death, after all, came as a tremendous surprise. We did not know till then how much faith we had put in his delusions. We had taken his chances of life so much at his own valuation that his death, like the death of an old belief, shook the foundations of our society. A common bond was gone; the strong, effective, and respectable bond of a sentimental lie. All that day we mooned at our work, with suspicious looks and a disabused air. In our hearts we thought that in the matter of his departure Jimmy had acted in a perverse and unfriendly manner. He didn't back us up, as a shipmate should. In going he took away with himself the gloomy and solemn shadow in which our folly had posed, with humane satisfaction, as a tender arbiter of fate. And now we saw it was no such thing. It was just common foolishness; a silly and ineffectual meddling with issues of majestic import – that is, if Podmore was right. Perhaps he was? Doubt survived Jimmy; and, like a community of banded criminals disintegrated by a touch of grace, we were profoundly scandalized with each other. Men spoke unkindly to their best chums. Others refused to speak at all. Singleton only was not surprised. 'Dead – is he? Of course,' he said, pointing at the island right abeam; for the calm still held the ship spell-bound within sight of Flores. Dead – of course. *He* wasn't surprised. Here was the land, and there, on the fore-hatch and waiting for the sailmaker – there was that corpse. Cause and effect. And for the first time that voyage, the old seaman became quite cheery and garrulous, explaining and illustrating from the stores of experience how, in sickness, the sight of an island (even a very small one) is generally more fatal than the view of a continent. But he couldn't explain why.

Jimmy was to be buried at five, and it was a long day till then – a day of mental disquiet and even of physical disturbance. We took no interest in our work and, very properly, were rebuked for it. This, in our constant state of hungry irritation, was exasperating. Donkin worked with his brow bound in a dirty rag, and looked so ghastly that Mr Baker was touched with compassion at the sight of this plucky suffering. 'Ough! You, Donkin! Put down your work and go lay-up this watch. You look ill.' 'I am bad, sir – in my 'ead,' he said in a subdued voice, and vanished speedily. This annoyed many, and they thought the mate 'bloomin' soft today'. Captain Allistoun could be seen on the poop watching the sky to the south-west, and it soon got to be known about the decks that the barometer had begun to fall in the night, and that a breeze might be expected before long. This, by a subtle association of ideas, led to violent quarrelling as to the exact moment of Jimmy's death. Was it before or after 'that 'ere glass started down'? It was impossible to know, and it caused much contemptuous growling at one another. All of a sudden there was a great tumult forward. Pacific Knowles and good-tempered Davis had come to blows over it. The watch below interfered with spirit, and for ten minutes there was a noisy scrimmage round the hatch, where, in the balancing shade of the sails, Jimmy's body wrapped up in a white blanket, was watched over by the sorrowful Belfast, who, in his desolation, disdained the fray. When the noise had ceased, and the passions had calmed into surly silence, he stood up at the head of the swathed body, lifting both arms on high, cried with pained indignation: 'You ought to be ashamed of yourselves! . . .' We were.

Belfast took his bereavement very hard. He gave proofs of unextinguishable devotion. It was he, and no other man, who would help the sailmaker to prepare what was left of Jimmy for a solemn surrender to the insatiable sea. He arranged the weights carefully at the feet: two holystones, an old anchor-shackle without its pin, some broken links of a worn-out stream cable. He arranged them this way, then that. 'Bless my soul! you aren't afraid he will chafe his heel?' said the sailmaker, who hated the job. He pushed the needle, puffing furiously, with his head in a cloud of tobacco smoke; he turned the flaps over, pulled at the stitches, stretched at the canvas. 'Lift his shoulders. . . . Pull to you a bit. . . . So – o – o. Steady.' Belfast obeyed, pulled, lifted, overcome with sorrow, dropping tears on the tarred twine. 'Don't you drag the canvas too taut over his poor face, Sails,' he entreated tearfully. 'What are you fashing yourself for? He will be comfortable enough,' assured the sailmaker, cutting the thread after the last stitch, which came about the middle of Jimmy's forehead. He rolled up the remaining canvas, put away the needles. 'What makes you take on so?' he asked. Belfast looked down at the long package of grey sailcloth. 'I pulled him out,' he whispered, 'and he did not want to go. If I had sat up with him last night he would have kept alive for me . . . but something made me tired.' The sailmaker took vigorous draws at his pipe and mumbled: 'When I . . . West India Station . . . In the *Blanche* frigate . . . Yellow Jack . . . sewed in twenty men a week . . . Portsmouth-Devonport men – townies – knew their fathers, mothers, sisters – the whole boiling of 'em. Thought nothing of it. And these niggers like this one – you don't know where it comes from. Got nobody. No use to nobody. Who will miss him?' 'I do – I pulled him out,' mourned Belfast dismally.

On two planks nailed together and apparently resigned and still under the folds of the Union Jack with a white border, James Wait, carried aft by four men, was deposited slowly, with his feet pointing at an open port. A swell had set in from the westward, and following on the roll of the ship, the red ensign, at half-mast, darted out and collapsed again on the grey sky, like a tongue of flickering fire; Charley tolled the bell; and at every swing to starboard the whole vast semi-circle of steely waters visible on that side seemed to come up with a rush to the edge of the port, as if impatient to get at our Jimmy. Everyone was there but Donkin, who was too ill to come; the Captain and Mr Creighton stood bareheaded on the break of the poop; Mr Baker, directed by the master, who had said to him gravely: 'You know more about the prayer book than I do,' came out of the cabin door quickly and a little embarrassed. All the caps went off. He began to read in a low tone, and with his usual harmlessly menacing utterance, as though he had been for the last time reproving confidentially that dead seaman at his feet. The men listened in scattered groups; they leaned on the fife rail, gazing on the deck; they held their chins in their hands thoughtfully, or, with crossed arms and one knee slightly bent, hung their heads in an attitude of upright meditation. Wamibo dreamed. Mr Baker read on, grunting reverently at the turn of every page. The words, missing the unsteady hearts of men, rolled out to wander without a home upon the heartless sea; and James Wait, silenced for ever, lay uncritical and passive under the hoarse murmur of despair and hopes.

Two men made ready and waited for those words that send so many of our brothers to their last plunge. Mr Baker began the passage. 'Stand by,' muttered the boatswain. Mr Baker read out: 'To the deep,' and paused. The men lifted the inboard end of the planks, the boatswain snatched off the Union Jack, and James Wait did not move. 'Higher,' muttered the boatswain angrily. All the heads were raised; every man stirred uneasily, but James Wait gave no sign of going. In death and swathed up for all eternity, he yet seemed to cling to the ship with the grip of an undying fear. 'Higher! Lift!'

whispered the boatswain, fiercely. 'He won't go,' stammered one of the men, shakily, and both appeared ready to drop everything. Mr Baker waited, burying his face in the book, and shuffling his feet nervously. All the men looked profoundly disturbed; from their midst a faint humming noise spread out – growing louder. . . . 'Jimmy!' cried Belfast in a wailing tone, and there was a second of shuddering dismay.

'Jimmy, be a man!' he shrieked, passionately. Every mouth was wide open, not an eyelid winked. He stared wildly, twitching all over; he bent his body forward like a man peering at a horror. 'Go!' he shouted, and sprang out of the crowd with his arm extended. 'Go, Jimmy! – Jimmy, go! Go!' His fingers touched the head of the body, and the grey package started reluctantly to whizz off the lifted planks all at once, with the suddenness of a flash of lightning. The crowd stepped forward like one man; a deep Ah – h – h! came out vibrating from the broad chests. The ship rolled as if relieved of an unfair burden; the sails flapped. Belfast, supported by Archie, gasped hysterically; and Charley, who anxious to see Jimmy's last dive, leaped headlong on the rail, was too late to see anything but the faint circle of a vanishing ripple.

Mr Baker, perspiring abundantly, read out the last prayer in a deep rumour of excited men and fluttering sails. 'Amen!' he said in an unsteady growl, and closed the book.

'Square the yards!' thundered a voice above his head. All hands gave a jump; one or two dropped their caps; Mr Baker looked up surprised. The master, standing on the break of the poop, pointed to the westward. 'Breeze coming,' he said. 'Man the weather braces.' Mr Baker crammed the book hurriedly into his pocket. 'Forward, there – let go the foretack!' he hailed joyfully, bareheaded and brisk; 'Square the foreyard, you port-watch!' 'Fair wind – fair wind,' muttered the men going to the braces. 'What did I tell you?' mumbled old Singleton, flinging down coil after coil with hasty energy; 'I knowed it – he's gone and here it comes.'

It came with the sound of a lofty and powerful sigh. The sails filled, the ship gathered way, and the waking sea began to murmur sleepily of home to the ears of men.

That night, while the ship rushed foaming to the northward before a freshening gale, the boatswain unbosomed himself to the petty officers' berth: 'The chap was nothing but trouble,' he said, 'from the moment he came aboard – d'ye remember – that night in Bombay? Been bullying all that softy crowd – cheeked the old man – we had to go fooling all over a half-drowned ship to save him. Dam' nigh a mutiny all for him – and now the mate abused me like a pickpocket for forgetting to dab a lump of grease on them planks. So I did, but you ought to have known better, too, than to leave a nail sticking up – hey, Chips?'

'And you ought to have known better than to chuck all my tools overboard for 'im, like a skeary greenhorn,' retorted the morose carpenter. 'Well – he's gone after 'em now,' he added in an unforgiving tone. 'On the China Station, I remember once, the Admiral he says to me . . .' began the sailmaker.

A week afterwards the *Narcissus* entered the chops of the Channel.

Under white wings she skimmed low over the blue sea like a great tired bird speeding to its nest. The clouds raced with her mastheads; they rose astern enormous and white, soared to the zenith, flew past, and, falling down the wide curve of the sky, seemed to dash headlong into the sea – the clouds swifter than the ship, more free, but without a home. The coast to welcome her stepped out of space into the sunshine. The lofty headlands trod masterfully into the sea; the wide bays smiled in the light; the shadows of homeless clouds ran along the sunny plains, leaped over valleys, without a check darted up the hills, rolled down the slopes; and the sunshine pursued them with patches of running brightness. On the brows of dark cliffs white lighthouses shone in pillars of light. The Channel glittered like a blue mantle shot with gold and starred by the silver of the capping seas. The *Narcissus* rushed past the headlands and the bays. Outward-bound vessels crossed her track, lying over, and with their masts stripped for a slogging fight with the hard sou'-wester. And, inshore, a string of smoking steamboats waddled, hugging the coast, like migrating and amphibious monsters, distrustful of the restless waves.

At night the headlands retreated, the bays advanced into one unbroken line of gloom. The lights of the earth mingled with the lights of heaven; and above the tossing lanterns of a trawling fleet a great lighthouse shone steadily, like an enormous riding light burning above a vessel of fabulous dimensions. Below its steady glow, the coast, stretching away straight and black, resembled the high side of an indestructible craft riding motionless upon the immortal and unresting sea. The dark land lay alone in the midst of waters, like a mighty ship bestarred with vigilant lights – a ship carrying the burden of millions of lives – a ship freighted with dross and with jewels, with gold and with steel. She towered up immense and strong, guarding priceless traditions and untold suffering, sheltering glorious memories and base forgetfulness, ignoble virtues and splendid transgressions. A great ship! For ages had the ocean battered in vain her enduring sides; she was there when the world was vaster and darker, when the sea was great and mysterious, and ready to surrender the prize of fame to audacious men. A ship mother of fleets and nations! The great flagship of the race; stronger than the storms! and anchored in the open sea.

The *Narcissus*, heeling over to off-shore gusts, rounded the South Foreland, passed through the Downs, and, in tow, entered the river. Shorn of the glory of her white wings, she wound obediently after the tug through the maze of invisible channels. As she passed them the red-painted light-vessels, swung at their moorings, seemed for an instant to sail with great speed in the rush of tide, and the next moment were left hopelessly behind. The big buoys on the tails of banks slipped past her sides very low, and, dropping in her wake, tugged at their chains like fierce watch-dogs. The reach narrowed; from both sides, the land approached the ship. She went steadily up the river. On the riverside slopes the houses appeared in groups – seemed to stream down the declivities at a run to see her pass, and, checked by the mud of the foreshore, crowded on the banks. Farther on, the tall factory chimneys appeared in insolent bands and watched her go by, like a straggling crowd of slim giants, swaggering and upright under the black plummets of smoke, cavalierly aslant. She swept round the bends; an impure breeze shrieked a welcome between her stripped spars; and the land, closing in, stepped between the ship and the sea.

A low cloud hung before her – a great opalescent and tremulous cloud, that seemed to rise from the steaming brows of millions of men. Long drifts of smoky vapours soiled it with livid trails; it throbbed to the beat of millions of hearts, and from it cáme an immense and lamentable murmur – the murmur of millions of lips praying, cursing, sighing, jeering – the undying murmur of folly, regret, and hope exhaled by the crowds of the anxious earth. The *Narcissus* entered the cloud; the shadows deepened; on all sides there was the clang of iron, the sound of mighty blows, shrieks, yells. Black barges drifted stealthily on the murky stream. A mad jumble of begrimed walls loomed up vaguely in the smoke, bewildering and mournful, like a vision of disaster. The tugs backed and filled in the stream, to hold the ship steady at the dock-gates; from her bows two lines went through the air whistling, and struck at the land viciously, like a pair of snakes. A bridge broke in two before her, as if by enchantment; big hydraulic capstans began to turn all by themselves, as though animated by a mysterious and unholy spell. She moved through a narrow lane of water between two low walls of granite, and men with check-ropes in their hands kept pace with her, walking on the broad flag-stones. A group waited impatiently on each side of the vanished bridge: rough heavy men in caps; sallow-faced men in high hats; two bareheaded women; ragged children, fascinated, and with wide eyes. A cart coming at a jerky trot pulled up sharply. One of the women screamed at the silent ship: 'Hallo, Jack!' without looking at anyone in particular, and all hands looked at her from the forecastle head. 'Stand clear! Stand clear of that rope!' cried the dockmen, bending over the stone posts. The crowd murmured, stamped where they stood. 'Let go your quarter-checks! Let go!' sang out a ruddy-faced old man on the quay. The ropes splashed heavily falling in the water, and the *Narcissus* entered the dock.

The stony shores ran away right and left in straight lines, enclosing a sombre and rectangular pool. Brick walls rose high above the water – soulless walls, staring through hundreds of windows as troubled and dull as the eyes of over-fed brutes. At their base monstrous iron cranes crouched, with chains hanging from their long necks, balancing cruel-looking hooks over the decks of lifeless ships. A noise of wheels rolling over stones, the thump of heavy things falling, the racket of feverish winches, the grinding of strained chains, floated on the air. Between high buildings the dust of all the continents soared in short flights; and a penetrating smell of perfumes and dirt, of spices and hides, of things costly and of things filthy, pervaded the space, made for it an atmosphere precious and disgusting. The *Narcissus* came gently into her berth; the shadows of soulless walls fell upon her, the dust of all the continents leaped upon her deck, and a swarm of strange men, clambering up her sides, took possession of her in the name of the sordid earth. She had ceased to live.

A toff in a black coat and high hat scrambled with agility, came up to the second mate, shook hands, and said: 'Hallo Herbert.' It was his brother. A lady appeared suddenly. A real lady, in a black dress and with a parasol.

She looked extremely elegant in the midst of us, and as strange as if she had fallen there from the sky. Mr Baker touched his cap to her. It was the master's wife. And very soon the Captain, dressed very smartly and in a white shirt, went with her over the side. We didn't recognize him at all till, turning on the quay, he called to Mr Baker: 'Don't forget to wind up the chronometers tomorrow morning.' An underhand lot of seedy-looking chaps with shifty eyes wandered in and out of the forecastle looking for a job – they said. 'More likely for something to steal,' commented Knowles, cheerfully. Poor beggars. Who cared? Weren't we home! But Mr Baker went for one of them who had given him some cheek, and we were delighted. Everything was delightful. 'I've finished aft, sir,' called out Mr Creighton. 'No water in the well, sir,' reported for the last time the carpenter, sounding-rod in hand. Mr Baker glanced along the decks at the expectant group of sailors, glanced aloft at the yards. 'Ough! That will do, men,' he grunted. The group broke up. The voyage was ended.

Rolled-up beds went flying over the rail; lashed chests went sliding down the gangway – mighty few of both at that. 'The rest is having a cruise off the Cape,' explained Knowles enigmatically to a dock-loafer with whom he had struck a sudden friendship. Men ran, calling to one another, hailing utter strangers to 'lend a hand with the dunnage', then with sudden decorum approached the mate to shake hands before going ashore. 'Good-bye, sir,' they repeated in various tones. Mr Baker grasped hard palms, grunted in a friendly manner at everyone, his eyes twinkled. 'Take care of your money, Knowles. Ough! Soon get a nice wife if you do.' The lame man was delighted. 'Good-bye, sir,' said Belfast, with emotion, wringing the mate's hand, and looked up with swimming eyes. 'I thought I would take 'im ashore with me,' he went on, plaintively. Mr Baker did not understand, but said kindly: 'Take care of yourself, Craik,' and the bereaved Belfast went over the rail mourning and alone.

Mr Baker, in the sudden peace of the ship, moved about solitary and grunting, trying door-handles, peering into dark places, never done – a model chief mate! No one waited for him ashore. Mother dead; father and two brothers, Yarmouth fishermen, drowned together on the Dogger Bank; sister married and unfriendly. Quite a lady. Married to the leading tailor of a little town, and its leading politician, who did not think his sailor brother-in-law quite respectable enough for him. Quite a lady, quite a lady, he thought, sitting down for a moment's rest on the quarter-hatch. Time enough to go ashore and get a bite and sup, and a bed somewhere. He didn't like to part with a ship. No one to think about then. The darkness of a misty evening fell, cold and damp, upon the deserted deck; and Mr Baker sat smoking, thinking of all the successive ships to whom through many long years he had given the best of a seaman's care. And never a command in sight. Not once! 'I haven't somehow the cut of a skipper about me,' he meditated, placidly, while the shipkeeper (who had taken possession of the galley), a wizened old man with bleared eyes, cursed him in whispers for 'hanging about so'. 'Now, Creighton,' he pursued the unenvious train of thought, 'quite a gentleman . . . swell friends . . . will get on. Fine young fellow . . . a little more experience.' He got up and shook himself. 'I'll be back first thing tomorrow morning for the hatches. Don't you let them touch anything before I come, shipkeeper,' he called out. Then, at last, he also went ashore – a model chief mate!

The men scattered by the dissolving contact of the land came together once more in the shipping office. 'The *Narcissus* pays off,' shouted outside a glazed door a brass-bound old fellow with a crown and the capitals B.T. on his cap. A lot trooped in at once but many were late. The room was large, whitewashed, and bare; a counter surmounted by a brass-wire grating fenced off a third of the dusty space, and behind the grating a pasty-faced clerk with his hair parted in the middle, had the quick, glittering eyes and the vivacious, jerky movements of a caged bird. Poor Captain Allistoun also in there, and sitting before a little table with piles of gold and notes on it, appeared subdued by his captivity. Another Board of Trade bird was perching on a high stool near the door: an old bird that did not mind the chaff of elated sailors. The crew of the *Narcissus*, broken up into knots, pushed in the corners. They had new shore togs, smart jackets that looked as if they had been shaped with an axe, glossy trousers that seemed made of crumpled sheet-iron, collarless flannel shirts, shiny new boots. They tapped on shoulders, button-holed one another, asked: 'Where did you sleep last night?' whispered gaily, slapped their thighs with bursts of subdued laughter. Most had clean, radiant faces; only one or two turned up dishevelled and sad; the two young Norwegians looked tidy, meek, and altogether of a promising material for the kind ladies who patronize the Scandinavian Home. Wamibo, still in his working clothes, dreamed, upright and burly in the middle of the room, and, when Archie came in, woke up for a smile. But the wide-awake clerk called out a name, and the paying-off business began.

One by one they came up to the pay-table to get the wages of their glorious and obscure toil. They swept the money with care into broad palms, rammed it trustfully into trousers' pockets, or, turning their backs on the table, reckoned with difficulty in the hollow of their stiff hands. 'Money right? Sign the release. There – there,' repeated the clerk, impatiently. 'How stupid those sailors are!' he thought. Singleton came up, venerable – and uncertain as to daylight; brown drops of tobacco juice hung in his white beard; his hands, that never hesitated in the great light of the open sea, could hardly find the small pile of gold in the profound darkness of the shore. 'Can't write?' said the clerk, shocked. 'Make a mark, then.' Singleton painfully sketched in a heavy cross, blotted the page. 'What a disgusting old brute,' muttered the clerk. Somebody opened the door for him, and the patriarchal seaman passed through unsteadily, without as much as a glance at any of us.

Archie displayed a pocket-book. He was chaffed. Belfast, who looked wild, as though he had already luffed up through a public-house or two, gave signs of emotion and wanted to speak to the Captain privately. The master was surprised. They spoke through the wires, and we could hear the Captain saying: 'I've given it up to the Board of Trade.' 'I should've liked to get something of his,' mumbled Belfast. 'But you can't, my man. It's given up, locked and sealed, to the Marine Office,' expostulated the master; and Belfast stood back, with drooping mouth and troubled eyes. In a pause of the business we heard the master and the clerk talking. We caught: 'James Wait – deceased – found no papers of any kind – no relations – no trace – the Office must hold his wages then.' Donkin entered. He seemed out of breath, was grave, full of business. He went straight to the desk, talked with animation to the clerk, who thought him an intelligent man. They discussed the account, dropping h's against one another as if for a wager – very friendly. Captain Allistoun paid. 'I give you a bad discharge,' he said, quietly. Donkin raised his voice: 'I don't want your bloomin' discharge – keep it. I'm goin' ter 'ave a job ashore.' He turned to us. 'No more bloomin' sea fur me,' he said, aloud. All looked at him. He had better clothes, had an easy air, appeared more at home than any of us; he stared with assurance, enjoying the effect of his declaration. 'Yuss. I 'ave friends well off. That's more'n you got. But I am a man. Yer shipmates for all that. Who's comin' fur a drink?'

No one moved. There was a silence; a silence of blank faces and stony looks. He waited a moment, smiled bitterly, and went to the door. There he faced round once more. 'You won't? You bloomin' lot of yrpocrits. No? What 'ave I done to yer? Did I bully yer? Did I 'urt yer? Did I? . . . You won't drink? . . . No! . . . Then may ye die of thirst, every mother's son of yer! Not one of yer 'as the sperrit of a bug. Ye're the scum of the world. Work and starve!'

He went out, and slammed the door with such violence that the old Board of Trade bird nearly fell off his perch.

'He's mad,' declared Archie. 'No! No! He's drunk,' insisted Belfast, lurching about, and in a maudlin tone. Captain Allistoun sat smiling thoughtfully at the cleared pay-table.

Outside, on Tower Hill, they blinked, hesitated clumsily, as if blinded by the strange quality of the hazy light, as if discomposed by the view of so many men; and they who could hear one another in the howl of gales seemed deafened and distracted by the dull roar of the busy earth. 'To the Black Horse! To the Black Horse!' cried some. 'Let us have a drink together before we part.' They crossed the road, clinging to one another. Only Charley and Belfast wandered off alone. As I came up I saw a red-faced, blowsy woman, in a grey shawl, and with dusty, fluffy hair, fall on Charley's neck. It was his mother. She slobbered over him: 'O, my boy! My boy!' 'Leggo of me,' said Charley. 'Leggo, mother!' I was passing him at the time, and over the untidy head of the blubbering woman he gave me a humorous smile and a glance ironic, courageous, and profound, that seemed to put all my knowledge of life to shame. I nodded and passed on, but heard him say again, good-naturedly: 'If you leggo of me this minyt – ye shall 'ave a bob for a drink out of my pay.' In the next few steps I came upon Belfast. He caught my arm with tremulous enthusiasm. 'I couldn't go wi' 'em,' he stammered, indicating by a nod our noisy crowd, that drifted slowly along the other sidewalk. 'When I think of Jimmy . . . Poor Jim! When I think of him I have no heart for drink. You were his chum, too . . . but I pulled him out . . . didn't I? Short wool he had. . . . Yes. And I stole the blooming pie. . . . He wouldn't go. . . . He wouldn't go for nobody.' He burst into tears. 'I never touched him – never – never!' he sobbed. 'He went for me like . . . like . . . a lamb.'

I disengaged myself gently. Belfast's crying fits generally ended in a fight with someone, and I wasn't anxious to stand the brunt of his inconsolable sorrow. Moreover, two bulky policemen stood near by, looking at us with a disapproving and incorruptible gaze. 'So long!' I said, and went on my way.

But at the corner I stopped to take my last look at the crew of the *Narcissus*. They were swaying irresolute and noisy on the broad flagstones before the Mint. They were bound for the Black Horse, where men in fur caps, with brutal faces and in shirt sleeves, dispense out of varnished barrels the illusions of strength, mirth, happiness; the illusion of splendour and poetry of life, to the paid-off crews of southern-going ships. From afar I saw them discoursing, with jovial eyes and clumsy gestures, while the sea of life thundered into their ears ceaseless and unheeded. And swaying about there on the white stones, surrounded by the hurry and clamour of men, they appeared to be creatures of another kind – lost, alone, forgetful, and doomed; they were like castaways, like reckless and joyous castaways, like mad castaways making merry in the storm and upon an insecure ledge of a treacherous rock. The roar of the town resembled the roar of topping breakers, merciless and strong, with a loud voice and cruel purpose; but overhead the clouds broke; a flood of sunshine streamed down the walls of grimy houses. The dark knot of seamen drifted in sunshine. To the left of them the trees in Tower Gardens sighed. The stones of the Tower gleaming, seemed to stir in the play of light, as if remembering suddenly all the great joys and sorrows of the past, the fighting prototypes of these men; press-gangs; mutinous cries; the wailing of women by the riverside, and the shouts of men welcoming victories. The sunshine of heaven fell like a gift of grace on the mud of the earth, on the remembering and mute stones, on greed, selfishness; on the anxious faces of forgetful men. And to the right of the dark group the stained front of the Mint, cleansed by the flood of light, stood out for a moment dazzling and white like a marble palace in a fairy tale. The crew of the *Narcissus* drifted out of sight.

I never saw them again. The sea took some, the steamers took others, the graveyards of the earth will account for the rest. Singleton has no doubt taken with him the long record of his faithful work into the peaceful depths of a hospitable sea. And Donkin, who never did a decent day's work in his life, no doubt earns his living by discoursing with filthy eloquence upon the right of labour to live. So be it! Let the earth and the sea each have its own.

A gone shipmate, like any other man, is gone for ever; and I never met one of them again. But at times the spring-flood of memory sets with force up the dark River of the Nine Bends. Then on the waters of the forlorn stream drifts a ship – a shadowy ship manned by a crew of Shades. They pass and make a sign, in a shadowy hail. Haven't we, together and upon the immortal sea, wrung out a meaning from our sinful lives? Good-bye, brothers! You were a good crowd. As good a crowd as ever fisted with wild cries the beating canvas of a heavy foresail; or tossing aloft, invisible in the night, gave back yell for yell to a westerly gale.

TYPHOON

TO
R. B. Cunninghame Graham

CHAPTER 1

Captain MacWhirr, of the steamer *Nan-Shan*, had a physiognomy that, in the order of material appearances, was the exact counterpart of his mind: it presented no marked characteristics of firmness or stupidity; it had no pronounced characteristics whatever; it was simply ordinary, irresponsive, and unruffled.

The only thing his aspect might have been said to suggest, at times, was bashfulness; because he would sit, in business offices ashore, sunburnt and smiling faintly, with downcast eyes. When he raised them, they were perceived to be direct in their glance and of blue colour. His hair was fair and extremely fine, clasping from temple to temple the bald dome of his skull in a clamp as of fluffy silk. The hair of his face, on the contrary, carroty and flaming, resembled a growth of copper wire clipped short to the line of the lip; while, no matter how close he shaved, fiery metallic gleams passed, when he moved his head, over the surface of his cheeks. He was rather below the medium height, a bit round-shouldered, and so sturdy of limb that his clothes always looked a shade too tight for his arms and legs. As if unable to grasp what is due to the difference of latitudes, he wore a brown bowler hat, a complete suit of a brownish hue, and clumsy black boots. These harbour togs gave to his thick figure an air of stiff and uncouth smartness. A thin silver watch-chain looped his waistcoat, and he never left his ship for the shore without clutching in his powerful, hairy fist an elegant umbrella of the very best quality, but generally unrolled. Young Jukes, the chief mate, attending his commander to the gangway, would sometimes venture to say, with the greatest gentleness, 'Allow me, sir' – and possessing himself of the umbrella deferentially, would elevate the ferrule, shake the folds, twirl a neat furl in a jiffy, and hand it back; going through the performance with a face of such portentous gravity, that Mr Solomon Rout, the chief engineer, smoking his morning cigar over the skylight, would turn away his head in order to hide a smile. 'Oh! aye! The blessed gamp ... Thank 'ee, Jukes, thank 'ee,' would mutter Captain MacWhirr, heartily, without looking up.

Having just enough imagination to carry him through each successive day, and no more, he was tranquilly sure of himself; and from the very same cause he was not in the least conceited. It is your imaginative superior who is touchy, overbearing, and difficult to please; but every ship Captain MacWhirr commanded was the floating abode of harmony and peace. It was, in truth, as impossible for him to take a flight of fancy as it would be for a watchmaker to put together a chronometer with nothing except a two-pound hammer and a whip-saw in the way of tools. Yet the uninteresting lives of men so entirely given to the actuality of the bare existence have their mysterious side. It was impossible in Captain MacWhirr's case, for instance, to understand what under heaven could have induced that perfectly satisfactory son of a petty grocer in Belfast to run away to sea. And yet he had done that very thing at the age of fifteen. It was enough, when you thought it over, to give you the idea of an immense, potent, and invisible hand thrust into the ant-heap of the earth, laying hold of shoulders, knocking heads together, and setting the unconscious faces of the multitude towards inconceivable goals and in undreamt-of directions.

His father never really forgave him for this undutiful stupidity. 'We could have got on without him,' he used to say later on, 'but there's the business. And he an only son, too!' His mother wept very much after his disappearance. As it had never occurred to him to leave word behind, he was mourned over for dead till, after eight months, his first letter arrived from Talcahuano. It was short, and contained the statement: 'We had very fine weather on our passage out.' But evidently, in the writer's mind, the only important intelligence was to the effect that his captain had, on the very day of writing, entered him regularly on the ship's articles as Ordinary Seaman. 'Because I can do the work,' he explained. The mother again wept copiously, while the remark, 'Tom's an ass,' expressed the emotions of the father. He was a corpulent man, with a gift for sly chaffing, which to the end of his life he exercised in his intercourse with his son, a little pityingly, as if upon a half-witted person.

MacWhirr's visits to his home were necessarily rare, and in the course of years he dispatched other letters to his parents, informing them of his successive promotions and of his movements upon the vast earth. In these missives could be found sentences like this: 'The heat here is very great.' Or: 'On Christmas day at 4 p.m. we fell in with some icebergs.' The old people ultimately became acquainted with a good many names of ships, and with the names of the skippers who commanded them – with the names of Scots and English shipowners – with the names of seas, oceans, straits, promontories – with outlandish names of lumber-ports, of rice-ports, of cotton-ports – with the names of islands – with the name of their son's young woman. She was called Lucy. It did not suggest itself to him to mention whether he thought the name pretty. And then they died.

The great day of MacWhirr's marriage came in due course, following shortly upon the great day when he got his first command.

All these events had taken place many years before the morning when, in the chart-room of the steamer *Nan-Shan*, he stood confronted by the fall of a barometer he had no reason to distrust. The fall – taking into account the excellence of the instrument, the time of the year, and the ship's position on the terrestrial globe – was of a nature ominously prophetic; but the red face of the man betrayed no sort of inward disturbance. Omens were as nothing to him, and he was unable to discover the message of a prophecy till the fulfilment· had brought it home to his very door. 'That's a fall, and no mistake,' he thought. 'There must be some uncommonly dirty weather knocking about.'

The *Nan-Shan* was on her way from the southward to the treaty port of Fu-chau, with some cargo in her lower holds, and two hundred Chinese coolies returning to their village homes in the province of Fo-kien, after a few years of work in various tropical colonies. The morning was fine, the oily sea heaved without a sparkle, and there was a queer white misty patch in the sky like a halo of the sun. The fore-deck, packed with Chinamen, was full of sombre clothing, yellow faces, and pigtails, sprinkled over with a good many naked shoulders, for there was no wind, and the heat was close. The coolies lounged, talked, smoked, or stared over the rail; some, drawing water over the side, sluiced each other; a few slept on hatches, while several small parties of six sat on their heels surrounding iron trays with plates of rice and tiny teacups; and every single Celestial of them was carrying with him all he had in the world – a wooden chest with a ringing lock and brass on the corners, containing the savings of his labours: some clothes of ceremony, sticks of incense, a little opium maybe, bits of nameless rubbish of conventional value, and a small hoard of silver dollars, toiled for in coal-lighters, won in gambling-houses or in petty trading, grubbed out of the earth, sweated out in mines, on railway lines, in deadly jungle, under heavy burdens – amassed patiently, guarded with care, cherished fiercely.

A cross swell had set in from the direction of Formosa Channel about ten o'clock, without disturbing these passengers much, because the *Nan-Shan*, with her flat bottom, rolling chocks on bilges, and great breadth of beam, had the reputation of an exceptionally steady ship in a sea-way. Mr Jukes, in moments of expansion on shore, would proclaim loudly that the 'old girl was as good as she was pretty'. It would never have occurred to Captain MacWhirr to express his favourable opinion so loud or in terms so fanciful.

She was a good ship, undoubtedly, and not old either. She had been built in Dumbarton less than three years before, to the order of a firm of merchants in Siam – Messrs Sigg and Son. When she lay afloat, finished in every detail and ready to take up the work of her life, the builders contemplated her with pride.

'Sigg has asked us for a reliable skipper to take her out,' remarked one of the partners; and the other, after reflecting for a while, said: 'I think MacWhirr is ashore just at present.' 'Is he? Then wire him at once. He's the very man,' declared the senior, without a moment's hesitation.

Next morning MacWhirr stood before them unperturbed, having travelled from London by the midnight express after a sudden but undemonstrative parting with his wife. She was the daughter of a superior couple who had seen better days.

'We had better be going together over the ship, Captain,' said the senior partner; and the three men started to view the perfections of the *Nan-Shan* from stem to stern, and from her keelson to the trucks of her two stumpy pole-masts.

Captain MacWhirr had begun by taking off his coat, which he hung on the end of a steam windlass embodying all the latest improvements.

'My uncle wrote of you favourably by yesterday's mail to our good friends – Messrs Sigg, you know – and doubtless they'll continue you out there in command,' said the junior partner. 'You'll be able to boast of being in charge of the handiest boat of her size on the coast of China, Captain,' he added.

'Have you? Thank 'ee,' mumbled vaguely MacWhirr, to whom the view of a distant eventuality could appeal no more than the beauty of a wide landscape to a purblind tourist; and his eyes happening at the moment to be at rest upon the lock of the cabin door, he walked up to it, full of purpose, and began to rattle the handle vigorously, while he observed, in his low, earnest voice, 'You can't trust the workmen nowadays. A brand-new lock, and it won't act at all. Stuck fast. See? See?'

As soon as they found themselves alone in their office across the yard: 'You praised that fellow up to Sigg. What is it you see in him?' asked the nephew, with faint contempt.

'I admit he has nothing of your fancy skipper about him, if that's what you mean,' said the elder man, curtly. 'Is the foreman of the joiners on the *Nan-Shan* outside? . . . Come in, Bates. How is it that you let Tait's people put us off with a defective lock on the cabin door? The Captain could see directly he set eye on it. Have it replaced at once. The little straws, Bates . . . the little straws . . .'

The lock was replaced accordingly, and a few days afterwards the *Nan-Shan* steamed out to the East, without MacWhirr having offered any further remark as to her fittings, or having been heard to utter a single word hinting at pride in his ship, gratitude for his appointment, or satisfaction at his prospects.

With a temperament neither loquacious nor taciturn he found very little occasion to talk. There were matters of duty, of course – directions, orders, and so on; but the past being to his mind done with, and the future not there yet, the more general actualities of the day required no comment – because facts can speak for themselves with overwhelming precision.

Old Mr Sigg liked a man of few words, and one that 'you could be sure would not try to improve upon his instructions'. MacWhirr, satisfying these requirements, was continued in command of the *Nan-Shan*, and applied himself to the careful navigation of his ship in the China seas. She had come out on a British register, but after some time Messrs Sigg judged it expedient to transfer her to the Siamese flag.

At the news of the contemplated transfer Jukes grew restless, as if under a sense of personal affront. He went about grumbling to himself, and uttering short scornful laughs. 'Fancy having a ridiculous Noah's Ark elephant in the ensign of one's ship,' he said once at the engine-room door. 'Dash me if I can stand it: I'll throw up the billet. Don't it make *you* sick, Mr Rout?' The chief engineer only cleared his throat with the air of a man who knows the value of a good billet.

The first morning the new flag floated over the stern of the *Nan-Shan* Jukes stood looking at it bitterly from the bridge. He struggled with his feelings for a while, and then remarked, 'Queer flag for a man to sail under, sir.'

'What's the matter with the flag?' inquired Captain MacWhirr. 'Seems all right to me.' And he walked across to the end of the bridge to have a good look.

'Well, it looks queer to me,' burst out Jukes, greatly exasperated, and flung off the bridge.

Captain MacWhirr was amazed at these manners. After a while he stepped quietly into the chart-room, and opened his International Signal Code-book at the plate where the flags of all the nations are correctly figured in gaudy rows. He ran his finger over them, and when he came to Siam he contemplated with great attention the red field and the white elephant. Nothing could be more simple; but to make sure he brought the book out on the bridge for the purpose of comparing the coloured drawing with the real thing at the flag-staff astern. When next Jukes, who was carrying on the duty that day with a sort of suppressed fierceness, happened on the bridge, his commander observed:

'There's nothing amiss with that flag.'

'Isn't there?' mumbled Jukes, falling on his knees before a deck-locker and jerking therefrom viciously a spare lead-line.

'No. I looked up the book. Length twice the breadth and the elephant exactly in the middle. I thought the people ashore would know how to make the local flag. Stands to reason. You were wrong, Jukes ...'

'Well, sir,' began Jukes, getting up excitedly, ' all I can say – ' He fumbled for the end of the coil of line with trembling hands.

'That's all right.' Captain MacWhirr soothed him, sitting heavily on a little canvas folding-stool he greatly affected. 'All you have to do is to take care they don't hoist the elephant upside-down before they get quite used to it.'

Jukes flung the new lead-line over on the fore-deck with a loud 'Here you are, bos'n – don't forget to wet it thoroughly,' and turned with immense resolution towards his commander; but Captain MacWhirr spread his elbows on the bridge-rail comfortably.

'Because it would be, I suppose, understood as a signal of distress,' he went on. 'What do you think? That elephant there, I take it, stands for something in the nature of the Union Jack in the flag ...'

'Does it!' yelled Jukes, so that every head on the *Nan-Shan*'s decks looked towards the bridge. Then he sighed, and with sudden resignation: 'It would certainly be a damn distressful sight,' he said, meekly.

Later in the day he accosted the chief engineer with a confidential, 'Here, let me tell you the old man's latest.'

Mr Solomon Rout (frequently alluded to as Long Sol, Old Sol, or Father Rout), from finding himself almost invariably the tallest man on board every ship he joined, had acquired the habit of a stooping, leisurely condescension. His hair was scant and sandy, his flat cheeks were pale, his bony wrists and long scholarly hands were pale, too, as though he had lived all his life in the shade.

He smiled from on high at Jukes, and went on smoking and glancing about quietly, in the manner of a kind uncle lending an ear to the tale of an excited schoolboy. Then, greatly amused but impassive, he asked:

'And did you throw up the billet?'

'No,' cried Jukes, raising a weary, discouraged voice above the harsh buzz of the *Nan-Shan*'s friction winches. All of them were hard at work, snatching slings of cargo, high up, to the end of long derricks, only, as it seemed, to let them rip down recklessly by the run. The cargo chains groaned in the gins, clinked on coamings, rattled over the side; and the whole ship quivered, with her long grey flanks smoking in wreaths of steam. 'No,' cried Jukes, 'I didn't. What's the good? I might just as well fling my resignation at this bulkhead. I don't believe you can make a man like that understand anything. He simply knocks me over.'

At that moment Captain MacWhirr, back from the shore, crossed the deck, umbrella in hand, escorted by a mournful, self-possessed Chinaman, walking behind in paper-soled silk shoes, and who also carried an umbrella.

The master of the *Nan-Shan*, speaking just audibly and gazing at his boots as his manner was, remarked that it would be necessary to call at Fu-chau this trip, and desired Mr Rout to have steam up tomorrow afternoon at one o'clock sharp. He pushed back his hat to wipe his forehead, observing at the same time that he hated going ashore anyhow; while overtopping him Mr Rout, without deigning a word, smoked austerely, nursing his right elbow in the palm of his left hand. Then Jukes was directed in the same subdued voice to keep the forward 'tween-deck clear of cargo. Two hundred coolies were going to be put down there. The Bun Hin Company were sending that lot home. Twenty-five bags of rice would be coming off in a sampan directly, for stores. All seven-years'-men they were, said Captain MacWhirr, with a camphor-wood chest to every man. The carpenter should be set to work nailing three-inch battens along the deck below, fore and aft, to keep these boxes from shifting in a sea-way. Jukes had better look to it at once. 'D'ye hear, Jukes?' This Chinaman here was coming with the ship as far as Fu-chau – a sort of interpreter he would be. Bun Hin's clerk he was, and wanted to have a look at the space. Jukes had better take him forward. 'D'ye hear, Jukes?'

Jukes took care to punctuate these instructions in proper places with the obligatory 'Yes, sir', ejaculated without enthusiasm. His brusque 'Come along, John; make look see' set the Chinaman in motion at his heels.

'Wanchee look see, all same look see can do,' said Jukes, who having no talent for foreign languages mangled the very pidgin-English cruelly. He pointed at the open hatch. 'Catchee number one piecie place to sleep in. Eh?'

He was gruff, as became his racial superiority, but not unfriendly. The Chinaman, gazing sad and speechless into the darkness of the hatchway, seemed to stand at the head of a yawning grave.

'No catchee rain down there – savee?' pointed out Jukes. 'Suppose all'ee same fine weather, one piecie coolie-man come topside,' he pursued, warming up imaginatively. 'Make so – Phooooo!' He expanded his chest and blew out his cheeks. 'Savee, John? Breathe – fresh air. Good. Eh? Washee him piecie pants, chow-chow top-side – see, John?'

With his mouth and hands he made exuberant motions of eating rice and washing clothes; and the Chinaman, who concealed his distrust of this pantomime under a collected demeanour tinged by a gentle and refined melancholy, glanced out of his almond eyes from Jukes to the hatch and back again. 'Velly good,' he murmured, in a disconsolate undertone, and hastened smoothly along the decks, dodging obstacles in his course. He disappeared, ducking low under a sling of ten dirty gunny-bags full of some costly merchandise and exhaling a repulsive smell.

Captain MacWhirr meantime had gone on the bridge, and into the chart-room, where a letter, commenced two days before, awaited termination. These long letters began with the words, 'My darling wife,' and the steward, between the scrubbing of the floors and the dusting of chronometer-boxes, snatched at every opportunity to read them. They interested him much more than they possibly could the woman for whose eye they were intended; and this for the reason that they related in minute detail each successive trip of the *Nan-Shan*.

Her master, faithful to facts, which alone his consciousness reflected, would set them down with painstaking care upon many pages. The house in a northern suburb to which these pages were addressed had a bit of garden before the bow-windows, a deep porch of good appearance, coloured glass with imitation lead frame in the front door. He paid five-and-forty pounds a year for it, and did not think the rent too high, because Mrs MacWhirr (a pretentious person with a scraggy neck and a disdainful manner) was admittedly ladylike, and in the neighbourhood considered as 'quite superior'. The only secret of her life was her abject terror of the time when her husband would come home to stay for good. Under the same roof there dwelt also a daughter called Lydia and a son, Tom. These two were but slightly acquainted with their father. Mainly, they knew him as a rare but privileged visitor, who of an evening smoked his pipe in the dining-room and slept in the house. The lanky girl, upon the whole, was rather ashamed of him; the boy was frankly and utterly indifferent in a straightforward, delightful, unaffected way manly boys have.

And Captain MacWhirr wrote home from the coast of China twelve times every year, desiring quaintly to be 'remembered to the children', and subscribing himself 'your loving husband', as calmly as if the words so long used by so many men were, apart from their shape, worn-out things, and of a faded meaning.

The China seas north and south are narrow seas. They are seas full of everyday, eloquent facts, such as islands, sand-banks, reefs, swift and change-able currents – tangled facts that nevertheless speak to a seaman in clear and definite language. Their speech appealed to Captain MacWhirr's sense of realities so forcibly that he had given up his state-room below and practically lived all his days on the bridge of his ship, often having his meals sent up, and sleeping at night in the chart-room. And he indited there his home letters. Each of them, without exception, contained the phrase, 'The weather has been very fine this trip,' or some other form of a statement to that effect. And this statement, too, in its wonderful persistence, was of the same perfect accuracy as all the others they contained.

Mr Rout likewise wrote letters; only no one on board knew how chatty he could be pen in hand, because the chief engineer had enough imagination to keep his desk locked. His wife relished his style greatly. They were a childless couple, and Mrs Rout, a big, high-bosomed jolly woman of forty, shared with Mr Rout's toothless and venerable mother a little cottage near Teddington. She would run over her correspondence, at breakfast, with lively eyes, and scream out interesting passages in a joyous voice at the deaf old lady, prefacing each extract by the warning shout, 'Solomon says!' She

had the trick of firing off Solomon's utterances also upon strangers, astonishing them easily by the unfamiliar text and the unexpectedly jocular vein
of these quotations. On the day the new curate called for the first time at the
cottage, she found occasion to remark, 'As Solomon says: "the engineers that
go down to the sea in ships behold the wonders of sailor nature" '; when a
change in the visitor's countenance made her stop and stare.

'Solomon . . . Oh! . . . Mrs Rout,' stuttered the young man, very red in
the face, 'I must say . . . I don't . . .'

'He's my husband,' she announced in a great shout, throwing herself back
in the chair. Perceiving the joke, she laughed immoderately with a handkerchief to her eyes, while he sat wearing a forced smile, and, from his
inexperience of jolly women, fully persuaded that she must be deplorably
insane. They were excellent friends afterwards; for, absolving her from
irreverent intention, he came to think she was a very worthy person indeed;
and he learned in time to receive without flinching other scraps of Solomon's
wisdom.

'For my part,' Solomon was reported by his wife to have said once, 'give
me the dullest ass for a skipper before a rogue. There is a way to take a fool;
but a rogue is smart and slippery.' This was an airy generalization drawn
from the particular case of Captain MacWhirr's honesty, which, in itself,
had the heavy obviousness of a lump of clay. On the other hand, Mr Jukes,
unable to generalize, unmarried, and unengaged, was in the habit of opening
his heart after another fashion to an old chum and former shipmate, actually
serving as second officer on board an Atlantic liner.

First of all he would insist upon the advantages of the Eastern trade,
hinting at its superiority to the Western ocean service. He extolled the sky,
the seas, the ships, and the easy life of the Far East. The *Nan-Shan*, he
affirmed, was second to none as a sea-boat.

'We have no brass-bound uniforms, but then we are like brothers here,'
he wrote. 'We all mess together and live like fighting-cocks . . . All the chaps
of the black-squad are as decent as they make that kind, and old Sol, the
Chief, is a dry stick. We are good friends. As to our old man, you could not
find a quieter skipper. Sometimes you would think he hadn't sense enough
to see anything wrong. And yet it isn't that. Can't be. He has been in
command for a good few years now. He doesn't do anything actually foolish,
and gets his ship along all right without worrying anybody. I believe he
hasn't brains enough to enjoy kicking up a row. I don't take advantage of
him. I would scorn it. Outside the routine of duty he doesn't seem to
understand more than half of what you tell him. We get a laugh out of this
at times; but it is dull, too, to be with a man like this – in the long run. Old
Sol says he hasn't much conversation. Conversation! O Lord! He never talks.
The other day I had been yarning under the bridge with one of the engineers,
and he must have heard us. When I came up to take my watch, he steps out
of the chart-room and has a good look all round, peeps over at the sidelights,
glances at the compass, squints upwards at the stars. That's his regular
performance. By-and-by he says: "Was that you talking just now in the port
alleyway?" "Yes, sir." "With the third engineer?" "Yes, sir." He walks off
to starboard, and sits under the dodger on a little camp-stool of his, and for

half an hour perhaps he makes no sound, except that I heard him sneeze once. Then after a while I hear him getting up over there, and he strolls across to port, where I was. "I can't understand what you can find to talk about," says he. "Two solid hours. I am not blaming you. I see people ashore at it all day long, and then in the evening they sit down and keep at it over the drinks. Must be saying the same things over and over again. I can't understand."

'Did you ever hear anything like that? And he was so patient about it. It made me quite sorry for him. But he is exasperating, too, sometimes. Of course one would not do anything to vex him even if it were worth while. But it isn't. He's so jolly innocent that if you were to put your thumb to your nose and wave your fingers at him he would only wonder gravely to himself what got into you. He told me once quite simply that he found it very difficult to make out what made people always act so queerly. He's too dense to trouble about, and that's the truth.'

Thus wrote Mr Jukes to his chum in the Western ocean trade, out of the fulness of his heart and the liveliness of his fancy.

He had expressed his honest opinion. It was not worth while trying to impress a man of that sort. If the world had been full of such men, life would have probably appeared to Jukes an unentertaining and unprofitable business. He was not alone in his opinion. The sea itself, as if sharing Mr Jukes's good-natured forbearance, had never put itself out to startle the silent man, who seldom looked up, and wandered innocently over the waters with the only visible purpose of getting food, raiment, and house-room for three people ashore. Dirty weather he had known, of course. He had been made wet, uncomfortable, tired in the usual way, felt at the time and presently forgotten. So that upon the whole he had been justified in reporting fine weather at home. But he had never been given a glimpse of immeasurable strength and of immoderate wrath, the wrath that passes exhausted but never appeased – the wrath and fury of the passionate sea. He knew it existed, as we know that crime and abominations exist; he had heard of it as a peaceable citizen in a town hears of battles, famines, and floods, and yet knows nothing of what these things mean – though, indeed, he may have been mixed up in a street row, have gone without his dinner once, or been soaked to the skin in a shower. Captain MacWhirr had sailed over the surface of the oceans as some men go skimming over the years of existence to sink gently into a placid grave, ignorant of life to the last, without ever having been made to see all it may contain of perfidy, of violence, and of terror. There are on sea and land such men thus fortunate – or thus disdained by destiny or by the sea.

CHAPTER 2

Observing the steady fall of the barometer, Captain MacWhirr thought, 'There's some dirty weather knocking about.' This is precisely what he thought. He had had an experience of moderately dirty weather – the term dirty as applied to the weather implying only moderate discomfort to the seaman. Had he been informed by an indisputable authority that the end of the world was to be finally accomplished by a castastrophic disturbance of the atmosphere, he would have assimilated the information under the simple idea of dirty weather, and no other, because he had no experience of cataclysms, and belief does not necessarily imply comprehension. The wisdom of his country had pronounced by means of an Act of Parliament that before he could be considered as fit to take charge of a ship he should be able to answer certain simple questions on the subject of circular storms such as hurricanes, cyclones, typhoons; and apparently he had answered them, since he was now in command of the *Nan-Shan* in the China seas during the season of typhoons. But if he had answered he remembered nothing of it. He was, however, conscious of being made uncomfortable by the clammy heat. He came out on the bridge, and found no relief to this oppression. The air seemed thick. He gasped like a fish, and began to believe himself greatly out of sorts.

The *Nan-Shan* was ploughing a vanishing furrow upon the circle of the sea that had the surface and the shimmer of an undulating piece of grey silk. The sun, pale and without rays, poured down leaden heat in a strangely indecisive light, and the Chinamen were lying prostrate about the decks. Their bloodless, pinched, yellow faces were like the faces of bilious invalids. Captain MacWhirr noticed two of them especially, stretched out on their backs below the bridge. As soon as they had closed their eyes they seemed dead. Three others, however, were quarrelling barbarously away forward; and one big fellow, half naked, with herculean shoulders, was hanging limply over a winch; another, sitting on the deck, his knees up and his head drooping sideways in a girlish attitude, was plaiting his pigtail with infinite languor depicted in his whole person and in the very movement of his fingers. The smoke struggled with difficulty out of the funnel, and instead of streaming away spread itself out like an infernal sort of cloud, smelling of sulphur and raining soot all over the decks.

'What the devil are you doing there, Mr Jukes?' asked Captain MacWhirr.

This unusual form of address, though mumbled rather than spoken, caused the body of Mr Jukes to start as though it had been prodded under the fifth rib. He had had a low bench brought on the bridge, and sitting on it, with a length of rope curled about his feet and a piece of canvas stretched over his knees, was pushing a sail-needle vigorously. He looked up, and his surprise gave to his eyes an expression of innocence and candour.

'I am only roping some of that new set of bags we made last trip for whipping up coals,' he remonstrated, gently. 'We shall want them for the next coaling, sir.'

'What became of the others?'

'Why, worn out of course, sir.'

Captain MacWhirr, after glaring down irresolutely at his chief mate, disclosed the gloomy and cynical conviction that more than half of them had been lost overboard, 'if only the truth was known', and retired to the other end of the bridge. Jukes, exasperated by this unprovoked attack, broke the needle at the second stitch, and dropping his work got up and cursed the heat in a violent undertone.

The propeller thumped, the three Chinamen forward had given up squabbling very suddenly, and the one who had been plaiting his tail clasped his legs and stared dejectedly over his knees. The lurid sunshine cast faint and sickly shadows. The swell ran higher and swifter every moment, and the ship lurched heavily in the smooth, deep hollows of the sea.

'I wonder where that beastly swell comes from,' said Jukes aloud, recovering himself after a stagger.

'North-east,' grunted the literal MacWhirr, from his side of the bridge. 'There's some dirty weather knocking about. Go and look at the glass.'

When Jukes came out of the chart-room, the cast of his countenance had changed to thoughtfulness and concern. He caught hold of the bridge-rail and stared ahead.

The temperature in the engine-room had gone up to a hundred and seventeen degrees. Irritated voices were ascending through the skylight and through the fiddle of the stokehold in a harsh and resonant uproar, mingled with angry clangs and scrapes of metal, as if men with limbs of iron and throats of bronze had been quarrelling down there. The second engineer was falling foul of the stokers for letting the steam go down. He was a man with arms like a blacksmith, and generally feared; but that afternoon the stokers were answering him back recklessly, and slammed the furnace doors with the fury of despair. Then the noise ceased suddenly, and the second engineer appeared, emerging out of the stokehold streaked with grime and soaking wet like a chimney-sweep coming out of a well. As soon as his head was clear of the fiddle he began to scold Jukes for not trimming properly the stokehold ventilators; and in answer Jukes made with his hands deprecatory soothing signs meaning: No wind – can't be helped – you can see for yourself. But the other wouldn't hear reason. His teeth flashed angrily in his dirty face. He didn't mind, he said, the trouble of punching their blanked heads down there, blank his soul, but did the condemned sailors think you could keep steam up in the God-forsaken boilers simply by knocking the blanked stokers about? No, by George! You had to get some draught, too – may he be everlastingly blanked for a swab-headed deck-hand if you didn't! And the chief, too, rampaging before the steam-gauge and carrying on like a lunatic up and down the engine-room ever since noon. What did

Jukes think he was stuck up there for, if he couldn't get one of his decayed, good-for-nothing deck-cripples to turn the ventilators to the wind?

The relations of the 'engine-room' and the 'deck' of the *Nan-Shan* were, as is known, of a brotherly nature; therefore Jukes leaned over and begged the other in a restrained tone not to make a disgusting ass of himself; the skipper was on the other side of the bridge. But the second declared mutinously that he didn't care a rap who was on the other side of the bridge, and Jukes, passing in a flash from lofty disapproval into a state of exaltation, invited him in unflattering terms to come up and twist the beastly things to please himself, and catch such wind as a donkey of his sort could find. The second rushed up to the fray. He flung himself at the port ventilator as though he meant to tear it out bodily and toss it overboard. All he did was to move the cowl round a few inches, with an enormous expenditure of force, and seemed spent in the effort. He leaned against the back of the wheelhouse, and Jukes walked up to him.

'Oh, Heavens!' ejaculated the engineer in a feeble voice. He lifted his eyes to the sky, and then let his glassy stare descend to meet the horizon that, tilting up to an angle of forty degrees, seemed to hang on a slant for a while and settled down slowly. 'Heavens! Phew! What's up, anyhow?'

Jukes, straddling his long legs like a pair of compasses, put on an air of superiority. 'We're going to catch it this time,' he said. 'The barometer is tumbling down like anything, Harry. And you trying to kick up that silly row . . .'

The word 'barometer' seemed to revive the second engineer's mad animosity. Collecting afresh all his energies, he directed Jukes in a low and brutal tone to shove the unmentionable instrument down his gory throat. Who cared for his crimson barometer? It was the steam – the steam – that was going down; and what between the firemen going faint and the chief going silly, it was worse than a dog's life for him; he didn't care a tinker's curse how soon the whole show was blown out of the water. He seemed on the point of having a cry, but after regaining his breath he muttered darkly, 'I'll faint them,' and dashed off. He stopped upon the fiddle long enough to shake his fist at the unnatural daylight, and dropped into the dark hole with a whoop.

When Jukes turned, his eyes fell upon the rounded back and the big red ears of Captain MacWhirr, who had come across. He did not look at his chief officer, but said at once, 'That's a very violent man, that second engineer.'

'Jolly good second, anyhow,' grunted Jukes. 'They can't keep up steam,' he added, rapidly, and made a grab at the rail against the coming lurch.

Captain MacWhirr, unprepared, took a run and brought himself up with a jerk by an awning stanchion.

'A profane man,' he said, obstinately. 'If this goes on, I'll have to get rid of him the first chance.'

'It's the heat,' said Jukes. 'The weather's awful. It would make a saint swear. Even up here I feel exactly as if I had my head tied up in a woollen blanket.'

Captain MacWhirr looked up. 'D'ye mean to say, Mr Jukes, you ever had your head tied up in a blanket? What was that for?'

'It's a manner of speaking, sir,' said Jukes, stolidly.

'Some of you fellows do go on! What's that about saints swearing? I wish you wouldn't talk so wild. What sort of saint would that be that would swear? No more saint than yourself, I expect. And what's a blanket got to do with it – or the weather either . . . The heat does not make me swear – does it? It's filthy bad temper. That's what it is. And what's the good of your talking like this?'

Thus Captain MacWhirr expostulated against the use of images in speech, and at the end electrified Jukes by a contemptuous snort, followed by words of passion and resentment: 'Damme! I'll fire him out of the ship if he don't look out.'

And Jukes, incorrigible, thought: 'Goodness me! Somebody's put a new inside to my old man. Here's temper, if you like. Of course it's the weather; what else? It would make an angel quarrelsome – let alone a saint.'

All the Chinamen on deck appeared at their last gasp.

At its setting the sun had a diminished diameter and an expiring brown, rayless glow, as if millions of centuries elapsing since the morning had brought it near its end. A dense bank of cloud became visible to the northward; it had a sinister dark olive tint, and lay low and motionless upon the sea, resembling a solid obstacle in the path of the ship. She went floundering towards it like an exhausted creature driven to its death. The coppery twilight retired slowly, and the darkness brought out overhead a swarm of unsteady, big stars, that, as if blown upon, flickered exceedingly and seemed to hang very near the earth. At eight o'clock Jukes went into the chart-room to write up the ship's log.

He copied neatly out of the rough-book the number of miles, the course of the ship, and in the column for 'wind' scrawled the word 'calm' from top to bottom of the eight hours since noon. He was exasperated by the continuous, monotonous rolling of the ship. The heavy inkstand would slide away in a manner that suggested perverse intelligence in dodging the pen. Having written in the large space under the head of 'Remarks' 'Heat very oppressive', he stuck the end of the pen-holder in his teeth, pipe fashion, and mopped his face carefully.

'Ship rolling heavily in a high cross-swell,' he began again, and commented to himself, 'Heavily is no word for it.' Then he wrote: 'Sunset threatening with a low bank of clouds to N. and E. Sky clear overhead.'

Sprawling over the table with arrested pen, he glanced out of the door, and in that frame of his vision he saw all the stars flying upwards between the teak-wood jambs on a black sky. The whole lot took flight together and disappeared, leaving only a blackness flecked with white flashes, for the sea was as black as the sky and speckled with foam afar. The stars that had flown to the roll came back on the return swing of the ship, rushing downwards in their glittering multitude, not of fiery points, but enlarged to tiny discs brilliant with a clear wet sheen.

Jukes watched the flying big stars for a moment, and then wrote: '8 p.m. Swell increasing. Ship labouring and taking water on her decks. Battened down the coolies for the night. Barometer still falling.' He paused, and thought to himself, 'Perhaps nothing whatever'll come of it.' And then he closed resolutely his entries: 'Every appearance of a typhoon coming on.'

On going out he had to stand aside, and Captain MacWhirr strode over the doorstep without saying a word or making a sign.

'Shut the door, Mr Jukes, will you?' he cried from within.

Jukes turned back to do so, muttering ironically: 'Afraid to catch cold, I suppose.' It was his watch below, but he yearned for communion with his kind; and he remarked cheerily to the second mate: 'Doesn't look so bad, after all – does it?'

The second mate was marching to and fro on the bridge, tripping down with small steps one moment, and the next climbing with difficulty the shifting slope of the deck. At the sound of Jukes's voice he stood still, facing forward, but made no reply.

'Hallo! That's a heavy one,' said Jukes, swaying to meet the long roll till his lowered hand touched the planks. This time the second mate made in his throat a noise of an unfriendly nature.

He was an oldish, shabby little fellow, with bad teeth and no hair on his face. He had been shipped in a hurry in Shanghai, that trip when the second officer brought from home had delayed the ship three hours in port by contriving (in some manner Captain MacWhirr could never understand) to fall overboard into an empty coal-lighter lying alongside, and had to be sent ashore to the hospital with concussion of the brain and a broken limb or two.

Jukes was not discouraged by the unsympathetic sound, 'The Chinamen must be having a lovely time of it down there,' he said. 'It's lucky for them the old girl has the easiest roll of any ship I've ever been in. There now! This one wasn't so bad.'

'You wait,' snarled the second mate.

With his sharp nose, red at the tip, and his thin pinched lips, he always looked as though he were raging inwardly; and he was concise in his speech to the point of rudeness. All his time off duty he spent in his cabin with the door shut, keeping so still in there that he was supposed to fall asleep as soon as he had disappeared; but the man who came in to wake him for his watch on deck would invariably find him with his eyes wide open, flat on his back in the bunk, and glaring irritably from a soiled pillow. He never wrote any letters, did not seem to hope for news from anywhere; and though he had been heard once to mention West Hartlepool, it was with extreme bitterness, and only in connexion with the extortionate charges of a boarding-house. He was one of those men who are picked up at need in the ports of the world. They are competent enough, appear hopelessly hard up, show no evidence of any sort of vice, and carry about them all the signs of manifest failure. They come aboard on an emergency, care for no ship afloat, live in their own atmosphere of casual connexion amongst their shipmates who know nothing of them, and make up their minds to leave at inconvenient times. They clear out with no words of leave-taking in some God-forsaken port other men would fear to be stranded in, and go ashore in company of a shabby sea-chest, corded like a treasure-box, and with an air of shaking the ship's dust off their feet.

'You wait,' he repeated, balanced in great swings with his back to Jukes, motionless and implacable.

'Do you mean to say we are going to catch it hot?' asked Jukes with boyish interest.

'Say? ... I say nothing. You don't catch me,' snapped the little second mate, with a mixture of pride, scorn, and cunning, as if Jukes's question had been a trap cleverly detected. 'Oh, no! None of you here shall make a fool of me if I know it,' he mumbled to himself.

Jukes reflected rapidly that this second mate was a mean little beast, and in his heart he wished poor Jack Allen had never smashed himself up in the coal-lighter. The far-off blackness ahead of the ship was like another night seen through the starry night of the earth – the starless night of the immensities beyond the created universe, revealed in its appalling stillness through a low fissure in the glittering sphere of which the earth is the kernel.

'Whatever there might be about,' said Jukes, 'we are steaming straight into it.'

'*You've* said it,' caught up the second mate, always with his back to Jukes. 'You've said it, mind – not I.'

'Oh, go to Jericho!' said Jukes, frankly; and the other emitted a triumphant little chuckle.

'You've said it,' he repeated.

'And what of that?'

'I've known some real good men get into trouble with their skippers for saying a damn sight less,' answered the second mate feverishly. 'Oh, no! You don't catch me.'

'You seem deucedly anxious not to give yourself away,' said Jukes, completely soured by such absurdity. 'I wouldn't be afraid to say what I think.'

'Aye, to me. That's no great trick. I am nobody, and well I know it.'

The ship, after a pause of comparative steadiness, started upon a series of rolls, one worse than the other, and for a time Jukes, preserving his equilibrium, was too busy to open his mouth. As soon as the violent swinging had quieted down somewhat, he said: 'This is a bit too much of a good thing. Whether anything is coming or not I think she ought to be put head on to that swell. The old man is just gone in to lie down. Hang me if I don't speak to him.'

But when he opened the door of the chart-room he saw his captain reading a book. Captain MacWhirr was not lying down; he was standing up with one hand grasping the edge of the bookshelf and the other holding open before his face a thick volume. The lamp wriggled in the gimbals, the loosened books toppled from side to side on the shelf, the long barometer swung in jerky circles, the table altered its slant every moment. In the midst of all this stir and movement Captain MacWhirr, holding on, showed his eyes above the upper edge, and asked, 'What's the matter?'

'Swell getting worse, sir.'

'Noticed that in here,' muttered Captain MacWhirr. 'Anything wrong?'

Jukes, inwardly disconcerted by the seriousness of the eyes looking at him over the top of the book, produced an embarrassed grin.

'Rolling like old boots,' he said, sheepishly.

'Aye! Very heavy – very heavy. What do you want?'

At this Jukes lost his footing and began to flounder.

'I was thinking of our passengers,' he said, in the manner of a man clutching at a straw.

'Passengers?' wondered the Captain, gravely. 'What passengers?'

'Why, the Chinamen, sir,' explained Jukes, very sick of this conversation.

'The Chinamen! Why don't you speak plainly? Couldn't tell what you meant. Never heard a lot of coolies spoken of as passengers before. Passengers, indeed! What's come to you?'

Captain MacWhirr, closing the book on his forefinger, lowered his arm and looked completely mystified. 'Why are you thinking of the Chinamen, Mr Jukes?' he inquired.

Jukes took a plunge, like a man driven to it. 'She's rolling her decks full of water, sir. Thought you might put her head on perhaps – for a while. Till this goes down a bit – very soon, I dare say. Head to the eastward. I never knew a ship roll like this.'

He held on in the doorway, and Captain MacWhirr, feeling his grip on the shelf inadequate, made up his mind to let go in a hurry, and fell heavily on the couch.

'Head to the eastward?' he said, struggling to sit up. 'That's more than four points off her course.'

'Yes, sir. Fifty degrees . . . Would just bring her head far enough round to meet this . . .'

Captain MacWhirr was now sitting up. He had not dropped the book, and he had not lost his place.

'To the eastward?' he repeated, with dawning astonishment. 'To the . . . Where do you think we are bound to? You want me to haul a full-powered steamship four points off her course to make the Chinamen comfortable! Now, I've heard more than enough of mad things done in the world – but this . . . If I didn't know you Jukes, I would think you were in liquor. Steer four points off . . . And what afterwards? Steer four points over the other way, I suppose, to make the course good. What put it into your head that I would start to tack a steamer as if she were a sailing-ship?'

'Jolly good thing she isn't,' threw in Jukes, with bitter readiness. 'She would have rolled every blessed stick out of her this afternoon.'

'Aye! And you just would have had to stand and see them go,' said Captain MacWhirr, showing a certain animation. 'It's a dead calm, isn't it?'

'It is, sir. But there's something out of the common coming, for sure.'

'Maybe. I suppose you have a notion I should be getting out of the way of that dirt,' said Captain MacWhirr, speaking with the utmost simplicity of manner and tone, and fixing the oilcloth on the floor with a heavy stare. Thus he noticed neither Jukes's discomfiture nor the mixture of vexation and astonished respect on his face.

'Now, here's this book,' he continued with deliberation, slapping his thigh with the closed volume. 'I've been reading the chapter on the storms there.'

This was true. He had been reading the chapter on the storms. When he had entered the chart-room, it was with no intention of taking the book down. Some influence in the air – the same influence, probably, that caused the steward to bring without orders the Captain's sea-boots and oilskin coat up to the chart-room – had as it were guided his hand to the shelf; and without taking the time to sit down he had waded with a conscious effort into the terminology of the subject. He lost himself amongst advancing semicircles, left- and right-hand quadrants, the curves of the tracks, the probable bearing of the centre, the shifts of wind, and the readings of barometer. He tried to bring all these things into a definite relation to himself, and ended by becoming contemptuously angry with such a lot of words and with so much advice, all head-work and supposition, without a glimmer of certitude.

'It's the damnedest thing, Jukes,' he said. 'If a fellow was to believe all that's in there, he would be running most of his time all over the sea trying to get behind the weather.'

Again he slapped his leg with the book; and Jukes opened his mouth, but said nothing.

'Running to get behind the weather! Do you understand that, Mr Jukes? It's the maddest thing!' ejaculated Captain MacWhirr, with pauses, gazing at the floor profoundly. 'You would think an old woman had been writing this. It passes me. If that thing means anything useful, then it means that I should at once alter the course away, away to the devil somewhere, and come booming down on Fu-chau from the northward at the tail of this dirty weather that's supposed to be knocking about in our way. From the north! Do you understand, Mr Jukes? Three hundred extra miles to the distance, and a pretty coal bill to show. I couldn't bring myself to do that if every word in there was gospel truth, Mr Jukes. Don't you expect me . . .'

And Jukes, silent, marvelled at this display of feeling and loquacity.

'But the truth is that you don't know if the fellow is right, anyhow. How can you tell what a gale is made of till you get it? He isn't aboard here, is he? Very well. Here he says that the centre of them things bears eight points off the wind; but we haven't got any wind, for all the barometer falling. Where's his centre now?'

'We will get the wind presently,' mumbled Jukes.

'Let it come, then,' said Captain MacWhirr, with dignified indignation. 'It's only to let you see, Mr Jukes, that you don't find everything in books. All these rules for dodging breezes and circumventing the winds of heaven, Mr Jukes, seem to me the maddest thing, when you come to look at it sensibly.'

He raised his eyes, saw Jukes gazing at him dubiously, and tried to illustrate his meaning.

'About as queer as your extraordinary notion of dodging the ship head to sea, for I don't know how long, to make the Chinamen comfortable; whereas all we've got to do is to take them to Fu-chau, being timed to get there before noon on Friday. If the weather delays me – very well. There's your log-book to talk straight about the weather. But suppose I went swinging off my course and came in two days late and they asked me: "Where have

you been all that time, Captain?" What could I say to that? "Went around
to dodge the bad weather," I would say. "It must've been damn bad," they
would say. "Don't know," I would have to say; "I've dodged clear of it." See
that, Jukes? I have been thinking it all out this afternoon.'

He looked up again in his unseeing, unimaginative way. No one had ever
heard him say so much at one time. Jukes, with his arms open in the
doorway, was like a man invited to behold a miracle. Unbounded wonder
was the intellectual meaning of his eye, while incredulity was seated in his
whole countenance.

'A gale is a gale, Mr Jukes,' resumed the Captain, 'and a full-powered
steamship has got to face it. There's just so much dirty weather knocking
about the world and the proper thing is to go through it with none of what
old Captain Wilson of the *Melita* calls "storm strategy". The other day
ashore I heard him hold forth about it to a lot of shipmasters who came in
and sat at a table next to mine. It seemed to me the greatest nonsense. He
was telling them how he out-manoeuvred, I think he said, a terrific gale so
that it never came nearer than fifty miles to him. A neat piece of head-work
he called it. How he knew there was a terrific gale fifty miles off beats me
altogether. It was like listening to a crazy man. I would have thought
Captain Wilson was old enough to know better.'

Captain MacWhirr ceased for a moment, then said, 'It's your watch
below, Mr Jukes?'

Jukes came to himself with a start. 'Yes, sir.'

'Leave orders to call me at the slightest change,' said the Captain. He
reached up to put the book away, and tucked his legs upon the couch. 'Shut
the door so that it don't fly open, will you? I can't stand a door banging.
They've put a lot of rubbishy locks into this ship, I must say.'

Captain MacWhirr closed his eyes.

He did so to rest himself. He was tired, and he experienced that state of
mental vacuity which comes at the end of an exhaustive discussion that had
liberated some belief matured in the course of meditative years. He had
indeed been making his confession of faith, had he only known it; and its
effect was to make Jukes, on the other side of the door, stand scratching his
head for a good while.

Captain MacWhirr opened his eyes.

He thought he must have been asleep. What was that loud noise? Wind?
Why had he not been called? The lamp wriggled in its gimbals, the barometer
swung in circles, the table altered its slant every moment; a pair of limp sea-
boots with collapsed tops went sliding past the couch. He put out his hand
instantly, and captured one.

Jukes's face appeared in a crack of the door: only his face, very red, with
staring eyes. The flame of the lamp leaped, a piece of paper flew up, a rush
of air enveloped Captain MacWhirr. Beginning to draw on the boot, he
directed an expectant gaze at Jukes's swollen, excited features.

'Came on like this,' shouted Jukes, 'five minutes ago . . . all of a sudden.'

The head disappeared with a bang, and a heavy splash and patter of drops
swept past the closed door as if a pailful of melted lead had been flung
against the house. A whistling could be heard now upon the deep vibrating

noise outside. The stuffy chart-room seemed as full of draughts as a shed. Captain MacWhirr collared the other sea-boot on its violent passage along the floor. He was not flustered, but he could not find at once the opening for inserting his foot. The shoes he had flung off were scurrying from end to end of the cabin, gambolling playfully over each other like puppies. As soon as he stood up he kicked at them viciously, but without effect.

He threw himself into the attitude of a lunging fencer, to reach after his oilskin coat; and afterwards he staggered all over the confined space while he jerked himself into it. Very grave, straddling his legs far apart, and stretching his neck, he started to tie deliberately the strings of his sou'wester under his chin, with thick fingers that trembled slightly. He went through all the movements of a woman putting on her bonnet before a glass, with a strained, listening attention, as though he had expected every moment to hear the shout of his name in the confused clamour that had suddenly beset his ship. Its increase filled his ears while he was getting ready to go out and confront whatever it might mean. It was tumultuous and very loud – made up of the rush of the wind, the crashes of the sea, with that prolonged deep vibration of the air, like the roll of an immense and remote drum beating the charge of the gale.

He stood for a moment in the light of the lamp, thick, clumsy, shapeless in his panoply of combat, vigilant and red-faced.

'There's a lot of weight in this,' he muttered.

As soon as he attempted to open the door the wind caught it. Clinging to the handle, he was dragged out over the doorstep, and at once found himself engaged with the wind in a sort of personal scuffle whose object was the shutting of that door. At the last moment a tongue of air scurried in and licked out the flame of the lamp.

Ahead of the ship he perceived a great darkness lying upon a multitude of white flashes; on the starboard beam a few amazing stars drooped, dim and fitful, above an immense waste of broken seas, as if seen through a mad drift of smoke.

On the bridge a knot of men, indistinct and toiling, were making great efforts in the light of the wheelhouse windows that shone mistily on their heads and backs. Suddenly darkness closed upon one pane, then on another. The voices of the lost group reached him after the manner of men's voices in a gale, in shreds and fragments of forlorn shouting snatched past the ear. All at once Jukes appeared at his side, yelling, with his head down.

'Watch – put in – wheelhouse shutters – glass – afraid – blow in.'

Jukes heard his commander upbraiding.

'This – come – anything – warning – call me.'

He tried to explain, with the uproar pressing on his lips.

'Light air – remained – bridge – sudden – north-east – could turn – thought – you – sure – hear.'

They had gained the shelter of the weather-cloth, and could converse with raised voices, as people quarrel.

'I got the hands along to cover up all the ventilators. Good job I had remained on deck. I didn't think you would be asleep, and so ... What did you say, sir? What?'

'Nothing,' cried Captain MacWhirr. 'I said – all right.'

'By all the powers! We've got it this time,' observed Jukes in a howl.

'You haven't altered her course?' inquired Captain MacWhirr, straining his voice.

'No, sir. Certainly not. Wind came out right ahead. And here comes the head sea.'

A plunge of the ship ended in a shock as if she had landed her forefoot upon something solid. After a moment of stillness a lofty flight of sprays drove hard with the wind upon their faces.

'Keep her at it as long as we can,' shouted Captain MacWhirr.

Before Jukes had squeezed the salt water out of his eyes all the stars had disappeared.

CHAPTER 3

Jukes was as ready a man as any half-dozen young mates that may be caught by casting a net upon the waters; and though he had been somewhat taken aback by the startling viciousness of the first squall, he had pulled himself together on the instant, had called out the hands, and had rushed them along to secure such openings about the deck as had not been already battened down earlier in the evening. Shouting in his fresh, stentorian voice, 'Jump, boys, and bear a hand!' he led in the work, telling himself the while that he had 'just expected this'.

But at the same time he was growing aware that this was rather more than he had expected. From the first stir of the air felt on his cheek the gale seemed to take upon itself the accumulated impetus of an avalanche. Heavy sprays enveloped the *Nan-Shan* from stem to stern, and instantly in the midst of her regular rolling she began to jerk and plunge as though she had gone mad with fright.

Jukes thought, 'This is no joke.' While he was exchanging explanatory yells with his captain, a sudden lowering of the darkness came upon the night, falling before their vision like something palpable. It was as if the masked lights of the world had been turned down. Jukes was uncritically glad to have his captain at hand. It relieved him as though that man had, by simply coming on deck, taken most of the gale's weight upon his shoulders. Such is the prestige, the privilege, and the burden of command.

Captain MacWhirr could expect no relief of that sort from anyone on earth. Such is the loneliness of command. He was trying to see, with that watchful manner of a seaman who stares into the wind's eye as if into the eye of an adversary, to penetrate the hidden intention and guess the aim and force of the thrust. The strong wind swept at him out of a vast obscurity; he felt under his feet the uneasiness of his ship, and he could not even discern the shadow of her shape. He wished it were not so; and very still he waited, feeling stricken by a blind man's helplessness.

To be silent was natural to him, dark or shine. Jukes, at his elbow, made himself heard yelling cheerily in the gusts, 'We must have got the worst of it at once, sir.' A faint burst of lightning quivered all round, as if flashed into a cavern – into a black and secret chamber of the sea, with a floor of foaming crests.

It unveiled for a sinister, fluttering moment a ragged mass of clouds hanging low, the lurch of the long outlines of the ship, the black figures of men caught on the bridge, heads forward, as if petrified in the act of butting. The darkness palpitated down upon all this, and then the real thing came at last.

It was something formidable and swift, like the sudden smashing of a vial of wrath. It seemed to explode all round the ship with an overpowering concussion and a rush of great waters, as if an immense dam had been blown up to windward. In an instant the men lost touch of each other. This is the disintegrating power of a great wind: it isolates one from one's kind. An earthquake, a landslip, an avalanche, overtake a man incidentally, as it were – without passion. A furious gale attacks him like a personal enemy, tries to grasp his limbs, fastens upon his mind, seeks to rout his very spirit out of him.

Jukes was driven away from his commander. He fancied himself whirled a great distance through the air. Everything disappeared – even, for a moment, his power of thinking; but his hand had found one of the rail-stanchions. His distress was by no means alleviated by an inclination to disbelieve the reality of this experience. Though young, he had seen some bad weather, and had never doubted his ability to imagine the worst; but this was so much beyond his powers of fancy that it appeared incompatible with the existence of any ship whatever. He would have been incredulous about himself in the same way, perhaps, had he not been so harassed by the necessity of exerting a wrestling effort against a force trying to tear him away from his hold. Moreover, the conviction of not being utterly destroyed returned to him through the sensations of being half-drowned, bestially shaken, and partly choked.

It seemed to him he remained there precariously alone with the stanchion for a long, long time. The rain poured on him, flowed, drove in sheets. He breathed in gasps; and sometimes the water he swallowed was fresh and sometimes it was salt. For the most part he kept his eyes shut tight, as if suspecting his sight might be destroyed in the immense flurry of the elements. When he ventured to blink hastily, he derived some moral support from the green gleam on the starboard light shining feebly upon the flight of rain and sprays. He was actually looking at it when its ray fell upon the uprearing sea which put it out. He saw the head of the wave topple over, adding the mite of its crash to the tremendous uproar raging around him, and almost at the same instant the stanchion was wrenched away from his embracing arms. After a crushing thump on his back he found himself suddenly afloat and borne upwards. His first irresistible notion was that the whole China Sea had climbed on the bridge. Then, more sanely, he concluded himself gone overboard. All the time he was being tossed, flung, and rolled in great volumes of water, he kept on repeating mentally, with the utmost precipitation, the words: 'My God! My God! My God! My God!'

All at once, in a revolt of misery and despair, he formed the crazy resolution to get out of that. And he began to thresh about with his arms and legs. But as soon as he commenced his wretched struggles he discovered that he had become somehow mixed up with a face, an oilskin coat, somebody's boots. He clawed ferociously, all these things in turn, lost them, found them again, lost them once more, and finally was himself caught in the firm clasp of a pair of stout arms. He returned the embrace closely round a thick solid body. He had found his captain.

They tumbled over and over, tightening their hug. Suddenly the water let them down with a brutal bang; and, stranded against the side of the wheelhouse, out of breath and bruised, they were left to stagger up in the wind and hold on where they could.

Jukes came out of it rather horrified, as though he had escaped some unparalleled outrage directed at his feelings. It weakened his faith in himself. He started shouting aimlessly to the man he could feel near him in that fiendish blackness, 'Is it you, sir? Is it you, sir?' till his temples seemed ready to burst. And he heard in answer a voice, as if crying far away, as if screaming to him fretfully from a very great distance, the one word 'Yes!' Other seas swept again over the bridge. He received them defencelessly right over his bare head, with both his hands engaged in holding.

The motion of the ship was extravagant. Her lurches had an appalling helplessness; she pitched as if taking a header into a void, and seemed to find a wall to hit every time. When she rolled she fell on her side headlong, and she would be righted back by such a demolishing blow that Jukes felt her reeling as a clubbed man reels before he collapses. The gale howled and scuffled about gigantically in the darkness, as though the entire world were one black gully. At certain moments the air streamed against the ship as if sucked through a tunnel with a concentrated solid force of impact that seemed to lift her clean out of the water and keep her up for an instant with only a quiver running through her from end to end. And then she would begin her tumbling again as if dropped back into a boiling cauldron. Jukes tried hard to compose his mind and judge things coolly.

The sea, flattened down in the heavier gusts, would uprise and overwhelm both ends of the *Nan-Shan* in snowy rushes of foam, expanding wide, beyond both rails, into the night. And on this dazzling sheet, spread under the blackness of the clouds and emitting a bluish glow, Captain MacWhirr could catch a desolate glimpse of a few tiny specks black as ebony, the tops of the hatches, the battened companions, the heads of the covered winches, the foot of a mast. This was all he could see of his ship. Her middle structure, covered by the bridge which bore him, his mate, the closed wheelhouse where a man was steering shut up with the fear of being swept overboard together with the whole thing in one great crash – her middle structure was like a half-tide rock awash upon a coast. It was like an outlying rock with the water boiling up, streaming over, pouring off, beating round – like a rock in the surf to which shipwrecked people cling before they let go – only it rose, it sank, it rolled continuously, without respite and rest, like a rock that should have miraculously struck adrift from a coast and gone wallowing upon the sea.

The *Nan-Shan* was being looted by the storm with a senseless, destructive fury: trysails torn out of the extra gaskets, double-lashed awnings blown away, bridge swept clean, weather-cloths burst, rails twisted, light-screens smashed – and two of the boats had gone already. They had gone unheard and unseen, melting, as it were, in the shock and smother of the wave. It was only later, when upon the white flash of another high sea hurling itself amidships, Jukes had a vision of two pairs of davits leaping black and empty out of the solid blackness, with one overhauled fall flying and an iron-bound block capering in the air, that he became aware of what had happened within about three yards of his back.

He poked his head forward, groping for the ear of his commander. His lips touched it – big, fleshy, very wet. He cried in an agitated tone, 'Our boats are going now, sir.'

And again he heard that voice, forced and ringing feebly, but with a penetrating effect of quietness in the enormous discord of noises, as if sent out from some remote spot of peace beyond the black wastes of the gale; again he heard a man's voice – the frail and indomitable sound that can be made to carry an infinity of thought, resolution, and purpose, that shall be pronouncing confident words on the last day, when heavens fall, and justice is done – again he heard it, and it was crying to him, as if from very, very far – 'All right.'

He thought he had not managed to make himself understood. 'Our boats – I say boats – the boats, sir! Two gone!'

The same voice, within a foot of him and yet so remote, yelled sensibly, 'Can't be helped.'

Captain MacWhirr had never turned his face, but Jukes caught some more words on the wind.

'What can – expect – when hammering through – such – Bound to leave – something behind – stands to reason.'

Watchfully Jukes listened for more. No more came. This was all Captain MacWhirr had to say; and Jukes could picture to himself rather than see the broad squat back before him. An impenetrable obscurity pressed down upon the ghostly glimmers of the sea. A dull conviction seized upon Jukes that there was nothing to be done.

If the steering-gear did not give way, if the immense volumes of water did not burst the deck in or smash one of the hatches, if the engines did not give up, if way could be kept on the ship against this terrific wind, and she did not bury herself in one of these awful seas, of whose white crests alone, topping high above her bows, he could now and then get a sickening glimpse – then there was a chance of her coming out of it. Something within him seemed to turn over, bringing uppermost the feeling that the *Nan-Shan* was lost.

'She's done for,' he said to himself, with a surprising mental agitation, as though he had discovered an unexpected meaning in this thought. One of these things was bound to happen. Nothing could be prevented now, and nothing could be remedied. The men on board did not count, and the ship could not last. This weather was too impossible.

Jukes felt an arm thrown heavily over his shoulders; and to this overture he responded with great intelligence by catching hold of his captain round the waist.

They stood clasped thus in the blind night, bracing each other against the wind, cheek to cheek and lip to ear, in the manner of two hulks lashed stem to stern together.

And Jukes heard the voice of his commander hardly any louder than before, but nearer, as though, starting to march athwart the prodigious rush of the hurricane, it had approached him, bearing that strange effect of quietness like the serene glow of a halo.

'D'ye know where the hands got to?' it asked, vigorous and evanescent at the same time, overcoming the strength of the wind, and swept away from Jukes instantly.

Jukes didn't know. They were all on the bridge when the real force of the hurricane struck the ship. He had no idea where they had crawled to. Under the circumstances they were nowhere, for all the use that could be made of them. Somehow the Captain's wish to know distressed Jukes.

'Want the hands, sir?' he cried, apprehensively.

'Ought to know,' asserted Captain MacWhirr. 'Hold hard.'

They held hard. An outburst of unchained fury, a vicious rush of the wind absolutely steadied the ship; she rocked only, quick and light like a child's cradle, for a terrific moment of suspense, while the whole atmosphere, as it seemed, streamed furiously past her, roaring away from the tenebrous earth.

It suffocated them, and with eyes shut they tightened their grasp. What from the magnitude of the shock might have been a column of water running upright in the dark, butted against the ship, broke short, and fell on her bridge, crushingly, from on high, with a dead burying weight.

A flying fragment of that collapse, a mere splash, enveloped them in one swirl from their feet over their heads, filling violently their ears, mouths, and nostrils with salt water. It knocked out their legs, wrenched in haste at their arms, seethed away swiftly under their chins; and opening their eyes, they saw the piled-up masses of foam dashing to and fro amongst what looked like the fragments of a ship. She had given way as if driven straight in. Their panting hearts yielded, too, before the tremendous blow; and all at once she sprang up again to her desperate plunging, as if trying to scramble out from under the ruins.

The seas in the dark seemed to rush from all sides to keep her back where she might perish. There was hate in the way she was handled, and a ferocity in the blows that fell. She was like a living creature thrown to the rage of a mob: hustled terribly, struck at, borne up, flung down, leaped upon. Captain MacWhirr and Jukes kept hold of each other, deafened by the noise, gagged by the wind; and the great physical tumult beating about their bodies, brought, like an unbridled display of passion, a profound trouble to their souls. One of these wild and appalling shrieks that are heard at times passing mysteriously overhead in the steady roar of a hurricane, swooped, as if borne on wings, upon the ship, and Jukes tried to outscream it.

'Will she live through this?'

The cry was wrenched out of his breast. It was as unintentional as the birth of a thought in the head, and he heard nothing of it himself. It all became extinct at once – thought, intention, effort – and of his cry the inaudible vibration added to the tempest waves of the air.

He expected nothing from it. Nothing at all. For indeed what answer could be made? But after a while he heard with amazement the frail and resisting voice in his ear, the dwarf sound, unconquered in the giant tumult.

'She may!'

It was a dull yell, more difficult to seize than a whisper. And presently the voice returned again, half submerged in the vast crashes, like a ship battling against the waves of an ocean.

'Let's hope so!' it cried – small, lonely, and unmoved, a stranger to the visions of hope or fear; and it flickered into disconnected words: 'Ship ... This ... Never – Anyhow ... for the best,' Jukes gave it up.

Then, as if it had come suddenly upon the one thing fit to withstand the power of a storm, it seemed to gain force and firmness for the last broken shouts:

'Keep on hammering ... builders ... good men ... And chance it ... engines ... Rout ... good man.'

Captain MacWhirr removed his arm from Jukes's shoulders, and thereby ceased to exist for his mate, so dark it was; Jukes, after a tense stiffening of every muscle, would let himself go limp all over. The gnawing of profound discomfort existed side by side with an incredible disposition to somnolence, as though he had been buffeted and worried into drowsiness. The wind would get hold of his head and try to shake it off his shoulders; his clothes, full of water, were as heavy as lead, cold and dripping like an armour of melting ice: he shivered – it lasted a long time; and with his hands closed hard on his hold, he was letting himself sink slowly into the depths of bodily misery. His mind became concentrated upon himself in an aimless, idle way, and when something pushed lightly at the back of his knees he nearly, as the saying is, jumped out of his skin.

In the start forward he bumped the back of Captain MacWhirr, who didn't move; and then a hand gripped his thigh. A lull had come, a menacing lull of the wind, the holding of a stormy breath – and he felt himself pawed all over. It was the boatswain. Jukes recognized these hands, so thick and enormous that they seemed to belong to some new species of man.

The boatswain had arrived on the bridge, crawling on all fours against the wind, and had found the chief mate's legs with the top of his head. Immediately he crouched and began to explore Jukes's person upwards with prudent, apologetic touches, as became an inferior.

He was an ill-favoured, undersized, gruff sailor of fifty, coarsely hairy, short-legged, long-armed, resembling an elderly ape. His strength was immense; and in his great lumpy paws, bulging like brown boxing-gloves on the end of furry forearms, the heaviest objects were handled like playthings. Apart from the grizzled pelt on his chest, the menacing demeanour, and the hoarse voice, he had none of the classical attributes of his rating. His good nature almost amounted to imbecility: the men did what they liked with him, and he had not an ounce of initiative in his character, which was easy-going and talkative. For these reasons Jukes disliked him; but Captain MacWhirr, to Jukes's scornful disgust, seemed to regard him as a first-rate petty officer.

He pulled himself up by Jukes's coat, taking that liberty with the greatest moderation, and only so far as it was forced upon him by the hurricane.

'What is it, bos'n, what is it?' yelled Jukes, impatiently. What could that fraud of a bos'n want on the bridge? The typhoon had got on Jukes's nerves. The husky bellowings of the other, though unintelligible, seemed to suggest a state of lively satisfaction. There could be no mistake. The old fool was pleased with something.

The boatswain's other hand had found some other body, for in a changed tone he began to inquire: 'Is it you, sir? Is it you, sir?' The wind strangled his howls.

'Yes!' cried Captain MacWhirr.

CHAPTER 4

All that the boatswain, out of a superabundance of yells, could make clear to Captain MacWhirr was the bizarre intelligence that 'All them Chinamen in the fore 'tween deck have fetched away, sir.'

Jukes to leeward could hear these two shouting within six inches of his face, as you may hear on a still night half a mile away two men conversing across a field. He heard Captain MacWhirr's exasperated 'What? What?' and the strained pitch of the other's hoarseness. 'In a lump . . . seen them myself . . . Awful sight, sir . . . thought . . . tell you.'

Jukes remained indifferent, as if rendered irresponsible by the force of the hurricane, which made the very thought of action utterly vain. Besides, being very young, he had found the occupation of keeping his heart completely steeled against the worst so engrossing that he had come to feel an overpowering dislike towards any other form of activity whatever. He was not scared; he knew this because, firmly believing he would never see another sunrise, he remained calm in that belief.

These are the moments of do-nothing heroics to which even good men surrender at times. Many officers of ships can no doubt recall a case in their experience when just such a trance of confounded stoicism would come all at once over a whole ship's company. Jukes, however, had no wide experience of men or storms. He conceived himself to be calm – inexorably calm; but as a matter of fact he was daunted; not abjectly, but only so far as a decent man may, without becoming loathsome to himself.

It was rather like a forced-on numbness of spirit. The long, long stress of a gale does it; the suspense of the interminably culminating catastrophe; and there is a bodily fatigue in the mere holding on to existence within the excessive tumult; a searching and insidious fatigue that penetrates deep into a man's breast to cast down and sadden his heart, which is incorrigible, and of all the gifts of the earth – even before life itself – aspires to peace.

Jukes was benumbed much more than he supposed. He held on – very wet, very cold, stiff in every limb; and in a momentary hallucination of swift visions (it is said that a drowning man thus reviews all his life) he beheld all sorts of memories altogether unconnected with his present situation. He remembered his father, for instance: a worthy businessman, who at an unfortunate crisis in his affairs went quietly to bed and died forthwith in a state of resignation. Jukes did not recall these circumstances, of course, but remaining otherwise unconcerned he seemed to see distinctly the poor man's face; a certain game of nap played when quite a boy in Table Bay on board a ship, since lost with all hands; the thick eyebrows of his first skipper; and without any emotion, as he might years ago have walked listlessly into her room and found her sitting there with a book, he remembered his mother – dead, too, now – the resolute woman, left badly off, who had been very firm in his bringing up.

It could not have lasted more than a second, perhaps not so much. A heavy arm had fallen about his shoulders; Captain MacWhirr's voice was speaking his name into his ear.

'Jukes! Jukes!'

He detected the tone of deep concern. The wind had thrown its weight on the ship, trying to pin her down amongst the seas. They made a clean breach over her, as over a deep-swimming log; and the gathered weight of crashes menaced monstrously from afar. The breakers flung out of the night with a ghostly light on their crests – the light of sea-foam that in a ferocious, boiling-up pale flash showed upon the slender body of the ship the toppling rush, the downfall, and the seething mad scurry of each wave. Never for a moment could she shake herself clear of the water; Jukes, rigid, perceived in her motion the ominous sign of haphazard floundering. She was no longer struggling intelligently. It was the beginning of the end; and the note of busy concern in Captain MacWhirr's voice sickened him like an exhibition of blind and pernicious folly.

The spell of the storm had fallen upon Jukes. He was penetrated by it, absorbed by it; he was rooted in it with a rigour of dumb attention. Captain MacWhirr persisted in his cries, but the wind got between them like a solid wedge. He hung round Jukes's neck as heavy as a millstone, and suddenly the sides of their heads knocked together.

'Jukes! Mr Jukes, I say!'

He had to answer that voice that would not be silenced. He answered in the customary manner: ' . . . Yes, sir.'

And directly, his heart, corrupted by the storm that breeds a craving for peace, rebelled against the tyranny of training and command.

Captain MacWhirr had his mate's head fixed firm in the crook of his elbow, and pressed it to his yelling lips mysteriously. Sometimes Jukes would break in, admonishing hastily: 'Look out, sir!' or Captain MacWhirr would bawl an earnest exhortation to 'Hold hard, there!' and the whole black universe seemed to reel together with the ship. They paused. She floated yet. And Captain MacWhirr would resume his shouts. ' . . . Says . . . whole lot . . . fetched away . . . Ought to see . . . what's the matter.'

Directly the full force of the hurricane had struck the ship, every part of her deck became untenable; and the sailors, dazed and dismayed, took shelter in the port alleyway under the bridge. It had a door aft, which they shut; it was very black, cold, and dismal. At each heavy fling of the ship they would groan all together in the dark, and tons of water could be heard scuttling about as if trying to get at them from above. The boatswain had been keeping up a gruff talk, but a more unreasonable lot of men, he said afterwards, he had never been with. They were snug enough there, out of harm's way, and not wanted to do anything, either; and yet they did nothing but grumble and complain peevishly like so many sick kids. Finally, one of them said that if there had been at least some light to see each other's noses by, it wouldn't be so bad. It was making him crazy, he declared, to lie there in the dark waiting for the blamed hooker to sink.

'Why don't you step outside, then, and be done with it at once?' the boatswain turned on him.

This called up a shout of execration. The boatswain found himself overwhelmed with reproaches of all sorts. They seemed to take it ill that a lamp was not instantly created for them out of nothing. They would whine after a light to get drowned by – anyhow! And though the unreason of their revilings was patent – since no one could hope to reach the lamp-room, which was forward – he became greatly distressed. He did not think it was decent of them to be nagging at him like this. He told them so, and was met by general contumely. He sought refuge, therefore, in an embittered silence. At the same time their grumbling and sighing and muttering worried him greatly, but by-and-by it occurred to him that there were six globe lamps hung in the 'tween-deck, and that there could be no harm in depriving the coolies of one of them.

The *Nan-Shan* had an athwartship coal-bunker, which, being at times used as cargo space, communicated by an iron door with the fore 'tween-deck. It was empty then, and its manhole was the foremost one in the alleyway. The boatswain could get in, therefore, without coming out on deck at all; but to his great surprise he found he could induce no one to help him in taking off the manhole cover. He groped for it all the same, but one of the crew lying in his way refused to budge.

'Why, I only want to get you that blamed light you are crying for,' he expostulated, almost pitifully.

Somebody told him to go and put his head in a bag. He regretted he could not recognize the voice, and that it was too dark to see, otherwise, as he said, he would have put a head on *that* son of a sea-cook, anyway, sink or swim. Nevertheless, he had made up his mind to show them he could get a light, if he were to die for it.

Through the violence of the ship's rolling, every movement was dangerous. To be lying down seemed labour enough. He nearly broke his neck dropping into the bunker. He fell on his back, and was sent shooting helplessly from side to side in the dangerous company of a heavy iron bar – a coal-trimmer's slice probably – left down there by somebody. This thing made him as nervous as though it had been a wild beast. He could not see it, the inside of the bunker coated with coal-dust being perfectly and impenetrably black; but he heard it sliding and clattering, and striking here and there, always in the neighbourhood of his head. It seemed to make an extraordinary noise, too – to give heavy thumps as though it had been as big as a bridge girder. This was remarkable enough for him to notice while he was flung from port to starboard and back again, and clawing desperately the smooth sides of the bunker in the endeavour to stop himself. The door into the 'tween-deck not fitting quite true, he saw a thread of dim light at the bottom.

Being a sailor, and a still active man, he did not want much of a chance to regain his feet; and as luck would have it, in scrambling up he put his hand on the iron slice, picking it up as he rose. Otherwise he would have been afraid of the thing breaking his legs, or at least knocking him down again. At first he stood still. He felt unsafe in this darkness that seemed to make the ship's motion unfamiliar, unforeseen, and difficult to counteract. He felt so much shaken for a moment that he dared not move for fear of 'taking charge again'. He had no mind to get battered to pieces in that bunker.

He had struck his head twice; he was dazed a little. He seemed to hear yet so plainly the clatter and bangs of the iron slice flying about his ears that he tightened his grip to prove to himself he had it there safely in his hand. He was vaguely amazed at the plainness with which down there he could hear the gale raging. Its howls and shrieks seemed to take on, in the emptiness of the bunker, something of the human character, of human rage and pain – being not vast but infinitely poignant. And there were, with every roll, thumps, too – profound, ponderous thumps, as if a bulk object of five-ton weight or so had got play in the hold. But there was no such thing in the cargo. Something on deck? Impossible. Or alongside? Couldn't be.

He thought all this quickly, clearly, competently, like a seaman, and in the end remained puzzled. This noise, though, came deadened from outside, together with the washing and pouring of water on deck above his head. Was it the wind? Must be. It made down there a row like the shouting of a big lot of crazed men. And he discovered in himself a desire for a light, too – if only to get drowned by – and a nervous anxiety to get out of that bunker as quickly as possible.

He pulled back the bolt: the heavy iron plate turned on its hinges; and it was as though he had opened the door to the sounds of the tempest. A gust of hoarse yelling met him: the air was still; and the rushing of water overhead was covered by a tumult of strangled, throaty shrieks that produced an effect of desperate confusion. He straddled his legs the whole width of the doorway and stretched his neck. And at first he perceived only what he had come to seek: six small yellow flames swinging violently on the great body of the dusk.

It was stayed like the gallery of a mine, with a row of stanchions in the middle, and cross-beams overhead, penetrating into the gloom ahead – indefinitely. And to port there loomed, like the caving in of one of the sides, a bulky mass with a slanting outline. The whole place, with the shadows and the shapes, moved all the time. The boatswain glared: the ship lurched to starboard, and a great howl came from that mass that had the slant of fallen earth.

Pieces of wood whizzed past. Planks, he thought, inexpressibly startled, and flinging back his head. At his feet a man went sliding over, open-eyed, on his back, straining with uplifted arms for nothing: and another came bounding like a detached stone with his head between his legs and his hands clenched. His pigtail whipped in the air; he made a grab at the boatswain's legs, and from his opened hand a bright white disc rolled against the boatswain's foot. He recognized a silver dollar, and yelled at it with astonishment. With a precipitated sound of trampling and shuffling of bare feet, and with guttural cries, the mound of writhing bodies piled up to port detached itself from the ship's side and sliding, inert and struggling, shifted to starboard, with a dull, brutal thump. The cries ceased. The boatswain heard a long moan through the roar and whistling of the wind; he saw an inextricable confusion of heads and shoulders, naked soles kicking upwards, fists raised, tumbling backs, legs, pigtails, faces.

'Good Lord!' he cried, horrified, and banged-to the iron door upon this vision.

This was what he had come on the bridge to tell. He could not keep it to himself; and on board ship there is only one man to whom it is worth while to unburden yourself. On his passage back the hands in the alleyway swore at him for a fool. Why didn't he bring that lamp? What the devil did the coolies matter to anybody? And when he came out, the extremity of the ship made what went on inside of her appear of little moment.

At first he thought he had left the alleyway in the very moment of her sinking. The bridge ladders had been washed away, but an enormous sea filling the after-deck floated him up. After that he had to lie on his stomach for some time, holding to a ring-bolt, getting his breath now and then, and swallowing salt water. He struggled farther on his hands and knees, too frightened and distracted to turn back. In this way he reached the after-part of the wheelhouse. In that comparatively sheltered spot he found the second mate. The boatswain was pleasantly surprised – his impression being that everybody on deck must have been washed away a long time ago. He asked eagerly where the captain was.

The second mate was lying low, like a malignant little animal under a hedge.

'Captain? Gone overboard, after getting us into this mess.' The mate, too, for all he knew or cared. Another fool. Didn't matter. Everybody was going by-and-by.

The boatswain crawled out again into the strength of the wind; not because he much expected to find anybody, he said, but just to get away from 'that man'. He crawled out as outcasts go to face an inclement world. Hence his great joy at finding Jukes and the Captain. But what was going on in the 'tween-deck was to him a minor matter by that time. Besides, it was difficult to make yourself heard. But he managed to convey the idea that the Chinamen had broken adrift together with their boxes, and that he had come up on purpose to report this. As to the hands, they were all right. Then, appeased, he subsided on the deck in a sitting posture, hugging with his arms and legs the stand of the engine-room telegraph – an iron casting as thick as a post. When that went, why, he expected he would go, too. He gave no more thought to the coolies.

Captain MacWhirr had made Jukes understand that he wanted him to go down below – to see.

'What am I to them, sir?' And the trembling of his whole wet body caused Jukes's voice to sound like bleating.

'See first ... Bos'n ... says ... adrift.'

'That bos'n is a confounded fool,' howled Jukes, shakily.

The absurdity of the demand made upon him revolted Jukes. He was as unwilling to go as if the moment he had left the deck the ship were sure to sink.

'I must know ... can't leave ...'

'They'll settle, sir.'

'Fight ... bos'n says they fight ... Why? Can't have ... fighting ... board ship ... Much rather keep you here ... case ... I should ... washed overboard myself ... Stop it ... some way. You see and tell me ... through engine-room tube. Don't want you ... come up here ... too often. Dangerous ... moving about ... deck.'

Jukes, held with his head in chancery, had to listen to what seemed horrible suggestions.

'Don't want ... you get lost ... so long ... ship isn't ... Rout ... Good man ... Ship ... many ... through this ... all right yet.'

All at once Jukes understood he would have to go.

'Do you think she may?' he screamed.

But the wind devoured the reply, out of which Jukes heard only the one word, pronounced with great energy ' ... Always....'

Captain MacWhirr released Jukes, and bending over the boatswain yelled, 'Get back with the mate.' Jukes only knew that the arm was gone off his shoulders. He was dismissed with his orders – to do what? He was exasperated into letting go his hold carelessly, and on the instant was blown away. It seemed to him that nothing could stop him from being blown right over the stern. He flung himself down hastily, and the boatswain, who was following, fell on him.

'Don't you get up yet, sir,' cried the boatswain. 'No hurry!'

A sea swept over. Jukes understood the boatswain to splutter that the bridge ladders were gone. 'I'll lower you down, sir, by your hands,' he screamed. He shouted also something about the smoke-stack being as likely to go overboard as not. Jukes thought it very possible, and imagined the fires out, the ship helpless.... The boatswain by his side kept on yelling. 'What? What is it?' Jukes cried distressfully; and the other repeated, 'What would my old woman say if she saw me now?'

In the alleyway, where a lot of water had got in and splashed in the dark, the men were still as death, till Jukes stumbled against one of them and cursed him savagely for being in the way. Two or three voices then asked, eager and weak, 'Any chance for us, sir?'

'What's the matter with you fools?' he said, brutally. He felt as though he could throw himself down amongst them and never move any more. But they seemed cheered; and in the midst of obsequious warnings, 'Look out! Mind that manhole lid, sir,' they lowered him into the bunker. The boatswain tumbled down after him, and as soon as he had picked himself up he remarked, 'She would say, "Serve you right, you old fool, for going to sea." '

The boatswain had some means, and made a point of alluding to them frequently. His wife – a fat woman – and two grown-up daughters kept a greengrocer's shop in the East End of London.

In the dark, Jukes, unsteady on his legs, listened to a faint thunderous patter. A deadened screaming went on steadily at his elbow, as it were; and from above the louder tumult of the storm descended upon these near sounds. His head swam. To him, too, in that bunker, the motion of the ship seemed novel and menacing, sapping his resolution as though he had never been afloat before.

He had half a mind to scramble out again; but the remembrance of Captain MacWhirr's voice made this impossible. His orders were to go and see. What was the good of it, he wanted to know. Enraged, he told himself he would see – of course. But the boatswain, staggering clumsily, warned him to be careful how he opened that door; there was a blamed fight going on. And Jukes, as if in great bodily pain, desired irritably to know what the devil they were fighting for.

'Dollars! Dollars, sir. All their rotten chests got burst open. Blamed money skipping all over the place, and they are tumbling after it head over heels – tearing and biting like anything. A regular little hell in there.'

Jukes convulsively opened the door. The short boatswain peered under his arm.

One of the lamps had gone out, broken perhaps. Rancorous, guttural cries burst out loudly on their ears, and a strange panting sound, the working of all these straining breasts. A hard blow hit the side of the ship: water fell above with a stunning shock, and in the forefront of the gloom, where the air was reddish and thick, Jukes saw a head bang the deck violently, two thick calves waving on high, muscular arms twined round a naked body, a yellow-face, open-mouthed and with a set wild stare, look up and slide away. An empty chest clattered turning over; a man fell head first with a jump, as if lifted by a kick; and farther off, indistinct, others streamed like a mass of rolling stones down a bank, thumping the deck with their feet and flourishing their arms wildly. The hatchway ladder was loaded with coolies swarming on it like bees on a branch. They hung on the steps in a crawling, stirring cluster, beating madly with their fists the underside of the battened hatch, and the headlong rush of the water above was heard in the intervals of their yelling. The ship heeled over more, and they began to drop off: first one, then two, then all the rest went away together, falling straight off with a great cry.

Jukes was confounded. The boatswain, with gruff anxiety, begged him, 'Don't you go in there, sir.'

The whole place seemed to twist upon itself, jumping incessantly the while; and when the ship rose to a sea Jukes fancied that all these men would be shot upon him in a body. He backed out, swung the door to, and with trembling hands pushed at the bolt....

As soon as his mate had gone Captain MacWhirr, left alone on the bridge, sidled and staggered as far as the wheelhouse. Its door being hinged forward, he had to fight the gale for admittance, and when at last he managed to enter, it was with an instantaneous clatter and a bang, as though he had been fired through the wood. He stood within, holding on to the handle.

The steering-gear leaked steam, and in the confined space the glass of the binnacle made a shiny oval of light in a thin white fog. The wind howled, hummed, whistled, with sudden booming gusts that rattled the doors and shutters in the vicious patter of sprays. Two coils of lead-line and a small canvas bag hung on a long lanyard, swung wide off, and came back clinging to the bulkheads. The gratings underfoot were nearly afloat; with every sweeping blow of a sea, water squirted violently through the cracks all round the door, and the man at the helm had flung down his cap, his coat, and stood propped against the gear-casing in a striped cotton shirt open on his breast. The little brass wheel in his hands had the appearance of a bright and fragile toy. The cords of his neck stood hard and lean, a dark patch lay in the hollow of his throat, and his face was still and sunken as in death.

Captain MacWhirr wiped his eyes. The sea that had nearly taken him overboard had, to his great annoyance, washed his sou'wester hat off his bald head. The fluffy, fair hair, soaked and darkened, resembled a mean skein of cotton threads festooned round his bare skull. His face, glistening with sea-water, had been made crimson with the wind, with the sting of sprays. He looked as though he had come off sweating from before a furnace.

'You here?' he muttered, heavily.

The second mate had found his way into the wheelhouse some time before. He had fixed himself in a corner with his knees up, a fist pressed against each temple; and this attitude suggested rage, sorrow, resignation, surrender, with a sort of concentrated unforgiveness. He said mournfully and defiantly, 'Well, it's my watch below now: ain't it?'

The steam gear clattered, stopped, clattered again; and the helmsman's eyeballs seemed to project out of a hungry face as if the compass card behind the binnacle glass had been meat. God knows how long he had been left there to steer, as if forgotten by all his shipmates. The bells had not been struck; there had been no reliefs; the ship's routine had gone down wind; but he was trying to keep her head north-north-east. The rudder might have been gone for all he knew, the fires out, the engines broken down, the ship ready to roll over like a corpse. He was anxious not to get muddled and lose control of her head, because the compass-card swung far both ways, wriggling on the pivot, and sometimes seemed to whirl right round. He suffered from mental stress. He was horribly afraid, also, of the wheelhouse going. Mountains of water kept on tumbling against it. When the ship took one of her desperate dives the corners of his lips twitched.

Captain MacWhirr looked up at the wheelhouse clock. Screwed to the bulk-head, it had a white face on which the black hands appeared to stand quite still. It was half past one in the morning.

'Another day,' he muttered to himself.

The second mate heard him, and lifting his head as one grieving amongst ruins, 'You won't see it break,' he exclaimed. His wrists and his knees could be seen to shake violently. 'No, by God! You won't. . . .'

He took his face again between his fists.

The body of the helmsman had moved slightly, but his head didn't budge on his neck – like a stone head fixed to look one way from a column. During a roll that all but took his booted legs from under him, and in the very stagger to save himself, Captain MacWhirr said austerely, 'Don't you pay any attention to what that man says.' And then, with an indefinable change of tone, very grave, he added, 'He isn't on duty.'

The sailor said nothing.

The hurricane boomed, shaking the little place, which seemed air-tight; and the light of the binnacle flickered all the time.

'You haven't been relieved,' Captain MacWhirr went on, looking down. 'I want you to stick to the helm, though, as long as you can. You've got the hang of her. Another man coming here might make a mess of it. Wouldn't do. No child's play. And the hands are probably busy with a job down below. . . . Think you can?'

The steering-gear leaped into an abrupt short clatter, stopped smouldering like an ember; and the still man, with a motionless gaze, burst out, as if all the passion in him had gone into his lips: 'By Heavens, sir! I can steer for ever if nobody talks to me.'

'Oh! aye! All right. . . .' The Captain lifted his eyes for the first time to the man, ' . . . Hackett.'

And he seemed to dismiss this matter from his mind. He stooped to the engine-room speaking-tube, blew in, and bent his head. Mr Rout below answered, and at once Captain MacWhirr put his lips to the mouthpiece.

With the uproar of the gale around him he applied alternately to his lips and his ear, and the engineer's voice mounted to him, harsh and as if out of the heat of an engagement. One of the stokers was disabled, the others had given in, the second engineer and the donkey-man were firing-up. The third engineer was standing by the steam-valve. The engines were being tended by hand. How was it above?

'Bad enough. It mostly rests with you,' said Captain MacWhirr. Was the mate down there yet? No? Well, he would be presently. Would Mr Rout let him talk through the speaking-tube? – through the deck speaking-tube, because he – the Captain – was going out again on the bridge directly. There was some trouble amongst the Chinamen. They were fighting, it seemed. Couldn't allow fighting anyhow. . . .

Mr Rout had gone away, and Captain MacWhirr could feel against his ear the pulsation of the engines, like the beat of the ship's heart. Mr Rout's voice down there shouted something distantly. The ship pitched headlong, the pulsation leaped with a hissing tumult, and stopped dead. Captain MacWhirr's face was impassive, and his eyes were fixed aimlessly on the crouching shape of the second mate. Again Mr Rout's voice cried out in the depths, and the pulsating beats recommenced, with slow strokes – growing swifter.

Mr Rout had returned to the tube. 'It don't matter much what they do,' he said, hastily; and then, with irritation, 'She takes these dives as if she never meant to come up again.'

'Awful sea,' said the Captain's voice from above.

'Don't let me drive her under,' barked Solomon Rout up the pipe.

'Dark and rain. Can't see what's coming,' uttered the voice. 'Must – keep – her – moving – enough to steer – and chance it,' it went on to state distinctly.

'I am doing as much as I dare.'

'We are – getting – smashed up – a good deal up here,' proceeded the voice mildly. 'Doing – fairly well – though. Of course, if the wheelhouse should go. . . .'

Mr Rout, bending an attentive ear, muttered peevishly something under his breath.

But the deliberate voice up there became animated to ask: 'Jukes turned up yet?' Then, after a short wait, 'I wish he would bear a hand. I want him to be done and come up here in case of anything. To look after the ship. I am all alone. The second mate's lost. . . .'

'What?' shouted Mr Rout into the engine-room, taking his head away. Then up the tube he cried, 'Gone overboard?' and clapped his ear to.

'Lost his nerve,' the voice from above continued in a matter-of-fact tone. 'Damned awkward circumstances.'

Mr Rout, listening with bowed neck, opened his eyes wide at this. However, he heard something like the sounds of a scuffle and broken exclamations coming down to him. He strained his hearing; and all the time Beale, the third engineer, with his arms uplifted, held between the palms of his hands the rim of a little black wheel projecting at the side of a big copper pipe. He seemed to be poising it above his head, as though it were a correct attitude in some sort of game.

To steady himself, he pressed his shoulder against the white bulkhead, one knee bent, and a sweat-rag tucked in his belt hanging on his hip. His smooth cheek was begrimed and flushed, and the coal dust on his eyelids, like the black pencilling of a make-up, enhanced the liquid brilliance of the whites, giving to his youthful face something of a feminine, exotic, and fascinating aspect. When the ship pitched he would with hasty movements of his hands screw hard at the little wheel.

'Gone crazy,' began the Captain's voice suddenly in the tube. 'Rushed at me . . . Just now. Had to knock him down . . . This minute. You heard, Mr Rout?'

'The devil!' muttered Mr Rout. 'Look out, Beale!'

His shout rang out like the blast of a warning trumpet, between the iron walls of the engine-room. Painted white, they rose high into the dusk of the skylight, sloping like a roof; and the whole lofty space resembled the interior of a monument, divided by floors of iron grating, with lights flickering at different levels, and a mass of gloom lingering in the middle, within the columnar stir of machinery under the motionless swelling of the cylinders.

A loud and wild resonance, made up of all the noises of the hurricane, dwelt in the still warmth of the air. There was in it the smell of hot metal, of oil, and a slight mist of steam. The blows of the sea seemed to traverse it in an unringing, stunning shock, from side to side.

Gleams, like pale long flames, trembled upon the polish of metal; from the flooring below the enormous crank-heads emerged in their turns with a flash of brass and steel – going over; while the connecting-rods, big-jointed, like skeleton limbs, seemed to thrust them down and pull them up again with an irresistible precision. And deep in the half-light other rods dodged deliberately to and fro, crossheads nodded, discs of metal rubbed smoothly against each other, slow and gentle, in a commingling of shadows and gleams.

Sometimes all those powerful and unerring movements would slow down simultaneously, as if they had been the functions of a living organism, stricken suddenly by the blight of languor; and Mr Rout's eyes would blaze darker in his long sallow face. He was fighting this fight in a pair of carpet slippers. A short shiny jacket barely covered his loins, and his white wrists protruded far out of the tight sleeves, as though the emergency had added to his stature, had lengthened his limbs, augmented his pallor, hollowed his eyes.

He moved, climbing high up, disappearing low down, with a restless, purposeful industry, and when he stood still, holding the guard-rail in front of the starting-gear, he would keep glancing to the right at the steam-gauge, at the water-gauge, fixed upon the white wall in the light of a swaying lamp. The mouths of two speaking-tubes gaped stupidly at his elbow, and the dial of the engine-room telegraph resembled a clock of large diameter, bearing on its face curt words instead of figures. The grouped letters stood out heavily black, around the pivot-head of the indicator, emphatically symbolic of loud exclamations: AHEAD, ASTERN, SLOW, HALF, STAND BY; and the fat black hand pointed downwards to the word FULL, which, thus singled out, captured the eye as a sharp cry secures attention.

The wood-encased bulk of the low-pressure cylinder, frowning portly from above, emitted a faint wheeze at every thrust, and except for that low hiss the engines worked their steel limbs headlong or slow with a silent, determined smoothness. And all this, the white walls, the moving steel, the floor plates under Solomon Rout's feet, the floors of iron grating above his head, the dusk and the gleams, uprose and sank continuously, with one accord, upon the harsh wash of the waves against the ship's side. The whole loftiness of the place, booming hollow to the great voice of the wind, swayed at the top like a tree, would go over bodily, as if borne down this way and that by the tremendous blasts.

'You've got to hurry up,' shouted Mr Rout, as soon as he saw Jukes appear in the stokehold doorway.

Jukes's glance was wandering and tipsy; his red face was puffy, as though he had overslept himself. He had had an arduous road, and had travelled over it with immense vivacity, the agitation of his mind corresponding to the exertions of his body. He had rushed up out of the bunker, stumbling in the dark alleyway amongst a lot of bewildered men who, trod upon, asked

'What's up, sir?' in awed mutters all round him – down the stokehold ladder, missing many iron rungs in his hurry, down into a place deep as a well, black as Tophet, tipping over back and forth like a see-saw. The water in the bilges thundered at each roll, and lumps of coal skipped to and fro, from end to end, rattling like an avalanche of pebbles on a slope of iron.

Somebody in there moaned with pain, and somebody else could be seen crouching over what seemed the prone body of a dead man; a lusty voice blasphemed; and the glow under each fire-door was like a pool of flaming blood radiating quietly in a velvety blackness.

A gust of wind struck upon the nape of Jukes's neck and next moment he felt it streaming about his wet ankles. The stokehold ventilators hummed; in front of the six fire-doors two wild figures, stripped to the waist, staggered and stooped, wrestling with two shovels.

'Hallo! Plenty of draught now,' yelled the second engineer at once, as though he had been all the time looking out for Jukes. The donkeyman, a dapper little chap with a dazzling fair skin and a tiny, gingery moustache, worked in a sort of mute transport. They were keeping a full head of steam, and a profound rumbling, as of an empty furniture van trotting over a bridge, made a sustained bass to all the other noises of the place.

'Blowing off all the time,' went on yelling the second. With a sound as of a hundred scoured saucepans, the orifice of a ventilator spat upon his shoulder a sudden gush of salt water, and he volleyed a stream of curses upon all things on earth including his own soul, ripping and raving, and all the time attending to his business. With a sharp clash of metal the ardent pale glare of the fire opened upon his bullet head, showing his spluttering lips, his insolent face, and with another clang closed like the white-hot wink of an iron eye.

'Where's the blooming ship? Can you tell me? blast my eyes! Under water – or what? It's coming down here in tons. Are the condemned cowls gone to Hades? Hey? Don't you know anything – you jolly sailor-man you . . .?'

Jukes, after a bewildered moment, had been helped by a roll to dart through; and as soon as his eyes took in the comparative vastness, peace, and brilliance of the engine-room, the ship, setting her stern heavily in the water, sent him charging head down upon Mr Rout.

The chief's arm, long like a tentacle, and straightening as if worked by a spring, went out to meet him, and deflected his rush into a spin towards the speaking-tubes. At the same time Mr Rout repeated earnestly:

'You've got to hurry up, whatever it is.'

Jukes yelled 'Are you there, sir?' and listened. Nothing. Suddenly the roar of the wind fell straight into his ear, but presently a small voice shoved aside the shouting hurricane quietly.

'You, Jukes? – Well?'

Jukes was ready to talk: it was only time that seemed to be wanting. It was easy enough to account for everything. He could perfectly imagine the coolies battened down in the reeking 'tween-deck, lying sick and scared between the rows of chests. Then one of these chests – or perhaps several at once – breaking loose in a roll, knocking out others, sides splitting, lids flying open, and all these clumsy Chinamen rising up in a body to save their property. Afterwards every fling of the ship would hurl that tramping, yelling mob here and there, from side to side, in a whirl of smashed wood, torn clothing, rolling dollars. A struggle once started, they would be unable to stop themselves. Nothing could stop them now except main force. It was a disaster. He had seen it, and that was all he could say. Some of them must be dead, he believed. The rest would go on fighting . . .

He sent up his words, tripping over each other, crowding the narrow tube. They mounted as if into a silence of an enlightened comprehension dwelling alone up there with a storm. And Jukes wanted to be dismissed from the face of that odious trouble intruding on the great need of the ship.

CHAPTER 5

He waited. Before his eyes the engines turned with slow labour, that in the moment of going off into a mad fling would stop dead at Mr Rout's shout, 'Look out, Beale!' They paused in an intelligent immobility, stilled in mid-stroke, a heavy crank arrested on the cant, as if conscious of danger and the passage of time. Then, with a 'Now, then!' from the chief, and the sound of a breath expelled through clenched teeth, they would accomplish the interrupted revolution and begin another.

There was the prudent sagacity of wisdom and the deliberation of enormous strength in their movements. This was their work – this patient coaxing of a distracted ship over the fury of the waves and into the very eye of the wind. At times Mr Rout's chin would sink on his breast, and he watched them with knitted eyebrows as if lost in thought.

The voice that kept the hurricane out of Jukes's ear began: 'Take the hands with you . . .' and left off unexpectedly.

.'What could I do with them, sir?'

A harsh, abrupt, imperious clang exploded suddenly. The three pairs of eyes flew up to the telegraph dial to see the hand jump from FULL to STOP as if snatched by a devil. And then these three men in the engine-room had the intimate sensation of a check upon the ship, of a strange shrinking, as if she had gathered herself for a desperate leap.

'Stop her!' bellowed Mr Rout.

Nobody – not even Captain MacWhirr, who alone on deck had caught sight of a white line of foam coming on at such a height that he couldn't believe his eyes – nobody was to know the steepness of that sea and the awful depth of the hollow the hurricane had scooped out behind the running wall of water.

It raced to meet the ship, and, with a pause, as of girding the loins, the *Nan-Shan* lifted her bows and leaped. The flames in all the lamps sank, darkening the engine-room. One went out. With a tearing crash and a swirling, raving tumult, tons of water fell upon the deck, as though the ship had darted under the foot of a cataract.

Down there they looked at each other, stunned.

'Swept from end to end, by God!' bawled Jukes.

She dipped into the hollow straight down, as if going over the edge of the world. The engine-room toppled forward menacingly, like the inside of a tower nodding in an earthquake. An awful racket, of iron things falling, came from the stokehold. She hung on this appalling slant long enough for Beale to drop on his hands and knees and begin to crawl as if he meant to fly on all fours out of the engine-room, and for Mr Rout to turn his head slowly, rigid, cavernous, with the lower jaw dropping. Jukes had shut his eyes, and his face in a moment became hopelessly blank and gentle, like the face of a blind man.

At last she rose slowly, staggering, as if she had to lift a mountain with her bows.

Mr Rout shut his mouth; Jukes blinked; and little Beale stood up hastily.

'Another one like this, and that's the last of her,' cried the chief.

He and Jukes looked at each other, and the same thought came into their heads. The Captain! Everything must have been swept away. Steering-gear gone – ship like a log. All over directly.

'Rush!' ejaculated Mr Rout thickly, glaring with enlarged, doubtful eyes at Jukes, who answered him by an irresolute glance.

The clang of the telegraph gong soothed them instantly. The black hand dropped in a flash from STOP to FULL.

'Now then, Beale!' cried Mr Rout.

The steam hissed low. The piston-rods slid in and out. Jukes put his ear to the tube. The voice was ready for him. It said: 'Pick up all the money. Bear a hand now. I'll want you up here.' And that was all.

'Sir?' called up Jukes. There was no answer.

He staggered away like a defeated man from the field of battle. He had got, in some way or other, a cut above his left eyebrow – a cut to the bone. He was not aware of it in the least: quantities of the China Sea, large enough to break his neck for him, had gone over his head, had cleaned, washed, and salted that wound. It did not bleed, but only gaped red; and this gash over the eye, his dishevelled hair, the disorder of his clothes, gave him the aspect of a man worsted in a fight with fists.

'Got to pick up the dollars.' He appealed to Mr Rout, smiling pitifully at random.

'What's that?' asked Mr Rout, wildly, 'Pick up ...? I don't care ...' Then, quivering in every muscle, but with an exaggeration of paternal tone, 'Go away now, for God's sake. You deck people'll drive me silly. There's that second mate been going for the old man. Don't you know? You fellows are going wrong for want of something to do ...'

At these words Jukes discovered in himself the beginnings of anger. Want of something to do – indeed ... Full of hot scorn against the chief, he turned to go the way he had come. In the stokehold the plump donkeyman toiled with his shovel mutely, as if his tongue had been cut out; but the second was carrying on like a noisy, undaunted maniac, who had preserved his skill in the art of stoking under a marine boiler.

'Hallo, you wandering officer! Hey! Can't you get some of your slush-slingers to wind up a few of them ashes? I am getting choked with them there. Curse it! Hallo! Hey! Remember the articles: *Sailors and firemen to assist each other*. Hey! D'ye hear?'

Jukes was climbing out frantically, and the other, lifting up his face after him, howled, 'Can't you speak? What are you poking about here for? What's your game anyhow?'

A frenzy possessed Jukes. By the time he was back amongst the men in the darkness of the alleyway, he felt ready to wring all their necks at the slightest sign of hanging back. The very thought of it exasperated him. *He* couldn't hang back. They shouldn't.

The impetuosity with which he came amongst them carried them along. They had already been excited and startled at all his comings and goings – by the fierceness and rapidity of his movements; and more felt than seen in his rushes, he appeared formidable – busied with matters of life and death that brooked no delay. At his first word he heard them drop into the bunker one after another obediently, with heavy thumps.

They were not clear as to what would have to be done. 'What is it? What is it?' they were asking each other. The boatswain tried to explain; the sounds of a great scuffle surprised them: and the mighty shocks, reverberating awfully in the black bunker, kept them in mind of their danger. When the boatswain threw open the door it seemed that an eddy of the hurricane, stealing through the iron sides of the ship, had set all these bodies whirling like dust: there came to them a confused uproar, a tempestuous tumult, a fierce mutter, gusts of screams dying away, and the tramping of feet mingling with the blows of the sea.

For a moment they glared amazed, blocking the doorway. Jukes pushed through them brutally. He said nothing, and simply darted in. Another lot of coolies on the ladder, struggling suicidally to break through the battened hatch to a swamped deck, fell off as before, and he disappeared under them like a man overtaken by a landslide.

The boatswain yelled excitedly: 'Come along. Get the mate out. He'll be trampled to death. Come on.'

They charged in, stamping on breasts, on fingers, on faces, catching their feet in heaps of clothing, kicking broken wood; but before they could get hold of him Jukes emerged waist deep in a multitude of clawing hands. In the instant he had been lost to view, all the buttons of his jacket had gone, its back had got split up to the collar, his waistcoat had been torn open. The central struggling mass of Chinamen went over to the roll, dark, indistinct, helpless, with a wild gleam of many eyes in the dim light of the lamps.

'Leave me alone – damn you. I am all right,' screeched Jukes. 'Drive them forward. Watch your chance when she pitches. Forward with 'em. Drive them against the bulkhead. Jam 'em up.'

The rush of the sailors into the seething 'tween-deck was like a splash of cold water into a boiling cauldron. The commotion sank for a moment.

The bulk of Chinamen were locked in such a compact scrimmage that, linking their arms and aided by an appalling dive of the ship, the seamen sent it forward in one great shove, like a solid block. Behind their backs small clusters and loose bodies tumbled from side to side.

The boatswain performed prodigious feats of strength. With his long arms open, and each great paw clutching at a stanchion, he stopped the rush of seven entwined Chinamen rolling like a boulder. His joints cracked; he said 'Ha!' and they flew apart. But the carpenter showed the greater intelligence. Without saying a word to anybody he went back into the alleyway, to fetch several coils of cargo gear he had seen there – chain and rope. With these life-lines were rigged.

There was really no resistance. The struggle, however it began, had turned into a scramble of blind panic. If the coolies had started up after their scattered dollars they were by that time fighting only for their footing. They took each other by the throat merely to save themselves from being hurled about. Whoever got a hold anywhere would kick at the others who caught at his legs and hung on, till a roll sent them flying together across the deck.

The coming of the white devils was a terror. Had they come to kill? The individuals torn out of the ruck became very limp in the seamen's hands: some, dragged aside by the heels, were passive, like dead bodies, with open, fixed eyes. Here and there a coolie would fall on his knees as if begging for mercy; several, whom the excess of fear made unruly, were hit with hard fists between the eyes, and cowered; while those who were hurt submitted to rough handling, blinking rapidly without a plaint. Faces streamed with blood; there were raw places on the shaven heads, scratches, bruises, torn wounds, gashes. The broken porcelain out of the chests was mostly responsible for the latter. Here and there a Chinaman, wild-eyed, with his tail unplaited, nursed a bleeding sole.

They had been ranged closely, after having been shaken into submission, cuffed a little to allay excitement, addressed in gruff words of encouragement that sounded like promises of evil. They sat on the deck in ghastly, drooping rows, and at the end the carpenter, with two hands to help him, moved busily from place to place, setting taut and hitching the life-lines. The boatswain, with one leg and one arm embracing a stanchion, struggled with a lamp pressed to his breast, trying to get a light, and growling all the time like an industrious gorilla. The figures of seamen stooped repeatedly, with the movements of gleaners, and everything was being flung into the bunker: clothing, smashed wood, broken china, and the dollars, too, gathered up in men's jackets. Now and then a sailor would stagger towards the doorway with his arms full of rubbish; and dolorous, slanting eyes followed his movements.

With every roll of the ship the long rows of sitting Celestials would sway forward brokenly, and her headlong dives knocked together the line of shaven polls from end to end. When the wash of water rolling on the deck died away for a moment, it seemed to Jukes, yet quivering from his exertions, that in his mad struggle down there he had overcome the wind somehow: that a silence had fallen upon the ship, a silence in which the sea struck thunderously at her sides.

Everything had been cleared out of the 'tween-deck – all the wreckage, as the men said. They stood erect and tottering above the level of heads and drooping shoulders. Here and there a coolie sobbed for his breath. Where the high light fell, Jukes could see the salient ribs of one, the yellow, wistful face of another; bowed necks; or would meet a dull stare directed at his face. He was amazed that there had been no corpses; but the lot of them seemed at their last gasp, and they appeared to him more pitiful than if they had been all dead.

Suddenly one of the coolies began to speak. The light came and went on his lean, straining face; he threw his head up like a baying hound. From the bunker came the sounds of knocking and the tinkle of some dollars rolling loose; he stretched out his arm, his mouth yawned black, and the incomprehensible guttural hooting sounds, that did not seem to belong to a human language, penetrated Jukes with a strange emotion as if a brute had tried to be eloquent.

Two more started mouthing what seemed to Jukes fierce denunciations; the others stirred with grunts and growls. Jukes ordered the hands out of the 'tween-decks hurriedly. He left last himself, backing through the door, while the grunts rose to a loud murmur and hands were extended after him as after a malefactor. The boatswain shot the bolt, and remarked uneasily, 'Seems as if the wind had dropped, sir.'

The seamen were glad to get back into the alleyway. Secretly each of them thought that at the last moment he could rush out on deck – and that was a comfort. There is something horribly repugnant in the idea of being drowned under a deck. Now they had done with the Chinamen, they again became conscious of the ship's position.

Jukes on coming out of the alleyway found himself up to the neck in the noisy water. He gained the bridge, and discovered he could detect obscure shapes as if his sight had become prenaturally acute. He saw faint outlines. They recalled not the familiar aspect of the *Nan-Shan*, but something remembered – an old dismantled steamer he had seen years ago rotting on a mudbank. She recalled that wreck.

There was no wind, not a breath, except the faint currents created by the lurches of the ship. The smoke tossed out of the funnel was settling down upon her deck. He breathed it as he passed forward. He felt the deliberate throb of the engines, and heard small sounds that seemed to have survived the great uproar: the knocking of broken fittings, the rapid tumbling of some piece of wreckage on the bridge. He perceived dimly the squat shape of his captain holding on to a twisted bridge-rail, motionless and swaying as if rooted to the planks. The unexpected stillness of the air oppressed Jukes.

'We have done it, sir,' he gasped.

'Thought you would,' said Captain MacWhirr.

'Did you?' murmured Jukes to himself.

'Wind fell all at once,' went on the Captain.

Jukes burst out: 'If you think it was an easy job —'

But his captain, clinging to the rail, paid no attention. 'According to the books the worst is not over yet.'

'If most of them hadn't been half dead with sea-sickness and fright, not one of us would have come out of that 'tween-deck alive,' said Jukes.

'Had to do what's fair by them,' mumbled MacWhirr, stolidly. 'You don't find everything in books.'

'Why, I believe they would have risen on us if I hadn't ordered the hands out of that pretty quick,' continued Jukes with warmth.

After the whisper of their shouts, their ordinary tones, so distinct, rang out very loud to their ears in the amazing stillness of the air. It seemed to them they were talking in a dark and echoing vault.

Through a jagged aperture in the dome of clouds the light of a few stars fell upon the black sea, rising and falling confusedly. Sometimes the head of a watery cone would topple on board and mingle with the rolling flurry of foam on the swamped deck; and the *Nan-Shan* wallowed heavily at the bottom of a circular cistern of clouds. This ring of dense vapours, gyrating madly round the calm of the centre, encompassed the ship like a motionless and unbroken wall of an aspect inconceivably sinister. Within, the sea, as if agitated by an internal commotion, leaped in peaked mounds that jostled each other, slapping heavily against her sides; and a low moaning sound, the infinite plaint of the storm's fury, came from beyond the limits of the menacing calm. Captain MacWhirr remained silent, and Jukes's ready ear caught suddenly the faint, long-drawn roar of some immense wave rushing unseen under that thick blackness, which made the appalling boundary of his vision.

'Of course,' he started resentfully, 'they thought we had caught at the chance to plunder them. Of course! You said – pick up the money. Easier said than done. They couldn't tell what was in our heads. We came in, smash – right into the middle of them. Had to do it by a rush.'

'As long as it's done . . .' mumbled the Captain, without attempting to look at Jukes. 'Had to do what's fair.'

'We shall find yet there's the devil to pay when this is over,' said Jukes, feeling very sore. 'Let them only recover a bit, and you'll see. They will fly at our throats, sir. Don't forget sir, she isn't a British ship now. These brutes know it well, too. The damned Siamese flag.'

'We are on board, all the same,' remarked Captain MacWhirr.

'The trouble's not over yet,' insisted Jukes, prophetically, reeling and catching on. 'She's a wreck,' he added, faintly.

'The trouble's not over yet,' assented Captain MacWhirr, half aloud . . . 'Look out for her a minute.'

'Are you going off the deck, sir?' asked Jukes, hurriedly, as if the storm were sure to pounce upon him as soon as he had been left alone with the ship.

He watched her, battered and solitary, labouring heavily in a wild scene of mountainous black waters lit by the gleams of distant worlds. She moved slowly, breathing into the still core of the hurricane the excess of her strength in a white cloud of steam – and the deep-toned vibration of the escape was like the defiant trumpeting of a living creature of the sea impatient for the renewal of the contest. It ceased suddenly. The still air moaned. Above Jukes's head a few stars shone into a pit of black vapours. The inky edge of the cloud-disc frowned upon the ship under the patch of glittering sky. The stars, too, seemed to look at her intently, as if for the last time, and the cluster of their splendour sat like a diadem on a lowering brow.

Captain MacWhirr had gone into the chart-room. There was no light there; but he could feel the disorder of that place where he used to live tidily. His armchair was upset. The books had tumbled out on the floor: he scrunched a piece of glass under his boot. He groped for the matches, and found a box on a shelf with a deep ledge. He struck one and, puckering the corners of his eyes, held out the little flame towards the barometer whose glittering top of glass and metals nodded at him continuously.

It stood very low – incredibly low, so low that Captain MacWhirr grunted. The match went out, and hurriedly he extracted another, with thick, stiff fingers.

Again a little flame flared up before the nodding glass and metal of the top. His eyes looked at it narrowed with attention, as if expecting an imperceptible sign. With his grave face he resembled a booted and misshapen pagan burning incense before the oracle of a Joss. There was no mistake. It was the lowest reading he had ever seen in his life.

Captain MacWhirr emitted a low whistle. He forgot himself till the flame diminished to a blue spark, burnt his fingers, and vanished. Perhaps something had gone wrong with the thing!

There was an aneroid glass screwed above the couch. He turned that way, struck another match, and discovered the white face of the other instrument looking at him from the bulkhead, meaningly, not to be gainsaid, as though the wisdom of men were made unerring by the indifference of matter. There was no room for doubt now. Captain MacWhirr pshawed at it, and threw the match down.

The worst was to come, then – and if the books were right this worst would be very bad. The experience of the last six hours had enlarged his conception of what heavy weather could be like. 'It'll be terrific,' he pronounced, mentally. He had not consciously looked at anything by the light of the matches except at the barometer; and yet somehow he had seen that his water-bottle and the two tumblers had been flung out of their stand. It seemed to give him a more intimate knowledge of the tossing the ship had gone through. 'I wouldn't have believed it,' he thought. And his table had been cleared, too; his rulers, his pencils, the inkstand – all the things that had their safe appointed places – they were gone, as if a mischievous hand had plucked them out one by one and flung them on the wet floor. The hurricane had broken in upon the orderly arrangements of his privacy. This had never happened before, and the feeling of dismay reached the very seat of his composure. And the worst was to come yet! He was glad the trouble in the 'tween-deck had been discovered in time. If the ship had to go after all, then, at least, she wouldn't be going to the bottom with a lot of people in her fighting teeth and claw. That would have been odious. And in that feeling there was a humane intention and a vague sense of the fitness of things.

These instantaneous thoughts were yet in their essence heavy and slow, partaking of the nature of the man. He extended his hand to put back the matchbox in its corner of the shelf. There were always matches there – by his order. The steward had his instructions impressed upon him long before. 'A box . . . just there, see? Not so very full . . . where I can put my hand on it, steward. Might want a light in a hurry. Can't tell on board ship *what* you might want in a hurry. Mind, now.'

And of course on his side he would be careful to put it back in its place scrupulously. He did so now, but before he removed his hand it occurred to him that perhaps he would never have occasion to use that box any more. The vividness of the thought checked him and for an infinitesimal fraction of a second his fingers closed again on the small object as though it had been the symbol of all these little habits that chain us to the weary round of life. He released it at last, and letting himself fall on the settee, listened for the first sounds of returning wind.

Not yet. He heard only the wash of water, the heavy splashes, the dull shocks of the confused seas boarding his ship from all sides. She would never have a chance to clear her decks.

But the quietude of the air was startlingly tense and unsafe, like a slender hair holding a sword suspended over his head. By this awful pause the storm penetrated the defences of the man and unsealed his lips. He spoke out in the solitude and the pitch darkness of the cabin, as if addressing another being awakened within his breast.

'I shouldn't like to lose her,' he said half aloud.

He sat unseen, apart from the sea, from his ship, isolated, as if withdrawn from the very current of his own existence, where such freaks as talking to himself surely had no place. His palms reposed on his knees, he bowed his short neck and puffed heavily, surrendering to a strange sensation of weariness he was not enlightened enough to recognize for the fatigue of mental stress.

From where he sat he could reach the door of a washstand locker. There should have been a towel there. There was. Good . . . He took it out, wiped his face, and afterwards went on rubbing his wet head. He towelled himself with energy in the dark, and then remained motionless with the towel on his knees. A moment passed, of a stillness so profound that no one could have guessed there was a man sitting in that cabin. Then a murmur arose.

'She may come out of it, yet.'

When Captain MacWhirr came out on deck, which he did brusquely, as though he had suddenly become conscious of having stayed away too long, the calm had lasted already more than fifteen minutes – long enough to make itself intolerable even to his imagination. Jukes, motionless on the forepart of the bridge, began to speak at once. His voice, blank and forced as though he were talking through hard-set teeth, seemed to flow away on all sides into the darkness, deepening again upon the sea.

'I had the wheel relieved. Hackett began to sing out that he was done. He's lying in there alongside the steering-gear with a face like death. At first I couldn't get anybody to crawl out and relieve the poor devil. That bos'n's worse than no good, I always said. Thought I would have had to go myself and haul out one of them by the neck.'

'Ah, well,' muttered the Captain. He stood watchful by Jukes's side.

'The second mate's in there, too, holding his head. Is he hurt, sir?'

'No – crazy,' said Captain MacWhirr, curtly.

'Looks as if he had a tumble, though.'

'I had to give him a push,' explained the Captain.

Jukes gave an impatient sigh.

'It will come very sudden,' said Captain MacWhirr, 'and from over there, I fancy. God only knows though. These books are only good to muddle your head and make you jumpy. It will be bad, and there's an end. If we only can steam her round in time to meet it . . .'

A minute passed. Some of the stars winked rapidly and vanished.

'You left them pretty safe?' began the Captain abruptly, as though the silence were unbearable.

'Are you thinking of the coolies, sir? I rigged lifelines all ways across that 'tween-deck.'

'Did you? Good idea, Mr Jukes.'

'I didn't . . . think you cared to . . . know,' said Jukes – the lurching of the ship cut his speech as though somebody had been jerking him around while he talked – 'how I got on with . . . that infernal job. We did it. And it may not matter in the end.'

'Had to do what's fair, for all – they are only Chinamen. Give them the same chance with ourselves – hang it all. She isn't lost yet. Bad enough to be shut up below in a gale —'

'That's what I thought when you gave me the job, sir,' interjected Jukes, moodily.

'– without being battered to pieces,' pursued Captain MacWhirr with rising vehemence. 'Couldn't let that go on in my ship, if I knew she hadn't five minutes to live. Couldn't bear it, Mr Jukes.'

A hollow echoing noise, like that of a shout rolling in a rocky chasm, approached the ship and went away again. The last star, blurred, enlarged, as if returning to the fiery mist of its beginning, struggled with the colossal depth of blackness hanging over the ship – and went out.

'Now for it!' muttered Captain MacWhirr. 'Mr Jukes.'

'Here, sir.'

The two men were growing indistinct to each other.

'We must trust her to go through it and come out on the other side. That's plain and straight. There's no room for Captain Wilson's storm-strategy here.'

'No, sir.'

'She will be smothered and swept again for hours,' mumbled the Captain. 'There's not much left by this time above deck for the sea to take away – unless you or me.'

'Both, sir,' whispered Jukes, breathlessly.

'You are always meeting trouble half-way, Jukes,' Captain MacWhirr remonstrated quaintly. 'Though it's a fact that the second mate is no good. D'ye hear, Mr Jukes? You would be left alone if . . .'

Captain MacWhirr interrupted himself, and Jukes, glancing on all sides, remained silent.

'Don't you be put out by anything,' the Captain continued, mumbling rather fast. 'Keep her facing it. They may say what they like, but the heaviest seas run with the wind. Facing it – always facing it – that's the way to get through. You are a young sailor. Face it. That's enough for any man. Keep a cool head.'

'Yes, sir,' said Jukes, with a flutter of the heart.

In the next few seconds the Captain spoke to the engine-room and got an answer.

For some reason Jukes experienced an access of confidence, a sensation that came from outside like a warm breath, and made him feel equal to every demand. The distant muttering of the darkness stole into his ears. He noted it unmoved, out of that sudden belief in himself, as a man safe in a shirt of mail would watch a point.

The ship laboured without intermission amongst the black hills of water, paying with this hard tumbling the price of her life. She rumbled in her depths, shaking a white plummet of steam into the night, and Jukes's thought skimmed like a bird through the engine-room, where Mr Rout – good man – was ready. When the rumbling ceased it seemed to him that there was a pause of every sound, a dead pause in which Captain MacWhirr's voice rang out startlingly.

'What's that? A puff of wind?' – it spoke much louder than Jukes had ever heard it before – 'On the bow. That's right. She may come out of it yet.'

The mutter of the winds drew near apace. In the forefront could be distinguished a drowsy waking plaint passing on, and far off the growth of a multiple clamour, marching and expanding. There was the throb as of many drums in it, a vicious rushing note, and like the chant of a tramping multitude.

Jukes could no longer see his captain distinctly. The darkness was absolutely piling itself upon the ship. At most he made out movements, a hint of elbows spread out, of a head thrown up.

Captain MacWhirr was trying to do up the top button of his oilskin coat with unwonted haste. The hurricane, with its power to madden the seas, to sink ships, to uproot trees, to overturn strong walls and dash the very birds of the air to the ground, had found this taciturn man in its path, and, doing its utmost, had managed to wring out a few words. Before the renewed wrath of winds swooped on his ship, Captain MacWhirr was moved to declare, in a tone of vexation, as it were: 'I wouldn't like to lose her.'

He was spared that annoyance.

CHAPTER 6

On a bright sunshiny day, with the breeze chasing her smoke far ahead, the *Nan-Shan* came into Fu-chau. Her arrival was at once noticed on shore, and the seamen in harbour said: 'Look! Look at that steamer. What's that? Siamese – isn't she? Just look at her!'

She seemed, indeed, to have been used as a running target for the secondary batteries of a cruiser. A hail of minor shells could not have given her upper works a more broken, torn, and devastated aspect: and she had about her the worn, weary air of ships coming from the far ends of the world – and indeed with truth, for in her short passage she had been very far; sighting, verily, even the coast of the Great Beyond, whence no ship ever returns to give up her crew to the dust of the earth. She was incrusted and grey with salt to the trucks of her masts and to the top of her funnel; as though (as some facetious seaman said) 'the crowd on board had fished her out somewhere from the bottom of the sea and brought her in here for salvage'. And further, excited by the felicity of his own wit, he offered to give five pounds for her – 'as she stands'.

Before she had been quite an hour at rest, a meagre little man, with a red-tipped nose and a face cast in an angry mould, landed from a sampan on the quay of the Foreign Concession, and incontinently turned to shake his fist at her.

A tall individual, with legs much too thin for a rotund stomach, and with watery eyes, strolled up and remarked, 'Just left her – eh? Quick work.'

He wore a soiled suit of blue flannel with a pair of dirty cricketing shoes; a dingy grey moustache drooped from his lip, and daylight could be seen in two places between the rim and the crown of his hat.

'Hallo! what are you doing here?' asked the ex second mate of the *Nan-Shan*, shaking hands hurriedly.

'Standing by for a job – chance worth taking – got a quiet hint,' explained the man with the broken hat, in jerky, apathetic wheezes.

The second shook his fist again at the *Nan-Shan*. 'There's a fellow there that ain't fit to have the command of a scow,' he declared, quivering with passion, while the other looked about listlessly.

'Is there?'

But he caught sight on the quay of a heavy seaman's chest, painted brown under a fringed sailcloth cover, and lashed with new manila line. He eyed it with awakened interest.

'I would talk and raise trouble if it wasn't for that damned Siamese flag. Nobody to go to – or I would make it hot for him. The fraud! Told his chief engineer – that's another fraud for you – I had lost my nerve. The greatest lot of ignorant fools that ever sailed the seas. No! You can't think ...'

'Got your money all right?' inquired his seedy acquaintance suddenly.

'Yes. Paid me off on board,' raged the second mate. ' "Get your breakfast on shore," says he.'

'Mean skunk!' commented the tall man, vaguely, and passed his tongue on his lips. 'What about having a drink of some sort?'

'He struck me,' hissed the second mate.

'No! Struck! You don't say?' The man in blue began to bustle about sympathetically. 'Can't possibly talk here. I want to know all about it. Struck – eh? Let's get a fellow to carry your chest. I know a quiet place where they have some bottled beer . . .'

Mr Jukes, who had been scanning the shore through a pair of glasses, informed the chief engineer afterwards that 'our late second mate hasn't been long in finding a friend. A chap looking uncommonly like a bummer. I saw them walk away together from the quay.'

The hammering and banging of the needful repairs did not disturb Captain MacWhirr. The steward found in the letter he wrote, in a tidy chart-room, passages of such absorbing interest that twice he was nearly caught in the act. But Mrs MacWhirr, in the drawing-room of the forty-pound house, stifled a yawn – perhaps out of self-respect – for she was alone.

She reclined in a plush-bottomed and gilt hammock-chair near a tiled fireplace, with Japanese fans on the mantel and a glow of coals in the grate. Lifting her hands, she glanced wearily here and there into the many pages. It was not her fault they were so prosy, so completely uninteresting – from 'My darling wife' at the beginning, to 'Your loving husband' at the end. She couldn't be really expected to understand all these ship affairs. She was glad, of course, to hear from him, but she had never asked herself why, precisely.

. . . They are called typhoons . . . The mate did not seem to like it . . . Not in books . . . Couldn't think of letting it go on . . .

The paper rustled sharply. '. . . A calm that lasted more than twenty minutes,' she read perfunctorily; and the next words her thoughtless eyes caught, on the top of another page, were: 'see you and the children again . . .'. She had a movement of impatience. He was always thinking of coming home. He had never had such a good salary before. What was the matter now?

It did not occur to her to turn back overleaf to look. She would have found it recorded there that between 4 and 6 a.m. on 25 December Captain MacWhirr did actually think that his ship could not possibly live another hour in such a sea, and that he would never see his wife and children again. Nobody was to know this (his letters got mislaid so quickly) – nobody whatever but the steward, who had been greatly impressed by that disclosure. So much so, that he tried to give the cook some idea of the 'narrow squeak we all had' by saying solemnly, 'The old man himself had a damn poor opinion of our chance.'

'How do you know?' asked, contemptuously, the cook, an old soldier. 'He hasn't told you, maybe?'

'Well, he did give me a hint to that effect,' the steward brazened it out.

'Get along with you! He will be coming to tell *me* next,' jeered the old cook, over his shoulder.

Mrs MacWhirr glanced farther, on the alert.

... Do what's fair ... Miserable objects ... Only three, with a broken leg each, and one ... Thought had better keep the matter quiet ... hope to have done the fair thing ...

She let fall her hands. No: there was nothing more about coming home. Must have been merely expressing a pious wish. Mrs MacWhirr's mind was set at ease, and a black marble clock, priced by the local jeweller at £3 18s. 6d., had a discreet stealthy tick.

The door flew open, and a girl in the long-legged, short-frocked period of existence, flung into the room. A lot of colourless, rather lanky hair was scattered over her shoulders. Seeing her mother, she stood still, and directed her pale prying eyes upon the letter.

'From father,' murmured Mrs MacWhirr. 'What have you done with your ribbon?'

The girl put her hands up to her head and pouted.

'He's well,' continued Mrs MacWhirr, languidly. 'At least I think so. He never says.' She had a little laugh. The girl's face expressed a wandering indifference, and Mrs MacWhirr surveyed her with fond pride.

'Go and get your hat,' she said after a while. 'I am going out to do some shopping. There is a sale at Linom's.'

'Oh, how jolly!' uttered the child, impressively, in unexpectedly grave vibrating tones, and bounded out of the room.

It was a fine afternoon, with a grey sky and dry sidewalks. Outside the draper's Mrs MacWhirr smiled upon a woman in a black mantle of generous proportions armoured in jet and crowned with flowers blooming falsely above a bilious matronly countenance. They broke into a swift little babble of greetings and exclamations both together, very hurried, as if the street were ready to yawn open and swallow all that pleasure before it could be expressed.

Behind them the high glass doors were kept on the swing. People couldn't pass, men stood aside waiting patiently, and Lydia was absorbed in poking the end of her parasol between the stone flags. Mrs MacWhirr talked rapidly.

'Thank you very much. He's not coming home yet. Of course it's very sad to have him away, but it's such a comfort to know he keeps so well.' Mrs MacWhirr drew breath. 'The climate there agrees with him,' she added, beamingly, as if poor MacWhirr had been away touring in China for the sake of his health.

Neither was the chief engineer coming home yet. Mr Rout knew too well the value of a good billet.

'Solomon says wonders will never cease,' cried Mrs Rout joyously at the old lady in her armchair by the fire. Mr Rout's mother moved slightly, her withered hands lying in black halfmittens on her lap.

The eyes of the engineer's wife fairly danced on the paper. 'That captain of the ship he is in – a rather simple man, you remember, mother? – has done something rather clever, Solomon says.'

'Yes, my dear,' said the old woman meekly, sitting with bowed silvery head, and that air of inward stillness characteristic of very old people who seem lost in watching the last flickers of life. 'I think I remember.'

Solomon Rout, Old Sol, Father Sol, the Chief, 'Rout, good man' – Mr Rout, the condescending and paternal friend of youth, had been the baby of her many children – all dead by this time. And she remembered him best as a boy of ten – long before he went away to serve his apprenticeship in some great engineering works in the North. She had seen so little of him since, she had gone through so many years, that she had now to retrace her steps very far back to recognize him plainly in the mist of time. Sometimes it seemed that her daughter-in-law was talking of some strange man.

Mrs Rout junior was disappointed. 'H'm. H'm.' She turned the page. 'How provoking! He doesn't say what it is. Says I couldn't understand how much there was in it. Fancy! What could it be so very clever? What a wretched man not to tell us!'

She read on without further remark soberly, and at last sat looking into the fire. The chief wrote just a word or two of the typhoon; but something had moved him to express an increased longing for the companionship of the jolly woman.

If it hadn't been that mother must be looked after, I would send you your passage-money today. You could set up a small house out here. I would have a chance to see you sometimes then. We are not growing younger . . .

'He's well, mother,' sighed Mrs Rout, rousing herself.

'He always was a strong healthy boy,' said the old woman, placidly.

But Mr Jukes's account was really animated and very full. His friend in the Western Ocean trade imparted it freely to the other officers of his liner. 'A chap I know writes to me about an extraordinary affair that happened on board his ship in that typhoon – you know – that we read of in the papers two months ago. It's the funniest thing! Just see for yourself what he says. I'll show you his letter.'

There were phrases in it calculated to give the impression of light-hearted, indomitable resolution. Jukes had written them in good faith, for he felt thus when he wrote. He described with lurid effect the scenes in the 'tween-deck.

. . . It struck me in a flash that those confounded Chinamen couldn't tell we weren't a desperate kind of robbers. 'Tisn't good to part the Chinaman from his money if he is the stronger party. We need have been desperate indeed to go thieving in such weather, but what could these beggars know of us? So, without thinking of it twice, I got the hands away in a jiffy. Our work was done – that the old man had set his heart on. We cleared out without staying to inquire how they felt. I am convinced that if they had not been so unmercifully shaken, and afraid – each individual one of them – to stand up, we would have been torn to pieces. Oh! It was pretty complete,

I can tell you; and you may run to and fro across the Pond to the end of time before you find yourself with such a job on your hands.

After this he alluded professionally to the damage done to the ship, and went on thus:

It was when the weather quietened down that the situation became confoundedly delicate. It wasn't made any better by us having been lately transferred to the Siamese flag; though the skipper can't see that it makes any difference – 'as long as *we* are on board' – he says. There are feelings that this man simply hasn't got – and there's an end of it. You might just as well try to make a bedpost understand. But apart from this it is an infernally lonely state for a ship to be going about the China seas with no proper consuls, not even a gunboat of her own anywhere, nor a body to go to in case of some trouble.

My notion was to keep these Johnnies under hatches for another fifteen hours or so; as we weren't much farther than that from Fu-chau. We would find there, most likely, some sort of a man-of-war, and once under her guns we were safe enough; for surely any skipper of a man-of-war – English, French, or Dutch – would see white men through as far as row on board goes. We could get rid of them and their money afterwards by delivering them to their Mandarin or Taotai, or whatever they call these chaps in goggles you see being carried about in sedan-chairs through their stinking streets.

The old man wouldn't see it somehow. He wanted to keep the matter quiet. He got that notion into his head, and a steam windlass couldn't drag it out of him. He wanted as little fuss made as possible, for the sake of the ship's name and for the sake of the owners – 'for the sake of all concerned', says he, looking at me very hard. It made me angry hot. Of course you couldn't keep a thing like that quiet; but the chests had been secured in the usual manner and were safe enough for any earthly gale, while this had been an altogether fiendish business I couldn't give you even an idea of.

Meantime, I could hardly keep on my feet. None of us had a spell of any sort for nearly thirty hours, and there the old man sat rubbing his chin, rubbing the top of his head, and so bothered he didn't even think of pulling his long boots off.

'I hope, sir,' says I, 'you won't be letting them out on deck before we make ready for them in some shape or other.' Not, mind you, that I felt very sanguine about controlling these beggars if they meant to take charge. A trouble with a cargo of Chinamen is no child's play. I was damn tired, too. 'I wish,' said I, 'you would let us throw the whole lot of these dollars down to them and leave them to fight it out amongst themselves, while we get a rest.'

'Now you talk wild, Jukes,' says he, looking up in his slow way that makes you ache all over, somehow. 'We must plan out something that would be fair to all parties.'

I had no end of work on hand, as you may imagine, so I set the hands going, and then I thought I would turn in a bit. I hadn't been asleep in my bunk ten minutes when in rushes the steward and begins to pull at my leg.

'For God's sake, Mr Jukes, come out! Come on deck quick, sir. Oh, do come out!'

The fellow scared all the sense out of me. I didn't know what had happened: another hurricane – or what. Could hear no wind.

'The Captain's letting them out. Oh, he is letting them out! Jump on deck, sir, and save us. The chief engineer has just run below for his revolver.'

That's what I understood the fool to say. However, Father Rout swears he went in there only to get a clean pocket-handkerchief. Anyhow, I made one jump into my trousers and flew on deck aft. There was certainly a good deal of noise going on forward of the bridge. Four of the hands with the bos'n were at work abaft. I passed up to them some of the rifles all the ships on the China coast carry in the cabin, and led them on the bridge. On the way I ran against Old Sol, looking startled and sucking at an unlighted cigar.

'Come along,' I shouted to him.

We charged, the seven of us, up to the chart-room. All was over. There stood the old man with his sea-boots still drawn up to the hips and in shirt-sleeves – got warm thinking it out, I suppose. Bun-hin's dandy clerk at his elbow, as dirty as a sweep, was still green in the face. I could see directly I was in for something.

'What the devil are these monkey tricks, Mr Jukes?' asks the old man, as angry as ever he could be. I tell you frankly it made me lose my tongue. 'For God's sake, Mr Jukes,' says he, 'do take away these rifles from the men. Somebody's sure to get hurt before long if you don't. Damme, if this ship isn't worse than Bedlam! Look sharp now. I want you up here to help me and Bun-hin's Chinaman to count that money. You wouldn't mind lending a hand, too, Mr Rout, now you are here. The more of us the better.'

He had settled it all in his mind while I was having a snooze. Had we been an English ship, or only going to land our cargo of coolies in an English port, like Hong Kong, for instance, there would have been no end of inquiries and bother, claims for damages, and so on. But these Chinamen know their officials better than we do.

The hatches had been taken off already, and they were all on deck after a night and a day down below. It made you feel queer to see so many gaunt, wild faces together. The beggars stared about at the sky, at the sea, at the ship, as though they had expected the whole thing to have been blown to pieces. And no wonder! They had had a doing that would have shaken the soul out of a white man. But then they say a Chinaman has no soul. He has, though, something about him that is deuced tough. There was a fellow (amongst others of the badly hurt) who had had his eye all but knocked out. It stood out of his head the size of half a hen's egg. This would have laid out a white man on his back for a month: and yet there was that chap elbowing here and there in the crowd and talking to the others as if nothing had been the matter. They made a great hubbub amongst themselves, and whenever the old man showed his bald head on the foreside of the bridge, they would all leave off jawing and look at him from below.

It seems that after he had done his thinking he made that Bun-hin's fellow go down and explain to them the only way they could get their money back. He told me afterwards that, all the coolies having worked in the same place and for the same length of time, he reckoned he would be doing the fair thing by them as near as possible if he shared all the cash we had picked up equally among the lot. You couldn't tell one man's dollars from another's, he said, and if you asked each man how much money he brought on board he was afraid they would lie, and he would find himself a long way short. I think he was right there. As to giving up the money to any Chinese official he could scare up in Fu-chau, he said he might just as well put the lot in his own pocket at once for all the good it would be to them. I suppose they thought so, too.

We finished the distribution before dark. It was rather a sight: the sea running high, the ship a wreck to look at, these Chinamen staggering up on the bridge one by one for their share, and the old man still booted, and in his shirt-sleeves, busy paying out at the chart-room door, perspiring like anything, and now and then coming down sharp on myself or Father Rout about one thing or another not quite to his mind. He took the share of those who were disabled himself to them on the

No. 2 hatch. There were three dollars left over, and these went to the three most damaged coolies, one to each. We turned-to afterwards, and shovelled out on deck heaps of wet rags, all sorts of fragments of things without shape, and that you couldn't give a name to, and let them settle the ownership themselves.

This certainly is coming as near as can be to keeping the thing quiet for the benefit of all concerned. What's your opinion, you pampered mail-boat swell? The old chief says that this was plainly the only thing that could be done. The skipper remarked to me the other day, 'There are things you find nothing about in books.' I think that he got out of it very well for such a stupid man.

NOSTROMO

A Tale of
the Seaboard

AUTHOR'S NOTE

Nostromo is the most anxiously meditated of the longer novels which belong to the period following upon the publication of the *Typhoon* volume of short stories.

I don't mean to say that I became then conscious of any impending change in my mentality and in my attitude toward the tasks of my writing life. And perhaps there was never any change, except in that mysterious, extraneous thing which has nothing to do with the theories of art; a subtle change in the nature of the inspiration; a phenomenon for which I can not in any way be held responsible. What, however, did cause me some concern was that after finishing the last story of the *Typhoon* volume it seemed somehow that there was nothing more in the world to write about.

This so strangely negative but disturbing mood lasted some little time; and then, as with many of my longer stories, the first hint for *Nostromo* came to me in the shape of a vagrant anecdote completely destitute of valuable details.

As a matter of fact in 1875 or '76, when very young, in the West Indies or rather in the Gulf of Mexico, for my contacts with land were short, few, and fleeting, I heard the story of some man who was supposed to have stolen single-handed a whole lighterful of silver, somewhere on the Tierra Firme seaboard during the troubles of a revolution.

On the face of it this was something of a feat. But I heard no details, and having no particular interest in crime *qua* crime I was not likely to keep that one in my mind. And I forgot it till twenty-six or -seven years afterwards I came upon the very thing in a shabby volume picked up outside a second-hand bookshop. It was the life story of an American seaman written by himself with the assistance of a journalist. In the course of his wanderings that American sailor worked for some months on board a schooner, the master and owner of which was the thief of whom I had heard in my very young days. I have no doubt of that because there could hardly have been two exploits of that peculiar kind in the same part of the world and both connected with a South American revolution.

The fellow had actually managed to steal a lighter with silver, and this, it seems, only because he was implicitly trusted by his employers who must have been singularly poor judges of character. In the sailor's story he is represented as an unmitigated rascal, a small cheat, stupidly ferocious, morose, of mean appearance, and altogether unworthy of the greatness this opportunity had thrust upon him. What was interesting was that he would boast of it openly.

He used to say: 'People think I make a lot of money in this schooner of mine. But that is nothing. I don't care for that. Now and then I go away quietly and lift a bar of silver. I must get rich slowly – you understand.'

There was also another curious point about the man. Once in the course of some quarrel the sailor threatened him: 'What's to prevent me reporting ashore what you have told me about that silver?'

The cynical ruffian was not alarmed in the least. He actually laughed. 'You fool, if you dare talk like that on shore about me you will get a knife stuck in your back. Every man, woman, and child in that port is my friend. And who's to prove the lighter wasn't sunk? I didn't show you where the silver is hidden. Did I? So you know nothing. And suppose I lied? Eh?'

Ultimately the sailor, disgusted with the sordid meanness of that impenitent thief, deserted from the schooner. The whole episode takes about three pages of his autobiography. Nothing to speak of; but as I looked them over, the curious confirmation of the few casual words heard in my early youth evoked the memories of that distant time when everything was so fresh, so surprising, so venturesome, so interesting; bits of strange coasts under the stars, shadows of hills in the sunshine, men's passions in the dusk, gossip half-forgotten, faces grown dim. . . . Perhaps, perhaps, there still was in the world something to write about. Yet I did not see anything at first in the mere story. A rascal steals a large parcel of a valuable commodity – so people say. It's either true or untrue; and in any case it has no value in itself. To invent a circumstantial account of the robbery did not appeal to me, because my talents not running that way I did not think that the game was worth the candle. It was only when it dawned upon me that the purloiner of the treasure need not necessarily be a confirmed rogue, that he could be even a man of character, an actor, and possibly a victim in the changing scenes of a revolution, it was only then that I had the first vision of a twilight country which was to become the province of Sulaco, with its high shadowy Sierra and its misty Campo for mute witnesses of events flowing from the passions of men short-sighted in good and evil.

Such are in very truth the obscure origins of *Nostromo* – the book. From that moment, I suppose, it had to be. Yet even then I hesitated, as if warned by the instinct of self-preservation from venturing on a distant and toilsome journey into a land full of intrigues and revolutions. But it had to be done.

It took the best part of the years 1903–4 to do; with many intervals of renewed hesitation, lest I should lose myself in the ever-enlarging vistas opening before me as I progressed deeper in my knowledge of the country. Often, also, when I had thought myself to a standstill over the tangled-up affairs of the Republic, I would, figuratively speaking, pack my bag, rush away from Sulaco for a change of air, and write a few pages of *The Mirror of the Sea*. But generally, as I've said before, my sojourn on the continent of Latin America, famed for its hospitality, lasted for about two years. On my return I found (speaking somewhat in the style of Captain Gulliver) my family all well, my wife heartily glad to learn that the fuss was all over, and our small boy considerably grown during my absence.

My principal authority for the history of Costaguana is, of course, my venerated friend, the late Don José Avellanos, Minister to the Courts of England and Spain, etc., etc., in his impartial and eloquent *History of Fifty Years of Misrule*. That work was never published – the reader will discover why – and I am in fact the only person in the world possessed of its contents. I have mastered them in not a few hours of earnest meditation, and I hope that my accuracy will be trusted. In justice to myself, and to allay the fears of prospective readers, I beg to point out that the few historical allusions are never dragged in for the sake of parading my unique erudition, but that each of them is closely related to actuality; either throwing a light on the nature of current events or affecting directly the fortunes of the people of whom I speak.

As to their own histories I have tried to set them down, Aristocracy and People, men and women, Latin and Anglo-Saxon, bandit and politician, with as cool a hand as was possible in the heat and clash of my own conflicting emotions. And after all this is also the story of their conflicts. It is for the reader to say how far they are deserving of interest in their actions and in the secret purposes of their hearts revealed in the bitter necessities of the time. I confess that, for me, that time is the time of firm friendships and unforgotten hospitalities. And in my gratitude I must mention here Mrs Gould, 'the first lady of Sulaco', whom we may safely leave to the secret devotion of Dr Monygham, and Charles Gould, the Idealist-creator of Material Interests whom we must leave to his Mine – from which there is no escape in this world.

About Nostromo, the second of the two racially and socially contrasted men, both captured by the silver of the San Tomé Mine, I feel bound to say something more.

I did not hesitate to make that central figure an Italian. First of all the thing is perfectly credible: Italians were swarming into the Occidental Province at the time, as anybody who will read further can see; and secondly, there was no one who could stand so well by the side of Giorgio Viola, the Garibaldino, the Idealist of the old, humanitarian revolutions. For myself I needed there a man of the People as free as possible from his class-conventions and all settled modes of thinking. This is not a side-snarl at conventions. My reasons were not moral but artistic. Had he been an Anglo-Saxon he would have tried to get into local politics. But Nostromo does not aspire to be a leader in a personal game. He does not want to raise himself above the mass. He is content to feel himself a power – within the People.

But mainly Nostromo is what he is because I received the inspiration for him in my early days from a Mediterranean sailor. Those who have read certain pages of mine will see at once what I mean when I say that Dominic, the *padrone* of the *Tremolino*, might under given circumstances have been a Nostromo. At any rate Dominic would have understood the younger man perfectly – if scornfully. He and I were engaged together in a rather absurd adventure, but the absurdity does not matter. It is a real satisfaction to think that in my very young days there must, after all, have been something in me worthy to command that man's half-bitter fidelity, his half-ironic devotion. Many of Nostromo's speeches I have heard first in Dominic's voice. His hand on the tiller and his fearless eyes roaming the horizon from within the monkish hood shadowing his face, he would utter the usual exordium of his remorseless wisdom: '*Vous autres gentilhommes!*' in a caustic tone that hangs on my ear yet. Like Nostromo! 'You *hombres finos!*' Very much like

Nostromo. But Dominic the Corsican nursed a certain pride of ancestry from which my Nostromo is free; for Nostromo's lineage had to be more ancient still. He is a man with the weight of countless generations behind him and no parentage to boast of ... Like the People.

In his firm grip on the earth he inherits, in his improvidence and generosity, in his lavishness with his gifts, in his manly vanity, in the obscure sense of his greatness, and in his faithful devotion with something despairing as well as desperate in its impulses, he is a Man of the People, their very own unenvious force, disdaining to lead but ruling from within. Years afterwards, grown older as the famous Captain Fidanza, with a stake in the country, going about his many affairs followed by respectful glances in the modernized streets of Sulaco, calling on the widow of the *cargador*, attending the Lodge, listening in unmoved silence to anarchist speeches at the meeting, the enigmatical patron of the new revolutionary agitation, the trusted, the wealthy comrade Fidanza with the knowledge of his moral ruin locked up in his breast, he remains essentially a man of the People. In his mingled love and scorn of life and in the bewildered conviction of having been betrayed, of dying betrayed he hardly knows by what or by whom, he is still of the People, their undoubted Great Man – with a private history of his own.

One more figure of those stirring times I would like to mention: and that is Antonia Avellanos – the 'beautiful Antonia'. Whether she is a possible variation of Latin-American girlhood I wouldn't dare to affirm. But, for me, she *is*. Always a little in the background by the side of her father (my venerated friend) I hope she has yet relief enough to make intelligible what I am going to say. Of all the people who had seen with me the birth of the Occidental Republic, she is the only one who has kept in my memory the aspect of continued life. Antonia the Aristocrat and Nostromo the Man of the People are the artisans of the New Era, the true creators of the New State; he by his legendary and daring feat, she, like a woman, simply by the force of what she is: the only being capable of inspiring a sincere passion in the heart of a trifler.

If anything could induce me to revisit Sulaco (I should hate to see all these changes) it would be Antonia. And the true reason for that – why not be frank about it? – the true reason is that I have modelled her on my first love. How we, a band of tallish schoolboys, the chums of her two brothers, how we used to look up to that girl just out of the schoolroom herself, as the standard-bearer of a faith to which we all were born but which she alone knew how to hold aloft with an unflinching hope! She had perhaps more glow and less serenity in her soul than Antonia, but she was an uncompromising Puritan of patriotism with no taint of the slightest worldliness in her thoughts. I was not the only one in love with her; but it was I who had to hear oftenest her scathing criticism of my levities – very much like poor Decoud – or stand the brunt of her austere, unanswerable invective. She did not quite understand – but never mind. That afternoon when I came in, a shrinking yet defiant sinner, to say the final good-bye I received a hand-squeeze that made my heart leap and saw a tear that took my breath away. She was softened at the last as though she had suddenly perceived (we were such children still!) that I was really going away for good, going very far away – even as far as Sulaco, lying unknown, hidden from our eyes in the darkness of the Placid Gulf.

That's why I long sometimes for another glimpse of the 'beautiful Antonia' (or can it be the Other?) moving in the dimness of the great cathedral, saying a short prayer at the tomb of the first and last Cardinal-Archbishop of Sulaco, standing absorbed in filial devotion before the monument of Don José Avellanos, and, with a lingering, tender, faithful glance at the medallion-memorial to Martin Decoud, going out serenely into the sunshine of the Plaza with her upright carriage and her white head; a relic of the past disregarded by men awaiting impatiently the Dawns of other New Eras, the coming of more Revolutions.

But this is the idlest of dreams; for I did understand perfectly well at the time that the moment the breath left the body of the Magnificent Capataz, the Man of the People, freed at last from the toils of love and wealth, there was nothing more for me to do in Sulaco.

J.C.

October 1917

PART ONE
THE SILVER OF THE MINE

CHAPTER 1

In the time of Spanish rule, and for many years afterwards, the town of Sulaco – the luxuriant beauty of the orange gardens bears witness to its antiquity – had never been commercially anything more important than a coasting port with a fairly large local trade in ox-hides and indigo. The clumsy deep-sea galleons of the conquerors that, needing a brisk gale to move at all, would lie becalmed, where your modern ship built on clipper lines forges ahead by the mere flapping of her sails, had been barred out of Sulaco by the prevailing calms of its vast gulf. Some harbours of the earth are made difficult of access by the treachery of sunken rocks and the tempests of their shores. Sulaco had found an inviolable sanctuary from the temptations of a trading world in the solemn hush of the deep Golfo Placido as if within an enormous semi-circular and unroofed temple open to the ocean, with its walls of lofty mountains hung with the mourning draperies of cloud.

On one side of this broad curve in the straight seaboard of the Republic of Costaguana, the last spur of the coast range forms an insignificant cape whose name is Punta Mala. From the middle of the gulf the point of the land itself is not visible at all; but the shoulder of a steep hill at the back can be made out faintly like a shadow on the sky.

On the other side, what seems to be an isolated patch of blue mist floats lightly on the glare of the horizon. This is the peninsula of Azuera, a wild chaos of sharp rocks and stony levels cut about by vertical ravines. It lies far out to sea like a rough head of stone stretched from a green-clad coast at the end of a slender neck of sand covered with thickets of thorny scrub. Utterly waterless, for the rainfall runs off at once on all sides into the sea, it has not soil enough – it is said – to grow a single blade of grass, as if it were blighted by a curse. The poor, associating by an obscure instinct of consolation the ideas of evil and wealth, will tell you that it is deadly because of its forbidden treasures. The common folk of the neighbourhood, peons of the *estancias, vaqueros* of the seaboard plains, tame Indians coming miles to market with a bundle of sugar-cane or a basket of maize worth about threepence, are well aware that heaps of shining gold lie in the gloom of the deep precipices cleaving the stony levels of Azuera. Tradition has it that many adventurers of olden time had perished in the search. The story goes also that within men's memory two wandering sailors – *Americanos*, perhaps, but *gringos* of some sort for certain – talked over a gambling, good-for-nothing *mozo,* and the three stole a donkey to carry for them a bundle of dry sticks, a water-skin, and provisions enough to last a few days. Thus accompanied, and with revolvers at their belts, they had started to chop their way with machetes through the thorny scrub on the neck of the peninsula.

On the second evening an upright spiral of smoke (it could only have been from their camp-fire) was seen for the first time within memory of man standing up faintly upon the sky above a razor-backed ridge on the stony head. The crew of a coasting schooner, lying becalmed three miles off the shore, stared at it with amazement till dark. A Negro fisherman, living in a lonely hut in a little bay near by, had seen the start and was on the lookout for some sign. He called to his wife just as the sun was about to set. They had watched the strange portent with envy, incredulity, and awe.

The impious adventurers gave no other sign. The sailors, the Indian, and the stolen *burro* were never seen again. As to the *mozo*, a Sulaco man – his wife paid for some Masses, and the poor four-footed beast, being without sin, had been probably permitted to die; but the two *gringos*, spectral and alive, are believed to be dwelling to this day amongst the rocks, under the fatal spell of their success. Their souls cannot tear themselves away from their bodies mounting guard over the discovered treasure. They are now rich and hungry and thirsty – a strange theory of tenacious *gringo* ghosts suffering in their starved and parched flesh of defiant heretics, where a Christian would have renounced and been released.

These, then, are the legendary inhabitants of Azuera guarding its forbidden wealth; and the shadow on the sky on one side, with the round patch of blue haze blurring the bright skirt of the horizon on the other, mark the two outermost points of the bend which bears the name of Golfo Placido, because never a strong wind had been known to blow upon its waters.

On crossing the imaginary line drawn from Punta Mala to Azuera the ships from Europe bound to Sulaco lose at once the strong breezes of the ocean. They become the prey of capricious airs that play with them for thirty hours at a stretch sometimes. Before them the head of the calm gulf is filled on most days of the year by a great body of motionless and opaque clouds. On the rare clear mornings another shadow is cast upon the sweep of the gulf. The dawn breaks high behind the towering and serrated wall of the Cordillera, a clear-cut vision of dark peaks rearing their steep slopes on a lofty pedestal of forest rising from the very edge of the shore. Amongst them the white head of Higuerota rises majestically upon the blue. Bare clusters of enormous rocks sprinkle with tiny black dots the smooth dome of snow.

Then, as the midday sun withdraws from the gulf the shadow of the mountains, the clouds begin to roll out of the lower valleys. They swathe in sombre tatters the naked crags of precipices above the wooded slopes, hide the peaks, smoke in stormy trails across the snows of Higuerota. The Cordillera is gone from you as if it had dissolved itself into great piles of grey and black vapours that travel out slowly to seaward and vanish into thin air all along the front before the blazing heat of the day. The wasting edge of the cloud-bank always strives for, but seldom wins, the middle of the gulf. The sun – as the sailors say – is eating it up. Unless perchance a sombre thunder-head breaks away from the main body to career all over the gulf till it escapes into the offing beyond Azuera, where it bursts suddenly into flame and crashes like a sinister pirate-ship of the air, hove-to above the horizon, engaging the sea.

At night the body of clouds advancing higher up the sky smothers the whole quiet gulf below with an impenetrable darkness, in which the sound of the falling showers can be heard beginning and ceasing abruptly – now here, now there. Indeed, these cloudy nights are proverbial with the seamen along the whole west coast of a great continent. Sky, land, and sea disappear together out of the world when the Placido – as the saying is – goes to sleep under its black poncho. The few stars left below the seaward frown of the vault shine feebly as into the mouth of a black cavern. In its vastness your ship floats unseen under your feet, her sails flutter invisible above your head. The eye of God Himself – they add with grim profanity – could not find out what work a man's hand is doing in there; and you would be free to call the devil to your aid with impunity if even his malice were not defeated by such a blind darkness.

The shores on the gulf are steep-to all round; three uninhabited islets basking in the sunshine just outside the cloud veil, and opposite the entrance to the harbour of Sulaco, bear the name of 'The Isabels'.

There is the Great Isabel; the Little Isabel, which is round; and Hermosa, which is the smallest.

That last is no more than a foot high, and about seven paces across, a mere flat top of a grey rock which smokes like a hot cinder after a shower, and where no man would care to venture a naked sole before sunset. On the Little Isabel an old ragged palm with a thick bulging trunk rough with spines, a very witch amongst palm trees, rustles a dismal bunch of dead leaves above the coarse sand. The Great Isabel has a spring of fresh water issuing from the overgrown side of a ravine. Resembling an emerald green wedge of land a mile long, and laid flat upon the sea, it bears two forest trees standing close together, with a wide spread of shade at the foot of their smooth trunks. A ravine extending the whole length of the island is full of bushes; and presenting a deep tangled cleft on the high side spreads itself out on the other into a shallow depression abutting on a small strip of sandy shore.

From that low end of the Great Isabel the eye plunges through an opening two miles away, as abrupt as if chopped with an axe out of the regular sweep of the coast, right into the harbour of Sulaco. It is an oblong, lake-like piece of water. On one side the short wooded spurs and valleys of the Cordillera come down at right angles to the very strand; on the other the open view of the great Sulaco plain passes into the opal mystery of great distances overhung by dry haze. The town of Sulaco itself – tops of walls, a great cupola, gleams of white miradors in a vast grove of orange trees – lies between the mountains and the plain, at some little distance from its harbour and out of the direct line of sight from the sea.

CHAPTER 2

The only sign of commercial activity within the harbour, visible from the beach of the Great Isabel, is the square blunt end of the wooden jetty which the Oceanic Steam Navigation Company (the O.S.N. of familiar speech) had thrown over the shallow part of the bay soon after they had resolved to make of Sulaco one of their ports of call for the Republic of Costaguana. The State possesses several harbours on its long seaboard, but except Cayta, an important place, all are either small and inconvenient inlets in an iron-bound coast – like Esmeralda, for instance, sixty miles to the south – or else mere open roadsteads exposed to the winds and fretted by the surf.

Perhaps the very atmospheric conditions which had kept away the merchant fleets of bygone ages induced the O.S.N. Company to violate the sanctuary of peace sheltering the calm existence of Sulaco. The variable airs sporting lightly with the vast semicircle of waters within the head of Azuera could not baffle the steam power of their excellent fleet. Year after year the black hulls of their ships had gone up and down the coast, in and out, past Azuera, past the Isabels, past Punta' Mala – disregarding everything but the tyranny of time. Their names, the names of all mythology, became the household words of a coast that had never been ruled by the gods of Olympus. The *Juno* was known only for her comfortable cabins amidships, the *Saturn* for the geniality of her captain and the painted and gilt luxuriousness of her saloon, whereas the *Ganymede* was fitted out mainly for cattle transport, and to be avoided by coastwise passengers. The humblest Indian in the obscurist village on the coast was familiar with the *Cerberus*, a little black puffer without charm or living accommodation to speak of, whose mission was to creep inshore along the wooded beaches close to mighty ugly rocks, stopping obligingly before every cluster of huts to collect produce, down to three-pound parcels of indiarubber bound in a wrapper of dry grass.

And as they seldom failed to account for the smallest package, rarely lost a bullock, and had never drowned a single passenger, the name of the O.S.N. stood very high for trustworthiness. People declared that under the Company's care their lives and property were safer on the water than in their own houses on shore.

The O.S.N.'s superintendent in Sulaco for the whole Costaguana section of the service was very proud of his Company's standing. He resumed it in a saying which was very often on his lips, 'We never make mistakes.' To the Company's officers it took the form of a severe injunction, 'We must make no mistakes. I'll have no mistakes here, no matter what Smith may do at his end.'

Smith, on whom he had never set eyes in his life, was the other superintendent of the service, quartered some fifteen hundred miles away from Sulaco. 'Don't talk to me of your Smith.'

Then, calming down suddenly, he would dismiss the subject with studied negligence.

'Smith knows no more of this continent than a baby.'

'Our excellent Señor Mitchell' for the business and official world of Sulaco; 'Fussy Joe' for the commanders of the Company's ships, Captain Joseph Mitchell prided himself on his profound knowledge of men and things in the country – *cosas de Costaguana*. Amongst these last he accounted as most unfavourable to the orderly working of his Company the frequent changes of government brought about by revolutions of the military type.

The political atmosphere of the Republic was generally stormy in these days. The fugitive patriots of the defeated party had the knack of turning up again on the coast with half a steamer's load of small arms and ammunition. Such resourcefulness Captain Mitchell considered as perfectly wonderful in view of their utter destitution at the time of flight. He had observed that 'they never seemed to have enough change about them to pay for their passage ticket out of the country'. And he could speak with knowledge; for on a memorable occasion he had been called upon to save the life of a dictator, together with the lives of a few Sulaco officials – the political chief, the director of the customs, and the head of police – belonging to an overturned government. Poor Señor Ribiera (such was the dictator's name) had come pelting eighty miles over mountain tracks after the lost battle of Socorro, in the hope of out-distancing the fatal news – which, of course, he could not manage to do on a lame mule. The animal, moreover, expired under him at the end of the Alameda, where the military band plays sometimes in the evenings between the revolutions. 'Sir,' Captain Mitchell would pursue with portentous gravity, 'the ill-timed end of that mule attracted attention to the unfortunate rider. His features were recognized by several deserters from the Dictatorial army amongst the rascally mob already engaged in smashing the windows of the Intendencia.'

Early on the morning of that day the local authorities of Sulaco had fled for refuge to the O.S.N. Company's offices, a strong building near the shore end of the jetty, leaving the town to the mercies of a revolutionary rabble; and as the Dictator was execrated by the populace on account of the severe recruitment law his necessities had compelled him to enforce during the struggle, he stood a chance of being torn to pieces. Providentially, Nostromo – invaluable fellow – with some Italian workmen, imported to work upon the National Central Railway, was at hand, and managed to snatch him away – for the time at least. Ultimately, Captain Mitchell succeeded in taking everybody off in his own gig to one of the Company's steamers – it was the *Minerva* – just then, as luck would have it, entering the harbour.

He had to lower these gentlemen at the end of a rope out of a hole in the wall at the back, while the mob which, pouring out of the town, had spread itself all along the shore, howled and foamed at the foot of the building in front. He had to hurry them then the whole length of the jetty; it had been a desperate dash, neck or nothing – and again it was Nostromo, a fellow in a thousand, who, at the head, this time, of the Company's body of lightermen, held the jetty against the rushes of the rabble, thus giving the fugitives time to reach the gig lying ready for them at the other end with the Company's flag at the stern. Sticks, stones, shots flew; knives, too, were thrown. Captain Mitchell exhibited willingly the long cicatrice of a cut over his left ear and temple, made by a razor-blade fastened to a stick – a weapon, he explained, very much in favour with the 'worst kind of nigger out here'.

Captain Mitchell was a thick, elderly man, wearing high, pointed collars and short side-whiskers, partial to white waistcoats, and really very communicative under his air of pompous reserve.

'These gentlemen,' he would say, staring with great solemnity, 'had to run like rabbits, sir. I ran like a rabbit myself. Certain forms of death are – er – distasteful to a – a – er – respectable man. They would have pounded me to death, too. A crazy mob, sir, does not discriminate. Under providence we owed our preservation to my Capataz de Cargadores, as they called him in the town, a man who, when I discovered his value, sir, was just the bos'n of an Italian ship, a big Genoese ship, one of the few European ships that ever came to Sulaco with a general cargo before the building of the National Central. He left her on account of some very respectable friends he made here, his own countrymen, but also, I suppose, to better himself. Sir, I am a pretty good judge of character. I engaged him to be the foreman of our lightermen, and caretaker of our jetty. That's all that he was. But without him Señor Ribiera would have been a dead man. This Nostromo, sir, a man absolutely above reproach, became the terror of all the thieves in the town. We were infested, infested, overrun, sir, here at that time by *ladrones* and *matreros*, thieves and murderers from the whole province. On this occasion they had been flocking into Sulaco for a week past. They had scented the end, sir. Fifty per cent of that murdering mob were professional bandits from the Campo, sir, but there wasn't one that hadn't heard of Nostromo. As to the town *leperos*, sir, the sight of his black whiskers and white teeth was enough for them. They quailed before him, sir. That's what the force of character will do for you.'

It could very well be said that it was Nostromo alone who saved the lives of these gentlemen. Captain Mitchell, on his part, never left them till he had seen them collapse, panting, terrified, and exasperated, but safe, on the luxuriant velvet sofas in the first-class saloon of the *Minerva*. To the very last he had been careful to address the ex-Dictator as 'Your Excellency'.

'Sir, I could do no other. The man was down – ghastly, livid, one mass of scratches.'

The *Minerva* never let go her anchor that call. The superintendent ordered her out of the harbour at once. No cargo could be landed, of course, and the passengers for Sulaco naturally refused to go ashore. They could hear the firing and see plainly the fight going on at the edge of the water. The repulsed mob devoted its energies to an attack upon the Custom House, a dreary, unfinished-looking structure with many windows two hundred yards away from the O.S.N. Offices, and the only other building near the harbour. Captain Mitchell, after directing the commander of the *Minerva* to land 'these gentlemen' in the first port of call outside Costaguana, went back in his gig to see what could be done for the protection of the Company's property. That and the property of the railway were preserved by the European residents; that is, by Captain Mitchell himself and the staff of engineers building the road, aided by the Italian and Basque workmen who rallied faithfully round their English chiefs. The Company's lightermen, too, natives of the Republic, behaved very well under their Capataz. An outcast lot of very mixed blood, mainly Negroes, everlastingly at feud with the other customers of low grog shops in the town, they embraced with delight this opportunity to settle their personal scores under such favourable auspices. There was not one of them that had not, at some time or other, looked with terror at Nostromo's revolver poked very close at his face, or been otherwise daunted by Nostromo's resolution. He was 'much of a man', their Capataz was, they said, too scornful in his temper ever to utter abuse, a tireless taskmaster, and the more to be feared because of his aloofness. And behold! there he was that day, at their head, condescending to make jocular remarks to this man or the other.

Such leadership was inspiriting, and in truth all the harm the mob managed to achieve was to set fire to one – only one – stack of railway-sleepers, which, being creosoted, burned well. The main attack on the railway yards, on the O.S.N. Offices, and especially on the Custom House, whose strong-room, it was well known, contained a large treasure in silver ingots, failed completely. Even the little hotel kept by old Giorgio, standing alone half-way between the harbour and the town, escaped looting and destruction, not by a miracle, but because with the safes in view they had neglected it at first, and afterwards found no leisure to stop. Nostromo, with his *cargadores*, was pressing them too hard then.

CHAPTER 3

It might have been said that there he was only protecting his own. From the first he had been admitted to live in the intimacy of the family of the hotel-keeper who was a countryman of his. Old Giorgio Viola, a Genoese with a shaggy white leonine head – often called simply 'the Garibaldino' (as Mohammedans are called after their prophet) – was, to use Captain Mitchell's own words, the 'respectable married friend' by whose advice Nostromo had left his ship to try for a run of shore luck in Costaguana.

The old man, full of scorn for the populace, as your austere republican so often is, had disregarded the preliminary sounds of trouble. He went on that day as usual pottering about the *casa* in his slippers, muttering angrily to himself his contempt of the non-political nature of the riot, and shrugging his shoulders. In the end he was taken unawares by the out-rush of the rabble. It was too late then to remove his family, and, indeed, where could he have run to with the portly Signora Teresa and two little girls on that great plain? So, barricading every opening, the old man sat down sternly in the middle of the darkened café with an old shot-gun on his knees. His wife sat on another chair by his side, muttering pious invocations to all the saints of the calendar.

The old republican did not believe in saints, or in prayers, or in what he called 'priest's religion'. Liberty and Garibaldi were his divinities; but he tolerated 'superstition' in women, preserving in these matters a lofty and silent attitude.

His two girls, the eldest fourteen, and the other two years younger, crouched on the sanded floor, on each side of the Signora Teresa, with their heads on their mother's lap, both scared, but each in her own way, the dark-haired Linda indignant and angry, the fair Giselle, the younger, bewildered and resigned. The Patrona removed her arms, which embraced her daughters, for a moment to cross herself and wring her hands hurriedly. She moaned a little louder.

'Oh! Gian' Battista, why art thou not here? Oh! why art thou not here?'

She was not then invoking the saint himself, but calling upon Nostromo, whose patron he was. And Giorgio, motionless on the chair by her side, would be provoked by these reproachful and distracted appeals.

'Peace, woman! Where's the sense of it? There's his duty,' he murmured in the dark; and she would retort, panting:

'Eh! I have no patience. Duty! What of the woman who has been like a mother to him? I bent my knee to him this morning; don't you go out, Gian' Battista – stop in the house, Battistino – look at those two little innocent children!'

Mrs Viola was an Italian, too, a native of Spezzia, and though considerably younger than her husband, already middle-aged. She had a handsome face, whose complexion had turned yellow because the climate of Sulaco did not suit her at all. Her voice was a rich contralto. When, with her arms folded tight under her ample bosom, she scolded the squat, thick-legged China girls handling linen, plucking fowls, pounding corn in wooden mortars amongst the mud outbuildings at the back of the house, she could bring out such an impassioned, vibrating, sepulchral note that the chained watch-dog bolted into his kennel with a great rattle. Luis, a cinnamon-coloured mulatto with a sprouting moustache and thick, dark lips, would stop sweeping the café with a broom of palm-leaves to let a gentle shudder run down his spine. His languishing almond eyes would remain closed for a long time.

This was the staff of the Casa Viola, but all these people had fled early that morning at the first sounds of the riot, preferring to hide on the plain rather than trust themselves in the house; a preference for which they were in no way to blame, since, whether true or not, it was generally believed in the town that the Garibaldino had some money buried under the clay floor of the kitchen. The dog, an irritable, shaggy brute, barked violently and whined plaintively in turns at the back, running in and out of his kennel as rage or fear prompted him.

Bursts of great shouting rose and died away, like wild gusts of wind on the plain round the barricaded house; the fitful popping of shots grew louder above the yelling. Sometimes there were intervals of unaccountable stillness outside, and nothing could have been more gaily peaceful than the narrow bright lines of sunlight from the cracks in the shutters, ruled straight across the café over the disarranged chairs and tables to the wall opposite. Old Giorgio had chosen that bare, whitewashed room for a retreat. It had only one window, and its only door swung out upon the track of thick dust fenced by aloe hedges between the harbour and the town, where clumsy carts used to creak along behind slow yokes of oxen guided by boys on horseback.

In a pause of stillness Giorgio cocked his gun. The ominous sound wrung a low moan from the rigid figure of the woman sitting by his side. A sudden outbreak of defiant yelling quite near the house sank all at once to a confused murmur of growls. Somebody ran along; the loud catching of his breath was heard for an instant passing the door; there were hoarse mutters and footsteps near the wall; a shoulder rubbed against the shutter, effacing the bright lines of sunshine pencilled across the whole breadth of the room. Signora Teresa's arms thrown about the kneeling forms of her daughters embraced them closer with a convulsive pressure.

The mob, driven away from the Custom House, had broken up into several bands, retreating across the plain in the direction of the town. The subdued crash of irregular volleys fired in the distance was answered by faint yells far away. In the intervals the single shots rang feebly, and the low, long, white building blinded in every window seemed to be the centre of a turmoil widening in a great circle about its closed-up silence. But the cautious movements and whispers of a routed party seeking a momentary shelter behind the wall made the darkness of the room, striped by threads of quiet sunlight, alight with evil, stealthy sounds. The Violas had them in their ears as though invisible ghosts hovering about their chairs had consulted in mutters as to the advisability of setting fire to this foreigner's *casa*.

It was trying to the nerves. Old Viola had risen slowly, gun in hand, irresolute, for he did not see how he could prevent them. Already voices could be heard talking at the back. Signora Teresa was beside herself with terror.

'Ah! the traitor! the traitor!' she mumbled, almost inaudibly. 'Now we are going to be burnt; and I bent my knee to him. No! he must run at the heels of his English.'

She seemed to think that Nostromo's mere presence in the house would have made it perfectly safe. So far, she, too, was under the spell of that reputation the Capataz de Cargadores had made for himself by the waterside, along the railway line, with the English, and with the populace of Sulaco. To his face, and even against her husband, she invariably affected to laugh it to scorn, sometimes good-naturedly, more often with a curious bitterness. But then women are unreasonable in their opinions, as Giorgio used to remark calmly on fitting occasions. On this occasion, with his gun held at ready before him, he stooped down to his wife's head, and, keeping his eyes steadfastly on the barricaded door, he breathed out into her ear that Nostromo would have been powerless to help. What could two men shut up in a house do against twenty or more bent upon setting fire to the roof? Gian' Battista was thinking of the *casa* all the time, he was sure.

'He think of the *casa*! He!' gasped Signora Viola, crazily. She struck her breast with her open hands. 'I know him. He thinks of nobody but himself.'

A discharge of firearms nearby made her throw her head back and close her eyes. Old Giorgio set his teeth hard under his white moustache, and his eyes began to roll fiercely. Several bullets struck the end of the wall together; pieces of plaster could be heard falling outside; a voice screamed 'Here they come!' and after a moment of uneasy silence there was a rush of running feet along the front.

Then the tension of old Giorgio's attitude relaxed, and a smile of contemptuous relief came upon his lips of an old fighter with a leonine face. These were not a people striving for justice, but thieves. Even to defend his life against them was a sort of degradation for a man who had been one of Garibaldi's immortal thousand in the conquest of Sicily. He had an immense scorn for this outbreak of scoundrels and *leperos*, who did not know the meaning of the word 'liberty'.

He grounded his old gun, and, turning his head, glanced at the coloured lithograph of Garibaldi in a black frame on the white wall; a thread of strong sunshine cut it perpendicularly. His eyes, accustomed to the luminous twilight, made out the high colouring of the face, the red of the shirt, the outlines of the square shoulders, the black patch of the Bersagliere hat with cock's feathers curling over the crown. An immortal hero! This was your liberty; it gave you not only life, but immortality as well!

For that one man his fanaticism had suffered no diminution. In the moment of relief from the apprehension of the greatest danger, perhaps, his family had been exposed to in all their wanderings, he had turned to the picture of his old chief, first and only, then laid his hand on his wife's shoulder.

The children kneeling on the floor had not moved. Signora Teresa opened her eyes a little, as though he had awakened her from a very deep and dreamless slumber. Before he had time in his deliberate way to say a reassuring word she jumped up, with the children clinging to her, one on each side, gasped for breath, and let out a hoarse shriek.

It was simultaneous with the bang of a violent blow struck on the outside of the shutter. They could hear suddenly the snorting of a horse, the restive tramping of hoofs on the narrow, hard path in front of the house; the toe of a boot struck at the shutter again; a spur jingled at every blow, and an excited voice shouted, 'Hola! hola, in there!'

CHAPTER 4

All the morning Nostromo had kept his eye from afar on the Casa Viola, even in the thick of the hottest scrimmage near the Custom House. 'If I see smoke rising over there,' he thought to himself, 'they are lost.' Directly the mob had broken he pressed with a small band of Italian workmen in that direction, which, indeed, was the shortest line towards the town. That part of the rabble he was pursuing seemed to think of making a stand under the house; a volley fired by his followers from behind an aloe hedge made the rascals fly. In a gap chopped out for the rails of the harbour branch-line Nostromo appeared, mounted on his silver-grey mare. He shouted, sent after them one shot from his revolver, and galloped up to the café window. He had an idea that old Giorgio would choose that part of the house for a refuge.

His voice had penetrated to them, sounding breathlessly hurried: '*Hola! vecchio! O, vecchio!* Is it all well with you in there?'

'You see –' murmured old Viola to his wife.

Signora Teresa was silent now. Outside Nostromo laughed.

'I can hear the *padrona* is not dead.'

'You have done your best to kill me with fear,' cried Signora Teresa. She wanted to say something more, but her voice failed her.

Linda raised her eyes to her face for a moment, but old Giorgio shouted apologetically:

'She is a little upset.'

Outside Nostromo shouted back with another laugh:

'She cannot upset me.'

Signora Teresa found her voice.

'It is what I say. You have no heart – and you have no conscience, Gian' Battista –'

They heard him wheel his horse away from the shutters. The party he led were babbling excitedly in Italian and Spanish, inciting each other to the pursuit. He put himself at their head, crying, '*Avanti!*'

'He has not stopped very long with us. There is no praise from strangers to be got here,' Signora Teresa said, tragically. '*Avanti!* Yes! That is all he cares for. To be first somewhere – somehow – to be first with these English. They will be showing him to everybody. "This is our Nostromo!"' She laughed ominously. 'What a name! What is that? Nostromo? He would take a name that is properly no word from them.'

Meantime Giorgio, with tranquil movements, had been unfastening the door; the flood of light fell on Signora Teresa, with her two girls gathered to her side, a picturesque woman in a pose of maternal exaltation. Behind her the wall was dazzlingly white, and the crude colours of the Garibaldi lithograph paled in the sunshine.

Old Viola, at the door, moved his arm upwards as if referring all his quick, fleeting thoughts to the picture of his old chief on the wall. Even when he was cooking for the '*signori inglesi*' – the engineers (he was a famous cook, though the kitchen was a dark place) – he was, as it were, under the eye of the great man who had led him in a glorious struggle where, under the walls of Gaeta, tyranny would have expired for ever had it not been for that accursed Piedmontese race of kings and ministers. When sometimes a frying-pan caught fire during a delicate operation with some shredded onions, and the old man was seen backing out of the doorway, swearing and coughing violently in an acrid cloud of smoke, the name of Cavour – the arch intriguer sold to kings and tyrants – could be heard involved in imprecations against the China girls, cooking in general, and the brute of a country where he was reduced to live for the love of liberty that traitor had strangled.

Then Signora Teresa, all in black, issuing from another door, advanced, portly and anxious, inclining her fine, black-browed head, opening her arms, and crying in a profound tone –

'Giorgio! thou passionate man! *Misericordia divina!* In the sun like this! He will make himself ill.'

At her feet the hens made off in all directions, with immense strides; if there were any engineers from up the line staying in Sulaco, a young English face or two would appear at the billiard-room occupying one end of the house; but at the other end, in the café, Luis, the mulatto, took good care not to show himself. The Indian girls, with hair like flowing black manes, and dressed only in a shift and short petticoat, stared dully from under the square-cut fringes on their foreheads; the noisy frizzling of fat had stopped, the fumes floated upwards in sunshine, a strong smell of burnt onions hung in the drowsy heat, enveloping the house; and the eye lost itself in a vast flat expanse of grass to the west, as if the plain between the Sierra overtopping Sulaco and the coast range away there towards Esmeralda had been as big as half the world.

Signora Teresa, after an impressive pause, remonstrated:

'Eh, Giorgio! Leave Cavour alone and take care of yourself now we are lost in this country all alone with the two children, because you cannot live under a king.'

And while she looked at him she would sometimes put her hand hastily to her side with a short twitch of her fine lips and a knitting of her black, straight eyebrows like a flicker of angry pain or an angry thought on her handsome, regular features.

It was pain; she suppressed the twinge. It had come to her first a few years after they had left Italy to emigrate to America and settle at last in Sulaco after wandering from town to town, trying shopkeeping in a small way here and there; and once an organized enterprise of fishing – in Maldonado – for Giorgio, like the great Garibaldi, had been a sailor in his time.

Sometimes she had no patience with pain. For years its gnawing had been part of the landscape embracing the glitter of the harbour under the wooded spurs of the range; and the sunshine itself was heavy and dull – heavy with pain – not like the sunshine of her girlhood, in which middle-aged Giorgio had wooed her gravely and passionately on the shores of the gulf of Spezzia.

'You go in at once, Giorgio,' she directed. 'One would think you do not wish to have any pity on me – with four Signori Inglesi staying in the house.'

'*Va bene, va bene,*' Giorgio would mutter.

He obeyed. The Signori Inglesi would require their midday meal presently. He had been one of the immortal and invincible band of liberators who had made the mercenaries of tyranny fly like chaff before a hurricane, '*un uragano terribile*'. But that was before he was married and had children; and before tyranny had reared its head again amongst the traitors who had imprisoned Garibaldi, his hero.

There were three doors in the front of the house, and each afternoon the

Garibaldino could be seen at one or another of them with his big bush of white hair, his arms folded, his legs crossed, leaning back his leonine head against the lintel, and looking up the wooded slopes of the foothills at the snowy dome of Higuerota. The front of his house threw off a black long rectangle of shade, broadening slowly over the soft ox-cart track. Through the gaps, chopped out in the oleander hedges, the harbour branch railway, laid out temporarily on the level of the plain, curved away its shining parallel ribbons on a belt of scorched and withered grass within sixty yards of the end of the house. In the evening the empty material trains of flat cars circled round the dark green grove of Sulaco, and ran, undulating slightly with white jets of steam, over the plain towards the Casa Viola, on their way to the railway yards by the harbour. The Italian drivers saluted him from the footplate with raised hand, while the Negro brakesmen sat carelessly on the brakes, looking straight forward, with the rims of their big hats flapping in the wind. In return Giorgio would give a slight sideways jerk of the head, without unfolding his arms.

On this memorable day of the riot his arms were not folded on his chest. His hand grasped the barrel of the gun grounded on the threshold; he did not look up once at the white dome of Higuerota, whose cool purity seemed to hold itself aloof from a hot earth. His eyes examined the plain curiously. Tall trails of dust subsided here and there. In a speckless sky the sun hung clear and blinding. Knots of men ran headlong; others made a stand; and the irregular rattle of firearms came rippling to his ears in the fiery, still air. Single figures on foot raced desperately. Horsemen galloped towards each other, wheeled round together, separated at speed. Giorgio saw one fall, rider and horse disappearing as if they had galloped into a chasm, and the movements of the animated scene were like the passages of a violent game played upon the plain by dwarfs mounted and on foot, yelling with tiny throats, under the mountain that seemed a colossal embodiment of silence. Never before had Giorgio seen this bit of plain so full of active life; his gaze could not take in all its details at once; he shaded his eyes with his hand, till suddenly the thundering of many hoofs near by startled him.

A troop of horses had broken out of the fenced paddock of the Railway Company. They came on like a whirlwind, and dashed over the line snorting, kicking, squealing in a compact, piebald, tossing mob of bay, brown, grey backs, eyes staring, necks extended, nostrils red, long tails streaming. As soon as they had leaped upon the road the thick dust flew upwards from under their hoofs, and within six yards of Giorgio only a brown cloud with vague forms of necks and cruppers rolled by, making the soil tremble on its passage.

Viola coughed, turning his face away from the dust, and shaking his head slightly.

'There will be some horse-catching to be done before tonight,' he muttered.

In the square of sunlight falling through the door Signora Teresa, kneeling before the chair, had bowed her head, heavy with a twisted mass of ebony hair streaked with silver, into the palm of her hands. The black lace shawl she used to drape about her face dropped to the ground by her side. The two girls had got up, hand-in-hand, in short skirts, their loose hair falling in disorder. The younger had thrown her arm across her eyes, as if afraid to face the light. Linda, with her hand on the other's shoulder, stared fearlessly. Viola looked at his children.

The sun brought out the deep lines on his face, and, energetic in expression, it had the immobility of a carving. It was impossible to discover what he thought. Bushy grey eyebrows shaded his dark glance.

'Well! And do you not pray like your mother?'

Linda pouted, advancing her red lips, which were almost too red; but she had admirable eyes, brown, with a sparkle of gold in the irises, full of intelligence and meaning, and so clear that they seemed to throw a glow upon her thin, colourless face. There were bronze glints in the sombre clusters of her hair, and the eyelashes, long and coal black, made her complexion appear still more pale.

'Mother is going to offer up a lot of candles in the church. She always does when Nostromo has been away fighting. I shall have some to carry up to the Chapel of the Madonna in the Cathedral.'

She said all this quickly, with great assurance, in an animated, penetrating voice. Then, giving her sister's shoulder a slight shake, she added:

'And she will be made to carry one, too!'

'Why made?' inquired Giorgio, gravely. 'Does she not want to?'

'She is timid,' said Linda, with a little burst of laughter. 'People notice her fair hair as she goes along with us. They call out after her, "Look at the *rubia*! Look at the *rubiacita*!" They call out in the streets. She is timid.'

'And you? You are not timid – eh?' the father pronounced, slowly.

She tossed back all her dark hair.

'Nobody calls out after me.'

Old Giorgio contemplated his children thoughtfully. There was two years difference between them. They had been born to him late, years after the boy had died. Had he lived he would have been nearly as old as Gian' Battista – he whom the English called Nostromo; but as to his daughters, the severity of his temper, his advancing age, his absorption in his memories, had prevented his taking much notice of them. He loved his children, but girls belong more to the mother, and much of his affection had been expended in the worship and service of liberty.

When quite a youth he had deserted from a ship trading to La Plata, to enlist in the navy of Montevideo, then under the command of Garibaldi. Afterwards, in the Italian legion of the Republic struggling against the encroaching tyranny of Rosas, he had taken part, on great plains, on the banks of immense rivers, in the fiercest fighting perhaps the world had ever known. He had lived amongst men who had declaimed about liberty, suffered for liberty, died for liberty, with a desperate exaltation, and with their eyes turned towards an oppressed Italy. His own enthusiasm had been fed on scenes of carnage, on the examples of lofty devotion, on the din of armed struggle, on the inflamed language of proclamations. He had never parted from the chief of his choice – the fiery apostle of independence – keeping by his side in America and in Italy till after the fatal day of Aspromonte, when the treachery of kings, emperors, and ministers had been revealed to the world in the wounding and imprisonment of his hero – a catastrophe that had instilled into him a gloomy doubt of ever being able to understand the ways of divine justice.

He did not deny it, however. It required patience, he would say. Though he disliked priests, and would not put his foot inside a church for anything, he believed in God. Were not the proclamations against tyrants addressed to the peoples in the name of God and liberty? 'God for men – religions for women, he muttered sometimes. In Sicily, an Englishman who had turned up in Palermo after its evacuation by the army of the king, had given him a Bible in Italian – the publication of the British and Foreign Bible Society, bound in a dark leather cover. In periods of political adversity, in the pauses of silence when the revolutionists issued no proclamations, Giorgio earned his living with the first work that came to hand – as sailor, as dock labourer on the quays of Genoa, once as a hand on a farm in the hills above Spezzia – and in his spare time he studied the thick volume. He carried it with him into battles. Now it was his only reading, and in order not to be deprived of it (the print was small) he had consented to accept the present of a pair of silver-mounted spectacles from Señora Emilia Gould, the wife of the Englishman who managed the silver mine in the mountains three leagues from the town. She was the only Englishwoman in Sulaco.

Giorgio Viola had a great consideration for the English. This feeling, born on the battlefields of Uruguay, was forty years old at the very least. Several of them had poured their blood for the cause of freedom in America, and the first he had ever known he remembered by the name of Samuel; he commanded a Negro company under Garibaldi, during the famous siege of Montevideo, and died heroically with his Negroes at the fording of the Boyana. He, Giorgio, had reached the rank of ensign – *alferez* – and cooked for the general. Later, in Italy, he, with the rank of lieutenant, rode with the staff and still cooked for the general. He had cooked for him in Lombardy through the whole campaign; on the march to Rome he had lassoed his beef in the Campagna after the American manner; he had been wounded in the defence of the Roman Republic; he was one of the four fugitives who, with the general, carried out of the woods the inanimate body of the general's wife into the farmhouse where she died, exhausted by the hardships of that terrible retreat. He had survived that disastrous time to attend his general in Palermo when the Neapolitan shells from the castle crashed upon the town. He had cooked for him on the field of Volturno after fighting all day. And everywhere he had seen Englishmen in the front rank of the army of freedom. He respected their nation because they loved Garibaldi. Their very countesses and princesses had kissed the general's hands in London, it was said. He could well believe it; for the nation was noble, and the man was a saint. It was enough to look once at his face to see the divine force of faith in him and his great pity for all that was poor, suffering, and oppressed in this world.

The spirit of self-forgetfulness, the simple devotion to a vast humanitarian idea which inspired the thought and stress of that revolutionary time, had left its mark upon Giorgio in a sort of austere contempt for all personal advantage. This man, whom the lowest class in Sulaco suspected of having a buried hoard in his kitchen, had all his life despised money. The leaders of his youth had lived poor, had died poor. It had been a habit of his mind to disregard tomorrow. It was engendered partly by an existence of excitement, adventure, and wild warfare. But mostly it was a matter of principle. It did not resemble the carelessness of a *condottiere*, it was a puritanism of conduct, born of stern enthusiasm like the puritanism of religion.

This stern devotion to a cause had cast a gloom upon Giorgio's old age. It cast a gloom because the cause seemed lost. Too many kings and emperors flourished yet in the world which God had meant for the people. He was sad because of his simplicity. Though always ready to help his countrymen, and greatly respected by the Italian emigrants wherever he lived (in his exile he called it), he could not conceal from himself that they cared nothing for the wrongs of down-trodden nations. They listened to his tales of war readily, but seemed to ask themselves what he had got out of it after all. There was nothing that they could see. 'We wanted nothing, we suffered for the love of all humanity!' he cried out furiously sometimes, and the powerful voice, the blazing eyes, the shaking of the white mane, the brown, sinewy hand pointing upwards as if to call heaven to witness, impressed his hearers. After the old man had broken off abruptly with a jerk of the head and a movement of the arm, meaning clearly, 'But what's the good of talking to you?' they nudged each other. There was in old Giorgio an energy of feeling, a personal quality of conviction, something they called *'terribilità'* – 'an old lion', they used to say of him. Some slight incident, a chance word would set him off talking on the beach to the Italian fishermen of Maldonado, in the little shop he kept afterwards (in Valparaiso) to his countrymen customers; of an evening, suddenly, in the café at one end of the Casa Viola (the other was reserved for the English engineers) to the select clientele of engine-drivers and foremen of the railway shops.

With their handsome, bronzed, lean faces, shiny black ringlets, glistening eyes, broad-chested, bearded, sometimes a tiny gold ring in the lobe of the ear, the aristocracy of the railway works listened to him, turning away from their cards or dominoes. Here and there a fair-haired Basque studied his hand meantime, waiting without protest. No native of Costaguana intruded there. This was the Italian stronghold. Even the Sulaco policemen on a night patrol let their horses pace softly by, bending low in the saddle to glance through the window at the heads in a fog of smoke; and the drone of old Giorgio's declamatory narrative seemed to sink behind them into the plain. Only now and then the assistant of the chief of police, some broad-faced, brown little gentleman, with a great deal of Indian in him, would put in an appearance. Leaving his man outside with the horses he advanced with a confident, sly smile, and without a word up to the long trestle table. He pointed to one of the bottles on the shelf; Giorgio, thrusting his pipe into his mouth abruptly, served him in person. Nothing would be heard but the slight jingle of the spurs. His glass emptied, he would take a leisurely, scrutinizing look all round the room, go out, and ride away slowly, circling towards the town.

CHAPTER 5

In this way only was the power of the local authorities vindicated amongst the great body of strong-limbed foreigners who dug the earth, blasted the rocks, drove the engines for the 'progressive and patriotic undertaking'. In these very words eighteen months before the Excellentissimo Señor don Vincente Ribiera, the Dictator of Costaguana, had described the National Central Railway in his great speech at the turning of the first sod.

He had come on purpose to Sulaco, and there was a one-o'clock dinner-party, a *convité* offered by the O.S.N. Company on board the *Juno* after the function on shore. Captain Mitchell had himself steered the cargo lighter, all draped with flags, which, in tow of the *Juno*'s steam launch, took the Excellentissimo from the jetty to the ship. Everybody of note in Sulaco had been invited – the one or two foreign merchants, all the representatives of the old Spanish families then in town, the great owners of estates on the plain, grave, courteous, simple men, *caballeros* of pure descent, with small hands and feet, conservative, hospitable, and kind. The Occidental Province was their stronghold; their Blanco party' had triumphed now; it was their President-Dictator, a Blanco of the Blancos, who sat smiling urbanely between the representatives of two friendly foreign powers. They had come with him from Sta Marta to countenance by their presence the enterprise in which the capital of their countries was engaged.

The only lady of that company was Mrs Gould, the wife of Don Carlos, the administrator of the San Tomé silver mine. The ladies of Sulaco were not advanced enough to take part in the public life to that extent. They had come out strongly at the great ball at the Intendencia the evening before, but Mrs Gould alone had appeared, a bright spot in the group of black coats behind the President-Dictator, on the crimson cloth-covered stage erected under a shady tree on the shore of the harbour, where the ceremony of turning the first sod had taken place. She had come off in the cargo lighter, full of notabilities, sitting under the flutter of gay flags, in the place of honour by the side of Captain Mitchell, who steered, and her clear dress gave the only true festive note to the sombre gathering in the long, gorgeous saloon of the *Juno*.

The head of the chairman of the railway board (from London), handsome and pale in a silvery mist of white hair and clipped beard, hovered near her shoulder attentive, smiling, and fatigued. The journey from London to Sta Marta in mail boats and the special carriages of the Sta Marta coast-line (the only railway so far) had been tolerable – even pleasant – quite tolerable. But the trip over the mountains to Sulaco was another sort of experience, in an old *diligencia* over impassable roads skirting awful precipices.

'We have been upset twice in one day on the brink of very deep ravines,' he was telling Mrs Gould in an undertone. 'And when we arrived here at last I don't know what we should have done without your hospitality. What an out-of-the-way place Sulaco is! – and for a harbour, too! Astonishing!'

'Ah, but we are very proud of it. It used to be historically important. The highest ecclesiastical court, for two viceroyalties, sat here in the olden time,' she instructed him with animation.

'I am impressed. I didn't mean to be disparaging. You seem very patriotic.'

'The place is lovable, if only by its situation. Perhaps you don't know what an old resident I am.'

'How old, I wonder,' he murmured, looking at her with a slight smile. Mrs Gould's appearance was made youthful by the mobile intelligence of her face. 'We can't give you your ecclesiastical court back again; but you shall have more steamers, a railway, a telegraph-cable – a future in the great world which is worth infinitely more than any amount of ecclesiastical past. You shall be brought in touch with something greater than two viceroyalties. But I had no notion that a place on a sea-coast could remain so isolated from the world. If it had been a thousand miles inland now – most remarkable! Has anything ever happened here for a hundred years before today?'

While he talked in a slow, humorous tone, she kept her little smile. Agreeing ironically, she assured him that certainly not – nothing ever happened in Sulaco. Even the revolutions, of which there had been two in her time, had respected the repose of the place. Their course ran in the more populous southern parts of the Republic, and in the great valley of Sta Marta, which was like one great battlefield of the parties, with the possession of the capital for a prize and an outlet to another ocean. They were more advanced over there. Here in Sulaco they heard only the echoes of these great questions, and, of course, their official world changed each time, coming to them over their rampart of mountains which he himself had traversed in an old *diligencia*, with such a risk to life and limb.

The chairman of the railway had been enjoying her hospitality for several days, and he was really grateful for it. It was only since he had left Sta Marta that he had utterly lost touch with the feeling of European life on the background of his exotic surroundings. In the capital he had been the guest of the Legation, and had been kept busy negotiating with the members of Don Vincente's Government – cultured men, men to whom the conditions of civilized business were not unknown.

What concerned him most at the time was the acquisition of land for the railway. In the Sta Marta Valley, where there was already one line in existence, the people were tractable, and it was only a matter of price. A commission had been nominated to fix the values, and the difficulty resolved itself into the judicious influencing of the Commissioners. But in Sulaco – the Occidental Province for whose very development the railway was intended – there had been trouble. It had been lying for ages ensconced behind its natural barriers, repelling modern enterprise by the precipices of its mountain range, by its shallow harbour opening into the everlasting calms of a gulf full of clouds, by the benighted state of mind of the owners of its fertile territory – all these aristocratic old Spanish families, all these Don Ambrosios this and Don Fernandos that, who seemed actually to dislike and distrust the coming of the railway over their lands. It had happened that some of the surveying parties scattered all over the province had been warned off with threats of violence. In other cases outrageous pretensions as to price had been raised. But the man of railways prided himself on being equal to every emergency. Since he was met by the inimical sentiment of blind conservatism in Sulaco he would meet it by sentiment, too, before taking his stand on his right alone. The Government was bound to carry out its part of the contract with the board of the new railway company, even if it had to use force for the purpose. But he desired nothing less than an armed disturbance in the smooth working of his plans. They were much too vast and far reaching, and too promising to leave a stone unturned; and so he imagined to get the President-Dictator over there on a tour of ceremonies and speeches, culminating in a great function at the turning of the first sod by the harbour shore. After all he was their own creature – that Don Vincente. He was the embodied triumph of the best elements in the State. These were facts, and, unless facts meant nothing, Sir John argued to himself, such a man's influence must be real, and his personal action would produce the conciliatory effect he required. He had succeeded in arranging the trip with the help of a very clever advocate, who was known in Sta Marta as the agent of the Gould silver mine, the biggest thing in Sulaco, and even in the whole Republic. It was indeed a fabulously rich mine. Its so-called agent, evidently a man of culture and ability, seemed, without official position, to possess an extraordinary influence in the highest Government spheres. He was able to assure Sir John that the President-Dictator would make the journey. He regretted, however, in the course of the same conversation, that General Montero insisted upon going, too.

General Montero, whom the beginning of the struggle had found an obscure army captain employed on the wild eastern frontier of the State, had thrown in his lot with the Ribiera party at a moment when special circumstances had given that small adhesion a fortuitous importance. The fortunes of war served him marvellously, and the victory of Río Seco (after a day of desperate fighting) put a seal to his success. At the end he emerged General, Minister of War, and the military head of the Blanco party, although there was nothing aristocratic in his descent. Indeed, it was said that he and his brother, orphans, had been brought up by the munificence of a famous European traveller, in whose service their father had lost his life. Another story was that their father had been nothing but a charcoal burner in the woods, and their mother a baptized Indian woman from the far interior.

However that might be, the Costaguana Press was in the habit of styling Montero's forest march from his commandancia to join the Blanco forces at the beginning of the troubles, the 'most heroic military exploit of modern times'. About the same time, too, his brother had turned up from Europe, where he had gone apparently as secretary to a consul. Having, however, collected a small band of outlaws, he showed some talent as guerrilla chief and had been rewarded at the pacification by the post of Miliary Commandant of the capital.

The Minister of War, then, accompanied the Dictator. The board of the

O.S.N. Company, working hand-in-hand with the railway people for the good of the Republic, had on this important occasion instructed Captain Mitchell to put the mailboat *Juno* at the disposal of the distinguished party. Don Vincente, journeying south from Sta Marta, had embarked at Cayta, the principal port of Costaguana, and came to Sulaco by sea. But the chairman of the railway company had courageously crossed the mountains in a ramshackle *diligencia*, mainly for the purpose of meeting his engineer-in-chief engaged in the final survey of the road.

For all the indifference of a man of affairs to nature, whose hostility can always be overcome by the resources of finance, he could not help being impressed by his surroundings during his halt at the surveying camp established at the highest point his railway was to reach. He spent the night there, arriving just too late to see the last dying glow of sunlight upon the snowy flank of Higuerota. Pillared masses of black basalt framed like an open portal a portion of the white field lying aslant against the west. In the transparent air of the high altitudes everything seemed very near, steeped in a clear stillness as in an imponderable liquid; and with his ear ready to catch the first sound of the expected *diligencia* the engineer-in-chief, at the door of a hut of rough stones, had contemplated the changing hues on the enormous side of the mountain, thinking that in this sight, as in a piece of inspired music, there could be found together the utmost delicacy of shaded expression and a stupendous magnificence of effect.

Sir John arrived too late to hear the magnificent and inaudible strain sung by the sunset amongst the high peaks of the Sierra. It had sung itself out into the breathless pause of deep dusk before, climbing down the fore wheel of the *diligencia* with stiff limbs, he shook hands with the engineer.

They gave him his dinner in a stone hut like a cubical boulder, with no door or windows in its two openings; a bright fire of sticks (brought on muleback from the first valley below) burning outside sent in a wavering glare; and two candles in tin candlesticks – lighted, it was explained to him, in his honour – stood on a sort of rough camp table, at which he sat on the right hand of the chief. He knew how to be amiable; and the young men of the engineering staff, for whom the surveying of the railway track had the glamour of the first steps on the path of life, sat there, too, listening modestly, with their smooth faces tanned by the weather, and very pleased to witness so much affability in so great a man.

Afterwards, late at night, pacing to and fro outside, he had a long talk with his chief engineer. He knew him well of old. This was not the first undertaking in which their gifts, as elementally different as fire and water, had worked in conjunction. From the contact of these two personalities, who had not the same vision of the world, there was generated a power for the world's service – a subtle force that could set in motion mighty machines, men's muscles, and awaken also in human breasts an unbounded devotion to the task. Of the young fellows at the table, to whom the survey of the track was like the tracing of the path of life, more than one would be called to meet death before the work was done. But the work would be done: the force would be almost as strong as a faith. Not quite, however. In the silence of the sleeping camp upon the moonlit plateau forming the top of the pass like the floor of a vast arena surrounded by the basalt walls of precipices, two strolling figures in thick ulsters stood still, and the voice of the engineer pronounced distinctly the words:

'We can't move mountains!'

Sir John, raising his head to follow the pointing gesture, felt the full force of the words. The white Higuerota soared out of the shadows of rock and earth like a frozen bubble under the moon. All was still, till near by, behind the wall of a corral for the camp animals, built roughly of loose stones in the form of a circle, a pack mule stamped his forefoot and blew heavily twice.

The engineer-in-chief had used the phrase in answer to the chairman's tentative suggestion that the tracing of the line could, perhaps, be altered in deference to the prejudices of the Sulaco landowners. The chief engineer believed that the obstinacy of men was the lesser obstacle. Moreover, to combat that they had the great influence of Charles Gould, whereas tunnelling under Higuerota would have been a colossal undertaking.

'Ah, yes! Gould. What sort of a man is he?'

Sir John had heard much of Charles Gould in Sta Marta, and wanted to know more. The engineer-in-chief assured him that the administrator of the San Tomé silver mine had an immense influence over all these Spanish Dons. He had also one of the best houses in Sulaco, and the Gould hospitality was beyond all praise.

'They received me as if they had known me for years,' he said. 'The little lady is kindness personified. I stayed with them for a month. He helped me to organize the surveying parties. His practical ownership of the San Tomé silver mine gives him a special position. He seems to have the ear of every provincial authority apparently, and, as I said, he can wind all the *hidalgos* of the province round his little finger. If you follow his advice the difficulties will fall away, because he wants the railway. Of course, you must be careful in what you say. He's English, and besides he must be immensely wealthy. The Holroyd house is in with him in that mine, so you may imagine –'

He interrupted himself as, from before one of the little fires burning outside the low wall of the corral, arose the figure of a man wrapped in a poncho up to the neck. The saddle which he had been using for a pillow made a dark patch on the ground against the red glow of embers.

'I shall see Holroyd himself on my way back through the States,' said Sir John. 'I've ascertained that he, too, wants the railway.'

The man who, perhaps disturbed by the proximity of the voices, had arisen from the ground, struck a match to light a cigarette. The flame showed a bronzed, black-whiskered face, a pair of eyes gazing straight; then, rearranging his wrappings, he sank full length and laid his head again on the saddle.

'That's our camp-master, whom I must send back to Sulaco now we are going to carry our survey into the Sta Marta Valley,' said the engineer. 'A most useful fellow, lent me by Captain Mitchell of the O.S.N. Company. It was very good of Mitchell. Charles Gould told me I couldn't do better than take advantage of the offer. He seems to know how to rule all these muleteers and peons. We had not the slightest trouble with our people. He shall escort your *diligencia* right into Sulaco with some of our railway peons. The road is bad. To have him at hand may save you an upset or two. He promised me to take care of your person all the way down as if you were his father.'

This camp-master was the Italian sailor whom all the Europeans in Sulaco, following Captain Mitchell's mispronunciation, were in the habit of calling Nostromo. And indeed, taciturn and ready, he did take excellent care of his charge at the bad parts of the road, as Sir John himself acknowledged to Mrs Gould afterwards.

CHAPTER 6

At that time Nostromo had been already long enough in the country to raise to the highest pitch Captain Mitchell's opinion of the extraordinary value of his discovery. Clearly he was one of those invaluable subordinates whom to possess is a legitimate cause of boasting. Captain Mitchell plumed himself upon his eye for men – but he was not selfish – and in the innocence of his pride was already developing that mania for 'lending you my Capataz de Cargadores' which was to bring Nostromo into personal contact, sooner or later, with every European in Sulaco, as a sort of universal factotum – a prodigy of efficiency in his own sphere of life.

'The fellow is devoted to me, body and soul!' Captain Mitchell was given to affirm; and though nobody, perhaps, could have explained why it should be so, it was impossible on a survey of their relation to throw doubt on that statement, unless, indeed, one were a bitter, eccentric character like Dr Monygham – for instance – whose short, hopeless laugh expressed somehow an immense mistrust of mankind. Not that Dr Monygham was a prodigal either of laughter or of words. He was bitterly taciturn when at his best. At his worst people feared the open scornfulness of his tongue. Only Mrs Gould could keep his unbelief in men's motives within due bounds; but even to her (on an occasion not connected with Nostromo, and in a tone which for him was gentle), even to her, he had said once, 'Really, it is most unreasonable to demand that a man should think of other people so much better than he is able to think of himself.'

And Mrs Gould had hastened to drop the subject. There were strange rumours of the English doctor. Years ago, in the time of Guzman Bento, he had been mixed up, it was whispered, in a conspiracy which was betrayed and, as people expressed it, drowned in blood. His hair had turned grey, his hairless, seamed face was of a brick-dust colour; the large check pattern of his flannel shirt and his old stained Panama hat were an established defiance to the conventionalities of Sulaco. Had it not been for the immaculate cleanliness of his apparel he might have been taken for one of those shiftless Europeans that are a moral eyesore to the respectability of a foreign colony in almost every exotic part of the world. The young ladies of Sulaco, adorning with clusters of pretty faces the balconies along the Street of the Constitution, when they saw him pass, with his limping gait and bowed head, a short linen jacket drawn on carelessly over the flannel check shirt, would remark to each other, 'Here is the Señor Doctor going to call on Doña Emilia. He has got his little coat on.' The inference was true. Its deeper meaning was hidden from their simple intelligence. Moreover, they expended no store of thought on the doctor. He was old, ugly, learned – and a little *loco* – mad, if not a bit of a sorcerer, as the common people suspected him of being. The little white jacket was in reality a concession to Mrs Gould's humanizing influence. The doctor, with his habit of sceptical, bitter speech, had no other means of showing his profound respect for the character of the woman who was known in the country as the English Señora. He presented this tribute very seriously indeed; it was no trifle for a man of his habits. Mrs Gould felt that, too, perfectly. She would never have thought of imposing upon him this marked show of deference.

She kept her old Spanish house (one of the finest specimens in Sulaco) open for the dispensation of the small graces of existence. She dispensed them with simplicity and charm because she was guided by an alert perception of values. She was highly gifted in the art of human intercourse which consists in delicate shades of self-forgetfulness and in the suggestion of universal comprehension. Charles Gould (the Gould family, established in Costaguana for three generations, always went to England for their education and for their wives) imagined that he had fallen in love with a girl's sound common sense like any other man, but these were not exactly the reasons why, for instance, the whole surveying camp, from the youngest of the young men to their mature chief, should have found occasion to allude to Mrs Gould's house so frequently amongst the high peaks of the Sierra. She would have protested that she had done nothing for them, with a low laugh and a surprised widening of her grey eyes, had anybody told her how convincingly she was remembered on the edge of the snow-line above Sulaco. But directly, with a little capable air of setting her wits to work, she would have found an explanation. 'Of course, it was such a surprise for these boys to find any sort of welcome here. And I suppose they are homesick. I suppose everybody must be always just a little homesick.'

She was always sorry for homesick people.

Born in the country, as his father before him, spare and tall, with a flaming moustache, a neat chin, clear blue eyes, auburn hair, and a thin, fresh, red face, Charles Gould looked like a new arrival from over the sea. His grandfather had fought in the cause of independence under Bolívar, in that famous English legion which on the battlefield of Carabobo had been saluted by the great Liberator as Saviours of his country. One of Charles Gould's uncles had been the elected President of that very province of Sulaco (then called a State) in the days of Federation, and afterwards had been put up against the wall of a church and shot by the order of the barbarous Unionist general, Guzman Bento. It was the same Guzman Bento who, becoming later Perpetual President, famed for his ruthless and cruel tyranny, reached his apotheosis in the popular legend of a sanguinary land-haunting spectre whose body had been carried off by the devil in person from the brick mausoleum in the nave of the Church of Assumption in Sta Marta. Thus, at least, the priests explained its disappearance to the barefooted multitude that streamed in, awestruck, to gaze at the hole in the side of the ugly box of bricks before the great altar.

Guzman Bento of cruel memory had put to death great numbers of people besides Charles Gould's uncle; but with a relative martyred in the cause of aristocracy, the Sulaco Oligarchs (this was the phraseology of Guzman Bento's time; now they were called Blancos, and had given up the federal idea), which meant the families of pure Spanish descent, considered Charles as one of themselves. With such a family record, no one could be more of a Costaguanero than Don Carlos Gould; but his aspect was so characteristic that in the talk of common people he was just the Inglés – the Englishman of Sulaco. He looked more English than a casual tourist, a sort of heretic pilgrim, however, quite unknown in Sulaco. He looked more English than the last arrived batch of young railway engineers, than anybody out of the hunting-field pictures in the numbers of *Punch* reaching his wife's drawing-room two months or so after date. It astonished you to hear him talk Spanish (Castillan, as the natives say) or the Indian dialect of the country-people so naturally. His accent had never been English; but there was something so indelible in all these ancestral Goulds – liberators, explorers, coffee planters, merchants, revolutionists – of Costaguana, that he, the only representative of the third generation in a continent possessing its own style of horsemanship, went on looking thoroughly English even on horseback. This is not said of him in the mocking spirit of the *llaneros* – men of the great plains – who think that no one in the world knows how to sit a horse but themselves. Charles Gould, to use the suitably lofty phrase, rode like a centaur. Riding for him was not a special form of exercise; it was a natural faculty, as walking straight is to all men sound of mind and limb; but, all the same, when cantering beside the rutty ox-cart track to the mine he looked in his English clothes and with his imported saddlery as though he had come this moment to Costaguana at his easy swift *pasotrote*, straight out of some green meadow at the other side of the world.

His way would lie along the old Spanish road – the Camino Real of popular speech – the only remaining vestige of a fact and name left by that royalty old Giorgio Viola hated, and whose very shadow had departed from the land; for the big equestrian statue of Charles IV at the entrance of the Alameda, towering white against the trees, was only known to the folk from the country and to the beggars of the town that slept on the steps around the pedestal, as the Horse of Stone. The other Carlos, turning off to the left with a rapid clatter of hoofs on the disjointed pavement – Don Carlos Gould, in his English clothes, looked as incongruous, but much more at home than the kingly cavalier reining in his steed on the pedestal above the sleeping *leperos*, with his marble arm raised towards the marble rim of a plumed hat.

The weather-stained effigy of the mounted king, with its vague suggestion of a saluting gesture, seemed to present an inscrutable breast to the political changes which had robbed it of its very name; but neither did the other horseman, well known to the people, keen and alive on his well-shaped, slate-coloured beast with a white eye, wear his heart on the sleeve of his English coat. His mind preserved its steady poise as if sheltered in the passionless stability of private and public decencies at home in Europe. He accepted with a like calm the shocking manner in which the Sulaco ladies smothered their faces with pearl powder till they looked like white plaster casts with beautiful living eyes, the peculiar gossip of the town, and the continuous political changes, the constant 'saving of the country', which to his wife seemed a puerile and bloodthirsty game of murder and rapine played with terrible earnestness by depraved children. In the early days of her Costaguana life, the little lady used to clench her hands with exasperation at not being able to take the public affairs of the country as seriously as the incidental atrocity of methods deserved. She saw in them a comedy of naïve pretences, but hardly anything genuine except her own appalled indignation. Charles, very quiet and twisting his long moustaches, would decline to discuss them at all. Once, however, he observed to her gently:

'My dear, you seem to forget that I was born here.'

These few words made her pause as if they had been a sudden revelation. Perhaps the mere fact of being born in the country did make a difference. She had a great confidence in her husband; it had always been very great. He had struck her imagination from the first by his unsentimentalism, by that very quietude of mind which she had erected in her thought for a sign of perfect competency in the business of living. Don José Avellanos, their neighbour across the street, a statesman, a poet, a man of culture, who had represented his country at several European Courts (and had suffered untold indignities as a state prisoner in the time of the tyrant Guzman Bento), used to declare in Doña Emilia's drawing-room that Carlos had all the English qualities of character with a truly patriotic heart.

Mrs Gould, raising her eyes to her husband's thin, red and tan face, could not detect the slightest quiver of a feature at what he must have heard said of his patriotism. Perhaps he had just dismounted on his return from the mine; he was English enough to disregard the hottest hours of the day. Basilio, in a livery of white linen and a red sash, had squatted for a moment behind his heels to unstrap the heavy, blunt spurs in the patio; and then the Señor Administrator would go up the staircase into the gallery. Rows of plants in pots, ranged on the balustrade between the pilasters of the arches, screened the *corredor* with their leaves and flowers from the quadrangle below, whose paved space is the true hearthstone of a South American house, where the quiet hours of domestic life are marked by the shifting of light and shadow on the flagstones.

Señor Avellanos was in the habit of crossing the patio at five o'clock almost every day. Don José chose to come over at tea-time because the English rite at Doña Emilia's house reminded him of the time when he lived in London as Minister Plenipotentiary to the Court of St James. He did not like tea; and, usually, rocking his American chair, his neat little shiny boots crossed on the foot-rest, he would talk on and on with a sort of complacent virtuosity wonderful in a man of his age, while he held the cup in his hands for a long time. His close-cropped head was perfectly white; his eyes coal-black.

On seeing Charles Gould step into the *sala* he would nod provisionally and go on to the end of the oratorial period. Only then he would say:

'Carlos, my friend, you have ridden from San Tomé in the heat of the day. Always the true English activity. No? What?'

He drank up all the tea at once in one draught. This performance was invariably followed by a slight shudder and a low, involuntary 'br-r-r-r', which was not covered by the hasty exclamation, 'Excellent!'

Then giving up the empty cup into his young friend's hand, extended with a smile, he continued to expatiate upon the patriotic nature of the San Tomé mine for the simple pleasure of talking fluently, it seemed, while his reclining body jerked backwards and forwards in a rocking-chair of the sort exported from the United States. The ceiling of the largest drawing-room of the Casa Gould extended its white level far above his head. The loftiness dwarfed the mixture of heavy, straight-backed Spanish chairs of brown wood with leathern seats, and European furniture, low, and cushioned all over, like squat little monsters gorged to bursting with steel springs and horsehair. There were knick-knacks on little tables, mirrors let into the wall above marble consoles, square spaces of carpet under the two groups of armchairs, each presided over by a deep sofa; smaller rugs scattered all over the floor of red tiles; three windows from ceiling down to the ground, opening on a balcony, and flanked by the perpendicular folds of the dark hangings. The stateliness of ancient days lingered between the four high, smooth walls, tinted a delicate primrose-colour; and Mrs Gould, with her little head and shining coils of hair, sitting in a cloud of muslin and lace before a slender mahogany table, resembled a fairy posed lightly before dainty philtres dispensed out of vessels of silver and porcelain.

Mrs Gould knew the history of the San Tomé mine. Worked in the early days mostly by means of lashes on the backs of slaves, its yield had been paid for in its own weight of human bones. Whole tribes of Indians had perished in the exploitation; and then the mine was abandoned, since with this primitive method it had ceased to make a profitable return, no matter how many corpses were thrown into its maw. Then it became forgotten. It was rediscovered after the War of Independence. An English company obtained the right to work it, and found so rich a vein that neither the exactions of successive governments, nor the periodical raids of recruiting officers upon the population of paid miners they had created, could discourage their perseverance. But in the end, during the long turmoil of *pronunciamientos* that followed the death of the famous Guzman Bento, the native miners, incited to revolt by the emissaries sent out from the capital, had risen upon their English chiefs and murdered them to a man. The decree of confiscation which appeared immediately afterwards in the *Diario Oficial*, published in Sta Marta, began with the words:

Justly incensed at the grinding oppression of foreigners, actuated by sordid motives of gain rather than by love for a country where they come impoverished to seek their fortunes, the mining population of San Tomé, etc. . . .

and ended with the declaration:

The chief of the State has resolved to exercise to the full his power of clemency. The mine, which by every law, international, human, and divine, reverts now to the Government as national property, shall remain closed till the sword drawn for the sacred defence of liberal principles has accomplished its mission of securing the happiness of our beloved country.

And for many years this was the last of the San Tomé mine. What advantage that Government had expected from the spoliation, it is impossible to tell now. Costaguana was made with difficulty to pay a beggarly money compensation to the families of the victims, and then the matter dropped out of diplomatic dispatches. But afterwards another Government bethought itself of that valuable asset. It was an ordinary Costaguana Government – the fourth in six years – but it judged of its opportunities sanely. It remembered the San Tomé mine with a secret conviction of its worthlessness in their own hands, but with an ingenious insight into the various uses a silver mine can be put to, apart from the sordid process of extracting the metal from under the ground. The father of Charles Gould, for a long time one of the most wealthy merchants of Costaguana, had already lost a considerable part of his fortune in forced loans to the successive Governments. He was a man of calm judgement, who never dreamed of pressing his claims; and when, suddenly, the perpetual concession of the San Tomé mine was offered to him in full settlement, his alarm became extreme. He was versed in the ways of Governments. Indeed, the intention of this affair, though no doubt deeply meditated in the closet, lay open on the surface of the document presented urgently for his signature. The third and most important clause stipulated that the concession-holder should pay at once to the Government five years' royalties on the estimated output of the mine.

Mr Gould, senior, defended himself from this fatal favour with many arguments and entreaties, but without success. He knew nothing of mining; he had no means to put his concession on the European market; the mine as a working concern did not exist. The buildings had been burnt down, the mining plant had been destroyed, the mining population had disappeared from the neighbourhood years and years ago; the very road had vanished under a flood of tropical vegetation as effectually as if swallowed by the sea; and the main gallery had fallen in within a hundred yards from the entrance. It was no longer an abandoned mine; it was a wild, inaccessible, and rocky gorge of the Sierra, where vestiges of charred timber, some heaps of smashed bricks, and a few shapeless pieces of rusty iron could have been found under the matted mass of thorny creepers covering the ground. Mr Gould, senior, did not desire the perpetual possession of that desolate locality; in fact, the mere vision of it arising before his mind in the still watches of the night had the power to exasperate him into hours of hot and agitated insomnia.

It so happened, however, that the Finance Minister of the time was a man to whom, in years gone by, Mr Gould had, unfortunately, declined to grant some small pecuniary assistance, basing his refusal on the ground that the applicant was a notorious gambler and cheat, besides being more than half suspected of a robbery with violence on a wealthy *ranchero* in a remote country district, where he was actually exercising the function of a judge.

Now, after reaching his exalted position, that politician had proclaimed his intention to repay evil with good to Señor Gould – the poor man. He affirmed and re-affirmed this resolution in the drawing-rooms of Sta Marta, in a soft and implacable voice, and with such malicious glances that Mr Gould's best friends advised him earnestly to attempt no bribery to get the matter dropped. It would have been useless. Indeed, it would not have been a very safe proceeding. Such was also the opinion of a stout, loud-voiced lady of French extraction, the daughter, she said, of an officer of high rank (*officier supérieur de l'armée*), who was accommodated with lodgings within the walls of a secularized convent next door to the Ministry of Finance. That florid person, when approached on behalf of Mr Gould in a proper manner, and with a suitable present, shook her head despondently. She was good-natured, and her despondency was genuine. She imagined she could not take money in consideration of something she could not accomplish. The friend of Mr Gould, charged with the delicate mission, used to say afterwards that she was the only honest person closely or remotely connected with the Government he had ever met. 'No go,' she had said with a cavalier, husky intonation which was natural to her, and using turns of expression more suitable to a child of parents unknown than to the orphaned daughter of a general officer. 'No; it's no go. *Pas moyen, mon garçon. C'est dommage, tout de même. Ah! zut! Je ne vole pas mon monde. Je ne suis pas ministre – moi! Vous pouvez emporter votre petit sac.*'

For a moment, biting her carmine lip, she deplored inwardly the tyranny of the rigid principles governing the sale of her influence in high places. Then, significantly, and with a touch of impatience, '*Allez*,' she added, '*et dites bien à votre bonhomme – entendez-vous? – qu'il faut avaler la pilule.*'

After such a warning there was nothing for it but to sign and pay. Mr Gould had swallowed the pill, and it was as though it had been compounded of some subtle poison that acted directly on his brain. He became at once mine-ridden, and as he was well read in light literature it took to his mind the form of the Old Man of the Sea fastened upon his shoulders. He also began to dream of vampires. Mr Gould exaggerated to himself the disadvantages of his new position, because he viewed it emotionally. His position in Costaguana was no worse than before. But man is a desperately conservative creature, and the extravagant novelty of this outrage upon his purse distressed his sensibilities. Everybody around him was being robbed by the grotesque and murderous bands that played their game of governments and revolutions after the death of Guzman Bento. His experience had taught him that, however short the plunder might fall of their legitimate expectations, no gang in possession of the Presidential Palace would be so incompetent as to suffer itself to be baffled by the want of a pretext. The first casual colonel of the barefooted army of scarecrows that came along was able to expose with force and precision to any mere civilian his titles to a sum of ten thousand dollars; the while his hope would be immutably fixed upon a gratuity, at any rate, of no less than a thousand. Mr Gould knew that very well, and, armed with resignation, had waited for better times. But to be robbed under the forms of legality and business was intolerable to his imagination. Mr Gould, the father, had one fault in his sagacious and honourable character: he attached too much importance to form. It is a failing common to mankind, whose views are tinged by prejudices. There was for him in that affair a malignancy of perverted justice which, by means of a moral shock, attacked his vigorous physique. 'It will end by killing me,' he used to affirm many times a day. And, in fact, since that time he began to suffer from fever, from liver pains, and mostly from a worrying inability to think of anything else. The Finance Minister could have formed no conception of the profound subtlety of his revenge. Even Mr Gould's letters to his fourteen-year-old boy Charles, then away in England for his education, came at last to talk of practically nothing but the mine. He groaned over the injustice, the persecution, the outrage of that mine; he occupied whole pages in the exposition of the fatal consequences attaching to the possession of that mine from every point of view, with every dismal inference, with words of horror at the apparently eternal character of that curse. For the Concession had been granted to him and his descendants for ever. He implored his son never to return to Costaguana, never to claim any part of his inheritance there, because it was tainted by the infamous Concession; never to touch it, never to approach it, to forget that America existed, and pursue a mercantile career in Europe. And each letter ended with bitter self-reproaches for having stayed too long in that cavern of thieves, intriguers, and brigands.

To be told repeatedly that one's future is blighted because of the possession of a silver mine is not, at the age of fourteen, a matter of prime importance as to its main statement; but in its form it is calculated to excite a certain amount of wonder and attention. In course of time the boy, at first only puzzled by the angry jeremiads, but rather sorry for his dad, began to turn the matter over in his mind in such moments as he could spare from play and study. In about a year he had evolved from the lecture of the letters a definite conviction that there was a silver mine in the Sulaco province of the Republic of Costaguana, where poor Uncle Harry had been shot by soldiers a great many years before. There was also connected closely with that mine a thing called the 'iniquitous Gould Concession', apparently written on a paper which his father desired ardently to 'tear and fling into the faces' of presidents, members of judicature, and ministers of State. And this desire persisted, though the names of these people, he noticed, seldom remained the same for a whole year together. This desire (since the thing was iniquitous) seemed quite natural to the boy, though why the affair was iniquitous he did not know. Afterwards, with advancing wisdom, he managed to clear the plain truth of the business from the fantastic intrusions of the Old Man of the Sea, vampires, and ghouls, which had lent to his father's correspondence the flavour of a gruesome Arabian Nights tale. In the end, the growing youth attained to as close an intimacy with the San Tomé mine as the old man who wrote these plaintive and enraged letters on the other side of the sea. He had been made several times already to pay heavy fines for neglecting to work the mine, he reported, besides other sums extracted from him on account of future royalties, on the ground that a man with such a valuable concession in his pocket could not refuse his financial assistance to the Government of the Republic. The last of his fortune was passing away from him against worthless receipts, he wrote, in a rage, whilst he was being pointed out as an individual who had known how to secure enormous advantages from the necessities of his country. And the young man in Europe grew more and more interested in that thing which could provoke such a tumult of words and passion.

He thought of it every day; but he thought of it without bitterness. It might have been an unfortunate affair for his poor dad, and the whole story threw a queer light upon the social and political life of Costaguana. The view he took of it was sympathetic to his father, yet calm and reflective. His personal feelings had not been outraged, and it is difficult to resent with proper and durable indignation the physical or mental anguish of another organism, even if that other organism is one's own father. By the time he was twenty Charles Gould had, in his turn, fallen under the spell of the San Tomé mine. But it was another form of enchantment, more suitable to his youth, into whose magic formula there entered hope, vigour, and self-confidence, instead of weary indignation and despair. Left after he was twenty to his own guidance (except for the severe injunction not to return to Costaguana), he had pursued his studies in Belgium and France with the idea of qualifying for a mining engineer. But this scientific aspect of his labours remained vague and imperfect in his mind. Mines had acquired for him a dramatic interest. He studied their peculiarities from a personal point of view, too, as one would study the varied characters of men. He visited them as one goes with curiosity to call upon remarkable persons. He visited mines in Germany, in Spain, in Cornwall. Abandoned workings had for him strong fascination. Their desolation appealed to him like the sight of human misery, whose causes are varied and profound. They might have been worthless, but also they might have been misunderstood. His future wife was the first, and perhaps the only person to detect this secret mood which governed the profoundly sensible, almost voiceless attitude of this man towards the world of material things. And at once her delight in him, lingering with half-open wings like those birds that cannot rise easily from a flat level, found a pinnacle from which to soar up into the skies.

They had become acquainted in Italy, where the future Mrs Gould was staying with an old and pale aunt who, years before, had married a middle-aged, impoverished Italian marquis. She now mourned that man, who had known how to give up his life to the independence and unity of his country, who had known how to be as enthusiastic in his generosity as the youngest of those who fell for that very cause of which old Giorgio Viola was a drifting relic, as a broken spar is suffered to float away disregarded after a naval victory. The Marchesa led a still, whispering existence, nun-like in her black robes and a white band over the forehead, in a corner of the first floor of an ancient and ruinous palace, whose big, empty halls downstairs sheltered under their painted ceilings the harvests, the fowls, and even the cattle, together with the whole family of the tenant farmer.

The two young people had met in Lucca. After that meeting Charles Gould visited no mines, though they went together in a carriage, once, to see some marble quarries, where the work resembled mining in so far that it also was the tearing of the raw material of treasure from the earth. Charles Gould did not open his heart to her in any set speeches. He simply went on

acting and thinking in her sight. This is the true method of sincerity. One
of his frequent remarks was, 'I think sometimes that poor father takes a
wrong view of that San Tomé business.' And they discussed that opinion
long and earnestly, as if they could influence a mind across half the globe;
but in reality they discussed it because the sentiment of love can enter into
any subject and live ardently in remote phrases. For this natural reason
these discussions were precious to Mrs Gould in her engaged state. Charles
feared that Mr Gould, senior, was wasting his strength and making himself
ill by his efforts to get rid of the Concession. 'I fancy that this is not the kind
of handling it requires,' he mused aloud, as if to himself. And when she
wondered frankly that a man of character should devote his energies to
plotting and intrigues, Charles would remark, with a gentle concern that
understood her wonder, 'You must not forget that he was born there.'

She would set her quick mind to work upon that, and then make the
inconsequent retort, which he accepted as perfectly sagacious, because, in
fact, it was so –

'Well, and you? You were born there, too.'

He knew his answer.

'That's different. I've been away ten years. Dad never had such a long
spell; and it was more than thirty years ago.'

She was the first person to whom he opened his lips after receiving the
news of his father's death.

'It has killed him!' he said.

He had walked straight out of town with the news, straight out before
him in the noonday sun on the white road, and his feet had brought him
face to face with her in the hall of the ruined *palazzo*, a room magnificent
and naked, with here and there a long strip of damask, black with damp and
age, hanging down on a bare panel of the wall. It was furnished with exactly
one gilt armchair, with a broken back, and an octagon columnar stand
bearing a heavy marble vase ornamented with sculptured masks and garlands
of flowers, and cracked from top to bottom. Charles Gould was dusty with
the white dust of the road lying on his boots, on his shoulders, on his cap
with two peaks. Water dripped from under it all over his face, and he
grasped a thick oaken cudgel in his bare right hand.

She went very pale under the roses of her big straw hat, gloved, swinging
a clear sunshade, caught just as she was going out to meet him at the bottom
of the hill, where three poplars stand near the wall of a vineyard.

'It has killed him!' he repeated. 'He ought to have had many years yet.
We are a long-lived family.'

She was too startled to say anything; he was contemplating with a
penetrating and motionless stare the cracked marble urn as though he had
resolved to fix its shape for ever in his memory. It was only when, turning
suddenly to her, he blurted out twice, 'I've come to you – I've come straight
to you –,' without being able to finish his phrase, that the great pitifulness
of that lonely and tormented death in Costaguana came to her with the full
force of its misery. He caught hold of her hand, raised it to his lips, and at
that she dropped her parasol to pat him on the cheek, murmured 'Poor boy',
and began to dry her eyes under the downward curve of her hat-brim, very

small in her simple, white frock, almost like a lost child crying in the degraded grandeur of the noble hall, while he stood by her, again perfectly motionless in the contemplation of the marble urn.

Afterwards they went out for a long walk, which was silent till he exclaimed suddenly:

'Yes. But if he had only grappled with it in a proper way!'

And then they stopped. Everywhere there were long shadows lying on the hills, on the roads, on the enclosed fields of olive trees; the shadows of poplars, of wide chestnuts, of farm buildings, of stone walls; and in mid-air the sound of a bell, thin and alert, was like the throbbing pulse of the sunset glow. Her lips were slightly parted as though in surprise that he should not be looking at her with his usual expression. His usual expression was unconditionally approving and attentive. He was in his talks with her the most anxious and deferential of dictators, an attitude that pleased her immensely. It affirmed her power without detracting from her dignity. That slight girl, with her little feet, little hands, little face attractively overweighted by great coils of hair; with a rather large mouth, whose mere parting seemed to breathe upon you the fragrance of frankness and generosity, had the fastidious soul of an experienced woman. She was, before all things and all flatteries, careful of her pride in the object of her choice. But now he was actually not looking at her at all; and his expression was tense and irrational, as is natural in a man who elects to stare at nothing past a young girl's head.

'Well, yes. It was iniquitous. They corrupted him thoroughly, the poor old boy. Oh! why wouldn't he let me go back to him? But now I shall know how to grapple with this.'

After pronouncing these words with immense assurance, he glanced down at her, and at once fell a prey to distress, incertitude, and fear.

The only thing he wanted to know now, he said, was whether she did love him enough – whether she would have the courage to go with him so far away? He put these questions to her in a voice that trembled with anxiety – for he was a determined man.

She did. She would. And immediately the future hostess of all the Europeans in Sulaco had the physical experience of the earth falling away from under her. It vanished completely, even to the very sound of the bell. When her feet touched the ground again, the bell was still ringing in the valley; she put her hands up to her hair, breathing quickly, and glanced up and down the stony lane. It was reassuringly empty. Meantime, Charles, stepping with one foot into a dry and dusty ditch, picked up the open parasol, which had bounded away from them with a martial sound of drum taps. He handed it to her soberly, a little crestfallen.

They turned back, and after she had slipped her hand on his arm, the first words he pronounced were:

'It's lucky that we shall be able to settle in a coast town. You've heard its name. It is Sulaco. I am so glad poor Father did get that house. He bought a big house there years ago, in order that there should always be a Casa Gould in the principal town of what used to be called the Occidental Province. I lived there once, as a small boy, with my dear mother, for a

whole year, while poor Father was away in the United States on business.
You shall be the new mistress of the Casa Gould.'

And later, in the inhabited corner of the Palazzo above the vineyards, the
marble hills, the pines and olives of Lucca, he also said:

'The name of Gould has been always highly respected in Sulaco. My
uncle Harry was chief of the State for some time, and has left a great name
amongst the first families. By this I mean the pure Creole families, who take
no part in the miserable farce of governments. Uncle Harry was no adventurer. In Costaguana we Goulds are no adventurers. He was of the country,
and he loved it, but he remained essentially an Englishman in his ideas. He
made use of the political cry of his time. It was Federation. But he was no
politician. He simply stood up for social order out of pure love for rational
liberty and from his hate of oppression. There was no nonsense about him.
He went to work in his own way because it seemed right, just as I feel I
must lay hold of that mine.'

In such words he talked to her because his memory was very full of the
country of his childhood, his heart of his life with that girl, and his mind of
the San Tomé Concession. He added that he would have to leave her for a
few days to find an American, a man from San Francisco, who was still
somewhere in Europe. A few months before he had made his acquaintance
in an old historic German town, situated in a mining district. The American
had his womankind with him, but seemed lonely while they were sketching
all day long the old doorways and the turreted corners of the medieval
houses. Charles Gould had with him the inseparable companionship of the
mine. The other man was interested in mining enterprises, knew something
of Costaguana, and was no stranger to the name of Gould. They had talked
together with some intimacy which was made possible by the difference of
their ages. Charles wanted now to find that capitalist of shrewd mind and
accessible character. His father's fortune in Costaguana, which he had
supposed to be still considerable, seemed to have melted in the rascally
crucible of revolutions. Apart from some ten thousand pounds deposited in
England, there appeared to be nothing left except the house in Sulaco, a
vague right of forest exploitation in a remote and savage district, and the
San Tomé Concession, which had attended his poor father to the very brink
of the grave.

He explained those things. It was late when they parted. She had never
before given him such a fascinating vision of herself. All the eagerness of
youth for a strange life, for great distances, for a future in which there was
an air of adventure, of combat – a subtle thought of redress and conquest,
had filled her with an intense excitement, which she returned to the giver
with a more open and exquisite display of tenderness.

He left her to walk down the hill, and directly he found himself alone he
became sober. That irreparable change a death makes in the course of our
daily thoughts can be felt in a vague and poignant discomfort of mind. It
hurt Charles Gould to feel that never more, by no effort of will, would he
be able to think of his father in the same way he used to think of him when
the poor man was alive. His breathing image was no longer in his power.
This consideration, closely affecting his own identity, filled his breast with

a mournful and angry desire for action. In this his instinct was unerring. Action is consolatory. It is the enemy of thought and the friend of flattering illusions. Only in the conduct of our action can we find the sense of mastery over the Fates. For his action, the mine was obviously the only field. It was imperative sometimes to know how to disobey the solemn wishes of the dead. He resolved firmly to make his disobedience as thorough (by way of atonement) as it well could be. The mine had been the cause of an absurd moral disaster; its working must be made a serious and moral success. He owed it to the dead man's memory. Such were the – properly speaking – emotions of Charles Gould. His thoughts ran upon the means of raising a large amount of capital in San Francisco or elsewhere; and incidentally there occurred to him also the general reflection that the counsel of the departed must be an unsound guide. Not one of them could be aware beforehand what enormous changes the death of any given individual may produce in the very aspect of the world.

The latest phase in the history of the mine Mrs Gould knew from personal experience. It was in essence the history of her married life. The mantle of the Goulds' hereditary position in Sulaco had descended amply upon her little person; but she would not allow the peculiarities of the strange garment to weigh down the vivacity of her character, which was the sign of no mere mechanical sprightliness, but of an eager intelligence. It must not be supposed that Mrs Gould's mind was masculine. A woman with a masculine mind is not a being of superior efficiency; she is simply a phenomenon of imperfect differentiation – interestingly barren and without importance. Doña Emilia's intelligence being feminine led her to achieve the conquest of Sulaco, simply by lighting the way for her unselfishness and sympathy. She could converse charmingly, but she was not talkative. The wisdom of the heart having no concern with the erection or demolition of theories any more than with the defence of prejudices, has no random words at its command. The words it pronounces have the value of acts of integrity, tolerance, and compassion. A woman's true tenderness, like the true virility of man, is expressed in action of a conquering kind. The ladies of Sulaco adored Mrs Gould. 'They still look upon me as something of a monster,' Mrs Gould had said pleasantly to one of the three gentlemen from San Francisco she had to entertain in her new Sulaco house just about a year after her marriage.

They were her first visitors from abroad, and they had come to look at the San Tomé mine. She jested most agreeably, they thought; and Charles Gould, besides knowing thoroughly what he was about, had shown himself a real hustler. These facts caused them to be well disposed towards his wife. An unmistakable enthusiasm, pointed by a slight flavour of irony, made her talk of the mine absolutely fascinating to her visitors, and provoked them to grave and indulgent smiles in which there was a good deal of deference. Perhaps had they known how much she was inspired by an idealistic view of success they would have been amazed at the state of her mind as the Spanish–American ladies had been amazed at the tireless activity of her body. She would – in her own words – have been for them 'something of a monster'. However, the Goulds were in essentials a reticent couple, and their guests departed without the suspicion of any other purpose but simple profit in the working of a silver mine. Mrs Gould had out her own carriage, with two white mules, to drive them down to the harbour, whence the *Ceres* was to carry them off into the Olympus of plutocrats. Captain Mitchell had snatched at the occasion of leave-taking to remark to Mrs Gould, in a low, confidential mutter, 'This marks an epoch.'

Mrs Gould loved the patio of her Spanish house. A broad flight of stone steps was overlooked silently from a niche in the wall by a Madonna in blue robes with the crowned child sitting on her arm. Subdued voices ascended in the early mornings from the paved well of the quadrangle, with the stamping of horses and mules led out in pairs to drink at the cistern. A tangle of slender bamboo stems drooped its narrow, blade-like leaves over the square pool of water, and the fat coachman sat muffled up on the edge, holding lazily the ends of halters in his hand. Barefooted servants passed to and fro, issuing from dark, low doorways below; two laundry girls with baskets of washed linen; the baker with the tray of bread made for the day; Leonarda – her own *camerista* – bearing high up, swung from her hand raised above her raven black head, a bunch of starched underskirts dazzlingly white in the slant of sunshine. Then the old porter would hobble in, sweeping the flagstones, and the house was ready for the day. All the lofty rooms on three sides of the quadrangle opened into each other and into the *corredor*, with its wrought-iron railings and a border of flowers, whence, like the lady of the medieval castle, she could witness from above all the departures and arrivals of the Casa, to which the sonorous arched gateway lent an air of stately importance.

She had watched her carriage roll away with the three guests from the north. She smiled. Their three arms went up simultaneously to their three hats. Captain Mitchell, the fourth, in attendance, had already begun a pompous discourse. Then she lingered. She lingered, approaching her face to the clusters of flowers here and there as if to give time to her thoughts to catch up with her slow footsteps along the straight vista of the corridor.

A fringed Indian hammock from Aroa, gay with coloured featherwork, had been swung judiciously in a corner that caught the early sun; for the mornings are cool in Sulaco. The cluster of *flor de noche buena* blazed in great masses before the open glass doors of the reception-rooms. A big green parrot, brilliant like an emerald in a cage that flashed like gold, screamed out ferociously, '*Viva Costaguana!*' then called twice mellifluously, '*Leonarda! Leonarda!*' in imitation of Mrs Gould's voice, and suddenly took refuge in immobility and silence. Mrs Gould reached the end of the gallery and put her head through the door of her husband's room.

Charles Gould, with one foot on a low wooden stool, was already strapping his spurs. He wanted to hurry back to the mine. Mrs Gould, without coming in, glanced about the room. One tall, broad bookcase, with glass doors, was full of books; but in the other, without shelves, and lined with red baize, were arranged firearms: Winchester carbines, revolvers, a couple of shot-guns, and even two pairs of double-barrelled holster pistols. Between them, by itself, upon a strip of scarlet velvet, hung an old cavalry sabre, once the property of Don Enrique Gould, the hero of the Occidental Province, presented by Don José Avellanos, the hereditary friend of the family.

Otherwise, the plastered white walls were completely bare, except for a water-colour sketch of the San Tomé mountain – the work of Doña Emilia herself. In the middle of the red-tiled floor stood two long tables littered with plans and papers, a few chairs, and a glass show-case containing specimens of ore from the mine. Mrs Gould, looking at all these things in turn, wondered aloud why the talk of these wealthy and enterprising men discussing the prospects, the working, and the safety of the mine rendered her so impatient and uneasy, whereas she could talk of the mine by the hour with her husband with unwearied interest and satisfaction.

And dropping her eyelids expressively, she added:

'What do *you* feel about it, Charley?'

Then, surprised at her husband's silence, she raised her eyes, opened wide, as pretty as pale flowers. He had done with the spurs, and, twisting his moustache with both hands, horizontally, he contemplated her from the height of his long legs with a visible appreciation of her appearance. The consciousness of being thus contemplated pleased Mrs Gould.

'They are considerable men,' he said.

'I know. But have you listened to their conversation? They don't seem to have understood anything they have seen here.'

'They have seen the mine. They have understood that to some purpose,' Charles Gould interjected, in defence of the visitors; and then his wife mentioned the name of the most considerable of the three. He was considerable in finance and in industry. His name was familiar to many millions of people. He was so considerable that he would never have travelled so far away from the centre of his activity if the doctors had not insisted, with veiled menaces, on his taking a long holiday.

'Mr Holroyd's sense of religion,' Mrs Gould pursued, 'was shocked and disgusted at the tawdriness of the dressed-up saints in the cathedral – the worship, he called it, of wood and tinsel. But it seemed to me that he looked upon his own God as a sort of influential partner, who gets his share of profits in the endowment of churches. That's a sort of idolatry. He told me he endowed churches every year, Charley.'

'No end of them,' said Mr Gould, marvelling inwardly at the mobility of her physiognomy. 'All over the country. He's famous for that sort of munificence.'

'Oh, he didn't boast,' Mrs Gould declared, scrupulously. 'I believe he's really a good man, but so stupid! A poor Chulo who offers a little silver arm or leg to thank his god for a cure is as rational and more touching.'

'He's at the head of immense silver and iron interests,' Charles Gould observed.

'Ah, yes! The religion of silver and iron. He's a very civil man, though he looked awfully solemn when he first saw the Madonna on the staircase, who's only wood and paint; but he said nothing to me. My dear Charley, I heard those men talk among themselves. Can it be that they really wish to become, for an immense consideration, drawers of water and hewers of wood to all the countries and nations of the earth?'

'A man must work to some end,' Charles Gould said, vaguely.

Mrs Gould, frowning, surveyed him from head to foot. With his riding-breeches, leather leggings (an article of apparel never before seen in Costaguana), a Norfolk coat of grey flannel, and those great flaming moustaches, he suggested an officer of cavalry turned gentleman farmer. This combination was gratifying to Mrs Gould's tastes. 'How thin the poor boy is!' she thought. 'He overworks himself.' But there was no denying that his fine-drawn, keen red face, and his whole, long-limbed, lank person had an air of breeding and distinction. And Mrs Gould relented.

'I only wondered what you felt,' she murmured, gently.

During the last few days, as it happened, Charles Gould had been kept too busy thinking twice before he spoke to have paid much attention to the state of his feelings. But theirs was a successful match, and he had no difficulty in finding his answer.

'The best of my feelings are in your keeping, my dear,' he said lightly; and there was so much truth in that obscure phrase that he experienced towards her at the moment a great increase of gratitude and tenderness.

Mrs Gould, however, did not seem to find this answer in the least obscure. She brightened up delicately; already he had changed his tone.

'But there are facts. The worth of the mine – as a mine – is beyond doubt. It shall make us very wealthy. The mere working of it is a matter of technical knowledge, which I have – which ten thousand other men in the world have. But its safety, its continued existence as an enterprise, giving a return to men – to strangers, comparative strangers – who invest money in it, is left altogether in my hands. I have inspired confidence in a man of wealth and position. You seem to think this perfectly natural – do you? Well, I don't know. I don't know why I have; but it is a fact. This fact makes everything possible, because without it I would never have thought of disregarding my father's wishes. I would never have disposed of the Concession as a speculator disposes of a valuable right to a company – for cash and shares, to grow rich eventually if possible, but at any rate to put some money at once in his pocket. No. Even if it had been feasible – which I doubt – I would not have done so. Poor Father did not understand. He was afraid I would hang on to the ruinous thing, waiting for just some such chance, and waste my life miserably. That was the true sense of his prohibition, which we have deliberately set aside.'

They were walking up and down the corridor. Her head just reached to his shoulder. His arm, extended downwards, was about her waist. His spurs jingled slightly.

'He had not seen me for ten years. He did not know me. He parted from me for my sake, and he would never let me come back. He was always talking in his letters of leaving Costaguana, of abandoning everything and making his escape. But he was too valuable a prey. They would have thrown him into one of their prisons at the first suspicion.'

His spurred feet clinked slowly. He was bending over his wife as they walked. The big parrot, turning its head askew, followed their pacing figures with a round, unblinking eye.

'He was a lonely man. Ever since I was ten years old he used to talk to me as if I had been grown up. When I was in Europe he wrote to me every month. Ten, twelve pages every month of my life for ten years. And, after all, he did not know me! Just think of it – ten whole years away; the years I was growing up into a man. He could not know me. Do you think he could?'

Mrs Gould shook her head negatively; which was just what her husband had expected from the strength of the argument. But she shook her head negatively only because she thought that no one could know her Charles – really know him for what he was but herself. The thing was obvious. It could be felt. It required no argument. And poor Mr Gould, senior, who had died too soon to ever hear of their engagement, remained too shadowy a figure for her to be credited with knowledge of any sort whatever.

'No, he did not understand. In my view this mine could never have been a thing to sell. Never! After all his misery I simply could not have touched it for money alone,' Charles Gould pursued: and she pressed her head to his shoulder approvingly.

These two young people remembered the life which had ended wretchedly just when their own lives had come together in that splendour of hopeful love, which to the most sensible minds appears like a triumph of good over all the evils of the earth. A vague idea of rehabilitation had entered the plan of their life. That it was so vague as to elude the support of argument made it only the stronger. It had presented itself to them at the instant when the woman's instinct of devotion and the man's instinct of activity receive from the strongest of illusions their most powerful impulse. The very prohibition imposed the necessity of success. It was as if they had been morally bound to make good their vigorous view of life against the unnatural error of weariness and despair. If the idea of wealth was present to them it was only so far as it was bound with that other success. Mrs Gould, an orphan from early childhood and without fortune, brought up in an atmosphere of intellectual interests, had never considered the aspects of great wealth. They were too remote, and she had not learned that they were desirable. On the other hand, she had not known anything of absolute want. Even the very poverty of her aunt, the Marchesa, had nothing intolerable to a refined mind; it seemed in accord with a great grief; it had the austerity of a sacrifice offered to a noble idea. Thus even the most legitimate touch of materialism was wanting in Mrs Gould's character. The dead man of whom she thought with tenderness (because he was Charley's father), and with some impatience (because he had been weak), must be put completely in the wrong. Nothing else would do to keep their prosperity without a stain on its only real, on its immaterial side!

Charles Gould, on his part, had been obliged to keep the idea of wealth well to the fore; but he brought it forward as a means, not as an end. Unless the mine was good business it could not be touched. He had to insist on that aspect of the enterprise. It was his lever to move men who had capital. And Charles Gould believed in the mine. He knew everything that could be known of it. His faith in the mine was contagious, though it was not served by a great eloquence; but businessmen are frequently as sanguine and imaginative as lovers. They are affected by a personality much oftener than people would suppose; and Charles Gould, in his unshaken assurance, was absolutely convincing. Besides, it was a matter of common knowledge to the men to whom he addressed himself that mining in Costaguana was a game that could be made considerably more than worth the candle. The men of affairs knew that very well. The real difficulty in touching it was elsewhere. Against that there was an implication of calm and implacable resolution in Charles Gould's very voice. Men of affairs venture sometimes on acts that the common judgement of the world would pronounce absurd; they make their decisions on apparently impulsive and human grounds. 'Very well,' had said the considerable personage to whom Charles Gould on his way out through San Francisco had lucidly exposed his point of view. 'Let us suppose that the mining affairs of Sulaco are taken in hand. There would then be in it: first, the house of Holroyd, which is all right; then, Mr Charles Gould, a citizen of Costaguana, who is also all right; and, lastly, the Government of the Republic. So far this resembles the first start of the Atacama nitrate fields, where there was a financing house, a gentleman of the name of Edwards, and – a Government; or, rather, two Governments – two South American Governments. And you know what came of it. War came of it; devastating and prolonged war came of it, Mr Gould. However, here we possess the advantage of having only one South American Government hanging around for plunder out of the deal. It is an advantage; but then there are degrees of badness, and that Government is the Costaguana Government.'

Thus spoke the considerable personage, the millionaire endower of churches on a scale befitting the greatness of his native land – the same to whom the doctors used the language of horrid and veiled menaces. He was a big-limbed, deliberate man, whose quiet burliness lent to an ample silk-faced frock-coat a superfine dignity. His hair was iron grey, his eyebrows were still black, and his massive profile was the profile of a Caesar's head on an old Roman coin. But his parentage was German and Scotch and English, with remote strains of Danish and French blood, giving him the temperament of a Puritan and an insatiable imagination of conquest. He was completely unbending to his visitor, because of the warm introduction the visitor had brought from Europe, and because of an irrational liking for earnestness and determination wherever met, to whatever end directed.

'The Costaguana Government shall play its hand for all it's worth – and don't you forget it, Mr Gould. Now, what is Costaguana? It is the bottomless pit of ten-per-cent loans and other fool investments. European capital had been flung into it with both hands for years. Not ours, though. We in this country know just about enough to keep indoors when it rains. We can sit and watch. Of course, some day we shall step in. We are bound to. But there's no hurry. Time itself has got to wait on the greatest country in the whole of God's Universe. We shall be giving the word for everything: industry, trade, law, journalism, art, politics, and religion, from Cape Horn clear over to Smith's Sound, and beyond, too, if anything worth taking hold of turns up at the North Pole. And then we shall have the leisure to take in hand the outlying islands and continents of the earth. We shall run the world's business whether the world likes it or not. The world can't help it – and neither can we, I guess.'

By this he meant to express his faith in destiny in words suitable to his intelligence, which was unskilled in the presentation of general ideas. His intelligence was nourished on facts; and Charles Gould, whose imagination had been permanently affected by the one great fact of a silver mine, had no objection to this theory of the world's future. If it had seemed distasteful for a moment it was because the sudden statement of such vast eventualities dwarfed almost to nothingness the actual matter in hand. He and his plans and all the mineral wealth of the Occidental Province appeared suddenly robbed of every vestige of magnitude. The sensation was disagreeable; but Charles Gould was not dull. Already he felt that he was producing a favourable impression; the consciousness of that flattering fact helped him to a vague smile, which his big interlocutor took for a smile of discreet and admiring assent. He smiled quietly, too; and immediately Charles Gould, with that mental agility mankind will display in defence of a cherished hope, reflected that the very apparent insignificance of his aim would help him to success. His personality and his mine would be taken up because it was a matter of no great consequence, one way or another, to a man who referred his action to such a prodigious destiny. And Charles Gould was not humiliated by this consideration, because the thing remained as big as ever for him. Nobody else's vast conceptions of destiny could diminish the aspect of his desire for the redemption of the San Tomé mine. In comparison to the correctness of his aim, definite in space and absolutely attainable within a limited time, the other man appeared for an instant as a dreamy idealist of no importance.

The great man, massive and benignant, had been looking at him thoughtfully; when he broke the short silence it was to remark that concessions flew about thick in the air of Costaguana. Any simple soul that just yearned to be taken in could bring down a concession at the first shot.

'Our consuls get their mouths stopped with them,' he continued, with a twinkle of genial scorn in his eyes. But in a moment he became grave. 'A conscientious, upright man, that cares nothing for boodle, and keeps clear of their intrigues, conspiracies, and factions, soon gets his passports. See that, Mr Gould? *Persona non grata*. That's the reason our Government is never properly informed. On the other hand, Europe must be kept out of this continent, and for proper interference on our part the time is not yet ripe, I dare say. But we here – we are not this country's Government, neither are we simple souls. Your affair is all right. The main question for us is whether the second partner, and that's you, is the right sort to hold his own against the third and unwelcome partner, which is one or another of the high and mighty robber gangs that run the Costaguana Government. What do you think, Mr Gould, eh?'

He bent forward to look steadily into the unflinching eyes of Charles Gould, who, remembering the large box full of his father's letters, put the accumulated scorn and bitterness of many years into the tone of his answer:

'As far as the knowledge of these men and their methods and their politics is concerned, I can answer for myself. I have been fed on that sort of knowledge since I was a boy. I am not likely to fall into mistakes from excess of optimism.'

'Not likely, eh? That's all right. Tact and a stiff upper lip is what you'll want; and you could bluff a little on the strength of your backing. Not too much, though. We will go with you as long as the thing runs straight. But we won't be drawn into any large trouble. This is the experiment which I am willing to make. There is some risk, and we will take it; but if you can't keep up your end, we will stand our loss, of course, and then – we'll let the thing go. This mine can wait; it has been shut up before, you know. You must understand that under no circumstances will we consent to throw good money after bad.'

Thus the great personage had spoken then, in his own private office, in a great city where other men (very considerable in the eyes of a vain populace) waited with alacrity upon a wave of his hand. And rather more than a year later, during his unexpected appearance in Sulaco, he had emphasized his uncompromising attitude with a freedom of sincerity permitted to his wealth and influence. He did this with the less reserve, perhaps, because the inspection of what had been done, and more still the way in which successive steps had been taken, had impressed him with the conviction that Charles Gould was perfectly capable of keeping up his end.

'This young fellow,' he thought to himself, 'may yet become a power in the land.'

This thought flattered him, for hitherto the only account of this young man he could give to his intimates was:

'My brother-in-law met him in one of these one-horse old German towns, near some mines, and sent him on to me with a letter. He's one of the Costaguana Goulds, pure-bred Englishmen, but all born in the country. His uncle went into politics, was the last Provincial President of Sulaco, and got shot after a battle. His father was a prominent businessman in Sta Marta, tried to keep clear of their politics, and died ruined after a lot of revolutions. And that's your Costaguana in a nutshell.'

Of course, he was too great a man to be questioned as to his motives, even by his intimates. The outside world was at liberty to wonder respectfully at the hidden meaning of his actions. He was so great a man that his lavish patronage of the 'purer forms of Christianity' (which in its naïve form of church-building amused Mrs Gould) was looked upon by his fellow-citizens as the manifestation of a pious and humble spirit. But in his own circles of the financial world the taking up of such a thing as the San Tomé mine was regarded with respect, indeed, but rather as a subject for discreet jocularity. It was a great man's caprice. In the great Holroyd building (an enormous pile of iron, glass, and blocks of stone at the corner of two streets, cobwebbed aloft by the radiation of telegraph wires) the heads of principal departments exchanged humorous glances, which meant that they were not let into the secrets of the San Tomé business. The Costaguana mail (it was never large – one fairly heavy envelope) was taken unopened straight into the great man's room, and no instructions dealing with it had ever been issued thence. The office whispered that he answered personally – and not by dictation either, but actually writing in his own hand, with pen and ink, and, it was to be supposed, taking a copy in his own private press copybook, inaccessible to profane eyes. Some scornful young men, insignificant pieces of minor machinery in that eleven-storey-high workshop of great affairs, expressed frankly their private opinion that the great chief had done at last something silly, and was ashamed of his folly; others, elderly and insignificant, but full of romantic reverence for the business that had devoured their best years, used to mutter darkly and knowingly that this was a portentous sign; that the Holroyd connexion meant by-and-by to get hold of the whole Republic of Costaguana, lock, stock, and barrel. But, in fact, the hobby theory was the right one. It interested the great man to attend personally to the San Tomé mine; it interested him so much that he allowed this hobby to give a direction to the first complete holiday he had taken for quite a startling number of years. He was not running a great enterprise there; no mere railway board or industrial corporation. He was running a man! A success would have pleased him very much on refreshingly novel grounds; but, on the other side of the same feeling, it was incumbent upon him to cast it off utterly at the first sign of failure. A man may be thrown off. The papers had unfortunately trumpeted all over the land his journey to Costaguana. If he was pleased at the way Charles Gould was going on, he infused an added grimness into his assurances of support. Even at the very last interview, half an hour or so before he rolled out of the patio, hat in hand, behind Mrs Gould's white mules, he had said in Charles's room:

'You go ahead in your own way, and I shall know how to help you as long as you hold your own. But you may rest assured that in a given case we shall know how to drop you in time.'

To this Charles Gould's only answer had been: 'You may begin sending out the machinery as soon as you like.'

And the great man had liked this imperturbable assurance. The secret of it was that to Charles Gould's mind these uncompromising terms were agreeable. Like this the mine preserved its identity, with which he had endowed it as a boy; and it remained dependent on himself alone. It was a serious affair, and he, too, took it grimly.

'Of course,' he said to his wife, alluding to this last conversation with the departed guest, while they walked slowly up and down the corridor, followed by the irritated eye of the parrot – 'of course, a man of that sort can take up a thing or drop it when he likes. He will suffer from no sense of defeat. He may have to give in, or he may have to die tomorrow, but the great silver and iron interests shall survive, and some day shall get hold of Costaguana along with the rest of the world.'

They had stopped near the cage. The parrot, catching the sound of a word belonging to his vocabulary, was moved to interfere. Parrots are very human.

'*Viva Costaguana!*' he shrieked, with intense self-assertion, and, instantly ruffling up his feathers, assumed an air of puffed-up somnolence behind the glittering wires.

'And do you believe that, Charley?' Mrs Gould asked. 'This seems to me most awful materialism, and –'

'My dear, it's nothing to me,' interrupted her husband, in a reasonable tone. 'I make use of what I see. What's it to me whether his talk is the voice of destiny or simply a bit of claptrap eloquence? There's a good deal of eloquence of one sort or another produced in both Americas. The air of the

New World seems favourable to the art of declamation. Have you forgotten how dear Avellanos can hold forth for hours here –?'

'Oh, but that's different,' protested Mrs Gould, almost shocked. The allusion was not to the point. Don José was a dear good man, who talked very well, and was enthusiastic about the greatness of the San Tomé mine. 'How can you compare them, Charles?' she exclaimed, reproachfully. 'He has suffered – and yet he hopes.'

The working competence of men – which she never questioned – was very surprising to Mrs Gould, because upon so many obvious issues they showed themselves strangely muddleheaded.

Charles Gould, with a careworn calmness which secured for him at once his wife's anxious sympathy, assured her that he was not comparing. He was an American himself, after all, and perhaps he could understand both kinds of eloquence – 'if it were worth while to try,' he added, grimly. But he had breathed the air of England longer than any of his people had done for three generations, and really he begged to be excused. His poor father could be eloquent, too. And he asked his wife whether she remembered a passage in one of his father's last letters where Mr Gould had expressed the conviction that 'God looked wrathfully at these countries, or else He would let some ray of hope fall through a rift in the appalling darkness of intrigue, bloodshed, and crime that hung over the Queen of Continents'.

Mrs Gould had not forgotten. 'You read it to me, Charley,' she murmured. 'It was a striking pronouncement. How deeply your father must have felt its terrible sadness!'

'He did not like to be robbed. It exasperated him,' said Charles Gould. 'But the image will serve well enough. What is wanted here is law, good faith, order, security. Anyone can declaim about these things, but I pin my faith to material interests. Only let the material interests once get a firm footing, and they are bound to impose the conditions on which alone they can continue to exist. That's how your money-making is justified here in the face of lawlessness and disorder. It is justified because the security which it demands must be shared with an oppressed people. A better justice will come afterwards. That's your ray of hope.' His arm pressed her slight form closer to his side for a moment. 'And who knows whether in that sense even the San Tomé mine may not become that little rift in the darkness which poor Father despaired of ever seeing?'

She glanced up at him with admiration. He was competent; he had given a vast shape to the vagueness of her unselfish ambitions.

'Charley,' she said, 'you are splendidly disobedient.'

He left her suddenly in the *corredor* to go and get his hat, a soft, grey sombrero, an article of national costume which combined unexpectedly well with his English get-up. He came back, a riding-whip under his arm, buttoning up a dogskin glove; his face reflected the resolute nature of his thoughts. His wife had waited for him at the head of the stairs, and before he gave her the parting kiss he finished the conversation:

'What should be perfectly clear to us,' he said, 'is the fact that there is no going back. Where could we begin life afresh? We are in now for all that there is in us.'

He bent over her upturned face very tenderly and a little remorsefully. Charles Gould was competent because he had no illusions. The Gould Concession had to fight for life with such weapons as could be found at once in the mire of corruption that was so universal as to almost lose its significance. He was prepared to stoop for his weapons. For a moment he felt as if the silver mine, which had killed his father, had decoyed him further than he meant to go; and with the roundabout logic of emotions, he felt that the worthiness of his life was bound up with success. There was no going back.

CHAPTER 7

Mrs Gould was too intelligently sympathetic not to share that feeling. It made life exciting, and she was too much of a woman not to like excitement. But it frightened her, too, a little; and when Don José Avellanos, rocking in the American chair, would go so far as to say, 'Even, my dear Carlos, if you had failed; even if some untoward event were yet to destroy your work – which God forbid! – you would have deserved well of your country,' Mrs Gould would look up from the tea-table profoundly at her unmoved husband stirring the spoon in the cup as though he had not heard a word.

Not that Don José anticipated anything of the sort. He could not praise enough dear Carlos's tact and courage. His English, rock-like quality of character was his best safeguard, Don José affirmed; and, turning to Mrs Gould, 'As to you, Emilia, my soul' – he would address her with the familiarity of his age and old friendship – 'you are as true a patriot as though you had been born in our midst.'

This might have been less or more than the truth. Mrs Gould, accompanying her husband all over the province in the search for labour, had seen the land with a deeper glance than a true-born Costaguanera could have done. In her travel-worn riding habit, her face powdered white like a plaster cast, with a further protection of a small silk mask during the heat of the day, she rode on a well-shaped, light-footed pony in the centre of a little cavalcade. Two *mozos de campo*, picturesque in great hats, with spurred bare heels, in white embroidered *calzoneras*, leather jackets, and striped ponchos, rode ahead with carbines across their shoulders, swaying in unison to the pace of the horses. A tropilla of pack mules brought up the rear in charge of a thin brown muleteer, sitting his long-eared beast very near the tail, legs thrust far forward, the wide brim of his hat set far back, making a sort of halo for his head. An old Costaguana officer, a retired senior major of humble origin, but patronized by the first families on account of his Blanco opinions, had been recommended by Don José for commissary and organizer of that expedition. The points of his grey moustache hung far below his chin, and, riding on Mrs Gould's left hand, he looked about with kind eyes, pointing out the features of the country, telling the names of the little *pueblos* and of the estates, of the smooth-walled *haciendas* like long fortresses crowning the knolls above the level of the Sulaco Valley. It unrolled itself, with green young crops, plains, woodland, and gleams of water, park-like, from the blue vapour of the distant sierra to an immense quivering horizon of grass and sky, where big white clouds seemed to fall slowly into the darkness of their own shadows.

Men ploughed with wooden ploughs and yoked oxen, small on a boundless expanse, as if attacking immensity itself. The mounted figures of *vaqueros* galloped in the distance, and the great herds fed with all their horned heads one way, in one single wavering line as far as eye could reach across the broad *potreros*. A spreading cotton-wool tree shaded a thatched *ranche* by the road; the trudging files of burdened Indians, taking off their hats, would lift sad, mute eyes to the cavalcade raising the dust of the crumbling *camino real* made by the hands of their enslaved forefathers. And Mrs Gould, with each day's journey, seemed to come nearer to the soul of the land in the tremendous disclosure of this interior unaffected by the slight European veneer of the coast towns, a great land of plain and mountain and people, suffering and mute, waiting for the future in a pathetic immobility of patience.

She knew its sights and its hospitality, dispensed with a sort of slumbrous dignity in those great houses presenting long, blind walls and heavy portals to the windswept pastures. She was given the head of the tables, where masters and dependants sat in a simple and patriarchal state. The ladies of the house would talk softly in the moonlight under the orange trees of the courtyards, impressing upon her the sweetness of their voices and the something mysterious in the quietude of their lives. In the morning the gentlemen, well mounted in braided sombreros and embroidered riding-suits, with much silver on the trappings of their horses, would ride forth to escort the departing guests before committing them, with grave good-byes, to the care of God at the boundary pillars of their estates. In all these households she could hear stories of political outrage; friends, relatives, ruined, impris-oned, killed in the battles of senseless civil wars, barbarously executed in ferocious proscriptions, as though the government of the country had been a struggle of lust between bands of absurd devils let loose upon the land with sabres and uniforms and grandiloquent phrases. And on all the lips she found a weary desire for peace, the dread of officialdom with its nightmarish parody of administration without law, without security, and without justice.

She bore a whole two months of wandering very well; she had that power of resistance to fatigue which one discovers here and there in some quite frail-looking women with surprise – like a state of possession by a remarkably stubborn spirit. Don Pepe – the old Costaguana major – after much display of solicitude for the delicate lady, had ended by conferring upon her the name of the 'Never-tired Señora'. Mrs Gould was indeed becoming a Costaguanera. Having acquired in southern Europe a knowledge of true peasantry, she was able to appreciate the great worth of the people. She saw the man under the silent, sad-eyed beast of burden. She saw them on the road carrying loads, lonely figures upon the plain, toiling under great straw hats, with their white clothing flapping about their limbs in the wind; she remembered the villages by some group of Indian women at the fountain impressed upon her memory, by the face of some young Indian girl with a melancholy and sensual profile, raising an earthenware vessel of cool water at the door of a dark hut with a wooden porch cumbered with great brown jars. The solid wooden wheels of an ox-cart, halted with its shafts in the dust, showed the strokes of the axe; and a party of charcoal carriers, with each man's load resting above his head on the top of the low mud wall, slept stretched in a row within the strip of shade.

The heavy stonework of bridges and churches left by the conquerors proclaimed the disregard of human labour, the tribute-labour of vanished nations. The power of king and church was gone, but at the sight of some heavy ruinous pile overtopping from a knoll the low mud walls of a village, Don Pepe would interrupt the tale of his campaigns to exclaim:

'Poor Costaguana! Before, it was everything for the padres, nothing for the people; and now it is everything for these great *políticos* in Sta Marta, for Negroes and thieves.'

Charles talked with the *alcaldes*, with the *fiscales*, with the principal people in towns, and with the *caballeros* on the estates. The *comandantes* of the districts offered him escorts – for he could show an authorization from the Sulaco political chief of the day. How much the document had cost him in gold twenty-dollar pieces was a secret between himself, a great man in the United States (who condescended to answer the Sulaco mail with his own hand), and a great man of another sort, with a dark olive complexion and shifty eyes, inhabiting then the Palace of the Intendencia in Sulaco, and who piqued himself on his culture and Europeanism generally in a rather French style because he had lived in Europe for some years – in exile, he said. However, it was pretty well known that just before this exile he had incautiously gambled away all the cash in the Custom House of a small port where a friend in power had procured for him the post of sub-collector. That youthful indiscretion had, amongst other inconveniences, obliged him to earn his living for a time as a café waiter in Madrid; but his talents must have been great, after all, since they had enabled him to retrieve his political fortunes so splendidly. Charles Gould, exposing his business with an imperturbable steadiness, called him Excellency.

The provincial Excellency assumed a weary superiority, tilting his chair far back near an open window in the true Costaguana manner. The military band happened to be braying operatic selections on the *plaza* just then, and twice he raised his hand imperatively for silence in order to listen to a favourite passage.

'Exquisite, delicious!' he murmured; while Charles Gould waited, standing by with inscrutable patience. 'Lucia, Lucia di Lammermoor! I am passionate for music. It transports me. Ha! the divine – ha! – Mozart. Sì! divine . . . What is it you were saying?'

Of course, rumours had reached him already of the newcomer's intentions. Besides, he had received an official warning from Sta Marta. His manner was intended simply to conceal his curiosity and impress his visitor. But after he had locked up something valuable in the drawer of a large writing-desk in a distant part of the room, he became very affable, and walked back to his chair smartly.

'If you intend to build villages and assemble a population near the mine, you shall require a decree of the Minister of the Interior for that,' he suggested in a businesslike manner.

'I have already sent a memorial,' said Charles Gould, steadily, 'and I reckon now confidently upon your Excellency's favourable conclusions.'

The Excellency was a man of many moods. With the receipt of the money a great mellowness had descended upon his simple soul. Unexpectedly he fetched a deep sigh.

'Ah, Don Carlos! What we want is advanced men like you in the province. The lethargy – the lethargy of these aristocrats! The want of public spirit! The absence of all enterprise! I, with my profound studies in Europe, you understand –'

With one hand thrust into his swelling bosom, he rose and fell on his toes, and for ten minutes, almost without drawing breath, went on hurling himself intellectually to the assault of Charles Gould's polite silence; and when, stopping abruptly, he fell back into his chair, it was as though he had been beaten off from a fortress. To save his dignity he hastened to dismiss this silent man with a solemn inclination of the head and the words, pronounced with moody, fatigued condescension:

'You may depend upon my enlightened goodwill as long as your conduct as a good citizen deserves it.'

He took up a paper fan and began to cool himself with a consequential air, while Charles Gould bowed and withdrew. Then he dropped the fan at once, and stared with an appearance of wonder and perplexity at the closed door for quite a long time. At last he shrugged his shoulders as if to assure himself of his disdain. Cold, dull. No intellectuality. Red hair. A true Englishman. He despised him.

His face darkened. What meant this unimpressed and frigid behaviour? He was the first of the successive politicians sent out from the capital to rule the Occidental Province whom the manner of Charles Gould in official intercourse was to strike as offensively independent.

Charles Gould assumed that if the appearance of listening to deplorable balderdash must form part of the price he had to pay for being left unmolested, the obligation of uttering balderdash personally was by no means included in the bargain. He drew the line there. To these provincial autocrats, before whom the peaceable population of all classes had been accustomed to tremble, the reserve of that English-looking engineer caused an uneasiness which swung to and fro between cringing and truculence. Gradually all of them discovered that, no matter what party was in power, that man remained in most effective touch with the higher authorities in Sta Marta.

This was a fact, and it accounted perfectly for the Goulds being by no means so wealthy as the engineer-in-chief on the new railway could legitimately suppose. Following the advice of Don José Avellanos, who was a man of good counsel (though rendered timid by his horrible experiences of Guzman Bento's time), Charles Gould had kept clear of the capital; but in the current gossip of the foreign residents there he was known (with a good deal of seriousness underlying the irony) by the nickname of 'King of Sulaco'. An advocate of the Costaguana Bar, a man of reputed ability and good character, member of the distinguished Moraga family possessing extensive estates in the Sulaco Valley, was pointed out to strangers, with a shade of mystery and respect, as the agent of the San Tomé mine – 'political, you know'. He was tall, black-whiskered, and discreet. It was known that he had easy access to ministers, and that the numerous Costaguana generals were always anxious to dine at his house. Presidents granted him audience with facility. He corresponded actively with his maternal uncle, Don José Avellanos; but his letters – unless those expressing formally his dutiful affection – were seldom entrusted to the Costaguana post office. There the envelopes are opened, indiscriminately, with the frankness of a brazen and childish impudence characteristic of some Spanish–American Governments. But it must be noted that at about the time of the reopening of the San Tomé mine the muleteer who had been employed by Charles Gould in his preliminary travels on the Campo added his small train of animals to the thin stream of traffic carried over the mountain passes between the Sta Marta upland and the Valley of Sulaco. There are no travellers by that arduous and unsafe route unless under very exceptional circumstances, and the state of inland trade did not visibly require additional transport facilities; but the man seemed to find his account in it. A few packages were always found for him whenever he took the road. Very brown and wooden, in goatskin breeches with the hair outside, he sat near the tail of his own smart mule, his great hat turned against the sun, an expression of blissful vacancy on his long face, humming day after day a love-song in a plaintive key, or, without a change of expression, letting out a yell at his small *tropilla* in front. A round little guitar hung high up on his back; and there was a place scooped out artistically in the wood of one of his pack-saddles where a tightly rolled piece of paper could be slipped in, the wooden plug replaced, and the coarse canvas nailed on again. When in Sulaco it was his practice to smoke and doze all day long (as though he had no care in the world) on a stone bench outside the doorway of the Casa Gould and facing the windows of the Avellanos house. Years and years ago his mother had been chief laundry-woman in that family – very accomplished in the matter of clear-starching. He himself had been born on one of their *haciendas*. His name was Bonifacio, and Don José, crossing the street about five o'clock to call on Doña Emilia, always acknowledged his humble salute by some movement of hand or head. The porters of both houses conversed lazily with him in tones of grave intimacy. His evenings he devoted to gambling and to calls in a spirit of generous festivity upon the *peyne d'oro* girls in the more remote side streets of the town. But he, too, was a discreet man.

CHAPTER 8

Those of us whom business or curiosity took to Sulaco in these years before the first advent of the railway can remember the steadying effect of the San Tomé mine upon the life of that remote province. The outward appearances had not changed then as they have changed since, as I am told, with cable cars running along the streets of the Constitution, and carriage roads far into the country, to Rincón and other villages, where the foreign merchants and the *ricos* generally have their modern villas, and a vast railway goods-yard by the harbour, which has a quayside, a long range of warehouses, and quite serious, organized labour troubles of its own.

Nobody had ever heard of labour troubles then. The Cargadores of the port formed, indeed, an unruly brotherhood of all sorts of scum, with a patron saint of their own. They went on strike regularly (every bullfight day), a form of trouble that even Nostromo at the height of his prestige could never cope with efficiently; but the morning after each fiesta, before the Indian market-women had opened their mat parasols on the *plaza*, when the snows of Higuerota gleamed pale over the town on a yet black sky, the appearance of a phantom-like horseman mounted on a silver-grey mare solved the problem of labour without fail. His steed paced the lanes of the slums and the weed-grown enclosures within the old ramparts, between the black, lightless cluster of huts, like cow-byres, like dog-kennels. The horse-man hammered with the butt of a heavy revolver at the doors of low *pulperías*, of obscene lean-to sheds sloping against the tumble-down piece of a noble wall, at the wooden sides of dwellings so flimsy that the sound of snores and sleepy mutters within could be heard in the pauses of the thundering clatter of his blows. He called out men's names menacingly from the saddle, once, twice. The drowsy answers – grumpy, conciliating, savage, jocular, or deprecating – came out into the silent darkness in which the horseman sat still, and presently a dark figure would flit out coughing in the still air. Sometimes a low-toned woman cried through the window-hole softly, 'He's coming directly, *señor*,' and the horseman waited silent on a motionless horse. But if perchance he had to dismount, then, after a while, from the door of that hovel or of that *pulpería*, with a ferocious scuffle and stifled imprecations, a *cargador* would fly out head first and hands abroad, to sprawl under the forelegs of the silver-grey mare, who only pricked forward her sharp little ears. She was used to that work; and the man, picking himself up, would walk away hastily from Nostromo's revolver, reeling a little along the street and snarling low curses. At sunrise Captain Mitchell, coming out anxiously in his night attire on to the wooden balcony running the whole length of the O.S.N. Company's lonely building by the shore, would see the lighters already under way, figures moving busily about the cargo cranes, perhaps hear the invaluable Nostromo, now dismounted and in the checked shirt and red sash of a Mediterranean sailor, bawling orders from the end of the jetty in a stentorian voice. A fellow in a thousand!

The material apparatus of perfected civilization which obliterates the individuality of old towns under the stereotyped conveniences of modern life had not intruded as yet; but over the worn-out antiquity of Sulaco, so characteristic with its stuccoed houses and barred windows, with the great yellowy-white walls of abandoned convents behind the rows of sombre green cypresses, that fact – very modern in its spirit – the San Tomé mine had already thrown its subtle influence. It had altered, too, the outward character of the crowds on feast days on the *plaza* before the open portal of the cathedral, by the number of white ponchos with a green stripe affected as holiday wear by the San Tomé miners. They had also adopted white hats with green cord and braid – articles of good quality, which could be obtained in the storehouse of the administration for very little money. A peaceable *cholo* wearing these colours (unusual in Costaguana) was somehow very seldom beaten to within an inch of his life on a charge of disrespect to the town police; neither ran he much risk of being suddenly lassoed on the road by a recruiting party of *lanceros* – a method of voluntary enlistment looked upon as almost legal in the Republic. Whole villages were known to have volunteered for the army in that way; but, as Don Pepe would say with a hopeless shrug to Mrs Gould, 'What would you! Poor people! *Pobrecitos! Pobrecitos!* But the State must have its soldiers.'

Thus professionally spoke Don Pepe, the fighter, with pendent moustaches, a nut-brown, lean face, and a clean run of a cast-iron jaw, suggesting the type of a cattleherd horseman from the great Llanos of the South. 'If you will listen to an old officer of Paez, *señores*,' was the exordium of all his speeches in the Aristocratic Club of Sulaco, where he was admitted on account of his past services to the extinct cause of Federation. The club, dating from the days of the proclamation of Costaguana's independence, boasted many names of liberators amongst its first founders. Suppressed arbitrarily innumerable times by various Governments, with memories of proscriptions and of at least one wholesale massacre of its members, sadly assembled for a banquet by the order of a zealous military *comandante* (their bodies were afterwards stripped naked and flung into the *plaza* out of the windows by the lowest scum of the populace), it was again flourishing, at that period, peacefully. It extended to strangers the large hospitality of the cool, big rooms of its historic quarters in the front part of a house, once the residence of a high official of the Holy Office. The two wings, shut up, crumbled behind the nailed doors, and what may be described as a grove of young orange trees grown in the unpaved *patio* concealed the utter ruin of the back part facing the gate. You turned in from the street, as if entering a secluded orchard, where you came upon the foot of a disjointed staircase, guarded by a moss-stained effigy of some saintly bishop, mitred and staffed, and bearing the indignity of a broken nose meekly, with his fine stone hands crossed on his breast. The chocolate-coloured faces of servants with mops of black hair peeped at you from above; the click of billiard balls came to your ears, and ascending the steps, you would perhaps see in the first *sala*, very stiff upon a straight-backed chair, in a good light, Don Pepe moving his long moustaches as he spelt his way, at arm's length, through an old Sta Marta newspaper. His horse – a stony-hearted but persevering black brute with a hammer head – you would have seen in the street dozing motionless under an immense saddle, with its nose almost touching the kerbstone of the sidewalk.

Don Pepe, when 'down from the mountain', as the phrase, often heard in Sulaco, went, could also be seen in the drawing-room of the Casa Gould. He sat with modest assurance at some distance from the tea-table. With his knees close together, and a kindly twinkle of drollery in his deep-set eyes, he would throw his small and ironic pleasantries into the current of conversation. There was in that man a sort of sane, humorous shrewdness, and a vein of genuine humanity so often found in simple old soldiers of proved courage who have seen much desperate service. Of course he knew nothing whatever of mining, but his employment was of a special kind. He was in charge of the whole population in the territory of the mine, which extended from the head of the gorge to where the cart-track from the foot of the mountain enters the plain, crossing a stream over a little wooden bridge painted green – green, the colour of hope, being also the colour of the mine.

It was reported in Sulaco that up there 'at the mountain' Don Pepe walked about precipitous paths, girt with a great sword and in a shabby uniform with tarnished bullion epaulettes of a senior major. Most miners being Indians, with big wild eyes, addressed him as 'Taita' (father), as these barefooted people of Costaguana will address anybody who wears shoes; but it was Basilio, Mr Gould's own *mozo* and the head servant of the Casa, who, in all good faith and from a sense of propriety, announced him once in the solemn words, 'El Señor Gobernador has arrived.'

Don José Avellanos, then in the drawing-room, was delighted beyond measure at the aptness of the title, with which he greeted the old major banteringly as soon as the latter's soldierly figure appeared in the doorway. Don Pepe only smiled in his long moustaches, as much as to say, 'You might have found a worse name for an old soldier.'

And 'El Señor Gobernador' he had remained, with his small jokes upon his function and upon his domain, where he affirmed with humorous exaggeration to Mrs Gould:

'No two stones could come together anywhere without the Gobernador hearing the click, *señora*.'

And he would tap his ear with the tip of his forefinger knowingly. Even when the number of the miners alone rose to over six hundred he seemed to know each of them individually, all the innumerable Josés, Manuels, Ignacios, from the villages *primero – segundo* – or *tercero* (there were three mining villages) under his government. He could distinguish them not only by their flat, joyless faces, which to Mrs Gould looked all alike, as if run into the same ancestral mould of suffering and patience, but apparently also by the infinitely graduated shades of reddish-brown, of blackish-brown, of coppery-brown backs, as the two shifts, stripped to linen drawers and leather skull-caps, mingled together with a confusion of naked limbs, of shouldered picks, swinging lamps, in a great shuffle of sandalled feet on the open plateau before the entrance of the main tunnel. It was a time of pause. The Indian boys leaned idly against the long line of little cradle wagons standing empty; the screeners and ore-breakers squatted on their heels smoking long cigars; the great wooden shoots slanting over the edge of the tunnel plateau were silent; and only the ceaseless, violent rush of water in the open flumes could be heard, murmuring fiercely, with the splash and rumble of revolving turbine-wheels, and the thudding march of the stamps pounding to powder the treasure rock on the plateau below. The heads of gangs, distinguished by brass medals hanging on their bare breasts, marshalled their squads; and at last the mountain would swallow one half of the silent crowd, while the other half would move off in long files down the zigzag paths leading to the bottom of the gorge. It was deep; and, far below, a thread of vegetation winding between the blazing rock faces resembled a slender green cord, in which three lumpy knots of banana patches, palm-leaf roots, and shady trees marked the Village One, Village Two, Village Three, housing the miners of the Gould Concession.

Whole families had been moving from the first towards the spot in the Higuerota range, whence the rumour of work and safety had spread over the pastoral Campo, forcing its way also, even as the waters of a high flood, into the nooks and crannies of the distant blue walls of the Sierras. Father first, in a pointed straw hat, then the mother with the bigger children, generally also a diminutive donkey, all under burdens, except the leader himself, or perhaps some grown girl, the pride of the family, stepping barefooted and straight as an arrow, with braids of raven hair, a thick, haughty profile, and no load to carry but the small guitar of the country and a pair of soft leather sandals tied together on her back. At the sight of such parties strung out on the cross trails between the pastures, or camped by the side of the royal road, travellers on horseback would remark to each other:

'More people going to the San Tomé mine. We shall see others tomorrow.'

And spurring on in the dusk they would discuss the great news of the province, the news of the San Tomé mine. A rich Englishman was going to work it – and perhaps not an Englishman, *Quién sabe!* A foreigner with much money. Oh, yes, it had begun. A party of men who had been to Sulaco with a herd of black bulls for the next *corrida* had reported that from the porch of the *posada* in Rincón, only a short league from the town, the lights on the mountain were visible, twinkling above the trees. And there was a woman seen riding a horse sideways, not in the chair seat, but upon a sort of saddle, and a man's hat on her head. She walked about, too, on foot up the mountain paths. A woman engineer, it seemed she was.

'What an absurdity! Impossible, *señor!*'

'*Sí! Sí! Una americana del Norte.*'

'Ah, well! if your worship is informed. *Una Americana*; it need be something of that sort.'

And they would laugh a little with astonishment and scorn, keeping a wary eye on the shadows of the road, for one is liable to meet bad men when travelling late on the Campo.

And it was not only the men that Don Pepe knew so well, but he seemed able, with one attentive, thoughtful glance, to classify each woman, girl, or growing youth of his domain. It was only the small fry that puzzled him sometimes. He and the padre could be seen frequently side by side, meditative and gazing across the street of a village at a lot of sedate brown children, trying to sort them out, as it were, in low, consulting tones, or else they would together put searching questions as to the parentage of some small, staid urchin met wandering, naked and grave, along the road with a cigar in his baby mouth, and perhaps his mother's rosary, purloined for purposes of ornamentation, hanging in a loop of beads low down on his rotund little stomach. The spiritual and temporal pastors of the mine flock were very good friends. With Dr Monygham, the medical pastor, who had accepted the charge from Mrs Gould, and lived in the hospital building, they were on not so intimate terms. But no one could be on intimate terms with El Señor Doctor, who, with his twisted shoulders, drooping head, sardonic mouth, and side-long bitter glance, was mysterious and uncanny. The other two authorities worked in harmony. Father Román, dried-up, small, alert, wrinkled, with big round eyes, a sharp chin, and a great snuff-taker, was an old campaigner, too; he had shriven many simple souls on the battlefields of the Republic, kneeling by the dying on hillsides, in the long grass, in the gloom of the forests, to hear the last confession with the smell of gunpowder smoke in his nostrils, the rattle of muskets, the hum and spatter of bullets in his ears. And where was the harm if, at the presbytery, they had a game with a pack of greasy cards in the early evening, before Don Pepe went his last rounds to see that all the watchmen of the mine – a body organized by himself – were at their posts? For that last duty before he slept Don Pepe did actually gird his old sword on the veranda of an unmistakable American white frame-house, which Father Román called the presbytery. Near by, a long, low, dark building, steeple-roofed, like a vast barn with a wooden cross over the gable, was the miners' chapel. There Father Román said Mass every day before a sombre altarpiece representing the Resurrection, the grey slab of the tombstone balanced on one corner, a figure soaring upwards, long-limbed and livid, in an oval of pallid light, and a helmeted brown legionary smitten down, right across the bituminous foreground. 'This picture, my children, *muy linda e maravillosa*,' Father Román would say to some of his flock, 'which you behold here through the munificence of the wife of our Señor Administrador, has been painted in Europe, a country of saints and miracles, and much greater than our Costaguana.' And he would take a pinch of snuff with unction. But when once an inquisitive spirit desired to know in what direction this Europe was situated, whether up or down the coast, Father Román, to conceal his perplexity, became very reserved and severe. 'No doubt it is extremely far away. But ignorant sinners like you of the San Tomé mine should think earnestly of everlasting punishment instead of inquiring into the magnitude of the earth, with its countries and populations altogether beyond your understanding.'

With a 'Good night, Padre;' 'Good night, Don Pepe,' the Gobernador would go off, holding up his sabre against his side, his body bent forward, with a long, plodding stride in the dark. The jocularity proper to an innocent card game for a few cigars or a bundle of yerba was replaced at once by the stern duty mood of an officer setting out to visit the outposts of an encamped army. One loud blast of the whistle that hung from his neck provoked instantly a great shrilling of responding whistles, mingled with the barking of dogs, that would calm down slowly at last, away up at the head of the gorge; and in the stillness two *serenos*, on guard by the bridge, would appear walking noiselessly towards him. On one side of the road a long frame-building – the store – would be closed and barricaded from end to end; facing it another white frame-house, still longer, and with a veranda – the hospital – would have lights in the two windows of Dr Monygham's quarters. Even the delicate foliage of a clump of pepper trees did not stir, so breathless would be the darkness warmed by the radiation of the over-heated rocks. Don Pepe would stand still for a moment with the two motionless *serenos* before him, and, abruptly, high up on the sheer face of the mountain, dotted with single torches, like drops of fire fallen from the two great blazing clusters of lights above, the ore shoots would begin to rattle. The great clattering, shuffling noise, gathering speed and weight, would be caught up by the walls of the gorge, and sent upon the plain in a growl of thunder. The *pasadero* in Rincón swore that on calm nights, by listening intently, he could catch the sound in his doorway as of a storm in the mountains.

To Charles Gould's fancy it seemed that the sound must reach the uttermost limits of the province. Riding at night towards the mine, it would meet him at the edge of a little wood just beyond Rincón. There was no mistaking the growling mutter of the mountain pouring its stream of treasure under the stamps; and it came to his heart with the peculiar force of a proclamation thundered forth over the land and the marvellousness of an accomplished fact fulfilling an audacious desire. He had heard this desire. He had heard this very sound in his imagination on that far-off evening when his wife and himself, after a tortuous ride through a strip of forest, had reined in their horses near the stream, and had gazed for the first time upon the jungle-grown solitude of the gorge. The head of a palm rose here and there. In a high ravine round the corner of the San Tomé mountain (which is square like a blockhouse) the thread of a slender waterfall flashed bright and glassy through the dark green of the heavy fronds of tree-ferns. Don Pepe, in attendance, rode up, and, stretching his arm up the gorge, had declared with mock solemnity, 'Behold the very paradise of snakes, *señora*.'

And then they had wheeled their horses and ridden back to sleep that night at Rincón. The *alcalde* – an old, skinny Moreno, a sergeant of Guzman Bento's time – had cleared respectfully out of his house with his three pretty daughters, to make room for the foreign *señora* and their worships the *caballeros*. All he asked Charles Gould (whom he took for a mysterious and official person) to do for him was to remind the supreme Government – *el Gobierno supremo* – of a pension (amounting to about a dollar a month) to which he believed himself entitled. It had been promised to him, he affirmed, straightening his bent back martially, 'many years ago, for my valour in the wars with the wild *indios* when a young man, *señor*'.

The waterfall existed no longer. The tree-ferns that had luxuriated in its spray had dried around the dried-up pool, and the high ravine was only a big trench half filled up with the refuse of excavations and tailings. The torrent, dammed up above, sent its water rushing along the open flumes of scooped tree trunks striding on trestle-legs to the turbines working the stamps on the lower plateau – the *mesa grande* of the San Tomé mountain. Only the memory of the waterfall, with its amazing fernery, like a hanging garden above the rocks of the gorge, was preserved in Mrs Gould's water-colour sketch; she had made it hastily one day from a cleared patch in the bushes, sitting in the shade of a roof of straw erected for her on three rough poles under Don Pepe's direction.

Mrs Gould had seen it all from the beginning: the clearing of the wilderness, the making of the road, the cutting of new paths up the cliff face of San Tomé. For weeks together she had lived on the spot with her husband; and she was so little in Sulaco during that year that the appearance of the Gould carriage on the Alameda would cause a social excitement. From the heavy family coaches full of stately *señoras* and black-eyed *señoritas* rolling solemnly in the shaded alley white hands were waved towards her with animation in a flutter of greetings. Doña Emilia was 'down from the mountain'.

But not for long. Doña Emilia would be gone 'up to the mountain' in a day or two, and her sleek carriage mules would have an easy time of it for another long spell. She had watched the erection of the first frame-house put up on the lower *mesa* for an office and Don Pepe's quarters; she heard with a thrill of thankful emotion the first wagon-load of ore rattle down the then only shoot; she had stood by her husband's side perfectly silent, and gone cold all over with excitement at the instant when the first battery of only fifteen stamps was put in motion for the first time. On the occasion when the fires under the first set of retorts in their shed had glowed far into the night she did not retire to rest on the rough cadre set up for her in the as yet bare frame-house till she had seen the first spongy lump of silver yielded to the hazards of the world by the dark depths of the Gould Concession; she had laid her unmercenary hands, with an eagerness that made them tremble, upon the first silver ingot turned out still warm from the mould; and by her imaginative estimate of its power she endowed that lump of metal with a justificative conception, as though it were not a mere fact, but something far-reaching and impalpable, like the true expression of an emotion or the emergence of a principle.

Don Pepe, extremely interested too, looked over her shoulder with a smile that, making longitudinal folds on his face, caused it to resemble a leathern mask with a benignantly diabolic expression.

'Would not the *muchachos* of Hernandez like to get hold of this insignificant object, that looks, *por Dios*, very much like a piece of tin?' he remarked, jocularly.

Hernandez, the robber, had been an inoffensive, small *ranchero*, kidnapped with circumstances of peculiar atrocity from his home during one of the civil wars, and forced to serve in the army. There his conduct as soldier was exemplary, till, watching his chance, he killed his colonel, and managed to get clear away. With a band of deserters, who chose him for their chief, he had taken refuge beyond the wild and waterless Bolson de Tonoro. The *haciendas* paid him blackmail in cattle and horses; extraordinary stories were told of his powers and of his wonderful escapes from capture. He used to ride, single-handed, into the villages and the little towns on the Campo, driving a pack mule before him, with two revolvers in his belt, go straight to the shop or store, select what he wanted, and ride away unopposed because of the terror his exploits and his audacity inspired. Poor country people he usually left alone; the upper class were often stopped on the roads and robbed; but any unlucky official that fell into his hands was sure to get a severe flogging. The army officers did not like his name to be mentioned in their presence. His followers, mounted on stolen horses, laughed at the pursuit of the regular cavalry sent to hunt them down, and whom they took pleasure to ambush most scientifically in the broken ground of their own fastness. Expeditions had been fitted out; a price had been put upon his head; even attempts had been made, treacherously of course, to open negotiations with him, without in the slightest way affecting the even tenor of his career. At last, in true Costaguana fashion, the Fiscal of Tonoro, who was ambitious of the glory of having reduced the famous Hernandez, offered him a sum of money and a safe conduct out of the country for the betrayal of his band. But Hernandez evidently was not of the stuff of which the distinguished military politicians and conspirators of Costaguana are made. This clever but common device (which frequently works like a charm in putting down revolutions) failed with the chief of vulgar Salteadores. It promised well for the Fiscal at first, but ended very badly for the squadron of *lanceros* posted (by the Fiscal's directions) in a fold of the ground into which Hernandez had promised to lead his unsuspecting followers. They came, indeed, at the appointed time, but creeping on their hands and knees through the bush, and only let their presence be known by a general discharge of firearms, which emptied many saddles. The troopers who escaped came riding very hard into Tonoro. It is said that their commanding officer (who, being better mounted, rode far ahead of the rest) afterwards got into a state of despairing intoxication and beat the ambitious Fiscal severely with the flat of his sabre in the presence of his wife and daughters, for bringing this disgrace upon the National Army. The highest civil official of Tonoro, falling to the ground in a swoon, was further kicked all over the body and rowelled with sharp spurs about the neck and face because of the great sensitiveness of his military colleague. This gossip of the inland Campo, so characteristic of the rulers of the country with its story of oppression, inefficiency, fatuous methods, treachery, and savage brutality, was perfectly known to Mrs Gould. That it should be accepted with no indignant comment by people of intelligence, refinement, and character as something inherent in the nature of things was one of the symptoms of degradation that had the power to exasperate her almost to the verge of despair. Still looking at the ingot of silver, she shook her head at Don Pepe's remark:

'If it had not been for the lawless tyranny of your Government, Don Pepe, many an outlaw now with Hernandez would be living peaceably and happy by the honest work of his hands.'

'*Señora*,' cried Don Pepe, with enthusiasm, 'it is true! It is as if God had given you the power to look into the very breasts of people. You have seen them working round you, Doña Emilia – meek as lambs, patient like their own *burros*, brave like lions. I have led them to the very muzzles of guns

– I, who stand here before you, *señora* – in the time of Paez, who was full of generosity, and in courage only approached by the uncle of Don Carlos here, as far as I know. No wonder there are bandits in the Campo when there are none but thieves, swindlers, and sanguinary *macaques* to rule us in Sta Marta. However, all the same, a bandit is a bandit, and we shall have a dozen good straight Winchesters to ride with the silver down to Sulaco.'

Mrs Gould's ride with the first silver escort to Sulaco was the closing episode of what she called 'my camp life' before she had settled in her townhouse permanently, as was proper and even necessary for the wife of the administrator of such an important institution as the San Tomé mine. For the San Tomé mine was to become an institution, a rallying-point for everything in the province that needed order and stability to live. Security seemed to flow upon this land from the mountain-gorge. The authorities of Sulaco had learned that the San Tomé mine could make it worth their while to leave things and people alone. This was the nearest approach to the rule of common sense and justice Charles Gould felt it possible to secure at first. In fact, the mine, with its organization, its population growing fiercely attached to their position of privileged safety, with its armoury, with its Don Pepe, with its armed body of *serenos* (where, it was said, many an outlaw and deserter – and even some members of Hernandez's band – had found a place), the mine was a power in the land. As a certain prominent man in Sta Marta had exclaimed with a hollow laugh, once, when discussing the line of action taken by the Sulaco authorities at a time of political crisis:

'You call these men Government officials? They? Never! They are officials of the mine – officials of the Concession – I tell you.'

The prominent man (who was then a person in power, with a lemon-coloured face and a very short and curly, not to say woolly, head of hair) went so far in his temporary discontent as to shake his yellow fist under the nose of his interlocutor, and shriek:

'Yes! All! Silence! All! I tell you! The political *jefe*, the chief of the police, the chief of the customs, the general, all, all are the officials of that Gould.'

Thereupon an intrepid but low and argumentative murmur would flow on for a space in the ministerial cabinet, and the prominent man's passion would end in a cynical shrug of the shoulders. After all, he seemed to say, what did it matter as long as the minister himself was not forgotten during his brief day of authority? But all the same, the unofficial agent of the San Tomé mine, working for a good cause, had his moments of anxiety, which were reflected in his letters to Don José Avellanos, his maternal uncle.

'No sanguinary *macaque* from Sta Marta shall set foot on that part of Costaguana which lies beyond the San Tomé bridge,' Don Pepe used to assure Mrs Gould. 'Except, of course, as an honoured guest – for our Señor Administrador is a deep *político*.' But to Charles Gould, in his own room, the old Major would remark with a grim and soldierly cheeriness, 'We are all playing our heads at this game.'

Don José Avellanos would mutter '*Imperium in imperio*, Emilia, my soul,' with an air of profound self-satisfaction which, somehow, in a curious way, seemed to contain a queer admixture of bodily discomfort. But that, perhaps, could only be visible to the initiated.

And for the initiated it was a wonderful place, this drawing-room of the Casa Gould, with its momentary glimpses of the master – El Señor Administrador – older, harder, mysteriously silent, with the lines deepened on his English, ruddy, out-of-doors complexion; flitting on his thin cavalryman's legs across the doorways, either just 'back from the mountain' or with jingling spurs and riding-whip under his arm, on the point of starting 'for the mountain'. Then Don Pepe, modestly martial in his chair, the *llanero* who seemed somehow to have found his martial jocularity, his knowledge of the world, and his manner perfect for his station, in the midst of savage armed contests with his kind; Avellanos, polished and familiar, the diplomatist with his loquacity covering much caution and wisdom in delicate advice, with his manuscript of a historical work on Costaguana, entitled *Fifty Years of Misrule*, which, at present, he thought it was not prudent (even if it were possible) 'to give to the world'; these three, and also Doña Emilia amongst them, gracious, small, and fairy-like, before the glittering tea-set, with one common master-thought in their heads, with one common feeling of a tense situation, with one ever-present aim to preserve the inviolable character of the mine at every cost. And there was also to be seen Captain Mitchell, a little apart, near one of the long windows, with an air of old-fashioned neat old bachelorhood about him, slightly pompous, in a white waistcoat, a little disregarded and unconscious of it; utterly in the dark, and imagining himself to be in the thick of things. The good man, having spent a clear thirty years of his life on the high seas before getting what he called a 'shore billet', was astonished at the importance of transactions (other than relating to shipping) which take place on dry land. Almost every event out of the usual daily course 'marked an epoch' for him or else was 'history'; unless with his pomposity struggling with a discomfited droop of his rubicund, rather handsome face, set off by snow-white close hair and short whiskers, he would mutter:

'Ah, that! That, sir, was a mistake.'

The reception of the first consignment of San Tomé silver for shipment to San Francisco in one of O.S.N. Company's mailboats had, of course, 'marked an epoch' for Captain Mitchell. The ingots packed in boxes of stiff ox-hide with plaited handles, small enough to be carried easily by two men, were brought down by the *serenos* of the mine walking in careful couples down the half mile or so of steep, zigzag paths to the foot of the mountain. There they would be loaded into a string of two-wheeled carts, resembling roomy coffers with a door at the back, and harnessed tandem with two mules each, waiting under the guard of armed and mounted *serenos*. Don Pepe padlocked each door in succession, and at the signal of his whistle the string of carts would move off, closely surrounded by the clank of spur and carabine, with jolts and cracking of whips, with a sudden deep rumble over the boundary bridge ('into the land of thieves and sanguinary *macaques*', Don Pepe defined that crossing); hats bobbing in the first light of the dawn, on the heads of cloaked figures; Winchesters on hip; bridle hands protruding lean and brown from under the falling folds of the ponchos. The convoy skirting a little wood, along the mine trail, between the mud huts and low walls of Rincón, increased its pace on the *camino real*, mules urged to speed, escort galloping, Don Carlos riding alone ahead of a dust storm affording a vague vision of long ears of mules, of fluttering little green and white flags stuck upon each cart; of raised arms in a mob of sombreros with the white gleam of ranging eyes; and Don Pepe, hardly visible in the rear of that rattling dust trail, with a stiff seat and impassive face, rising and falling rhythmically on a ewe-necked silverbitted black brute with a hammer head.

The sleepy people in the little clusters of huts, in the small *ranchos* near the road, recognized by the headlong sound the charge of the San Tomé silver escort towards the crumbling wall of the city on the Campo side. They came to the doors to see it dash by over ruts and stones, with a clatter and clank and cracking of whips, with the reckless rush and precise driving of a field battery hurrying into action, and the solitary English figure of the Señor Administrador riding far ahead in the lead.

In the fenced roadside paddocks loose horses galloped wildly for a while; the heavy cattle stood up breast deep in the grass, lowing mutteringly at the flying noise; a meek Indian villager would glance back once and hasten to shove his loaded little donkey bodily against a wall, out of the way of the San Tomé silver escort going to the sea; a small knot of chilly *leperos* under the Stone Horse of the Alameda would mutter: '*Caramba!*' on seeing it take a wide curve at a gallop and dart into the empty street of the Constitution; for it was considered the correct thing, the only proper style by the mule-drivers of the San Tomé mine to go through the waking town from end to end without a check in the speed as if chased by a devil.

The early sunshine glowed on the delicate primrose, pale pink, pale blue fronts of the big houses with all their gates shut yet, and no face behind the iron bars of the windows. In the whole sunlit range of empty balconies along the street only one white figure would be visible high up above the clear pavement – the wife of the Señor Administrador – leaning over to see the escort go by to the harbour, a mass of heavy, fair hair twisted up negligently on her little head, and a lot of lace about the neck of her muslin wrapper. With a smile to her husband's single, quick, upward glance, she would watch the whole thing stream past below her feet with an orderly uproar, till she answered by a friendly sign the salute of the galloping Don Pepe, the stiff, deferential inclination with a sweep of the hat below the knee.

The string of padlocked carts lengthened, the size of the escort grew bigger as the years went on. Every three months an increasing stream of treasure swept through the streets of Sulaco on its way to the strong room in the O.S.N. Company's building by the harbour, there to await shipment for the north. Increasing in volume, and of immense value also; for, as Charles Gould told his wife once with some exultation, there had never been seen anything in the world to approach the vein of the Gould Concession. For them both, each passing of the escort under the balconies of the Casa Gould was like another victory gained in the conquest of peace for Sulaco.

No doubt the initial action of Charles Gould had been helped at the beginning by a period of comparative peace which occurred just about that time; and also by the general softening of manners as compared with the epoch of civil wars whence had emerged the iron tyranny of Guzman Bento of fearful memory. In the contests that broke out at the end of his rule (which had kept peace in the country for a whole fifteen years) there was more fatuous imbecility, plenty of cruelty and suffering still, but much less of the old-time fierce and blindly ferocious political fanaticism. It was all more vile, more base, more contemptible, and infinitely more manageable in the very outspoken cynicism of motives. It was more clearly a brazen-faced scramble for a constantly diminishing quantity of booty; since all enterprise had been stupidly killed in the land. Thus it came to pass that the province of Sulaco, once the field of cruel party vengeances, had become in a way one of the considerable prizes of political career. The great of the earth (in Sta Marta) reserved the posts in the old Occidental State to those nearest and dearest to them: nephews, brothers, husbands of favourite sisters, bosom friends, trusty supporters – or prominent supporters of whom perhaps they were afraid. It was the blessed province of great opportunities and of largest salaries; for the San Tomé mine had its own unofficial pay list, whose items and amounts, fixed in consultation by Charles Gould and Señor Avellanos, were known to a prominent businessman in the United States, who for twenty minutes or so in every month gave his undivided attention to Sulaco affairs. At the same time the material interests of all sorts, backed up by the influence of the San Tomé mine, were quietly gathering substance in that part of the Republic. If, for instance, the Sulaco Collectorship was generally understood, in the political world of the capital, to open the way to the Ministry of Finance, and so on for every official post, then, on the other hand, the despondent business circles of the Republic had come to consider the Occidental Province as the promised land of safety, especially if a man managed to get on good terms with the administration of the mine. 'Charles Gould; excellent fellow! Absolutely necessary to make sure of him before taking a single step. Get an introduction to him from Moraga if you can – the agent of the King of Sulaco, don't you know.'

No wonder, then, that Sir John, coming from Europe to smooth the path for his railway, had been meeting the name (and even the nickname) of Charles Gould at every turn in Costaguana. The agent of the San Tomé Administration in Sta Marta (a polished, well-informed gentleman, Sir John thought him) had certainly helped so greatly in bringing about the presidential tour that he began to think that there was something in the faint whispers hinting at the immense occult influence of the Gould Concession. What was currently whispered was this – that the San Tomé Administration had, in part, at least, financed the last revolution, which had brought into a five-year dictatorship Don Vincente Ribiera, a man of culture and of unblemished character, invested with a mandate of reform by the best elements of the State. Serious, well-informed men seemed to believe the fact, to hope for better things, for the establishment of legality, of good faith and order in public life. So much the better, then, thought Sir John. He worked always on a great scale; there was a loan to the State, and a project for systematic colonization of the Occidental Province, involved in one vast scheme with the construction of the National Central Railway. Good faith, order, honesty, peace, were badly wanted for this great development of material interests. Anybody on the side of these things, and especially if able to help, had an importance in Sir John's eyes. He had not been disappointed in the 'King of Sulaco'. The local difficulties had fallen away, as the engineer-in-chief had foretold they would, before Charles Gould's mediation. Sir John had been extremely fêted in Sulaco, next to the President-Dictator, a fact which might have accounted for the evident ill-humour General Montero displayed at lunch given on board the *Juno* just before she was to sail, taking away from Sulaco the President-Dictator and the distinguished foreign guests in his train.

The Excellentissimo ('the hope of honest men', as Don José had addressed him in a public speech delivered in the name of the Provincial Assembly of Sulaco) sat at the head of the long table; Captain Mitchell, positively stony-eyed and purple in the face with the solemnity of this 'historical event', occupied the foot as the representative of the O.S.N. Company in Sulaco, the hosts of that informal function, with the captain of the ship and some minor officials from the shore around him. Those cheery, swarthy little gentlemen cast jovial side-glances at the bottles of champagne beginning to pop behind the guests' backs in the hands of the ship's stewards. The amber wine creamed up to the rims of the glasses.

Charles Gould had his place next to a foreign envoy, who, in a listless undertone, had been talking to him fitfully of hunting and shooting. The well-nourished, pale face, with an eyeglass and drooping yellow moustache, made the Señor Administrador appear by contrast twice as sunbaked, more flaming red, a hundred times more intensely and silently alive. Don José Avellanos touched elbows with the other foreign diplomat, a dark man with a quiet, watchful, self-confident demeanour, and a touch of reserve. All etiquette being laid aside on the occasion, General Montero was the only one there in full uniform, so stiff with embroideries in front that his broad chest seemed protected by a cuirass of gold. Sir John at the beginning had got away from high places for the sake of sitting near Mrs Gould.

The great financier was trying to express to her his grateful sense of her hospitality and of his obligation to her husband's 'enormous influence in this part of the country', when she interrupted him by a low 'Hush!' The President was going to make an informal pronouncement.

The Excellentissimo was on his legs. He said only a few words, evidently deeply felt, and meant perhaps mostly for Avellanos – his old friend – as to the necessity of unremitting effort to secure the lasting welfare of the country emerging after this last struggle, he hoped, into a period of peace and material prosperity.

Mrs Gould, listening to the mellow, slightly mournful voice, looking at this rotund, dark, spectacled face, at the short body, obese to the point of infirmity, thought that this man of delicate and melancholy mind, physically almost a cripple, coming out of his retirement into a dangerous strife at the call of his fellows, had the right to speak with the authority of his self-sacrifice. And yet she was made uneasy. He was more pathetic than promising, this first civilian Chief of the State Costaguana had ever known, pronouncing, glass in hand, his simple watchwords of honesty, peace, respect for law, political good faith abroad and at home – the safeguards of national honour.

He sat down. During the respectful, appreciative buzz of voices that followed the speech, General Montero raised a pair of heavy, drooping eyelids and rolled his eyes with a sort of uneasy dullness from face to face. The military backwoods hero of the party, though secretly impressed by the sudden novelties and splendours of his position (he had never been on board a ship before, and had hardly ever seen the sea except from a distance), understood by a sort of instinct the advantage his surly, unpolished attitude of a savage fighter gave him amongst all these refined Blanco aristocrats. But why was it that nobody was looking at him? he wondered to himself angrily. He was able to spell out the print of newspapers, and knew that he had performed the 'greatest military exploit of modern times'.

'My husband wanted the railway,' Mrs Gould said to Sir John in the general murmur of resumed conversations. 'All this brings nearer the sort of future we desire for the country, which has waited for it in sorrow long enough, God knows. But I will confess that the other day, during my afternoon drive when I suddenly saw an Indian boy ride out of a wood with the red flag of a surveying party in his hand, I felt something of a shock. The future means change – an utter change. And yet even here there are simple and picturesque things that one would like to preserve.'

Sir John listened, smiling. But it was his turn now to hush Mrs Gould.

'General Montero is going to speak,' he whispered, and almost immediately added, in comic alarm, 'Heavens! he's going to propose my own health, I believe.'

General Montero had risen with a jingle of steel scabbard and a ripple of glitter on his gold-embroidered breast; a heavy sword-hilt appeared at his side above the edge of the table. In this gorgeous uniform, with his bull neck, his hooked nose flattened on the tip upon a blue-black, dyed moustache, he looked like a disguised and sinister *vaquero*. The drone of his voice had a strangely rasping, soulless ring. He floundered, lowering, through a few vague sentences; then suddenly raising his big head and his voice together, burst out harshly:

'The honour of the country is in the hands of the army. I assure you I shall be faithful to it.' He hesitated till his roaming eyes met Sir John's face, upon which he fixed a lurid, sleepy glance; and the figure of the lately negotiated loan came into his mind. He lifted his glass. 'I drink to the health of the man who brings us a million and a half of pounds.'

He tossed off his champagne, and sat down heavily with a half-surprised, half-bullying look all round the faces in the profound, as if appalled, silence which succeeded the felicitous toast. Sir John did not move.

'I don't think I am called upon to rise,' he murmured to Mrs Gould. 'That sort of thing speaks for itself.' But Don José Avellanos came to the rescue with a short oration, in which he alluded pointedly to England's goodwill towards Costaguana – 'a goodwill', he continued, significantly, 'of which I, having been in my time accredited to the Court of St James, am able to speak with some knowledge.'

Only then Sir John thought fit to respond, which he did gracefully in bad French, punctuated by bursts of applause and the 'Hear! Hears!' of Captain Mitchell, who was able to understand a word now and then. Directly he had done, the financier of railways turned to Mrs Gould:

'You were good enough to say that you intended to ask me for something,' he reminded her, gallantly. 'What is it? Be assured that any request from you would be considered in the light of a favour to myself.'

She thanked him by a gracious smile. Everybody was rising from the table.

'Let us go on deck,' she proposed, 'where I'll be able to point out to you the very object of my request.'

An enormous national flag of Costaguana, diagonal red and yellow, with two green palm trees in the middle, floated lazily at the mainmast head of the *Juno*. A multitude of fireworks being let off in their thousands at the water's edge in honour of the President kept up a mysterious crepitating noise half round the harbour. Now and then a lot of rockets, swishing upwards invisibly, detonated overhead with only a puff of smoke in the bright sky. Crowds of people could be seen between the town gate and the harbour, under the bunches of multicoloured flags fluttering on tall poles. Faint bursts of military music would be heard suddenly, and the remote sound of shouting. A knot of ragged Negroes at the end of the wharf kept on loading and firing a small iron cannon time after time. A greyish haze of dust hung thin and motionless against the sun.

Don Vincente Ribiera made a few steps under the deck-awning, leaning on the arm of Señor Avellanos; a wide circle was formed round him, where the mirthless smile of his dark lips and the sightless glitter of his spectacles could be seen turning amiably from side to side. The informal function arranged on purpose on board the *Juno* to give the President-Dictator an opportunity to meet intimately some of his most notable adherents in Sulaco was drawing to an end. On one side, General Montero, his bald head covered now by a plumed cocked hat, remained motionless on a skylight seat, a pair of big gauntleted hands folded on the hilt of the sabre standing upright between his legs. The white plume, the coppery tint of his broad face, the blue-black of the moustaches under the curved beak, the mass of gold on sleeves and breast, the high shining boots with enormous spurs, the working nostrils, the imbecile and domineering stare of the glorious victor of Río Seco had in them something ominous and incredible; the exaggeration of a cruel caricature, the fatuity of solemn masquerading, the atrocious grotesqueness of some military idol of Aztec conception and European bedecking, awaiting the homage of worshippers. Don José approached diplomatically this weird and inscrutable portent, and Mrs Gould turned her fascinated eyes away at last.

Charles, coming up to take leave of Sir John, heard him say, as he bent over his wife's hand, 'Certainly. Of course, my dear Mrs Gould, for a protégé of yours! Not the slightest difficulty. Consider it done.'

Going ashore in the same boat with the Goulds, Don José Avellanos was very silent. Even in the Gould carriage he did not open his lips for a long time. The mules trotted slowly away from the wharf between the extended hands of the beggars, who for that day seemed to have abandoned in a body the portals of churches. Charles Gould sat on the back seat and looked away upon the plain. A multitude of booths made of green boughs, of rushes, of odd pieces of plank eked out with bits of canvas had been erected all over it for the sale of cana, of dulces, of fruit, of cigars. Over little heaps of glowing charcoal Indian women, squatting on mats, cooked food in black earthen pots, and boiled the water for the maté gourds, which they offered in soft, caressing voices to the country people. A racecourse had been staked out for the *vaqueros*; and away to the left, from where the crowd was massed thickly about a huge temporary erection, like a circus tent of wood with a conical grass roof, came the resonant twanging of harp strings, the sharp ping of guitars, with the grave drumming throb of an Indian gombo pulsating steadily through the shrill choruses of the dancers.

Charles Gould said presently:

'All this piece of land belongs now to the Railway Company. There will be no more popular feasts held here.'

Mrs Gould was rather sorry to think so. She took this opportunity to mention how she had just obtained from Sir John the promise that the house occupied by Giorgio Viola should not be interfered with. She declared she could never understand why the survey engineers ever talked of demolishing that old building. It was not in the way of the projected harbour branch of the line in the least.

She stopped the carriage before the door to reassure at once the old Genoese, who came out bare-headed and stood by the carriage step. She talked to him in Italian, of course, and he thanked her with calm dignity. An old Garibaldino was grateful to her from the bottom of his heart for keeping the roof over the heads of his wife and children. He was too old to wander any more.

'And is it for ever, *signora*?' he asked.

'For as long as you like.'

'*Bene*. Then the place must be named. It was not worth while before.'

He smiled ruggedly, with a running together of wrinkles at the corners of his eyes. 'I shall set about the painting of the name tomorrow.'

'And what is it going to be, Giorgio?'

'Albergo d'Italia Una,' said the old Garibaldino, looking away for a moment. 'More in memory of those who have died,' he added, 'than for the country stolen from us soldiers of liberty by the craft of that accursed Piedmontese race of kings and ministers.'

Mrs Gould smiled slightly, and, bending over a little, began to inquire about his wife and children. He had sent them into town on that day. The *padrona* was better in health; many thanks to the *signora* for inquiring.

People were passing in twos and threes, in whole parties of men and women attended by trotting children. A horseman mounted on a silver-grey mare drew rein quietly in the shade of the house after taking off his hat to the party in the carriage, who returned smiles and familiar nods. Old Viola, evidently very pleased with the news he had just heard, interrupted himself for a moment to tell him rapidly that the house was secured, by the kindness of the English *signora*, for as long as he liked to keep it. The other listened attentively, but made no response.

When the carriage moved on he took off his hat again, a grey sombrero with a silver cord and tassels. The bright colours of a Mexican serape twisted on the cantle, the enormous silver buttons on the embroidered leather jacket, the row of tiny silver buttons down the seam of the trousers, the snowy linen, a silk sash with embroidered ends, the silver plates on headstall and saddle, proclaimed the unapproachable style of the famous Capataz de Cargadores – a Mediterranean sailor – got up with more finished splendour than any well-to-do young *ranchero* of the Campo had ever displayed on a high holiday.

'It is a great thing for me,' murmured old Giorgio, still thinking of the house, for now he had grown weary of change. 'The *signora* just said a word to the Englishman.'

'The old Englishman who has enough money to pay for a railway? He is going off in an hour,' remarked Nostromo, carelessly. '*Buon viaggio*, then. I've guarded his bones all the way from the Entrada pass down to the plain and into Sulaco, as though he had been my own father.'

Old Giorgio only moved his head sideways absently. Nostromo pointed after the Goulds' carriage, nearing the grass-grown gate in the old town wall that was like a wall of matted jungle.

'And I have sat alone at night with my revolver in the Company's warehouse time and again by the side of that other Englishman's heap of silver, guarding it as though it had been my own.'

Viola seemed lost in thought. 'It is a great thing for me,' he repeated again, as if to himself.

'It is,' agreed the magnificent Capataz de Cargadores, calmly. 'Listen, *vecchio* – go in and bring me out a cigar, but don't look for it in my room. There's nothing there.'

Viola stepped into the café and came out directly, still absorbed in his idea, and tendered him a cigar, mumbling thoughtfully in his moustache, 'Children growing up – and girls, too! Girls!' He sighed and fell silent.

'What, only one?' remarked Nostromo, looking down with a sort of comic inquisitiveness at the unconscious old man. 'No matter,' he added, with lofty negligence; 'one is enough till another is wanted.'

He lit it and let the match drop from his passive fingers. Giorgio Viola looked up, and said abruptly:

'My son would have been just such a fine young man as you, Gian' Battista, if he had lived.'

'What? Your son? But you are right, *padrone*. If he had been like me he would have been a man.'

He turned his horse slowly, and paced on between the booths, checking the mare almost to a standstill now and then for children, for the groups of people from the distant Campo, who stared after him with admiration. The Company's lightermen saluted him from afar; and the greatly envied Capataz de Cargadores advanced, amongst murmurs of recognition and obsequious greetings, towards the huge circus-like erection. The throng thickened; the guitars tinkled louder; other horsemen sat motionless, smoking calmly above the heads of the crowd; it eddied and pushed before the doors of the high-roofed building, whence issued a shuffle and thumping of feet in time to the dance music vibrating and shrieking with a racking rhythm, overhung by the tremendous, sustained, hollow roar of the gombo. The barbarous and imposing noise of the big drum, that can madden a crowd, and that even

Europeans cannot hear without a strange emotion, seemed to draw Nostromo on to its source, while a man, wrapped up in a faded, torn poncho, walked by his stirrup, and, buffeted right and left, begged 'his worship' insistently for employment on the wharf. He whined, offering the Señor Capataz half his daily pay for the privilege of being admitted to the swaggering fraternity of *cargadores*; the other half would be enough for him, he protested. But Captain Mitchell's right-hand man – 'invaluable for our work – a perfectly incorruptible fellow' – after looking down critically at the ragged *mozo*, shook his head without a word in the uproar going on around.

The man fell back; and a little farther on Nostromo had to pull up. From the doors of the dance-hall men and women emerged tottering, streaming with sweat, trembling in every limb, to lean, panting, with staring eyes and parted lips, against the wall of the structure, where the harps and guitars played on with mad speed in an incessant roll of thunder. Hundreds of hands clapped in there; voices shrieked, and then all at once would sink low, chanting in unison the refrain of a love song, with a dying fall. A red flower, flung with a good aim from somewhere in the crowd, struck the resplendent Capataz on the cheek.

He caught it as it fell, neatly, but for some time did not turn his head. When at last he condescended to look round, the throng near him had parted to make way for a pretty Morenita, her hair held up by a small golden comb, who was walking towards him in the open space.

Her arms and neck emerged plump and bare from a snowy chemisette; the blue woollen skirt, with all the fullness gathered in front, scanty on the hips and tight across the back, disclosed the provoking action of her walk. She came straight on and laid her hand on the mare's neck with a timid, coquettish look upwards out of the corner of her eyes.

'*Querido*,' she murmured, caressingly, 'why do you pretend not to see me when I pass?'

'Because I don't love thee any more,' said Nostromo, deliberately, after a moment of reflective silence.

The hand on the mare's neck trembled suddenly. She dropped her head before all the eyes in the wide circle formed round the generous, the terrible, the inconstant Capataz de Cargadores, and his Morenita.

Nostromo, looking down, saw tears beginning to fall down her face.

'Has it come, then, ever beloved of my heart?' she whispered. 'Is it true?'

'No,' said Nostromo, looking away carelessly. 'It was a lie. I love thee as much as ever.'

'Is that true?' she cooed, joyously, her cheeks still wet with tears.

'It is true.'

'True on the life?'

'As true as that; but thou must not ask me to swear it on the Madonna that stands in thy room.' And the Capataz laughed a little in response to the grins of the crowd.

She pouted – very pretty – a little uneasy.

'No, I will not ask for that. I can see love in your eyes.' She laid her hand on his knee. 'Why are you trembling like this? From love?' she continued, while the cavernous thundering of the gombo went on without a pause. 'But if you love her as much as that, you must give your Paquita a gold-mounted rosary of beads for the neck of her Madonna.'

'No,' said Nostromo, looking into her uplifted, begging eyes, which suddenly turned stony with surprise.

'No? Then what else will your worship give me on the day of the fiesta?' she asked, angrily; 'so as not to shame me before all these people.'

'There is no shame for thee in getting nothing from thy lover for once.'

'True! The shame is your worship's – my poor lover's,' she flared up, sarcastically.

Laughs were heard at her anger, at her retort. What an audacious spitfire she was! The people aware of this scene were calling out urgently to others in the crowd. The circle round the silver-grey mare narrowed slowly.

The girl went off a pace or two, confronting the mocking curiosity of the eyes, then flung back to the stirrup, tiptoeing, her enraged face turned up to Nostromo with a pair of blazing eyes. He bent low to her in the saddle.

'Juan,' she hissed, 'I could stab thee to the heart!'

The dreaded Capataz de Cargadores, magnificent and carelessly public in his amours, flung his arm round her neck and kissed her spluttering lips. A murmur went round.

'A knife!' he demanded at large, holding her firmly by the shoulder.

Twenty blades flashed out together in the circle. A young man in holiday attire, bounding in, thrust one in Nostromo's hand and bounded back into the ranks, very proud of himself. Nostromo had not even looked at him.

'Stand on my foot,' he commanded the girl, who, suddenly subdued, rose lightly, and when he had her up, encircling her waist, her face near to his, he pressed the knife into her little hand.

'No, Morenita! You shall not put me to shame,' he said. 'You shall have your present; and so that everyone should know who is your lover today, you may cut all the silver buttons off my coat.'

There were shouts of laughter and applause at this witty freak, while the girl passed the keen-blade, and the impassive rider jingled in his palm the increasing hoard of silver buttons. He eased her to the ground with both her hands full. After whispering for a while with a very strenuous face, she walked away, staring haughtily, and vanished into the crowd.

The circle had broken up, and the lordly Capataz de Cargadores, the indispensable man, the tried and trusty Nostromo, the Mediterranean sailor come ashore casually to try his luck in Costaguana, rode slowly towards the harbour. The *Juno* was just then swinging round; and even as Nostromo reined up again to look on, a flag ran up on the improvised flagstaff erected in an ancient and dismantled little fort at the harbour entrance. Half a battery of field guns had been hurried over there from the Sulaco barracks for the purpose of firing the regulation salutes for the President-Dictator and the War Minister. As the mail-boat headed through the pass, the badly timed reports announced the end of Don Vincente Ribiera's first official visit to Sulaco, and for Captain Mitchell the end of another 'historic occasion'. Next time when the 'Hope of honest men' was to come that way, a year and a half later, it was unofficially, over the mountain tracks, fleeing after a defeat on a lame mule, to be only just saved by Nostromo from an ignominious death at the hands of a mob. It was a very different event, of which Captain Mitchell used to say:

'It was history – history, sir! And that fellow of mine, Nostromo, you know, was right in it. Absolutely making history, sir.'

But this event, creditable to Nostromo, was to lead immediately to another, which could not be classed either as 'history' or as 'a mistake' in Captain Mitchell's phraseology. He had another word for it.

'Sir,' he used to say afterwards, 'that was no mistake. It was a fatality. A misfortune, pure and simple, sir. And that poor fellow of mine was right in it – right in the middle of it! A fatality, if ever there was one – and to my mind he has never been the same man since.'

PART TWO
THE ISABELS

CHAPTER 1

Through good and evil report in the varying fortune of that struggle which Don José had characterized in the phrase, 'the fate of national honesty trembles in the balance', the Gould Concession, '*Imperium in Imperio*', had gone on working; the square mountain had gone on pouring its treasure down the wooden shoots to the unresting batteries of stamps; the lights of San Tomé had twinkled night after night upon the great, limitless shadow of the Campo; every three months the silver escort had gone down to the sea as if neither war nor its consequences could ever affect the ancient Occidental State secluded beyond its high barrier of the Cordillera. All the fighting took place on the other side of that mighty wall of serrated peaks lorded over by the white dome of Higuerota and as yet unbreached by the railway, of which only the first part, the easy Campo part from Sulaco to the Ivie Valley at the foot of the pass, had been laid. Neither did the telegraph line cross the mountains yet; its poles, like slender beacons on the plain, penetrated into the forest fringe of the foothills cut by the deep avenue of the track; and its wire ended abruptly in the construction camp at a white deal table supporting a Morse apparatus, in a long hut of planks with a corrugated-iron roof overshadowed by gigantic cedar trees – the quarters of the engineer in charge of the advance section.

The harbour was busy, too, with the traffic in railway material, and with the movements of troops along the coast. The O.S.N. Company found much occupation for its fleet. Costaguana had no navy, and, apart from a few coastguard cutters, there were no national ships except a couple of old merchant steamers used as transports.

Captain Mitchell, feeling more and more in the thick of history, found time for an hour or so during an afternoon in the drawing-room of the Casa Gould, where, with a strange ignorance of the real forces at work around him, he professed himself delighted to get away from the strain of affairs. He did not know what he would have done without his invaluable Nostromo, he declared. Those confounded Costaguana politics gave him more work – he confided to Mrs Gould – than he had bargained for.

Don José Avellanos had displayed in the service of the endangered Ribiera Government an organizing activity and an eloquence of which the echoes reached even Europe. For, after the new loan to the Ribiera Government, Europe had become interested in Costaguana. The Sala of the Provincial Assembly (in the Municipal Buildings of Sulaco), with its portraits of the Liberators on the walls and an old flag of Cortés preserved in a glass case above the President's chair, had heard all these speeches – the early one containing the impassioned declaration 'Militarism is the enemy', the famous one of the 'trembling balance' delivered on the occasion of the vote for the raising of a second Sulaco regiment in the defence of the reforming Government; and when the provinces again displayed their old flags (proscribed in Guzman Bento's time) there was another of those great orations, when Don José greeted these old emblems of the war of Independence, brought out again in the name of new Ideals. The old idea of Federalism had disappeared. For his part he did not wish to revive old political doctrines. They were perishable. They died. But the doctrine of political rectitude was immortal. The second Sulaco regiment, to whom he was presenting this flag, was going to show its valour in a contest for order, peace, progress; for the establishment of national self-respect without which – he declared with energy – 'we are a reproach and a byword amongst the powers of the world'.

Don José Avellanos loved his country. He had served it lavishly with his fortune during his diplomatic career, and the later story of his captivity and barbarous ill-usage under Guzman Bento was well known to his listeners. It was a wonder that he had not been a victim of the ferocious and summary executions which marked the course of that tyranny; for Guzman had ruled the country with the sombre imbecility of political fanaticism. The power of Supreme Government had become in his dull mind an object of strange worship, as if it were some sort of cruel deity. It was incarnated in himself, and his adversaries, the Federalists, were the supreme sinners, objects of hate, abhorrence, and fear, as heretics would be to a convinced Inquisitor. For years he had carried about at the tail of the Army of Pacification, all over the country, a captive band of such atrocious criminals, who considered themselves most unfortunate at not having been summarily executed. It was a diminishing company of nearly naked skeletons, loaded with irons, covered with dirt, with vermin, with raw wounds, all men of position, of education, of wealth, who had learned to fight amongst themselves for scraps of rotten beef thrown to them by soldiers, or to beg a Negro cook for a drink of muddy water in pitiful accents. Don José Avellanos, clanking his chains amongst the others, seemed only to exist in order to prove how much hunger, pain, degradation, and cruel torture a human body can stand without parting with the last spark of life. Sometimes interrogatories, backed by some primitive method of torture, were administered to them by a commission of officers hastily assembled in a hut of sticks and branches, and made pitiless by the fear for their own lives. A lucky one or two of that spectral company of prisoners would perhaps be led tottering behind a bush to be shot by a file of soldiers. Always an army chaplain – some unshaven, dirty man, girt with a sword and with a tiny cross embroidered in white cotton on the left breast of a lieutenant's uniform – would follow, cigarette in the corner of the mouth, wooden stool in hand, to hear the confession and give absolution; for the Citizen Saviour of the Country (Guzman Bento was called thus officially in petitions) was not averse from the exercise of rational clemency. The irregular report of the firing squad would be heard, followed sometimes by a single finishing shot; a little bluish cloud of smoke would float up above the green bushes, and the Army of Pacification would move on over the savannas, through the forests, crossing rivers, invading rural *pueblos*, devastating the *haciendas* of the horrid aristocrats, occupying the inland towns in the fulfilment of its patriotic mission, and leaving behind a united land wherein the evil taint of Federalism could no longer be detected in the smoke of burning houses and the smell of spilt blood.

Don José Avellanos had survived that time.

Perhaps, when contemptuously signifying to him his release, the Citizen Saviour of the Country might have thought this benighted aristocrat too broken in health and spirit and fortune to be any longer dangerous. Or, perhaps, it may have been a simple caprice. Guzman Bento, usually full of fanciful fears and brooding suspicions, had sudden accesses of unreasonable self-confidence when he perceived himself elevated on a pinnacle of power and safety beyond the reach of mere mortal plotters. At such times he would impulsively command the celebration of a solemn Mass of thanksgiving which would be sung in great pomp in the cathedral of Sta Marta by the trembling, subservient Archbishop of his creation. He heard it sitting in a gilt armchair placed before the high altar, surrounded by the civil and military heads of his Government. The unofficial world of Sta Marta would crowd into the cathedral, for it was not quite safe for anybody of mark to stay away from these manifestations of presidential piety. Having thus acknowledged the only power he was at all disposed to recognize as above himself, he would scatter acts of political grace in a sardonic wantonness of clemency. There was no other way left now to enjoy his power but by seeing his crushed adversaries crawl impotently into the light of day out of the dark, noisome cells of the Collegio. Their harmlessness fed his insatiable vanity, and they could always be got hold of again. It was the rule for all women of their families to present thanks afterwards in a special audience. The incarnation of that strange god: El Gobierno Supremo, received them standing, cocked hat on head, and exhorted them in a menacing mutter to show their gratitude by bringing up their children in fidelity to the democratic form of government, 'which I have established for the happiness of our country'. His front teeth having been knocked out in some accident of his former herdsman's life, his utterance was spluttering and indistinct. He had been working for Costaguana alone in the midst of treachery and opposition. Let it cease now lest he should become weary of forgiving!

Don José Avellanos had known this forgiveness.

He was broken in health and fortune deplorably enough to present a truly gratifying spectacle to the supreme chief of democratic institutions. He retired to Sulaco. His wife had an estate in that province, and she nursed him back to life out of the house of death and captivity. When she died, their daughter, an only child, was old enough to devote herself to 'poor papa'.

Miss Avellanos, born in Europe and educated partly in England, was a tall, grave girl, with a self-possessed manner, a wide, white forehead, a wealth of rich brown hair, and blue eyes.

The other young ladies of Sulaco stood in awe of her character and accomplishments. She was reputed to be terribly learned and serious. As to pride, it was well known that all the Corbeláns were proud, and her mother was a Corbelán. Don José Avellanos depended very much upon the devotion of his beloved Antonia. He accepted it in the benighted way of men, who, though made in God's image, are like stone idols without sense before the smoke of certain burnt offerings. He was ruined in every way, but a man possessed of passion is not a bankrupt in life. Don José Avellanos desired passionately for his country: peace, prosperity, and (as the end of the preface to *Fifty Years of Misrule* has it) 'an honourable place in the comity of civilized nations'. In this last phrase the Minister Plenipotentiary, cruelly humiliated by the bad faith of his Government towards the foreign bond-holders, stands disclosed in the patriot.

The fatuous turmoil of greedy factions succeeding the tyranny of Guzman Bento seemed to bring his desire to the very door of opportunity. He was too old to descend personally into the centre of the arena at Sta Marta. But the men who acted there sought his advice at every step. He himself thought that he could be most useful at a distance, 'in Sulaco. His name, his connexions, his former position, his experience commanded the respect of his class. The discovery that this man, living in dignified poverty in the Corbelán town residence (opposite the Casa Gould), could dispose of material means towards the support of the cause increased his influence. It was his open letter of appeal that decided the candidature of Don Vincente Ribiera for the Presidency. Another of these informal State papers drawn up by Don José (this time in the shape of an address from the Province) induced that scrupulous constitutionalist to accept the extraordinary powers conferred upon him for five years by an overwhelming vote of congress in Sta Marta. It was a specific mandate to establish the prosperity of the people on the basis of firm peace at home, and to redeem the national credit by the satisfaction of all just claims abroad.

In the afternoon the news of that vote had reached Sulaco by the usual roundabout postal way through Cayta, and up the coast by steamer. Don José, who had been waiting for the mail in the Gould's drawing room, got out of the rocking-chair, letting his hat fall off his knees. He rubbed his silvery, short hair with both hands, speechless with the excess of joy.

'Emilia, my soul,' he had burst out, 'let me embrace you! Let me – '

Captain Mitchell, had he been there, would no doubt have made an apt remark about the dawn of a new era; but if Don José thought something of the kind, his eloquence failed him on this occasion. The inspirer of that revival of the Blanco party tottered where he stood. Mrs Gould moved forward quickly and, as she offered her cheek with a smile to her old friend, managed very cleverly to give him the support of her arm he really needed.

Don José had recovered himself at once, but for a time he could do no more than murmur, 'Oh, you two patriots! Oh, you two patriots!' – looking from one to the other. Vague plans of another historical work, wherein all the devotions to the regeneration of the country he loved would be enshrined for the reverent worship of posterity, flitted through his mind. The historian who had enough elevation of soul to write of Guzman Bento: 'Yet this monster, imbrued in the blood of his countrymen, must not be held unreservedly to the execration of future years. It appears to be true that he, too, loved his country. He had given it twelve years of peace; and, absolute master of lives and fortunes as he was, he died poor. His worst fault, perhaps, was not his ferocity, but his ignorance'; the man who could write thus of a cruel persecutor (the passage occurs in his *History of Misrule*) felt at the foreshadowing of success an almost boundless affection for his two helpers, for these two young people from over the sea.

Just as years ago, calmly, from the conviction of practical necessity, stronger than any abstract political doctrine, Henry Gould had drawn the sword, so now, the times being changed, Charles Gould had flung the silver of the San Tomé into the fray. The Inglés of Sulaco, the 'Costaguana Englishman' of the third generation, was as far from being a political intriguer as his uncle from a revolutionary swashbuckler. Springing from the instinctive uprightness of their natures their action was reasoned. They saw an opportunity and used the weapon to hand.

Charles Gould's position – a commanding position in the background of that attempt to retrieve the peace and the credit of the Republic – was very clear. At the beginning he had had to accommodate himself to existing circumstances of corruption so naïvely brazen as to disarm the hatred of a man courageous enough not to be afraid of its irresponsible potency to ruin everything it touched. It seemed to him too contemptible for hot anger even. He made use of it with a cold, fearless scorn, manifested rather than concealed by the forms of stony courtesy which did away with much of the ignominy of the situation. At bottom, perhaps, he suffered from it, for he was not a man of cowardly illusions, but he refused to discuss the ethical view with his wife. He trusted that, though a little disenchanted, she would be intelligent enough to understand that his character safeguarded the enterprise of their lives as much or more than his policy. The extraordinary development of the mine had put a great power into his hands. To feel that prosperity always at the mercy of unintelligent greed had grown irksome to him. To Mrs Gould it was humiliating. At any rate, it was dangerous. In the confidential communications passing between Charles Gould, the King of Sulaco, and the head of the silver and steel interests far away in California, the conviction was growing that any attempt made by men of education and integrity ought to be discreetly supported. 'You may tell your friend Avellanos that I think so,' Mr Holroyd had written at the proper moment from his inviolable sanctuary within the eleven-storey-high factory of great affairs. And shortly afterwards, with a credit opened by the Third Southern Bank (located next door but one to the Holroyd Building), the Ribierist party in Costaguana took a practical shape under the eye of the administrator of the San Tomé mine. And Don José, the hereditary friend of the Gould family, could say: 'Perhaps, my dear Carlos, I shall not have believed in vain.'

CHAPTER 2

After another armed struggle, decided by Montero's victory of Río Seco, had been added to the tale of civil wars, the 'honest men', as Don José called them, could breathe freely for the first time in half a century. The Five-

Year-Mandate law became the basis of that regeneration, the passionate desire and hope for which had been like the elixir of everlasting youth for Don José Avellanos.

And when it was suddenly – and not quite unexpectedly – endangered by that 'brute Montero', it was a passionate indignation that gave him a new lease of life, as it were. Already at the time of the President-Dictator's visit to Sulaco, Moraga had sounded a note of warning from Sta Marta about the War Minister. Montero and his brother made the subject of an earnest talk between the Dictator-President and the Nestor-inspirer of the party. But Don Vincente, a doctor of philosophy from the Cordova University, seemed to have an exaggerated respect for military ability, whose mysteriousness – since it appeared to be altogether independent of intellect – imposed upon his imagination. The Victor of Río Seco was a popular hero. His services were so recent that the President-Dictator quailed before the obvious charge of political ingratitude. Great regenerating transactions were being initiated – the fresh loan, a new railway line, a vast colonization scheme. Anything that could unsettle the public opinion in the capital was to be avoided. Don José bowed to these arguments and tried to dismiss from his mind the gold-laced portent in boots, and with a sabre, made meaningless now at last, he hoped, in the new order of things.

Less than six months after the President-Dictator's visit, Sulaco learned with stupefaction of the military revolt in the name of national honour. The Minister of War, in a barrack-square allocution to the officers of the artillery regiment he had been inspecting, had declared the national honour sold to foreigners. The Dictator, by his weak compliance with the demands of the European powers – for the settlement of long outstanding money claims – had showed himself unfit to rule. A letter from Moraga explained afterwards that the initiative, and even the very text, of the incendiary allocution came, in reality, from the other Montero, the ex-*guerrillero*, the Commandante de Plaza. The energetic treatment of Dr Monygham, sent for in haste 'to the mountain', who came galloping three leagues in the dark, saved Don José from a dangerous attack of jaundice.

After getting over the shock, Don José refused to let himself be prostrated. Indeed, better news succeeded at first. The revolt in the capital had been suppressed after a night of fighting in the streets. Unfortunately, both the Monteros had been able to make their escape south, to their native province of Entre-Montes. The hero of the forest march, the victor of Río Seco, had been received with frenzied acclamations in Nicoya, the provincial capital. The troops in garrison there had gone to him in a body. The brothers were organizing an army, gathering malcontents, sending emissaries primed with patriotic lies to the people, and with promises of plunder to the wild *llaneros*. Even a Monterist press had come into existence, speaking oracularly of the secret promises of support given by 'our great sister Republic of the North' against the sinister land-grabbing designs of European powers, cursing in every issue the 'miserable Ribiera', who had plotted to deliver his country, bound hand and foot, for a prey to foreign speculators.

Sulaco, pastoral and sleepy, with its opulent Campo and the rich silver mine, heard the din of arms fitfully in its fortunate isolation. It was nevertheless in the very forefront of the defence with men and money; but the very rumours reached it circuitously – from abroad even, so much was it cut off from the rest of the Republic, not only by natural obstacles, but also by the vicissitudes of the war. The Monteristos were besieging Cayta, an important postal link. The overland couriers ceased to come across the mountains, and no muleteer would consent to risk the journey at last; even Bonifacio on one occasion failed to return from Sta Marta, either not daring to start, or perhaps captured by the parties of the enemy raiding the country between the Cordillera and the capital. Monterist publications, however, found their way into the province, mysteriously enough; and also Monterist emissaries preaching death to aristocrats in the villages and towns of the Campo. Very early, at the beginning of the trouble, Hernandez, the bandit, had proposed (through the agency of an old priest of a village in the wilds) to deliver two of them to the Ribierist authorities in Tonoro. They had come to offer him a free pardon and the rank of colonel from General Montero in consideration of joining the rebel army with his mounted band. No notice was taken at the time of the proposal. It was joined, as an evidence of good faith, to a petition praying the Sulaco Assembly for permission to enlist, with all his followers, in the forces being then raised in Sulaco for the defence of the Five-Year Mandate of regeneration. The petition, like everything else, had found its way into Don José's hands. He had showed to Mrs Gould these pages of dirty-greyish rough paper (perhaps looted in some village store), covered with the crabbed, illiterate handwriting of the old padre, carried off from his hut by the side of a mud-walled church to be the secretary of the dreaded Salteador. They had both bent in the lamplight of the Gould drawing-room over the document containing the fierce and yet humble appeal of the man against the blind and stupid barbarity turning an honest *ranchero* into a bandit. A postscript of the priest stated that, but for being deprived of his liberty for ten days, he had been treated with humanity and the respect due to his sacred calling. He had been, it appears, confessing and absolving the chief and most of the band, and he guaranteed the sincerity of their good disposition He had distributed heavy penances, no doubt in the way of litanies and fasts; but he argued shrewdly that it would be difficult for them to make their peace with God durably till they had made peace with men.

Never before, perhaps, had Hernandez's head been in less jeopardy than when he petitioned humbly for permission to buy a pardon for himself and his gang of deserters by armed service. He could range afar from the waste lands protecting his fastness, unchecked, because there were no troops left in the whole province. The usual garrison of Sulaco had gone south to the war, with its brass band playing the 'Bolívar March' on the bridge of one of the O.S.N. Company's steamers. The great family coaches drawn up along the shore of the harbour were made to rock on the high leathern springs by the enthusiasm of the *señoras* and the *señoritas* standing up to wave their lace handkerchiefs, as lighter after lighter packed full of troops left the end of the jetty.

Nostromo directed the embarkation, under the superintendence of Captain Mitchell, red-faced in the sun, conspicuous in a white waistcoat, representing the allied and anxious goodwill of all the material interests of civilization. General Barrios, who commanded the troops, assured Don José on parting that in three weeks he would have Montero in a wooden cage drawn by three pair of oxen ready for a tour through all the towns of the Republic.

'And then, *señora*,' he continued baring his curly iron-grey head to Mrs Gould in her landau – 'and then, *señora*, we shall convert our swords into ploughshares and grow rich. Even I, myself, as soon as this little business is settled, shall open a *fundación* on some land I have on the *llanos* and try to make a little money in peace and quietness. *Señora* you know, all Costaguana knows – what do I say? – this whole South American continent knows, that Pablo Barrios has had his fill of military glory.'

Charles Gould was not present at the anxious and patriotic send-off. It was not his part to see the soldiers embark. It was neither his part, nor his inclination, nor his policy. His part, his inclination, and his policy were united in one endeavour to keep unchecked the flow of treasure he had started singlehanded from the re-opened scar in the flank of the mountain. As the mine developed he had trained for himself some native help. There were foremen, artificers, and clerks, with Don Pepe for the *gobernador* of the mining population. For the rest his shoulders alone sustained the whole weight of the '*Imperium in Imperio*', the great Gould Concession whose mere shadow had been enough to crush the life out of his father.

Mrs Gould had no silver mine to look after. In the general life of the Gould Concession she was respected by her two lieutenants, the doctor and the priest, but she fed her woman's love for excitement on events whose significance was purified to her by the fire of her imaginative purpose. On that day she had brought the Avellanos, father and daughter, down to the harbour with her.

Amongst his other activities of that stirring time, Don José had become the chairman of a Patriotic Committee which had armed a great proportion of troops in the Sulaco command with an improved model of a military rifle. It had been just discarded for something still more deadly by one of the great European powers. How much of the market-price for second-hand weapons was covered by the voluntary contributions of the principal families, and how much came from those funds Don José was understood to command abroad, remained a secret which he alone could have disclosed; but the *ricos*, as the populace called them, had contributed under the pressure of their Nestor's eloquence. Some of the more enthusiastic ladies had been moved to bring offerings of jewels into the hands of the man who was the life and soul of the party.

There were moments when both his life and his soul seemed overtaxed by so many years of undiscouraged belief in regeneration. He appeared almost inanimate, sitting rigidly by the side of Mrs Gould in the landau, with his fine, old, clean-shaven face of a uniform tint as if modelled in yellow wax, shaded by a soft felt hat, the dark eyes looking out fixedly. Antonia, the beautiful Antonia, as Miss Avellanos was called in Sulaco, leaned back, facing them; and her full figure, the grave oval of her face with full red lips, made her look more mature than Mrs Gould, with her mobile expression and small, erect person under a slightly swaying sunshade.

Whenever possible Antonia attended her father; her recognized devotion weakened the shocking effect of her scorn for the rigid conventions regulating the life of Spanish–American girlhood. And, in truth, she was no longer girlish. It was said that she often wrote State papers from her father's dictation, and was allowed to read all the books in his library. At the receptions – where the situation was saved by the presence of a very decrepit old lady (a relation of the Corbeláns), quite deaf and motionless in an armchair – Antonia could hold her own in a discussion with two or three men at a time. Obviously she was not the girl to be content with peeping through a barred window at a cloaked figure of a lover ensconced in a doorway opposite – which is the correct form of Costaguana courtship. It was generally believed that with her foreign upbringing and foreign ideas the learned and proud Antonia would never marry – unless, indeed, she married a foreigner from Europe or North America, now that Sulaco seemed on the point of being invaded by all the world.

CHAPTER 3

When General Barrios stopped to address Mrs Gould, Antonia raised negligently her hand holding an open fan, as if to shade from the sun her head, wrapped in a light lace shawl. The clear gleam of her blue eyes gliding behind the black fringe of eyelashes paused for a moment upon her father, then travelled farther to the figure of a young man of thirty at most, of medium height, rather thick-set, wearing a light overcoat. Bearing down with the open palm of his hand upon the knob of a flexible cane, he had been looking on from a distance; but directly he saw himself noticed, he approached quietly and put his elbow over the door of the landau.

The shirt collar, cut low in the neck, the big bow of his cravat, the style of his clothing, from the round hat to the varnished shoes, suggested an idea of French elegance; but otherwise he was the very type of a fair Spanish creole. The fluffy moustache and the short, curly, golden beard did not conceal his lips, rosy, fresh, almost pouting in expression. His full, round face was of that warm, healthy creole white which is never tanned by its native sunshine. Martin Decoud was seldom exposed to the Costaguana sun under which he was born. His people had been long settled in Paris, where he had studied law, had dabbled in literature, had hoped now and then in moments of exaltation to become a poet like that other foreigner of Spanish blood, José Maria Heredia. In other moments he had, to pass the time, condescended to write articles on European affairs for the *Semenario*, the principal newspaper in Sta Marta, which printed them under the heading 'From our special correspondent', though the authorship was an open secret. Everybody in Costaguana, where the tale of compatriots in Europe is jealously kept, knew that it was 'the son Decoud', a talented young man, supposed to be moving in the higher spheres of Society. As a matter of fact, he was an idle boulevardier in touch with some smart journalists, made free of a few newspaper offices, and welcomed in the pleasure-haunts of pressmen. This life, whose dreary superficiality is covered by the glitter of universal *blague*, like the stupid clowning of a harlequin by the spangles of a motley costume, induced in him a Frenchified – but most un-French – cosmopolitanism, in reality a mere barren indifferentism posing as intellectual superiority. Of his own country he used to say to his French associates: 'Imagine an atmosphere of *opéra bouffe* in which all the comic business of stage statesmen, brigands, etc., etc., all their farcical stealing, intriguing, and stabbing is done in dead earnest. It is screamingly funny, the blood flows all the time, and the actors believe themselves to be influencing the fate of the universe. Of course, government in general, any government anywhere, is a thing of exquisite comicality to a discerning mind; but really we Spanish –Americans do overstep the bounds. No man of ordinary intelligence can take part in the intrigues of *une farce macabre*. However, these Ribierists, of whom we hear so much just now, are really trying in their own comical way to make the country habitable, and even to pay some of its debts. My friends, you had better write up Señor Ribiera all you can in kindness to your own bondholders. Really, if what I am told in my letters is true, there is some chance for them at last.'

And he would explain with railing verve what Don Vincente Ribiera stood for – a mournful little man oppressed by his own good intentions, the significance of battles won, who Montero was (*un grotesque vaniteux et féroce*), and the manner of the new loan connected with railway development, and the colonization of vast tracts of land in one great financial scheme.

And his French friends would remark that evidently this little fellow Decoud *connaissait la question à fond*. An important Parisian review asked him for an article on the situation. It was composed in a serious tone and in a spirit of levity. Afterwards he asked one of his intimates:

'Have you read my thing about the regeneration of Costaguana – *une bonne blague, hein?*'

He imagined himself Parisian to the tips of his fingers. But far from being that he was in danger of remaining a sort of nondescript dilettante all his life. He had pushed the habit of universal raillery to a point where it blinded him to the genuine impulses of his own nature. To be suddenly selected for the executive member of the patriotic small-arms committee of Sulaco seemed to him the height of the unexpected, one of those fantastic moves of which only his 'dear countrymen' were capable.

'It's like a tile falling on my head. I – I – executive member! It's the first I hear of it! What do I know of military rifles? *C'est funambulesque!*' he had exclaimed to his favourite sister; for the Decoud family – except the old father and mother – used the French language amongst themselves. 'And you should see the explanatory and confidential letter! Eight pages of it – no less!'

This letter, in Antonia's handwriting, was signed by Don José who appealed to the 'young and gifted Costaguanero' on public grounds, and privately opened his heart to his talented godson, a man of wealth and leisure, with wide relations, and by his parentage and bringing-up worthy of all confidence.

'Which means,' Martin commented, cynically, to his sister, 'that I am not likely to misappropriate the funds, or go blabbing to our Chargé d'Affaires here.'

The whole thing was being carried out behind the back of the War Minister, Montero, a mistrusted member of the Ribiera Government, but difficult to get rid of at once. He was not to know anything of it till the troops under Barrios's command had the new rifle in their hands. The President-Dictator, whose position was very difficult, was alone in the secret.

'How funny!' commented Martin's sister and confidant; to which the brother, with an air of best Parisian *blague*, had retorted:

'It's immense! The idea of that Chief of the State engaged, with the help of private citizens, in digging a mine under his own indispensable War Minister. No! We are unapproachable!' And he laughed immoderately.

Afterwards his sister was surprised at the earnestness and ability he displayed in carrying out his mission, which circumstances made delicate, and his want of special knowledge rendered difficult. She had never seen Martin take so much trouble about anything in his whole life.

'It amuses me,' he had explained, briefly. 'I am beset by a lot of swindlers trying to sell all sorts of gaspipe weapons. They are charming; they invite me to expensive luncheons; I keep up their hopes; it's extremely entertaining. Meanwhile, the real affair is being carried through in quite another quarter.'

When the business was concluded he declared suddenly his intention of seeing the precious consignment delivered safely in Sulaco. The whole burlesque business, he thought, was worth following up to the end. He mumbled his excuses, tugging at his golden beard, before the acute young lady who (after the first wide stare of astonishment) looked at him with narrowed eyes, and pronounced slowly:

'I believe you want to see Antonia.'

'What Antonia?' asked the Costaguana boulevardier, in a vexed and disdainful tone. He shrugged his shoulders, and spun round on his heel. His sister called out after him joyously:

'The Antonia you used to know when she wore her hair in two plaits down her back.'

He had known her some eight years since, shortly before the Avellanos had left Europe for good, as a tall girl of sixteen, youthfully austere, and of a character already so formed that she ventured to treat slightingly his pose of disabused wisdom. On one occasion, as though she had lost all patience, she flew out at him about the aimlessness of his life and the levity of his opinions. He was twenty then, an only son, spoiled by his adoring family. This attack disconcerted him so greatly that he had faltered in his affection of amused superiority before that insignificant chit of a school-girl. But the impression left was so strong that ever since all the girl friends of his sisters recalled to him Antonia Avellanos by some faint resemblance, or by the great force of contrast. It was, he told himself, like a ridiculous fatality. And, of course, in the news the Decouds received regularly from Costaguana, the name of their friends, the Avellanos, cropped up frequently – the arrest and the abominable treatment of the ex-Minister, the dangers and hardships endured by the family, its withdrawal in poverty to Sulaco, the death of the mother.

The Monterist *pronunciamiento* had taken place before Martin Decoud reached Costaguana. He came out in a roundabout way, through Magellan's Straits by the main line and the West Coast Service of the O.S.N. Company. His precious consignment arrived just in time to convert the first feelings of consternation into a mood of hope and resolution. Publicly he was made much of by the *familias principales*. Privately Don José, still shaken and weak, embraced him with tears in his eyes.

'You have come out yourself! No less could be expected from a Decoud. Alas! our worst fears have been realized,' he moaned, affectionately. And again he hugged his godson. This was indeed the time for men of intellect and conscience to rally round the endangered cause.

It was then that Martin Decoud, the adopted child of Western Europe, felt the absolute change of atmosphere. He submitted to being embraced and talked to without a word. He was moved in spite of himself by that note of passion and sorrow unknown on the more refined stage of European politics. But when the tall Antonia, advancing with her light step in the dimness of the big bare *sala* of the Avellanos house, offered him her hand (in her emancipated way), and murmured, 'I am glad to see you here, Don Martin,' he felt how impossible it would be to tell these two people that he had intended to go away by the next month's packet. Don José, meantime, continued his praises. Every accession added to public confidence, and, besides, what an example to the young men at home from the brilliant defender of the country's regeneration, the worthy expounder of the party's political faith before the world! Everybody had read the magnificent article in the famous *Parisian Review*. The world was now informed: and the author's appearance at this moment was like a public act of faith. Young Decoud felt overcome by a feeling of impatient confusion. His plan had been to return by way of the United States through California, visit Yellowstone Park, see Chicago, Niagara, have a look at Canada, perhaps make a short stay in New York, a longer one in Newport, use his letters of introduction. The pressure of Antonia's hand was so frank, the tone of her voice was so unexpectedly unchanged in its approving warmth, that all he found to say after his low bow was:

'I am inexpressibly grateful for your welcome; but why need a man be thanked for returning to his native country? I am sure Doña Antonia does not think so.'

'Certainly not, *señor*,' she said, with that perfectly calm openness of manner which characterized all her utterances. 'But when he returns, as you return, one may be glad – for the sake of both.'

Martin Decoud said nothing of his plans. He not only never breathed a word of them to anyone, but only a fortnight later asked the mistress of the Casa Gould (where he had of course obtained admission at once), leaning forward in his chair with an air of well-bred familiarity, whether she could not detect in him that day a marked change – an air, he explained, of more excellent gravity. At this Mrs Gould turned her face full towards him with the silent inquiry of slightly widened eyes and the merest ghost of a smile, a habitual movement with her, which was very fascinating to men by something subtly devoted, finely self-forgetful in its lovely readiness of attention. Because, Decoud continued imperturbably, he felt no longer an idle cumberer of the earth. She was, he assured her, actually beholding at that moment the Journalist of Sulaco. At once Mrs Gould glanced towards Antonia, posed upright in the corner of a high, straight-backed Spanish sofa, a large black fan waving slowly against the curves of her fine figure, the tips of crossed feet peeping from under the hem of the black skirt. Decoud's eyes also remained fixed there, while in an undertone he added that Miss Avellanos was quite aware of his new and unexpected vocation, which in Costaguana was generally the speciality of half-educated Negroes and wholly penniless lawyers. Then, confronting with a sort of urbane effrontery Mrs Gould's gaze, now turned sympathetically upon himself, he breathed out the words, '*Pro patria!*'

What had happened was that he had all at once yielded to Don José's pressing entreaties to take the direction of a newspaper that would 'voice the aspirations of the province'. It had been Don José's old and cherished idea. The necessary plant (on a modest scale) and a large consignment of paper had been received from America some time before; the right man alone was wanted. Even Señor Moraga in Sta Marta had not been able to find one, and the matter was now becoming pressing; some organ was absolutely needed to counteract the effect of the lies disseminated by the Monterist Press: the atrocious calumnies, the appeals of the people calling upon them to rise with their knives in their hands and put an end once for all to the Blancos, to these Gothic remnants, to these sinister mummies, these impotent *paralíticos*, who plotted with foreigners for the surrender of the lands and the slavery of the people.

The clamour of this 'Negro Liberalism' frightened Señor Avellanos. A newspaper was the only remedy. And now that the right man had been found in Decoud, great black letters appeared painted between the windows above the arcaded ground floor of a house on the Plaza. It was next to Anzani's great emporium of boots, silks, ironware, muslins, wooden toys, tiny silver arms, legs, heads, hearts (for ex-voto offerings), rosaries, champagne, women's hats, patent medicines, even a few dusty books in paper covers and mostly in the French language. The big black letters formed the words 'Offices of the *Porvenir*'. From these offices a single folded sheet of Martin's journalism issued three times a week; and the sleek yellow Anzani prowling in a suit of ample black and carpet slippers, before the many doors of his establishment, greeted by a deep, side-long inclination of his body the Journalist of Sulaco going to and fro on the business of his august calling.

CHAPTER 4

Perhaps it was in the exercise of his calling that he had come to see the troops depart. The *Porvenir* of the day after next would no doubt relate the event, but its editor, leaning his side against the landau, seemed to look at nothing. The front rank of the company of infantry drawn up three deep across the shore-end of the jetty when pressed too close would bring their bayonets to the charge ferociously, with an awful rattle; and then the crowd of spectators swayed back bodily, even under the noses of the big white mules. Notwithstanding the great multitude there was only a low, muttering noise; the dust hung in a brown haze, in which the horsemen, wedged in the throng here and there, towered from the hips upwards, gazing all one way over the heads. Almost every one of them had mounted a friend, who steadied himself with both hands grasping his shoulders from behind; and the rims of their hats touching, made like one disc sustaining the cones of two pointed crowns with a double face underneath. A hoarse *mozo* would bawl out something to an acquaintance in the ranks, or a woman would shriek suddenly the word *Adiôs!* followed by the Christian name of a man.

General Barrios, in a shabby blue tunic and white peg-top trousers falling upon strange red boots, kept his head uncovered and stooped slightly, propping himself up with a thick stick. No! He had earned enough military glory to satiate any man, he insisted to Mrs Gould, trying at the same time to put an air of gallantry into his attitude. A few jetty hairs hung sparsely from his upper lip, he had a salient nose, a thin, long jaw, and a black silk patch over one eye. His other eye, small and deep-set, twinkled erratically in all directions, aimlessly affable. The few European spectators, all men, who had naturally drifted into the neighbourhood of the Gould carriage, betrayed by the solemnity of their faces their impression that the general must have had too much punch (Swedish punch, imported in bottles by Anzani) at the Amarilla Club before he had started with his Staff on a furious ride to the harbour. But Mrs Gould bent forward, self-possessed, and declared her conviction that still more glory awaited the general in the near future.

'*Señora!*' he remonstrated, with great feeling, 'in the name of God, reflect! How can there be any glory for a man like me in overcoming that bald-headed *embustero* with the dyed moustaches?'

Pablo Ignacio Barrios, son of a village *alcalde*, general of division, commanding in chief the Occidental Military district, did not frequent the higher society of the town. He preferred the unceremonious gatherings of men where he could tell jaguar-hunt stories, boast of his powers with the lasso, with which he could perform extremely difficult feats of the sort 'no married man should attempt', as the saying goes amongst the *llaneros*; relate tales of

extraordinary night rides, encounters with wild bulls, struggles with croc-
odiles, adventures in the great forests, crossings of swollen rivers. And it was
not mere boastfulness that prompted the general's reminiscences, but a
genuine love of that wild life which he had led in his young days before he
turned his back for ever on the thatched roof of the parental *tolderia* in the
woods. Wandering away as far as Mexico he had fought against the French
by the side (as he said) of Juarez, and was the only military man of
Costaguana who had ever encountered European troops in the field. That
fact shed a great lustre upon his name till it became eclipsed by the rising
star of Montero. All his life he had been an inveterate gambler. He alluded
himself quite openly to the current story how once, during some campaign
(when in command of a brigade), he had gambled away his horses, pistols
and accoutrements, to the very epaulettes, playing *monte* with his colonels
the night before the battle. Finally, he had sent under escort his sword (a
presentation sword, with a gold hilt) to the town in the rear of his position
to be immediately pledged for five hundred pesetas with a sleepy and
frightened shopkeeper. By daybreak he had lost the last of that money, too,
when his only remark, as he rose calmly, was, 'Now let us go and fight to
the death.' From that time he had become aware that a general could lead
his troops into battle very well with a simple stick in his hand. 'It has been
my custom ever since,' he would say.

He was always overwhelmed with debts; even during the periods of
splendour in his varied fortunes of a Costaguana general, when he held high
military commands, his gold-laced uniforms were almost always in pawn
with some tradesman. And at last, to avoid the incessant difficulties of
costume caused by the anxious lenders, he had assumed a disdain of military
trappings, an eccentric fashion of shabby old tunics, which had become like
a second nature. But the faction Barrios joined needed to fear no political
betrayal. He was too much of a real soldier for the ignoble traffic of buying
and selling victories. A member of the foreign diplomatic body in Sta Marta
had once passed a judgement upon him: 'Barrios is a man of perfect honesty,
and even of some talent for war, *mais il manque de tenue.*' After the triumph
of the Ribierists he had obtained the reputedly lucrative Occidental command
mainly through the exertions of his creditors (the Sta Marta shopkeepers
all great politicians), who moved heaven and earth in his interest publicly,
and privately besieged Señor Moraga, the influential agent of the San Tomé
mine, with the exaggerated lamentations that if the general were passed
over, 'we shall all be ruined'. An incidental but favourable mention of his
name in Mr Gould senior's long correspondence with his son had something
to do with his appointment, too; but most of all undoubtedly his established
political honesty. No one questioned the personal bravery of the Tiger-killer
as the populace called him. He was, however, said to be unlucky in the field
– but this was to be the beginning of an era of peace. The soldiers liked him
for his humane temper, which was like a strange and precious flower
unexpectedly blooming on the hotbed of corrupt revolutions; and when he
rode slowly through the streets during some military display, the contemptuous good humour of his solitary eye roaming over the crowds extorted the
acclamations of the populace. The women of that class especially seemed

positively fascinated by the long dropping nose, the peaked chin, the heavy lower lip, the black silk eye-patch and band slanting rakishly over the forehead. His high rank always procured an audience of *caballeros* for his sporting stories, which he detailed very well with a simple, grave enjoyment. As to the society of ladies, it was irksome by the restraints it imposed without any equivalent, as far as he could see. He had not, perhaps, spoken three times on the whole to Mrs Gould since he had taken up his high command; but he had observed her frequently riding with the Señor Administrador, and had pronounced that there was more sense in her little bridle-hand than in all the female heads in Sulaco. His impulse had been to be very civil on parting to a woman who did not wobble in the saddle, and happened to be the wife of a personality very important to a man always short of money. He even pushed his attentions so far as to desire the aide-de-camp at his side (a thick-set, short captain with a Tartar physiognomy) to bring along a corporal with a file of men in front of the carriage, lest the crowd in its backward surges would 'incommode the mules of the *señora*'. Then, turning to the small knot of silent Europeans looking on within earshot, he raised his voice protectingly:

'*Señores*, have no apprehension. Go on quietly making your Ferro Carril – your railways, your telegraphs. Your – There's enough wealth in Costaguana to pay for everything – or else you would not be here. Ha! ha! Don't mind this little *picardía* of my friend Montero. In a little while you shall behold his dyed moustaches through the bars of a strong wooden cage. *Sí, señores!* Fear nothing, develop the country, work, work!'

The little group of engineers received this exhortation without a word, and after waving his hand at them loftily, he addressed himself again to Mrs Gould:

'That is what Don José says we must do. Be enterprising! Work! Grow rich! To put Montero in a cage is my work; and when that insignificant piece of business is done, then, as Don José wishes us, we shall grow rich, one and all, like so many Englishmen, because it is money that saves a country, and –'

But a young officer in a very new uniform, hurrying up from the direction of the jetty, interrupted his interpretation of Señor Avellanos's ideals. The general made a movement of impatience; the other went on talking to him insistently, with an air of respect. The horses of the Staff had been embarked, the steamer's gig was awaiting the general at the boat steps; and Barrios, after a fierce stare of his one eye, began to take leave. Don José roused himself for an appropriate phrase pronounced mechanically. The terrible strain of hope and fear was telling on him, and he seemed to husband the last sparks of his fire for those oratorical efforts of which even the distant Europe was to hear. Antonia, her red lips firmly closed, averted her head behind the raised fan; and young Decoud, though he felt the girl's eyes upon him, gazed away persistently, hooked on his elbow, with a scornful and complete detachment. Mrs Gould heroically concealed her dismay at the appearance of men and events so remote from her racial conventions, dismay too deep to be uttered in words even to her husband. She understood his voiceless reserve better now. Their confidential intercourse fell, not in moments of privacy, but precisely in public, when the quick meeting of their glances would comment upon some fresh turn of events. She had gone to his school of uncompromising silence, the only one possible, since so much that seemed shocking, weird, and grotesque in the working out of their purposes had to be accepted as normal in this country. Decidedly, the stately Antonia looked more mature and infinitely calm; but she would never have known how to reconcile the sudden sinkings of her heart with an amiable mobility of expression.

Mrs Gould smiled a good-bye at Barrios, nodded round to the Europeans (who raised their hats simultaneously) with an engaging invitation, 'I hope to see you all presently, at home'; then said nervously to Decoud, 'Get in, Don Martin,' and heard him mutter to himself in French, as he opened the carriage door, '*Le sort en est jeté.*' She heard him with a sort of exasperation. Nobody ought to have known better than himself that the first cast of dice had been already thrown long ago in a most desperate game. Distant acclamations, words of command yelled out, and a roll of drums on the jetty greeted the departing general. Something like a slight faintness came over her, and she looked blankly at Antonia's still face, wondering what would happen to Charley if that absurd man failed. '*A la casa, Ignacio,*' she cried at the motionless broad back of the coachman, who gathered the reins without haste, mumbling to himself under his breath, '*Sí, la casa. Sí, sí, niña.*'

The carriage rolled noiselessly on the soft track, the shadows fell long on the dusty little plain interspersed with dark bushes, mounds of turned-up earth, low wooden buildings with iron roofs of the Railway Company; the sparse row of telegraph poles strode obliquely clear of the town, bearing a single, almost invisible wire far into the great *campo* – like a slender, vibrating feeler of that progress waiting outside for a moment of peace to enter and twine itself about the weary heart of the land.

The café window of the Albergo d'Italia Una was full of sunburnt, whiskered faces of railway men. But at the other end of the house, the end of the Signori Inglesi, old Giorgio, at the door with one of his girls on each side, bared his bushy head, as white as the snows of Higuerota. Mrs Gould stopped the carriage. She seldom failed to speak to the protégé; moreover, the excitement, the heat, and the dust had made her thirsty. She asked for a glass of water. Giorgio sent the children indoors for it, and approached with pleasure expressed in his whole rugged countenance. It was not often that he had occasion to see his benefactress, who was also an Englishwoman – another title to his regard. He offered some excuses for his wife. It was a bad day with her; her oppressions – he tapped his own broad chest. She could not move from her chair that day.

Decoud, ensconced in the corner of his seat, observed gloomily Mrs Gould's old revolutionist, then, offhand:

'Well, and what do you think of it all, Garibaldino?'

Old Giorgio, looking at him with some curiosity, said civilly that the troops had marched very well. One-eyed Barrios and his officers had done wonders with the recruits in a short time. Those *indos*, only caught the other day, had gone swinging past in double-quick time, like *bersaglieri*; they looked well fed, too, and had whole uniforms. 'Uniforms!' he repeated with a half-smile of pity. A look of grim retrospect stole over his piercing, steady eyes. It had been otherwise in his time when men fought against tyranny, in the forests of Brazil, or on the plains of Uruguay, starving on half-raw beef without salt, half naked, with often only a knife tied to a stick for a weapon. 'And yet we used to prevail against the oppressor,' he concluded, proudly.

His animation fell; the slight gesture of his hand expressed discouragement; but he added that he had asked one of the sergeants to show him the new rifle. There was no such weapon in his fighting days; and if Barrios could not –

'Yes, yes,' broke in Don José, almost trembling with eagerness. 'We are safe. The good Señor Viola is a man of experience. Extremely deadly – is it not so? You have accomplished your mission admirably, my dear Martin.'

Decoud, lolling back moodily, contemplated old Viola.

'Ah! Yes. A man of experience. But who are you for, really, in your heart?'

Mrs Gould leaned over to the children. Linda had brought out a glass of water on a tray, with extreme care; Giselle presented her with a bunch of flowers gathered hastily.

'For the people,' declared old Viola, sternly.

'We are all for the people – in the end.'

'Yes,' muttered old Viola, savagely. 'And meantime they fight for you. Blind. *Esclavos!*'

At that moment young Scarfe of the railway staff emerged from the door of the part reserved for the Signori Inglesi. He had come down to head-quarters from somewhere up the line on a light engine, and had had just time to get a bath and change his clothes. He was a nice boy, and Mrs Gould welcomed him.

'It's a delightful surprise to see you, Mrs Gould. I've just come down. Usual luck. Missed everything, of course. This show is just over, and I hear there has been a great dance at Don Juste Lopez's last night. Is it true?'

'The young patricians,' Decoud began suddenly in his precise English, 'have indeed been dancing before they started off to the war with the Great Pompey.'

Young Scarfe stared, astounded. 'You haven't met before,' Mrs Gould intervened. 'Mr Decoud – Mr Scarfe.'

'Ah! But we are not going to Pharsalia,' protested Don José, with nervous haste, also in English. 'You should not jest like this, Martin.'

Antonia's breast rose and fell with a deeper breath. The young engineer was utterly in the dark. 'Great what?' he muttered, vaguely.

'Luckily, Montero is not a Caesar,' Decoud continued. 'Not the two Monteros put together would make a decent parody of a Caesar.' He crossed his arms on his breast, looking at Señor Avellanos, who had returned to his immobility. 'It is only you, Don José, who are a genuine old Roman – *vir Romanus* – eloquent and inflexible.'

Since he had heard the name of Montero pronounced, young Scarfe had been eager to express his simple feelings. In a loud and youthful tone he hoped that this Montero was going to be licked once for all and done with.

There was no saying what would happen to the railway if the revolution got the upper hand. Perhaps it would have to be abandoned. It would not be the first railway gone to pot in Costaguana. 'You know, it's one of their so-called national things,' he ran on, wrinkling up his nose as if the world had a suspicious flavour to his profound experience of South American affairs. And, of course, he chatted with animation, it had been such an immense piece of luck for him at his age to get appointed on the staff 'of a big thing like that – don't you know'. It would give him the pull over a lot of chaps all through life, he asserted. 'Therefore – down with Montero! Mrs Gould.' His artless grin disappeared slowly before the unanimous gravity of the faces turned upon him from the carriage; only that 'old chap', Don José, presenting a motionless, waxy profile, stared straight on as if deaf. Scarfe did not know the Avellanos very well. They did not give balls, and Antonia never appeared at a ground-floor window, as some other young ladies used to do attended by elder women, to chat with the *caballeros* on horseback in the Calle. The stares of these creoles did not matter much; but what on earth had come to Mrs Gould? She said, 'Go on, Ignacio,' and gave him a slow inclination of the head. He heard a short laugh from that round-faced, Frenchified fellow. He coloured up to the eyes, and stared at Giorgio Viola, who had fallen back with the children, hat in hand.

'I shall want a horse presently,' he said with some asperity to the old man.

'*Sí, señor*. There are plenty of horses,' murmured the Garibaldino, smoothing absently, with his brown hands, the two heads, one dark with bronze glints, the other fair with a coppery ripple, of the two girls by his side. The returning stream of sightseers raised a great dust on the road. Horsemen noticed the group. 'Go to your mother,' he said. 'They are growing up as I am growing older, and there is nobody –'

He looked at the young engineer and stopped, as if awakened from a dream; then, folding his arms on his breast, took up his usual position, leaning back in the doorway with an upward glance fastened on the white shoulder of Higuerota far away.

In the carriage Martin Decoud, shifting his position as though he could not make himself comfortable, muttered as he swayed towards Antonia, 'I suppose you hate me.' Then in a loud voice he began to congratulate Don José upon all the engineers being convinced Ribierists. The interest of all those foreigners was gratifying. 'You have heard this one. He is an enlightened well-wisher. It is pleasant to think that the prosperity of Costaguana is of some use to the world.'

'He is very young,' Mrs Gould remarked quietly.

'And so very wise for his age,' retorted Decoud. 'But here we have the naked truth from the mouth of that child. You are right. Don José. The natural treasures of Costaguana are of importance to the progressive Europe represented by this youth, just as three hundred years ago the wealth of our Spanish fathers was a serious object to the rest of Europe – as represented by the bold buccaneers. There is a curse of futility upon our character: Don Quixote and Sancho Panza, chivalry and materialism, high-sounding sentiments and a supine morality, violent efforts for an idea and a sullen acquiescence in every form of corruption. We convulsed a continent for our independence only to become the passive prey of a democratic parody, the helpless victims of scoundrels and cut-throats, our institutions a mockery, our laws a farce – a Guzman Bento our master! And we have sunk so low that when a man like you has awakened our conscience, a stupid barbarian of a Montero – Great Heavens! a Montero! – becomes a deadly danger, and an ignorant, boastful *indio*, like Barrios, is our defender.'

But Don José, disregarding the general indictment as though he had not heard a word of it, took up the defence of Barrios. The man was competent enough for his special task in the plan of campaign. It consisted in an offensive movement, with Cayta as base, upon the flank of the revolutionist forces advancing from the south against Sta Marta, which was covered by another army with the President-Dictator in its midst. Don José became quite animated with a great flow of speech, bending forward anxiously under the steady eyes of his daughter. Decoud, as if silenced by so much ardour, did not make a sound. The bells of the city were striking the hour of *Oración* when the carriage rolled under the old gateway facing the harbour like a shapeless monument of leaves and stones. The rumble of wheels under the sonorous arch was traversed by a strange, piercing shriek, and Decoud, from his back seat, had a view of the people behind the carriage trudging along the road outside, all turning their heads, in sombreros and rebozos, to look at a locomotive which rolled quickly out of sight behind Giorgio Viola's house, under a white trail of steam that seemed to vanish in the breathless, hysterically prolonged scream of warlike triumph. And it was all like a fleeting vision, the shrieking ghost of a railway engine fleeing across the frame of the archway, behind the startled movement of the people streaming back from a military spectacle with silent footsteps on the dust of the road. It was a material train returning from the Campo to the palisaded yards. The empty cars rolled lightly on the single track; there was no rumble of wheels, no tremor on the ground. The engine-driver, running past the Casa Viola with the salute of an uplifted arm, checked his speed smartly before entering the yard; and when the ear-splitting screech of the steam-whistle for the brakes had stopped, a series of hard, battering shocks, mingled with the clanking of chain-couplings, made a tumult of blows and shaken fetters under the vault of the gate.

CHAPTER 5

The Gould carriage was the first to return from the harbour to the empty town. On the ancient pavement, laid out in patterns, sunk into ruts and holes, the portly Ignacio, mindful of the springs of the Parisian-built landau, had pulled up to a walk, and Decoud in his corner contemplated moodily the inner aspect of the gate. The squat turreted sides held up between them a mass of masonry with bunches of grass growing at the top, and a grey, heavily scrolled armorial shield of stone above the apex of the arch with the arms of Spain nearly smoothed out as if in readiness for some new device typical of the impending progress.

The explosive noise of the railway trucks seemed to augment Decoud's irritation. He muttered something to himself, then began to talk aloud in curt, angry phrases thrown at the silence of the two women. They did not look at him at all; while Don José, with his semi-translucent, waxy complexion, overshadowed by the soft grey hat, swayed a little to the jolts of the carriage by the side of Mrs Gould.

'This sound puts a new edge on a very old truth.'

Decoud spoke in French, perhaps because of Ignacio on the box above him; the old coachman, with his broad back filling a short, silver-braided jacket, had a big pair of ears, whose thick rims stood well away from his cropped head.

'Yes, the noise outside the city wall is new, but the principle is old.'

He ruminated his discontent for a while, then began afresh with a sidelong glance at Antonia:

'No, but just imagine our forefathers in morions and corselets drawn up outside this gate, and a band of adventurers just landed from their ships in the harbour there. Thieves, of course. Speculators, too. Their expeditions, each one, were the speculations of grave and reverend persons in England. That is history, as that absurd sailor Mitchell is always saying.'

'Mitchell's arrangements for the embarkation of the troops were excellent!' exclaimed Don José.

'That! – that! oh, that's really the work of that Genoese seaman! But to return to my noises; there used to be in the old days the sound of trumpets outside that gate. War trumpets! I'm sure they were trumpets. I have read somewhere that Drake, who was the greatest of these men, used to dine alone in his cabin on board ship to the sound of trumpets. In those days this town was full of wealth. Those men came to take it. Now the whole land is like a treasure-house, and all these people are breaking into it, whilst we are cutting each other's throats. The only thing that keeps them out is mutual jealousy. But they'll come to an agreement some day – and by the time we've settled our quarrels and become decent and honourable, there'll be nothing left for us. It has always been the same. We are a wonderful people, but it has always been our fate to be' – he did not say 'robbed', but added, after a pause – 'exploited!'

Mrs Gould said, 'Oh, this is unjust!' And Antonia interjected, 'Don't answer him, Emilia. He is attacking me.'

'You surely do not think I was attacking Don Carlos!' Decoud answered.

And then the carriage stopped before the door of the Casa Gould. The young man offered his hand to the ladies. They went in first together; Don José walked by the side of Decoud, and the gouty old porter tottered after them with some light wraps on his arm.

Don José slipped his hand under the arm of the journalist of Sulaco.

'The *Porvenir* must have a long and confident article upon Barrios and the irresistibleness of his army of Cayta! The moral effect should be kept up in the country. We must cable encouraging extracts to Europe and the United States to maintain a favourable impression abroad.'

Decoud muttered, 'Oh, yes, we must comfort our friends, the speculators.'

The long open gallery was in shadow, with its screen of plants in vases along the balustrade, holding out motionless blossoms, and all the glass doors of the reception-rooms thrown open. A jingle of spurs died out at the farther end.

Basilio, standing aside against the wall, said in a soft tone to the passing ladies, 'The Señor Administrador is just back from the mountain.'

In the great *sala*, with its groups of ancient Spanish and modern European furniture making as if different centres under the high white spread of the ceiling, the silver and porcelain of the tea-service gleamed along a cluster of dwarf chairs, like a bit of a lady's boudoir, putting in a note of feminine and intimate delicacy.

Don José in his rocking-chair placed his hat on his lap, and Decoud walked up and down the whole length of the room passing between tables loaded with knick-knacks and almost disappearing behind the high backs of leathern sofas. He was thinking of the angry face of Antonia; he was confident that he would make his peace with her. He had not stayed in Sulaco to quarrel with Antonia.

Martin Decoud was angry with himself. All he saw and heard going on around him exasperated the preconceived views of his European civilization. To contemplate revolutions from the distance of the Parisian Boulevards was quite another matter. Here on the spot it was not possible to dismiss their tragic comedy with the expression, '*Quelle farce!*'

The reality of the political action, such as it was, seemed closer, and acquired poignancy by Antonia's belief in the cause. Its crudeness hurt his feelings. He was surprised at his own sensitiveness.

'I suppose I am more of a Costaguanero than I would have believed possible,' he thought to himself.

His disdain grew like a reaction of his scepticism against the action into which he was forced by his infatuation for Antonia. He soothed himself by saying he was not a patriot, but a lover.

The ladies came in bareheaded, and Mrs Gould sank low before the little tea-table. Antonia took up her usual place at the reception hour – the corner of a leathern couch, with a rigid grace in her pose and a fan in her hand. Decoud, swerving from the straight line of his march, came to lean over the high back of her seat.

For a long time he talked into her ear from behind, softly, with a half smile and an air of apologetic familiarity. Her fan lay half grasped on her knees. She never looked at him. His rapid utterance grew more and more insistent and caressing. At last he ventured a slight laugh.

'No, really. You must forgive me. One must be serious sometimes.' He paused. She turned her head a little; her blue eyes glided slowly towards him, slightly upwards, mollified and questioning.

'You can't think I am serious when I call Montero a *gran' bestia* every second day in the *Porvenir*? That is not a serious occupation. No occupation is serious, not even when a bullet through the heart is the penalty of failure!'

Her hand closed firmly on her fan.

'Some reason, you understand, I mean some sense, may creep into thinking; some glimpse of truth. I mean some effective truth, for which there is no room in politics or journalism. I happen to have said what I thought. And you are angry! If you do me the kindness to think a little you will see that I spoke like a patriot.'

She opened her red lips for the first time, not unkindly.

'Yes, but you never see the aim. Men must be used as they are. I suppose nobody is really disinterested, unless, perhaps you, Don Martin.'

'God forbid! It's the last thing I should like you to believe of me.' He spoke lightly, and paused.

She began to fan herself with a slow movement without raising her hand. After a time he whispered passionately:

'Antonia!'

She smiled, and extended her hand after the English manner towards Charles Gould, who was bowing before her; while Decoud, with his elbows spread on the back of the sofa, dropped his eyes and murmured, '*Bonjour.*'

The Señor Administrador of the San Tomé mine bent over his wife for a moment. They exchanged a few words, of which only the phrase, 'The greatest enthusiasm,' pronounced by Mrs Gould, could be heard.

'Yes,' Decoud began in a murmur. 'Even he!'

'This is sheer calumny,' said Antonia, not very severely.

'You just ask him to throw his mine into the melting-pot for the great cause,' Decoud whispered.

Don José had raised his voice. He rubbed his hands cheerily. The excellent aspect of the troops and the great quantity of new deadly rifles on the shoulders of those brave men seemed to fill him with an ecstatic confidence.

Charles Gould, very tall and thin before his chair, listened, but nothing could be discovered in his face except a kind and deferential attention.

Meantime, Antonia had risen, and, crossing the room, stood looking out of one of the three long windows giving on the street. Decoud followed her. The window was thrown open, and he leaned against the thickness of the wall. The long folds of the damask curtain, falling straight from the broad brass cornice, hid him partly from the room. He folded his arms on his breast, and looked steadily at Antonia's profile.

The people returning from the harbour filled the pavements; the shuffle of sandals and a low murmur of voices ascended to the window. Now and then a coach rolled slowly along the disjointed roadway of the Calle de la Constitución. There were not many private carriages in Sulaco; at the most crowded hour on the Alameda they could be counted with one glance of the eye. The great family arks swayed on high leathern springs, full of pretty powdered faces in which the eyes looked intensely alive and black. And first Don Juste Lopez, the President of the Provincial Assembly, passed with his three lovely daughters, solemn in a black frock-coat and stiff white tie, as when directing a debate from a high tribune. Though they all raised their eyes, Antonia did not make the usual greeting gesture of a fluttered hand, and they affected not to see the two young people, Costaguaneros with European manners, whose eccentricities were discussed behind the barred windows of the first families in Sulaco. And then the widowed Señora Gavilaso de Valdes rolled by, handsome and dignified, in a great machine in which she used to travel to and from her country house, surrounded by an armed retinue in leather suits and big sombreros, with carbines at the bows of their saddles. She was a woman of most distinguished family, proud, rich, and kind-hearted. Her second son, Jaime, had just gone off on the Staff of Barrios. The eldest, a worthless fellow of a moody disposition, filled Sulaco with the noise of his dissipations, and gambled heavily at the club. The two youngest boys, with yellow Ribierist cockades in their caps, sat on the front seat. She, too, affected not to see the Señor Decoud talking publicly with Antonia in defiance of every convention. And he not even her *novio* as far as the world knew! Though, even in that case, it would have been scandal enough. But the dignified old lady, respected and admired by the first families, would have been still more shocked if she could have heard the words they were exchanging.

'Did you say I lost sight of the aim? I have only one aim in the world.'

She made an almost imperceptible negative movement of her head, still staring across the street at the Avellanos's house, grey, marked with decay, and with iron bars like a prison.

'And it would be so easy of attainment,' he continued, 'this aim which, whether knowingly or not, I have always had in my heart – ever since the day when you snubbed me so horribly once in Paris, you remember.'

A slight smile seemed to move the corner of the lip that was on his side.

'You know you were a very terrible person, a sort of Charlotte Corday in a schoolgirl's dress; a ferocious patriot. I suppose you would have stuck a knife into Guzman Bento?'

She interrupted him. 'You do me too much honour.'

'At any rate,' he said, changing suddenly to a tone of bitter levity, 'you would have sent me to stab him without compunction.'

'Ah, *par exemple!*' she murmured in a shocked tone.

'Well,' he argued, mockingly, 'you do keep me here writing deadly nonsense. Deadly to me! It has already killed my self-respect. And you may imagine,' he continued, his tone passing into light banter, 'that Montero, should he be successful, would get even with me in the only way such a brute can get even with a man of intelligence who condescends to call him a *gran' bestia* three times a week. It's a sort of intellectual death; but there is the other one in the background for a journalist of my ability.'

'If he is successful!' said Antonia, thoughtfully.

'You seem satisfied to see my life hang on a thread,' Decoud replied, with a broad smile. 'And the other Montero, the "my trusted brother" of the proclamations, the *guerrillero* – haven't I written that he was taking the guests' overcoats and changing plates in Paris at our Legation in the intervals of spying on our refugees there, in the time of Rojas? He will wash out that sacred truth in blood. In my blood! Why do you look annoyed? This is simply a bit of the biography of one of our great men. What do you think he will do to me? There is a certain convent wall round the corner of the Plaza, opposite the door of the Bull Ring. You know? Opposite the door with the inscription, "Intrada de la Sombra". Appropriate, perhaps! That's where the uncle of our host gave up his Anglo-South-American soul. And, note, he might have run away. A man who has fought with weapons may run away. You might have let me go with Barrios if you had cared for me. I would have carried one of those rifles, in which Don José believes, with the greatest satisfaction, in the ranks of poor peons and *indios*, that know nothing either of reason or politics. The most forlorn hope in the most forlorn army on earth would have been safer than that for which you made me stay here. When you make war you may retreat, but not when you spend your time in inciting poor ignorant fools to kill and to die.'

His tone remained light, and as if unaware of his presence she stood motionless, her hands clasped lightly, the fan hanging down from her interlaced fingers. He waited for a while, and then:

'I shall go to the wall,' he said, with a sort of jocular desperation.

Even that declaration did not make her look at him. Her head remained still, her eyes fixed upon the house of the Avellanos, whose clipped pilasters, broken cornices, the whole degradation of dignity was hidden now by the gathering dusk of the street. In her whole figure her lips alone moved, forming the words:

'Martin, you will make me cry.'

He remained silent for a minute, startled, as if overwhelmed by a sort of awed happiness, with the lines of the mocking smile still stiffened about his mouth, and incredulous surprise in his eyes. The value of a sentence is in the personality which utters it, for nothing new can be said by man or woman; and those were the last words, it seemed to him, that could ever have been spoken by Antonia. He had never made it up with her so completely in all their intercourse of small encounters; but even before she had time to turn towards him, which she did slowly with a rigid grace, he had begun to plead:

'My sister is only waiting to embrace you. My father is transported with joy. I won't say anything of my mother! Our mothers were like sisters. There is the mail-boat for the south next week – let us go. That Morago is a fool! A man like Montero is bribed. It's the practice of the country. It's tradition – it's politics. Read *Fifty Years of Misrule*.'

'Leave poor papa alone, Don Martin. He believes –'

'I have the greatest tenderness for your father,' he began, hurriedly. 'But I love you, Antonia! And Morago has miserably mismanaged this business. Perhaps your father did, too; I don't know. Montero was bribable. Why, I suppose he only wanted his share of this famous loan for national development. Why didn't the stupid Sta Marta people give him a mission to Europe, or something? He would have taken five years' salary in advance, and gone on loafing in Paris, this stupid, ferocious *indio!*'

'The man,' she said, thoughtfully, and very calm before this outburst, 'was intoxicated with vanity. We had all the information, not from Morago only; from others, too. There was his brother intriguing, too.'

'Oh, yes!' he said. 'Of course you know. You know everything. You read all the correspondence, you write all the papers – all those State papers that are inspired here, in this room, in blind deference to a theory of political purity. Hadn't you Charles Gould before your eyes? "Rey de Sulaco!" He and his mine are the practical demonstration of what could have been done. Do you think he succeeded by his fidelity to a theory of virtue? And all those railway people, with their honest work! Of course, their work is honest! But what if you cannot work honestly till the thieves are satisfied? Could he not, a gentleman, have told this Sir John what's-his-name that Montero had to be bought off – he and all his Negro liberals hanging on to his gold-laced sleeve? He ought to have been bought off with his own stupid weight of gold – his weight of gold, I tell you, boots, sabre, spurs, cocked hat, and all.'

She shook her head slightly. 'It was impossible,' she murmured.

'He wanted the whole lot? What?'

She was facing him now in the deep recess of the window, very close and motionless. Her lips moved rapidly. Decoud, leaning his back against the wall, listened with crossed arms and lowered eyelids. He drank the tones of her even voice, and watched the agitated life of her throat, as if waves of emotion had run from her heart to pass out into the air in her reasonable words. He also had his aspirations, he aspired to carry her away out of these deadly futilities of *pronunciamientos* and reforms. All this was wrong – utterly wrong; but she fascinated him, and sometimes the sheer sagacity of a phrase would break the charm, replace the fascination by a sudden unwilling thrill of interest. Some women hovered, as it were, on the threshold of genius, he reflected. They did not want to know, or think, or understand. Passion stood for all that, and he was ready to believe that some startlingly profound remark, some appreciation of character, or a judgement upon an event, bordered on the miraculous. In the mature Antonia he could see with an extraordinary vividness the austere schoolgirl of the earlier days. She seduced his attention; sometimes he could not restrain a murmur of assent; now and then he advanced an objection quite seriously. Gradually they began to argue; the curtain half hid them from the people in the *sala*.

Outside it had grown dark. From the deep trench of shadow between the houses, lit up vaguely by the glimmer of street lamps, ascended the evening silence of Sulaco; the silence of a town with a few carriages, of unshod horses, and a softly sandalled population. The windows of the Casa Gould flung their shining parallelograms upon the house of the Avellanos. Now and then a shuffle of feet passed below with the pulsating red glow of a cigarette at the foot of the walls; and the night air, as if cooled by the snows of Higuerota, refreshed their faces.

'We Occidentals,' said Martin Decoud, using the usual term the provincials of Sulaco applied to themselves, 'have been always distinct and separated. As long as we hold Cayta nothing can reach us. In all our troubles no army has marched over those mountains. A revolution in the central provinces isolates us at once. Look how complete it is now! The news of Barrios's movement will be cabled to the United States, and only in that way will it reach Sta Marta by the cable from the other seaboard. We have the greatest riches, the greatest fertility, the purest blood in our great families, the most laborious population. The Occidental Province should stand alone. The early Federalism was not bad for us. Then came this union which Don Henrique Gould resisted. It opened the road to tyranny; and, ever since, the rest of Costaguana hangs like a millstone round our necks. The Occidental territory is large enough to make any man's country. Look at the mountains! Nature itself seems to cry to us "Separate!" '

She made an energetic gesture of negation. A silence fell.

'Oh, yes, I know it's contrary to the doctrine laid down in the *History of Fifty Years' Misrule*. I am only trying to be sensible. But my sense seems always to give you cause for offence. Have I startled you very much with this perfectly reasonable aspiration?'

She shook her head. No, she was not startled, but the idea shocked her early convictions. Her patriotism was larger. She had never considered that possibility.

'It may yet be the means of saving some of your convictions,' he said prophetically.

She did not answer. She seemed tired. They leaned side by side on the rail of the little balcony, very friendly, having exhausted politics, giving themselves up to the silent feeling of their nearness, in one of those profound pauses that fall upon the rhythm of passion. Towards the *plaza* end of the street the glowing coals in the *brazeros* of the market women cooking their evening meal gleamed red along the edge of the pavement. A man appeared without a sound in the light of a street lamp, showing the coloured inverted triangle of his bordered poncho, square on his shoulders, hanging to a point below his knees. From the harbour end of the *calle* a horseman walked his soft-stepping mount, gleaming silver-grey abreast each lamp under the dark shape of the rider.

'Behold the illustrious Capataz de Cargadores,' said Decoud, gently, 'coming in all his splendour after his work is done. The next great man of Sulaco after Don Carlos Gould. But he is good-natured, and let me make friends with him.'

'Ah, indeed!' said Antonia. 'How did you make friends?'

'A journalist ought to have his finger on the popular pulse, and this man is one of the leaders of the populace. A journalist ought to know remarkable men – and this man is remarkable in his way.'

'Ah, yes!' said Antonia, thoughtfully. 'It is known that this Italian has a great influence.'

The horseman had passed below them, with a gleam of dim light on the shining broad quarters of the grey mare, on a bright heavy stirrup, on a long silver spur; but the short flick of yellowish flame in the dusk was powerless against the muffled-up mysteriousness of the dark figure with an invisible face concealed by a great sombrero.

Decoud and Antonia remained leaning over the balcony, side by side, touching elbows, with their heads overhanging the darkness of the street, and the brilliantly lighted *sala* at their backs. This was a *tête-à-tête* of extreme impropriety; something of which in the whole extent of the Republic only the extraordinary Antonia could be capable – the poor, motherless girl, never accompanied, with a careless father, who had thought only of making her learned. Even Decoud himself seemed to feel that this was as much as he could expect of having her to himself till – till the revolution was over and he could carry her off to Europe, away from the endlessness of civil strife, whose folly seemed even harder to bear than its ignominy. After one

Montero there would be another, the lawlessness of a populace of all colours and races, barbarism, irremediable tyranny. As the great Liberator Bolívar had said in the bitterness of his spirit, 'America is ungovernable. Those who worked for her independence have ploughed the sea.' He did not care, he declared boldly; he seized every opportunity to tell her that though she had managed to make a Blanco journalist of him, he was no patriot. First of all, the word had no sense for cultured minds, to whom the narrowness of every belief is odious; and secondly, in connexion with the everlasting troubles of this unhappy country it was hopelessly besmirched; it had been the cry of dark barbarism, the cloak of lawlessness, of crimes, of rapacity, of simple thieving.

He was surprised at the warmth of his own utterance. He had no need to drop his voice; it had been low all the time, a mere murmur in the silence of dark houses with their shutters closed early against the night air, as is the custom of Sulaco. Only the *sala* of the Casa Gould flung out defiantly the blaze of its four windows, the bright appeal of light in the whole dumb obscurity of the street. And the murmur on the little balcony went on after a short pause.

'But we are labouring to change all that,' Antonia protested. 'It is exactly what we desire. It is our object. It is the great cause. And the word you despise has stood also for sacrifice, for courage, for constancy, for suffering. Papa, who –'

'Ploughing the sea,' interrupted Decoud, looking down.

There was below the sound of hasty and ponderous footsteps.

'Your uncle, the Grand Vicar of the cathedral, has just turned under the gate,' observed Decoud. 'He said Mass for the troops in the Plaza this morning. They had built for him an altar of drums, you know. And they brought outside all the painted blocks to take the air. All the wooden saints stood militarily in a row at the top of the great flight of steps. They looked like a gorgeous escort attending the Vicar-General. I saw the great function from the windows of the *Porvenir*. He is amazing, your uncle, the last of the Corbeláns. He glittered exceedingly in his vestments with a great crimson velvet cross down his back. And all the time our saviour Barrios sat in the Amarilla Club drinking punch at an open window. *Esprit fort* – our Barrios. I expected every moment your uncle to launch an excommunication there and then at the black eye-patch in the window across the Plaza. But not at all. Ultimately the troops marched off. Later Barrios came down with some of the officers, and stood with his uniform all unbuttoned, discoursing at the edge of the pavement. Suddenly your uncle appeared, no longer glittering, but all black, at the cathedral door with that threatening aspect he has – you know, like a sort of avenging spirit. He gives one look, strides over straight at the group of uniforms, and leads away the general by the elbow. He walked him for a quarter of an hour in the shade of a wall. Never let go his elbow for a moment, talking all the time with exaltation, and gesticulating with a long black arm. It was a curious scene. The officers seemed struck with astonishment. Remarkable man, your missionary uncle. He hates an infidel much less than a heretic, and prefers a heathen many times to an infidel. He condescends graciously to call me a heathen, sometimes, you know.'

Antonia listened with her hands over the balustrade, opening and shutting the fan gently; and Decoud talked a little nervously, as if afraid that she would leave him at the first pause. Their comparative isolation, the precious sense of intimacy, the slight contact of their arms, affected him softly; for now and then a tender inflection crept into the flow of his ironic murmurs.

'Any slight sign of favour from a relative of yours is welcome, Antonia. And perhaps he understands me, after all! But I know him, too, our Padre Corbelán. The idea of political honour, justice, and honesty for him consists in the restitution of the confiscated Church property. Nothing else could have drawn that fierce converter of savage Indians out of the wilds to work for the Ribierist cause! Nothing else but that wild hope! He would make a *pronunciamiento* himself for such an object against any Government if he could only get followers! What does Don Carlos Gould think of that? But, of course, with his English impenetrability, nobody can tell what he thinks. Probably he thinks of nothing apart from his mine; of his "*Imperium in Imperio*". As to Mrs Gould, she thinks of her schools, of her hospitals, of the mothers with the young babies, of every sick old man in the three villages. If you were to turn your head now you would see her extracting a report from that sinister doctor in a check shirt – what's his name? Monygham – or else catechizing Don Pepe or perhaps listening to Padre Román. They are all down here today – all her ministers of state. Well, she is a sensible woman, and perhaps Don Carlos is a sensible man. It's a part of solid English sense not to think too much; to see only what may be of practical use at the moment. These people are not like ourselves. We have no political reason; we have political passions – sometimes. What is a conviction? A particular view of our personal advantage either practical or emotional. No one is a patriot for nothing. The word serves us well. But I am clear-sighted, and I shall not use that word to you, Antonia! I have no patriotic illusions. I have only the supreme illusion of a lover.'

He paused, then muttered almost inaudibly, 'That can lead one very far, though.'

Behind their backs the political tide that once in every twenty-four hours set with a strong flood through the Gould drawing-room could be heard, rising higher in a hum of voices. Men had been dropping in singly, or in twos and threes: the higher officials of the province, engineers of the railway, sunburnt and in tweeds, with the frosted head of their chief smiling with slow, humorous indulgence amongst the young eager faces. Scarfe, the lover of fandangos, had already slipped out in search of some dance, no matter where, on the outskirts of the town. Don Juste Lopez, after taking his daughters home, had entered solemnly, in a black creased coat buttoned up under his spreading brown beard. The few members of the Provincial Assembly present clustered at once around their President to discuss the news of the war and the last proclamation of the rebel Montero, the miserable Montero, calling in the name of a 'a justly incensed democracy' upon all the Provincial Assemblies of the Republic to suspend their sittings till his sword had made peace and the will of the people could be consulted. It was practically an invitation to dissolve: an unheard-of audacity of that evil madman.

The indignation ran high in the knot of deputies behind José Avellanos. Don José, lifting up his voice, cried out to them over the high back of his chair, 'Sulaco has answered by sending today an army upon his flank. If all the other provinces show only half as much patriotism as we, Occidentals–'

A great outburst of acclamations covered the vibrating treble of the life and soul of the party. Yes! Yes! This was true! A great truth! Sulaco was in the forefront as ever! It was a boastful 'tumult, the hopefulness inspired by the event of the day breaking out amongst those *caballeros* of the Campo thinking of their herds, of their lands, of the safety of their families. Everything was at stake. . . . No! It was impossible that Montero should succeed! This criminal, this shameless *indio*! The clamour continued for some time, everybody else in the room looking towards the group where Don Juste had put on his air of impartial solemnity as if presiding at a sitting of the Provincial Assembly. Decoud had turned round at the noise, and, leaning his back on the balustrade, shouted into the room with all the strength of his lungs, '*Gran' bestia!*'

This unexpected cry had the effect of stilling the noise. All the eyes were directed to the window with an approving expectation; but Decoud had already turned his back upon the room, and was again leaning out over the quiet street.

'This is the quintessence of my journalism; this is the supreme argument,' he said to Antonia. 'I have invented this definition, this last word on a great question. But I am no patriot. I am no more of a patriot than the Capataz of the Sulaco Cargadores, this Genoese who has done such great things for this harbour – this active usher-in of the material implements for our progress. You have heard Captain Mitchell confess over and over again that till he got this man he could never tell how long it would take to unload a ship. That is bad for progress. You have seen him pass by after his labours on his famous horse to dazzle the girls in some ballroom with an earthen floor. He is a fortunate fellow! His work is an exercise of personal powers; his leisure is spent in receiving the marks of extraordinary adulation. And he likes it, too. Can anybody be more fortunate? To be feared and admired is –'

'And are these your highest aspirations, Don Martin?' interrupted Antonia.

'I was speaking of a man of that sort,' said Decoud, curtly. 'The heroes of the world have been feared and admired. What more could he want?'

Decoud had often felt his familiar habit of ironic thought fall shattered against Antonia's gravity. She irritated him as if she, too, had suffered from that inexplicable feminine obtuseness which stands so often between a man and a woman of the more ordinary sort. But he overcame his vexation at once. He was very far from thinking Antonia ordinary, whatever verdict his scepticism might have pronounced upon himself. With a touch of penetrating tenderness in his voice he assured her that his only aspiration was to a felicity so high that it seemed almost unrealizable on this earth.

She coloured invisibly, with a warmth against which the breeze from the sierra seemed to have lost its cooling power in the sudden melting of the snows. His whisper could not have carried so far, though there was enough ardour in his tone to melt a heart of ice. Antonia turned away abruptly, as if to carry his whispered assurance into the room behind, full of light, noisy with voices.

The tide of political speculation was beating high within the four walls of the great *sala*, as if driven beyond the marks by a great gust of hope. Don Juste's fan-shaped beard was still the centre of loud and animated discussions. There was a self-confident ring in all the voices. Even the few Europeans around Charles Gould – a Dane, a couple of Frenchmen, a discreet fat German, smiling, with down-cast eyes, the representatives of those material interests that had got a footing in Sulaco under the protecting might of the San Tomé mine – had infused a lot of good humour into their deference. Charles Gould, to whom they were paying their court, was the visible sign of the stability that could be achieved on the shifting ground of revolutions. They felt hopeful about their various undertakings. One of the two Frenchmen, small, black, with glittering eyes lost in an immense growth of bushy beard, waved his tiny brown hands and delicate wrists. He had been travelling in the interior of the province for a syndicate of European capitalists. His forcible '*Monsieur l'Administrateur*' returning every minute shrilled above the steady hum of conversations. He was relating his discoveries. He was ecstatic. Charles Gould glanced down at him courteously.

At a given moment of these necessary receptions it was Mrs Gould's habit to withdraw quietly into a little drawing-room, especially her own, next to the great *sala*. She had risen, and, waiting for Antonia, listened with a slightly worried graciousness to the engineer-in-chief of the railway, who stooped over her, relating slowly, without the slightest gesture, something apparently amusing, for his eyes had a humorous twinkle. Antonia, before she advanced into the room to join Mrs Gould, turned her head over her shoulder towards Decoud, only for a moment.

'Why should any one of us think his aspirations unrealizable?' she said, rapidly.

'I am going to cling to mine to the end, Antonia,' he answered, through clenched teeth, then bowed very low, a little distantly.

The engineer-in-chief had not finished telling his amusing story. The humours of railway building in South America appealed to his keen appreciation of the absurd, and he told his instances of ignorant prejudice and as ignorant cunning very well. Now, Mrs Gould gave him all her attention as he walked by her side escorting the ladies out of the room. Finally all three passed unnoticed through the glass doors in the gallery. Only a tall priest stalking silently in the noise of the *sala* checked himself to look after them. Father Corbelán, whom Decoud had seen from the balcony turning into the gateway of the Casa Gould, had addressed no one since coming in. The long, skimpy soutane accentuated the tallness of his stature; he carried his powerful torso thrown forward; and the straight, black bar of his joined eyebrows, the pugnacious outline of the bony face, the white spot of a scar on the bluish shaven cheeks (a testimonial to his apostolic zeal from a party of unconverted Indians), suggested something unlawful behind his priest-hood, the idea of a chaplain of bandits.

He separated his bony knotted hands clasped behind his back, to shake his finger at Martin.

Decoud had stepped into the room after Antonia. But he did not go far. He had remained just within, against the curtain, with an expression of not quite genuine gravity, like a grown-up person taking part in a game of children. He gazed quietly at the threatening finger.

'I have watched your reverence converting General Barrios by a special sermon on the Plaza,' he said, without making the slightest movement.

'What miserable nonsense!' Father Corbelán's deep voice resounded all over the room, making all the heads turn on the shoulders. 'The man is a drunkard. *Señores*, the God of your General is a bottle!'

His contemptuous, arbitrary voice caused an uneasy suspension of every sound, as if the self-confidence of the gathering had been staggered by a blow. But nobody took up Father Corbelán's declaration.

It was known that Father Corbelán had come out of the wilds to advocate the sacred rights of the Church with the same fanatical fearlessness with which he had gone preaching to blood-thirsty savages, devoid of human compassion or worship of any kind. Rumours of legendary proportions told of his successes as a missionary beyond the eye of Christian men. He had baptized whole nations of Indians, living with them like a savage himself. It was related that the padre used to ride with his Indians for days, half naked, carrying a bullock-hide shield, and, no doubt, a long lance, too – who knows? That he had wandered clothed in skins, seeking for proselytes somewhere near the snow line of the Cordillera. Of these exploits Padre Corbelán himself was never known to talk. But he made no secret of his opinion that the politicians of Sta Marta had harder hearts and more corrupt minds than the heathen to whom he had carried the word of God. His injudicious zeal for the temporal welfare of the Church was damaging the Ribierist cause. It was common knowledge that he had refused to be made titular bishop of the Occidental diocese till justice was done to a despoiled Church. The political *jefe* of Sulaco (the same dignitary whom Captain Mitchell saved from the mob afterwards) hinted with naïve cynicism that doubtless their Excellencies the Ministers sent the padre over the mountains to Sulaco in the worst season of the year in the hope that he would be frozen to death by the icy blasts of the high *páramos*. Every year a few hardy muleteers – men inured to exposure – were known to perish in that way. But what would you have? Their Excellencies possibly had not realized what a tough priest he was. Meantime, the ignorant were beginning to murmur that the Ribierist reforms meant simply the taking away of the land from the people. Some of it was to be given to foreigners who made the railway; the greater part was to go to the padres.

These were the results of the Grand Vicar's zeal. Even from the short allocution to the troops on the Plaza (which only the first ranks could have heard) he had not been able to keep out his fixed idea of an outraged Church waiting for reparation from a penitent country. The political *jefe* had been exasperated. But he could not very well throw the brother-in-law of Don

José into the prison of the Cabildo. The chief magistrate, an easy-going and popular official, visited the Casa Gould, walking over after sunset from the Intendencia, unattended, acknowledging with dignified courtesy the salutations of high and low alike. That evening he had walked up straight to Charles Gould and had hissed out to him that he would have liked to deport the Grand Vicar out of Sulaco, anywhere, to some desert island, to the Isabels, for instance. 'The one without water preferably – eh, Don Carlos?' he had added in a tone between jest and earnest. This uncontrollable priest, who had rejected his offer of the episcopal palace for a residence and preferred to hang his shabby hammock amongst the rubble and spiders of the sequestrated Dominican Convent, had taken into his head to advocate an unconditional pardon for Hernandez the Robber! And this was not enough; he seemed to have entered into communication with the most audacious criminal the country had known for years. The Sulaco police knew, of course, what was going on. Padre Corbelán had got hold of that reckless Italian, the Capataz de Cargadores, the only man fit for such an errand, and had sent a message through him. Father Corbelán had studied in Rome, and could speak Italian. The Capataz was known to visit the old Dominican Convent at night. An old woman who served the Grand Vicar had heard the name of Hernandez pronounced; the only last Saturday afternoon the Capataz had been observed galloping out of town. He did not return for two days. The police would have laid the Italian by the heels if it had not been for fear of the *cargadores*, a turbulent body of men, quite apt to raise a tumult. Nowadays it was not so easy to govern Sulaco. Bad characters flocked into it, attracted by the money in the pockets of the railway workmen. The populace was made restless by Father Corbelán's discourses. And the first magistrate explained to Charles Gould that now the province was stripped of troops any outbreak of lawlessness would find the authorities with their boots off, as it were.

Then he went away moodily to sit in an armchair, smoking a long, thin cigar, not very far from Don José, with whom, bending over sideways, he exchanged a few words from time to time. He ignored the entrance of the priest, and whenever Father Corbelán's voice was raised behind him, he shrugged his shoulders impatiently.

Father Corbelán had remained quite motionless for a time with that something vengeful in his immobility which seemed to characterize all his attitudes. A lurid glow of strong convictions gave its peculiar aspect to the black figure. But its fierceness became softened as the padre, fixing his eyes upon Decoud, raised his long, black arm slowly, impressively:

'And you – you are a perfect heathen,' he said, in a subdued, deep voice.

He made a step nearer, pointing a forefinger at the young man's breast. Decoud, very calm, felt the wall behind the curtain with the back of his head. Then, with his chin tilted well up, he smiled.

'Very well,' he agreed with the slightly weary nonchalance of a man well used to these passages. 'But is it perhaps that you have not discovered yet what is the God of my worship? It was an easier task with our Barrios.'

The priest suppressed a gesture of discouragement. 'You believe neither in stick nor stone,' he said.

'Nor bottle,' added Decoud without stirring. 'Neither does the other of your reverence's confidants. I mean the Capataz of the Cargadores. He does not drink. Your reading of my character does honour to your perspicacity. But why call me a heathen?'

'True,' retorted the priest. 'You are ten times worse. A miracle could not convert you.'

'I certainly do not believe in miracles,' said Decoud, quietly. Father Corbelán shrugged his high, broad shoulders doubtfully.

'A sort of Frenchman – godless – a materialist,' he pronounced slowly, as if weighing the terms of a careful analysis. 'Neither the son of his own country nor of any other,' he continued, thoughtfully.

'Scarcely human, in fact,' Decoud commented under his breath, his head at rest against the wall, his eyes gazing up at the ceiling.

'The victim of this faithless age,' Father Corbelán resumed in a deep but subdued voice.

'But of some use as a journalist.' Decoud changed his pose and spoke in a more animated tone. 'Has your worship neglected to read the last number of the *Porvenir*? I assure you it is just like the others. On the general policy it continues to call Montero a *gran' bestia*, and stigmatize his brother, the *guerrillero*, for a combination of lacquey and spy. What could be more effective? In local affairs it urges the Provincial Government to enlist bodily into the national army the band of Hernandez the Robber – who is apparently the protégé of the Church – or at least of the Great Vicar. Nothing could be more sound.'

The priest nodded and turned on the heels of his square-toed shoes with big steel buckles. Again, with his hands clasped behind his back, he paced to and fro, planting his feet firmly. When he swung about, the skirt of his soutane was inflated slightly by the brusqueness of his movements.

The great *sala* had been emptying itself slowly. When the Jefe Politico rose to go, most of those still remaining stood up suddenly in sign of respect, and Don José Avellanos stopped the rocking of his chair. But the good-natured First Official made a deprecatory gesture, waved his hand to Charles Gould, and went out discreetly.

In the comparative peace of the room the screaming '*Monsieur l'Administrateur*' of the frail, hairy Frenchman seemed to acquire a preternatural shrillness. The explorer of the Capitalist syndicate was still enthusiastic. 'Ten million dollars' worth of copper practically in sight, *Monsieur l'Administrateur*. Ten millions in sight! And a railway coming – a railway! They will never believe my report. *C'est trop beau.*' He fell a prey to a screaming ecstasy, in the midst of sagely nodding heads, before Charles Gould's imperturbable calm.

And only the priest continued his pacing, flinging round the skirt of his soutane at each end of his beat. Decoud murmured to him ironically: 'Those gentlemen talk about their gods.'

Father Corbelán stopped short, looked at the journalist of Sulaco fixedly for a moment, shrugged his shoulders slightly, and resumed his plodding walk of an obstinate traveller.

And now the Europeans were dropping off from the group around Charles

Gould till the Administrator of the Great Silver Mine could be seen in his whole lank length, from head to foot, left stranded by the ebbing tide of his guests on the great square of carpet, as it were a multi-coloured shoal of flowers and arabesques under his brown boots. Father Corbelán approached the rocking-chair of Don José Avellanos.

'Come, brother,' he said, with kindly brusqueness and a touch of relieved impatience a man may feel at the end of a perfectly useless ceremony. '*A la Casa! A la Casa!* This has been all talk. Let us now go and think and pray for guidance from Heaven.'

He rolled his black eyes upwards. By the side of the frail diplomatist – the life and soul of the party – he seemed gigantic, with a gleam of fanaticism in the glance. But the voice of the party, or, rather, its mouthpiece, the 'son Decoud' from Paris, turned journalist for the sake of Antonia's eyes, knew very well that it was not so, that he was only a strenuous priest with one idea, feared by the women and execrated by the men of the people. Martin Decoud, the dilettante in life, imagined himself to derive an artistic pleasure from watching the picturesque extreme of wrong-headedness into which an honest, almost sacred, conviction may drive a man. 'It is like madness. It must be – because it's self-destructive,' Decoud had said to himself often. It seemed to him that every conviction, as soon as it became effective, turned into that form of dementia the gods send upon those they wish to destroy. But he enjoyed the bitter flavour of that example with the zest of a connoisseur in the art of his choice. Those two men got on well together, as if each had felt respectively that a masterful conviction, as well as utter scepticism, may lead a man very far on the by-paths of political action.

Don José obeyed the touch of the big hairy hand. Decoud followed out the brothers-in-law. And there remained only one visitor in the vast empty *sala*, bluishly hazy with tobacco smoke, a heavy-eyed, round-cheeked man, with a drooping moustache, a hide merchant from Esmeralda, who had come overland to Sulaco, riding with a few peons across the coast range. He was very full of his journey, undertaken mostly for the purpose of seeing the Señor Administrador of San Tomé in relation to some assistance he required in his hide-exporting business. He hoped to enlarge it greatly now that the country was going to be settled. It was going to be settled, he repeated several times, degrading by a strange, anxious whine the sonority of the Spanish language, which he pattered rapidly, like some sort of cringing jargon. A plain man could carry on his little business now in the country, and even think of enlarging it – with safety. Was it not so? He seemed to beg Charles Gould for a confirmatory word, a grunt of assent, a simple nod even.

He could get nothing. His alarm increased, and in the pauses he would dart his eyes here and there; then, loth to give up, he would branch off into feeling allusion to the dangers of his journey. The audacious Hernandez, leaving his usual haunts, had crossed the Campo of Sulaco, and was known to be lurking in the ravines of the coast range. Yesterday, when distant only a few hours from Sulaco, the hide merchant and his servants had seen three men on the road arrested suspiciously, with their horses' heads together. Two of these rode off at once and disappeared in a shallow *quebrada* to the left. 'We stopped,' continued the man from Esmeralda, 'and I tried to hide behind a small bush. But none of my *mozos* would go forward to find out what it meant, and the third horseman seemed to be waiting for us to come up. It was no use. We had been seen. So we rode slowly on, trembling. He let us pass – a man on a grey horse with his hat down on his eyes – without a word of greeting; but by-and-by we heard him galloping after us. We faced about, but that did not seem to intimidate him. He rode up at speed, and touching my foot with the toe of his boot, asked me for a cigar, with a blood-curdling laugh. He did not seem armed, but when he put his hand back to reach for the matches I saw an enormous revolver strapped to his waist. I shuddered. He had very fierce whiskers, Don Carlos, and as he did not offer to go on we dared not move. At last, blowing the smoke of my cigar into the air through his nostrils, he said, "*Señor*, it would be perhaps better for you if I rode behind your party. You are not very far from Sulaco now. Go you with God." What would you? We went on. There was no resisting him. He might have been Hernandez himself; though my servant, who has been many times to Sulaco by sea, assured me that he had recognized him very well for the Capataz of the Steamship Company's *cargadores*. Later, that same evening, I saw that very man at the corner of the Plaza talking to a girl, a Morenita, who stood by the stirrup with her hand on the grey horse's mane.'

'I assure you, Señor Hirsch,' murmured Charles Gould, 'that you ran no risk on this occasion.'

'That may be, *señor*, though I tremble yet. A most fierce man – to look at. And what does it mean? A person employed by the Steamship Company talking with *salteadores* – no less, *señor*; the other horsemen were *salteadores* – in a lonely place, and behaving like a robber himself! A cigar is nothing, but what was there to prevent him asking me for my purse?'

'No, no, Señor Hirsch,' Charles Gould murmured, letting his glance stray away a little vacantly from the round face, with its hooked beak upturned towards him in an almost childlike appeal. 'If it was the Capataz de Cargadores you met – and there is no doubt, is there? – you were perfectly safe.'

'Thank you. You are very good. A very fierce-looking man, Don Carlos. He asked me for a cigar in a most familiar manner. What would have happened if I had not had a cigar? I shudder yet. What business had he to be talking with robbers in a lonely place?'

But Charles Gould, openly preoccupied now, gave not a sign, made no sound. The impenetrability of the embodied Gould Concession had its surface shades. To be dumb is merely a fatal affliction; but the King of Sulaco had words enough to give him all the mysterious weight of a taciturn force. His silences, backed by the power of speech, had as many shades of significance as uttered words in the way of assent, of doubt, of negation – even of simple comment. Some seemed to say plainly, 'Think it over'; others meant clearly 'Go ahead,' a simple, low 'I see', with an affirmative nod, at the end of a patient listening half-hour was the equivalent of a verbal contract, which men had learned to trust implicitly, since behind it all there was the great San Tomé mine, the head and front of the material interests, so strong that it depended on no man's goodwill in the whole length and breadth of the

Occidental Province – that is, on no goodwill which it could not buy ten times over. But to the little hook-nosed man from Esmeralda, anxious about the export of hides, the silence of Charles Gould portended a failure. Evidently this was no time for extending a modest man's business. He enveloped in a swift mental malediction the whole country, with all its inhabitants, partisans of Ribiera and Montero alike; and there were incipient tears in his mute anger at the thought of the innumerable ox-hides going to waste upon the dreamy expanse of the Campo, with its single palms rising like ships at sea within the perfect circle of the horizon, its clumps of heavy timber motionless like solid islands of leaves above the running waves of grass. There were hides there, rotting, with no profit to anybody – rotting where they had been dropped by men called away to attend the urgent necessities of political revolutions. The practical, mercantile soul of Señor Hirsch rebelled against all that foolishness, while he was taking a respectful but disconcerted leave of the might and majesty of the San Tomé mine in the person of Charles Gould. He could not restrain a heart-broken murmur, wrung out of his very aching heart, as it were.

'It is a great, great foolishness, Don Carlos, all this. The price of hides in Hamburg is gone up – up. Of course the Ribierist Government will do away with all that – when it gets established firmly. Meantime –'

He sighed.

'Yes, meantime,' repeated Charles Gould, inscrutably.

The other shrugged his shoulders. But he was not ready to go yet. There was a little matter he would like to mention very much if permitted. It appeared he had some good friends in Hamburg (he murmured the name of the firm) who were very anxious to do business, in dynamite, he explained. A contract for dynamite with the San Tomé mine, and then, perhaps, later on, other mines, which were sure to – The little man from Esmeralda was ready to enlarge, but Charles interrupted him. It seemed as though the patience of the Señor Administrador was giving way at last.

'Señor Hirsch,' he said, 'I have enough dynamite stored up at the mountain to send it down crashing into the valley' – his voice rose a little – 'to send half Sulaco into the air if I liked.'

Charles Gould smiled at the round, startled eyes of the dealer in hides, who was murmuring hastily, 'Just so. Just so.' And now he was going. It was impossible to do business in explosives with an Administrador so well provided and so discouraging. He had suffered agonies in the saddle and had exposed himself to the atrocities of the bandit Hernandez for nothing at all. Neither hides nor dynamite – and the very shoulders of the enterprising Israelite expressed dejection. At the door he bowed low to the engineer-in-chief. But at the bottom of the stairs in the patio he stopped short, with his podgy hand over his lips in an attitude of meditative astonishment.

'What does he want to keep so much dynamite for?' he muttered. 'And why does he talk like this to me?'

The engineer-in-chief, looking in at the door of the empty *sala*, whence the political tide had ebbed out to the last insignificant drop, nodded familiarly to the master of the house, standing motionless like a tall beacon amongst the deserted shoals of furniture.

'Good night, I am going. Got my bike downstairs. The railway will know where to go for dynamite should we get short at any time. We have done cutting and chopping for a while now. We shall begin soon to blast our way through.'

'Don't come to me,' said Charles Gould, with perfect serenity. 'I shan't have an ounce to spare for anybody. Not an ounce. Not for my own brother, if I had a brother, and he were the engineer-in-chief of the most promising railway in the world.'

'What's that?' asked the engineer-in-chief, with equanimity. 'Unkindness?'

'No,' said Charles Gould, stolidly. 'Policy.'

'Radical, I should think,' the engineer-in-chief observed from the doorway.

'Is that the right name?' Charles Gould said, from the middle of the room.

'I mean, going to the roots, you know,' the engineer explained, with an air of enjoyment.

'Why, yes,' Charles pronounced, slowly. 'The Gould Concession has struck such deep roots in this country, in this province, in that gorge of the mountains, that nothing but dynamite shall be allowed to dislodge it from there. It's my choice. It's my last card to play.'

The engineer-in-chief whistled low. 'A pretty game,' he said, with a shade of discretion. 'And have you told Holroyd of that extraordinary trump card you hold in your hand?'

'Card only when it's played; when it falls at the end of the game. Till then you may call it a – a –'

'Weapon,' suggested the railway man.

'No. You may call it rather an argument,' corrected Charles Gould, gently. 'And that's how I've presented it to Mr Holroyd.'

'And what did he say to it?' asked the engineer, with undisguised interest.

'He' – Charles Gould spoke after a slight pause – 'he said something about holding on like grim death and putting our trust in God. I should imagine he must have been rather startled. But then' – pursued the Administrador of the San Tomé mine – 'but then, he is very far away, you know, and, as they say in this country, God is very high above.'

The engineer's appreciative laugh died away down the stairs, where the Madonna with the Child on her arm seemed to look after his shaking broad back from her shallow niche.

CHAPTER 6

A profound stillness reigned in the Casa Gould. The master of the house, walking along the corridor, opened the door of his room, and saw his wife sitting in a big armchair – his own smoking armchair – thoughtful, contemplating her little shoes. And she did not raise her eyes when he walked in.

'Tired?' asked Charles Gould.

'A little,' said Mrs Gould. Still without looking up, she added with feeling, 'There is an awful sense of unreality about all this.'

Charles Gould, before the long table strewn with papers, on which lay a hunting crop and a pair of spurs, stood looking at his wife: 'The heat and dust must have been awful this afternoon by the waterside,' he murmured, sympathetically. 'The glare on the water must have been simply terrible.'

'One could close one's eyes to the glare,' said Mrs Gould. 'But, my dear Charley, it is impossible for me to close my eyes to our position; to this awful . . . '

She raised her eyes and looked at her husband's face, from which all sign of sympathy or any other feeling had disappeared. 'Why don't you tell me something?' she almost wailed.

'I thought you had understood me perfectly from the first,' Charles Gould said, slowly. 'I thought we had said all there was to say a long time ago. There is nothing to say now. There were things to be done. We have done them; we have gone on doing them. There is no going back now. I don't suppose that, even from the first, there was really any possible way back. And, what's more, we can't even afford to stand still.'

'Ah, if one only knew how far you mean to go,' said his wife, inwardly trembling, but in an almost playful tone.

'Any distance, any length, of course,' was the answer, in a matter-of-fact tone, which caused Mrs Gould to make another effort to repress a shudder.

She stood up, smiling graciously, and her little figure seemed to be diminished still more by the heavy mass of her hair and the long train of her gown.

'But always to success,' she said, persuasively.

Charles Gould, enveloping her in the steely blue glance of his attentive eyes, answered without hesitation:

'Oh, there is no alternative.'

He put an immense assurance into his tone. As to the words, this was all that his conscience would allow him to say.

Mrs Gould's smile remained a shade too long upon her lips. She murmured:

'I will leave you; I've a slight headache. The heat, the dust, were indeed – I suppose you are going back to the mine before the morning?'

'At midnight,' said Charles Gould. 'We are bringing down the silver tomorrow. Then I shall take three whole days off in town with you.'

'Ah, you are going to meet the escort. I shall be on the balcony at five o'clock to see you pass. Till then, good-bye.'

Charles Gould walked rapidly round the table, and, seizing her hands, bent down, pressing them both to his lips. Before he straightened himself up again to his full height she had disengaged one to smooth his cheek with a light touch, as if he were a little boy.

'Try to get some rest for a couple of hours,' she murmured, with a glance at a hammock stretched in a distant part of the room. Her long train swished softly after her on the red tiles. At the door she looked back.

Two big lamps with unpolished glass globes bathed in a soft and abundant light the four white walls of the room, with a glass case of arms, the brass hilt of Henry Gould's cavalry sabre on its square of velvet, and the water-colour sketch of the San Tomé gorge. And Mrs Gould, gazing at the last in its black wooden frame, sighed out:

'Ah, if we had left it alone, Charley!'

'No,' Charles Gould said, moodily; 'it was impossible to leave it alone.'

'Perhaps it was impossible,' Mrs Gould admitted, slowly. Her lips quivered a little, but she smiled with an air of dainty bravado. 'We have disturbed a good many snakes in that Paradise, Charley, haven't we?'

'Yes, I remember,' said Charles Gould, 'it was Don Pepe who called the gorge the Paradise of snakes. No doubt we have disturbed a great many. But remember, my dear, that it is not now as it was when you made that sketch.' He waved his hand towards the small water-colour hanging alone upon the great bare wall. 'It is no longer a Paradise of snakes. We have brought mankind into it, and we cannot turn our backs upon them to go and begin a new life elsewhere.'

He confronted his wife with a firm, concentrated gaze, which Mrs Gould returned with a brave assumption of fearlessness before she went out, closing the door gently after her.

In contrast with the white glaring room the dimly lit corridor had a restful mysteriousness of a forest glade, suggested by the stems and the leaves of the plants ranged along the balustrade of the open side. In the streaks of light falling through the open doors of the reception-rooms, the blossoms, white and red and pale lilac, came out vivid with the brilliance of flowers in a stream of sunshine; and Mrs Gould, passing on, had the vividness of a figure seen in the clear patches of sun that chequer the gloom of open glades in the woods. The stones in the rings upon her hand pressed to her forehead glittered in the lamplight abreast of the door of the *sala*.

'Who's there?' she asked, in a startled voice. 'Is that you, Basilio?' She looked in, and saw Martin Decoud walking about, with an air of having lost something, amongst the chairs and tables.

'Antonia has forgotten her fan in here,' said Decoud, with a strange air of distraction; 'so I entered to see.'

But, even as he said this, he had obviously given up his search, and walked straight towards Mrs Gould, who looked at him with doubtful surprise.

'*Señora*,' he began, in a low voice.

'What is it, Don Martin?' asked Mrs Gould. And then she added, with a slight laugh, 'I am so nervous today,' as if to explain the eagerness of the question.

'Nothing immediately dangerous,' said Decoud, who now could not conceal his agitation. 'Pray don't distress yourself. No, really, you must not distress yourself.'

Mrs Gould, with her candid eyes very wide open, her lips composed into a smile, was steadying herself in the doorway with a little bejewelled hand.

'Perhaps you don't know how alarming you are, appearing like this unexpectedly –'

'I! Alarming!' he protested, sincerely vexed and surprised. 'I assure you that I am not in the least alarmed myself. A fan is lost; well, it will be found again. But I don't think it is here. It is a fan I am looking for. I cannot understand how Antonia could – Well! Have you found it, *amigo?*'

'No, *señor,*' said behind Mrs Gould the soft voice of Basilio, the head servant of the Casa. 'I don't think the *señorita* could have left it in this house at all.'

'Go and look for it in the patio again. Go now, my friend; look for it on the step's under the gate; examine every flagstone; search for it till I come down again. . . . That fellow' – he addressed himself in English to Mrs Gould – 'is always stealing up behind one's back on his bare feet. I set him to look for that fan directly I came in to justify my reappearance, my sudden return.'

He paused and Mrs Gould said, amiably, 'You are always welcome.' She paused for a second, too. 'But I am waiting to learn the cause of your return.'

Decoud affected suddenly the utmost nonchalance.

'I can't bear to be spied upon. Oh, the cause? Yes, there is a cause; there is something else that is lost besides Antonia's favourite fan. As I was walking home after seeing Don José and Antonia to their house, the Capataz de Cargadores, riding down the street, spoke to me.'

'Has anything happened to the Violas?' inquired Mrs Gould.

'The Violas? You mean the Old Garibaldino who keeps the hotel where the engineers live? Nothing happened there. The Capataz said nothing of them; he only told me that the telegraphist of the Cable Company was walking on the Plaza, bareheaded, looking out for me. This is news from the interior, Mrs Gould. I should rather say rumours of news.'

'Good news?' said Mrs Gould in a low voice.

'Worthless, I should think. But if I must define them, I would say bad. They are to the effect that a two days' battle had been fought near Sta Marta, and that the Ribierists are defeated. It must have happened a few days ago – perhaps a week. The rumour has just reached Cayta, and the man in charge of the cable station there has telegraphed the news to his colleague here. We might just as well have kept Barrios in Sulaco.'

'What's to be done now?' murmured Mrs Gould.

'Nothing. He's at sea with the troops. He will get to Cayta in a couple of days' time and learn the news there. What he will do then, who can say? Hold Cayta? Offer his submission to Montero? Disband his army – this last most likely, and go himself in one of the O.S.N. Company's steamers, north or south – to Valparaiso or to San Francisco, no matter where. Our Barrios has a great practice in exiles and repatriations, which mark the points in the political game.'

Decoud, exchanging a steady stare with Mrs Gould, added, tentatively, as it were, 'And yet, if we had Barrios with his 2,000 improved rifles here, something could have been done.'

'Montero victorious, completely victorious!' Mrs Gould breathed out in a tone of unbelief.

'A canard, probably. That sort of bird is hatched in great numbers in such times as these. And even if it were true? Well, let us put things at their worst, let us say it is true.'

'Then everything is lost,' said Mrs Gould, with the calmness of despair.

Suddenly she seemed to divine, she seemed to see Decoud's tremendous excitement under its cloak of studied carelessness. It was, indeed, becoming visible in his audacious and watchful stare, in the curve, half-reckless, half-contemptuous, of his lips. And a French phrase came upon them as if, for this Costaguanero of the Boulevard, that had been the only forcible language: 'Non, Madame. Rien n'est perdu.'

It electrified Mrs Gould out of her benumbed attitude, and she said, vivaciously:

'What would you think of doing?'

But already there was something of mockery in Decoud's suppressed excitement.

'What would you expect a true Costaguanero to do? Another revolution, of course. On my word of honour, Mrs Gould, I believe I am a true *hijo del país*, a true son of the country, whatever Father Corbelán may say. And I'm not so much of an unbeliever as not to have faith in my own ideas, in my own remedies, in my own desires.'

'Yes,' said Mrs Gould, doubtfully.

'You don't seem convinced,' Decoud went on again in French. 'Say, then, in my passions.'

Mrs Gould received this addition unflinchingly. To understand it thoroughly she did not require to hear his muttered assurance:

'There is nothing I would not do for the sake of Antonia. There is nothing I am not prepared to undertake. There is no risk I am not ready to run.'

Decoud seemed to find a fresh audacity in this voicing of his thoughts. 'You would not believe me if I were to say that it is the love of the country which –'

She made a sort of discouraged protest with her arm, as if to express that she had given up expecting that motive from anyone.

'A Sulaco revolution,' Decoud pursued in a forcible undertone. 'The Great Cause may be served here, on the very spot of its inception, in the place of its birth, Mrs Gould.'

Frowning, and biting her lower lip thoughtfully, she made a step away from the door.

'You are not going to speak to your husband?' Decoud arrested her anxiously.

'But you will need his help?'

'No doubt,' Decoud admitted without hesitation. 'Everything turns upon the San Tomé mine, but I would rather he didn't know anything as yet of my – my hopes.'

A puzzled look came upon Mrs Gould's face, and Decoud, approaching, explained confidentially:

'Don't you see, he's such an idealist.'

Mrs Gould flushed pink, and her eyes grew darker at the same time.

'Charley an idealist!' she said, as if to herself, wonderingly. 'What on earth do you mean?'

'Yes,' conceded Decoud, 'it's a wonderful thing to say with the sight of the San Tomé mine, the greatest fact in the whole of South America, perhaps, before our very eyes. But look even at that, he has idealized this fact to a point –' He paused. 'Mrs Gould, are you aware to what point he has idealized the existence, the worth, the meaning of the San Tomé mine? Are you aware of it?'

He must have known what he was talking about.

The effect he expected was produced. Mrs Gould, ready to take fire, gave it up suddenly with a low little sound that resembled a moan.

'What do you know?' she asked in a feeble voice.

'Nothing,' answered Decoud, firmly. 'But, then, don't you see, he's an Englishman?'

'Well, what of that?' asked Mrs Gould.

'Simply that he cannot act or exist without idealizing every simple feeling, desire, or achievement. He could not believe his own motives if he did not make them first a part of some fairy tale. The earth is not quite good enough for him, I fear. Do you excuse my frankness? Besides, whether you excuse it or not, it is part of the truth of things which hurts the – what do you call them? – the Anglo-Saxon's susceptibilities, and at the present moment I don't feel as if I could treat seriously either his conception of things or – if you allow me to say so – or yet yours.'

Mrs Gould gave no sign of being offended. 'I suppose Antonia understands you thoroughly?'

'Understands? Well, yes. But I am not sure that she approves. That, however, makes no difference. I am honest enough to tell you that, Mrs Gould.'

'Your idea, of course, is separation,' she said.

'Separation, of course,' declared Martin. 'Yes; separation of the whole Occidental Province from the rest of the unquiet body. But my true idea, the only one I care for, is not to be separated from Antonia.'

'And that is all?' asked Mrs Gould, without severity.

'Absolutely. I am not deceiving myself about my motives. She won't leave Sulaco for my sake, therefore Sulaco must leave the rest of the Republic to its fate. Nothing could be clearer than that. I like a clearly defined situation. I cannot part with Antonia, therefore the one and indivisible Republic of Costaguana must be made to part with its western province. Fortunately it happens to be also a sound policy. The richest, the most fertile part of this land may be saved from anarchy. Personally, I care little, very little; but it's a fact that the establishment of Montero in power would mean death to me. In all the proclamations of general pardon which I have seen, my name, with a few others, is specially excepted. The brothers hate me, as you know very well, Mrs Gould; and behold, here is the rumour of them having won a battle. You say that supposing it is true, I have plenty of time to run away.'

The slight, protesting murmur on the part of Mrs Gould made him pause for a moment, while he looked at her with a sombre and resolute glance.

'Oh, but I would, Mrs Gould. I would run away if it served that which at present is my only desire. I am courageous enough to say that, and to do it, too. But women, even our women, are idealists. It is Antonia that won't run away. A novel sort of vanity.'

'You call it vanity,' said Mrs Gould, in a shocked voice.

'Say pride, then, which, Father Corbelán would tell you, is a mortal sin. But I am not proud. I am simply too much in love to run away. At the same time I want to live. There is no love for a dead man. Therefore it is necessary that Sulaco should not recognize the victorious Montero.'

'And you think my husband will give you his support?'

'I think he can be drawn into it, like all idealists, when he once sees a sentimental basis for his action. But I wouldn't talk to him. Mere clear facts won't appeal to his sentiment. It is much better for him to convince himself in his own way. And, frankly, I could not, perhaps, just now pay sufficient respect to either his motives or even, perhaps, to yours, Mrs Gould.'

It was evident that Mrs Gould was very determined not to be offended. She smiled vaguely, while she seemed to think the matter over. As far as she could judge from the girl's half-confidences, Antonia understood that young man. Obviously there was promise of safety in his plan, or rather in his idea. Moreover, right or wrong, the idea could do no harm. And it was quite possible, also, that the rumour was false.

'You have some sort of a plan,' she said.

'Simplicity itself. Barrios has started, let him go on then; he will hold Cayta, which is the door of the sea route to Sulaco. They cannot send a sufficient force over the mountains. No; not even to cope with the band of Hernandez. Meantime we shall organize our resistance here. And for that, this very Hernandez will be useful. He has defeated troops as a bandit; he will no doubt accomplish the same thing if he is made a colonel or even a general. You know the country well enough not to be shocked by what I say, Mrs Gould. I have heard you assert that this poor bandit was the living, breathing example of cruelty, injustice, stupidity, and oppression, that ruin men's souls as well as their fortunes in this country. Well, there would be some poetical retribution in that man arising to crush the evils which had driven an honest *ranchero* into a life of crime. A fine idea of retribution in that, isn't there?'

Decoud had dropped easily into English, which he spoke with precision, very correctly, but with too many *z* sounds.

'Think also of your hospitals, of your schools, of your ailing mothers and feeble old men, of all that population which you and your husband have brought into the rocky gorge of San Tomé. Are you not responsible to your conscience for all these people? Is it not worth while to make another effort, which is not at all so desperate as it looks, rather than –'

Decoud finished his thought with an upward toss of the arm, suggesting annihilation; and Mrs Gould turned away her head with a look of horror.

'Why don't you say all this to my husband?' she asked, without looking at Decoud, who stood watching the effect of his words.

'Ah! But Don Carlos is so English,' he began. Mrs Gould interrupted:

'Leave that alone, Don Martin. He's as much a Costaguanero – No! He's more of a Costaguanero than yourself.'

'Sentimentalist, sentimentalist,' Decoud almost cooed, in a tone of gentle and soothing deference. 'Sentimentalist, after the amazing manner of your people. I have been watching El Rey de Sulaco since I came here on a fool's errand, and perhaps impelled by some treason of fate lurking behind the unaccountable turns of a man's life. But I don't matter, I am not a sentimentalist, I cannot endow my personal desires with a shining robe of silk and jewels. Life is not for me a moral romance derived from the tradition of a pretty fairy tale. No, Mrs Gould; I am practical. I am not afraid of my motives. But, pardon me, I have been rather carried away. What I wish to say is that I have been observing. I won't tell you what I have discovered–'

'No. That is unnecessary,' whispered Mrs Gould, once more averting her head.

'It is. Except one little fact, that your husband does not like me. It's a small matter, which, in the circumstances, seems to acquire a perfectly ridiculous importance. Ridiculous and immense; for, clearly, money is required for my plan,' he reflected; then added, meaningly, 'and we have two sentimentalists to deal with.'

'I don't know that I understand you, Don Martin,' said Mrs Gould, coldly, preserving the low key of their conversation. 'But, speaking as if I did, who is the other?'

'The great Holroyd in San Francisco, of course,' Decoud whispered, lightly. 'I think you understand me very well. Women are idealists; but then they are so perspicacious.'

But whatever was the reason of that remark, disparaging and complimentary at the same time, Mrs Gould seemed not to pay attention to it. The name of Holroyd had given a new tone to her anxiety.

'The silver escort is coming down to the harbour tomorrow; a whole six months' working, Don Martin!' she cried in dismay.

'Let it come down, then,' breathed out Decoud, earnestly, almost into her ear.

'But if the rumour should get about, and especially if it turned out true, troubles might break out in the town,' objected Mrs Gould.

Decoud admitted that it was possible. He knew well the town children of the Sulaco Campo: sullen, thievish, vindictive, and bloodthirsty, whatever great qualities their brothers of the plain might have had. But then there was that other sentimentalist, who attached a strangely idealistic meaning to concrete facts. This stream of silver must be kept flowing north to return in the form of financial backing from the great house of Holroyd. Up at the mountain in the strong-room of the mine the silver bars were worth less for his purpose than so much lead, from which at least bullets may be run. Let it come down to the harbour, ready for shipment.

The next north-going steamer would carry it off for the very salvation of the San Tomé mine, which has produced so much treasure. And, moreover, the rumour was probably false, he remarked, with much conviction in his hurried tone.

'Besides, *señora*,' concluded Decoud, 'we may suppress it for many days. I have been talking with the telegraphist in the middle of the Plaza Mayor; thus I am certain that we could not have been overheard. There was not even a bird in the air near us. And also let me tell you something more. I have been making friends with this man called Nostromo, the Capataz. We had a conversation this very evening, I walking by the side of his horse as he rode slowly out of the town just now. He promised me that if a riot took place for any reason – even for the most political of reasons, you understand – his *cargadores*, an important part of the populace, you will admit, should be found on the side of the Europeans.'

'He has promised you that?' Mrs Gould inquired, with interest. 'What made him make that promise to you?'

'Upon my word, I don't know,' declared Decoud, in a slightly surprised tone. 'He certainly promised me that, but now you ask me why I certainly could not tell you his reasons. He talked with his usual carelessness, which, if he had been anything else but a common sailor, I would call a pose or an affectation.'

Decoud, interrupting himself, looked at Mrs Gould curiously.

'Upon the whole,' he continued, 'I suppose he expects something to his advantage from it. You mustn't forget that he does not exercise his extraordinary power over the lower classes without a certain amount of personal risk and without a great profusion in spending his money. One must pay in some way or other for such a solid thing as individual prestige. He told me after we made friends at a dance, in a *posada* kept by a Mexican just outside the walls, that he had come here to make his fortune. I suppose he looks upon his prestige as a sort of investment.'

'Perhaps he prizes it for its own sake,' Mrs Gould said in a tone as if she were repelling an undeserved aspersion. 'Viola, the Garibaldino, with whom he has lived for some years, calls him the Incorruptible.'

'Ah! he belongs to the group of your protégés out there towards the harbour, Mrs Gould. *Muy bien*. And Captain Mitchell calls him wonderful. I have heard no end of tales of his strength, his audacity, his fidelity. No end of fine things. H'm! incorruptible! It is indeed a name of honour for the Capataz of the Cargadores of Sulaco. Incorruptible! Fine, but vague. However, I suppose he's sensible, too. And I talked to him upon that sane and practical assumption.'

'I prefer to think him disinterested, and therefore trustworthy,' Mrs Gould said, with the nearest approach to curtness it was in her nature to assume.

'Well, if so, then the silver will be still more safe. Let it come down, *señora*. Let it come down, so that it may go north and return to us in the shape of credit.'

Mrs Gould glanced along the corridor towards the door of her husband's room. Decoud, watching her as if she had his fate in her hands, detected an almost imperceptible nod of assent. He bowed with a smile, and, putting his hand into the breast pocket of his coat, pulled out a fan of light feathers set upon painted leaves of sandal-wood. 'I had it in my pocket,' he murmured, triumphantly, 'for a plausible pretext.' He bowed again. 'Good night, *señora*.'

Mrs Gould continued along the corridor away from her husband's room. The fate of the San Tomé mine was lying heavy upon her heart. It was a long time now since she had begun to fear it. It had been an idea. She had watched it with misgivings turning into a fetish, and now the fetish had grown into a monstrous and crushing weight. It was as if the inspiration of their early years had left her heart to turn into a wall of silver-bricks, erected by the silent work of evil spirits, between her and her husband. He seemed to dwell alone within a circumvallation of precious metal, leaving her outside with her school, her hospital, the sick mothers, and the feeble old men, mere insignificant vestiges of the initial inspiration. 'Those poor people!' she murmured to herself.

Below she heard the voice of Martin Decoud in the patio speaking loudly: 'I have found Doña Antonia's fan, Basilio. Look, here it is!'

CHAPTER 7

It was part of what Decoud would have called his sane materialism that he did not believe in the possibility of friendship between man and woman.

The one exception he allowed confirmed, he maintained, that absolute rule. Friendship was possible between brother and sister, meaning by friendship the frank unreserve, as before another human being, of thoughts and sensations; all the objectless and necessary sincerity of one's innermost life trying to react upon the profound sympathies of another existence.

His favourite sister, the handsome, slightly arbitrary, and resolute angel, ruling the father and mother Decoud in the first-floor apartments of a very fine Parisian house, was the recipient of Martin Decoud's confidences as to his thoughts, actions, purposes, doubts, and even failures....

Prepare our little circle in Paris for the birth of another South American Republic. One more or less, what does it matter? They may come into the world like evil flowers on a hotbed of rotten institutions; but the seed of this one has germinated in your brother's brain, and that will be enough for your devoted assent. I am writing this to you by the light of a single candle, in a sort of inn, near the harbour, kept by an Italian called Viola, a protégé of Mrs Gould. The whole building, which, for all I know, may have been contrived by a Conquistador farmer of the pearl fishery three hundred years ago, is perfectly silent. So is the plain between the town and the harbour; silent, but not so dark as the house, because the pickets of Italian workmen guarding the railway have lighted little fires all along the line. It was not so quiet around here yesterday. We had an awful riot – a sudden outbreak of the populace, which was not suppressed till late today. Its object, no doubt, was loot, and that was defeated, as you must have learned already from the cablegram sent via San Francisco and New York last night, when the cables were still open. You have read already there that the energetic action of the Europeans of the railway has saved the town from destruction, and you may believe that. I wrote out the cable myself. We have no Reuter's agency man here. I have also fired at the mob from the windows of the club, in company with some other young men of position. Our object was to keep the Calle de la Constitución clear for the exodus of the ladies and children, who have taken refuge on board a couple of cargo ships now in the harbour here. That was yesterday. You should also have learned from the cable that the missing President, Ribiera, who had disappeared after the battle of Sta Marta, has turned up here in Sulaco by one of those strange coincidences that are almost incredible, riding on a lame mule into the very midst of the street fighting. It appears that he had fled, in company with a muleteer called Bonifacio, across the mountains from the threats of Montero into the arms of an enraged mob.

The Capataz of Cargadores, that Italian sailor of whom I have written to you before, has saved him from an ignoble death. That man seems to have a particular talent for being on the spot whenever there is something picturesque to be done.

He was with me at four o'clock in the morning at the offices of the *Porvenir*, where he had turned up so early in order to warn me of the coming trouble, and also to assure me that he would keep his *cargadores* on the side of order. When the full daylight came we were looking together at the crowd on foot and on horseback, demonstrating on the Plaza and shying stones at the windows of the Intendencia. Nostromo (that is the name they call him by here) was pointing out to me his *cargadores* interspersed in the mob.

The sun shines late upon Sulaco, for it has first to climb above the mountains. In that clear morning light, brighter than twilight, Nostromo saw right across the vast Plaza, at the end of the street beyond the cathedral, a mounted man apparently in difficulties with a yelling knot of *leperos*. At once he said to me, 'That's a stranger. What is it they are doing to him?' Then he took out the silver whistle he is in the habit of using on the wharf (this man seems to disdain the use of any metal less precious than silver) and blew into it twice, evidently a preconcerted signal for his *cargadores*. He ran out immediately, and they rallied round him. I ran out, too, but was too late to follow them and help in the rescue of the stranger, whose animal had fallen. I was set upon at once as a hated aristocrat, and was only too glad to get into the club, where Don Jaime Berges (you may remember him visiting at our house in Paris some three years ago) thrust a sporting gun into my hands. They were already firing from the windows. There were little heaps of cartridges lying about on the open card-tables. I remember a couple of overturned chairs, some bottles rolling on the floor amongst the packs of cards scattered suddenly as the *caballeros* rose from their game to open fire upon the mob. Most of the young men had spent the night at the club in the expectation of some such disturbance. In two of the candelabra, on the consoles, the candles were burning down in their sockets. A large iron nut, probably stolen from the railway workshops, flew in from the street as I entered, and broke one of the large mirrors set in the wall. I noticed also one of the club servants tied up hand and foot with the cords of the curtain and flung in a corner. I have a vague recollection of Don Jaime assuring me hastily that the fellow had been detected putting poison into the dishes at supper. But I remember distinctly he was shrieking for mercy, without stopping at all, continuously, and so absolutely disregarded that nobody even took the trouble to gag him. The noise he made was so disagreeable that I had half a mind to do it myself. But there was no time to waste on such trifles. I took my place at one of the windows and began firing.

I didn't learn till later in the afternoon whom it was that Nostromo, with his *cargadores* and some Italian workmen as well, had managed to save from those drunken rascals. That man has a peculiar talent when anything striking to the imagination has to be done. I made that remark to him afterwards when we met after some sort of order had been restored in the town, and the answer he made rather surprised me. He said quite moodily, 'And how much do I get for that, *señor*?' Then it dawned upon me that perhaps this man's vanity has been satiated by the adulation of the common people and the confidence of his superiors!

Decoud paused to light a cigarette, then, with his head still over his writing, he blew a cloud of smoke, which seemed to rebound from the paper. He took up the pencil again.

That was yesterday evening on the Plaza, while he sat on the steps of the cathedral, his hands between his knees, holding the bridle of his famous silver-grey mare. He had led his body of *cargadores* splendidly all day long. He looked fatigued. I don't know how I looked. Very dirty, I suppose. But I suppose I also looked pleased. From the time the fugitive President had been got off to the s.s. *Minerva*, the tide of success had turned against the mob. They had been driven off the harbour, and out of the better streets of the town, into their own maze of ruins and *tolderías*. You must understand that this riot, whose primary object was undoubtedly the getting hold of the San Tomé silver stored in the lower rooms of the Custom House (besides the general looting of the *ricos*), had acquired a political colouring from the fact of two Deputies to the Provincial Assembly, Señores Gamacho and Fuentes, both from Bolson, putting themselves at the head of it – late in the afternoon, it is true, when the mob, disappointed in their hopes of loot, made a stand in the narrow streets to the cries of '*Viva la libertad!* Down with Feudalism!' (I wonder what they imagine feudalism to be?) 'Down with the Goths and Paralytics.' I suppose the Señores Gamacho and Fuentes knew what they were doing. They are prudent gentlemen. In the Assembly they called themselves Moderates, and opposed every energetic measure with philanthropic pensiveness. At the first rumours of Montero's victory, they began to show a subtle change of the pensive temper, and began to defy poor Don Juste Lopez in his Presidential tribune with an effrontery to which the poor man could only respond by a dazed smoothing of his beard and the ringing of the Presidential bell. Then, when the downfall of the Ribierist cause became confirmed beyond the shadow of a doubt, they have blossomed into convinced Liberals, acting together as if they were Siamese twins, and ultimately taking charge, as it were, of the riot in the name of Monterist principles.

Their last move of eight o'clock last night was to organize themselves into a Monterist Committee which sits, as far as I know, in a *posada* kept by a retired Mexican bull-fighter, a great politician, too, whose name I have forgotten. Thence they have issued a communication to us, the Goths and Paralytics of the Amarilla Club (who have our own committee), inviting us to come to some provisional understanding for a truce, in order, they have the impudence to say, that the noble cause of Liberty 'should not be stained by the criminal excesses of Conservative selfishness'! As I came out to sit with Nostromo on the cathedral steps the club was busy considering a proper reply in the principal room, littered with exploded cartridges, with a lot of broken glass, blood smears, candlesticks, and all sorts of wreckage on the floor. But all this is nonsense. Nobody in the town has any real power except the railway engineers, whose men occupy the dismantled houses acquired by the Company for their town station on one side of the Plaza, and Nostromo, whose *cargadores* were sleeping under the arcades along the front of Anzani's shops. A fire of broken furniture out of the Intendencia saloons, mostly gilt, was burning on the Plaza, in a high flame swaying right upon the statue of Charles IV. The dead body of a man was lying on the steps of the pedestal, his arms thrown wide open, and his sombrero covering his face – the attention of some friend, perhaps. The light of the flame touched the foliage of the first trees on the Alameda, and played on the end of a side-street near by, blocked up by a jumble of ox-carts and dead bullocks. Sitting on one of the carcases, a *lepero*, muffled up, smoked a cigarette. It was a truce, you understand. The only other living being on the Plaza besides ourselves was a *cargador* walking to and fro, with a long, bare knife in his hand, like a sentry before the Arcades, where his friends were sleeping. And the only other spot of light in the dark town were the lighted windows of the club, at the corner of the Calle.

After having written so far, Don Martin Decoud, the exotic dandy of the

Parisian boulevard, got up and walked across the sanded floor of the café at one end of the Albergo of United Italy, kept by Giorgio Viola, the old companion of Garibaldi. The highly coloured lithograph of the Faithful Hero seemed to look dimly, in the light of one candle, at the man with no faith in anything except the truth of his own sensations. Looking out of the window, Decoud was met by a darkness so impenetrable that he could see neither the mountains nor the town, nor yet the buildings near the harbour; and there was not a sound, as if the tremendous obscurity of the Placid Gulf, spreading from the waters over the land, had made it dumb as well as blind. Presently Decoud felt a light tremor of the floor and a distant clank of iron. A bright white light appeared, deep in the darkness, growing bigger with a thundering noise. The rolling stock usually kept on the sidings in Rincón was being run back to the yards for safe keeping. Like a mysterious stirring of the darkness behind the headlight of the engine, the train passed in a gust of hollow uproar, by the end of the house, which seemed to vibrate all over in response. And nothing was clearly visible but, on the end of the last flat car, a Negro, in white trousers and naked to the waist, swinging a blazing torch basket incessantly with a circular movement of his bare arm. Decoud did not stir.

Behind him, on the back of the chair from which he had risen, hung his elegant Parisian overcoat, with a pearl-grey silk lining. But when he turned back to come to the table the candlelight fell upon a face that was grimy and scratched. His rosy lips were blackened with heat, the smoke of gun-powder. Dirt and rust tarnished the lustre of his short beard. His shirt collar and cuffs were crumpled; the blue silken tie hung down his breast like a rag; a greasy smudge crossed his white brow. He had not taken off his clothing nor used water, except to snatch a hasty drink greedily, for some forty hours. An awful restlessness had made him its own, had marked him with all the signs of desperate strife, and put a dry, sleepless stare into his eyes. He murmured to himself in a hoarse voice, 'I wonder if there's any bread here,' looked vaguely about him, then dropped into the chair and took the pencil up again. He became aware he had not eaten anything for many hours.

It occurred to him that no one could understand him so well as his sister. In the most sceptical heart there lurks at such moments, when the chances of existence are involved, a desire to leave a correct impression of the feelings, like a light by which the action may be seen when personality is gone, gone where no light of investigation can ever reach the truth which every death takes out of the world. Therefore, instead of looking for something to eat, or trying to snatch an hour or so of sleep, Decoud was filling the pages of a large pocket-book with a letter to his sister.

In the intimacy of that intercourse he could not keep out his weariness, his great fatigue, the close touch of his bodily sensations. He began again as if he were talking to her. With almost an illusion of her presence, he wrote the phrase, 'I am very hungry.'

I have the feeling of a great solitude around me [he continued]. Is it, perhaps, because I am the only man with a definite idea in his head, in the complete collapse of every resolve, intention, and hope about me? But the solitude is also very real. All the engineers are out, and have been for two days, looking after the property of the National Central Railway, of that great Costaguana undertaking which is to put money into the pockets of Englishmen, Frenchmen, Americans, Germans, and God knows who else. The silence about me is ominous. There is above the middle part of this house a sort of first floor, with narrow openings like loopholes for windows, probably used in old times for the better defence against the savages, when the persistent barbarism of our native continent did not wear the black coats of politicians, but went about yelling, half-naked, with bows and arrows in its hands. The woman of the house is dying up there, I believe, all alone with her old husband. There is a narrow staircase, the sort of staircase one man could easily defend against a mob, leading up there, and I have just heard, through the thickness of the wall, the old fellow going down into their kitchen for something or other. It was a sort of noise a mouse might make behind the plaster of a wall. All the servants they had ran away yesterday and have not returned yet, if ever they do. For the rest, there are only two children here, two girls. The father has sent them downstairs, and they have crept into this café, perhaps because I am here. They huddle together in a corner, in each other's arms; I just noticed them a few minutes ago, and I feel more lonely than ever.

Decoud turned half round in his chair, and asked, 'Is there any bread here?'

Linda's dark head was shaken negatively in response, above the fair head of her sister nestling on her breast.

'You couldn't get me some bread?' insisted Decoud. The child did not move; he saw her large eyes stare at him very dark from the corner. 'You're not afraid of me?' he said.

'No,' said Linda, 'we are not afraid of you. You came here with Gian' Battista.'

'You mean Nostromo?' said Decoud.

'The English call him so, but that is no name either for man or beast,' said the girl, passing her hand gently over her sister's hair.

'But he lets people call him so,' remarked Decoud.

'Not in this house,' retorted the child.

'Ah! well, I shall call him the Capataz then.'

Decoud gave up the point, and after writing steadily for a while turned round again.

'When do you expect him back?' he asked.

'After he brought you here he rode off to fetch the Señor Doctor from the town for mother. He will be back soon.'

'He stands a good chance of getting shot somewhere on the road,' Decoud murmured to himself audibly; and Linda declared in her high-pitched voice:

'Nobody would dare to fire a shot at Gian' Battista.'

'You believe that,' asked Decoud, 'do you?'

'I know it,' said the child, with conviction. 'There is no one in this place brave enough to attack Gian' Battista.'

'It doesn't require much bravery to pull a trigger behind a bush,' muttered Decoud to himself. 'Fortunately, the night is dark, or there would be but little chance of saving the silver of the mine.'

He turned again to his pocket-book, glanced back through the pages, and again started his pencil.

That was the position yesterday, after the *Minerva* with the fugitive President had gone out of harbour, and the rioters had been driven back into the side-lanes of the town. I sat on the steps of the cathedral with Nostromo, after sending out the cable message for the information of a more or less attentive world. Strangely enough, though the offices of the Cable Company are in the same building as the *Porvenir*, the mob, which has thrown my presses out of the window and scattered the type all over the Plaza, has been kept from interfering with the instruments on the other side of the courtyard. As I sat talking with Nostromo, Bernhardt, the telegraphist, came out from under the Arcades with a piece of paper in his hand. The little man had tied himself up to an enormous sword and was hung all over with revolvers. He is ridiculous, but the bravest German of his size that ever tapped the key of a Morse transmitter. He had received the message from Cayta reporting the transports with Barrios's army just entering the port, and ending with the words, 'The greatest enthusiasm prevails.' I walked off to drink some water at the fountain, and I was shot at from the Alameda by somebody hiding behind a tree. But I drank, and didn't care; with Barrios in Cayta and the great Cordillera between us and Montero's victorious army I seemed, notwithstanding Messrs Gamacho and Fuentes, to hold my new State in the hollow of my hand. I was ready to sleep, but when I got as far as the Casa Gould I found the patio full of wounded laid out on straw. Lights were burning, and in that enclosed courtyard on that hot night a faint odour of chloroform and blood hung about. At one end Dr Monygham, the doctor of the mine, was dressing the wounds; at the other, near the stairs, Father Corbelán kneeling, listened to the confession of a dying *cargador*. Mrs Gould was walking about through these shambles with a large bottle in one hand and a lot of cotton wool in the other. She just looked at me and never even winked. Her *camerista* was following her, also holding a bottle, and sobbing gently to herself.

I busied myself for some time in fetching water from the cistern for the wounded. Afterwards I wandered upstairs, meeting some of the first ladies of Sulaco, paler than I had even seen them before, with bandages over their arms. Not all of them had fled to the ships. A good many had taken refuge for the day in the Casa Gould. On the landing a girl, with her hair half down, was kneeling against the wall under the niche where stands a Madonna in blue robes and a gilt crown on her head. I think it was the eldest Miss Lopez; I couldn't see her face, but I remember looking at the high French heel of her little shoe. She did not make a sound, she did not stir, she was not sobbing; she remained there, perfectly still, all black against the white wall, a silent figure of passionate piety. I am sure she was no more frightened than the other white-faced ladies I met carrying bandages. One was sitting on the top step tearing a piece of linen hastily into strips – the young wife of an elderly man of fortune here. She interrupted herself to wave her hand to my bow, as though she were in her carriage on the Alameda. The women of our country are worth looking at during a revolution. The rouge and pearl powder fall off, together with that passive attitude towards the outer world which education, tradition, custom impose upon them from the earliest infancy. I thought of your face, which from your infancy had the stamp of intelligence instead of that patient and resigned cast which appears when some political commotion tears down the veil of cosmetics and usage.

In the great *sala* upstairs a sort of Junta of Notables was sitting, the remnant of the vanished Provincial Assembly. Don Juste Lopez had had half his beard singed off at the muzzle of a trabuco loaded with slugs, of which every one missed him, providentially. And as he turned his head from side to side it was exactly as if there had been two men inside his frock-coat, one nobly whiskered and solemn, the other untidy and scared.

They raised a cry of 'Decoud! Don Martin!' at my entrance. I asked them, 'What are you deliberating upon, gentlemen?' There did not seem to be any president, though Don José Avellanos sat at the head of the table. They all answered together, 'On the preservation of life and property.' 'Till the new officials arrive,' Don Juste explained to me, with the solemn side of his face offered to my view. It was as if a stream of water had been poured upon my glowing idea of a new State. There was a hissing sound in my ears, and the room grew dim, as if suddenly filled with vapour.

I walked up to the table blindly, as though I had been drunk. 'You are deliberating upon surrender,' I said. They all sat still, with their noses over the sheet of paper each had before him, God only knows why. Only Don José hid his face in his hands, muttering, 'Never, never!' But as I looked at him, it seemed to me that I could have blown him away with my breath, he looked so frail, so weak, so worn out. Whatever happens, he will not survive. The deception is too great for a man of his age; and hasn't he seen the sheets of *Fifty Years of Misrule*, which we have begun printing on the presses of the *Porvenir*, littering the Plaza, floating in the gutters, fired out as wads for trabucos loaded with handfuls of type, blown in the wind, trampled in the mud? I have seen pages floating upon the very waters of the harbour. It would be unreasonable to expect him to survive. It would be cruel.

'Do you know,' I cried, 'what surrender means to you, to your women, to your children, to your property?'

I declaimed for five minutes without drawing breath, it seems to me, harping on our best chances, on the ferocity of Montero, whom I made out to be as great a beast as I have no doubt he would like to be if he had intelligence enough to conceive a systematic reign of terror. And then for another five minutes or more I poured out an impassioned appeal to their courage and manliness, with all the passion of my love for Antonia. For·if ever man spoke well, it would be from a personal feeling, denouncing an enemy, defending himself, or pleading for what really may be dearer than life. My dear girl, I absolutely thundered at them. It seemed as if my voice would burst the walls asunder, and when I stopped I saw all their scared eyes looking at me dubiously. And that was all the effect I had produced! Only Don José's head had sunk lower and lower on his breast. I bent my ear to his withered lips, and made out his whisper, something like, 'In God's name, then, Martin, my son!' I don't know exactly. There was the name of God in it, I am certain. It seems to me I have caught his last breath – the breath of his departing soul on his lips.

He lives yet, it is true. I have seen him since; but it was only a senile body, lying on its back, covered to the chin, with open eyes, and so still that you might have said it was breathing no longer. I left him thus, with Antonia kneeling by the side of the bed, just before I came to this Italian's *posada*, where the ubiquitous death is also waiting. But I know that Don José has really died there, in the Casa Gould, with that whisper urging me to attempt what no doubt his soul, wrapped up in the sanctity of diplomatic treaties and solemn declarations, must have abhorred. I had exclaimed very loud, 'There is never any God in a country where men will not help themselves.'

Meanwhile, Don Juste had begun a pondered oration whose solemn effect was spoiled by the ridiculous disaster to his beard. I did not wait to make it out. He seemed to argue that Montero's (he called him The General) intentions were probably not evil, though, he went on, 'that distinguished man' (only a week ago we used to call him a *gran' bestia*) 'was perhaps mistaken as to the true means'. As you may imagine, I didn't stay to hear the rest. I know the intentions of Montero's brother, Pedrito, the *guerrillero*, whom I exposed in Paris, some years ago, in a café frequented by South American students, where he tried to pass himself off for a Secretary of Legation. He used to come in and talk for hours, twisting his felt hat in his hairy paws, and his ambition seemed to become a sort of Duc de Morny to a sort of Napoleon. Already, then, he used to talk of his brother in inflated terms. He seemed fairly safe from being found out, because the students, all of the Blanco families, did not, as you may imagine, frequent the Legation. It was only Decoud, a man without faith and principles, as they used to say, that went in there sometimes for the sake of the fun, as it were to an assembly of trained monkeys. I know his intentions. I have seen him change the plates at table. Whoever is allowed to live on in terror, I must die the death.

No, I didn't stay to the end to hear Don Juste Lopez trying to persuade himself in a grave oration of the clemency and justice, and honesty, and purity of the brothers Montero. I went out abruptly to seek Antonia. I saw her in the gallery. As I opened the door, she extended to me her clasped hands.

'What are they doing in there?' she asked.

'Talking,' I said, with my eyes looking into hers.

'Yes, yes, but —'

'Empty speeches,' I interrupted her. 'Hiding their fears behind imbecile hopes. They are all great Parliamentarians there – on the English model, as you know.' I was so furious that I could hardly speak. She made a gesture of despair.

Through the door I held a little ajar behind me, we heard Don Juste's measured mouthing monotone go on from phrase to phrase, like a sort of awful and solemn madness.

'After all, the Democratic aspirations have, perhaps, their legitimacy. The ways of human progress are inscrutable, and if the fate of the country is in the hand of Montero, we ought —'

I crashed the door to on that; it was enough; it was too much. There was never a beautiful face expressing more horror and despair than the face of Antonia. I couldn't bear it; I seized her wrists.

'Have they killed my father in there?' she asked.

Her eyes blazed with indignation, but as I looked on, fascinated, the light in them went out.

'It is a surrender,' I said. And I remember I was shaking her wrists I held apart in my hands. 'But it's more than talk. Your father told me to go on in God's name.'

My dear girl, there is that in Antonia which would make me believe in the feasibility of anything. One look at her face is enough to set my brain on fire. And yet I love her as any other man would – with the heart, and with that alone. She is more to me than his Church to Father Corbelán (the Grand Vicar disappeared last night from the town; perhaps gone to join the band of Hernandez). She is more to me than his precious mine to that sentimental Englishman. I won't speak of his wife. She may have been sentimental once. The San Tomé mine stands now between those two people. 'Your father himself, Antonia,' I repeated; 'your father, do you understand? has told me to go on.'

She averted her face, and in a pained voice —

'He has?' she cried. 'Then, indeed, I fear he will never speak again.'

She freed her wrists from my clutch and began to cry in her handkerchief. I disregarded her sorrow; I would rather see her miserable than not see her at all, never any more; for whether I escaped or stayed to die, there was for us no coming together, no future. And that being so, I had no pity to waste upon the passing moments of her sorrow. I sent her off in tears to fetch Doña Emilia and Don Carlos, too. Their sentiment was necessary to the very life of my plan; the sentimentalism of the people that will never do anything for the sake of their passionate desire, unless it comes to them clothed in the fair robes of an idea.

Late at night we formed a small junta of four – the two women, Don Carlos, and myself – in Mrs Gould's blue-and-white boudoir.

El Rey de Sulaco thinks himself, no doubt, a very honest man. And so he is, if one could look behind his taciturnity. Perhaps he thinks that this alone makes his honesty unstained. Those Englishmen live on illusions which somehow or other help them to get a firm hold of the substance. When he speaks it is by a rare 'yes' or 'no' that seems as impersonal as the words of an oracle. But he could not impose on me by his dumb reserve. I knew what he had in his head; he has his mine in his head; and his wife had nothing in her head but his precious person, which he has bound up with the Gould Concession and tied to that little woman's neck. No matter. The thing was to make him present the affair to Holroyd (the Steel and Silver King) in such a manner as to secure his financial support. At that time last night, just twenty-four hours ago, we thought the silver of the mine safe in the Custom House vaults till the north-bound steamer came to take it away. And as long as the treasure flowed north, without a break, that utter sentimentalist, Holroyd, would not drop his idea of introducing, not only justice, industry, peace, to the benighted continents, but also that pet dream of his of a purer form of Christianity. Later on, the principal European really in Sulaco, the engineer-in-chief of the railway, came riding up the *calle*, from the harbour, and was admitted to our conclave. Meantime, the Junta of the Notables in the great *sala* was still deliberating; only, one of them had run out in the corridor to ask the servant whether something to eat couldn't be sent in. The first words the engineer-in-chief said as he came into the boudoir were, 'What is your house, dear Mrs Gould? A war hospital below, and apparently a restaurant above. I saw them carrying trays full of good things into the *sala*.'

'And here, in this boudoir,' I said, 'you behold the inner cabinet of the Occidental Republic that is to be.'

He was so preoccupied that he didn't smile at that, he didn't even look surprised.

He told us that he was attending to the general dispositions for the defence of the railway property at the railway yards when he was sent for to go into the railway telegraph office. The engineer of the railhead, at the foot of the mountains, wanted to talk to him from his end of the wire. There was nobody in the office but himself and the operator of the railway telegraph, who read off the clicks aloud as the tape coiled its length upon the floor. And the purport of that talk, clicked nervously from a wooden shed in the depths of the forests, had informed the chief that President Ribiera had been, or was being, pursued. This was news, indeed, to all of us in Sulaco. Ribiera himself, when rescued, revived, and soothed by us, had been inclined to think that he had not been pursued.

Ribiera had yielded to the urgent solicitations of his friends, and had left the headquarters of his discomfited army alone, under the guidance of Bonifacio, the muleteer, who had been willing to take the responsibility with the risk. He had departed at daybreak of the third day. His remaining forces had melted away during the night. Bonifacio and he rode hard on horses towards the Cordillera; then they obtained mules, entered the passes, and crossed the Paramo of Ivie just before a freezing blast swept over that stony plateau, burying in a drift of snow the little shelter-hut of stones in which they had spent the night. Afterwards poor Ribiera had many adventures, got separated from his guide, lost his mount, struggled down to the Campo on foot, and if he had not thrown himself on the mercy of a *ranchero* would have perished a long way from Sulaco. That man, who, as a matter of fact, recognized him at once, let him have a fresh mule, which the fugitive, heavy and unskilful, had ridden to death. And it was true he had been pursued by a party commanded by no less a person than Pedro Montero, the brother of the general. The cold wind of the Paramo luckily caught the pursuers on the top of the pass. Some few men, and all the animals, perished in the icy blast. The stragglers died, but the main body kept on. They found poor Bonifacio lying half-dead at the foot of a snow slope, and bayoneted him promptly in the true Civil War style. They would have had Ribiera, too, if they had not, for some reason or other, turned off the track of the old *camino real*, only to lose their way in the forests at the foot of the lower slopes. And there they were at last, having stumbled in unexpectedly upon the construction camp. The engineer at the railhead told his chief by wire that he had Pedro Montero absolutely there, in the very office, listening to the clicks. He was going to take possession of Sulaco in the name of the Democracy. He was very overbearing. His men slaughtered some of the Railway Company's cattle without asking leave, and went to work broiling the meat on the embers. Pedrito made many pointed inquiries as to the silver mine, and what had become of the product of the last six months' working. He had said peremptorily, 'Ask your chief up there by wire, he ought to know; tell him that Don Pedro Montero, Chief of the Campo and Minister of the Interior of the new Government, desires to be correctly informed.'

He had his feet wrapped up in blood-stained rags, a lean, haggard face, ragged beard and hair, and had walked in limping, with a crooked branch of a tree for a staff. His followers were, perhaps, in a worse plight, but apparently they had not thrown away their arms, and, at any rate, not all their ammunition. Their lean faces filled the door and the windows of the telegraph hut. As it was at the same time, the bedroom of the engineer-in-charge there, Montero had thrown himself on his clean blankets and lay there shivering and dictating requisitions to be transmitted by wire to Sulaco. He demanded a train of cars to be sent down at once to transport his men up.

'To this I answered from my end,' the engineer-in-chief related to us, 'that I dared not risk the rolling-stock in the interior, as there had been attempts to wreck trains all along the line several times. I did that for your sake, Gould,' said the chief engineer. 'The answer to this was, in the words of my subordinate, "The filthy brute on my bed said, 'Suppose I were to have you shot?' " ' To which my subordinate, who, it appears, was himself operating, remarked that it would not bring the cars up. Upon that, the other, yawning, said, "Never mind, there is no lack of horses on the Campo." And, turning over, went to sleep on Harris's bed.'

This is why, my dear girl, I am a fugitive tonight. The last wire from railhead says that Pedro Montero and his men left at daybreak, after feeding on asado beef all night. They took all the horses; they will find more on the road; they'll be here in less than thirty hours, and thus Sulaco is no place either for me or the great store of silver belonging to the Gould Concession.

But that is not the worst. The garrison of Esmeralda has gone over to the victorious party. We have heard this by means of the telegraphist of the Cable Company, who came to the Casa Gould in the early morning with the news. In fact, it was so early that the day had not yet quite broken over Sulaco. His colleague in Esmeralda had called him up to say that the garrison, after shooting some of their officers, had taken possession of a Government steamer laid up in the harbour. It is really a heavy blow for me. I thought I could depend on every man in this province. It was a mistake. It was a Monterist Revolution in Esmeralda, just such as was attempted in Sulaco, only that *that* one came off. The telegraphist was signalling to Bernhardt all the time, and his last transmitted words were, 'They are bursting in the door, and taking possession of the cable office. You are cut off. Can do no more.'

But, as a matter of fact, he managed somehow to escape the vigilance of his captors, who had tried to stop the communication with the outer world. He did manage it. How it was done I don't know, but a few hours afterwards he called up Sulaco again, and what he said was, 'The insurgent army has taken possession of the Government transport in the bay and are filling her with troops, with the intention of going round the coast to Sulaco. Therefore look out for yourselves. They will be ready to start in a few hours, and may be upon you before daybreak.'

This is all he could say. They drove him away from his instrument this time for good, because Bernhardt has been calling up Esmeralda ever since without getting an answer.

After setting these words down in the pocket-book which he was filling up for the benefit of his sister, Decoud lifted his head to listen. But there were no sounds, neither in the room nor in the house, except the drip of the water from the filter into the vast earthenware jar under the wooden stand. And outside the house there was a great silence. Decoud lowered his head again over the pocket-book.

I am not running away, you understand [he wrote on]. I am simply going away with that great treasure of silver which must be saved at all costs. Pedro Montero from the Campo and the revolted garrison of Esmeralda from the sea are converging upon it. That it is there lying ready for them is only an accident. The real objective is the San Tomé mine itself, as you may well imagine; otherwise the Occidental Province would have been, no doubt, left alone for many weeks, to be gathered at leisure into the arms of the victorious party. Don Carlos Gould will have enough to do to save his mine, with its organization and its people; this '*Imperium in Imperio*', this wealth-producing thing, to which his sentimentalism attaches a strange idea of justice. He holds to it as some men hold to the idea of love or revenge. Unless I am much mistaken in the man, it must remain inviolate or perish by an act of his will alone. A passion has crept into his cold and idealistic life. A passion which I can only comprehend intellectually. A passion that is not like the passions we know, we men of another blood. But it is as dangerous as any of ours.

His wife has understood it, too. That is why she is such a good ally of mine. She seizes upon all my suggestions with a sure instinct that in the end they make for the safety of the Gould Concession. And he defers to her because he trusts her perhaps, but I fancy more rather as if he wished to make up for some subtle wrong, for that sentimental unfaithfulness which surrenders her happiness, her life, to the seduction of an idea. The little woman has discovered that he lives for the mine rather than for her. But let them be. To each his fate, shaped by passion or sentiment. The principal thing is that she has backed up my advice to get the silver out of the town, out of the country, at once, at any cost, at any risk. Don Carlos's mission is to preserve unstained the fair name of his mine; Mrs Gould's mission is to save him from the effects of that cold and overmastering passion, which she dreads more than if it were an infatuation for another woman. Nostromo's mission is to save the silver. The plan is to load it into the largest of the Company's lighters, and send it across the gulf to a small port out of Costaguana territory just on the other side of the Azuera, where the first northbound steamer will get orders to pick it up. The waters here are calm. We shall slip away into the darkness of the gulf before the Esmeralda rebels arrive; and by the time the day breaks over the ocean we shall be out of sight, invisible, hidden by Azuera, which itself looks from the Sulaco shore like a faint blue cloud on the horizon.

The incorruptible Capataz de Cargadores is the man for that work; and I, the man with a passion, but without a mission, I go with him to return – to play my part in the farce to the end, and, if successful, to receive my reward, which no one but Antonia can give me.

I shall not see her again now before I depart. I left her, as I have said, by Don José's bedside. The street was dark, the houses shut up, and I walked out of the town in the night. Not a single street-lamp had been lit for two days, and the archway of the gate was only a mass of darkness in the vague form of a tower, in which I heard low, dismal groans that seemed to answer the murmurs of a man's voice.

I recognized something impassive and careless in the tone, characteristic of that Genoese sailor who, like me, has come casually here to be drawn into the events for which his scepticism as well as mine seems to entertain a sort of passive contempt. The only thing he seems to care for, as far as I have been able to discover, is to be well spoken of. An ambition fit for noble souls, but also a profitable one for an exceptionally intelligent scoundrel. Yes. His very words, 'To be well spoken of. *Sí, señor.*' He does not seem to make any difference between speaking and thinking. Is it sheer naïveness or the practical point of view, I wonder? Exceptional individualities always interest me, because they are true to the general formula expressing the moral state of humanity.

He joined me on the harbour road after I had passed them under the dark archway without stopping. It was a woman in trouble he had been talking to. Through discretion I kept silent while he walked by my side. After a time he began to talk himself. It was not what I expected. It was only an old woman, an old lace-maker, in search of her son, one of the street-sweepers employed by the municipality. Friends had come the day before at daybreak to the door of their hovel calling him out. He had gone with them, and she had not seen him since; so she had left the food she had been preparing half-cooked on the extinct embers and had crawled out as far as the harbour, where she had heard that some town *mozos* had been killed on the morning of the riot. One of the *cargadores* guarding the Custom House had brought out a lantern, and had helped her to look at the few dead left lying about there. Now she was creeping back, having failed in her search. So she sat down on the stone seat under the arch, moaning, because she was very tired. The Capataz had questioned her, and after hearing her broken and groaning tale had advised her to go and look amongst the wounded in the patio of the Casa Gould. He had also given her a quarter dollar, he mentioned carelessly.

'Why did you do that?' I asked. 'Do you know her?'

'No, *señor.* I don't suppose I have ever seen her before. How should I? She has not probably been out in the streets for years. She is one of those old women that you find in this country at the back of huts, crouching over fireplaces, with a stick on the ground by their side, and almost too feeble to drive away the stray dogs from their cooking-pots. *Caramba!* I could tell by her voice that death had forgotten her. But, old or young, they like money, and will speak well of the man who gives it to them.' He laughed a little. '*Señor*, you should have felt the clutch of her paw as I put the piece in her palm.' He paused. 'My last, too,' he added.

I made no comment. He's known for his liberality and his bad luck at the game of *monte*, which keeps him as poor as when he first came here.

'I suppose, Don Martin,' he began, in a thoughtful, speculative tone, 'that the Señor Administrador of San Tomé will reward me some day if I save his silver?'

I said that it could not be otherwise, surely. He walked on, muttering to himself. '*Sí, sí*, without doubt, without doubt; and, look you, Señor Martin, what it is to be well spoken of! There is not another man that could have been even thought of for such a thing. I shall get something great for it some day. And let it come soon,' he mumbled. 'Time passes in this country as quick as anywhere else.'

This, *soeur chérie*, is my companion in the great escape for the sake of the great cause. He is more naïve than shrewd, more masterful than crafty, more generous with his personality than the people who make use of him are with their money. At least, that is what he thinks himself with more pride than sentiment. I am glad I have made friends with him. As a companion he acquires more importance than he ever had as a sort of minor genius in his way – as an original Italian sailor whom I allowed to come in in the small hours and talk familiarly to the editor of the *Porvenir* while the paper was going through the press. And it is curious to have met a man for whom the value of life seems to consist in personal prestige.

I am waiting for him here now. On arriving at the *posada* kept by Viola we found the children alone down below, and the old Genoese shouted to his countryman to go and fetch the doctor. Otherwise we would have gone on to the wharf, where it appears Captain Mitchell with some volunteer Europeans and a few picked *cargadores* are loading the lighter with the silver that must be saved from Montero's clutches in order to be used for Montero's defeat. Nostromo galloped furiously back towards the town. He has been long gone already. This delay gives me time to talk to you. By the time this pocket-book reaches your hands much will have happened. But now it is a pause under the hovering wing of death in that silent house buried in the black night, with this dying woman, the two children crouching without a sound, and that old man whom I can hear through the thickness of the wall passing up and down with a light rubbing noise no louder than a mouse. And I, the only other with them, don't really know whether to count myself with the living or with the dead. '*Quién sabe?*' as the people here are prone to say in answer to every question. But no! feeling for you is certainly not dead, and the whole thing, the house, the dark night, the silent children in this dim room, my very presence here – all this is life, must be life, since it is so much like a dream.

With the writing of the last line there came upon Decoud a moment of sudden and complete oblivion. He swayed over the table as if struck by a bullet. The next moment he sat up, confused, with the idea that he had heard his pencil roll on the floor. The low door of the café, wide open, was filled with the glare of a torch in which was visible half of a horse, switching its tail against the leg of a rider with a long iron spur strapped to the naked heel. The two girls were gone, and Nostromo, standing in the middle of the room, looked at him from under the round brim of the sombrero low down over his brow.

'I have brought that sour-faced English doctor in Señora Gould's carriage,' said Nostromo. 'I doubt if, with all his wisdom, he can save the Padrona this time. They have sent for the children. A bad sign that.'

He sat down on the end of a bench. 'She wants to give them her blessing, I suppose.'

Dazedly Decoud observed that he must have fallen sound asleep, and Nostromo said, with a vague smile, that he had looked in at the window and had seen him lying still across the table with his head on his arms. The English *señora* had also come in the carriage, and went upstairs at once with the doctor. She had told him not to wake up Don Martin yet; but when they sent for the children he had come into the café.

The half of the horse with its half of the rider swung round outside the door; the torch of tow and resin in the iron basket which was carried on a stick at the saddle-bow flared right into the room for a moment, and Mrs Gould entered hastily with a very white, tired face. The hood of her dark, blue cloak had fallen back. Both men rose.

'Teresa wants to see you, Nostromo,' she said.

The Capataz did not move. Decoud, with his back to the table, began to button up his coat.

'The silver, Mrs Gould, the silver,' he murmured in English. 'Don't forget that the Esmeralda garrison have got a steamer. They may appear at any moment at the harbour entrance.'

'The doctor says there is no hope,' Mrs Gould spoke rapidly, also in English. 'I shall take you down to the wharf in my carriage and then come back to fetch away the girls.' She changed swiftly into Spanish to address Nostromo. 'Why are you wasting time? Old Giorgio's wife wishes to see you.'

'I am going to her, *señora*,' muttered the Capataz.

Dr Monygham now showed himself, bringing back the children. To Mrs Gould's inquiring glance he only shook his head and went outside at once, followed by Nostromo.

The horse of the torch-bearer, motionless, hung his head low, and the rider had dropped the reins to light a cigarette. The glare of the torch played on the front of the house crossed by the big black letters of its inscription in which only the word ITALIA was lighted fully. The patch of wavering glare reached as far as Mrs Gould's carriage waiting on the road, with the yellow-faced, portly Ignacio apparently dozing on the box. By his side Basilio, dark and skinny, held a Winchester carbine in front of him, with both hands, and peered fearfully into the darkness. Nostromo touched lightly the doctor's shoulder.

'Is she really dying, Señor Doctor?'

'Yes,' said the doctor, with a strange twitch of his scarred cheek. 'And why she wants to see you I cannot imagine.'

'She has been like that before,' suggested Nostromo, looking away.

'Well, Capataz, I can assure you she will never be like that again,' snarled Dr Monygham. 'You may go to her or stay away. There is very little to be got from talking to the dying. But she told Doña Emilia in my hearing that she has been like a mother to you ever since you first set foot ashore here.'

'*Sí!* And she never had a good word to say for me to anybody. It is more as if she could not forgive me for being alive, and such a man, too, as she would have liked her son to be.'

'Maybe!' exclaimed a mournful deep voice near them. 'Women have their own ways of tormenting themselves.' Giorgio Viola had come out of the house. He threw a heavy black shadow in the torchlight, and the glare fell on his big face, on the great bushy head of white hair. He motioned the Capataz indoors with his extended arm.

Dr Monygham, after busying himself with a little medicament box of polished wood on the seat of the landau, turned to old Giorgio and thrust into his big, trembling hand one of the glass-stoppered bottles out of the case.

'Give her a spoonful of this now and then, in water,' he said. 'It will make her easier.'

'And there is nothing more for her?' asked the old man, patiently.

'No. Not on earth,' said the doctor, with his back to him, clicking the lock of the medicine case.

Nostromo slowly crossed the large kitchen, all dark but for the glow of a heap of charcoal under the heavy mantel of the cooking-range, where water was boiling in an iron pot with a loud bubbling sound. Between the two walls of a narrow staircase a bright light streamed from the sick-room above; and the magnificent Capataz de Cargadores stepping noiselessly in soft leather sandals, bushy whiskered, his muscular neck and bronzed chest bare in the open check shirt, resembled a Mediterranean sailor just come ashore from some wine- or fruit-laden felucca. At the top he paused, broad shouldered, narrow hipped, and supple, looking at the large bed, like a white couch of state, with a profusion of snowy linen, amongst which the Padrona sat unpropped and bowed, her handsome, black-browed face bent over her chest. A mass of raven hair with only a few white threads in it covered her shoulders; one thick strand fallen forward half veiled her cheek. Perfectly motionless in that pose, expressing physical anxiety and unrest, she turned her eyes alone towards Nostromo.

The Capataz had a red sash wound many times round his waist, and a heavy silver ring on the forefinger of the hand he raised to give a twist to his moustache.

'Their revolutions, their revolutions,' gasped Señora Teresa. 'Look, Gian' Battista, it has killed me at last!'

Nostromo said nothing, and the sick woman with an upward glance insisted. 'Look, this one has killed me, while you were away fighting for what did not concern you, foolish man.'

'Why talk like this?' mumbled the Capataz between his teeth. 'Will you never believe in my good sense? It concerns me to keep on being what I am: every day alike.'

'You never change, indeed,' she said, bitterly. 'Always thinking of yourself and taking your pay out in fine words from those who care nothing for you.'

There was between them an intimacy of antagonism as close in its way as the intimacy of accord and affection. He had not walked along the way of Teresa's expectations. It was she who had encouraged him to leave his ship, in the hope of securing a friend and defender for the girls. The wife of old Giorgio was aware of her precarious health, and was haunted by the fear of her aged husband's loneliness and the unprotected state of the children. She had wanted to annex that apparently quiet and steady young man, affectionate and pliable, an orphan from his tenderest age, as he had told her, with no ties in Italy except an uncle, owner and master of a felucca, from whose ill-usage he had run away before he was fourteen. He had seemed to her courageous, a hard worker, determined to make his way in the world. From gratitude and the ties of habit he would become like a son to herself and Giorgio; and then, who knows, when Linda had grown up . . . Ten years' difference between husband and wife was not so much. Her own great man was nearly twenty years older than herself. Gian' Battista was an attractive young fellow, besides; attractive to men, women, and children, just by that profound quietness of personality which, like a serene twilight, rendered more seductive the promise of his vigorous form and the resolution of his conduct.

Old Giorgio, in profound ignorance of his wife's views and hopes, had a great regard for his young countryman. 'A man ought not to be tame,' he used to tell her, quoting the Spanish proverb in defence of the splendid Capataz. She was growing jealous of his success. He was escaping from her, she feared. She was practical, and he seemed to her to be an absurd spend-thrift of these qualities which made him so valuable. He got too little for them. He scattered them with both hands amongst too many people, she thought. He laid no money by. She railed at his poverty, his exploits, his adventures, his loves, and his reputation; but in her heart she had never given him up, as though, indeed, he had been her son.

Even now, ill as she was, ill enough to feel the chill, black breath of the approaching end, she had wished to see him. It was like putting out her benumbed hand to regain her hold. But she had presumed too much on her strength. She could not command her thoughts; they had become dim, like her vision. The words faltered on her lips, and only the paramount anxiety and desire of her life seemed to be too strong for death.

The Capataz said, 'I have heard these things many times. You are unjust, but it does not hurt me. Only now you do not seem to have much strength to talk, and I have but little time to listen. I am engaged in a work of very great moment.'

She made an effort to ask him whether it was true that he had found time to go and fetch a doctor for her. Nostromo nodded affirmatively.

She was pleased: it relieved her sufferings to know that the man had condescended to do so much for those who really wanted his help. It was a proof of his friendship. Her voice became stronger.

'I want a priest more than a doctor,' she said, pathetically. She did not move her head; only her eyes ran into the corners to watch the Capataz standing by the side of her bed. 'Would you go to fetch a priest for me now? Think! A dying woman asks you!'

Nostromo shook his head resolutely. He did not believe in priests in their sacerdotal character. A doctor was an efficacious person; but a priest, as priest, was nothing, incapable of doing either good or harm. Nostromo did not even dislike the sight of them as old Giorgio did. The utter uselessness of the errand was what struck him most.

'Padrona,' he said, 'you have been like this before, and got better after a few days. I have given you already the very last moments I can spare. Ask Señora Gould to send you one.'

He was feeling uneasy at the impiety of this refusal. The Padrona believed in priests, and confessed herself to them. But all women did that. It could not be of much consequence. And yet his heart felt oppressed for a moment – at the thought what absolution would mean to her if she believed in it only ever so little. No matter. It was quite true that he had given her already the very last moment he could spare.

'You refuse to go?' she gasped. 'Ah! you are always yourself, indeed.'

'Listen to reason, Padrona,' he said. 'I am needed to save the silver of the mine. Do you hear? A greater treasure than the one which they say is guarded by ghosts and devils in Azuera. It is true. I am resolved to make this the most desperate affair I was ever engaged on in my whole life.'

She felt a despairing indignation. The supreme test had failed. Standing above her, Nostromo did not see the distorted features of her face, distorted by a paroxysm of pain and anger. Only she began to tremble all over. Her bowed head shook. The broad shoulders quivered.

'Then God, perhaps, will have mercy upon me! But do you look to it, man, that you get something for yourself out of it, besides the remorse that shall overtake you some day.'

She laughed feebly. 'Get riches at least for once, you indispensable, admired Gian' Battista, to whom the peace of a dying woman is less than the praise of people who have given you a silly name – and nothing besides – in exchange for your soul and body.'

The Captain de Cargadores swore to himself under his breath.

'Leave my soul alone, Padrona, and I shall know how to take care of my body. Where is the harm of people having need of me? What are you envying me that I have robbed you and the children of? Those very people you are throwing in my teeth have done more for old Giorgio than they ever thought of doing for me.'

He struck his breast with his open palm; his voice had remained low though he had spoken in a forcible tone. He twisted his moustaches one after another, and his eyes wandered a little about the room.

'Is it my fault that I am the only man for their purposes? What angry nonsense are you talking, mother? Would you rather have me timid and foolish, selling water-melons on the market-place or rowing a boat for passengers along the harbour, like a soft Neapolitan without courage or reputation? Would you have a young man live like a monk? I do not believe it. Would you want a monk for your eldest girl? Let her grow. What are you afraid of? You have been angry with me for everything I did for years; ever since you first spoke to me, in secret from old Giorgio, about your Linda. Husband to one and brother to the other, did you say? Well, why not! I like the little ones, and a man must marry some time. But ever since that time you have been making little of me to everyone. Why? Did you think you could put a collar and chain on me as if I were one of the watchdogs they keep over there in the railway yards? Look here, Padrona, I am the same man who came ashore one evening and sat down in the thatched ranche you lived in at that time on the other side of the town and told you all about himself. You were not unjust to me then. What has happened since? I am no longer an insignificant youth. A good name, Giorgio says, is a treasure, Padrona.'

'They have turned your head with their praises,' gasped the sick woman. 'They have been paying you with words. Your folly shall betray you into poverty, misery, starvation. The very *leperos* shall laugh at you – the great Capataz.'

Nostromo stood for a time as if struck dumb. She never looked at him. A self-confident, mirthless smile passed quickly from his lips, and then he backed away. His disregarded figure sank down beyond the doorway. He descended the stairs backwards, with the usual sense of having been somehow baffled by this woman's disparagement of this reputation he had obtained and desired to keep.

Downstairs in the big kitchen a candle was burning, surrounded by the shadows of the walls, of the ceiling, but no ruddy glare filled the open square of the outer door. The carriage with Mrs Gould and Don Martin, preceded by the horseman bearing the torch, had gone on to the jetty. Dr Monygham, who had remained, sat on the corner of a hard wood table near the candlestick, his seamed, shaved face inclined sideways, his arms crossed on his breast, his lips pursed up, and his prominent eyes glaring stonily upon the floor of black earth. Near the overhanging mantel of the fireplace where the pot of water was still boiling violently, old Giorgio held his chin in his hand, one foot advanced, as if arrested by a sudden thought.

'*Adios, viejo,*' said Nostromo, feeling the handle of his revolver in the belt and loosening his knife in its sheath. He picked up a blue poncho lined with red from the table, and put it over his head. '*Adios,* look after the things in my sleeping-room, and if you hear from me no more, give up the box to Paquita. There is not much of value there, except my new serape from Mexico, and a few silver buttons on my best jacket. No matter! The things will look well enough on the next lover she gets, and the man need not be afraid I shall linger on earth after I am dead, like those *gringos* that haunt the Azuera.'

Dr Monygham twisted his lips into a bitter smile. After old Giorgio, with an almost imperceptible nod and without a word, had gone up the narrow stairs, he said:

'Why, Capataz! I thought you could never fail in anything.'

Nostromo, glancing contemptuously at the doctor, lingered in the doorway rolling a cigarette, then struck a match, and, after lighting it, held the burning piece of wood above his head till the flame nearly touched his fingers.

'No wind!' he muttered to himself. 'Look here, *señor* – do you know the nature of my undertaking?'

Dr Monygham nodded sourly.

'It is as if I were taking up a curse upon me, Señor Doctor. A man with a treasure on this coast will have every knife raised against him in every place upon the shore. You see that, Señor Doctor? I shall float along with a spell upon my life till I meet somewhere the north-bound steamer of the Company, and then indeed they will talk about the Capataz of the Sulaco Cargadores from one end of America to another.'

Dr Monygham laughed his short, throaty laugh. Nostromo turned round in the doorway.

'But if your worship can find any other man ready and fit for such business I will stand back. I am not exactly tired of my life, though I am so poor that I can carry all I have with myself on my horse's back.'

'You gamble too much, and never say "no" to a pretty face, Capataz,' said Dr Monygham, with sly simplicity. 'That's not the way to make a fortune. But nobody that I know ever suspected you of being poor. I hope you have made a good bargain in case you come back safe from this adventure.'

'What bargain would your worship have made?' asked Nostromo, blowing the smoke out of his lips through the doorway.

Dr Monygham listened up the staircase for a moment before he answered, with another of his short, abrupt laughs:

'Illustrious Capataz, for taking the curse of death upon my back, as you call it, nothing else but the whole treasure would do.'

Nostromo vanished out of the doorway with a grunt of discontent at this jeering answer. Dr Monygham heard him gallop away. Nostromo rode furiously in the dark. There were lights in the buildings of the O.S.N. Company near the wharf, but before he got there he met the Gould carriage. The horseman preceded it with the torch, whose light showed the white mules trotting, the portly Ignacio driving, and Basilio with the carbine on the box. From the dark body of the landau Mrs Gould's voice cried, 'They are waiting for you, Capataz!' She was returning, chilly and excited, with Decoud's pocket-book still held in her hand. He had confided it to her to send to his sister. 'Perhaps my last words to her,' he had said, pressing Mrs Gould's hand.

The Capataz never checked his speed. At the head of the wharf vague figures with rifles leapt to the head of his horse; other closed upon him – *cargadores* of the company posted by Captain Mitchell on the watch. At a word from him they fell back with subservient murmurs, recognizing his voice. At the other end of the jetty, near a cargo crane, in a dark group with glowing cigars, his name was pronounced in a tone of relief. Most of the Europeans in Sulaco were there, rallied round Charles Gould, as if the silver of the mine had been the emblem of a common cause, the symbol of the supreme importance of material interests. They had loaded it into the lighter with their own hands. Nostromo recognized Don Carlos Gould, a thin, tall shape, standing a little apart and silent, to whom another tall shape, the engineer-in-chief, said aloud, 'If it must be lost, it is a million times better that it should go to the bottom of the sea.'

Martin Decoud called out from the lighter, '*Au revoir, messieurs*, till we clasp hands again over the new-born Occidental Republic.' Only a subdued murmur responded to his clear, ringing tones; and then it seemed to him that the wharf was floating away into the night; but it was Nostromo, who was already pushing against a pile with one of the heavy sweeps. Decoud did not move; the effect was that of being launched into space. After a splash or two there was not a sound but the thud of Nostromo's feet leaping about the boat. He hoisted the big sail; a breath of wind fanned Decoud's cheek. Everything had vanished but the light of the lantern Captain Mitchell had hoisted upon the post at the end of the jetty to guide Nostromo out of the harbour.

The two men, unable to see each other, kept silent till the lighter, slipping before the fitful breeze, passed out between almost invisible headlands into the still deeper darkness of the gulf. For a time the lantern on the jetty shone after them. The wind failed, then fanned up again, but so faintly that the big, half-decked boat slipped along with no more noise than if she had been suspended in the air.

'We are out in the gulf now,' said the calm voice of Nostromo. A moment after he added, 'Señor Mitchell has lowered the light.'

'Yes,' said Decoud; 'nobody can find us now.'

A great recrudescence of obscurity embraced the boat. The sea in the gulf was as black as the clouds above. Nostromo, after striking a couple of matches to get a glimpse of the boat-compass he had with him in the lighter, steered by the feel of the wind on his cheek.

It was a new experience for Decoud, this mysteriousness of the great waters spread out strangely smooth, as if their restlessness had been crushed by the weight of that dense night. The Placido was sleeping profoundly under its black poncho.

The main thing now for success was to get away from the coast and gain the middle of the gulf before day broke. The Isabels were somewhere at hand. 'On your left as you look forward, *señor*,' said Nostromo, suddenly. When his voice ceased, the enormous stillness, without light or sound, seemed to affect Decoud's senses like a powerful drug. He didn't even know at times whether he were asleep or awake. Like a man lost in slumber, he heard nothing, he saw nothing. Even his hand held before his face did not exist for his eyes. The change from the agitation, the passions and the dangers, from the sights and sounds of the shore, was so complete that it would have resembled death had it not been for the survival of his thoughts. In this foretaste of eternal peace they floated vivid and light, like unearthly clear dreams of earthly things that may haunt the souls freed by death from the misty atmosphere of regrets and hopes. Decoud shook himself, shuddered a bit, though the air that drifted past him was warm. He had the strangest sensation of his soul having just returned into his body from the circumambient darkness in which land, sea, sky, the mountains, and the rocks were as if they had not been.

Nostromo's voice was speaking, though he, at the tiller, was also as if he were not. 'Have you been asleep, Don Martin? *Caramba!* If it were possible I would think that I, too, have dozed off. I have a strange notion somehow of having dreamt that there was a sound of blubbering, a sound a sorrowing man could make, somewhere near this boat. Something between a sigh and a sob.'

'Strange!' muttered Decoud, stretched upon the pile of treasure boxes covered by many tarpaulins. 'Could it be that there is another boat near us in the gulf? We could not see it, you know.'

Nostromo laughed a little at the absurdity of the idea. They dismissed it from their minds. The solitude could almost be felt. And when the breeze ceased, the blackness seemed to weigh upon Decoud like a stone.

'This is overpowering,' he muttered. 'Do we move at all, Capataz?'

'Not so fast as a crawling beetle tangled in the grass,' answered Nostromo, and his voice seemed deadened by the thick veil of obscurity that felt warm and hopeless all about them. There were long periods when he made no sound, invisible and inaudible as if he had mysteriously stepped out of the lighter.

In the featureless night Nostromo was not even certain which way the lighter headed after the wind had completely died out. He peered for the islands. There was not a hint of them to be seen, as if they had sunk to the bottom of the gulf. He threw himself down by the side of Decoud at last, and whispered into his ear that if daylight caught them near the Sulaco shore through want of wind, it would be possible to sweep the lighter behind the cliff at the high end of the Great Isabel, where she would lie concealed.

Decoud was surprised at the grimness of his anxiety. To him the removal of the treasure was a political move. It was necessary for several reasons that it should not fall into the hands of Montero, but here was a man who took another view of this enterprise. The *caballeros* over there did not seem to have the slightest idea of what they had given him to do. Nostromo, as if affected by the gloom around, seemed nervously resentful. Decoud was surprised. The Capataz, indifferent to those dangers that seemed obvious to his companion, allowed himself to become scornfully exasperated by the deadly nature of the trust put, as a matter of course, into his hands. It was more dangerous, Nostromo said, with a laugh and a curse, than sending a man to get the treasure that people said was guarded by devils and ghosts in the deep ravines of Azuera. 'Señor,' he said, 'we must catch the steamer at sea. We must keep out in the open looking for her till we have eaten and drunk all that has been put on board here. And if we miss her by some mischance, we must keep away from the land till we grow weak, and perhaps mad, and die, and drift dead, until one or another of the steamers of the Compania comes upon the boat with the two dead men who have saved the treasure. That, *señor*, is the only way to save it; for, don't you see? for us to come to the land anywhere in a hundred miles along this coast with this silver in our possession is to run the naked breast against the point of a knife. This thing has been given to me like a deadly disease. If men discover it I am dead, and you, too, *señor*, since you would come with me. There is enough silver to make a whole province rich, let alone a seaboard *pueblo* inhabited by thieves and vagabonds. *Señor*, they would think that heaven itself sent these riches into their hands, and would cut our throats without hesitation. I would trust no fair words from the best man around the shores of this wild gulf. Reflect that, even by giving up the treasure at the first demand, we would not be able to save our lives. Do you understand this, or must I explain?'

'No, you needn't explain,' said Decoud, a little listlessly. 'I can see it well enough myself, that the possession of this treasure is very much like a deadly disease for men situated as we are. But it had to be removed from Sulaco, and you were the man for the task.'

'I was; but I cannot believe,' said Nostromo, 'that its loss would have impoverished Don Carlos Gould very much. There is more wealth in the mountain. I have heard it rolling down the shoots on quiet nights when I used to ride to Rincón to see a certain girl, after my work at the harbour was done. For years the rich rocks have been pouring down with a noise like thunder, and the miners say that there is enough at the heart of the mountain to thunder on for years and years to come. And yet, the day before yesterday, we have been fighting to save it from the mob, and tonight I am sent out with it into this darkness, where there is no wind to get away with; as if it were the last lot of silver on earth to get bread for the hungry with. Ha! ha! Well, I am going to make it the most famous and desperate affair of my life – wind or no wind. It shall be talked about when the little children are grown up and the grown men are old. Aha! the Monterists must not get hold of it, I am told, whatever happens to Nostromo the Capataz; and they shall not have it, I tell you, since it has been tied for safety round Nostromo's neck.'

'I see it,' murmured Decoud. He saw, indeed, that his companion had his own peculiar view of this enterprise.

Nostromo interrupted his reflections upon the way men's qualities are made use of, without any fundamental knowledge of their nature, by the proposal they should slip the long oars out and sweep the lighter in the direction of the Isabels. It wouldn't do for daylight to reveal the treasure floating within a mile or so of the harbour entrance. The denser the darkness generally, the smarter were the puffs of wind on which he had reckoned to make his way; but tonight the gulf, under its poncho of clouds, remained breathless, as if dead rather than asleep.

Don Martin's soft hands suffered cruelly, tugging at the thick handle of the enormous oar. He stuck to it manfully, setting his teeth. He, too, was in the toils of an imaginative existence, and that strange work of pulling a lighter seemed to belong naturally to the inception of a new state, and acquired an ideal meaning from his love for Antonia. For all their efforts, the heavily laden lighter hardly moved. Nostromo could be heard swearing to himself between the regular splashes of the sweeps. 'We are making a crooked path,' he muttered to himself. 'I wish I could see the islands.'

In his unskilfulness Don Martin over-exerted himself. Now and then a sort of muscular faintness would run from the tips of his aching fingers through every fibre of his body, and pass off in a flush of heat. He had fought, talked, suffered mentally and physically, exerting his mind and body for the last forty-eight hours without intermission. He had had no rest, very little food, no pause in the stress of his thoughts and his feelings. Even his love for Antonia, whence he drew his strength and his inspiration, had reached the point of tragic tension during their hurried interview by Don José's bedside. And now, suddenly, he was thrown out of all this into a dark gulf, whose very gloom, silence, and breathless peace added a torment to the necessity for physical exertion. He imagined the lighter sinking to the bottom with an extraordinary shudder of delight. 'I am on the verge of delirium,' he thought. He mastered the trembling of all his limbs, of his breast, the inward trembling of all his body exhausted of its nervous force.

'Shall we rest, Capataz?' he proposed in a careless tone. 'There are many hours of night yet before us.'

'True. It is but a mile or so, I suppose. Rest your arms, *señor*, if that is what you mean. You will find no other sort of rest, I can promise you, since you let yourself be bound to this treasure whose loss would make no poor man poorer. No, *señor*; there is no rest till we find a north-bound steamer, or else some ship finds us drifting about stretched out dead upon the Englishman's silver. Or rather – no; *por Dios*! I shall cut down the gunwale with the axe right to the water's edge before thirst and hunger rob me of my strength. By all the saints and devils I shall let the sea have the treasure rather than give it up to any stranger. Since it was the good pleasure of the *caballeros* to send me off on such an errand, they shall learn I am just the man they take me for.'

Decoud lay on the silver boxes panting. All his active sensations and feelings from as far back as he could remember seemed to him the maddest of dreams. Even his passionate devotion to Antonia into which he had worked himself up out of the depths of his scepticism had lost all appearance of reality. For a moment he was the prey of an extremely languid but not unpleasant indifference.

'I am sure they didn't mean you to take such a desperate view of this affair,' he said.

'What was it, then? A joke?' snarled the man, who on the pay-sheets of the O.S.N. Company's establishment in Sulaco was described as 'Foreman of the wharf' against the figure of his wages. 'Was it for a joke they woke me up from my sleep after two days of street fighting to make me stake my life upon a bad card? Everybody knows, too, that I am not a lucky gambler.'

'Yes, everybody knows of your good luck with women, Capataz,' Decoud propitiated his companion in a weary drawl.

'Look here, *señor*,' Nostromo went on. 'I never even remonstrated about this affair. Directly I heard what was wanted I saw what a desperate affair it must be, and I made up my mind to see it out. Every minute was of importance. I had to wait for you first. Then, when we arrived at the Italia Una, old Giorgio shouted to me to go for the English doctor. Later on, that poor dying woman wanted to see me, as you know. *Señor*, I was reluctant to go. I felt already this cursed silver growing heavy upon my back, and I was afraid that, knowing herself to be dying, she would ask me to ride off again for a priest. Father Corbelán, who is fearless, would have come at a word; but Father Corbelán is far away, safe with the band of Hernandez, and the populace, that would have liked to tear him to pieces, are much incensed against the priests. Not a single fat padre would have consented to put his head out of his hiding-place tonight to save a Christian soul, except, perhaps, under my protection. That was in her mind. I pretended I did not believe she was going to die. *Señor*, I refused to fetch a priest for a dying woman. . . .'

Decoud was heard to stir.

'You did, Capataz!' he exclaimed. His tone changed. 'Well, you know – it was rather fine.'

'You do not believe in priests, Don Martin? Neither do I. What was the use of wasting time? But she – she believes in them. The thing sticks in my throat. She may be dead already, and here we· are floating helpless with no wind at all. Curse on all superstition. She died thinking I deprived her of Paradise, I suppose. It shall be the most desperate affair of my life.'

Decoud remained lost in reflection. He tried to analyse the sensations awakened by what he had been told. The voice of the Capataz was heard again:

'Now, Don Martin, let us take up the sweeps and try to find the Isabels. It is either that or sinking the lighter if the day overtakes us. We must not forget that the steamer from Esmeralda with the soldiers may be coming along. We will pull straight on now. I have discovered a bit of a candle here, and we must take the risk of a small light to make a course by the boat compass. There is not enough wind to blow it out – may the curse of Heaven fall upon this blind gulf!'

A small flame appeared burning quite straight. It showed fragmentarily the stout ribs and planking in the hollow, empty part of the lighter. Decoud could see Nostromo standing up to pull. He saw him as high as the red sash on his waist, with a gleam of a white-handled revolver and the wooden haft of a long knife protruding on his left side. Decoud nerved himself for the effort of rowing. Certainly there was not enough wind to blow the candle out, but its flame swayed a little to the slow movement of the heavy boat. It was so big that with their utmost efforts they could not move it quicker than about a mile an hour. This was sufficient, however, to sweep them amongst the Isabels long before daylight came. There was a good six hours of darkness before them, and the distance from the harbour to the Great Isabel did not exceed two miles. Decoud put this heavy toil to the account of the Capataz's impatience. Sometimes they paused, and then strained their ears to hear the boat from Esmeralda. In this perfect quiétness a steamer moving would have been heard from far off. As to seeing anything it was out of the question. They could not see each other. Even the lighter's sail, which remained set, was invisible. Very often they rested.

'*Caramba!*' said Nostromo, suddenly, during one of those intervals when they lolled idly against the heavy handles of the sweeps. 'What is it? Are you distressed, Don Martin?'

Decoud assured him that he was not distressed in the least. Nostromo for a time kept perfectly still, and then in a whisper invited Martin to come aft.

With lips touching Decoud's ear he declared his belief that there was somebody else besides themselves upon the lighter. Twice now he had heard the sound of stifled sobbing.

'*Señor,*' he whispered with awed wonder, 'I am certain that there is somebody weeping in this lighter.'

Decoud had heard nothing. He expressed his incredulity. However, it was easy to ascertain the truth of the matter.

'It is most amazing,' muttered Nostromo. 'Could anybody have concealed himself on board while the lighter was lying alongside the wharf?'

'And you say it was like sobbing?' asked Decoud, lowering his voice, too. 'If he is weeping, whoever he is he cannot be very dangerous.'

Clambering over the precious pile in the middle, they crouched low on the foreside of the mast and groped under the half-deck. Right forward, in the narrowest part, their hands came upon the limbs of a man, who remained as silent as death. Too startled themselves to make a sound, they dragged him aft by one arm and the collar of his coat. He was limp – lifeless.

The light of the bit of candle fell upon a round, hook-nosed face with black moustaches and little side-whiskers. He was extremely dirty. A greasy growth of beard was sprouting on the shaven parts of the cheeks. The thick lips were slightly parted, but the eyes remained closed. Decoud, to his immense astonishment, recognized Señor Hirsch, the hide merchant from Esmeralda. Nostromo, too, had recognized him. And they gazed at each other across the body, lying with its naked feet higher than its head, in an absurd pretence of sleep, faintness, or death.

CHAPTER 8

For a moment, before this extraordinary find, they forgot their own concerns and sensations. Señor Hirsch's sensations as he lay there must have been those of extreme terror. For a long time he refused to give a sign of life, till at last Decoud's objurgations, and, perhaps more, Nostromo's impatient suggestion that he should be thrown overboard, as he seemed to be dead, induced him to raise one eyelid first, and then the other.

It appeared that he had never found a safe opportunity to leave Sulaco. He lodged with Anzani, the universal storekeeper, on the Plaza Mayor. But when the riot broke out he had made his escape from his host's house before daylight, and in such a hurry that he had forgotten to put on his shoes. He had run out impulsively in his socks, and with his hat in his hand, into the garden of Anzani's house. Fear gave him the necessary agility to climb over several low walls, and afterwards he blundered into the overgrown cloisters of the ruined Franciscan convent in one of the by-streets. He forced himself into the midst of matted bushes with the recklessness of desperation, and this accounted for his scratched body and his torn clothing. He lay hidden there all day, his tongue cleaving to the roof of his mouth with all the intensity of thirst engendered by heat and fear. Three times different bands of men invaded the place with shouts and imprecations, looking for Father Corbelán; but towards the evening, still lying on his face in the bushes, he thought he would die from the fear of silence. He was not very clear as to what had induced him to leave the place, but evidently he had got out and slunk successfully out of town along the deserted back lanes. He wandered in the darkness near the railway, so maddened by apprehension that he dared not even approach the fires of the pickets of Italian workmen guarding the line. He had a vague idea evidently of finding refuge in the railway yards, but the dogs rushed upon him, barking; men began to shout; a shot was fired at random. He fled away from the gates. By the merest accident, as it happened, he took the direction of the O.S.N. Company's offices. Twice he stumbled upon the bodies of men killed during the day. But everything living frightened him much more. He crouched, crept, crawled, made dashes, guided by a sort of animal instinct, keeping away from every light and from every sound of voices. His idea was to throw himself at the feet of Captain Mitchell and beg for shelter in the Company's offices. It was all dark there as he approached on his hands and knees, but suddenly someone on guard challenged loudly, '*Quién vive?*' There were more dead men lying about, and he flattened himself down at once by the side of a cold corpse. He heard a voice saying, 'Here is one of those wounded rascals crawling about. Shall I go and finish him?' And another voice objected that it was not safe to go out without a lantern upon such an errand; perhaps it was only some Negro liberal looking for a chance to stick a knife into the stomach of an honest man. Hirsch didn't stay to hear any more, but crawling away to the end of the wharf, hid himself amongst a lot of empty casks. After a while some people came along, talking, and with glowing cigarettes. He did not stop to ask himself whether they would be likely to do him any harm, but bolted incontinently along the jetty, saw a lighter lying moored at the end, and threw himself into it. In his desire to find cover he crept right forward under the half-deck, and he had remained there more dead than alive, suffering agonies of hunger and thirst, and almost fainting with terror, when he heard numerous footsteps and the voices of the Europeans who came in a body escorting the wagon-load of treasure, pushed along the rails by a squad of *cargadores*. He understood perfectly what was being done from the talk, but did not disclose his presence from the fear that he would not be allowed to remain. His only idea at the time, overpowering and masterful, was to get away from this terrible Sulaco. And now he regretted it very much. He had heard Nostromo talk to Decoud, and wished himself back on shore. He did not desire to be involved in any desperate affair – in a situation where one could not run away. The involuntary groans of his anguished spirit had betrayed him to the sharp ears of the Capataz.

They had propped him up in a sitting posture against the side of the lighter, and he went on with the moaning account of his adventures till his voice broke, his head fell foward. 'Water,' he whispered, with difficulty. Decoud held one of the cans to his lips. He revived after an extraordinarily short time, and scrambled up to his feet wildly. Nostromo, in an angry and threatening voice, ordered him forward. Hirsch was one of those men whom fear lashes like a whip, and he must have had an appalling idea of the Capataz's ferocity. He displayed an extraordinary agility in disappearing forward into the darkness. They heard him getting over the tarpaulin; then there was the sound of a heavy fall, followed by a weary sigh. Afterwards all was still in the fore-part of the lighter, as though he had killed himself in his headlong tumble. Nostromo shouted in a menacing voice:

'Lie still there! Do not move a limb. If I hear as much as a loud breath from you I shall come over there and put a bullet through your head.'

The mere presence of a coward, however passive, brings an element of treachery into a dangerous situation. Nostromo's nervous impatience passed into gloomy thoughtfulness. Decoud, in an undertone, as if speaking to himself, remarked that, after all, this bizarre event made no great difference. He could not conceive what harm the man could do. At most he would be in the way, like an inanimate and useless object – like a block of wood, for instance.

'I would think twice before getting rid of a piece of wood,' said Nostromo, calmly. 'Something may happen unexpectedly where you could make use of it. But in an affair like ours a man like this ought to be thrown overboard. Even if he were as brave as a lion we would not want him here. We are not running away for our lives. *Señor*, there is no harm in a brave man trying to save himself with ingenuity and courage; but you have heard his tale, Don Martin. His being here is a miracle of fear –' Nostromo paused. 'There is no room for fear in this lighter,' he added through his teeth.

Decoud had no answer to make. It was not a position for argument, for a display of scruples or feelings. There were a thousand ways in which a panic-stricken man could make himself dangerous. It was evident that Hirsch could not be spoken to, reasoned with, or persuaded into a rational line of conduct. The story of his own escape demonstrated that clearly enough. Decoud thought that it was a thousand pities the wretch had not died of fright. Nature, who had made him what he was, seemed to have calculated cruelly how much he could bear in the way of atrocious anguish without actually expiring. Some compassion was due to so much terror. Decoud, though imaginative enough for sympathy, resolved not to interfere with any action that Nostromo would take. But Nostromo did nothing. And the fate of Señor Hirsch remained suspended in the darkness of the gulf at the mercy of events which could not be foreseen.

The Capataz, extending his hand, put out the candle suddenly. It was to Decoud as if his companion had destroyed, by a single touch, the world of affairs, of loves, of revolution, where his complacent superiority analysed fearlessly all motives and all passions, including his own.

He gasped a little. Decoud was affected by the novelty of his position. Intellectually self-confident, he suffered from being deprived of the only weapon he could use with effect. No intelligence could penetrate the darkness of the Placid Gulf. There remained only one thing he was certain of, and that was the overweening vanity of his companion. It was direct, uncomplicated, naïve, and effectual. Decoud, who had been making use of him, had tried to understand his man thoroughly. He had discovered a complete singleness of motive behind the varied manifestations of a consistent character. This was why the man remained so astonishingly simple in the jealous greatness of his conceit. And now there was a complication. It was evident that he resented having been given a task in which there were so many chances of failure. 'I wonder,' thought Decoud, 'how he would behave if I were not here.'

He heard Nostromo mutter again, 'No! there is no room for fear on this lighter. Courage itself does not seem good enough. I have a good eye and a steady hand; no man can say he ever saw me tired or uncertain what to do; but *por Dios*, Don Martin, I have been sent out into this black calm on a business where neither a good eye, nor a steady hand, nor judgement are any use. . . .' He swore a string of oaths in Spanish and Italian under his breath. 'Nothing but sheer desperation will do for this affair.'

These words were in strange contrast to the prevailing peace – to this almost stolid stillness of the gulf. A shower fell with an abrupt whispering sound all round the boat, and Decoud took off his hat, and, letting his head get wet, felt greatly refreshed. Presently a steady little draught of air caressed his cheek. The lighter began to move, but the shower distanced it. The drops ceased to fall upon his head and hands, the whispering died out in the distance. Nostromo emitted a grunt of satisfaction, and grasping the tiller, chirruped softly, as sailors do, to encourage the wind. Never for the last three days had Decoud felt less the need for what the Capataz would call desperation.

'I fancy I hear another shower on the water,' he observed in a tone of quiet content. 'I hope it will catch us up.'

Nostromo ceased chirruping at once. 'You hear another shower?' he said, doubtfully. A sort of thinning of the darkness seemed to have taken place, and Decoud could see now the outline of his companion's figure, and even the sail came out of the night like a square block of dense snow.

The sound which Decoud had detected came along the water harshly. Nostromo recognized that noise partaking of a hiss and a rustle which spreads out on all sides of a steamer making her way through a smooth water on a quiet night. It could be nothing else but the captured transport with troops from Esmeralda. She carried no lights. The noise of her steaming, growing louder every minute, would stop at times altogether, and then begin again abruptly, and sound startlingly nearer, as if that invisible vessel, whose position could not be precisely guessed, were making straight for the lighter. Meantime, that last kept on sailing slowly and noiselessly before a breeze so faint that it was only by leaning over the side and feeling the water slip through his fingers that Decoud convinced himself they were moving at all. His drowsy feeling had departed. He was glad to know that the lighter was moving. After so much stillness the noise of the steamer seemed uproarious and distracting. There was a weirdness in not being able to see her. Suddenly all was still. She had stopped, but so close to them that the steam, blowing off, sent its rumbling vibration right over their heads.

'They are trying to make out where they are,' said Decoud in a whisper. Again he leaned over and put his fingers into the water. 'We are moving quite smartly,' he informed Nostromo.

'We seem to be crossing her bows,' said the Capataz in a cautious tone. 'But this is a blind game with death. Moving on is of no use. We mustn't be seen or heard.'

His whisper was hoarse with excitement. Of all his face there was nothing visible but a gleam of white eyeballs. His fingers gripped Decoud's shoulder. 'That is the only way to save this treasure from this steamer full of soldiers. Any other would have carried lights. But you observe there is not a gleam to show us where she is.'

Decoud stood as if paralysed; only his thoughts were wildly active. In the space of a second he remembered the desolate glance of Antonia as he left her at the bedside of her father in the gloomy house of Avellanos, with shuttered windows, but all the doors standing open, and deserted by all the servants except an old Negro at the gate. He remembered the Casa Gould on his last visit, the arguments, the tones of his voice, the impenetrable attitude of Charles, Mrs Gould's face so blanched with anxiety and fatigue that her eyes seemed to have changed colour, appearing nearly black by contrast. Even whole sentences of the proclamation which he meant to make Barrios issue from his headquarters at Cayta as soon as he got there passed through his mind; the very germ of the new State, the Separationist proclamation which he had tried before he left to read hurriedly to Don José, stretched out on his bed under the fixed gaze of his daughter. God knows whether the old statesman had understood it; he was unable to speak, but he had certainly lifted his arm off the coverlet; his hand had moved as if to make the sign of the cross in the air, a gesture of blessing, of consent. Decoud had that very draft in his pocket, written in pencil on several loose sheets of paper, with the heavily printed heading, 'Administration of the San Tomé Silver Mine. Sulaco. Republic of Costaguana.' He had written it furiously, snatching page after page on Charles Gould's table. Mrs Gould had looked several times over his shoulder as he wrote; but the Señor Administrador, standing straddle-legged, would not even glance at it when it was finished. He had waved it away firmly. It must have been scorn, and not caution, since he never made a remark about the use of the Administration's paper for such a compromising document. And that showed his disdain, the true English disdain of common prudence, as if everything outside the range of their own thoughts and feelings were unworthy of serious recognition. Decoud had the time in a second or two to become furiously angry with Charles Gould, and even resentful against Mrs Gould, in whose care, tacitly it is true, he had left the safety of Antonia. Better perish a thousand times than owe your preservation to such people, he exclaimed mentally. The grip of Nostromo's fingers never removed from his shoulder, tightening fiercely, recalled him to himself.

'The darkness is our friend,' the Capataz murmured into his ear. 'I am going to lower the sail, and trust our escape to this black gulf. No eyes could make us out lying silent with a naked mast. I will do it now, before this steamer closes still more upon us. The faint creak of a block would betray us and the San Tomé treasure into the hands of those thieves.'

He moved about as warily as a cat. Decoud heard no sound; and it was only by the disappearance of the square blotch of darkness that he knew the yard had come down, lowered as carefully as if it had been made of glass. Next moment he heard Nostromo's quiet breathing by his side.

'You had better not move at all from where you are, Don Martin,' advised the Capataz, earnestly. 'You might stumble or displace something which would make a noise. The sweeps and the punting poles are lying about. Move not for your life. *Por Dios*, Don Martin,' he went on in a keen but friendly whisper, 'I am so desperate that if I didn't know your worship to be a man of courage, capable of standing stock still whatever happens, I would drive my knife into your heart.'

A deathlike stillness surrounded the lighter. It was difficult to believe that there was near a steamer full of men with many pairs of eyes peering from her bridge for some hint of land in the night. Her steam had ceased blowing off, and she remained stopped too far off apparently for any other sound to reach the lighter.

'Perhaps you would, Capataz,' Decoud began in a whisper. 'However, you need not trouble. There are other things than the fear of your knife to keep my heart steady. It shall not betray you. Only, have you forgotten – '

'I spoke to you openly as to a man as desperate as myself,' explained the Capataz. 'The silver must be saved from the Monterists. I told Captain Mitchell three times that I preferred to go alone. I told Don Carlos Gould, too. It was in the Casa Gould. They had sent for me. The ladies were there; and when I tried to explain why I did not wish to have you with me, they promised me, both of them great rewards for your safety. A strange way to talk to a man you are sending out to an almost certain death. Those gentlefolk do not seem to have sense enough to understand what they are giving one to do. I told them I could do nothing for you. You would have been safer with the bandit Hernandez. It would have been possible to ride out of the town with no greater risk than a chance shot sent after you in the dark. But it was as if they had been deaf. I had to promise I would wait for you under the harbour gate. I did wait. And now because you are a brave man you are as safe as the silver. Neither more nor less.'

At that moment, as if by way of comment upon Nostromo's words, the invisible steamer went ahead at half speed only, as could be judged by the leisurely beat of her propeller. The sound shifted its place markedly, but without coming nearer. It even grew a little more distant right abeam of the lighter, and ceased again.

'They are trying for a sight of the Isabels,' muttered Nostromo, 'in order to make for the harbour in a straight line and seize the Custom House with the treasure in it. Have you ever seen the Commandant of Esmeralda, Sotillo? A handsome fellow, with a soft voice. When I first came here I used to see him in the Calle talking to the *señoritas* at the windows of the houses, and showing his white teeth all the time. But one of my *cargadores*, who had been a soldier, told me that he had once ordered a man to be flayed alive in the remote Campo, where he was sent recruiting amongst the people of the *estancias*. It has never entered his head that the *compañia* had a man capable of baffling his game.'

The murmuring loquacity of the Capataz disturbed Decoud like a hint of weakness. And yet, talkative resolution may be as genuine as grim silence.

'Sotillo is not baffled so far,' he said. 'Have you forgotten that crazy man forward?'

Nostromo had not forgotten Señor Hirsch. He reproached himself bitterly for not having visited the lighter carefully before leaving the wharf. He reproached himself for not having stabbed and flung Hirsch overboard at the very moment of discovery without even looking at his face. That would have been consistent with the desperate character of the affair. Whatever happened, Sotillo *was* already baffled. Even if that wretch, now as silent as death, did anything to betray the nearness of the lighter, Sotillo – if Sotillo it was in command of the troops on board – would be still baffled of his plunder.

'I have an axe in my hand,' Nostromo whispered, wrathfully, 'that in three strokes would cut through the side down to the water's edge. Moreover, each lighter has a plug in the stern, and I know exactly where it is. I feel it under the sole of my foot.'

Decoud recognized the ring of genuine determination in the nervous murmurs, the vindictive excitement of the famous Capataz. Before the steamer, guided by a shriek or two (for there could be no more than that, Nostromo said, gnashing his teeth audibly), could find the lighter there would be plenty of time to sink this treasure tied up round his neck.

The last words he hissed into Decoud's ear. Decoud said nothing. He was perfectly convinced. The usual characteristic quietness of the man was gone. It was not equal to the situation as he conceived it. Something deeper, something unsuspected by everyone, had come to the surface. Decoud, with careful movements, slipped off his overcoat and divested himself of his boots; he did not consider himself bound in honour to sink with the treasure. His object was to get down to Barrios, in Cayta, as the Capataz knew very well; and he, too, meant, in his own way, to put into that attempt all the desperation of which he was capable. Nostromo muttered, 'True, true! You are a politician, *señor*. Rejoin the army, and start another revolution.' He pointed out, however, that there was a little boat belonging to every lighter fit to carry two men, if not more. Theirs was towing behind.

Of that Decoud had not been aware. Of course, it was too dark to see, and it was only when Nostromo put his hand upon its painter fastened to a cleat in the stern that he experienced a full measure of relief. The prospect of finding himself in the water and swimming, overwhelmed by ignorance and darkness, probably in a circle, till he sank from exhaustion, was revolting. The barren and cruel futility of such an end intimidated his affectation of careless pessimism. In comparison to it, the chance of being left floating in a boat, exposed to thirst, hunger, discovery, imprisonment, execution, presented itself with an aspect of amenity worth securing even at the cost of some self-contempt. He did not accept Nostromo's proposal that he should get into the boat at once. 'Something sudden may overwhelm us, *señor*,' the Capataz remarked promising faithfully, at the same time, to let go the painter at the moment when the necessity became manifest.

But Decoud assured him lightly that he did not mean to take to the boat till the very last moment, and that then he meant the Capataz to come along, too. The darkness of the gulf was no longer for him the end of all things. It was part of a living world since, pervading it, failure and death could be felt at your elbow. And at the same time it was a shelter. He exulted in its impenetrable obscurity. 'Like a wall, like a wall,' he muttered to himself.

The only thing which checked his confidence was the thought of Señor Hirsch. Not to have bound and gagged him seemed to Decoud now the height of improvident folly. As long as the miserable creature had the power to raise a yell he was a constant danger. His abject terror was mute now, but there was no saying from what cause it might suddenly find vent in shrieks.

This very madness of fear which both Decoud and Nostromo had seen in the wild and irrational glances, and in the continuous twitchings of his mouth, protected Señor Hirsch from the cruel necessities of this desperate affair. The moment of silencing him for ever had passed. As Nostromo remarked, in answer to Decoud's regrets, it was too late! It could not be done without noise, especially in the ignorance of the man's exact position. Wherever he had elected to crouch and tremble, it was too hazardous to go near him. He would begin probably to yell for mercy. It was much better to leave him quite alone since he was keeping so still. But to trust to his silence became every moment a greater strain upon Decoud's composure.

'I wish, Capataz, you had not let the right moment pass,' he murmured.

'What! To silence him for ever! I thought it good to hear first how he came to be here. It was too strange. Who could imagine that it was all an accident? Afterwards, *señor*, when I saw you giving him water to drink, I could not do it. Not after I had seen you holding up the can to his lips as though he were your brother. *Señor*, that sort of necessity must not be thought of too long. And yet it would have been no cruelty to take away from him his wretched life. It is nothing but fear. Your compassion saved him then, Don Martin, and now it is too late. It couldn't be done without noise.'

In the steamer they were keeping a perfect silence, and the stillness was so profound that Decoud felt as if the slightest sound conceivable must travel unchecked and audible to the end of the world. What if Hirsch coughed or sneezed? To feel himself at the mercy of such an idiotic contingency was too exasperating to be looked upon with irony. Nostromo too, seemed to be getting restless. Was it possible, he asked himself, that the steamer, finding the night too dark altogether, intended to remain stopped where she was till daylight? He began to think that this, after all, was the real danger. He was afraid that the darkness, which was his protection, would, in the end, cause his undoing.

Sotillo, as Nostromo had surmised, was in command on board the transport. The events of the last forty-eight hours in Sulaco were not known to him; neither was he aware that the telegraphist in Esmeralda had managed to warn his colleague in Sulaco. Like a good many officers of the troops garrisoning the province, Sotillo had been influenced in his adoption of the Ribierist cause by the belief that it had the enormous wealth of the Gould Concession on its side. He had been one of the frequenters of the Casa Gould, where he had aired his Blanco convictions and his ardour for reform before Don José Avellanos, casting frank, honest glances towards Mrs Gould and Antonia the while. He was known to belong to a good family persecuted and impoverished during the tyranny of Guzman Bento. The opinions he expressed appeared eminently natural and proper in a man of his parentage and antecedents. And he was not a deceiver; it was perfectly natural for him to express elevated sentiments while his whole faculties were taken up with what seemed then a solid and practical notion – the notion that the husband of Antonia Avellanos would be, naturally, the intimate friend of the Gould Concession. He even pointed this out to Anzani once, when negotiating the sixth or seventh small loan in the gloomy, damp apartment with enormous iron bars, behind the principal shop in the whole row under the Arcades. He hinted to the universal shopkeeper at the excellent terms he was on with the emancipated *señorita*, who was like a sister to the Englishwoman. He would advance one leg and put his arms akimbo, posing for Anzani's inspection, and fixing him with a haughty stare.

'Look, miserable shopkeeper! How can a man like me fail with any woman, let alone an emancipated girl living in scandalous freedom?' he seemed to say.

His manner in the Casa Gould was, of course, very different – devoid of all truculence, and even slightly mournful. Like most of his countrymen, he was carried away by the sound of fine words, especially if uttered by himself. He had no convictions of any sort upon anything except as to the irresistible power of his personal advantages. But that was so firm that even Decoud's appearance in Sulaco, and his intimacy with the Goulds and the Avellanos, did not disquiet him. On the contrary, he tried to make friends with that rich Costaguanero from Europe in the hope of borrowing a large sum by-and-by. The only guiding motive of his life was to get money for the satisfaction of his expensive tastes, which he indulged recklessly, having no self-control. He imagined himself a master of intrigue, but his corruption was as simple as an animal instinct. At times, in solitude, he had his moments of ferocity, and also on such occasions as, for instance, when alone in a room with Anzani trying to get a loan.

He had talked himself into the command of the Esmeralda garrison. That small seaport had its importance as the station of the main submarine cable connecting the Occidental Provinces with the outer world, and the junction with it of the Sulaco branch. Don José Avellanos proposed him, and Barrios, with a rude and jeering guffaw, had said, 'Oh, let Sotillo go. He is a very good man to keep guard over the cable, and the ladies of Esmeralda ought to have their turn.' Barrios, an indubitably brave man, had no great opinion of Sotillo.

It was through the Esmeralda cable alone that the San Tomé mine could be kept in constant touch with the great financier, whose tacit approval made the strength of the Ribierist movement. This movement had its adversaries even there. Sotillo governed Esmeralda with repressive severity till the adverse course of events upon the distant theatre of civil war forced upon him the reflection that, after all, the great silver mine was fated to become the spoil of the victors. But caution was necessary. He began by assuming a dark and mysterious attitude towards the faithful Ribierist municipality of Esmeralda. Later on, the information that the commandant was holding assemblies of officers in the dead of night (which had leaked out somehow) caused those gentlemen to neglect their civil duties altogether, and remain shut up in their houses. Suddenly one day all the letters from Sulaco by the overland courier were carried off by a file of soldiers from the post office to the Comandancia, without disguise, concealment, or apology. Sotillo had heard through Cayta of the final defeat of Ribiera.

This was the first open sign of the change in his convictions. Presently notorious democrats, who had been living till then in constant fear of arrest, leg irons, and even floggings, could be observed going in and out at the great door of the Comandancia, where the horses of the orderlies doze under their heavy saddles, while the men, in ragged uniforms and pointed straw hats, lounge on a bench, with their naked feet stuck out beyond the strip of shade; and a sentry, in a red baize coat with holes at the elbows, stands at the top of the steps glaring haughtily at the common people, who uncover their heads to him as they pass.

Sotillo's ideas did not soar above the care for his personal safety and the chance of plundering the town in his charge, but he feared that such a late adhesion would earn but scant gratitude from the victors. He had believed just a little too long in the power of the San Tomé mine. The seized correspondence had confirmed his previous information of a large amount of silver ingots lying in the Sulaco Custom House. To gain possession of it would be a clear Monterist move; a sort of service that would have to be rewarded. With the silver in his hands he could make terms for himself and his soldiers. He was aware neither of the riots, nor of the President's escape to Sulaco and the close pursuit led by Montero's brother, the *guerrillero*. The game seemed in his own hands. The initial moves were the seizure of the cable telegraph office and the securing of the Government steamer lying in the narrow creek which is the harbour of Esmeralda. The last was effected without difficulty by a company of soldiers swarming with a rush over the gangways as she lay alongside the quay; but the lieutenant charged with the duty of arresting the telegraphist halted on the way before the only café in Esmeralda, where he distributed some brandy to his men, and refreshed himself at the expense of the owner, a known Ribierist. The whole party became intoxicated, and proceeded on their mission up the street yelling and firing random shots at the windows. This little festivity, which might have turned out dangerous to the telegraphist's life, enabled him in the end to send his warning to Sulaco. The lieutenant, staggering upstairs with a drawn sabre, was before long kissing him on both cheeks in one of those swift changes of mood peculiar to a state of drunkenness. He clasped the telegraphist close round the neck, assuring him that all the officers of the Esmeralda garrison were going to be made colonels, while tears of happiness streamed down his sodden face. Thus it came about that the town major, coming along later, found the whole party sleeping on the stairs and in passages, and the telegraphist (who scorned this chance of escape) very busy clicking the key of the transmitter. The major led him away bareheaded, with his hands tied behind his back, but concealed the truth from Sotillo, who remained in ignorance of the warning despatched to Sulaco.

The colonel was not the man to let any sort of darkness stand in the way of the planned surprise. It appeared to him a dead certainty; his heart was set upon his object with an ungovernable, childlike impatience. Ever since the steamer had rounded Punta Mala, to enter the deeper shadow of the gulf, he had remained on the bridge in a group of officers as excited as himself. Distracted between the coaxings and menaces of Sotillo and his Staff, the miserable commander of the steamer kept her moving with as much prudence as they would let him exercise. Some of them had been drinking heavily, no doubt; but the prospect of laying hands on so much wealth made them absurdly foolhardy, and, at the same time, extremely anxious. The old major of the battalion, a stupid, suspicious man, who had never been afloat in his life, distinguished himself by putting out suddenly the binnacle light, the only one allowed on board for the necessities of navigation. He could not understand of what use it could be for finding the way. To the vehement protestations of the ship's captain, he stamped his foot and tapped the handle of his sword. 'Aha! I have unmasked you,' he cried, triumphantly. 'You are tearing your hair from despair at my acuteness. Am I a child to believe that a light in that brass box can show you where the harbour is? I am an old soldier, I am. I can smell a traitor a league off. You wanted the gleam to betray our approach to your friend the Englishman. A thing like that show you the way! What a miserable lie! *Que picardía!* You Sulaco people are all in the pay of those foreigners. You deserve to be run through the body with my sword.' Other officers, crowding round, tried to calm his indignation, repeating persuasively, 'No, no! This is an appliance of the mariners, major. This is no treachery.' The captain of the transport flung himself face downwards on the bridge, and refused to rise. 'Put an end to me at once,' he repeated in a stifled voice. Sotillo had to interfere.

The uproar and confusion on the bridge became so great that the helmsman fled from the wheel. He took refuge in the engine-room, and alarmed the engineers, who, disregarding the threats of the soldiers set on guard over them, stopped the engines, protesting that they would rather be shot than run the risk of being drowned down below.

This was the first time Nostromo and Decoud heard the steamer stop. After order had been restored, and the binnacle lamp relighted, she went ahead again, passing wide of the lighter in her search for the Isabels. The group could not be made out, and, at the pitiful entreaties of the captain, Sotillo allowed the engines to be stopped again to wait for one of those periodical lightenings of darkness caused by the shifting of the cloud canopy spread above the waters of the gulf.

Sotillo, on the bridge, muttered from time to time angrily to the captain. The other, in an apologetic and cringing tone, begged *su merced* the colonel to take into consideration the limitations put upon human faculties by the darkness of the night. Sotillo swelled with rage and impatience. It was the chance of a lifetime.

'If your eyes are of no more use to you than this, I shall have them put out,' he burst out.

The captain of the steamer made no answer, for just then the mass of the Great Isabel loomed up darkly after a passing shower, then vanished, as if swept away by a wave of greater obscurity preceding another downpour. This was enough for him. In the voice of a man come back to life again, he informed Sotillo that in an hour he would be alongside the Sulaco wharf. The ship was put then full speed on the course, and a great bustle of preparation for landing arose among the soldiers on her deck.

It was heard distinctly by Decoud and Nostromo. The Capataz understood its meaning. They had made out the Isabels, and were going on now in a straight line for Sulaco. He judged that they would pass close; but believed that lying still like this, with the sail lowered, the lighter could not be seen. 'No, not even if they rubbed sides with us,' he muttered.

The rain began to fall again; first like a wet mist, then with a heavier touch, thickening into a smart, perpendicular downpour; and the hiss and thump of the approaching steamer was coming extremely near. Decoud, with his eyes full of water, and lowered head, asked himself how long it would be before she drew past, when unexpectedly he felt a lurch. An inrush of foam broke swishing over the stern, simultaneously with a crack of timbers and a staggering shock. He had the impression of an angry hand laying hold of the lighter and dragging it along to destruction. The shock, of course, had knocked him down, and he found himself rolling in a lot of water at the bottom of the lighter. A violent churning went on alongside; a strange and amazed voice cried out something above him in the night. He heard a piercing shriek for help from Señor Hirsch. He kept his teeth hard set all the time. It was a collision!

The steamer had struck the lighter obliquely, heeling her over till she was half swamped, starting some of her timbers, and swinging her head parallel to her own course with the force of the blow. The shock of it on board of her was hardly perceptible. All the violence of that collision was, as usual, felt only on board the smaller craft. Even Nostromo himself thought that this was perhaps the end of his desperate adventure. He, too, had been flung away from the long tiller, which took charge of the lurch. Next moment the steamer would have passed on, leaving the lighter to sink or swim after having shouldered her thus out of her way, and without even getting a glimpse of her form, had it not been that, being deeply laden with stores and the great number of people on board, her anchor was low enough to hook itself into one of the wire shrouds of the lighter's mast. For the space of two or three gasping breaths that new rope held against the sudden strain. It was this that gave Decoud the sensation of the snatching pull, dragging the lighter away to destruction. The cause of it, of course, was inexplicable to him. The whole thing was so sudden that he had no time to think. But all his sensations were perfectly clear; he had kept complete possession of himself; in fact, he was even pleasantly aware of that calmness at the very moment of being pitched head first over the transom, to struggle on his back in a lot of water. Señor Hirsch's shriek he had heard and recognized while he was regaining his feet, always with that mysterious sensation of being dragged headlong through the darkness. Not a word, not a cry escaped him; he had no time to see anything; and following upon the despairing screams for help, the dragging motion ceased so suddenly that he staggered forward with open arms and fell against the pile of treasure boxes. He clung to them instinctively, in the vague apprehension of being flung about again; and immediately he heard another lot of shrieks for help, prolonged and despairing, not near him at all, but unaccountably in the distance, away from the lighter altogether, as if some spirit in the night were mocking at Señor Hirsch's terror and despair.

Then all was still – as still as when you wake up in your bed in a dark room from a bizarre and agitated dream. The lighter rocked slightly; the rain was still falling. Two groping hands took hold of his bruised sides from behind, and the Capataz's voice whispered, in his ear, 'Silence, for your life! Silence! The steamer has stopped.'

Decoud listened. The gulf was dumb. He felt the water nearly up to his knees. 'Are we sinking?' he asked in a faint breath.

'I don't know,' Nostromo breathed back to him. '*Señor*, make not the slightest sound.'

Hirsch, when ordered forward by Nostromo, had not returned into his first hiding-place. He had fallen near the mast, and had no strength to rise; moreover, he feared to move. He had given himself up for dead, but not on any rational grounds. It was simply a cruel and terrifying feeling. Whenever he tried to think what would become of him his teeth would start chattering violently. He was too absorbed in the utter misery of his fear to take notice of anything.

Though he was stifling under the lighter's sail which Nostromo had unwittingly lowered on top of him, he did not even dare to put out his head till the very moment of the steamer striking. Then, indeed, he leaped right out, spurred on to new miracles of bodily vigour by this new shape of danger. The inrush of water when the lighter heeled over unsealed his lips. His shriek, 'Save me!' was the first distinct warning of the collision for the people on board the steamer. Next moment the wire shroud parted and the released anchor swept over the lighter's forecastle. It came against the breast of Señor Hirsch, who simply seized hold of it, without in the least knowing what it was, but curling his arms and legs upon the part above the fluke with an invincible, unreasonable tenacity. The lighter yawed off wide, and the steamer, moving on, carried him away, clinging hard, and shouting for help. It was some time, however, after the steamer had stopped that his position was discovered. His sustained yelping for help seemed to come from somebody swimming in the water. At last a couple of men went over the bows and hauled him on board. He was carried straight off to Sotillo on the bridge. His examination confirmed the impression that some craft had been run over and sunk, but it was impracticable on such a dark night to look for the positive proof of floating wreckage. Sotillo was more anxious than ever now to enter the harbour without loss of time; the idea that he had destroyed the principal object of his expedition was too intolerable to be accepted. This feeling made the story he had heard appear the more incredible. Señor Hirsch, after being beaten a little for telling lies, was thrust into the chartroom. But he was beaten only a little. His tale had taken the heart out of Sotillo's Staff, though they all repeated round their chief, 'Impossible! impossible!' with the exception of the old major, who triumphed gloomily.

'I told you; I told you,' he mumbled. 'I could smell some treachery, some *diablería* a league off.'

Meantime, the steamer had kept on her way towards Sulaco where only the truth of that matter could be ascertained. Decoud and Nostromo heard the loud churning of her propeller diminish and die out; and then, with no useless words, busied themselves in making for the Isabels. The last shower had brought with it a gentle but steady breeze. The danger was not over yet, and there was no time for talk. The lighter was leaking like a sieve. They splashed in the water at every step. The Capataz put into Decoud's hands the handle of the pump which was fitted at the side aft, and at once, without question or remark, Decoud began to pump in utter forgetfulness of every desire but that of keeping the treasure afloat. Nostromo hoisted the sail, flew back to the tiller, pulled at the sheet like mad. The short flare of a match (they had been kept dry in a tight tin box, though the man himself was completely wet), the vivid flare of a match, disclosed to the toiling Decoud the eagerness of his face, bent low over the box of the compass, and the attentive stare of his eyes. He knew now where he was, and he hoped to run the sinking lighter ashore in the shallow cove where the high, cliff-like end of the Great Isabel is divided in two equal parts by a deep and overgrown ravine.

Decoud pumped without intermission. Nostromo steered without relaxing for a second the intense, peering effort of his stare. Each of them was as if utterly alone with his task. It did not occur to them to speak. There was nothing in common between them but the knowledge that the damaged lighter must be slowly but surely sinking. In that knowledge, which was like the crucial test of their desires, they seemed to have become completely estranged, as if they had discovered in the very shock of the collision that the loss of the lighter would not mean the same thing to them both. This common danger brought their differences in aim, in view, in character, and in position, into absolute prominence in the private vision of each. There was no bond of conviction, of common idea; they were merely two adventurers pursuing each his own adventure, involved in the same imminence of deadly peril. Therefore they had nothing to say to each other. But this peril, this only incontrovertible truth in which they shared, seemed to act as an inspiration to their mental and bodily powers.

There was certainly something almost miraculous in the way the Capataz made the cove with nothing but the shadowy hint of the island's shape and the vague gleam of a small sandy strip for a guide. Where the ravine opens between the cliffs, and a slender, shallow rivulet meanders out of the bushes to lose itself in the sea, the lighter was run ashore; and the two men, with a taciturn, undaunted energy, began to discharge her precious freight, carrying each ox-hide box up the bed of the rivulet beyond the bushes to a hollow place which the caving in of the soil had made below the roots of a large tree. Its big smooth trunk leaned like a falling column far over the trickle of water running amongst the loose stones.

A couple of years before Nostromo had spent a whole Sunday, all alone, exploring the island. He explained this to Decoud after their task was done, and they sat, weary in every limb, with their legs hanging down the low bank, and their backs against the tree, like a pair of blind men aware of each other and their surroundings by some indefinable sixth sense.

'Yes,' Nostromo repeated, 'I never forget a place I have carefully looked at once.' He spoke slowly, almost lazily, as if there had been a whole leisurely life before him, instead of the scanty two hours before daylight. The existence of the treasure, barely concealed in this improbable spot, laid a burden of secrecy upon every contemplated step, upon every intention and plan of future conduct. He felt the partial failure of this desperate affair entrusted to the great reputation he had known how to make for himself. However, it was also a partial success. His vanity was half appeased. His nervous irritation had subsided.

'You never know what may be of use,' he pursued with his usual quietness of tone and manner. 'I spent a whole miserable Sunday in exploring this crumb of land.'

'A misanthropic sort of occupation,' muttered Decoud, viciously. 'You had no money, I suppose, to gamble with, and to fling about amongst the girls in your usual haunts, Capataz.'

'*È vero!*' exclaimed the Capataz, surprised into the use of his native tongue by so much perspicacity. 'I had not! Therefore I did not want to go amongst those beggarly people accustomed to my generosity. It is looked for from the Capataz of the Cargadores, who are the rich men, and, as it were, the *caballeros* amongst the common people. I don't care for cards but as a pastime; and as to those girls that boast of having opened their doors to my knock, you know I wouldn't look at any one of them twice except for what the people would say. They are queer, the good people of Sulaco, and I have got much useful information simply by listening patiently to the talk of the women that everybody believed I was in love with. Poor Teresa could never understand that. On that particular Sunday, *señor*, she scolded so that I went out of the house swearing that I would never darken their door again unless to fetch away my hammock and my chest of clothes. *Señor*, there is nothing more exasperating than to hear a woman you respect rail against your good reputation when you have not a single brass coin in your pocket. I untied one of the small boats and pulled myself out of the harbour with nothing but three cigars in my pocket to help me spend the day on this island. But the water of this rivulet you hear under your feet is cool and sweet and good, *señor*, both before and after a smoke.' He was silent for a while, then added reflectively, 'That was the first Sunday after I brought the white-whiskered English *rico* all the way down the mountains from the Paramo on the top of the Entrada Pass – and in the coach, too! No coach had gone up or down that mountain road within the memory of man, *señor*, till I brought this one down in charge of fifty peons working like one man with ropes, pickaxes, and poles under my direction. That was the rich Englishman who, as people say, pays for the making of this railway. He was very pleased with me. But my wages were not due till the end of the month.'

He slid down the bank suddenly. Decoud heard the splash of his feet in the brook and followed his footsteps down the ravine. His form was lost among the bushes till he had reached the strip of sand under the cliff. As often happens in the gulf when the showers during the first part of the night had been frequent and heavy, the darkness had thinned considerably towards the morning though there were no signs of daylight as yet.

The cargo-lighter, relieved of its precious burden, rocked feebly, half-afloat, with her fore-foot on the sand. A long rope stretched away like a black cotton thread across the strip of white beach to the grapnel Nostromo had carried ashore and hooked to the stem of a tree-like shrub in the very opening of the ravine.

There was nothing for Decoud but to remain on the island. He received from Nostromo's hands whatever food the foresight of Captain Mitchell had put on board the lighter and deposited it temporarily in the little dinghy which on their arrival they had hauled up out of sight amongst the bushes. It was to be left with him. The island was to be a hiding-place, not a prison; he could pull out to a passing ship. The O.S.N. Company's mail boats passed close to the islands when going into Sulaco from the north. But the *Minerva*, carrying off the ex-president, had taken the news up north of the disturbances in Sulaco. It was possible that the next steamer down would get instructions to miss the port altogether since the town, as far as the *Minerva*'s officers knew, was for the time being in the hands of the rabble. This would mean that there would be no steamer for a month, as far as the mail service went; but Decoud had to take his chance of that. The island was his only shelter from the proscription hanging over his head. The Capataz was, of course, going back. The unloaded lighter leaked much less, and he thought that she would keep afloat as far as the harbour.

He passed to Decoud, standing knee-deep alongside, one of the two spades which belonged to the equipment of each lighter for use when ballasting ships. By working with it carefully as soon as there was daylight enought to see, Decoud could loosen a mass of earth and stones overhanging the cavity in which they had deposited the treasure, so that it would look as if it had fallen naturally. It would cover up not only the cavity, but even all traces of their work, the footsteps, the displaced stones, and even the broken bushes.

'Besides, who would think of looking either for you or the treasure here?' Nostromo continued, as if he could not tear himself away from the spot. 'Nobody is ever likely to come here. What could any man want with this piece of earth as long as there is room for his feet on the mainland! The people in this country are not curious. There are even no fishermen here to intrude upon your worship. All the fishing that is done in the gulf goes on near Zapiga, over there. *Señor*, if you are forced to leave this island before anything can be arranged for you, do not try to make for Zapiga. It is a settlement of thieves and *matreros*, where they would cut your throat promptly for the sake of your gold watch and chain. And, *señor*, think twice before confiding in anyone whatever; even in the officers of the Company's steamers, if you ever get on board one. Honesty alone is not enough for security. You must look to discretion and prudence in a man. And always remember, *señor*, before you open your lips for a confidence, that this treasure may be left safely here for hundreds of years. Time is on its side, *señor*. And silver is an incorruptible metal that can be trusted to keep its value for ever . . . . An incorruptible metal,' he repeated, as if the idea had given him a profound pleasure.

'As some men are said to be,' Decound pronounced, inscrutably, while the Capataz, who busied himself in baling out the lighter with a wooden bucket, went on throwing the water over the side with a regular splash. Decoud, incorrigible in his scepticism, reflected, not cynically, but with general satisfaction, that this man was made incorruptible by his enormous vanity, that finest form of egoism which can take on the aspect of every virtue.

Nostromo ceased baling and, as if struck with a sudden thought, dropped the bucket with a clatter into the lighter.

'Have you any message?' he asked in a lowered voice. 'Remember, I shall be asked questions.'

'You must find the hopeful words that ought to be spoken to the people in town. I trust for that your intelligence and your experience, Capataz. You understand?'

'*Sí, señor* . . . For the ladies.'

'Yes, yes,' said Decoud, hastily. 'Your wonderful reputation will make them attach great value to your words; therefore be careful what you say. I am looking forward,' he continued, feeling the fatal touch of contempt for himself to which his complex nature was subject, 'I am looking forward to a glorious and successful ending to my mission. Do you hear, Capataz? Use the words glorious and successful when you speak to the *señorita*. Your own mission is accomplished gloriously and successfully. You have indubitably saved the silver of the mine. Not only this silver, but probably all the silver that shall ever come out of it.'

Nostromo detected the ironic tone. 'I dare say, Señor Don Martin,' he

said, moodily. 'There are very few things that I am not equal to. Ask the
foreign *signori*. I, a man of the people, who cannot always understand what
you mean. But as to this lot which I must leave here, let me tell you that I
would believe it in greater safety if you had not been with me at all.'

An exclamation escaped Decoud, and a short pause followed. 'Shall I go
back with you to Sulaco?' he asked in an angry tone.

'Shall I strike you dead with my knife where you stand?' retorted
Nostromo, contemptuously. 'It would be the same thing as taking you to
Sulaco. Come, *señor*. Your reputation is in your politics, and mine is bound
up with the fate of this silver. Do you wonder I wish there had been no
other man to share my knowledge? I wanted no one with me, *señor*.'

'You could not have kept the lighter afloat without me,' Decoud almost
shouted. 'You would have gone to the bottom with her.'

'Yes,' uttered Nostromo, slowly; 'alone.'

Here was a man, Decoud reflected, that seemed as though he would have
preferred to die rather than deface the perfect form of his egoism. Such a
man was safe. In silence he helped the Capataz to get the grapnel on board.
Nostromo cleared the shelving shore with one push of the heavy oar, and
Decoud found himself solitary on the beach like a man in a dream. A sudden
desire to hear a human voice once more seized upon his heart. The lighter
was hardly distinguishable from the black water upon which she floated.

'What do you think has become of Hirsch?' he shouted.

'Knocked overboard and drowned,' cried Nostromo's voice confidently out
of the black wastes of sky and sea around the islet. 'Keep close in the ravine,
señor. I shall try to come out to you in a night or two.'

A slight swishing rustle showed that Nostromo was setting the sail. It
filled all at once with a sound as of a single loud drum-tap. Decoud went
back to the ravine. Nostromo, at the tiller, looked back from time to time at
the vanishing mass of the Great Isabel, which, little by little, merged into
the uniform texture of the night. At last, when he turned his head again, he
saw nothing but a smooth darkness, like a solid wall.

Then he, too, experienced that feeling of solitude which had weighed
heavily on Decoud after the lighter had slipped off the shore. But while the
man on the island was oppressed by a bizarre sense of unreality affecting
the very ground upon which he walked, the mind of the Capataz of the
Cargadores turned alertly to the problem of future conduct. Nostromo's
faculties, working on parallel lines, enabled him to steer straight, to keep a
look-out for Hermosa, near which he had to pass, and to try to imagine
what would happen tomorrow in Sulaco. Tomorrow, or, as a matter of fact,
today, since the dawn was not very far, Sotillo would find out in what way
the treasure had gone. A gang of *cargadores* had been employed in loading
it into a railway truck from the Custom House store-rooms, and running
the truck on to the wharf. There would be arrests made, and certainly before
noon Sotillo would know in what manner the silver had left Sulaco, and
who it was that took it out.

Nostromo's intention had been to sail right into the harbour; but at this
thought by a sudden touch of the tiller he threw the lighter into the wind
and checked her rapid way. His re-appearance with the very boat would

raise suspicions, would cause surmises, would absolutely put Sotillo on the track. He himself would be arrested; and once in the Calabozo there was no saying what they would do to him to make him speak. He trusted himself, but he stood up to look round. Near by, Hermosa showed low its white surface as flat as a table, with the slight run of the sea raised by the breeze washing over its edges noisily. The lighter must be sunk at once.

He allowed her to drift with her sail aback. There was already a good deal of water in her. He allowed her to drift towards the harbour entrance, and, letting the tiller swing about, squatted down and busied himself in loosening the plug. With that out she would fill very quickly, and every lighter carried a little iron ballast – enough to make her go down when full of water. When he stood up again the noisy wash about the Hermosa sounded far away, almost inaudible; and already he could make out the shape of land about the harbour entrance. This was a desperate affair, and he was a good swimmer. A mile was nothing to him, and he knew of an easy place for landing just below the earthworks of the old abandoned fort. It occurred to him with a peculiar fascination that this fort was a good place in which to sleep the day through after so many sleepless nights.

With one blow of the tiller he unshipped for the purpose, he knocked the plug out, but did not take the trouble to lower the sail. He felt the water welling up heavily about his legs before he leaped on to the taffrail. There, upright and motionless, in his shirt and trousers only, he stood waiting. When he had felt her settle he sprang far away with a mighty splash.

At once he turned his head. The gloomy, clouded dawn from behind the mountains showed him on the smooth waters the upper corner of the sail, a dark wet triangle of canvas waving slightly to and fro. He saw it vanish, as if jerked under, and then struck out for the shore.

PART THREE
THE LIGHTHOUSE

CHAPTER 1

Directly the cargo boat had slipped away from the wharf and got lost in the darkness of the harbour the Europeans of Sulaco separated, to prepare for the coming of the Monterist régime, which was approaching Sulaco from the mountains, as well as from the sea.

This bit of manual work in loading the silver was their last concerted action. It ended the three days of danger, during which, according to the newspaper press of Europe, their energy had preserved the town from the calamities of popular disorder. At the shore end of the jetty, Captain Mitchell said good night and turned back. His intention was to walk the planks of the wharf till the steamer from Esmeralda turned up. The engineers of the railway staff, collecting their Basque and Italian workmen, marched them away to the railway yards, leaving the Custom House, so well defended on the first day of the riot, standing open to the four winds of heaven. Their men had conducted themselves bravely and faithfully during the famous 'three days' of Sulaco. In a great part this faithfulness and that courage had been exercised in self-defence rather than in the cause of those material interests to which Charles Gould had pinned his faith. Amongst the cries of the mob not the least loud had been the cry of death to foreigners. It was, indeed, a lucky circumstance for Sulaco that the relations of those imported workmen with the people of the country had been uniformly bad from the first.

Dr Monygham, going to the door of Viola's kitchen, observed this retreat marking the end of the foreign interference, this withdrawal of the army of material progress from the field of Costaguana revolutions.

Algarroba torches carried on the outskirts of the moving body sent their penetrating aroma into his nostrils. Their light, sweeping along the front of the house, made the letters of the inscription, 'Albergo d'Italia Una', leap out black from end to end of the long wall. His eyes blinked in the clear blaze. Several young men, mostly fair and tall, shepherding this mob of dark bronzed heads, surmounted by the glint of slanting rifle barrels, nodded to him familiarly as they went by. The doctor was a well-known character. Some of them wondered what he was doing there. Then, on the flank of their workmen they tramped on, following the line of rails.

'Withdrawing your people from the harbour?' said the doctor, addressing himself to the chief engineer of the railway, who had accompanied Charles Gould so far on his way to the town, walking by the side of the horse, with his hand on the saddlebow. They had stopped just outside the open door to let the workmen cross the road.

'As quick as I can. We are not a political faction,' answered the engineer, meaningly. 'And we are not going to give our new rulers a handle against the railway. You approve me, Gould?'

'Absolutely,' said Charles Gould's impassive voice, high up and outside the dim parallelogram of light falling on the road through the open door.

With Sotillo expected from one side, and Pedro Montero from the other, the engineer-in-chief's only anxiety now was to avoid a collision with either. Sulaco, for him, was a railway station, a terminus, workshops, a great accumulation of stores. As against the mob the railway defended its property, but politically the railway was neutral. He was a brave man; and in that spirit of neutrality he had carried proposals of truce to the self-appointed chiefs of the popular party, the deputies Fuentes and Gamacho. Bullets were still flying about when he had crossed the Plaza on that mission, waving above his head a white napkin belonging to the table linen of the Amarilla Club.

He was rather proud of this exploit; and reflecting that the doctor, busy all day with the wounded in the *patio* of the Casa Gould, had not had time to hear the news, he began a succinct narrative. He had communicated to them the intelligence from the Construction Camp as to Pedro Montero. The brother of the victorious general, he had assured them, could be expected at Sulaco at any time now. This news (as he anticipated), when shouted out of the window by Señor Gamacho, induced a rush of the mob along the Campo Road towards Rincón. The two deputies also, after shaking hands with him effusively, mounted and galloped off to meet the great man. 'I have misled them a little as to the time,' the chief engineer confessed. 'However hard he rides, he can scarcely get here before the morning. But my object is attained. I've secured several hours' peace for the losing party. But I did not tell them anything about Sotillo, for fear they would take it into their heads to try to get hold of the harbour again, either to oppose him or welcome him – there's no saying which. There was Gould's silver, on which rests the remnant of our hopes. Decoud's retreat had to be thought of, too. I think the railway has done pretty well by its friends without compromising itself hopelessly. Now the parties must be left to themselves.'

'Costaguana for the Costaguaneros,' interjected the doctor, sardonically. 'It is a fine country, and they have raised a fine crop of hates, vengeance, murder, and rapine – those sons of the country.'

'Well, I am one of them,' Charles Gould's voice sounded, calmly, 'and I must be going on to see to my own crop of trouble. My wife has driven straight on, doctor?'

'Yes. All was quiet on this side. Mrs Gould has taken the two girls with her.'

Charles Gould rode on, and the engineer-in-chief followed the doctor indoors.

'That man is calmness personified,' he said, appreciatively, dropping on a bench, and stretching his well-shaped legs in cycling stockings nearly across the doorway. 'He must be extremely sure of himself.'

'If that's all he is sure of, then he is sure of nothing,' said the doctor. He had perched himself again on the end of the table. He nursed his cheek in the palm of one hand, while the other sustained the elbow. 'It is the last thing a man ought to be sure of.' The candle, half-consumed and burning dimly with. a long wick, lighted up from below his inclined face, whose expression affected by the drawn-in cicatrices in the cheeks, had something vaguely unnatural, an exaggerated remorseful bitterness. As he sat there he had the air of meditating upon sinister things. The engineer-in-chief gazed at him for a time before he protested.

'I really don't see that. For me there seems to be nothing else. However –'

He was a wise man, but he could not quite conceal his contempt for that sort of paradox; in fact, Dr Monygham was not liked by the Europeans of Sulaco. His outward aspect of an outcast, which he preserved even in Mrs Gould's drawing-room, provoked unfavourable criticism. There could be no doubt of his intelligence; and as he had lived for over twenty years in the country, the pessimism of his outlook could not be altogether ignored. But instinctively, in self-defence of their activities and hopes, his hearers put it to the account of some hidden imperfection in the man's character. It was known that many years before, when quite young, he had been made by Guzman Bento chief medical officer of the army. Not one of the Europeans then in the service of Costaguana had been so much liked and trusted by the fierce old Dictator.

Afterwards his story was not so clear. It lost itself amongst the innumerable tales of conspiracies and plots against the tyrant as a stream is lost in an arid belt of sandy country before it emerges, diminished and troubled, perhaps, on the other side. The doctor made no secret of it that he had lived for years in the wildest parts of the Republic, wandering with almost unknown Indian tribes in the great forests of the far interior where the great rivers have their sources. But it was mere aimless wandering; he had written nothing, collected nothing, brought nothing for science out of the twilight of the forests, which seemed to cling to his battered personality limping about Sulaco, where it had drifted in casually, only to get stranded on the shores of the sea.

It was also known that he had lived in a state of destitution till the arrival of the Goulds from Europe. Don Carlos and Doña Emilia had taken up the mad English doctor, when it became apparent that for all his savage independence he could be tamed by kindness. Perhaps it was only hunger that had tamed him. In years gone by he had certainly been acquainted with Charles Gould's father in Sta Marta; and now, no matter what were the dark passages of his history, as the medical officer of the San Tomé mine he became a recognized personality. He was recognized, but not unreservedly accepted. So much defiant eccentricity and such an outspoken scorn for mankind seemed to point to mere recklessness of judgement, the bravado of guilt. Besides, since he had become again of some account, vague whispers had been heard that years ago, when fallen into disgrace and thrown into prison by Guzman Bento at the time of the so-called Great Conspiracy, he had betrayed some of his best friends amongst the conspirators. Nobody pretended to believe that whisper; the whole story of the Great Conspiracy was hopelessly involved and obscure; it is admitted in Costaguana that there never had been a conspiracy except in the diseased imagination of the Tyrant; and, therefore, nothing and no one to betray; though the most distinguished

Costaguaneros had been imprisoned and executed upon that accusation. The procedure had dragged on for years, decimating the better class like a pestilence. The mere expression of sorrow for the fate of executed kinsmen had been punished with death. Don José Avellanos was perhaps the only one living who knew the whole story of those unspeakable cruelties. He had suffered from them himself, and he, with a shrug of the shoulders and a nervous, jerky gesture of the arm, was wont to put away from him, as it were, every allusion to it. But whatever the reason, Dr Monygham, a personage in the administration of the Gould Concession, treated with reverent awe by the miners, and indulged in his peculiarities by Mrs Gould, remained somehow outside the pale.

It was not from any liking for the doctor that the engineer-in-chief had lingered in the inn upon the plain. He liked old Viola much better. He had come to look upon the Albergo d'Italia Una as a dependence of the railway. Many of his subordinates had their quarters there. Mrs Gould's interest in the family conferred upon it a sort of distinction. The engineer-in-chief, with an army of workers under his orders, appreciated the moral influence of the old Garibaldino upon his countrymen. His austere, old-world Republicanism had a severe, soldier-like standard of faithfulness and duty, as if the world were a battlefield where men had to fight for the sake of universal love and brotherhood, instead of a more or less large share of booty.

'Poor old chap!' he said, after he had heard the doctor's account of Teresa. 'He'll never be able to keep the place going by himself. I shall be sorry.'

'He's quite alone up there,' grunted Dr Monygham, with a toss of his heavy head towards the narrow staircase. 'Every living soul has cleared out, and Mrs Gould took the girls away just now. It might not be over-safe for them out here before very long. Of course, as a doctor I can do nothing more here; but she has asked me to stay with old Viola, and as I have no horse to get back to the mine, where I ought to be, I made no difficulty to stay. They can do without me in the town.'

'I have a good mind to remain with you, doctor, till we see whether anything happens tonight at the harbour,' declared the engineer-in-chief. 'He must not be molested by Sotillo's soldiery, who may push on as far as this at once. Sotillo used to be very cordial to me at the Goulds' and at the club. How that man'll ever dare to look any of his friends here in the face I can't imagine.'

'He'll no doubt begin by shooting some of them to get over the first awkwardness,' said the doctor. 'Nothing in this country serves better your military man who has changed sides than a few summary executions.' He spoke with a gloomy positiveness that left no room for protest. The engineer-in-chief did not attempt any. He simply nodded several times regretfully, then said:

'I think we shall be able to mount you in the morning, doctor. Our peons have recovered some of our stampeded horses. By riding hard and taking a wide circuit by Los Hatos and along the edge of the forest, clear of Rincón altogether, you may hope to reach the San Tomé bridge without being interfered with. The mine is just now, to my mind, the safest place for anybody at all compromised. I only wish the railway was as difficult to touch.'

'Am I compromised?' Dr Monygham brought out slowly after a short silence.

'The whole Gould Concession is compromised. It could not have remained for ever outside the political life of the country – if those convulsions may be called life. The thing is – can it be touched? The moment was bound to come when neutrality would become impossible, and Charles Gould understood this well. I believe he is prepared for every extremity. A man of his sort has never contemplated remaining indefinitely at the mercy of ignorance and corruption. It was like being a prisoner in a cavern of *banditti* with the price of your ransom in your pocket, and buying your life from day to day. Your mere safety, not your liberty, mind, doctor. I know what I am talking about. The image at which you shrug your shoulders is perfectly correct, especially if you conceive such a prisoner endowed with the power of replenishing his pocket by means as remote from the faculties of his captors as if they were magic. You must have understood that as well as I do, doctor. He was in the position of the goose with the golden eggs. I broached this matter to him as far back as Sir John's visit here. The prisoner of stupid and greedy *banditti* is always at the mercy of the first imbecile ruffian, who may blow out his brains in a fit of temper or for some prospect of an immediate big haul. The tale of killing the goose with the golden eggs has not been evolved for nothing out of the wisdom of mankind. It is a story that will never grow old. That is why Charles Gould in his deep, dumb way has countenanced the Ribierist Mandate, the first public act that promised him safety on other than venal grounds. Ribierism has failed, as everything merely rational fails in this country. But Gould remains logical in wishing to save this big lot of silver. Decoud's plan of a counter-revolution may be practicable or not, it may have a chance, or it may not have a chance. With all my experience of this revolutionary continent, I can hardly yet look at their methods seriously. Decoud has been reading to us his draft of a proclamation, and talking very well for two hours about his plan of action. He had arguments which should have appeared solid enough if we, members of old, stable political and national organizations, were not startled by the mere idea of a new State evolved like this out of the head of a scoffing young man fleeing for his life, with a proclamation in his pocket, to a rough, jeering, half-bred swash-buckler, who in this part of the world is called a general. It sounds like a comic fairy tale – and behold, it may come off; because it is true to the very spirit of the country.'

'Is the silver gone off, then?' asked the doctor, moodily.

The chief engineer pulled out his watch. 'By Captain Mitchell's reckoning – and he ought to know – it has been gone long enough now to be some three or four miles outside the harbour; and, as Mitchell says, Nostromo is the sort of seaman to make the best of his opportunities.' Here the doctor grunted so heavily that the other changed his tone.

'You have a poor opinion of that move, doctor? But why? Charles Gould has got to play his game out, though he is not the man to formulate his conduct even to himself, perhaps, let alone to others. It may be that the game has been partly suggested to him by Holroyd; but it accords with his character, too; and that is why it has been so successful. Haven't they come to calling him "El Rey de Sulaco" in Sta Marta? A nickname may be the best record of a success. That's what I call putting the face of a joke upon the body of a truth. My dear sir, when I first arrived in Sta Marta I was struck by the way all those journalists, demagogues, members of Congress, and all those generals and judges cringed before a sleepy-eyed advocate without practice simply because he was the plenipotentiary of the Gould Concession. Sir John when he came out was impressed, too.'

'A new State, with that plump dandy, Decoud, for the first President,' mused Dr Monygham, nursing his cheek and swinging his legs all the time.

'Upon my word, and why not?' the chief engineer retorted in an unexpectedly earnest and confidential voice. It was as if something subtle in the air of Costaguana had inoculated him with the local faith in *pronunciamientos*. All at once he began to talk, like an expert revolutionist, of the instrument ready to hand in the intact army at Cayta, which could be brought back in a few days to Sulaco if only Decoud managed to make his way at once down the coast. For the military chief there was Barrios, who had nothing but a bullet to expect from Montero, his former professional rival and bitter enemy. Barrios's concurrence was assured. As to his army, it had nothing to expect from Montero either; not even a month's pay. From that point of view the existence of the treasure was of enormous importance. The mere knowledge that it had been saved from the Monterists would be a strong inducement for the Cayta troops to embrace the cause of the new State.

The doctor turned round and contemplated his companion for some time.

'This Decoud, I see, is a persuasive young beggar,' he remarked at last. 'And pray is it for this, then, that Charles Gould has let the whole lot of ingots go out to sea in charge of that Nostromo?'

'Charles Gould,' said the engineer-in-chief, 'has said no more about his motive than usual. You know, he doesn't talk. But we all here know his motive, and he has only one – the safety of the San Tomé mine with the preservation of the Gould Concession in the spirit of his compact with Holroyd. Holroyd is another uncommon man. They understand each other's imaginative side. One is thirty, the other nearly sixty, and they have been made for each other. To be a millionaire, and such a millionaire as Holroyd, is like being eternally young. The audacity of youth reckons upon what it fancies an unlimited time at its disposal; but a millionaire has unlimited means in his hand – which is better. One's time on earth is an uncertain quantity, but about the long reach of millions there is no doubt. The introduction of a pure form of Christianity into this continent is a dream for a youthful enthusiast, and I have been trying to explain to you why Holroyd at fifty-eight is like a man on the threshold of life, and better, too. He's not a missionary, but the San Tomé mine holds just that for him. I assure you, in sober truth, that he could not manage to keep this out of a strictly business conference upon the finances of Costaguana he had with Sir John a couple of years ago. Sir John mentioned it with amazement in a letter he wrote to me here, from San Francisco, when on his way home. Upon my word, doctor, things seem to be worth nothing by what they are in themselves. I begin to believe that the only solid thing about them is the spiritual value which everyone discovers in his own form of activity –'

'Bah!' interrupted the doctor, without stopping for an instant the idle swinging movement of his legs. 'Self-flattery. Food for that vanity which makes the world go round. Meantime, what do you think is going to happen to the treasure floating about the gulf with the great Capataz and the great politician?'

'Why are you uneasy about it, doctor?'

'I uneasy! And what the devil is it to me? I put no spiritual value into my desires, or my opinions, or my actions. They have not enough vastness to give me room for self-flattery. Look, for instance, I should certainly have liked to ease the last moments of that poor woman. And I can't. It's impossible. Have you met the impossible face to face – or have you, the Napoleon of railways, no such word in your dictionary?'

'Is she bound to have a very bad time of it?' asked the chief engineer, with humane concern.

Slow, heavy footsteps moved across the planks above the heavy hard wood beams of the kitchen. Then down the narrow opening of the staircase made in the thickness of the wall, and narrow enough to be defended by one man against twenty enemies, came the murmur of two voices, one faint and broken, the other deep and gentle answering it, and in its graver tone covering the weaker sound.

The two men remained still and silent till the murmurs ceased, then the doctor shrugged his shoulders and muttered:

'Yes, she's bound to. And I could do nothing if I went up now.'

A long period of silence above and below ensued.

'I fancy,' began the engineer, in a subdued voice, 'that you mistrust Captain Mitchell's Capataz.'

'Mistrust him!' muttered the doctor through his teeth. 'I believe him capable of anything – even of the most absurd fidelity. I am the last person he spoke to before he left the wharf, you know. The poor woman up there wanted to see him, and I let him go up to her. The dying must not be contradicted, you know. She seemed then fairly calm and resigned, but the scoundrel in those ten minutes or so has done or said something which seems to have driven her into despair. You know,' went on the doctor, hesitatingly, 'women are so very unaccountable in every position, and at all times of life, that I thought sometimes she was in a way, don't you see? in love with him – the Capataz. The rascal has his own charm indubitably, or he would not have made the conquest of all the populace of the town. No, no, I am not absurd. I may have given a wrong name to some strong sentiment for him on her part, to an unreasonable and simple attitude a woman is apt to take up emotionally towards a man. She used to abuse him to me frequently, which, of course, is not inconsistent with my idea. Not at all. It looked to me as if she were always thinking of him. He was something important in her life. You know, I have seen a lot of those people. Whenever I came down from the mine Mrs Gould used to ask me to keep my eye on them. She likes Italians; she has lived a long time in Italy, I believe, and she took a special fancy to that old Garibaldino. A remarkable chap enough. A rugged and dreamy character, living in the republicanism of his young days as if in a cloud. He has encouraged much of the Capataz's confounded nonsense – the high-strung, exalted old beggar!'

'What sort of nonsense?' wondered the chief engineer. 'I found the Capataz always a very shrewd and sensible fellow, absolutely fearless, and remarkably useful. A perfect handyman. Sir John was greatly impressed by his resourcefulness and attention when he made that overland journey from Sta Marta. Later on, as you might have heard, he rendered us a service by disclosing to the then chief of police the presence in the town of some professional thieves, who came from a distance to wreck and rob our monthly pay train. He has certainly organized the lighterage service of the harbour for the O.S.N. Company with great ability. He knows how to make himself obeyed, foreigner though he is. It is true that the *cargadores* are strangers here, too, for the most part – immigrants, *isleños*.'

'His prestige is his fortune,' muttered the doctor, sourly.

'The man has proved his trustworthiness up to the hilt on innumerable occasions and in all sorts of ways,' argued the engineer. 'When this question of the silver arose, Captain Mitchell naturally was very warmly of the opinion that his Capataz was the only man fit for the trust. As a sailor, of course, I suppose so. But as a man, don't you know, Gould, Decoud, and myself judged that it didn't matter in the least who went. Any boatman would have done just as well. Pray, what could a thief do with such a lot of ingots? If he ran off with them he would have in the end to land somewhere, and how could he conceal his cargo from the knowledge of the people ashore? We dismissed that consideration from our minds. Moreover, Decoud was going. There have been occasions when the Capataz has been more implicitly trusted.'

'He took a slightly different view,' the doctor said. 'I heard him declare in this very room that it would be the most desperate affair of his life. He made a sort of verbal will here in my hearing, appointing old Viola his executor; and, by Jove! do you know, he – he's not grown rich by his fidelity to you good people of the railway and the harbour. I suppose he obtains some – how do you say that? – some spiritual value for his labours, or else I don't know why the devil he should be faithful to you, Gould, Mitchell, or anybody else. He knows this country well. He knows, for instance, that Gamacho, the Deputy from Javira, has been nothing else but a *tramposo* of the commonest sort, a petty pedlar of the Campo, till he managed to get enough goods on credit from Anzani to open a little store in the wilds, and got himself elected by the drunken *mozos* that hang about the *estancias* and the poorest sort of *rancheros* who were in his debt. And Gamacho, who tomorrow will be probably one of our high officials, is a stranger, too – an *isleño*. He might have been a *cargador* on the O.S.N. wharf had he not (the *posadero* of Rincón is ready to swear it) murdered a pedlar in the woods and stolen his pack to begin life on. And do you think that Gamacho, then, would have ever become a hero with the democracy of this place, like our Capataz? Of course not. He isn't half the man. No; decidedly, I think that Nostromo is a fool.'

The doctor's talk was distasteful to the builder of railways. 'It is impossible to argue that point,' he said, philosophically. 'Each man has his gifts. You should have heard Gamacho haranguing his friends in the street. He has a howling voice, and he shouted like mad, lifting his clenched fist right above his head, and throwing his body half out of the window. At every pause the rabble below yelled, "Down with the Oligarchs! *Viva la libertad*!" Fuentes inside looked extremely miserable. You know, he is the brother of Jorge Fuentes, who has been Minister of the Interior for six months or so, some few years back. Of course, he has no conscience; but he is a man of birth and education – at one time the director of the Customs of Cayta. That idiot-brute Gamacho fastened himself upon him with his following of the lowest rabble. His sickly fear of that ruffian was the most rejoicing sight imaginable.'

He got up and went to the door to look out towards the harbour. 'All quiet,' he said; 'I wonder if Sotillo really means to turn up here?'

CHAPTER 2

Captain Mitchell, pacing the wharf, was asking himself the same question. There was always the doubt whether the warning of the Esmeralda telegraphist – a fragmentary and interrupted message – had been properly understood. However, the good man had made up his mind not to go to bed till daylight, if even then. He imagined himself to have rendered an enormous service to Charles Gould. When he thought of the saved silver he rubbed his hands together with satisfaction. In his simple way he was proud at being a party to this extremely clever expedient. It was he who had given it a practical shape by suggesting the possibility of intercepting at sea the northbound steamer. And it was advantageous to his Company, too, which would have lost a valuable freight if the treasure had been left ashore to be confiscated. The pleasure of disappointing the Monterists was also very great. Authoritative by temperament and the long habit of command, Captain Mitchell was no democrat. He even went so far as to profess a contempt for parliamentarism itself. 'His Excellency Don Vincente Ribiera,' he used to say, 'whom I and that fellow of mine, Nostromo, had the honour, sir, and the pleasure of saving from a cruel death, deferred too much to his Congress. It was a mistake – a distinct mistake, sir.'

The guileless old seaman superintending the O.S.N. service imagined that the last three days had exhausted every startling surprise the political life of Costaguana could offer. He used to confess afterwards that the events which followed surpassed his imagination. To begin with, Sulaco (because of the seizure of the cables and the disorganization of the steam service) remained for a whole fortnight cut off from the rest of the world like a besieged city.

'One would not have believed it possible; but so it was, sir. A full fortnight.'

The account of the extraordinary things that happened during that time, and the powerful emotions he experienced, acquired a comic impressiveness from the pompous manner of his personal narrative. He opened it always by assuring his hearer that he was 'in the thick of things from first to last'. Then he would begin by describing the getting away of the silver, and his natural anxiety lest 'his fellow' in charge of the lighter should make some mistake. Apart from the loss of so much precious metal, the life of Señor Martin Decoud, an agreeable, wealthy, and well-informed young gentleman, would have been jeopardized through his falling into the hands of his political enemies. Captain Mitchell also admitted that in his solitary vigil on the wharf he had felt a certain measure of concern for the future of the whole country.

'A feeling, sir,' he exclaimed, 'perfectly comprehensible in a man properly grateful for the many kindnesses received from the best families of merchants and other native gentlemen of independent means, who, barely saved by us from the excesses of the mob, seemed, to my mind's eye, destined to become the prey in person and fortune of the native soldiery, which, as is well known, behave with regrettable barbarity to the inhabitants during their civil commotions. And then, sir, there were the Goulds, for both of whom, man and wife, I could not but entertain the warmest feelings deserved by their hospitality and kindness. I felt, too, the dangers of the gentlemen of the Amarilla Club, who had made me honorary member, and had treated me with uniform regard and civility, both in my capacity of Consular Agent and as Superintendent of an important Steam Service. Miss Antonia Avellanos, the most beautiful and accomplished young lady whom it had ever been my privilege to speak to, was not a little in my mind, I confess. How the interests of my Company would be affected by the impending change of officials claimed a large share of my attention, too. In short, sir, I was extremely anxious and very tired, as you may suppose, by the exciting and memorable events in which I had taken my little part. The Company's building containing my residence was within five minutes' walk, with the attraction of some supper and of my hammock (I always take my nightly rest in a hammock, as the most suitable to the climate); but somehow, sir, though evidently I could do nothing for anyone by remaining about, I could not tear myself away from that wharf, where the fatigue made me stumble painfully at times. The night was excessively dark – the darkest I remember in my life; so that I began to think that the arrival of the transport from Esmeralda could not possibly take place before daylight, owing to the difficulty of navigating the gulf. The mosquitoes bit like fury. We have been infested here with mosquitoes before the late improvements; a peculiar harbour brand sir, renowned for its ferocity. They were like a cloud about my head, and I shouldn't wonder that but for their attacks I would have dozed off as I walked up and down, and got a heavy fall. I kept on smoking cigar after cigar, more to protect myself from being eaten up alive than from any real relish for the weed. Then, sir, when perhaps for the twentieth time I was approaching my watch to the lighted end in order to see the time, and observing with surprise that it wanted yet ten minutes to midnight, I heard the splash of a ship's propeller – an unmistakable sound to a sailor's ear on such a calm night. It was faint indeed, because they were advancing with precaution and dead slow, both on account of the darkness and from their desire of not revealing too soon their presence: a very unnecessary care, because, I verily believe, in all the enormous extent of this harbour I was the only living soul about. Even the usual staff of watchmen and others had been absent from their posts for several nights owing to the disturbances. I stood stock still, after dropping and stamping out my cigar – a circumstance highly agreeable, I should think, to the mosquitoes, if I may judge from the state of my face next morning. But that was a trifling inconvenience in comparison with the brutal proceedings I became victim of on the part of Sotillo. Something utterly inconceivable, sir; more like the proceedings of a maniac than the action of a sane man, however lost to all sense of honour and decency. But Sotillo was furious at the failure of his thievish scheme.'

In this Captain Mitchell was right. Sotillo was indeed infuriated. Captain Mitchell, however, had not been arrested at once; a vivid curiosity induced him to remain on the wharf (which is nearly four hundred feet long) to see, or rather hear, the whole process of disembarkation. Concealed by the railway truck used for the silver, which had been run back afterwards to the shore end of the jetty, Captain Mitchell saw the small detachment thrown forward, pass by, taking different directions upon the plain. Meantime, the troops were being landed and formed into a column, whose head crept up gradually so close to him that he made it out, barring nearly the whole width of the wharf, only a very few yards from him. Then the low, shuffling, murmuring, clinking sounds ceased, and the whole mass remained for about an hour motionless and silent, awaiting the return of the scouts. On land nothing was to be heard except the deep baying of the mastiffs at the railway yards, answered by the faint barking of the curs infesting the outer limits of the town. A detached knot of dark shapes stood in front of the head of the column.

Presently the picket at the end of the wharf began to challenge in undertones single figures approaching from the plain. Those messengers sent back from the scouting parties flung to their comrades brief sentences and passed on rapidly, becoming lost in the great motionless mass, to make their report to the Staff. It occurred to Captain Mitchell that his position could become disagreeable and perhaps dangerous, when suddenly, at the head of the jetty, there was a shout of command, a bugle call, followed by a stir and a rattling of arms, and a murmuring noise that ran right up the column. Near by a loud voice directed hurriedly, 'Push that railway car out of the way!' At the rush of bare feet to execute the order Captain Mitchell skipped back a pace or two; the car, suddenly impelled by many hands, flew away from him along the rails, and before he knew what had happened he found himself surrounded and seized by his arms and the collar of his coat.

'We have caught a man hiding here, *mi teniente!*' cried one of his captors.

'Hold him on one side till the rearguard comes along,' answered the voice. The whole column streamed past Captain Mitchell at a run, the thundering noise of their feet dying away suddenly on the shore. His captors held him tightly, disregarding his declaration that he was an Englishman and his loud demands to be taken at once before their commanding officer. Finally he lapsed into dignified silence. With a hollow rumble of wheels on the planks a couple of field guns, dragged by hand, rolled by. Then, after a small body of men had marched past escorting four or five figures which walked in advance, with a jingle of steel scabbards, he felt a tug at his arms, and was ordered to come along. During the passage from the wharf to the Custom House it is to be feared that Captain Mitchell was subjected to certain indignities at the hands of the soldiers – such as jerks, thumps on the neck forcible application of the butt of a rifle to the small of his back. Their ideas of speed were not in accord with his notion of his dignity. He became flustered, flushed, and helpless. It was as if the world were coming to an end.

The long building was surrounded by troops, which were already piling arms by companies and preparing to pass the night lying on the ground in their ponchos with their sacks under their heads. Corporals moved with swinging lanterns posting sentries all round the walls wherever there was a door or an opening. Sotillo was taking his measures to protect his conquest as if it had indeed contained the treasure. His desire to make his fortune at one audacious stroke of genius had overmastered his reasoning faculties. He would not believe in the possibility of failure; the mere hint of such a thing made his brain reel with rage. Every circumstance pointing to it appeared incredible. The statement of Hirsch, which was so absolutely fatal to his hopes, could by no means be admitted. It is true, too, that Hirsch's story had been told so incoherently, with such excessive signs of distraction, that it really looked improbable. It was extremely difficult, as the saying is, to make head or tail of it. On the bridge of the steamer, directly after his rescue, Sotillo and his officers, in their impatience and excitement, would not give the wretched man time to collect such few wits as remained to him. He ought to have been quieted, soothed, and reassured, whereas he had been roughly handled, cuffed, shaken, and addressed in menacing tones. His struggles, his wriggles, his attempts to get down on his knees, followed by the most violent efforts to break away, as if he meant incontinently to jump overboard, his shrieks and shrinkings and cowering wild glances had filled them first with amazement, then with a doubt of his genuineness, as men are wont to suspect the sincerity of every great passion. His Spanish, too, became so mixed up with German that the better half of his statements remained incomprehensible. He tried to propitiate them by calling them *hochwohlgeborene Herren*, which in itself sounded suspicious. When admonished sternly not to trifle he repeated his entreaties and protestations of loyalty and innocence again in German, obstinately, because he was not aware in what language he was speaking. His identity, of course, was perfectly known as an inhabitant of Esmeralda, but this made the matter no clearer. As he kept on forgetting Decoud's name, mixing him up with several other people he had seen in the Casa Gould, it looked as if they all had been in the lighter together; and for a moment Sotillo thought that he had drowned every prominent Ribierist of Sulaco. The improbability of such a thing threw a doubt upon the whole statement. Hirsch was either mad or playing a part – pretending fear and distraction on the spur of the moment to cover the truth. Sotillo's rapacity, excited to the highest pitch by the prospect of

an immense booty, could believe in nothing adverse. This Jew might have
been very much frightened by the accident, but he knew where the silver
was concealed, and had invented this story, with his Jewish cunning, to put
him entirely off the track as to what had been done.

Sotillo had taken up his quarters on the upper floor in a vast apartment
with heavy black beams. But there was no ceiling, and the eye lost itself in
the darkness under the high pitch of the roof. The thick shutters stood open.
On a long table could be seen a large inkstand, some stumpy, inky quill
pens, and two square wooden boxes, each holding half a hundredweight of
sand. Sheets of grey coarse official paper bestrewed the floor. It must have
been a room occupied by some higher official of the Customs, because a
large leathern armchair stood behind the table, with other high-backed
chairs scattered about. A net hammock was swung under one of the beams
– for the official's afternoon siesta, no doubt. A couple of candles stuck into
tall iron candlesticks gave a dim reddish light. The colonel's hat, sword, and
revolver lay between them, and a couple of his more trusty officers lounged
gloomily against the table. The colonel threw himself into the armchair, and
a big Negro with a sergeant's stripes on his ragged sleeve, kneeling down,
pulled off his boots. Sotillo's ebony moustache contrasted violently with the
livid colouring of his cheeks. His eyes were sombre and as if sunk very far
into his head. He seemed exhausted by his perplexities, languid with
disappointment; but when the sentry on the landing thrust his head in to
announce the arrival of a prisoner, he revived at once.

'Let him be brought in,' he shouted, fiercely.

The door flew open, and Captain Mitchell, bareheaded, his waitcoat open,
the bow of his tie under his ear, was hustled into the room.

Sotillo recognized him at once. He could not have hoped for a more
precious capture; here was a man who could tell him, if he chose, everything
he wished to know – and directly the problem of how best to make him talk
to the point presented itself to his mind. The resentment of a foreign nation
had no terrors for Sotillo. The might of the whole armed Europe would not
have protected Captain Mitchell from insults and ill-usage, so well as the
quick reflection of Sotillo that this was an Englishman who would most
likely turn obstinate under bad treatment, and become quite unmanageable.
At all events, the colonel smoothed the scowl on his brow.

'What! The excellent Señor Mitchell!' he cried, in affected dismay. The
pretended anger of his swift advance and of his shout, 'Release the *caballero*
at once,' was so effective that the astounded soldiers positively sprang away
from their prisoner. Thus suddenly deprived of forcible support, Captain
Mitchell reeled as though about to fall. Sotillo took him familiarly under the
arm, led him to a chair, waved his hand at the room. 'Go out, all of you,'
he commanded.

When they had been left alone he stood looking down, irresolute and
silent, watching till Captain Mitchell had recovered his power of speech.

Here in his very grasp was one of the men concerned in the removal of
the silver. Sotillo's temperament was of that sort that he experienced an
ardent desire to beat him; just as formerly when negotiating with difficulty
a loan from the cautious Anzani, his fingers itched to take the shopkeeper

by the throat. As to Captain Mitchell, the suddenness, unexpectedness, and general inconceivableness of this experience had confused his thoughts. Moreover, he was physically out of breath.

'I've been knocked down three times between this and the wharf,' he gasped out at last. 'Somebody shall be made to pay for this.' He had certainly stumbled more than once, and had been dragged along for some distance before he could regain his stride. With his recovered breath his indignation seemed to madden him. He jumped up, crimson, all his white hair bristling, his eyes glaring vengefully, and shook violently the flaps of his ruined waistcoat before the disconcerted Sotillo. 'Look! Those uniformed thieves of yours downstairs have robbed me of my watch.'

The old sailor's aspect was very threatening. Sotillo saw himself cut off from the table on which his sabre and revolver were lying.

'I demand restitution and apologies,' Mitchell thundered at him, quite beside himself. 'From you! Yes, from you!'

For the space of a second or so the colonel stood with a perfectly stony expression of face; then, as Captain Mitchell flung out an arm towards the table as if to snatch up the revolver, Sotillo, with a yell of alarm, bounded to the door and was gone in a flash, slamming it after him. Surprise calmed Captain Mitchell's fury. Behind the closed door Sotillo shouted on the landing, and there was a great tumult of feet on the wooden staircase.

'Disarm him! Bind him!' the colonel could be heard vociferating.

Captain Mitchell had just the time to glance once at the windows, with three perpendicular bars of iron each and some twenty feet from the ground, as he well knew, before the door flew open and the rush upon him took place. In an incredibly short time he found himself bound with many turns of a hide rope to a high-backed chair, so that his head alone remained free. Not till then did Sotillo, who had been leaning in the doorway trembling visibly, venture again within. The soldiers, picking up from the floor the rifles they had dropped to grapple with the prisoner, filed out of the room. The officers remained leaning on their swords and looking on.

'The watch! the watch!' raved the colonel, pacing to and fro like a tiger in a cage. 'Give me that man's watch.'

It was true, that when searched for arms in the hall downstairs, before being taken into Sotillo's presence, Captain Mitchell had been relieved of his watch and chain; but at the colonel's clamour it was produced quickly enough, a corporal bringing it up, carried carefully in the palms of his joined hands. Sotillo snatched it, and pushed the clenched fist from which it dangled close to Captain Mitchell's face.

'Now then! You arrogant Englishman! You dare to call the soldiers of the army thieves! Behold your watch.'

He flourished his fist as if aiming blows at the prisoner's nose. Captain Mitchell, helpless as a swathed infant, looked anxiously at the sixty-guinea gold half-chronometer, presented to him years ago by a Committee of Underwriters for saving a ship from total loss by fire. Sotillo, too, seemed to perceive its valuable appearance. He became silent suddenly, stepped aside to the table, and began a careful examination in the light of the candles.

He had never seen anything so fine. His officers closed in and craned their necks behind his back.

He became so interested that for an instant he forgot his precious prisoner. There is always something childish in the rapacity of the passionate, clear-minded, Southern races, wanting in the misty idealism of the Northerners, who at the smallest encouragement dream of nothing less than the conquest of the earth. Sotillo was fond of jewels, gold trinkets, of personal adornment. After a moment he turned about, and with a commanding gesture made all his officers fall back. He laid down the watch on the table, then, negligently, pushed his hat over it.

'Ha!' he began, going up very close to the chair. 'You dare call my valiant soldiers of the Esmeralda regiment, thieves. You dare! What impudence! You foreigners come here to rob our country of its wealth. You never have enough! Your audacity knows no bounds.'

He looked towards the officers, among whom there was an approving murmur. The older major was moved to declare:

'*Sí, mi coronel*. They are all traitors.'

'I shall say nothing,' continued Sotillo, fixing the motionless and powerless Mitchell with an angry but uneasy stare. 'I shall say nothing of your treacherous attempt to get possession of my revolver to shoot me while I was trying to treat you with consideration you did not deserve. You have forfeited your life. Your only hope is in my clemency.

He watched for the effect of his words, but there was no obvious sign of fear on Captain Mitchell's face. His white hair was full of dust, which covered also the rest of his helpless person. As if he had heard nothing, he twitched an eyebrow to get rid of a bit of straw which hung amongst the hairs.

Sotillo advanced one leg and put his arms akimbo. 'It is you, Mitchell,' he said, emphatically, 'who are the thief, not my soldiers!' He pointed at his prisoner a forefinger with a long, almond-shaped nail. 'Where is the silver of the San Tomé mine? I ask you, Mitchell, where is the silver that was deposited in this Custom House? Answer me that! You stole it. You were a party to stealing it. It was stolen from the Government. Aha! you think I do not know what I say; but I am up to your foreign tricks. It is gone, the silver! No? Gone in one of your *lanchas*, you miserable man! How dared you?'

This time he produced his effect. 'How on earth could Sotillo know that?' thought Mitchell. His head, the only part of his body that could move, betrayed his surprise by a sudden jerk.

'Ha! you tremble,' Sotillo shouted, suddenly. 'It is a conspiracy. It is a crime against the State. Did you not know that the silver belongs to the Republic till the Government claims are satisfied? Where is it? Where have you hidden it, you miserable thief?'

At this question Captain Mitchell's sinking spirits revived. In whatever incomprehensible manner Sotillo had already got his information about the lighter, he had not captured it. That was clear. In his outraged heart, Captain Mitchell had resolved that nothing would induce him to say a word while he remained so disgracefully bound, but his desire to help the escape of the silver made him depart from this resolution. His wits were very much at work. He detected in Sotillo a certain air of doubt, of irresolution.

'That man,' he said to himself, 'is not certain of what he advances.' For all his pomposity in social intercourse, Captain Mitchell could meet the realities of life in a resolute and ready spirit. Now he had got over the first shock of the abominable treatment he was cool and collected enough. The immense contempt he felt for Sotillo steadied him, and he said oracularly, 'No doubt it is well concealed by this time.'

Sotillo, too, had time to cool down. '*Muy bien*, Mitchell,' he said in a cold and threatening manner. 'But can you produce the Government receipt for the royalty and the Custom House permit of embarkation, hey? Can you? No. Then the silver has been removed illegally, and the guilty shall be made to suffer, unless it is produced within five days from this.' He gave orders for the prisoner to be unbound and locked up in one of the smaller rooms downstairs. He walked about the room, moody and silent, till Captain Mitchell, with each of his arms held by a couple of men, stood up, shook himself, and stamped his feet.

'How did you like to be tied up, Mitchell?' he asked, derisively.

'It is the most incredible, abominable use of power!' Captain Mitchell declared in a loud voice. 'And whatever your purpose, you shall gain nothing from it, I can promise you.'

The tall colonel, livid, with his coal-black ringlets and moustache, crouched, as it were, to look into the eyes of the short, thick-set, red-faced prisoner with rumpled white hair.

'That we shall see. You shall know my power a little better when I tie you up to a *potalón* outside in the sun for a whole day.' He drew himself up haughtily, and made a sign for Captain Mitchell to be led away.

'What about my watch?' cried Captain Mitchell, hanging back from the efforts of the men pulling him towards the door.

Sotillo turned to his officers. 'No! But only listen to this *pícaro, caballeros*,' he pronounced with affected scorn, and was answered by a chorus of derisive laughter. 'He demands his watch!' ... He ran up again to Captain Mitchell, for the desire to relieve his feelings by inflicting blows and pain upon this Englishman was very strong within him. 'Your watch! You are a prisoner in war time, Mitchell! In war time! You have no rights and no property! *Caramba!* The very breath in your body belongs to me. Remember that.'

'Bosh!' said Captain Mitchell, concealing a disagreeable impression.

Down below, in a great hall, with the earthen floor and with a tall mound thrown up by white ants in a corner, the soldiers had kindled a small fire with broken chairs and tables near the arched gateway, through which the faint murmur of the harbour waters on the beach could be heard. While Captain Mitchell was being led down the staircase, an officer passed him, running up to report to Sotillo the capture of more prisoners. A lot of smoke hung about in the vast gloomy place, the fire crackled, and, as if through a haze, Captain Mitchell made out, surrounded by short soldiers with fixed bayonets, the heads of three tall prisoners – the doctor, the engineer-in-chief, and the white leonine mane of old Viola, who stood half-turned away from the others with his chin on his breast and his arms crossed. Mitchell's astonishment knew no bounds. He cried out; the other two exclaimed also. But he hurried on, diagonally, across the big cavern-like hall. Lots of thoughts, surmises, hints of caution, and so on, crowded his head to distraction.

'Is he actually keeping you?' shouted the chief engineer, whose single eyeglass glittered in the firelight.

An officer from the top of the stairs was shouting urgently, 'Bring them all up – all three.'

In the clamour of voices and the rattle of arms, Captain Mitchell made himself heard imperfectly: 'By heavens! the fellow has stolen my watch.'

The engineer-in-chief on the staircase resisted the pressure long enough to shout, 'What? What did you say?'

'My chronometer!' Captain Mitchell yelled violently at the very moment of being thrust head foremost through a small door into a sort of cell, perfectly black, and so narrow that he fetched up against the opposite wall. The door had been instantly slammed. He knew where they had put him. This was the strong-room of the Custom House, whence the silver had been removed only a few hours earlier. It was almost as narrow as a corridor, with a small square aperture, barred by a heavy grating, at the distant end. Captain Mitchell staggered for a few steps, then sat down on the earthen floor with his back to the wall. Nothing, not even a gleam of light from anywhere, interfered with Captain Mitchell's meditation. He did some hard but not very extensive thinking. It was not of a gloomy cast. The old sailor, with all his small weaknesses and absurdities, was constitutionally incapable of entertaining for any length of time a fear of his personal safety. It was not so much firmness of soul as the lack of a certain kind of imagination – the kind whose undue development caused intense suffering to Señor Hirsch; that sort of imagination which adds the blind terror of bodily suffering and of death, envisaged as an accident to the body alone, strictly – to all the other apprehensions on which the sense of one's existence is based. Unfortunately, Captain Mitchell had not much penetration of any kind; characteristic, illuminating trifles of expression, action, or movement, escaped him completely. He was too pompously and innocently aware of his own existence to observe that of others. For instance, he could not believe that Sotillo had been really afraid of him, and this simply because it would never have entered into his head to shoot anyone except in the most pressing case of self-defence. Anybody could see he was not a murdering kind of man, he reflected quite gravely. Then why this preposterous and insulting charge? he asked himself. But his thoughts mainly clung around the astounding and unanswerable question: How the devil the fellow got to know that the silver had gone off in the lighter? It was obvious that he had not captured it. And, obviously, he could not have captured it! In this last conclusion Captain Mitchell was misled by the assumption drawn from his observation of the weather during his long vigil on the wharf. He thought that there had been much more wind than usual that night in the gulf; whereas, as a matter of fact, the reverse was the case.

'How in the name of all that's marvellous did that confounded fellow get wind of the affair?' was the first question he asked directly after the bang, clatter, and flash of the open door (which was closed again almost before he could lift his dropped head) informed him that he had a companion of captivity. Dr Monygham's voice stopped muttering curses in English and Spanish.

'Is that you, Mitchell?' he made answer, surlily. 'I struck my forehead against this confounded wall with enough force to fell an ox. Where are you?'

Captain Mitchell, accustomed to the darkness, could make out the doctor stretching out his hands blindly.

'I am sitting here on the floor. Don't fall over my legs,' Captain Mitchell's voice announced with great dignity of tone. The doctor, entreated not to walk about in the dark, sank down to the ground, too. The two prisoners of Sotillo, with their heads nearly touching, began to exchange confidences.

'Yes,' the doctor related in a low tone to Captain Mitchell's vehement curiosity, 'we have been nabbed in old Viola's place. It seems that one of their pickets, commanded by an officer, pushed as far as the town gate. They had orders not to enter, but to bring along every soul they could find on the plain. We had been talking in there with the door open, and no doubt they saw the glimmer of our light. They must have been making their approaches for some time. The engineer laid himself on a bench in a recess by the fireplace, and I went upstairs to have a look. I hadn't heard any sound from there for a long time. Old Viola, as soon as he saw me come up, lifted his arm for silence. I stole in on tiptoe. By Jove, his wife was lying down and had gone to sleep. The woman had actually dropped off to sleep! "Señor Doctor," Viola whispers to me, "it looks as if her oppression was going to get better." "Yes," I said, very much surprised; "your wife is a wonderful woman, Giorgio." Just then a shot was fired in the kitchen, which made us jump and cower as if at a thunder-clap. It seems that the party of soldiers had stolen quite close up, and one of them had crept up to the door. He looked in, thought there was no one there, and, holding his rifle ready, entered quietly. The chief told me that he had just closed his eyes for a moment. When he opened them, he saw the man already in the middle of the room peering into the dark corners. The chief was so startled that, without thinking, he made one leap from the recess right out in front of the fireplace. The soldier, no less startled, up with his rifle and pulls the trigger, deafening and singeing the engineer, but in his flurry missing him completely. But, look what happens! At the noise of the report the sleeping woman sat up, as if moved by a spring, with a shriek, "The children, Gian' Battista! Save the children!" I have it in my ears now. It was the truest cry of distress I ever heard. I stood as if paralysed, but the old husband ran across to the bedside, stretching out his hands. She clung to them! I could see her eyes go glazed; the old fellow lowered her down on the pillows and then looked round at me. She was dead! All this took less than five minutes, and then I ran down to see what was the matter. It was no use thinking of any resistance. Nothing we two could say availed with the officer, so I volunteered to go up with a couple of soldiers and fetch down old Viola. He was sitting at the foot of the bed, looking at his wife's face, and did not seem to hear what I said; but after I had pulled the sheet over her head, he got up and followed us downstairs quietly, in a sort of thoughtful way. They marched us off along the road, leaving the door open and the candle burning. The chief engineer strode on without a word, but I looked back once or twice at the feeble gleam. After we had gone some considerable distance, the Garibaldino, who was walking by my side, suddenly said, "I have buried many men on battlefields on this continent. The priests talk of consecrated ground! Bah! All the earth made by God is holy; but the sea, which knows nothing of kings and priests and tyrants, is the holiest of all. Doctor! I should like to bury her in the sea. No mummeries, candles, incense, no holy water mumbled over by priests. The spirit of liberty is upon the waters." . . . Amazing old man. He was saying all this is an undertone as if talking to himself.'

'Yes, yes,' interrupted Captain Mitchell, impatiently. 'Poor old chap! But have you any idea how the ruffian Sotillo obtained his information? He did not get hold of any of our *cargadores* who helped with the truck, did he? But no, it is impossible! These were picked men we've had in our boats for these five years, and I paid them myself specially for the job, with instructions to keep out of the way for twenty-four hours at least. I saw them with my own eyes march on with the Italians to the railway yards. The chief promised to give them rations as long as they wanted to remain there.'

'Well,' said the doctor, slowly, 'I can tell you that you may say good-bye for ever to your best lighter, and to the Capataz of Cargadores.'

At this, Captain Mitchell scrambled up to his feet in the excess of his excitement. The doctor, without giving him time to exclaim, stated briefly the part played by Hirsch during the night.

Captain Mitchell was overcome. 'Drowned!' he muttered, in a bewildered and appalled whisper. 'Drowned!' Afterwards he kept still, apparently listening, but too absorbed in the news of the catastrophe to follow the doctor's narrative with attention.

The doctor had taken up an attitude of perfect ignorance, till at last Sotillo was induced to have Hirsch brought in to repeat the whole story, which was got out of him again with the greatest difficulty, because every moment he would break out into lamentations. At last, Hirsch was led away, looking more dead than alive, and shut up in one of the upstairs rooms to be close at hand. Then the doctor, keeping up his character of a man not admitted to the inner councils of the San Tomé Administration, remarked that the story sounded incredible. Of course, he said, he couldn't tell what had been the action of the Europeans, as he had been exclusively occupied with his own work in looking after the wounded, and also in attending Don José Avellanos. He had succeeded in assuming so well a tone of impartial indifference that Sotillo seemed to be completely deceived. Till then a show of regular inquiry had been kept up; one of the officers sitting at the table wrote down the questions and the answers, the others, lounging about the room, listened attentively, puffing at their long cigars and keeping their eyes on the doctor. But at that point Sotillo ordered everybody out.

CHAPTER 3

Directly they were alone, the colonel's severe official manner changed. He rose and approached the doctor. His eyes shone with rapacity and hope; he became confidential. 'The silver might have been indeed put on board the lighter, but it was not conceivable that it should have been taken out to sea.' The doctor, watching every word, nodded slightly, smoking with apparent relish the cigar which Sotillo had offered him as a sign of his friendly intentions. The doctor's manner of cold detachment from the rest of the Europeans led Sotillo on, till, from conjecture to conjecture, he arrived at hinting that in his opinion this was a put-up job on the part of Charles Gould, in order to get hold of that immense treasure all to himself. The doctor, observant and self-possessed, muttered, 'He is very capable of that.'

Here Captain Mitchell exclaimed with amazement, amusement, and indignation, 'You said that of Charles Gould!' Disgust, and even some suspicion, crept into his tone, for to him, too, as to other Europeans, there appeared to be something dubious about the doctor's personality.

'What on earth made you say that to this watch-stealing scoundrel?' he asked. 'What's the object of an infernal lie of that sort? That confounded pickpocket was quite capable of believing you.'

He snorted. For a time the doctor remained silent in the dark.

'Yes, that is exactly what I did say,' he uttered at last, in a tone which would have made it clear enough to a third party that the pause was not of a reluctant but of a reflective character. Captain Mitchell thought that he had never heard anything so brazenly impudent in his life.

'Well, well!' he muttered to himself, but he had not the heart to voice his thoughts. They were swept away by others full of astonishment and regret. A heavy sense of discomfiture crushed him: the loss of the silver, the death of Nostromo, which was really quite a blow to his sensibilities, because he had become attached to his Capataz as people get attached to their inferiors from love of ease and almost unconscious gratitude. And when he thought of Decoud being drowned, too, his sensibility was almost overcome by this miserable end. What a heavy blow for that poor young woman! Captain Mitchell did not belong to the species of crabbed old bachelors; on the contrary, he liked to see young men paying attentions to young women. It seemed to him a natural and proper thing. Proper especially. As to sailors, it was different; it was not their place to marry, he maintained, but it was on moral grounds as a matter of self-denial, for, he explained, life on board ship is not fit for a woman even at best, and if you leave her on shore, first of all it is not fair, and next she either suffers from it or doesn't care a bit, which, in both cases, is bad. He couldn't have told what upset him most – Charles Gould's immense material loss, the death of Nostromo, which was a heavy loss to himself, or the idea of that beautiful and accomplished young woman being plunged into mourning.

'Yes,' the doctor, who had been apparently reflecting some more, began again, 'he believed me right enough. I thought he would have hugged me. "*Sí, sí*," he said, "he will write to that partner of his, the rich *americano* in San Francisco, that it is all lost. Why not? There is enough to share with many people." '

'But this is perfectly imbecile!' cried Captain Mitchell.

The doctor remarked that Sotillo *was* imbecile, and that his imbecility was ingenious enough to lead him completely astray. He had helped him only but a little way.

'I mentioned,' the doctor said, 'in a sort of casual way, that treasure is generally buried in the earth rather than being set afloat upon the sea. At this my Sotillo slapped his forehead. "*Por Dios*, yes," he said; "they must have buried it on the shores of this harbour somewhere before they sailed out." '

'Heavens and earth!' muttered Captain Mitchell, 'I should not have believed that anybody could be ass enough –' He paused, then went on mournfully: 'But what's the good of all this? It would have been a clever enough lie if the lighter had been still afloat. It would have kept that inconceivable idiot perhaps from sending out the steamer to cruise in the gulf. That was the danger that worried me no end.' Captain Mitchell sighed profoundly.

'I had an object,' the doctor pronounced, slowly.

'Had you?' muttered Captain Mitchell. 'Well, that's lucky, or else I would have thought that you went on fooling him for the fun of the thing. And perhaps that was your object. Well, I must say I personally wouldn't condescend to that sort of thing. It is not to my taste. No, no. Blackening a friend's character is not my idea of fun, if it were to fool the greatest blackguard on earth.'

Had it not been for Captain Mitchell's depression, caused by the fatal news, his disgust of Dr Monygham would have taken a more outspoken shape; but he thought to himself that now it really did not matter what that man, whom he had never liked, would say and do.

'I wonder,' he grumbled, 'why they have shut us up together, or why Sotillo should have shut you up at all, since it seems to me you have been fairly chummy up there?'

'Yes, I wonder?' said the doctor, grimly.

Captain Mitchell's heart was so heavy that he would have preferred for the time being a complete solitude to the best of company. But any company would have been preferable to the doctor's, at whom he had always looked askance as a sort of beachcomber of superior intelligence partly reclaimed from his abased state. That feeling led him to ask:

'What has that ruffian done with the other two?'

'The chief engineer he would have let go in any case,' said the doctor. 'He wouldn't like to have a quarrel with the railway upon his hands. Not just yet, at any rate. I don't think, Captain Mitchell, that you understand exactly what Sotillo's position is –'

'I don't see why I should bother my head about it,' snarled Captain Mitchell.

'No,' assented the doctor, with the same grim composure. 'I don't see why you should. It wouldn't help a single human being in the world if you thought ever so hard upon any subject whatever.'

'No,' said Captain Mitchell, simply, and with evident depression. 'A man locked up in a confounded dark hole is not much use to anybody.'

'As to old Viola,' the doctor continued, as though he had not heard, 'Sotillo released him for the same reason he is presently going to release you.'

'Eh? What?' exclaimed Captain Mitchell, staring like an owl in the darkness. 'What is there in common between me and old Viola? More likely because the old chap has no watch and chain for the pickpocket to steal. And I tell you what, Dr Monygham,' he went on with rising choler, 'he will find it more difficult than he thinks to get rid of me. He will burn his fingers over that job yet, I can tell you. To begin with, I won't go without my watch, and as to the rest – we shall see. I dare say it is no great matter for you to be locked up. But Joe Mitchell is a different kind of man, sir. I don't mean to submit tamely to insult and robbery. I am a public character, sir.'

And then Captain Mitchell became aware that the bars of the opening had become visible, a black grating upon a square of grey. The coming of the day silenced Captain Mitchell as if by the reflection that now in all the future days he would be deprived of the invaluable services of his Capataz. He leaned against the wall with his arms folded on his breast, and the doctor walked up and down the whole length of the place with his peculiar hobbling gait, as if slinking about on damaged feet. At the end farthest from the grating he would be lost altogether in the darkness. Only the slight limping shuffle could be heard. There was an air of moody detachment in that painful prowl kept up without a pause. When the door of the prison was suddenly flung open and his name shouted out he showed no surprise. He swerved sharply in his walk, and passed out at once, as though much depended upon his speed; but Captain Mitchell remained for some time with his shoulders against the wall, quite undecided in the bitterness of his spirit whether it wouldn't be better to refuse to stir a limb in the way of protest. He had half a mind to get himself carried out, but after the officer at the door had shouted three or four times in tones of remonstrance and surprise he condescended to walk out.

Sotillo's manner had changed. The colonel's offhand civility was slightly irresolute, as though he were in doubt if civility were the proper course in this case. He observed Captain Mitchell attentively before he spoke from the big armchair behind the table in a condescending voice:

'I have concluded not to detain you, Señor Mitchell. I am of a forgiving disposition. I make allowances. Let this be a lesson to you, however.'

The peculiar dawn of Sulaco, which seems to break far away to the westward and creep back into the shade of the mountains, mingled with the reddish light of the candles. Captain Mitchell, in sign of contempt and indifference, let his eyes roam all over the room, and he gave a hard stare to the doctor, perched already on the casement of one of the windows, with his eyelids lowered, careless and thoughtful – or perhaps ashamed.

Sotilla, ensconced in the vast armchair, remarked, 'I should have thought that the feelings of a *caballero* would have dictated to you an appropriate reply.'

He waited for it, but Captain Mitchell remaining mute, more from extreme resentment than from reasoned intention, Sotillo hesitated, glanced towards the doctor, who looked up and nodded, then went on with a slight effort:

'Here, Señor Mitchell, is your watch. Learn how hasty and unjust has been your judgement of my patriotic soldiers.'

Lying back in his seat, he extended his arm over the table and pushed the watch away slightly. Captain Mitchell walked up with undisguised eagerness, put it to his ear, then slipped it into his pocket coolly.

Sotillo seemed to overcome an immense reluctance. Again he looked aside at the doctor, who stared at him unwinkingly.

But as Captain Mitchell was turning away, without as much as a nod or a glance, he hastened to say:

'You may go and wait downstairs for the Señor Doctor, whom I am going to liberate, too. You foreigners are insignificant, to my mind.'

He forced a slight, discordant laugh out of himself, while Captain Mitchell, for the first time, looked at him with some interest.

'The law shall take note later on of your transgressions,' Sotillo hurried on. 'But as for me, you can live free, unguarded, unobserved. Do you hear, Señor Mitchell? You may depart to your affairs. You are beneath my notice. My attention is claimed by matters of the very highest importance.'

Captain Mitchell was very nearly provoked to an answer. It displeased him to be liberated insultingly; but want of sleep, prolonged anxieties, a profound disappointment with the fatal ending of the silver-saving business weighed upon his spirits. It was as much as he could do to conceal his uneasiness, not about himself perhaps, but about things in general. It occurred to him distinctly that something underhand was going on. As he went out he ignored the doctor pointedly.

'A brute!' said Sotillo, as the door shut.

Dr Monygham slipped off the window-sill, and, thrusting his hands into the pockets of the long, grey dust coat he was wearing, made a few steps into the room.

Sotillo got up, too, and, putting himself in the way, examined him from head to foot.

'So your countrymen do not confide in you very much, Señor Doctor. They do not love you, eh? Why is that, I wonder?'

The doctor, lifting his head, answered by a long, lifeless stare and the words, 'Perhaps because I have lived too long in Costaguana.'

Sotillo had a gleam of white teeth under the black moustache.

'Aha! But you love yourself,' he said, encouragingly.

'If you leave them alone,' the doctor said, looking with the same lifeless stare at Sotillo's handsome face, 'they will betray themselves very soon. Meantime, I may try to make Don Carlos speak?'

'Ah, Señor Doctor,' said Sotillo, wagging his head, 'you are a man of quick intelligence. We were made to understand each other.' He turned away. He could bear no longer that expressionless and motionless stare, which seemed to have a sort of impenetrable emptiness like the black depth of an abyss.

Even in a man utterly devoid of moral sense there remains an appreciation of rascality which, being conventional, is perfectly clear. Sotillo thought that Dr Monygham, so different from all Europeans, was ready to sell his countrymen and Charles Gould, his employer, for some share of the San Tomé silver. Sotillo did not despise him for that. The colonel's want of moral sense was of a profound and innocent character. It bordered upon stupidity, moral stupidity. Nothing that served his ends could appear to him really reprehensible. Nevertheless, he despised Dr Monygham. He had for him an immense and satisfactory contempt. He despised him with all his heart because he did not mean to let the doctor have any reward at all. He despised him, not as a man without faith and honour, but as a fool. Dr Monygham's insight into his character had deceived Sotillo completely. Therefore he thought the doctor a fool.

Since his arrival in Sulaco the colonel's ideas had undergone some modification.

He no longer wished for a political career in Montero's administration. He had always doubted the safety of that course. Since he had learned from the chief engineer that at daylight most likely he would be confronted by Pedro Montero his misgivings on that point had considerably increased. The *guerrillero* brother of the general – the Pedrito of popular speech – had a reputation of his own. He wasn't safe to deal with. Sotillo had vaguely planned seizing not only the treasure but the town itself, and then negotiating at leisure. But in the face of facts learned from the chief engineer (who had frankly disclosed to him the whole situation) his audacity, never of a very dashing kind, had been replaced by a most cautious hesitation.

'An army – an army crossed the mountains under Pedrito already,' he had repeated, unable to hide his consternation. 'If it had not been that I am given the news by a man of your position I would never have believed it. Astonishing!'

'An armed force,' corrected the engineer, suavely.

His aim was attained. It was to keep Sulaco clear of any armed occupation for a few hours longer, to let those whom fear impelled leave the town. In the general dismay there were families hopeful enough to fly upon the road towards Los Hatos, which was left open by the withdrawal of the armed rabble under Señores Fuentes and Gamacho, to Rincón, with their enthusiastic welcome for Pedro Montero. It was a hasty and risky exodus, and it was said that Hernandez, occupying with his band the woods about Los Hatos, was receiving the fugitives. That a good many people he knew were contemplating such a flight had been well known to the chief engineer.

Father Corbelán's efforts in the cause of that most pious robber had not been altogether fruitless. The political chief of Sulaco had yielded at the last moment to the urgent entreaties of the priest, had signed a provisional nomination appointing Hernandez a general, and calling upon him officially in his new capacity to preserve order in the town. The fact is that the political chief, seeing the situation desperate, did not care what he signed.

It was the last official document he signed before he left the palace of the Intendencia for the refuge of the O.S.N. Company's office. But even had he meant his act to be effective it was already too late. The riot which he feared and expected broke out in less than an hour after Father Corbelán had left him. Indeed, Father Corbelán, who had appointed a meeting with Nostromo in the Dominican Convent, where he had his residence in one of the cells, never managed to reach the place. From the Intendencia he had gone straight on to the Avellanos's house to tell his brother-in-law, and though he stayed there no more than half an hour he had found himself cut off from his ascetic abode. Nostromo, after waiting there for some time, watching uneasily the increasing uproar in the street, had made his way to the offices of the *Porvenir*, and stayed there till daylight, as Decoud had mentioned in the letter to his sister. Thus the Capataz, instead of riding towards the Los Hatos woods as bearer of Hernandez's nomination, had remained in town to save the life of the President-Dictator, to assist in repressing the outbreak of the mob, and at last to sail out with the silver of the mine.

But Father Corbelán, escaping to Hernandez, had the document in his pocket, a piece of official writing turning a bandit into a general in a memorable last official act of the Ribierist party, whose watchwords were honesty, peace, and progress. Probably neither the priest nor the bandit saw the irony of it. Father Corbelán must have found messengers to send into the town, for early on the second day of the disturbances there were rumours of Hernandez being on the road to Los Hatos ready to receive those who would put themselves under his protection. A strange-looking horseman, elderly and audacious, had appeared in the town, riding slowly while his eyes examined the fronts of the houses, as though he had never seen such high buildings before. Before the cathedral he had dismounted, and, kneeling in the middle of the Plaza, his bridle over his arm and his hat lying in front of him on the ground, had bowed his head, crossing himself and beating his breast for some little time. Remounting his horse, with a fearless but not unfriendly look round the little gathering formed about his public devotions, he had asked for the Casa Avellanos. A score of hands were extended in answer, with fingers pointing up the Calle de la Constitución.

The horseman had gone on with only a glance of casual curiosity upwards to the windows of the Amarilla Club at the corner. His stentorian voice shouted periodically in the empty street, 'Which is the Casa Avellanos?' till an answer came from the scared porter, and he disappeared under the gate. The letter he was bringing, written by Father Corbelán with a pencil by the camp-fire of Hernandez, was addressed to Don José, of whose critical state the priest was not aware. Antonia read it, and, after consulting Charles Gould, sent it on for the information of the gentlemen garrisoning the Amarilla Club. For herself, her mind was made up; she would rejoin her uncle; she would entrust the last day – the last hours perhaps – of her father's life to the keeping of the bandit, whose existence was a protest against the irresponsible tyranny of all parties alike, against the moral darkness of the land. The gloom of Los Hatos woods was preferable; a life of hardships in the train of a robber band less debasing. Antonia embraced with all her soul her uncle's obstinate defiance of misfortune. It was grounded in the belief in the man whom she loved.

In his message the Vicar-General answered upon his head for Hernandez's fidelity. As to his power, he pointed out that he had remained unsubdued for so many years. In that letter Decoud's idea of the new Occidental State (whose flourishing and stable condition is a matter of common knowledge now) was for the first time made public and used as an argument. Hernandez, ex-bandit and the last general of Ribierist creation, was confident of being able to hold the tract of country between the woods of Los Hatos and the coast range till that devoted patriot, Don Martin Decoud, could bring General Barrios back to Sulaco for the reconquest of the town.

'Heaven itself wills it. Providence is on our side,' wrote Father Corbelán; there was no time to reflect upon or to controvert his statement; and if the discussion started upon the reading of that letter in the Amarilla Club was violent, it was also short-lived. In the general bewilderment of the collapse some jumped at the idea with joyful astonishment as upon the amazing discovery of a new hope. Others became fascinated by the prospect of immediate personal safety for their women and children. The majority caught at it as a drowning man catches at a straw. Father Corbelán was unexpectedly offering them a refuge from Pedrito Montero with his *llaneros* allied to Señores Fuentes and Gamacho with their armed rabble.

All the latter part of the afternoon an animated discussion went on in the big rooms of the Amarilla Club. Even those members posted at the windows with rifles and carbines to guard the end of the street in case of an offensive return of the populace shouted their opinions and arguments over their shoulders. As dusk fell Don Juste Lopez, inviting those *caballeros* who were of his way of thinking to follow him, withdrew into the corridor, where at a little table in the light of two candles he busied himself in composing an address, or rather a solemn declaration to be presented to Pedrito Montero by a deputation of such members of Assembly as had elected to remain in town. His idea was to propitiate him in order to save the form at least of parliamentary institutions. Seated before a blank sheet of paper, a goose-quill in his hand, and surged upon from all sides, he turned to the right and to the left, repeating with solemn insistence:

'*Caballeros*, a moment of silence! A moment of silence! We ought to make it clear that we bow in all good faith to the accomplished facts.'

The utterance of that phrase seemed to give him a melancholy satisfaction. The hubbub of voices round him was growing strained and hoarse. In the sudden pauses the excited grimacing of the faces would sink all at once into the stillness of profound dejection.

Meantime, the exodus had begun. Carretas full of ladies and children rolled swaying across the Plaza, with men walking or riding by their side; mounted parties followed on mules and horses; the poorest were setting out on foot, men and women carrying bundles, clasping babies in their arms, leading old people, dragging along the bigger children. When Charles Gould, after leaving the doctor and the engineer at the Casa Viola, entered the town by the harbour gate, all those that had meant to go were gone, and the others had barricaded themselves in their houses. In the whole dark street there was only one spot of flickering lights and moving figures, where the Señor Administrador recognized his wife's carriage waiting at the door of the Avellanos's house. He rode up, almost unnoticed, and looked on without a word while some of his own servants came out of the gate carrying Don José Avellanos, who, with closed eyes and motionless features, appeared perfectly lifeless. His wife and Antonia walked on each side of the improvised stretcher, which was put at once into the carriage. The two women embraced; while from the other side of the landau Father Corbelán's emissary, with his ragged beard all streaked with grey, and high, bronzed cheek-bones, stared, sitting upright in the saddle. Then Antonia, dry-eyed, got in by the side of the stretcher, and, after making the sign of the cross rapidly, lowered a thick veil upon her face. The servants and the three or four neighbours who had come to assist, stood back, uncovering their heads. On the box, Ignacio, resigned now to driving all night (and to having perhaps his throat cut before daylight) looked back surlily over his shoulder.

'Drive carefully,' cried Mrs Gould in a tremulous voice.

'*Sí*, carefully, *sí niña*,' he mumbled, chewing his lips, his round leathery cheeks quivering. And the landau rolled slowly out of the light.

'I will see them as far as the ford,' said Charles Gould to his wife. She stood on the edge of the sidewalk with her hands clasped lightly, and nodded to him as he followed after the carriage. And now the windows of the Amarilla Club were dark. The last spark of resistance had died out. Turning his head at the corner, Charles Gould saw his wife crossing over to their own gate in the lighted patch of the street. One of their neighbours, a well-known merchant and landowner of the province, followed at her elbow, talking with great gestures. As she passed in all the lights went out in the street, which remained dark and empty from end to end.

The houses of the vast Plaza were lost in the night. High up, like a star, there was a small gleam in one of the towers of the cathedral; and the equestrian statue gleamed pale against the black trees of the Alameda, like a ghost of royalty haunting the scenes of revolution. The rare prowlers they met ranged themselves against the wall. Beyond the last houses the carriage rolled noiselessly on the soft cushion of dust, and with a greater obscurity a feeling of freshness seemed to fall from the foliage of the trees bordering the country road. The emissary from Hernandez's camp pushed his horse close to Charles Gould.

'*Caballero*,' he said in an interested voice, 'you are he whom they call the King of Sulaco, the master of the mine? Is it not so?'

'Yes, I am the master of the mine,' answered Charles Gould.

The man cantered for a time in silence, then said, 'I have a brother, a *sereno* in your service in the San Tomé valley. You have proved yourself a just man. There had been no wrong done to anyone since you called upon the people to work in the mountains. My brother says that no official of the Government, no oppressor of the Campo, had been seen on your side of the stream. Your own officials do not oppress the people in the gorge. Doubtless they are afraid of your severity. You are a just man and a powerful one,' he added.

He spoke in an abrupt, independent tone, but evidently he was communicative with a purpose. He told Charles Gould that he had been a *ranchero* in one of the lower valleys, far south, a neighbour of Hernandez in the old days, and godfather to his eldest boy; one of those who joined him in his resistance to the recruiting raid which was the beginning of all their misfortunes. It was he that, when his *compadre* had been carried off, had buried his wife and children, murdered by the soldiers.

'*Sí, señor,*' he muttered, hoarsely, 'I and two or three others, the lucky ones left at liberty, buried them all in one grave near the ashes of their ranch, under the tree that had shaded its roof.'

It was to him, too, that Hernandez came after he had deserted, three years afterwards. He had still his uniform on with the sergeant's stripes on the sleeve, and the blood of his colonel upon his hands and breast. Three troopers followed him, of those who had started in pursuit but had ridden on for liberty. And he told Charles Gould how he and a few friends, seeing those soldiers, lay in ambush behind some rocks ready to pull the trigger on them, when he recognized his *compadre* and jumped up from cover, shouting his name, because he knew that Hernandez could not have been coming back on an errand of injustice and oppression. Those three soldiers, together with the party who lay behind the rocks, had formed the nucleus of the famous band and he, the narrator, had been the favourite lieutenant of Hernandez for many, many years. He mentioned proudly that the officials had put a price upon his head, too; but it did not prevent it getting sprinkled with grey upon his shoulders. And now he had lived long enough to see his *compadre* made a general.

He had a burst of muffled laughter. 'And now from robbers we have become soldiers. But look, *caballero,* all those who made us soldiers and him a general! Look at these people!'

Ignacio shouted. The light of the carriage lamps, running along the nopal hedges that crowned the bank on each side, flashed upon the scared faces of people standing aside in the road, sunk deep, like an English country lane, into the soft soil of the Campo. They cowered; their eyes glistened very big for a second; and then the light, running on, fell upon the half-denuded roots of a big tree, on another stretch of nopal hedge, caught up another bunch of faces glaring back apprehensively. Three women – of whom one was carrying a child – and a couple of men in civilian dress – one armed with a sabre and another with a gun – were grouped about a donkey carrying two bundles tied up in blankets. Farther on Ignacio shouted again to pass a carreta, a long wooden box on two high wheels, with the door at the back swinging open. Some ladies in it must have recognized the white mules, because they screamed out, 'Is it you, Doña Emilia?'

At the turn of the road the glare of a big fire filled the short stretch vaulted over by the branches meeting overhead. Near the ford of a shallow stream a roadside *rancho* of woven rushes and a roof of grass had been set on fire by accident, and the flames, roaring viciously, lit up an open space blocked with horses, mules, and a distracted, shouting crowd of people. When Ignacio pulled up, several ladies on foot assailed the carriage, begging Antonia for a seat. To their clamour she answered by pointing silently to her father.

'I must leave you here,' said Charles Gould, in the uproar. The flames leaped up sky-high, and in the recoil from the scorching heat across the road the stream of fugitives pressed against the carriage. A middle-aged lady dressed in black silk, but with a coarse manta over her head and a rough branch for a stick in her hand, staggered against the front wheel. Two young girls, frightened and silent, were clinging to her arms. Charles Gould knew her very well.

'*Misericordia!* We are getting terribly bruised in this crowd!' she exclaimed, smiling up courageously to him. 'We have started on foot. All our servants ran away yesterday to join the democrats. We are going to put ourselves under the protection of Father Corbelán, of your sainted uncle, Antonia. He has wrought a miracle in the heart of a most merciless robber. A miracle!'

She raised her voice gradually up to a scream as she was borne along by the pressure of people getting out of the way of some carts coming up out of the ford at a gallop, with loud yells and cracking of whips. Great masses of sparks mingled with black smoke flew over the road; the bamboos of the walls detonated in the fire with the sound of an irregular fusillade. And then the bright blaze sank suddenly, leaving only a red dusk crowded with aimless dark shadows drifting in contrary directions; the noise of voices seemed to die away with the flame; and the tumult of heads, arms, quarrelling, and imprecations passed on fleeing into the darkness.

'I must leave you now,' repeated Charles Gould to Antonia. She turned her head slowly and uncovered her face. The emissary and *compadre* of Hernandez spurred his horse close up.

'Has not the master of the mine any message to send to Hernandez, the master of the Campo?'

The truth of the comparison struck Charles Gould heavily. In his determined purpose he held the mine, and the indomitable bandit held the Campo by the same precarious tenure. They were equals before the lawlessness of the land. It was impossible to disentangle one's activity from its debasing contacts. A close-meshed net of crime and corruption lay upon the whole country. An immense and weary discouragement sealed his lips for a time.

'You are a just man,' urged the emissary of Hernandez. 'Look at those people who made my *compadre* a general and have turned us all into soldiers. Look at those oligarchs fleeing for life, with only the clothes on their backs. My *compadre* does not think of that, but our followers may be wondering greatly, and I would speak for them to you. Listen, *señor!* For many months now the Campo has been our own. We need ask no man for anything; but soldiers must have their pay to live honestly when the wars are over. It is believed that your soul is so just that a prayer from you would cure the sickness of every beast, like the orison of the upright judge. Let me have some words from your lips that would act like a charm upon the doubts of our *partida*, where all are men.'

'Do you hear what he says?' Charles Gould said in English to Antonia.

'Forgive us our misery!' she exclaimed, hurriedly. 'It is your character that is the inexhaustible treasure which may save us all yet; your character, Carlos, not your wealth. I entreat you to give this man your word that you will accept any arrangement my uncle may make with their chief. One word. He will want no more.'

On the site of the roadside hut there remained nothing but an enormous heap of embers, throwing afar a darkening red glow, in which Antonia's face appeared deeply flushed with excitement. Charles Gould, with only a short hesitation, pronounced the required pledge. He was like a man who had ventured on a precipitous path with no room to turn, where the only chance of safety is to press forward. At that moment he understood it thoroughly as he looked down at Don José stretched out, hardly breathing, by the side of the erect Antonia, vanquished in a lifelong struggle with the powers of moral darkness, whose stagnant depths breed monstrous crimes and monstrous illusions. In a few words the emissary from Hernandez expressed his complete satisfaction. Stoically Antonia lowered her veil, resisting the longing to inquire about Decoud's escape. But Ignacio leered morosely over his shoulder.

'Take a good look at the mules, *mi amo*,' he grumbled. 'You shall never see them again!'

CHAPTER 4

Charles Gould turned towards the town. Before him jagged peaks of the Sierra came out all black in the clear dawn. Here and there a muffled *lepero* whisked round the corner of a grass-grown street before the ringing hoofs of his horse. Dogs barked behind the walls of the gardens; and with the colourless light the chill of the snows seemed to fall from the mountains upon the disjointed pavements and the shuttered houses with broken cornices and the plaster peeling in patches between the flat pilasters of the fronts. The daybreak struggled with the gloom under the arcades on the Plaza, with no signs of country people disposing their goods for the day's market, piles of fruit, bundles of vegetables ornamented with flowers, on low benches under enormous mat umbrellas; with no cheery early-morning bustle of villagers, women, children, and loaded donkeys. Only a few scattered knots of revolutionists stood in the vast space, looking all one way from under their slouched hats for some sign of news from Rincón. The largest of those groups turned about like one man as Charles Gould passed, and shouted, '*Viva la libertad!*' after him in a menacing tone.

Charles Gould rode on, and turned into the archway of his house. In the patio littered with straw, a *practicante*, one of Dr Monygham's native assistants, sat on the ground with his back against the rim of the fountain, fingering a guitar discreetly, while two girls of the lower class, standing up before him, shuffled their feet a little and waved their arms, humming a popular dance tune. Most of the wounded during the two days of rioting had been taken away already by their friends and relations, but several figures could be seen sitting up balancing their bandaged heads in time to the music. Charles Gould dismounted. A sleepy *mozo* coming out of the bakery door took hold of the horse's bridle; the *practicante* endeavoured to conceal his guitar hastily; the girls, unabashed, stepped back smiling; and Charles Gould, on his way to the staircase, glanced into a dark corner of the patio at another group, a mortally wounded *cargador* with a woman kneeling by his side; she mumbled prayers rapidly, trying at the same time to force a piece of orange between the stiffening lips of the dying man.

The cruel futility of things stood unveiled in the levity and sufferings of that incorrigible people; the cruel futility of lives and of deaths thrown away in the vain endeavour to attain an enduring solution of the problem. Unlike Decoud, Charles Gould could not play lightly a part in a tragic farce. It was tragic enough for him in all conscience, but he could see no farcical element. He suffered too much under a conviction of irremediable folly. He was too severely practical and too idealistic to look upon its terrible humours with amusement, as Martin Decoud, the imaginative materialist, was able to do in the dry light of his scepticism. To him, as to all of us, the compromises with his conscience appeared uglier than ever in the light of failure. His taciturnity, assumed with a purpose, had prevented him from tampering openly with his thoughts; but the Gould Concession had insidiously corrupted his judgement. He might have known, he said to himself, leaning over the balustrade of the corridor, that Ribierism could never come to anything. The mine had corrupted his judgement by making him sick of bribing and intriguing merely to have his work left alone from day to day. Like his father, he did not like to be robbed. It exasperated him. He had persuaded himself that, apart from higher considerations, the backing up of Don José's hopes of reform was good business. He had gone forth into the senseless fray as his poor uncle, whose sword hung on the wall of his study, had gone forth – in the defence of the commonest decencies of organized society. Only his weapon was the wealth of the mine, more far-reaching and subtle than an honest blade of steel fitted into a simple brass guard.

More dangerous to the wielder, too, this weapon of wealth, double-edged with the cupidity and misery of mankind, steeped in all the voices of self-indulgence as in a concoction of poisonous roots, tainting the very cause for which it is drawn, always ready to turn awkwardly in the hand. There was nothing for it now but to go on using it. But he promised himself to see it shattered into small bits before he let it be wrenched from his grasp.

After all, with his English parentage and English upbringing, he perceived that he was an adventurer in Costaguana, the descendant of adventurers enlisted in a foreign legion, of men who had sought fortune in a revolutionary war, who had planned revolutions, who had believed in revolutions. For all the uprightness of his character, he had something of an adventurer's easy morality which takes count of personal risk in the ethical appraising of his action. He was prepared, if need be, to blow up the whole San Tomé mountain sky high out of the territory of the Republic. This resolution expressed the tenacity of his character, the remorse of that subtle conjugal infidelity through which his wife was no longer the sole mistress of his thoughts, something of his father's imaginative weakness, and something, too, of the spirit of a buccaneer throwing a lighted match into the magazine rather than surrender his ship.

Down below in the patio the wounded *cargador* had breathed his last. The woman cried out once, and her cry, unexpected and shrill, made all the wounded sit up. The *practicante* scrambled up to his feet, and, guitar in hand, gazed steadily in her direction with elevated eyebrows. The two girls – sitting now one on each side of their wounded relative, with their knees drawn up and long cigars between their lips – nodded at each other significantly.

Charles Gould, looking down over the balustrade, saw three men dressed ceremoniously in black frock-coats with white shirts, and wearing European round hats, enter the patio from the street. One of them, head and shoulders taller than the two others, advanced with marked gravity, leading the way. This was Don Juste Lopez, accompanied by two of his friends, members of Assembly, coming to call upon the Administrador of the San Tomé mine at this early hour. They saw him, too, waved their hands to him urgently, walking up the stairs as if in procession.

Don Juste, astonishingly changed by having shaved off altogether his damaged beard, had lost with it nine-tenths of his outward dignity. Even at that time of serious preoccupation Charles Gould could not help noting the revealed ineptitude in the aspect of the man. His companions looked crestfallen and sleepy. One kept on passing the tip of his tongue over his parched lips; the other's eyes strayed dully over the tiled floor of the corridor, while Don Juste, standing a little in advance, harangued the Señor Administrador of the San Tomé mine. It was his firm opinion that forms had to be observed. A new governor is always visited by deputations from the Cabildo, which is the Municipal Council, from the Consulado, the Commercial Board, and it was proper that the Provincial Assembly should send a deputation, too, if only to assert the existence of parliamentary institutions. Don Juste proposed that Don Carlos Gould, as the most prominent citizen of the province, should join the Assembly's deputation. His position was exceptional, his personality known through the length and breadth of the whole Republic. Official courtesies must not be neglected, if they are gone through with a bleeding heart. The acceptance of accomplished facts may save yet the precious vestiges of parliamentary institutions. Don Juste's eyes glowed dully; he believed in parliamentary institutions – and the convinced drone of his voice lost itself in the stillness of the house like the deep buzzing of some ponderous insect.

Charles Gould had turned round to listen patiently, leaning his elbow on the balustrade. He shook his head a little, refusing, almost touched by the anxious gaze of the President of the Provincial Assembly. It was not Charles Gould's policy to make the San Tomé mine a party to any formal proceedings.

'My advice, *señores*, is that you should wait for your fate in your houses. There is no necessity for you to give yourselves up formally into Montero's hands. Submission to the inevitable, as Don Juste calls it, is all very well, but when the inevitable is called Pedrito Montero there is no need to exhibit pointedly the whole extent of your surrender. The fault of this country is the want of measure in political life. Flat acquiescence in illegality, followed by sanguinary reaction – that, *señores*, is not the way to a stable and prosperous future.'

Charles Gould stopped before the sad bewilderment of the faces, the wondering, anxious glances of the eyes. The feeling of pity for those men, putting all their trust into words of some sort, while murder and rapine stalked over the land, had betrayed him into what seemed empty loquacity. Don Juste murmured:

'You are abandoning us, Don Carlos ... And yet, parliamentary institutions –'

He could not finish from grief. For a moment he put his hand over his eyes. Charles Gould, in his fear of empty loquacity, made no answer to the charge. He returned in silence their ceremonious bows. His taciturnity was his refuge. He understood that what they sought was to get the influence of the San Tomé mine on their side. They wanted to go on a conciliating errand to the victor under the wing of the Gould Concession. Other public bodies – the Cabildo, the Consulado – would be coming, too, presently, seeking the support of the most stable, the most effective force they had ever known to exist in their province.

The doctor, arriving with his sharp, jerky walk, found that the master had retired into his own room with orders not to be disturbed on any account. But Dr Monygham was not anxious to see Charles Gould at once. He spent some time in a rapid examination of his wounded. He gazed down upon each in turn, rubbing his chin between the thumb and forefinger; his steady stare met without expression their silently inquisitive look. All these cases were doing well; but when he came to the dead *cargador* he stopped a little longer, surveying not the man who had ceased to suffer, but the woman kneeling in silent contemplation of the rigid face, with its pinched nostrils and a white gleam in the imperfectly closed eyes. She lifted her head slowly, and said in a dull voice:

'It is not long since he had become a *cargador* – only a few weeks. His worship the Capataz had accepted him after many entreaties.'

'I am not responsible for the great Capataz,' muttered the doctor, moving off.

Directing his course upstairs towards the door of Charles Gould's room, the doctor at the last moment hesitated; then, turning away from the handle with a shrug of his uneven shoulders, slunk off hastily along the corridor in search of Mrs Gould's *camerista*.

Leonarda told him that the *señora* had not risen yet. The *señora* had given into her charge the girls belonging to that Italian *posadero*. She, Leonarda, had put them to bed in her own room. The fair girl had cried herself to sleep, but the dark one – the bigger – had not closed her eyes yet. She sat up in bed clutching the sheets right up under her chin and staring before her like a little witch. Leonarda did not approve of the Viola children being admitted to the house. She made this feeling clear by the indifferent tone in which she inquired whether their mother was dead yet. As to the *señora*, she must be asleep. Ever since she had gone into her room after seeing the departure of Doña Antonia with her dying father, there had been no sound behind her door.

The doctor, rousing himself out of profound reflection, told her abruptly to call her mistress at once. He hobbled off to wait for Mrs Gould in the *sala*. He was very tired, but too excited to sit down. In this great drawing-room, now empty, in which his withered soul had been refreshed after many arid years and his outcast spirit had accepted silently the toleration of many side-glances, he wandered haphazard amongst the chairs and tables till Mrs Gould, enveloped in a morning wrapper, came in rapidly.

'You know that I never approved of the silver being sent away,' the doctor began at once, as a preliminary to the narrative of his night's adventures in association with Captain Mitchell, the engineer-in-chief, and old Viola, at Sotillo's headquarters. To the doctor, with his special conception of this political crisis, the removal of the silver had seemed an irrational and ill-omened measure. It was as if a general were sending the best part of his troops away on the eve of battle upon some recondite pretext. The whole lot of ingots might have been concealed somewhere where they could have been got at for the purpose of staving off the dangers which were menacing the security of the Gould Concession. The Administrador had acted as if the immense and powerful prosperity of the mine had been founded on methods of probity, on the sense of usefulness. And it was nothing of the kind. The method followed had been the only one possible. The Gould Concession had ransomed its way through all those years. It was a nauseous process. He quite understood that Charles Gould had got sick of it and had left the old path to back up that hopeless attempt at reform. The doctor did not believe in the reform of Costaguana. And now the mine was back again in its old path, with the disadvantage that henceforth it had to deal not only with the greed provoked by its wealth, but with the resentment awakened by the attempt to free itself from its bondage to moral corruption. That was the penalty of failure. What made him uneasy was that Charles Gould seemed to him to have weakened at the decisive moment when a frank return to the old methods was the only chance. Listening to Decoud's wild scheme had been a weakness.

The doctor flung up his arms, exclaiming, 'Decoud! Decoud!' He hobbled about the room with slight, angry laughs. Many years ago both his ankles had been seriously damaged in the course of a certain investigation conducted in the castle of Sta Marta by a commission composed of military men. Their nomination had been signified to them unexpectedly at the dead of night, with scowling brow, flashing eyes, and in a tempestuous voice, by Guzman Bento. The old tyrant, maddened by one of his sudden accesses of suspicion, mingled spluttering appeals to their fidelity with imprecations and horrible menaces. The cells and casements of the castle on the hill had been already filled with prisoners. The commission was charged now with the task of discovering the iniquitous conspiracy against the Citizen-Saviour of his country.

The dread of the raving tyrant translated itself into a hasty ferocity of procedure. The Citizen-Saviour was not accustomed to wait. A conspiracy had to be discovered. The courtyards of the castle resounded with the clanking of leg-irons, sounds of blows, yells of pain; and the commission of high officers laboured feverishly, concealing their distress and apprehensions from each other, and especially from their secretary, Father Berón, an army chaplain, at that time very much in the confidence of the Citizen-Saviour.

That priest was a big round-shouldered man, with an unclean-looking, overgrown tonsure on the top of his flat head, of a dingy, yellow complexion, softly fat, with greasy stains all down the front of his lieutenant's uniform, and a small cross embroidered in white cotton on his left breast. He had a heavy nose and a pendant lip. Dr Monygham remembered him still. He remembered him against all the force of his will striving its utmost to forget. Father Berón had been adjoined to the commission by Guzman Bento expressly for the purpose that his enlightened zeal should assist them in their labours. Dr Monygham could by no manner of means forget the zeal of Father Berón, or his face, or the pitiless, monotonous voice in which he pronounced the words, 'Will you confess now?'

The memory did not make him shudder, but it had made of him what he was in the eyes of respectable people, a man careless of common decencies, something between a clever vagabond and a disreputable doctor. But not all respectable people would have had the necessary delicacy of sentiment to understand with what trouble of mind and accuracy of vision Dr Monygham, medical officer of the San Tomé mine, remembered Father Berón, army chaplain, and once a secretary of a military commission. After all these years Dr Monygham, in his rooms at the end of the hospital building in the San Tomé gorge, remembered Father Berón as distinctly as ever. He remembered that priest at night, sometimes, in his sleep. On such nights the doctor waited for daylight with a candle lighted, and walking the whole length of his rooms to and fro, staring down at his bare feet, his arms hugging his sides tightly. He would dream of Father Berón sitting at the end of a long black table, behind which, in a row, appeared the heads, shoulders, and epaulettes of the military members, nibbling the feather of a quill pen, and listening with weary and impatient scorn to the protestations of some prisoner calling heaven to witness of his innocence, till he burst out, 'What's the use of wasting time over that miserable nonsense! Let me take him outside for a while.' And Father Berón would go outside after the clanking prisoner, led away between two soldiers. Such interludes happened on many days, many times, with many prisoners. When the prisoner returned he was ready to make a full confession, Father Berón would declare, leaning forward with that dull, surfeited look which can be seen in the eyes of gluttonous persons after a heavy meal.

The priest's inquisitorial instincts suffered but little from the want of classical apparatus of the Inquisition. At no time of the world's history have men been at a loss how to inflict mental and bodily anguish upon their fellow-creatures. This aptitude came to them in the growing complexity of their passions and the early refinement of their ingenuity. But it may safely be said that primeval man did not go to the trouble of inventing tortures. He was indolent and pure of heart. He brained his neighbour ferociously with a stone axe from necessity and without malice. The stupidest mind may invent a rankling phrase or brand the innocent with a cruel aspersion. A piece of string and a ramrod; a few muskets in combination with a length of hide rope; or even a simple mallet of heavy, hard wood applied with a swing to human fingers or to the joints of a human body is enough for the infliction of the most exquisite torture. The doctor had been a very stubborn prisoner, and, as natural consequence of that 'bad disposition' (so Father Berón called it), his subjugation had been very crushing and very complete. That is why the limp in his walk, the twist of his shoulders, the scars on his cheeks were so pronounced. His confessions, when they came at last, were very complete, too. Sometimes on the nights when he walked the floor, he wondered, grinding his teeth with shame and rage, at the fertility of his imagination when stimulated by a sort of pain which makes truth, honour, self-respect, and life itself matters of little moment.

And he could not forget Father Berón with his monotonous phrase, 'Will you confess now?' reaching him in an awful iteration and lucidity of meaning through the delirious incoherence of unbearable pain. He could not forget. But that was not the worst. Had he met Father Berón in the street after all these years Dr Monygham was sure he would have quailed before him. This contingency was not to be feared now. Father Berón was dead; but the sickening certitude prevented Dr Monygham from looking anybody in the face.

Dr Monygham had become, in a manner, the slave of a ghost. It was obviously impossible to take his knowledge of Father Berón home to Europe. When making his extorted confessions to the Military Board, Dr Monygham was not seeking to avoid death. He longed for it. Sitting half-naked for hours on the wet earth of his prison, and so motionless that the spiders, his companions, attached their webs to his matted hair, he consoled the misery of his soul with acute reasonings that he had confessed to crimes enough for a sentence of death – that they had gone too far with him to let him live to tell the tale.

But, as if by a refinement of cruelty, Dr Monygham was left for months to decay slowly in the darkness of his grave-like prison. It was no doubt hoped that it would finish him off without the trouble of an execution; but Dr Monygham had an iron constitution. It was Guzman Bento who died, not by the knife thrust of a conspirator, but from a stroke of apoplexy, and Dr Monygham was liberated hastily. His fetters were struck off by the light of a candle, which, after months of gloom, hurt his eyes so much that he had to cover his face with his hands. He was raised up. His heart was beating violently with the fear of this liberty. When he tried to walk the extraordinary lightness of his feet made him giddy, and he fell down. Two sticks were thrust into his hands, and he was pushed out of the passage. It was dusk; candles glimmered already in the windows of the officers' quarters round the courtyard; but the twilight sky dazed him by its enormous and over-whelming brilliance. A thin poncho hung over his naked, bony shoulders; the rags of his trousers came down no lower than his knees; an eighteen months' growth of hair fell in dirty grey locks on each side of his sharp cheek-bones. As he dragged himself past the guard-room door, one of the soldiers, lolling outside, moved by some obscure impulse, leaped forward with a strange laugh and rammed a broken old straw hat on his head. And Dr Monygham, after having tottered, continued on his way. He advanced one stick, then one maimed foot, then the other stick; the other foot followed only a very short distance along the ground, toilfully, as though it were almost too heavy to be moved at all; and yet his legs under the hanging angles of the poncho appeared no thicker than the two sticks in his hands. A ceaseless trembling agitated his bent body, all his wasted limbs, his bony head, the conical ragged crown of the sombrero, whose ample flat rim rested on his shoulders.

In such conditions of manner and attire did Dr Monygham go forth to take possession of his liberty. And these conditions seemed to bind him indissolubly to the land of Costaguana like an awful procedure of naturalization, involving him deep in the national life, far deeper than any amount of success and honour could have done. They did away with his Europeanism; for Dr Monygham had made himself an ideal conception of his disgrace. It was a conception eminently fit and proper for an officer and a gentleman. Dr Monygham, before he went out to Costaguana, had been surgeon in one of Her Majesty's regiments of foot. It was a conception which took no account of physiological facts or reasonable arguments; but it was not stupid for all that. It was simple. A rule of conduct resting mainly on severe rejections is necessarily simple. Dr Monygham's view of what it behoved him to do was severe; it was an ideal view, in so much that it was the imaginative exaggeration of a correct feeling. It was also, in its force, influence, and persistency, the view of an eminently loyal nature.

There was a great fund of loyalty in Dr Monygham's nature. He had settled it all on Mrs Gould's head. He believed her worthy of every devotion. At the bottom of his heart he felt an angry uneasiness before the prosperity of the San Tomé mine, because its growth was robbing her of all peace of mind. Costaguana was no place for a woman of that kind. What could Charles Gould have been thinking of when he brought her out there! It was outrageous! And the doctor had watched the course of events with a grim and distant reserve which, he imagined, his lamentable history imposed upon him.

Loyalty to Mrs Gould could not, however, leave out of account the safety of her husband. The doctor had contrived to be in town at the critical time because he mistrusted Charles Gould. He considered him hopelessly infected with the madness of revolutions. That is why he hobbled in distress in the drawing-room of the Casa Gould on that morning, exclaiming, 'Decoud, Decoud!' in a tone of mournful irritation.

Mrs Gould, her colour heightened, and with glistening eyes, looked straight before her at the sudden enormity of that disaster. The finger-tips on one hand rested lightly on a low little table by her side, and the arm trembled right up to the shoulder. The sun, which looks late upon Sulaco, issuing in all the fullness of its power high up on the sky from behind the dazzling snow-edge of Higuerota, had precipitated the delicate, smooth, pearly greyness of light, in which the town lies steeped during the early hours, into sharp-cut masses of black shade and spaces of hot, blinding glare. Three long rectangles of sunshine fell through the windows of the *sala*; while just across the street the front of the Avellanos's house appeared very sombre in its own shadow seen through the flood of light.

A voice said at the door, 'What of Decoud?'

It was Charles Gould. They had not heard him coming along the corridor. His glance just glided over his wife and struck full at the doctor.

'You have brought some news, doctor?'

Dr Monygham blurted it all at once, in the rough. For some time after he had done, the Administrador of the San Tomé mine remained looking at him without a word. Mrs Gould sank into a low chair with her hands lying on her lap. A silence reigned between those three motionless persons. Then Charles Gould spoke:

'You must want some breakfast.'

He stood aside to let his wife pass first. She caught up her husband's hand and pressed it as she went out, raising the handkerchief to her eyes. The sight of her husband had brought Antonia's position to her mind, and she could not contain her tears at the thought of the poor girl. When she rejoined the two men in the dining-room after having bathed her face, Charles Gould was saying to the doctor across the table:

'No, there does not seem any room for doubt.'

And the doctor assented.

'No, I don't see myself how we could question that wretched Hirsch's tale. It's only too true, I fear.'

She sat down desolately at the head of the table and looked from one to the other. The two men, without absolutely turning their heads away, tried to avoid her glance. The doctor even made a show of being hungry; he seized his knife and fork, and began to eat with emphasis, as if on the stage. Charles Gould made no pretence of the sort; with his elbows raised squarely, he twisted both ends of his flaming moustaches – they were so long that his hands were quite away from his face.

'I am not surprised,' he muttered, abandoning his moustaches and throwing one arm over the back of the chair. His face was calm with that immobility of expression which betrays the intensity of a mental struggle. He felt that this accident had brought to a point all the consequences involved in his line of conduct, with its conscious and subconscious intentions. There must be an end now of this silent reserve, of that air of impenetrability behind which he had been safeguarding his dignity. It was the least ignoble form of dissembling forced upon him by that parody of civilized institutions which offended his intelligence, his uprightness, and his sense of right. He was like his father. He had no ironic eye. He was not amused at the absurdities that prevail in this world. They hurt him in his innate gravity. He felt that the miserable death of that poor Decoud took from him his inaccessible position of a force in the background. It committed him openly unless he wished to throw up the game – and that was impossible. The material interests required from him the sacrifice of his aloofness – perhaps his own safety too. And he reflected that Decoud's separationist plan had not gone to the bottom with the lost silver.

The only thing that was not changed was his position towards Mr Holroyd. The head of silver and steel interests had entered into Costaguana affairs with a sort of passion. Costaguana had become necessary to his existence; in the San Tomé mine he had found the imaginative satisfaction which other minds would get from drama, from art, or from a risky and fascinating sport. It was a special form of the great man's extravagance, sanctioned by a moral intention, big enough to flatter his vanity. Even in this aberration of his genius he served the progress of the world. Charles Gould felt sure of being understood with precision and judged with the indulgence of their common passion. Nothing now could surprise or startle this great man. And Charles Gould imagined himself writing a letter to San Francisco in some such words: '. . . The men at the head of the movement are dead or have fled; the civil organization of the province is at an end for the present; the Blanco party in Sulaco has collapsed inexcusably, but in the characteristic manner of this country. But Barrios, untouched in Cayta, remains still available. I am forced to take up openly the plan of a provincial revolution as the only way of placing the enormous material interests involved in the prosperity and peace of Sulaco in a position of permanent safety. . . .' That was clear. He saw these words as if written in letters of fire upon the wall at which he was gazing abstractedly.

Mrs Gould watched his abstraction with dread. It was a domestic and frightful phenomenon that darkened and chilled the house for her like a thunder-cloud passing over the sun. Charles Gould's fits of abstraction depicted the energetic concentration of a will haunted by a fixed idea. A man haunted by a fixed idea is insane. He is dangerous even if that idea is an idea of justice; for may he not bring the heaven down pitilessly upon a loved head? The eyes of Mrs Gould, watching her husband's profile, filled with tears again. And again she seemed to see the despair of the unfortunate Antonia.

'What would I have done if Charley had been drowned while we were engaged?' she exclaimed, mentally, with horror. Her heart turned to ice, while her cheeks flamed up as if scorched by the blaze of a funeral pyre consuming all her earthly affections. The tears burst out of her eyes.

'Antonia will kill herself!' she cried out.

This cry fell into the silence of the room with strangely little effect. Only the doctor, crumbling up a piece of bread, with his head inclined on one side, raised his face, and the few long hairs sticking out of his shaggy eyebrows stirred in a slight frown. Dr Monygham thought quite sincerely that Decoud was a singularly unworthy object for any woman's affection. Then he lowered his head again, with a curl of his lip, and his heart full of tender admiration for Mrs Gould.

'She thinks of that girl,' he said to himself; 'she thinks of the Viola children; she thinks of me; of the wounded; of the miners; she always thinks of everybody who is poor and miserable! But what will she do if Charles gets the worst of it in this infernal scrimmage those confounded Avellanos have drawn him into? No one seems to be thinking of her.'

Charles Gould, staring at the wall, pursued his reflections subtly.

'I shall write to Holroyd that the San Tomé mine is big enough to take in hand the making of a new State. It'll please him. It'll reconcile him to the risk.'

But was Barrios really available? Perhaps. But he was inaccessible. To send off a boat to Cayta was no longer possible, since Sotillo was master of the harbour, and had a steamer at his disposal. And now, with all the democrats in the province up, and every Campo township in a state of disturbance, where could he find a man who would make his way successfully

overland to Cayta with a message, a ten day's ride at least; a man of courage
and resolution, who would avoid arrest or murder, and if arrested would
faithfully eat the paper? The Capataz de Cargadores would have been just
such a man. But the Capataz of the Cargadores was no more.

And Charles Gould, withdrawing his eyes from the wall, said gently,
'That Hirsch! What an extraordinary thing! Saved himself by clinging to
the anchor, did he? I had no idea that he was still in Sulaco. I thought he
had gone back overland to Esmeralda more than a week ago. He came here
once to talk to me about his hide business and some other things. I made it
clear to him that nothing could be done.'

'He was afraid to start back on account of Hernandez being about,'
remarked the doctor.

'And but for him we might not have known anything of what has
happened,' marvelled Charles Gould.

Mrs Gould cried out:

'Antonia must not know! She must not be told. Not now.'

'Nobody's likely to carry the news,' remarked the doctor. 'It's no one's
interest. Moreover, the people here are afraid of Hernandez as if he were
the devil.' He turned to Charles Gould. 'It's even awkward, because if you
wanted to communicate with the refugees you could find no messenger.
When Hernandez was ranging hundreds of miles away from here the Sulaco
populace used to shudder at the tales of him roasting his prisoners alive.'

'Yes,' murmured Charles Gould; 'Captain Mitchell's Capataz was the
only man in the town who had seen Hernandez eye to eye. Father Corbelán
employed him. He opened the communications first. It is a pity that – '

His voice was covered by the booming of the great bell of the cathedral.
Three single strokes, one after another, burst out explosively, dying away
in deep and mellow vibrations. And then all the bells in the tower of every
church, convent, or chapel in town, even those that had remained shut up
for years, pealed out together with a crash. In this furious flood of metallic
uproar there was a power of suggesting images of strife and violence which
blanched Mrs Gould's cheek. Basilio, who had been waiting at table,
shrinking within himself, clung to the sideboard with chattering teeth. It
was impossible to hear yourself speak.

'Shut these windows!' Charles Gould yelled at him, angrily. All the other
servants, terrified at what they took for the signal of a general massacre, had
rushed upstairs, tumbling over each other, men and women, the obscure and
generally invisible population of the ground floor on the four sides of the
patio. The women, screaming '*Misericordia!*' ran right into the room, and,
falling on their knees against the walls, began to cross themselves convulsively.
The staring heads of men blocked the doorway in an instant – *mozos* from
the stable, gardeners, nondescript helpers living on the crumbs of the
munificent house – and Charles Gould beheld all the extent of his domestic
establishment, even to the gatekeeper. This was a half-paralysed old man,
whose long white locks fell down to his shoulders: an heirloom taken up by
Charles Gould's familial piety. He could remember Henry Gould, an
Englishman and a Costaguanero of the second generation, chief of the Sulaco
province; he had been his personal *mozo* years and years ago in peace and

war; had been allowed to attend his master in prison; had, on the fatal morning, followed the firing squad; and, peeping from behind one of the cypresses growing along the wall of the Franciscan Convent, had seen, with his eyes starting out of his head, Don Enrique throw up his hands and fall with his face in the dust. Charles Gould noted particularly the big patriarchal head of that witness in the rear of the other servants. But he was surprised to see a shrivelled old hag or two, of whose existence within the walls of his house he had not been aware. They must have been the mothers, or even the grandmothers, of some of his people. There were a few children, too, more or less naked, crying and clinging to the legs of their elders. He had never before noticed any sign of a child in his patio. Even Leonarda, the *camerista*, came in a fright, pushing through, with her spoiled, pouting face of a favourite maid, leading the Viola girls by the hand. The crockery rattled on table and sideboard, and the whole house seemed to sway in the deafening wave of sound.

CHAPTER 5

During the night the expectant populace had taken possession of all the belfries in the town in order to welcome Pedrito Montero, who was making his entry after having slept the night in Rincón. And first came straggling in through the land gate the armed mob of all colours, complexions, types, and states of raggedness, calling themselves the Sulaco National Guard, and commanded by Señor Gamacho. Through the middle of the street streamed, like a torrent of rubbish, a mass of straw hats, ponchos, gun-barrels, with an enormous green and yellow flag flapping in their midst, in a cloud of dust, to the furious beating of drums. The spectators recoiled against the walls of the houses shouting their '*Vivas!*' Behind the rabble could be seen the lances of the cavalry, the 'army' of Pedro Montero. He advanced between Señores Fuentes and Gamacho at the head of his *llaneros*, who had accomplished the feat of crossing the Paramos of the Higuerota in a snow-storm. They rode four abreast, mounted on confiscated Campo horses, clad in the heterogeneous stock of roadside stores they had looted hurriedly in their rapid ride through the northern part of the province; for Pedro Montero had been in a great hurry to occupy Sulaco. The handkerchiefs knotted loosely around their bare throats were glaringly new, and all the right sleeves of their cotton shirts had been cut off close to the shoulder for greater freedom in throwing the *lazo*. Emaciated greybeards rode by the side of lean dark youths, marked by all the hardships of campaigning, with strips of raw beef twined round the crowns of their hats, and huge iron spurs fastened to their naked heels. Those that in the passes of the mountain had lost their lances had provided themselves with the goads used by the Campo cattlemen: slender shafts of palm fully ten feet long, with a lot of loose rings jingling under the ironshod point. They were armed with knives and revolvers. A haggard fearlessness characterized the expression of all these sun-blacked countenances; they glared down haughtily with their scorched eyes at the crowd, or, blinking upwards insolently, pointed out to each other some particular head amongst the women at the windows. When they had ridden into the Plaza and caught sight of the equestrian statue of the King dazzlingly white in the sunshine, towering enormous and motionless above the surges of the crowd, with its eternal gesture of saluting, a murmur of surprise ran through their ranks. 'What is that saint in the big hat?' they asked each other.

They were a good sample of the cavalry of the plains with which Pedro Montero had helped so much the victorious career of his brother the general. The influence which that man, brought up in coast towns, acquired in a short time over the plainsmen of the Republic can be ascribed only to a genius for treachery of so effective a kind that it must have appeared to those violent men but little removed from a state of utter savagery, as the perfection of sagacity and virtue. The popular lore of all nations testified that duplicity and cunning, together with bodily strength, were looked upon, even more than courage, as heroic virtues by primitive mankind. To overcome your adversary was the great affair of life. Courage was taken for granted. But the use of intelligence awakened wonder and respect. Stratagems, providing they did not fail, were honourable; the easy massacre of an unsuspecting enemy evoked no feelings but those of gladness, pride, and admiration. Not perhaps that primitive men were more faithless than their descendants of today, but that they went straighter to their aim, and were more artless in their recognition of success as the only standard of morality.

We have changed since. The use of intelligence awakens little wonder and less respect. But the ignorant and barbarous plainsmen engaging in civil strife followed willingly a leader who often managed to deliver their enemies bound, as it were, into their hands. Pedro Montero had a talent for lulling his adversaries into a sense of security. And as men learn wisdom with extreme slowness, and are always ready to believe promises that flatter their secret hopes, Pedro Montero was successful time after time. Whether only a servant or some inferior official in the Costaguana Legation in Paris, he had rushed back to his country directly he heard that his brother had emerged from the obscurity of his frontier *comandancia*. He had managed to deceive by his gift of plausibility the chiefs of the Ribierist movement in the capital, and even the acute agent of the San Tomé mine had failed to understand him thoroughly. At once he had obtained an enormous influence over his brother. They were very much alike in appearance, both bald, with bunches of crisp hair above their ears, arguing the presence of some Negro blood. Only Pedro was smaller than the general, more delicate altogether, with an ape-like faculty for imitating all the outward signs of refinement and distinction, and with a parrot-like talent for languages. Both brothers had received some elementary instruction by the munificence of a great European traveller, to whom their father had been a body-servant during his journeys in the interior of the country. In General Montero's case it enabled him to rise from the ranks. Pedrito, the younger, incorrigibly lazy and slovenly, had drifted aimlessly from one coast town to another, hanging about counting-houses, attaching himself to strangers as a sort of *valet de place*, picking up an easy and disreputable living. His ability to read did nothing for him but fill his head with absurd visions. His actions were usually determined by motives so improbable in themselves as to escape the penetration of a rational person.

Thus at first sight the agent of the Gould Concession in Sta Marta had credited him with the possession of sane views, and even with a restraining power over the general's everlastingly discontented vanity. It could never have entered his head that Pedrito Montero, lackey or inferior scribe, lodged in the garrets of the various Parisian hotels where the Costaguana Legation used to shelter its diplomatic dignity, had been devouring the lighter sort of historical works in the French language, such, for instance, as the books of Imbert de Saint Amand upon the Second Empire. But Pedrito had been struck by the splendour of a brilliant court, and had conceived the idea of an existence for himself where, like the Duc de Morny, he would associate the command of every pleasure with the conduct of political affairs and enjoy power supremely in every way. Nobody could have guessed that. And yet this was one of the immediate causes of the Monterist Revolution. This will appear less incredible by the reflection that the fundamental causes were the same as ever, rooted in the political immaturity of the people, in the indolence of the upper classes and the mental darkness of the lower.

Pedrito Montero saw in the elevation of his brother the road wide open to his wildest imaginings. This was what made the Monterist *pronunciamiento* so unpreventable. The general himself probably could have been bought off, pacified with flatteries, dispatched on a diplomatic mission to Europe. It was his brother who had egged him on from first to last. He wanted to become the most brilliant statesman of South America. He did not desire supreme power. He would have been afraid of its labour and risk, in fact. Before all, Pedrito Montero, taught by his European experience, meant to acquire a serious fortune for himself. With this object in view he obtained from his brother, on the very morrow of the successful battle, the permission to push on over the mountains and take possession of Sulaco. Sulaco was the land of future prosperity, the chosen land of material progress, the only province in the Republic of interest to European capitalists. Pedrito Montero, following the example of the Duc de Morny, meant to have his share of this prosperity. This is what he meant literally. Now his brother was master of the country, whether as president, dictator, or even as Emperor – why not as an Emperor? – he meant to demand a share in every enterprise – in railways, in mines, in sugar estates, in cotton mills, in land companies, in each and every undertaking – as the price of his protection. The desire to be on the spot early was the real cause of the celebrated ride over the mountains with some two hundred *llaneros*, an enterprise of which the dangers had not appeared at first clearly to his impatience. Coming from a series of victories, it seemed to him that a Montero had only to appear to be master of the situation. This illusion had betrayed him into a rashness of which he was becoming aware. As he rode at the head of his *llaneros* he regretted that there were so few of them. The enthusiasm of the populace

reassured him. They yelled *'Viva Montero! Viva Pedrito!'* In order to make
them still more enthusiastic, and from the natural pleasure he had in
dissembling, he dropped the reins on his horse's neck, and with a tremendous
effect of familiarity and confidence slipped his hands under the arms of
Señores Fuentes and Gamacho. In that posture, with a ragged town *mozo*
holding his horse by the bridle, he rode triumphantly across the Plaza to the
door of the Intendencia. Its old gloomy walls seemed to shake in the
acclamations that rent the air and covered the crashing peals of the cathedral
bells.

Pedro Montero, the brother of the general, dismounted into a shouting
and perspiring throng of enthusiasts whom the ragged Nationals were
pushing back fiercely. Ascending a few steps he surveyed the large crowd
gaping at him and the bullet-speckled walls of the houses opposite lightly
veiled by a sunny haze of dust. The word 'PORVENIR' in immense black
capitals, alternating with broken windows, stared at him across the vast
space; and he thought with delight of the hour of vengeance, because he was
very sure of laying his hands upon Decoud. On his left hand, Gamacho, big
and hot, wiping his hairy wet face, uncovered a set of yellow fangs in a grin
of stupid hilarity. On his right, Señor Fuentes, small and lean, looked on
with compressed lips. The crowd stared literally open-mouthed, lost in eager
stillness, as though they had expected the great *guerrillero*, the famous
Pedrito, to begin scattering at once some sort of visible largesse. What he
began was a speech. He began it with the shouted word 'Citizens!' which
reached even those in the middle of the Plaza. Afterwards the greater part
of the citizens remained fascinated by the orator's action alone, his tip-toeing,
the arms flung above his head with the fists clenched, a hand laid flat upon
the heart, the silver gleam of rolling eyes, the sweeping, pointing, embracing
gestures, a hand laid familiarly on Gamacho's shoulder; a hand waved
formally towards the little black-coated person of Señor Fuentes, advocate
and politician and a true friend of the people. The *'Vivas!'* of those nearest
to the orator bursting out suddenly propagated themselves irregularly to the
confines of the crowd, like flames running over dry grass, and expired in the
opening of the streets. In the intervals, over the swarming Plaza brooded a
heavy silence, in which the mouth of the orator went on opening and
shutting, and detached phrases – 'The happiness of the people', 'Sons of the
country', 'The entire world, *el mundo entiero*' – reached even the packed
steps of the cathedral with a feeble clear ring, thin as the buzzing of a
mosquito. But the orator struck his breast; he seemed to prance between his
two supporters. It was the supreme effort of his peroration. Then the two
smaller figures disappeared from the public gaze and the enormous Gamacho,
left alone, advanced, raising his hat high above his head. Then he covered
himself proudly and yelled out, *'Ciudadanos!'* A dull roar greeted Señor
Gamacho, ex-pedlar of the Campo, Comandante of the National Guard.

Upstairs Pedrito Montero walked about rapidly from one wrecked room
of the Intendencia to another, snarling incessantly:

'What stupidity! What destruction!'

Señor Fuentes, following, would relax his taciturn disposition to murmur:
'It is all the work of Gamacho and his Nationals'; and then, inclining his

head on his left shoulder, would press together his lips so firmly that a little hollow would appear at each corner. He had his nomination for Political Chief of the town in his pocket, and was all impatience to enter upon his functions.

In the long audience-room, with its tall mirrors all starred by stones, the hangings torn down, and the canopy over the platform at the upper end pulled to pieces, the vast, deep muttering of the crowd and the howling voice of Gamacho speaking just below reached them through the shutters as they stood idly in dimness and desolation.

'The brute!' observed his Excellency Don Pedro Montero through clenched teeth. 'We must contrive as quickly as possible to send him and his Nationals out there to fight Hernandez.'

The new Jefe Político only jerked his head sideways, and took a puff at his cigarette in sign of his agreement with his method for ridding the town of Gamacho and his inconvenient rabble.

Pedrito Montero looked with disgust at the absolutely bare floor, and at the belt of heavy gilt picture-frames running round the room, out of which the remnants of torn and slashed canvases fluttered like dingy rags.

'We are not barbarians,' he said.

This was what said his Excellency, the popular Pedrito, the *guerrillero* skilled in the art of laying ambushes, charged by his brother at his own demand with the organization of Sulaco on democratic principles. The night before, during the consultation with his partisans, who had come out to meet him in Rincón, he had opened his intentions to Señor Fuentes:

'We shall organize a popular vote, by yes or no, confiding the destinies of our beloved country to the wisdom and valiance of my heroic brother, the invincible general. A plebiscite. Do you understand?'

And Señor Fuentes, puffing out his leathery cheeks, had inclined his head slightly to the left, letting a thin, bluish jet of smoke escape through his pursed lips. He had understood.

His Excellency was exasperated at the devastation. Not a single chair, table, sofa, *étagère*, or console had been left in the state rooms of the Intendencia. His Excellency, though twitching all over with rage, was restrained from bursting into violence by a sense of his remoteness and isolation. His heroic brother was very far away. Meantime, how was he going to take his siesta? He had expected to find comfort and luxury in the Intendencia after a year of hard camp life, ending with the hardships and privations of the daring dash upon Sulaco – upon the province which was worth more in wealth and influence than all the rest of the Republic's territory. He would get even with Gamacho by-and-by. And Señor Gamacho's oration, delectable to popular ears, went on in the heat and glare of the Plaza like the uncouth howlings of an inferior sort of devil cast into a white-hot furnace. Every moment he had to wipe his streaming face with his bare fore-arm; he had flung off his coat, and had turned up the sleeves of his shirt high above the elbows; but he kept on his head the large cocked hat with white plumes. His ingenuousness cherished this sign of his rank as Comandante of the National Guard. Approving and grave murmurs greeted his periods. His opinion was that war should be declared at once

against France, England, Germany, and the United States, who, by introducing railways, mining enterprises, colonization, and under such other
shallow pretences, aimed at robbing poor people of their lands, and with the
help of these Goths and paralytics, the aristocrats would convert them into
toiling and miserable slaves. And the *leperos*, flinging about the corners of
their dirty white mantas, yelled their approbation. General Montero,
Gamacho howled with conviction, was the only man equal to the patriotic
task. They assented to that, too.

The morning was wearing on; there were already signs of disruption,
currents and eddies in the crowd. Some were seeking the shade of the walls
and under the trees of the Alameda. Horsemen spurred through, shouting;
groups of sombreros set level on heads against the vertical sun were drifting
away into the streets, where the open doors of *pulperías* revealed an enticing
gloom resounding with the gentle tinkling of guitars. The National Guards
were thinking of siesta, and the eloquence of Gamacho, their chief, was
exhausted. Later on, when, in the cooler hours of the afternoon, they tried
to assemble again for further consideration of public affairs, detachments of
Montero's cavalry camped on the Alameda charged them without parley, at
speed, with long lances levelled at their flying backs as far as the ends of the
streets. The National Guards of Sulaco were surprised by this proceeding.
But they were not indignant. No Costaguanero had ever learned to question
the eccentricities of a military force. They were part of the natural order of
things. This must be, they concluded, some kind of administrative measure,
no doubt. But the motive of it escaped their unaided intelligence, and their
chief and orator, Gamacho, Comandante of the National Guard, was lying
drunk and asleep in the bosom of his family. His bare feet were upturned
in the shadows repulsively, in the manner of a corpse. His eloquent mouth
had dropped open. His youngest daughter, scratching her head with one
hand, with the other waved a green bough over his scorched and peeling
face.

CHAPTER 6

The declining sun had shifted the shadows from west to east amongst the
houses of the town. It had shifted them upon the whole extent of the immense
Campo, with the white walls of its *haciendas* on the knolls dominating the
green distances; with its grass-thatched *ranchos* crouching in the folds of
ground by the banks of streams; with the dark islands of clustered trees on
a clear sea of grass, and the precipitous range of the Cordillera, immense
and motionless, emerging from the billows of the lower forests like the barren
coast of a land of giants. The sunset rays striking the snow-slope of Higuerota
from afar gave it an air of rosy youth, while the serrated mass of distant
peaks remained black, as if calcined in the fiery radiance. The undulating

surface of the forests seemed powdered with pale gold dust; and away there, beyond Rincón, hidden from the town by two wooded spurs, the rocks of the San Tomé gorge, with the flat wall of the mountain itself crowned by gigantic ferns, took on warm tones of brown and yellow, with red rusty streaks, and the dark green clumps of bushes rooted in crevices. From the plain the stamp sheds and the houses of the mine appeared dark and small, high up, like the nests of birds clustered on the ledges of a cliff. The zigzag paths resembled faint tracings scratched on the wall of a cylopean blockhouse. To the two *serenos* of the mine on patrol duty, strolling, carbine in hand, and watchful eyes, in the shade of the trees lining the stream near the bridge, Don Pepe, descending the path from the upper plateau, appeared no bigger than a large beetle.

With his air of aimless, insect-like going to and fro upon the face of the rock, Don Pepe's figure kept on descending steadily, and, when near the bottom, sank at last behind the roofs of store-houses, forges, and workshops. For a time the pair of *serenos* strolled back and forth before the bridge, on which they had stopped a horseman holding a large white envelope in his hand. Then Don Pepe, emerging in the village street from amongst the houses, not a stone's throw from the frontier bridge, approached, striding in wide dark trousers tucked into boots, a white linen jacket, sabre at his side, and revolver at his belt. In this disturbed time nothing could find the Señor Gobernador with his boots off, as the saying is.

At a slight nod from one of the *serenos*, the man, a messenger from the town, dismounted, and crossed the bridge, leading his horse by the bridle.

Don Pepe received the letter from his other hand, slapped his left side and his hips in succession, feeling for his spectacle case. After settling the heavy silver-mounted affair astride his nose, and adjusting it carefully behind his ears, he opened the envelope, holding it up at about a foot in front of his eyes. The paper he pulled out contained some three lines of writing. He looked at them for a long time. His grey moustache moved slightly up and down, and the wrinkles, radiating at the corners of his eyes, ran together. He nodded serenely. '*Bueno,*' he said. 'There is no answer.'

Then, in his quiet, kindly way, he engaged in a cautious conversation with the man, who was willing to talk cheerily, as if something lucky had happened to him recently. He had seen from a distance Sotillo's infantry camped along the shore of the harbour on each side of the Custom House. They had done no damage to the buildings. The foreigners of the railway remained shut up within the yards. They were no longer anxious to shoot poor people. He cursed the foreigners; then he reported Montero's entry and the rumours of the town. The poor were going to be made rich now. That was very good. More he did not know, and, breaking into propitiatory smiles, he intimated that he was hungry and thirsty. The old major directed him to go to the *alcalde* of the first village. The man rode off, and Don Pepe, striding slowly in the direction of a little wooden belfry, looked over a hedge into a little garden, and saw Father Román sitting in a white hammock slung between two orange trees in front of the presbytery.

An enormous tamarind shaded with its dark foliage the whole white frame-house. A young Indian girl with long hair, big eyes, and small hands and feet, carried out a wooden chair, while a thin old woman, crabbed and vigilant, watched her all the time from the veranda.

Don Pepe sat down in the chair and lighted a cigar; the priest drew in an immense quantity of snuff out of the hollow of his palm. On his reddish-brown face, worn, hollowed as if crumbled, the eyes, fresh and candid, sparkled like two black diamonds.

Don Pepe, in a mild and humorous voice, informed Father Román that Pedrito Montero, by the hand of Señor Fuentes, had asked him on what terms he would surrender the mine in proper working order to a legally constituted commission of patriotic citizens, escorted by a small military force. The priest cast his eyes up to heaven. However, Don Pepe continued, the *mozo* who brought the letter said that Don Carlos Gould was alive, and so far unmolested.

Father Román expressed in a few words his thankfulness at hearing of the Señor Administrador's safety.

The hour of oration had gone by in the silvery ringing of a bell in the little belfry. The belt of forest closing the entrance of the valley stood like a screen between the low sun and the street of the village. At the other end of the rocky gorge, between the walls of basalt and granite, a forest-clad mountain, hiding all the range from the San Tomé dwellers, rose steeply, lighted up and leafy to the very top. Three small rosy clouds hung motionless overhead in the great depth of blue. Knots of people sat in the street between the wattled huts. Before the *casa* of the *alcalde*, the foremen of the night-shift, already assembled to lead their men, squatted on the ground in a circle of leather skull-caps, and, bowing their bronze backs, were passing round the gourd of maté. The *mozo* from the town, having fastened his horse to a wooden post before the door, was telling them the news of Sulaco as the blackened gourd of the decoction passed from hand to hand. The grave *alcalde* himself, in a white waistcloth and a flowered chintz gown with sleeves, open wide upon his naked stout person with an effect of a gaudy bathing robe, stood by, wearing a rough beaver hat at the back of his head, and grasping a tall staff with a silver knob in his hand. These insignia of his dignity had been conferred upon him by the Administration of the mine, the fountain of honour, of prosperity, and peace. He had been one of the first immigrants into this valley; his sons and sons-in-law worked within the mountain which seemed with its treasures to pour down the thundering ore shoots of the upper *mesa*, the gifts of well-being, security, and justice upon the toilers. He listened to the news from the town with curiosity and indifference, as if concerning another world than his own. And it was true that they appeared to him so. In a very few years the sense of belonging to a powerful organization had been developed in these harassed, half-wild Indians. They were proud of, and attached to, the mine. It had secured their confidence and belief. They invested it with a protecting and invincible virtue as though it were a fetish made by their own hands, for they were ignorant, and in other respects did not differ appreciably from the rest of mankind which puts infinite trust in its own creations. It never entered the *alcalde*'s head that the mine could fail in its protection and force. Politics were good enough for people of the town and the Campo. His yellow, round face, with wide nostrils, and motionless in expression, resembled a fierce full moon. He listened to the excited vapourings of the *mozo* without misgivings, without surprise, without any active sentiment whatever.

Padre Román sat dejectedly balancing himself, his feet just touching the ground, his hands gripping the edge of the hammock. With less confidence, but as ignorant as his flock, he asked the major what did he think was going to happen now.

Don Pepe, bolt upright in the chair, folded his hands peacefully on the hilt of his sword, standing perpendicular between his thighs, and answered that he did not know. The mine could be defended against any force likely to be sent to take possession. On the other hand, from the arid character of the valley, when the regular supplies from the Campo had been cut off, the population of the three villages could be starved into submission. Don Pepe exposed these contingencies with serenity to Father Román, who, as an old campaigner, was able to understand the reasoning of a military man. They talked with simplicity and directness. Father Román was saddened at the idea of his flock being scattered or else enslaved. He had no illusions as to their fate, not from penetration, but from long experience of political atrocities, which seemed to him fatal and unavoidable in the life of a State. The working of the usual public institutions presented itself to him most distinctly as a series of calamities overtaking private individuals and flowing logically from each other through hate, revenge, folly, and rapacity, as though they had been part of a divine dispensation. Father Román's clear-sightedness was served by an uninformed intelligence; but his heart, preserving its tenderness amongst scenes of carnage, spoliation, and violence, abhorred these calamities the more as his association with the victims was closer. He entertained towards the Indians of the valley feelings of paternal scorn. He had been marrying, baptizing, confessing, absolving, and burying the workers of the San Tomé mine with dignity and unction for five years or more; and he believed in the sacredness of these ministrations, which made them his own in a spiritual sense. They were dear to his sacerdotal supremacy. Mrs Gould's earnest interest in the concerns of these people enhanced their importance in the priest's eyes, because it really augmented his own. When talking over with her the innumerable Marias and Brigidas of the villages, he felt his own humanity expand. Padre Román was incapable of fanaticism to an almost reprehensible degree. The English *señora* was evidently a heretic; but at the same time she seemed to him wonderful and angelic. Whenever that confused state of his feelings occurred to him, while strolling, for instance, his breviary under his arm, in the wide shade of the tamarind, he would stop short to inhale with a strong snuffling noise a large quantity of snuff, and shake his head profoundly. At the thought of what might befall the illustrious *señora* presently, he became gradually overcome with dismay. He voiced it in an agitated murmur. Even Don Pepe lost his serenity for a moment. He leaned forward stiffly.

'Listen, Padre. The very fact that those thieving *macaques* in Sulaco are trying to find out the price of my honour proves that Señor Don Carlos and all in the Casa Gould are safe. As to my honour, that also is safe, as every man, woman, and child knows. But the Negro liberals who have snatched the town by surprise do not know that. *Bueno.* Let them sit and wait. While they wait they can do no harm.'

And he regained his composure. He regained it easily, because whatever happened his honour of an old officer of Paez was safe. He had promised Charles Gould that at the approach of an armed force he would defend the gorge just long enough to give himself time to destroy scientifically the whole plant, buildings, and workshops of the mine with heavy charges of dynamite; block with ruins the main tunnel, break down the pathways, blow up the dam of the water-power, shatter the famous Gould Concession into fragments, flying sky-high out of a horrified world. The mine had got hold of Charles Gould with a grip as deadly as ever it had laid upon his father. But this extreme resolution had seemed to Don Pepe the most natural thing in the world. His measures had been taken with judgement. Everything was prepared with a careful completeness. And Don Pepe folded his hands pacifically on his sword hilt, and nodded at the priest. In his excitement, Father Román had flung snuff in handfuls at his face, and, all besmeared with tobacco, roundeyed, and beside himself, had got out of the hammock to walk about, uttering exclamations.

Don Pepe stroked his grey and pendant moustache, whose fine ends hung far below the clean-cut line of his jaw, and spoke with a conscious pride in his reputation.

'So, Padre, I don't know what will happen. But I know that as long as I am here Don Carlos can speak to that *macaque*, Pedrito Montero, and threaten the destruction of the mine with perfect assurance that will be taken seriously. For people know me.'

He began to turn the cigar in his lips a little nervously, and went on:

'But that is talk – good for the *políticos.* I am a military man. I do not know what may happen. But I know what ought to be done – the mine should march upon the town with guns, axes, knives tied up to sticks – *por Dios.* That is what should be done. Only –'

His folded hands twitched on the hilt. The cigar turned faster in the corner of his lips.

'And who should lead but I? Unfortunately – observe – I have given my word of honour to Don Carlos not to let the mine fall into the hands of these thieves. In war – you know this, Padre – the fate of battles is uncertain, and whom could I leave here to act for me in case of defeat? The explosives are ready. But it would require a man of high honour, of intelligence, of judgement, of courage, to carry out the prepared destruction. Somebody I can trust with my honour as I can trust myself. Another old officer of Paez, for instance. Or – or – perhaps one of Paez's old chaplains would do.'

He got up, long, lank, upright, hard, with his martial moustache and the bony structure of his face, from which the glance of the sunken eyes seemed to transfix the priest, who stood still, an empty wooden snuff-box held upside down in his hand, and glared back, speechless, at the governor of the mine.

CHAPTER 7

At about that time, in the Intendencia of Sulaco, Charles Gould was assuring Pedrito Montero, who had sent a request for his presence there, that he would never let the mine pass out of his hands for the profit of a Government who had robbed him of it. The Gould Concession could not be resumed. His father had not desired it. The son would never surrender it. He would never surrender it alive. And once dead, where was the power capable of resuscitating such an enterprise in all its vigour and wealth out of the ashes and ruin of destruction? There was no such power in the country. And where was the skill and capital abroad that would condescend to touch such an ill-omened corpse? Charles Gould talked in the impassive tone which had for many years served to conceal his anger and contempt. He suffered. He was disgusted with what he had to say. It was too much like heroics. In him the strictly practical instinct was in profound discord with the almost mystic view he took of his right. The Gould Concession was symbolic of abstract justice. Let the heavens fall. But since the San Tomé mine had developed its world-wide fame his threat had enough force and effectiveness to reach the rudimentary intelligence of Pedro Montero, wrapped up as it was in the futilities of historical anecdotes. The Gould Concession was a serious asset in the country's finance, and, what was more, in the private budgets of many officials as well. It was traditional. It was known. It was said. It was credible. Every Minister of Interior drew a salary from the San Tomé mine. It was natural. And Pedrito intended to be Minister of the Interior and President of the Council in his brother's Government. The Duc de Morny had occupied those high posts during the Second French Empire with conspicuous advantage to himself.

A table, a chair, a wooden bedstead had been procured for His Excellency, who, after a short siesta, rendered absolutely necessary by the labours and the pomps of his entry into Sulaco, had been getting hold of the administrative machine by making appointments, giving orders, and signing proclamations. Alone with Charles Gould in the audience room, His Excellency managed with his well-known skill to conceal his annoyance and consternation. He had begun at first to talk loftily of confiscation, but the want of all proper feeling and mobility in the Señor Administrador's features ended by affecting adversely his power of masterful expression. Charles Gould had repeated: 'The Government can certainly bring about the destruction of the San Tomé mine if it likes; but without me it can do nothing else.' It was an alarming pronouncement, and well calculated to hurt the sensibilities of a politician whose mind is bent upon the spoils of victory. And Charles Gould said also that the destruction of the San Tomé mine would cause the ruin of other undertakings, the withdrawal of European capital, the withholding, most probably, of the last instalment of the foreign loan. That stony fiend of a man said all these things (which were accessible to His Excellency's intelligence) in a cold-blooded manner which made one shudder.

A long course of reading historical works, light and gossipy in tone, carried out in garrets of Parisian hotels, sprawling on an untidy bed, to the neglect of his duties, menial or otherwise, had affected the manners of Pedro Montero. Had he seen around him the splendour of the old Intendencia, the magnificent hangings, the gilt furniture ranged along the walls; had he stood upon a daïs on a noble square of red carpet, he would have probably been very dangerous from a sense of success and elevation. But in this sacked and devasted residence, with the three pieces of common furniture huddled up in the middle of the vast apartment, Pedrito's imagination was subdued by a feeling of insecurity and impermanence. That feeling and the firm attitude of Charles Gould who had not once, so far, pronounced the word 'Excellency', diminished him in his own eyes. He assumed the tone of an enlightened man of the world, and begged Charles Gould to dismiss from his mind every cause for alarm. He was now conversing, he reminded him, with the brother of the master of the country, charged with a reorganizing mission. The trusted brother of the master of the country, he repeated. Nothing was farther from the thoughts of that wise and patriotic hero than ideas of destruction. 'I entreat you, Don Carlos, not to give way to your anti-democratic prejudices,' he cried, in a burst of condescending effusion.

Pedrito Montero surprised one at first sight by the vast development of his bald forehead, a shiny yellow expanse between the crinkly coal-black tufts of hair without any lustre, the engaging form of his mouth, and an unexpectedly cultivated voice. But his eyes, very glistening as if freshly painted on each side of his hooked nose, had a round, hopeless, birdlike stare when opened fully. Now, however, he narrowed them agreeably, throwing his square chin up and speaking with closed teeth slightly through the nose, with what he imagined to be the manner of a *grand seigneur*.

In that attitude, he declared suddenly that the highest expression of democracy was Caesarism: the imperial rule based upon the direct popular vote. Caesarism was conservative. It was strong. It recognized the legitimate needs of democracy which requires orders, titles, and distinctions. They would be showered upon deserving men. Caesarism was peace. It was progressive. It secured prosperity of a country. Pedrito Montero was carried away. Look at what the Second Empire had done for France. It was a régime which delighted to honour men of Don Carlos's stamp. The Second Empire fell, but that was because its chief was devoid of that military genius which had raised General Montero to the pinnacle of fame and glory. Pedrito elevated his hand jerkily to help the idea of pinnacle, of fame. 'We shall have many talks yet. We shall understand each other thoroughly, Don Carlos!' he cried in a tone of fellowship. Republicanism had done its work. Imperial democracy was the power of the future. Pedrito, the *guerrillero*, showing his hand, lowered his voice forcibly. A man singled out by his fellow-citizens for the honourable nickname of El Rey de Sulaco could not but receive a full recognition from an imperial democracy as a great captain of industry and a person of weighty counsel, whose popular designation would be soon replaced by a more solid title. 'Eh, Don Carlos? No! What do you say? Conde de Sulaco – Eh? – or marquis . . .'

He ceased. The air was cool on the Plaza, where a patrol of cavalry rode round and round without penetrating into the streets, which resounded with shouts and the strumming of guitars issuing from the open doors of *pulperías*. The orders were not to interfere with the enjoyments of the people. And above the roofs, next to the perpendicular lines of the cathedral towers, the snowy curve of Higuerota blocked a large space of darkening blue sky before the windows of the Intendencia. After a time Pedrito Montero, thrusting his hand in the bosom of his coat, bowed his head with slow dignity. The audience was over.

Charles Gould on going out passed his hand over his forehead as if to disperse the mists of an oppressive dream, whose grotesque extravagance leaves behind a subtle sense of bodily danger and intellectual decay. In the passages and on the staircases of the old palace Montero's troopers lounged about insolently, smoking and making way for no one; the clanking of sabres and spurs resounded all over the building. Three silent groups of civilians in severe black waited in the main gallery, formal and helpless, a little huddled up, each keeping apart from the others, as if in the exercise of a public duty they had been overcome by a desire to shun the notice of every eye. These were the deputations waiting for their audience. The one from the Provincial Assembly, more restless and uneasy in its corporate expression, was overtopped by the big face of Don Juste Lopez, soft and white, with prominent eyelids and wreathed in impenetrable solemnity as if in a dense cloud. The President of the Provincial Assembly, coming bravely to save the last shred of parliamentary institutions (on the English model), averted his eyes from the Administrador of the San Tomé mine as a dignified rebuke of his little faith in that only saving principle.

The mournful severity of that reproof did not affect Charles Gould, but he was sensible to the glances of the others directed upon him without reproach, as if only to read their own fate upon his face. All of them had talked, shouted, and declaimed in the great *sala* of the Casa Gould. The feeling of compassion for those men, struck with a strange impotence in the toils of moral degradation, did not induce him to make a sign. He suffered from his fellowship in evil with them too much. He crossed the Plaza unmolested. The Amarilla Club was full of festive ragamuffins. Their frowsy heads protruded from every window, and from within came drunken shouts, the thumping of feet, and the twanging of harps. Broken bottles strewed the pavement below. Charles Gould found the doctor still in his house.

Dr Monygham came away from the crack in the shutter through which he had been watching the street.

'Ah! You are back at last!' he said in a tone of relief. 'I have been telling Mrs Gould that you were perfectly safe, but I was not by an means certain that the fellow would have let you go.'

'Neither was I,' confessed Charles Gould, laying his hat on the table.

'You will have to take action.'

The silence of Charles Gould seemed to admit that this was the only course. This was as far as Charles Gould was accustomed to go towards expressing his intentions.

'I hope you did not warn Montero of what you mean to do,' the doctor said, anxiously.

'I tried to make him see that the existence of the mine was bound up with my personal safety,' continued Charles Gould, looking away from the doctor, and fixing his eyes upon the water-colour sketch upon the wall.

'He believed you?' the doctor asked, eagerly.

'God knows!' said Charles Gould. 'I owed it to my wife to say that much. He is well enough informed. He knows that I have Don Pepe there. Fuentes must have told him. They know that the old major is perfectly capable of blowing up the San Tomé mine without hesitation or compunction. Had it not been for that I don't think I'd have left the Intendencia a free man. He would blow everything up from loyalty and from hate – from hate of these Liberals, as they call themselves. Liberals! The words one knows so well have a nightmarish meaning in this country. Liberty, democracy, patriotism, government – all of them have a flavour of folly and murder. Haven't they, doctor? . . . I alone can restrain Don Pepe. If they were to – to do away with me, nothing could prevent him.'

'They will try to tamper with him,' the doctor suggested, thoughtfully.

'It is very possible,' Charles Gould said very low, as if speaking to himself, and still gazing at the sketch of the San Tomé gorge upon the wall. 'Yes, I expect they will try that.' Charles Gould looked for the first time at the doctor. 'It would give me time,' he added.

'Exactly,' said Dr Monygham, suppressing his excitement. 'Especially if Don Pepe behaves diplomatically. Why shouldn't he give them some hope of success? Eh? Otherwise you wouldn't gain so much time. Couldn't he be instructed to –'

Charles Gould, looking at the doctor steadily, shook his head, but the doctor continued with a certain amount of fire:

'Yes, to enter into negotiations for the surrender of the mine. It is a good notion. You would mature your plan. Of course, I don't ask what it is. I don't want to know. I would refuse to listen to you if you tried to tell me. I am not fit for confidences.'

'What nonsense!' muttered Charles Gould, with displeasure.

He disapproved of the doctor's sensitiveness about that far-off episode of his life. So much memory shocked Charles Gould. It was like morbidness. And again he shook his head. He refused to tamper with the open rectitude of Don Pepe's conduct, both from taste and from policy. Instructions would have to be either verbal or in writing. In either case they ran the risk of being intercepted. It was by no means certain that a messenger could reach the mine; and, besides, there was no one to send. It was on the tip of Charles's tongue to say that only the late Capataz de Cargadores could have been employed with some chance of success and the certitude of discretion. But he did not say that. He pointed out to the doctor that it would have been bad policy. Directly Don Pepe let it be supposed that he could be bought over, the Administrador's personal safety and the safety of his friends would become endangered. For there would be then no reason for moderation. The incorruptibility of Don Pepe was the essential and restraining fact. The doctor hung his head and admitted that in a way it was so.

He couldn't deny to himself that the reasoning was sound enough. Don Pepe's usefulness consisted in his unstained character. As to his own usefulness, he reflected bitterly, it was also his own character. He declared to Charles Gould that he had the means of keeping Sotillo from joining his forces with Montero, at least for the present.

'If you had had all this silver here,' the doctor said, 'or even if it had been known to be at the mine, you could have bribed Sotillo to throw off his recent Monterism. You could have induced him either to go away in his steamer or even to join you.'

'Certainly not that last,' Charles Gould declared, firmly. 'What could one do with a man like that, afterwards – tell me, doctor? The silver is gone, and I am glad of it. It would have been an immediate and strong temptation. The scramble for that visible plunder would have precipitated a disastrous ending. I would have had to defend it, too. I am glad we've removed it – even if it is lost. It would have been a danger and a curse.'

'Perhaps he is right,' the doctor, an hour later, said hurriedly to Mrs Gould, whom he met in the corridor. 'The thing is done, and the shadow of the treasure may do just as well as the substance. Let me try to serve you to the whole extent of my evil reputation. I am off now to play my game of betrayal with Sotillo, and keep him off the town.'

She put out both her hands impulsively. 'Dr Monygham, you are running a terrible risk,' she whispered, averting from his face her eyes, full of tears, for a short glance at the door of her husband's room. She pressed both his hands, and the doctor stood as if rooted to the spot, looking down at her, and trying to twist his lips into a smile.

'Oh, I know you will defend my memory,' he uttered at last, and ran tottering down the stairs across the patio, and out of the house. In the street he kept up a great pace with his smart hobbling walk, a case of instruments under his arm. He was known for being *loco*. Nobody interfered with him. From under the seaward gate, across the dusty, arid plain, interspersed with low bushes, he saw, more than a mile away, the ugly enormity of the Custom House, and the two or three other buildings which at that time constituted the seaport of Sulaco. Far away to the south groves of palm trees edged the curve of the harbour shore. The distant peaks of the Cordillera had lost their identity of clear-cut shapes in the steadily deepening blue of the eastern sky. The doctor walked briskly. A darkling shadow seemed to fall upon him from the zenith. The sun had set. For a time the snows of Higuerota continued to glow with the reflected glory of the west. The doctor, holding a straight course for the Custom House, appeared lonely, hopping amongst the dark bushes like a tall bird with a broken wing.

Tints of purple, gold, and crimson were mirrored in the clear water of the harbour. A long tongue of land, straight as a wall, with the grass-grown ruins of the fort making a sort of rounded green mound, plainly visible from the inner shore, closed its circuit; while beyond the Placid Gulf repeated those splendours of colouring on a greater scale and with a more sombre magnificence. The great mass of cloud filling the head of the gulf had long red smears amongst its convoluted folds of grey and black, as of a floating mantle stained with blood. The three Isabels, overshadowed and clear cut in a great smoothness confounding the sea and sky, appeared suspended, purple-black, in the air. The little wavelets seemed to be tossing tiny red sparks upon the sandy beaches. The glassy bands of water along the horizon gave out a fiery red glow, as if fire and water had been mingled together in the vast bed of the ocean.

At last the conflagration of sea and sky, lying embraced and still in a flaming contact upon the edge of the world, went out. The red sparks in the water vanished together with the stains of blood in the black mantle draping the sombre head of the Placid Gulf; a sudden breeze sprang up and died out after rustling heavily the growth of bushes on the ruined earthwork of the fort. Nostromo woke up from a fourteen hours' sleep, and arose full length from his lair in the long grass. He stood knee deep amongst the whispering undulations of the green blades with the lost air of a man just born into the world. Handsome, robust, and supple, he threw back his head, flung his arms open, and stretched himself with a slow twist of the waist and a leisurely growling yawn of white teeth, as natural and free from evil in the moment of waking as a magnificent and unconscious wild beast. Then, in the suddenly steadied glance fixed upon nothing from under a thoughtful frown, appeared the man.

CHAPTER 8

After landing from his swim Nostromo had scrambled up, all dripping, into the main quadrangle of the old fort; and there, amongst ruined bits of walls and rotting remnants of roofs and sheds, he had slept the day through. He had slept in the shadow of the mountains, in the white blaze of noon, in the stillness and solitude of that overgrown piece of land between the oval of the harbour and the spacious semi-circle of the gulf. He lay as if dead. A *rey zamuro*, appearing like a tiny black speck in the blue, stooped, circling prudently with a stealthiness of flight startling in a bird of that great size. The shadow of his pearly-white body, of his black-tipped wings, fell on the grass no more silently than he alighted himself on a hillock of rubbish within three yards of that man, lying as still as a corpse. The bird stretched his bare neck, craned his bald head, loathsome in the brilliance of varied colouring, with an air of voracious anxiety towards the promising stillness of that prostrate body. Then, sinking his head deeply into his soft plumage, he settled himself to wait. The first thing upon which Nostromo's eyes fell on waking was this patient watcher for the signs of death and corruption. When the man got up the vulture hopped away in great, side-long, fluttering jumps. He lingered for a while, morose and reluctant, before he rose, circling noiselessly with a sinister droop of beak and claws.

Long after he had vanished, Nostromo, lifting his eyes up to the sky, muttered, 'I am not dead yet.'

The Capataz of the Sulaco Cargadores had lived in splendour and publicity up to the very moment, as it were, when he took charge of the lighter containing the treasure of silver ingots.

The last act he had performed in Sulaco was in complete harmony with his vanity, and as such perfectly genuine. He had given his last dollar to an old woman moaning with the grief and fatigue of a dismal search under the arch of the ancient gate. Performed in obscurity and without witnesses, it had still the characteristics of splendour and publicity, and was in strict keeping with his reputation. But this awakening in solitude, except for the watchful vulture, amongst the ruins of the fort, had no such characteristics. His first confused feeling was exactly this – that it was not in keeping. It was more like the end of things. The necessity of living concealed somehow, for God knows how long, which assailed him on his return to consciousness, made everything that had gone before for years appear vain and foolish, like a flattering dream come suddenly to an end.

He climbed the crumbling slope of the rampart, and, putting aside the bushes, looked upon the harbour. He saw a couple of ships at anchor upon the sheet of water reflecting the last gleams of light, and Sotillo's steamer moored to the jetty. And behind the pale long front of the Custom House, there appeared the extent of the town like a grove of thick timber on the plain with a gateway in front, and the cupolas, towers, and miradors rising above the trees, all dark, as if surrendered already to the night. The thought that it was no longer open to him to ride through the streets, recognized by everyone, great and little, as he used to do every evening on his way to play *monte* in the *posada* of the Mexican Domingo; or to sit in the place of honour, listening to songs and looking at dances, made it appear to him as a town that had no existence.

For a long time he gazed on, then let the parted bushes spring back, and, crossing over to the other side of the fort, surveyed the vaster emptiness of the great gulf. The Isabels stood out heavily upon the narrowing long band of red in the west, which gleamed low between their black shapes, and the Capataz thought of Decoud alone there with the treasure. That man was the only one who cared whether he fell into the hands of the Monterists or not, the Capataz reflected bitterly. And that merely would be an anxiety for his own sake. As to the rest, they neither knew nor cared. What he had heard Giorgio Viola say once was very true. Kings, ministers, aristocrats, the rich in general, kept the people in poverty and subjection; they kept them as they kept dogs, to fight and hunt for their service.

The darkness of the sky had descended to the line of the horizon, enveloping the whole gulf, the islets, and the lover of Antonia alone with the treasure on the Great Isabel. The Capataz, turning his back on these things invisible and existing, sat down and took his face between his fists. He felt the pinch of poverty for the first time in his life. To find himself without money after a run of bad luck at *monte* in the low, smoky room of Domingo's *posada*, where the fraternity of *cargadores* gambled, sang, and danced of an evening; to remain with empty pockets after a burst of public generosity to some *peyne d'oro* girl or other (for whom he did not care), had none of the humiliation of destitution. He remained rich in glory and reputation. But since it was no longer possible for him to parade the streets of the town, and be hailed with respect in the usual haunts of his leisure, this sailor felt himself destitute indeed.

His mouth was dry. It was dry with heavy sleep and extremely anxious thinking, as it had never been dry before. It may be said that Nostromo tasted the dust and ashes of the fruit of life into which he had bitten deeply in his hunger for praise. Without removing his head from between his fists, he tried to spit before him – 'Tfui' – and muttered a curse upon the selfishness of all the rich people.

Since everything seemed lost in Sulaco (and that was the feeling of his waking), the idea of leaving the country altogether had presented itself to Nostromo. At that thought he had seen, like the beginning of another dream, a vision of steep and tideless shores, with dark pines on the heights and white houses low down near a very blue sky. He saw the quays of a big port, where the coasting feluccas, with their lateen sails outspread like motionless wings, enter gliding silently between the end of long moles of squared blocks that project angularly towards each other, hugging a cluster of shipping to the superb bosom of a hill covered with palaces. He remembered these sights not without some filial emotion, though he had been habitually and severely beaten as a boy on one of these feluccas by a short-necked, shaven Genoese, with a deliberate and distrustful manner, who (he firmly believed) had cheated him out of his orphan's inheritance. But it is mercifully decreed that the evils of the past should appear but faintly in retrospect. Under the sense of loneliness, abandonment, and failure, the idea of return to these things appeared tolerable. But, what? Return? With bare feet and head, with one check shirt and a pair of cotton *calzoneros* for all worldly possessions?

The renowned Capataz, his elbows on his knees and a fist dug into each cheek, laughed with self-derision, as he had spat with disgust, straight out before him into the night. The confused and intimate impressions of universal dissolution which beset a subjective nature at any strong check to its ruling passion had a bitterness approaching that of death itself. He was simple. He was as ready to become the prey of any belief, superstition, or desire as a child.

The facts of his situation he could appreciate like a man with a distinct experience of the country. He saw them clearly. He was as if sobered after a long bout of intoxication. His fidelity had been taken advantage of. He had persuaded the body of *cargadores* to side with the Blancos against the rest of the people; he had had interviews with Don José; he had been made use of by Father Corbelán for negotiating with Hernandez; it was known that Don Martin Decoud had admitted him to a sort of intimacy, so that he had been free of the offices of the *Porvenir*. All these things had flattered him in the usual way. What did he care about their politics? Nothing at all. And at the end of it all – Nostromo here and Nostromo there – where is Nostromo? Nostromo can do this and that – work all day and ride all night – behold! he found himself a marked Ribierist for any sort of vengeance

Gamacho, for instance, would choose to take, now the Montero party had, after all, mastered the town. The Europeans had given up; the *caballeros* had given up. Don Martin had indeed explained it was only temporary – that he was going to bring Barrios to the rescue. Where was that now – with Don Martin (whose ironic manner of talk had always made the Capataz feel vaguely uneasy) stranded on the Great Isabel? Everybody had given up. Even Don Carlos had given up. The hurried removal of the treasure out to sea meant nothing else than that. The Capataz de Cargadores, on a revulsion of subjectiveness, exasperated almost to insanity, beheld all his world without faith and courage. He had been betrayed!

With the boundless shadows of the sea behind him, out of his silence and immobility, facing the lofty shapes of the lower peaks crowded around the white, misty sheen of Higuerota, Nostromo laughed aloud again, sprang abruptly to his feet, and stood still. He must go. But where?

'There is no mistake. They keep us and encourage us as if we were dogs born to fight and hunt for them. The *vecchio* is right,' he said, slowly and scathingly. He remembered old Giorgio taking his pipe out of his mouth to throw these words over his shoulder at the café, full of engine-drivers and fitters from the railway workshops. This image fixed his wavering purpose. He would try to find old Giorgio if he could. God knows what might have happened to him! He made a few steps, then stopped again and shook his head. To the left and right, in front and behind him, the scrubby bush rustled mysteriously in the darkness.

'Teresa was right, too,' he added in a low tone touched with awe. He wondered whether she was dead in her anger with him or still alive. As if in answer to this thought, half of remorse and half of hope, with a soft flutter and oblique flight, a big owl, whose appalling cry: 'Ya-acabo! Ya-acabo! – it is finished; it is finished' – announces calamity and death in the popular belief, drifted vaguely like a large dark ball across his path. In the downfall of all the realities that made his force, he was affected by the superstition, and shuddered slightly. Signora Teresa must have died, then. It could mean nothing else. The cry of the ill-omened bird, the first sound he was to hear on his return, was a fitting welcome for his betrayed individuality. The unseen powers which he had offended by refusing to bring a priest to a dying woman were lifting up their voice against him. She was dead. With admirable and human consistency he referred everything to himself. She had been a woman of good counsel always. And the bereaved old Giorgio remained stunned by his loss just as he was likely to require the advice of his sagacity. The blow would render the dreamy old man quite stupid for a time.

As to Captain Mitchell, Nostromo, after the manner of trusted subordinates, considered him as a person fitted by education perhaps to sign papers in an office and to give orders, but otherwise of no use whatever, and something of a fool. The necessity of winding round his little finger, almost daily, the pompous and testy self-importance of the old seaman had grown irksome with use to Nostromo. At first it had given him an inward satisfaction. But the necessity of overcoming small obstacles becomes wearisome to a self-confident personality as much by the certitude of success as by the monotony of effort. He mistrusted his superior's proneness to fussy action. That old Englishman had no judgement, he said to himself. It was useless to suppose that, acquainted with the true state of the case, he would keep it to himself. He would talk of doing impracticable things. Nostromo feared him as one would fear saddling one's self with some persistent worry. He had no discretion. He would betray the treasure. And Nostromo had made up his mind that the treasure should not be betrayed.

The word had fixed itself tenaciously in his intelligence. His imagination had seized upon the clear and simple notion of betrayal to account for the dazed feeling of enlightenment as to being done for, of having inadvertently gone out of his existence on an issue in which his personality had not been taken into account. A man betrayed is a man destroyed. Signora Teresa (may God have her soul!) had been right. He had never been taken into account. Destroyed! Her white form sitting up bowed in bed, the falling black hair, the wide-browed suffering face raised to him, the anger of her denunciations appeared to him now majestic with the awfulness of inspiration and of death. For it was not for nothing that the evil bird had uttered its lamentable shriek over his head. She was dead – may God have her soul!

Sharing in the anti-priestly freethought of the masses, his mind used the pious formula from the superficial force of habit, but with a deep-seated sincerity. The popular mind is incapable of scepticism; and that incapacity delivers their helpless strength to the wiles of swindlers and to the pitiless enthusiasms of leaders inspired by visions of a high destiny. She was dead. But would God consent to receive her soul? She had died without confession or absolution, because he had not been willing to spare her another moment of his time. His scorn of priests as priests remained; but after all, it was impossible to know whether what they affirmed was not true. Power, punishment, pardon are simple and credible notions. The magnificent Capataz de Cargadores, deprived of certain simple realities, such as the admiration of women, the adulation of men, the admired publicity of his life, was ready to feel the burden of sacrilegious guilt descend upon his shoulders.

Bareheaded, in a thin shirt and drawers, he felt the lingering warmth of the fine sand under the soles of his feet. The narrow strand gleamed far ahead in a long curve, defining the outline of this wild side of the harbour. He flitted along the shore like a pursued shadow between the sombre palm-groves and the sheet of water lying as still as death on his right hand. He strode with headlong haste in the silence and solitude as though he had forgotten all prudence and caution. But he knew that on this side of the water he ran no risk of discovery. The only inhabitant was a lonely, silent, apathetic Indian in charge of the *palmarías*, who brought sometimes a load of coconuts to the town for sale. He lived without a woman in an open shed, with a perpetual fire of dry sticks smouldering near an old canoe lying bottom up on the beach. He could be easily avoided.

The barking of the dogs about that man's *ranche* was the first thing that checked his speed. He had forgotten the dogs. He swerved sharply, and plunged into the palm-grove, as into a wilderness of columns in an immense hall, whose dense obscurity seemed to whisper and rustle faintly high above his head. He traversed it, entered a ravine, climbed to the top of a steep ridge free of trees and bushes.

From there, open and vague in the starlight, he saw the plain between the town and the harbour. In the woods above some night-bird made a strange drumming noise. Below beyond the *palmaría* on the beach, the Indian's dogs continued to bark uproariously. He wondered what had upset them so much, and, peering down from his elevation, was surprised to detect unaccountable movements of the ground below, as if several oblong pieces of the plain had been in motion. Those dark, shifting patches, alternately catching and eluding the eye, altered their place always away from the harbour, with a suggestion of consecutive order and purpose. A light dawned upon him. It was a column of infantry on a night march towards the higher broken country at the foot of the hills. But he was too much in the dark about everything for wonder and speculation.

The plain had resumed its shadowy immobility. He descended the ridge and found himself in the open solitude, between the harbour and the town. Its spaciousness, extended indefinitely by an effect of obscurity, rendered more sensible his profound isolation. His pace became slower. No one waited for him; no one thought of him; no one expected or wished his return. 'Betrayed! Betrayed!' he muttered to himself. No one cared. He might have been drowned by this time. No one would have cared – unless, perhaps, the children, he thought to himself. But they were with the English *signora*, and not thinking of him at all.

He wavered in his purpose of making straight for the Casa Viola. To what end? What could he expect there? His life seemed to fail him in all its details, even to the scornful reproaches of Teresa. He was aware painfully of his reluctance. Was it that remorse which she had prophesied with, what he saw now, was her last breath?

Meantime, he had deviated from the straight course, inclining by a sort of instinct to the left, towards the jetty and the harbour, the scene of his daily labours. The great length of the Custom House loomed up all at once like the wall of a factory. Not a soul challenged his approach, and his curiosity became excited as he passed cautiously towards the front by the unexpected sight of two lighted windows.

They had the fascination of a lonely vigil kept by some mysterious watcher up there, those two windows shining dimly upon the harbour in the whole vast extent of the abandoned building. The solitude could almost be felt. A strong smell of wood smoke hung about in a thin haze, which was faintly perceptible to his raised eyes against the glitter of the stars. As he advanced in the profound silence, the shrilling of innumerable cicadas in the dry grass seemed positively deafening to his strained ears. Slowly, step by step, he found himself in the great hall, sombre and full of acrid smoke.

A fire built against the staircase had burnt down impotently to a low heap of embers. The hard wood had failed to catch; only a few steps at the bottom smouldered, with a creeping glow of sparks defining their charred edges. At the top he saw a streak of light from an open door. It fell upon the vast landing, all foggy with a slow drift of smoke. That was the room. He climbed the stairs, then checked himself, because he had seen within the shadow of a man cast upon one of the walls. It was a shapeless, high-shouldered shadow of somebody standing still, with lowered head, out of his line of sight. The Capataz, remembering that he was totally unarmed, stepped aside, and, effacing himself upright in a dark corner, waited with his eyes fixed on the door.

The whole enormous ruined barrack of a place, unfinished, without ceilings under its lofty roof, was pervaded by the smoke swaying to and fro in the faint cross-draughts playing in the obscurity of many lofty rooms and barnlike passages. Once one of the swinging shutters came against the wall with a single sharp crack, as if pushed by an impatient hand. A piece of paper scurried out from somewhere, rustling along the landing. The man, whoever he was, did not darken the lighted doorway. Twice the Capataz, advancing a couple of steps out of his corner, craned his neck in the hope of catching sight of what he could be at, so quietly, in there. But every time he saw only the distorted shadow of broad shoulders and bowed head. He was doing apparently nothing, and stirred not from the spot, as though he were meditating – or, perhaps, reading a paper. And not a sound issued from the room.

Once more the Capataz stepped back. He wondered who it was – some Monterist? But he dreaded to show himself. To discover his presence on shore, unless after many days, would, he believed, endanger the treasure. With his own knowledge possessing his whole soul, it seemed impossible that anybody in Sulaco should fail to jump at the right surmise. After a couple of weeks or so it would be different. Who could tell he had not returned overland from some port beyond the limits of the Republic? The existence of the treasure confused his thoughts with a peculiar sort of anxiety, as though his life had become bound up with it. It rendered him timorous for a moment before that enigmatic, lighted door. Devil take the fellow! He did not want to see him. There would be nothing to learn from his face, known or unknown. He was a fool to waste his time there in waiting.

Less than five minutes after entering the place the Capataz began his retreat. He got away down the stairs with perfect success, gave one upward look over his shoulder at the light on the landing, and ran stealthily across the hall. But at the very moment he was turning out of the great door, with his mind fixed upon escaping the notice of the man upstairs, somebody he had not heard coming briskly along the front ran full into him. Both muttered a stifled exclamation of surprise, and leaped back and stood still, each indistinct to the other. Nostromo was silent. The other man spoke first, in an amazed and deadened tone.

'Who are you?'

Already Nostromo had seemed to recognize Dr Monygham. He had no doubt now. He hesitated the space of a second. The idea of bolting without a word presented itself to his mind. No use! An inexplicable repugnance to pronounce the name by which he was known kept him silent a little longer. At last he said in a low voice:

'A *cargador*.'

He walked up to the other. Dr Monygham had received a shock. He flung his arms up and cried out his wonder aloud, forgetting himself before the marvel of this meeting. Nostromo angrily warned him to moderate his voice. The Custom House was not so deserted as it looked. There was somebody in the lighted room above.

There is no more evanescent quality in an accomplished fact than its wonderfulness. Solicited incessantly by the considerations affecting its fears and desires, the human mind turns naturally away from the marvellous side of events. And it was in the most natural way possible that the doctor asked this man whom only two minutes before he believed to have been drowned in the gulf:

'You have seen somebody up there? Have you?'

'No, I have not seen him.'

'Then how do you know?'

'I was running away from his shadow when we met.'

'His shadow?'

'Yes. His shadow in the lighted room,' said Nostromo, in a contemptuous tone. Leaning back with folded arms at the foot of the immense building, he dropped his head, biting his lips slightly, and not looking at the doctor. 'Now,' he thought to himself, 'he will begin asking me about the treasure.'

But the doctor's thoughts were concerned with an event not as marvellous as Nostromo's appearance, but in itself much less clear. Why had Sotillo taken himself off with his whole command with this suddenness and secrecy? What did this move portend? However, it dawned upon the doctor that the man upstairs was one of the officers left behind by the disappointed colonel to communicate with him.

'I believe he is waiting for me,' he said.

'It is possible.'

'I must see. Do not go away yet, Capataz.'

'Go away where?' muttered Nostromo.

Already the doctor had left him. He remained leaning against the wall, staring at the dark water of the harbour; the shrilling of cicadas filled his ears. An invincible vagueness coming over his thoughts took from them all power to determine his will.

'Capataz! Capataz!' the doctor's voice called urgently from above.

The sense of betrayal and ruin floated upon his sombre indifference as upon a sluggish sea of pitch. But he stepped out from under the wall, and, looking up, saw Dr Monygham leaning out of a lighted window.

'Come up and see what Sotillo has done. You need not fear the man up here.'

He answered by a slight, bitter laugh. Fear a man! The Capataz of the Sulaco Cargadores fear a man! It angered him that anybody should suggest such a thing. It angered him to be disarmed and skulking and in danger because of the accursed treasure, which was of so little account to the people who had tied it round his neck. He could not shake off the worry of it. To Nostromo the doctor represented all these people. . . . And he had never even asked after it. Not a word of inquiry about the most desperate undertaking of his life.

Thinking these thoughts, Nostromo passed again through the cavernous hall, where the smoke was considerably thinned, and went up the stairs, not so warm to his feet now, towards the streak of light at the top. The doctor appeared in it for a moment, agitated and impatient.

'Come up! Come up!'

At the moment of crossing the doorway the Capataz experienced a shock of surprise. The man had not moved. He saw his shadow in the same place. He started, then stepped in with a feeling of being about to solve a mystery.

It was very simple, For an infinitesimal fraction of a second, against the light of two flaring and guttering candles, through a blue, pungent, thin haze which made his eyes smart, he saw the man standing, as he had imagined him, with his back to the door, casting an enormous and distorted shadow upon the wall. Swifter than a flash of lightning followed the impression of his constrained, toppling attitude – the shoulders projecting forward, the head sunk low upon the breast. Then he distinguished the arms behind his back, and wrenched so terribly that the two clenched fists, lashed together, had been forced up higher than the shoulder-blades. From there his eyes traced in one instantaneous glance the hide rope going upwards from the tied wrists over a heavy beam and down to a staple in the wall. He did not want to look at the rigid legs, at the feet hanging down nervelessly, with their bare toes some six inches above the floor, to know that the man had been given the estrapade till he had swooned. His first impulse was to dash forward and sever the rope at one blow. He felt for his knife. He had no knife – not even a knife. He stood quivering, and the doctor, perched on the edge of the table, facing thoughtfully the cruel and lamentable sight, his chin in his hand, uttered, without stirring:

'Tortured – and shot dead through the breast – getting cold.'

This information calmed the Capataz. One of the candles flickering in the socket went out. 'Who did this?' he asked.

'Sotillo, I tell you. Who else? Tortured – of course. But why shot?' The doctor looked fixedly at Nostromo, who shrugged his shoulders slightly. 'And mark, shot suddenly, on impulse. It is evident. I wish I had his secret.'

Nostromo had advanced, and stooped slightly to look. 'I seem to have seen that face somewhere,' he muttered. 'Who is he?'

The doctor turned his eyes upon him again. 'I may yet come to envying his fate. What do you think of that, Capataz, eh?'

But Nostromo did not even hear these words. Seizing the remaining light, he thrust it under the drooping head. The doctor sat oblivious, with a lost gaze. Then the heavy iron candlestick, as if struck out of Nostromo's hand, clattered on the floor.

'Hullo!' exclaimed the doctor, looking up with a start. He could hear the Capataz stagger against the table and gasp. In the sudden extinction of the light within, the dead blackness sealing the window-frames became alive with stars to his sight.

'Of course, of course,' the doctor muttered to himself in English. 'Enough to make him jump out of his skin.'

Nostromo's heart seemed to force itself into his throat. His head swam. Hirsch! The man was Hirsch! He held on tight to the edge of the table.

'But he was hiding in the lighter,' he almost shouted. His voice fell. 'In the lighter, and – and –'

'And Sotillo brought him in,' said the doctor. 'He is no more startling to you than you were to me. What I want to know is how he induced some compassionate soul to shoot him.'

'So Sotillo knows –' began Nostromo, in a more equable voice.

'Everything!' interrupted the doctor.

The Capataz was heard striking the table with his fist. 'Everything? What are you saying, there? Everything? Know everything? It is impossible! Everything?'

'Of course. What do you mean by impossible? I tell you I have heard this Hirsch questioned last night, here, in this very room. He knew your name, Decoud's name, and all about the loading of the silver. . . . The lighter was cut in two. He was grovelling in abject terror before Sotillo, but he remembered that much. What do you want more? He knew least about himself. They found him clinging to their anchor. He must have caught at it just as the lighter went to the bottom.'

'Went to the bottom?' repeated Nostromo, slowly. 'Sotillo believes that? *Bueno!*'

The doctor, a little impatiently, was unable to imagine what else anybody could believe. Yes, Sotillo believed that the lighter was sunk, and the Capataz de Cargadores, together with Martin Decoud and perhaps one or two other political fugitives, had been drowned.

'I told you well, Señor Doctor,' remarked Nostromo at that point, 'that Sotillo did not know everything.'

'Eh? What do you mean?'

'He did not know I was not dead.'

'Neither did we.'

'And you did not care – none of you *caballeros* on the wharf – once you got off a man of flesh and blood like yourselves on a fool's business that could not end well.'

'You forget, Capataz, I was not on the wharf. And I did not think well of the business. So you need not taunt me. I tell you what, man, we had but little leisure to think of the dead. Death stands near behind us all. You were gone.'

'I went, indeed!' broke in Nostromo. 'And for the sake of what – tell me?'

'Ah! that is your own affair,' the doctor said, roughly. 'Do not ask me.'

Their flowing murmurs paused in the dark. Perched on the edge of the table with slightly averted faces, they felt their shoulders touch, and their eyes remained directed towards an upright shape nearly lost in the obscurity of the inner part of the room, that with projecting head and shoulders, in ghastly immobility, seemed intent on catching every word.

'*Muy bien!*' Nostromo muttered at last. 'So be it. Teresa was right. It is my own affair.'

'Teresa is dead,' remarked the doctor, absently, while his mind followed a new line of thought suggested by what might have been called Nostromo's return to life. 'She died, the poor woman.'

'Without a priest?' the Capataz asked, anxiously.

'What a question! Who could have got a priest for her last night?'

'May God keep her soul!' ejaculated Nostromo, with a gloomy and hopeless fervour which had no time to surprise Dr Monygham, before, reverting to their previous conversation, he continued in a sinister tone, '*Sí*, Señor Doctor. As you were saying, it is my own affair. A very desperate affair.'

'There are no two men in this part of the world that could have saved themselves by swimming as you have done,' the doctor said, admiringly.

And again there was silence between those two men. They were both reflecting, and the diversity of their natures made their thoughts born from their meeting swing afar from each other. The doctor, impelled to risky action by his loyalty to the Goulds, wondered with thankfulness at the chain of accident which had brought that man back where he would be of the greatest use in the work of saving the San Tomé mine. The doctor was loyal to the mine. It presented itself to his fifty-years-old eyes in the shape of a little woman in a soft dress with a long train, with a head attractively overweighted by a great mass of fair hair and the delicate preciousness of her inner worth, partaking of a gem and a flower, revealed in every attitude of her person. As the dangers thickened round the San Tomé mine this illusion acquired force, permanency, and authority. It claimed him at last! This claim, exalted by a spiritual detachment from the usual sanctions of hope and reward, made Dr Monygham's thinking, acting, individuality, extremely dangerous to himself and to others, all his scruples vanishing in the proud feeling that his devotion was the only thing that stood between an admirable woman and a frightful disaster.

It was a sort of intoxication which made him utterly indifferent to Decoud's fate, but left his wits perfectly clear for the appreciation of Decoud's political idea. It was a good idea – and Barrios was the only instrument of its realization. The doctor's soul, withered and shrunk by the shame of a moral disgrace, became implacable in the expansion of its tenderness. Nostromo's return was providential. He did not think of him humanely, as of a fellow-creature just escaped from the jaws of death. The Capataz for him was the only possible messenger to Cayta. The very man. The doctor's misanthropic mistrust of mankind (the bitterer because based on personal failure) did not lift him sufficiently above common weaknesses. He was under the spell of an established reputation. Trumpeted by Captain Mitchell, grown in repetition, and fixed in general assent, Nostromo's faithfulness had never been questioned by Dr Monygham as a fact. It was not likely to be questioned now he stood in desperate need of it himself. Dr Monygham was human; he accepted the popular conception of the Capataz's incorruptibility simply because no word or fact had ever contradicted a mere affirmation. It seemed to be a part of the man, like his whiskers or his teeth. It was impossible to conceive him otherwise. The question was whether he would consent to go on such a dangerous and desperate errand. The doctor was observant enough to have become aware from the first of something peculiar in the man's temper. He was no doubt sore about the loss of the silver.

'It will be necessary to take him into my fullest confidence,' he said to himself, with a certain acuteness of insight into the nature he had to deal with.

On Nostromo's side the silence had been full of black irresolution, anger, and mistrust. He was the first to break it, however.

'The swimming was no great matter,' he said. 'It is what went before – and what comes after that –'

He did not quite finish what he meant to say, breaking off short, as though his thought had butted against a solid obstacle. The doctor's mind pursued its own schemes with Machiavellian subtlety. He said as sympathetically as he was able:

'It is unfortunate, Capataz. But no one would think of blaming you. Very unfortunate. To begin with, the treasure ought never to have left the mountain. But it was Decoud who – however, he is dead. There is no need to talk of him.'

'No,' assented Nostromo, as the doctor paused, 'there is no need to talk of dead men. But I am not dead yet.'

'You are all right. Only a man of your intrepidity could have saved himself.'

In this Dr Monygham was sincere. He esteemed highly the intrepidity of that man, whom he valued but little, being disillusioned as to mankind in general, because of the particular instance in which his own manhood had failed. Having had to encounter single-handed during his period of eclipse many physical dangers, he was well aware of the most dangerous element common to them all: of the crushing, paralysing sense of human littleness, which is what really defeats a man struggling with natural forces, alone, far from the eyes of his fellows. He was eminently fit to appreciate the mental image he made for himself of the Capataz, after hours of tension and anxiety, precipitated suddenly into an abyss of waters and darkness, without earth or sky, and confronting it not only with an undismayed mind, but with sensible success. Of course, the man was an incomparable swimmer, that was known, but the doctor judged that this instance testified to a still greater intrepidity of spirit. It was pleasing to him; he augured well from it for the success of the arduous mission with which he meant to entrust the Capataz so marvellously restored to usefulness. And in a tone vaguely gratified, he observed:

'It must have been terribly dark!'

'It was the worst darkness of the Golfo,' the Capataz assented, briefly. He was mollified by what seemed a sign of some faint interest in such things as had befallen him, and dropped a few descriptive phrases with an affected and curt nonchalance. At that moment he felt communicative. He expected the continuance of that interest which, whether accepted or rejected, would have restored to him his personality – the only thing lost in that desperate affair. But the doctor, engrossed by a desperate adventure of his own, was terrible in the pursuit of his idea. He let an exclamation of regret escape him.

'I could almost wish you had shouted and shown a light.'

This unexpected utterance astounded the Capataz by its character of cold-blooded atrocity. It was as much as to say, 'I wish you had shown yourself a coward; I wish you had had your throat cut for your pains.' Naturally he referred it to himself, whereas it related only to the silver, being uttered simply and with many mental reservations. Surprise and rage rendered him speechless, and the doctor pursued, practically unheard by Nostromo, whose stirred blood was beating violently in his ears.

'For I am convinced Sotillo in possession of the silver would have turned short round and made for some small port abroad. Economically it would have been wasteful, but still less wasteful than having it sunk. It was the next best thing to having it at hand in some safe place, and using part of it to buy up Sotillo. But I doubt whether Don Carlos would have ever made up his mind to it. He is not fit for Costaguana, and that is a fact, Capataz.'

The Capataz had mastered the fury that was like a temper in his ears in time to hear the name of Don Carlos. He seemed to have come out of it a changed man – a man who spoke thoughtfully in a soft and even voice.

'And would Don Carlos have been content if I had surrendered this treasure?'

'I would not wonder if they were all of that way of thinking now,' the doctor said, grimly. 'I was never consulted. Decoud had it his own way. Their eyes are opened by this time, I should think. I for one know that if that silver turned up this moment miraculously ashore I would give it to Sotillo. And, as things stand, I would be approved.'

'Turned up miraculously,' repeated the Capataz very low; then raised his voice. 'That, *señor*, would be a greater miracle than any saint could perform.'

'I believe you, Capataz,' said the doctor, drily.

He went on to develop his view of Sotillo's dangerous influence upon the situation. And the Capataz, listening as if in a dream, felt himself of as little account as the indistinct, motionless shape of the dead man whom he saw upright under the beam, with his air of listening also, disregarded, forgotten, like a terrible example of neglect.

'Is it for an unconsidered and foolish whim that they came to me, then?' he interrupted, suddenly. 'Had I not done enough for them to be of some account, *por Dios*? Is it that the *hombres finos* – the gentlemen – need not think as long as there is a man of the people ready to risk his body and soul? Or, perhaps, we have no souls – like dogs?'

'There was Decoud, too, with his plan,' the doctor reminded him again.

'*Sí!* And the rich man in San Francisco who had something to do with that treasure, too – what do I know? No! I have heard too many things. It seems to me that everything is permitted to the rich.'

'I understand, Capataz,' the doctor began.

'What Capataz?' broke in Nostromo, in a forcible but even voice. 'The Capataz is undone, destroyed. There is no Capataz. Oh, no! You will find the Capataz no more.'

'Come, this is childish!' remonstrated the doctor; and the other calmed down suddenly.

'I have been indeed like a little child,' he muttered.

And as his eyes met again the shape of the murdered man suspended in his awful immobility, which seemed the uncomplaining immobility of attention, he asked, wondering gently:

'Why did Sotillo give the estrapade to this pitiful wretch? Do you know? No torture could have been worse than his fear. Killing I can understand.

His anguish was intolerable to behold. But why should he torment him like this? He could tell no more.'

'No; he could tell nothing more. Any sane man would have seen that. He had told him everything. But I tell you what it is, Capataz. Sotillo would not believe what he was told. Not everything.'

'What is it he would not believe? I cannot understand.'

'I can, because I have seen the man. He refuses to believe that the treasure is lost.'

'What?'· the Capataz cried out in a discomposed tone.

'That startles you – eh?'

'Am I to understand, *señor*,' Nostromo went on in a deliberate and, as it were, watchful tone, 'that Sotillo thinks the treasure has been saved by some means?'

'No! no! That would be impossible,' said the doctor, with conviction; and Nostromo emitted a grunt in the dark. 'That would be impossible. He thinks that the silver was no longer in the lighter when she was sunk. He has convinced himself that the whole show of getting it away to sea· is a mere sham got up to deceive Gamacho and his Nationals, Pedrito Montero, Señor Fuentes, our new Jefe Político, and himself, too. Only, he says, he is no such fool.'

'But he is devoid of sense. He is the greatest imbecile that ever called himself a colonel in this country of evil,' growled Nostromo.

'He is no more unreasonable than many sensible men,' said the doctor. 'He has convinced himself that the treasure can be found because he desires passionately to possess himself of it. And he is also afraid of his officers turning upon him and going over to Pedrito, whom he has not the courage either to fight or trust. Do you see that, Capataz? He need fear no desertion as long as some hope remains of that enormous plunder turning up. I have made it my business to keep this very hope up.'

'You have!' the Capataz de Cargadores repeated cautiously. 'Well, that is wonderful. And how long do you think you are going to keep it up?'

'As long as I can.'

'What does that mean?'

'I can tell you exactly. As long as I live,' the doctor retorted in a stubborn voice. Then, in a few words, he described the story of his arrest and the circumstances of his release. 'I was going back to that silly scoundrel when we met,' he concluded.

Nostromo had listened with profound attention. 'You have made up your mind, then, to a speedy death,' he muttered through his clenched teeth.

'Perhaps, my illustrious Capataz,' the doctor said, testily. 'You are not the only one here who can look an ugly death in the face.'

'No doubt,' mumbled Nostromo, loud enough to be overheard. 'There may be even more than two fools in this place. Who knows?'

'And that is my affair,' said the doctor, curtly.

'As taking out the accursed silver to sea was my affair,' retorted Nostromo. 'I see. *Bueno*. Each of us has his reasons. But you were the last man I conversed with before I started, and you talked to me as if I were a fool.'

Nostromo had a great distaste for the doctor's sardonic treatment of his great reputation. Decoud's faintly ironic recognition used to make him uneasy; but the familiarity of a man like Don Martin was flattering, whereas the doctor was a nobody. He could remember him a penniless outcast, slinking about the streets of Sulaco, without a single friend or acquaintance, till Don Carlos Gould took him into the service of the mine.

'You may be very wise,' he went on, thoughtfully, staring into the obscurity of the room, pervaded by the gruesome enigma of the tortured and murdered Hirsch. 'But I am not such a fool as when I started. I have learned one thing since, and that is that you are a dangerous man.'

Dr Monygham was too startled to do more than exclaim:

'What is it you say?'

'If he could speak he would say the same thing,' pursued Nostromo, with a nod of his shadowy head silhouetted against the starlit window.

'I do not understand you,' said Dr Monygham faintly.

'No? Perhaps, if you had not confirmed Sotillo in his madness, he would have been in no haste to give the estrapade to that miserable Hirsch.'

The doctor started at the suggestion. But his devotion, absorbing all his sensibilities, had left his heart steeled against remorse and pity. Still, for complete relief, he felt the necessity of repelling it loudly and contemptuously.

'Bah! You dare to tell me that, with a man like Sotillo. I confess I did not give a thought to Hirsch. If I had it would have been useless. Anybody can see that the luckless wretch was doomed from the moment he caught hold of the anchor. He was doomed, I tell you! Just as I myself am doomed – most probably.'

This is what Dr Monygham said in answer to Nostromo's remark, which was plausible enough to prick his conscience. He was not a callous man. But the necessity, the magnitude, the importance of the task he had taken upon himself dwarfed all merely humane considerations. He had undertaken it in a fanatical spirit. He did not like it. To lie, to deceive, to circumvent even the basest of mankind was odious to him. It was odious to him by training, instinct, and tradition. To do these things in the character of a traitor was abhorrent to his nature and terrible to his feelings. He had made that sacrifice in a spirit of abasement. He had said to himself bitterly, 'I am the only one fit for that dirty work.' And he believed this. He was not subtle. His simplicity was such that, though he had no sort of heroic idea of seeking death, the risk, deadly enough, to which he exposed himself, had a sustaining and comforting effect. To that spiritual state the fate of Hirsch presented itself as part the general atrocity of things. He considered that episode practically. What did it mean? Was it a sign of some dangerous change in Sotillo's delusion? That the man should have been killed like this was what the doctor could not understand.

'Yes. But why shot?' he murmured to himself.

Nostromo kept very still.

CHAPTER 9

Distracted between doubts and hopes, dismayed by the sound of bells pealing out the arrival of Pedrito Montero, Sotillo had spent the morning in battling with his thoughts; a contest to which he was unequal, from the vacuity of his mind and the violence of his passions. Disappointment, greed, anger, and fear made a tumult in the colonel's breast louder than the din of bells in the town. Nothing he had planned had come to pass. Neither Sulaco nor the silver of the mine had fallen into his hands. He had performed no military exploit to secure his position, and had obtained no enormous booty to make off with. Pedrito Montero, either as friend or foe, filled him with dread. The sound of bells maddened him.

Imagining at first that he might be attacked at once, he had made his battalion stand to arms on the shore. He walked to and fro all the length of the room, stopping sometimes to gnaw the finger-tips of his right hand with a lurid sideways glare fixed on the floor; then, with a sullen, repelling glance all round, he would resume his tramping in savage aloofness. His hat, horse-whip, sword, and revolver were lying on the table. His officers, crowding the window giving the view of the town gate, disputed amongst themselves the use of his field-glass bought last year on long credit from Anzani. It passed from hand to hand, and the possessor for the time being was besieged by anxious inquiries.

'There is nothing; there is nothing to see!' he would repeat, impatiently.

There was nothing. And when the picket in the bushes near the Casa Viola had been ordered to fall back upon the main body, no stir of life appeared on the stretch of dusty and arid land between the town and the waters of the port. But late in the afternoon a horseman issuing from the gate was made out riding up fearlessly. It was an emissary from Señor Fuentes. Being all alone he was allowed to come on. Dismounting at the great door he greeted the silent bystanders with cheery impudence, and begged to be taken up at once to the 'muy valiente' colonel.

Señor Fuentes, on entering upon his functions of Jefe Político, had turned his diplomatic abilities to getting hold of the harbour as well as of the mine. The man he pitched upon to negotiate with Sotillo was a Notary Public, whom the revolution had found languishing in the common jail on a charge of forging documents. Liberated by the mob along with the other 'victims of Blanco tyranny', he had hastened to offer his services to the new Government.

He set out determined to display much zeal and eloquence in trying to induce Sotillo to come into town alone for a conference with Pedrito Montero. Nothing was farther from the colonel's intentions. The mere fleeting idea of trusting himself into the famous Pedrito's hands had made him feel unwell several times. It was out of the question – it was madness. And to put himself in open hostility was madness, too. It would render impossible a systematic search for that treasure, for that wealth of silver which he seemed to feel somewhere about, to scent somewhere near.

But where? Where? Heavens! Where? Oh! why had he allowed that doctor to go! Imbecile that he was. But no! It was the only right course, he reflected distractedly, while the messenger waited downstairs chatting agreeably to the officers. It was in that scoundrelly doctor's true interest to return with positive information. But what if anything stopped him? A general prohibition to leave the town, for instance! There would be patrols!

The colonel, seizing his head in his hands, turned in his tracks as if struck with vertigo. A flash of craven inspiration suggested to him an expedient not unknown to European statesmen when they wish to delay a difficult negotiation. Booted and spurred, he scrambled into the hammock with undignified haste. His handsome face had turned yellow with the strain of weighty cares. The ridge of his shapely nose had grown sharp; the audacious nostrils appeared mean and pinched. The velvety, caressing glance of his fine eyes seemed dead and even decomposed; for these almond-shaped, languishing orbs had become inappropriately bloodshot with much sinister sleeplessness. He addressed the surprised envoy of Señor Fuentes in a deadened, exhausted voice. It came pathetically feeble from under a pile of ponchos, which buried his elegant person right up to the black moustaches, uncurled, pendant, in sign of bodily prostration, and mental incapacity. Fever, fever – a heavy fever had overtaken the '*muy valiente*' colonel. A wavering wildness of expression, caused by the passing spasms of a slight colic which had declared itself suddenly, and the rattling teeth of repressed panic, had a genuineness which impressed the envoy. It was a cold fit. The colonel explained that he was unable to think, to listen, to speak. With an appearance of superhuman effort the colonel gasped out that he was not in a state to return a suitable reply or to execute any of his Excellency's orders. But tomorrow! Tomorrow! Ah! tomorrow! Let his Excellency Don Pedro be without uneasiness. The brave Esmeralda Regiment held the harbour, held – And closing his eyes, he rolled his aching head like a half-delirious invalid under the inquisitive stare of the envoy, who was obliged to bend down over the hammock in order to catch the painful and broken accents. Meantime, Colonel Sotillo trusted that his Excellency's humanity would permit the doctor, the English doctor, to come out of town with his case of foreign remedies to attend upon him. He begged anxiously his worship the *caballero* now present for the grace of looking in as he passed the Casa Gould, and informing the English doctor, who was probably there, that his services were immediately required by Colonel Sotillo, lying ill of fever in the Custom House. Immediately. Most urgently required. Awaited with extreme impatience. A thousand thanks. He closed his eyes wearily and would not open them again, lying perfectly still, deaf, dumb, insensible, overcome, vanquished, crushed, annihilated by the fell disease.

But as soon as the other had shut after him the door of the landing, the colonel leaped out with a fling of both feet in an avalanche of woollen coverings. His spurs having become entangled in a perfect welter of ponchos he nearly pitched on his head, and did not recover his balance till the middle of the room. Concealed behind the half-closed jalousies he listened to what went on below.

The envoy had already mounted, and turning to the morose officers occupying the great doorway, took off his hat formally.

'*Caballeros*,' he said, in a very loud tone, 'allow me to recommend you to take great care of your colonel. It has done me much honour and gratification to have seen you all, a fine body of men exercising the soldierly virtue of patience in this exposed situation, where there is much sun, and no water to speak of, while a town full of wine and feminine charms is ready to embrace you for the brave men you are. *Caballeros*, I have the honour to salute you. There will be much dancing tonight in Sulaco. Good-bye!'

But he reined in his horse and inclined his head sideways on seeing the old major step out, very tall and meagre, in a straight narrow coat coming down to his ankles as if it were the casing of the regimental colours rolled round their staff.

The intelligent old warrior, after enunciating in a dogmatic tone the general proposition that the 'world was full of traitors', went on pronouncing deliberately a panegyric upon Sotillo. He ascribed to him with leisurely emphasis every virtue under heaven, summing it all up in an absurd colloquialism current amongst the lower class of Occidentals (especially about Esmeralda). 'And,' he concluded, with a sudden rise in the voice, 'a man of many teeth – "*hombre de muchos dientes*". *Sí, señor*. As to us,' he pursued, portentous and impressive, 'your worship is beholding the finest body of officers in the Republic, men unequalled for valour and sagacity, "*y hombres de muchos dientes*".'

'What? All of them?' inquired the disreputable envoy of Señor Fuentes, with a faint, derisive smile.

'*Todos. Sí, señor*,' the major affirmed, gravely, with conviction. 'Men of many teeth.'

The other wheeled his horse to face the portal resembling the high gate of a dismal barn. He raised himself in his stirrups, extended one arm. He was a facetious scoundrel, entertaining for these stupid Occidentals a feeling of great scorn natural in a native from the central provinces. The folly of Esmeraldians especially aroused his amused contempt. He began an oration upon Pedro Montero, keeping a solemn countenance. He flourished his hand as if introducing him to their notice. And when he saw every face set, all the eyes fixed upon his lips, he began to shout a sort of catalogue of perfections: 'Generous, valorous, affable, profound' – he snatched off his hat enthusiastically – 'a statesman, an invincible chief of partisans –' He dropped his voice startlingly to a deep, hollow note – 'and a dentist.'

He was off instantly at a smart walk; the rigid straddle of his legs, the turned-out feet, the stiff back, the rakish slant of the sombrero above the square, motionless set of the shoulders expressing an infinite, awe-inspiring impudence.

Upstairs, behind the jalousies, Sotillo did not move for a long time. The audacity of the fellow appalled him. What were his officers saying below? They were saying nothing. Complete silence. He quaked. It was not thus that he had imagined himself at that stage of the expedition. He had seen himself triumphant, unquestioned, appeased, the idol of the soldiers, weighing in secret complacency the agreeable alternatives of power and wealth open to his choice. Alas! How different! Distracted, restless, supine, burning with fury, or frozen with terror, he felt a dread as fathomless as the sea creep upon him from every side. That rogue of a doctor had to come out with his information. That was clear. It would be of no use to him – alone. He could do nothing with it. Malediction! The doctor would never come out. He was probably under arrest already, shut up together with Don Carlos. He laughed aloud insanely. Ha! ha! ha! ha! It was Pedrito Montero who would get the information. Ha! ha! ha! ha! – and the silver. Ha!

All at once, in the midst of the laugh, he became motionless and silent as if turned into stone. He, too, had a prisoner. A prisoner who must, must know the real truth. He would have to be made to speak. And Sotillo, who all that time had not quite forgotten Hirsch, felt an inexplicable reluctance at the notion of proceeding to extremities.

He felt a reluctance – part of that unfathomable dread that crept on all sides upon him. He remembered reluctantly, too, the dilated eyes of the hide merchant, his contortions, his loud sobs and protestations. It was not compassion or even mere nervous sensibility. The fact was that though Sotillo did never for a moment believe his story – he could not believe it; nobody could believe such nonsense – yet those accents of despairing truth impressed him disagreeably. They made him feel sick. And he suspected also that the man might have gone mad with fear. A lunatic is a hopeless subject. Bah! A pretence. Nothing but a pretence. He would know how to deal with that.

He was working himself up to the right pitch of ferocity. His fine eyes squinted slightly; he clapped his hands; a barefooted orderly appeared noiselessly; a corporal, with his bayonet hanging on his thigh and a stick in his hand.

The colonel gave his orders, and presently the miserable Hirsch, pushed in by several soldiers, found him frowning awfully in a broad armchair, hat on head, knees wide apart, arms akimbo, masterful, imposing, irresistible, haughty, sublime, terrible.

Hirsch, with his arms tied behind his back, had been bundled violently into one of the smaller rooms. For many hours he remained apparently forgotten, stretched lifelessly on the floor. From that solitude, full of despair and terror, he was torn out brutally, with kicks and blows, passive, sunk in hebetude. He listened to threats and admonitions, and afterwards made his usual answers to questions, with his chin sunk on his breast, his hands tied behind his back, swaying a little in front of Sotillo, and never looking up. When he was forced to hold up his head, by means of a bayonet-point prodding him under the chin, his eyes had a vacant, trance-like stare, and drops of perspiration as big as peas were seen hailing down the dirt, bruises, and scratches of his white face. Then they stopped suddenly.

Sotillo looked at him in silence. 'Will you depart from your obstinacy, you rogue?' he asked. Already a rope, whose one end was fastened to Señor Hirsch's wrists, had been thrown over a beam, and three soldiers held the other end, waiting. He made no answer. His heavy lower lip hung stupidly. Sotillo made a sign. Hirsch was jerked up off his feet, and a yell of despair and agony burst out in the room, filled the passage of the great buildings, rent the air outside, caused every soldier of the camp along the shore to look up at the windows, started some of the officers in the hall babbling excitedly, with shining eyes; others, setting their lips, looked gloomily at the floor.

Sotillo, followed by the soldiers, had left the room. The sentry on the landing presented arms. Hirsch went on screaming all alone behind the half-closed jalousies while the sunshine, reflected from the water of the harbour, made an ever-running ripple of light high up on the wall. He screamed with uplifted eyebrows and a wide-open mouth – incredibly wide, black, enormous, full of teeth – comical.

In the still burning air of the windless afternoon he made the waves of agony travel as far as the O.S.N. Company's offices. Captain Mitchell on the balcony, trying to make out what went on generally, had heard him faintly but distinctly, and the feeble and appalling sound lingered in his ears after he had retreated indoors with blanched cheeks. He had been driven off the balcony several times during that afternoon.

Sotillo, irritable, moody, walked restlessly about, held consultations with his officers, gave contradictory orders in this shrill clamour pervading the whole empty edifice. Sometimes there would be long and awful silences. Several times he had entered the torture-chamber where his sword, horse-whip, revolver, and field-glass were lying on the table, to ask with forced calmness, 'Will you speak the truth now? No? I can wait.' But he could not afford to wait much longer. That was just it. Every time he went in and came out with a slam of the door, the sentry on the landing presented arms, and got in return a black, venomous, unsteady glance, which, in reality, saw nothing at all, being merely the reflection of the soul within – a soul of gloomy hatred, irresolution, avarice, and fury.

The sun had set when he went in once more. A soldier carried in two lighted candles and slunk out, shutting the door without noise.

'Speak, thou Jewish child of the devil! The silver! The silver, I say! Where is it? Where have you foreign rogues hidden it? Confess or –'

A slight quiver passed up the taut rope from the racked limbs, but the body of Señor Hirsch, enterprising businessman from Esmeralda, hung under the heavy beam perpendicular and silent, facing the colonel awfully. The inflow of the night air, cooled by the snows of the Sierra, spread gradually a delicious freshness through the close heat of the room.

'Speak – thief – scoundrel – *picaro* – or –'

Sotillo had seized the riding-whip, and stood with his arm lifted up. For a word, for one little word, he felt he would have knelt, cringed, grovelled on the floor before the drowsy, conscious stare of those fixed eyeballs starting out of the grimy, dishevelled head that drooped very still with its mouth closed askew. The colonel ground his teeth with rage and struck. The rope vibrated leisurely to the blow, like the long string of a pendulum starting from a rest. But no swinging motion was imparted to the body of Señor Hirsch, the well-known hide merchant on the coast. With a convulsive effort of the twisted arms it leaped up a few inches, curling upon itself like a fish on the end of a line. Señor Hirsch's head was flung back on his straining throat; his chin trembled. For a moment the rattle of his chattering teeth pervaded the vast, shadowy room, where the candles made a patch of light round the two flames burning side by side. And as Sotillo, staying his raised hand, waited for him to speak, with the sudden flash of a grin and a straining forward of the wrenched shoulders, he spat violently into his face.

The uplifted whip fell, and the colonel sprang back with a low cry of dismay, as if aspersed by a jet of deadly venom. Quick as thought he snatched up his revolver, and fired twice. The report and the concussion of the shots seemed to throw him at once from ungovernable rage into idiotic stupor. He stood with drooping jaw and stony eyes. What had he done, *sangre de Dios!* What had he done? He was basely appalled at his impulsive act, sealing for ever these lips from which so much was to be extorted. What could he say? How could he explain? Ideas of headlong flight somewhere, anywhere, passed through his mind; even the craven and absurd notion of hiding under the table occurred to his cowardice. It was too late; his officers had rushed in tumultuously, in a great clatter of scabbards, clamouring, with astonishment and wonder. But since they did not immediately proceed to plunge their swords into his breast, the brazen side of his character asserted itself. Passing the sleeve of his uniform over his face, he pulled himself together. His truculent glance turned slowly here and there, checked the noise where it fell; and the stiff body of the late Señor Hirsch, merchant, after swaying imperceptibly, made a half turn, and came to a rest in the midst of awed murmurs and uneasy shuffling.

A voice remarked loudly, 'Behold a man who will never speak again.' And another, from the back row of faces, timid and pressing, cried out:

'Why did you kill him, *mi coronel?*'

'Because he has confessed everything,' answered Sotillo, with the hardihood of desperation. He felt himself cornered. He brazened it out on the strength of his reputation with very fair success. His hearers thought him very capable of such an act. They were disposed to believe his flattering tale. There is no credulity so eager and blind as the credulity of covetousness, which, in its universal extent, measures the moral misery and the intellectual destitution of mankind. Ah! he had confessed everything, this fractious Jew, this *bribón.* Good! Then he was no longer wanted. A sudden dense guffaw was heard from the senior captain – a big-headed man, with little round eyes and monstrously fat cheeks which never moved. The old major, tall and fantastically ragged like a scarecrow, walked round the body of the late Señor Hirsch, muttering to himself with ineffable complacency that like this there was no need to guard against any future treacheries of that scoundrel. The others stared, shifting from foot to foot, and whispering short remarks to each other.

Sotillo buckled on his sword and gave curt, peremptory orders to hasten the retirement decided upon in the afternoon. Sinister, impressive, his sombrero pulled right down upon his eyebrows, he marched first through the door in such disorder of mind that he forgot utterly to provide for Dr Monygham's possible return. As the officers trooped out after him, one or two looked back hastily at the late Señor Hirsch, merchant from Esmeralda, left swinging rigidly at rest, alone with the two burning candles. In the emptiness of the room the burly shadow of head and shoulders on the wall had an air of life.

Below, the troops fell in silently and moved off by companies without drum or trumpet. The old scarecrow major commanded the rearguard; but the party he left behind with orders to fire the Custom House (and 'burn the carcass of the treacherous Jew where it hung') failed somehow in their haste to set the staircase properly alight. The body of the late Señor Hirsch dwelt alone for a time in the dismal solitude of the unfinished building, resounding weirdly with sudden slams and clicks of doors and latches, with rustling scurries of torn papers, and the tremulous sighs that at each gust of wind passed under the high roof. The light of the two candles burning before the perpendicular and breathless immobility of the late Señor Hirsch threw a gleam afar over land and water, like a signal in the night. He remained to startle Nostromo by his presence, and to puzzle Dr Monygham by the mystery of his atrocious end.

'But why shot?' the doctor again asked himself, audibly. This time he was answered by a dry laugh from Nostromo.

'You seem much concerned at a very natural thing, Señor Doctor. I wonder why? It is very likely that before long we shall all get shot one after another, if not by Sotillo, then by Pedrito, or Fuentes, or Gamacho. And we may even get the estrapade, too, or worse – *quién sabe?* – with your pretty tale of the silver you put into Sotillo's head.'

'It was in his head already,' the doctor protested. 'I only –'

'Yes. And you only nailed it there so that the devil himself –'

'That is precisely what I meant to do,' caught up the doctor.

'That is what you meant to do. *Bueno*. It is as I say. You are a dangerous man.'

Their voices, which without rising had been growing quarrelsome, ceased suddenly. The late Señor Hirsch, erect and shadowy against the stars, seemed to be waiting attentive, in impartial silence.

But Dr Monygham had no mind to quarrel with Nostromo. At this supremely critical point of Sulaco's fortunes it was borne upon him at last that this man was really indispensable, more indispensable than ever the infatuation of Captain Mitchell, his proud discoverer, could conceive, far beyond what Decoud's best dry raillery about 'my illustrious friend, the unique Capataz de Cargadores', had ever intended. The fellow was unique. He was not 'one in a thousand'. He was absolutely the only one. The doctor surrendered. There was something in the genius of that Genoese seaman which dominated in the destinies of great enterprises and of many people, the fortunes of Charles Gould, the fate of an admirable woman. At this last thought the doctor had to clear his throat before he could speak.

In a completely changed tone he pointed out to the Capataz that, to begin with, he personally ran no great risk. As far as everybody knew he was dead. It was an enormous advantage. He had only to keep out of sight in the Casa Viola, where the old Garibaldino was known to be alone – with his dead wife. The servants had all run away. No one would think of searching for him there, or anywhere else on earth, for that matter.

'That would be very true,' Nostromo spoke up, bitterly, 'if I had not met you.'

For a time the doctor kept silent. 'Do you mean to say that you think I may give you away?' he asked in an unsteady voice. 'Why? Why should I do that?'

'What do I know? Why not? To gain a day perhaps. It would take Sotillo a day to give me the estrapade, and try some other things perhaps, before he puts a bullet through my heart – as he did to that poor wretch here. Why not?'

The doctor swallowed with difficulty. His throat had gone dry in a moment. It was not from indignation. The doctor, pathetically enough, believed that he had forfeited the right to be indignant with anyone – for anything. It was simple dread. Had the fellow heard his story by some chance? If so, there was an end of his usefulness in that direction. The indispensable man escaped his influence, because of that indelible blot which made him fit for dirty work. A feeling as of sickness came upon the doctor. He would have given anything to know, but he dared not clear up the point. The fanaticism of his devotion, fed on the sense of his abasement, hardened his heart in sadness and scorn.

'Why not, indeed? he re-echoed, sardonically. 'Then the safe thing for you is to kill me on the spot. I would defend myself. But you may just as well know I am going about unarmed.'

'*Por Dios!*' said the Capataz, passionately. 'You fine people are all alike. All dangerous. All betrayers of the poor who are your dogs.'

'You do not understand,' began the doctor, slowly.

'I understand you all!' cried the other with a violent movement, as shadowy to the doctor's eyes as the persistent immobility of the late Señor Hirsch. 'A poor man amongst you has got to look after himself. I say that you do not care for those that serve you. Look at me! After all these years, suddenly, here I find myself like one of these curs that bark outside the walls – without a kennel or a dry bone for my teeth. *Caramba!*' But he relented with a contemptuous fairness. 'Of course,' he went on, quietly, 'I do not suppose that you would hasten to give me up to Sotillo, for example. It is not that. It is that I am nothing! Suddenly –' He swung his arm downwards. 'Nothing to anyone,' he repeated.

The doctor breathed freely. 'Listen, Capataz,' he said, stretching out his arm almost affectionately towards Nostromo's shoulder. 'I am going to tell you a very simple thing. You are safe because you are needed. I would not give you away for any conceivable reason, because I want you.'

In the dark Nostromo bit his lip. He had heard enough of that. He knew what that meant. No more of that for him. But he had to look after himself now, he thought. And he thought, too, that it would not be prudent to part in anger from his companion. The doctor, admitted to be a great healer, had, amongst the populace of Sulaco, the reputation of being an evil sort of man. It was based solidly on his personal appearance, which was strange, and on his rough ironic manner – proofs visible, sensible, and incontrovertible of the doctor's malevolent disposition. And Nostromo was of the people. So he only grunted incredulously.

'You, to speak plainly, are the only man,' the doctor pursued. 'It is in your power to save this town and . . . everybody from the destructive rapacity of men who –'

'No, *señor*,' said Nostromo, sullenly. 'It is not in my power to get the treasure back for you to give up to Sotillo, or Pedrito, or Gamacho. What do I know?'

'Nobody expects the impossible,' was the answer.

'You have said it yourself – nobody,' muttered Nostromo, in a gloomy, threatening tone.

But Dr Monygham, full of hope, disregarded the enigmatic words and the threatening tone. To their eyes, accustomed to obscurity, the late Señor Hirsch, growing more distinct, seemed to have come nearer. And the doctor lowered his voice in exposing his scheme as though afraid of being overheard.

He was taking the indispensable man into his fullest confidence. Its implied flattery and suggestion of great risks came with a familiar sound to the Capataz. His mind, floating in irresolution and discontent, recognized it with bitterness. He understood well that the doctor was anxious to save the San Tomé mine from annihilation. He would be nothing without it. It was his interest. Just as it had been the interest of Señor Decoud, of the Blancos, and of the Europeans to get his Cargadores on their side. His thought became arrested upon Decoud. What would happen to him?

Nostromo's prolonged silence made the doctor uneasy. He pointed out, quite unnecessarily, that though for the present he was safe, he could not live concealed for ever. The choice was between accepting the mission to Barrios, with all its dangers and difficulties, and leaving Sulaco by stealth, ingloriously, in poverty.

'None of your friends could reward you and protect you just now, Capataz. Not even Don Carlos himself.'

'I would have none of your protection and none of your rewards. I only wish I could trust your courage and your sense. When I return in triumph, as you say, with Barrios, I may find you all destroyed. You have the knife at your throat now.'

It was the doctor's turn to remain silent in the contemplation of horrible contingencies.

'Well, we would trust your courage and your sense. And you, too, have a knife at your throat.'

'Ah! And whom am I to thank for that? What are your politics and your mines to me – your silver and your constitutions – your Don Carlos this, and Don José that –'

'I don't know,' burst out the exasperated doctor. 'There are innocent people in danger whose little finger is worth more than you or I and all the Ribierists together. I don't know. You should have asked yourself before you allowed Decoud to lead you into all this. It was your place to think like a man; but if you did not think, then try to act like a man now. Did you imagine Decoud cared very much for what would happen to you?'

'No more than you care for what will happen to me,' muttered the other.

'No; I care for what will happen to you as little as I care for what will happen to myself.'

'And all this because you are such a devoted Ribierist?' Nostromo said in an incredulous tone.

'All this because I am such a devoted Ribierist,' repeated Dr Monygham, grimly.

Again Nostromo, gazing abstractedly at the body of the late Señor Hirsch, remained silent, thinking that the doctor was a dangerous person in more than one sense. It was impossible to trust him.

'Do you speak in the name of Don Carlos?' he asked at last.

'Yes. I do,' the doctor said, loudly, without hesitation. 'He must come forward now. He must,' he added in a mutter, which Nostromo did not catch.

'What did you say, *señor*?'

The doctor started. 'I say that you must be true to yourself, Capataz. It would be worse than folly to fail now.'

'True to myself,' repeated Nostromo. 'How do you know that I would not be true to myself if I told you to go to the devil with your propositions?'

'I do not know. Maybe you would,' the doctor said, with a roughness of tone intended to hide the sinking of his heart and the faltering of his voice. 'All I know is that you had better get away from here. Some of Sotillo's men may turn up here looking for me.'

He slipped off the table, listened intently. The Capataz, too, stood up.

'Suppose I went to Cayta, what would you do meantime?' he asked.

'I would go to Sotillo directly you had left – in the way I am thinking of.'

'A very good way – if only that engineer-in-chief consents. Remind him, *señor*, that I looked after the old rich Englishman who pays for the railway, and that I saved the lives of some of his people that time when a gang of thieves came from the south to wreck one of his pay-trains. It was I who discovered it all at the risk of my life, by pretending to enter into their plans. Just as you are doing with Sotillo.'

'Yes. Yes, of course. But I can offer him better arguments,' the doctor said, hastily. 'Leave it to me.'

'Ah, yes! True. I am nothing.'

'Not at all. You are everything.'

They moved a few paces towards the door. Behind them the late Señor Hirsch preserved the immobility of a disregarded man.

'That will be all right. I know what to say to the engineer,' pursued the doctor, in a low tone. 'My difficulty will be with Sotillo.'

And Dr Monygham stopped short in the doorway as if intimidated by the difficulty. He had made the sacrifice of his life. He considered this a fitting opportunity. But he did not want to throw his life away too soon. In his quality of betrayer of Don Carlos's confidence, he would have ultimately to indicate the hiding-place of the treasure. That would be the end of his deception, and the end of himself as well, at the hands of the infuriated colonel. He wanted to delay him to the very last moment; and he had been racking his brains to invent some place of concealment at once plausible and difficult of access.

He imparted his trouble to Nostromo, and concluded:

'Do you know what, Capataz? I think that when the time comes and some information must be given, I shall indicate the Great Isabel. That is the best place I can think of. What is the matter?'

A low exclamation had escaped Nostromo. The doctor waited, surprised, and after a moment of profound silence, heard a thick voice stammer out 'Utter folly', and stop with a gasp.

'Why folly?'

'Ah! You do not see it,' began Nostromo, scathingly, gathering scorn as he went on. 'Three men in half an hour would see that no ground had been disturbed anywhere on that island. Do you think that such a treasure can be buried, without leaving traces of the work – eh! Señor Doctor? Why, you would not gain half a day more before having your throat cut by Sotillo. The Isabel! What stupidity! What miserable invention! Ah! you are all alike, you fine men of intelligence. All you are fit for is to betray men of the people into undertaking deadly risks for objects that you are not even sure about. If it comes off you get the benefit. If not, then it does not matter. He is only a dog. Ah! *Madre de Dios*, I would –' He shook his fists above his head.

The doctor was overwhelmed at first by this fierce, hissing vehemence.

'Well! It seems to me on your own showing that the men of the people are no mean fools, too,' he said, sullenly. 'No, but come. You are so clever. Have you a better place?'

Nostromo had calmed down as quickly as he had flared up.

'I am clever enough for that,' he said, quietly, almost with indifference. 'You want to tell him of a hiding-place big enough to take days in ransacking – a place where a treasure of silver ingots can be buried without leaving a sign on the surface.'

'And close at hand,' the doctor put in.

'Just so, *señor*. Tell him it is sunk.'

'This has the merit of being the truth,' the doctor said, contemptuously. 'He will not believe it.'

'You tell him that it is sunk where he may hope to lay his hands on it, and he will believe you quick enough. Tell him it has been sunk in the harbour in order to be recovered afterwards by divers. Tell him you found out that I had orders from Don Carlos Gould to lower the cases quietly overboard somewhere in a line between the end of the jetty and the entrance. The depth is not too great there. He has no divers, but he has a ship, boats, ropes, chains, sailors – of a sort. Let him fish for the silver. Let him set his fools to drag backwards and forwards and crossways while he sits and watches till his eyes drop out of his head.'

'Really, this is an admirable idea,' muttered the doctor.

'*Sí*. You tell him that, and see whether he will not believe you! He will spend days in rage and torment – and still he will believe. He will have no thought for anything else. He will not give up till he is driven off – why, he may even forget to kill you. He will neither eat nor sleep. He –'

'The very thing! The very thing!' the doctor repeated in an excited whisper. 'Capataz, I begin to believe that you are a great genius in your way.'

Nostromo had paused; then began again in a changed tone, sombre, speaking to himself as though he had forgotten the doctor's existence.

'There is something in a treasure that fastens upon a man's mind. He will pray and blaspheme and still persevere, and will curse the day he ever heard of it, and will let his last hour come upon him unawares, still believing that he missed it only by a foot. He will see it every time he closes his eyes. He will never forget it till he is dead – and even then – Doctor, did you ever hear of the miserable *gringos* on Azuera, that cannot die? Ha! ha! Sailors like myself. There is no getting away from a treasure that once fastens upon your mind.'

'You are a devil of a man, Capataz. It is the most plausible thing.'

Nostromo pressed his arm.

'It will be worse for him than thirst at sea or hunger in a town full of people. Do you know what that is? He shall suffer greater torments than he inflicted upon that terrified wretch who had no invention. None! none! Not like me. I could have told Sotillo a deadly tale for very little pain.'

He laughed wildly and turned in the doorway towards the body of the late Señor Hirsch, an opaque long blotch in the semi-transparent obscurity of the room between the two tall parallelograms of the windows full of stars.

'You man of fear!' he cried. 'You shall be avenged by me – Nostromo. Out of my way, doctor! Stand aside – or, by the suffering soul of a woman dead without confession, I will strangle you with my two hands.'

He bounded downwards into the black, smoky hall. With a grunt of astonishment, Dr Monygham threw himself recklessly into the pursuit. At the bottom of the charred stairs he had a fall, pitching forward on his face with a force that would have stunned a spirit less intent upon a task of love and devotion. He was up in a moment, jarred, shaken, with a queer impression of the terrestrial globe having been flung at his head in the dark. But it wanted more than that to stop Dr Monygham's body, possessed by the exaltation of self-sacrifice; a reasonable exaltation, determined not to lose whatever advantage chance put into its way. He ran with headlong, tottering swiftness, his arms going like a windmill in his effort to keep his balance on his crippled feet. He lost his hat; the tails of his open gaberdine flew behind him. He had no mind to lose sight of the indispensable man. But it was a long time, and a long way from the Custom House, before he managed to seize his arm from behind, roughly, out of breath.

'Stop! Are you mad?'

Already Nostromo was walking slowly, his head dropping, as if checked in his pace by the weariness of irresolution.

'What is that to you? Ah! I forgot you want me for something. Always. *Siempre Nostromo*.'

'What do you mean by talking of strangling me?' panted the doctor.

'What do I mean? I mean that the king of the devils himself has sent you out of this town of cowards and talkers to meet me tonight of all the nights of my life.'

Under the starry sky the Albergo d'Italia Una emerged, black and low, breaking the dark level of the plain. Nostromo stopped altogether.

'The priests say he is a tempter, do they not?' he added, through his clenched teeth.

'My good man, you drivel. The devil has nothing to do with this. Neither has the town, which you may call by what name you please. But Don Carlos. Gould is neither a coward nor an empty talker. You will admit that?' He waited. 'Well?'

'Could I see Don Carlos?'

'Great heavens! No! Why? What for?' exclaimed the doctor in agitation. 'I tell you it is madness. I will not let you go into the town for anything.'

'I must.'

'You must not!' hissed the doctor, fiercely, almost beside himself with the fear of the man doing away with his usefulness for an imbecile whim of some sort. 'I tell you you shall not. I would rather –'

He stopped at a loss for words, feeling fagged out, powerless, holding on to Nostromo's sleeve, absolutely for support after his run.

'I am betrayed!' muttered the Capataz to himself; and the doctor, who overheard the last word, made an effort to speak calmly.

'That is exactly what would happen to you. You would be betrayed.'

He thought with a sickening dread that the man was so well known that he could not escape recognition. The house of the Señor Administrador was beset by spies, no doubt. And even the very servants of the *casa* were not to be trusted. 'Reflect, Capataz,' he said, impressively.... 'What are you laughing at?'

'I am laughing to think that if somebody that did not approve of my presence in town, for instance – you understand, *señor doctor* – if somebody were to give me up to Pedrito, it would not be beyond my power to make friends even with him. It is true. What do you think of that?'

'You are man of infinite resource, Capataz,' said Dr Monygham, dismally, 'I recognize that. But the town is full of talk about you; and those few *cargadores* that are not in hiding with the railway people have been shouting *"Viva Montero!"* on the Plaza all day.'

'My poor *cargadores*!' muttered Nostromo. 'Betrayed! Betrayed!'

'I understand that on the wharf you were pretty free in laying about you with a stick amongst your poor *cargadores*,' the doctor said in a grim tone, which showed that he was recovering from his exertions. 'Make no mistake. Pedrito is furious at Señor Ribiera's rescue, and at having lost the pleasure of shooting Decoud. Already there are rumours in the town of the treasure having been spirited away. To have missed that does not please Pedrito either; but let me tell you that if you had all the silver in your hand for your ransom it would not save you.'

Turning swiftly, and catching the doctor by the shoulders, Nostromo thrust his face close to his.

'*Maladetta!* You follow me speaking of the treasure. You have sworn my ruin. You were the last man who looked upon me before I went out with it. And Sidoni the engine-driver says you have an evil eye.'

'He ought to know. I saved his broken leg for him last year,' the doctor said, stoically. He felt on his shoulders the weight of these hands famed amongst the populace for snapping thick ropes and bending horseshoes. 'And to you I offer the best means of saving yourself – let me go – and of retrieving your great reputation. You boasted of making the Capataz de Cargadores

famous from one end of America to the other about this wretched silver. But
I bring you a better opportunity – let me go, *hombre!*'

Nostromo released him abruptly, and the doctor feared that the indispensable man would run off again. But he did not. He walked on slowly. The
doctor hobbled by his side till, within a stone's throw from the Casa Viola,
Nostromo stopped again.

Silent in inhospitable darkness, the Casa Viola seemed to have changed
its nature; his home appeared to repel him with an air of hopeless and
inimical mystery. The doctor said:

'You will be safe there. Go in, Capataz.'

'How can I go in?' Nostromo seemed to ask himself in a low, inward
tone. 'She cannot unsay what she said, and I cannot undo what I have done.'

'I tell you it is all right. Viola is all alone in there. I looked in as I came
out of the town. You will be perfectly safe in that house till you leave it to
make your name famous on the Campo. I am going now to arrange for your
departure with the engineer-in-chief, and I shall bring you news here long
before daybreak.'

Dr Monygham, disregarding, or perhaps fearing to penetrate the meaning
of Nostromo's silence, clapped him lightly on the shoulder, and starting off
with his smart, lame walk, vanished utterly at the third or fourth hop in the
direction of the railway track. Arrested between the two wooden posts for
people to fasten their horses to, Nostromo did not move, as if he, too, had
been planted solidly in the ground. At the end of half an hour he lifted his
head to the deep baying of the dogs at the railway yards, which had burst
out suddenly, tumultuous and deadened as if coming out from under the
plain. That lame doctor with the evil eye had got there pretty fast.

Step by step Nostromo approached the Albergo d'Italia Una, which he
had never known so lightless, so silent, before. The door, all black in the
pale wall, stood open as he had left it twenty-four hours before, when he
had nothing to hide from the world. He remained before it, irresolute, like
a fugitive, like a man betrayed. Poverty, misery, starvation! Where had he
heard these words? The anger of a dying woman had prophesied that fate
for his folly. It looked as if it would come true very quickly. And the *leperos*
would laugh – she had said. Yes, they would laugh if they knew that the
Capataz de Cargadores was at the mercy of the mad doctor whom they could
remember, only a few years ago, buying cooked food from a stall on the
Plaza for a copper coin – like one of themselves.

At that moment the notion of seeking Captain Mitchell passed through
his mind. He glanced in the direction of the jetty and saw a small gleam of
light in the O.S.N. Company's building. The thought of lighted windows
was not attractive. Two lighted windows had decoyed him into the empty
Custom House, only to fall into the clutches of that doctor. No! He would
not go near lighted windows again on that night. Captain Mitchell was
there. And what could he be told? That doctor would worm it all out of him
as if he were a child.

On the threshold he called out 'Giorgio!' in an undertone. Nobody
answered. He stepped in. '*Olá! viejo!* Are you there? . . .' In the impenetrable
darkness his head swam with the illusion that the obscurity of the kitchen

was as vast as the Placid Gulf, and that the floor dipped forward like a sinking lighter. '*Olá! viejo!*' he repeated, falteringly, swaying where he stood. His hand, extended to steady himself, fell upon the table. Moving a step forward, he shifted it, and felt a box of matches under his fingers. He fancied he had heard a quiet sigh. He listened for a moment, holding his breath; then, with trembling hands, tried to strike a light.

The tiny piece of wood flamed up quite blindingly at the end of his fingers, raised above his blinking eyes. A concentrated glare fell upon the leonine white head of old Giorgio against the black fireplace – showed him leaning forward in a chair in staring immobility, surrounded, overhung, by great masses of shadow, his legs crossed, his cheek in his hand, an empty pipe in the corner of his mouth. It seemed hours before he attempted to turn his face; at the very moment the match went out, and he disappeared, overwhelmed by the shadows, as if the walls and roof of the desolate house had collapsed upon his white head in ghostly silence.

Nostromo heard him stir and utter dispassionately the words:

'It may have been a vision.'

'No,' he said, softly. 'It is no vision, old man.'

A strong chest voice asked in the dark:

'Is that you I hear, Giovann' Battista?'

'*Sì, viejo.* Steady. Not so loud.'

After his release by Sotillo, Giorgio Viola, attended to the very door by the good-natured engineer-in-chief, had re-entered his house, which he had been made to leave almost at the very moment of his wife's death. All was still. The lamp above was burning. He nearly called out to her by name; and the thought that no call from him would ever again evoke the answer of her voice, made him drop heavily into the chair with a loud groan, wrung out by the pain as of a keen blade piercing his breast.

The rest of the night he made no sound. The darkness turned to grey, and on the colourless, clear, glassy dawn the jagged sierra stood out flat and opaque, as if cut out of paper.

The enthusiastic and severe soul of Giorgio Viola, sailor, champion of oppressed humanity, enemy of kings, and, by the grace of Mrs Gould, hotel-keeper of the Sulaco harbour, had descended into the open abyss of desolation amongst the shattered vestiges of his past. He remembered his wooing between two campaigns a single short week in the season of gathering olives. Nothing approached the grave passion of that time but the deep, passionate sense of his bereavement. He discovered all the extent of his dependence upon the silenced voice of that woman. It was her voice that he missed. Abstracted, busy, lost in inward contemplation, he seldom looked at his wife in those later years. The thought of his girls was a matter of concern, not of consolation. It was her voice that he would miss. And he remembered the other child – the little boy who died at sea. Ah! a man would have been something to lean upon. And, alas! even Gian' Battista – he of whom, and of Linda, his wife had spoken to him so anxiously before she dropped off into her last sleep on earth, he on whom she had called aloud to save the children, just before she died – even he was dead!

And the old man, bent forward, his head in his hand, sat through the day in immobility and solitude. He never heard the brazen roar of the bells in town. When it ceased the earthenware filter in the corner of the kitchen kept on its swift musical drip, drip into the great porous jar below.

Towards sunset he got up, and with slow movements disappeared up the narrow staircase. His bulk filled it; and the rubbing of his shoulders made a small noise as of a mouse running behind the plaster of a wall. While he remained up there the house was as dumb as a grave. Then, with the same faint rubbing noise, he descended. He had to catch at the chairs and tables to regain his seat. He seized his pipe off the high mantel of the fireplace – but made no attempt to reach the tobacco – thrust it empty into the corner of his mouth, and sat down again in the same staring pose. The sun of Pedrito's entry into Sulaco, the last sun of Señor Hirsch's life, the first of Decoud's solitude on the Great Isabel, passed over the Albergo d'Italia Una on its way to the west. The tinkling drip, drip of the filter had ceased, the lamp upstairs had burnt itself out, and the night beset Giorgio Viola and his dead wife with its obscurity and silence that seemed invincible till the Capataz de Cargadores, returning from the dead, put them to flight with the splutter and flare of a match.

'*Sí, viejo.* It is me. Wait.'

Nostromo, after barricading the door and closing the shutters carefully, groped upon a shelf for a candle, and lit it.

Old Viola had risen. He followed with his eyes in the dark the sounds made by Nostromo. The light disclosed him standing without support, as if the mere presence of that man who was loyal, brave, incorruptible, who was all his son would have been, were enough for the support of his decaying strength.

He extended his hand grasping the briar-wood pipe, whose bowl was charred on the edge, and knitted his bushy eyebrows heavily at the light.

'You have returned,' he said, with shaky dignity. 'Ah! Very well! I –'

He broke off. Nostromo, leaning back against the table, his arms folded on his breast, nodded at him slightly.

'You thought I was drowned! No! The best dog of the rich, of the aristocrats, of these fine men who can only talk and betray the people, is not dead yet.'

The Garibaldino, motionless, seemed to drink in the sound of the well-known voice. His head moved slightly once as if in sign of approval; but Nostromo saw clearly that the old man understood nothing of the words. There was no one to understand; no one he could take into the confidence of Decoud's fate, of his own, into the secret of the silver. That doctor was an enemy of the people – a tempter. . . .

Old Giorgio's heavy frame shook from head to foot with the effort to overcome his emotion at the sight of that man, who had shared the intimacies of his domestic life as though he had been a grown-up son.

'She believed you would return,' he said, solemnly.

Nostromo raised his head.

'She was a wise woman. How could I fail to come back –?'

He finished the thought mentally: 'Since she has prophesied for me an end of poverty, misery, and starvation.' These words of Teresa's anger, from the circumstances in which they had been uttered, like the cry of a soul prevented from making its peace with God, stirred the obscure superstition of personal fortune from which even the greatest genius amongst men of adventure and action is seldom free. They reigned over Nostromo's mind with the force of a potent malediction. And what a curse it was that which her words had laid upon him! He had been orphaned so young that he could remember no other woman whom he called mother. Henceforth there would be no enterprise in which he would not fail. The spell was working already. Death itself would elude him now.... He said violently:

'Come, *viejo*! Get me something to eat. I am hungry! *Sangre de Dios!* The emptiness of my belly makes me lightheaded.'

With his chin dropped again upon his bare breast above his folded arms, barefooted, watching from under a gloomy brow the movements of old Viola foraging amongst the cupboards, he seemed as if indeed fallen under a curse – a ruined and sinister Capataz.

Old Viola walked out of a dark corner, and, without a word, emptied upon the table out of his hollowed palms a few dry crusts of bread and half a raw onion.

While the Capataz began to devour his beggar's fare, taking up with stony-eyed voracity piece after piece lying by his side, the Garibaldino went off, and squatting down in another corner filled an earthenware mug with red wine out of a wicker-covered demijohn. With a familiar gesture, as when serving customers in the café, he had thrust his pipe between his teeth to have his hands free.

The Capataz drank greedily. A slight flush deepened the bronze of his cheek. Before him, Viola, with a turn of his white and massive head towards the staircase, took his empty pipe out of his mouth, and pronounced slowly:

'After the shot was fired down here, which killed her as surely as if the bullet had struck her oppressed heart, she called upon you to save the children. Upon you, Gian' Battista.'

The Capataz looked up.

'Did she do that, Padrone? To save the children! They are with the English *señora*, their rich benefactress. Hey! old man of the people. Thy benefactress....'

'I am old,' muttered Giorgio Viola. 'An Englishwoman was allowed to give a bed to Garibaldi lying wounded in prison. The greatest man that ever lived. A man of the people, too – a sailor. I may let another keep a roof over my head. *Sì* ... I am old. I may let her. Life lasts too long sometimes.'

'And she herself may not have a roof over her head before many days are out, unless I ... What do you say? Am I to keep a roof over her head? Am I to try – and save all the Blancos together with her?'

'You shall do it,' said old Viola in a strong voice. 'You shall do it as my son would have....'

'Thy son, *viejo*! ... There never has been a man like thy son. Ha, I must try.... But what if it were only a part of the curse to lure me on? ... And so she called upon me to save – and then –?'

'She spoke no more.' The heroic follower of Garibaldi, at the thought of the eternal stillness and silence fallen upon the shrouded form stretched out on the bed upstairs, averted his face and raised his hand to his furrowed brow. 'She was dead before I could seize her hands,' he stammered out, pitifully.

Before the wide eyes of the Capataz, staring at the doorway of the dark staircase, floated the shape of the Great Isabel, like a strange ship in distress, freighted with enormous wealth and the solitary life of a man. It was impossible for him to do anything. He could only hold his tongue, since there was no one to trust. The treasure would be lost, probably – unless Decoud.... And his thought came abruptly to an end. He perceived that he could not imagine in the least what Decoud was likely to do.

Old Viola had not stirred. And the motionless Capataz dropped his long, soft eyelashes, which gave to the upper part of his fierce, black-whiskered face a touch of feminine ingenuousness. The silence had lasted for a long time.

'God rest her soul!' he murmured, gloomily.

CHAPTER 10

The next day was quiet in the morning, except for the faint sound of firing to the northward, in the direction of Los Hatos. Captain Mitchell had listened to it from his balcony anxiously. The phrase, 'In my delicate position as the only consular agent then in the port, everything, sir, everything was a just cause for anxiety,' had its place in the more or less stereotyped relation of the 'historical events' which for the next few years was at the service of distinguished strangers visiting Sulaco. The mention of the dignity and neutrality of the flag, so difficult to preserve in his position, 'right in the thick of these events between the lawlessness of that piratical villain Sotillo and the more regularly established but scarcely less atrocious tyranny of his Excellency Don Pedro Montero', came next in order. Captain Mitchell was not the man to enlarge upon mere dangers much. But he insisted that it was a memorable day. On that day, towards dusk, he had seen 'that poor fellow of mine – Nostromo. The sailor whom I discovered, and, I may say, made, sir. The man of the famous ride to Cayta, sir. An historical event, sir!'

Regarded by the O.S.N. Company as an old and faithful servant, Captain Mitchell was allowed to attain the term of his usefulness in ease and dignity at the head of the enormously extended service. The augmentation of the establishment, with its crowds of clerks, an office in town, the old office in the harbour, the division into departments – passenger, cargo, lighterage, and so on – secured a greater leisure for his last years in the regenerated Sulaco, the capital of the Occidental Republic. Liked by the natives for his good nature and the formality of his manner, self-important and simple, known for years as a 'friend of our country,' he felt himself a personality of mark in the town. Getting up early for a turn in the market-place while the gigantic shadow of Higuerota was still lying upon the fruit and flower stalls piled up with masses of gorgeous colouring, attending easily to current affairs, welcomed in houses, greeted by ladies on the Alameda, with his entry into all the clubs and a footing in the Casa Gould, he led his privileged old bachelor, man-about-town existence with great comfort and solemnity. But on mail-boat days he was down at the Harbour Office at an early hour, with his own gig, manned by a smart crew in white and blue, ready to dash off and board the ship directly she showed her bows between the harbour heads.

It would be into the Harbour Office that he would lead some privileged passenger he had brought off in his own boat, and invite him to take a seat for a moment while he signed a few papers. And Captain Mitchell, seating himself at his desk, would keep on talking hospitably:

'There isn't much time if you are to see everything in a day. We shall be off in a moment. We'll have lunch at the Amarilla Club – though I belong also to the Anglo-American – mining engineers and businessmen, don't you know – and to the Mirliflores as well, a new club – English, French, Italians, all sorts – lively young fellows mostly, who wanted to pay a compliment to an old resident, sir. But we'll lunch at the Amarilla. Interest you, I fancy. Real thing of the country. Men of the first families. The President of the Occidental Republic himself belongs to it, sir. Fine old bishop with a broken nose in the patio. Remarkable piece of statuary, I believe. Cavaliere Parrochetti – you know Parrochetti, the famous Italian sculptor – was working here for two years – thought very highly of our old bishop.... There! I am very much at your service now.'

Proud of his experience, penetrated by the sense of historical importance of men, events, and buildings, he talked pompously in jerky periods, with slight sweeps of his short, thick arm, letting nothing 'escape the attention' of his privileged captive.

'Lot of building going on, as you observe. Before the Separation it was a plain of burnt grass smothered in clouds of dust, with an ox-cart track to our Jetty. Nothing more. This is the Harbour Gate. Picturesque, is it not? Formerly the town stopped short there. We enter now the Calle de la Constitución. Observe the old Spanish houses. Great dignity. Eh? I suppose it's just as it was in the time of the Viceroys, except for the pavement. Wood blocks now. Sulaco National Bank there, with the sentry boxes each side of the gate. Casa Avellanos this side, with all the ground-floor windows shuttered. A wonderful woman lives there – Miss Avellanos – the beautiful Antonia. A character, sir! A historical woman! Opposite – Casa Gould. Noble gateway. Yes, *the* Goulds of the original Gould Concession, that all the world knows of now. I hold seventeen of the thousand-dollar shares in the Consolidated San Tomé mines. All the poor savings of my lifetime, sir, and it will be enough to keep me in comfort to the end of my days at home when I retire. I got in on the ground floor, you see. Don Carlos, great friend of mine. Seventeen shares – quite a little fortune to leave behind one, too. I have a niece – married a parson – most worthy man, incumbent of a small parish in Sussex; no end of children. I was never married myself. A sailor should exercise self-denial. Standing under that very gateway, sir, with some young engineer-fellows, ready to defend that house where we had received so much kindness and hospitality, I saw the first and last charge of Pedrito's horsemen upon Barrios's troops, who had just taken the Harbour Gate. They could not stand the new rifles brought out by that poor Decoud. It was a murderous fire. In a moment the street became blocked with a mass of dead men and horses. They never came on again.'

And all day Captain Mitchell would talk like this to his more or less willing victim:

'The Plaza. I call it magnificent. Twice the area of Trafalgar Square.'

From the very centre, in the blazing sunshine, he pointed out the buildings:

'The Intendencia, now President's Palace – Cabildo, where the Lower Chamber of Parliament sits. You notice the new houses on that side of the Plaza? Compañia Anzani, a great general store, like those cooperative things at home. Old Anzani was murdered by the National Guards in front of his safe. It was even for that specific crime that the deputy Gamacho, commanding the Nationals, a bloodthirsty and savage brute, was executed publicly by garrotte upon the sentence of a court-martial ordered by Barrios. Anzani's nephews converted the business into a company. All that side of the Plaza had been burnt; used to be colonnaded before. A terrible fire, by the light of which I saw the last of the fighting, the *llaneros* flying, the Nationals throwing their arms down, and the miners of San Tomé, all Indians from the Sierra, rolling by like a torrent to the sound of pipes and cymbals, green flags flying, a wild mass of men in white ponchos and green hats, on foot, on mules, on donkeys. Such a sight, sir, will never be seen again. The miners, sir, had marched upon the town. Don Pepe leading on his black horse, and their very wives in the rear on *burros*, screaming encouragement, sir, and beating tambourines. I remember one of these women had a green parrot seated on her shoulder, as calm as a bird of stone. They had just saved their Señor Administrador; for Barrios, though he ordered the assault at once, at night, too, would have been too late. Pedrito Montero had Don Carlos led out to be shot – like his uncle many years ago – and then, as Barrios said afterwards, "Sulaco would not have been worth fighting for." Sulaco without the Concession was nothing; and there were tons and tons of dynamite distributed all over the mountain with detonators arranged, and an old priest, Father Román, standing by to annihilate the San Tomé mine at the first news of failure. Don Carlos had made up his mind not to leave it behind, and he had the right men to see to it, too.'

Thus Captain Mitchell would talk in the middle of the Plaza, holding over his head a white umbrella with a green lining; but inside the cathedral, in the dim light, with a faint scent of incense floating in the cool atmosphere, and here and there a kneeling female figure, black or all white, with a veiled head, his lowered voice became solemn and impressive.

'Here,' he would say, pointing to a niche in the wall of the dusky aisle, 'you see the bust of Don José Avellanos, "Patriot and Statesman", as the inscription says, "Minister to Courts of England and Spain, etc., etc., died in the woods of Los Hatos worn out with his life-long struggle for Right and Justice at the dawn of the New Era." A fair likeness. Parrochetti's work from some old photographs and a pencil sketch by Mrs Gould. I was well acquainted with that distinguished Spanish–American of the old school, a true *hidalgo*, beloved by everybody who knew him. The marble medallion in the wall, in the antique style, representing a veiled woman seated with her hands clasped loosely over her knees, commemorates that unfortunate young gentleman who sailed out with Nostromo on that fatal night, sir. See, "To the memory of Martin Decoud, his betrothed Antonia Avellanos." Frank, simple, noble. There you have that lady, sir, as she is. An exceptional woman. Those who thought she would give way to despair were mistaken, sir. She has been blamed in many quarters for not having taken the veil. It was expected of her. But Doña Antonia is not the stuff they make nuns of. Bishop Corbelán, her uncle, lives with her in the Corbelán town house. He is a fierce sort of priest, everlastingly worrying the Government about the old Church lands and convents. I believe they think a lot of him in Rome. Now let us go to the Amarilla Club, just across the Plaza, to get some lunch.'

Directly outside the cathedral on the very top of the noble flight of steps, his voice rose pompously, his arm found again its sweeping gesture.

'*Porvenir*, over there on that first floor, above those French plate-glass shop-fronts; our biggest daily. Conservative, or, rather, I should say, Parliamentary. We have the Parliamentary party here of which the actual Chief of the State, Don Juste Lopez, is the head; a very sagacious man, I think. A first-rate intellect, sir. The Democratic party in opposition rests mostly, I am sorry to say, on these socialistic Italians, sir, with their secret societies, *camorras*, and such-like. There are lots of Italians settled here on the railway lands, dismissed navvies, mechanics, and so on, all along the trunk line. There are whole villages of Italians on the Campo. And the natives, too, are being drawn into these ways . . . American bar? Yes. And over there you can see another. New Yorkers mostly frequent that one – Here we are at the Amarilla. Observe the bishop at the foot of the stairs to the right as we go in.'

And the lunch would begin and terminate its lavish and leisurely course at a little table in the gallery, Captain Mitchell nodding, bowing, getting up to speak for a moment to different officials in black clothes, merchants in jackets, officers in uniform, middle-aged *caballeros* from the Campo – sallow, little, nervous men, and fat, placid, swarthy men, and Europeans or North Americans of superior standing, whose faces looked very white amongst the majority of dark complexions and black, glistening eyes.

Captain Mitchell would lie back in the chair, casting around looks of satisfaction, and tender over the table a case full of thick cigars.

'Try a weed with your coffee. Local tobacco. The black coffee you get at the Amarilla, sir, you don't meet anywhere in the world. We get the bean from a famous cafeteria in the foot-hills, whose owner sends three sacks every year as a present to his fellow members in remembrance of the fight against Gamacho's Nationals, carried on from these very windows by the *caballeros*. He was in town at the time, and took part, sir, to the bitter end. It arrives on three mules – not in the common way, by rail; no fear! – right into the patio, escorted by mounted peons, in charge of the Mayoral of his estate, who walks upstairs, booted and spurred, and delivers it to our committee formally with the words, "For the sake of those fallen the third of May." We call it "Tres de Mayo', coffee. Taste it.'

Captain Mitchell, with an expression as though making ready to hear a sermon in a church, would lift the tiny cup to his lips. And the nectar would be sipped to the bottom during a restful silence in a cloud of cigar smoke.

'Look at this man in black just going out,' he would begin, leaning forward hastily. 'This is the famous Hernandez, Minister of War. *The Times*'s special correspondent, who wrote that striking series of letters calling the Occidental Republic the "Treasure House of the World", gave a whole article to him and the force he has organized – the renowned Carabineers of the Campo.'

Captain Mitchell's guest, staring curiously, would see a figure in a long-tailed black coat walking gravely, with downcast eyelids in a long, composed face, a brow furrowed horizontally, a pointed head, whose grey hair, thin at the top, combed down carefully on all sides and rolled at the ends, fell low on the neck and shoulders. This, then, was the famous bandit of whom Europe had heard with interest. He put on a high-crowned sombrero with a wide flat brim; a rosary of wooden beads was twisted about his right wrist. And Captain Mitchell would proceed:

'The protector of the Sulaco refugees from the rage of Pedrito. As general of cavalry with Barrios he distinguished himself at the storming of Tonoro, where Señor Fuentes was killed with the last remnant of the Monterists. He is the friend and humble servant of Bishop Corbelán. Hears three Masses every day. I bet you he will step into the cathedral to say a prayer or two on his way home to his siesta.'

He took several puffs at his cigar in silence; then, in his best important manner, pronounced:

'The Spanish race, sir, is prolific of remarkable characters in every rank of life.... I propose we go now into the billiard-room, which is cool, for a quiet chat. There's never anybody there till after five. I could tell you episodes of the Separationist revolution that would astonish you. When the great heat's over, we'll take a turn on the Alameda.'

The programme went on relentless, like a law of Nature. The turn on the Alameda was taken with slow steps and stately remarks.

'All the great world of Sulaco here, sir,' Captain Mitchell bowed right and left with no end of formality; then with animation, 'Doña Emilia, Mrs Gould's carriage. Look. Always white mules. The kindest, most gracious woman the sun ever shone upon. A great position, sir. A great position. First lady in Sulaco – far before the President's wife. And worthy of it.' He took off his hat; then, with a studied change of tone, added, negligently, that the man in black by her side, with a high white collar and a scarred, snarly face, was Dr Monygham, Inspector of State Hospitals, chief medical officer of the Consolidated San Tomé mines. 'A familiar of the house. Everlastingly there. No wonder. The Goulds made him. Very clever man and all that, but I never liked him. Nobody does. I can recollect him limping about the streets in a check shirt and native sandals with a water-melon under his arm – all he would get to eat for the day. A big-wig now, sir, and as nasty as ever. However ... There's no doubt he played his part fairly well at the time. He saved us all from the deadly incubus of Sotillo, where a more particular man might have failed –'

His arm went up.

'The equestrian statue that used to stand on the pedestal over there has been removed. It was an anachronism,' Captain Mitchell commented, obscurely. 'There is some talk of replacing it by a marble shaft commemorative of Separation, with angels of peace at the four corners, and bronze Justice holding an even balance, all gilt, on the top. Cavaliere Parrochetti was asked to make a design, which you can see framed under glass in the Municipal Sala: Names are to be engraved all round the base. Well! They could do no better than begin with the name of Nostromo. He has done for Separation as much as anybody else, and,' added Captain Mitchell, 'has got less than many others by it – when it comes to that.' He dropped on to a stone seat under a tree, and tapped invitingly at the place by his side. 'He carried to Barrios the letters from Sulaco which decided the General to abandon Cayta for a time, and come back to our help here by sea. The transports were still in harbour fortunately. Sir, I did not even know that my Capataz de Cargadores was alive. I had no idea. It was Dr Monygham who came upon him, by chance, in the Custom House, evacuated an hour or two before by the wretched Sotillo. I was never told; never given a hint, nothing – as if I were unworthy of confidence. Monygham arranged it all. He went to the railway yards, and got admission to the engineer-in-chief, who, for the sake of the Goulds as much as for anything else, consented to let an engine make a dash down the line, one hundred and eighty miles, with Nostromo aboard. It was the only way to get him off. In the Construction Camp at the rail-head, he obtained a horse, arms, some clothing, and started alone on that marvellous ride – four hundred miles in six days, through a disturbed country, ending by the feat of passing through the Monterist lines outside Cayta. The history of that ride, sir, would make a most exciting book. He carried all our lives in his pocket. Devotion, courage, fidelity, intelligence were not enough. Of course, he was perfectly fearless and incorruptible. But a man was wanted that would know how to succeed. He was that man, sir. On the fifth of May, being practically a prisoner in the Harbour Office of my Company, I suddenly heard the whistle of an engine in the railway yards, a quarter of a mile away. I could not believe my ears. I made one jump on to the balcony, and beheld a locomotive under a great head of steam run out of the yard gates, screeching like mad, enveloped in a white cloud, and then, just abreast of old Viola's inn, check almost to a standstill. I made out, sir, a man – I couldn't tell who – dash out of the Albergo d'Italia Una, climb into the cab, and then, sir, that engine seemed positively to leap clear of the house, and was gone in the twinkling of an eye. As you blow a candle out, sir! There was a first-rate driver on the foot-plate, sir, I can tell you. They were fired heavily upon by the National Guards in Rincón and one other place. Fortunately the line had not been torn up. In four hours they reached the Construction Camp. Nostromo had his start.... The rest you know. You've got only to look around you. There are people on this Alameda that ride in their carriages, or even are alive at all today, because years ago I engaged a runaway Italian sailor for a foreman of our wharf simply on the strength of his looks. And that's a fact. You can't get over it, sir. On the seventeenth of May, just twelve days after I saw the man from the Casa Viola get on the engine, and wondered what it meant, Barrios's transports were entering this harbour, and the "Treasure House of the World", as *The Times* man calls Sulaco in his book, was saved intact for civilization – for a great future, sir. Pedrito, with Hernandez on the west, and the San Tomé miners pressing on the land gate, was not able to oppose the landing. He had been sending messages to Sotillo for a week to join him. Had Sotillo done so there would have been massacres and proscription that would have left no man or woman of position alive. But that's where Dr Monygham comes in. Sotillo, blind and deaf to everything, stuck on board his steamer watching the dragging for silver, which he believed to be sunk at the bottom of the harbour. They say that for the last three days he was out of his mind raving and foaming with disappointment at getting nothing, flying about the deck, and yelling curses at the boats with the drags, ordering them in, and then suddenly stamping his foot and crying out, "And yet it is there! I see it! I feel it!"

'He was preparing to hang Dr Monygham (whom he had on board) at the end of the after-derrick, when the first of Barrios's transports, one of our own ships at that, steamed right in, and ranging close alongside opened a small-arm fire without as much preliminaries as a hail. It was the completest surprise in the world, sir. They were too astounded at first to bolt below. Men were falling right and left like ninepins. It's a miracle that Monygham, standing on the after-hatch with the rope already round his neck, escaped being riddled through and through like a sieve. He told me since that he had given himself up for lost, and kept on yelling with all the strength of his lungs: "Hoist a white flag! Hoist a white flag!" Suddenly an old major of the Esmeralda regiment, standing by, unsheathed his sword with a shriek: "Die, perjured traitor!" and ran Sotillo clean through the body, just before he fell himself shot through the head.'

Captain Mitchell stopped for a while.

'Begad, sir! I could spin you a yarn for hours. But it's time we started off to Rincón. It would not do for you to pass through Sulaco and not see the lights of the San Tomé mine, a whole mountain ablaze like a lighted palace above the dark Campo. It's a fashionable drive.... But let me tell you one little anecdote, sir; just to show you. A fortnight or more later, when Barrios, declared Generalissimo, was gone in pursuit of Pedrito away south, when the Provisional Junta, with Don Juste Lopez at its head, had promulgated the new Constitution, and our Don Carlos Gould was packing up his trunks bound on a mission to San Francisco and Washington (the United States, sir, were the first great power to recognize the Occidental Republic) – a fortnight later, I say, when we were beginning to feel that our heads were safe on our shoulders, if I may express myself so, a prominent man, a large shipper by our line, came to see me on business, and, says he, the first thing: "I say, Captain Mitchell, is that fellow" (meaning Nostromo) "still the Capataz of your *cargadores* or not?" "What's the matter?" says I. "Because, if he is, then I don't mind; I send and receive a good lot of cargo by your ships; but I have observed him several days loafing about the wharf, and just now he stopped me as cool as you please, with a request for a cigar. Now, you know, my cigars are rather special, and I can't get them so easily as all that." "I hope you stretched a point," I said, very gently. "Why, yes. But it's a confounded nuisance. The fellow's everlastingly cadging for smokes." Sir, I turned my eyes away, and then asked, "Weren't you one of the prisoners in the *cabildo*?" "You know very well I was, and in chains, too," says he. "And under a fine of fifteen thousand dollars?" He coloured, sir, because it got about that he fainted from fright when they came to arrest him, and then behaved before Fuentes in a manner to make the very *policianos*, who had dragged him there by the hair of his head, smile at his cringing. "Yes," he says, in a sort of shy way. "Why?" "Oh, nothing. You stood to lose a tidy bit," says I, "even if you saved your life.... But what can I do for you?" He never even saw the point. Not he. And that's how the world wags, sir.'

He rose a little stiffly, and the drive to Rincón would be taken with only one philosophical remark, uttered by the merciless cicerone, with his eyes fixed upon the lights of San Tomé, that seemed suspended in the dark night between earth and heaven.

'A great power, this, for good and evil, sir. A great power.'

And the dinner of the Mirliflores would be eaten, excellent as to cooking, and leaving upon the traveller's mind an impression that there were in Sulaco many pleasant, able young men with salaries apparently too large for their discretion, and amongst them a few, mostly Anglo-Saxon, skilled in the art of, as the saying is, 'taking a rise' out of his kind host.

With a rapid, jingling drive to the harbour in a two-wheeled machine (which Captain Mitchell called a curricle) behind a fleet and scraggy mule beaten all the time by an obviously Neapolitan driver, the cycle would be nearly closed before the lighted-up offices of the O.S.N. Company, remaining open so late because of the steamer. Nearly – but not quite.

'Ten o'clock. Your ship won't be ready to leave till half past twelve, if by then. Come in for a brandy-and-soda and one more cigar.'

And in the superintendent's private room the privileged passenger by the *Ceres*, or *Juno*, or *Pallas*, stunned and as it were annihilated mentally by a sudden surfeit of sights, sounds, names, facts, and complicated information imperfectly apprehended, would listen like a tired child to a fairy tale; would hear a voice, familiar and surprising in its pompousness, tell him, as if from another world, how there was 'in this very harbour' an international naval demonstration, which put an end to the Costaguana-Sulaco War. How the United States cruiser, *Powhattan*, was the first to salute the Occidental flag – white, with a wreath of green laurel in the middle encircling a yellow amarilla flower. Would hear how General Montero, in less than a month after proclaiming himself Emperor of Costaguana, was shot dead (during a solemn and public distribution of orders and crosses) by a young artillery officer, the brother of his then mistress.

'The abominable Pedrito, sir, fled the country,' the voice would say. And it would continue: 'A captain of one of our ships told me lately that he recognized Pedrito the Guerrillero, arrayed in purple slippers and a velvet smoking-cap with a gold tassel, keeping a disorderly house in one of the southern ports.'

'Abominable Pedrito! Who the devil was he?' would wonder the distinguished bird of passage hovering on the confines of waking and sleep with resolutely open eyes and a faint but amiable curl upon his lips, from between which stuck out the eighteenth or twentieth cigar of that memorable day.

'He appeared to me in this very room like a haunting ghost, sir' – Captain Mitchell was talking of his Nostromo with true warmth of feeling and a touch of wistful pride. 'You may imagine, sir, what an effect it produced on me. He had come round by sea with Barrios, of course. And the first thing he told me after I became fit to hear him was that he had picked up the lighter's boat floating in the gulf! He seemed quite overcome by the circumstance. And a remarkable enough circumstance it was, when you remember that it was then sixteen days since the sinking of the silver. At once I could see he was another man. He stared at the wall, sir, as if there had been a spider or something running about there. The loss of the silver preyed on his mind. The first thing he asked me about was whether Doña Antonia had heard yet of Decoud's death. His voice trembled. I had to tell him that Doña Antonia, as a matter of fact, was not then back in town yet. Poor girl! And just as I was making ready to ask him a thousand questions, with a sudden, "Pardon me, *señor*," he cleared out of the office altogether. I did not see him again for three days. I was terribly busy, you know. It seems that he wandered about in and out of the town, and on two nights turned up to sleep in the baracoons of the railway people. He seemed absolutely indifferent to what went on. I asked him on the wharf, "When are you going to take hold again, Nostromo? There will be plenty of work for the *cargadores* presently."

' "*Señor*," says he, looking at me in a slow, inquisitive manner, "would it surprise you to hear that I am too tired to work just yet? And what work could I do now? How can I look my *cargadores* in the face after losing a lighter?"

'I begged him not to think any more about the silver, and he smiled. A smile that went to my heart, sir. "It was no mistake," I told him. "It was a fatality. A thing that could not be helped." "*Sí, sí!*" he said, and turned away. I thought it best to leave him alone for a bit to get over it. Sir, it took him years really, to get over it. I was present at his interview with Don Carlos. I must say that Gould is rather a cold man. He had to keep a tight hand on his feelings, dealing with thieves and rascals, in constant danger of ruin for himself and wife for so many years, that it had become a second nature. They looked at each other for a long time. Don Carlos asked what he could do for him, in his quiet, reserved way.

' "My name is known from one end of Sulaco to the other," he said, as quiet as the other. "What more can you do for me?" That was all that passed on that occasion. Later, however, there was a very fine coasting schooner for sale, and Mrs Gould and I put our heads together to get her bought and presented to him. It was done, but he paid all the price back within the next three years. Business was booming all along this seaboard, sir. Moreover, that man always succeeded in everything except in saving the silver. Poor Doña Antonia, fresh from her terrible experiences in the woods of Los Hatos, had an interview with him, too. Wanted to hear about Decoud: what they said, what they did, what they thought up to the last on that fatal night. Mrs Gould told me his manner was perfect for quietness and sympathy. Miss Avellanos burst into tears only when he told her how Decoud had happened to say that his plan would be a glorious success. . . . And there's no doubt, sir, that it is. It is a success.'

The cycle was about to close at last. And while the privileged passenger, shivering with the pleasant anticipation of his berth, forgot to ask himself what on earth Decoud's plan could be, Captain Mitchell was saying, 'Sorry we must part so soon. Your intelligent interest made this a pleasant day to me. I shall see you now on board. You had a glimpse of the "Treasure House of the World". A very good name that.' And the coxswain's voice at the door, announcing that the gig was ready, closed the cycle.

Nostromo had, indeed, found the lighter's boat, which he had left on the Great Isabel with Decoud, floating empty far out in the gulf. He was then on the bridge of the first of Barrios's transports, and within an hour's steaming from Sulaco. Barrios, always delighted with a feat of daring and a good judge of courage, had taken a great liking to the Capataz. During the passage round the coast the General kept Nostromo near his person, addressing him frequently in that abrupt and boisterous manner which was the sign of his high favour.

Nostromo's eyes were the first to catch, broad on the bow, the tiny, elusive dark speck, which, alone with the forms of the Three Isabels right ahead, appeared on the flat, shimmering emptiness of the gulf. There are times when no fact should be neglected as insignificant; a small boat so far from the land might have had some meaning worth finding out. At a nod of consent from Barrios the transport swept out of her course, passing near enough to ascertain that no one manned the little cockle-shell. It was merely a common small boat gone adrift with her oars in her. But Nostromo, to whose mind Decoud had been insistently present for days, had long before recognized with excitement the dinghy of the lighter.

There could be no question of stopping to pick up that thing. Every minute of time was momentous with the lives and futures of a whole town. The head of the leading ship, with the General on board, fell off to her course. Behind her, the fleet of transports, scattered haphazard over a mile or so in the offing, like the finish of an ocean race, pressed on, all black and smoking on the western sky.

'*Mi General,*' Nostromo's voice rang out loud, but quiet, from behind a group of officers, 'I should like to save that little boat. *Por Dios*, I know her. She belongs to my Company.'

'And, *por Dios,*' guffawed Barrios, in a noisy, good-humoured voice, 'you belong to me. I am going to make you a captain of cavalry directly we get within sight of a horse again.'

'I can swim far better than I can ride, *mi General,*' cried Nostromo, pushing through to the rail with a set stare in his eyes. 'Let me – '

'Let you? What a conceited fellow that is,' bantered the General, jovially, without even looking at him. 'Let him go! Ha! ha! ha! He wants me to admit that we cannot take Sulaco without him! Ha! ha! ha! Would you like to swim off to her, my son?'

A tremendous shout from one end of the ship to the other stopped his guffaw. Nostromo had leaped overboard; and his black head bobbed up far away already from the ship. The General muttered an appalled '*Cielo!* Sinner that I am!' in a thunderstruck tone. One anxious glance was enough to show him that Nostromo was swimming with perfect ease; and then he thundered terribly, 'No! no! We shall not stop to pick up this impertinent fellow. Let him drown – that mad Capataz.'

Nothing short of main force would have kept Nostromo from leaping overboard. That empty boat, coming out to meet him mysteriously, as if rowed by an invisible spectre, exercised the fascination of some sign, of some warning, seemed to answer in a startling and enigmatic way the persistent thought of a treasure and of a man's fate. He would have leaped if there had been death in that half mile of water. It was as smooth as a pond, and for some reason sharks are unknown in the Placid Gulf, though on the other side of the Punta Mala the coastline swarms with them.

The Capataz seized hold of the stern and blew with force. A queer, faint feeling had come over him while he swam. He had got rid of his boots and coat in the water. He hung on for a time, regaining his breath. In the distance the transports, more in a bunch now, held on straight for Sulaco, with their air of friendly contest, of nautical sport, of a regatta; and the united smoke of their funnels drove like a thin, sulphurous fogbank right over his head. It was his daring, his courage, his act that had set these ships in motion upon the sea, hurrying on to save the lives and fortunes of the Blancos, the taskmasters of the people; to save the San Tomé mine; to save the children.

With a vigorous and skilful effort he clambered over the stern. The very boat! No doubt of it; no doubt whatever. It was the dinghy of the lighter No. 3 – the dinghy left with Martin Decoud on the Great Isabel so that he should have some means to help himself if nothing could be done for him from the shore. And here she had come out to meet him empty and inexplicable. What had become of Decoud? The Capataz made a minute examination. He looked for some scratch, for some mark, for some sign. All he discovered was a brown stain on the gunwale abreast of the thwart. He bent his face over it and rubbed hard with his finger. Then he sat down in the stern sheets, passive, with knees close together and legs aslant.

Streaming from head to foot, with his hair and whiskers hanging lank and dripping and a lustreless stare fixed upon the bottom boards, the Capataz of the Sulaco Cargadores resembled a drowned corpse come up from the bottom to idle away the sunset hour in a small boat. The excitement of his adventurous ride, the excitement of the return in time, of achievement, of success, all these excitements centred round the associated ideas of the great treasure and of the only other man who knew of its existence, had departed from him. To the very last moment he had been cudgelling his brains as to how he could manage to visit the Great Isabel without loss of time and undetected. For the idea of secrecy had come to be connected with the treasure so closely that even to Barrios himself he had refrained from mentioning the existence of Decoud and of the silver on the island. The letters he carried to the General, however, made brief mention of the loss of the lighter, as having its bearing upon the situation in Sulaco. In the circumstances, the one-eyed tiger-slayer, scenting battle from afar, had not wasted his time in making inquiries from the messenger. In fact, Barrios, talking with Nostromo, assumed that both Don Martin Decoud and the ingots of San Tomé were lost together, and Nostromo, not questioned directly, had kept silent, under the influence of some indefinable form of resentment and distrust. Let Don Martin speak of everything with his own lips – was what he told himself mentally.

And now, with the means of gaining the Great Isabel thrown thus in his way at the earliest possible moment, his excitement had departed, as when the soul takes flight leaving the body inert upon an earth it knows no more. Nostromo did not seem to know the gulf. For a long time even his eyelids did not flutter once upon the glazed emptiness of his stare. Then slowly, without a limb having stirred, without a twitch of muscle or quiver of an eyelash, an expression, a living expression came upon the still features, deep thought crept into the empty stare – as if an outcast soul, a quiet, brooding soul, finding that untenanted body in its way, had come in stealthily to take possession.

The Capataz frowned: and in the immense stillness of sea, islands, and coast, of cloud-forms on the sky and trails of light upon the water, the knitting of that brow had the emphasis of a powerful gesture. Nothing else budged for a long time; then the Capataz shook his head and again surrendered himself to the universal repose of all visible things. Suddenly he seized the oars and with one movement made the dinghy spin round, head-on to the Great Isabel. But before he began to pull he bent once more over the brown stain on the gunwale.

'I know that thing,' he muttered to himself, with a sagacious jerk of the head. 'That's blood.'

His stroke was long, vigorous, and steady. Now and then he looked over his shoulder at the Great Isabel, presenting its low cliff to his anxious gaze like an impenetrable face. At last the stem touched the strand. He flung rather than dragged the boat up the little beach. At once, turning his back upon the sunset, he plunged with long strides into the ravine, making the water of the stream spurt and fly upwards at every step, as if spurning its shallow, clear, murmuring spirit with his feet. He wanted to save every moment of daylight.

A mass of earth, grass, and smashed bushes had fallen down very naturally from above upon the cavity under the leaning tree. Decoud had attended to the concealment of the silver as instructed, using the spade with some intelligence. But Nostromo's half-smile of approval changed into a scornful curl of the lip by the sight of the spade itself flung there in full view, as if in utter carelessness or sudden panic, giving away the whole thing. Ah! They were all alike in their folly, these *hombres finos* that invented laws and governments and barren tasks for the people.

The Capataz picked up the spade, and with the feel of the handle in his palm the desire to have a look at the horse-hide boxes of treasure came upon him suddenly. In a very few strokes he uncovered the edges and corners of several; then, clearing away more earth, became aware that one of them had been slashed with a knife.

He exclaimed at that discovery in a stifled voice, and dropped on his knees with a look of irrational apprehension over one shoulder, then over the other. The stiff hide had closed, and he hesitated before he pushed his hand through the long slit and felt the ingots inside. There they were. One, two, three. Yes, four gone. Taken away. Four ingots. But who? Decoud? Nobody else. And why? For what purpose? For what cursed fancy? Let him explain. Four ingots carried off in a boat, and – blood!

In the face of the open gulf, the sun, clear, unclouded unaltered, plunged into the waters in a grave and untroubled mystery of self-immolation consummated.far from all mortal eyes, with an infinite majesty of silence and peace. Four ingots short! – and blood!

The Capataz got up slowly.

'He might simply have cut his hand,' he muttered. 'But, then – '

He sat down on the soft earth, unresisting, as if he had been chained to the treasure, his drawn-up legs clasped in his hands with an air of hopeless submission, like a slave set on guard. Once only he lifted his head smartly: the rattle of hot musketry fire had reached his ears, like pouring from on high a stream of dry peas upon a drum. After listening for a while, he said, half aloud:

'He will never come back to explain.'

And he lowered his head again.

'Impossible!' he muttered, gloomily.

The sounds of firing died out. The loom of a great conflagration in Sulaco flashed up red above the coast, played on the clouds at the head of the gulf, seemed to touch with a ruddy and sinister reflection the forms of the Three Isabels. He never saw it, though he raised his head.

'But then I cannot know,' he pronounced, distinctly, and remained silent and staring for hours.

He could not know. Nobody was to know. As might have been supposed, the end of Don Martin Decoud never became a subject of speculation for anyone except Nostromo. Had the truth of the facts been known, there would always have remained the question Why? Whereas the version of his death at the sinking of the lighter had no uncertainty of motive. The young apostle of Separation had died striving for his idea by an ever-lamented accident. But the truth was that he died from solitude, the enemy known but to few on this earth, and whom only the simplest of us are fit to withstand. The brilliant Costaguanero of the boulevards had died from solitude and want of faith in himself and others.

For some good and valid reasons beyond mere human comprehension, the sea-birds of the gulf shun the Isabels. The rocky head of Azuera is their haunt, whose stony levels and chasms resound with their wild and tumultuous clamour as if they were for ever quarrelling over the legendary treasure.

At the end of his first day on the Great Isabel, Decoud, turning in his lair of coarse grass, under the shade of a tree, said to himself:

'I have not seen as much as one single bird all day.'

And he had not heard a sound, either, all day but that one now of his own muttering voice. It had been a day of absolute silence – the first he had known in his life. And he had not slept a wink. Not for all these wakeful nights and the days of fighting, planning, talking; not for all that last night of danger and hard physical toil upon the gulf, had he been able to close his eyes for a moment. And yet from sunrise to sunset he had been lying prone on the ground, either on his back or on his face.

He stretched himself, and with slow steps descended into the gully to spend the night by the side of the silver. If Nostromo returned – as he might have done at any moment – it was there that he would look first; and night would, of course, be the proper time for an attempt to communicate. He remembered with profound indifference that he had not eaten anything yet since he had been left alone on the island.

He spent the night open-eyed, and when the day broke he ate something with the same indifference. The brilliant 'Son Decoud', the spoiled darling of the family, the lover of Antonia and journalist of Sulaco, was not fit to grapple with himself single-handed. Solitude from mere outward condition of existence becomes very swiftly a state of soul in which the affectations of irony and scepticism have no place. It takes possession of the mind, and drives forth the thought into the exile of utter unbelief. After three days of waiting for the sight of some human face, Decoud caught himself entertaining a doubt of his own individuality. It had merged into the world of cloud and water, of natural forces and forms of nature. In our activity alone do we find the sustaining illusion of an independent existence as against the whole scheme of things of which we form a helpless part. Decoud lost all belief in the reality of his action past and to come. On the fifth day an immense melancholy descended upon him palpably. He resolved not to give himself up to these people in Sulaco, who had beset him, unreal and terrible, like jibbering and obscene spectres. He saw himself struggling feebly in their midst, and Antonia, gigantic and lovely like an allegorical statue, looking on with scornful eyes at his weakness.

Not a living being, not a speck of distant sail, appeared within the range of his vision; and, as if to escape from his solitude, he absorbed himself in his melancholy. The vague consciousness of a misdirected life given up to impulses whose memory left a bitter taste in his mouth was the first moral sentiment of his manhood. But at the same time he felt no remorse. What should he regret? He had recognized no other virtue than intelligence, and had erected passions into duties. Both his intelligence and his passion were swallowed up easily in this great unbroken solitude of waiting without faith. Sleeplessness had robbed his will of all energy, for he had not slept seven hours in the seven days. His sadness was the sadness of a sceptical mind. He beheld the universe as a succession of incomprehensible images. Nostromo was dead. Everything had failed ignominiously. He no longer dared to think of Antonia. She had not survived. But if she survived he could not face her. And all exertion seemed senseless.

On the tenth day, after a night spent without even dozing off once (it had occurred to him that Antonia could not possibly have ever loved a being so impalpable as himself), the solitude appeared like a great void, and the silence of the gulf like a tense, thin cord to which he hung suspended by both hands, without fear, without surprise, without any sort of emotion whatever. Only towards the evening, in the comparative relief of coolness, he began to wish that this cord would snap. He imagined it snapping with a report as of a pistol – a sharp, full crack. And that would be the end of him. He contemplated that eventuality with pleasure, because he dreaded the sleepless nights in which the silence, remaining unbroken in the shape of a cord to which he hung with both hands, vibrated with senseless phrases, always the same but utterly incomprehensible, about Nostromo, Antonia, Barrios, and proclamations mingled into an ironical and senseless buzzing. In the daytime he could look at the silence like a still cord stretched to breaking-point, with his life, his vain life, suspended to it like a weight.

'I wonder whether I would hear it snap before I fell,' he asked himself.

The sun was two hours above the horizon when he got up, gaunt, dirty, white-faced, and looked at it with his red-rimmed eyes. His limbs obeyed him slowly, as if full of lead, yet without tremor; and the effect of that physical condition gave to his movements an unhesitating, deliberate dignity. He acted as if accomplishing some sort of rite. He descended into the gully; for the fascination of all that silver, with its potential power, survived alone outside of himself. He picked up the belt with the revolver, that was lying there, and buckled it round his waist. The cord of silence could never snap on the island. It must let him fall and sink into the sea, he thought. And sink! He was looking at the loose earth covering the treasure. In the sea! His aspect was that of a somnambulist. He lowered himself down on his knees slowly and went on grubbing with his fingers with industrious patience till he uncovered one of the boxes. Without a pause, as if doing some work done many times before, he slit it open and took four ingots, which he put in his pockets. He covered up the exposed box again and step by step came out of the gully. The bushes closed after him with a swish.

It was on the third day of his solitude that he had dragged the dinghy near the water with an idea of rowing away somewhere, but had desisted partly at the whisper of lingering hope that Nostromo would return, partly from conviction of utter uselessness of all effort. Now she wanted only a slight shove to be set afloat. He had eaten a little every day after the first, and had some muscular strength left yet. Taking up the oars slowly, he pulled away from the cliff of the Great Isabel, that stood behind him warm with sunshine, as if with the heat of life, bathed in a rich light from head to foot as if in a radiance of hope and joy. He pulled straight towards the setting sun. When the gulf had grown dark, he ceased rowing and flung the sculls in. The hollow clatter they made in falling was the loudest noise he had ever heard in his life. It was a revelation. It seemed to recall him from far away. Actually the thought, 'Perhaps I may sleep tonight,' passed through his mind. But he did not believe it. He believed in nothing; and he remained sitting on the thwart.

The dawn from behind the mountains put a gleam into his unwinking eyes. After a clear daybreak the sun appeared splendidly above the peaks of the range. The great gulf burst into a glitter all around the boat; and in this glory of merciless solitude the silence appeared again before him, stretched taut like a dark, thin string.

His eyes looked at it while, without haste, he shifted his seat from the thwart to the gunwale. They looked at it fixedly, while his hand, feeling about his waist, unbuttoned the flap of the leather case, drew the revolver, cocked it, brought it forward pointing at his breast, pulled the trigger, and, with convulsive force, sent the still-smoking weapon hurtling through the air. His eyes looked at it while he fell forward and hung with his breast on the gunwale and the fingers of his right hand hooked under the thwart. They looked –

'It is done,' he stammered out, in a sudden flow of blood. His last thought was: 'I wonder how Capataz died.' The stiffness of the fingers relaxed, and the lover of Antonia Avellanos rolled overboard without having heard the cord of silence snap in the solitude of the Placid Gulf, whose glittering surface remained untroubled by the fall of his body.

A victim of the disillusioned weariness which is the retribution meted out to intellectual audacity, the brilliant Don Martin Decoud, weighted by the bars of San Tomé silver, disappeared without a trace, swallowed up in the immense indifference of things. His sleepless, crouching figure was gone from the side of the San Tomé silver; and for a time the spirits of good and evil that hover near every concealed treasure of the earth might have thought that this one had been forgotten by all mankind. Then, after a few days, another form appeared striding away from the setting sun to sit motionless and awake in the narrow black gully all through the night, in nearly the same pose, in the same place in which had sat that other sleepless man who had gone away for ever so quietly in a small boat, about the time of sunset. And the spirits of good and evil that hover about a forbidden treasure understood well that the silver of San Tomé was provided now with a faithful and lifelong slave.

The magnificent Capataz de Cargadores, victim of the disenchanted vanity which is the reward of audacious action, sat in the weary pose of a hunted outcast through a night of sleeplessness as tormenting as any known to Decoud, his companion in the most desperate affair of his life. And he wondered how Decoud had died. But he knew the part he had played himself. First a woman, then a man, abandoned each in their last extremity, for the sake of this accursed treasure. It was paid for by a soul lost and by a vanished life. The blank stillness of awe was succeeded by a gust of immense pride. There was no one in the world but Gian' Battista Fidanza, Capataz de Cargadores, the incorruptible and faithful Nostromo, to pay such a price.

He had made up his mind that nothing should be allowed now to rob him of his bargain. Nothing. Decoud had died. But how? That he was dead he had not a shadow of a doubt. But four ingots? . . . What for? Did he mean to come for more – some other time?

The treasure was putting forth its latent power. It troubled the clear mind of the man who had paid the price. He was sure that Decoud was dead. The island seemed full of that whisper. Dead? Gone! And he caught himself listening for the swish of bushes and the splash of the footfalls in the bed of the brook. Dead! The talker, the *novio* of Doña Antonia!

'Ha!' he murmured, with his head on his knees, under the livid clouded dawn breaking over the liberated Sulaco and upon the gulf as grey as ashes. 'It is to her that he will fly. To her that he will fly!'

And four ingots! Did he take them in revenge, to cast a spell, like the angry woman who had prophesied remorse and failure, and yet had laid upon him the task of saving the children? Well, he had saved the children. He had defeated the spell of poverty and starvation. He had done it all alone – or perhaps helped by the devil. Who cared? He had done it, betrayed as he was, and saving by the same stroke the San Tomé mine, which appeared to him hateful and immense, lording it by its vast wealth over the valour, the toil, the fidelity of the poor, over war and peace, over the labours of the town, the sea, and the Campo.

The sun lit up the sky behind the peaks of the Cordillera. The Capataz looked down for a time upon the fall of loose earth, stones, and smashed bushes, concealing the hiding place of the silver.

'I must grow rich very slowly,' he meditated, aloud.

CHAPTER 11

Sulaco outstripped Nostromo's prudence, growing rich swiftly on the hidden treasures of the earth, hovered over by the anxious spirits of good and evil, torn out by the labouring hands of the people. It was like a second youth, like a new life, full of promise, of unrest, of toil, scattering lavishly its wealth to the four corners of an excited world. Material changes swept along in the train of material interests. And other changes more subtle, outwardly unmarked, affected the minds and hearts of the workers. Captain Mitchell had gone home to live on his savings invested in the San Tomé mine; and Dr Monygham had grown older, with his head steel-grey and the unchanged expression of his face, living on the inexhaustible treasure of his devotion drawn upon in the secret of his heart like a store of unlawful wealth.

The Inspector-General of State Hospitals (whose maintenance is a charge upon the Gould Concession), Official Adviser on Sanitation to the Municipality, Chief Medical Officer of the San Tomé Consolidated Mines (whose territory, containing gold, silver, copper, lead, cobalt, extends for miles along the foothills of the Cordillera), had felt poverty-stricken, miserable, and starved during the prolonged, second visit the Goulds paid to Europe and the United States of America. Intimate of the *casa*, proved friend, a bachelor without ties and without establishment (except of the professional sort), he had been asked to take up his quarters in the Gould house. In the eleven months of their absence the familiar rooms, recalling at every glance the woman to whom he had given all his loyalty, had grown intolerable. As the day approached for the arrival of the mail boat *Hermes* (the latest addition to the O.S.N. Company's splendid fleet), the doctor hobbled about more vivaciously, snapped more sardonically at simple and gentle out of sheer nervousness.

He packed up his modest trunk with speed, with fury, with enthusiasm, and saw it carried out past the old porter at the gate of the Casa Gould with delight, with intoxication; then, as the hour approached, sitting alone in the great landau behind the white mules, a little sideways, his drawn-in face positively venomous with the effort of self-control, and holding a pair of new gloves in his left hand, he drove to the harbour.

His heart dilated within him so, when he saw the Goulds on the deck of the *Hermes*, that his greetings were reduced to a casual mutter. Driving back to town, all three were silent. And in the patio the doctor, in a more natural manner said:

'I'll leave you now to yourselves. I'll call tomorrow if I may?'

'Come to lunch, dear Dr Monygham, and come early,' said Mrs Gould, in her travelling dress and her veil down, turning to look at him at the foot of the stairs; while at the top of the flight the Madonna, in blue robes and child on her arm, seemed to welcome her with an aspect of pitying tenderness.

'Don't expect to find me at home,' Charles Gould warned him. 'I'll be off early to the mine.'

After lunch, Doña Emilia and the Señor Doctor came slowly through the inner gateway of the patio. The large gardens of the Casa Gould, surrounded by high walls, and the red-tile slopes of neighbouring roofs, lay open before them, with masses of shade under the trees and level surfaces of sunlight upon the lawns. A triple row of old orange trees surrounded the whole. Barefooted, brown gardeners, in snowy white shirts and wide *calzoneras*, dotted the grounds, squatting over flowerbeds, passing between the trees, dragging slender india-rubber tubes across the gravel of the paths; and the fine jets of water crossed each other in graceful curves, sparkling in the sunshine with a slight pattering noise upon the bushes, and an effect of showered diamonds upon the grass.

Doña Emilia, holding up the train of a clear dress, walked by the side of Dr Monygham, in a longish black coat and severe black bow on an immaculate shirt-front. Under a shady clump of trees, where stood scattered little tables and wicker easy-chairs, Mrs Gould sat down in a low and ample seat.

'Don't go yet,' she said to Dr Monygham, who was unable to tear himself away from the spot. His chin nestling within the points of his collar, he devoured her stealthily with his eyes, which, luckily were round and hard like clouded marbles, and incapable of disclosing his sentiments. His pitying emotion at the marks of time upon the face of that woman, the air of frailty and weary fatigue that had settled upon the eyes and temples of the 'Never-tired Señora' (as Don Pepe years ago used to call her with admiration), touched him almost to tears. 'Don't go yet. Today is all my own,' Mrs Gould urged, gently. 'We are not back yet officially. No one will come. It's only tomorrow that the windows of the Casa Gould are to be lit up for a reception.'

The doctor dropped into a chair.

'Giving a *tertulia*?' he said, with a detached air.

'A simple greeting for all the kind friends who care to come.'

'And only tomorrow?'

'Yes. Charles would be tired out after a day at the mine, and so I – It would be good to have him to myself for one evening on our return to this house I love. It has seen all my life.'

'Ah, yes!' snarled the doctor, suddenly. 'Women count time from the marriage feast. Didn't you live a little before?'

'Yes; but what is there to remember? There were no cares.'

Mrs Gould sighed. And as two friends, after a long separation, will revert to the most agitated period of their lives, they began to talk of the Sulaco Revolution. It seemed strange to Mrs Gould that people who had taken part in it seemed to forget its memory and its lesson.

'And yet,' struck in the doctor, 'we who played our part in it had our reward. Don Pepe, though superannuated, still can sit a horse. Barrios is drinking himself to death in jovial company away somewhere on his *fundación* beyond the Bolson de Tonoro. And the heroic Father Román – I imagine the old padre blowing up systematically the San Tomé mine, uttering a pious exclamation at every bang, and taking handfuls of snuff between the explosions – the heroic Padre Román says that he is not afraid of the harm Holroyd's missionaries can do to his flock, as long as *he* is alive.'

Mrs Gould shuddered a little at the allusion to the destruction that had come so near to the San Tomé mine.

'Ah, but you, dear friend?'

'I did the work I was fit for.'

'You faced the most cruel dangers of all. Something more than death.'

'No, Mrs Gould! Only death – by hanging. And I am rewarded beyond my deserts.'

Noticing Mrs Gould's gaze fixed upon him, he dropped his eyes.

'I've made my career – as you see,' said the Inspector-General of State Hospitals, taking up lightly the lapels of his superfine black coat. The doctor's self-respect, marked inwardly by the almost complete disappearance from his dreams of Father Berón, appeared visibly in what, by contrast with former carelessness, seemed an immoderate cult of personal appearance. Carried out within severe limits of form and colour, and in perpetual freshness, this change of apparel gave to Dr Monygham an air at the same time professional and festive; while his gait and the unchanged crabbed character of his face acquired from it a startling force of incongruity.

'Yes,' he went on. 'We all had our rewards – the engineer-in-chief, Captain Mitchell –'

'We saw him,' interrupted Mrs Gould, in her charming voice. 'The poor dear man came up from the country on purpose to call on us in our hotel in London. He comported himself with great dignity, but I fancy he regrets Sulaco. He rambled feebly about "historical events" till I felt I could have a cry.'

'H'm,' grunted the doctor; 'getting old, I suppose. Even Nostromo is getting older – though he is not changed. And, speaking of that fellow, I wanted to tell you something –'

For some time the house had been full of murmurs, of agitation. Suddenly the two gardeners, busy with rose trees at the side of the garden arch, fell upon their knees with bowed heads on the passage of Antonia Avellanos, who appeared walking beside her uncle.

Invested with the red hat after a short visit to Rome, where he had been invited by the Propaganda, Father Corbelán, missionary to the wild Indians, conspirator, friend and patron of Hernandez the robber, advanced with big, slow strides, gaunt and leaning forward, with his powerful hands clasped behind his back. The first Cardinal-Archbishop of Sulaco had preserved his fanatical and morose air; the aspect of a chaplain of bandits. It was believed that his unexpected elevation to the purple was a counter-move to the Protestant invasion of Sulaco organized by the Holroyd Missionary Fund. Antonia, the beauty of her face as if a little blurred, her figure slightly fuller, advanced with her light walk and her high serenity, smiling from a distance at Mrs Gould. She had brought her uncle over to see dear Emilia, without ceremony, just for a moment before the siesta.

When all were seated again, Dr Monygham, who had come to dislike heartily everybody who approached Mrs Gould with any intimacy, kept aside, pretending to be lost in profound meditation. A louder phrase of Antonia made him lift his head.

'How can we abandon, groaning under oppression, those who have been our countrymen only a few years ago, who *are* our countrymen now?' Miss Avellanos was saying. 'How can we remain blind, and deaf without pity to the cruel wrongs suffered by our brothers? There is a remedy.'

'Annex the rest of Costaguana to the order and prosperity of Sulaco,' snapped the doctor. 'There is no other remedy.'

'I am convinced, Señor Doctor,' Antonia said, with the earnest calm of invincible resolution, 'that this was from the first poor Martin's intention.'

'Yes, but the material interests will not let you jeopardize their development for a mere idea of pity and justice,' the doctor muttered, grumpily. 'And it is just as well perhaps.'

The Cardinal-Archbishop straightened up his gaunt, bony frame.

'We have worked for them; we have made them, these material interests of the foreigners,' the last of the Corbeláns uttered in a deep, denunciatory tone.

'And without them you are nothing,' cried the doctor from the distance. 'They will not let you.'

'Let them beware then, lest the people, prevented from their aspirations, should rise and claim their share of the wealth and their share of the power,' the popular Cardinal-Archbishop of Sulaco declared, significantly, menacingly.

A silence ensued, during which his Eminence stared, frowning at the ground, and Antonia, graceful and rigid in her chair, breathed calmly in the strength of her convictions. Then the conversation took a social turn, touching on the visit of the Goulds to Europe. The Cardinal-Archbishop, when in Rome, had suffered from neuralgia in the head all the time. It was the climate – the bad air.

When uncle and niece had gone away, with the servants again falling on their knees, and the old porter, who had known Henry Gould, almost totally blind and impotent now, creeping up to kiss his Eminence's extended hand, Dr Monygham, looking after them, pronounced the one word:

'Incorrigible!'

Mrs Gould, with a look upwards, dropped wearily on her lap her white hands flashing with the gold and stones of many rings.

'Conspiring. Yes!' said the doctor. 'The last of the Avellanos and the last of the Corbeláns are conspiring with the refugees from Sta Marta that flock here after every revolution. The Café Lambroso at the corner of the Plaza is full of them; you can hear their chatter across the street like the noise of a parrot-house. They are conspiring for the invasion of Costaguana. And do you know where they go for strength, for the necessary force? To the secret societies amongst the immigrants and natives, where Nostromo – I should say Captain Fidanza – is the great man. What gives him that position? Who can say? Genius? He has genius. He is greater with the populace than ever he was before. It was as if he had some secret power; some mysterious means to keep up his influence. He holds conferences with the Archbishop, as in those old days which you and I remember. Barrios is useless. But for a military head they have the pious Hernandez. And they may raise the country with the new cry of wealth for the people.'

'Will there be never any peace? Will there be no rest?' Mrs Gould whispered. 'I thought that we –'

'No!' interrupted the doctor. 'There is no peace and no rest in the development of material interests. They have their law, and their justice. But it is founded on expediency, and is inhuman; it is without rectitude, without the continuity and the force that can be found only in a moral principle. Mrs Gould, the time approaches when all that the Gould Concession stands for shall weigh as heavily upon the people as the barbarism, cruelty, and misrule of a few years back.'

'How can you say that, Dr Monygham?' she cried out, as if hurt in the most sensitive place of her soul.

'I can say what is true,' the doctor insisted, obstinately. 'It'll weigh as heavily, and provoke resentment, bloodshed, and vengeance, because the men have grown different. Do you think that now the mine would march upon the town to save their Señor Administrador? Do you think that?'

She pressed the backs of her entwined hands on her eyes and murmured hopelessly:

'Is it this we have worked for, then?'

The doctor lowered his head. He could follow her silent thought. Was it for this that her life had been robbed of all the intimate felicities of daily affection which her tenderness needed as the human body needs air to breathe? And the doctor, indignant with Charles Gould's blindness, hastened to change the conversation.

'It is about Nostromo that I wanted to talk to you. Ah! that fellow has some continuity and force. Nothing will put an end to him. But never mind that. There's something inexplicable going on – or perhaps only too easy to explain. You know, Linda is practically the lighthouse keeper of the Great Isabel light. The Garibaldino is too old now. His part is to clean the lamps and to cook in the house; but he can't get up the stairs any longer. The black-eyed Linda sleeps all day and watches the light all night. Not all day, though. She is up towards five in the afternoon, when our Nostromo, whenever he is in harbour with his schooner, comes out on his courting visit, pulling in a small boat.'

'Aren't they married yet?' Mrs Gould asked. 'The mother wished it, as far as I can understand, while Linda was yet quite a child. When I had the girls with me for a year or so during the War of Separation, that extraordinary Linda used to declare quite simply that she was going to be Gian' Battista's wife.'

'They are not married yet,' said the doctor, curtly. 'I have looked after them a little.'

'Thank you, dear Dr Monygham,' said Mrs Gould; and under the shade of the big trees her little, even teeth gleamed in a youthful smile of gentle malice. 'People don't know how really good you are. You will not let them know, as if on purpose to annoy me, who have put my faith in your good heart long ago.'

The doctor, with a lifting up of his upper lip, as though he were longing to bite, bowed stiffly in his chair. With the utter absorption of a man to whom love comes late, not as the most splendid of illusions, but like an enlightening and priceless misfortune, the sight of that woman (of whom he had been deprived for nearly a year) suggested ideas of adoration, of kissing the hem of her robe. And this excess of feeling translated itself into an augmented grimness of speech.

'I am afraid of being overwhelmed by too much gratitude. However, these people interest me. I went out several times to the Great Isabel light to look after old Giorgio.'

He did not tell Mrs Gould that it was because he found there, in her absence, the relief of an atmosphere of congenial sentiment in old Giorgio's austere admiration for the 'English signora – the benefactress'; in black-eyed Linda's voluble, torrential, passionate affection for 'our Doña Emilia – that angel'; in the white-throated, fair Giselle's adoring upward turn of the eyes, which then glided towards him with a sidelong, half-arch, half-candid glance, which made the doctor exclaim to himself mentally, 'If I weren't what I am, old and ugly, I would think the minx is making eyes at me. And perhaps she is. I dare say she would make eyes at anybody.' Dr Monygham said nothing of this to Mrs Gould, the providence of the Viola family, but reverted to what he called 'our great Nostromo'.

'What I wanted to tell you is this: Our great Nostromo did not take much notice of the old man and the children for some years. It's true, too, that he was away on his coasting voyages certainly ten months out of the twelve. He was making his fortune, as he told Captain Mitchell once. He seems to have done uncommonly well. It was only to be expected. He is a man full of resource, full of confidence in himself, ready to take chances and risks of every sort. I remember being in Mitchell's office one day, when he came in with that calm, grave air he always carries everywhere. He had been away trading in the Gulf of California, he said, looking straight past us at the wall, as his manner is, and was glad to see on his return that a lighthouse was being built on the cliff of the Great Isabel. Very glad, he repeated. Mitchell explained that it was the O.S.N. Company who were building it, for the convenience of the mail service, on his own advice. Captain Fidanza was good enough to say that it was excellent advice. I remember him twisting up his moustaches and looking all around the cornice of the room before he proposed that old Giorgio should be made the keeper of that light.'

'I heard of this. I was consulted at the time,' Mrs Gould said. 'I doubted whether it would be good for these girls to be shut up on that island as if in a prison.'

'The proposal fell in with the old Garibaldino's humour. As to Linda, any place was lovely and delightful enough for her as long as it was Nostromo's suggestion. She could wait for her Gian' Battista's good pleasure there as well as anywhere else. My opinion is that she was always in love with that incorruptible Capataz. Moreover, both father and sister were anxious to get Giselle away from the attentions of a certain Ramirez.'

'Ah!' said Mrs Gould, interested. 'Ramirez? What sort of man is that?'

'Just a *mozo* of the town. His father was a *cargador*. As a lanky boy he ran about the wharf in rags, till Nostromo took him up and made a man of him. When he got a little older, he put him into a lighter and very soon gave him charge of the No. 3 boat – the boat which took the silver away, Mrs Gould. Nostromo selected that lighter for the work because she was the best sailing and the strongest boat of all the Company's fleet. Young Ramirez was one of the five *cargadores* entrusted with the removal of the treasure from the Custom House on that famous night. As the boat he had charge of was sunk, Nostromo, on leaving the Company's service, recommended him to Captain Mitchell for his successor. He had trained him in the routine of work perfectly, and thus Mr Ramirez, from a starving waif, becomes a man and the Capataz of the Sulaco *cargadores*.'

'Thanks to Nostromo,' said Mrs Gould, with warm approval.

'Thanks to Nostromo,' repeated Dr Monygham. 'Upon my word, the fellow's power frightens me when I think of it. That our poor old Mitchell was only too glad to appoint somebody trained to the work, who saved him trouble, is not surprising. What is wonderful is the fact that the Sulaco *cargadores* accepted Ramirez for their chief, simply because such was Nostromo's good pleasure. Of course, he is not a second Nostromo, as he fondly imagined he would be; but still, the position was brilliant enough. It emboldend him to make up to Giselle Viola, who, you know, is the recognized beauty of the town. The old Garibaldino, however, took a violent dislike to him. I don't know why. Perhaps because he was not a model of perfection like his Gian' Battista, the incarnation of the courage, the fidelity, the honour of "the people". Signor Viola does not think much of Sulaco natives. Both of them, the old Spartan and that white-faced Linda, with her red mouth and coal-black eyes, were looking rather fiercely after the fair one. Ramirez was warned off. Father Viola, I am told, threatened him with his gun once.'

'But what of Giselle herself?' asked Mrs Gould.

'She's a bit of a flirt, I believe,' said the doctor. 'I don't think she cared much one way or another. Of course she likes men's attentions. Ramirez was not the only one, let me tell you, Mrs Gould. There was one engineer, at least, on the railway staff who got warned off with a gun, too. Old Viola does not allow any trifling with his honour. He has grown uneasy and suspicious since his wife died. He was very pleased to remove his youngest girl away from the town. But look what happens, Mrs Gould. Ramirez, the honest, lovelorn swain, is forbidden the island. Very well. He respects the prohibition, but naturally turns his eyes frequently towards the Great Isabel. It seems as though he had been in the habit of gazing late at night upon the light. And during these sentimental vigils he discovers that Nostromo, Captain Fidanza that is, returns very late from his visits to the Violas. As late as midnight at times.'

The doctor paused and stared meaningly at Mrs Gould.

'Yes, But I don't understand,' she began, looking puzzled.

'Now comes the strange part,' went on Dr Monygham. 'Viola, who is king on his island, will allow no visitor on it after dark. Even Captain Fidanza has got to leave after sunset, when Linda has gone up to tend the light. And Nostromo goes away obediently. But what happens afterwards? What does he do in the gulf between half past six and midnight? He has been seen more than once at that late hour pulling quietly into the harbour. Ramirez is devoured by jealousy. He dare not approach old Viola; but he plucked up courage to rail Linda about it on Sunday morning as she came on the mainland to hear Mass and visit her mother's grave. There was a scene on the wharf, which, as a matter of fact, I witnessed. It was early morning. He must have been waiting for her on purpose. I was there by the merest chance, having been called to an urgent consultation by the doctor of the German gunboat in the harbour. She poured wrath, scorn, and flame upon Ramirez, who seemed out of his mind. It was a strange sight, Mrs Gould: the long jetty, with this raving *cargador* in his crimson sash and the girl all in black, at the end; the early Sunday-morning quiet of the harbour in the shade of the mountains; nothing but a canoe or two moving between the ships at anchor, and the German gunboat's gig coming to take me off. Linda passed me within a foot. I noticed her wild eyes. I called out to her. She never heard me. She never saw me. But I looked at her face. It was awful in its anger and wretchedness.'

Mrs Gould sat up, opening her eyes very wide.

'What do you mean, Dr Monygham? Do you mean to say that you suspect the younger sister?'

'*Quién sabe!* Who can tell?' said the doctor, shrugging his shoulders like a born Costaguanero. 'Ramirez came up to me on the wharf. He reeled – he looked insane. He took his head into his hands. He had to talk to someone – simply had to. Of course for all his mad state he recognized me. People know me well here. I have lived too long amongst them to be anything else but the evil-eyed doctor, who can cure all the ills of the flesh, and bring bad luck by a glance. He came up to me. He tried to be calm. He tried to make it out that he wanted merely to warn me against Nostromo. It seems that Captain Fidanza at some secret meeting or other had mentioned me as the worst despiser of all the poor – of the people. It's very possible. He honours me with his undying dislike. And a word from the great Fidanza may be quite enough to send some fool's knife into my back. The Sanitary Commission I preside over is not in favour with the populace. "Beware of him, Señor Doctor. Destroy him, Señor Doctor," Ramirez hissed right into my face. And then he broke out. "That man," he spluttered, "has cast a spell upon both these girls." As to himself, he had said too much. He must run away now – run away and hide somewhere. He moaned tenderly about Giselle, and then called her names that cannot be repeated. If he thought she could be made to love him by any means, he would carry her off from the island. Off into the woods. But it was no good ... He strode away, flourishing his arms above his head. Then I noticed an old Negro who had been sitting behind a pile of cases, fishing from the wharf. He wound up his lines and slunk away at once. But he must have heard something, and must have talked, too, because some of the old Garibaldino's railway friends, I suppose, warned him against Ramirez. At any rate, the father had been warned. But Ramirez has disappeared from the town.'

'I feel I have a duty towards these girls,' said Mrs Gould, uneasily. 'Is Nostromo in Sulaco now?'

'He is, since last Sunday.'

'He ought to be spoken to – at once.'

'Who will dare speak to him? Even the love-mad Ramirez runs away from the mere shadow of Captain Fidanza.'

'I can. I will,' Mrs Gould declared. 'A word will be enough for a man like Nostromo.'

The doctor smiled sourly.

'He must end this situation which lends itself to – I can't believe it of that child,' pursued Mrs Gould.

'He's very attractive,' muttered the doctor, gloomily.

'He'll see it, I am sure. He must put an end to all this by marrying Linda at once,' pronounced the first lady of Sulaco with immense decision.

Through the garden gate emerged Basilio, grown fat and sleek, with an elderly hairless face, wrinkles at the corners of his eyes, and his jet-black, coarse hair plastered down smoothly. Stooping carefully behind an ornamental clump of bushes, he put down with precaution a small child he had been carrying on his shoulder – his own and Leonarda's last born. The pouting, spoiled *camerista* and the head *mozo* of the Casa Gould had been married for some years now.

He remained squatting on his heels for a time, gazing fondly at his offspring, which returned his stare with imperturbable gravity; then, solemn and respectable, walked down the path.

'What is it, Basilio?' asked Mrs Gould.

'A telephone call came through from the office of the mine. The master remains to sleep at the mountain tonight.'

Dr Monygham had got up and stood looking away. A profound silence reigned for a time under the shade of the biggest trees in the lovely gardens of the Casa Gould.

'Very well, Basilio,' said Mrs Gould. She watched him walk away along the path, step aside behind the flowering bush, and reappear with the child seated on his shoulder. He passed through the gateway between the garden and the patio with measured steps, careful of his light burden.

The doctor, with his back to Mrs Gould, contemplated a flower-bed away in the sunshine. People believed him scornful and soured. The truth of his nature consisted in his capacity for passion and in the sensitiveness of his temperament. What he lacked was the polished callousness of men of the world, the callousness from which springs an easy tolerance for oneself and others; the tolerance wide as poles asunder from true sympathy and human compassion. This want of callousness accounted for his sardonic turn of mind and his biting speeches.

In profound silence, and glaring viciously at the brilliant flower-bed, Dr Monygham poured mental imprecations on Charles Gould's head. Behind him the immobility of Mrs Gould added to the grace of her seated figure the charm of art, of an attitude caught and interpreted for ever. Turning abruptly, the doctor took his leave.

Mrs Gould leaned back in the shade of the big trees planted in a circle. She leaned back with her eyes closed and her white hands lying idle on the arms of her seat. The half-light under the thick mass of leaves brought out the youthful prettiness of her face; made the clear, light fabrics and white lace of her dress appear luminous. Small and dainty, as if radiating a light of her own in the deep shade of the interlaced boughs, she resembled a good fairy, weary with a long career of well-doing, touched by the withering suspicion of the uselessness of her labours, the powerlessness of her magic.

Had anybody asked her what she was thinking, alone in the garden of the *casa*, with her husband at the mine and house closed to the street like an empty dwelling, her frankness would have had to evade the question. It had come into her mind that for life to be large and full, it must contain the care of the past and of the future in every passing moment of the present. Our daily work must be done to the glory of the dead, and for the good of those who come after. She thought that, and sighed without opening her eyes – without moving at all. Mrs Gould's face became set and rigid for a second, as if to receive, without flinching, a great wave of loneliness that swept over her head. And it came into her mind too, that no one would ever ask her with solicitude what she was thinking of. No one. No one, but perhaps the man who had just gone away. No; no one who could be answered with careless sincerity in the ideal perfection of confidence.

The word 'incorrigible' – a word lately pronounced by Dr Monygham – floated into her still and sad immobility. Incorrigible in his devotion to the great silver mine was the Señor Administrador! Incorrigible in his hard, determined service of the material interest to which he had pinned his faith in the triumph of order and justice. Poor boy! She had a clear vision of the great hairs on his temples. He was perfect – perfect. What more could she have expected? It was a colossal and lasting success; and love was only a short moment of forgetfulness, a short intoxication, whose delight one remembered with a sense of sadness, as if it had been a deep grief lived through. There was something inherent in the necessities of successful action which carried with it the moral degradation of the idea. She saw the San Tomé mountain hanging over the Campo, over the whole land, feared, hated, wealthy; more soulless than any tyrant, more pitiless and autocratic than the worst Government; ready to crush innumerable lives in the expansion of its greatness. He did not see it. He could not see it. It was not his fault. He was perfect, perfect; but she would never have him to herself. Never; not for one short hour altogether to herself in this old Spanish house she loved so well!

Incorrigible, the last of the Corbeláns, the last of the Avellanos, the doctor had said; but she saw clearly the San Tomé mine possessing, consuming, burning up the life of the last of the Costaguana Goulds; mastering the energetic spirit of the son as it had mastered the lamentable weakness of the father. A terrible success for the last of the Goulds. The last! She had hoped for a long, long time, that perhaps – but no! There were to be no more. An immense desolation, the dread of her own continued life, descended upon the first lady of Sulaco. With a prophetic vision she saw herself surviving alone the degradation of her young ideal of life, of love, of work – all alone in the Treasure House of the World. The profound, blind, suffering expression of a painful dream settled on her face with its closed eyes. In the indistinct voice of an unlucky sleeper, lying passive in the grip of a merciless nightmare, she stammered out aimlessly the words:

'Material interest.'

CHAPTER 12

Nostromo had been growing rich very slowly. It was an effect of his prudence. He could command himself even when thrown off his balance. And to become the slave of a treasure with full self-knowledge is an occurrence rare and mentally disturbing. But it was also in a great part because of the difficulty of converting it into a form in which it could become available. The mere act of getting it away from the island piecemeal, little by little, was surrounded by difficulties, by the dangers of imminent detection. He had to visit the Great Isabel in secret, between his voyages along the coast, which were the ostensible source of his fortune. The crew of his own schooner were to be feared as if they had been spies upon their dreaded captain. He did not dare stay too long in port. When his coaster was unloaded, he hurried away on another trip, for he feared arousing suspicion even by a day's delay. Sometimes during a week's stay, or more, he could only manage one visit to the treasure. And that was all. A couple of ingots. He suffered through his fears as much as through his prudence. To do things by stealth humiliated him. And he suffered most from the concentration of his thought upon the treasure.

A transgression, a crime, entering a man's existence, eats it up like a malignant growth, consumes it like a fever. Nostromo had lost his peace; the genuineness of all his qualities was destroyed. He felt it himself, and often cursed the silver of San Tomé. His courage, his magnificence, his leisure, his work, everything was as before, only everything was a sham. But the treasure was real. He clung to it with a more tenacious, mental grip. But he hated the feel of the ingots. Sometimes, after putting away a couple of them in his cabin – the fruit of a secret night expedition to the Great Isabel

– he would look fixedly at his fingers, as if surprised they had left no stain on his skin.

He had found means of disposing of the silver bars in distant ports. The necessity to go far afield made his coasting voyages long, and caused his visits to the Viola household to be rare and far between. He was fated to have his wife from there. He had said so once to Giorgio himself. But the Garibaldino had put the subject aside with a majestic wave of his hand, clutching a smouldering black briar-root pipe. There was plenty of time; he was not the man to force his girls upon anybody.

As time went on, Nostromo discovered his preference for the younger of the two. They had some profound similarities of nature, which must exist for complete confidence and understanding, no matter what outward differences of temperament there may be to exercise their own fascination of contrast. His wife would have to know his secret or else life would be impossible. He was attracted by Giselle, with her candid gaze and white throat, pliable, silent, fond of excitement under her quiet indolence; whereas Linda, with her intense, passionately pale face, energetic, all fire and words, touched with gloom and scorn, a chip off the old block, true daughter of the austere republican, but with Teresa's voice, inspired him with a deep-seated mistrust. Moreover, the poor girl could not conceal her love for Gian' Battista. He could see it would be violent, exacting, suspicious, uncompromising – like her soul. Giselle, by her fair but warm beauty, by the surface placidity of her nature holding a promise of submissiveness, by the charm of her girlish mysteriousness, excited his passion and allayed his fears as to the future.

His absences from Sulaco were long. On returning from the longest of them, he made out lighters loaded with blocks of stone lying under the cliff of the Great Isabel; cranes and scaffolding above; workmen's figures moving about, and a small lighthouse already rising from its foundations on the edge of the cliff.

At this unexpected, undreamt-of, startling sight, he thought himself lost irretrievably. What could save him from detection now? Nothing! He was struck with amazed dread at this turn of chance, that would kindle a far-reaching light upon the only secret spot of his life; that life whose very essence, value, reality, consisted in its reflection from the admiring eyes of men. All of it but that thing which was beyond common comprehension; which stood between him and the power that hears and gives effect to the evil intention of curses. It was dark. Not every man had such a darkness. And they were going to put a light there. A light! He saw it shining upon disgrace, poverty, contempt. Somebody was sure to . . . Perhaps somebody had already . . .

The incomparable Nostromo, the Capataz, the respected and feared Captain Fidanza, the unquestioned patron of secret societies, a republican like old Giorgio, and a revolutionist at heart (but in another manner), was on the point of jumping overboard from the deck of his own schooner. That man, subjective almost to insanity, looked suicide deliberately in the face. But he never lost his head. He was checked by the thought that this was no escape. He imagined himself dead, and the disgrace, the shame going on.

Or, rather, properly speaking, he could not imagine himself dead. He was possessed too strongly by the sense of his own existence, a thing of infinite duration in its changes, to grasp the notion of finality. The earth goes on for ever.

And he was courageous. It was a corrupt courage, but it was as good for his purposes as the other kind. He sailed close to the cliff of the Great Isabel, throwing a penetrating glance from the deck at the mouth of the ravine, tangled in an undisturbed growth of bushes. He sailed close enough to exchange hails with the workmen, shading their eyes on the edge of the sheer drop of the cliff overhung by the jib-head of a powerful crane. He perceived that none of them had any occasion even to approach the ravine where the silver lay hidden; let alone to enter it. In the harbour he learned that no one slept on the island. The labouring gangs returned to port every evening, singing chorus songs in the empty lighters towed by a harbour tug. For the moment he had nothing to fear.

But afterwards? he asked himself. Later, when a keeper came to live in the cottage that was being built some hundred and fifty yards back from the low light-tower, and four hundred or so from the dark, shaded, jungly ravine, containing the secret of his safety, of his influence, of his magnificence, of his power over the future, of his defiance of ill-luck, of every possible betrayal from rich and poor alike – what then? He could never shake off the treasure. His audacity, greater than that of other men, had welded that vein of silver into his life. And the feeling of fearful and ardent subjection, the feeling of his slavery – so irremediable and profound that often, in his thoughts, he compared himself to the legendary *gringos*, neither dead nor alive, bound down to their conquest of unlawful wealth on Azuera – weighed heavily on the independent Captain Fidanza, owner and master of a coasting schooner, whose smart appearance (and fabulous good luck in trading) were so well known along the western seaboard of a vast continent.

Fiercely whiskered and grave, a shade less supple in his walk, the vigour and symmetry of his powerful limbs lost in the vulgarity of a brown tweed suit, made by Jews in the slums of London, and sold by the clothing department of the Compañía Anzani, Captain Fidanza was seen in the streets of Sulaco attending to his business, as usual, that trip. And, as usual. he allowed it to get about that he had made a great profit on his cargo. It was a cargo of salt fish, and Lent was approaching. He was seen in tramcars going to and fro between the town and the harbour; he talked with people in a café or two in his measured, steady voice. Captain Fidanza was *seen*. The generation that would know nothing of the famous ride to Cayta was not born yet.

Nostromo, the miscalled Capataz de Cargadores, had made for himself, under his rightful name, another public existence, but modified by the new conditions, less picturesque, more difficult to keep up in the increased size and varied population of Sulaco, the progressive capital of the Occidental Republic.

Captain Fidanza, unpicturesque, but always a little mysterious, was recognized quite sufficiently under the lofty glass and iron roof of the Sulaco railway station. He took a local train, and got out in Rincón, where he visited the widow of the *cargador* who had died of his wounds (at the dawn of the New Era, like Don José Avellanos) in the patio of the Casa Gould. He consented to sit down and drink a glass of cool lemonade in the hut, while the woman, standing up, poured a perfect torrent of words to which he did not listen. He left some money with her, as usual. The orphaned children, growing up and well schooled, calling him uncle, clamoured for his blessing. He gave that, too; and in the doorway paused for a moment to look at the flat face of the San Tomé mountain with a faint frown. This slight contraction of his bronzed brow casting a marked tinge of severity upon his usual unbending expression, was observed at the Lodge which he attended – but went away before the banquet. He wore it at the meeting of some good comrades, Italians and Occidentals, assembled in his honour under the presidency of an indigent, sickly, somewhat hunchbacked little photographer, with a white face and a magnanimous soul dyed crimson by a bloodthirsty hate of all capitalists, oppressors of the two hemispheres. The heroic Giorgio Viola, old revolutionist, would have understood nothing of his opening speech; and Captain Fidanza, lavishly generous as usual to some poor comrades, made no speech at all. He had listened, frowning with his mind far away, and walked off unapproachable, silent, like a man full of cares.

His frown deepened as, in the early morning, he watched the stone-masons go off to the Great Isabel, in lighters loaded with squared blocks of stone, enough to add another course to the squat light-tower. That was the rate of the work. One course per day.

And Captain Fidanza meditated. The presence of strangers on the island would cut him completely off the treasure. It had been difficult and dangerous enough before. He was afraid, and he was angry. He thought with the resolution of a master and the cunning of a cowed slave. Then he went ashore.

He was a man of great resource and ingenuity; and, as usual, the expedient he found at a critical moment was effective enough to alter the situation radically. He had the gift of evolving safety out of the very danger, this incomparable Nostromo, this 'fellow in a thousand'. With Giorgio established on the Great Isabel, there would be no need for concealment. He would be able to go openly, in daylight, to see his daughters – one of his daughters – and stay late talking to the old Garibaldino. Then in the dark ... Night after night ... He would dare to grow rich quicker now. He yearned to clasp, embrace, absorb, subjugate in unquestioned possession this treasure, whose tyranny had weighed upon his mind, his actions, his very sleep.

He went to see his friend Captain Mitchell – and the thing was done as Dr Monygham had related to Mrs Gould. When the project was mooted to the Garibaldino, something like the faint reflection, the dim ghost of a very ancient smile, stole under the white and enormous moustaches of the old hater of kings and ministers. His daughters were the object of his anxious care. The younger, especially. Linda, with her mother's voice, had taken more her mother's place. Her deep, vibrating 'Eh, Padre?' seemed, but for the change of the word, the very echo of the impassioned, remonstrating 'Eh, Giorgio?' of poor Signora Teresa. It was his fixed opinion that the town was no proper place for his girls. The infatuated but guileless Ramirez was the object of his profound aversion, as resuming the sins of the country whose people were blind, vile *esclavos*.

On his return from his next voyage, Captain Fidanza found the Violas settled in the light-keeper's cottage. His knowledge of Giorgio's idiosyncrasies had not played him false. The Garibaldino had refused to entertain the idea of any companion whatever, except his girls. And Captain Mitchell, anxious to please his poor Nostromo, with that felicity of inspiration which only true affection can give, had formally appointed Linda Viola as under-keeper of the Isabel's Light.

'The light is private property,' he used to explain. 'It belongs to my Company. I've the power to nominate whom I like, and Viola it shall be. It's about the only thing Nostromo – a man worth his weight in gold, mind you – has ever asked me to do for him.'

Directly his schooner was anchored opposite the New Custom House, with its sham air of a Greek temple, flat-roofed, with a colonnade, Captain Fidanza went pulling his small boat out of the harbour, bound for the Great Isabel, openly in the light of a declining day, before all men's eyes, with a sense of having mastered the fates. He must establish a regular position. He would ask him for his daughter now. He thought of Giselle as he pulled. Linda loved him, perhaps, but the old man would be glad to keep the eldest, who had his wife's voice.

He did not pull for the narrow strand where he had landed with Decoud, and afterwards alone on his first visit to the treasure. He made for the beach at the other end, and walked up the regular and gentle slope of the wedge-shaped island. Giorgio Viola, whom he saw from afar, sitting on a bench under the front wall of the cottage, lifted his arm slightly to his loud hail. He walked up. Neither of the girls appeared.

'It is good here,' said the old man, in his austere, far-away manner.

Nostromo nodded; then after a short silence:

'You saw my schooner pass in not two hours ago? Do you know why I am here before, so to speak, my anchor has fairly bitten into the ground of this port of Sulaco?'

'You are welcome like a son,' the old man declared, quietly, staring away upon the sea.

'Ah! thy son. I know. I am what thy son would have been. It is well, *viejo*. It is a very good welcome. Listen, I have come to ask you for –'

A sudden dread came upon the fearless and incorruptible Nostromo. He dared not utter the name in his mind. The slight pause only imparted a marked weight and solemnity to the changed end of the phrase.

'For my wife!' . . . His heart was beating fast. 'It is time you –'

The Garibaldino arrested him with an extended arm. 'That was left for you to judge.'

He got up slowly. His beard, unclipped since Teresa's death, thick, snow-white, covered his powerful chest. He turned his head to the door, and called out in his strong voice:

'Linda.'

Her answer came sharp and faint from within; and the appalled Nostromo stood up, too, but remained mute, gazing at the door. He was afraid. He was not afraid of being refused the girl he loved – no mere refusal could stand between him and a woman he desired – but the shining spectre of the treasure rose before him, claiming his allegiance in a silence that could not be gainsaid. He was afraid, because, neither dead nor alive, like the *gringos* on Azuera, he belonged body and soul to the unlawfulness of his audacity. He was afraid of being forbidden the island. He was afraid, and said nothing.

Seeing the two men standing up side by side to await her, Linda stopped in the doorway. Nothing could alter the passionate dead whiteness of her face; but her black eyes seemed to catch and concentrate all the light of the low sun in a flaming spark within the black depths, covered at once by the slow descent of heavy eyelids.

'Behold thy husband, master, and benefactor.' Old Viola's voice resounded with a force that seemed to fill the whole gulf.

She stepped forward with her eyes nearly closed, like a sleep-walker in a beatific dream.

Nostromo made a superhuman effort. 'It is time, Linda, we two were betrothed,' he said, steadily, in his level, careless, unbending tone.

She put her hand into his offered palm, lowering her head, dark with bronze glints, upon which her father's hand rested for a moment.

'And so the soul of the dead is satisfied.'

This came from Giorgio Viola, who went on talking for a while of his dead wife; while the two, sitting side by side, never looked at each other. Then the old man ceased; and Linda, motionless, began to speak.

'Ever since I felt I lived in the world, I have lived for you alone, Gian' Battista. And that you knew! You knew it . . . Battistino.'

She pronounced the name exactly with her mother's intonation. A gloom as of the grave covered Nostromo's heart.

'Yes. I knew,' he said.

The heroic Garibaldino sat on the same bench bowing his hoary head, his old soul dwelling alone with its memories, tender and violent, terrible and dreary – solitary on the earth full of men.

And Linda, his best-loved daughter, was saying, 'I was yours ever since I can remember. I had only to think of you for the earth to become empty to my eyes. When you were there, I could see no one else. I was yours. Nothing is changed. The world belongs to you, and you let me live in it . . .' She dropped her low, vibrating voice to a still lower note, and found other things to say – torturing for the man at her side. Her murmur ran on ardent and voluble. She did not seem to see her sister, who came out with an altar-cloth she was embroidering in her hands, and passed in front of them, silent, fresh, fair, with a quick glance and a faint smile, to sit a little away on the other side of Nostromo.

The evening was still. The sun sank almost to the edge of a purple ocean; and the white lighthouse, livid against the background of clouds filling the head of the gulf, bore the lantern red and glowing, like a live ember kindled by the fire of the sky. Giselle, indolent and demure, raised the altar-cloth from time to time to hide nervous yawns, as of a young panther.

Suddenly Linda rushed at her sister, and, seizing her head, covered her face with kisses. Nostromo's brain reeled. When she left her, as if stunned by the violent caresses, with her hands lying in her lap, the slave of the treasure felt as if he could shoot that woman. Old Giorgio lifted his leonine head.

'Where are you going, Linda?'

'To the light, *padre mio.*'

'*Sì, sì* – to your duty.'

He got up, too, looked after his eldest daughter; then, in a tone whose festive note seemed the echo of a mood lost in the night of ages:

'I am going to cook something. Aha! Son! The old man knows where to find a bottle of wine, too.'

He turned to Giselle, with a change to austere tenderness.

'And you, little one, pray not to the God of priests and slaves, but to the God of orphans, of the oppressed, of the poor, of little children, to give thee a man like this one for a husband.'

His hand rested heavily for a moment on Nostromo's shoulder; then he went in. The hopeless slave of the San Tomé silver felt at these words the venomous fangs of jealousy biting deep into his heart. He was appalled by the novelty of the experience, by its force, by its physical intimacy. A husband! A husband for her! And yet it was natural that Giselle should have a husband at some time or other. He had never realized that before. In discovering that her beauty could belong to another he felt as though he could kill this one of old Giorgio's daughters also. He muttered moodily:

'They say you love Ramirez.'

She shook her head without looking at him. Coppery glints rippled to and fro on the wealth of her gold hair. Her smooth forehead had the soft, pure sheen of a priceless pearl in the splendour of the sunset, mingling the gloom of starry spaces, the purple of the sea, and the crimson of the sky in a magnificent stillness.

'No,' she said, slowly. 'I never loved him. I think I never . . . He loves me – perhaps.'

The seduction of her slow voice died out of the air, and her raised eyes remained fixed on nothing, as if indifferent and without thought.

'Ramirez told you he loved you?' asked Nostromo, restraining himself.

'Ah! once – one evening . . .'

'The miserable . . . Ha!'

He had jumped up as if stung by a gad-fly, and stood before her mute with anger.

'*Misericordia Divina!* You, too, Gian' Battista! Poor wretch that I am!' she lamented in ingenuous tones. 'I told Linda, and she scolded – she scolded. Am I to live blind, dumb, and deaf in this world? And she told father, who took down his gun and cleaned it. Poor Ramirez! Then you came, and she told you.'

He looked at her. He fastened his eyes upon the hollow of her white throat, which had the invincible charm of things young, palpitating, delicate, and alive. Was this the child he had known? Was it possible? It dawned upon him that in these last years he had really seen very little – nothing – of her. Nothing. She had come into the world like a thing unknown. She had come upon him unawares. She was a danger. A frightful danger. The instinctive mood of fierce determination that had never failed him before the perils of this life added its steady force to the violence of his passion. She, in a voice that recalled to him the song of running water, the tinkling of a silver bell, continued:

'And between you three you have brought me here into this captivity to the sky and water. Nothing else. Sky and water. Oh, *Santissima Madre*. My hair shall turn grey on this tedious island. I could hate you, Gian' Battista!'

He laughed loudly. Her voice enveloped him like a caress. She bemoaned her fate, spreading unconsciously, like a flower its perfume in the coolness of the evening, the indefinable seduction of her person. Was it her fault that nobody ever had admired Linda? Even when they were little, going out with their mother to Mass, she remembered that people took no notice of Linda, who was fearless, and chose instead to frighten her, who was timid, with their attention. It was her hair like gold, she supposed.

He broke out:

'Your hair like gold, and your eyes like violets, and your lips like the rose; your round arms, your white throat. ...'

Imperturbable in the indolence of her pose, she blushed deeply all over to the roots of her hair. She was not conceited. She was no more self-conscious than a flower. But she was pleased. And perhaps even a flower loves to hear itself praised. He glanced down, and added, impetuously:

'Your little feet!'

Leaning back against the rough stone wall of the cottage, she seemed to bask languidly in the warmth of the rosy flush. Only her lowered eyes glanced at her little feet.

'And so you are going at last to marry our Linda. She is terrible. Ah! now she will understand better since you have told her you love her. She will not be so fierce.'

'*Chica!*' said Nostromo 'I have not told her anything.'

'Then make haste. Come tomorrow. Come and tell her, so that I may have some peace from her scolding and – perhaps – who knows ...'

'Be allowed to listen to your Ramirez, eh? Is that it? You ...'

'Mercy of God! How violent you are, Giovanni,' she said, unmoved. 'Who is Ramirez ... Ramirez ... Who is he?' she repeated, dreamily, in the dusk and gloom of the clouded gulf, with a low red streak in the west like a hot bar of glowing iron laid across the entrance of a world sombre as a cavern, where the magnificent Capataz de Cargardores had hidden his conquests of love and wealth.

'Listen, Giselle,' he said, in measured tones; 'I will tell no word of love to your sister. Do you want to know why?'

'Alas! I could not understand perhaps, Giovanni. Father says you are not like other men; that no one has ever understood you properly; that the rich will be surprised yet ... Oh! saints in heaven! I am weary.'

She raised her embroidery to conceal the lower part of her face, then let it fall on her lap. The lantern was shaded on the land side, but slanting away from the dark column of the lighthouse they could see the long shaft of light, kindled by Linda, go out to strike the expiring glow in a horizon of purple and red.

Giselle Viola, with her head resting against the wall of the house, her eyes half closed, and her little feet, in white stockings and black slippers, crossed over each other, seemed to surrender herself, tranquil and fatal, to the gathering dusk. The charm of her body, the promising mysteriousness of her indolence, went out into the night of the Placid Gulf like a fresh and intoxicating fragrance spreading out in the shadows, impregnating the air. The incorruptible Nostromo breathed her ambient seduction in the tumultuous heaving of his breast. Before leaving the harbour he had thrown off the store clothing of Captain Fidanza, for greater ease in the long pull out to the islands. He stood before her in the red sash and check shirt as he used to appear on the Company's wharf – a Mediterranean sailor come ashore to try his luck in Costaguana. The dusk of purple and red enveloped him, too – close, soft, profound, as no more than fifty yards from that spot it had gathered evening after evening about the self-destructive passion of Don Martin Decoud's utter scepticism, flaming up to death in solitude.

'You have got to hear,' he began at last, with perfect self-control. 'I shall say no word of love to your sister, to whom I am betrothed from this evening, because it is you that I love. It is you! . . .'

The dusk let him see yet the tender and voluptuous smile that came instinctively upon her lips shaded for love and kisses, freeze hard in the drawn, haggard lines of terror. He could not restrain himself any longer. While she shrank from his approach, her arms went out to him, abandoned and regal in the dignity of her languid surrender. He held her head in his two hands, and showered rapid kisses upon the upturned face that gleamed in the purple dusk. Masterful and tender, he was entering slowly upon the fullness of his possession. And he perceived that she was crying. Then the incomparable Capataz, the man of careless loves, became gentle and caressing, like a woman to the grief of a child. He murmured to her fondly. He sat down by her and nursed her fair head on his breast. He called her his star and his little flower.

It had grown dark. From the living-room of the light-keeper's cottage, where Giorgio, one of the Immortal Thousand, was bending his leonine and heroic head over a charcoal fire, there came the sound of sizzling and the aroma of an artistic *frittura*.

In the obscure disarray of that thing, happening like a cataclysm, it was in her feminine head that some gleam of reason survived. He was lost to the world in their embraced stillness. But she said, whispering into his ear:

'God of mercy! What will become of me – here – now – between this sky and this water I hate? Linda, Linda – I see her! . . .' She tried to get out of his arms, suddenly relaxed at the sound of that name. But there was no one approaching their black shapes, enlaced and struggling on the white background of the wall. 'Linda! Poor Linda! I tremble! I shall die of fear before my poor sister Linda, betrothed today to Giovanni – my lover! Giovanni, you must have been mad! I cannot understand you! You are not like other men! I will not give you up – never – only to God himself! But why have you done this blind, mad, cruel, frightful thing?'

Released, she hung her head, let fall her hands. The altar-cloth, as if tossed by a great wind, lay far away from them, gleaming white on the black ground.

'From fear of losing my hope of you,' said Nostromo.

'You knew that you had my soul! You know everything! It was made for you! But what could stand between you and me? What? Tell me!' she repeated, without impatience, in superb assurance.

'Your dead mother,' he said, very low.

'Ah! . . . Poor mother! She has always . . . She is a saint in heaven now, and I cannot give you up to her. No, Giovanni. Only to God alone. You were mad – but it is done. Oh! what have you done? Giovanni, my beloved, my life, my master, do not leave me here in this grave of clouds. You cannot leave me now. You must take me away – at once – this instant – in the little boat. Giovanni, carry me off tonight, from my fear of Linda's eyes, before I have to look at her again.'

She nestled close to him. The slave of the San Tomé silver felt the weight as of chains upon his limbs, a pressure as of a cold hand upon his lips. He struggled against the spell.

'I cannot,' he said. 'Not yet. There is something that stands between us two and the freedom of the world.'

She pressed her form closer to his side with subtle and naïve instinct of seduction.

'You rave, Giovanni – my lover!' she whispered, engagingly. 'What can there be? Carry me off – in thy very hands – to Doña Emilia – away from here. I am not very heavy.'

It seemed as though she expected him to lift her up at once in his two palms. She had lost the notion of all impossibility. Anything could happen on this night of wonder. As he made no movement, she almost cried aloud:

'I tell you I am afraid of Linda!' And still he did not move. She became quiet and wily. 'What can there be?' she asked coaxingly.

He felt her warm, breathing, alive, quivering in the hollow of his arm. In the exulting consciousness of his strength, and the triumphant excitement of his mind, he struck out for his freedom.

'A treasure,' he said. All was still. She did not understand. 'A treasure. A treasure of silver to buy a gold crown for thy brow.'

'A treasure?' she repeated in a faint voice, as if from the depths of a dream. 'What is it you say?'

She disengaged herself gently. He got up and looked down at her, aware of her face, of her hair, her lips, the dimples on her cheeks – seeing the fascination of her person in the night of the gulf as if in the blaze of noonday. Her nonchalant and seductive voice trembled with the excitement of admiring awe and ungovernable curiosity.

'A treasure of silver!' she stammered out. Then pressed on faster: 'What? Where? How did you get it, Giovanni?'

He wrestled with the spell of captivity. It was as if striking a heroic blow that he burst out:

'Like a thief!'

The densest blackness of the Placid Gulf seemed to fall upon his head. He could not see her now. She had vanished into a long, obscure, abysmal silence, whence her voice came back to him after a time with a faint glimmer, which was her face.

'I love you! I love you!'

These words gave him an unwonted sense of freedom; they cast a spell stronger than the accursed spell of the treasure; they changed his weary subjection to that dead thing into an exulting conviction of his power. He would cherish her, he said, in a splendour as great as Doña Emilia's. The rich lived on wealth stolen from the people, but he had taken from the rich nothing – nothing that was not lost to them already by their folly and their betrayal. For he had been betrayed – he said – deceived, tempted. She believed him. . . . He had kept the treasure for purposes of revenge; but now he cared nothing for it. He cared only for her. He would put her beauty in a palace on a hill crowned with olive trees – a white palace above a blue sea. He would keep her there like a jewel in a casket. He would get land for her – her own land fertile with vines and corn – to set her little feet upon. He kissed them. . . . He had already paid for it all with the soul of a woman and the life of a man. . . . The Capataz de Cargadores tasted the supreme intoxication of his generosity. He flung the mastered treasure superbly at her feet in the impenetrable darkness of the gulf, in the darkness defying – as men said – the knowledge of God and the wit of the devil. But she must let him grow rich first – he warned her.

She listened as if in a trance. Her finger stirred in his hair. He got up from his knees reeling, weak, empty, as though he had flung his soul away.

'Make haste, then,' she said. 'Make haste, Giovanni, my lover, my master, for I will give thee up to no one but God. And I am afraid of Linda.'

He guessed at her shudder, and swore to do his best. He trusted the courage of her love. She promised to be brave in order to be loved always – far away in a white palace upon a hill above a blue sea. Then with a timid, tentative eagerness she murmured:

'Where is it? Where? Tell me that, Giovanni.'

He opened his mouth and remained silent – thunderstruck.

'Not that! Not that!' he gasped out, appalled at the spell of secrecy that had kept him dumb before so many people falling upon his lips again with unimpaired force. Not even to her. Not even to her. It was too dangerous. 'I forbid thee to ask,' he cried at her, deadening cautiously the anger of his voice.

He had not regained his freedom. The spectre of the unlawful treasure arose, standing by her side like a figure of silver, pitiless and secret, with a finger on its pale lips. His soul died within him at the vision of himself creeping in presently along the ravine, with the smell of earth, of damp foliage in his nostrils – creeping in, determined in a purpose that numbed his breast, and creeping out again loaded with silver, with his ears alert to every sound. It must be done on this very night – that work of a craven slave!

He stooped low, pressed the hem of her skirt to his lips, with a muttered command:

'Tell him I would not stay,' and was gone suddenly from her, silent, without as much as a footfall in the dark night.

She sat still, her head resting indolently against the wall, and her little feet in white stockings and black slippers crossed over each other. Old Giorgio, coming out, did not seem to be surprised at the intelligence as much as she had vaguely feared. For she was full of inexplicable fear now – fear of everything and everybody except of her Giovanni and his treasure. But that was incredible.

The heroic Garibaldino accepted Nostromo's abrupt departure with a sagacious indulgence. He remembered his own feelings, and exhibited a masculine penetration of the true state of the case.

'*Va bene*. Let him go. Ha! ha! No matter how fair the woman, it galls a little. Liberty, liberty. There's more than one kind! He has said the great word, and son Gian' Battista is not tame.' He seemed to be instructing the motionless and scared Giselle . . . 'A man should not be tame,' he added, dogmatically out of the doorway. Her stillness and silence seemed to displease him. 'Do not give way to the enviousness of your sister's lot,' he admonished her, very grave, in his deep voice.

Presently he had to come to the door again to call in his younger daughter. It was late. He shouted her name three times before she even moved her head. Left alone, she had become the helpless prey of astonishment. She walked into the bedroom she shared with Linda like a person profoundly asleep. That aspect was so marked that even old Giorgio, spectacled, raising his eyes from the Bible, shook his head as she shut the door behind her.

She walked right across the room without looking at anything, and sat down at once by the open window. Linda, stealing down from the tower in the exuberance of her happiness, found her with a lighted candle at her back, facing the black night full of sighing gusts of wind and the sound of distant showers – a true night of the gulf, too dense for the eye of God and the wiles of the devil. She did not turn her head at the opening of the door.

There was something in that immobility which reached Linda in the depths of her paradise. The elder sister guessed angrily: the child is thinking of that wretched Ramirez. Linda longed to talk. She said in her arbitrary voice, 'Giselle!' and was not answered by the slightest movement.

The girl that was going to live in a palace and walk on ground of her own was ready to die with terror. Not for anything in the world would she have turned her head to face her sister. Her heart was beating madly. She said with subdued haste:

'Do not speak to me. I am praying.'

Linda, disappointed, went out quietly; and Giselle sat on, unbelieving, lost, dazed, patient, as if waiting for the confirmation of the incredible. The hopeless blackness of the clouds seemed part of a dream, too. She waited.

She did not wait in vain. The man whose soul was dead within him, creeping out of the ravine, weighted with silver, had seen the gleam of the lighted window, and could not help retracing his steps from the beach.

On that impenetrable background, obliterating the lofty mountains by the seaboard, she saw the slave of the San Tomé silver, as if by an extraordinary power of a miracle. She accepted his return as if henceforth the world could hold no surprise for all eternity.

She rose, compelled and rigid, and began to speak long before the light from within fell upon the face of the approaching man.

'You have come back to carry me off. It is well! Open thy arms, Giovanni, my lover. I am coming.'

His prudent footsteps stopped, and with his eyes glistening wildly, he spoke in a harsh voice:

'Not yet. I must grow rich slowly.' . . . A threatening note came into his tone. 'Do not forget that you have a thief for your lover.'

'Yes! Yes!' she whispered, hastily. 'Come nearer! Listen! Do not give me up, Giovanni! Never, never! . . . I will be patient! . . .'

Her form drooped consolingly over the low casement towards the slave of the unlawful treasure. The light in the room went out, and weighted with silver, the magnificent Capataz clasped her round her white neck in the darkness of the gulf as a drowning man clutches at a straw.

CHAPTER 13

On the day Mrs Gould was going, in Dr Monygham's words, to 'give a *tertulia*', Captain Fidanza went down the side of his schooner lying in Sulaco harbour, calm, unbending, deliberate in the way he sat down in his dinghy and took up his sculls. He was later than usual. The afternoon was well advanced before he landed on the beach of the Great Isabel, and with a steady pace climbed the slope of the island.

From a distance he made out Giselle sitting in a chair tilted back against the end of the house, under the window of the girl's room. She had her embroidery in her hands, and held it well up to her eyes. The tranquillity of that girlish figure exasperated the feeling of perpetual struggle and strife he carried in his breast. He became angry. It seemed to him that she ought to hear the clanking of his fetters – his silver fetters, from afar. And while ashore that day, he had met the doctor with the evil eye, who had looked at him very hard.

The raising of her eyes mollified him. They smiled in their flower-like freshness straight upon his heart. Then she frowned. It was a warning to be cautious. He stopped some distance away, and in a loud, indifferent tone, said:

'Good day, Giselle. Is Linda up yet?'

'Yes. She is in the big room with father.'

He approached then, and, looking through the window into the bedroom for fear of being detected by Linda returning there for some reason, he said, moving only his lips:

'You love me?'

'More than my life.' She went on with her embroidery under his contemplating gaze and continued to speak, looking at her work, 'Or I could not live. I could not, Giovanni. For this life is like death. Oh, Giovanni, I shall perish if you do not take me away.'

He smiled carelessly. 'I will come to the window when it's dark,' he said.

'No, don't, Giovanni. Not tonight. Linda and father have been talking together for a long time today.'

'What about?'

'Ramirez, I fancy I heard. I do not know. I am afraid. I am always afraid. It is like dying a thousand times a day. Your love is to me like your treasure to you. It is there, but I can never get enough of it.

He looked at her very still. She was beautiful. His desire had grown within him. He had two masters now. But she was incapable of sustained emotion. She was sincere in what she said, but she slept placidly at night. When she saw him she flamed up always. Then only an increased taciturnity marked the change in her. She was afraid of betraying herself. She was afraid of pain, of bodily harm, of sharp words, of facing anger, and witnessing violence. For her soul was light and tender with a pagan sincerity in its impulses. She murmured:

'Give up the palazzo, Giovanni, and the vineyard on the hills, for which we are starving our love.'

She ceased, seeing Linda standing silent at the corner of the house.

Nostromo turned to his affianced wife with a greeting, and was amazed at her sunken eyes, at her hollow cheeks, at the air of illness and anguish in her face.

'Have you been ill?' he asked, trying to put some concern into this question.

Her black eyes blazed at him. 'Am I thinner?' she asked.

'Yes – perhaps – a little.'

'And older?'

'Every day counts – for all of us.'

'I shall go grey, I fear, before the ring is on my finger,' she said, slowly, keeping her gaze fastened upon him.

She waited for what he would say, rolling down her turned-up sleeves.

'No fear of that,' he said, absently.

She turned away as if it had been something final, and busied herself with household cares while Nostromo talked with her father. Conversation with the old Garibaldino was not easy. Age had left his faculties unimpaired, only they seemed to have withdrawn somewhere deep within him. His answers were slow in coming, with an effect of august gravity. But that day he was more animated, quicker; there seemed to be more life in the old lion. He was uneasy for the integrity of his honour. He believed Sidoni's warning as to Ramirez's designs upon his younger daughter. And he did not trust her. She was flighty. He said nothing of his cares to 'Son Gian' Battista'. It was a touch of senile vanity. He wanted to show that he was equal yet to the task of guarding alone the honour of his house.

Nostromo went away early. As soon as he had disappeared, walking towards the beach, Linda stepped over the threshold and, with a haggard smile, sat down by the side of her father.

Ever since that Sunday, when the infatuated and desperate Ramirez had waited for her on the wharf, she had no doubts whatever. The jealous ravings of that man were no revelation. They had only fixed with precision, as with a nail driven into her heart, that sense of unreality and deception which, instead of bliss and security, she had found in her intercourse with her promised husband. She had passed on, pouring indignation and scorn upon Ramirez; but, that Sunday, she nearly died of wretchedness and shame, lying on the carved and lettered stone of Teresa's grave, subscribed for by the engine-drivers and the fitters of the railway workshops, in sign of their respect for the hero of Italian Unity. Old Viola had not been able to carry out his desire of burying his wife in the sea; and Linda wept upon the stone.

The gratuitous outrage appalled her. If he wished to break her heart – well and good. Everything was permitted to Gian' Battista. But why trample upon the pieces; why seek to humiliate her spirit? Aha! He could not break that. She dried her tears. And Giselle! Giselle! The little one that, ever since she could toddle, had always clung to her skirt for protection. What duplicity! But she could not help it probably. When there was a man in the case the poor featherheaded wretch could not help herself.

Linda had a good share of the Viola stoicism. She resolved to say nothing. But woman-like she put passion into her stoicism. Giselle's short answers, prompted by fearful caution, drove her beside herself by their curtness that resembled disdain. One day she flung herself upon the chair in which her indolent sister was lying and impressed the mark of her teeth at the base of the whitest neck in Sulaco. Giselle cried out. But she had her share of the Viola heroism. Ready to faint with terror, she only said, in a lazy voice, '*Madre de Dios!* Are you going to eat me alive, Linda?' And this outburst passed off leaving no trace upon the situation. 'She knows nothing. She cannot know anything,' reflected Giselle. 'Perhaps it is not true. It cannot be true,' Linda tried to persuade herself.

But when she saw Captain Fidanza for the first time after her meeting with the distracted Ramirez, the certitude of her misfortune returned. She watched him from the doorway go away to his boat, asking herself stoically, 'Will they meet tonight?' She made up her mind not to leave the tower for a second. When he had disappeared she came out and sat down by her father.

The venerable Garibaldino felt, in his own words, 'a young man yet'. In one way or another a good deal of talk about Ramirez had reached him of late; and his contempt and dislike of that man who obviously was not what his son would have been, had made him restless. He slept very little now; but for several nights past instead of reading – or only sitting, with Mrs Gould's silver spectacles on his nose, before the open Bible, he had been prowling actively all about the island with his old gun, on watch over his honour.

Linda, laying her thin brown hand on his knee, tried to soothe his excitement. Ramirez was not in Sulaco. Nobody knew where he was. He was gone. His talk of what he would do meant nothing.

'No,' the old man interrupted. 'But son Gian' Battista told me – quite of himself – that the cowardly *esclavo* was drinking and gambling with the rascals of Zapiga, over there on the north side of the gulf. He may get some of the worst scoundrels of that scoundrelly town of Negroes to help him in his attempt upon the little one. . . . But I am not so old. No!'

She argued earnestly against the probability of any attempt being made; and at last the old man fell silent, chewing his white moustache. Women had their obstinate notions which must be honoured – his poor wife was like that, and Linda resembled her mother. It was not seemly for a man to argue. 'Maybe. Maybe,' he mumbled.

She was by no means easy in her mind. She loved Nostromo. She turned her eyes upon Giselle, sitting at a distance, with something of maternal tenderness, and the jealous anguish of a rival outraged in her defeat. Then she rose and walked over to her.

'Listen – you,' she said, roughly.

The invincible candour of the gaze, raised up all violet and dew, excited her rage and admiration. She had beautiful eyes – the *chica* – this vile thing of white flesh and black deception. She did not know whether she wanted to tear them out with shouts of vengeance or cover up their mysterious and shameless innocence with kisses of pity and love. And suddenly they became empty, gazing blankly at her, except for a little fear not quite buried deep enough with all the other emotions in Giselle's heart.

Linda said, 'Ramirez is boasting in town that he will carry you off from the island.'

'What folly!' answered the other, and in a perversity born of long restraint, she added: 'He is not the man,' in a jesting tone with a trembling audacity.

'No?' said Linda, through her clenched teeth. 'Is he not? Well, then, look to it; because father has been walking about with a loaded gun at night.'

'It is not good for him. You must tell him not to, Linda. He will not listen to me.'

'I shall say nothing – never any more – to anybody,' cried Linda, passionately.

This could not last, thought Giselle. Giovanni must take her away soon – the very next time he came. She would not suffer these terrors for ever so much silver. To speak with her sister made her ill. But she was not uneasy at her father's watchfulness. She had begged Nostromo not to come to the window that night. He had promised to keep away for this once. And she did not know, could not guess or imagine, that he had another reason for coming on the island.

Linda had gone straight to the tower. It was time to light up. She unlocked the little door, and went heavily up the spiral staircase, carrying her love for the magnificent Capataz de Cargadores like an ever-increasing load of shameful fetters. No; she could not throw it off. No; let Heaven dispose of these two. And moving about the lantern, filled with twilight and the sheen of the moon, with careful movements she lighted the lamp. Then her arms fell along her body.

'And with our mother looking on,' she murmured. 'My own sister – the *chica*!'

The whole refracting apparatus, with its brass fittings and rings of prisms, glittered and sparkled like a dome-shaped shrine of diamonds, containing not a lamp, but some sacred flame, dominating the sea. And Linda, the keeper, in black, with a pale face, drooped low in a wooden chair, alone with her jealousy, far above the shames and passions of the earth. A strange, dragging pain, as if somebody were pulling her about brutally by her dark hair with bronze glints, made her put her hands up to her temples. They would meet. They would meet. And she knew where, too. At the window. The sweat of torture fell in drops on her cheeks, while the moonlight in the offing closed as if with a colossal bar of silver the entrance of the Placid Gulf – the sombre cavern of clouds and stillness in the surf-fretted seaboard.

Linda Viola stood up suddenly with a finger on her lip. He loved neither her nor her sister. The whole thing seemed so objectless as to frighten her, and also give her some hope. Why did he not carry her off? What prevented him? He was incomprehensible. What were they waiting for? For what end were these two lying and deceiving? Not for the ends of their love. There was no such thing. The hope of regaining him for herself made her break her vow of not leaving the tower that night. She must talk at once to her father, who was wise, and would understand. She ran down the spiral stairs. At the moment of opening the door at the bottom she heard the sound of the first shot ever fired on the Great Isabel.

She felt a shock, as though the bullet had struck her breast. She ran on without pausing. The cottage was dark. She cried at the door, 'Giselle! Giselle!' then dashed round the corner and screamed her sister's name at the open window, without getting an answer; but as she was rushing, distracted, round the house, Giselle came out of the door, and darted past her, running silently, her hair loose, and her eyes staring straight ahead. She seemed to skim along the grass as if on tiptoe, and vanished.

Linda walked on slowly, with her arms stretched out before her. All was still on the island; she did not know where she was going. The tree under which Martin Decoud spent his last days, beholding life like a succession of senseless images, threw a large blotch of black shade upon the grass. Suddenly she saw her father, standing quietly all alone in the moonlight.

The Garibaldino – big, erect, with his snow-white hair and beard – had a monumental repose in his immobility, leaning upon a rifle. She put her hand upon his arm lightly. He never stirred.

'What have you done?' she asked, in her ordinary voice.

'I have shot Ramirez – *infame!*' he answered, with his eyes directed to where the shade was blackest. 'Like a thief he came, and like a thief he fell. The child had to be protected.'

He did not offer to move an inch, to advance a single step. He stood there, rugged and unstirring, like a statue of an old man guarding the honour of his house. Linda removed her trembling hand from his arm, firm and steady like an arm of stone, and, without a word, entered the blackness of the shade. She saw a stir of formless shapes on the ground, and stopped short. A murmur of despair and tears grew louder to her strained hearing.

'I entreated you not to come tonight. Oh, my Giovanni! And you promised. Oh! Why – why did you come, Giovanni?'

It was her sister's voice. It broke on a heartrending sob. And the voice of the resourceful Capataz de Cargadores, master and slave of the San Tomé treasure, who had been caught unawares by old Giorgio while stealing across the open towards the ravine to get some more silver, answered careless and cool, but sounding startlingly weak from the ground.

'It seemed as though I could not live through the night without seeing thee once more – my star, my little flower.'

The brilliant *tertulia* was just over, the last guests had departed, and the Señor Administrador had gone to his room already, when Dr Monygham, who had been expected in the evening but had not turned up, arrived driving along the woodblock pavement under the electric-lamps of the deserted Calle de la Constitución, and found the great gateway of the *casa* still open.

He limped in, stumped up the stairs, and found the fat and sleek Basilio on the point of turning off the lights in the *sala*. The prosperous majordomo remained open-mouthed at this late invasion.

'Don't put out the lights,' commanded the doctor. 'I want to see the *señora*.'

'The *señora* is in the Señor Administrador's *cancillaría*,' said Basilio, in an unctuous voice. The Señor Administrador starts for the mountain in an hour. There is some trouble with the workmen to be feared, it appears. A shameless people without reason and decency. And idle, *señor*. Idle.'

'You are shamelessly lazy and imbecile yourself,' said the doctor, with that faculty for exasperation which made him so generally beloved. 'Don't put the lights out.'

Basilio retired with dignity. Dr Monygham, waiting in the brilliantly lighted *sala*, heard presently a door close at the farther end of the house. A jingle of spurs died out. The Señor Administrador was off to the mountain.

With a measured swish of her long train, flashing with jewels and the shimmer of silk, her delicate head bowed as if under the weight of a mass of fair hair, in which the silver threads were lost, the 'first lady of Sulaco', as Captain Mitchell used to describe her, moved along the lighted corridor, wealthy beyond great dreams of wealth, considered, loved, respected, honoured, and as solitary as any human being had ever been, perhaps, on this earth.

The doctor's 'Mrs Gould! One minute!' stopped her with a start at the door of the lighted and empty *sala*. From the similarity of mood and circumstance, the sight of the doctor, standing there all alone amongst the groups of furniture, recalled to her emotional memory her unexpected meeting with Martin Decoud; she seemed to hear in the silence the voice of that man, dead miserably so many years ago, pronounce the words, 'Antonia left her fan here.' But it was the doctor's voice that spoke, a little altered by his excitement. She remarked his shining eyes.

'Mrs Gould, you are wanted. Do you know what has happened? You remember what I told you yesterday about Nostromo. Well, it seems that a *lancha*, a decked boat, coming from Zapiga, with four Negroes in her, passing close to the Great Isabel, was hailed from the cliff by a woman's voice – Linda's, as a matter of fact – commanding them (it's a moonlight night) to go round to the beach and take up a wounded man to the town. The *patron* (from whom I've heard all this), of course, did so at once. He told me that when they got round to the low side of the Great Isabel, they found Linda Viola waiting for them. They followed her: she led them under a tree not far from the cottage. There they found Nostromo lying on the ground with his head in the younger girl's lap, and father Viola standing some distance off leaning on his gun. Under Linda's direction they got a table out of the cottage for a stretcher, after breaking off the legs. They are here, Mrs Gould. I mean Nostromo and – and Giselle. The Negroes brought him in to the first-aid hospital near the harbour. He made the attendant send for me. But it is not me he wanted to see – it was you, Mrs Gould! It was you.'

'Me?' whispered Mrs Gould, shrinking a little.

'Yes, you!' the doctor burst out. 'He begged me – his enemy, as he thinks – to bring you to him at once. It seems he has something to say to you alone.'

'Impossible!' murmured Mrs Gould.

'He said to me, "Remind her that I have done something to keep a roof over her head." ... Mrs Gould,' the doctor pursued, in the greatest excitement. 'Do you remember the silver? The silver in the lighter – that was lost!'

Mrs Gould remembered. But she did not say she hated the mere mention of that silver. Frankness personified, she remembered with an exaggerated horror that for the first and last time of her life she had concealed the truth from her husband about that very silver. She had been corrupted by her fears at that time, and she had never forgiven herself. Moreover, that silver, which would never have come down if her husband had been made acquainted with the news brought by Decoud, had been in a roundabout way nearly the cause of Dr Monygham's death. And these things appeared to her very dreadful.

'Was it lost, though?' the doctor exclaimed. 'I've always felt that there was a mystery about our Nostromo ever since. I do believe he wants now, at the point of death –'

'The point of death,' repeated Mrs Gould.

'Yes. Yes ... He wants perhaps to tell you something concerning that silver which –'

'Oh, no! No!' exclaimed Mrs Gould, in a low voice. 'Isn't it lost and done with? Isn't there enough treasure without it to make everybody in the world miserable?'

The doctor remained still, in a submissive, disappointed silence. At last he ventured, very low:

'And there is that Viola girl, Giselle. What are we to do? It looks as though father and sister had –'

Mrs Gould admitted that she felt in duty bound to do her best for these girls.

'I have a volante here,' the doctor said. 'If you don't mind getting into that –'

He waited, all impatience, till Mrs Gould reappeared, having thrown over her dress a grey cloak with a deep hood.

It was thus that, cloaked and monastically hooded over her evening costume, this woman, full of endurance and compassion, stood by the side of the bed on which the splendid Capataz de Cargadores lay stretched out motionless on his back. The whiteness of sheets and pillows gave a sombre and energetic relief to his bronzed face, to the dark, nervous hands, so good on a tiller, upon a bridle, and on a trigger, lying open and idle upon a white coverlet.

'She is innocent,' the Capataz was saying in a deep and level voice, as though afraid that a louder word would break the slender hold his spirit still kept upon his body. 'She is innocent. It is I alone. But no matter. For these things I would answer to no man or woman alive.'

He paused. Mrs Gould's face, very white within the shadow of the hood, bent over him with an invincible and dreary sadness. And the low sobs of Giselle Viola, kneeling at the end of the bed, her gold hair with coppery gleams loose and scattered over the Capataz's feet, hardly troubled the silence of the room.

'Ha! Old Giorgio – the guardian of thine honour! Fancy the Vecchio coming upon me so light of foot, so steady of aim. I myself could have done no better. But the price of a charge of powder might have been saved. The honour was safe . . . *Señora*, she would have followed to the end of the world Nostromo the thief . . . I have said the word. The spell is broken!'

A low moan from the girl made him cast his eyes down.

'I cannot see her. . . . No matter,' he went on, with the shadow of the old magnificent carelessness in his voice. 'One kiss is enough, if there is no time for more. An airy soul, *señora*! Bright and warm, like sunshine – soon clouded, and soon serene. They would crush it there between them. *Señora*, cast on her the eye of your compassion, as famed from one end of the land to the other as the courage and daring of the man who speaks to you. She will console herself in time. And even Ramirez is not a bad fellow. I am not angry. No! It is not Ramirez who overcame the Capataz of the Sulaco Cargadores.' He paused, made an effort, and in a louder voice, a little wildly, declared:

'I die betrayed – betrayed by –'

But he did not say by whom or by what he was dying betrayed.

'She would not have betrayed me,' he began again, opening his eyes very wide. 'She was faithful. We were going very far – very soon. I could have torn myself away from that accursed treasure for her. For that child I would have left boxes and boxes of it – full. And Decoud took four. Four ingots. Why? *Picardía!* To betray me? How could I give back the treasure with four ingots missing? They would have said I had purloined them. The doctor would have said that. Alas! it holds me yet!'

Mrs Gould bent low, fascinated – cold with apprehension.

'What became of Don Martin on that night, Nostromo?'

'Who knows! I wondered what would become of me. Now I know. Death was to come upon me unawares. He went away! He betrayed me. And you think I have killed him! You are all alike, you fine people. The silver has killed me. It has held me. It holds me yet. Nobody knows where it is. But you are the wife of Don Carlos, who put it into my hands and said, "Save it on your life." And when I returned, and you all thought it was lost, what do I hear? It was nothing of importance. Let it go. Up, Nostromo, the faithful, and ride away to save us, for dear life!'

'Nostromo!' Mrs Gould whispered, bending very low. 'I, too, have hated the idea of that silver from the bottom of my heart.'

'Marvellous! – that one of you should hate the wealth that you know so well how to take from the hands of the poor. The world rests upon the poor, as old Giorgio says. You have been always good to the poor. But there is something accursed in wealth. *Señora*, shall I tell you where the treasure is? To you alone . . . Shining! Incorruptible!'

A pained, involuntary reluctance lingered in his tone, in his eyes, plain to the woman with the genius of sympathetic intuition. She averted her glance from the miserable subjection of the dying man, appalled, wishing to hear no more of the silver.

'No, Capataz,' she said. 'No one misses it now. Let it be lost for ever.'

After hearing these words, Nostromo closed his eyes, uttered no word, made no movement. Outside the door of the sick-room Dr Monygham, excited to the highest pitch, his eyes shining with eagerness, came up to the two women.

'Now, Mrs Gould,' he said, almost brutally in his impatience, 'tell me, was I right? There is a mystery. You have got the word of it, have you not? He told you –'

'He told me nothing,' said Mrs Gould, steadily.

The light of his temperamental enmity to Nostromo went out of Dr Monygham's eyes. He stepped back submissively. He did not believe Mrs Gould. But her word was law. He accepted her denial like an inexplicable fatality affirming the victory of Nostromo's genius over his own. Even before that woman, whom he loved with secret devotion, he had been defeated by the magnificent Capataz de Cargadores, the man who had lived his own life on the assumption of unbroken fidelity, rectitude, and courage!

'Pray send at once somebody for my carriage,' spoke Mrs Gould from within her hood. Then, turning to Giselle Viola, 'Come nearer me, child; come closer. We will wait here.'

Giselle Viola, heartbroken and childlike, her face veiled in her falling hair, crept up to her side. Mrs Gould slipped her hand through the arm of the unworthy daughter of old Viola, the immaculate republican, the hero without a stain. Slowly, gradually, as a withered flower droops, the head of the girl, who would have followed a thief to the end of the world, rested on the shoulder of Doña Emilia, the first lady of Sulaco, the wife of the Señor Administrador of the San Tomé mine. And Mrs Gould, feeling her suppressed sobbing, nervous and excited, had the first and only moment of bitterness in her life. It was worthy of Dr Monygham himself.

'Console yourself, child. Very soon he would have forgotten you for his treasure.'

'*Señora*, he loved me. He loved me,' Giselle whispered, despairingly. 'He loved me as no one had ever been loved before.'

'I have been loved, too,' Mrs Gould said in a severe tone.

Giselle clung to her convulsively. 'Oh, *señora*, but you shall live adored to the end of your life,' she sobbed out.

Mrs Gould kept an unbroken silence till the carriage arrived. She helped in the half-fainting girl. After the doctor had shut the door of the landau, she leaned over to him.

'You can do nothing?' she whispered.

'No, Mrs Gould. Moreover, he won't let us touch him. It does not matter. I just had one look . . . Useless.'

But he promised to see old Viola and the other girl that very night. He could get the police-boat to take him off to the island. He remained in the street, looking after the landau rolling away slowly behind the white mules.

The rumour of some accident – an accident to Captain Fidanza – had been spreading along the new quays with their rows of lamps and the dark shapes of towering cranes. A knot of night-prowlers – the poorest of the poor – hung about the door of the first-aid hospital, whispering in the moonlight of the empty street.

There was no one with the wounded man but the pale photographer, small, frail, bloodthirsty, the hater of capitalists, perched on a high stool near the head of the bed with his knees up and his chin in his hands. He had been fetched by a comrade who, working late on the wharf, had heard from a Negro belonging to a *lancha* that Captain Fidanza had been brought ashore mortally wounded.

'Have you any dispositions to make, comrade?' he asked, anxiously. 'Do not forget that we want money for our work. The rich must be fought with their own weapons.'

Nostromo made no answer. The other did not insist, remaining huddled up on the stool, shock-headed, wildly hairy, like a hunchbacked monkey. Then, after a long silence:

'Comrade Fidanza,' he began, solemnly, 'you have refused all aid from that doctor. Is he really a dangerous enemy of the people?'

In the dimly lit room Nostromo rolled his head slowly on the pillow and opened his eyes, directing at the weird figure perched by his bedside a glance of enigmatic and profound inquiry. Then his head rolled back, his eyelids fell, and the Capataz de Cargadores died without a word or moan after an hour of immobility, broken by short shudders testifying to the most atrocious sufferings.

Dr Monygham, going out in the police-galley to the islands, beheld the glitter of the moon upon the gulf and the high black shape of the Great Isabel sending a shaft of light afar, from under the canopy of clouds.

'Pull easy,' he said, wondering what he would find there. He tried to imagine Linda and her father, and discovered a strange reluctance within himself. 'Pull easy,' he repeated.

From the moment he fired at the thief of his honour, Giorgio Viola had not stirred from the spot. He stood, his old gun grounded, his hand grasping the barrel near the muzzle. After the *lancha* carrying off Nostromo for ever from her had left the shore, Linda, coming up, stopped before him. He did not seem to be aware of her presence, but when, losing her forced calmness, she cried out: 'Do you know whom you have killed?' he answered: 'Ramirez the vagabond.'

White, and staring insanely at her father, Linda laughed in his face. After a time he joined her faintly in a deep-toned and distant echo of her peals. Then she stopped, and the old man spoke as if startled:

'He cried out in son Gian' Battista's voice.'

The gun fell from his opened hand, but the arm remained extended for a moment as if still supported. Linda seized it roughly.

'You are too old to understand. Come into the house.'

He let her lead him. On the threshold he stumbled heavily, nearly coming to the ground together with his daughter. His excitement, his activity of the last few days, had been like the flare of a dying lamp. He caught at the back of his chair.

'In son Gian' Battista's voice,' he repeated in a severe tone. 'I heard him – Ramirez – the miserable –'

Linda helped him into the chair, and, bending low, hissed into his ear:

'You have killed Gian' Battista.'

The old man smiled under his thick moustache. Women had strange fancies.

'Where is the child?' he asked, surprised at the penetrating chilliness of the air and the unwonted dimness of the lamp by which he used to sit up half the night with the open Bible before him.

Linda hesitated a moment, then averted her eyes.

'She is asleep,' she said. 'We shall talk of her tomorrow.'

She could not bear to look at him. He filled her with terror and with an almost unbearable feeling of pity. She had observed the change that came over him. He would never understand what he had done; and even to her the whole thing remained incomprehensible. He said with difficulty:

'Give me the book.'

Linda laid on the table the closed volume in its worn leather cover, the Bible given him ages ago by an Englishman in Palermo.

'The child had to be protected,' he said, in a strange, mournful voice.

Behind his chair Linda wrung her hands, crying without noise. Suddenly she started for the door. He heard her move.

'Where are you going?' he asked.

'To the light,' she answered, turning round to look at him balefully.

'The light! *Sì* – duty.'

Very upright, white-haired, leonine, heroic in his absorbed quietness, he felt in the pocket of his red shirt for the spectacles given him by Doña Emilia. He put them on. After a long period of immobility he opened the book, and from on high looked through the glasses at the small print in double columns. A rigid, stern expression settled upon his features with a slight frown, as if in response to some gloomy thought or unpleasant sensation. But he never detached his eyes from the book while he swayed forward, gently, gradually, till his snow-white head rested upon the open pages. A wooden clock ticked methodically on the white-washed wall, and growing slowly cold the Garibaldino lay alone, rugged undecayed, like an old oak uprooted by a treacherous gust of wind.

The light of the Great Isabel burned unfailing above the lost treasure of the San Tomé mine. Into the bluish sheen of a night without stars the lantern sent out a yellow beam towards the far horizon. Like a black speck upon the shining panes, Linda, crouching in the outer gallery, rested her head on the rail. The moon, drooping in the western board, looked at her radiantly.

Below, at the foot of the cliff, the regular splash of oars from a passing boat ceased, and Dr Monygham stood up in the stern sheets.

'Linda!' he shouted, throwing back his head. 'Linda!'

Linda stood up. She had recognized the voice.

'Is he dead?' she cried, bending over.

'Yes, my poor girl. I am coming round,' the doctor answered from below. 'Pull to the beach,' he said to the rowers.

Linda's black figure detached itself upright on the light of the lantern with her arms raised above her head as though she were going to throw herself over.

'It is I who loved you,' she whispered, with a face as set and white as marble in the moonlight. 'I! Only I! She will forget thee, killed miserably for her pretty face. I cannot understand. I cannot understand. But I shall never forget thee. Never!'

She stood silent and still, collecting her strength to throw all her fidelity, her pain, bewilderment, and despair into one great cry.

'Never! Gian' Battista!'

Dr Monygham, pulling round in the police-galley, heard the name pass over his head. It was another of Nostromo's triumphs, the greatest, the most enviable, the most sinister of all. In that true cry of undying passion that seemed to ring aloud from Punta Mala to Azuera and away to the bright line of the horizon, overhung by a big white cloud shining like a mass of solid silver, the genius of the magnificent Capataz de Cargadores dominated the dark gulf containing his conquests of treasure and love.

THE SECRET AGENT

A Simple Tale

AUTHOR'S NOTE

The origin of *The Secret Agent*: subject, treatment, artistic purpose, and every other motive that may induce an author to take up his pen, can, I believe, be traced to a period of mental and emotional reaction.

The actual facts are that I began this book impulsively and wrote it continuously. When in due course it was bound and delivered to the public gaze I found myself reproved for having produced it at all. Some of the admonitions were severe, others had a sorrowful note. I have not got them textually before me but I remember perfectly the general argument, which was very simple; and also my surprise at its nature. All this sounds a very old story now! And yet it is not such a long time ago. I must conclude that I had still preserved much of my pristine innocence in the year 1907. It seems to me now that even an artless person might have foreseen that some criticisms would be based on the ground of sordid surroundings and the moral squalor of the tale.

That of course is a serious objection. It was not universal. In fact it seems ungracious to remember so little reproof amongst so much intelligent and sympathetic appreciation; and I trust that the readers of this Preface will not hasten to put it down to wounded vanity or a natural disposition to ingratitude. I suggest that a charitable heart could very well ascribe my choice to natural modesty. Yet it isn't exactly modesty that makes me select reproof for the illustration of my case. No, it isn't exactly modesty. I am not at all certain that I am modest; but those who have read so far through my work will credit me with enough decency, tact, *savoir-faire*, what you will, to prevent me from making a song for my own glory out of the words of other people. No! The true motive of my selection lies in quite a different trait. I have always had a propensity to justify my action. Not to defend. To justify. Not to insist that I was right but simply to explain that there was no perverse intention, no secret scorn for the natural sensibilities of mankind at the bottom of my impulses.

That kind of weakness is dangerous only so far that it exposes one to the risk of becoming a bore; for the world generally is not interested in the motives of any overt act but in its consequences. Man may smile and smile but he is not an investigating animal. He loves the obvious. He shrinks from explanations. Yet I will go on with mine. It's obvious that I need not have written that book. I was under no necessity to deal with that subject; using the word subject both in the sense of the tale itself and in the larger one of a special manifestation in the life of mankind. This I fully admit. But the thought of elaborating mere ugliness in order to shock, or even simply to surprise my readers by a change of front, has never entered my head. In making this statement I expect to be believed, not only on the evidence of my general character but also for the reason, which anybody can see, that the whole treatment of the tale, its inspiring indignation and underlying pity and contempt, prove my detachment from the squalor and sordidness which lie simply in the outward circumstances of the setting.

The inception of *The Secret Agent* followed immediately on a two years' period of intense absorption in the task of writing that remote novel, *Nostromo*, with its far-off Latin-American atmosphere; and the profoundly personal *Mirror of the Sea*. The first an intense creative effort on what I suppose will always remain my largest canvas, the second an unreserved attempt to unveil for a moment the profounder intimacies of the sea and the formative influences of nearly half my lifetime. It was a period, too, in which my sense of the truth of things was attended by a very intense imaginative and emotional readiness which, all genuine and faithful to facts as it was, yet made me feel (the task once done) as if I were left behind, aimless amongst mere husks of sensations and lost in a world of other, of inferior, values.

I don't know whether I really felt that I wanted a change, change in my imagination, in my vision, and in my mental attitude. I rather think that a change in the fundamental mood had already stolen over me unawares. I don't remember anything definite happening. With *The Mirror of the Sea* finished in the full consciousness that I had dealt honestly with myself and my readers in every line of that book, I gave myself up to a not unhappy pause. Then, while I was yet standing still, as it were, and certainly not thinking of going out of my way to look for anything ugly, the subject of *The Secret Agent* – I mean the tale – came to me in the shape of a few words uttered by a friend in a casual conversation about anarchists or rather anarchist activities; how brought about I don't remember now.

I remember, however, remarking on the criminal futility of the whole thing, doctrine, action, mentality; and on the contemptible aspect of the half-crazy pose as of a brazen cheat exploiting the poignant miseries and passionate credulities of a mankind always so tragically eager for self-destruction. That was what made for me its philosophical pretences so unpardonable. Presently, passing to particular instances, we recalled the already old story of the attempt to blow up the Greenwich Observatory; a blood-stained inanity of so fatuous a kind that it was impossible to fathom its origin by any reasonable or even unreasonable process of thought. For perverse unreason has its own logical processes. But that outrage could not be laid hold of mentally in any sort of way, so that one remained faced by the fact of a man blown to bits for nothing even most remotely resembling an idea, anarchistic or other. As to the outer wall of the Observatory it did not show as much as the faintest crack.

I pointed all this out to my friend who remained silent for a while and then remarked in his characteristically casual and omniscient manner: 'Oh, that fellow was half an idiot. His sister committed suicide afterwards.' These were absolutely the only words that passed between us; for extreme surprise at this unexpected piece of information kept me dumb for a moment and he began at once to talk of something else. It never occurred to me later to ask how he arrived at his knowledge. I am sure that if he had seen once in his life the back of an anarchist that must have been the whole extent of his connexion with the underworld. He was, however, a man who liked to talk with all sorts of people, and he may have gathered those illuminating facts at second or third hand, from a crossing-sweeper, from a retired police officer, from some vague man in his club, or even, perhaps from a Minister of State met at some public or private reception.

Of the illuminating quality there could be no doubt whatever. One felt like walking out of a forest on to a plain – there was not much to see but one had plenty of light. No, there was not much to see and, frankly, for a considerable time I didn't even attempt to perceive anything. It was only the illuminating impression that remained. It remained satisfactory but in a passive way. Then, about a week later, I came upon a book which as far as I know had never attained any prominence, the rather summary recollections of an Assistant Commissioner of Police, an obviously able man with a strong religious strain in his character who was appointed to his post at the time of the dynamite outrages in London, away back in the eighties. The book was fairly interesting, very discreet of course; and I have by now forgotten the bulk of its contents. It contained no revelations, it ran over the surface agreeably, and that was all. I won't even try to explain why I should have been arrested by a little passage of about seven lines, in which the author (I believe his name was Anderson) reproduced a short dialogue held in the Lobby of the House of Commons after some unexpected anarchist outrage, with the Home Secretary. I think it was Sir William Harcourt then. He was very much irritated and the official was very apologetic. The phrase, amongst the three which passed between them, that struck me most was Sir W. Harcourt's angry sally: 'All that's very well. But your idea of secrecy over there seems to consist of keeping the Home Secretary in the dark.' Characteristic enough of Sir W. Harcourt's temper but not much in itself. There must have been, however, some sort of atmosphere in the whole incident because all of a sudden I felt myself stimulated. And then ensued in my mind what a student of chemistry would best understand from the analogy of the addition of the tiniest little drop of the right kind, precipitating the process of crystallization in a test tube containing some colourless solution.

It was at first for me a mental change, disturbing a quieted-down imagination, in which strange forms, sharp in outline but imperfectly apprehended, appeared and claimed attention as crystals will do by their bizarre and unexpected shapes. One fell to musing before the phenomenon – even of the past: of South America, a continent of crude sunshine and brutal revolutions, of the sea, the vast expanse of salt waters, the mirror of heaven's frowns and smiles, the reflector of the world's light. Then the vision of an enormous town presented itself, of a monstrous town more populous than some continents and in its man-made might as if indifferent to heaven's frowns and smiles; a cruel devourer of the world's light. There was room enough there to place any story, depth enough for any passion, variety enough there for any setting, darkness enough to bury five millions of lives.

Irresistibly the town became the background for the ensuing period of deep and tentative meditations. Endless vistas opened before me in various directions. It would take years to find the right way! It seemed to take years! . . . Slowly the dawning conviction of Mrs Verloc's maternal passion grew up to a flame between me and that background, tingeing it with its secret ardour and receiving from it in exchange some of its own sombre colouring. At last the story of Winnie Verloc stood out complete from the days of her childhood to the end, unproportioned as yet, with everything still on the first plan, as it were; but ready now to be dealt with. It was a matter of about three days.

This book is *that* story, reduced to manageable proportions, its whole course suggested and centred round the absurd cruelty of the Greenwich Park explosion. I had there a task I will not say arduous but of the most absorbing difficulty. But it had to be done. It was a necessity. The figures grouped about Mrs Verloc and related directly or indirectly to her tragic suspicion that 'life doesn't stand much looking into', are the outcome of that very necessity. Personally I have never had any doubt of the reality of Mrs Verloc's story; but it had to be disengaged from its obscurity in that immense town, it had to be made credible, I don't mean so much as to her soul but as to her surroundings, not so much as to her psychology but as to her humanity. For the surroundings hints were not lacking. I had to fight hard to keep at arm's length the memories of my solitary and nocturnal walks all over London in my early days, lest they should rush in and overwhelm each page of the story as these emerged one after another from a mood as serious in feeling and thought as any in which I ever wrote a line. In that respect I really think that *The Secret Agent* is a perfectly genuine piece of work. Even the purely artistic purpose, that of applying an ironic method to a subject of that kind, was formulated with deliberation and in the earnest belief that ironic treatment alone would enable me to say all I felt I would have to say in scorn as well as in pity. It is one of the minor satisfactions of my writing life that having taken that resolve I did manage, it seems to me, to carry it right through to the end. As to the personages whom the absolute necessity of the case – Mrs Verloc's case – brings out in front of the London background, from them, too, I obtained those little satisfactions which really count for so much against the mass of oppressive doubts that haunt so persistently every attempt at creative work. For instance, of Mr Vladimir himself (who was fair game for a caricatural presentation) I was gratified to hear that an experienced man of the world had said 'that Conrad must have been in touch with that sphere or else has an excellent intuition of things', because Mr Vladimir was 'not only possible in detail but quite right in essentials'. Then a visitor from America informed me that all sorts of revolutionary refugees in New York would have it that the book was written by somebody who knew a lot about them. This seemed to me a very high compliment, considering that, as a matter of hard fact, I had seen even less of their kind than the omniscient friend who gave me the first suggestion for the novel. I have no doubt, however, that there had been moments during the writing of the book when I was an extreme revolutionist, I won't say more convinced than they but certainly cherishing a more concentrated purpose than any of them had ever done in the whole course of his life. I don't say this to boast. I was simply attending to my business. In the matter of all my books I have always attended to my business. I have attended to it with complete self-surrender. And this statement, too, is not a boast. I could not have done otherwise. It would have bored me too much to make-believe.

The suggestions for certain personages of the tale, both law-abiding and lawless, came from various sources which, perhaps, here and there, some reader may have recognized. They are not very recondite. But I am not concerned here to legitimize any of those people, and even as to my general view of the moral reactions as between the criminal and the police all I will venture to say is that it seems to me to be at least arguable.

The twelve years that have elapsed since the publication of the book have not changed my attitude. I do not regret having written it. Lately, circumstances, which have nothing to do with the general tenor of this preface, have compelled me to strip this tale of the literary robe of indignant scorn it has cost me so much to fit on it decently, years ago. I have been forced, so to speak, to look upon its bare bones. I confess that it makes a grisly skeleton. But still I will submit that telling Winnie Verloc's story to its anarchistic end of utter desolation, madness, and despair, and telling it as I have told it here, I have not intended to commit a gratuitous outrage on the feelings of mankind.

J. C.

1920

CHAPTER 1

Mr Verloc, going out in the morning, left his shop nominally in charge of his brother-in-law. It could be done, because there was very little business at any time, and practically none at all before the evening. Mr Verloc cared but little about his ostensible business. And, moreover, his wife was in charge of his brother-in-law.

The shop was small, and so was the house. It was one of those grimy brick houses which existed in large quantities before the era of reconstruction dawned upon London. The shop was a square box of a place, with the front glazed in small panes. In the daytime the door remained closed; in the evening it stood discreetly but suspiciously ajar.

The window contained photographs of more or less undressed dancing girls; nondescript packages in wrappers like patent medicines; closed yellow paper envelopes, very flimsy, and marked two and six in heavy black figures; a few numbers of ancient French comic publications hung across a string as if to dry; a dingy blue china bowl, a casket of black wood, bottles of marking ink, and rubber stamps; a few books with titles hinting at impropriety; a few apparently old copies of obscure newspapers, badly printed, with titles like the *Torch*, the *Gong* – rousing titles. And the two gas-jets inside the panes were always turned low, either for economy's sake or for the sake of the customers.

These customers were either very young men, who hung about the window for a time before slipping in suddenly; or men of a more mature age, but looking generally as if they were not in funds. Some of that last kind had the collars of their overcoats turned right up to their moustaches, and traces of mud on the bottom of their nether garments, which had the appearance of being much worn and not very valuable. And the legs inside them did not, as a general rule, seem of much account either. With their hands plunged deep in the side pockets of their coats, they dodged in sideways, one shoulder first, as if afraid to start the bell going.

The bell, hung on the door by means of a curved ribbon of steel, was difficult to circumvent. It was hopelessly cracked; but of an evening, at the slightest provocation, it clattered behind the customer with impudent virulence.

It clattered; and at that signal, through the dusty glass door behind the painted deal counter, Mr Verloc would issue hastily from the parlour at the back. His eyes were naturally heavy; he had an air of having wallowed, fully dressed, all day on an unmade bed. Another man would have felt such an appearance a distinct disadvantage. In a commercial transaction of the retail order much depends on the seller's engaging and amiable aspect. But Mr Verloc knew his business, and remained undisturbed by any sort of aesthetic doubt about his appearance. With a firm, steady-eyed impudence, which seemed to hold back the threat of some abominable menace, he would proceed to sell over the counter some object looking obviously and scandalously not worth the money which passed in the transaction: a small cardboard box with apparently nothing inside, for instance, or one of those carefully closed yellow flimsy envelopes, or a soiled volume in paper covers with a promising title. Now and then it happened that one of the faded, yellow dancing girls would get sold to an amateur, as though she had been alive and young.

Sometimes it was Mrs Verloc who would appear at the call of the cracked bell. Winnie Verloc was a young woman with a full bust, in a tight bodice, and with broad hips. Her hair was very tidy. Steady-eyed like her husband, she preserved an air of unfathomable indifference behind the rampart of the counter. Then the customer of comparatively tender years would get suddenly disconcerted at having to deal with a woman, and with rage in his heart would proffer a request for a bottle of marking ink, retail value sixpence (price in Verloc's shop one and sixpence), which, once outside, he would drop stealthily into the gutter.

The evening visitors – the men with collars turned up and soft hats rammed down – nodded familiarly to Mrs Verloc, and with a muttered greeting, lifted up the flap at the end of the counter in order to pass into the back parlour, which gave access to a passage and to a steep flight of stairs. The door of the shop was the only means of entrance to the house in which Mr Verloc carried on his business of a seller of shady wares, exercised his vocation of a protector of society, and cultivated his domestic virtues. These last were pronounced. He was thoroughly domesticated. Neither his spiritual, nor his mental, nor his physical needs were of the kind to take him much abroad. He found at home the ease of his body and the peace of his conscience, together with Mrs Verloc's wifely attentions and Mrs Verloc's mother's deferential regard.

Winnie's mother was a stout, wheezy woman, with a large brown face. She wore a black wig under a white cap. Her swollen legs rendered her inactive. She considered herself to be of French descent, which might have been true; and after a good many years of married life with a licensed victualler of the more common sort, she provided for the years of widowhood by letting furnished apartments for gentlemen near Vauxhall Bridge Road in a square once of some splendour and still included in the district of Belgravia. This topographical fact was of some advantage in advertising her rooms; but the patrons of the worthy widow were not exactly of the fashionable kind. Such as they were, her daughter Winnie helped to look after them. Traces of the French descent which the widow boasted of were apparent in Winnie, too. They were apparent in the extremely neat and artistic arrangement of her glossy dark hair. Winnie had also other charms: her youth; her full, rounded form; her clear complexion; the provocation of her unfathomable reserve, which never went so far as to prevent conversation, carried on on the lodger's part with animation, and on hers with an equable amiability. It must be that Mr Verloc was susceptible to these fascinations. Mr Verloc was an intermittent patron. He came and went without any very apparent reason. He generally arrived in London (like the influenza) from the Continent, only he arrived unheralded by the Press; and his visitations set in with great severity. He breakfasted in bed, and remained wallowing there with an air of quiet enjoyment till noon every day – and sometimes even to a later hour. But when he went out he seemed to experience a great difficulty in finding his way back to his temporary home in the Belgravian square. He left it late, and returned to it early – as early as three or four in the morning; and on waking up at ten addressed Winnie, bringing in the breakfast tray, with jocular, exhausted civility, in the hoarse, failing tones of a man who had been talking vehemently for many hours together. His prominent, heavy-lidded eyes rolled sideways amorously and languidly, the bedclothes were pulled up to his chin, and his dark smooth moustache covered his thick lips capable of much honeyed banter.

In Winnie's mother's opinion Mr Verloc was a very nice gentleman. From her life's experience gathered in various 'business houses' the good woman had taken into her retirement an ideal of gentlemanliness as exhibited by the patrons of private-saloon bars. Mr Verloc approached that ideal; he attained it, in fact.

'Of course, we'll take over your furniture, mother,' Winnie had remarked.

The lodging-house was to be given up. It seems it would not answer to carry it on. It would have been too much trouble for Mr Verloc. It would not have been convenient for his other business. What his business was he did not say; but after his engagement to Winnie he took the trouble to get up before noon, and descending the basement stairs, make himself pleasant to Winnie's mother in the breakfast-room downstairs where she had her motionless being. He stroked the cat, poked the fire, had his lunch served to him there. He left its slightly stuffy cosiness with evident reluctance, but, all the same, remained out till the night was far advanced. He never offered to take Winnie to theatres, as such a nice gentleman ought to have done. His evenings were occupied. His work was in a way political, he told Winnie once. She would have, he warned her, to be very nice to his political friends. And with her straight, unfathomable glance she answered that she would be so, of course.

How much more he told her as to his occupation it was impossible for Winnie's mother to discover. The married couple took her over with the furniture. The mean aspect of the shop surprised her. The change from the Belgravian square to the narrow street in Soho affected her legs adversely. They became of an enormous size. On the other hand, she experienced a complete relief from material cares. Her son-in-law's heavy good nature inspired her with a sense of absolute safety. Her daughter's future was obviously assured, and even as to her son Stevie she need have no anxiety. She had not been able to conceal from herself that he was a terrible encumbrance, that poor Stevie. But in view of Winnie's fondness for her delicate brother, and of Mr Verloc's kind and generous disposition, she felt that the poor boy was pretty safe in this rough world. And in her heart of hearts she was not perhaps displeased that the Verlocs had no children. As that circumstance seemed perfectly indifferent to Mr Verloc, and as Winnie found an object of quasi-maternal affection in her brother, perhaps this was just as well for poor Stevie.

For he was difficult to dispose of, that boy. He was delicate and, in a frail way, good-looking, too, except for the vacant droop of his lower lip. Under our excellent system of compulsory education he had learned to read and write, notwithstanding the unfavourable aspect of the lower lip. But as errand-boy he did not turn out a great success. He forgot his messages; he was easily diverted from the straight path of duty by the attractions of stray cats and dogs, which he followed down narrow alleys into unsavoury courts; by the comedies of the street, which he contemplated open-mouthed, to the detriment of his employer's interests; or by the dramas of fallen horses, whose pathos and violence induced him sometimes to shriek piercingly in a crowd, which disliked to be disturbed by sounds of distress in its quiet enjoyment of the national spectacle. When led away by a grave and protecting policeman, it would often become apparent that poor Stevie had forgotten his address – at least for a time. A brusque question caused him to stutter to the point of suffocation. When startled by anything perplexing he used to squint horribly. However, he never had any fits (which was encouraging); and before the natural outburst of impatience on the part of his father he could always, in his childhood's days, run for protection behind the short skirts of his sister Winnie. On the other hand, he might have been suspected of hiding a fund of reckless naughtiness. When he had reached the age of fourteen a friend of his late father, an agent for a foreign preserved milk firm, having given him an opening as office-boy, he was discovered one foggy afternoon, in his chief's absence, busy letting off fireworks on the staircase. He touched off in quick succession a set of fierce rockets, angry catherine wheels, loudly exploding squibs – and the matter might have turned out very serious. An awful panic spread through the whole building. Wild-eyed, choking clerks stampeded through the passages full of smoke; silk hats and elderly businessmen could be seen rolling independently down the stairs. Stevie did not seem to derive any personal gratification from what he had done. His motives for this stroke of originality were difficult to discover. It was only later on that Winnie obtained from him a misty and confused confession. It seems that two other office-boys in the building had worked upon his feelings by tales of injustice and oppression till they had wrought his compassion to the pitch of that frenzy. But his father's friend, of course, dismissed him summarily as likely to ruin his business. After that altruistic exploit Stevie was to put to help wash the dishes in the basement kitchen, and to black the boots of the gentlemen patronizing the Belgravian mansion. There was obviously no future in such work. The gentlemen tipped him a shilling now and then. Mr Verloc showed himself the most generous of lodgers. But altogether all that did not amount to much either in the way of gain or prospects; so that when Winnie announced her engagement to Mr Verloc her mother could not help wondering, with a sigh and a glance towards the scullery, what would become of poor Stephen now.

It appeared that Mr Verloc was ready to take him over together with his wife's mother and with the furniture, which was the whole visible fortune of the family. Mr Verloc gathered everything as it came to his broad, good-natured breast. The furniture was disposed to the best advantage all over the house, but Mrs Verloc's mother was confined to two back rooms on the first floor. The luckless Stevie slept in one of them. By this time a growth of thin fluffy hair had come to blur, like a golden mist, the sharp line of his small lower jaw. He helped his sister with blind love and docility in her household duties. Mr Verloc thought that some occupation would be good for him. His spare time he occupied by drawing circles with compass and pencil on a piece of paper. He applied himself to that pastime with great industry, with his elbows spread out and bowed low over the kitchen table. Through the open door of the parlour at the back of the shop Winnie, his sister, glanced at him from time to time with maternal vigilance.

CHAPTER 2

Such was the house, the household, and the business Mr Verloc left behind him on his way westward at the hour of half past ten in the morning. It was unusually early for him; his whole person exhaled the charm of almost dewy freshness; he wore his blue cloth overcoat unbuttoned; his boots were shiny; his cheeks, freshly shaven, had a sort of gloss; and even his heavy-lidded eyes, refreshed by a night of peaceful slumber, sent out glances of comparative alertness. Through the park railings these glances beheld men and women riding in the Row, couples cantering past harmoniously, others advancing sedately at a walk, loitering groups of three or four, solitary horsemen looking unsociable, and solitary women followed at a long distance by a groom with a cockade to his hat and a leather belt over his tight-fitting coat. Carriages went bowling by, mostly two-horse broughams, with here and there a victoria with the skin of some wild beast inside and a woman's face and hat emerging above the folded hood. And a peculiarly London sun – against which nothing could be said except that it looked bloodshot – glorified all this by its state. It hung at a moderate elevation above Hyde Park Corner with an air of punctual and benign vigilance. The very pavement under Mr Verloc's feet had an old-gold tinge in that diffused light, in which neither wall, nor tree, nor beast, nor man cast a shadow. Mr Verloc was going westward through a town without shadows in an atmosphere of powdered old gold. There were red, coppery gleams on the roofs of houses, on the corners of walls, on the panels of carriages, on the very coats of the horses, and on the broad back of Mr Verloc's overcoat, where they produced a dull effect of rustiness. But Mr Verloc was not in the least conscious of having got rusty. He surveyed through the park railings the evidences of the town's opulence and luxury with an approving eye. All these people had to be protected. Protection is the first necessity of opulence and luxury. They had to be protected; and their horses, carriages, houses, servants had to be protected; and the source of their wealth had to be protected in the heart of the city and the heart of the country; the whole social order favourable to their hygienic idleness had to be protected against the shallow enviousness of unhygienic labour. It had to – and Mr Verloc would have rubbed his hands with satisfaction had he not been constitutionally averse from every superfluous exertion. His idleness was not hygienic, but it suited him very well. He was in a manner devoted to it with a sort of inert fanaticism, or perhaps rather with a fanatical inertness. Born of industrious parents for a life of toil, he had embraced indolence from an impulse as profound as inexplicable and as imperious as the impulse which directs a man's preference for one particular woman in a given thousand. He was too lazy even for a mere demagogue, for a workman orator, for a leader of labour. It was too much trouble. He required a more perfect form of ease; or it might have been that he was the victim of a philosophical unbelief in the effectiveness of every human effort. Such a form of indolence requires, implies, a certain amount of intelligence. Mr Verloc was not devoid of intelligence – and at the notion of a menaced social order he would perhaps have winked to himself if there had not been an effort to make in that sign of scepticism. His big, prominent eyes were not well adapted to winking. They were rather of the sort that closes solemnly in slumber with majestic effect.

Undemonstrative and burly in a fat-pig style, Mr Verloc, without either rubbing his hands with satisfaction or winking sceptically at his thoughts, proceeded on his way. He trod the pavement heavily with his shiny boots, and his general get-up was that of a well-to-do mechanic in business for himself. He might have been anything from a picture-frame maker to a locksmith; an employer of labour in a small way. But there was also about him an indescribable air which no mechanic could have acquired in the practice of his handicraft however dishonestly exercised: the air common to men who live on the vices, the follies, or the baser fears of mankind; the air of moral nihilism common to keepers of gambling hells and disorderly houses; to private detectives and inquiry agents; to drink sellers and, I should say, to the sellers of invigorating electric belts and to the inventors of patent medicines. But of that last I am not sure, not having carried my investigations so far into the depths. For all I know, the expression of these last may be perfectly diabolic. I shouldn't be surprised. What I want to affirm is that Mr Verloc's expression was by no means diabolic.

Before reaching Knightsbridge, Mr Verloc took a turn to the left out of the busy main thoroughfare, uproarious with the traffic of swaying omnibuses and trotting vans, in the almost silent, swift flow of hansoms. Under his hat, worn with a slight backward tilt, his hair had been carefully brushed into respectful sleekness; for his business was with an embassy. And Mr Verloc, steady like a rock – a soft kind of rock – marched now along a street which could with every propriety be described as private. In its breadth, emptiness, and extent it had the majesty of inorganic nature, of matter that never dies. The only reminder of mortality was a doctor's brougham arrested in august solitude close to the kerbstone. The polished knockers of the doors gleamed as far as the eye could reach, the clean windows shone with a dark opaque lustre. And all was still. But a milk cart rattled noisily across the distant perspective; a butcher boy, driving with the noble recklessness of a charioteer at Olympic Games, dashed round the corner sitting high above a pair of red wheels. A guilty-looking cat issuing from under the stones ran for a while in front of Mr Verloc, then dived into another basement; and a thick police constable, looking a stranger to every emotion, as if he, too, were part of inorganic nature, surging apparently out of a lamp-post, took not the slightest notice of Mr Verloc. With a turn to the left Mr Verloc pursued his way along a narrow street by the side of a yellow wall which, for some inscrutable reason, had No. 1 Chesham Square written on it in black letters. Chesham Square was at least sixty yards away, and Mr Verloc, cosmopolitan enough not to be deceived by London's topographical mysteries, held on steadily, without a sign of surprise or indignation. At last, with business-like persistency, he reached the Square, and made diagonally for the number 10. This belonged to an imposing carriage gate in a high, clean wall between two houses, of which one rationally enough bore the number 9 and the other was numbered 37; but the fact that this last belonged to Porthill Street, a street well known in the neighbourhood, was proclaimed by an inscription placed above the ground-floor windows by whatever highly efficient authority is charged with the duty of keeping track of London's strayed houses. Why powers are not asked of Parliament (a short Act would do) for compelling those edifices to return where they belong is one of the mysteries of municipal administration. Mr Verloc did not trouble his head about it, his mission in life being the protection of the social mechanism, not its perfectionment or even its criticism.

It was so early that the porter of the Embassy issued hurriedly out of his lodge still struggling with the left sleeve of his livery coat. His waistcoat was red, and he wore knee-breeches, but his aspect was flustered. Mr Verloc, aware of the rush on his flank, drove it off by simply holding out an envelope stamped with the arms of the Embassy, and passed on. He produced the same talisman also to the footman who opened the door, and stood back to let him enter the hall.

A clear fire burned in a tall fireplace, and an elderly man standing with his back to it, in evening dress and with a chain round his neck, glanced up from the newspaper he was holding spread out in both hands before his calm and severe face. He didn't move; but another lackey, in brown trousers and clawhammer coat edged with thin yellow cord, approaching Mr Verloc listened to the murmur of his name, and turning round on his heel in silence, began to walk, without looking back once. Mr Verloc, thus led along a ground-floor passage to the left of the great carpeted staircase, was suddenly motioned to enter a quite small room furnished with a heavy writing-table and a few chairs. The servant shut the door, and Mr Verloc remained alone. He did not take a seat. With his hat and stick held in one hand he glanced about, passing his other podgy hand over his uncovered sleek head.

Another door opened noiselessly, and Mr Verloc immobilizing his glance in that direction saw at first only black clothes. The bald top of a head, and a drooping dark grey whisker on each side of a pair of wrinkled hands. The person who had entered was holding a batch of papers before his eyes and walked up to the table with a rather mincing step, turning the papers over the while. Privy Councillor Wurmt, Chancelier d'Ambassade, was rather shortsighted. This meritorious official, laying the papers on the table, disclosed a face of pasty complexion and of melancholy ugliness surrounded by a lot of fine, long, dark grey hairs, barred heavily by thick and bushy eyebrows. He put on a black-framed pince-nez upon a blunt and shapeless nose, and seemed struck by Mr Verloc's appearance. Under the enormous eyebrows his weak eyes blinked pathetically through the glasses.

He made no sign of greeting; neither did Mr Verloc who certainly knew his place; but a subtle change about the general outlines of his shoulders and back suggested a slight bending of Mr Verloc's spine under the vast surface of his overcoat. The effect was of unobtrusive deference.

'I have here some of your reports,' said the bureaucrat in an unexpectedly soft and weary voice, and pressing the tip of his forefinger on the papers with force. He paused; and Mr Verloc, who had recognized his own handwriting very well, waited in an almost breathless silence. 'We are not very satisfied with the attitude of the police here,' the other continued, with every appearance of mental fatigue.

The shoulders of Mr Verloc, without actually moving, suggested a shrug. And for the first time since he left his home that morning his lips opened.

'Every country has its police,' he said, philosophically. But as the official of the Embassy went on blinking at him steadily he felt constrained to add: 'Allow me to observe that I have no means of action upon the police here.'

'What is desired,' said the man of papers, 'is the occurrence of something definite which should stimulate their vigilance. That is within your province – is it not so?'

Mr Verloc made no answer except by a sigh, which escaped him involuntarily, for instantly he tried to give his face a cheerful expression. The official blinked doubtfully, as if affected by the dim light of the room. He repeated vaguely:

'The vigilance of the police – and the severity of the magistrates. The general leniency of the judicial procedure here, and the utter absence of all repressive measures, are a scandal to Europe. What is wished for just now is the accentuation of the unrest – of the fermentation which undoubtedly exists –'

'Undoubtedly, undoubtedly,' broke in Mr Verloc in a deep, deferential bass of an oratorical quality, so utterly different from the tone in which he had spoken before that his interlocutor remained profoundly surprised. 'It exists to a dangerous degree. My reports for the last twelve months make it sufficiently clear.'

'Your reports for the last twelve months,' State Councillor Wurmt began in his gentle and dispassionate tone, 'have been read by me. I failed to discover why you wrote them at all.'

A sad silence reigned for a time. Mr Verloc seemed to have swallowed his tongue, and the other gazed at the papers on the table fixedly. At last he gave them a slight push.

'The state of affairs you expose there is assumed to exist as the first condition of your employment. What is required at present is not writing, but the bringing to light of a distinct, significant fact – I would almost say of an alarming fact.'

'I need not say that all my endeavours shall be directed to that end,' Mr Verloc said, with convinced modulations in his conversational husky tone. But the sense of being blinked at watchfully behind the blind glitter of these eyeglasses on the other side of the table disconcerted him. He stopped short with a gesture of absolute devotion. The useful hard-working, if obscure member of the Embassy had an air of being impressed by some newly born thought.

'You are very corpulent,' he said.

This observation, really of a psychological nature, and advanced with the modest hesitation of an officeman more familiar with ink and paper than with the requirements of active life, stung Mr Verloc in the manner of a rude personal remark. He stepped back a pace.

'Eh? What were you pleased to say?' he exclaimed, with husky resentment.

The Chancelier d'Ambassade, entrusted with the conduct of this interview, seemed to find it too much for him.

'I think,' he said, 'that you had better see Mr Vladimir. Yes, decidedly I think you ought to see Mr Vladimir. Be good enough to wait here,' he added, and went out with mincing steps.

At once Mr Verloc passed his hand over his hair. A slight perspiration had broken out of his forehead. He let the air escape from his pursed-up lips like a man blowing at a spoonful of hot soup. But when the servant in brown appeared at the door silently, Mr Verloc had not moved an inch from the place he had occupied throughout the interview. He had remained motionless, as if feeling himself surrounded by pitfalls.

He walked along a passage lighted by a lonely gas-jet, then up a flight of winding stairs, and through a glazed and cheerful corridor on the first floor. The footman threw open a door, and stood aside. The feet of Mr. Verloc felt a thick carpet. The room was large, with three windows; and a young man with a shaven, big face, sitting in a roomy armchair before a vast mahogany writing-table, said in French to the Chancelier d'Ambassade, who was going out with the papers in his hand:

'You are quite right, *mon cher*. He's fat – the animal.'

Mr Vladimir, First Secretary, had a drawing-room reputation as an agreeable and entertaining man. He was something of a favourite in society. His wit consisted in discovering droll connexions between incongruous ideas; and when talking in that strain he sat well forward on his seat, with his left hand raised, as if exhibiting his funny demonstrations between the thumb and forefinger, while his round and clean-shaven face wore an expression of merry perplexity.

But there was no trace of merriment or perplexity in the way he looked at Mr Verloc. Lying far back in the deep armchair, with squarely spread elbows, and throwing one leg over a thick knee, he had with his smooth and rosy countenance the air of a preternaturally thriving baby that will not stand nonsense from anybody.

'You understand French, I suppose?' he said.

Mr Verloc stated huskily that he did. His whole vast bulk had a forward inclination. He stood on the carpet in the middle of the room, clutching his hat and stick in one hand; the other hung lifelessly by his side. He muttered unobtrusively somewhere deep down in his throat something about having done his military service in the French artillery. At once, with contemptuous perversity, Mr Vladimir changed the language, and began to speak idiomatic English without the slightest trace of a foreign accent.

'Ah! Yes. Of course. Let's see. How much did you get for obtaining the design of the improved breech-block of their new field-gun?'

'Five years' rigorous confinement in a fortress,' Mr Verloc answered, unexpectedly, but without any sign of feeling.

'You got off easily,' was Mr Vladimir's comment. 'And, anyhow, it served you right for letting yourself get caught. What made you go in for that sort of thing – eh?'

Mr Verloc's husky conversational voice was heard speaking of youth, of a fatal infatuation for an unworthy –

'Aha! *Cherchez la femme*,' Mr Vladimir deigned to interrupt, unbending, but without affability; there was, on the contrary, a touch of grimness in his condescension. 'How long have you been employed by the Embassy here?' he asked.

'Ever since the time of the late Baron Stott-Wartenheim,' Mr Verloc answered in subdued tones, and protruding his lips sadly, in sign of sorrow for the deceased diplomat. The First Secretary observed this play of physiognomy steadily.

'Ah! ever since. . . . Well! What have you got to say for yourself? he asked, sharply.

Mr Verloc answered with some surprise that he was not aware of having anything special to say. He had been summoned by a letter – And he plunged his hand busily into the side pocket of his overcoat, but before the mocking, cynical watchfulness of Mr Vladimir, concluded to leave it there.

'Bah!' said the latter. 'What do you mean by getting out of condition like this? You haven't got even the physique of your profession. You – a member of a starving proletariat – never! You – a desperate socialist or anarchist – which is it?'

'Anarchist,' stated Mr Verloc in a deadened tone.

'Bosh!' went on Mr Vladimir, without raising his voice. 'You startled old Wurmt himself. You wouldn't deceive an idiot. They all are that by-the-by, but you seem to me simply impossible. So you began your connexion with us by stealing the French gun designs. And you got yourself caught. That must have been very disagreeable to our Government. You don't seem to be very smart.'

Mr Verloc tried to exculpate himself huskily.

'As I've had occasion to observe before, a fatal infatuation for an unworthy – '

Mr Vladimir raised a large, white, plump hand.

'Ah, yes. The unlucky attachment – of your youth. She got hold of the money, and then sold you to the police – eh?'

The doleful change in Mr Verloc's physiognomy, the momentary drooping of his whole person, confessed that such was the regrettable case. Mr Vladimir's hand clasped the ankle reposing on his knee. The sock was of dark blue silk.

'You see, that was not very clever of you. Perhaps you are too susceptible.'

Mr Verloc intimated in a throaty, veiled murmur that he was no longer young.

'Oh! That's a failing which age does not cure,' Mr Vladimir remarked, with sinister familiarity. 'But no! You are too fat for that. You could not have come to look like this if you had been at all susceptible. I'll tell you what I think is the matter: you are a lazy fellow. How long have you been drawing pay from this Embassy?'

'Eleven years,' was the answer, after a moment of sulky hesitation. 'I've been charged with several missions to London while His Excellency Baron Stott-Wartenheim was still Ambassador in Paris. Then by his Excellency's instructions I settled down in London. I am English.'

'You are! Are you? Eh?'

'A natural-born British subject,' Mr Verloc said, stolidly. 'But my father was French, and so – '

'Never mind explaining,' interrupted the other. 'I daresay you could have been legally a Marshal of France and a Member of Parliament in England – and then, indeed, you would have been of some use to our Embassy.'

This flight of fancy provoked something like a faint smile on Mr Verloc's face. Mr. Vladimir retained an imperturbable gravity.

'But, as I've said, you are a lazy fellow; you don't use your opportunities. In the time of Baron Stott-Wartenheim we had a lot of soft-headed people running this Embassy. They caused fellows of your sort to form a false conception of the nature of a secret service fund. It is my business to correct this misapprehension by telling you what the secret service is not. It is not a philanthropic institution. I've had you called here on purpose to tell you this.'

Mr Vladimir observed the forced expression of bewilderment on Verloc's face, and smiled sarcastically.

'I see that you understand me perfectly. I daresay you are intelligent enough for your work. What we want now is activity – activity.'

On repeating this last word Mr Vladimir laid a long white forefinger on the edge of the desk. Every trace of huskiness disappeared from Verloc's voice. The nape of his gross neck became crimson above the velvet collar of his overcoat. His lips quivered before they came widely open.

'If you'll only be good enough to look up my record,' he boomed out in his great, clear, oratorical bass, 'you'll see I gave a warning only three months ago on the occasion of the Grand Duke Romuald's visit to Paris, which was telegraphed from here to the French police, and –'

'Tut, tut!' broke out Mr Vladimir, with a frowning grimace. 'The French police had no use for your warning. Don't roar like this. What the devil do you mean?'

With a note of proud humility Mr Verloc apologized for forgetting himself. His voice, famous for years at open-air meetings and at workmen's assemblies in large halls, had contributed, he said, to his reputation of a good and trustworthy comrade. It was, therefore, a part of his usefulness. It had inspired confidence in his principles. 'I was always put up to speak by the leaders at a critical moment,' Mr Verloc declared, with obvious satisfaction. There was no uproar above which he could not make himself heard, he added; and suddenly he made a demonstration.

'Allow me,' he said. With lowered forehead, without looking up, swiftly and ponderously, he crossed the room to one of the french windows. As if giving way to an uncontrollable impulse, he opened it a little. Mr Vladimir, jumping up amazed from the depths of the armchair, looked over his shoulder; and below, across the courtyard of the Embassy, well beyond the open gate, could be seen the broad back of a policeman watching idly the gorgeous perambulator of a wealthy baby being wheeled in state across the Square.

'Constable!' said Mr Verloc, with no more effort than if he were whispering; and Mr Vladimir burst into a laugh on seeing the policeman spin round as if prodded by a sharp instrument. Mr Verloc shut the window quietly, and returned to the middle of the room.

'With a voice like that,' he said, putting on the husky conversational pedal, 'I was naturally trusted. And I knew what to say, too.'

Mr Vladimir, arranging his cravat, observed him in the glass over the mantelpiece.

'I daresay you have the social revolutionary jargon by heart well enough,' he said, contemptuously. '*Vox et. . . .* You haven't even studied Latin – have you?'

'No,' growled Mr Verloc. 'You did not expect me to know it. I belong to the million. Who knows Latin? Only a few hundred imbeciles who aren't fit to take care of themselves.'

For some thirty seconds longer Mr Vladimir studied in the mirror the fleshy profile, the gross bulk, of the man behind him. And at the same time he had the advantage of seeing his own face, clean-shaved and round, rosy about the gills, and with the thin, sensitive lips formed exactly for the utterance of those delicate witticisms which had made him such a favourite in the very highest society. Then he turned, and advanced into the room with such determination that the very ends of his quaintly old-fashioned bow necktie seemed to bristle with unspeakable menaces. The movement was so swift and fierce that Mr Verloc, casting an oblique glance, quailed inwardly. 'Aha! You dare be impudent,' Mr Vladimir began, with an amazingly guttural intonation not only utterly un-English, but absolutely un-European, and startling even to Mr Verloc's experience of cosmopolitan slums. 'You dare! Well, I am going to speak plain English to you. Voice won't do. We have no use for your voice. We don't want a voice. We want facts – startling facts – damn you,' he added, with a sort of ferocious discretion, right into Mr Verloc's face.

'Don't you try to come over me with your Hyperborean manners,' Mr Verloc defended himself, huskily, looking at the carpet. At this his interlocutor, smiling mockingly above the bristling bow of his necktie, switched the conversation into French.

'You give yourself for an *agent provocateur*. The proper business of an *agent provocateur* is to provoke. As far as I can judge from your record kept here, you have done nothing to earn your money for the last three years.'

'Nothing!' exclaimed Verloc, stirring not a limb, and not raising his eyes, but with the note of sincere feeling in his tone. 'I have several times prevented what might have been – '

'There is a proverb in this country which says prevention is better than cure,' interrupted Mr Vladimir, throwing himself into the armchair. 'It is stupid in a general way. There is no end to prevention. But it is characteristic. They dislike finality in this country. Don't you be too English. And in this particular instance, don't be absurd. The evil is already here. We don't want prevention – we want cure.'

He paused, turned to the desk, and turning over some papers lying there, spoke in a changed, business-like tone, without looking at Mr Verloc.

'You know, of course, of the International Conference assembled in Milan?'

Mr Verloc intimated hoarsely that he was in the habit of reading the daily papers. To a further question his answer was that, of course, he understood what he read. At this Mr Vladimir, smiling faintly at the documents he was still scanning one after another, murmured 'As long as it is not written in Latin, I suppose.'

'Or Chinese,' added Mr Verloc, stolidly.

'H'm. Some of your revolutionary friends' effusions are written in a *charabia* every bit as incomprehensible as Chinese – ' Mr Vladimir let fall disdainfully a grey sheet of printed matter. 'What are all these leaflets headed F.P., with a hammer, pen, and torch crossed? What does it mean, this F.P.?'

Mr Verloc approached the imposing writing-table.

'The Future of the Proletariat. It's society,' he explained, standing ponderously by the side of the armchair, 'not anarchist in principle, but open to all shades of revolutionary opinion.'

'Are you in it?'

'One of the Vice-Presidents,' Mr Verloc breathed out heavily; and the First Secretary of the Embassy raised his head to look at him.

'Then you ought to be ashamed of yourself,' he said, incisively. 'Isn't your society capable of anything else but printing this prophetic bosh in blunt type on this filthy paper – eh? Why don't you do something? Look here. I've this matter in hand now, and I tell you plainly that you will have to earn your money. The good old Stott-Wartenheim times are over. No work, no pay.'

Mr Verloc felt a queer sensation of faintness in his stout legs. He stepped back one pace, and blew his nose loudly.

He was, in truth, startled and alarmed. The rusty London sunshine struggling clear of the London mist shed a lukewarm brightness into the First Secretary's private room: and in the silence Mr Verloc heard against a window-pane the faint buzzing of a fly – his first fly of the year – heralding better than any number of swallows the approach of spring. The useless fussing of that tiny, energetic organism affected unpleasantly this big man threatened in his indolence.

In the pause Mr Vladimir formulated in his mind a series of disparaging remarks concerning Mr Verloc's face and figure. The fellow was unexpectedly vulgar, heavy, and impudently unintelligent. He looked uncommonly like a master plumber come to present his bill. The First Secretary of the

Embassy, from his occasional excursions into the field of American humour, had formed a special notion of that class of mechanic as the embodiment of fraudulent laziness and incompetency.

This was then the famous and trusty secret agent, so secret that he was never designated otherwise but by the symbol △ in the late Baron Stott-Wartenheim's official, semi-official, and confidential correspondence; the celebrated agent △ whose warnings had the power to change the schemes and the dates of royal, imperial, grand-ducal journeys, and sometimes cause them to be put off altogether! This fellow! And Mr Vladimir indulged mentally in an enormous and derisive fit of merriment, partly at his own astonishment, which he judged naïve, but mostly at the expense of the universally regretted Baron Stott-Wartenheim. His late Excellency, whom the august favour of his Imperial master had imposed as Ambassador upon several reluctant Ministers of Foreign Affairs, had enjoyed in his life-time a fame for an owlish, pessimistic gullibility. His Excellency had the social revolution on the brain. He imagined himself to be a diplomatist set apart by a special dispensation to watch the end of diplomacy, and pretty nearly the end of the world, in a horrid, democratic upheaval. His prophetic and doleful dispatches had been for years the joke of Foreign Offices. He was said to have exclaimed on his deathbed (visited by his Imperial friend and master): 'Unhappy Europe! Thou shalt perish by the moral insanity of thy children!' He was fated to be the victim of the first humbugging rascal that came along, thought Mr Vladimir, smiling vaguely at Mr Verloc.

'You ought to venerate the memory of Baron Stott-Wartenheim,' he exclaimed, suddenly.

The lowered physiognomy of Mr Verloc expressed a sombre and weary annoyance.

'Permit me to observe to you,' he said, 'that I came here because I was summoned by a peremptory letter. I have been here only twice before in the last eleven years, and certainly never at eleven in the morning. It isn't very wise to call me up like this. There is just a chance of being seen. And that would be no joke for me.'

Mr Vladimir shrugged his shoulders.

'It would destroy my usefulness,' continued the other hotly.

'That's your affair,' murmured Mr Vladimir, with soft brutality. 'When you cease to be useful you shall cease to be employed. Yes. Right off. Cut short. You shall – ' Mr Vladimir, frowning, paused, at a loss for a sufficiently idiomatic expression, and instantly brightened up, with a grin of beautifully white teeth. 'You shall be chucked,' he brought out, ferociously.

Once more Mr Verloc had to react with all the force of his will against that sensation of faintness running down one's legs which once upon a time had inspired some poor devil with the felicitous expression: 'My heart went down into my boots.' Mr Verloc, aware of the sensation, raised his head bravely.

Mr Vladimir bore the look of heavy inquiry with perfect serenity.

'What we want is to administer a tonic to the Conference in Milan,' he said, airily. 'Its deliberations upon international action for the suppression of political crime don't seem to get anywhere. England lags. This country is absurd with its sentimental regard for individual liberty. It's intolerable to think that all your friends have got only to come over to – '

'In that way I have them all under my eye,' Mr Verloc interrupted, huskily.

'It would be much more to the point to have them all under lock and key. England must be brought into line. The imbecile bourgeoisie of this country make themselves the accomplices of the very people whose aim is to drive them out of their houses to starve in ditches. And they have the political power still, if they only had the sense to use it for their preservation. I suppose you agree that the middle classes are stupid?'

Mr Verloc agreed hoarsely.

'They are.'

'They have no imagination. They are blinded by an idiotic vanity. What they want just now is a jolly good scare. This is the psychological moment to set your friends to work. I have had you called here to develop to you my idea.'

And Mr Vladimir developed his idea from on high, with scorn and condescension, displaying at the same time an amount of ignorance as to the real aims, thoughts, and methods of the revolutionary world which filled the silent Mr Verloc with inward consternation. He confounded causes with effects more than was excusable; the most distinguished propagandists with impulsive bomb throwers; assumed organization where in the nature of things it could not exist; spoke of the social revolutionary party one moment as of a perfectly disciplined army, where the words of chiefs was supreme, and at another as if it had been the loosest association of desperate brigands that ever camped in a mountain gorge. Once Mr Verloc had opened his mouth for a protest, but the raising of a shapely, large white hand arrested him. Very soon he became too appalled to even try to protest. He listened in a stillness of dread which resembled the immobility of profound attention.

'A series of outrages,' Mr Vladimir continued, calmly, 'executed here in this country; not only *planned* here – that would not do – they would not mind. Your friends could set half the Continent on fire without influencing the public opinion here in favour of a universal repressive legislation. They will not look outside their backyard here.'

Mr Verloc cleared his throat, but his heart failed him, and he said nothing.

'These outrages need not be especially sanguinary,' Mr Vladimir went on, as if delivering a scientific lecture, 'but they must be sufficiently startling – effective. Let them be directed against buildings, for instance. What is the fetish of the hour that all the bourgeoisie recognize – eh, Mr Verloc?'

Mr Verloc opened his hands and shrugged his shoulders slightly.

'You are too lazy to think,' was Mr Vladimir's comment upon that gesture. 'Pay attention to what I say. The fetish of today is neither royalty nor religion. Therefore the palace and the church should be left alone. You understand what I mean, Mr Verloc?'

The dismay and the scorn of Mr Verloc found vent in an attempt at levity.

'Perfectly. But what of the Embassies? A series of attacks on the various Embassies,' he began; but he could not withstand the cold, watchful stare of the First Secretary.

'You can be facetious, I see,' the latter observed, carelessly. 'That's all right. It may enliven your oratory at socialistic congresses. But this room is no place for it. It would be infinitely safer for you to follow carefully what I am saying. As you are being called upon to furnish facts instead of cock-and-bull stories, you had better try to make your profit off what I am taking the trouble to explain to you. The sacrosanct fetish of today is science. Why don't you get some of your friends to go for that wooden-faced panjandrum – eh? Is it not part of these institutions which must be swept away before the F.P. comes along?'

Mr Verloc said nothing. He was afraid to open his lips lest a groan should escape him.

'This is what you should try for. An attempt upon a crowned head or on a president is sensational enough in a way, but not so much as it used to be. It has entered into the general conception of the existence of all chiefs of state. It's almost conventional – especially since so many presidents have been assassinated. Now let us take an outrage upon – say, a church. Horrible enough at first sight, no doubt, and yet not so effective as a person of an ordinary mind might think. No matter how revolutionary and anarchist in inception, there would be fools enough to give such an outrage the character of a religious manifestation. And that would detract from the especial alarming significance we wish to give to the act. A murderous attempt on a restaurant or a theatre would suffer in the same way from the suggestion of non-political passion; the exasperation of a hungry man, an act of social revenge. All this is used up; it is no longer instructive as an object lesson in revolutionary anarchism. Every newspaper has ready made phrases to explain such manifestations away. I am about to give you the philosophy of bomb throwing from my point of view; from the point of view you pretend to have been serving for the last eleven years. I will try not to talk above your head. The sensibilities of the class you are attacking are soon blunted. Property seems to them an indestructible thing. You can't count upon their emotions either of pity or fear for very long. A bomb outrage to have any influence on public opinion now must go beyond the intention of vengeance or terrorism. It must be purely destructive. It must be that, and only that, beyond the faintest suspicion of any other object. You anarchists should make it clear that you are perfectly determined to make a clean sweep of the whole social creation. But how to get that appallingly absurd notion into the heads of the middle classes so that there should be no mistake? That's the question. By directing your blows at something outside the ordinary passions of humanity is the answer. Of course, there is art. A bomb in the National Gallery would make some noise. But it would not be serious enough. Art has never been their fetish. It's like breaking a few back windows in a man's house; whereas, if you want to make him really sit up, you must try at least to raise the roof. There would be some screaming of course, but from whom? Artists – art critics and such like – people of no account. Nobody minds what they say. But there is learning – science. Any imbecile that has got an income believes in that. He does not know why, but he believes it matters somehow. It is the sacrosanct fetish. All the damned professors are radicals at heart. Let them know that their great panjandrum has got to go, too, to make room for the Future of the Proletariat. A howl from all these intellectual idiots is bound to help forward the labours of the Milan Conference. They will be writing to the papers. Their indignation would be above suspicion, no material interests being openly at stake, and it will alarm every selfishness of the class which should be impressed. They believe that in some mysterious way science is at the source of their material prosperity. They do. And the absurd ferocity of such a demonstration will affect them more profoundly than the mangling of a whole street – or theatre – full of their own kind. To that last they can always say: "Oh! it's mere class hate." But what is one to say to an act of destructive ferocity so absurd as to be incomprehensible, inexplicable, almost unthinkable; in fact, mad? Madness alone is truly terrifying, inasmuch as you cannot placate it either by threats, persuasion, or bribes. Moreover, I am a civilized man. I would never dream of directing you to organize a mere butchery, even if I expected the best results from it. But I wouldn't expect from a butchery the result I want. Murder is always with us. It is almost an institution. The demonstration must be against learning – science. But not every science will do. The attack must have all the shocking senselessness of gratuitous blasphemy. Since bombs are your means of expression, it would be really telling if one could throw a bomb into pure mathematics. But that is impossible. I have been trying to educate you; I have expounded to you the higher philosophy of your usefulness, and suggested to you some serviceable arguments. The practical application of my teaching interests *you* mostly. But from the moment I have undertaken to interview you I have also given some attention to the practical aspect of the question. What do you think of having a go at astronomy?'

For sometime already Mr Verloc's immobility by the side of the armchair resembled a state of collapsed coma – a sort of passive insensibility interrupted by slight convulsive starts, such as may be observed in the domestic dog having a nightmare on the hearthrug. And it was in an uneasy, doglike growl that he repeated the word:

'Astronomy.'

He had not recovered thoroughly as yet from the state of bewilderment brought about by the effort to follow Mr Vladimir's rapid, incisive utterance. It had overcome his power of assimilation. It had made him angry. This anger was complicated by incredulity. And suddenly it dawned upon him that all this was an elaborate joke. Mr. Vladimir exhibited his white teeth in a smile, with dimples on his round, full face posed with a complacent inclination above the bristling bow of his necktie. The favourite of intelligent society women had assumed his drawing-room attitude accompanying the delivery of delicate witticisms. Sitting well forward, his white hand upraised, he seemed to hold delicately between his thumb and forefinger the subtlety of his suggestion.

'There could be nothing better. Such an outrage combines the greatest possible regard for humanity with the most alarming display of ferocious imbecility. I defy the ingenuity of journalists to persuade their public that any given member of the proletariat can have a personal grievance against astronomy. Starvation itself could hardly be dragged in there – eh? And there are other advantages. The whole civilized world has heard of Greenwich. The very boot-blacks in the basement of Charing Cross Station knows something of it. See?'

The features of Mr Vladimir, so well known in the best society by their humorous urbanity, beamed with cynical self-satisfaction, which would have astonished the intelligent women his wit entertained so exquisitely. 'Yes,' he continued, with a contemptuous smile, 'the blowing up of the first meridian is bound to raise a howl of execration.'

'A difficult business,' Mr Verloc mumbled, feeling that this was the only safe thing to say.

'What is the matter? Haven't you the whole gang under your hand? The very pick of the basket? That old terrorist Yundt is here. I see him walking about Piccadilly in his green havelock almost every day. And Michaelis, the ticket-of-leave apostle – you don't mean to say you don't know where he is? Because if you don't, I can tell you,' Mr Vladimir went on menacingly. 'If you imagine that you are the only one in the secret fund list, you are mistaken.'

This perfectly gratuitous suggestion caused Mr Verloc to shuffle his feet slightly.

'And the whole Lausanne lot – eh? Haven't they been flocking over here at the first hint of the Milan Conference? This is an absurd country.'

'It will cost money,' Mr Verloc said, by a sort of instinct.

'That cock won't fight,' Mr Vladimir retorted, with an amazingly genuine English accent. 'You'll get your screw every month, and no more till something happens. And if nothing happens very soon you won't get even that. What's your ostensible occupation? What are you supposed to live by?'

'I keep a shop,' answered Mr Verloc.

'A shop? What sort of shop?'

'Stationery, newspapers. My wife – '

'Your what?' interrupted Mr Vladimir in his guttural Central Asian tones.

'My wife.' Mr Verloc raised his husky voice slightly. 'I am married.'

'That be damned for a yarn,' exclaimed the other in unfeigned astonishment. 'Married! And you a professed anarchist, too! What is this confounded nonsense? But I suppose it's merely a manner of speaking. Anarchists don't marry. It's well known. They can't. It would be apostasy.'

'My wife isn't one,' Mr Verloc mumbled, sulkily. 'Moreover, it's no concern of yours.'

'Oh, yes, it is,' snapped Mr Vladimir. 'I am beginning to be convinced that you are not at all the man for the work you've been employed on. Why, you must have discredited yourself completely in your own world by your marriage. Couldn't you have managed without? This is your virtuous attachment – eh? What with one sort of attachment and another you are doing away with your usefulness.'

Mr Verloc, puffing out his cheeks, let the air escape violently, and that was all. He had armed himself with patience. It was not to be tried much longer. The First Secretary became suddenly very curt, detached, final.

'You may go now,' he said. 'A dynamite outrage must be provoked. I give you a month. The sittings of the Conference are suspended. Before it reassembles again something must have happened here, or your connexion with us ceases.'

He changed the note once more with an unprincipled versatility.

'Think over my philosophy, Mr – Mr – Verloc,' he said, with a sort of chaffing condescension, waving his hand towards the door. 'Go for the first meridian. You don't know the middle classes as well as I do. Their sensibilities are jaded. The first meridian. Nothing better, and nothing easier, I should think.'

He had got up, and with his thin sensitive lips twitching humorously, watched in the glass over the mantelpiece Mr Verloc backing out of the room heavily, hat and stick in hand. The door closed.

The footman in trousers, appearing suddenly in the corridor, led Mr Verloc another way out and through a small door in the corner of the courtyard. The porter standing at the gate ignored his exit completely; and Mr Verloc retraced the path of his morning's pilgrimage as if in a dream – an angry dream. This detachment from the material world was so complete that, though the mortal envelope of Mr Verloc had not hastened unduly along the streets, that part of him to which it would be unwarrantably rude to refuse immortality, found itself at the shop door all at once, as borne from west to east on the wings of a great wind. He walked straight behind the counter, and sat down on a wooden chair that stood there. No one appeared to disturb his solitude. Stevie, put into a green baize apron, was now sweeping and dusting upstairs, intent and conscientious, as though he were playing at it; and Mrs Verloc, warned in the kitchen by the clatter of the cracked bell, had merely come to the glazed door of the parlour, and putting the curtain aside a little, had peered into the dim shop. Seeing her husband sitting there shadowy and bulky, with his hat tilted far back on his head, she had at once returned to her stove. An hour or more later she took the green baize apron off her brother Stevie, and instructed him to wash his hands and face in the peremptory tone she had used in that connexion for fifteen years or so – ever since she had, in fact, ceased to attend to the boy's hands and face herself. She spared presently a glance away from her dishing-up for the inspection of that face and those hands which Stevie, approaching the kitchen table, offered for her approval with an air of self-assurance hiding a perpetual residue of anxiety. Formerly the anger of the father was the supremely effective sanction of these rites, but Mr Verloc's placidity in domestic life would have made all mention of anger incredible – even to poor Stevie's nervousness. The theory was that Mr Verloc would have been inexpressibly pained and shocked by any deficiency of cleanliness at meal times. Winnie after the death of her father found considerable consolation in the feeling that she need no longer tremble for poor Stevie. She could not bear to see the boy hurt. It maddened her. As a little girl she had often faced with blazing eyes the irascible licensed victualler in defence of her brother. Nothing now in Mrs Verloc's appearance could lead one to suppose that she was capable of a passionate demonstration.

She finished her dishing-up. The table was laid in the parlour. Going to the foot of the stairs she screamed out 'Mother!' Then opening the glazed door leading to the shop, 'Adolf!' Mr Verloc had not changed his position;

he had not apparently stirred a limb for an hour and a half. He got up heavily, and came to his dinner in his overcoat and with his hat on, without uttering a word. His silence in itself had nothing startlingly unusual in this household, hidden in the shades of the sordid street seldom touched by the sun, behind the dim shop with its wares of disreputable rubbish. Only that day Mr Verloc's taciturnity was so obviously thoughtful that the two women were impressed by it. They sat silent themselves, keeping a watchful eye on poor Stevie, lest he should break out into one of his fits of loquacity. He faced Mr Verloc across the table, and remained very good and quiet, staring vacantly. The endeavour to keep him from making himself objectionable in any way to the master of the house put no inconsiderable anxiety into these two women's lives. 'That boy,' as they alluded to him softly between themselves, had been a source of that sort of anxiety almost from the very day of his birth. The late licensed victualler's humiliation at having such a very peculiar boy for a son manifested itself by a propensity to brutal treatment; for he was a person of fine sensibilities, and his sufferings as a man and a father were perfectly genuine. Afterwards Stevie had to be kept from making himself a nuisance to the single gentlemen lodgers, who are themselves a queer lot, and are easily aggrieved. And there was always the anxiety of his mere existence to face. Visions of a workhouse infirmary for her child had haunted the old woman in the basement breakfast-room of the decayed Belgravian house. 'If you had not found such a good husband, my dear,' she used to say to her daughter, 'I don't know what would have become of that poor boy.'

Mr Verloc extended as much recognition to Stevie as a man not particularly fond of animals may give to his wife's beloved cat; and this recognition, benevolent and perfunctory, was essentially of the same quality. Both women admitted to themselves that not much more could be reasonably expected. It was enough to earn for Mr Verloc the old woman's reverential gratitude. In the early days, made sceptical by the trials of friendless life, she used sometimes to ask anxiously: 'You don't think, my dear, that Mr Verloc is getting tired of seeing Stevie about?' To this Winnie replied habitually by a slight toss of her head. Once, however, she retorted, with a rather grim pertness: 'He'll have to get tired of me first.' A long silence ensued. The mother, with her feet propped up on a stool, seemed to be trying to get to the bottom of that answer, whose feminine profundity had struck her all of a heap. She had never really understood why Winnie had married Mr Verloc. It was very sensible of her, and evidently had turned out for the best, but her girl might have naturally hoped to find somebody of a more suitable age. There had been a steady young fellow, only son of a butcher in the next street, helping his father in business, with whom Winnie had been walking out with obvious gusto. He was dependent on his father, it is true; but the business was good, and his prospects excellent. He took her girl to the theatre on several evenings. Then just as she began to dread to hear of their engagement (for what could she have done with that big house alone, with Stevie on her hands), that romance came to an abrupt end, and Winnie went about looking very dull. But Mr Verloc, turning up providentially to occupy the first-floor front bedroom, there had been no more question of the young butcher. It was clearly providential.

CHAPTER 3

'. . . All idealization makes life poorer. To beautify it is to take away its character of complexity – it is to destroy it. Leave that to the moralists, my boy. History is made by men, but they do not make it in their heads. The ideas that are born in their consciousness play an insignificant part in the march of events. History is dominated and determined by the tool and the production – by the force of economic conditions. Capitalism has made socialism, and the laws made by the capitalist for the protection of property are responsible for anarchism. No one can tell what form the social organization may take in the future. Then why indulge in prophetic phantasies? At best they can only interpret the mind of the prophet, and can have no objective value. Leave that pastime to the moralists, my boy.'

Michaelis, the ticket-of-leave apostle, was speaking in an even voice, a voice that wheezed as if deadened and oppressed by the layer of fat on his chest. He had come out of a highly hygienic prison round like a tub, with an enormous stomach and distended cheeks of a pale, semi-transparent complexion, as though for fifteen years the servants of an outraged society had made a point of stuffing him with fattening foods in a damp and lightless cellar. And ever since he had never managed to get his weight down as much as an ounce.

It was said that for three seasons running a very wealthy old lady had sent him for a cure to Marienbad – where he was about to share the public curiosity once with a crowned head – but the police on that occasion ordered him to leave within twelve hours. His martyrdom was continued by forbidding him all access to the healing waters. But he was resigned now.

With his elbow presenting no appearance of a joint, but more like a bend in a dummy's limb, thrown over the back of a chair, he leaned forward slightly over his short and enormous thighs to spit into the grate.

'Yes! I had the time to think things out a little,' he added without emphasis. 'Society has given me plenty of time for meditation.'

On the other side of the fireplace, in the horse-hair armchair where Mrs Verloc's mother was generally privileged to sit, Karl Yundt giggled grimly, with a faint black grimace of a toothless mouth. The terrorist, as he called himself, was old and bald, with a narrow, snow-white wisp of a goatee hanging limply from his chin. An extraordinary expression of underhand malevolence survived in his extinguished eyes. When he rose painfully the thrusting forward of a skinny groping hand deformed by gouty swellings suggested the effort of a moribund murderer summoning all his remaining strength for a last stab. He leaned on a thick stick, which trembled under his other hand. 'I have always dreamed,' he mouthed, fiercely, 'of a band of men absolute in their resolve to discard all scruples in the choice of means, strong enough to give themselves frankly the name of destroyers, and free from the taint of that resigned pessimism which rots the world. No pity for anything on earth, including themselves, and death enlisted for good and all in the service of humanity – that's what I would have liked to see.'

His little bald head quivered, imparting a comical vibration to the wisp of white goatee. His enunciation would have been almost totally unintelligible to a stranger. His worn-out passion, resembling in its impotent fierceness the excitement of a senile sensualist, was badly served by a dried throat and toothless gums which seemed to catch the tip of his tongue. Mr Verloc, established in the corner of the sofa at the other end of the room, emitted two hearty grunts of assent.

The old terrorist turned slowly his head on his skinny neck from side to side.

'And I could never get as many as three such men together. So much for your rotten pessimism,' he snarled at Michaelis, who uncrossed his thick legs similar to bolsters, and slid his feet abruptly under his chair in sign of exasperation.

He a pessimist! Preposterous! He cried out that the charge was outrageous. He was so far from pessimism that he saw already the end of all private property coming along logically, unavoidably, by the mere development of its inherent viciousness. The possessors of property had not only to face the awakened proletariat, but they had also to fight amongst themselves. Yes. Struggle, warfare, was the condition of private ownership. It was fatal. Ah! he did not depend upon emotional excitement to keep up his belief, no declamations, no anger, no visions of blood-red flags waving, or metaphorical lurid suns of vengeance rising above the horizon of a doomed society. Not he! Cold reason, he boasted, was the basis of his optimism. Yes optimism –

His laborious wheezing stopped, then, after a gasp or two, he added:

'Don't you think that, if I had not been the optimist I am, I could not have found in fifteen years some means to cut my throat? And, in the last instance, there were always the walls of my cell to dash my head against.'

The shortness of breath took all fire, all animation out of his voice; his great, pale cheeks hung like filled pouches, motionless, without a quiver; but in his blue eyes, narrowed as if peering, there was the same look of confident shrewdness, a little crazy in its fixity, they must have had while the indomitable optimist sat thinking at night in his cell. Before him, Karl Yundt remained standing, one wing of his faded greenish havelock thrown back cavalierly over his shoulder. Seated in front of the fireplace, Comrade Ossipon, ex-medical student, the principal writer of the F.P. leaflets, stretched out his robust legs, keeping the soles of his boots turned up to the glow in the grate. A bush of crinkly yellow hair topped his red, freckled face, with a flattened nose and prominent mouth cast in the rough mould of the Negro type. His almond-shaped eyes leered languidly over the high cheek-bones. He wore a grey flannel shirt, the loose ends of a black silk tie hung down the buttoned breast of his serge coat; and his head resting on the back of his chair, his throat largely exposed, he raised to his lips a cigarette in a long wooden tube, puffing jets of smoke straight up at the ceiling.

Michaelis pursued his idea – *the* idea of his solitary reclusion – the thought vouchsafed to his captivity and growing like a faith revealed in visions. He talked to himself, indifferent to the sympathy or hostility of his hearers, indifferent indeed to their presence, from the habit he had acquired of thinking aloud hopefully in the solitude of the four whitewashed walls of his cell, in the sepulchral silence of the great blind pile of bricks near a river, sinister and ugly like a colossal mortuary for the socially drowned.

He was no good in discussion, not because any amount of argument could shake his faith, but because the mere fact of hearing another voice disconcerted him painfully, confusing his thoughts at once – these thoughts that for so many years, in a mental solitude more barren than a waterless desert, no living voice had ever combated, commented, or approved.

No one interrupted him now, and he made again the confession of his faith, mastering him irresistible and complete like an act of grace: the secret of fate discovered in the material side of life; the economic condition of the world responsible for the past and shaping the future; the source of all ideas, guiding the mental development of mankind and the very impulses of their passion –

A harsh laugh from Comrade Ossipon cut the tirade dead short in a sudden faltering of the tongue and a bewildered unsteadiness of the apostle's mildly exalted eyes. He closed them slowly for a moment, as if to collect his routed thoughts. A silence fell; but what with the two gas-jets over the table and the glowing grate the little parlour behind Mr Verloc's shop had become frightfully hot. Mr Verloc, getting off the sofa with ponderous reluctance, opened the door leading into the kitchen to get more air, and thus disclosed the innocent Stevie, seated very good and quiet at a deal table, drawing circles, circles; innumerable circles, concentric, eccentric; a coruscating whirl of circles that by their tangled multitude of repeated curves, uniformity of form, and confusion of intersecting lines suggested a rendering of cosmic chaos, the symbolism of a mad art attempting the inconceivable. The artist never turned his head; and in all his soul's application to the task his back quivered, his thin neck, sunk into a deep hollow at the base of the skull, seemed ready to snap.

Mr Verloc, after a grunt of disapproving surprise, returned to the sofa. Alexander Ossipon got up, tall in his threadbare blue serge suit under the low ceiling, shook off the stiffness of long immobility, and strolled away into the kitchen (down two steps) to look over Stevie's shoulder. He came back, pronouncing oracularly: 'Very good. Very characteristic, perfectly typical.'

'What's very good?' grunted, inquiringly, Mr Verloc, settled again in the corner of the sofa. The other explained his meaning negligently, with a shade of condescension and a toss of his head towards the kitchen:

'Typical of this form of degeneracy – these drawings, I mean.'

'You would call that lad a degenerate, would you?' mumbled Mr Verloc.

Comrade Alexander Ossipon – nicknamed the Doctor, ex-medical student without a degree; afterwards wandering lecturer to working-men's associations upon the socialistic aspects of hygiene; author of a popular quasi-medical study (in the form of a cheap pamphlet seized promptly by the police) entitled *The Corroding Vices of the Middle Classes*; special delegate of the more or less mysterious Red Committee, together with Karl Yundt and Michaelis for the work of literary propaganda – turned upon the obscure familiar of at least two Embassies that glance of insufferable, hopelessly dense sufficiency which nothing but the frequentation of science can give to the dullness of common mortals.

'That's what he may be called scientifically. Very good type, too, altogether, of that sort of degenerate. It's good enough to glance at the lobes of his ears. If you read Lombroso – '

Mr Verloc, moody and spread largely on the sofa, continued to look down the row of his waistcoat buttons; but his cheeks became tinged by a faint blush. Of late even the merest derivative of the word science (a term in itself inoffensive and of indefinite meaning) had the curious power of evoking a definitely offensive mental vision of Mr Vladimir, in his body as he lived, with an almost supernatural clearness. And this phenomenon deserving justly to be classed amongst the marvels of science, induced in Mr Verloc an emotional state of dread and exasperation tending to express itself in violent swearing. But he said nothing. It was Karl Yundt who was heard, implacable to his last breath.

'Lombroso is an ass.'

Comrade Ossipon met the shock of this blasphemy by an awful, vacant stare. And the other, his extinguished eyes without gleams blackening the deep shadows under the great, bony forehead, mumbled, catching the tip of his tongue between his lips at every second word as though he were chewing it angrily:

'Did you ever see such an idiot? For him the criminal is the prisoner. Simple, is it not? What about those who shut him up there – forced him in there? Exactly. Forced him in there. And what is crime? Does he know that, this imbecile who has made his way in this world of gorged fools by looking at the ears and teeth of a lot of poor, luckless devils? Teeth and ears mark the criminal? Do they? And what about the law that marks him still better – the pretty branding instrument invented by the overfed to protect themselves against the hungry? Red-hot applications on their vile skins – hey? Can't you smell and hear from here the thick hide of the people burn and sizzle? That's how criminals are made for your Lombrosos to write their silly stuff about.'

The knob of his stick and his legs shook together with passion, whilst the trunk, draped in the wings of the havelock, preserved his historic attitude of defiance. He seemed to sniff the tainted air of social cruelty, to strain his ear for its atrocious sounds. There was an extraordinary force of suggestion in this posturing. The all but moribund veteran of dynamite wars had been a great actor in his time – actor on platforms, in secret assemblies, in private interviews. The famous terrorist had never in his life raised personally as much as his little finger against the social edifice. He was no man of action; he was not even an orator of torrential eloquence, sweeping the masses along in the rushing noise and foam of a great enthusiasm. With a more subtle intention, he took the part of an insolent and venomous evoker of sinister impulses which lurk in the blind envy and exasperated vanity of ignorance, in the suffering and misery of poverty, in all the hopeful and noble illusions of righteous anger, pity, and revolt. The shadow of his evil gift clung to him yet like the smell of a deadly drug in an old vial of poison, emptied now, useless, ready to be thrown away upon the rubbish-heap of things that had served their time.

Michaelis, the ticket-of-leave apostle, smiled vaguely with his glued lips; his pasty moon face drooped under the weight of melancholy assent. He had been a prisoner himself. His own skin had sizzled under the red-hot brand, he murmured softly. But Comrade Ossipon, nicknamed the Doctor, had got over the shock by that time.

'You don't understand,' he began, disdainfully, but stopped short, intimidated by the dead blackness of the cavernous eyes in the face turned slowly towards him with a blind stare, as if guided only by the sound. He gave the discussion up, with a slight shrug of the shoulders.

Stevie, accustomed to move about disregarded, had got up from the kitchen table, carrying off his drawing to bed with him. He had reached the parlour door in time to receive in full the shock of Karl Yundt's eloquent imagery. The sheet of paper covered with circles dropped out of his fingers, and he remained staring at the old terrorist, as if rooted suddenly to the spot by his morbid horror and dread of physical pain. Stevie knew very well that hot iron applied to one's skin hurt very much. His scared eyes blazed with indignation: it would hurt terribly. His mouth dropped open.

Michaelis by staring unwinkingly at the fire had regained that sentiment of isolation necessary for the continuity of his thought. His optimism had begun to flow from his lips. He saw Capitalism doomed in its cradle, born with the poison of the principle of competition in its system. The great capitalists devouring the little capitalists, concentrating the power and the tools of production in great masses, perfecting industrial processes, and in the madness of self-aggrandizement only preparing, organizing, enriching, making ready the lawful inheritance of the suffering proletariat. Michaelis pronounced the great word 'Patience' – and his clear blue glance, raised to the low ceiling of Mr Verloc's parlour, had a character of seraphic trustfulness. In the doorway Stevie, calmed, seemed sunk in hebetude.

Comrade Ossipon's face twitched with exasperation.

'Then it's no use doing anything – no use whatever.'

'I don't say that,' protested Michaelis, gently. His vision of truth had grown so intense that the sound of a strange voice failed to rout it this time. He continued to look down at the red coals. Preparation for the future was necessary, and he was willing to admit that the great change would perhaps come in the upheaval of a revolution. But he argued that revolutionary propaganda was a delicate work of high conscience. It was the education of the masters of the world. It should be as careful as the education given to kings. He would have it advance its tenets cautiously, even timidly, in our ignorance of the effect that may be produced by any given economic change upon the happiness, the morals, the intellect, the history of mankind. For history is made with tools, not with ideas; and everything is changed by economic conditions – art, philosophy, love, virtue – truth itself!

The coals in the grate settled down with a slight crash; and Michaelis, the hermit of visions in the desert of a penitentiary, got up impetuously. Round like a distended balloon, he opened his short, thick arms, as if in a pathetically hopeless attempt to embrace and hug to his breast a self-regenerated universe. He gasped with ardour.

'The future is as certain as the past – slavery, feudalism, individualism, collectivism. This is the statement of a law, not an empty prophecy.'

The disdainful pout of Comrade Ossipon's thick lips accentuated the negro type of his face.

'Nonsense,' he said, calmly enough. 'There is no law and no certainty. The teaching propaganda be hanged. What the people knows does not matter, were its knowledge ever so accurate. The only thing that matters to us is the emotional state of the masses. Without emotion there is no action.'

He paused, then added with modest firmness:

'I am speaking now to you scientifically – scientifically – Eh? What did you say, Verloc?'

'Nothing,' growled from the sofa Mr Verloc, who, provoked by the abhorrent sound, had merely muttered a 'Damn.'

The venomous spluttering of the old terrorist without teeth was heard.

'Do you know how I would call the nature of the present economic conditions? I would call it cannibalistic. That's what it is! They are nourishing their greed on the quivering flesh and the warm blood of the people – nothing else.'

Stevie swallowed the terrifying statement with an audible gulp, and at once, as though it had been swift poison, sank limply in a sitting posture on the steps of the kitchen door.

Michaelis gave no signs of having heard anything. His lips seemed glued together for good; not a quiver passed over his heavy cheeks. With troubled eyes he looked for his round, hard hat, and put it on his round head. His round and obese body seemed to float low between the chairs under the sharp elbow of Karl Yundt. The old terrorist, raising an uncertain and clawlike hand, gave a swaggering tilt to a black felt sombrero shading the hollows and ridges of his wasted face. He got in motion slowly, striking the floor with his stick at every step. It was rather an affair to get him out of the house because, now and then, he would stop, as if to think, and did not offer to move again till impelled forward by Michaelis. The gentle apostle grasped his arm with brotherly care; and behind them, his hands in his pockets, the robust Ossipon yawned vaguely. A blue cap with a patent leather peak set well at the back of his yellow bush of hair gave him the aspect of a Norwegian sailor bored with the world after a thundering spree. Mr Verloc saw his guests off the premises, attending them bareheaded, his heavy overcoat hanging open, his eyes on the ground.

He closed the door behind their backs with restrained violence, turned the key, shot the bolt. He was not satisfied with his friends. In the light of Mr Vladimir's philosophy of bomb throwing they appeared hopelessly futile. The part of Mr Verloc in revolutionary politics having been to observe, he could not all at once, either in his own home or in larger assemblies, take the initiative of action. He had to be cautious. Moved by the just indignation of a man well over forty, menaced in what is dearest to him – his repose and his security – he asked himself scornfully what else could have been expected from such a lot, this Karl Yundt, this Michaelis – this Ossipon.

Pausing in his intention to turn off the gas burning in the middle of the shop, Mr Verloc descended into the abyss of moral reflections. With the insight of a kindred temperament he pronounced his verdict. A lazy lot – this Karl Yundt, nursed by a blear-eyed old woman, a woman he had years ago enticed away from a friend, and afterwards had tried more than once to shake off into the gutter. Jolly lucky for Yundt that she had persisted in coming up time after time, or else there would have been no one now to help him out of the bus by the Green Park railings, where that spectre took its constitutional crawl every fine morning. When that indomitable snarling old witch died the swaggering spectre would have to vanish, too – there would be an end to fiery Karl Yundt. And Mr Verloc's morality was offended also by the optimism of Michaelis, annexed by his wealthy old lady, who had taken lately to sending him to a cottage she had in the country. The ex-prisoner could moon about the shady lanes for days together in a delicious and humanitarian idleness. As to Ossipon, that beggar was sure to want for nothing as long as there were silly girls with savings-bank books in the world. And Mr Verloc, temperamentally identical with his associates, drew fine distinctions in his mind on the strength of insignificant differences. He drew them with a certain complacency, because the instinct of conventional respectability was strong within him, being only overcome by his dislike of all kinds of recognized labour – a temperamental defect which he shared with a large proportion of revolutionary reformers of a given social state. For obviously one does not revolt against the advantages and opportunities of that state, but against the price which must be paid for the same in the coin of accepted morality, self-restraint, and toil. The majority of revolutionists are the enemies of discipline and fatigue mostly. There are natures, too, to whose sense of justice the price exacted looms up monstrously enormous, odious, oppressive, worrying, humiliating, extortionate, intolerable. Those are the fanatics. The remaining portion of social rebels is accounted for by vanity, the mother of all noble and vile illusions, the companion of poets, reformers, charlatans, prophets, and incendiaries.

Lost for a whole minute in the abyss of meditation, Mr Verloc did not reach the depth of these abstract considerations. Perhaps he was not able. In any case he had not the time. He was pulled up painfully by the sudden recollection of Mr Vladimir, another of his associates, whom in virtue of subtle moral affinities he was capable of judging correctly. He considered him as dangerous. A shade of envy crept into his thoughts. Loafing was all very well for these fellows, who knew not Mr Vladimir, and had women to fall back upon; whereas he had a woman to provide for –

At this point, by a simple association of ideas, Mr Verloc was brought face to face with the necessity of going to bed some time or other that evening. Then why not go now – at once? He sighed. The necessity was not so normally pleasurable as it ought to have been for a man of his age and temperament. He dreaded the demon of sleeplessness, which he felt had marked him for its own. He raised his arm, and turned off the flaring gas-jet above his head.

A bright band of light fell through the parlour door into the part of the shop behind the counter. It enabled Mr Verloc to ascertain at a glance the number of silver coins in the till. These were but few; and for the first time since he opened his shop he took a commercial survey of its value. This survey was unfavourable. He had gone into trade for no commercial reasons. He had been guided in the selection of this peculiar line of business by an instinctive leaning towards shady transactions, where money is picked up easily. Moreover, it did not take him out of his own sphere – the sphere which is watched by the police. On the contrary, it gave him a publicly confessed standing in that sphere, and as Mr Verloc had unconfessed relations which made him familiar with yet careless of the police, there was a distinct advantage in such a situation. But as a means of livelihood it was by itself insufficient.

He took the cash-box out of the drawer, and turning to leave the shop, became aware that Stevie was still downstairs.

What on earth is he doing there? Mr Verloc asked himself. What's the meaning of these antics? He looked dubiously at his brother-in-law, but he did not ask him for information. Mr Verloc's intercourse with Stevie was limited to the casual mutter of a morning, after breakfast, 'My boots,' and even that was more a communication at large of a need than a direct order or request. Mr Verloc perceived with some surprise that he did not know really what to say to Stevie. He stood still in the middle of the parlour, and looked into the kitchen in silence. Nor yet did he know what would happen if he did say anything. And this appeared very queer to Mr Verloc in view of the fact, borne upon him suddenly, that he had to provide for this fellow, too. He had never given a moment's thought till then to that aspect of Stevie's existence.

Positively he did not know how to speak to the lad. He watched him gesticulating and murmuring in the kitchen. Stevie prowled round the table like an excited animal in a cage. A tentative 'Hadn't you better go to bed now?' produced no effect whatever; and Mr Verloc, abandoning the stony contemplation of his brother-in-law's behaviour, crossed the parlour wearily, cash-box in hand. The cause of the general lassitude he felt while climbing the stairs being purely mental, he became alarmed by its inexplicable character. He hoped he was not sickening for anything. He stopped on the dark landing to examine his sensations. But a slight and continuous sound of snoring pervading the obscurity interfered with their clearness. The sound came from his mother-in-law's room. Another one to provide for, he thought – and on this thought walked into the bedroom.

Mrs Verloc had fallen asleep with the lamp (no gas was laid upstairs) turned up full on the table by the side of the bed. The light thrown down by the shade fell dazzlingly on the white pillow sunk by the weight of her head reposing with closed eyes and dark hair done up in several plaits for the night. She woke up with the sound of her name in her ears, and saw her husband standing over her.

'Winnie! Winnie!'

At first she did not stir, lying very quiet and looking at the cash-box in Mr Verloc's hand. But when she understood that her brother was 'capering all over the place downstairs' she swung out in one sudden movement on to the edge of the bed. Her bare feet, as if poked through the bottom of an unadorned, sleeved calico sack buttoned tightly at neck and wrists, felt over the rug for the slippers while she looked upward into her husband's face.

'I don't know how to manage him,' Mr Verloc explained, peevishly. 'Won't do to leave him downstairs alone with the lights.'

She said nothing, glided across the room swiftly, and the door closed upon her white form.

Mr Verloc deposited the cash-box on the night table, and began the operation of undressing by flinging his overcoat on to a distant chair. His coat and waistcoat followed. He walked about the room in his stockinged feet, and his burly figure, with the hands worrying nervously at his throat, passed and repassed across the long strip of looking-glass in the door of his wife's wardrobe. Then after slipping his braces off his shoulders he pulled up violently the venetian blind, and leaned his forehead against the cold window-pane – a fragile film of glass stretched between him and the enormity of cold, black, wet, muddy, inhospitable accumulation of bricks, slates, and stones, things in themselves unlovely and unfriendly to man.

Mr Verloc felt the latent unfriendliness of all out of doors with a force approaching to positive bodily anguish. There is no occupation that fails a man more completely than that of a secret agent of police. It's like your horse suddenly falling dead under you in the midst of an uninhabited and thirsty plain. The comparison occurred to Mr Verloc because he had sat astride various army horses in his time, and had now the sensation of an incipient fall. The prospect was as black as the window-pane against which he was leaning his forehead. And suddenly the face of Mr Vladimir, clean-shaved and witty, appeared enhaloed in the glow of its rosy complexion like a sort of pink seal impressed on the fatal darkness.

This luminous and mutilated vision was so ghastly physically that Mr Verloc started away from the window, letting down the venetian blind with a great rattle. Discomposed and speechless with the apprehension of more such visions, he beheld his wife re-enter the room and get into bed in a calm, business-like manner which made him feel hopelessly lonely in the world. Mrs Verloc expressed her surprise at seeing him up yet.

'I don't feel very well,' he muttered, passing his hands over his moist brow.

'Giddiness?'

'Yes. Not at all well.'

Mrs Verloc, with all the placidity of an experienced wife, expressed a confident opinion as to the cause, and suggested the usual remedies; but her husband, rooted in the middle of the room, shook his lowered head sadly.

'You'll catch cold standing there,' she observed.

Mr Verloc made an effort, finished undressing, and got into bed. Down below in the quiet, narrow street measured footsteps approached the house, then died away, unhurried and firm, as if the passer-by had started to pace out all eternity, from gas-lamp to gas-lamp in a night without end; and the drowsy ticking of the old clock on the landing became distinctly audible in the bedroom.

Mrs Verloc, on her back, and staring at the ceiling, made a remark.

'Takings very small today.'

Mr Verloc, in the same position, cleared his throat as if for an important statement, but merely inquired:

'Did you turn off the gas downstairs?'

'Yes; I did,' answered Mrs Verloc, conscientiously. 'That poor boy is in a very excited state tonight,' she murmured, after a pause which lasted for three ticks of the clock.

Mr Verloc cared nothing for Stevie's excitement, but he felt horribly wakeful, and dreaded facing the darkness and silence that would follow the extinguishing of the lamp. This dread led him to make the remark that Stevie had disregarded his suggestion to go to bed. Mrs Verloc, falling into the trap, started to demonstrate at length to her husband that this was not 'impudence' of any sort, but simply 'excitement'. There was no young man of his age in London more willing and docile than Stephen, she affirmed; none more affectionate and ready to please, and even useful, as long as people did not upset his poor head. Mrs Verloc, turning towards her recumbent husband, raised herself on her elbow, and hung over him in her anxiety that he should believe Stevie to be a useful member of the family. That ardour of protecting compassion exalted morbidly in her childhood by the misery of another child tinged her sallow cheeks with a faint dusky blush, made her big eyes gleam under the dark lids. Mrs Verloc then looked younger; she looked as young as Winnie used to look, and much more animated than the Winnie of the Belgravian mansion days had ever allowed herself to appear to gentlemen lodgers. Mr Verloc's anxieties had prevented him from attaching any sense to what his wife was saying. It was as if her voice was talking on the other side of a very thick wall. It was her aspect that recalled him to himself.

He appreciated this woman, and the sentiment of this appreciation, stirred by a display of something resembling emotion, only added another pang to his mental anguish. When her voice ceased he moved uneasily, and said:

'I haven't been feeling well for the last few days.'

He might have meant this as an opening to a complete confidence; but Mrs Verloc laid her head on the pillow again, and staring upward, went on:

'That boy hears too much of what is talked about here. If I had known they were coming tonight I would have seen to it that he went to bed at the same time I did. He was out of his mind with something he overheard about eating people's flesh and drinking blood. What's the good of talking like that?'

There was a note of indignant scorn in her voice. Mr Verloc was fully responsive now.

'Ask Karl Yundt,' he growled, savagely.

Mrs Verloc, with great decision, pronounced Karl Yundt 'a disgusting old man'. She declared openly her affection for Michaelis. Of the robust Ossipon, in whose presence she always felt uneasy behind an attitude of stony reserve, she said nothing whatever. And continuing to talk of that brother, who had been for so many years an object of care and fears:

'He isn't fit to hear what's said here. He believes it's all true. He knows no better. He gets into his passions over it.'

Mr Verloc made no comment.

'He glared at me, as if he didn't know who I was, when I went downstairs. His heart was going like a hammer. He can't help being excitable. I woke mother up, and asked her to sit with him till he went to sleep. It isn't his fault. He's no trouble when he's left alone.'

Mr Verloc made no comment.

'I wish he had never been to school,' Mrs Verloc began again, brusquely. 'He's always taking away those newspapers from the window to read. He gets a red face poring over them. We don't get rid of a dozen numbers in a month. They only take up room in the front window. And Mr Ossipon brings every week a pile of these F.P. tracts to sell at a halfpenny each. I wouldn't give a halfpenny for the whole lot. It's silly reading – that's what it is. There's no sale for it. The other day Stevie got hold of one, and there was a story in it of a German soldier officer tearing half-off the ear of a recruit, and nothing was done to him for it. The brute! I couldn't do anything with Stevie that afternoon. The story was enough, too, to make one's blood boil. But what's the use of printing things like that? We aren't German slaves here, thank God. It's not our business – is it?'

Mr Verloc made no reply.

'I had to take the carving knife from the boy,' Mrs Verloc continued, a little sleepily now. 'He was shouting and stamping and sobbing. He can't stand the notion of any cruelty. He would have stuck that officer like a pig if he had seen him then. It's true, too! Some people don't deserve much mercy.' Mrs Verloc's voice ceased, and the expression of her motionless eyes became more and more contemplative and veiled during the long pause. 'Comfortable, dear?' she asked in a faint, far-away voice. 'Shall I put out the light now?'

The dreary conviction that there was no sleep for him held Mr Verloc mute and hopelessly inert in his fear of darkness. He made a great effort.

'Yes. Put it out,' he said at last in a hollow tone.

CHAPTER 4

Most of the thirty or so little tables covered by red cloths with a white design stood ranged at right angles to the deep brown wainscoting of the underground hall. Bronze chandeliers with many globes depended from the low, slightly vaulted ceiling, and the fresco paintings ran flat and dull all round the walls without windows, representing scenes of the chase and of outdoor revelry in medieval costumes. Varlets in green jerkins brandished hunting knives and raised on high tankards of foaming beer.

'Unless I am very much mistaken, you are the man who would know the inside of this confounded affair,' said the robust Ossipon, leaning over, his elbows far out on the table and his feet tucked back completely under his chair. His eyes stared with wild eagerness.

An upright semi-grand piano near the door, flanked by two palms in pots, executed suddenly all by itself a valse tune with aggressive virtuosity. The din it raised was deafening. When it ceased, as abruptly as it had started, the be-spectacled, dingy little man who faced Ossipon behind a heavy glass mug full of beer emitted calmly what had the sound of a general proposition.

'In principle what one of us may or may not know as to any given fact can't be a matter for inquiry to the others.'

'Certainly not,' Comrade Ossipon agreed in a quiet undertone. 'In principle.'

With his big florid face held between his hands he continued to stare hard, while the dingy little man in spectacles coolly took a drink of beer and stood the glass mug back on the table. His flat, large ears departed widely from the sides of his skull, which looked frail enough for Ossipon to crush between thumb and forefinger; the dome of the forehead seemed to rest on the rim of the spectacles; the flat cheeks, of a greasy, unhealthy complexion, were merely smudged by the miserable poverty of a thin dark whisker. The lamentable inferiority of the whole physique was made ludicrous by the supremely self-confident bearing of the individual. His speech was curt, and he had a particularly impressive manner of keeping silent.

Ossipon spoke again from between his hands in a mutter.

'Have you been out much today?'

'No. I stayed in bed all the morning,' answered the other. 'Why?'

'Oh! Nothing,' said Ossipon, gazing earnestly and quivering inwardly with the desire to find out something, but obviously intimidated by the little man's overwhelming air of unconcern. When talking with this comrade – which happened but rarely – the big Ossipon suffered from a sense of moral and even physical insignificance. However, he ventured another question. 'Did you walk down here?'

'No; omnibus,' the little man answered, readily enough. He lived far away in Islington, in a small house down a shabby street, littered with straw and dirty paper, where out of school hours a troop of assorted children ran and squabbled with a shrill, joyless, rowdy clamour. His single back room, remarkable for having an extremely large cupboard, he rented furnished from two elderly spinsters, dressmakers in a humble way with a clientele of servant girls mostly. He had a heavy padlock put on the cupboard, but otherwise he was a model lodger, giving no trouble, and requiring practically no attendance. His oddities were that he insisted on being present when his room was being swept, and that when he went out he locked his door, and took the key away with him.

Ossipon had a vision of these round black-rimmed spectacles progressing along the streets on the top of an omnibus, their self-confident glitter falling here and there on the walls of houses or lowered upon the heads of the unconscious stream of people on the pavements. The ghost of a sickly smile altered the set of Ossipon's thick lips at the thought of the walls nodding, of people running for life at the sight of those spectacles. If they had only known! What a panic! He murmured interrogatively: 'Been sitting long here?'

'An hour or more,' answered the other, negligently, and took a pull at the dark beer. All his movements – the way he grasped the mug, the act of drinking, the way he set the heavy glass down and folded his arms – had a firmness, an assured precision which made the big and muscular Ossipon, leaning forward with staring eyes and protruding lips, look the picture of eager indecision.

'An hour,' he said. 'Then it may be you haven't heard yet the news I've heard just now – in the street. Have you?'

The little man shook his head negatively the least bit. But as he gave no indication of curiosity Ossipon ventured to add that he had heard it just outside the place. A newspaper boy had yelled the thing under his very nose, and not being prepared for anything of that sort, he was very much startled and upset. He had to come in there with a dry mouth. 'I never thought of finding you here,' he added, murmuring steadily, with his elbows planted on the table.

'I come here sometimes,' said the other, preserving his provoking coolness of demeanour.

'It's wonderful that you of all people should have heard nothing of it,' the big Ossipon continued. His eyelids snapped nervously upon the shining eyes. 'You of all people,' he repeated, tentatively. This obvious restraint argued an incredible and inexplicable timidity of the big fellow before the calm little man, who again lifted the glass mug, drank, and put it down with brusque and assured movements. And that was all. Ossipon, after waiting for something, word or sign, that did not come, made an effort to assume a sort of indifference.

'Do you,' he said, deadening his voice still more, 'give your stuff to anybody who's up to asking you for it?'

'My absolute rule is never to refuse anybody – as long as I have a pinch by me,' answered the little man with decision.

'That's a principle?' commented Ossipon.

'It's a principle.'

'And you think it's sound?'

The large round spectacles, which gave a look of staring self-confidence to the sallow face, confronted Ossipon like sleepless, unwinking orbs flashing a cold fire.

'Perfectly. Always. Under every circumstance. What could stop me? Why should I not? Why should I think twice about it?'

Ossipon gasped, as it were, discreetly.

'Do you mean to say you would hand it over to a tec if one came to ask you for your wares?'

The other smiled faintly.

'Let them come and try it on, and you will see,' he said. 'They know me, but I know also every one of them. They won't come near me – not they.'

His thin, livid lips snapped together firmly. Ossipon began to argue.

'But they could send someone – rig a plant on you. Don't you see? Get the stuff from you in that way, and then arrest you with the proof in their hands.'

'Proof of what? Dealing in explosives without a licence perhaps.' This was meant for a contemptuous jeer, though the expression of the thin, sickly face remained unchanged, and the utterance was negligent. 'I don't think there's one of them anxious to make that arrest. I don't think they could get one of them to apply for a warrant. I mean one of the best. Not one.'

'Why?' Ossipon asked.

'Because they know very well I take care never to part with the last handful of my wares. I've it always by me.' He touched the breast of his coat lightly. 'In a thick glass flask,' he added.

'So I have been told,' said Ossipon, with a shade of wonder in his voice. 'But I didn't know if – '

'They know,' interrupted the little man, crisply, leaning against the straight chair back, which rose higher than his fragile head. 'I shall never be arrested. The game isn't good enough for any policeman of them all. To deal with a man like me you require, sheer, naked, inglorious heroism.'

Again his lips closed with a self-confident snap. Ossipon repressed a movement of impatience.

'Or recklessness – or simply ignorance,' he retorted. 'They've only to get somebody for the job who does not know you carry enough stuff in your pocket to blow yourself and everything within sixty yards of you to pieces.'

'I never affirmed I could not be eliminated,' rejoined the other. 'But that wouldn't be an arrest. Moreover, it's not so easy as it looks.'

'Bah!' Ossipon contradicted. 'Don't be too sure of that. What's to prevent half a dozen of them jumping upon you from behind in the street? With your arms pinned to your sides you could do nothing – could you?'

'Yes; I could. I am seldom out in the streets after dark,' said the little man, impassively, 'and never very late. I walk always with my right hand closed round the india-rubber ball which I have in my trouser pocket. The pressing of this ball actuates a detonator inside the flask I carry in my pocket. It's the principle of the pneumatic instantaneous shutter for a camera lens. The tube leads up – '

With a swift, disclosing gesture he gave Ossipon a glimpse of an india-rubber tube, resembling a slender brown worm, issuing from the armhole of his waistcoat and plunging into the inner breast pocket of his jacket. His clothes, of a nondescript brown mixture, were threadbare and marked with stains, dusty in the folds, with ragged button-holes. 'The detonator is partly mechanical, partly chemical,' he explained, with casual condescension.

'It is instantaneous, of course?' murmured Ossipon, with a slight shudder.

'Far from it,' confessed the other, with a reluctance which seemed to twist his mouth dolorously. 'A full twenty seconds must elapse from the moment I press the ball till the explosion takes place.'

'Phew!' whistled Ossipon, completely appalled. 'Twenty seconds! Horrors! You mean to say that you could face that? I should go crazy – '

'Wouldn't matter if you did. Of course, it's the weak point of this special system, which is only for my own use. The worst is that the manner of exploding is always the weak point with us. I am trying to invent a detonator that would adjust itself to all conditions of action, and even to unexpected changes of conditions. A variable and yet perfectly precise mechanism. A really intelligent detonator.'

'Twenty seconds,' muttered Ossipon again. 'Ough! And then – '

With a slight turn of the head the glitter of the spectacles seemed to gauge the size of the beer saloon in the basement of the renowned Silenus Restaurant.

'Nobody in this room could hope to escape,' was the verdict of that survey. 'Nor yet this couple going up the stairs now.'

The piano at the foot of the staircase clanged through a mazurka with brazen impetuosity, as though a vulgar and impudent ghost were showing off. The keys sank and rose mysteriously. Then all became still. For a moment Ossipon imagined the overlighted place changed into a dreadful black hole belching horrible fumes choked with ghastly rubbish of smashed brickwork and mutilated corpses. He had such a distinct perception of ruin and death that he shuddered again. The other observed, with an air of calm sufficiency:

'In the last instance it is character alone that makes for one's safety. There are very few people in the world whose character is as well established as mine.'

'I wonder how you managed it,' growled Ossipon.

'Force of personality,' said the other, without raising his voice; and coming from the mouth of that obviously miserable organism the assertion caused the robust Ossipon to bite his lower lip. 'Force of personality,' he repeated, with ostentatious calm.

'I have the means to make myself deadly, but that by itself, you understand, is absolutely nothing in the way of protection. What is effective is the belief those people have in my will to use the means. That's their impression. It is absolute. Therefore I am deadly.'

'There are individuals of character amongst that lot, too,' muttered Ossipon ominously.

'Possibly. But it is a matter of degree obviously, since, for instance, I am not impressed by them. Therefore they are inferior. They cannot be otherwise. Their character is built upon conventional morality. It leans on the social order. Mine stands free from everything artificial. They are bound in all sorts of conventions. They depend on life, which, in this connexion, is a historical fact surrounded by all sorts of restraints and considerations, a complex, organized fact open to attack at every point; whereas I depend on death, which knows no restraint and cannot be attacked. My superiority is evident.'

'This is a transcendental way of putting it,' said Ossipon, watching the cold glitter of the round spectacles. 'I've heard Karl Yundt say much the same thing not very long ago.'

'Karl Yundt,' mumbled the other, contemptuously, 'the delegate of the International Red Committee, has been a posturing shadow all his life. There are three of you delegates, aren't there? I won't define the other two, as you are one of them. But what you say means nothing. You are the worthy delegates for revolutionary propaganda, but the trouble is not only that you are as unable to think independently as any respectable grocer or journalist of them all, but that you have no character whatever.'

Ossipon could not restrain a start of indignation.

'But what do you want from us?' he exclaimed in a deadened voice. 'What is it you are after yourself?'

'A perfect detonator,' was the peremptory answer. 'What are you making that face for? You see, you can't even bear the mention of something conclusive.'

'I am not making a face,' growled the annoyed Ossipon, bearishly.

'You revolutionists', the other continued, with leisurely self-confidence, 'are the slaves of the social convention, which is afraid of you; slaves of it as much as the very police that stands up in the defence of that convention. Clearly you are, since you want to revolutionize it. It governs your thought, of course, and your action, too, and thus neither your thought nor your action can ever be conclusive.' He paused, tranquil, with the air of close, endless silence, then almost immediately went on: 'You are not a bit better than the forces arrayed against you – than the police, for instance. The other day I came suddenly upon Chief Inspector Heat at the corner of Tottenham Court Road. He looked at me very steadily. But I did not look at him. Why should I give him more than a glance? He was thinking of many things – of his superiors, of his reputation, of the law courts, of his salary, of newspapers – of a hundred things. But I was thinking of my perfect detonator only. He meant nothing to me. He was as insignificant as – I can't call to mind anything insignificant enough to compare him with – except Karl Yundt perhaps. Like to like. The terrorist and the policeman both come from the same basket. Revolution, legality – counter moves to the same game; forms of idleness at bottom identical. He plays his little game – so do you propagandists. But I don't play; I work fourteen hours a day, and go hungry sometimes. My experiments cost money now and again, and then I must do without food for a day or two. You're looking at my beer. Yes. I have had two glasses already, and shall have another presently. This is a little holiday, and I celebrate it alone. Why not? I've the grit to work alone, quite alone, absolutely alone. I've worked alone for years.'

Ossipon's face had turned dusky red.

'At the perfect detonator – eh?' he sneered, very low.

'Yes,' retorted the other. 'It is a good definition. You couldn't find anything half so precise to define the nature of your activity with all your committees and delegations. It is I who am the true propagandist.'

'We won't discuss that point,' said Ossipon, with an air of rising above personal considerations. 'I am afraid I'll have to spoil your holiday for you, though. There's a man blown up in Greenwich Park this morning.'

'How do you know?'

'They have been yelling the news in the streets since two o'clock. I bought the paper, and just ran in here. Then I saw you sitting at this table. I've got it in my pocket now.'

He pulled the newspaper out. It was a good-sized, rosy sheet, as if flushed by the warmth of its own convictions which were optimistic. He scanned the pages rapidly.

'Ah! Here it is. Bomb in Greenwich Park. There isn't much so far. Half past eleven. Foggy morning. Effects of explosion felt as far as Romney Road and Park Place. Enormous hole in the ground under a tree filled with smashed roots and broken branches. All round fragments of a man's body blown to pieces. That's all. The rest's mere newspaper gup. No doubt a wicked attempt to blow up the Observatory, they say. H'm. That's hardly credible.'

He looked at the paper for a while longer in silence then passed it to the other, who, after gazing abstractedly at the print, laid it down without comment.

It was Ossipon who spoke first – still resentful.

'The fragments of only *one* man, you note. *Ergo*: blew *himself* up. That spoils your day off for you – don't it? Were you expecting that sort of move? I hadn't the slightest idea – not the ghost of a notion of anything of the sort being planned to come off here – in this country. Under the present circumstances it's nothing short of criminal.'

The little man lifted his thin black eyebrows with dispassionate scorn.

'Criminal! What is that? What *is* crime? What can be the meaning of such an assertion?'

'How am I to express myself? One must use the current words,' said Ossipon, impatiently. 'The meaning of this assertion is that this business may affect our position very adversely in this country. Isn't that crime enough for you? I am convinced you have been giving away some of your stuff lately.'

Ossipon stared hard. The other, without flinching, lowered and raised his head slowly.

'You have!' burst out the editor of the F.P. leaflets in an intense whisper. 'No! And are you really handing it over at large like this, for the asking, to the first fool that comes along?'

'Just so! The condemned social order has not been built up on paper and ink, and I don't fancy that a combination of paper and ink will ever put an end to it, whatever you may think. Yes, I would give the stuff with both hands to every man, woman, or fool that likes to come along. I know what you are thinking about. But I am not taking my cue from the Red Committee. I would see you all hounded out of here, or arrested – or beheaded for that matter – without turning a hair. What happens to us as individuals is not of the least consequence.'

He spoke carelessly, without heat, almost without feeling, and Ossipon, secretly much affected, tried to copy this detachment.

'If the police here knew their business they would shoot you full of holes with revolvers, or else try to sand-bag you from behind in broad daylight.'

The little man seemed already to have considered that point of view in his dispassionate, self-confident manner.

'Yes,' he assented with the utmost readiness. 'But for that they would have to face their own institutions. Do you see? That requires uncommon grit. Grit of a special kind.'

Ossipon blinked.

'I fancy that's exactly what would happen to you if you were to set up your laboratory in the States. They don't stand on ceremony with their institutions there.'

'I am not likely to go and see. Otherwise your remark is just,' admitted the other. 'They have more character over there, and their character is essentially anarchistic. Fertile ground for us, the States – very good ground. The great Republic has the root of the destructive matter in her. The collective temperament is lawless. Excellent. They may shoot us down, but – '

'You are too transcendental for me,' growled Ossipon, with moody concern.

'Logical,' protested the other. 'There are several kinds of logic. This is the enlightened kind. America is all right. It is this country that is dangerous, with her idealistic conception of legality. The social spirit of this people is wrapped up in scrupulous prejudices, and that is fatal to our work. You talk of England being our only refuge! So much the worse. Capua! What do we want with refuges? Here you talk, print, plot, and do nothing. I daresay it's very convenient for such Karl Yundts.'

He shrugged his shoulders slightly, then added with the same leisurely assurance: 'To break up the superstition and worship of legality should be our aim. Nothing would please me more than to see Inspector Heat and his likes take to shooting us down in broad daylight with the approval of the public. Half our battle would be won then; the disintegration of the old morality would have set in in its very temple. That is what you ought to aim at. But you revolutionists will never understand that. You plan the future, you lose yourselves in reveries of economical systems derived from what is; whereas what's wanted is a clean sweep and a clear start for a new conception of life. That sort of future will take care of itself if you will only make room for it. Therefore I would shovel my stuff in heaps at the corners of the streets if I had enough for that; and as I haven't, I do my best by perfecting a really dependable detonator.'

Ossipon, who had been mentally swimming in deep waters, seized upon the last word as if it were a saving plank.

'Yes. Your detonators. I shouldn't wonder if it weren't one of your detonators that made a clean sweep of the man in the park.'

A shade of vexation darkened the determined, sallow face confronting Ossipon.

'My difficulty consists precisely in experimenting practically with the various kinds. They must be tried, after all. Besides – '

Ossipon interrupted.

'Who could that fellow be? I assure you that we in London had no knowledge – Couldn't you describe the person you gave the stuff to?'

The other turned his spectacles upon Ossipon like a pair of searchlights.

'Describe him,' he repeated, slowly. 'I don't think there can be the slightest objection now. I will describe him to you in one word – Verloc.'

Ossipon, whom curiosity had lifted a few inches off his seat, dropped back, as if hit in the face.

'Verloc! Impossible.'

The self-possessed little man nodded slightly once.

'Yes. He's the person. You can't say that in this case I was giving my stuff to the first fool that came along. He was a prominent member of the group as far as I understand.'

'Yes,' said Ossipon. 'Prominent. No, not exactly. He was the centre for general intelligence, and usually received comrades coming over here. More useful than important. Man of no ideas. Years ago he used to speak at meetings – in France, I believe. Not very well, though. He was trusted by such men as Latorre, Moser, and all that lot. The only talent he showed really was his ability to elude the attentions of the police somehow. Here, for instance, he did not seem to be looked after very closely. He was regularly married, you know. I suppose it's with her money that he started that shop. Seemed to make it pay, too.'

Ossipon paused abruptly, muttered to himself 'I wonder what that woman will do now?' and fell into thought.

The other waited with ostentatious indifference. His parentage was obscure, and he was generally known only by his nickname of Professor. His title to that designation consisted in his having been once assistant demonstrator in chemistry at some technical institute. He quarrelled with the authorities upon a question of unfair treatment. Afterwards he obtained a post in the laboratory of a manufactory of dyes. There, too, he had been treated with revolting injustice. His struggles, his privations, his hard work to raise himself in the social scale, had filled him with such an exalted conviction of his merits that it was extremely difficult for the world to treat him with justice – the standard of that notion depending so much upon the patience of the individual. The Professor had genius, but lacked the great social virtue of resignation.

'Intellectually a nonentity,' Ossipon pronounced aloud, abandoning suddenly the inward contemplation of Mrs Verloc's bereaved person and business. 'Quite an ordinary personality. You are wrong in not keeping more in touch with the comrades, Professor,' he added in a reproving tone. 'Did he say anything to you – give you some idea of his intentions? I hadn't seen him for a month. It seems impossible that he should be gone.'

'He told me it was going to be a demonstration against a building,' said the Professor. 'I had to know that much to prepare the missile. I pointed out to him that I had hardly a sufficient quantity for a completely destructive result, but he pressed me very earnestly to do my best. As he wanted something that could be carried openly in the hand, I proposed to make use of an old one-gallon copal varnish can I happened to have by me. He was pleased at the idea. It gave me some trouble, because I had to cut out the bottom first and solder it on again afterwards. When prepared for use, the can enclosed a wide-mouthed, well-corked jar of thick glass packed around with some wet clay and containing sixteen ounces of X2 green powder. The detonator was connected with the screw top of the can. It was ingenious – a combination of time and shock. I explained the system to him. It was a thin tube of tin enclosing – '

Ossipon's attention had wandered.

'What do you think has happened?' he interrupted.

'Can't tell. Screwed the top on tight, which would make the connexion, and then forgot the time. It was set for twenty minutes. On the other hand, the time contact being made, a sharp shock would bring about the explosion at once. He either ran the time too close, or simply let the thing fall. The contact was made all right – that's clear to me at any rate. The system's worked perfectly. And yet you would think that a common fool in a hurry would be much more likely to forget to make the contact altogether. I was worrying myself about that sort of failure mostly. But there are more kinds of fools than one can guard against. You can't expect a detonator to be absolutely foolproof.'

He beckoned to a waiter. Ossipon sat rigid, with the abstracted gaze of mental travail. After the man had gone away with the money he roused himself, with an air of profound dissatisfaction.

'It's extremely unpleasant for me,' he mused. 'Karl has been in bed with bronchitis for a week. There's an even chance that he will never get up again. Michaelis is luxuriating in the country somewhere. A fashionable publisher has offered him five hundred pounds for a book. It will be a ghastly failure. He has lost the habit of consecutive thinking in prison, you know.'

The Professor on his feet, now buttoning his coat, looked about him with perfect indifference.

'What are you going to do?' asked Ossipon, wearily. He dreaded the blame of the Central Red Committee, a body which had no permanent place of abode, and of whose membership he was not exactly informed. If this affair eventuated in the stoppage of the modest subsidy allotted to the publication of the F.P. pamphlets, then indeed he would have to regret Verloc's inexplicable folly.

'Solidarity with the extremest form of action is one thing, and silly recklessness is another,' he said, with a sort of moody brutality. 'I don't know what came to Verloc. There's some mystery there. However, he's gone. You may take it as you like, but under the circumstances the only policy for the militant revolutionary group is to disclaim all connexion with this damned freak of yours. How to make the disclaimer convincing enough is what bothers me.'

The little man on his feet, buttoned up and ready to go, was no taller than the seated Ossipon. He levelled his spectacles at the latter's face point-blank.

'You might ask the police for a testimonial of good conduct. They know where every one of you slept last night. Perhaps if you asked them they would consent to publish some sort of official statement.'

'No doubt they are aware well enough that we had nothing to do with this,' mumbled Ossipon, bitterly. 'What they will say is another thing.' He remained thoughtful, disregarding the short, owlish, shabby figure standing by his side. 'I must lay hands on Michaelis at once, and get him to speak from his heart at one of our gatherings. The public has a sort of sentimental regard for that fellow. His name is known. And I am in touch with a few reporters on the big dailies. What he would say would be utter bosh, but he has a turn of talk that makes it go down all the same.'

'Like treacle,' interjected the Professor, rather low, keeping an impassive expression.

The perplexed Ossipon went on communing with himself half audibly, after the manner of a man reflecting in perfect solitude.

'Confounded ass! To leave such an imbecile business on my hands. And I don't even know if – '

He sat with compressed lips. The idea of going for news straight to the shop lacked charm. His notion was that Verloc's shop might have been turned already into a police trap. They will be bound to make some arrests, he thought, with something resembling virtuous indignation, for the even tenor of his revolutionary life was menaced by no fault of his. And yet unless he went there he ran the risk of remaining in ignorance of what perhaps it would be very material for him to know. Then he reflected that, if the man in the park had been so very much blown to pieces as the evening papers said, he could not have been identified. And if so, the police could have no special reason for watching Verloc's shop more closely than any other place known to be frequented by marked anarchists – no more reason, in fact, than for watching the doors of the Silenus. There would be a lot of watching all round, no matter where he went. Still –

'I wonder what I had better do now?' he muttered, taking counsel with himself.

A rasping voice at his elbow said, with sedate scorn:

'Fasten yourself upon the woman for all she's worth.'

After uttering these words the Professor walked away from the table. Ossipon, whom that piece of insight had taken unawares, gave one ineffectual start, and remained still, with a helpless gaze, as though nailed fast to the seat of his chair. The lonely piano, without as much as a music stool to help it, struck a few chords courageously, and beginning a selection of national airs, played him out at last to the tune of 'The Blue Bells of Scotland'. The painfully detached notes grew faint behind his back while he went slowly upstairs, across the hall, and into the street.

In front of the great doorway a dismal row of newspaper sellers standing clear of the pavement dealt out their wares from the gutter. It was a raw, gloomy day of the early spring; and the grimy sky, the mud of the streets, the rags of the dirty men harmonized excellently with the eruption of the damp, rubbishy sheets of paper soiled with printers' ink. The posters, maculated with filth, garnished like tapestry the sweep of the kerbstone. The trade in afternoon papers was brisk, yet, in comparison with the swift, constant march of foot traffic, the effect was of indifference, of a disregarded distribution. Ossipon looked hurriedly both ways before stepping out into the cross-currents, but the Professor was already out of sight.

CHAPTER 5

The Professor had turned into a street to the left, and walked along, with his head carried rigidly erect, in a crowd whose every individual almost overtopped his stunted stature. It was vain to pretend to himself that he was not disappointed. But that was mere feeling; the stoicism of his thought could not be disturbed by this or any other failure. Next time, or the time after next, a telling stroke would be delivered – something really startling – a blow fit to open the first crack in the imposing front of the great edifice of legal conceptions sheltering the atrocious injustice of society. Of humble origin, and with an appearance really so mean as to stand in the way of his considerable natural abilities, his imagination had been fired early by the tales of men rising from the depths of poverty to positions of authority and affluence. The extreme, almost ascetic purity of his thought, combined with an astounding ignorance of worldly conditions, had set before him a goal of power and prestige to be attained without the medium of arts, graces, tact, wealth – by sheer weight of merit alone. On that view he considered himself entitled to undisputed success. His father, a delicate dark enthusiast with a sloping forehead, had been an itinerant and rousing preacher of some obscure but rigid Christian sect – a man supremely confident in the privileges of his righteousness. In the son, individualist by temperament, once the science of colleges had replaced thoroughly the faith of conventicles, this moral attitude translated itself into a frenzied puritanism of ambition. He nursed it as something secularly holy. To see it thwarted opened his eyes to the true nature of the world, whose morality was artificial, corrupt and blasphemous. The way of even the most justifiable revolutions is prepared by personal impulses disguised into creeds. The Professor's indignation found in itself a final cause that absolved him from the sin of turning to destruction as the agent of his ambition. To destroy public faith in legality was the imperfect formula of his pedantic fanaticism; but the subconscious conviction that the framework of an established social order cannot be effectually shattered except by some form of collective or individual violence was precise and correct. He was a moral agent – that was settled in his mind. By exercising his agency with ruthless defiance he procured for himself the appearances of power and personal prestige. That was undeniable to his vengeful bitterness. It pacified its unrest; and in their own way the most ardent of revolutionaries are perhaps doing no more but seeking for peace in common with the rest of mankind – the peace of soothed vanity, of satisfied appetites, or perhaps of appeased conscience.

Lost in the crowd, miserable and undersized, he meditated confidently on his power, keeping his hand in the left pocket of his trousers, grasping lightly the indiarubber ball, the supreme guarantee of his sinister freedom: but after a while he became disagreeably affected by the sight of the roadway thronged with vehicles and of the pavement crowded with men and women. He was in a long, straight street, peopled by a mere fraction of an immense multitude; but all round him, on and on, even to the limits of the horizon hidden by the enormous piles of bricks, he felt the mass of mankind mighty in its numbers. They swarmed numerous like locusts, industrious like ants, thoughtless like a natural force, pushing on blind and orderly and absorbed, impervious to sentiment, to logic, to terror, too, perhaps.

That was the form of doubt he feared most. Impervious to fear! Often while walking abroad, when he happened also to come out of himself, he had such moments of dreadful and sane mistrust of mankind. What if nothing could move them? Such moments come to all men whose ambition aims at a direct grasp upon humanity – to artists, politicians, thinkers, reformers, or saints. A despicable emotional state this, against which solitude fortifies a superior character; and with severe exultation the Professor thought of the refuge of his room, with its padlocked cupboard, lost in a wilderness of poor houses, the hermitage of the perfect anarchist. In order to reach sooner the point where he could take his omnibus, he turned brusquely out of the populous street into a narrow and dusky alley paved with flagstones. On one side the low brick houses had in their dusty windows the sightless, moribund look of incurable decay – empty shells awaiting demolition. From the other side life had not departed wholly as yet. Facing the only gas-lamp yawned the cavern of a second-hand-furniture dealer, where, deep in the gloom of a sort of narrow avenue winding through a bizarre forest of wardrobes, with an undergrowth tangle of table legs, a tall pier-glass glimmered like a pool of water in a wood. An unhappy, homeless couch, accompanied by two unrelated chairs, stood in the open. The only human being making use of the alley besides the Professor, coming stalwart and erect from the opposite direction, checked his swinging pace suddenly.

'Hallo!' he said, and stood a little on one side watchfully.

The Professor had already stopped, with a ready half turn which brought his shoulders very near the other wall. His right hand fell lightly on the back of the outcast couch, the left remained purposefully plunged deep in the trousers pocket, and the roundness of the heavy rimmed spectacles imparted an owlish character to his moody, unperturbed face.

It was like a meeting in a side corridor of a mansion full of life. The stalwart man was buttoned up in a dark overcoat, and carried an umbrella. His hat, tilted back, uncovered a good deal of forehead, which appeared very white in the dusk. In the dark patches of the orbits the eyeballs glimmered piercingly. Long, drooping moustaches, the colour of ripe corn, framed with their points the square block of his shaved chin.

'I am not looking for you,' he said, curtly.

The Professor did not stir an inch. The blended noises of the enormous town sank down to an inarticulate low murmur. Chief Inspector Heat of the Special Crime Department changed his tone.

'Not in a hurry to get home?' he asked, with mocking simplicity.

The unwholesome-looking little moral agent of destruction exulted silently in the possession of personal prestige, keeping in check this man armed with the defensive mandate of a menaced society. More fortunate than Caligula, who wished that the Roman Senate had only one head for the better satisfaction of his cruel lust, he beheld in that one man all the forces he had set at defiance: the force of law, property, oppression, and injustice. He beheld all his enemies and fearlessly confronted them all in a supreme satisfaction of his vanity. They stood perplexed before him as if before a dreadful portent. He gloated inwardly over the chance of this meeting affirming his superiority over all the multitude of mankind.

It was in reality a chance meeting. Chief Inspector Heat had had a disagreeably busy day since his department received the first telegram from Greenwich a little before eleven in the morning. First of all, the fact of the outrage being attempted less than a week after he had assured a high official that no outbreak of anarchist activity was to be apprehended was sufficiently annoying. If he ever thought himself safe in making a statement, it was then. He had made that statement with infinite satisfaction to himself, because it was clear that the high official desired greatly to hear that very thing. He had affirmed that nothing of the sort could even be thought of without the department being aware of it within twenty-four hours; and he had spoken thus in his consciousness of being the great expert of his department. He had gone even so far as to utter words which true wisdom would have kept back. But Chief Inspector Heat was not very wise – at least not truly so. True wisdom, which is not certain of anything in this world of contradictions, would have prevented him from attaining his present position. It would have alarmed his superiors, and done away with his chances of promotion. His promotion had been very rapid.

'There isn't one of them, sir, that we couldn't lay our hands on at any time of night and day. We know what each of them is doing hour by hour,' he had declared. And the high official had deigned to smile. This was so obviously the right thing to say for an officer of Chief Inspector Heat's reputation that it was perfectly delightful. The high official believed the declaration, which chimed in with his idea of the fitness of things. His wisdom was of an official kind, or else he might have reflected upon a matter not of theory but of experience that in the close-woven stuff of relations between the conspirator and police there occur unexpected solutions of continuity, sudden holes in space and time. A given anarchist may be watched inch by inch and minute by minute, but a moment always comes when somehow all sight and touch of him are lost for a few hours, during which something (generally an explosion) more or less deplorable does happen. But the high official, carried away by his sense of fitness of things, had smiled, and now the recollection of that smile was very annoying to Chief Inspector Heat, principal expert in anarchist procedure.

This was not the only circumstance whose recollection depressed the usual serenity of the eminent specialist. There was another dating back only to that very morning. The thought that when called urgently to his Assistant Commissioner's private room he had been unable to conceal his astonishment was distinctly vexing. His instinct of a successful man had taught him long ago that, as a general rule, a reputation is built on manner as much as on achievement. And he felt that his manner when confronted with the telegram had not been impressive. He had opened his eyes widely, and had exclaimed 'Impossible!' exposing himself thereby to the unanswerable retort of a finger-tip laid forcibly on the telegram which the Assistant Commissioner, after reading it aloud, had flung on the desk. To be crushed, as it were, under the tip of a forefinger was an unpleasant experience. Very damaging, too! Furthermore, Chief Inspector Heat was conscious of not having mended matters by allowing himself to express a conviction.

'One thing I can tell you at once: none of our lot had anything to do with this.'

He was strong in his integrity of a good detective, but he saw now that an impenetrably attentive reserve towards this incident would have served his reputation better. On the other hand, he admitted to himself that it was difficult to preserve one's reputation if rank outsiders were going to take a hand in the business. Outsiders are the bane of the police as of other professions. The tone of the Assistant Commissioner's remarks had been sour enough to set one's teeth on edge.

And since breakfast Chief Inspector Heat had not managed to get anything to eat.

Starting immediately to begin his investigation on the spot, he had swallowed a good deal of raw, unwholesome fog in the park. Then he had walked over to the hospital; and when the investigation in Greenwich was concluded at last he had lost his inclination for food. Not accustomed, as the doctors are, to examine closely the mangled remains of human beings, he had been shocked by the sight disclosed to his view when a waterproof sheet had been lifted off a table in a certain apartment of the hospital.

Another waterproof sheet was spread over that table in the manner of a tablecloth with the corners turned up over a sort of mound – a heap of rags, scorched and bloodstained, half concealing what might have been an accumulation of raw material for a cannibal feast. It required considerable firmness of mind not to recoil before that sight. Chief Inspector Heat, an efficient officer of his department, stood his ground, but for a whole minute he did not advance. A local constable in uniform cast a sidelong glance, and said with stolid simplicity:

'He's all there. Every bit of him. It was a job.'

He had been the first man on the spot after the explosion. He mentioned the fact again. He had seen something like a heavy flash of lightning in the fog. At that time he was standing at the door of the King William Street Lodge talking to the keeper. The concussion made him tingle all over. He ran between the trees towards the Observatory. 'As fast as my legs would carry me,' he repeated twice.

Chief Inspector Heat, bending forward over the table in a gingerly and horrified manner, let him run on. The hospital porter and another man turned down the corners of the cloth, and stepped aside. The Chief Inspector's eyes searched the gruesome detail of that heap of mixed things, which seemed to have been collected in shambles and rag shops.

'You used a shovel,' he remarked, observing a sprinkling of small gravel, tiny brown bits of bark, and particles of splintered wood as fine as needles.

'Had to in one place,' said the stolid constable. 'I sent a keeper to fetch a spade. When he heard me scraping the ground with it he leaned his forehead against a tree, and was as sick as a dog.'

The Chief Inspector, stooping guardedly over the table, fought down the unpleasant sensation in his throat. The shattering violence of destruction which had made of that body a heap of nameless fragments affected his feelings with a sense of ruthless cruelty, though his reason told him the effect must have been as swift as a flash of lightning. The man, whoever he was, had died instantaneously; and yet it seemed impossible to believe that a human body could have reached that state of disintegration without passing through the pangs of inconceivable agony. No physiologist, and still less of a metaphysician, Chief Inspector Heat rose by the force of sympathy, which is a form of fear, above the vulgar conception of time. Instantaneous! He remembered all he had ever read in popular publications of long and terrifying dreams dreamed in the instant of waking; of the whole past life lived with frightful intensity by a drowning man as his doomed head bobs up, screaming, for the last time. The inexplicable mysteries of conscious existence beset Chief Inspector Heat till he evolved a horrible notion that ages of atrocious pain and mental torture could be contained between two successive winks of an eye. And meantime the Chief Inspector went on peering at the table with a calm face and the slightly anxious attention of an indigent customer bending over what may be called the by-products of a butcher's shop with a view to an inexpensive Sunday dinner. All the time his trained faculties of an excellent investigator, who scorns no chance of information, followed the self-satisfied, disjointed loquacity of the constable.

'A fair-haired fellow,' the last observed in a placid tone, and paused. 'The old woman who spoke to the sergeant noticed a fair-haired fellow coming out of Maze Hill Station.' He paused. 'And he was a fair-haired fellow. She noticed two men coming out of the station after the uptrain had gone on,' he continued, slowly. 'She couldn't tell if they were together. She took no particular notice of the big one, but the other was a fair, slight chap, carrying a tin varnish can in one hand.' The constable ceased.

'Know the woman?' muttered the Chief Inspector, with his eyes fixed on the table, and a vague notion in his mind of an inquest to be held presently upon a person likely to remain for ever unknown.

'Yes. She's housekeeper to a retired publican, and attends the chapel in Park Place sometimes,' the constable uttered weightily, and paused, with another oblique glance at the table. Then suddenly: 'Well, here he is – all of him I could see. Fair. Slight – slight enough. Look at that foot there. I picked up the legs first, one after another. He was that scattered you didn't know where to begin.'

The constable paused; the least flicker of an innocent, self-laudatory smile invested his round face with an infantile expression.

'Stumbled,' he announced, positively. 'I stumbled once myself, and pitched on my head, too, while running up. Them roots do stick out all about the place. Stumbled against the root of a tree and fell, and that thing he was carrying must have gone off right under his chest, I expect.'

The echo of the words 'Persons unknown' repeating itself in his inner consciousness bothered the Chief Inspector considerably. He would have liked to trace this affair back to its mysterious origin for his own information. He was professionally curious. Before the public he would have liked to vindicate the efficiency of his department by establishing the identity of that man. He was a loyal servant. That, however, appeared impossible. The first term of the problem was unreadable – lacked all suggestion but that of atrocious cruelty.

Overcoming his physical repugnance, Chief Inspector Heat stretched out his hand without conviction for the salving of his conscience, and took up the least soiled of the rags. It was a narrow strip of velvet with a larger triangular piece of dark blue cloth hanging from it. He held it up to his eyes; and the police constable spoke.

'Velvet collar. Funny the old woman should have noticed the velvet collar. Dark blue overcoat with a velvet collar, she has told us. He was the chap she saw, and no mistake. And here he is all complete, velvet collar and all. I don't think I missed a single piece as big as a postage stamp.'

At this point the trained faculties of the Chief Inspector ceased to hear the voice of the constable. He moved to one of the windows for better light. His face, averted from the room, expressed a startled, intense interest while he examined closely the triangular piece of broadcloth. By a sudden jerk he detached it, and only after stuffing it into his pocket turned round to the room, and flung the velvet collar back on the table.

'Cover up,' he directed the attendants, curtly, without another look, and, saluted by the constable, carried off his spoil hastily.

A convenient train whirled him up to town, alone and pondering deeply, in a third-class compartment. That singed piece of cloth was incredibly valuable, and he could not defend himself from astonishment at the casual manner it had come into his possession. It was as if Fate had thrust that clue into his hands. And after the manner of the average man, whose ambition is to command events, he began to mistrust such a gratuitous and accidental success – just because it seemed forced upon him. The practical value of success depends not a little on the way you look at it. But Fate looks at nothing. It has no discretion. He no longer considered it eminently desirable all round to establish publicly the identity of the man who had blown himself up that morning with such horrible completeness. But he was not certain of the view his department would take. A department is to those it employs a complex personality with ideas and even fads of its own. It depends on the loyal devotion of its servants, and the devoted loyalty of trusted servants is associated with a certain amount of affectionate contempt, which keeps it sweet, as it were. By a benevolent provision of Nature no man is a hero to his valet, or else the heroes would have to brush their own clothes. Likewise no department appears perfectly wise to the intimacy of its workers. A department does not know so much as some of its servants. Being a dispassionate organism, it can never be perfectly informed. It would not be good for its efficiency to know too much. Chief Inspector Heat got out of the train in a state of thoughtfulness entirely untainted with disloyalty, but not quite free of that jealous mistrust which so often springs on the ground of perfect devotion, whether to women or to institutions.

It was in this mental disposition, physically very empty, but still nauseated by what he had seen, that he had come upon the Professor. Under these conditions which make for irascibility in a sound, normal man, this meeting was specially unwelcome to Chief Inspector Heat. He had not been thinking of the Professor; he had not been thinking of any individual anarchist at all. The complexion of that case had somehow forced upon him the general idea of the absurdity of things human, which in the abstract is sufficiently annoying to an unphilosophical temperament, and in concrete instances becomes exasperating beyond endurance. At the beginning of his career Chief Inspector Heat had been concerned with the more energetic forms of thieving. He had gained his spurs in that sphere, and naturally enough had kept for it, after his promotion to another department, a feeling not very far removed from affection. Thieving was not a sheer absurdity. It was a form of human industry, perverse indeed, but still an industry exercised in an industrious world; it was work undertaken for the same reason as the work in potteries, in coal mines, in fields, in tool-grinding shops. It was labour, whose practical difference from the other forms of labour consisted in the nature of its risk, which did not lie in ankylosis, or lead poisoning, or fire-damp, or gritty dust, but in what may be briefly defined in its own special phraseology as 'Seven years' hard'. Chief Inspector Heat was, of course, not insensible to the gravity of moral differences. But neither were the thieves he had been looking after. They submitted to the severe sanctions of a morality familiar to Chief Inspector Heat with a certain resignation. They were his fellow-citizens gone wrong because of imperfect education, Chief Inspector Heat believed; but allowing for that difference, he could understand the mind of a burglar, because, as a matter of fact, the mind and the instincts of a burglar are of the same kind as the mind and the instincts of a police officer. Both recognize the same conventions, and have a working knowledge of each other's methods and of the routine of their respective trades. They understand each other, which is advantageous to both, and establishes a sort of amenity in their relations. Products of the same machine, one classed as useful and the other as noxious, they take the machine for granted in different ways, but with a seriousness essentially the same. The mind of Chief Inspector Heat was inaccessible to ideas of revolt. But his thieves were not rebels. His bodily vigour, his cool, inflexible manner, his courage, and his fairness, had secured for him much respect and some adulation in the sphere of his early successes. He had felt himself revered and admired. And Chief Inspector Heat, arrested within six paces of the anarchist nicknamed the Professor, gave a thought of regret to the world of thieves – sane, without morbid ideals, working by routine, respectful of constituted authorities, free from all taint of hate and despair.

After paying this tribute to what is normal in the constitution of society (for the idea of thieving appeared to his instinct as normal as the idea of property), Chief Inspector Heat felt very angry with himself for having stopped, for having spoken, for having taken that way at all on the ground of it being a short cut from the station to the headquarters. And he spoke again in his big, authoritative voice, which, being moderated, had a threatening character.

'You are not wanted, I tell you,' he repeated.

The anarchist did not stir. An inward laugh of derision uncovered not only his teeth but his gums as well, shook him all over, without the slightest sound. Chief Inspector Heat was led to add, against his better judgement:

'Not yet. When I want you I will know where to find you.'

Those were perfectly proper words, within the tradition and suitable to his character of a police officer addressing one of his special flock. But the reception they got departed from tradition and propriety. It was outrageous. The stunted, weakly figure before him spoke at last.

'I've no doubt the papers would give you an obituary notice then. You know best what that would be worth to you. I should think you can imagine easily the sort of stuff that would be printed. But you may be exposed to the unpleasantness of being buried together with me, though I suppose your friends would make an effort to sort us out as much as possible.'

With all his healthy contempt for the spirit dictating such speeches, the atrocious allusiveness of the words had its effect on Chief Inspector Heat. He had too much insight, and too much exact information as well, to dismiss them as rot. The dusk of this narrow lane took on a sinister tint from the dark, frail little figure, its back to the wall, and speaking with a weak, self-confident voice. To the vigorous, tenacious vitality of the Chief Inspector, the physical wretchedness of that being, so obviously not fit to live, was ominous; for it seemed to him that if he had the misfortune to be such a miserable object he would not have cared how soon he died. Life had such a strong hold upon him that a fresh wave of nausea broke out in slight perspiration upon his brow. The murmur of town life, the subdued rumble of wheels in the two invisible streets to the right and left, came through the curve of the sordid lane to his ears with a precious familiarity and an appealing sweetness. He was human. But Chief Inspector Heat was also a man, and he could not let such words pass.

'All this is good to frighten children with,' he said. 'I'll have you yet.'

It was very well said, without scorn, with an almost austere quietness.

'Doubtless,' was the answer; 'but there's no time like the present, believe me. For a man of real convictions this is a fine opportunity of self-sacrifice. You may not find another so favourable, so humane. There isn't even a cat near us, and these condemned old houses would make a good heap of bricks where you stand. You'll never get me at so little cost to life and property, which you are paid to protect.'

'You don't know who you're speaking to,' said Chief Inspector Heat, firmly. 'If I were to lay my hands on you now I would be no better than yourself.'

'Ah! The game!'

'You may be sure our side will win in the end. It may yet be necessary to make people believe that some of you ought to be shot at sight like mad dogs. Then that will be the game. But I'll be damned if I know what yours is. I don't believe you know yourselves. You'll never get anything by it.'

'Meantime, it's you who get something from it – so far. And you get it easily, too. I won't speak of your salary, but haven't you made your name simply by not understanding what we are after?'

'What are you after, then?' asked Chief Inspector Heat, with scornful haste, like a man in a hurry who perceives he is wasting his time.

The perfect anarchist answered by a smile which did not part his thin, colourless lips; and the celebrated Chief Inspector felt a sense of superiority which induced him to raise a warning finger.

'Give it up – whatever it is,' he said in an admonishing tone, but not so kindly as if he were condescending to give good advice to a cracksman of repute. 'Give it up. You'll find we are too many for you.'

The fixed smile on the Professor's lips wavered, as if the mocking spirit within had lost its assurance. Chief Inspector Heat went on:

'Don't you believe me – eh? Well, you've only got to look about you. We are. And anyway, you're not doing it well. You're always making a mess of it. Why, if the thieves didn't know their work better they would starve.'

The hint of an invincible multitude behind that man's back roused a sombre indignation in the breast of the Professor. He smiled no longer his enigmatic and mocking smile. The resisting power of numbers, the unattackable stolidity of a great multitude, was the haunting fear of his sinister loneliness. His lips trembled for some time before he managed to say in a strangled voice:

'I am doing my work better than you're doing yours.'

'That'll do now,' interrupted Chief Inspector Heat, hurriedly; and the Professor laughed right out this time. While still laughing he moved on; but he did not laugh long. It was a sad-faced, miserable little man who emerged from the narrow passage into the bustle of the broad thoroughfare. He walked with the nerveless gait of a tramp going on, still going on, indifferent to rain or sun in a sinister detachment from the aspects of sky and earth. Chief Inspector Heat, on the other hand, after watching him for a while, stepped out with the purposeful briskness of a man disregarding indeed the inclemencies of the weather, but conscious of having an authorized mission on this earth and the moral support of his kind. All the inhabitants of the immense town, the population of the whole country, and even the teeming millions struggling upon the planet, were with him – down to the very thieves and mendicants. Yes, the thieves themselves were sure to be with him in his present work. The consciousness of universal support in his general activity heartened him to grapple with the particular problem.

The problem immediately before the Chief Inspector was that of managing the Assistant Commissioner of his department, his immediate superior. This is the perennial problem of trusty and loyal servants; anarchism gave it its particular complexion, but nothing more. Truth to say, Chief Inspector Heat thought but little of anarchism. He did not attach undue importance to it, and could never bring himself to consider it seriously. It had more the character of disorderly conduct; disorderly without the human excuse of drunkenness, which at any rate implies good feeling and an amiable leaning towards festivity. As criminals, anarchists were distinctly no class – no class at all. And recalling the Professor, Chief Inspector Heat, without checking his swinging pace, muttered through his teeth:

'Lunatic.'

Catching thieves was another matter altogether. It had that quality of seriousness belonging to every form of open sport where the best man wins under perfectly comprehensible rules. There were no rules for dealing with anarchists. And that was distasteful to the Chief Inspector. It was all foolishness, but that foolishness excited the public mind, affected persons in high places, and touched upon international relations. A hard, merciless contempt settled rigidly on the Chief Inspector's face as he walked on. His mind ran over all the anarchists of his flock. Not one of them had half the spunk of this or that burglar he had known. Not half – not one tenth.

At headquarters the Chief Inspector was admitted at once to the Assistant Commissioner's private room. He found him, pen in hand, bent over a great table bestrewn with papers, as if worshipping an enormous double inkstand of bronze and crystal. Speaking-tubes resembling snakes were tied by the heads to the back of the Assistant Commissioner's wooden armchair, and their gaping mouths seemed ready to bite his elbows. And in this attitude he raised only his eyes, whose lids were darker than his face and very much creased. The reports had come in: every anarchist had been exactly accounted for.

After saying this he lowered his eyes, signed rapidly two single sheets of paper, and only then laid down his pen, and sat well back, directing an inquiring gaze at his renowned subordinate. The Chief Inspector stood it well, deferential but inscrutable.

'I daresay you were right,' said the Assistant Commissioner, 'in telling me at first that the London anarchists had nothing to do with this. I quite appreciate the excellent watch kept on them by your men. On the other hand, this, for the public, does not amount to more than a confession of ignorance.'

The Assistant Commissioner's delivery was leisurely, as it were cautious. His thought seemed to rest poised on a word before passing to another, as though words had been the stepping-stones for his intellect picking its way across the waters of error. 'Unless you have brought something useful from Greenwich,' he added.

The Chief Inspector began at once the account of his investigation in a clear, matter-of-fact manner. His superior turning his chair a little, and crossing his thin legs, leaned sideways on his elbow, with one hand shading his eyes. His listening attitude had a sort of angular and sorrowful grace. Gleams as of highly burnished silver played on the sides of his ebony black head when he inclined it slowly at the end.

Chief Inspector Heat waited with the appearance of turning over in his mind all he had just said, but, as a matter of fact, considering the advisability of saying something more. The Assistant Commissioner cut his hesitation short.

'You believe there were two men?' he asked, without uncovering his eyes.

The Chief Inspector thought it more than probable. In his opinion, the two men had parted from each other within a hundred yards from the Observatory walls. He explained also how the other man could have got out of the park speedily without being observed. The fog, though not very dense, was in his favour. He seemed to have escorted the other to the spot, and then to have left him there to do the job single-handed. Taking the time those two were seen coming out of Maze Hill Station by the old woman, and the time when the explosion was heard, the Chief Inspector thought that the other man might have been actually at the Greenwich Park Station, ready to catch the next train up, at the moment his comrade was destroying himself so thoroughly.

'Very thoroughly – eh?' murmured the Assistant Commissioner from under the shadow of his hand.

The Chief Inspector in a few vigorous words described the aspect of the remains. 'The coroner's jury will have a treat,' he added, grimly.

The Assistant Commissioner uncovered his eyes.

'We shall have nothing to tell them,' he remarked, languidly.

He looked up, and for a time watched the markedly noncommittal attitude of his Chief Inspector. His nature was one that is not easily accessible to illusions. He knew that a department is at the mercy of its subordinate officers, who have their own conceptions of loyalty. His career had begun in a tropical colony. He had liked his work there. It was police work. He had been very successful in tracking and breaking up certain nefarious secret societies amongst the natives. Then he took his long leave, and got married rather impulsively. It was a good match from a worldly point of view, but his wife formed an unfavourable opinion of the colonial climate on hearsay evidence. On the other hand, she had influential connexions. It was an excellent match. But he did not like the work he had to do now. He felt himself dependent on too many subordinates and too many masters. The near presence of that strange emotional phenomenon called public opinion weighed upon his spirits, and alarmed him by its irrational nature. No doubt that from ignorance he exaggerated to himself its power for good and evil – especially for evil; and the rough east winds of the English spring (which agreed with his wife) augmented his general mistrust of men's motives and of the efficiency of their organization. The futility of office work especially appalled him on those days so trying to his sensitive liver.

He got up, unfolding himself to his full height, and with a heaviness of step remarkable in so slender a man, moved across the room to the window. The panes streamed with rain, and the short street he looked down into lay wet and empty, as if swept clear suddenly by a great flood. It was a very trying day, choked in raw fog to begin with, and now drowned in cold rain. The flickering, blurred flames of gas-lamps seemed to be dissolving in a watery atmosphere. And the lofty pretensions of a mankind oppressed by the miserable indignities of the weather appeared as a colossal and hopeless vanity deserving of scorn, wonder, and compassion.

'Horrible, horrible!' thought the Assistant Commissioner to himself, with his face near the window-pane. 'We have been having this sort of thing now for ten days; no, a fortnight – a fortnight.' He ceased to think completely for a time. That utter stillness of his brain lasted about three seconds. Then he said, perfunctorily: 'You have set inquiries on foot for tracing that other man up and down the line?'

He had no doubt that everything needful had been done. Chief Inspector Heat knew, of course, thoroughly the business of man-hunting. And these were the routine steps, too, that would be taken as a matter of course by the merest beginner. A few inquiries amongst the ticket collectors and the porters of the two small railway stations would give additional details as to the appearance of the two men; the inspection of the collected tickets would show at once where they came from that morning. It was elementary, and could not have been neglected. Accordingly, the Chief Inspector answered that all this had been done directly the old woman had come forward with her deposition. And he mentioned the name of a station. 'That's where they came from, sir,' he went on. 'The porter who took the tickets at Maze Hill remembers two chaps answering to the description passing the barrier. They seemed to him two respectable working-men of a superior sort – sign painters or house decorators. The big man got out of a third-class compartment backward, with a bright tin can in his hand. On the platform he gave it to carry to the fair young fellow who followed him. All this agrees exactly with what the old woman told the police sergeant in Greenwich.'

The Assistant Commissioner, still with his face turned to the window, expressed his doubt as to these two men having had anything to do with the outrage. All this theory rested upon the utterances of an old charwoman who had been nearly knocked down by a man in a hurry. Not a very substantial authority indeed, unless on the ground of sudden inspiration, which was hardly tenable.

'Frankly now, could she have been really inspired?' he queried, with grave irony, keeping his back to the room, as if entranced by the contemplation of the town's colossal forms half lost in the night. He did not even look round when he heard the mutter of the word 'Providential' from the principal subordinate of his department, whose name, printed sometimes in the papers, was familiar to the great public as that of one of its zealous and hard-working protectors. Chief Inspector Heat raised his voice a little.

'Strips and bits of bright tin were quite visible to me,' he said. 'That's a pretty good corroboration.'

'And these men came from that little country station,' the Assistant Commissioner mused aloud, wondering. He was told that such was the name on two tickets out of three given up out of that train at Maze Hill. The third person who got out was a hawker from Gravesend well known to the porters. The Chief Inspector imparted that information in a tone of finality with some ill humour, as loyal servants will do in the consciousness of their fidelity and with the sense of the value of their loyal exertions. And still the Assistant Commissioner did not turn away from the darkness outside, as vast as a sea.

'Two foreign anarchists coming from that place,' he said, apparently to the window-pane. 'It's rather unaccountable.'

'Yes, sir. But it would be still more unaccountable if that Michaelis weren't staying in a cottage in the neighbourhood.'

At the sound of that name, falling unexpectedly into this annoying affair, the Assistant Commissioner dismissed brusquely the vague remembrance of his daily whist party at his club. It was the most comforting habit of his life, in a mainly successful display of his skill without the assistance of any subordinate. He entered his club to play from five to seven, before going home to dinner, forgetting for those two hours whatever was distasteful in his life, as though the game were a beneficent drug for allaying the pangs of moral discontent. His partners were the gloomily humorous editor of a celebrated magazine; a silent, elderly barrister with malicious little eyes; and a highly martial, simple-minded old Colonel with nervous brown hands. They were his club acquaintances merely. He never met them elsewhere except at the card-table. But they all seemed to approach the game in the spirit of co-sufferers, as if it were indeed a drug against the secret ills of existence; and every day as the sun declined over the countless roofs of the town, a mellow, pleasurable impatience, resembling the impulse of a sure and profound friendship, lightened his professional labours. And now this pleasurable sensation went out of him with something resembling a physical shock, and was replaced by a special kind of interest in his work of social protection – an improper sort of interest, which may be defined best as a sudden and alert mistrust of the weapon in his hand.

CHAPTER 6

The lady patroness of Michaelis, the ticket-of-leave apostle of humanitarian hopes, was one of the most influential and distinguished connexions of the Assistant Commissioner's wife, whom she called Annie, and treated still rather as a not very wise and utterly inexperienced young girl. But she had consented to accept him on a friendly footing, which was by no means the case with all of his wife's influential connexions. Married young and splendidly at some remote epoch of the past, she had had for a time a close view of great affairs, and even of some great men. She herself was a great lady. Old now in the number of her years, she had that sort of exceptional temperament which defies time with scornful disregard, as if it were a rather vulgar convention submitted to by the mass of inferior mankind. Many other conventions easier to set aside, alas! failed to obtain her recognition, also on temperamental grounds – either because they bored her, or else because they stood in the way of her scorns and sympathies. Admiration was a sentiment unknown to her (it was one of the secret griefs of her most noble husband against her) – first, as always more or less tainted with mediocrity, and next as being in a way an admission of inferiority. And both were frankly inconceivable to her nature. To be fearlessly outspoken in her opinions came easily to her, since she judged solely from the standpoint of her social position. She was equally untrammelled in her actions; and as her tactfulness proceeded from genuine humanity, her bodily vigour remained remarkable and her superiority was serene and cordial, three generations had admired her infinitely, and the last she was likely to see had pronounced her a wonderful woman. Meantime, intelligent, with a sort of lofty simplicity, and curious at heart, but not like many women merely of social gossip, she amused her age by attracting within her ken through the power of her great, almost historical, social prestige everything that rose above the dead level of mankind, lawfully or unlawfully, by position, wit, audacity, fortune or misfortune. Royal Highnesses, artists, men of science, young statesmen, and charlatans of all ages and conditions, who, unsubstantial and light, bobbing up like corks, show best the direction of the surface currents, had been welcomed in that house, listened to, penetrated, understood, appraised, for her own edification. In her own words, she liked to watch what the world was coming to. And as she had a practical mind her judgement of men and things, though based on special prejudices, was seldom totally wrong, and almost never wrong-headed. Her drawing-room was probably the only place in the wide world where an Assistant Commissioner of Police could meet a convict liberated on a ticket-of-leave on other than professional and offical ground. Who had brought Michaelis there one afternoon the Assistant Commissioner did not remember very well. He had a notion it must have been a certain Member of Parliament of illustrious parentage and unconventional sympathies, which were the standing joke of the comic papers. The notabilities and even the simple notorieties of the day brought each other freely to that temple of an old woman's not ignoble curiosity. You never could guess whom you were likely to come upon being received in semi-privacy within the faded blue silk and gilt frame screen, making a cosy nook for a couch and a few armchairs in the great drawing-room, with its hum of voices and the groups of people seated or standing in the light of six tall windows.

Michaelis had been the object of a revulsion of popular sentiment, the same sentiment which years ago had applauded the ferocity of the life sentence passed upon him for complicity in a rather mad attempt to rescue some prisoners from a police van. The plan of the conspirators had been to shoot down the horses and overpower the escort. Unfortunately, one of the police constables got shot, too. He left a wife and three small children, and the death of that man aroused through the length and breadth of a realm for whose defence, welfare, and glory men die every day as matter of duty, an outburst of furious indignation, of a raging, implacable pity for the victim. Three ring-leaders got hanged. Michaelis, young and slim, locksmith by trade, and great frequenter of evening schools, did not even know that anybody had been killed, his part with a few others being to force open the door at the back of the special conveyance. When arrested he had a bunch of skeleton keys in one pocket, a heavy chisel in another, and a short crowbar in his hand: neither more nor less than a burglar. But no burglar would have received such a heavy sentence. The death of the constable had made him miserable at heart, but the failure of the plot also. He did not conceal either of these sentiments from his empanelled countrymen, and that sort of compunction appeared shockingly imperfect to the crammed court. The judge on passing sentence commented feelingly upon the depravity and callousness of the young prisoner.

That made the groundless fame of his condemnation; the fame of his release was made for him on no better grounds by people who wished to exploit the sentimental aspect of his imprisonment either for purposes of their own or for no intelligible purpose. He let them do so in the innocence of his heart and the simplicity of his mind. Nothing that happened to him individually had any importance. He was like those saintly men whose personality is lost in the contemplation of their faith. His ideas were not in the nature of convictions. They were inaccessible to reasoning. They formed in all their contradictions and obscurities an invincible and humanitarian creed, which he confessed rather than preached, with an obstinate gentleness, a smile of pacific assurance on his lips, and his candid blue eyes cast down because the sight of faces troubled his inspiration developed in solitude. In that characteristic attitude, pathetic in his grotesque and incurable obesity which he had to drag like a galley slave's bullet to the end of his days, the Assistant Commissioner of Police beheld the ticket-of-leave apostle filling a privileged armchair within the screen. He sat there by the head of the old lady's couch, mild-voiced and quiet, with no more self-consciousness than a very small child, and with something of a child's charm – the appealing charm of trustfulness. Confident of the future, whose secret ways had been revealed to him within the four walls of a well-known penitentiary, he had no reason to look with suspicion upon anybody. If he could not give the great and curious lady a very definite idea as to what the world was coming to, he had managed without effort to impress her by his unembittered faith, by the sterling quality of his optimism.

A certain simplicity of thought is common to serene souls at both ends of the social scale. The great lady was simple in her own way. His views and beliefs had nothing in them to shock or startle her, since she judged them from the standpoint of her lofty position. Indeed, her sympathies were easily accessible to a man of that sort. She was not an exploiting capitalist herself; she was, as it were, above the play of economic conditions. And she had a great capacity of pity for the more obvious forms of common human miseries, precisely because she was such a complete stranger to them that she had to translate her conception into terms of mental suffering before she could grasp the notion of their cruelty. The Assistant Commissioner remembered very well the conversation between these two. He had listened in silence. It was something as exciting in a way, and even touching in its foredoomed futility, as the efforts at moral intercourse between the inhabitants of remote planets. But this grotesque incarnation of humanitarian passion appealed, somehow, to one's imagination. At last Michaelis rose, and taking the great lady's extended hand, shook it, retained it for a moment in his great cushioned palm with unembarrassed friendliness, and turned upon the semi-private nook of the drawing-room his back, vast and square, and as if distended under the short tweed jacket. Glancing about in serene benevolence, he waddled along to the distant door between the knots of other visitors. The murmur of conversations paused on his passage. He smiled innocently at a tall, brilliant girl, whose eyes met his accidentally, and went out unconscious of the glances following him across the room. Michaelis's first appearance in the world was a success – a success of esteem unmarred by a single murmur of derision. The interrupted conversations were resumed in their proper tone, grave or light. Only a well-set-up, long-limbed, active-looking man of forty talking with two ladies near a window remarked aloud, with an unexpected depth of feeling: 'Eighteen stone, I should say, and not five foot six. Poor fellow! It's terrible – terrible.'

The lady of the house, gazing absently at the Assistant Commissioner, left alone with her on the private side of the screen, seemed to be rearranging her mental impressions behind her thoughtful immobility of a handsome old face. Men with grey moustaches and full, healthy, vaguely smiling countenances approached, circling round the screen; two mature women with a matronly air of gracious resolution; a clean-shaved individual with sunken cheeks, and dangling a gold-mounted eye-glass on a broad black ribbon with an old-world, dandified effect. A silence deferential, but full of reserves, reigned for a moment, and then the great lady exclaimed, not with resentment, but with a sort of protesting indignation:

'And that officially is supposed to be a revolutionist! What nonsense.' She looked hard at the Assistant Commissioner, who murmured, apologetically: 'Not a dangerous one perhaps.'

'Not dangerous – I should think not indeed. He is a mere believer. It's the temperament of a saint,' declared the great lady in a firm tone. 'And they kept him shut up for twenty years. One shudders at the stupidity of it. And now they have let him out everybody belonging to him is gone away somewhere or dead. His parents are dead; the girl he was to marry has died while he was in prison; he has lost the skill necessary for his manual occupation. He told me all this himself with the sweetest patience; but then, he said, he had had plenty of time to think out things for himself. A pretty compensation! If that's the stuff revolutionists are made of some of us may well go on their knees to them,' she continued in a slightly bantering voice, while the banal society smiles hardened on the worldly faces turned towards her with conventional deference. 'The poor creature is obviously no longer in a position to take care of himself. Somebody will have to look after him a little.'

'He should be recommended to follow a treatment of some sort,' the soldierly voice of the active-looking man was heard advising earnestly from a distance. He was in the pink of condition for his age, and even the texture of his long frock coat had a character of elastic soundness, as if it were a living tissue. 'The man is virtually a cripple,' he added with unmistakable feeling.

Other voices, as if glad of the opening, murmured hasty compassion. 'Quite startling,' 'Monstrous,' 'Most painful to see.' The lank man, with the eyeglass on a broad ribbon, pronounced mincingly the word 'Grotesque,' whose justness was appreciated by those standing near him. They smiled at each other.

The Assistant Commissioner had expressed no opinion either then or later, his position making it impossible for him to ventilate any independent view of a ticket-of-leave convict. But, in truth, he shared the view of his wife's friend and patron that Michaelis was a humanitarian sentimentalist, a little mad, but upon the whole incapable of hurting a fly intentionally. So when that name cropped up suddenly in this vexing bomb affair he realized all the danger of it for the ticket-of-leave apostle, and his mind reverted at once to the old lady's well-established infatuation. Her arbitrary kindness would not brook patiently any interference with Michaelis's freedom. It was a deep, calm, convinced infatuation. She had not only felt him to be inoffensive, but she had said so, which last by a confusion of her absolutist mind became a sort of incontrovertible demonstration. It was as if the monstrosity of the man, with his candid infant's eyes and a fat angelic smile, had fascinated her. She had come to believe almost his theory of the future, since it was not repugnant to her prejudices. She disliked the new element of plutocracy in the social compound, and industrialism as a method of human development appeared to her singularly repulsive in its mechanical and unfeeling character. The humanitarian hopes of the mild Michaelis tended not towards utter destruction, but merely towards the complete economic ruin of the system. And she did not really see where was the moral harm of it. It would do away with all the multitude of the parvenus, whom she disliked and mistrusted, not because they had arrived anywhere (she denied that), but because of their profound unintelligence of the world, which was the primary cause of the crudity of their perceptions and the aridity of their hearts. With the annihilation of all capital they would vanish, too; but universal ruin (providing it was universal, as it was revealed to Michaelis) would leave the social values untouched. The disappearance of the last piece of money could not affect people of position. She could not conceive how it could affect her position, for instance. She had developed these discoveries to the Assistant Commissioner with all the serene fearlessness of an old woman who had escaped the blight of indifference. He had made for himself the rule to receive everything of that sort in a silence which he took care from policy and inclination not to make offensive. He had an affection for the aged disciple of Michaelis, a complex sentiment depending a little on her prestige, on her personality, but most of all on the instinct of flattered gratitude. He felt himself really liked in her house. She was kindness personified. And she was practically wise, too, after the manner of experienced women. She made his married life much easier than it would have been without her generously full recognition of his rights as Annie's husband. Her influence upon his wife, a woman devoured by all sorts of small selfishnesses, small envies, small jealousies, was excellent. Unfortunately, both her kindness and her wisdom were of unreasonable complexion, distinctly feminine, and difficult to deal with. She remained a perfect woman all along her full tale of years, and not as some of them do become – a sort of slippery, pestilential old man in petticoats. And it was as of a woman that he thought of her – the specially choice incarnation of the feminine, wherein is recruited the tender, ingenuous, and fierce bodyguard for all sorts of men who talk under the influence of an emotion, true or fraudulent; for preachers, seers, prophets, or reformers.

Appreciating the distinguished and good friend of his wife, and himself, in that way, the Assistant Commissioner became alarmed at the convict Michaelis's possible fate. Once arrested on suspicion of being in some way, however remote, a party to this outrage, the man could hardly escape being sent back to finish his sentence at least. And that would kill him; he would never come out alive. The Assistant Commissioner made a reflection extremely unbecoming his official position without being really creditable to his humanity.

'If the fellow is laid hold of again,' he thought, 'she will never forgive me.'

The frankness of such a secretly outspoken thought could not go without some derisive self-criticism. No man engaged in a work he does not like can preserve many saving illusions about himself. The distaste, the absence of glamour, extend from the occupation to the personality. It is only when our appointed activities seem by a lucky accident to obey the particular eagerness of our temperament that we can taste the comfort of complete self-deception. The Assistant Commissioner did not like his work at home. The police work he had been engaged on in a distant part of the globe had the saving character of an irregular sort of warfare or at least the risk and excitement of open-air sport. His real abilities, which were mainly of an administrative order, were combined with an adventurous disposition. Chained to a desk in the thick of four millions of men, he considered himself the victim of an ironic fate – the same, no doubt, which had brought about his marriage with a woman exceptionally sensitive in the matter of colonial climate, besides other limitations testifying to the delicacy of her nature – and her tastes. Though he judged his alarm sardonically he did not dismiss the improper thought from his mind. The instinct of self-preservation was strong within him. On the contrary, he repeated it mentally with profane emphasis and a fuller precision: 'Damn it! If that infernal Heat has his way the fellow'll die in prison smothered in his fat, and she'll never forgive me.'

His black, narrow figure, with the white band of the collar under the silvery gleams on the close-cropped hair at the back of the head, remained motionless. The silence had lasted such a long time that Chief Inspector Heat ventured to clear his throat. This noise produced its effect. The zealous and intelligent officer was asked by his superior, whose back remained turned to him immovably:

'You connect Michaelis with this affair?'

Chief Inspector Heat was very positive, but cautious.

'Well, sir,' he said, 'we have enough to go upon. A man like that has no business to be at large, anyhow.'

'You will want some conclusive evidence,' came the observation in a murmur.

Chief Inspector Heat raised his eyebrows at the black, narrow back, which remained obstinately presented to his intelligence and his zeal.

'There will be no difficulty in getting up sufficient evidence against *him*,' he said, with virtuous complacency. 'You may trust me for that, sir,' he added, quite unnecessarily, out of the fullness of his heart; for it seemed to him an excellent thing to have that man in hand to be thrown down to the public should it think fit to roar with any special indignation in this case. It was impossible to say yet whether it would roar or not. That in the last instance depended, of course, on the newspaper press. But in any case, Chief Inspector Heat, purveyor of prisons by trade, and a man of legal instincts, did logically believe that incarceration was the proper fate for every declared enemy of the law. In the strength of that conviction he committed a fault of tact. He allowed himself a little conceited laugh, and repeated:

'Trust me for that, sir.'

This was too much for the forced calmness under which the Assistant Commissioner had for upwards of eighteen months concealed his irritation with the system and the subordinates of his office. A square peg forced into a round hole, he had felt like a daily outrage that long-established smooth roundness into which a man of less sharply angular shape would have fitted himself, with voluptuous acquiescence, after a shrug or two. What he resented most was just the necessity of taking so much on trust. At the little laugh of Chief Inspector Heat's he spun swiftly on his heels, as if whirled away from the window-pane by an electric shock. He caught on the latter's face not only the complacency proper to the occasion lurking under the moustache, but the vestiges of experimental watchfulness in the round eyes, which had been, no doubt, fastened on his back, and now met his glance for a second before the intent character of their stare had the time to change to a merely startled appearance.

The Assistant Commissioner of Police had really some qualifications for his post. Suddenly his suspicion was awakened. It is but fair to say that his suspicions of the police methods (unless the police happened to be a semi-military body organized by himself) was not difficult to arouse. If it ever slumbered from sheer weariness, it was but lightly: and his appreciation of Chief Inspector Heat's zeal and ability, moderate in itself, excluded all notion of moral confidence. 'He's up to something,' he exclaimed, mentally, and at once became angry. Crossing over to his desk with headlong strides, he sat down violently. 'Here I am stuck in a litter of paper,' he reflected, with unreasonable resentment, 'supposed to hold all the threads in my hands, and yet I can but hold what is put in my hand, and nothing else. And they can fasten the other ends of the threads where they please.'

He raised his head, and turned towards his subordinate a long, meagre face with the accentuated features of an energetic Don Quixote.

'Now what is it you've got up your sleeve?'

The other stared. He stared without winking in a perfect immobility of his round eyes, as he was used to stare at the various members of the criminal class when, after being duly cautioned, they made their statements in the tones of injured innocence, or false simplicity, or sullen resignation. But behind that professional and stony fixity there was some surprise, too, for in such a tone, combining nicely the note of contempt and impatience, Chief Inspector Heat, the right-hand man of the department, was not used to be addressed. He began in a procrastinating manner, like a man taken unawares by a new and unexpected experience.

'What I've got against that man Michaelis you mean, sir?'

The Assistant Commissioner watched the bullet head; the points of that Norse rover's moustache, falling below the line of the heavy jaw; the whole full and pale physiognomy, whose determined character was marred by too much flesh; at the cunning wrinkles radiating from the outer corners of the eyes – and in that purposeful contemplation of the valuable and trusted officer he drew a conviction so sudden that it moved him like an inspiration.

'I have reason to think that when you came into this room,' he said in measured tones, 'it was not Michaelis who was in your mind; not principally - perhaps not at all.'

'You have reason to think, sir?' muttered Chief Inspector Heat with every appearance of astonishment, which up to a certain point was genuine enough. He had discovered in this affair a delicate and perplexing side, forcing upon the discoverer a certain amount of insincerity – that sort of insincerity which, under the names of skill, prudence, discretion, turns up at one point or another in most human affairs. He felt at the moment like a tight-rope artist might feel if suddenly, in the middle of the performance, the manager of the Music Hall were to rush out of the proper managerial seclusion and begin to shake the rope. Indignation, the sense of moral insecurity engendered by such a treacherous proceeding joined to the immediate apprehension of a broken neck, would, in the colloquial phrase, put him in a state. And there would be also some scandalized concern for his art, too, since a man must identify himself with something more tangible than his own personality, and establish his pride somewhere, either in his social position, or in the quality of the work he is obliged to do, or simply in the superiority of the idleness he may be fortunate enough to enjoy.

'Yes,' said the Assistant Commissioner; 'I have. I do not mean to say that you have not thought of Michaelis at all. But you are giving the fact you've mentioned a prominence which strikes me as not quite candid, Inspector Heat. If that is really the track of discovery, why haven't you followed it up at once, either personally or by sending one of your men to that village?'

'Do you think, sir, I have failed in my duty there?' the Chief Inspector asked, in a tone which he sought to make simply reflective. Forced unexpectedly to concentrate his faculties upon the task of preserving his balance, he had seized upon that point, and exposed himself to a rebuke; for the Assistant Commissioner, frowning slightly, observed that this was a very improper remark to make.

'But since you've made it,' he continued, coldly, 'I'll tell you that this is not my meaning.'

He paused, with a straight glance of his sunken eyes which was a full equivalent of the unspoken termination 'and you know it'. The head of the so-called Special Crimes Department debarred by his position from going out of doors personally in quest of secrets locked up in guilty breasts, had a propensity to exercise his considerable gifts for the detection of incriminating truth upon his own subordinates. That peculiar instinct could hardly be called a weakness. It was natural. He was a born detective. It had unconsciously governed his choice of a career, and if it ever failed him in life it was perhaps in the one exceptional circumstance of his marriage – which was also natural. It fed, since it could not roam abroad, upon the human material which was brought to it in its official seclusion. We can never cease to be ourselves.

His elbow on the desk, his thin legs crossed and nursing his cheek in the palm of his meagre hand, the Assistant Commissioner in charge of the Special Crimes branch was getting hold of the case with growing interest. His Chief Inspector, if not an absolutely worthy foeman of his penetration, was at any rate the most worthy of all within his reach. A mistrust of established reputations was strictly in character with the Assistant Commissioner's ability as detector. His memory evoked a certain old fat and wealthy native chief in the distant colony whom it was a tradition for the successive Colonial Governors to trust and make much of as a firm friend and supporter of the order and legality established by white men; whereas, when examined sceptically, he was found out to be principally his own good friend, and nobody else's. Not precisely a traitor, but still a man of many dangerous reservations in his fidelity, caused by a due regard for his own advantage, comfort, and safety. A fellow of some innocence in his naïve duplicity, but none the less dangerous. He took some finding out. He was physically a big man, too, and (allowing for the difference of colour, of course) Chief Inspector Heat's appearance recalled him to the memory of his superior. It was not the eyes nor yet the lips exactly. It was bizarre. But does not Alfred Wallace relate in his famous book on the Malay Archipelago how, amongst the Aru Islanders, he discovered in an old and naked savage with a sooty skin a peculiar resemblance to a dear friend at home?

For the first time since he took up his appointment the Assistant Commissioner felt as if he were going to do some real work for his salary. And that was a pleasurable sensation. 'I'll turn him inside out like an old glove,' thought the Assistant Commissioner, with his eyes resting pensively upon Chief Inspector Heat.

'No, that was not my thought,' he began again. 'There is no doubt about you knowing your business – no doubt at all; and that's precisely why I –' He stopped short, and changing his tone: 'What could you bring up against Michaelis of a definite nature? I mean apart from the fact that the two men under suspicion – you're certain there were two of them – came last from a railway station within three miles of the village where Michaelis is living now.'

'This by itself is enough for us to go upon, sir, with that sort of man,' said the Chief Inspector, with returning composure. The slight, approving movement of the Assistant Commissioner's head went far to pacify the resentful astonishment of the renowned officer. For Chief Inspector Heat was a kind man, an excellent husband, a devoted father; and the public and departmental confidence he enjoyed acting favourably upon an amiable nature, disposed him to feel friendly towards the successive Assistant Commissioners he had seen pass through that very room. There had been three in his time. The first one, a soldierly, abrupt, red-faced person, with white eyebrows and an explosive temper, could be managed with a silken thread. He left on reaching the age limit. The second, a perfect gentleman, knowing his own and everybody else's place to a nicety, on resigning to take up a higher appointment out of England got decorated for (really) Inspector Heat's services. To work with him had been a pride and a pleasure. The third, a bit of a dark horse from the first, was at the end of eighteen months something of a dark horse still to the department. Upon the whole Chief Inspector Heat believed him to be in the main harmless – odd-looking, but harmless. He was speaking now, and the Chief Inspector listened with outward deference (which means nothing, being a matter of duty) and inwardly with benevolent toleration.

'Michaelis reported himself before leaving London for the country?'

'Yes, sir. He did.'

'And what may he be doing there?' continued the Assistant Commissioner, who was perfectly informed on that point. Fitted with painful tightness into an old wooden armchair, before a worm-eaten oak table in an upstairs room of a four-roomed cottage with a roof of moss-grown tiles, Michaelis was writing night and day in a shaky, slanting hand that *Autobiography of a Prisoner* which was to be like a book of Revelation in the history of mankind. The conditions of confined space, seclusion, and solitude in a small four-roomed cottage were favourable to his inspiration. It was like being in prison, except that one was never disturbed for the odious purpose of taking exercise according to the tyrannical regulations of his old home in the penitentiary. He could not tell whether the sun still shone on the earth or not. The perspiration of the literary labour dropped from his brow. A delightful enthusiasm urged him on. It was the liberation of his inner life, the letting out of his soul into the wide world. And the zeal of his guileless vanity (first awakened by the offer of five hundred pounds from a publisher) seemed something predestined and holy.

'It would be, of course, most desirable to be informed exactly,' insisted the Assistant Commissioner, uncandidly.

Chief Inspector Heat, conscious of renewed irritation at this display of scrupulousness, said that the county police had been notified from the first of Michaelis's arrival, and that a full report could be obtained in a few hours. A wire to the superintendent –

Thus he spoke, rather slowly, while his mind seemed already to be weighing the consequences. A slight knitting of the brow was the outward sign of this. But he was interrupted by a question.

'You've sent that wire already?'

'No, sir,' he answered, as if surprised.

The Assistant Commissioner uncrossed his legs suddenly. The briskness of that movement contrasted with the casual way in which he threw out a suggestion.

'Would you think that Michaelis had anything to do with the preparation of that bomb, for instance?'

The Chief Inspector assumed a reflective manner.

'I wouldn't say so. There's no necessity to say anything at present. He associates with men who are classed as dangerous. He was made a delegate of the Red Committee less than a year after his release on licence. A sort of compliment, I suppose.'

And the Chief Inspector laughed a little angrily, a little scornfully. With a man of that sort scrupulousness was a misplaced and even an illegal sentiment. The celebrity bestowed upon Michaelis on his release two years ago by some emotional journalists in want of special copy had rankled ever since in his breast. It was perfectly legal to arrest that man on the barest suspicion. It was legal and expedient on the face of it. His two former chiefs would have seen the point, at once; whereas this one, without saying either yes or no, sat there, as if lost in a dream. Moreover, besides being legal and expedient, the arrest of Michaelis solved a little personal difficulty which worried Chief Inspector Heat somewhat. This difficulty had its bearing upon his reputation, upon his comfort, and even upon the efficient performance of his duties. For, if Michaelis no doubt knew something about this outrage, the Chief Inspector was fairly certain that he did not know too much. This was just as well. He knew much less – the Chief Inspector was positive – than certain other individuals he had in his mind, but whose arrest seemed to him inexpedient, besides being a more complicated matter, on account of the rules of the game. The rules of the game did not protect so much Michaelis, who was an ex-convict. It would be stupid not take advantage of legal facilities, and the journalists who had written him up with emotional gush would be ready to write him down with emotional indignation.

This prospect, viewed with confidence, had the attraction of a personal triumph for Chief Inspector Heat. And deep down in his blameless bosom of an average married citizen, almost unconscious but potent nevertheless, the dislike of being compelled by events to meddle with the desperate ferocity of the Professor had its say. This dislike had been strengthened by the chance meeting in the lane. The encounter did not leave behind with Chief Inspector Heat that satisfactory sense of superiority the members of the police force get from the unofficial but intimate side of their intercourse with the criminal classes, by which the vanity of power is soothed, and the vulgar love of domination over our fellow-creatures is flattered as worthily as it deserves.

The perfect anarchist was not recognized as a fellow-creature by Chief Inspector Heat. He was impossible – a mad dog to be left alone. Not that the Chief Inspector was afraid of him; on the contrary, he meant to have him some day. But not yet: he meant to get hold of him in his own time, properly and effectively, according to the rules of the game. The present was not the right time for attempting that feat, not the right time for many reasons, personal and of public service. This being the strong feeling of Inspector Heat, it appeared to him just and proper that this affair should be shunted off its obscure and inconvenient track, leading goodness knows where, into a quiet (and lawful) siding called Michaelis. And he repeated, as if reconsidering the suggestion conscientiously:

'The bomb. No, I would not say that exactly. We may never find that out. But it's clear that he is connected with this in some way, which we can find out without much trouble.'

His countenance had that look of grave, overbearing indifference once well known and much dreaded by the better sort of thieves. Chief Inspector Heat, though what is called a man, was not a smiling animal. But his inward state was that of satisfaction at the passively receptive attitude of the Assistant Commissioner, who murmured gently:

'And you really think that the investigation should be made in that direction?'

'I do, sir.'

'Quite convinced?'

'I am, sir. That's the true line for us to take.'

The Assistant Commissioner withdrew the support of his hand from his reclining head with a suddenness that, considering his languid attitude, seemed to menace his whole person with collapse. But, on the contrary, he sat up, extremely alert, behind the great writing-table on which his hand had fallen with the sound of a sharp blow.

'What I want to know is what put it out of your head till now.'

'Put it out of my head,' repeated the Chief Inspector very slowly.

'Yes. Till you were called into this room – you know.'

The Chief Inspector felt as if the air between his clothing and his skin had become unpleasantly hot. It was the sensation of an unprecedented and incredible experience.

'Of course,' he said, exaggerating the deliberation of his utterance to the utmost limits of possibility, 'if there is a reason, of which I know nothing, for not interfering with the convict Michaelis, perhaps it's just as well I didn't start the county police after him.'

This took such a long time to say that the unflagging attention of the Assistant Commissioner seemed a wonderful feat of endurance. His retort came without delay.

'No reason whatever that I know of. Come, Chief Inspector, this finessing with me is highly improper on your part – highly improper. And it's also unfair, you know. You shouldn't leave me to puzzle things out for myself like this. Really, I am surprised.'

He paused, then added smoothly: 'I need scarcely tell you that this conversation is altogether unofficial.'

These words were far from pacifying the Chief Inspector. The indignation of a betrayed tight-rope performer was strong within him. In his pride of a trusted servant he was affected by the assurance that the rope was not shaken for the purpose of breaking his neck, as by an exhibition of impudence. As if anybody were afraid! Assistant Commissioners come and go, but a valuable Chief Inspector is not an ephemeral office phenomenon. He was not afraid of getting a broken neck. To have his performance spoiled was more than enough to account for the glow of honest indignation. And as thought is no respecter of persons, the thought of Chief Inspector Heat took a threatening and prophetic shape. 'You, my boy,' he said to himself, keeping his round and habitually roving eyes fastened upon the Assistant Commissioner's face – 'you, my boy, you don't know your place, and your place won't know you very long either, I bet.'

As if in provoking answer to that thought, something like the ghost of an amiable smile passed on the lips of the Assistant Commissioner. His manner was easy and businesslike while he persisted in administering another shake to the tight rope.

'Let us come now to what you have discovered on the spot, Chief Inspector,' he said.

'A fool and his job are soon parted,' went on the train of prophetic thought in Chief Inspector Heat's head. But it was immediately followed by the reflection that a higher official, even when 'fired out' (this was the precise image), has still the time as he flies through the door to launch a nasty kick at the shin-bones of a subordinate. Without softening very much the basilisk nature of his stare, he said, impassively:

'We are coming to that part of my investigation, sir.'

'That's right. Well, what have you brought away from it?'

The Chief Inspector, who had made up his mind to jump off the rope, came to the ground with gloomy frankness.

'I've brought away an address,' he said, pulling out of his pocket without haste a singed rag of dark blue cloth. 'This belongs to the overcoat the fellow who got himself blown to pieces was wearing. Of course, the overcoat may not have been his, and may even have been stolen. But that's not at all probable if you look at this.'

The Chief Inspector, stepping up to the table, smoothed out carefully the rag of blue cloth. He had picked it up from the repulsive heap in the mortuary, because a tailor's name is found sometimes under the collar. It is not often of much use, but still – He only half expected to find anything useful, but certainly he did not expect to find – not under the collar at all, but stitched carefully on the under side of the lapel – a square piece of calico with an address written on it in marking ink.

The Chief Inspector removed his smoothing hand.

'I carried it off with me without anybody taking notice,' he said. 'I thought it best. It can always be produced if required.'

The Assistant Commissioner, rising a little in his chair, pulled the cloth over to his side of the table. He sat looking at it in silence. Only the number 32 and the name of Brett Street were written in marking ink on a piece of calico slightly larger than an ordinary cigarette paper. He was genuinely surprised.

'Can't understand why he should have gone about labelled like this,' he said, looking up at Chief Inspector Heat. 'It's a most extraordinary thing.'

'I met once in the smoking-room of a hotel an old gentleman who went about with his name and address sewn on in all his coats in case of an accident or sudden illness,' said the Chief Inspector. 'He professed to be eighty-four years old, but he didn't look his age. He told me he was also afraid of losing his memory suddenly, like those people he had been reading of in the papers.'

A question from the Assistant Commissioner, who wanted to know what was No. 32 Brett Street, interrupted that reminiscence abruptly. The Chief Inspector, driven down to the ground by unfair artifices, had elected to walk the path of unreserved openness. If he believed firmly that to know too much was not good for the department, the judicious holding back of knowledge was as far as his loyalty dared to go for the good of the service. If the Assistant Commissioner wanted to mismanage this affair nothing, of course, could prevent him. But, on his own part, he now saw no reason for a display of alacrity. So he answered concisely:

'It's a shop, sir.'

The Assistant Commissioner, with his eyes lowered on the rag of blue cloth, waited for more information. As that did not come he proceeded to obtain it by a series of questions propounded with gentle patience. Thus he acquired an idea of the nature of Mr Verloc's commerce, of his personal appearance, and heard at last his name. In a pause the Assistant Commissioner raised his eyes, and discovered some animation on the Chief Inspector's face. They looked at each other in silence.

'Of course,' said the latter, 'the department has no record of that man.'

'Did any of my predecessors have any knowledge of what you have told me now?' asked the Assistant Commissioner, putting his elbows on the table and raising his joined hands before his face, as if about to offer prayer, only that his eyes had not a pious expression.

'No, sir; certainly not. What would have been the object? That sort of man could never be produced publicly to any good purpose. It was sufficient for me to know who he was, and to make use of him in a way that could be used publicly.'

'And do you think that sort of private knowledge consistent with the official position you occupy?'

'Perfectly, sir. I think it's quite proper. I will take the liberty to tell you, sir, that it makes me what I am – and I am looked upon as a man who knows his work. It's a private affair of my own. A personal friend of mine in the French police gave me the hint that the fellow was an Embassy spy. Private friendship, private information, private use of it – that's how I look upon it.'

The Assistant Commissioner, after remarking to himself that the mental state of the renowned Chief Inspector seemed to affect the outline of his lower jaw, as if the lively sense of his high professional distinction had been located in that part of his anatomy, dismissed the point for the moment with a calm 'I see.' Then leaning his cheek on his joined hands:

'Well, then – speaking privately if you like – how long have you been in private touch with this Embassy spy?'

To this inquiry the private answer of the Chief Inspector, so private that it was never shaped into audible words, was:

'Long before you were even thought of for your place here.'

The so-to-speak public utterance was much more precise.

'I saw him for the first time in my life a little more than seven years ago, when two Imperial Highnesses and the Imperial Chancellor were on a visit here. I was put in charge of all the arrangements for looking after them. Baron Stott-Wartenheim was Ambassador then. He was a very nervous old gentleman. One evening, three days before the Guildhall Banquet, he sent word that he wanted to see me for a moment. I was downstairs, and the carriages were at the door to take the Imperial Highnesses and the Chanceller to the opera. I went up at once. I found the Baron walking up and down his bedroom in a pitiable state of distress, squeezing his hands together. He assured me he had the fullest confidence in our police and in my abilities, but he had there a man just come over from Paris whose information could be trusted implicitly. He wanted me to hear what that man had to say. He took me at once into a dressing-room next door, where I saw a big fellow in a heavy overcoat sitting all alone on a chair, and holding his hat and stick in one hand. The Baron said to him in French "Speak, my friend." The light in that room was not very good. I talked with him for some five minutes perhaps. He certainly gave me a piece of very startling news. Then the Baron took me aside nervously to praise him up to me, and when I turned round again I discovered that the fellow had vanished like a ghost. Got up and sneaked out down some back stairs, I suppose. There was no time to run after him, as I had to hurry off after the Ambassador down the great staircase, and see the party started safe for the opera. However, I acted upon the information that very night. Whether it was perfectly correct or not, it did look serious enough. Very likely it saved us from an ugly trouble on the day of the Imperial visit to the City.

'Some time later, a month or so after my promotion to Chief Inspector, my attention was attracted to a big burly man, I thought I had seen somewhere before, coming out in a hurry from a jeweller's shop in the Strand. I went after him, as it was on my way towards Charing Cross, and there seeing one of our detectives across the road, I beckoned him over, and pointed out the fellow to him, with instructions to watch his movements for a couple of days and then report to me. No later than next afternoon my man turned up to tell me that the fellow had married his landlady's daughter at a registrar's office that very day at 11.30 a.m., and had gone off with her to Margate for a week. Our man had seen the luggage being put on the cab. There were some old Paris labels on one of the bags. Somehow I couldn't get the fellow out of my head, and the very next time I had to go to Paris on service I spoke about him to that friend of mine in the Paris police. My friend said: "From what you tell me I think you must mean a rather well-known hanger-on and emissary of the Revolutionary Red Committee. He says he is an Englishman by birth. We have an idea that he has been for a good few years now a secret agent of one of the foreign Embassies in London." This woke up my memory completely. He was the vanishing fellow I saw sitting on a chair in Baron Stott-Wartenheim's bathroom. I told my friend that he was quite right. The fellow was a secret agent to my certain knowledge. Afterwards my friend took the trouble to ferret out the complete record of that man for me. I thought I had better know all there was to know; but I don't suppose you want to hear his history now, sir?'

The Assistant Commissioner shook his supported head. 'The history of your relations with that useful personage is the only thing that matters just now,' he said, closing his weary, deep-set eyes, and then opening them swiftly with a greatly refreshed glance.

'There's nothing official about them,' said the Chief Inspector, bitterly. 'I went into his shop one evening, told him who I was, and reminded him of our first meeting. He didn't as much as twitch an eyebrow. He said that he was married and settled now, and that all he wanted was not to be interfered with in his little business. I took it upon myself to promise him that, as long as he didn't go in for anything obviously outrageous, he would be left alone by the police. That was worth something to him, because a word from us to the Custom-House people would have been enough to get some of these packages he gets from Paris and Brussels opened in Dover, with confiscation to follow for certain, and perhaps a prosecution as well at the end of it.'

'That's a very precarious trade,' murmured the Assistant Commissioner. 'Why did he go in for that?'

The Chief Inspector raised scornful eyebrows dispassionately.

'Most likely got a connexion – friends on the Continent – amongst people who deal in such wares. They would be just the sort he would consort with. He's a lazy dog, too – like the rest of them.'

'What do you get from him in exchange for your protection?'

The Chief Inspector was not included to enlarge on the value of Mr Verloc's services.

'He would not be much good to anybody but myself. One has got to know a good deal beforehand to make use of a man like that. I can understand the sort of hint he can give. And when I want a hint he can generally furnish it to me.'

The Chief Inspector lost himself suddenly in a discreet reflective mood; and the Assistant Commissioner repressed a smile at the fleeting thought that the reputation of Chief Inspector Heat might possibly have been made in a great part by the Secret Agent Verloc.

'In a more general way of being of use, all our men of the Special Crimes section on duty at Charing Cross and Victoria have orders to take careful notice of anybody they may see with him. He meets the new arrivals frequently, and afterwards keeps track of them. He seems to have been told off for that sort of duty. When I want an address in a hurry, I can always get it from him. Of course, I know how to manage our relations. I haven't seen him to speak to three times in the last two years. I drop him a line, unsigned, and he answers me in the same way at my private address.'

From time to time the Assistant Commissioner gave an almost imperceptible nod. The Chief Inspector added that he did not suppose Mr Verloc to be deep in the confidence of the prominent members of the Revolutionary International Council, but that he was generally trusted of that there could be no doubt. 'Whenever I've had reason to think there was something in the wind,' he concluded, 'I've always found he could tell me something worth knowing.'

The Assistant Commissioner made a significant remark.

'He failed you this time.'

'Neither had I wind of anything in any other way,' retorted Chief Inspector Heat. 'I asked him nothing so he could tell me nothing. He isn't one of our men. It isn't as if he were in our pay.'

'No,' muttered the Assistant Commissioner. 'He's a spy in the pay of a foreign government. We could never confess to him.'

'I must do my work in my own way,' declared the Chief Inspector. 'When it comes to that I would deal with the devil himself, and take the consequences. There are things not fit for everybody to know.'

'Your idea of secrecy seems to consist in keeping the chief of your department in the dark. That's stretching it perhaps a little too far, isn't it? He lives over his shop?'

'Who – Verloc? Oh, yes. He lives over his shop. The wife's mother, I fancy, lives with them.'

'Is the house watched?'

'Oh, dear, no. It wouldn't do. Certain people who come there are watched. My opinion is that he knows nothing of this affair.'

'How do you account for this?' The Assistant Commissioner nodded at the cloth rag lying before him on the table.

'I don't account for it at all, sir. It's simply unaccountable. It can't be explained by what I know.' The Chief Inspector made those admissions with the frankness of a man whose reputation is established as if on a rock. 'At any rate not at this present moment. I think that the man who had most to do with it will turn out to be Michaelis.'

'You do?'

'Yes, sir; because I can answer for all the others.'

'What about that other man supposed to have escaped from the park?'

'I should think he's far away by this time,' opined the Chief Inspector.

The Assistant Commissioner looked hard at him, and rose suddenly, as though having made up his mind to some course of action. As a matter of fact, he had that very moment succumbed to a fascinating temptation. The Chief Inspector heard himself dismissed with instructions to meet his superior early next morning for further consultation upon the case. He listened with an impenetrable face, and walked out of the room with measured steps.

Whatever might have been the plans of the Assistant Commissioner they had nothing to do with the desk work, which was the bane of his existence because of its confined nature and apparent lack of reality. It could not have had, or else the general air of alacrity that came upon the Assistant Commissioner would have been inexplicable. As soon as he was left alone he looked for his hat impulsively, and put it on his head. Having done that, he sat down again to reconsider the whole matter. But as his mind was already made up, this did not take long. And before Chief Inspector Heat had gone very far on the way home, he also left the building.

CHAPTER 7

The Assistant Commissioner walked along a short and narrow street like a wet, muddy trench, then crossing a very broad thoroughfare entered a public edifice, and sought speech with a young private secretary (unpaid) of a great personage.

This fair, smooth-faced young man, whose symmetrically arranged hair gave him the air of a large and neat schoolboy, met the Assistant Commissioner's request with a doubtful look, and spoke with bated breath.

'Would he see you? I don't know about that. He has walked over from the House an hour ago to talk with the permanent Under-Secretary, and now he's ready to walk back again. He might have sent for him; but he does it for the sake of a little exercise, I suppose. It's all the exercise he can find time for while this session lasts. I don't complain; I rather enjoy these little strolls. He leans on my arm, and doesn't open his lips. But, I say, he's very tired, and – well – not in the sweetest of tempers just now.'

'It's in connexion with that Greenwich affair.'

'Oh! I say! He's very bitter against you people. But I will go and see, if you insist.'

'Do. That's a good fellow,' said the Assistant Commissioner.

The unpaid secretary admired this pluck. Composing for himself an innocent face, he opened a door, and went in with the assurance of a nice and privileged child. And presently he reappeared, with a nod to the Assistant Commissioner, who passing through the same door left open for him, found himself with the great personage in a large room.

Vast in bulk and stature, with a long white face, which, broadened at the base by a big double chin, appeared egg-shaped in the fringe of thin greyish whisker, the great personage seemed an expanding man. Unfortunate from a tailoring point of view, the crossfolds in the middle of a buttoned black coat added to the impression, as if the fastenings of the garment were tried to the utmost. From the head, set upward on a thick neck, the eyes, with puffy lower lids, stared with a haughty droop on each side of a hooked, aggressive nose, nobly salient in the vast pale circumference of the face. A shiny silk hat and a pair of worn gloves lying ready on the end of a long table looked expanded, too, enormous.

He stood on the hearthrug in big, roomy boots, and uttered no word of greeting.

'I would like to know if this is the beginning of another dynamite campaign,' he asked at once in a deep, very smooth voice. 'Don't go into details. I have no time for that.'

The Assistant Commissioner's figure before this big and rustic Presence had the frail slenderness of a reed addressing an oak. And indeed the unbroken record of that man's descent surpassed in the number of centuries the age of the oldest oak in the country.

'No. As far as one can be positive about anything I can assure you that it is not.'

'Yes. But your idea of assurances over there,' said the great man, with a contemptuous wave of his hand towards a window giving on the broad thoroughfare, 'seem to consist mainly in making the Secretary of State look a fool. I have been told positively in this very room less than a month ago that nothing of the sort was even possible.'

The Assistant Commissioner glanced in the direction of the window calmly.

'You will allow me to remark, Sir Ethelred, that so far I have had no opportunity to give you assurances of any kind.'

The haughty droop of the eyes was focused now upon the Assistant Commissioner.

'True,' confessed the deep, smooth voice. 'I sent for Heat. You are still rather a novice in your new berth. And how are you getting on over there?'

'I believe I am learning something every day.'

'Of course, of course. I hope you will get on.'

'Thank you, Sir Ethelred. I've learned something today, and even within the last hour or so. There is much in this affair of a kind that does not meet the eye in a usual anarchist outrage, even if one looked into it as deep as can be. That's why I am here.'

The great man put his arms akimbo, the backs of his big hands resting on his hips.

'Very well. Go on. Only no details, pray. Spare me the details.'

'You shall not be troubled with them, Sir Ethelred,' the Assistant Commissioner began, with a calm and untroubled assurance. While he was speaking the hands on the face of the clock behind the great man's back – a heavy, glistening affair of massive scrolls in the same dark marble as the mantelpiece, and with a ghostly, evanescent tick – had moved through the space of seven minutes. He spoke with a studious fidelity to a parenthetical manner, into which every little fact – that is, every detail – fitted with delightful ease. Not a murmur nor even a movement hinted at interruption. The great Personage might have been the statue of one of his own princely ancestors stripped of a crusader's war harness, and put into an ill-fitting frock coat. The Assistant Commissioner felt as though he were at liberty to talk for an hour. But he kept his head, and at the end of the time mentioned above he broke off with a sudden conclusion, which, reproducing the opening statement, pleasantly surprised Sir Ethelred by its apparent swiftness and force.'

'The kind of thing which meets us under the surface of this affair, otherwise without gravity, is unusual – in this precise form at least – and requires special treatment.'

The tone of Sir Ethelred was deepened, full of conviction.

'I should think so – involving the Ambassador of a foreign power!'

'Oh! The Ambassador!' protested the other, erect and slender, allowing himself a mere half smile. 'It would be stupid of me to advance anything of the kind. And it is absolutely unnecessary, because if I am right in my surmises, whether ambassador or hall porter it's a mere detail.'

Sir Ethelred opened a wide mouth, like a cavern, into which the hooked nose seemed anxious to peer; there came from it a subdued rolling sound, as from a distant organ with the scornful indignation stop.

'No! These people are too impossible. What do they mean by importing their method of Crim-Tartary here? A Turk would have more decency.'

'You forget, Sir Ethelred, that strictly speaking we know nothing positively – as yet.'

'No! But how would you define it? Shortly?'

'Barefaced audacity amounting to childishness of a peculiar sort.'

'We can't put up with the innocence of nasty little children,' said the great and expanded personage, expanding a little more, as it were. The haughty, drooping glance struck crushingly the carpet at the Assistant Commissioner's feet. 'They'll have to get a hard rap on the knuckles over this affair. We must be in a position to – What is your general idea, stated shortly? No need to go into details.'

'No, Sir Ethelred. In principle, I should lay it down that the existence of secret agents should not be tolerated, as tending to augment the positive dangers of the evil against which they are used. That the spy will fabricate his information as a mere commonplace. But in the sphere of political and revolutionary action, relying partly on violence, the professional spy has every facility to fabricate the very facts themselves, and will spread the double evil of emulation in one direction, and of panic, hasty legislation, unreflecting hate, in the other. However, this is an imperfect world –'

The deep-voiced Presence on the hearthrug, motionless, with big elbows stuck out, said hastily:

'Be lucid, please.'

'Yes, Sir Ethelred – An imperfect world. Therefore directly the character of this affair suggested itself to me, I thought it should be dealt with with special secrecy, and ventured to come over here.'

'That's right,' approved the great Personage, glancing down complacently over his double chin. 'I am glad there's somebody over at your shop who thinks that the Secretary of State may be trusted now and then.'

The Assistant Commissioner had an amused smile. 'I was really thinking that it might be better at this stage for Heat to be replaced by – '

'What! Heat? An ass – eh?' exclaimed the great man with distinct animosity.

'Not at all. Pray, Sir Ethelred, don't put that unjust interpretation on my remarks.'

'Then what? Too clever by half?'

'Neither – at least not as a rule. All the grounds of my surmises I have from him. The only thing I've discovered by myself is that he has been making use of that man privately. Who could blame him? He's an old police hand. He told me virtually that he must have tools to work with. It occurred to me that this tool should be surrendered to the Special Crimes division as a whole, instead of remaining the private property of Chief Inspector Heat. I extended my conception of our departmental duties to the suppression of the secret agent. But Chief Inspector Heat is an old departmental hand. He would accuse me of perverting its morality and attacking its efficiency. He would define it bitterly as protection extended to the criminal class of revolutionists. It would mean just that to him.'

'Yes. But what do you mean?'

'I mean to say, first, that there's but poor comfort in being able to declare that any given act of violence – damaging property of destroying life – is not the work of anarchism at all, but of something else altogether – some species of authorized scoundrelism. This, I fancy, is much more frequent than we suppose. Next, it's obvious that the existence of these people in the pay of foreign governments destroys in a measure the efficiency of our supervision. A spy of that sort can afford to be more reckless than the most reckless of conspirators. His occupation is free from all restraint. He's without as much faith as is necessary for complete negation, and without that much law is as implied in lawlessness. Thirdly, the existence of these species amongst the revolutionary groups, which we are reproached for harbouring here, does away with all certitude. You have received a reassuring statement from Chief Inspector Heat some time ago. It was by no means groundless – and yet this episode happens. I call it an episode, because this affair, I make bold to say, is episodic; it is no part of any general scheme, however wild. The very pecularities which surprise and perplex Chief Inspector Heat establish its character in my eyes. I am keeping clear of details, Sir Ethelred.'

The Personage on the hearthrug had been listening with profound attention.

'Just so. Be as concise as you can.'

The Assistant Commissioner intimated by an earnest, deferential gesture that he was anxious to be concise.

'There is a peculiar stupidity and feebleness in the conduct of this affair which gives me excellent hopes of getting behind it and finding there something else than an individual freak of fanaticism. For it is a planned thing, undoubtedly. The actual perpetrator seems to have been led by the hand to the spot, and then abandoned hurriedly to his own devices. The inference is that he was imported from abroad for the purpose of committing this outrage. At the same time one is forced to the conclusion that he did not know enough English to ask his way, unless one were to accept the fantastic theory that he was a deaf mute. I wonder now – But this is idle. He has destroyed himself by an accident, obviously. Not an extraordinary accident. But an extraordinary little fact remains: the address on his clothing discovered by the merest accident, too. It is an incredible little fact, so incredible that the explanation which will account for it is bound to touch the bottom of this affair. Instead of instructing Heat to go on with this case, my intention is to seek this explanation personally – by myself, I mean – where it may be picked up. That is in a certain shop in Brett Street, and on the lips of a certain secret agent once upon a time the confidential and trusted spy of the late Baron Stott-Wartenheim, Ambassador of a Great Power to the Court of St. James.'

The Assistant Commissioner paused, then added: 'Those fellows are a perfect pest.' In order to raise his drooping glance to the speaker's face, the Personage on the hearthrug had gradually tilted his head farther back, which gave him an aspect of extraordinary haughtiness.

'Why not leave it to Heat?'

'Because he is an old departmental hand. They have their own morality. My line of inquiry would appear to him an awful perversion of duty. For him the plain duty is to fasten the guilt upon as many prominent anarchists as he can on some slight indications he had picked up in the course of his investigation on the spot; whereas I, he would say, am bent upon vindicating their innocence. I am trying to be as lucid as I can in presenting this obscure matter to you without details.'

'He would, would he?' muttered the proud head of Sir Ethelred from its lofty elevation.

'I am afraid so – with an indignation and disgust of which you or I can have no idea. He's an excellent servant. We must not put an undue strain on his loyalty. That's always a mistake. Besides, I want a free hand – a freer hand than it would be perhaps advisable to give Chief Inspector Heat. I haven't the slightest wish to spare this man Verloc. He will, I imagine, be extremely startled to find his connexion with this affair, whatever it may be, brought home to him so quickly. Frightening him will not be very difficult. But our true objective lies behind him somewhere. I want your authority to give him such assurances of personal safety as I may think proper.'

'Certainly,' said the Personage on the hearthrug. 'Find out as much as you can; find it out in your own way.'

'I must set about it without loss of time, this very evening,' said the Assistant Commissioner.

Sir Ethelred shifted one hand under his coat tails, and tilting back his head, looked at him steadily.

'We'll have a late sitting tonight,' he said. 'Come to the House with your discoveries if we are not gone home. I'll warn Toodles to look out for you. He'll take you into my room.'

The numerous family and the wide connexions of the youthful-looking Private Secretary cherished for him the hope of an austere and exalted destiny. Meantime, the social sphere he adorned in his hours of idleness chose to pet him under the above nickname. And Sir Ethelred, hearing it on the lips of his wife and girls every day (mostly at breakfast-time), had conferred upon it the dignity of unsmiling adoption.

The Assistant Commissioner was surprised and gratified extremely.

'I shall certainly bring my discoveries to the House on the chance of you having the time to –'

'I won't have the time,' interrupted the great Personage. 'But I will see you. I haven't the time now – And you are going yourself?'

'Yes, Sir Ethelred. I think it the best way.'

The Personage had tilted his head so far back that, in order to keep the Assistant Commissioner under his observation, he had to nearly close his eyes.

'H'm. Ha! And how do you propose – Will you assume a disguise?'

'Hardly a disguise! I'll change my clothes, of course.'

'Of course,' repeated the great man, with a sort of absent-minded loftiness. He turned his big head slowly, and over his shoulder gave a haughty, oblique stare to the ponderous marble timepiece with the sly, feeble tick. The gilt hands had taken the opportunity to steal through no less than five and twenty minutes behind his back.

The Assistant Commissioner, who could not see them, grew a little nervous in the interval. But the great man presented to him a calm and undismayed face.

'Very well,' he said, and paused, as if in deliberate contempt of the official clock. 'But what first put you in motion in this direction?'

'I have been always of opinion,' began the Assistant Commissioner.

'Ah. Yes! Opinion. That's of course. But the immediate motive?'

'What shall I say, Sir Ethelred? A new man's antagonism to old methods. A desire to know something at first hand. Some impatience. It's my old work, but the harness is different. It has been chafing me a little in one or two tender places.'

'I hope you'll get on over there,' said the great man, kindly, extending his hand, soft to the touch, but broad and powerful like the hand of a glorified farmer. The Assistant Commissioner shook it, and withdrew.

In the outer room Toodles, who had been waiting perched on the edge of a table, advanced to meet him, subduing his natural buoyancy.

'Well? Satisfactory?' he asked, with airy importance.

'Perfectly. You've earned my undying gratitude,' answered the Assistant Commissioner, whose long face looked wooden in contrast with the peculiar character of the other's gravity, which seemed perpetually ready to break into ripples and chuckles.

'That's all right. But, seriously, you can't imagine how irritated he is by the attacks on his Bill for the Nationalization of Fisheries. They call it the beginning of social revolution. Of course, it is a revolutionary measure. But these fellows have no decency. The personal attacks – '

'I read the papers,' remarked the Assistant Commissioner.

'Odious? Eh? And you have no notion what a mass of work he has got to get through every day. He does it all himself. Seems unable to trust any one with these Fisheries.'

'And yet he's given a whole half hour to the consideration of my very small sprat,' interjected the Assistant Commissioner.

'Small! Is it? I'm glad to hear that. But it's a pity you didn't keep away, then. This fight takes it out of him frightfully. The man's getting exhausted. I feel it by the way he leans on my arm as we walk over. And, I say, is he safe in the streets? Mullins has been marching his men up here this afternoon. There's a constable stuck by every lamp-post, and every second person we meet between this and Palace Yard is an obvious tec. It will get on his nerves presently. I say, these foreign scoundrels aren't likely to throw something at him – are they? It would be a national calamity. The country can't spare him.'

'Not to mention yourself. He leans on your arm,' suggested the Assistant Commissioner, soberly. 'You would both go.'

'It would be an easy way for a young man to go down into history? Not so many British Ministers have been assassinated as to make it a minor incident. But seriously now – '

'I am afraid that if you want to go down into history you'll have to do something for it. Seriously, there's no danger whatever for both of you but from overwork.'

The sympathetic Toodles welcomed this opening for a chuckle.

'The Fisheries won't kill me. I am used to late hours,' he declared, with ingenuous levity. But, feeling an instant compunction, he began to assume an air of statesmanlike moodiness, as one draws on a glove. 'His massive intellect will stand any amount of work. It's his nerves that I am afraid of. The reactionary gang, with that abusive brute Cheeseman at their head, insult him every night.'

'If he will insist on beginning a revolution!' murmured the Assistant Commissioner.

'The time has come, and he is the only man great enough for the work,' protested the revolutionary Toodles, flaring up under the calm, speculative gaze of the Assistant Commissioner. Somewhere in a corridor a distant bell tinkled urgently, and with devoted vigilance the young man pricked up his ears at the sound. 'He's ready to go now,' he exclaimed in a whisper, snatched up his hat, and vanished from the room.

The Assistant Commissioner went out by another door in a less elastic manner. Again he crossed the wide thoroughfare, walked along the narrow street, and re-entered hastily his own departmental buildings. He kept up this accelerated pace to the door of his private room. Before he had closed it fairly his eyes sought his desk. He stood still for a moment, then walked up, looked all round on the floor, sat down in his chair, rang a bell, and waited.

'Chief Inspector Heat gone yet?'

'Yes, sir. Went away half an hour ago.'

He nodded. 'That will do.' And sitting still, with his hat pushed off his forehead, he thought that it was just like Heat's confounded cheek to carry off quietly the only piece of material evidence. But he thought this without animosity. Old and valued servants will take liberties. The piece of overcoat with the address sewn on was certainly not a thing to leave about. Dismissing from his mind this manifestation of Chief Inspector Heat's mistrust, he wrote and dispatched a note to his wife, charging her to make his apologies to Michaelis' great lady, with whom they were engaged to dine that evening.

The short jacket and the low, round hat he assumed in a sort of curtained alcove containing a washstand, a row of wooden pegs and a shelf, brought out wonderfully the length of his grave, brown face. He stepped back into the full light of the room, looking like the vision of a cool, reflective Don Quixote, with the sunken eyes of a dark enthusiast and a very deliberate manner. He left the scene of his daily labours quickly like an unobtrusive shadow. His descent into the street was like the descent into a slimy aquarium from which the water had been run off. A murky, gloomy dampness enveloped him. The walls of the houses were wet, the mud of the roadway glistened with an effect of phosphorescence, and when he emerged into the Strand out of a narrow street by the side of Charing Cross Station the genius of the locality assimilated him. He might have been but one more of the queer foreign fish that can be seen of an evening about there flitting round the dark corners.

He came to a stand on the very edge of the pavement, and waited. His exercised eyes had made out in the confused movements of lights and shadows thronging the roadway the crawling approach of a hansom. He gave no sign; but when the low step gliding along the curbstone came to his feet he dodged in skilfully in front of the big turning wheel, and spoke up through the little trap door almost before the man gazing supinely ahead from his perch was aware of having been boarded by a fare.

It was not a long drive. It ended by signal abruptly, nowhere in particular, between two lamp-posts before a large drapery establishment – a long range of shops already lapped up in sheets of corrugated iron for the night. Tendering a coin through the trap door the fare slipped out and away, leaving an effect of uncanny, eccentric ghostliness upon the driver's mind. But the size of the coin was satisfactory to his touch, and his education not being literary, he remained untroubled by the fear of finding it presently turned to a dead leaf in his pocket. Raised above the world of fares by the nature of his calling, he contemplated their action with a limited interest. The sharp pulling of his horse right round expressed his philosophy.

Meantime, the Assistant Commissioner was already giving his order to a waiter in a little Italian restaurant round the corner – one of those traps for the hungry, long and narrow, baited with a perspective of mirrors and white napery; without air, but with an atmosphere of their own – an atmosphere of fraudulent cookery mocking an abject mankind in the most pressing of its miserable necessities. In this immoral atmosphere the Assistant Commissioner, reflecting upon his enterprise, seemed to lose some more of his identity. He had a sense of loneliness, of evil freedom. It was rather pleasant. When, after paying for his short meal, he stood up and waited for his change, he saw himself in the sheet of glass, and was struck by his foreign appearance. He contemplated his own image with a melancholy and inquisitive gaze, then by sudden inspiration raised the collar of his jacket. This arrangement appeared to him commendable, and he completed it by giving an upward twist to the ends of his black moustache. He was satisfied by the subtle modification of his personal aspect caused by these small changes. 'That'll do very well,' he thought. 'I'll get a little wet, a little splashed – '

He became aware of the waiter at his elbow and of a small pile of silver coins on the edge of the table before him. The waiter kept one eye on it, while his other eye followed the long back of a tall, not very young girl, who passed up to a distant table looking perfectly sightless and altogether unapproachable. She seemed to be an habitual customer.

On going out the Assistant Commissioner made to himself the observation that the patrons of the place had lost in the frequentation of fraudulent cookery all their national and private characteristics. And this was strange, since the Italian restaurant is such a peculiarly British institution. But these people were as denationalized as the dishes set before them with every circumstance of unstamped respectability. Neither was their personality stamped in any way, professionally, socially, or racially. They seemed created for the Italian restaurant, unless the Italian restaurant had been perchance created for them. But that last hypothesis was unthinkable, since one could not place them anywhere outside those special establishments. One never met these enigmatical persons elsewhere. It was impossible to form a precise idea what occupations they followed by day and where they went to bed at night. And he himself had become unplaced. It would have been impossible for anybody to guess his occupation. As to going to bed, there was a doubt even in his own mind. Not indeed in regard to his domicile itself, but very much so in respect of the time when he would be able to return there. A pleasurable feeling of independence possessed him when he heard the glass doors swing to behind his back with a sort of imperfect baffled thud. He advanced at once into an immensity of greasy slime and damp plaster interspersed with lamps, and enveloped, oppressed, penetrated, choked, and suffocated by the blackness of a wet London night, which is composed of soot and drops of water.

Brett Street was not very far away. It branches off, narrow, from the side of an open triangular space surrounded by dark and mysterious houses, temples of petty commerce emptied of traders for the night. Only a fruiterer's stall at the corner made a violent blaze of light and colour. Beyond all was black, and the few people passing in that direction vanished at one stride beyond the glowing heaps of oranges and lemons. No footsteps echoed. They would never be heard of again. The adventurous head of the Special Crimes Department watched these disappearances from a distance with an interested eye. He felt light-hearted, as though he had been ambushed all alone in a jungle many thousands of miles away from departmental desks and official inkstands. This joyousness and dispersion of thought before a task of some importance seems to prove that this world of ours is not such a very serious affair after all. For the Assistant Commissioner was not constitutionally inclined to levity.

The policeman on the beat projected his sombre and moving form against the luminous glory of oranges and lemons, and entered Brett Street without haste. The Assistant Commissioner, as though he were a member of the criminal classes, lingered out of sight, awaiting his return. But this constable seemed to be lost for ever to the force. He never returned: must have gone out at the other end of Brett Street.

The Assistant Commissioner, reaching this conclusion, entered the street in his turn, and came upon a large van arrested in front of the dimly lit window-panes of a carter's eating-house. The man was refreshing himself inside, and the horses, their big heads lowered to the ground, fed out of nose-bags steadily. Farther on, on the opposite side of the street, another suspect patch of dim light issued from Mr Verloc's shop front, hung with papers, heaving with vague piles of cardboard boxes and the shapes of books. The Assistant Commissioner stood observing it across the roadway. There could be no mistake. By the side of the front window, encumbered by the shadows of nondescript things, the door, standing ajar, let escape on the pavement a narrow, clear streak of gaslight within.

Behind the Assistant Commissioner the van and horses, merged into one mass, seemed something alive – a square-backed black monster blocking half the street, with sudden iron-shod stampings, fierce jingles, and heavy, blowing sighs. The harshly festive, ill-omened glare of a large and prosperous public-house faced the other end of Brett Street across a wide road. This barrier of blazing lights, opposing the shadows gathered about the humble abode of Mr Verloc's domestic happiness, seemed to drive the obscurity of the street back upon itself, make it more sullen, brooding, and sinister.

CHAPTER 8

Having infused by persistent importunities some sort of heat into the chilly interest of several licensed victuallers (the acquaintances once upon a time of her late unlucky husband), Mrs Verloc's mother had at last secured her admission to certain almshouses founded by a wealthy innkeeper for the destitute widows of the trade.

This end, conceived in the astuteness of her uneasy heart, the old woman had pursued with secrecy and determination. That was the time when her daugher Winnie could not help passing a remark to Mr Verloc that 'mother has been spending half-crowns and five shillings almost every day this last week in cab fares'. But the remark was not made grudgingly. Winnie respected her mother's infirmities. She was only a little surprised at this sudden mania for locomotion. Mr Verloc, who was sufficiently magnificent in his way, had grunted the remark impatiently aside as interfering with his mediations. These were frequent, deep, and prolonged; they bore upon a matter more important than five shillings. Distinctly more important, and beyond all comparison more difficult to consider in all its aspects with philosophical serenity.

Her object attained in astute secrecy, the heroic old woman had made a clean breast of it to Mrs Verloc. Her soul was triumphant and her heart tremulous. Inwardly she quaked, because she dreaded and admired the calm, self-contained character of her daughter Winnie, whose displeasure was made redoubtable by a diversity of dreadful silences. But she did not allow her inward apprehensions to rob her of the advantage of venerable placidity conferred upon her outward person by her triple chin, the floating ampleness of her ancient form, and the impotent condition of her legs.

The shock of the information was so unexpected that Mrs Verloc, against her usual practice when addressed, interrupted the domestic occupation she was engaged upon. It was the dusting of the furniture in the parlour behind the shop. She turned her head towards her mother.

'Whatever did you want to do that for?' she exclaimed, in scandalized astonishment.

The shock must have been severe to make her depart from that distant and uninquiring acceptance of facts which was her force and her safeguard in life.

'Weren't you made comfortable enough here?'

She had lapsed into these inquiries, but next moment she saved the consistency of her conduct by resuming her dusting, while the old woman sat scared and dumb under her dingy white cap and lustreless dark wig.

Winnie finished the chair, and ran the duster along the mahogany at the back of the horsehair sofa on which Mr Verloc loved to take his ease in hat and overcoat. She was intent on her work, but presently she permitted herself another question.

'How in the world did you manage it, mother?'

As not affecting the inwardness of things, which it was Mrs Verloc's principle to ignore, this curiosity was excusable. It bore merely on the methods. The old woman welcomed it eagerly as bringing forward something that could be talked about with much sincerity.

She favoured her daughter by an exhaustive answer full of names and enriched by side-comments upon the ravages of time as observed in the alteration of human countenances. The names were principally the names of licensed victuallers – 'poor daddy's friends, my dear'. She enlarged with special appreciation on the kindness and condescension of a large brewer, a Baronet and an M.P., the Chairman of the Governors of the Charity. She expressed herself thus warmly because she had been allowed to interview by appointment his Private Secretary – 'a very polite gentleman, all in black, with a gentle, sad voice, but so very, very thin and quiet. He was like a shadow, my dear'.

Winnie, prolonging her dusting operations till the tale was told to the end, walked out of the parlour into the kitchen (down two steps) in her usual manner, without the slightest comment.

Shedding a few tears in sign of rejoicing at her daughter's mansuetude in this terrible affair, Mrs Verloc's mother gave play to her astuteness in the direction of her furniture, because it was her own; and sometimes she wished it hadn't been. Heroism is all very well, but there are circumstances when the disposal of a few tables and chairs, brass bedsteads, and so on, may be big with remote and disastrous consequences. She required a few pieces herself, the Foundation which, after many importunities, had gathered her to its charitable breast, giving nothing but bare planks and cheaply papered bricks to the objects of its solicitude. The delicacy guiding her choice to the least valuable and most dilapidated articles passed unacknowledged, because Winnie's philosophy consisted in not taking notice of the inside of facts; she assumed that mother took what suited her best. As to Mr Verloc, his intense meditation, like a sort of Chinese wall, isolated him completely from the phenomena of this world of vain effort and illusory appearances.

Her selection made, the disposal of the rest became a perplexing question in a particular way. She was leaving it in Brett Street, of course. But she had two children. Winnie was provided for by her sensible union with that excellent husband, Mr Verloc. Stevie was destitute – and a little peculiar. His position had to be considered before the claims of legal justice and even the promptings of partiality. The possession of the furniture would not be in any sense a provision. He ought to have it – the poor boy. But to give it to him would be like tampering with his position of complete dependence. It was a sort of claim which she feared to weaken. Moreover, the susceptibilities of Mr Verloc would perhaps not brook being beholden to his brother-in-law for the chairs he sat on. In a long experience of gentlemen lodgers, Mrs Verloc's mother had acquired a dismal but resigned notion of the fantastic side of human nature. What if Mr Verloc suddenly took it into his head to tell Stevie to take his blessed sticks somewhere out of that? A division, on the other hand, however carefully made, might give some cause of offence to Winnie. No. Stevie must remain destitute and dependent. And at the moment of leaving Brett Street she had said to her daughter: 'No use waiting till I am dead, is there? Everything I leave here is altogether your own now, my dear.'

Winnie, with her hat on, silent behind her mother's back, went on arranging the collar of the old woman's cloak. She got her handbag, an umbrella, with an impassive face. The time had come for the expenditure of the sum of three and sixpence on what might well be supposed the last cab-drive of Mrs Verloc's mother's life. They went out at the shop door.

The conveyance awaiting them would have illustrated the proverb that 'truth can be more cruel than caricature', if such a proverb existed. Crawling behind an infirm horse, a metropolitan hackney carriage drew up on wobbly wheels and with a maimed driver on the box. This last peculiarity caused some embarrassment. Catching sight of a hooked iron contrivance protruding from the left sleeve of the man's coat, Mrs Verloc's mother lost suddenly the heroic courage of these days. She really couldn't trust herself. 'What do you think, Winnie?' She hung back. The passionage expostulations of the big-faced cabman seemed to be squeezed out of a blocked throat. Leaning over from his box, he whispered with mysterious indignation. What was the matter now? Was it possible to treat a man so? His enormous and unwashed countenance flamed red in the muddy stretch of the street. Was it likely they would have given him a licence, he inquired desperately, if –

The police constable of the locality quieted him by a friendly glance; then addressing himself to the two women without marked consideration, said:

'He's been driving a cab for twenty years. I never knew him to have an accident.'

'Accident!' shouted the driver in a scornful whisper.

The policeman's testimony settled it. The modest assemblage of seven people, mostly under age, dispersed. Winnie followed her mother into the cab. Stevie climbed on the box. His vacant mouth and distressed eyes depicted the state of his mind in regard to the transactions which were taking place. In the narrow streets the progress of the journey was made sensible to those within by the near fronts of the houses gliding past slowly and shakily, with a great rattle and jingling of glass, as if about to collapse behind the cab; and the infirm horse, with the harness hung over his sharp backbone flapping very loose about his thighs, appeared to be dancing mincingly on his toes with infinite patience. Later on, in the wider space of Whitehall, all visual evidences of motion became imperceptible. The rattle and jingle of glass went on indefinitely in front of the long Treasury building – and time itself seemed to stand still.

At last Winnie observed: 'This isn't a very good horse.'

Her eyes gleamed in the shadow of the cab straight ahead, immovable. On the box, Stevie shut his vacant mouth first, in order to ejaculate earnestly: 'Don't.'

The driver, holding high the reins twisted around the hook, took no notice. Perhaps he had not heard. Stevie's breast heaved.

'Don't whip.'

The man turned slowly his bloated and sodden face of many colours bristling with white hairs. His little red eyes glistened with moisture. His big lips had a violent tint. They remained closed. With the dirty back of his whip-hand he rubbed the stubble sprouting on his enormous chin.

'You mustn't,' stammered out Stevie, violently, 'it hurts.'

'Mustn't whip,' queried the other in a thoughtful whisper, and immediately whipped. He did this, not because his soul was cruel and his heart evil, but because he had to earn his fare. And for a time the walls of St Stephen's, with its towers and pinnacles, contemplated in immobility and silence a cab that jingled. It rolled, too, however, But on the bridge there was a commotion. Stevie suddenly proceeded to get down from the box. There were shouts on the pavement, people ran forward, the driver pulled up, whispering curses of indignation and astonishment. Winnie lowered the window, and put her head out, white as a ghost. In the depths of the cab, her mother was exclaiming, in tones of anguish: 'Is that boy hurt? Is that boy hurt?'

Stevie was not hurt, he had not even fallen, but excitement as usual had robbed him of the power of connected speech. He could do no more than stammer at the window: 'Too heavy. Too heavy.' Winnie put out her hand on to his shoulder.

'Stevie! Get up on the box directly, and don't try to get down again.'

'No. No. Walk. Must walk.'

In trying to state the nature of that necessity he stammered himself into utter incoherence. No physical impossibility stood in the way of his whim. Stevie could have managed easily to keep pace with the infirm, dancing horse without getting out of breath. But his sister withheld her consent decisively. 'The idea! Whoever heard of such a thing! Run after a cab!' Her mother, frightened and helpless in the depth of the conveyance, entreated:

'Oh, don't let him, Winnie. He'll get lost. Don't let him.'

'Certainly not. What next! Mr Verloc will be sorry to hear of this nonsense, Stevie – I can tell you. He won't be happy at all.'

The idea of Mr Verloc's grief and unhappiness acting as usual powerfully upon Stevie's fundamentally docile disposition, he abandoned all resistance and climbed up again on the box, with a face of despair.

The cabby turned at him his enormous and inflamed countenance truculently. 'Don't you go for trying this silly game again, young fellow.'

After delivering himself thus in a stern whisper, strained almost to extinction, he drove on, ruminating solemnly. To his mind the incident remained somewhat obscure. But his intellect, though it had lost its pristine vivacity in the benumbing years of sedentary exposure to the weather, lacked not independence or sanity. Gravely he dismissed the hypothesis of Stevie being a drunken young nipper.

Inside the cab the spell of silence, in which the two women had endured shoulder to shoulder the jolting, rattling, and jingling of the journey, had been broken by Stevie's outbreak. Winnie raised her voice.

'You've done what you wanted, mother. You'll have only yourself to thank for it if you aren't happy afterwards. And I don't think you'll be. That I don't. Weren't you comfortable enough in the house? Whatever people'll think of us – you throwing yourself like this on a Charity?'

'My dear,' screamed the old woman earnestly above the noise, 'you've been the best of daughters to me. As to Mr Verloc – there – '

Words failing her on the subject of Mr Verloc's excellence, she turned her old tearful eyes to the roof of the cab. Then she averted her head on the pretence of looking out of the window, as if to judge of their progress. It was insignificant, and went on close to the curbstone. Night, the early dirty night, the sinister, noisy, hopeless, and rowdy night of South London, had overtaken her on her last cab drive. In the gas-light of the low-fronted shops her big cheeks glowed with an orange hue under a black and mauve bonnet.

Mrs Verloc's mother's complexion had become yellow by the effect of age and from a natural predisposition to biliousness, favoured by the trials of a difficult and worried existence, first as wife, then as widow. It was a complexion that under the influence of a blush would take on an orange tint. And this woman, modest indeed but hardened in the fires of adversity, of an age, moreover, when blushes are not expected, had positively blushed before her daughter. In the privacy of a four-wheeler, on her way to a charity cottage (one of a row) which by the exiguity of its dimensions and the simplicity of its accommodation, might well have been devised in kindness as a place of training for the still more straitened circumstances of the grave, she was forced to hide from her own child a blush of remorse and shame.

Whatever people will think? She knew very well what they did think, the people Winnie had in her mind – the old friends of her husband, and others too, whose interest she had solicited with such flattering success. She had not known before what a good beggar she could be. But she guessed very well what inference was drawn from her application. On account of that shrinking delicacy, which exists side by side with aggressive brutality in masculine nature, the inquiries into her circumstances had not been pushed very far. She had checked them by a visible compression of the lips and some display of an emotion determined to be eloquently silent. And the men would become suddenly incurious, after the manner of their kind. She congratulated herself more than once on having nothing to do with women, who being naturally more callous and avid of details, would have been anxious to be exactly informed by what sort of unkind conduct her daughter and son-in-law had driven her to that sad extremity. It was only before the Secretary of the great brewer M.P. and Chairman of the Charity, who, acting for his principal, felt bound to be conscientiously inquisitive as to the real circumstances of the applicant, that she had burst into tears outright and aloud, as a cornered woman will weep. The thin and polite gentleman, after contemplating her with an air of being 'struck all of a heap', abandoned his position under the cover of soothing remarks. She must not distress herself. The deed of the Charity did not absolutely specify 'childless widows'. In fact, it did not by any means disqualify her. But the discretion of the Committee must be an informed discretion. One could understand very well her unwillingness to be a burden, etc., etc. Thereupon, to his profound disappointment, Mrs Verloc's mother wept some more with an augmented vehemence.

The tears of that large female in a dark, dusty wig, and ancient silk dress festooned with dingy white cotton lace, were the tears of genuine distress. She had wept because she was heroic and unscrupulous and full of love for both her children. Girls frequently get sacrificed to the welfare of the boys. In this case she was sacrificing Winnie. By the suppression of truth she was slandering her. Of course, Winnie was independent, and need not care for the opinion of people that she would never see and who would never see her; whereas poor Stevie had nothing in the world he could call his own except his mother's heroism and unscrupulousness.

The first sense of security following on Winnie's marriage wore off in time (for nothing lasts), and Mrs Verloc's mother, in the seclusion of the back bedroom, had recalled the teaching of that experience which the world impresses upon a widowed woman. But she had recalled it without vain bitterness; her store of resignation amounted almost to dignity. She reflected stoically that everything decays, wears out, in this world; that the way of kindness should be made easy to the well disposed; that her daughter Winnie was a most devoted sister, and a very self-confident wife indeed. As regards Winnie's sisterly devotion, her stoicism flinched. She excepted that sentiment from the rule of decay affecting all things human and some things divine. She could not help it; not to do so would have frightened her too much. But in considering the conditions of her daughter's married state, she rejected firmly all flattering illusions. She took the cold and reasonable view that the less strain put on Mr Verloc's kindness the longer its effects were likely to last. That excellent man loved his wife, of course, but he would, no doubt, prefer to keep as few of her relations as was consistent with the proper display of that sentiment. It would be better if its whole effect were concentrated on poor Stevie. And the heroic old woman resolved on going away from her children as an act of devotion and as a move of deep policy.

The 'virtue' of this policy consisted in this (Mrs Verloc's mother was subtle in her way), that Stevie's moral claim would be strengthened. The poor boy – a good, useful boy, if a little peculiar – had not a sufficient standing. He had been taken over with his mother, somewhat in the same way as the furniture of the Belgravian mansion had been taken over, as if on the ground of belonging to her exclusively. What will happen, she asked herself (for Mrs Verloc's mother was in a measure imaginative), when I die? And when she asked herself that question it was with dread. It was also terrible to think that she would not then have the means of knowing what happened to the poor boy. But by making him over to his sister, by going thus away, she gave him the advantage of a directly dependent position. This was the more subtle sanction of Mrs Verloc's mother's heroism and unscrupulousness. Her act of abandonment was really an arrangement for settling her son permanently in life. Other people made material sacrifices for such an object, she in that way. It was the only way. Moreover, she would be able to see how it worked. Ill or well she would avoid the horrible incertitude on the death-bed. But it was hard, hard, cruelly hard.

The cab rattled, jingled, jolted; in fact, the last was quite extraordinary. By its disproportionate violence and magnitude it obliterated every sensation of onward movement; and the effect was of being shaken in a stationary apparatus like a medieval device for the punishment of crime, or some very new-fangled invention for the cure of a sluggish liver. It was extremely distressing; and the raising of Mrs Verloc's mother's voice sounded like a wail of pain.

'I know, my dear, you'll come to see me as often as you can spare the time. Won't you?'

'Of course,' answered Winnie, shortly, staring straight before her.

And the cab jolted in front of a steamy, greasy shop in a blaze of gas and in the smell of fried fish.

The old woman raised a wail again.

'And, my dear, I must see that poor boy every Sunday. He won't mind spending the day with his old mother – '

Winnie screamed out stolidly:

'Mind! I should think not. That poor boy will miss you something cruel. I wish you had thought a little of that, mother.'

Not think of it! The heroic woman swallowed a playful and inconvenient object like a billiard ball, which had tried to jump out of her throat. Winnie sat mute for a while, pouting at the front of the cab, then snapped out, which was an unusual tone with her:

'I expect I'll have a job with him at first, he'll be that restless – '

'Whatever you do, don't let him worry your husband, my dear.'

Thus they discussed on familiar lines the bearings of a new situation. And the cab jolted. Mrs Verloc's mother expressed some misgivings. Could Stevie be trusted to come all that way alone? Winnie maintained that he was much less 'absent-minded' now. They agreed as to that. It could not be denied. Much less – hardly at all. They shouted at each other in the jingle with comparative cheerfulness. But suddenly the maternal anxiety broke out afresh. There were two omnibuses to take, and a short walk between. It was too difficult! The old woman gave way to grief and consternation.

Winnie stared forward.

'Don't you upset yourself like this, mother. You must see him, of course.'

'No, my dear. I'll try not to.'

She mopped her streaming eyes.

'But you can't spare the time to come with him, and if he should forget himself and lose his way and somebody spoke to him sharply, his name and address may slip his memory, and he'll remain lost for days and days – '

The vision of a workhouse infirmary for poor Stevie – if only during inquiries – wrung her heart. For she was a proud woman. Winnie's stare had grown hard, intent, inventive.

'I can't bring him to you myself every week,' she cried. 'But don't you worry, mother. I'll see to it that he don't get lost for long.'

They felt a peculiar bump; a vision of brick pillars lingered before the rattling windows of the cab; a sudden cessation of atrocious jolting and uproarious jingling dazed the two women. What had happened? They sat motionless and scared in the profound stillness, till the door came open, and a rough, strained whispering was heard:

''Ere you are!'

A range of gabled little houses, each with one dim yellow window, on the ground floor, surrounded the dark open space of a grass plot planted with shrubs and railed off from the patchwork of lights and shadows in the wide road, resounding with the dull rumble of traffic. Before the door of one of these tiny houses – one without a light in the little downstairs window – the cab had come to a standstill. Mrs Verloc's mother got out first, backwards, with a key in her hand. Winnie lingered on the flagstone path to pay the cabman. Stevie, after helping to carry inside a lot of small parcels, came out and stood under the light of a gas-lamp belonging to the Charity. The cabman looked at the pieces of silver, which, appearing very minute in his big, grimy palm, symbolized the insignificant results which reward the ambitious courage and toil of a mankind whose day is short on this earth of evil.

He had been paid decently – four one-shilling pieces – and he contemplated them in perfect stillness, as if they had been the surprising terms of a melancholy problem. The slow transfer of that treasure to an inner pocket demanded much laborious groping in the depths of decayed clothing. His form was squat and without flexibility. Stevie, slender, his shoulders a little up, and his hands thrust deep in the side pockets of his warm overcoat, stood at the edge of the path, pouting.

The cabman, pausing in his deliberate movements, seemed struck by some misty recollection.

'Oh! 'Ere you are, young fellow,' he whispered. 'You'll know him again – won't you?'

Stevie was staring at the horse, whose hind quarters appeared unduly elevated by the effect of emancipation. The little stiff tail seemed to have been fitted in for a heartless joke; and at the other end the thin, flat neck, like a plank covered with old horse-hide, drooped to the ground under the weight of an enormous bony head. The ears hung at different angles, negligently; and the macabre figure of that mute dweller on the earth steamed straight up from ribs and backbone in the muggy stillness of the air.

The cabman struck lightly Stevie's breast with the iron hook protruding from a ragged, greasy sleeve.

'Look 'ere young feller. 'Ow'd *you* like to sit behind this 'oss up to two o'clock in the morning p'raps?'

Stevie looked vacantly into the fierce little eyes with red-edged lids.

'He ain't lame,' pursued the other, whispering with energy.

'He ain't got no sore places on 'im. 'Ere he is. 'Ow would *you* like – '

His strained, extinct voice invested his utterance with a character of vehement secrecy. Stevie's vacant gaze was changing slowly into dread.

'You may well look! Till three and four o'clock in the morning. Cold and 'ungry. Looking for fares. Drunks.'

His jovial purple cheeks bristled with white hairs; and like Virgil's Silenus, who, his face smeared with the juice of berries, discoursed of Olympian Gods to the innocent shepherds of Sicily, he talked to Stevie of domestic matters and the affairs of men whose sufferings are great and immortality by no means assured.

'I am a night cabby, I am,' he whispered, with a sort of boastful exasperation. 'I've got to take out what they will blooming well give me at the yard. I've got my missus and four kids at 'ome.'

The monstrous nature of that declaration of paternity seemed to strike the world dumb. A silence reigned, during which the flanks of the old horse, the steed of apocalyptic misery, smoked upwards in the light of the charitable gas-lamp.

The cabman grunted, then added in his mysterious whisper:

'This ain't an easy world.'

Stevie's face had been twitching for some time and at last his feelings burst out in their usual concise form.

'Bad! Bad!'

His gaze remained fixed on the ribs of the horse, self-conscious and sombre, as though he were afraid to look about him at the badness of the world. And his slenderness, his rosy lips and pale, clear complexion, gave him the aspect of a delicate boy, notwithstanding the fluffy growth of golden hair on his cheeks. He pouted in a scared way like a child. The cabman, short and broad, eyed him with his fierce little eyes that seemed to smart in a clear and corroding liquid.

''Ard on 'osses, but dam' sight 'arder on poor chaps like me,' he wheezed just audibly.

'Poor! Poor!' stammered out Stevie, pushing his hands deeper into his pockets with convulsive sympathy. He could say nothing; for the tenderness to all pain and all misery, the desire to make the horse happy and the cabman happy, had reached the point of a bizarre longing to take them to bed with him. And that, he knew, was impossible. For Stevie was not mad. It was, as it were, a symbolic longing; and at the same time it was very distinct, because springing from experience, the mother of wisdom. Thus when as a child he cowered in a dark corner scared, wretched, sore, and miserable with the black, black misery of the soul, his sister Winnie used to come along and carry him off to bed with her, as into a heaven of consoling peace. Stevie, though apt to forget mere facts, such as his name and address for instance, had a faithful memory of sensations. To be taken into a bed of compassion was the supreme remedy, with the only one disadvantage of being difficult of application on a large scale. And looking at the cabman, Stevie perceived this clearly, because he was reasonable.

The cabman went on with his leisurely preparations as if Stevie had not existed. He made as if to hoist himself on the box, but at the last moment, from some obscure motive, perhaps merely from disgust with carriage exercise, desisted. He approached instead the motionless partner of his labours, and stooping to seize the bridle, lifted up the big, weary head to the height of his shoulder with one effort of his right arm, like a feat of strength.

'Come on,' he whispered, secretly.

Limping, he led the cab away. There was an air of austerity in this departure, the scrunched gravel of the drive crying out under the slowly turning wheels, the horse's lean thighs moving with ascetic deliberation away from the light into the obscurity of the open space bordered dimly by the pointed roofs and the feebly shining windows of the little almshouses. The plaint of the gravel travelled slowly all round the drive. Between the lamps of the charitable gateway the slow cortège reappeared, lighted up for a moment, the short, thick man limping busily, with the horse's head held aloft in his fist, the lank animal walking in stiff and forlorn dignity, the dark, low box on wheels rolling behind comically with an air of waddling. They turned to the left. There was a pub down the street, within fifty yards of the gate.

Stevie, left alone beside the private lamp-post of the Charity, his hands thrust deep into his pockets, glared with vacant sulkiness. At the bottom of his pockets his incapable, weak hands were clinched hard into a pair of angry fists. In the face of anything which affected directly or indirectly his morbid dread of pain, Stevie ended by turning vicious. A magnanimous indignation swelled his frail chest to bursting, and caused his candid eyes to squint. Supremely wise in knowing his own powerlessness, Stevie was not wise enough to restrain his passions. The tenderness of his universal charity had two phases as indissolubly joined and connected as the reverse and obverse sides of a medal. The anguish of immoderate compassion was succeeded by the pain of an innocent but pitiless rage. Those two states expressing themselves outwardly by the same signs of futile bodily agitation, his sister Winnie soothed his excitement without ever fathoming its twofold character. Mrs Verloc wasted no portion of this transient life in seeking for fundamental information. This is a sort of economy having all the appearances and some of the advantages of prudence. Obviously it may be good for one not to know too much. And such a view accords very well with constitutional indolence.

On that evening on which it may be said that Mrs Verloc's mother having parted for good from her children had also departed this life, Winnie Verloc did not investigate her brother's psychology. The poor boy was excited, of course. After once more assuring the old woman on the threshold that she would know how to guard against the risk of Stevie losing himself for very long on his pilgrimages of filial piety, she took her brother's arm to walk away. Stevie did not even mutter to himself, but with the special sense of sisterly devotion developed in her earliest infancy, she felt that the boy was very much excited indeed. Holding tight to his arm, under the appearance of leaning on it, she thought of some words suitable to the occasion.

'Now, Stevie, you must look well after me at the crossings, and get first into the bus, like a good brother.'

This appeal to manly protection was received by Stevie with his usual docility. It flattered him. He raised his head and threw out his chest.

'Don't be nervous, Winnie. Mustn't be nervous! Bus all right,' he answered in a brusque, slurring stammer partaking of the timorousness of a child and the resolution of a man. He advanced fearlessly with the woman on his arm, but his lower lip dropped. Nevertheless, on the pavement of the squalid and wide thoroughfare, whose poverty in all the amenities of life stood foolishly exposed by a mad profusion of gas-lights, their resemblance to each other was so pronounced as to strike the casual passers-by.

Before the doors of the public-house at the corner, where the profusion of gas-light reached the height of positive wickedness, a four-wheeled cab standing by the curbstone, with no one on the box, seemed cast out into the gutter on account of irremediable decay. Mrs Verloc recognized the conveyance. Its aspect was so profoundly lamentable, with such a perfection of grotesque misery and weirdness of macabre detail, as if it were the Cab of Death itself, that Mrs Verloc, with that ready compassion of a woman for a horse (when she is not sitting behind him), exclaimed vaguely!

'Poor brute.'

Hanging back suddenly, Stevie inflicted an arresting jerk upon his sister.

'Poor! Poor!' he ejaculated appreciatively. 'Cabman poor, too. He told me himself.'

The contemplation of the infirm and lonely steed overcame him. Jostled, but obstinate, he would remain there, trying to express the view newly opened to his sympathies of the human and equine misery in close association. But it was very difficult. 'Poor brute, poor people!' was all he could repeat. It did not seem forcible enough, and he came to a stop with an angry splutter: 'Shame!' Stevie was no master of phrases, and perhaps for that very reason his thoughts lacked clearness and precision. But he felt with greater completeness and some profundity. That little word contained all his sense of indignation and horror at one sort of wretchedness having to feed upon the anguish of the other – at the poor cabman beating the poor horse in the name, as it were, of his poor kids at home. And Stevie knew what it was to be beaten. He knew it from experience. It was a bad world. Bad! Bad!

Mrs Verloc, his only sister, guardian, and protector, could not pretend to such depths of insight. Moreover, she had not experienced the magic of the cabman's eloquence. She was in the dark as to the inwardness of the word 'Shame'. And she said placidly:

'Come along, Stevie. You can't help that.'

The docile Stevie went along; but now he went along without pride, shamblingly, and muttering half words, and even words that would have been whole if they had not been made up of halves that did not belong to each other. It was as though he had been trying to fit all the words he could remember to his sentiments in order to get some sort of corresponding idea. And, as a matter of fact, he got it at last. He hung back to utter it at once.

'Bad world for poor people.'

Directly he had expressed that thought he became aware that it was familiar to him already in all its consequences. This circumstance strengthened his conviction immensely, but also augmented his indignation. Somebody, he felt, ought to be punished for it – punished with great severity. Being no sceptic, but a moral creature, he was in a manner at the mercy of his righteous passions.

'Beastly!' he added, concisely.

It was clear to Mrs Verloc that he was greatly excited.

'Nobody can help that,' she said. 'Do come along. Is that the way you're taking care of me?'

Stevie mended his pace obediently. He prided himself on being a good brother. His morality, which was very complete, demanded that from him. Yet he was pained at the information imparted by his sister Winnie – who was good. Nobody could help that! He came along gloomily, but presently he brightened up. Like the rest of mankind, perplexed by the mystery of the universe, he had his moments of consoling trust in the organized powers of the earth.

'Police,' he suggested, confidently.

'The police aren't for that,' observed Mrs Verloc, cursorily, hurrying on her way.

Stevie's face lengthened considerably. He was thinking. The more intense his thinking, the slacker was the droop of his lower jaw. And it was with an aspect of hopeless vacancy that he gave up his intellectual enterprise.

'Not for that?' he mumbled, resigned but surprised. 'Not for that?' He had formed for himself an ideal conception of the metropolitan police as a sort of benevolent institution for the suppression of evil. The notion of benevolence especially was very closely associated with his sense of the power of the men in blue. He had liked all police constables tenderly, with a guileless trustfulness. And he was pained. He was irritated, too, by a suspicion of duplicity in the members of the force. For Stevie was frank and as open as the day himself. What did they mean by pretending then? Unlike his sister, who put her trust in face values, he wished to go to the bottom of the matter. He carried on his inquiry by means of an angry challenge.

'What are they for then, Winn? What are they for? Tell me.'

Winnie disliked controversy. But fearing most a fit of black depression consequent on Stevie missing his mother very much at first, she did not altogether decline the discussion. Guiltless of all irony, she answered yet in a form which was not perhaps unnatural in the wife of Mr Verloc, Delegate of the Central Red Committee, personal friend of certain anarchists, and a votary of social revolution.

'Don't you know what the police are for, Stevie? They are there so that them as have nothing shouldn't take anything away from them who have.'

She avoided using the verb 'to steal,' because it always made her brother uncomfortable. For Stevie was delicately honest. Certain simple principles had been instilled into him so anxiously (on account of his 'queerness') that the mere names of certain transgressions filled him with horror. He had been always easily impressed by speeches. He was impressed and startled now, and his intelligence was very alert.

'What?' he asked at once, anxiously. 'Not even if they were hungry? Mustn't they?'

The two had paused in their walk.

'Not if they were ever so,' said Mrs Verloc, with the equanimity of a person untroubled by the problem of the distribution of wealth and exploring the perspective of the roadway for an omnibus of the right colour. 'Certainly not. But what's the use of talking about all that? You aren't ever hungry.'

She cast a swift glance at the boy, like a young man, by her side. She saw him amiable, attractive, affectionate, and only a little, a very little peculiar. And she could not see him otherwise, for he was connected with what there was of the salt of passion in her tasteless life – the passion of indignation, of courage, of pity, and even of self-sacrifice. She did not add: 'And you aren't likely ever to be as long as I live.' But she might very well have done so, since she had taken effectual steps to that end. Mr Verloc was a very good husband. It was her honest impression that nobody could help liking the boy. She cried out suddenly:

'Quick, Stevie. Stop that green bus.'

And Stevie, tremulous and important with his sister Winnie on his arm, flung up the other high above his head at the approaching bus, with complete success.

An hour afterwards Mr Verloc raised his eyes from a newspaper he was reading, or at any rate looking at, behind the counter, and in the expiring clatter of the door-bell beheld Winnie, his wife, enter and cross the shop on her way upstairs, followed by Stevie, his brother-in-law. The sight of his wife was agreeable to Mr Verloc. It was his idiosyncrasy. The figure of his brother-in-law remained imperceptible to him because of the morose thoughtfulness that lately had fallen like a veil between Mr Verloc and the appearances of the world of senses. He looked after his wife fixedly, without a word, as though she had been a phantom. His voice for home use was husky and placid, but now it was heard not at all. It was not heard at supper, to which he was called by his wife in the usual brief manner: 'Adolf.' He sat down to consume it without conviction, wearing his hat pushed far back on his head. It was not devotion to an outdoor life, but the frequentation of foreign cafés which was responsible for that habit, investing with a character of unceremonious impermanency Mr Verloc's steady fidelity to his own fireside. Twice at the clatter of the cracked bell he arose without a word, disappeared into the shop, and came back silently. During these absences Mrs Verloc, becoming acutely aware of the vacant place at her right hand, missed her mother very much and stared stonily; while Stevie, from the same reason, kept on shuffling his feet, as though the floor under the table were uncomfortably hot. When Mr Verloc returned to sit in his place, like the very embodiment of silence, the character of Mrs Verloc's stare underwent a subtle change, and Stevie ceased to fidget with his feet, because of his great and awed regard for his sister's husband. He directed at him glances of respectful compassion. Mr Verloc was sorry. His sister Winnie had impressed upon him (in the omnibus) that Mr Verloc would be found at home in a state of sorrow, and must not be worried. His father's anger, the irritability of gentlemen lodgers, and Mr Verloc's predisposition to immoderate grief, had been the main sanctions of Stevie's self-restraint. Of these sentiments, all easily provoked, but not always easy to understand, the last had the greatest moral efficiency – because Mr Verloc was *good*. His mother and his sister had established that ethical fact on an unshakable foundation. They had established, erected, consecrated it behind Mr Verloc's back, for reasons that had nothing to do with abstract morality. And Mr Verloc was not aware of it. It is but bare justice to him to say that he had no notion of appearing good to Stevie. Yet so it was. He was even the only man so qualified in Stevie's knowledge, because the gentlemen lodgers had been too transient and too remote to have anything very distinct about them but perhaps their boots; and as regards the disciplinary measures of his father, the desolation of his mother and sister shrank from setting up a theory of goodness before the victim. It would have been too cruel. And it was even possible that Stevie would not have believed them. As far as Mr Verloc was concerned, nothing could stand in the way of Stevie's belief. Mr Verloc was obviously yet mysteriously *good*. And the grief of a good man is august.

Stevie gave glances of reverential compassion to his brother-in-law. Mr Verloc was sorry. The brother of Winnie had never before felt himself in such close communion with the mystery of that man's goodness. It was an understandable sorry. And Stevie himself was sorry. He was very sorry. The same sort of sorrow. And his attention being drawn to this unpleasant state, Stevie shuffled his feet. His feelings were habitually manifested by the agitation of his limbs.

'Keep your feet quiet, dear,' said Mrs Verloc, with authority and tenderness; then turning towards her husband in an indifferent voice, the masterly achievement of instinctive tact: 'Are you going out tonight?' she asked.

The mere suggestion seemed repugnant to Mr Verloc. He shook his head moodily, and then sat still with downcast eyes, looking at the piece of cheese on his plate for a whole minute. At the end of that time he got up, and went out – went right out in the clatter of the shop-door bell. He acted thus inconsistently, not from any desire to make himself unpleasant, but because of an unconquerable restlessness. It was no earthly good going out. He could not find anywhere in London what he wanted. But he went out. He led a cortège of dismal thoughts along dark streets, through lighted streets, in and out of two flash bars, as if in a half-hearted attempt to make a night of it, and finally back again to his menaced home, where he sat down fatigued behind the counter, and they crowded urgently round him, like a pack of hungry black hounds. After locking up the house and putting out the gas he took them upstairs with him – a dreadful escort for a man going to bed. His wife had preceded him some time before, and with her ample form defined vaguely under the counterpane, her head on the pillow, and a hand under the cheek, offered to his distraction the view of early drowsiness arguing the possession of an equable soul. Her big eyes stared wide open, inert and dark against the snowy whiteness of the linen. She did not move.

She had an equable soul. She felt profoundly that things do not stand much looking into. She made her force and her wisdom of that instinct. But the taciturnity of Mr Verloc had been lying heavily upon her for a good many days. It was, as a matter of fact, affecting her nerves. Recumbent and motionless, she said placidly:

'You'll catch cold walking about in your socks like this.'

This speech, becoming the solicitude of the wife and the prudence of the woman, took Mr Verloc unawares. He had left his boots downstairs, but he had forgotten to put on his slippers, and he had been turning about the bedroom on noiseless pads like a bear in a cage. At the sound of his wife's voice he stopped and stared at her with a somnambulistic, expressionless gaze so long that Mrs Verloc moved her limbs slightly under the bedclothes. But she did not move her black head sunk in the white pillow, one hand under her cheek and the big, dark, unwinking eyes.

Under her husband's expressionless stare, and remembering her mother's empty room across the landing, she felt an acute pang of loneliness. She had never been parted from her mother before. They had stood by each other. She felt that they had, and she said to herself that now mother was gone – gone for good. Mrs Verloc had no illusions. Stevie remained, however. And she said:

'Mother's done what she wanted to do. There's no sense in it that I can see. I'm sure she couldn't have thought you had enough of her. It's perfectly wicked, leaving us like that.'

Mr Verloc was not a well-read person; his range of allusive phrases was limited, but there was a peculiar aptness in circumstances which made him think of rats leaving a doomed ship. He very nearly said so. He had grown suspicious and embittered. Could it be that the old woman had such an excellent nose? But the unreasonableness of such a suspicion was patent, and Mr Verloc held his tongue. Not altogether, however. He muttered, heavily:

'Perhaps it's just as well.'

He began to undress. Mrs Verloc kept very still, perfectly still, with her eyes fixed in a dreamy, quiet stare. And her heart for the fraction of a second seemed to stand still, too. That night she was 'not quite herself', as the saying is, and it was borne upon her with some force that a simple sentence may hold several diverse meanings – mostly disagreeable. *How* was it just as well? And why? But she did not allow herself to fall into the idleness of barren speculation. She was rather confirmed in her belief that things did not stand being looked into. Practical and subtle in her way, she brought Stevie to the front without loss of time, because in her the singleness of purpose had the unerring nature and the force of an instinct.

'What I am going to do to cheer up that boy for the first few days I'm sure I don't know. He'll be worrying himself from morning till night before he gets used to mother being away. And he's such a good boy. I couldn't do without him.'

Mr Verloc went on divesting himself of his clothing with the unnoticing inward concentration of a man undressing in the solitude of a vast and hopeless desert. For thus inhospitably did this fair earth, our common inheritance, present itself to the mental vision of Mr Verloc. All was so still without and within that the lonely ticking of the clock on the landing stole into the room as if for the sake of company.

Mr Verloc, getting into bed on his own side, remained prone and mute behind Mrs Verloc's back. His thick arms rested abandoned on the outside of the counterpane like dropped weapons, like discarded tools. At that moment he was within a hair's breadth of making a clean breast of it all to his wife. The moment seem propitious. Looking out of the corners of his eyes, he saw her ample shoulders draped in white, the back of her head, with the hair done for the night in three plaits tied up with black tapes at the ends. And he forbore. Mr Verloc loved his wife as a wife should be loved – that is, maritally, with the regard one has for one's chief possession. This head arranged for the night, those ample shoulders, had an aspect of familiar sacredness – the sacredness of domestic peace. She moved not, massive and shapeless like a recumbent statue in the rough; he remembered her wide-open eyes looking into the empty room. She was mysterious, with the mysteriousness of living beings. The far-famed secret agent △ of the late Baron Stott-Wartenheim's alarmist dispatches was not the man to break into such mysteries. He was easily intimidated. And he was also indolent, with the indolence which is so often the secret of good nature. He forbore touching that mystery out of love, timidity, and indolence. There would be always time enough. For several minutes he bore his sufferings silently in the drowsy silence of the room. And then he disturbed it by a resolute declaration.

'I am going on the Continent tomorrow.'

His wife might have fallen asleep already. He could not tell. As a matter of fact, Mrs Verloc had heard him. Her eyes remained very wide open, and she lay very still, confirmed in her instinctive conviction that things don't bear looking into very much. And yet it was nothing very unusual for Mr Verloc to take such a trip. He renewed his stock from Paris and Brussels. Often he went over to make his purchases personally. A little select connexion of amateurs was forming around the shop in Brett Street, a secret connexion eminently proper for any business undertaken by Mr Verloc, who, by a mystic accord of temperament and necessity, had been set apart to be a secret agent all his life.

He waited for a while, then added: 'I'll be away a week or perhaps a fortnight. Get Mrs Neale to come for the day.'

Mrs Neale was the charwoman of Brett Street. Victim of her marriage with a debauched joiner, she was oppressed by the needs of many infant children. Red-armed, and aproned in coarse sacking up to the armpits, she exhaled the anguish of the poor in a breath of soap-suds and rum, in the uproar of scrubbing, in the clatter of tin pails.

Mrs Verloc, full of deep purpose, spoke in the tone of the shallowest indifference.

'There is no need to have the woman here all day. I shall do very well with Stevie.'

She let the lonely clock on the landing count off fifteen ticks into the abyss of eternity, and asked:

'Shall I put the light out?'

Mr Verloc snapped at his wife huskily.

'Put it out.'

CHAPTER 9

Mr Verloc returning from the Continent at the end of ten days, brought back a mind evidently unrefreshed by the wonders of foreign travel and a countenance unlighted by the joys of homecoming. He entered in the clatter of the shop-bell with an air of sombre and vexed exhaustion. His bag in hand, his head lowered, he strode straight behind the counter, and let himself fall into the chair, as though he had tramped all the way from Dover. It was early morning. Stevie, dusting various objects displayed in the front windows, turned to gape at him with reverence and awe.

'Here!' said Mr Verloc, giving a slight kick to the gladstone bag on the floor; and Stevie flung himself upon it, seized it, bore it off with triumphant devotion. He was so prompt that Mr Verloc was distinctly surprised.

Already at the clatter of the shop-bell Mrs Neale, blackleading the parlour grate, had looked through the door, and rising from her knees had gone, aproned, and grimy with everlasting toil, to tell Mrs Verloc in the kitchen that 'there was the master come back'.

Winnie came no farther than the inner shop door.

'You'll want some breakfast,' she said from a distance.

Mr Verloc moved his hands slightly, as if overcome by an impossible suggestion. But once enticed into the parlour he did not reject the food set before him. He ate as if in a public place, his hat pushed off his forehead, the skirts of his heavy overcoat hanging in a triangle on each side of the chair. And across the length of the table covered with brown oilcloth Winnie, his wife, talked evenly at him the wifely talk, as artfully adapted, no doubt, to the circumstances of this return as the talk of Penelope to the return of the wandering Odysseus. Mrs Verloc, however, had done no weaving during her husband's absence. But she had had all the upstairs room cleaned thoroughly, had sold some wares, had seen Mr Michaelis several times. He had told her the last time that he was going away to live in a cottage in the country, somewhere on the London, Chatham, and Dover line. Karl Yundt had come, too, once, led under the arm by that 'wicked old house-keeper of his'. He was 'a disgusting old man'. Of Comrade Ossipon, whom she had received curtly, entrenched behind the counter with a stony face and a far-away gaze, she said nothing, her mental reference to the robust anarchist being marked by a short pause, with the faintest possible blush. And bringing in her brother Stevie as soon as she could into the current of domestic events, she mentioned that the boy had moped a good deal.

'It's all along of mother leaving us like this.'

Mr Verloc neither said 'Damn!' nor yet 'Stevie be hanged!' And Mrs Verloc, not let into the secret of his thoughts, failed to appreciate the generosity of this restraint.

'It isn't that he doesn't work as well as ever,' she continued. 'He's been making himself very useful. You'd think he couldn't do enough for us.'

Mr Verloc directed a casual and somnolent glance at Stevie, who sat on his right, delicate, pale-faced, his rosy mouth open vacantly. It was not a critical glance. It had no intention. And if Mr Verloc thought for a moment that his wife's brother looked uncommonly useless, it was only a dull and fleeting thought, devoid of that force and durability which enables sometimes a thought to move the world. Leaning back, Mr Verloc uncovered his head. Before his extended arm could put down the hat Stevie pounced upon it, and bore it off reverently into the kitchen. And again Mr Verloc was surprised.

'You could do anything with that boy, Adolf,' Mrs Verloc said, with her best air of inflexible calmness. 'He would go through fire for you. He – '

She paused attentive, her ear turned towards the door of the kitchen.

There Mrs Neale was scrubbing the floor. At Stevie's appearance she groaned lamentably, having observed that he could be induced easily to bestow for the benefit of her infant children the shilling his sister Winnie presented him with from time to time. On all fours amongst the puddles, wet and begrimed, like a sort of amphibious and domestic animal living in ashbins and dirty water, she uttered the usual exordium; 'It's all very well for you, kept doing nothing like a gentleman.' And she followed it with the everlasting plaint of the poor, pathetically mendacious, miserably authenticated by the horrible breath of cheap rum and soap-suds. She scrubbed hard, snuffling all the time, and talking volubly. And she was sincere. And on each side of her thin red nose her bleared, misty eyes swam in tears, because she felt really the want of some sort of stimulant in the morning.

In the parlour Mrs Verloc observed, with knowledge:

'There's Mrs Neale at it again with her harrowing tales about her little children. They can't be all so little as she makes them out. Some of them must be big enough by now to try to do something for themselves. It only makes Stevie angry.'

These words were confirmed by a thud as of a fist striking the kitchen table. In the normal evolution of his sympathy Stevie had become angry on discovering that he had no shilling in his pocket. In his inability to relieve at once Mrs Neale's 'little 'uns'' privations, he felt that somebody should be made to suffer for it. Mrs Verloc rose and went into the kitchen to 'stop that nonsense'. And she did it firmly but gently. She was well aware that directly

Mrs Neale received her money she went round the corner to drink ardent spirits in a mean and musty public-house – the unavoidable station on the *via dolorosa* of her life. Mrs Verloc's comment upon this practice had an unexpected profundity, as coming from a person disinclined to look under the surface of things. 'Of course, what is she to do to keep up? If I were like Mrs Neale I expect I wouldn't act any different.'

In the afternoon of the same day, as Mr Verloc, coming with a start out of the last of a long series of dozes before the parlour fire, declared his intention of going out for a walk, Winnie said from the shop:

'I wish you would take that boy out with you, Adolf.'

For the third time that day Mr Verloc was surprised. He stared stupidly at his wife. She continued in her steady manner. The boy, whenever he was not doing anything, moped in the house. It made her uneasy; it made her nervous, she confessed. And that from the calm Winnie sounded like exaggeration. But in truth, Stevie moped in the striking fashion of an unhappy domestic animal. He would go up on the dark landing, to sit on the floor at the foot of the tall clock, with his knees drawn up and his head in his hands. To come upon his pallid face, with its big eyes gleaming in the dusk, was discomposing; to think of him up there was uncomfortable.

Mr Verloc got used to the startling novelty of the idea. He was fond of his wife as a man should be – that is, generously. But a weighty objection presented itself to his mind, and he formulated it.

'He'll lose sight of me perhaps, and get lost in the street,' he said.

Mrs Verloc shook her head competently.

'He won't. You don't know him. That boy just worships you. But if you should miss him – '

Mrs Verloc paused for a moment, but only for a moment.

'You just go on, and have your walk out. Don't worry. He'll be all right. He's sure to turn up safe here before very long.'

This optimism procured for Mr Verloc his fourth surprise of the day.

'Is he?' he grunted doubtfully. But perhaps his brother-in-law was not such an idiot as he looked. His wife would know best. He turned away his heavy eyes, saying huskily: 'Well, let him come along, then,' and relapsed into the clutches of black care, that perhaps prefers to sit behind a horseman, but knows also how to tread close on the heels of people not sufficiently well off to keep horses – like Mr Verloc, for instance.

Winnie, at the shop door, did not see this fatal attendant upon Mr Verloc's walks. She watched the two figures down the squalid street, one tall and burly, the other slight and short, with a thin neck, and the peaked shoulders raised slightly under the large semi-transparent ears. The material of their overcoats was the same, their hats were black and round in shape. Inspired by the similarity of wearing apparel, Mrs Verloc gave rein to her fancy.

'Might be father and son,' she said to herself. She thought also that Mr Verloc was as much of a father as poor Stevie ever had in his life. She was aware also that it was her work. And with peaceful pride she congratulated herself on a certain resolution she had taken a few years before. It had cost her some effort, and even a few tears.

She congratulated herself still more on observing in the course of days that Mr Verloc seemed to be taking kindly to Stevie's companionship. Now, when ready to go out for his walk, Mr Verloc called aloud to the boy, in the spirit, no doubt, in which a man invites the attendance of the household dog, though, of course, in a different manner. In the house Mr Verloc could be detected staring curiously at Stevie a good deal. His own demeanour had changed. Taciturn still, he was not so listless. Mrs Verloc thought that he was rather jumpy at times. It might have been regarded as an improvement. As to Stevie, he moped no longer at the foot of the clock, but muttered to himself in corners instead in a threatening tone. When asked 'What is it you're saying, Stevie?' he merely opened his mouth, and squinted at his sister. At odd times he clenched his fists without apparent cause, and when discovered in solitude would be scowling at the wall, with the sheet of paper and the pencil given him for drawing circles lying blank and idle on the kitchen table. This was a change, but it was no improvement. Mrs Verloc, including all these vagaries under the general definition of excitement, began to fear that Stevie was hearing more than was good for him of her husband's conversations with his friends. During his 'walks' Mr Verloc, of course, met and conversed with various persons. It could hardly be otherwise. His walks were an integral part of his outdoor activities, which his wife had never looked deeply into. Mrs Verloc felt that the position was delicate, but she faced it with the same impenetrable calmness which impressed and even astonished the customers of the shop and made the other visitors keep their distance a little wonderingly. No! She feared that there were things not good for Stevie to hear of, she told her husband. It only excited the poor boy, because he could not help them being so. Nobody could.

It was in the shop. Mr Verloc made no comment. He made no retort, and yet the retort was obvious. But he refrained from pointing out to his wife that the idea of making Stevie the companion of his walks was her own, and nobody else's. At that moment, to an impartial observer, Mr Verloc would have appeared more than human in his magnanimity. He took down a small cardboard box from the shelf, peeped in to see that the contents were all right, and put it down gently on the counter. Not till that was done did he break the silence, to the effect that most likely Stevie would profit greatly by being sent out of town for a while; only he supposed his wife could not get on without him.

'Could not get on without him!' repeated Mrs Verloc, slowly. 'I couldn't get on without him if it were for his good! The idea! Of course, I can get on without him. But there's nowhere for him to go.'

Mr Verloc got out some brown paper and a ball of string; and meanwhile he muttered that Michaelis was living in a little cottage in the country. Michaelis wouldn't mind giving Stevie a room to sleep in. There were no visitors and no talk there. Michaelis was writing a book.

Mrs Verloc declared her affection for Michaelis; mentioned her abhorrence of Karl Yundt, 'nasty old man'; and of Ossipon she said nothing. As to Stevie, he could be no other than very pleased. Mr Michaelis was always so nice and kind to him. He seemed to like the boy. Well, the boy was a good boy.

'You, too, seem to have grown quite fond of him of late,' she added, after a pause, with her inflexible assurance.

Mr Verloc, tying up the cardboard box into a parcel for the post, broke the string by an injudicious jerk, and muttered several swear-words confidentially to himself. Then raising his tone to the usual husky mutter, he announced his willingness to take Stevie into the country himself, and leave him all safe with Michaelis.

He carried out this scheme on the very next day. Stevie offered no objection. He seemed rather eager, in a bewildered sort of way. He turned his candid gaze inquisitively to Mr Verloc's heavy countenance at frequent intervals, especially when his sister was not looking at him. His expression was proud, apprehensive, and concentrated, like that of a small child entrusted for the first time with a box of matches and the permission to strike a light. But Mrs Verloc, gratified by her brother's docility, recommended him not to dirty his clothes unduly in the country. At this Stevie gave his sister, guardian, and protector a look, which for the first time in his life seemed to lack the quality of perfect childlike trustfulness. It was haughtily gloomy. Mrs Verloc smiled.

'Goodness me! You needn't be offended. You know you do get yourself very untidy when you get a chance, Stevie.'

Mr Verloc was already gone some way down the street.

Thus in consequence of her mother's heroic proceedings, and of her brother's absence on this villegiature, Mrs Verloc found herself oftener than usual all alone not only in the shop, but in the house. For Mr Verloc had to take his walks. She was alone longer than usual on the day of the attempted bomb outrage in Greenwich Park, because Mr Verloc went out very early that morning and did not come back till nearly dusk. She did not mind being alone. She had no desire to go out. The weather was too bad, and the shop was cosier than the streets. Sitting behind the counter with some sewing, she did not raise her eyes from her work when Mr Verloc entered in the aggressive clatter of the bell. She had recognized his step on the pavement outside.

She did not raise her eyes, but as Mr Verloc, silent, and with his hat rammed down upon his forehead, made straight for the parlour door, she said, serenely:

'What a wretched day. You've been perhaps to see Stevie?'

'No! I haven't,' said Mr Verloc, softly, and slammed the glazed parlour door behind him with unexpected energy.

For some time Mrs Verloc remained quiescent, with her work dropped in her lap, before she put it away under the counter and got up to light the gas. This done, she went into the parlour on her way to the kitchen. Mr Verloc would want his tea presently. Confident of the power of her charms, Winnie did not expect from her husband in the daily intercourse of their married life a ceremonious amenity of address and courtliness of manner; vain and antiquated forms at best, probably never very exactly observed, discarded nowadays even in the highest spheres, and always foreign to the standards of her class. She did not look for courtesies from him. But he was a good husband, and she had a loyal respect for his rights.

Mrs Verloc would have gone through the parlour and on to her domestic duties in the kitchen with the perfect serenity of a woman sure of the power of her charms. But a slight, very slight, and rapid rattling sound grew upon her hearing. Bizarre and incomprehensible, it arrested Mrs Verloc's attention. Then as its character became plain to the ear she stopped short, amazed and concerned. Striking a match on the box she held in her hand, she turned on and lighted, above the parlour table, one of the two gas-burners, which, being defective, first whistled as if astonished, and then went on purring comfortably like a cat.

Mr Verloc, against his usual practice, had thrown off his overcoat. It was lying on the sofa. His hat, which he must also have thrown off, rested overturned under the edge of the sofa. He had dragged a chair in front of the fireplace, and his feet planted inside the fender, his head held between his hands, he was hanging low over the glowing grate. His teeth rattled with an ungovernable violence, causing his whole enormous back to tremble at the same rate. Mrs Verloc was startled.

'You've been getting wet,' she said.

'Not very,' Mr Verloc managed to falter out, in a profound shudder. By a great effort he suppressed the rattling of his teeth.

'I'll have you laid up on my hands,' she said, with genuine uneasiness.

'I don't think so,' remarked Mr Verloc, snuffling huskily.

He had certainly contrived somehow to catch an abominable cold between seven in the morning and five in the afternoon. Mrs Verloc looked at his bowed back.

'Where have you been today?' she asked.

'Nowhere,' answered Mr Verloc in a low, choked nasal tone. His attitude suggested aggrieved sulks or a severe headache. The unsufficiency and uncandidness of his answer became painfully apparent in the dead silence of the room. He snuffled apologetically, and added: 'I've been to the bank.'

Mrs Verloc became attentive.

'You have!' she said, dispassionately. 'What for?'

Mr Verloc mumbled, with his nose over the grate, and with marked unwillingness:

'Draw the money out!'

'What do you mean? All of it?'

'Yes. All of it.'

Mrs Verloc spread out with care the scanty tablecloth, got two knives and two forks out of the table drawer, and suddenly stopped in her methodical proceedings.

'What did you do that for?'

'May want it soon,' snuffled vaguely Mr Verloc, who was coming to the end of his calculated indiscretions.

'I don't know what you mean,' remarked his wife in a tone perfectly casual, but standing stock still between the table and the cupboard.

'You know you can trust me,' Mr Verloc remarked to the grate, with hoarse feeling.

Mrs Verloc turned slowly towards the cupboard, saying with deliberation:

'Oh, yes. I can trust you.'

And she went on with her methodical proceedings. She laid two plates, got the bread, the butter, going to and fro quietly between the table and the cupboard in the peace and silence of her home. On the point of taking out the jam, she reflected practically: 'He will be feeling hungry, having been away all day,' and she returned to the cupboard once more to get the cold beef. She set it under the purring gas-jet, and with a passing glance at her motionless husband hugging the fire, she went (down two steps) into the kitchen. It was only when coming back, carving knife and fork in hand, that she spoke again.

'If I hadn't trusted you I wouldn't have married you.'

Bowed under the overmantel, Mr Verloc, holding his head in both hands, seemed to have gone to sleep. Winnie made the tea, and called out in an undertone:

'Adolf.'

Mr Verloc got up at once, and staggered a little before he sat down at the table. His wife, examining the sharp edge of the carving knife, placed it on the dish, and called his attention to the cold beef. He remained insensible to the suggestion, with his chin on his breast.

'You should feed your cold,' Mrs Verloc said, dogmatically.

He looked up, and shook his head. His eyes were bloodshot and his face red. His fingers had ruffled his hair into a dissipated untidiness. Altogether he had a disreputable aspect, expressive of the discomfort, the irritation, and the gloom following a heavy debauch. But Mr Verloc was not a debauched man. In his conduct he was respectable. His appearance might have been the effect of a feverish cold. He drank three cups of tea, but abstained from food entirely. He recoiled from it with sombre aversion when urged by Mrs Verloc, who said at last:

'Aren't your feet wet? You had better put on your slippers. You aren't going out any more this evening.'

Mr Verloc intimated by morose grunts and signs that his feet were not wet, and that anyhow he did not care. The proposal as to slippers was disregarded as beneath his notice. But the question of going out in the evening received an unexpected development. It was not of going out in the evening that Mr Verloc was thinking. His thoughts embraced a vaster scheme. From moody and incomplete phrases it became apparent that Mr Verloc had been considering the expediency of emigrating. It was not very clear whether he had in his mind France or California.

The utter unexpectedness, improbability, and inconceivableness of such an event robbed this vague declaration of all its effect. Mrs Verloc, as placidly as if her husband had been threatening her with the end of the world, said:

'The idea!'

Mr Verloc declared himself sick and tired of everything, and besides – She interrupted him.

'You've a bad cold.'

It was indeed obvious that Mr Verloc was not in his usual state, physically and even mentally. A sombre irresolution held him silent for a while. Then he murmured a few ominous generalities on the theme of necessity.

'Will have to,' repeated Winnie, sitting calmly back, with folded arms, opposite her husband. 'I should like to know who's to make you. You ain't a slave. No one need be a slave in this country – and don't you make yourself one.' She paused, and with invincible and steady candour: 'The business isn't so bad,' she went on. 'You've a comfortable home.'

She glanced all round the parlour, from the corner cupboard to the good fire in the grate. Ensconced cosily behind the shop of doubtful wares, with the mysteriously dim window, and its door suspiciously ajar in the obscure and narrow street, it was in all essentials of domestic propriety and domestic comfort a respectable home. Her devoted affection missed out of it her brother Stevie, now enjoying a damp villegiature in the Kentish lanes under the care of Mr Michaelis. She missed him poignantly, with all the force of her protecting passion. This was the boy's home, too – the roof, the cupboard, the stoked grate. On this thought Mrs Verloc rose, and walking to the other end of the table, said in the fullness of her heart;

'And you are not tired of me.'

Mr Verloc made no sound. Winnie leaned on his shoulder from behind, and pressed her lips to his forehead. Thus she lingered. Not a whisper reached them from the outside world. The sound of footsteps on the pavement died out in the discreet dimness of the shop. Only the gas-jet above the table went on purring equably in the brooding silence of the parlour.

During the contact of that unexpected and lingering kiss Mr Verloc, gripping with both hands the edges of his chair, preserved a hieratic immobility. When the pressure was removed he let go the chair, rose, and went to stand before the fireplace. He turned no longer his back to the room. With his features swollen and an air of being drugged, he followed his wife's movements with his eyes.

Mrs Verloc went about serenely, clearing up the table. Her tranquil voice commented on the idea thrown out in a reasonable and domestic tone. It wouldn't stand examination. She condemned it from every point of view. But her only real concern was Stevie's welfare. He appeared to her thought in that connexion as sufficiently 'peculiar' not to be taken rashly abroad. And that was all. But talking round that vital point, she approached absolute vehemence in her delivery. Meanwhile, with brusque movements, she arrayed herself in an apron for the washing up of cups. And as if excited by the sound of her uncontradicted voice, she went so far as to say in a tone almost tart:

'If you go abroad you'll have to go without me.'

'You know I wouldn't,' said Mr Verloc, huskily, and the unresonant voice of his private life trembled with an enigmatical emotion.

Already Mrs Verloc was regretting her words. They had sounded more unkind than she meant them to be. They had also the unwisdom of unnecessary things. In fact, she had not meant them at all. It was a sort of phrase that is suggested by the demon of perverse inspiration. But she knew a way to make it as if it had not been.

She turned her head over her shoulder and gave that man planted heavily in front of the fireplace a glance, half arch, half cruel, out of her large eyes – a glance of which the Winnie of the Belgravian mansion days would have been incapable, because of her respectability and her ignorance. But the man was her husband now, and she was no longer ignorant. She kept it on him for a whole second, with her grave face motionless like a mask, while she said playfully:

'You couldn't. You would miss me too much.'

Mr Verloc started forward.

'Exactly,' he said in a louder tone, throwing his arms out and making a step towards her. Something wild and doubtful in his expression made it appear uncertain whether he meant to strangle or to embrace his wife. But Mrs Verloc's attention was called away from that manifestation by the clatter of the shop-bell.

'Shop, Adolf. You go.'

He stopped, his arms came down slowly.

'You go,' repeated Mrs Verloc. 'I've got my apron on.'

Mr Verloc obeyed woodenly, stony-eyed, and like an automaton whose face had been painted red. And this resemblance to a mechanical figure went so far that he had an automaton's absurd air of being aware of the machinery inside of him.

He closed the parlour door, and Mrs Verloc, moving briskly, carried the tray into the kitchen. She washed the cups and some other things before she stopped in her work to listen. No sound reached her. The customer was a long time in the shop. It was a customer, because if he had not been Mr Verloc would have taken him inside. Undoing the strings of her apron with a jerk, she threw it on a chair, and walked back to the parlour slowly.

At that precise moment Mr Verloc entered from the shop.

He had gone in red. He came out a strange papery white. His face, losing its drugged, feverish stupor, had in that short time acquired a bewildered and harassed expression. He walked straight to the sofa, and stood looking down at his overcoat lying there, as though he were afraid to touch it.

'What's the matter?' asked Mrs Verloc in a subdued voice. Through the door left ajar she could see that the customer was not gone yet.

'I find I'll have to go out this evening,' said Mr Verloc. He did not attempt to pick up his outer garment.

Without a word Winnie made for the shop, and shutting the door after her, walked in behind the counter. She did not look overtly at the customer till she had established herself comfortably on the chair. But by that time she had noted that he was tall and thin, and wore his moustaches twisted up. In fact, he gave the sharp points a twist just then. His long, bony face rose out of a turned-up collar. He was a little splashed, a little wet. A dark man, with the ridge of the cheek-bone well defined under the slightly hollow temple. A complete stranger. Not a customer, either.

Mrs Verloc looked at him placidly.

'You came over from the Continent?' she said after a time.

The long, thin stranger, without exactly looking at Mrs Verloc, answered only by a faint and peculiar smile.

Mrs Verloc's steady, incurious gaze rested on him.

'You understand English, don't you?'

'Oh, yes. I understand English.'

There was nothing foreign in his accent, except that he seemed in his slow enunciation to be taking pains with it. And Mrs Verloc, in her varied experience, had come to the conclusion that some foreigners could speak better English than the natives. She said, looking at the door of the parlour fixedly:

'You don't think perhaps of staying in England for good?'

The stranger gave her again a silent smile. He had a kindly mouth and probing eyes. And he shook his head a little sadly, it seemed.

'My husband will see you through all right. Meantime, for a few days you couldn't do better than take lodgings with Mr Guigliani. Continental Hotel it's called. Private. It's quiet. My husband will take you there.'

'A good idea,' said the thin, dark man, whose glance had hardened suddenly.

'You knew Mr Verloc before – didn't you? Perhaps in France?'

'I have heard of him,' admitted the visitor in his slow, painstaking tone, which yet had a certain curtness of intention.

There was a pause. Then he spoke again, in a far less elaborate manner.

'Your husband has not gone out to wait for me in the street by chance?'

'In the street!' repeated Mrs Verloc, surprised. 'He couldn't. There's no other door to the house.'

For a moment she sat impassive, then left her seat to go and peep through the glazed door. Suddenly she opened it, and disappeared into the parlour.

Mr Verloc had done no more than put on his overcoat. But why he should remain afterwards leaning over the table propped up on his two arms as though he were feeling giddy or sick, she could not understand. 'Adolf,' she called out half aloud; and when he had raised himself:

'Do you know that man?' she asked, rapidly.

I've heard of him,' whispered uneasily Mr Verloc, darting a wild glance at the door.

Mrs Verloc's fine, incurious eyes lighted up with a flash of abhorrence.

'One of Karl Yundt's friends – beastly old man.'

'No! No!' protested Mr Verloc, busy fishing for his hat. But when he got it from under the sofa he held it as if he did not know the use of a hat.

'Well – he's waiting for you,' said Mrs Verloc at last. 'I say, Adolf, he ain't one of them Embassy people you have been bothered with of late?'

'Bothered with Embassy people,' repeated Mr Verloc, with a heavy start of surprise and fear. 'Who's been talking to you of the Embassy people?'

'Yourself.'

'I! I! Talked of the Embassy to you!'

Mr Verloc seemed scared and bewildered beyond measure. His wife explained:

'You've been talking a little in your sleep of late, Adolf.'

'What – what did I say? What do you know?'

'Nothing much. It seemed mostly nonsense. Enough to let me guess that something worried you.'

Mr Verloc rammed his hat on his head. A crimson flood of anger ran over his face.

'Nonsense – eh? The Embassy people! I would cut their hearts out one after another. But let them look out. I've got a tongue in my head.'

He fumed, pacing up and down between the table and the sofa, his open overcoat catching against the angles. The red flood of anger ebbed out, and left his face all white, with quivering nostrils. Mrs Verdoc, for the purposes of practical existence, put down these appearances to the cold.

'Well,' she said, 'get rid of the man whoever he is, as soon as you can, and come back home to me. You want looking after for a day or two.'

Mr Verloc calmed down, and, with resolution imprinted on his pale face, had already opened the door, when his wife called him back in a whisper:

'Adolf! Adolf!' He came back, startled. 'What about that money you drew out?' she asked. 'You've got it in your pocket? Hadn't you better – '

Mr Verloc gazed stupidly into the palm of his wife's extended hand for some time before he slapped his brow.

'Money! Yes! Yes! I didn't know what you meant.'

He drew out of his breast-pocket a new pigskin pocket-book. Mrs Verloc received it without another word, and stood still till the bell, clattering after Mr Verloc and Mr Verloc's visitor, had quieted down. Only then she peeped in at the amount, drawing the notes out for the purpose. After this inspection she looked round thoughtfully, with an air of mistrust in the silence and solitude of the house. This abode of her married life appeared to her as lonely and unsafe as though it had been situated in the midst of a forest. No receptacle she could think of amongst the solid, heavy furniture seemed other but flimsy and particularly tempting to her conception of a house-breaker. It was an ideal conception, endowed with sublime faculties and a miraculous insight. The till was not to be thought of. It was the first spot a thief would make for. Mrs Verloc, unfastening hastily a couple of hooks, slipped the pocket-book under the bodice of her dress. Having thus disposed of her husband's capital, she was rather glad to hear the clatter of the door-bell, announcing an arrival. Assuming the fixed, unabashed stare and the stony expression reserved for the casual customer, she walked in behind the counter.

A man standing in the middle of the shop was inspecting it with a swift, cool, all-round glance. His eyes ran over the walls, took in the ceiling, noted the floor – all in a moment. The points of a long fair moustache fell below the line of the jaw. He smiled the smile of an old if distant acquaintance, and Mrs Verloc remembered having seen him before. Not a customer. She softened her 'customer stare' to mere indifference, and faced him across the counter.

He approached, on his side, confidentially, but not too markedly so.

'Husband at home, Mrs Verloc?' he asked in an easy, full tone.

'No. He's gone out.'

'I am sorry for that. I've called to get from him a little private information.'

This was the exact truth. Chief Inspector Heat had been all the way home and had even gone so far as to think of getting into his slippers, since practically he was, he told himself, chucked out of that case. He indulged in some scornful and in a few angry thoughts, and found the occupation so unsatisfactory that he resolved to seek relief out of doors. Nothing prevented him paying a friendly call on Mr Verloc, casually as it were. It was in the character of a private citizen that walking out privately he made use of his customary conveyances. Their general direction was towards Mr Verloc's home. Chief Inspector Heat respected his own private character so consistently that he took especial pains to avoid all the police constables on point and patrol duty in the vicinity of Brett Street. This precaution was much more necessary for a man of his standing than for an obscure Assistant Commissioner. Private Citizen Heat entered the street, manoeuvring in a way which in a member of the criminal classes would have been stigmatized as slinking. The piece of cloth picked up in Greenwich was in his pocket. Not that he had the slighest intention of producing it in his private capacity. On the contrary, he wanted to know just what Mr Verloc would be disposed to say voluntarily. He hoped Mr Verloc's talk would be of a nature to incriminate Michaelis. It was a conscientiously professional hope in the main, but not without its moral value. For Chief Inspector Heat was a servant of justice. Finding Mr Verloc from home, he felt disappointed.

'I would wait for him a little if I were sure he wouldn't be long,' he said.

Mrs Verloc volunteered no assurance of any kind.

'The information I need is quite private,' he repeated. 'You understand what I mean? I wonder if you could give me a notion where he's gone to?'

Mrs Verloc shook her head.

'Can't say.'

She turned away to range some boxes on the shelves behind the counter. Chief Inspector Heat looked at her thoughtfully for a time.

'I suppose you know who I am?' he said.

Mrs Verloc glanced over her shoulder. Chief Inspector Heat was amazed at her coolness.

'Come! You know I am in the police,' he said, sharply.

'I don't trouble my head much about it,' Mrs Verloc remarked, returning to the ranging of her boxes.

'My name is Heat. Chief Inspector Heat of the Special Crimes section.'

Mrs Verloc adjusted nicely in its place a small cardboard box, and turning round, faced him again, heavy-eyed, with idle hands hanging down. A silence reigned for a time.

'So your husband went out a quarter of an hour ago! And he didn't say when he would be back?'

'He didn't go out alone,' Mrs Verloc let fall negligently.

'A friend?'

Mrs Verloc touched the back of her hair. It was in perfect order.

'A stranger who called.'

'I see. What sort of man was that stranger? Would you mind telling me?'

Mrs Verloc did not mind. And when Chief Inspector Heat heard of a man dark, thin, with a long face and turned-up moustaches, he gave signs of perturbation, and exclaimed:

'Dash me if I didn't think so! He hasn't lost any time.'

He was intensely disgusted in the secrecy of his heart at the unofficial conduct of his immediate chief. But he was not quixotic. He lost all desire to await Mr Verloc's return. What they had gone out for he did not know, but he imagined it possible that they would return together. The case is not followed properly, it's being tampered with, he thought, bitterly.

'I am afraid I haven't time to wait for your husband,' he said.

Mrs Verloc received this declaration listlessly. Her detachment had impressed Chief Inspector Heat all along. At this precise moment it whetted his curiosity. Chief Inspector Heat hung in the wind, swayed by his passions like the most private of citizens.

'I think,' he said, looking at her steadily, 'that you could give me a pretty good notion of what's going on if you liked.'

Forcing her fine, inert eyes to return his gaze, Mrs Verloc murmured: 'Going on! What *is* going on?'

'Why, the affair I came to talk about a little with your husband.'

That day Mrs Verloc had glanced at a morning paper as usual. But she had not stirred out of doors. The newsboys never invaded Brett Street. It was not a street for their business. And the echo of their cries drifting along the populous thoroughfares, expired between the dirty brick walls without reaching the threshold of the shop. Her husband had not brought an evening paper home. At any rate she had not seen it. Mrs Verloc knew nothing whatever of any affair. And she said so, with a genuine note of wonder in her quiet voice.

Chief Inspector Heat did not believe for a moment in so much ignorance. Curtly, without amiability, he stated the bare fact.

Mrs Verloc turned away her eyes.

'I call it silly,' she pronounced, slowly. She paused. 'We ain't downtrodden slaves here.'

The Chief Inspector waited watchfully. Nothing more came.

'And your husband didn't mention anything to you when he came home?'

Mrs Verloc simply turned her face from right to left in sign of negation. A languid, baffling silence reigned in the shop. Chief Inspector Heat felt provoked beyond endurance.

'There was another small matter,' he began in a detached tone, 'which I wanted to speak to your husband about. There came into our hands a – a – what we believe is – a stolen overcoat.'

Mrs Verloc, with her mind specially aware of thieves that evening, touched lightly the bosom of her dress.

'We have lost no overcoat,' she said, calmly.

'That's funny,' continued Private Citizen Heat. 'I see you keep a lot of marking ink here – '

He took up a small bottle, and looked at it against the gas-jet in the middle of the shop.

'Purple – isn't it?' he remarked, setting it down again. 'As I said, it's strange. Because the overcoat has got a label sewn on the inside with your address written in marking ink.'

Mrs Verloc leaned over the counter with a low exclamation.

'That's my brother's, then.'

'Where's your brother? Can I see him?' asked the Chief Inspector, briskly. Mrs Verloc leaned a little more over the counter.

'No. He isn't here. I wrote that label myself.'

'Where's your brother now?'

'He's been away living with – a friend – in the country.'

'The overcoat comes from the country. And what's the name of the friend?'

'Michaelis,' confessed Mrs Verloc in an awed whisper.

The Chief Inspector let out a whistle. His eyes snapped.

'Just so. Capital. And your brother now, what's he like – a sturdy, darkish chap – eh?'

'Oh, no,' exclaimed Mrs Verloc, fervently. 'That must be the thief. Stevie's slight and fair.'

'Good,' said the Chief Inspector in an approving tone. And while Mrs Verloc, wavering between alarm and wonder, stared at him, he sought for information. Why have the address sewn like this inside the coat? And he heard that the mangled remains he had inspected that morning with extreme repugnance were those of a youth, nervous, absent-minded, peculiar, and also that the woman who was speaking to him had had the charge of that boy since he was a baby.

'Easily excitable?' he suggested.

'Oh, yes. He is. But how did he come to lose his coat – '

Chief Inspector Heat suddenly pulled out a pink newspaper he had bought less than half an hour ago. He was interested in horses. Forced by his calling into an attitude of doubt and suspicion towards his fellow-citizens, Chief Inspector Heat relieved the instinct of credulity implanted in the human breast by putting unbounded faith in the sporting prophets of that particular evening publication. Dropping the extra special on to the counter, he plunged his hand again into his pocket, and pulling out the piece of cloth fate had presented him with out of a heap of things that seemed to have been collected in shambles and rag shops, he offered it to Mrs Verloc for inspection.

'I suppose you recognize this?'

She took it mechanically in both her hands. Her eyes seemed to grow bigger as she looked.

'Yes,' she whispered, then raised her head, and staggered backward a little.

'Whatever for is it torn out like this?'

The Chief Inspector snatched across the counter the cloth out of her hands, and she sat heavily on the chair. He thought: identification's perfect. And in that moment he had a glimpse into the whole amazing truth. Verloc was the 'other man'.

'Mrs Verloc,' he said, 'it strikes me that you know more of this bomb affair than even you yourself are aware of.'

Mrs Verloc sat still, amazed, lost in boundless astonishment. What was the connexion? And she became so rigid all over that she was not able to turn her head at the clatter of the bell, which caused the private investigator Heat to spin round on his heel. Mr Verloc had shut the door, and for a moment the two men looked at each other.

Mr Verloc, without looking at his wife, walked up to the Chief Inspector, who was relieved to see him return alone.

'You here!' muttered Mr Verloc, heavily. 'Who are you after?'

'No one,' said Chief Inspector Heat in a low tone. 'Look here, I would like a word or two with you.'

Mr Verloc, still pale, had brought an air of resolution with him. Still he didn't look at his wife. He said:

'Come in here, then.' And he led the way into the parlour.

The door was hardly shut when Mrs Verloc, jumping up from the chair, ran to it as if to fling it open, but instead of doing so fell on her knees, with her ear to the keyhole. The two men must have stopped directly they were through, because she heard plainly the Chief Inspector's voice, though she could not see his finger pressed against her husband's breast emphatically.

'You are the other man, Verloc. Two men were seen entering the park.'

And the voice of Mr Verloc said:

'Well, take me now. What's to prevent you? You have the right.'

'Oh, no! I know too well who you have been giving yourself away to. He'll have to manage this little affair all by himself. But don't you make a mistake, it's I who found you out.'

Then she heard only muttering. Inspector Heat must have been showing to Mr Verloc the piece of Stevie's overcoat, because Stevie's sister, guardian, and protector heard her husband a little louder.

'I never noticed that she had hit upon that dodge.'

Again for a time Mrs Verloc heard nothing but murmurs, whose mysteriousness was less nightmarish to her brain than the horrible suggestions of shaped words. Then Chief Inspector Heat, on the other side of the door, raised his voice:

'You must have been mad.'

And Mr Verloc's voice answered, with a sort of gloomy fury:

'I have been mad for a month or more, but I am not mad now. It's all over. It shall all come out of my head, and hang the consequences.'

There was a silence, and then Private Citizen Heat murmured:

'What's coming out?'

'Everything,' exclaimed the voice of Mr Verloc, and then sank very low. After a while it rose again.

'You have known me for several years now, and you've found me useful, too. You know I was a straight man. Yes, straight.'

This appeal to old acquaintance must have been extremely distasteful to the Chief Inspector.

His voice took on a warning note.

'Don't you trust so much to what you have been promised. If I were you I would clear out. I don't think we will run after you.'

Mr Verloc was heard to laugh a little.

'Oh, yes; you hope the others will get rid of me for you – don't you? No, no; you don't shake me off now. I have been a straight man to those people too long, and now everything must come out.'

'Let it come out, then,' the indifferent voice of Chief Inspector Heat assented. 'But tell me now how did you get away?'

'I was making for Chesterfield Walk,' Mrs Verloc heard her husband's voice, 'when I heard the bang. I started running then. Fog. I saw no one till I was past the end of George Street. Don't think I met anyone till then.'

'So easy as that!' marvelled the voice of Chief Inspector Heat. 'The bang startled you, eh?'

'Yes; it came too soon,' confessed the gloomy, husky voice of Mr Verloc.

Mrs Verloc pressed her ear to the keyhole; her lips were blue, her hands cold as ice, and her pale face, in which the two eyes seemed like two black holes, felt to her as if it were enveloped in flames.

On the other side of the door the voices sank very low. She caught words now and then sometimes in her husband's voice, sometimes in the smooth tones of the Chief Inspector. She heard this last say:

'We believe he stumbled against the root of a tree?'

There was a husky, voluble murmur, which lasted for some time, and then the Chief Inspector, as if answering some inquiry, spoke emphatically:

'Of course. Blown to small bits: limbs, gravel, clothing, bones, splinters – all mixed up together. I tell you they had to fetch a shovel to gather him up with.'

Mrs Verloc sprang up suddenly from her crouching position, and stopping her ears, reeled to and fro between the counter and the shelves on the wall towards the chair. Her crazed eyes noted the sporting sheet left by the Chief Inspector, and as she knocked herself against the counter she snatched it up, fell into the chair, tore the optimistic, rosy sheet right across in trying to open it, then flung it on the floor. On the other side of the door, Chief Inspector Heat was saying to Mr Verloc, the secret agent:

'So your defence will be practically a full confession?'

'It will. I am going to tell the whole story.'

'You won't be believed as much as you fancy you will.'

And the Chief Inspector remained thoughtful. The turn this affair was taking meant the disclosure of many things – the laying waste of fields of knowledge, which, cultivated by a capable man, had a distinct value for the individual and for the society. It was sorry, sorry meddling. It would leave Michaelis unscathed; it would drag to light the Professor's home industry; disorganize the whole system of supervision; make no end of a row in the papers, which, from that point of view, appeared to him by a sudden illumination as invariably written by fools for the reading of imbeciles. Mentally he agreed with the words Mr Verloc let fall at last in answer to his last remark.

'Perhaps not. But it will upset many things. I have been a straight man, and I shall keep straight in this – '

'If they let you,' said the Chief Inspector, cynically. 'You will be preached to, no doubt, before they put you into the dock. And in the end you may get let in for a sentence that will surprise you. I wouldn't trust too much the gentleman who's been talking to you.'

Mr Verloc listened, frowning.

'My advice to you is to clear out while you may. I have no instructions. There are some of them,' continued Chief Inspector Heat, laying a peculiar stress on the word 'them', 'who think you are already out of the world.'

'Indeed!' Mr Verloc was moved to say. Though since his return from Greenwich he had spent most of his time sitting in the tap-room of an obscure little public-house, he could hardly have hoped for such favourable news.

'That's the impression about you.' The Chief Inspector nodded at him. 'Vanish. Clear out.'

'Where to?' snarled Mr Verloc. He raised his head, and gazing at the closed door of the parlour, muttered feelingly: 'I only wish you would take me away tonight. I would go quietly.'

'I daresay,' assented sardonically the Chief Inspector, following the direction of his glance.

The brow of Mr Verloc broke into slight moisture. He lowered his husky voice confidentially before the unmoved Chief Inspector.

'The lad was half-witted, irresponsible. Any court would have seen that at once. Only fit for the asylum. And that was the worst that would've happened to him if – '

The Chief Inspector, his hand on the door handle, whispered into Mr Verloc's face:

'He may've been half-witted, but you must have been crazy. What drove you off your head like this?'

Mr Verloc, thinking of Mr Vladimir, did not hesitate in the choice of words.

'A Hyperborean swine,' he hissed, forcibly. 'A what you might call a – a gentleman.'

The Chief Inspector, steady-eyed, nodded briefly his comprehension, and opened the door. Mrs Verloc, behind the counter, might have heard but did not see his departure, pursued by the aggressive clatter of the bell. She sat at her post of duty behind the counter. She sat rigidly erect in the chair with two dirty pink pieces of paper lying spread out at her feet. The palms of her hands were pressed convulsively to her face, with the tips of the fingers contracted against the forehead, as though the skin had been a mask which she was ready to tear off violently. The perfect immobility of her pose expressed the agitation of rage and despair, all the potential violence of tragic passions, better than any shallow display of shrieks, with the beating of a distracted head against the walls, could have done. Chief Inspector Heat, crossing the shop at his busy, swinging pace, gave her only a cursory glance. And when the cracked bell ceased to tremble on its curved ribbon of steel nothing stirred near Mrs Verloc, as if her attitude had the locking power of a spell. Even the butterfly-shaped gas flames posed on the ends of the suspended T-bracket burned without a quiver. In that shop of shady wares fitted with deal shelves painted a dull brown, which seemed to devour the sheen of the light, the gold circlet of the wedding ring on Mrs Verloc's left hand glittered exceedingly with the untarnished glory of a piece from some splendid treasure of jewels, dropped in a dust-bin.

CHAPTER 10

The Assistant Commissioner, driven rapidly in a hansom from the neighbourhood of Soho in the direction of Westminster, got out at the very centre of the Empire on which the sun never sets. Some stalwart constables, who did not seem particularly impressed by the duty of watching the august spot, saluted him. Penetrating through a portal by no means lofty into the precincts of the House which is *the* House, *par excellence*, in the minds of many millions of men, he was met at last by the volatile and revolutionary Toodles.

That neat and nice young man concealed his astonishment at the early appearance of the Assistant Commissioner, whom he had been told to look out for some time about midnight. His turning up so early he concluded to be the sign that things, whatever they were, had gone wrong. With an extremely ready sympathy, which in nice youngsters goes often with a joyous temperament, he felt sorry for the great Presence he called 'The Chief', and also for the Assistant Commissioner, whose face appeared to him more ominously wooden than ever before, and quite wonderfully long. 'What a queer, foreign-looking chap he is,' he thought to himself, smiling from a distance with friendly buoyancy. And directly they came together he began to talk with the kind intention of burying the awkwardness of failure under a heap of words. It looked as if the great assault threatened for that night were going to fizzle out. An inferior henchman of 'that brute Cheeseman' was up boring mercilessly a very thin House with some shamelessly cooked statistics. He, Toodles, hoped he would bore them into a count out every minute. But then he might be only marking time to let that guzzling Cheeseman dine at his leisure. Anyway, the Chief could not be persuaded to go home.

'He will see you at once, I think. He's sitting all alone in his room thinking of all the fishes of the sea,' concluded Toodles, airily. 'Come along.'

Notwithstanding the kindness of his disposition, the young private secretary (unpaid) was accessible to the common failings of humanity. He did not wish to harrow the feelings of the Assistant Commissioner, who looked to him uncommonly like a man who has made a mess of his job. But his curiosity was too strong to be restrained by mere compassion. He could not help, as they went along, to throw over his shoulder lightly:

'And your sprat?'

'Got him,' answered the Assistant Commissioner with a concision which did not mean to be repellent in the least.

'Good. You've no idea how these great men dislike to be disappointed in small things.'

After this profound observation the experienced Toodles seemed to reflect. At any rate he said nothing for quite two seconds. Then:

'I'm glad. But – I say – is it really such a very small thing as you make it out?'

'Do you know what may be done with a sprat?' the Assistant Commissioner asked in his turn.

'He's sometimes put into a sardine box,' chuckled Toodles, whose erudition on the subject of the fishing industry was fresh and, in comparison with his ignorance of all other industrial matters, immense. 'There are sardine canneries on the Spanish coast which – '

The Assistant Commissioner interrupted the apprentice statesman.

'Yes. Yes. But a sprat is also thrown away sometimes in order to catch a whale.'

'A whale. Phew!' exclaimed Toodles, with bated breath. 'You're after a whale, then?'

'Not exactly. What I am after is more like a dog-fish. You don't know perhaps what a dog-fish is like.'

'Yes; I do. We're buried in special books up to our necks – whole shelves full of them – with plates ... It's a noxious, rascally-looking, altogether detestable beast, with a sort of smooth face and moustaches.'

'Described to a T,' commended the Assistant Commissioner. 'Only mine is clean-shaven altogether. You've seen him. It's a witty fish.'

'I have seen him!' said Toodles, incredulously. 'I can't conceive where I could have seen him.'

'At the Explorers, I should say,' dropped the Assistant Commissioner, calmly. At the name of that extremely exclusive club Toodles looked scared, and stopped short.

'Nonsense,' he protested, but in an awestruck tone. 'What do you mean? A member?'

'Honorary,' muttered the Assistant Commissioner through his teeth.

'Heavens!'

Toodles looked so thunderstruck that the Assistant Commissioner smiled faintly.

'That's between ourselves strictly,' he said.

'That's the beastliest thing I've ever heard in my life,' declared Toodles, feebly, as if astonishment had robbed him of all his buoyant strength in a second.

The Assistant Commissioner gave him an unsmiling glance. Till they came to the door of the great man's room, Toodles preserved a scandalized and solemn silence, as though he were offended with the Assistant Commissioner for exposing such an unsavoury and disturbing fact. It revolutionized his idea of the Explorers' Club's extreme selectness, of its social purity. Toodles was revolutionary only in politics; his social beliefs and personal feelings he wished to preserve unchanged through all the years allotted to him on this earth which, upon the whole, he believed to be a nice place to live on.

He stood aside.

'Go in without knocking,' he said.

Shades of green silk fitted low over all the lights imparted to the room something of a forest's deep gloom. The haughty eyes were physically the great man's weak point. This point was wrapped up in secrecy. When an opportunity offered, he rested them conscientiously. The Assistant Commissioner entering saw at first only a big pale hand supporting a big head, and concealing the upper part of a big pale face. An open dispatch-box stood on the writing-table near a few oblong sheets of paper and a scattered handful of quill pens. There was absolutely nothing else on the large flat surface except a little bronze statuette draped in a toga, mysteriously watchful in its shadowy immobility. The Assistant Commissioner, invited to take a chair, sat down. In the dim light, the salient points of his personality, the long face, the black hair, his lankness, made him look more foreign than ever.

The great man manifested no surprise, no eagerness, no sentiment whatever. The attitude in which he rested his menaced eyes was profoundly meditative. He did not alter it the least bit. But his tone was not dreamy.

'Well! What is it that you've found out already? You came upon something unexpected on the first step.'

'Not exactly unexpected, Sir Ethelred. What I mainly came upon was a psychological state.'

The Great Presence made a slight movement.

'You must be lucid, please.'

'Yes, Sir Ethelred. You know no doubt that most criminals at some time or other feel an irresistible need of confessing – of making a clean breast of it to somebody – to anybody. And they do it often to the police. In that Verloc whom Heat wished so much to screen I've found a man in that particular psychological state. The man, figuratively speaking, flung himself on my breast. It was enough on my part to whisper to him who I was and to add "I know that you are at the bottom of this affair". It must have seemed miraculous to him that we should know already, but he took it all in the stride. The wonderfulness of it never checked him for a moment. There remained for me only to put to him the two questions: Who put you up to it? and Who was the man who did it? He answered the first with remarkable emphasis. As to the second question, I gather that the fellow with the bomb was his brother-in-law – quite a lad – a weak-minded creature. . . . It is rather a curious affair – too long perhaps to state fully just now.'

'What then have you learned?' asked the great man.

'First, I've learned that the ex-convict Michaelis had nothing to do with it, though indeed the lad had been living with him temporarily in the country up to eight o'clock this morning. It is more than likely that Michaelis knows nothing of it to this moment.'

'You are positive as to that?' asked the great man.

'Quite certain, Sir Ethelred. This fellow Verloc went there this morning, and took away the lad on the pretence of going out for a walk in the lanes. As it was not the first time that he did this, Michaelis could not have the slightest suspicion of anything unusual. For the rest, Sir Ethelred, the indignation of this man Verloc had left nothing in doubt – nothing whatever. He had been driven out of his mind almost by an extraordinary performance, which for you or me it would be difficult to take as seriously meant, but which produced a great impression obviously on him.'

The Assistant Commissioner then imparted briefly to the great man, who sat still, resting his eyes under the screen of his hand, Mr Verloc's appreciation of Mr Vladimir's proceedings and character. The Assistant Commissioner did not seem to refuse it a certain amount of competency. But the great personage remarked:

'All this seems very fantastic.'

'Doesn't it? One would think a ferocious joke. But our man took it seriously, it appears. He felt himself threatened. Formerly, you know, he was in direct communication with old Stott-Wartenheim himself, and had come to regard his services as indispensable. It was an extremely rude awakening. I imagine that he lost his head. He became angry and frightened. Upon my word, my impression is that he thought these Embassy people quite capable not only to throw him out but to give him away, too, in some manner or other – '

'How long were you with him?' interrupted the Presence from behind his big hand.

'Some forty minutes, Sir Ethelred, in a house of bad repute called Continental Hotel, closeted in a room which by-the-by I took for the night. I found him under the influence of that reaction which follows the effort of crime. The man cannot be defined as a hardened criminal. It is obvious that he did not plan the death of that wretched lad – his brother-in-law. That was a shock to him – I could see that. Perhaps he is a man of strong sensibilities. Perhaps he was even fond of the lad – who knows? He might have hoped that the fellow would get clear away; in which case it would have been almost impossible to bring this thing home to anyone. At any rate, he risked consciously nothing more but arrest for him.'

The Assistant Commissioner paused in his speculations to reflect for a moment.

'Though how, in that last case, he could hope to have his own share in the business concealed is more than I can tell,' he continued, in his ignorance of poor Stevie's devotion to Mr Verloc (who was *good*), and of his truly peculiar dumbness, which in the old affair of fireworks on the stairs had for many years resisted entreaties, coaxing, anger, and other means of investigation used by his beloved sister. For Stevie was loyal. . . . 'No, I can't imagine. It's possible that he never thought of that at all. It sounds an extravagant way of putting it, Sir Ethelred, but his state of dismay suggested to me an impulsive man who, after committing suicide with the notion that it would end all his troubles, had discovered that it did nothing of the kind.'

The Assistant Commissioner gave this definition in an apologetic voice. But in truth there is a sort of lucidity proper to extravagant language, and the great man was not offended. A slight jerky movement of the big body half lost in the gloom of the green silk shades, of the big head leaning on the big hand, accompanied an intermittent stifled but powerful sound. The great man had laughed.

'What have you done with him?'

The Assistant Commissioner answered very readily:

'As he seemed very anxious to get back to his wife in the shop I let him go, Sir Ethelred.'

'You did? But the fellow will disappear.'

'Pardon me. I don't think so. Where could he go to? Moreover, you must remember that he has got to think of the danger from his comrades, too. He's there at his post. How could he explain leaving it? But even if there were no obstacles to his freedom of action he would do nothing. At present he hasn't enough moral energy to take a resolution of any sort. Permit me also to point out that if I had detained him we would have been committed to a course of action on which I wished to know your precise intentions first.'

The great personage rose heavily, an imposing, shadowy form in the greenish gloom of the room.

'I'll see the Attorney-General tonight, and will send for you tomorrow morning. Is there anything more you'd wish to tell me now?'

The Assistant Commissioner had stood up also, slender and flexible.

'I think not, Sir Ethelred, unless I were to enter into details which – '

'No. No details, please.'

The great shadowy form seemed to shrink away as if in physical dread of details; then came forward, expanded, enormous, and weighty, offering a large hand. 'And you say that this man has got a wife?'

'Yes, Sir Ethelred,' said the Assistant Commissioner, pressing deferentially the extended hand. 'A genuine wife and a genuinely, respectably, marital relation. He told me that after his interview at the Embassy he would have thrown everything up, would have tried to sell his shop, and leave the country, only he felt certain that his wife would not even hear of going abroad. Nothing could be more characteristic of the respectable bond than that,' went on, with a touch of grimness, the Assistant Commissioner, whose own wife, too, had refused to hear of going abroad. 'Yes, a genuine wife. And the victim was a genuine brother-in-law. From a certain point of view we are here in the presence of a domestic drama.'

The Assistant Commissioner laughed a little; but the great man's thoughts seemed to have wandered far away, perhaps to the questions of his country's domestic policy, the battleground of his crusading valour against the paynim Cheeseman. The Assistant Commissioner withdrew quietly, unnoticed, as if already forgotten.

He had his own crusading instincts. This affair, which, in one way or another, disgusted Chief Inspector Heat, seemed to him a providentially given starting-point for a crusade. He had it much at heart to begin. He walked slowly home, meditating that enterprise on the way, and thinking over Mr Verloc's psychology in a composite mood of repugnance and satisfaction. He walked all the way home. Finding the drawing-room dark, he went upstairs, and spent some time between the bedroom and the dressing-room, changing his clothes, going to and fro with the air of a thoughtful somnambulist. But he shook it off before going out again to join his wife at the house of the great lady patroness of Michaelis.

He knew he would be welcomed there. On entering the smaller of the two drawing-rooms he saw his wife in a small group near the piano. A youngish composer in pass of becoming famous was discoursing from a music stool to two thick men whose backs looked old, and three slender women whose backs looked young. Behind the screen the great lady had only two persons with her: a man and a woman, who sat side by side on armchairs at the foot of her couch. She extended her hand to the Assistant Commissioner.

'I never hoped to see you here tonight. Annie told me – '

'Yes. I had no idea myself that my work would be over so soon.'

The Assistant Commissioner added in a low tone: 'I am glad to tell you that Michaelis is altogether clear of this – '

The patroness of the ex-convict received this assurance indignantly.

'Why? Were your people stupid enough to connect him with – '

'Not stupid,' interrupted the Assistant Commissioner, contradicting deferentially. 'Clever enough – quite clever enough for that.'

A silence fell. The man at the foot of the couch had stopped speaking to the lady, and looked on with a faint smile.

'I don't know whether you ever met before,' said the great lady.

Mr Vladimir and the Assistant Commissioner, introduced, acknowledged each other's existence with punctilious and guarded courtesy.

'He's been frightening me,' declared suddenly the lady who sat by the side of Mr Vladimir, with an inclination of the head towards that gentleman. The Assistant Commissioner knew the lady.

'You do not look frightened,' he pronounced, after surveying her conscientiously with his tired and equable gaze. He was thinking meantime to himself that in this house one met everybody sooner or later. Mr Vladimir's rosy countenance was wreathed in smiles, because he was witty, but his eyes remained serious, like the eyes of convinced man.

'Well, he tried to at least,' amended the lady.

'Force of habit perhaps,' said the Assistant Commissioner, moved by an irresistible inspiration.

'He has been threatening society with all sorts of horrors,' continued the lady, whose enunciation was caressing and slow, 'apropos of this explosion in Greenwich Park. It appears we all ought to quake in our shoes at what's coming if those people are not suppressed all over the world. I had no idea this was such a grave affair.'

Mr Vladimir, affecting not to listen, leaned towards the couch, talking amiably in subdued tones, but he heard the Assistant Commissioner say:

'I've no doubt that Mr Vladimir has a very precise notion of the true importance of this affair.'

Mr Vladimir asked himself what that confounded and intrusive policeman was driving at. Descended from generations victimized by the instruments of an arbitary power, he was racially, nationally, and individually afraid of the police. It was an inherited weakness, altogether independent of his judgement, of his reason, of his experience. He was born to it. But that sentiment, which resembled the irrational horror some people have of cats, did not stand in the way of his immense contempt for the English police. He finished the sentence addressed to the great lady, and turned slightly in his chair.

'You mean that we have a great experience of these people. Yes; indeed, we suffer greatly from that activity, while you' – Mr Vladimir hesitated for a moment, in smiling perplexity – 'While you suffer their presence gladly in your midst,' he finished, displaying a dimple in each clean-shaven cheek. Then he added more gravely: 'I may even say – because you do.'

When Mr Vladimir ceased speaking the Assistant Commissioner lowered his glance, and the conversation dropped. Almost immediately afterwards Mr Vladimir took leave. Directly his back was turned on the couch the Assistant Commissioner rose, too.

'I thought you were going to stay and take Annie home,' said the lady patroness of Michaelis.

'I find that I've yet a little work to do tonight.'

'In connexion –?'

'Well, yes – in a way.'

'Tell me, what is it really – this horror?'

'It's difficult to say what it is, but it may yet be a *cause célèbre*,' said the Assistant Commissioner.

He left the drawing-room hurriedly, and found Mr Vladimir still in the hall, wrapping up his throat carefully in a large silk handkerchief. Behind him a footman waited, holding his overcoat. Another stoody ready to open the door. The Assistant Commissioner was duly helped into his coat, and let out at once. After descending the front steps he stopped, as if to consider the way he should take. On seeing this through the door held open, Mr Vladimir lingered in the hall to get out a cigar and asked for a light. It was furnished to him by an elderly man out of livery with an air of calm solicitude. But the match went out; the footman then closed the door, and Mr Vladimir lighted his large Havana with leisurely care. When at last he got out of the house, he saw with disgust the 'confounded policeman' still standing on the pavement.

'Can he be waiting for me,' thought Mr Vladimir, looking up and down for some signs of a hansom. He saw none. A couple of carriages waited by the kerbstone, their lamps blazing steadily, the horses standing perfectly still, as if carved in stone, the coachmen sitting motionless under the big fur capes, without as much as a quiver stirring the white thongs of their big whips. Mr Vladimir walked on, and the 'confounded policeman' fell into step at his elbow. He said nothing. At the end of the fourth stride Mr Vladimir felt infuriated and uneasy. This could not last.

'Rotten weather,' he growled, savagely.

'Mild,' said the Assistant Commissioner without passion. He remained silent for a little while. 'We've got hold of a man called Verloc,' he announced, casually.

Mr Vladimir did not stumble, did not stagger back, did not change his stride. But he could not prevent himself from exclaiming: 'What?' The Assistant Commissioner did not repeat his statement. 'You know him,' he went on in the same tone.

Mr Vladimir stopped, and became guttural.

'What makes you say that?'

'I don't. It's Verloc who says that.'

'A lying dog of some sort,' said Mr Vladimir in somewhat Oriental phraseology. But in his heart he was almost awed by the miraculous cleverness of the English police. The change of his opinion on the subject was so violent that it made him for a moment feel slightly sick. He threw away his cigar, and moved on.

'What pleased me most in this affair,' the Assistant went on, talking slowly, 'is that it makes such an excellent starting-point for a piece of work which I've felt must be taken in hand – that is, the clearing out of this country of all the foreign political spies, police, and that sort of – of – dogs. In my opinion they are a ghastly nuisance; also an element of danger. But we can't very well seek them out individually. The only way is to make their employment unpleasant to their employers. The thing's becoming indecent. And dangerous, too, for us, here.'

Mr Vladimir stopped again for a moment.

'What do you mean?'

'The prosecution of this Verloc will demonstrate to the public both the danger and the indecency.'

'Nobody will believe what a man of that sort says,' said Mr Vladimir, contemptuously.

'The wealth and precision of detail will carry conviction to the great mass of the public,' advanced the Assistant Commissioner gently.

'So that is seriously what you mean to do.'

'We've got the man; we have no choice.'

'You will be only feeding up the lying spirit of these revolutionary scoundrels,' Mr Vladimir protested. 'What do you want to make a scandal for? – from morality – or what?'

Mr Vladimir's anxiety was obvious. The Assistant Commissioner, having ascertained in this way that there must be some truth in the summary statements of Mr Verloc, said indifferently:

'There's a practical side, too. We have really enough to do to look after the genuine article. You can't say we are not effective. But we don't intend to let ourselves be bothered by shams under any pretext whatever.'

Mr Vladimir's tone became lofty.

'For my part, I can't share your view. It is selfish. My sentiments for my own country cannot be doubted; but I've always felt that we ought to be good Europeans besides – I mean governments and men.'

'Yes,' said the Assistant Commissioner simply. 'Only you look at Europe from its other end. But,' he went on in a good-natured tone, 'the foreign governments cannot complain of the inefficiency of our police. Look at this outrage; a case specially difficult to trace inasmuch as it was a sham. In less than twelve hours we have established the identity of a man literally blown to shreds, have found the organizer of the attempt, and have had a glimpse of the inciter behind him. And we could have gone further; only we stopped at the limits of our territory.'

'So this instructive crime was planned abroad,' Mr Vladimir said, quickly. 'You admit it was planned abroad?'

'Theoretically. Theoretically only, on foreign territory; abroad only by a fiction,' said the Assistant Commissioner, alluding to the character of Embassies which are supposed to be part and parcel of the country to which they belong. 'But that's a detail. I talked to you of this business because it's your government that grumbles most at our police. You see that we are not so bad. I wanted particularly to tell you of our success.'

'I'm sure I'm very grateful,' muttered Mr Vladimir through his teeth.

'We can put our finger on every anarchist here,' went on the Assistant Commissioner, as though he were quoting Chief Inspector Heat. 'All that's wanted now is to do away with the *agent provocateur* to make everything safe.'

Mr Vladimir held up his hand to a passing hansom.

'You're not going in here,' remarked the Assistant Commissioner, looking at a building of noble proportions and hospitable aspect, with the light of a great hall falling through its glass doors on a broad flight of steps.

But Mr Vladimir, sitting, stony-eyed, inside the hansom, drove off without a word.

The Assistant Commissioner himself did not turn into the noble building. It was the Explorers' Club. The thought passed through his mind that Mr Vladimir, honorary member, would not be seen very often there in the future. He looked at his watch. It was only half past ten. He had had a very full evening.

CHAPTER 11

After Chief Inspector Heat had left him Mr Verloc moved about the parlour. From time to time he eyed his wife through the open door. 'She knows all about it now,' he thought to himself with commiseration for her sorrow and with some satisfaction as regarded himself. Mr. Verloc's soul, if lacking greatness perhaps, was capable of tender sentiments. The prospect of having to break the news to her had put him into a fever. Chief Inspector Heat had relieved him of the task. That was good as far as it went. It remained for him now to face her grief.

Mr Verloc had never expected to have to face it on account of death, whose catastrophic character cannot be argued away by sophisticated reasoning or persuasive eloquence. Mr Verloc never meant Stevie to perish with such abrupt violence. He did not mean him to perish at all. Stevie dead was a much greater nuisance than ever he had been when alive. Mr Verloc had augured a favourable issue to his enterprise, basing himself not on Stevie's intelligence, which sometimes plays queer tricks with a man, but on the blind docility and on the blind devotion of the boy. Though not much of a psychologist, Mr Verloc had gauged the depth of Stevie's fanaticism. He dared cherish the hope of Stevie walking away from the walls of the Observatory as he had been instructed to do, taking the way shown to him several times previously, and rejoining his brother-in-law, the wise and good Mr Verloc, outside the precincts of the park. Fifteen minutes ought to have been enough for the veriest fool to deposit the engine and walk away. And the Professor had guaranteed more than fifteen minutes. But Stevie had stumbled within five minutes of being left to himself. And Mr Verloc was shaken morally to pieces. He had foreseen everything but that. He had foreseen Stevie distracted and lost – sought for – found in some police station or provincial workhouse in the end. He had foreseen Stevie arrested, and was not afraid, because Mr Verloc had a great opinion of Stevie's loyalty, which had been carefully indoctrinated with the necessity of silence in the course of many walks. Like a peripatetic philosopher, Mr Verloc, strolling along the streets of London, had modified Stevie's view of the police by conversations full of subtle reasonings. Never had a sage a more attentive and admiring disciple. The submission and worship were so apparent that Mr Verloc had come to feel something like a liking for the boy. In any case, he had not foreseen the swift bringing home of his connexion. That his wife should hit upon the precaution of sewing the boy's address inside his overcoat was the last thing Mr Verloc would have thought of. One can't think of everything. That was what she meant when she said that he need not worry if he lost Stevie during their walks. She had assured him that the boy would turn up all right. Well, he had turned up with a vengeance!

'Well, well,' muttered Mr Verloc in his wonder. What did she mean by it? Spare him the trouble of keeping an anxious eye on Stevie? Most likely she had meant well. Only she ought to have told him of the precaution she had taken.

Mr Verloc walked behind the counter of the shop. His intention was not to overwhelm his wife with bitter reproaches. Mr Verloc felt no bitterness. The unexpected march of events had converted him to the doctrine of fatalism. Nothing could be helped now. He said:

'I didn't mean any harm to come to the boy.'

Mrs Verloc shuddered at the sound of her husband's voice. She did not uncover her face. The trusted secret agent of the late Baron Stott-Wartenheim looked at her for a time with a heavy, persistent, undiscerning glance. The torn evening paper was lying at her feet. It could not have told her much. Mr Verloc felt the need of talking to his wife.

'It's that damned Heat – eh?' he said. 'He upset you. He's a brute, blurting it out like this to a woman. I made myself ill thinking how to break it to you. I sat for hours in the little parlour of the Cheshire Cheese thinking over the best way. You understand I never meant any harm to come to that boy.'

Mr Verloc, the secret agent, was speaking the truth. It was his marital affection that had received the greatest shock from the premature explosion. He added:

'I didn't feel particularly gay sitting there and thinking of you.'

He observed another slight shudder of his wife, which affected his sensibility. As she persisted in hiding her face in her hands, he thought he had better leave her alone for a while. On this delicate impulse Mr Verloc withdrew into the parlour again, where the gas-jet purred like a contented cat. Mrs Verloc's wifely forethought had left the cold beef on the table with carving knife and fork and half a loaf of bread for Mr Verloc's supper. He noticed all these things now for the first time, and cutting himself a piece of bread and meat, began to eat.

His appetite did not proceed from callousness. Mr Verloc had not eaten any breakfast that day. He had left his home fasting. Not being an energetic man, he found his resolution in nervous excitement, which seemed to hold him mainly by the throat. He could not have swallowed anything solid. Michaelis's cottage was as destitute of provisions as the cell of a prisoner. The ticket-of-leave apostle lived on a little milk and crusts of stale bread. Moreover, when Mr Verloc arrived he had already gone upstairs after his frugal meal. Absorbed in the toil and delight of literary composition, he had not even answered Mr Verloc's shout up the little staircase.

'I am taking this young fellow home for a day or two.'

And, in truth, Mr Verloc did not wait for an answer, but had marched out of the cottage at once, followed by the obedient Stevie.

Now that all action was over and his fate taken out of his hands with unexpected swiftness, Mr Verloc felt terribly empty physically. He carved the meat, cut the bread, and devoured his supper standing by the table, and now and then casting a glance towards his wife. Her prolonged immobility disturbed the comfort of his reflection. He walked again into the shop, and came up very close to her. This sorrow with a veiled face made Mr Verloc uneasy. He expected, of course, his wife to be very much upset, but he wanted her to pull herself together. He needed all her assistance and all her loyalty in these new conjunctures his fatalism had already accepted.

'Can't be helped,' he said in a tone of gloomy sympathy. 'Come, Winnie, we've got to think of tomorrow. You'll want all your wits about you after I am taken away.'

He paused. Mrs Verloc's breast heaved convulsively. This was not reassuring to Mr Verloc, in whose view the newly created situation required from the two people most concerned in it calmness, decision, and other qualitites incompatible with the mental disorder of passionate sorrow. Mr Verloc was a humane man; he had come home prepared to allow every latitude to his wife's affection for her brother. Only he did not understand either the nature or the whole extent of that sentiment. And in this he was excusable, since it was impossible for him to understand it without ceasing to be himself. He was startled and disappointed, and his speech conveyed it by a certain roughness of tone.

'You might look at a fellow,' he observed after waiting a while.

As if forced through the hands covering Mrs Verloc's face the answer came, deadened, almost pitiful.

'I don't want to look at you as long as I live.'

'Eh? What!' Mr Verloc was merely startled by the superficial and literal meaning of this declaration. It was obviously unreasonable, the mere cry of exaggerated grief. He threw over it the mantle of his marital indulgence. The mind of Mr Verloc lacked profundity. Under the mistaken impression that the value of individuals consists in what they are in themselves, he could not possibly comprehend the value of Stevie in the eyes of Mrs Verloc. She was taking it confoundedly hard, he thought to himself. It was all the fault of that damned Heat. What did he want to upset the woman for? But she mustn't be allowed, for her own good, to carry on so till she got quite beside herself.

'Look here! You can't sit like this in the shop,' he said with affected severity, in which there was some real annoyance; for urgent practical matters must be talked over if they had to sit up all night. 'Somebody might come in at any minute,' he added, and waited again. No effect was produced, and the idea of the finality of death occurred to Mr Verloc during the pause. He changed his tone. 'Come. This won't bring him back,' he said, gently, feeling ready to take her in his arms and press her to his breast, where impatience and compassion dwelt side by side. But except for a short shudder Mrs Verloc remained apparently unaffected by the force of that terrible truism. It was Mr Verloc himself who was moved. He was moved in his simplicity to urge moderation by asserting the claims of his own personality.

'Do be reasonable, Winnie. What would it have been if you had lost me?'

He had vaguely expected to hear her cry out. But she did not budge. She leaned back a little, quieted down to a complete, unreadable stillness. Mr Verloc's heart began to beat faster with exasperation and something resembling alarm. He laid his hand on her shoulder, saying:

'Don't be a fool, Winnie.'

She gave no sign. It was impossible to talk to any purpose with a woman whose face one cannot see. Mr Verloc caught hold of his wife's wrists. But her hands seemed glued fast. She swayed forward bodily to his tug, and nearly went off the chair. Startled to feel her so helplessly limp, he was trying to put her back on the chair when she stiffened suddenly all over, tore herself out of his hands, ran out of the shop, across the parlour, and into the kitchen. This was very swift. He had just a glimpse of her face and that much of her eyes that he knew she had not looked at him.

It all had the appearance of a struggle for the possession of a chair, because Mr Verloc instantly took his wife's place in it. Mr Verloc did not cover his face with his hands, but a sombre thoughtfulness veiled his features. A term of imprisonment could not be avoided. He did not wish now to avoid it. A prison was a place as safe from certain unlawful vengeances as the grave, with this advantage, that in a prison there is room for hope. What he saw before him was a term of imprisonment, an early release, and then life abroad somewhere, such as he had contemplated already, in case of failure. Well, it was a failure, if not exactly the sort of failure he had feared. It had been so near success that he could have positively terrified Mr Vladimir out of his ferocious scoffing with this proof of occult efficiency. So at least it seemed now to Mr Verloc. His prestige with the Embassy would have been immense if – if his wife had not had the unlucky notion of sewing on the address inside Stevie's overcoat. Mr Verloc, who was no fool, had soon perceived the extraordinary character of the influence he had over Stevie, though he did not understand exactly its origin – the doctrine of his supreme wisdom and goodness inculcated by two anxious women. In all the eventualities he had foreseen Mr Verloc had calculated with correct insight on Stevie's instinctive loyalty and blind discretion. The eventuality he had not foreseen had appalled him as a humane man and a fond husband. From every other point of view it was rather advantageous. Nothing can equal the everlasting discretion of death. Mr Verloc, sitting perplexed and frightened in the small parlour of the Cheshire Cheese, could not help acknowledging that to himself, because his sensibility did not stand in the way of his judgement. Stevie's violent disintegration, however disturbing to think about, only assured the success; for, of course, the knocking down of a wall was not the aim of Mr Vladimir's menaces, but the production of a moral effect. With much trouble and distress on Mr Verloc's part the effect might be said to have been produced. When, however, most unexpectedly, it came home to roost in Brett Street, Mr Verloc, who had been struggling like a man in a nightmare for the preservation of his position, accepted the blow in the spirit of a convinced fatalist. The position was gone through no one's fault really. A small, tiny fact had done it. It was like slipping on a bit of orange peel in the dark and breaking your leg.

Mr Verloc drew a weary breath. He nourished no resentment against his wife. He thought: 'She will have to look after the shop while they keep me locked up.' And thinking also how cruelly she would miss Stevie at first, he felt greatly concerned about her health and spirits. How would she stand her solitude – absolutely alone in that house? It would not do for her to break down while he was locked up. What would become of the shop then? The shop was an asset. Though Mr Verloc's fatalism accepted his undoing as a secret agent, he had no mind to be utterly ruined, mostly, it must be owned, from regard for his wife.

Silent, and out of his line of sight in the kitchen, she frightened him. If only she had her mother with her. But that silly old woman – An angry dismay possessed Mr Verloc. He must talk with his wife. He could tell her certainly that a man does get desperate under certain circumstances. But he did not go incontinently to impart to her that information. First of all, it was clear to him that this evening was no time for business. He got up to close the street door and put the gas out in the shop.

Having thus assured a solitude around his hearth-stone Mr Verloc walked into the parlour, and glanced down into the kitchen. Mrs Verloc was sitting in the place where poor Stevie usually established himself of an evening with paper and pencil for the pastime of drawing those coruscations of innumerable circles suggesting chaos and eternity. Her arms were folded on the table, and her head was lying on her arms. Mr Verloc contemplated her back and the arrangement of her hair for a time, then walked away from the kitchen door. Mrs Verloc's philosophical, almost disdainful incuriosity, the foundation of their accord in domestic life, made it extremely difficult to get into contact with her, now this tragic necessity had arisen. Mr Verloc felt this difficulty acutely. He turned around the table in the parlour with his usual air of a large animal in a cage.

Curiosity being one of the forms of self-revelation, a systematically incurious person remains always partly mysterious. Every time he passed near the door Mr Verloc glanced at his wife uneasily. It was not that he was afraid of her. Mr Verloc imagined himself loved by that woman. But she had not accustomed him to make confidences. And the confidence he had to make was of a profound psychological order. How with his want of practice could he tell her what he himself felt but vaguely: that there are conspiracies of fatal destiny, that a notion grows in a mind sometimes till it acquires an outward existence, an independent power of its own, and even a suggestive voice? He could not inform her that a man may be haunted by a fat, witty, clean-shaved face till the wildest expedient to get rid of it appears a child of wisdom.

On this mental reference to a First Secretary of a great Embassy, Mr Verloc stopped in the doorway, and looking down into the kitchen with an angry face and clenched fists, addressed his wife.

'You don't know what a brute I had to deal with.'

He started off to make another perambulation of the table, then when he had come to the door again he stopped, glaring in from the height of two steps.

'A silly, jeering, dangerous brute, with no more sense than – After all these years! A man like me! And I have been playing my head at that game. You didn't know. Quite right, too. What was the good of telling you that I stood the risk of having a knife stuck into me any time these seven years we've been married? I am not a chap to worry a woman that's fond of me. You had no business to know.'

Mr Verloc took another turn round the parlour, fuming.

'A venomous beast,' he began again from the doorway. 'Drive me out into a ditch to starve for a joke. I could see he thought it was a damned good joke. A man like me! Look here! Some of the highest in the world got to thank me for walking on their two legs to this day. That's the man you've got married to, my girl!'

He perceived that his wife had sat up. Mrs Verloc's arms remained lying stretched on the table. Mr Verloc watched her back as if he could read there the effect of his words.

'There isn't a murdering plot for the last eleven years that I hadn't my finger in at the risk of my life. There's scores of these revolutionists I've sent off with their bombs in their blamed pockets, to get themselves caught on the frontier. The old Baron knew what I was worth to his country. And here suddenly a swine comes along – an ignorant, overbearing swine.'

Mr Verloc, stepping slowly down two steps, entered the kitchen, took a tumbler off the dresser, and holding it in his hand, approached the sink, without looking at his wife.

'It wasn't the old Baron who would have had the wicked folly of getting me to call on him at eleven in the morning. There are two or three in this town that, if they had seen me going in, would have made no bones about knocking me on the head sooner or later. It was a silly, murderous trick to expose for nothing a man – like me.'

Mr Verloc, turning on the tap above the sink, poured three glasses of water, one after another, down his throat to quench the fires of his indignation. Mr Vladimir's conduct was like a hot brand which set his internal economy in a blaze. He could not get over the disloyalty of it. This man, who would not work at the usual hard tasks which society sets to its humbler members, had exercised his secret industry with an indefatigable devotion. There was in Mr Verloc a fund of loyalty. He had been loyal to his employers, to the cause of social stability – and to his affections, too – as became apparent when, after standing the tumbler in the sink, he turned about, saying:

'If I hadn't thought of you I would have taken the bullying brute by the throat and rammed his head into the fireplace. I'd have been more than a match for that pink-faced, smooth-shaved – '

Mr Verloc neglected to finish the sentence, as if there could be no doubt of the terminal word. For the first time in his life he was taking that incurious woman into his confidence. The singularity of the event, the force and importance of the personal feelings aroused in the course of this confession, drove Stevie's fate clean out of Mr Verloc's mind. The boy's stuttering existence of fears and indignations, together with the violence of his end, had passed out of Mr Verloc's mental sight for a time. For that reason, when he looked up he was startled by the inappropriate character of his wife's stare. It was not a wild stare, and it was not inattentive, but its attention was peculiar and not satisfactory, inasmuch that it seemed concentrated upon some point beyond Mr Verloc's person. The impression was so strong that Mr Verloc glanced over his shoulder. There was nothing behind him: there was just the whitewashed wall. The excellent husband of Winnie Verloc saw no writing on the wall. He turned to his wife again, repeating, with some emphasis:

'I would have taken him by the throat. As true as I stand here, if I hadn't thought of you then I would have half choked the life out of the brute before I let him get up. And don't you think he would have been anxious to call the police – either. He wouldn't have dared. You understand why – don't you?'

He blinked at his wife knowingly.

'No,' said Mrs Verloc in an unresonant voice, and without looking at him at all. 'What are you talking about?'

A great discouragement, the result of fatigue, came upon Mr Verloc. He had had a very full day, and his nerves had been tried to the utmost. After a month of maddening worry, ending in an unexpected catastrophe, the storm-tossed spirit of Mr Verloc longed for repose. His career as a secret agent had come to an end in a way no one could have foreseen; only, now, perhaps he could manage to get a night's sleep at last. But looking at his wife, he doubted it. She was taking it very hard – not at all like herself, he thought. He made an effort to speak.

'You'll have to pull youself together, my girl,' he said, sympathetically. 'What's done can't be undone.'

Mrs Verloc gave a slight start, though not a muscle of her white face moved in the least. Mr Verloc, who was not looking at her, continued ponderously:

'You go to bed now. What you want is a good cry.'

This opinion had nothing to recommend it but the general consent of mankind. It is universally understood that, as if it were nothing more substantial than vapour floating in the sky, every emotion of a woman is bound to end in a shower. And it is very probable that had Stevie died in his bed under her despairing gaze, in her protecting arms, Mrs Verloc's grief would have found relief in a flood of bitter and pure tears. Mrs Verloc,

in common with other human beings, was provided with a fund of unconscious resignation sufficient to meet the normal manifestation of human
destiny. Without 'troubling her head about it,' she was aware that it 'did not
stand looking into very much'. But the lamentable circumstances of Stevie's
end, which to Mr Verloc's mind had only an episodic character, as part of
a greater disaster, dried her tears at their very source. It was the effect of
a white-hot iron drawn across her eyes; at the same time her heart, hardened
and chilled into a lump of ice, kept her body in an inward shudder, set her
features into a frozen, contemplative immobility addressed to a whitewashed
wall with no writing on it. The exigencies of Mrs Verloc's temperament,
which, when stripped of its philosophical reserve, was maternal and violent,
forced her to roll a series of thoughts in her motionless head. These thoughts
were rather imagined than expressed. Mrs Verloc was a woman of singularly
few words, either for public or private use. With the rage and dismay of a
betrayed woman, she reviewed the tenor of her life in visions concerned
mostly with Stevie's difficult existence from its earliest days. It was a life of
single purpose and of a noble unity of inspiration, like those rare lives that
have left their mark on the thoughts and feelings of mankind. But the visions
of Mrs Verloc lacked nobility and magnificence. She saw herself putting the
boy to bed by the light of a single candle on the deserted top floor of a
'business house', dark under the roof and scintillating exceedingly with lights
and cut glass at the level of the street like a fairy palace. That meretricious
splendour was the only one to be met in Mrs Verloc's visions. She remembered
brushing the boy's hair and tying his pinafores – herself in a pinafore still;
the consolations administered to a small and badly scared creature by another
creature nearly as small but not quite so badly scared; she had the vision of
the blows intercepted (often with her own head), of a door held desperately
shut against a man's rage (not for very long); of a poker flung once (not very
far), which stilled that particular storm into the dumb and awful silence
which follows a thunder-clap. And all these scenes of violence came and
went accompanied by the unrefined noise of deep vociferations proceeding
from a man wounded in his paternal pride, declaring himself obviously
accursed since one of his kids was a 'slobbering idjut and the other a wicked
she-devil'. It was of her that this had been said many years ago.

Mrs Verloc heard the words again in a ghostly fashion, and then the
dreary shadow of the Belgravian mansion descended upon her shoulders. It
was a crushing memory, an exhausting vision of countless breakfast trays
carried up and down innumerable stairs, of endless haggling over pence, of
the endless drudgery of sweeping, dusting, cleaning, from basement to attics;
while the impotent mother, staggering on swollen legs, cooked in a grimy
kitchen, and poor Stevie, the unconscious presiding genius of all their toil,
blacked the gentlemen's boots in the scullery. But this vision had a breath
of a hot London summer in it, and for a central figure a young man wearing
his Sunday best, with a straw hat on his dark head and a wooden pipe in
his mouth. Affectionate and jolly, he was a fascinating companion for a
voyage down the sparkling stream of life; only his boat was very small.
There was room in it for a girl-partner at the oar, but no accommodation
for passengers. He was allowed to drift away from the threshold of the

Belgravian mansion while Winnie averted her tearful eyes. He was not a lodger. The lodger was Mr Verloc, indolent and keeping late hours, sleepily jocular of a morning from under his bed-clothes, but with gleams of infatuation in his heavy-lidded eyes, and always with some money in his pockets. There was no sparkle of any kind on the lazy stream of his life. It flowed through secret places. But his barque seemed a roomy craft, and his taciturn magnanimity accepted as a matter of course the presence of passengers.

Mrs Verloc pursued the visions of seven years' security for Stevie loyally paid for on her part; of security growing into confidence, into a domestic feeling, stagnant and deep like a placid pool, whose guarded surface hardly shuddered on the occasional passage of Comrade Ossipon, the robust anarchist with shamelessly inviting eyes, whose glance had a corrupt clearness sufficient to enlighten any woman not absolutely imbecile.

A few seconds only had elapsed since the last word had been uttered aloud in the kitchen, and Mrs Verloc was staring already at the vision of an episode not more than a fortnight old. With eyes whose pupils were extremely dilated she stared at the vision of her husband and poor Stevie walking up Brett Street side by side away from the shop. It was the last scene of an existence created by Mrs Verloc's genius; an existence foreign to all grace and charm, without beauty and almost without decency, but admirable in the continuity of feeling and tenacity of purpose. And this last vision had such plastic relief, such nearness of form, such a fidelity of suggestive detail, that it wrung from Mrs Verloc an anguished and faint murmur, reproducing the supreme illusion of her life, an appalled murmur that died out on her blanched lips.

'Might have been father and son.'

Mr Verloc stopped, and raised a careworn face. 'Eh? What did you say?' he asked. Receiving no reply, he resumed his sinister tramping. Then with a menacing flourish of a thick, fleshy fist, he burst out:

'Yes. The Embassy people. A pretty lot, ain't they! Before a week's out I'll make some of them wish themselves twenty feet under ground. Eh? What?'

He glanced sideways, with his head down. Mrs Verloc gazed at the whitewashed wall. A blank wall – perfectly blank. A blankness to run at and dash your head against. Mrs Verloc remained immovably seated. She kept still as the population of half the globe would keep still in astonishment and despair, were the sun suddenly put out in the summer sky by the perfidy of a trusted providence.

'The Embassy,' Mr Verloc began again, after a preliminary grimace which bared his teeth wolfishly. 'I wish I could get loose in there with a cudgel for half an hour. I would keep on hitting till there wasn't a single unbroken bone left amongst the whole lot. But never mind, I'll teach them yet what it means trying to throw out a man like me to rot in the streets. I've a tongue in my head. All the world shall know what I've done for them. I am not afraid. I don't care. Everything'll come out. Every damned thing. Let them look out!'

In these terms did Mr Verloc declare his thirst for revenge. It was a very appropriate revenge. It was in harmony with the promptings of Mr Verloc's genius. It had also the advantage of being within the range of his powers and of adjusting itself easily to the practice of his life, which had consisted precisely in betraying the secret and unlawful proceedings of his fellowmen. Anarchists or diplomats were all one to him. Mr Verloc was temperamentally no respecter of persons. His scorn was equally distributed over the whole field of his operations. But as a member of a revolutionary proletariat – which he undoubtedly was – he nourished a rather inimical sentiment against social distinction.

'Nothing on earth can stop me now,' he added, and paused, looking fixedly at his wife, who was looking fixedly at a blank wall.

The silence in the kitchen was prolonged, and Mr Verloc felt disappointed. He had expected his wife to say something. But Mrs Verloc's lips, composed in their usual form, preserved a statuesque immobility like the rest of her face. And Mr Verloc was disappointed. Yet the occasion did not, he recognized, demand speech from her. She was a woman of very few words. For reasons involved in the very foundation of his psychology, Mr Verloc was inclined to put his trust in any woman who had given herself to him. Therefore he trusted his wife. Their accord was perfect, but it was not precise. It was a tacit accord, congenial to Mrs Verloc's incuriosity and to Mr Verloc's habits of mind, which were indolent and secret. They refrained from going to the bottom of facts and motives.

This reserve, expressing, in a way, their profound confidence in each other, introduced at the same time a certain element of vagueness into their intimacy. No system of conjugal relations is perfect. Mr Verloc presumed that his wife had understood him but he would have been glad to hear her say what she thought at the moment. It would have been a comfort.

There were several reasons why this comfort was denied him. There was a physical obstacle: Mrs Verloc had not sufficient command over her voice. She did not see any alternative between screaming and silence, and instinctively she chose the silence. Winnie Verloc was temperamentally a silent person. And there was the paralysing atrocity of the thought which occupied her. Her cheeks were blanched, her lips ashy, her immobility amazing. And she thought without looking at Mr Verloc: 'This man took the boy away to murder him. He took the boy from his home to murder him. He took the boy away from me to murder him!'

Mrs Verloc's whole being was racked by that inconclusive and maddening thought. It was in her veins, in her bones, in the roots of her hair. Mentally she assumed the biblical attitude of mourning – the covered face, the rent garments; the sound of wailing and lamentation filled her head. But her teeth were violently clenched, and her tearless eyes were hot with rage, because she was not a submissive creature. The protection she had extended over her brother had been in its origin of a fierce and indignant complexion. She had to love him with a militant love. She had battled for him – even against herself. His loss had the bitterness of defeat, with the anguish of a baffled passion. It was not an ordinary stroke of death. Moreover, it was not death that took Stevie from her. It was Mr Verloc who took him away. She had seen him. She had watched him, without raising a hand, take the boy away. And she had let him go, like – like a fool – a blind fool. Then after he had murdered the boy he came home to her. Just came home like any other man would come home to his wife. . . .

Through her set teeth Mrs Verloc muttered at the wall:

'And I thought he had caught a cold.'

Mr Verloc heard these words and appropriated them.

'It was nothing,' he said, moodily. 'I was upset. I was upset on your account.'

Mrs Verloc, turning her head slowly, transferred her stare from the wall to her husband's person. Mr Verloc, with the tips of his fingers between his lips, was looking on the ground.

'Can't be helped,' he mumbled, letting his hand fall. 'You must pull yourself together. You'll want all your wits about you. It is you who brought the police about our ears. Never mind, I won't say anything more about it,' continued Mr Verloc, magnanimously. 'You couldn't know.'

'I couldn't,' breathed out Mrs Verloc. It was as if a corpse had spoken. Mr Verloc took up the thread of his discourse.

'I don't blame you. I'll make them sit up. Once under lock and key it will be safe enough for me to talk – you understand. You must reckon on me being two years away from you,' he continued, in a tone of sincere concern. 'It will be easier for you than for me. You'll have something to do, while I – Look here, Winnie, what you must do is to keep this business going for two years. You know enough for that. You've a good head on you. I'll send you word when it's time to go about trying to sell. You'll have to be extra careful. The comrades will be keeping an eye on you all the time. You'll have to be as artful as you know how, and as close as the grave. No one must know what you are going to do. I have no mind to get a knock on the head or a stab in the back directly I am let out.'

Thus spoke Mr Verloc, applying his mind with ingenuity and forethought to the problems of the future. His voice was sombre, because he had a correct sentiment of the situation. Everything which he did not wish to pass had come to pass. The future had become precarious. His judgement, perhaps, had been momentarily obscured by his dread of Mr Vladimir's truculent folly. A man somewhat over forty may be excusably thrown into considerable disorder by the prospect of losing his employment, especially if the man is a secret agent of political police, dwelling secure in the consciousness of his high value and in the esteem of high personages. He was excusable.

Now the thing had ended in a crash. Mr Verloc was cool; but he was not cheerful. A secret agent who throws his secrecy to the winds from desire of vengeance, and flaunts his achievements before the public eye, becomes the mark for desperate and bloodthirsty indignations. Without unduly exaggerating the danger, Mr Verloc tried to bring it clearly before his wife's mind. He repeated that he had no intention of letting the revolutionists do away with him.

He looked straight into his wife's eyes. The enlarged pupils of the woman received his stare into their unfathomable depths.

'I am too fond of you for that,' he said, with a little nervous laugh.

A faint flush coloured Mrs Verloc's ghastly and motionless face. Having done with the visions of the past, she had not only heard, but had also understood the words uttered by her husband. By their extreme disaccord with her mental condition these words produced on her a slightly suffocating effect. Mrs Verloc's mental condition had the merit of simplicity; but it was not sound. It was governed too much by a fixed idea. Every nook and cranny of her brain was filled with the thought that this man, with whom she had lived without distaste for seven years, had taken the 'poor boy' away from her in order to kill him – the man to whom she had grown accustomed in body and mind; the man whom she had trusted, took the boy away to kill him! In its form, in its substance, in its effect, which was universal, altering even the aspect of inanimate things, it was a thought to sit still and marvel at for ever and ever. Mrs Verloc sat still. And across that thought (not across the kitchen) the form of Mr Verloc went to and fro, familiarly in hat and overcoat, stamping with his boots upon her brain. He was probably talking, too; but Mrs Verloc thought for the most part covered the voice.

Now and then, however, the voice would make itself heard. Several connected words emerged at times. Their purport was generally hopeful. On each of these occasions Mrs Verloc's dilated pupils, losing their far-off fixity, followed her husband's movements with the effect of black care and impenetrable attention. Well informed upon all matters relating to his secret calling, Mr Verloc augured well for the success of his plans and combinations. He really believed that it would be upon the whole easy for him to escape the knife of infuriated revolutionists. He had exaggerated the strength of their fury and the length of their arm (for professional purposes) too often to have many illusions one way or the other. For to exaggerate with judgement one must begin by measuring with nicety. He knew also how much virtue and how much infamy is forgotten in two years – two long years. His first really confidential discourse to his wife was optimistic from conviction. He also thought it good policy to display all the assurance he could muster. It would put heart into the poor woman. On his liberation, which, harmonizing with the whole tenor of his life, would be secret, of course, they would vanish together without loss of time. As to covering up the tracks, he begged his wife to trust him for that. He knew how it was to be done so that the devil himself –

He waved his hand. He seemed to boast. He wished only to put heart into her. It was a benevolent intention, but Mr Verloc had the misfortune not to be in accord with his audience.

The self-confident tone grew upon Mrs Verloc's ear which let most of the words go by; for what were words to her now? What could words do to her for good or evil in the face of her fixed idea? Her black glance followed that man who was asserting his impunity – the man who had taken poor Stevie from home to kill him somewhere. Mrs Verloc could not remember exactly where, but her heart began to beat very perceptibly.

Mr Verloc, in a soft and conjugal tone, was now expressing his firm belief that there were yet a good few years of quiet life before them both. He did not go into the question of means. A quiet life it must be and, as it were, nestling in the shade, concealed among men whose flesh is grass; modest, like the life of violets. The words used by Mr Verloc were: 'Lie low for a bit.' And far from England, of course. It was not clear whether Mr Verloc had in his mind Spain or South America; but at any rate somewhere abroad.

This last word, falling into Mrs Verloc's ear, produced a definite impression. This man was talking of going abroad. The impression was completely disconnected; and such is the force of mental habit that Mrs Verloc at once and automatically asked herself: 'And what of Stevie?'

It was a sort of forgetfulness; but instantly she became aware that there was no longer any occasion for anxiety on that score. There would never be any occasion any more. The poor boy had been taken out and killed. The poor boy was dead.

This shaking piece of forgetfulness stimulated Mrs Verloc's intelligence. She began to perceive certain consequences which would have surprised Mr Verloc. There was no need for her now to stay there, in that kitchen, in that house, with that man – since the boy was gone for ever. No need whatever. And on that Mrs Verloc rose as if raised by a spring. But neither could she see what there was to keep her in the world at all. And this inability arrested her. Mr Verloc watched her with marital solicitude.

'You're looking more like yourself,' he said, uneasily. Something peculiar in the blackness of his wife's eyes disturbed his optimism. At that precise moment Mrs Verloc began to look upon herself as released from all earthly ties. She had her freedom. Her contract with existence, as represented by that man standing over there, was at an end. She was a free woman. Had this view become in some way perceptible to Mr Verloc he would have been extremely shocked. In his affairs of the heart Mr Verloc had been always carelessly generous, yet always with no other idea than that of being loved for himself. Upon this matter, his ethical notions being in agreement with his vanity, he was completely incorrigible. That this should be so in the case of his virtuous and legal connexion he was perfectly certain. He had grown older, fatter, heavier, in the belief that he lacked no fascination for being loved for his own sake. When he saw Mrs Verloc starting to walk out of the kitchen without a word he was disappointed.

'Where are you going to?' he called out rather sharply. 'Upstairs?'

Mrs Verloc in the doorway turned at the voice. An instinct of prudence born of fear, the excessive fear of being approached and touched by that man, induced her to nod at him slightly (from the height of two steps), with a stir of the lips which the conjugal optimism of Mr Verloc took for a wan and uncertain smile.

'That's right,' he encouraged her gruffly. 'Rest and quiet's what you want. Go on. It won't be long before I am with you.'

Mrs Verloc, the free woman who had had really no idea where she was going to, obeyed the suggestion with rigid steadiness.

Mr Verloc watched her. She disappeared up the stairs. He was disappointed. There was that within him which would have been more satisfied if she had been moved to throw herself upon his breast. But he was generous and indulgent. Winnie was always undemonstrative and silent. Neither was Mr Verloc himself prodigal of endearments and words as a rule. But this was not an ordinary evening. It was an occasion when a man wants to be fortified and strengthened by open proofs of sympathy and affection. Mr

Verloc sighed, and put out the gas in the kitchen. Mr Verloc's sympathy with his wife was genuine and intense. It almost brought tears into his eyes as he stood in the parlour reflecting on the loneliness hanging over her head. In this mood Mr Verloc missed Stevie very much out of a difficult world. He thought mournfully of his end. If only that lad had not stupidly destroyed himself!

The sensation of unappeasable hunger, not unknown after the strain of a hazardous enterprise to adventurers of tougher fibre than Mr Verloc, overcame him again. The piece of roast beef, laid out in the likeness of funereal baked meats for Stevie's obsequies, offered itself largely to his notice. And Mr Verloc again partook. He partook ravenously, without restraint and decency, cutting thick slices with the sharp carving knife, and swallowing them without bread. In the course of that reflection it occurred to Mr Verloc that he was not hearing his wife move about the bedroom as he should have done. The thought of finding her perhaps sitting on the bed in the dark not only cut Mr Verloc's appetite, but also took from him the inclination to follow her upstairs just yet. Laying down the carving knife, Mr Verloc listened with careworn attention.

He was comforted by hearing her move at last. She walked suddenly across the room, and threw the window up. After a period of stillness up there, during which he figured her to himself with her head out, he heard the sash being lowered slowly. Then she made a few steps, and sat down. Every resonance of this house was familiar to Mr Verloc, who was thoroughly domesticated. When next he heard his wife's footsteps overhead he knew, as well as if he had seen her doing it, that she had been putting on her walking shoes. Mr Verloc wriggled his shoulders slightly at this ominous symptom, and moving away from the table, stood with his back to the fireplace, his head on one side, and gnawing perplexedly at the tips of his fingers. He kept track of her movements by the sound. She walked here and there violently, with abrupt stoppages, now before the chest of drawers, then in front of the wardrobe. An immense load of weariness, the harvest of a day of shocks and surprises, weighed Mr Verloc's energies to the ground.

He did not raise his eyes till he heard his wife descending the stairs. It was as he had guessed, she was dressed for going out.

Mrs Verloc was a free woman. She had thrown open the window of the bedroom either with the intention of screaming Murder! Help! or of throwing herself out. For she did not exactly know what use to make of her freedom. Her personality seemed to have been torn into two pieces, whose mental operations did not adjust themselves very well to each other. The street, silent and deserted from end to end, repelled her by taking sides with that man who was so certain of his impunity. She was afraid to shout lest no one should come. Obviously no one would come. Her instinct of self-preservation recoiled from the depth of the fall into that sort of slimy, deep trench. Mrs Verloc closed the window, and dressed herself to go out into the street by another way. She was a free woman. She had dressed herself thoroughly, down to the tying of a black veil over her face. As she appeared before him in the light of the parlour, Mr Verloc observed that she had even her little handbag hanging from her left wrist . . . Flying off to her mother, of course.

The thought that women were wearisome creatures after all presented itself to his fatigued brain. But he was too generous to harbour it for more than an instant. This man, hurt cruelly in his vanity, remained magnanimous in his conduct, allowing himself no satisfaction of a bitter smile or of a contemptuous gesture. With true greatness of soul, he only glanced at the wooden clock on the wall, and said in a perfectly calm but forcible manner:

'Five and twenty minutes past eight, Winnie. There's no sense in going over there so late. You will never manage to get back tonight.'

Before his extended hand Mrs Verloc had stopped short. He added, heavily: 'Your mother will be gone to bed before you get there. This is the sort of news that can wait.'

Nothing was further from Mrs Verloc's thoughts than going to her mother. She recoiled at the mere idea, and feeling a chair behind her, she obeyed the suggestion of the touch, and sat down. Her intention had been simply to get outside the door for ever. And if this feeling was correct, its mental form took an unrefined shape corresponding to her origin and station. 'I would rather walk the streets all the days of my life,' she thought. But this creature, whose moral nature had been subjected to a shock of which, in the physical order, the most violent earthquake of history could only be a faint and languid rendering, was at the mercy of mere trifles, of casual contacts. She sat down. With her hat and veil she had the air of a visitor, of having looked in on Mr Verloc for a moment. Her instant docility encouraged him, whilst her aspect of only temporary and silent acquiescence provoked him a little.

'Let me tell you, Winnie,' he said with authority, 'that your place is here this evening. Hang it all! you brought the damned police high and low about my ears. I don't blame you – but it's your doing all the same. You'd better take this confounded hat off. I can't let you go out, old girl,' he added in a softened voice.

Mrs Verloc's mind got hold of that declaration with morbid tenacity. The man who had taken Stevie out from under her very eyes to murder him in a locality whose name was at the moment not present to her memory would not allow her to go out. Of course he wouldn't. Now he had murdered Stevie he would never let her go. He would want to keep her for nothing. And on this characteristic reasoning, having all the force of insane logic, Mrs Verloc's disconnected wits went to work practically. She could slip by him, open the door, run out. But he would dash out after her, seize her round the body, drag her back into the shop. She could scratch, kick, and bite – and stab, too; but for stabbing she wanted a knife. Mrs Verloc sat still under her black veil, in her own house, like a masked and mysterious visitor of impenetrable intentions.

Mr Verloc's magnanimity was not more than human. She had exasperated him at last.

'Can't you say something? You have your own dodges for vexing a man. Oh, yes! I know your deaf-and-dumb trick. I've seen you at it before today. But just now it won't do. And to begin with, take this damned thing off. One can't tell whether one is talking to a dummy or to a live woman.'

He advanced, and stretching out his hand, dragged the veil off, unmasking a still unreadable face, against which his nervous exasperation was shattered like a glass bubble flung against a rock. 'That's better,' he said, to cover his momentary uneasiness, and retreated back to his old station by the mantelpiece. It never entered his head that his wife could give him up. He felt a little ashamed of himself, for he was fond and generous. What could he do? Everything had been said already. He protested vehemently.

'By heavens! You know that I hunted high and low. I ran the risk of giving myself away to find somebody for that accursed job. And I tell you again I couldn't find any one crazy enough or hungry enough. What do you take me for – a murderer, or what? The boy is gone. Do you think I wanted him to blow himself up? He's gone. His troubles are over. Ours are just going to begin, I tell you, precisely because he did blow himself up. I don't blame you. But just try to understand that it was a pure accident; as much an accident as if he had been run over by a bus while crossing the street.'

His generosity was not infinite, because he was a human being – and not a monster, as Mrs Verloc believed him to be. He paused, and a snarl lifting his moustaches above a gleam of white teeth gave him the expression of a reflective beast, not very dangerous – a slow beast with a sleek head, gloomier than a seal, and with a husky voice.

'And when it comes to that, it's as much your doing as mine. That's so. You may glare as much as you like. I know what you can do in that way. Strike me dead if I ever would have thought of the lad for that purpose. It was you who kept on shoving him in my way when I was half distracted with the worry of keeping the lot of us out of trouble. What the devil made you? One would think you were doing it on purpose. And I am damned if I know that you didn't. There's no saying how much of what's going on you have got hold of on the sly with your infernal don't-care-a-damn way of looking nowhere in particular, and saying nothing at all. . . .'

His husky, domestic voice ceased for a while. Mrs Verloc made no reply. Before that silence he felt ashamed of what he had said. But as often happens to peaceful men in domestic tiffs, being ashamed he pushed another point.

'You have a devilish way of holding your tongue sometimes,' he began again, without raising his voice. 'Enough to make some men go mad. It's lucky for you that I am not so easily put out as some of them would be by your deaf-and-dumb sulks. I am fond of you. But don't you go too far. This isn't the time for it. We ought to be thinking of what we've got to do. And I can't let you go out tonight, galloping off to your mother with some crazy tale or other about me. I won't have it. Don't you make any mistake about it: if you will have it that I killed the boy, then you've killed him as much as I.'

In sincerity of feeling and openness of statement, these words went far beyond anything that had ever been said in this home, kept up on the wages of a secret industry eked out by the sale of more or less secret wares: the poor expedients devised by a mediocre mankind for preserving an imperfect society from the dangers of moral and physical corruption, both secret, too, of their kind. They were spoken because Mr Verloc had felt himself really outraged; but the reticent decencies of this home life, nestling in a shady street behind a shop where the sun never shone, remained apparently undisturbed. Mrs Verloc heard him out with perfect propriety, and then rose from her chair in her hat and jacket like a visitor at the end of a call. She advanced towards her husband, one arm extended as if for a silent leave-taking. Her net veil dangling down by one end on the left side of her face gave an air of disorderly formality to her restrained movements. But when she arrived as far as the hearthrug, Mr Verloc was no longer standing there. He had moved off in the direction of the sofa, without raising his eyes to watch the effect of his tirade. He was tired, resigned in a truly marital spirit. But he felt hurt in the tender spot of his secret weakness. If she would go on sulking in that dreadful overcharged silence – why then she must. She was a master in that domestic art. Mr Verloc flung himself heavily upon the sofa, disregarding as usual the fate of his hat, which, as if accustomed to take care of itself, made for a safe shelter under the table.

He was tired. The last particle of his nervous force had been expended in the wonders and agonies of this day full of surprising failures coming at the end of a harassing month of scheming and insomnia. He was tired. A man isn't made of stone. Hang everything! Mr Verloc reposed characteris-tically, clad in his outdoor garments. One side of his open overcoat was lying partly on the ground. Mr Verloc wallowed on his back. But he longed for a more perfect rest – for sleep – for a few hours of delicious forgetfulness. That would come later. Provisionally he rested. And he thought: 'I wish she would give over this damned nonsense. It's exasperating.'

There must have been something imperfect in Mrs Verloc's sentiment of regained freedom. Instead of taking the way of the door she leaned back, with her shoulders against the tablet of the mantelpiece, as a wayfarer rests against a fence. A tinge of wildness in her aspect was derived from the black veil hanging like a rag against her cheek, and from the fixity of her black gaze where the light of the room was absorbed and lost without the trace of a single gleam. This woman, capable of a bargain the mere suspicion of which would have been infinitely shocking to Mr Verloc's idea of love, remained irresolute, as if scrupulously aware of something wanting on her part for the formal closing of the transaction.

On the sofa Mr Verloc wriggled his shoulders into perfect comfort, and from the fullness of his heart emitted a wish which was certainly as pious as anything likely to come from such a source.

'I wish to goodness,' he growled, huskily, 'I had never seen Greenwich Park or anything belonging to it.'

The veiled sound filled the small room with its moderate volume, well adapted to the modest nature of the wish. The waves of air of the proper length, propagated in accordance with correct mathematical formulas, flowed around all the inanimate things in the room, lapped against Mrs Verloc's head as if it had been a head of stone. And incredible as it may appear, the eyes of Mrs Verloc seemed to grow still larger. The audible wish of Mr Verloc's overflowing heart flowed into an empty place in his wife's memory. Greenwich Park. A park! That's where the boy was killed. A park – smashed branches, torn leaves, gravel, bits of brotherly flesh and bone, all spouting up together in the manner of a firework. She remembered now what she had heard, and she remembered it pictorially. They had to gather him up with the shovel. Trembling all over with irrepressible shudders, she saw before her the very implement with its ghastly load scraped up from the ground. Mrs Verloc closed her eyes desperately, throwing upon that vision the night of her eyelids, where after a rainlike fall of mangled limbs the decapitated head of Stevie lingered suspended alone, and fading out slowly like the last star of a pyrotechnic display. Mrs Verloc opened her eyes.

Her face was no longer stony. Anybody could have noted the subtle change on her features, in the stare of her eyes, giving her a new and startling expression; an expression seldom observed by competent persons under the conditions of leisure and security demanded for thorough analysis, but whose meaning could not be mistaken at a glance. Mrs Verloc's doubts as to the end of the bargain no longer existed; her wits no longer disconnected, were working under the control of her will. But Mr Verloc observed nothing. He was reposing in that pathetic condition of optimism induced by excess of fatigue. He did not want any more trouble – with his wife, too – of all people in the world. He had been unanswerable in his vindication. He was loved for himself. The present phase of her silence he interpreted favourably. This was the time to make it up with her. The silence had lasted long enough. He broke it by calling to her in an undertone:

'Winnie.'

'Yes,' answered obediently Mrs Verloc the free woman. She commanded her wits now, her vocal organs; she felt herself to be in an almost preternaturally perfect control of every fibre of her body. It was all her own, because the bargain was at an end. She was clear sighted. She had become cunning. She chose to answer him so readily for a purpose. She did not wish that man to change his position on the sofa which was very suitable to the circumstances. She succeeded. The man did not stir. But after answering him she remained leaning negligently against the mantelpiece in the attitude of a resting wayfarer. She was unhurried. Her brow was smooth. The head and shoulders of Mr Verloc were hidden from her by the high side of the sofa. She kept her eyes fixed on his feet.

She remained thus mysteriously still and suddenly collected till Mr Verloc was heard with an accent of marital authority, and moving slightly to make room for her to sit on the edge of the sofa.

'Come here,' he said in a peculiar tone, which might have been the tone of brutality, but was intimately known to Mrs Verloc as the note of wooing.

She started forward at once, as if she were still a loyal woman bound to that man by an unbroken contract. Her right hand skimmed slightly the end of the table, and when she had passed on towards the sofa the carving knife had vanished without the slightest sound from the side of the dish. Mr Verloc heard the creaky plank in the floor, and was content. He waited. Mrs Verloc was coming. As if the homeless soul of Stevie had flown for shelter straight to the breast of his sister, guardian and protector, the resemblance of her face with that of her brother grew at every step, even to the droop of the lower lip, even to the slight divergence of the eyes. But Mr Verloc did not see that. He was lying on his back and staring upwards. He saw partly on the ceiling and partly on the wall the moving shadow of an arm with a clenched hand holding a carving knife. It flickered up and down. Its movements were leisurely. They were leisurely enough for Mr Verloc to recognize the limb and the weapon.

They were leisurely enough for him to take in the full meaning of the portent, and to taste the flavour of death rising in his gorge. His wife had gone raving mad – murdering mad. They were leisurely enough for the first paralysing effect of this discovery to pass away before a resolute determination to come out victorious from the ghastly struggle with that armed lunatic. They were leisurely enough for Mr Verloc to elaborate a plan of defence, involving a dash behind the table, and the felling of the woman to the ground with a heavy wooden chair. But they were not leisurely enough to allow Mr Verloc the time to move either hand or foot. The knife was already planted in his breast. It met no resistance on its way. Hazard has such accuracies. Into that plunging blow, delivered over the side of the couch, Mrs Verloc had put all the inheritance of her immemorial and obscure descent, the simple ferocity of the age of caverns, and the unbalanced nervous fury of the age of bar-rooms. Mr Verloc, the secret agent, turning slightly on his side with the force of the blow, expired without stirring a limb, in the muttered sound of the word 'Don't' by way of protest.

Mrs Verloc had let go the knife, and her extraordinary resemblance to her late brother had faded, had become very ordinary now. She drew a deep breath, the first easy breath since Chief Inspector Heat had exhibited to her the labelled piece of Stevie's overcoat. She leaned forward on her folded arms over the wide of the sofa. She adopted that easy attitude not in order to watch or gloat over the body of Mr Verloc, but because of the undulatory and swinging movements of the parlour, which for some time behaved as though it were at sea in a tempest. She was giddy but calm. She had become a free woman with a perfection of freedom which left her nothing to desire and absolutely nothing to do, since Stevie's urgent claim on her devotion no longer existed. Mrs Verloc, who thought in images, was not troubled now by visions, because she did not think at all. And she did not move. She was a woman enjoying her complete irresponsibility and endless leisure, almost in the manner of a corpse. She did not move, she did not think. Neither did the mortal envelope of the late Mr Verloc reposing on the sofa. Except for the fact that Mrs Verloc breathed these two would have been perfectly in accord: that accord of prudent reserve without superfluous words, and sparing of signs, which had been the foundation of their respectable home life. For it had been respectable, covering by a decent reticence the problems that may arise in the practice of a secret profession and the commerce of shady wares. To the last its decorum had remained undisturbed by unseemly shrieks and other misplaced sincerities of conduct. And after the striking of the blow, this respectability was continued in immobility and silence.

Nothing moved in the parlour till Mrs Verloc raised her head slowly and looked at the clock with inquiring mistrust. She had become aware of a ticking sound in the room. It grew upon her ear, while she remembered clearly that the clock on the wall was silent, had no audible tick. What did it mean by beginning to tick so loudly all of a sudden? Its face indicated ten minutes to nine. Mrs Verloc cared nothing for time, and the ticking went on. She concluded it could not be the clock, and her sullen gaze moved along the walls, wavered, and became vague, while she strained her hearing to locate the sound. Tic, tic, tic.

After listening for some time Mrs Verloc lowered her gaze deliberately on her husband's body. Its attitude of repose was so homelike and familiar that she could do so without feeling embarrassed by any pronounced novelty in the phenomena of her home life. Mr Verloc was taking his habitual ease. He looked comfortable.

By the position of the body the face of Mr Verloc was not visible to Mrs Verloc, his widow. Her fine, sleepy eyes, travelling downward on the track of the sound, become contemplative on meeting a flat object of bone which protruded a little beyond the edge of the sofa. It was the handle of the domestic carving knife with nothing strange about it but its position at right angles to Mr Verloc's waistcoat and the fact that something dripped from it. Dark drops fell on the floorcloth one after another, with a sound of ticking growing fast and furious like the pulse of an insane clock. At its highest speed this ticking changed into a continuous sound of trickling. Mrs Verloc watched that transformation with shadows of anxiety coming and going on her face. It was a trickle, dark, swift, thin . . . Blood!

At this unforeseen circumstance Mrs Verloc abandoned her pose of idleness and irresponsibility.

With a sudden snatch at her skirts and a faint shriek she ran to the door, as if the trickle had been the first sign of a destroying flood. Finding the table in her way she gave it a push with both hands as though it had been alive, with such force that it went for some distance on its four legs, making a loud, scraping racket, whilst the big dish with the joint crashed heavily on the floor.

Then all became still. Mrs Verloc on reaching the door had stopped. A round hat disclosed in the middle of the floor by the moving of the table rocked slightly on its crown in the wind of her flight.

CHAPTER 12

Winnie Verloc, the widow of Mr Verloc, the sister of the late faithful Stevie (blown to fragments in a state of innocence and in the conviction of being engaged in a humanitarian enterprise), did not run beyond the door of the parlour. She had indeed run away so far from a mere trickle of blood, but that was a movement of instinctive repulsion. And there she had paused, with staring eyes and lowered head. As though she had run through long years in her flight across the small parlour, Mrs Verloc by the door was quite a different person from the woman who had been leaning over the sofa, a little swimmy in her head, but otherwise free to enjoy the profound calm of idleness and irresponsibility. Mrs Verloc was no longer giddy. Her head was steady. On the other hand, she was no longer calm. She was afraid.

If she avoided looking in the direction of her reposing husband it was not because she was afraid of him. Mr Verloc was not frightful to behold. He looked comfortable. Moreover, he was dead. Mrs Verloc entertained no vain delusions on the subject of the dead. Nothing brings them back, neither love nor hate. They can do nothing to you. They are as nothing. Her mental state was tinged by a sort of austere contempt for that man who had let himself be killed so easily. He had been the master of a house, the husband of a woman, and the murderer of her Stevie. And now he was of no account in every respect. He was of less practical account than the clothing on his body, than his overcoat, than his boots – than that hat lying on the floor. He was nothing. He was not worth looking at. He was even no longer the murderer of poor Stevie. The only murderer that would be found in the room when people came to look for Mr Verloc would be – herself!

Her hands shook so that she failed twice in the task of refastening her veil. Mrs Verloc was no longer a person of leisure and irresponsibility. She was afraid. The stabbing of Mr Verloc had been only a blow. It had relieved the pent-up agony of shrieks strangled in her throat, of tears dried up in her hot eyes, of the maddening and indignant rage at the atrocious part played by that man, who was less than nothing now, in robbing her of the boy. It had been an obscurely prompted blow. The blood trickling on the floor off the handle of the knife had turned it into an extremely plain case of murder. Mrs Verloc, who always refrained from looking deep into things, was compelled to look into the very bottom of this thing. She saw there no haunting face, no reproachful shade, no vision of remorse, no sort of ideal conception. She saw there an object. That object was the gallows. Mrs Verloc was afraid of the gallows.

She was terrified of them ideally. Having never set eyes on that last argument of men's justice except in illustrative woodcuts to a certain type of tales, she first saw them erect against a black and stormy background, festooned with chains and human bones, circled about by birds that peck at dead men's eyes. This was frightful enough, but Mrs Verloc, though not a well-informed woman, had a sufficient knowledge of the institutions of her country to know that gallows are no longer erected romantically on the banks of dismal rivers or on wind-swept headlands, but in the yards of jails. There within four high walls, as if into a pit, at dawn of day, the murderer was brought out to be executed, with a horrible quietness and, as the reports in the newspapers always said, 'in the presence of the authorities'. With her eyes staring on the floor, her nostrils quivering with anguish and shame, she imagined herself all alone amongst a lot of strange gentlemen in silk hats who were calmly proceeding about the business of hanging her by the neck. That – never! Never! And how was it done? The impossibility of imagining the details of such quiet execution added something maddening to her abstract terror. The newspapers never gave any details except one, but that one with some affectation was always there at the end of a meagre report. Mrs Verloc remembered its nature. It came with a cruel burning pain into her head, as if the words 'The drop given was fourteen feet' had been scratched on her brain with a hot needle. 'The drop given was fourteen feet.'

These words affected her physically, too. Her throat became convulsed in waves to resist strangulation; and the apprehension of the jerk was so vivid that she seized her head in both hands as if to save it from being torn off her shoulders. 'The drop given was fourteen feet.' No! that must never be. She could not stand *that*. The thought of it even was not bearable. She could not stand thinking of it. Therefore Mrs Verloc formed the resolution to go at once and throw herself into the river off one of the bridges.

This time she managed to refasten her veil. With her face as if masked, all black from head to foot except for some flowers in her hat, she looked up mechanically at the clock. She thought it must have stopped. She could not believe that only two minutes had passed since she had looked at it last. Of course not. It had been stopped all the time. As a matter of fact, only three minutes had elapsed from the moment she had drawn the first deep, easy breath after the blow, to this moment when Mrs Verloc formed the resolution to drown herself in the Thames. But Mrs Verloc could not believe that. She seemed to have heard or read that clocks and watches always stopped at the moment of murder for the undoing of the murderer. She did not care. 'To the bridge – and over I go.' ... But her movements were slow.

She dragged herself painfully across the shop, and had to hold on to the handle of the door before she found the necessary fortitude to open it. The street frightened her, since it led either to the gallows or to the river. She floundered over the doorstep head forward, arms thrown out, like a person falling over the parapet of a bridge. This entrance into the open air had a foretaste of drowning; a slimy dampness enveloped her, entered her nostrils, clung to her hair. It was not actually raining, but each gas lamp had a rusty little halo of mist. The van and horses were gone, and in the black street the curtained window of the carters' eating-house made a square patch of soiled blood-red light glowing faintly very near the level of the pavement. Mrs Verloc, dragging herself slowly towards it, thought that she was a very friendless woman. It was true. It was so true that, in a sudden longing to see some friendly face, she could think of no one else but of Mrs Neale, the charwoman. She had no acquaintances of her own. Nobody would miss her in a social way. It must not be imagined that the Widow Verloc had forgotten her mother. This was not so. Winnie had been a good daughter because she had been a devoted sister. Her mother had always leaned on her for support. No consolation or advice could be expected there. Now that Stevie was dead the bond seemed to be broken. She could not face the old woman with the horrible tale. Moreover, it was too far. The river was her present destination. Mrs Verloc tried to forget her mother.

Each step cost her an effort of will which seemed the last possible. Mrs Verloc had dragged herself past the red glow of the eating-house window. 'To the bridge – and over I go,' she repeated to herself with fierce obstinacy. She put out her hand just in time to steady herself against a lamp-post. 'I'll never get there before morning,' she thought. The fear of death paralysed her efforts to escape the gallows. It seemed to her she had been staggering in that street for hours. 'I'll never get there,' she thought. 'They'll find me knocking about the streets. It's too far.' She held on, panting under her black veil.

'The drop given was fourteen feet.'

She pushed the lamp-post away from her violently, and found herself walking. But another wave of faintness overtook her like a great sea, washing away her heart clean out of her breast. 'I will never get there,' she muttered, suddenly arrested, swaying lightly where she stood. 'Never.'

And perceiving the utter impossibility of walking as far as the nearest bridge, Mrs Verloc thought of a flight abroad.

It came to her suddenly. Murderers escaped. They escaped abroad. Spain or California. Mere names. The vast world created for the glory of man was only a vast blank to Mrs Verloc. She did not know which way to turn. Murderers had friends, relations, helpers – they had knowledge. She had nothing. She was the most lonely of murderers that ever struck a mortal blow. She was alone in London: and the whole town of marvels and mud, with its maze of streets and its mass of lights, was sunk in a hopeless night, rested at the bottom of a black abyss from which no unaided woman could hope to scramble out.

She swayed forward, and made a fresh start blindly, with an awful dread of falling down; but at the end of a few steps, unexpectedly, she found a sensation of support, of security. Raising her head, she saw a man's face peering closely at her veil. Comrade Ossipon was not afraid of strange women, and no feeling of false delicacy could prevent him from striking an acquaintance with a woman apparently very much intoxicated. Comrade Ossipon was interested in women. He held up this one between his two large palms, peering at her in a business-like way till he heard her say faintly 'Mr Ossipon!' and then he very nearly let her drop to the ground.

'Mrs Verloc!' he exclaimed. 'You here!'

It seemed impossible to him that she should have been drinking. But one never knows. He did not go into that question, but attentive not to discourage kind fate surrendering to him the widow of Comrade Verloc, he tried to draw her to his breast. To his astonishment she came quite easily, and even rested on his arm for a moment before she attempted to disengage herself. Comrade Ossipon would not be brusque with kind fate. He withdrew his arm in a natural way.

'You recognized me,' she faltered out, standing before him, fairly steady on her legs.

'Of course I did,' said Ossipon with perfect readiness. 'I was afraid you were going to fall. I've thought of you too often lately not to recognize you anywhere, at any time. I've always thought of you – ever since I first set eyes on you.'

Mrs Verloc seemed not to hear. 'You were coming to the shop?' she said, nervously.

'Yes; at once,' answered Ossipon. 'Directly I read the paper.'

In fact, Comrade Ossipon had been skulking for a good two hours in the neighbourhood of Brett Street, unable to make up his mind for a bold move. The robust anarchist was not exactly a bold conqueror. He remembered that Mrs Verloc had never responded to his glances by the slightest sign of encouragement. Besides, he thought the shop might be watched by the police, and Comrade Ossipon did not wish the police to form an exaggerated notion of his revolutionary sympathies. Even now he did not know precisely what to do. In comparison with his usual amatory speculations this was a big and serious undertaking. He ignored how much there was in it and how far he would have to go in order to get hold of what there was to get – supposing there was a chance at all. These perplexities checking his elation imparted to his tone a soberness well in keeping with the circumstances.

'May I ask you where you were going?' he inquired in a subdued voice.

'Don't ask me!' cried Mrs Verloc with a shuddering, repressed violence. All her strong vitality recoiled from the idea of death. 'Never mind where I was going. . . .'

Ossipon concluded that she was very much excited but perfectly sober. She remained silent by his side for a moment, then all at once she did something which he did not expect. She slipped her hand under his arm. He was startled by the act itself certainly, and quite as much, too, by the palpably resolute character of this movement. But this being a delicate affair, Comrade Ossipon behaved with delicacy. He contented himself by pressing the hand slightly against his robust ribs. At the same time he felt himself being impelled forward, and yielded to the impulse. At the end of Brett Street he became aware of being directed to the left. He submitted.

The fruiterer at the corner had put out the blazing glory of his oranges and lemons, and Brett Place was all darkness, interspersed with the misty halos of the few lamps defining its triangular shape, with a cluster of three lights on one stand in the middle. The dark forms of the man and woman glided slowly arm in arm along the walls with a loverlike and homeless aspect in the miserable night.

'What would you say if I were to tell you that I was going to find you?' Mrs Verloc asked, gripping his arm with force.

'I would say that you couldn't find anyone more ready to help you in your trouble,' answered Ossipon, with a notion of making tremendous headway. In fact, the progress of this delicate affair was almost taking his breath away.

'In my trouble!' Mrs Verloc repeated, slowly.

'Yes.'

'And do you know what my trouble is?' she whispered with strange intensity.

'Ten minutes after seeing the evening paper,' explained Ossipon with ardour, 'I met a fellow whom you may have seen once or twice at the shop perhaps, and I had a talk with him which left no doubt whatever in my mind. Then I started for here, wondering whether you – I've been fond of you beyond words ever since I set eyes on your face,' he cried, as if unable to command his feelings.

Comrade Ossipon assumed correctly that no woman was capable of wholly disbelieving such a statement. But he did not know that Mrs Verloc accepted it with all the fierceness the instinct of self-preservation imparts to the grip of a drowning person. To the widow of Mr Verloc the robust anarchist was like a radiant messenger of life.

They walked slowly, in step. 'I thought so,' Mrs Verloc murmured, faintly.

'You've read it in my eyes,' suggested Ossipon with great assurance.

'Yes,' she breathed out into his inclined ear.

'A love like mine could not be concealed from a woman like you,' he went on, trying to detach his mind from material considerations such as the business value of the shop, and the amount of money Mr Verloc might have left in the bank. He applied himself to the sentimental side of the affair. In his heart of hearts he was a little shocked at his success. Verloc had been a good fellow, and certainly a very decent husband as far as one could see. However, Comrade Ossipon was not going to quarrel with his luck for the sake of a dead man. Resolutely he suppressed his sympathy for the ghost of Comrade Verloc, and went on:

'I could not conceal it. I was too full of you. I daresay you could not help seeing it in my eyes. But I could not guess it. You were always so distant. . . .'

'What else did you expect?' burst out Mrs Verloc. 'I was a respectable woman – '

She paused, then added, as if speaking to herself, in sinister resentment: 'Till he made me what I am.'

Ossipon let that pass, and took up his running.

'He never did seem to me to be quite worthy of you,' he began, throwing loyalty to the winds. 'You were worthy of a better fate.'

Mrs Verloc interrupted bitterly:

'Better fate! He cheated me out of seven years of life.'

'You seemed to live so happily with him.' Ossipon tried to exculpate the lukewarmness of his past conduct. 'It's that what's made me timid. You seemed to love him. I was surprised – and jealous,' he added.

'Love him!' Mrs Verloc cried out in a whisper full of scorn and rage. 'Love him! I was a good wife to him. I am a respectable woman. You thought I loved him! You did! Look here, Tom – '

The sound of this name thrilled Comrade Ossipon with pride. For his name was Alexander, and he was called Tom by arrangement with the most familiar of his intimates. It was a name of friendship – of moments of expansion. He had no idea that she had ever heard it used by anybody. It was apparent that she had not only caught it, but had treasured it in her memory – perhaps in her heart.

'Look here, Tom! I was a young girl. I was done up. I was tired. I had two people depending on what I could do, and it did seem as if I couldn't do any more. Two people – mother and the boy. He was much more mine than mother's. I sat up nights and nights with him on my lap, all alone upstairs, when I wasn't more than eight years old myself. And then – He was mine, I tell you . . . You can't understand that. No man can understand it. What was I to do? There was a young fellow – '

The memory of the early romance with the young butcher survived, tenacious, like the image of a glimpsed ideal in that heart quailing before the fear of the gallows and full of revolt against death.

'That was the man I loved then,' went in the widow of Mr Verloc. 'I suppose he could see it in my eyes, too. Five and twenty shillings a week, and his father threatened to kick him out of the business if he made such a fool of himself as to marry a girl with a crippled mother and a crazy idiot of a boy on her hands. But he would hang about me, till one evening I found the courage to slam the door in his face. I had to do it. I loved him dearly.

Five and twenty shillings a week! There was that other man – a good lodger. What is a girl to do? Could I've gone on the streets? He seemed kind. He wanted me, anyhow. What was I to do with mother and that poor boy? Eh? I said yes. He seemed good-natured, he was freehanded, he had money, he never said anything. Seven years – seven years a good wife to him, the kind, the good, the generous, the – And he loved me. Oh, yes. He loved me till I sometimes wished myself – Seven years. Seven years a wife to him. And do you know what he was, that dear friend of yours? Do you know what he was? . . . He was a devil!'

The superhuman vehemence of that whispered statement completely stunned Comrade Ossipon. Winnie Verloc turning about held him by both arms, facing him under the falling mist in the darkness and solitude of Brett Place, in which all sounds of life seemed lost as if in a triangular well of asphalt and bricks, of blind houses and unfeeling stones.

'No; I didn't know,' he declared, with a sort of flabby stupidity, whose comical aspect was lost upon a woman haunted by the fear of the gallows, 'But I do now. I – I understand,' he floundered on, his mind speculating as to what sort of atrocities Verloc could have practised under the sleepy, placid appearances of his married estate. It was positively awful. 'I understand,' he repeated, and then by a sudden inspiration uttered an 'Unhappy woman!' of lofty commiseration instead of the more familiar 'Poor darling!' of his usual practice. This was no usual case. He felt conscious of something abnormal going on, while he never lost sight of the greatness of the stake. 'Unhappy, brave woman!'

He was glad to have discovered that variation; but he could discover nothing else. 'Ah, but he is dead now,' was the best he could do. And he put a remarkable amount of animosity into his guarded exclamation. Mrs Verloc caught at his arm with a sort of frenzy. 'You guessed then he was dead,' she murmured, as if beside herself. 'You! You guessed what I had to do. Had to!'

There were suggestions of triumph, relief, gratitude in the indefinable tone of these words. It engrossed the whole attention of Ossipon to the detriment of mere literal sense. He wondered what was up with her, why she had worked herself into this state of wild excitement. He even began to wonder whether the hidden causes of that Greenwich Park affair did not lie deep in the unhappy circumstances of the Verlocs' married life. He went so far as to suspect Mr Verloc of having selected that extraordinary manner of committing suicide. By Jove! that would account for the utter inanity and wrong-headedness of the thing. No anarchist manifestation was required by the circumstances. Quite the contrary; and Verloc was as well aware of that as any other revolutionist of his standing. What an immense joke if Verloc had simply made fools of the whole of Europe, of the revolutionary world, of the police, of the press, and of the cocksure Professor as well. Indeed, thought Ossipon, in astonishment, it seemed almost certain that he did! Poor beggar! It struck him as very possible that of that household of two it wasn't precisely the man who was the devil.

Alexander Ossipon, nicknamed the Doctor, was naturally inclined to think indulgently of his men friends. He eyed Mrs Verloc hanging on his arm. Of his women friends he thought in a specially practical way. Why Mrs Verloc should exclaim at his knowledge of Mr Verloc's death, which was no guess at all, did not disturb him beyond measure. Women often talked like lunatics. But he was curious to know how she had been informed. The papers could tell her nothing beyond the mere fact: the man blown to pieces in Greenwich Park not having been identified. It was inconceivable on any theory that Verloc should have given her an inkling of his intention – whatever it was. This problem interested Comrade Ossipon immensely. He stopped short. They had gone then along the three sides of Brett Place, and were near the end of Brett Street again.

'How did you first come to hear of it?' he asked in a tone he tried to render appropriate to the character of the revelations which had been made to him by the woman at his side.

She shook violently for a while before she answered in a listless voice:

'From the police. A chief inspector came. Chief Inspector Heat he said he was. He showed me – '

Mrs Verloc choked. 'Oh, Tom, they had to gather him up with a shovel.' Her breast heaved with dry sobs. In a moment Ossipon found his tongue.

'The police! Do you mean to say the police came already? That Chief Inspector Heat himself actually came to tell you.'

'Yes,' she confirmed in the same listless tone. 'He came. Just like this. He came. I didn't know. He showed me a piece of overcoat, and – Just like that. Do you know this? he says.'

'Heat! Heat! And what did he do?'

Mrs Verloc's head dropped. 'Nothing. He did nothing. He went away. The police were on that man's side,' she murmured tragically. 'Another one came, too.'

'Another – another inspector, do you mean?' asked Ossipon, in great excitement, and very much in the tone of a scared child.

'I don't know. He came. He looked like a foreigner. He may have been one of them Embassy people.'

Comrade Ossipin nearly collapsed under this new shock.

'Embassy! Are you aware what you are saying? What Embassy? What on earth do you mean by Embassy?'

'It's that place in Chesham Square. The people he cursed so. I don't know. What does it matter!'

'And that fellow, what did he do or say to you?'

'I don't remember ... Nothing ... I don't care. Don't ask me,' she pleaded in a wary voice.

'All right. I won't,' assented Ossipon, tenderly. And he meant it, too, not because he was touched by the pathos of the pleading voice, but because he felt himself losing his footing in the depths of this tenebrous affair. Police! Embassy! Phew! For fear of adventuring his intelligence into ways where its natural lights might fail to guide it safely he dismissed resolutely all suppositions, surmises, and theories out of his mind. He had the woman there, absolutely flinging herself at him, and that was the principal consideration. But after what he had heard nothing could astonish him any more. And when Mrs Verloc, as if startled suddenly out of a dream of safety, began to urge upon him wildly the necessity of an immediate flight on the Continent, he did not exclaim in the least. He simply said with unaffected regret that there was no train till the morning, and stood looking thoughtfully at her face, veiled in black net, in the light of a gas-lamp veiled in a gauze of mist.

Near him, her black form merged in the night, like a figure half chiselled out of a block of black stone. It was impossible to say what she knew, how deep she was involved with policemen and Embassies. But if she wanted to get away, it was not for him to object. He was anxious to be off himself. He felt that the business, the shop so strangely familiar to chief inspectors and members of foreign Embassies, was not the place for him. That must be dropped. But there was the rest. These savings. The money!

'You must hide me till the morning somewhere,' she said in a dismayed voice.

'Fact is, my dear, I can't take you where I live. I share the room with a friend.'

He was somewhat dismayed himself. In the morning the blessed tecs will be out in all the stations, no doubt. And if they once got hold of her, for one reason or another she would be lost to him indeed.

'But you must. Don't you care for me at all - at all? What are you thinking of?'

She said this violently, but she let her clasped hands fall in discouragement. There was a silence, while the mist fell, and darkness reigned undisturbed over Brett Place. Not a soul, not even the vagabond, lawless, and amorous soul of a cat, came near the man and the woman facing each other.

'It would be possible perhaps to find a safe lodging somewhere,' Ossipon spoke at last. 'But the truth is, my dear, I have not enough money to go and try with - only a few pence. We revolutionists are not rich.'

He had fifteen shillings in his pocket. He added:

'And there's the journey before us, too - first thing in the morning at that.'

She did not move, made no sound, and Comrade Ossipon's heart sank a little. Apparently she had no suggestion to offer. Suddenly she clutched at her breast, as if she had felt a sharp pain there.

'But I have,' she gasped. 'I have the money. I have enough money. Tom! Let us go from here.'

'How much have you got?' he inquired, without stirring to her tug; for he was a cautious man.

'I have the money, I tell you. All the money.'

'What do you mean by it? All the money there was in the bank, or what?' he asked, incredulously, but ready not to be surprised at anything in the way of luck.

'Yes, yes!' she said nervously. 'All there was. I've it all.'

'How on earth did you manage to get hold of it already?' he marvelled.

'He gave it to me,' she murmured, suddenly subdued and trembling. Comrade Ossipon put down his rising surprise with a firm hand.

'Why, then - we are saved,' he uttered slowly.

She leaned forward, and sank against his breast. He welcomed her there.

She had all the money. Her hat was in the way of very marked effusion; her veil, too. He was adequate in his manifestations, but no more. She received them without resistance and without abandonment, passively, as if only half-sensible. She freed herself from his lax embrace without difficulty.

'You will save me, Tom,' she broke out, recoiling, but still keeping her hold on him by the two lapels of his damp coat. 'Save me. Hide me. Don't let them have me. You must kill me first. I couldn't do it myself – I couldn't, I couldn't – not even for what I am afraid of.'

She was confoundedly bizarre, he thought. She was beginning to inspire him with an indefinite uneasiness. He said surlily, for he was busy with important thoughts:

'What the devil *are* you afraid of?'

'Haven't you guessed what I was driven to do!' cried the woman. Distracted by the vividness of her dreadful apprehensions, her head ringing with forceful words, that kept the horror of her position before her mind, she had imagined her incoherence to be clearness itself. She had no conscience of how little she had audibly said in the disjointed phrases completed only in her thought. She had felt the relief of a full confession, and she gave a special meaning to every sentence spoken by Comrade Ossipon, whose knowledge did not in the least resemble her own. 'Haven't you guessed what I was driven to do!' Her voice fell. 'You needn't be long in guessing then what I am afraid of,' she continued in a bitter and sombre murmur. 'I won't have it. I won't. I won't. I won't. You must promise to kill me first!' She shook the lapels of his coat. 'It must never be!'

He assured her curtly that no promises on his part were necessary, but he took good care not to contradict her in set terms, because he had had much to do with excited women, and he was inclined in general to let his experience guide his conduct in preference to applying his sagacity to each special case. His sagacity in this case was busy in other directions. Women's words fell into water, but the shortcomings of time-tables remained. The insular nature of Great Britain obtruded itself upon his notice in an odious form. 'Might just as well be put under lock and key every night,' he thought irritably, as nonplussed as though he had a wall to scale with the woman on his back. Suddenly he slapped his forehead. He had by dint of cudgelling his brains just thought of the Southampton–St Malo service. The boat left about midnight. There was a train at 10.30. He became cheery and ready to act.

'From Waterloo. Plenty of time. We are all right after all. . . . What's the matter now? This isn't the way,' he protested.

Mrs Verloc, having hooked her arm into his, was trying to drag him into Brett Street again.

'I've forgotten to shut the shop door as I went out,' she whispered, terribly agitated.

The shop and all that was in it had ceased to interest Comrade Ossipon. He knew how to limit his desires. He was on the point of saying 'What of that? Let it be,' but he refrained. He disliked argument about trifles. He even mended his pace considerably on the thought that she might have left the money in the drawer. But his willingness lagged behind her feverish impatience.

The shop seemed to be quite dark at first. The door stood ajar. Mrs Verloc, leaning against the front, grasped out:

'Nobody has been in. Look! The light – the light in the parlour.'

Ossipon, stretching his head forward, saw a faint gleam in the darkness of the shop.

'There is,' he said.

'I forgot it.' Mrs Verloc's voice came from behind her veil faintly. And as he stood waiting for her to enter first, she said louder: 'Go in and put it out – or I'll go mad.'

He made no immediate objection to this proposal, so strangely motivated. 'Where's all that money?' he asked.

'On me! Go, Tom. Quick! Put it out . . . Go in!' she cried, seizing him by both shoulders from behind.

Not prepared for a display of physical force, Comrade Ossipon stumbled far into the shop before her push. He was astonished at the strength of the woman and scandalized by her proceedings. But he did not retrace his steps in order to remonstrate with her severely in the street. He was beginning to be disagreeably impressed by her fantastic behaviour. Moreover, this or never was the time to humour the woman. Comrade Ossipon avoided easily the end of the counter, and approached calmly the glazed door of the parlour. The curtain over the panes being drawn back a little he, by a very natural impulse, looked in, just as he made ready to turn the handle. He looked in without a thought, without intention, without curiosity of any sort. He looked in because he could not help looking in. He looked in, and discovered Mr Verloc reposing quietly on the sofa.

A yell coming from the innermost depths of his chest died out unheard and transformed into a sort of greasy, sickly taste on his lips. At the same time the mental personality of Comrade Ossipon executed a frantic leap backwards. But his body, left thus without intellectual guidance, held on to the door handle with the unthinking force of an instinct. The robust anarchist did not even totter. And he stared, his face close to the glass, his eyes protruding out of his head. He would have given anything to get away, but his returning reason informed him that it would not do to let go the door handle. What was it – madness, a nightmare, or a trap into which he had been decoyed with fiendish artfulness? Why – what for? He did not know. Without any sense of guilt in his breast, in the full peace of his conscience as far as these people were concerned, the idea that he would be murdered for mysterious reasons by the couple Verloc passed not so much across his mind as across the pit of his stomach, and went out, leaving behind a trail of sickly faintness – an indisposition. Comrade Ossipon did not feel very well in a very special way for a moment – a long moment. And he stared. Mr Verloc lay very still meanwhile, simulating sleep for reasons of his own, while that savage woman of his was guarding the door – invisible and silent in the dark and deserted street. Was all this some sort of terrifying arrangement invented by the police for his especial benefit? His modesty shrank from that explanation.

But the true sense of the scene he was beholding came to Ossipon through the contemplation of the hat. It seemed an extraordinary thing, an ominous object, a sign. Black, and rim upward, it lay on the floor before the couch as if prepared to receive the contributions of pence from people who would come presently to behold Mr Verloc in the fullness of his domestic ease reposing on a sofa. From the hat the eyes of the robust anarchist wandered to the displaced table, gazed at the broken dish for a time, received a kind of optical shock from observing a white gleam under the imperfectly closed eyelids of the man on the couch. Mr Verloc did not seem so much asleep now as lying down with a bent head and looking insistently at his left breast. And when Comrade Ossipon had made out the handle of the knife he turned away from the glazed door, and retched violently.

The crash of the street door flung to made his very soul leap in a panic. This house with its harmless tenant could still be made a trap of – a trap of a terrible kind. Comrade Ossipon had no settled conception now of what was happening to him. Catching his thigh against the end of the counter, he spun round, staggered with a cry of pain, felt in the distracting clatter of the bell his arms pinned to his side by a convulsive hug, while the cold lips of a woman moved creepily on his very ear to form the words:

'Policeman! He has seen me!'

He ceased to struggle; she never let him go. Her hands had locked themselves with an inseparable twist of fingers on his robust back. While the footsteps approached, they breathed quickly, breast to breast, with hard, laboured breaths, as if theirs had been the attitude of a deadly struggle, while, in fact, it was the attitude of deadly fear. And the time was long.

The constable on the beat had in truth seen something of Mrs Verloc; only coming from the lighted thoroughfare at the other end of Brett Street, she had been no more to him than a flutter in the darkness. And he was not even quite sure that there had been a flutter. He had no reason to hurry up. On coming abreast of the shop he observed that it had been closed early. There was nothing very unusual in that. The men on duty had special instructions about that shop: what went on about there was not to be meddled with unless absolutely disorderly, but any observations made were to be reported. There were no observations to make; but from a sense of duty and for the peace of his conscience, owing also to that doubtful flutter of the darkness, the constable crossed the road, and tried the door. The spring latch, whose key was reposing for ever off duty in the late Mr Verloc's waistcoat pocket, held as well as usual. While the conscientious officer was shaking the handle, Ossipon felt the cold lips of the woman stirring again creepily against his very ear:

'If he comes in kill me – kill me, Tom.'

The constable moved away, flashing as he passed the light of his dark lantern, merely for form's sake, at the shop window. For a moment longer the man and the woman inside stood motionless, panting, breast to breast; then her fingers came unlocked, her arms fell by her side slowly. Ossipon leaned against the counter. The robust anarchist wanted support badly. This was awful. He was almost too disgusted for speech. Yet he managed to utter a plaintive thought, showing at least that he realized his position.

'Only a couple of minutes later and you'd have made me blunder against the fellow poking about here with his damned dark lantern.'

The widow of Mr Verloc, motionless in the middle of the shop, said insistently:

'Go in and put that light out, Tom. It will drive me crazy.'

She saw vaguely his vehement gesture of refusal. Nothing in the world would have induced Ossipon to go into the parlour. He was not superstitious, but there was too much blood on the floor; a beastly pool of it all round the hat. He judged he had been already too near that corpse for his peace of mind – for the safety of his neck, perhaps!

'At the meter then! There. Look. In that corner.'

The robust form of Comrade Ossipon, striding brusque and shadowy across the shop, squatted in a corner obediently; but this obedience was without grace. He fumbled nervously – and suddenly in the sound of a muttered curse the light behind the glazed door flicked out to a gasping, hysterical sigh of a woman. Night, the inevitable reward of men's faithful labours on this earth, night had fallen on Mr Verloc, the tried revolutionist – 'one of the old lot' – the humble guardian of society; the invaluable secret agent $\triangle$ of Baron Stott-Wartenheim's dispatches; a servant of law and order, faithful, trusted, accurate, admirable, with perhaps one single amiable weakness: the idealistic belief in being loved for himself.

Ossipon groped his way back through the stuffy atmosphere, as black as ink now, to the counter. The voice of Mrs Verloc, standing in the middle of the shop, vibrated after him in that blackness with a desperate protest.

'I will not be hanged, Tom. I will not—'

She broke off. Ossipon from the counter issued a warning: 'Don't shout like this,' then seemed to reflect profoundly. 'You did this thing quite by yourself?' he inquired in a hollow voice, but with an appearance of masterful calmness which filled Mrs Verloc's heart with grateful confidence in his protecting strength.

'Yes,' she whispered, invisible.

'I wouldn't have believed it possible,' he muttered. 'Nobody would.' She heard him move about and the snapping of a lock in the parlour door. Comrade Ossipon had turned the key on Mr Verloc's repose; and this he did not from reverence for its eternal nature or any other obscurely sentimental consideration, but for the precise reason that he was not at all sure that there was not someone else hiding somewhere in the house. He did not believe the woman, or rather he was incapable by now of judging what could be true, possible, or even probable on this astounding universe. He was terrified out of all capacity for belief or disbelief in regard to this extraordinary affair, which began with police inspectors and Embassies and would end goodness knows where – on the scaffold for someone. He was terrified at the thought that he could not prove the use he made of his time ever since seven o'clock, for he had been skulking about Brett Street. He was terrified at this savage woman who had brought him in there, and would probably saddle him with complicity, at least if he were not careful. He was terrified at the rapidity with which he had been involved in such danger – decoyed into it. It was some twenty minutes since he had met her – not more.

The voice of Mrs Verloc rose subdued, pleading piteously: 'Don't let them hang me, Tom! Take me out of the country. I'll work for you. I'll slave for you. I'll love you. I've no one in the world . . . Who would look at me if you don't!' She ceased for a moment; then in the depths of the loneliness made round her by an insignificant thread of blood trickling off the handle of a knife, she found a dreadful inspiration to her – who had been the respectable girl of the Belgravian mansion, the loyal, respectable wife of Mr Verloc. 'I won't ask you to marry me,' she breathed out in shamefaced accents.

She moved a step forward in the darkness. He was terrified at her. He would not have been surprised if she had suddenly produced another knife destined for his breast. He certainly would have made no resistance. He had really not enough fortitude in him just then to tell her to keep back. But he inquired in a cavernous, strange tone: 'Was he asleep?'

'No,' she cried, and went on rapidly: 'He wasn't. Not he. He had been telling me that nothing could touch him. After taking the boy away from under my very eyes to kill him – the loving, innocent, harmless lad. My own, I tell you. He was lying on the couch quite easy – after killing the boy – my boy. I would have gone on the streets to get out of his sight. And he says to me like this: "Come here," after telling me I had helped to kill the boy. You hear, Tom? He says like this: "Come here," after taking my very heart out of me along with the boy to smash in the dirt.'

She ceased, then dreamily repeated twice: 'Blood and dirt. Blood and dirt.' A great light broke upon Comrade Ossipon. It was that half-witted lad then who had perished in the park. And the fooling of everybody all round appeared more complete than ever – colossal. He exclaimed scientifically, in the extremity of his astonishment: 'The degenerate – by heavens!'

'Come here.' The voice of Mrs Verloc rose again. 'What did he think I was made of? Tell me, Tom. Come here! Me! Like this! I had been looking at the knife, and I thought I would come then if he wanted me so much. Oh, yes! I came – for the last time . . . With the knife.'

He was excessively terrified at her – the sister of the degenerate – a degenerate herself of a murdering type . . . or else of the lying type. Comrade Ossipon might have been said to be terrified scientifically in addition to all other kinds of fear. It was an immeasurable and composite funk, which from its very excess gave him in the dark a false appearance of calm and thoughtful deliberation. For he moved and spoke with difficulty, being as if half frozen in his will and mind – and no one could see his ghastly face. He felt half dead.

He leaped a foot high. Unexpectedly Mrs Verloc had desecrated the unbroken, reserved decency of her home by a shrill and terrible shriek.

'Help, Tom! Save me. I won't be hanged!'

He rushed forward, groping for her mouth with a silencing hand, and the shriek died out. But in his rush he had knocked her over. He felt her now clinging round his legs, and his terror reached its culminating point, became a sort of intoxication, entertained delusions, acquired the characteristics of delirium tremens. He positively saw snakes now. He saw the woman twined round him like a snake, not to be shaken off. She was not deadly. She was death itself – the companion of life.

Mrs Verloc, as if relieved by the outburst, was very far from behaving noisily now. She was pitiful.

'Tom, you can't throw me off now,' she murmured from the floor. 'Not unless you crush my head under your heel. I won't leave you.'

'Get up,' said Ossipon.

His face was so pale as to be quite visible in the profound black darkness of the shop; while Mrs Verloc, veiled, had no face, almost no discernible form. The trembling of something small and white, a flower in her hat, marked her place, her movements.

It rose in the blackness. She had got up from the floor, and Ossipon regretted not having run out at once into the street. But he perceived easily that it would not do. It would not do. She would run after him. She would pursue him shrieking till she sent every policeman within hearing in chase. And then goodness only knew what she would say of him. He was so frightened that for a moment the insane notion of strangling her in the dark passed through his mind. And he became more frightened than ever! She had him. He saw himself living in abject terror in some obscure hamlet in Spain or Italy; till some fine morning they found him dead, too, with a knife in his breast – like Mr Verloc. He sighed deeply. He dared not move. And Mrs Verloc waited in silence the good pleasure of her saviour, deriving comfort from his reflective silence.

Suddenly he spoke up in an almost natural voice. His reflections had come to an end.

'Let's get out, or we will lose the train.'

'Where are we going to, Tom?' she asked, timidly. Mrs Verloc was no longer a free woman.

'Let's get to Paris first, the best way we can ... Go out first, and see if the way's clear.'

She obeyed. Her voice came subdued through the cautiously opened door. 'It's all right.'

Ossipon came out. Notwithstanding his endeavours to be gentle, the cracked bell clattered behind the closed door in the empty shop, as if trying in vain to warn the reposing Mr Verloc of the final departure of his wife – accompanied by his friend.

In the hansom, they presently picked up, the robust anarchist became explanatory. He was still awfully pale, with eyes that seemed to have sunk a whole half-inch into his tense face. But he seemed to have thought of everything with extraordinary method.

'When we arrive,' he discoursed in a queer, monotonous tone, 'you must go into the station ahead of me, as if we did not know each other. I will take the tickets, and slip yours into your hand as I pass you. Then you will go into the first-class ladies' waiting-room, and sit there till ten minutes before the train starts. Then you come out. I will be outside. You go in first on the platform, as if you did not know me. There may be eyes watching there that know what's what. Alone you are only a woman going off by train. I am known. With me, you may be guessed at as Mrs Verloc running away. Do you understand, my dear?' he added with an effort.

'Yes,' said Mrs Verloc, sitting there against him in the hansom all rigid with the dread of the gallows and the fear of death. 'Yes, Tom.' And she added to herself, like an awful refrain: 'The drop given was fourteen feet.'

Ossipon, not looking at her, and with a face like a fresh plaster cast of himself after a wasting illness, said: 'By-the-by, I ought to have the money for the tickets now.'

Mrs Verloc, undoing some hooks of her bodice, while she went on staring ahead beyond the splashboard, handed over to him the new pigskin pocket-book. He received it without a word, and seemed to plunge it deep somewhere into his very breast. Then he slapped his coat on the outside.

All this was done without the exchange of a single glance; they were like two people looking out for the first sight of a desired goal. It was not till the hansom swung round a corner and towards the bridge that Ossipon opened his lips again.

'Do you know how much money there is in that thing?' he asked as if addressing slowly some hob-goblin sitting between the ears of the horse.

'No,' said Mrs Verloc. 'He gave it to me. I didn't count. I thought nothing of it at the time. Afterwards—'

She moved her right hand a little. It was so expressive that little movement of that right hand which had struck the deadly blow into a man's heart less than an hour before that Ossipon could not repress a shudder. He exaggerated it then purposely, and muttered:

'I am cold. I got chilled through.'

Mrs Verloc looked straight ahead at the perspective of her escape. Now and then, like a sable streamer blown across a road, the words 'The drop given was fourteen feet' got in the way of her tense stare. Through her black veil the whites of her big eyes gleamed lustrously like the eyes of a masked woman.

Ossipon's rigidity had something businesslike, a queer official expression. He was heard again all of a sudden, as though he had released a catch in order to speak.

'Look here! Do you know whether your – whether he kept his account at the bank in his own name or in some other name.'

Mrs Verloc turned upon him her masked face and the big white gleam of her eyes.

'Other name?' she said, thoughtfully.

'Be exact in what you say,' Ossipon lectured in the swift motion of the hansom. 'It's extremely important. I will explain to you. The bank has the numbers of these notes. If they were paid to him in his own name, then when his – his death becomes known, the notes may serve to track us since we have no other money. You have no other money on you?'

She shook her head negatively.

'None whatever?' he insisted.

'A few coppers.'

'It would be dangerous in that case. The money would have then to be dealt specially with. Very specially. We'd have perhaps to lose more than half the amount in order to get these notes changed in a certain safe place I know of in Paris. In the other case – I mean if he had his account and got paid out under some other name – say Smith, for instance – the money is perfectly safe to use. You understand? The bank has no means of knowing that Mr Verloc and, say, Smith are one and the same person. Do you see how important it is that you should make no mistake in answering me? Can you answer that query at all? Perhaps not. Eh?'

She said composedly:

'I remember now! He didn't bank in his own name. He told me once that it was on deposit in the name of Prozor.'

'You are sure?'

'Certain.'

'You don't think the bank had any knowledge of his real name? Or anybody in the bank or – '

She shrugged her shoulders.

'How can I know? Is it likely, Tom?'

'No. I suppose it's not likely. It would have been more comfortable to know . . . Here we are. Get out first, and walk straight in. Move smartly.'

He remained behind, and paid the cabman out of his own loose silver. The programme traced by his minute foresight was carried out. When Mrs Verloc, with her ticket for St Malo in her hand, entered the ladies' waiting-room, Comrade Ossipon walked into the bar, and in seven minutes absorbed three goes of hot brandy and water.

'Trying to drive out a cold,' he explained to the barmaid, with a friendly nod and a grimacing smile. Then he came out, bringing out from that festive interlude the face of a man who had drunk at the very Fountain of Sorrow. He raised his eyes to the clock. It was time. He waited.

Punctual, Mrs Verloc came out, with her veil down, and all black – black as commonplace death itself, crowned with a few cheap and pale flowers. She passed close to a little group of men who were laughing, but whose laughter could have been struck dead by a single word. Her walk was indolent, but her back was straight, and Comrade Ossipon looked after it in terror before making a start himself.

The train was drawn up, with hardly anybody about its row of open doors. Owing to the time of the year and to the abominable weather there were but few passengers. Mrs Verloc walked slowly along the line of empty compartments till Ossipon touched her elbow from behind.

'In here.'

She got in, and he remained on the platform looking about. She bent forward, and in a whisper:

'What is it, Tom? Is there any danger.'

'Wait a moment. There's the guard.'

She saw him accost the man in uniform. They talked for a while. She heard the guard say 'Very well, sir,' and saw him touch his cap. Then Ossipon came back, saying: 'I told him not to let anybody get into our compartment.'

She was leaning forward on her seat. 'You think of everything . . . You'll get me off, Tom?' she asked in a gust of anguish, lifting her veil brusquely to look at her saviour.

She had uncovered a face like adamant. And out of this face the eyes looked on, big, dry, enlarged, lightless, burnt out like two black holes in the white, shining globes.

'There is no danger,' he said, gazing into them with an earnestness almost rapt, which to Mrs Verloc, flying from the gallows, seemed to be full of force and tenderness. This devotion deeply moved her – and the adamantine face lost the stern rigidity of its terror. Comrade Ossipon gazed at it as no lover ever gazed at his mistress's face. Alexander Ossipon, anarchist, nicknamed the Doctor, author of a medical (and improper) pamphlet, late lecturer on the social aspects of hygiene to working men's clubs, was free from the trammels of conventional morality – but he submitted to the rule of science. He was scientific, and he gazed scientifically at that woman, the sister of a degenerate, a degenerate herself – of a murdering type. He gazed at her, and invoked Lombroso, as an Italian peasant recommends himself to his favourite saint. He gazed scientifically. He gazed at her cheeks, at her nose, at her eyes, at her ears ... Bad! ... Fatal! Mrs Verloc's pale lips parting, slightly relaxed under his passionately attentive gaze, he gazed also at her teeth ... Not a doubt remained ... a murdering type ... If Comrade Ossipon did not recommend his terrified soul to Lombroso, it was only because on scientific grounds he could not believe that he carried about him such a thing as a soul. But he had in him the scientific spirit, which moved him to testify on the platform of a railway station in nervous, jerky phrases.

'He was an extraordinary lad, that brother of yours. Most interesting to study. A perfect type in a way. Perfect!'

He spoke scientifically in his secret fear. And Mrs Verloc, hearing these words of commendation vouchsafed to her beloved dead, swayed forward with a flicker of light in her sombre eyes, like a ray of sunshine heralding a tempest of rain.

'He was that indeed,' she whispered, softly, with quivering lips. 'You took a lot of notice of him, Tom. I loved you for it.'

'It's almost incredible the resemblance there was between you two,' pursued Ossipon, giving a voice to his abiding dread, and trying to conceal his nervous, sickening impatience for the train to start. 'Yes, he resembled you.'

These words were not especially touching or sympathetic. But the fact of that resemblance insisted upon was enough in itself to act upon her emotions powerfully. With a little faint cry, and throwing her arms out, Mrs Verloc burst into tears at last.

Ossipon entered the carriage, hastily closed the door and looked out to see the time by the station clock. Eight minutes more. For the first three of these Mrs Verloc wept violently and helplessly without pause or interruption. Then she recovered somewhat, and sobbed gently in an abundant fall of tears. She tried to talk to her saviour, to the man who was the messenger of life.

'Oh, Tom! How could I fear to die after he was taken away from me so cruelly! How could I! How could I be such a coward!'

She lamented aloud her love of life, that life without grace or charm, and almost without decency, but of an exalted faithfulness of purpose, even unto murder. And, as often happens in the lament of poor humanity rich in suffering but indigent in words, the truth – the very cry of truth – was found in a worn and artificial shape picked up somewhere among the phrases of sham sentiment.

'How could I be so afraid of death! Tom, I tried. But I am afraid. I tried to do away with myself. And I couldn't. Am I hard? I suppose the cup of horrors was not full enough for such as me. Then when you came . . .'

She paused. Then in a gust of confidence and gratitude. 'I will live all my days for you, Tom!' she sobbed out.

'Go over into the other corner of the carriage, away from the platform,' said Ossipon, solicitously. She let her saviour settle her comfortably, and he watched the coming on of another crisis of weeping, still more violent than the first. He watched the symptoms with a sort of medical air, as if counting seconds. He heard the guard's whistle at last. An involuntary contraction of the upper lip bared his teeth with all the aspect of savage resolution as he felt the train beginning to move. Mrs Verloc heard and felt nothing, and Ossipon, her saviour, stood still. He felt the train roll quicker, rumbling heavily to the sound of the woman's loud sobs, and then crossing the carriage in two long strides he opened the door deliberately, and leaped out.

He had leaped out at the very end of the platform; and such was his determination in sticking to his desperate plan that he managed by a sort of miracle, performed almost in the air, to slam to the door of the carriage. Only then did he find himself rolling head over heels like a shot rabbit. He was bruised, shaken, pale as death, and out of breath when he got up. But he was calm, and perfectly able to meet the excited crowd of railwaymen who had gathered round him in a moment. He explained, in gentle and convincing tones, that his wife had started at a moment's notice for Brittany to her dying mother; that, of course, she was greatly upset, and he considerably concerned at her state; that he was trying to cheer her up, and had absolutely failed to notice at first that the train was moving out. To the general exclamation 'Why didn't you go on to Southampton, then, sir?' he objected the inexperience of a young sister-in-law left alone in the house with three small children, and her alarm at his absence, the telegraph offices being closed. He had acted on impulse. 'But I don't think I'll ever try that again,' he concluded; smiled all round; distributed some small change, and marched without a limp out of the station.

Outside, Comrade Ossipon, flush of safe banknotes as never before in his life, refused the offer of a cab.

'I can walk,' he said, with a little friendly laugh to the civil driver.

He could walk. He walked. He crossed the bridge. Later on the towers of the Abbey saw in their massive immobility the yellow bush of his hair passing under the lamps. The lights of Victoria saw him, too, and Sloane Square, and the railings of the park. And Comrade Ossipon once more found himself on a bridge. The river, a sinister marvel of still shadows and flowing gleams mingling below in a black silence, arrested his attention. He stood looking over the parapet for a long time. The clock tower boomed a brazen blast above his drooping head. He looked up at the dial . . . Half past twelve of a wild night in the Channel.

And again Comrade Ossipon walked. His robust form was seen that night in distant parts of the enormous town slumbering monstrously on a carpet of mud under a veil of raw mist. It was seen crossing the streets without life and sound, or diminishing in the interminable straight perspectives of shadowy houses bordering empty roadways lined by strings of gaslamps. He walked through Squares, Places, Ovals, Commons, through monotonous streets with unknown names where the dust of humanity settles inert and hopeless out of the stream of life. He walked. And suddenly turning into a strip of a front garden with a mangy grass plot, he let himself into a small grimy house with a latchkey he took out of his pocket.

He threw himself down on his bed all dressed, and lay still for a whole quarter of an hour. Then he sat up suddenly, drawing up his knees, and clasping his legs. The first dawn found him open-eyed, in that same posture. This man who could walk so long, so far, so aimlessly, without showing a sign of fatigue, could also remain sitting still for hours without stirring a limb or an eyelid. But when the late sun sent its rays into the room he unclasped his hands, and fell back on the pillow. His eyes stared at the ceiling. And suddenly they closed. Comrade Ossipon slept in the sunlight.

CHAPTER 13

The enormous iron padlock on the doors of the wall cupboard was the only object in the room on which the eye could rest without becoming afflicted by the miserable unloveliness of forms and the poverty of material. Unsaleable in the ordinary course of business on account of its noble proportions, it had been ceded to the Professor for a few pence by a marine dealer in the east of London. The room was large, clean, respectable, and poor with that poverty suggesting the starvation of every human need except mere bread. There was nothing on the walls but the paper, an expanse of arsenical green, soiled with indelible smudges here and there, and with stains resembling faded maps of uninhabited continents.

At a deal table near a window sat Comrade Ossipon, holding his head between his fists. The Professor, dressed in his only suit of shoddy tweeds, but flapping to and fro on the bare boards a pair of incredibly dilapidated slippers, had thrust his hands deep into the over-strained pockets of his jacket. He was relating to his robust guest a visit he had lately been paying to the Apostle Michaelis. The Perfect Anarchist had even been unbending a little.

'The fellow didn't know anything of Verloc's death. Of course! He never looks at the newspapers. They make him too sad, he says. But never mind. I walked into his cottage. Not a soul anywhere. I had to shout half a dozen times before he answered me. I thought he was fast asleep yet, in bed. But not at all. He had been writing his book for four hours already. He sat in that tiny cage in a litter of manuscript. There was a half-eaten raw carrot on the table near him. His breakfast. He lives on a diet of raw carrots and a little milk now.'

'How does he look on it?' asked Comrade Ossipon, listlessly.

'Angelic ... I picked up a handful of his pages from the floor. The poverty of reasoning is astonishing. He has no logic. He can't think consecutively. But that's nothing. He had divided his biography into three parts, entitled "Faith, Hope, Charity". He is elaborating now the idea of a world planned out like an immense and nice hospital, with gardens and flowers, in which the strong are to devote themselves to the nursing of the weak.'

The Professor paused.

'Conceive you this folly, Ossipon? The weak! The source of all evil on this earth!' he continued with his grim assurance. 'I told him that I dreamt of a world like shambles, where the weak would be taken in hand for utter extermination.

'Do you understand, Ossipon? The source of all evil! They are our sinister masters – the weak, the flabby, the silly, the cowardly, the faint of heart, and the slavish of mind. They have power. They are the multitude. Theirs is the kingdom of the earth. Exterminate, exterminate! That is the only way of progress. It is! Follow me, Ossipon. First the great multitude of the weak must go, then the only relatively strong. You see? First the blind, then the deaf and the dumb, then the halt and the lame – and so on. Every taint, every vice, every prejudice, every convention must meet its doom.'

'And what remains?' asked Ossipon in a stifled voice.

'I remain – if I am strong enough,' asserted the sallow little Professor, whose large ears, thin like membranes, and standing far out from the sides of his frail skull, took on suddenly a deep red tint.

'Haven't I suffered enough from this oppression of the weak?' he continued forcibly. Then tapping the breast-pocket of his jacket: 'And yet I *am* the force,' he went on. 'But the time! The time! Give me time! Ah! that multitude, too stupid to feel either pity or fear. Sometimes I think they have everything on their side. Everything – even death – my own weapon.'

'Come and drink some beer with me at the Silenus,' said the robust Ossipon after an interval of silence pervaded by the rapid flap, flap of the slippers on the feet of the Perfect Anarchist. This last accepted. He was jovial that day in his own peculiar way. He slapped Ossipon's shoulder.

'Beer! So be it! Let us drink and be merry, for we are strong, and tomorrow we die.'

He busied himself with putting on his boots, and talked meanwhile in his curt, resolute tones.

'What's the matter with you, Ossipon? You look glum and seek even my company. I hear that you are seen constantly in places where men utter foolish things over glasses of liquor. Why? Have you abandoned your collection of women? They are the weak who feed the strong – eh?'

He stamped one foot, and picked up his other laced boot, heavy, thick-soled, unblacked, mended many times. He smiled to himself grimly.

'Tell me, Ossipon, terrible man, has ever one of your victims killed herself for you – or are your triumphs so far incomplete – for blood alone puts a seal on greatness? Blood. Death. Look at history.'

'You be damned,' said Ossipon, without turning his head.

'Why? Let that be the hope of the weak, whose theology has invented hell for the strong. Ossipon, my feeling for you is amicable contempt. You couldn't kill a fly.'

But rolling to the feast on the top of the omnibus the Professor lost his high spirits. The contemplation of the multitudes thronging the pavements extinguished his assurance under a load of doubt and uneasiness which he could shake off after a period of seclusion in the room with the large cupboard closed by an enormous padlock.

'And so,' said over his shoulder Comrade Ossipon, who sat on the seat behind. 'And so Michaelis dreams of a world like a beautiful and cheery hospital.'

'Just so. An immense charity for the healing of the weak,' assented the Professor, sardonically.

'That's silly,' admitted Ossipon. 'You can't heal weakness. But after all Michaelis may not be so far wrong. In two hundred years doctors will rule the world. Science reigns already. It reigns in the shade maybe – but it reigns. And all science must culminate at last in the science of healing – not the weak, but the strong. Mankind wants to live – to live.'

'Mankind,' asserted the Professor with a self-confident glitter of his iron-rimmed spectacles, 'does not know what it wants.'

'But you do,' growled Ossipon. 'Just now you've been crying for time – time. Well, the doctors will serve you out your time – if you are good. You profess yourself to be one of the strong – because you carry in your pocket enough stuff to send yourself and, say, twenty other people into eternity. But eternity is a damned hole. It's time that you need. You – if you met a man who could give you for certain ten years of time, you would call him your master.'

'My device is: No God! No master,' said the Professor, sententiously, as he rose to get off the bus.

Ossipon followed. 'Wait till you are lying flat on your back at the end of your time,' he retorted, jumping off the footboard after the other. 'Your scurvy, shabby, mangy little bit of time,' he continued across the street, and hopping on to the curbstone.

'Ossipon, I think that you are a humbug,' the Professor said, opening masterfully the doors of the renowned Silenus. And when they had established themselves at a little table he developed further this gracious thought. 'You are not even a doctor. But you are funny. Your notion of a humanity universally putting out the tongue and taking the pill from pole to pole at the bidding of a few solemn jokers is worthy of the prophet. Prophecy! What's the good of thinking of what will be!' He raised his glass. 'To the destruction of what is,' he said calmly.

He drank and relapsed into his peculiarly close manner of silence. The thought of a mankind as numerous as the sands of the seashore, as indestructible, as difficult to handle, oppressed him. The sound of exploding bombs was lost in their immensity of passive grains without an echo. For instance, this Verloc affair. Who thought of it now?

Ossipon, as if suddenly compelled by some mysterious force, pulled a much-folded newspaper out of his pocket. The Professor raised his head at the rustle. 'What's that paper? Anything in it?' he asked.

Ossipon started like a scared somnambulist.

'Nothing. Nothing whatever. The thing's ten days old. I forgot it in my pocket, I suppose.'

But he did not throw the old thing away. Before returning it to his pocket he stole a glance at the last lines of a paragraph. They ran thus: '*An impenetrable mystery seems destined to hang for ever over this act of madness or despair.*'

Such were the end words of an item of news headed: 'Suicide of Lady Passenger from a cross-Channel Boat.' Comrade Ossipon was familiar with the beauties of its journalistic style. '*An impenetrable mystery seems destined to hang for ever . . .*' He knew every word by heart. '*An impenetrable mystery . . .*' And the robust anarchist, hanging his head on his breast, fell into a long reverie.

He was menaced by this thing in the very sources of his existence. He could not issue forth to meet his various conquests, those that he courted on benches in Kensington Gardens, and those he met near area railings, without the dread of beginning to talk to them of an impenetrable mystery destined . . . He was becoming scientifically afraid of insanity lying in wait for him amongst these lines. '*To hang for ever over.*' It was an obsession, a torture. He had lately failed to keep several of these appointments, whose note used to be an unbounded trustfulness in the language of sentiment and manly tenderness. The confiding disposition of various classes of women satisfied the needs of his self-love, and put some material means into his hand. He needed it to live. It was there. But if he could no longer make use of it, he ran the risk of starving his ideals and his body . . . '*This act of madness or despair.*'

'An impenetrable mystery' was sure 'to hang for ever' as far as all mankind was concerned. But what of that if he alone of all men could never get rid of the cursed knowledge? And Comrade Ossipon's knowledge was as precise as the newspaper man could make it – up to the very threshold of the '*mystery destined to hang for ever . . .*'

Comrade Ossipon was well informed. He knew what the gangway man of the steamer had seen: 'A lady in a black dress and a black veil, wandering at midnight alongside on the quay. "Are you going by the boat, ma'am," he had asked her, encouragingly. "This way." She seemed not to know what to do. He helped her on board. She seemed weak.'

And Ossipon knew also what the stewardess had seen: a lady in black with a white face standing in the middle of the empty ladies' cabin. The stewardess induced her to lie down there. The lady seemed quite unwilling to speak, and as if she were in some awful trouble. The next the stewardess knew she was gone from the ladies' cabin. The stewardess then went on deck to look for her, and Comrade Ossipon was informed that the good woman found the unhappy lady lying down in one of the hooded seats. Her eyes were open, but she would not answer anything that was said to her. She seemed very ill. The stewardess fetched the chief steward, and those two people stood by the side of the hooded seat consulting over their extraordinay and tragic passenger. They talked in audible whispers (for she seemed past hearing) of St Malo and the Consul there, of communicating with her people in England. Then they went away to arrange for her removal down below, for indeed by what they could see of her face she seemed to them to be dying. But Comrade Ossipon knew that behind that white mask of despair there was struggling against terror and despair a vigour of vitality, a love of life that could resist the furious anguish which drives to murder and the fear, the blind, mad fear of the gallows. He knew. But the stewardess and the chief steward knew nothing, except that when they came back for her in less than five minutes the lady in black was no longer in the hooded seat. She was nowhere. She was gone. It was then five o'clock in the morning, and it was no accident either. An hour afterwards one of the steamer's hands found a wedding ring left lying on the seat. It had stuck to the wood in a bit of wet, and its glitter caught the man's eye. There was a date, 24 June 1879, engraved inside. '*An impenetrable mystery is destined to hang for ever . . .*'

And Comrade Ossipon raised his bowed head, beloved of various humble women of these isles, Apollo-like in the sunniness of its bush of hair.

The Professor had grown restless meantime. He rose.

'Stay,' said Ossipon, hurriedly. 'Here, what do you know of madness and despair?'

The Professor passed the tip of his tongue on his dry, thin lips, and said doctorally:

'There are no such things. All passion is lost now. The world is mediocre, limp, without force. And madness and despair are a force. And force is a crime in the eyes of the fools, the weak and the silly who rule the roost. You are mediocre. Verloc, whose affair the police has managed to smother so nicely, was mediocre. And the police murdered him. He was mediocre. Everybody is mediocre. Madness and despair! Give me that for a lever, and I'll move the world. Ossipon, you have my cordial scorn. You are incapable of conceiving even what the fat-fed citizen would call a crime. You have no force.' He paused, smiling sardonically under the fierce glitter of his thick glasses.

'And let me tell you that this little legacy they say you've come into has not improved your intelligence. You sit at your beer like a dummy. Good-bye.'

'Will you have it?' said Ossipon, looking up with an idiotic grin.

'Have what?'

'The legacy. All of it.'

The incorruptible Professor only smiled. His clothes were all but falling off him, his boots, shapeless with repairs, heavy like lead, let water in at every step. He said:

'I will send you by-and-by a small bill for certain chemicals which I shall order tomorrow. I need them badly. Understood – eh?'

Ossipon lowered his head slowly. He was alone. '*An impenetrable mystery . . .*' It seemed to him that suspended in the air before him he saw his own brain pulsating to the rhythm of an impenetrable mystery. It was diseased clearly. '. . . *This act of madness or despair.*'

The mechanical piano near the door played through a valse cheekily, then fell silent all at once, as if gone grumpy.

Comrade Ossipon, nicknamed the Doctor went out of the Silenus beer-hall. At the door he hesitated, blinking at a not too splendid sunlight – and the paper with the report of the suicide of a lady was in his pocket. His heart was beating against it. The suicide of a lady – *'this act of madness or despair'*.

He walked along the street without looking where he put his feet; and he walked in a direction which would not bring him to the place of appointment with another lady (an elderly nursery governess putting her trust in an Apollo-like ambrosial head). He was walking away from it. He could face no woman. It was ruin. He could neither think, work, sleep, nor eat. But he was beginning to drink with pleasure, with anticipation, with hope. It was ruin. His revolutionary career, sustained by the sentiment and trustfulness of many women, was menaced by an impenetrable mystery – the mystery of a human brain pulsating wrongfully to the rhythm of journalistic phrases. '. . . *Will hang for ever over this act* . . .' – it was inclining towards the gutter – '. . . *of madness or despair.*'

'I am seriously ill, he muttered to himself with scientific insight. Already his robust form, with an Embassy's secret-service money (inherited from Mr Verloc) in his pockets, was marching in the gutter as if in training for the task of an inevitable future. Already he bowed his broad shoulders, his head of ambrosial locks, as if ready to receive the leather yoke of the sandwich board. As on that night, more than a week ago, Comrade Ossipon walked without looking where he put his feet, feeling no fatigue, feeling nothing, seeing nothing, hearing not a sound. '*An impenetrable mystery* . . .' He walked disregarded. '. . . *This act of madness or despair.*'

And the incorruptible Professor walked, too, averting his eyes from the odious multitude of mankind. He had no future. He disdained it. He was a force. His thoughts caressed the images of ruin and destruction. He walked frail, insignificant, shabby, miserable – and terrible in the simplicity of his idea calling madness and despair to the regeneration of the world. Nobody looked at him. He passed on unsuspected and deadly, like a pest in the street full of men.